Pink Knight

An Epic Adventure in Time and Space
and a Tale of Enduring Love

C J Harvey

authorHOUSE®

AuthorHouse™ UK
1663 Liberty Drive
Bloomington, IN 47403 USA
www.authorhouse.co.uk
Phone: 0800.197.4150

Published by AuthorHouse 01/31/2019

ISBN: 978-1-7283-8164-0 (sc)
ISBN: 978-1-7283-8163-3 (hc)
ISBN: 978-1-7283-8162-6 (e)

Print information available on the last page.

Any people depicted in stock imagery provided by Getty Images are models,
and such images are being used for illustrative purposes only.
Certain stock imagery © Getty Images.

This book is printed on acid-free paper.

Contents

To my grandson

Kai Gopsill

PART ONE

1986 – 2004

CHAPTER 1

A New Discovery

1986

Ashley Bonner was nearly five years old and had dark brown hair, light brown eyes and was quite slim and tall for his age. He liked to wake up before everyone else in the house, get dressed and sit in the enclosed front porch to watch the sun rising over the houses opposite; or at least to watch the sky lighten into a new day. In the summer months he would often be up as early as 4 o'clock in the morning. He loved the summer as the garden was always so full of birds and buzzing bees. Ashley especially liked the butterflies as he could go right up to them before they flew away. He made sure the bird feeder was well stocked with fat balls for the birds and would remind his dad to buy some more if they were running low.

There was something fascinating about the morning sky that was attractive to Ashley. Pink was a special colour for him as it made him feel good and full of extra energy. He felt that something special was happening to him whenever the sky looked pink. He didn't understand what that something special could be as he was still too young to know. But it would not be long before he would get to understand.

He first noticed pink tints appearing in the daytime sky when he was four years old and asked his mum lots of children's questions. And mummy was always very patient and answered them all, after a fashion. Mummy Lillian remembers his early questions about the sky colour and why it sometimes turned pink. She thought this was just a childish awareness and mix-up in colour identification. She thought nothing of Ashley's habit of disappearing around a bush in the park to suddenly reappear literally yards away. Children do move so quickly. You can't take your eyes off them for an instant.

Daddy Alex was a quiet man. He was a computer technician in the main railway offices in Birmingham. Mummy Lillian was a teacher in a secondary school with her main subjects as the sciences. She had done a BSc in physics at Aston University followed by a one year PGCE training course. She was also very gentle and easy going in her manner.

When Ashley was two and a half years old his baby sister Katy arrived just after Easter. He thought she cried a lot at first. Lillian then voluntarily gave up teaching to remain with her children full time.

Daddy Alex had then also found a new and better job with the MoD up in Sutton Coldfield. He had a special interest in computers and had picked up a lot from the Micro-tech courses he had been sent on during his years with the railways. He drove an old Rover 45, but Lillian had to get rid of her VW golf when she gave up teaching. With one salary coming in they considered it prudent to have just the one car.

Alex's dad Eric was tall and slim for his 62 years, and he worked part time as a driver for a day care centre in Sutton Coldfield. Being a widower he was a frequent visitor at Lillian and Alex's place. He was especially fond of his grandson, but also doted on his granddaughter Katy. Lillian's mom and dad, Beryl and David Jones, were both alive and well and lived in Aberdare, South Wales. Because of the distance, or so they said, they didn't visit very often and then in the summer only, rarely staying the night. They had been with their daughter Lillian for only one Christmas, and that was before Ashley was born. They tended to favour Brenda more often. Brenda was their other daughter. She lived with her husband Ron Davies in Aberporth near Cardigan, where they ran a small B&B together. This was very handy for Lillian as the sisters were very close and visited each other several times a year. Aberporth is a lovely coastal village with two lovely beaches. Dogs were allowed on only one of these, the inland one that flooded at every tide.

Because the B&B did well in the summer months, Lillian tended to avoid visiting Brenda during these busy periods. Of course, if there was any slack weekend Brenda would ring Lillian and Alex and invite them to come over which was usually taken up with relish. Sometimes Eric would accompany them as well. He would drive up in his own car as he preferred to leave early before lunch the next day or early morning of the next. It was a three hour drive to Birmingham.

Ashley's birthday was in September so he started school when he was just five. By now Katy was two and a half years old and she just adored her big brother. The tantrums had mostly gone though brother and sister still had their little fights over possession of a particular toy. Poor Ashley never had a chance in hell of winning against his precocious little sister. Katy had a way about her that was very persuasive. More like organising things to her advantage and convincing Ashley to do what she wanted. Ashley loved his sister Katy, and having a gentle nature didn't mind this in the least.

They loved their granddad Eric and he was over every week on an evening or two as he only lived a couple of miles up the road. Katy was the apple of his eye and he let her boss him around too. He would often give Ashley a wink when Katy was up to her organising tricks. They played catch-the-ball in the back garden where you stood on one leg if you missed a catch in the round. Eric remarked to Lillian that Ashley never missed catching the ball even when it was not thrown quite straight towards him. He always seemed to be able to dash to where the ball went and catch it with ease. Eric would even distract him by pointing to something in the sky before chucking the ball, but Ashley still caught the ball easily.

Daddy Alex was a bit of a gardener and the two long flower beds in the back garden were full of hardy-herbaceous shrubs that required very little maintenance. Alex especially liked Euphorbias and Hostas and had many different varieties of each. Then there were the Fuchsias and Dahlias, the Cannas and the Lavender, and of course, the Azalea and the Rhododendron bushes. He also had his preferred ground cover plants in the Sedum, Primula-Wanda and London-Pride. There were also quite a few fancy plastic containers on the patio that had Geraniums and Marigolds in them for a good summer bedding of colour. But Alex was especially fond of trees. He loved his winter-flowering Cherry trees and even persuaded some of the neighbours in their cul-de-sac to have at least one. These tended to blossom over the winter months from November to March which added a beautiful splash of colour at a time of grey days. These, along with the Viburnum bushes with their pink and white blooms and the yellow Winter-Jasmine added that extra colour to liven up the dull days of winter. There was not much gardening to be done during these months but Ashley was always ready and willing to give his dad a hand whenever the chance came along. He seemed to take to gardening and was keen to help his dad with any outside work.

It was in the summer of '86 when Ashley was nearly five and just about to start school that it first became noticeable. At the time they were visiting Ron and Brenda in Aberporth and were out on a coastal path walk. They were strolling leisurely along when Lillian remarked to Alex what a lovely day it was and how beautifully blue the sky looked.

"But mummy," chirped up Ashley, "it also looks pink sometimes."

"Yes my dear," said Lillian, "but that is only in the mornings and evenings when the sun is low. We do get such lovely colours then don't we dear?"

"No mummy," reiterated Ashley, "also at other times too, if I want it to."

Lillian thought about Ashley's remarks and made a mental note to get Ashley's eyes checked for colour vision when they were back at home in Birmingham. Or perhaps he was just getting mixed up with his colours. After all he was not quite five years old and had yet to start school.

They carried on with their pleasant walk past the old railway carriages that had been deposited at various locations on the hillside, and which had been converted into quaint little homes with porches and green houses attached and with such pretty well kept gardens in bloom around them.

Ashley kept running ahead and seemed to be really enjoying the outing. At one point he came running back to the group with something held between finger and thumb of his right hand. It was a pretty yellow butterfly and quite small. It was one of those that tend to dash about ever so quickly. He was holding it with both wings folded back and held it up to show his mum.

"Look mummy, I caught a butterfly. Isn't it pretty?"

"Yes my dear," said Lillian, "but I think you should let it go, it is so much prettier when it is sitting on a flower, don't you think?"

When Ashley let it go it flew off into the wind and was soon out of sight. Ashley darted off up the path again to carry on his search of the exciting discoveries that he knew were waiting just around the next corner.

It was Alex who made the remark that the yellow butterfly was an extremely difficult one to catch, even with a net. He just wondered how Ashley had managed to catch it and then in such a manner that he did it no injury at all. He made a mental note to ask his son how he had caught it so easily when they got back from their stroll. But with so much going on, and Brenda and Ron being such good company, it was only in the car going back to Birmingham in the evening that Alex remembered to ask. Ashley's reply was a simple one.

"Oh daddy" he said, "it was just flying very slowly, so it was quite easy for me to catch it as I did." Daddy had no reply to that but spent the rest of the night thinking just what it could mean. Did Ashley have a special talent or just a very quick eye? He would discuss it with Lillian when he got the chance.

But of course, the next few days after the August bank holiday were taken up with preparations for Ashley's start in the Reception at St Barnabas' School on Spring Lane. And also the arrangements for his fifth birthday party on the eighth of September. And so the days went by and the questions faded.

Ashley loved school and as usual was up early well before anyone else each morning; including weekends. On school days he had so many things to tell his mum and dad every evening, and they just loved to listen to all his enthusiasm. Katy would ask repeatedly when she also could go to school like her brother.

Ashley had good reports from his teacher Miss Bums, a young NQT, newly qualified teacher, and whom Ashley simply adored. It was always Miss Bums said to do this, and Miss Burns said to do that. One of her reports was that Ashley was always the first to finish his work. But more important, that he was always helpful in the class and gentle towards the other children.

Children are all very possessive and snatched toys off one another, usually resulting in tears for one. Ashley would somehow, as if magically, go up to the crying child and give the snatched toy back; to the utter bewilderment of the snatcher. Miss Bums said it was wonderful how comforting Ashley always was towards any child in tears.

And so time passed. Christmas came and went, as did Easter and soon it was time again for the ending of the school's third term and the beginning of the summer holidays. It was at about this time that Ashley began catching little birds in his cupped hands and bringing them in to the house to show his mum. It was usually the birds that came regularly to the fat ball feeder in the back garden. There were Blue tits, Great tits, Willow tits, Dunnocks, Robins, Chaffinches and Sparrows, and a few others. But he never kept hold of them for long, never for more than a minute or two before letting them go free again.

Lillian never ever saw her five year old son actually catch one of these. It always seemed that the bird was one minute at the feeder, and the next instant Ashley was running up the garden with it cupped in his hands calling out excitedly. On one of their bookshelves was a Collins' book on British birds from which they tried to identify the bird in Ashley's hands.

"I think we ought to get a small cage from the pet shop" said Lillian, "then we can really see what we've caught before letting it go free."

"Oh yes please mummy," said Ashley, "but it might have babies at home so how long can we keep it?"

"Only an hour or two my dear," said mummy, "and we can put some seed and water in the cage for it to have its tea."

"Do you think it will come back to our garden after we let it go," said Ashley.

"Oh, I'm sure it will know that we intended it no harm," said mummy Lillian, "birds are quite clever like that you know."

So the very next day Lillian took Ashley and Katy to the pet shop on Church road and they chose a nice small shiny wire birdcage. The woman serving them asked what bird they intended to keep in it, whereupon Ashley piped up, "All the birds in our garden." Lillian just rolled her eyes upward and smiled at the woman, who winked back at her with a big smile too. And that is exactly what Ashley did during the days that followed. It was a puzzle that Lillian and Alex had yet to solve. During the summer holidays the family went to Barry Island for a day's outing and all had a lovely swim in the waters of the shallow cove. The cove was so sheltered from the winds that the sands got quite warm in the sun. The tide came in about mid-day and the children screamed with delight as they tried to protect their sand castles from the invading sea. Of course, daddy Alex also got into the thrill of the game which excited the children even further. Here again Alex noticed how quick Ashley was in building his section of their protection wall. Finally, it was one big wave that crashed right up the beach, nearly up to where Lillian was sitting on the beach rug that washed away all their heroic efforts in a trice.

It was a long journey there in the Rover but on the return they had planned to stop off in Aberdare for an overnight visit to Lillian's parents. They were ready and waiting and were ever so pleased to see them, especially their two lovely grandchildren. Ashley and Katy had a room specially set up for them. It was a big house on Clifton Street with lots of different levels. Lillian and Brenda had grown up in it all those years ago and had many pleasant memories. There had been a few improvements, like an extra bath and shower room with toilet. Lillian's dad was very good at redecorating and had just finished doing up three of the rooms. There was even a room that resembled a dungeon with iron bars in the door which used to be a coal storage room in the old days. Lillian and Alex didn't mention about Ashley's talent for catching birds and butterflies since they could hardly understand it themselves. It was a pleasant twenty four hours and they said their goodbyes and left for home the following evening.

They also managed two weekend visits that summer to Ron and Brenda in Aberporth. And both times the grownups discussed Ashley. It was Ron who suggested a discreet investigation by Lillian and Alex. They must plan it carefully so as not to cause Ashley any concern. Ron thought that Ashley might have a special gift, which must be kept within the family for now. Since Ashley was nearly six years old, it might be worth probing gently to ascertain a few more facts. Was the boy's insistence of the occasional daytime pink sky a clue worth following?

Lillian and Alex thought that Ashley was too young to have to undergo a lengthy questioning session. So they decided on a pattern of the odd question here and there and with plenty of days in between. They must make it seem like an ordinary conversation between parent and child. They regularly discussed the type of questions to be asked but couldn't yet decide when to actually go about it. The last thing they wanted was to alarm their son into thinking that something about his behaviour was not quite right.

So it wasn't until just before Christmas when Ashley was already six years old that Lillian actually spoke to him on the subject. They were at the kitchen table and Katy was with them doing her usual drawing and colouring. Ashley was also at the same table and was looking at the Robin he had just caught and put into the shiny birdcage. Lillian then quite casually asked Ashley what colour the sky had been when he caught the Robin.

"Oh, just a light rosy pink mummy," said Ashley without taking his eyes off the Robin.

"And when the sky turns rosy pink," asked mummy "what happens to all the birds in the garden?" "Silly mummy," said Ashley, "they all fly very slowly of course."

"That's wonderful darling," said mummy, "and do you know what makes the sky rosy pink?"

"Why, I do of course," said Ashley, "whenever I want it to. But it makes me very deaf and I don't like that."

"When the sky is rosy pink can you see mummy in the kitchen?" asked Lillian.

"Oh yes mummy," said Ashley, "but you are always standing very still. I think I'll let Mr Robin go now mummy. I don't think he's happy in there. Katy, do you want to come out with me to open the cage and let him fly away?"

"Oh yes," said Katy "and can I carry the cage as well?"

And off the two went without a care in the world.

Lillian now had some facts to add to her list to show Alex. She also rang Ron and Brenda to tell them about her latest conversation with Ashley. Ron thought it was definitely something to do with the colour pink and suggested the next line of questioning follow up on what else took on a rosy pink hue. He had a suspicion of what might be happening but didn't think it possible. Such things were only found in science fiction. Lillian also had vague thoughts in a similar direction, but as a passing thought only. She definitely needed to probe a bit deeper but not just yet; perhaps much later on in a week or so.

There was a long thoughtful pause when Lillian told Alex of her conversation with Ashley. Alex said he couldn't believe what he was hearing. He just didn't think such things could happen in our world. But then there were stranger things happening all around us that we didn't understand either. As an avid reader of books on cosmology and the universe theories, Alex had read about Einstein's theories on the variation of the pace of time in space when travelling at great speeds. But that was out there not here on the flat ground of our Earth.

Lillian also had an interest in physics. Her degree touched on the fringes of astrophysics but that was very long ago. When she was still in teaching and ran her tutorial sessions with the sixth formers, they always seemed especially fascinated when Lillian brought the subject around to cosmological theories. It was the physicist JBS Haldane who said that the science of cosmology was not only stranger than we suppose, but stranger than we *can* suppose. It was certainly a strange world and it seemed as though it was about to explode right here in the home of the Bonner family.

Lillian and Alex thought it might be a good idea to probe into their respective family histories in case some sort of a precedent existed. So Alex's dad Eric was brought into the picture. He expressed surprise at the thought but couldn't remember any strange occurrences ever having taken place to him or his parents before him. He said that he could now understand how it was that Ashley at the early age of four had been so good at catching the ball whenever they played ball games in the back garden. He must have had this gift even then.

It was in the Easter holidays that the Bonner family went to spend a weekend in Aberdare with

Lillian's parents Beryl and David. They just didn't know what to think when told of the purpose of this special fact finding visit. They were quite conservative and religiously minded and were rather surprised and a bit horrified by it all. They were not in the least bit science minded and therefore expressed puzzlement and a bit of disbelief at what they had just been told. When asked if there was ever anything strange in their family history, they came out with stories of an Uncle Peter who was a bit mad and had to be put in an institution. He was always seen to be scribbling numbers in note books. On hot days he would wrap up in blankets and say he was defying the heat. It would be the opposite in freezing weather. Apart from this, there was nothing else that was unusual that they could remember. Both of their own parents had lived well into their early eighties, and apart from the aches and pains in their joints brought on by the ageing process, had lived fairly healthy lives right to the end. In fact Beryl's mum never saw a dentist in all her years and had all her teeth in perfect condition when she died at the age of eighty two. They said that perhaps this was just a phase in Ashley's growing up that would pass. They had heard of poltergeist activity caused by the minds of disturbed young children going through an adjustment phase in their lives. These youngsters had caused TV sets to malfunction, and had even made objects fall off mantel shelves and bureaux among lots of other strange goings on. They had been told by their church that it was known and accepted as a phase in the development of some young people and had nothing to do with the spirit world. They were sure that Lillian and Alex had nothing to worry about and that Ashley would develop into a clean living young man.

Ashley was now a happy-go-lucky six year old and a very good looking little boy. He was doing very well in Year One at St. Barnabas' and his new teacher, an elderly Mrs Preston, had a special liking for him. She considered Ashley the best and politest child in her class. The other children thought the same and all wanted to be his friend.

By Easter Ashley could read quite well and had become an avid reader. Lillian bought him lots of children's story books to read but he seemed to need something a bit more challenging and exciting. So Lillian went up into the attic and brought down two boxes of her old Enid Blyton books that she had read as a child. There must have been about thirty dusty and damp smelling books in the pile. There were also a few hard cover books among them and Ashley chose a pale blue one and began to flick through the pages. It was called 'A Book of Naughty Children' and had illustrations to each short story. Although Ashley could read, he preferred the way his mum read to him. She made the stories come alive and sound so much more exciting. There was another pale green hard back called 'A Second Book of Naughty children' that became another favourite. One of Ashley's favourite stories was in the first book and was called 'Boastful Bill'. It was about a boy who bragged that he could do everything. In the end he had to be saved because he couldn't even swim. All these stories had a happy outcome with a lesson to be learned from each, and was quite character building. Ashley would eventually outgrow these and progress to the Famous Five series. He still liked to watch his programs on TV. Thomas the Tank Engine and Scooby Doo were among his favourite programs.

By the time of the summer holidays Ashley didn't catch as many birds for his cage as he used to. It was usually at the insistence of Katy when she saw a bird at the feeder that he did so. Lillian noted that Ashley was doing all the things a normal child would do and she was pleased with his development along the lines of an average healthy enquiring mind.

One day Ashley was alone with granddad Eric in the back garden. They were looking at the flowers and Ashley said he could name most of them. His daddy had been teaching him the names when he helped with the weeding.

"I'm going to have a big garden of my own with lots and lots of bright colours," said Ashley to his granddad.

"And what is your favourite flower, Ashley?" asked Eric.

At this Ashley paused before answering.

"I think I like them all together," said Ashley "because they look so jolly with so many colours"

"You know Ashley," said Eric, "can you tell me something? Just when you go to catch one of the birds for Katy and the sky turns pink, does the grass in the garden also look pink?"

"Oh that too is a rosy colour," said Ashley, "but much darker."

"Can you make the sky any other colour Ashley?" asked granddad Eric.

"It only goes red," said Ashley, "and sometimes very dark red and then a bit foggy as well. And I can't hear anything at all then."

"Would you mind if we played a new game of catch the ball, Ashley?" said Eric, "I want to see how good you really are at catching the ball."

"Oh lovely" said Ashley, "how do we play it granddad?"

"Well," said Eric, "I am going to stand in the middle of the garden and throw the ball in any direction I like and you must try and catch it. You can use your talent of making the sky pink or even deep red and foggy if you wish. Do you want to play?"

Ashley said that would be fun and could they start right away.

It was a mild day with a gentle breeze from the west with plenty of cloud clusters drifting across a pale blue sky. The air was fresh and it seemed that they might have a fairly decent summer. Ashley was standing near the newly planted Flagpole-Cherry tree on one side of the garden.

Eric held the ball in the palm of his hand, called out "ready," then turned and threw the ball with some force in the direction away from Ashley. The next instant, according to Eric, there was Ashley smiling and holding the near football-sized ball in both hands just about ten feet away.

Granddad Eric clapped his hands and rushed up to Ashley, knelt down and gave him a big hug and a kiss. There were tears in his eyes.

"Granddad, why are you crying," said Ashley, "are you sad?"

"No my darling boy," said Eric, "I've got tears in my eyes because you have made me so proud and I love you so very much."

"Oh granddad," said Ashley, "I love you also. You are the best granddad ever. Can we play some more?"

"Of course" said Eric, "but first tell me what colour you made the sky when you caught the ball?"

"It was dark red and a little bit foggy all around the garden," said Ashley.

Eric made a mental note of this to report back to the family. He reckoned that it was probably the quickest that Ashley had had to move to date.

"Right," said Eric, "this time I'm going to throw the ball as before but I want to see how close to me you can catch it. Now stand back a little bit further."

Then with a quick "ready, steady and go" Eric turned and threw the ball straight at the flagpole cherry tree. Eric blinked and there was Ashley standing two feet from him holding the ball in two hands and smiling. This time Eric couldn't contain himself. He got all choked up and the tears flowed freely as he hugged his little wizard of a grandson, not quite seven years old.

"I think I've punctured the ball," said Ashley. "I had to jump up and my finger poked it as I caught it."

Sure enough, when Eric examined the ball which was of the thick rubberised type, it appeared to have a puncture mark as though a small spike had been driven through it! The ball felt quite deflated. Eric knelt down beside his grandson and checked both his hands for any injury.

"Which finger did you hurt Ashley?" asked Eric.

Ashley held up his left index finger. There was not a mark on it.

"Oh, it didn't get hurt granddad," said Ashley, "it just felt like it was going into something soft and squishy. Can we get another ball, I promise not to poke it again. I nearly didn't catch it because it was so foggy."

They came into the house then and Eric made a glass of blackcurrant squash for Ashley and a mug of tea for himself. They also had a biscuit from the biscuit tin. Lillian came downstairs with Katy after doing the ironing and went into the kitchen to make Katy a drink and herself a cup of coffee. Eric joined her there and they had a whispered conversation. Eric told her what had transpired in the garden with the ball game with Ashley. It only confirmed what they had already suspected. Somehow Ashley could make the pace of time go slower for everyone but himself. And the degree of that slowdown was dependent upon the urgency of action that he required. But there seemed to be a new factor in the running. And that was that the greater that Ashley caused time to slow down the less clearly was he able to see. Under these conditions a sort of dense fog seemed to surround everything making it difficult for Ashley to see clearly.

Eric said that there was another new development. Something they could never have imagined. He showed Lillian the ball and the puncture mark and explained how it had happened. He stressed that Ashley seemed to have poked his finger into the ball without any injury to himself. He repeated Ashley's description about the ball feeling soft and squishy when he poked it. The fact that Ashley could do this must mean that the relativity of the atom structure of Ashley and the ball must have been such under those time variation conditions as to give the finger a tremendous mechanical advantage in strength over the ball. Lillian thought that this difference in structural makeup must apply to all material in the slowed down world. Lillian stared out the kitchen window deep in thought. She wondered what it all meant for Ashley in the long term. There must be a purpose for him to have been given such a gift. She wondered how that other mother had felt so very long ago when learning that her son too had a special gift. Lillian wondered what the future had in store for Ashley as she wiped the wetness from around her eyes.

"There is another thing too," said Eric, bringing her back to the present from her deep thoughts. "I think that Ashley had to jump at least seven feet up in the air to catch the ball the last time I threw it. I'm six feet tall and I threw the ball with my arm raised high. Ashley caught the ball barely two feet from where I stood, so he must have had to leap that high to catch it."

"Well," said Lillian, "that would be a part of the extra mechanical advantage he would possess when he puts the world into a go-slow status. I think that in the light of all this we must consider making Ashley aware that he has a special power and that he must be careful how he uses it. I think we should test his strength over material objects to make him aware just what he can do. But I feel we ought to wait till he is a bit older. I want him to lead as normal a childhood for as long as possible before he is lost to us."

There were shallow tears in Lillian's eyes as she said this. She knew Alex would agree with her and she couldn't wait to tell him when he came home that evening. She must also ring Brenda in Wales and arrange a mini-conference sometime soon. Lillian expressed her concern to Eric that Ashley might unintentionally do an injury to someone or something when in his time-dilation status. What would happen if he tripped during his time-warp and bumped into someone? Broken bones could result. So far he had never injured any of the birds he had caught. They had obviously been caught while Ashley was in time dilation. He had also caught butterflies which had never suffered any ill effects either. But accidents could happen.

When Alex came home that night and when Lillian told him her fears he too had a melancholy look on his face. Of course they rang Brenda that same evening and agreed to meet the following weekend which was the August bank holiday. Eric said he'd like to come along too if there was room at Brenda's. There was, and so it was all arranged. He would drive down in his own car of course.

They didn't think it was worth telling Lillian's mum and dad in Aberdare as they hadn't shown much interest the last time they'd been told about Ashley. They had thought it was just a growing up phase and had said so quite assuredly.

"Don't worry," David had said, "it is just a growing up phase and will surely pass."

Lillian didn't like the way they had put forward their poltergeist 'disturbed youth' theory. She felt they wouldn't be any help and thought it was pointless worrying them unnecessarily.

When she informed Ashley and Katy that they were all going to Aunty Brenda's for the Bank Holiday weekend there were shouts of glee. They loved their aunty and uncle but more important they loved the seaside.

That night in bed Lillian wept bitterly and clung close to Alex.

"O Alex," she cried, "what is to become of our dear little boy? I do so fear for him."

Alex didn't say anything. He just hugged Lillian closer to him and let his own wetness mingle with hers.

The month of August had so far enjoyed lovely weather and the Bank Holiday weekend proved no different. Alex drove down with his little family on the Friday afternoon. He had taken half the day off work as was usual for the bank holidays. Brenda and Ron's B&B was having a low period and they were only half full. Eric would arrive in time for breakfast next morning. He liked to drive as early in the mornings as possible. He'd probably leave Birmingham about six in the morning if not a bit earlier. He would do the same when he left on Monday morning for the return journey. Lillian and Alex planned to stay till Tuesday afternoon.

Earlier in the year Ron had bought Brenda a puppy dog from the kennels near Cardigan. It was a King Charles Cavalier spaniel and was then four months old. He was brown and white being of the standard Blenheim colouring. They had named him Barclay, the same as the bank. He was a lovely playful chap, and both Katy and Ashley fell in love with him instantly. They simply had to take him out whenever they got the chance. Which was just as well as it gave the grownups a chance to talk.

Again it was Ron who suggested that they should get Ashley to undertake a series of tests. Ashley was nearly seven years old now but possessed the maturity of a much older child. Perhaps this was a part of the gift he had been given. Ashley seemed to possess a calmness of outlook about him that showed a maturity beyond his years.

Eric said that he had carried out those ball-throwing experiments with Ashley in the garden in Birmingham and had found him to be quite at ease about it all. In fact Ashley had gloried in showing off his skills and had wanted to continue with the game as he then saw it.

Ron said that they needed to know whether there might be other facets to Ashley's gift. Under his rosy pink conditions how high was he able to leap and how far? With the mechanical advantage that came with time dilation, did he possess extraordinary power to lift and move heavy objects and if so, how heavy? What about bending things? For instance, would he be able to bend a steel rod? To establish limits one would need to set up a series of experiments with steel rods of varying lengths and thickness. And then there was the fact of the punctured ball. Ron wondered if Ashley could similarly poke a hole in a plate made of wood, pottery or even metal.

Alex said he would need quite some time to prepare all these experiments. The weight lifting tasks could be arranged in a gym when no one else was around. Or perhaps they could borrow some weights from a friend who was into body building at home. He'd think of something. They would have to improvise as they went along depending on what they found Ashley capable of achieving.

Pieces of wood could be got from a timber yard and then prepared accordingly. Small steel plate sections and rods could be a problem. Alex said he had a boat builder friend who could probably help or point them in the right direction. However, all this would take a few months to arrange at the very least.

The other big concern was on how long Ashley could remain in the time dilation zone at any one time. Would he suffer adverse effects by remaining there too long? And was he continuously ageing within this slowed time zone while everything and everyone else was practically at a standstill?

The big question was whether to let Ashley in on the purpose of these tests or to pretend it was all just a game. Lillian said that she was all for letting Ashley know the true purpose behind the tests and so to getting his full participation. She was certain that Ashley must have already indulged his curiosity and experimented with his gifted powers at some stage. She knew that she herself would have done so if she had been in his situation. He was an intelligent boy and was bound to have guessed that he was different. It was up to them as a family to ensure that Ashley didn't abuse his gift and not use it for anything wicked or nasty. Perhaps some of the planned experiments might prove unnecessary if Ashley already knew the answers they sought. Lillian said she would take it upon herself to pursue this with Ashley over the next few months.

When Katy and Ashley returned from their walk with Barclay they found all the adults in the B&B's TV lounge enjoying a drink and chatting merrily. Katy said that they had let Barclay off the lead and had played on the doggie beach. She said that he didn't like the water at all and wouldn't jump in to fetch his ball after the first time. She thought he could do with a bath as he had sand all over his belly. Brenda said she would wait till he dried out before giving him a good brushing down. That should get him clean enough as he didn't like being bathed either.

Ashley looked at everyone in the room and then smiled up at his mum.

"You don't have to worry mum," he said, "I will never do anything to hurt anyone."

The grownups simply looked at one another surprised at Ashley's words. Could he read minds as well?

And so was to begin a period of discovery for Ashley, but more so for his family.

September arrived and Ashley turned seven. Although it was just a party for family members, Ashley was pleasantly surprised when grandma Beryl and granddad David turned up quite unexpectedly from Aberdare. They seemed anxious to be included in whatever was going on in Ashley's life. They had not only brought Ashley a present but had one for little Katy as well, just so she wouldn't feel left out. Lillian thought this was a very thoughtful gesture from her mum and dad. She felt sorry she hadn't included them in the last round of discussions at Brenda and Ron's last month. Unfortunately, both Brenda and Ron couldn't get away due to a full booking at the B&B, but they did phone and have a long chat with everyone, off peak of course.

With Beryl and David agreeing to stay the night, Lillian had the opportunity later that evening to bring them up to date with regard to what they planned for Ashley. It was David who suggested that they add one more test to the list.

"We're sorry about our response regarding Ashley last Easter," said David, "it was such a surprise for us and at the time we just couldn't understand any of it and said the first thing that came into our minds to try and ease your own fears. Of course we have had time to reflect and now believe you have a specially gifted boy. Can you find it in your heart to forgive an old man his prejudices and include us in all your future plans regarding our lovely grandson?"

"No problem David," said Alex, "you're in this whether you like it or not. We were going to fill you in with the latest after we had carried out our list of tests and knew exactly all that Ashley was capable of. We just didn't want to cause you any concern prematurely. I'm glad you are here now"

After being brought up to date David suggested again that perhaps they ought to add another item to the list of tests. And that was to see if Ashley possessed the power to move an object with his mind alone. Telekinesis as they called it. He had read about a Russian woman who had this power of causing a compass needle to deflect simply by concentrating her mind on it. The article also said she could cause a small circular object to roll on a table without touching it.

Lillian said that she suspected that Ashley was either very perceptive or that he could read their minds. Was he also telepathic? She told her parents that Ashley always seemed to anticipate the things they said. He was also a very understanding little boy.

It was then that Lillian had a tearful moment and again expressed her fears at what was to become of her dear little boy.

The living room door opened and Ashley walked in still dressed in his pyjamas and crawled onto his mother's lap.

"Don't worry mum," he said, "I'm never going to leave you. We are all going to live happily ever after just like in the books. You'll see."

And with that he gave everyone in the room another goodnight kiss and went back up to bed.

"Do you know," said Lillian wiping her eyes, "that's the first time he's called me mum. It was always mummy up until this moment. Our little Ashley is growing up ever so fast into the young man he is to become. And I wonder where this is taking him?"

Everyone kept their thoughts to themselves.

Eric said it was late and it was time he scooted off. Saying goodnight to all he asked Alex to see him out. They had a hurried conversation at the front door before Eric got into his car and drove off home.

Next morning at the breakfast table all was as it should be. Katy was chattering away as usual and getting prettier by the day. She had lovely curls that Lillian had to spend long moments on every day. Ashley seemed to have an increasingly mischievous expression. Sometimes Lillian could swear that he looked like a little pixie from one of his story books. They finished their bowl of cornflakes and glass of milk and were excused from the table. The adults continued with a hearty breakfast of eggs, bacon and toast followed by cups of tea or coffee. For some reason Alex preferred to drink only tea.

Of course, the conversation reverted to that of the evening before.

"Don't rush the boy," said David. "Let things move along gradually. I think you may get a lead from Ashley himself. I'm sure the boy understands far more than we give him credit for. If anything, let his mother be the one he confides in. Encourage him in that direction. At the same time Alex, do go ahead with the preparation of the tests you mentioned."

Lillian said it was all settled and that they should now talk of other matters. She felt that everything they said was somehow picked up by Ashley. Perhaps he possessed an additional form of communication unknown to them. Telepathy and mind reading were not impossible.

That evening they all went out for dinner to The Fox a local pub which did a fantastic carvery meal for just under a fiver per person. The Bonner family were regulars there and were recognised as soon as they joined the waiting queue. They gave their name and table requirement for six and were told it would be a twenty minute wait. So they went into the bar area and sat at a corner table while Alex and David went up to the bar to get the drinks.

Katy and Ashley loved coming here mainly because they could choose the vegetables they liked. The cheese cauliflower was one of Katy's favourites. Ashley liked the roasters and the parsnips.

The drinks had hardly arrived when the waitress called out their name.

"My, that was quick" said Beryl quite pleased, "it's hardly been ten minutes."

It was a lovely meal and the turkey was nice and juicy. As was the gammon and the roast beef. You could have a bit of each if you so wished, but Alex usually stayed with just turkey as did Lillian and the kids. David and Beryl went for a bit of each. No one had room for a pudding afterwards though Ashley asked if Katy and he could have some ice cream from the freezer when they got back home.

"What a good idea," said David, "and we can also have some of your special home brewed coffee nice and strong. The stuff they serve at restaurants and pubs is not always to my liking."

So the day ended on a very pleasant and sated note. All in all Lillian reckoned that it had been a very pleasant weekend. She was sure her parents had enjoyed their visit after so long a time away. Both had got on famously with Katy, and Lillian saw that they were quite taken with her. They were bound to want to visit more often now, if only to see their lovely granddaughter. And of course to see how things went with Ashley their gifted grandson.

They left for Aberdare after another good breakfast next morning. There were hugs and kisses all around and lots of arm waving as Beryl and David reversed down the drive and drove away. They promised to ring as soon as they arrived back home.

In another two weeks it would be Ashley's birthday and Lillian had arranged a swim party for Ashley and some of his school friends at the Crystal Leisure Centre in Stourbridge. Ashley had chosen this venue because it had a wave making machine. It also had a beach style shallow end for toddlers, a flowing water channel and two water chutes, not forgetting the restaurant for their little party afterwards. Ashley was very well liked in school and had invited all the boys in his class. He was still a bit iffy about girls, as all young boys are at that age. His birthday on September 8th actually fell on a Friday so the party was arranged for the next day. It would also be the end of the first week back at school after the summer holidays.

The day turned out nice and sunny and Ashley was quite excited and looking forward to his party. It was a brilliant success and all fifteen children had a great time. Katy brought along her friend Rehana who lived two doors away and was a frequent visitor. Afterwards they had refreshments in the restaurant and were all given party bags of goodies to take home. Many of the parents had stayed and joined in the swim. All thanked Lillian for a wonderful time and said how much they enjoyed being there. Some had never been there before and said they were glad they had found out about it and would be returning often with their own kids in the future.

That night Ashley thanked his mum again for his party and said he had something to show her the next day. This time he did call her mummy. He was not so grown up after all.

Katy would start school in the January term as she would be five at Easter. Though there was the option of sending her to the school on one day each week, Lillian had decided against this as she felt it should be all or nothing. She had strong views regarding the educational establishment but kept these to herself. Her policy was one of 'the-less-said-the-better'.

The next morning Lillian and the children went to church as usual for the Sunday morning service. On the stroll home through Rookery Park, Ashley said he had something to show his mum. He led them to a large oak tree near the centre of the park and showed them a hole in the trunk about four feet from the ground.

"It's a hole for birds or squirrels to nest in," said Ashley, "but they haven't used it yet. Do you think it needs to be higher up mum? I made it last year."

Lillian looked at Katy and asked her if she would like to play on the swings for a bit. Katy was off like a shot before Lillian had finished her sentence.

"Did you make this hole yourself?" said Lillian to Ashley.

"O yes mum," said Ashley, "I made this one and some more in those other trees as well for the birds."

"And how did you manage that my son" asked Lillian.

"When I make the sky go pink the tree gets very soft and I just put my hand into it like it was play dough," said Ashley. "Do you want me to show you by making a new hole?"

"Yes please," said Lillian looking over her shoulder to see that Katy was playing happily on the swings.

Ashley walked to another tree nearby and said "Will this one be alright, mummy?"

Lillian said it was okay and the next thing she saw Ashley with his hand buried up to his wrist in the bark of the tree.

"See mum," he said, "I pushed my hand straight in when the tree was soft. Now my hand is stuck. But I can easily make the hole bigger again any time I want. See."

And the next thing his hand was out and the hole looked much wider. When Lillian looked into the hole she could see that there was quite a large pocket inside all smooth and rounded.

"When I put my hand inside", said Ashley, "I move it round and round slowly to make a nice big home for the birds to nest. I then take my hand out and make the entry hole smaller by pushing the edges inwards a little. The tree feels just like it was made of play dough".

"That's wonderful dear." said Lillian, "but I don't think you should make many more as it could hurt the tree. Also, little children like Katy could put their hand into the hole and get stuck. But I'm glad you showed me how you did it. I must tell daddy all this too. You can make a nest for the birds in the tree in our back garden but it needs to be higher up for the birds to feel safe. We will have to ask daddy to put the ladder against the tree for you to reach up higher."

Ashley then went on to explain how careful he had to be when touching things in the pink zone as he could easily damage them. He said he had to be especially careful with regard to living things. When he caught a bird he made sure he held it ever so gently. One little squeeze and it could suffer a broken bone or two. And to further his argument he took his mum to the kiddies play area. He went right up to the railings perimeter and pointed out some dent marks. There were quite a few of these at intervals on the top metal strip.

"See mummy, I did these when I was little, years ago when you used to bring me here to play," said Ashley.

Lillian had a flash back of her little toddler running around among the various slides and frames. And how he would often just walk or run alongside the inside of the play area running his hand across the railings.

Now she walked with Ashley looking carefully. There were numerous little dents and impressions in the railings. Some were in the vertical bars and others in the thicker top rail. Lillian stopped to look at something that was different. When she looked closely there was definitely a set of teeth impressions in the top rail. She ran her fingers over the marks and asked Ashley if they were his also. They could have been made by someone hammering a steel chisel on it just there.

"O yes, those are mine," said Ashley, "I think I must have been three or four years old then. I nearly bit through it then when the sky suddenly went rosy pink for an instant all of its own. I think someone else made it pink. Do you think there are other boys who can also do things like me mummy?"

"I don't really know. Perhaps there are. I only hope they are as nice as you and as careful," said Lillian.

When they got back home again Alex asked if they'd had a nice time. Lillian went into the kitchen to make a cup of tea and he put his arm around her.

"What is it dear, you have a funny look, have you seen a ghost?"

"No dear," said Lillian "but our son has just been showing me things in the park that he did years ago". And with that opening she went on to tell Alex what Ashley had shown her. Also of Ashley's question whether there might be someone else with a similar gift or power.

Katy was playing in her room. They could hear her thumping about upstairs. The very next moment Ashley was standing beside them with a big smile on his face.

"Mummy I think there is someone else. I can hear someone's thoughts quite clearly when I am in the pink zone. A voice has just been trying to tell me that I have to learn about lots of things before I am ready. But I don't understand what it is that I'm to be ready for," said Ashley.

Then to his dad he said. "You can do all those tests on me, dad. I think I know a lot of what I can do but I feel there must be much more. I'll tell you as I find out new things. There's this thing too. When I think about something new, the answer comes to me of its own accord quite soon. It's as if someone can read my thoughts and just gives me the answer."

And so it was that Ashley had long conversations with his mum and dad when Katy was not around. One by one he began to list and give details of all the things that he could do.

And they were most enlightening. Especially as they came from the lips of a precocious four foot tall seven years old boy.

CHAPTER 2

Tests

1989

Although it took dad nearly a year to prepare for the major parts of the testing, there was a lot that I could show him at home. The good thing for me was that whenever I was in the 'pink' zone no one could see or hear me. For that matter neither could I hear any sounds either. It was an absolute silence. Yet it was at this time that I could recognise thoughts that were definitely not my own.

I was learning about a lot of things quite suddenly. It was as though someone was tutoring me on a telepathic wavelength. I was beginning to know things that I had not seen or experienced personally in my seven and a half years. But I was still quite exhilarated about the whole scenario. I could pick up a book and know the meaning of words I had not read before. I found I was an extremely quick learner. Let me give just one example.

It was early one morning. Mom and dad were still asleep. So was Katy. I was sitting in the front porch watching the sky blossoming as the dawn swelled to light. I did this often. And then the tip of the sun peeped over those far away rooftops. And I started to wonder what the sun was made of and what made it move over the land. I then heard these telepathic thoughts rushing through my head and almost immediately I understood everything about the sun, the moon, the planets, the stars, the galaxies, the vastness of space, the size of our universe and all that was beyond. It was nice to know that the earth was round and not flat as I had thought. No chance of falling off it.

I was also beginning to get some fun out of it. I suppose you could call it a bit of harmless fun in that I would play tricks on the other kids at school. Like at dinner times in the mess hall. When the boy sitting next to me at the long table would pick up his drink for a sip I would go 'pink' and simply take the juice carton out of his hand and put it back on the table. You should have seen the look of surprise on his face when he looked at his empty hand.

Katy started school in January 1989 in the reception class. Katy was four but would be five years old at Easter, so was classed as 'a rising five'. She was ever so keen to begin although she didn't start school till the third week of the term. But she would be ready every morning just the same and come with mom and me to the school as though she were about to start lessons. When she did start she came home that first day full of stories of her teacher Mrs Hunt. I told Katy that Mrs Hunt used to be my reception teacher as well when I first started school two years ago. That was before she got married and changed her name from Miss Burns to Mrs Hunt. I didn't see Katy at all in school as we had different areas. The reception children were not allowed to mix with the rest of the school in their first term. But I did wait for Katy at the end of school if mom wasn't already there.

There are two boys who are my best friends. They are Rory Jacobs and David Matthews. Rory lives in the next road to mine and we are often in each other's houses over weekends. He has two other brothers but they are much too young to join in our play. His mum is nice. She always makes me feel special. I think her name is Margaret but I've only ever heard Rory's dad call her Maggie. Rory's dad doesn't talk to us kids much apart from a welcoming hello. He doesn't seem to mind us playing near him if we don't make too much noise, except when the football is on the telly. Then he tells us to go and play upstairs or if it is nice to play out in the back.

David lives quite far from us but gets to school about a half an hour early. I think both his mum and dad have to get to work in the morning so one of them drops him off on their way. David has a talent for drawing. He can draw horses brilliantly and I have one of his pencil drawings on my bedroom wall at home. He can also draw comic book stories which he is very good at and which makes him quite popular at school. Mr Briars the head teacher says that he wished David was as good at his school work as he was at art. David also likes to draw portraits of people. I've seen one of 'Bristles' as we call our head teacher and it really was quite good. Except that David had given him a longer nose and slightly bigger ears. He did look funny. David got into real trouble when Bristles accidentally found out from another member of staff. I think the staff looked kindly on David from then on. We were in the same Year Two class and our teacher was Miss Sales. She had a good sense of humour and didn't mind us singing the Rod Stewart song 'I am sailing' when she was on playground duty.

"Really Miss Sales you must put a stop to this behaviour" said Bristles on many occasions. But she always said it was good clean fun, and besides didn't he think the children sang it quite well.

David really did have trouble with his class work and both Rory and I would help him as much as we could. I tried not to use my 'pink' talent in school if I could help it. But conditions were to change.

There was a stairs monitor who was a bit of a bossy boots. He was Jimmy Marshall, a boy much bigger than us and in Year Three. The problem was that he had a friend called Mike Marrs who was just like him and they always seemed to roam about together. Mike the Martian would do whatever 'General' Marshall told him even though he was the elder by a year.

For some reason the 'General' would pick on David whenever he got the chance. Or pass remarks to taunt him.

"Hey Picasso" he would call out so everyone could hear, "done any more portraits of staff recently or are you too scared?"

David didn't ever respond. He would just looked down and walk on.

One day as David was returning to PE class and approached to go up the stairs he was met by the 'General' at the bottom of the stairs. There were no other kids around and the 'General' demanded to know where David was going. He had no right to ask this so David ignored him as usual and continued towards the first step. Jimmy Marshall was a bully and didn't like to be ignored so he put his foot out and tripped David so that he had to grab the stair rail to stop his fall. In the process he dropped all his books. Jimmy Marshall just laughed and walked away. David was very angry but didn't tell anyone. But I knew all about it because I could read David's mind. I decided to play a prank on the bully. I had an idea.

And so it was that Jimmy Marshall began to look ill.

Over the next few days at school I would go into 'pink' mode and very gently place a spot on Jimmy's face with a red permanent Magic-Marker Felt pen. The first day at playtime I put a tiny red spot on his forehead just above his left eyebrow. Jimmy didn't notice it at all nor did anyone else think anything of this one little spot. The next day I put two bigger spots on the back of his neck. This time some of the other children mentioned it to him but he didn't believe them. By the end of the week he had a spot on the tip of his nose, one on his chin, two on his forehead, one beside each ear and two on the back of his neck.

Now Jimmy began to get a bit worried. He really thought something was the matter with him. The following week the marks had faded but I soon marked them up again and added a few more. The teacher sent him to report to the school nurse. Nurse Angela Stephens was fairly new to the school and quite young and pretty. She was very friendly and we all liked her. Some of the bigger boys had a sort of a crush on her and were always finding an excuse to visit the sick room.

When Jimmy walked in and showed her the spots she asked when they first showed up and if he had any on other parts of his body. Jimmy said he wasn't sure so he was asked to remove his shirt. He did so while she had her back turned and this was when I went 'pink' again and covered his chest and back with about twenty or so spots. I was back outside the door and could see everything. It was a simple job as both seemed to be frozen in time, almost anyway. No one ever saw me at these times.

Jimmy was in trouble. Nurse Angela saw the spots on Jimmy's back and decided to clean one with a sterile wipe soaked in surgical spirit. When the spot wiped clean she immediately realised that the spots had been put there by a marker pen and assumed that this was a ruse by Jimmy just to come in to see her. She was not at all amused by it. And so Jimmy was reported to headmaster 'Bristles'. The outcome was that Jimmy was no longer stair monitor and was given detention for a whole week.

I did feel a bit sorry for him especially since no one seemed to care, not even his friend Mike. And he did seem to have lost some of his bullying air. So I asked David to draw a fun portrait of him with all his spots. It was a very good drawing and Rory, David and I went over to him while he was at detention one evening and presented it to him. We were not sure what his reaction would be but were pleasantly surprised when he gave a sheepish smile and said thanks to David.

"Thanks Picasso, I mean David" he said. "It's really very good. My mum will like it. I'll put it on my bedroom wall. Also, I'm sorry for being mean to you."

"That's all right" said David, "see you around General, I mean Jimmy."

Gradually over the next few weeks and months there seemed to be a friendship developing between David and Jimmy. He gradually came to be liked by quite a few of the other children in his year group. In fact I took a distant sort of liking to him myself.

To this day Jimmy is puzzled over those red spots and of course no one ever told him, nor could they.

I still find it surprising that I can move around in the 'pink' zone while everything else is at a near standstill. I know that I must be very careful not to be rough with anything I touch as this could be disastrous. But I do like to watch the birds in their very slow motion flight. It looks so majestic in its execution. I also know that no one can see or hear me then. When I had placed each spot on Jimmy it was as though I were marking up a life-sized sculpture in a museum.

14

When I first encountered the 'pink' zone it seemed to happen on its own. I wondered then why it was so quiet and everything was so still. And yet I could move quite normally. At first the 'pink' zone would switch on and off at random. But once I realised it had something to do with me I found I could will it on and off as I wished. I found that most materials were like soft putty for me in the pink zone. I then had to be careful how I touched things. If I picked up a pen and held it too tight, I found that it acquired a dent in it as though it had been squeezed by a pair of very hot pliers. The railings in the park play area were one area where I used to experiment by squeezing them out of shape. I could also bend the railings and then straighten them back again. Of course none of this was possible when I was in the normal everyday blue sky status. I did try to bend the railing once in normal mode but found I couldn't. Not even the least little bit. I must have been about four years old then.

It was by accident that I began to make holes in trees. I was picking at the bark of a tree as kids often do when suddenly the 'pink' zone turned on. I found that my finger seemed to be pushing on something like putty so I forced it in. When I pulled it out there was a neat little hole in the tree trunk. So I simply enlarged it a little so birds could nest in it. I was quite pleased with myself. And so I began making other larger holes in nearly every tree in the park. When I showed these to my mom she was impressed but suggested that the birds may have liked them a bit higher up the trees.

Back home in our own garden I would catch the birds that came to our 'fat ball' feeder. I would wait till a bird was pecking away, then go 'pink' and simply walk up to the feeder, reach up and gently take hold of the bird. Katy loved me to do this and often told me which one to catch. I think the Robin was her favourite as she would keep it in our cage the longest. We seldom kept them for more than an hour or two at a time. Mum made sure of this. The same birds came to the feeder so they got used to my gentle treatment, especially since there was always plenty of bird seed in the cage.

Going into 'pink' mode was simply a thought process for me. I just had to desire it and it would happen. I don't know how but it did. The same was the case when I wanted to get back to normal again. There were different levels of 'pink' and these would depend upon how urgent my desire was for slowing things down. The colour scale went towards 'rosy pink' and darker, but then my vision would begin to blur and the world became more and more foggy. It would appear as though the land was covered in a dense fog. I now try to avoid entering this zone and 'jump' back the moment I notice it getting slightly misty. However I did get the impression that when I entered this dense foggy zone there was someone or something not very far away trying to communicate.

I did tests for dad on several occasions and he made notes in his little pocket diary. I lifted some very heavy gym style weights. I found that I had to go into the foggy zone to lift the heaviest ones.

The one I couldn't lift was so heavy that I left my hand impression on the lifting bar. I think if I had tried harder the bar would have got squashed thin instead. Dad said that I had gone beyond what he had expected.

Another test was to see how far I could throw a cricket ball. This test showed some unexpected results. We were in the park and Dad gave me the ball and asked me to throw it as far as I could. I went into the pink mode and threw with all my strength. But the moment the ball left my hand it slowed and became suspended in mid air just like everything else. When I came back to normal time the ball flew through the air with a hissing noise and fell at the other end of the park. Then dad asked me to just throw the ball without going pink. Again I threw it with all my strength but this time it didn't go very far at all. I was rather disappointed. Dad made notes in his diary.

Dad never made me do more than one or two tests each month. The one I liked took place at our kitchen table. It still has the burn mark upon it. We were into the summer holidays again and dad came home from work one evening with a rusty piece of round metal bar. It was two inches in diameter and about six inches long and felt quite heavy. Dad asked me to have a go and see what I could do with it. I picked it up and made funny faces pretending to use all my little boy strength to bend it. We had a good laugh and then dad said to try it in the pink zone. I did and bent it double quite easily. When I put it back on the table again it felt quite warm. Dad picked it up and looked at it from all sides. He said it had got warm from the bending action. Then dad asked me to see what else I could do with it. I told him that it would feel like putty in the pink zone so he asked me to make something, anything. So I went pink and squeezed and pulled and pinched the piece till I had made a crude four legged animal with pointed ears and a stubby tail. It had felt like thick hard moulding clay. I came out of pink and put it on the table. When dad went to pick it up he dropped it again and said it was too hot to hold. It hadn't been hot for me before but when I felt it now it certainly was too hot for me too. He quickly got some oven gloves and put it on a hotplate. Too late, there was a burn mark on our lovely Ikea table surface. When mom saw it she said it was an event that would be forever 'burned' in her memory. We all laughed at that.

It was the August Bank holiday weekend and we were by the sea at Aberporth and staying with Aunty Brenda and Uncle Ron. It was after we had finished dinner and were sitting around the dining table that Uncle Ron asked me if I would play a special game of cards. Uncle Ron had already taught me to play rummy, sly donkey and beggar-my-neighbour so I thought we were to play one of those.

15

"This is a different game" said Uncle Ron, "it's to do with your gift. We want to see if you can correctly guess the cards as I deal them out."

So he dealt one card face down to each person at the table; to mom, dad, Katy, Aunty Brenda and granddad Eric, and one for himself. Katy said she didn't know the game so could she leave the table and go play with Barclay instead, which was just as well as I found it hard to explain things to her.

I looked at the back of each card in turn and my mind was a total blank. There was no way I knew what any of the cards were. I said so to Uncle Ron.

Then he picked up his card, looked at it and asked me if I could now tell him his card. I told him right away that it was the ten of Hearts. And I was right. He asked me how I knew.

"Because you told me Uncle Ron," I said. "The moment you saw your card you told me what it was telepathically even though you didn't know you were doing so."

I did the same with each of the other cards. And I was right every time.

I then asked if I could do some tests of my own. I wanted to reverse the process and see if I could tell them telepathically what the card was that I was looking at. I said I would first like to try this with one of them at a time. Dad was to be first. I picked the first card, a Jack of Spades. There was a moment of silence before Uncle Ron named the card correctly.

Dad said that all he got was that it was a dark coloured card, nothing more. Uncle Ron said he had got it straight away but waited to see if anyone else had as well. I then said I would do it again and for anyone to guess. And this time I said the name of the card in my head as I looked at it.

"Three of Hearts," they all shouted out together and they were right. I told them what I had done and dad suggested that we do this a few more times before trying a telepathic conversation. Mom said that it seemed as though I had spoken to her quite normally. I said 'I love you mom' in my head and mom smiled back and said, "I love you too son," which meant mom had heard me loud and clear.

"I heard that too son," said dad and this was repeated by Aunty Brenda and Uncle Ron.

We played a few more rounds of the card guessing game and I got it right every time.

And now I was ready for the next test. Dad suggested that I communicate with only one person at a time, even though the others may be able to listen in. He suggested I begin with mom.

'I love it here at Aunty Brenda's, it is so fresh and bright,' I said in my thoughts.

'I love it here too,' came back mom's thought response loud and clear.

'Can we have a dog like Barclay mom?'

'That might be possible son, but who will walk it, groom it, feed it and be responsible for it.'

'I will mom. I'm really much more grown up than my eight years.'

'We shall have to talk it over with daddy and Katy first. There are a lot of things to consider. Perhaps we can get one in a year or two.'

'I was only making conversation mom. I wonder if dad, aunt and uncle have also heard our chat'

I could see them nodding with smiles on their faces.

"I could hear your thoughts son," said dad, "but not anything from your mom. Did mom say you could have a dog?"

"No dad," I said, "mom said we would all have to talk it over as there were a lot of things to consider first."

So we had established that I could communicate telepathically with each of them and them with me, but not with each other. Actually, they were not strictly communicating with me in a telepathic manner, but rather it was my ability to read their minds that allowed us to have such a conversation. However, I could not confine my telepathic transmissions to any particular person. So my side of the conversation with mom was anything but private.

It was Uncle Ron who made the next suggestion. And that was for us to establish the distances over which it was possible to hold a telepathic conversation. Perhaps they might be able to receive my thoughts but could I receive theirs? After all there would be thousands of other working minds in between.

It was suggested by mom that we call it a day and have a cup of tea before lunch after which we could all go for a nice long walk on the coastal path. It was only then that I noticed that I had a dull ache in my head behind my left eye. I said as much telepathically and all said that I should have a lie down and rest. Dad seemed to think that telepathy might actually cause a strain on the brain's normal functioning. Or perhaps it was a process that I had not got used to and might therefore need to go through a 'learning' and 'practice' stage. In fact it took me nearly three years to really master the technique without the after-effects. Dad was so right.

Mom then said that her parents had wanted to be kept up to date with regard to my progress and she ought to ring them to let them know about today's developments. All agreed so Aunt Brenda rang granddad's home in Aberdare and granddad David answered. He said they were all fine and how nice of her to call. Aunt Brenda said what the call was about and that they were all here at the B&B. She then handed the phone to mom who asked if the extension upstairs was still working. Grandma Beryl answered that she was already upstairs on the other phone. Then mom gave a detailed rundown of my progress up to the card games of a few moments ago. Mom stressed that they should not discuss this with anyone ever. It must remain a family secret. Mom said she would ring them every month to give a progress report whether there were any new developments or not. Beryl thanked her daughter and then asked to speak to me.

'My dear, dear Ashley,' she said with genuine affection. 'I'm so proud to be your grandma. I think you are very special and I shall pray to God to guide you so that whatever you are meant to do that you do it wisely and justly. We shall try to come up and see you all in the next holidays and then we can talk a lot more.'

I thanked her and said it would be nice to see her again. After I said goodbye I passed the phone back to mom. I thought about Katy being the only one in the family not in the know but I realised she was much too young to be trusted with such a secret. Later when I mentioned this thought to mom and dad they agreed that the time was not yet right for Katy to know.

When we went into the lounge we were met by a lovely sight. Katy was sitting on the rocker and Barclay was fast asleep on her lap. He was on his back with legs up in the air and long fluffy ears dangling downwards. I think he also had a smile on his face as did Katy. Mom couldn't resist grabbing her digital camera and taking a picture. But the flash woke Barclay and up he jumped and ran around us wagging his tail. I thought with wonder at all the love bottled up inside something so small. And he never seemed to run out of it either. His affection was always like a gushing fountain. And he was ever ready to lick you to death.

After I had about an hours rest in the room that I shared with Katy, Aunty Brenda treated us to a lovely chicken salad lunch with strawberry ice cream for afters. She even let us kids put squirty cream on top of ours with a good squeeze of chocolate sauce. The grownups all had coffee in the lounge afterwards and they decided to wait another hour before venturing out for our planned walk on the coastal path.

All through lunch I found I could block my mind to everyone's thoughts quite easily and also to prevent my thinking from reaching out to them. I suppose I was able to control my telepathic transmissions in the same way that I could control my entry into and out of the 'pink' zone.

Aunty Brenda didn't come on the walk with us as she said she had some guests arriving that evening and wanted be around to welcome them, even though she had two of her staff on reception. Of course Katy made sure that Barclay came too. It was a lovely day and we just strolled along, sometimes in single file. Barclay was very good and tended to stay quite close to us. Even when he did get a bit ahead he would stop every once in a while and look back to see where we were. His tail was like a white flag waving to and fro as he trotted ahead.

We must have walked for about an hour before we came to the lane up to Tresaith village. Uncle Ron suggested we take this to get to the Ffordd Tresaith road that would take us back on a direct route to Aberporth just over a mile away. There was a big black cloud partway over the sky and it looked ever so threatening. But dad said that the forecast had said it would remain dry all day. Mom said that didn't mean a thing as the weathermen often got it wrong. Besides this was just one big black cloud on its own and couldn't be part of any weatherman's predictions. So we made the walk back a little bit faster than a stroll. Katy and I kept looking over our shoulders to see the progress of the cloud. It was definitely getting closer. It was exciting to see if it would catch us up before we got home. We came to an old church halfway back to Aberporth and dad said he wanted to have a look around it. Dad had a thing about churches and was hoping to write a book about all the different churches in England. The church was locked so we wandered around looking at the dates on the gravestones in the churchyard. That was when it suddenly started to pour down with rain. We all ran towards the Lych-gate amid screams of laughter and stood underneath this shelter till the black cloud passed us by. Barclay of course got soaked in the rain and when he came into the shelter he sprayed us all when he shook himself dry; to the accompaniment of a scream and a sideways jump from mom. He just looked up at her and wagged his tail as if to say 'didn't you enjoy that?'

Until a moment before I had no idea what a Lych-gate was. But suddenly the whole history unfolded in my mind. I now knew the purpose of it and when it was first made a part of the churchyard. I even knew that the longest wait by a funeral coffin in the covered gate had been three and a half hours; the vicar having apparently forgotten his schedule. I had got used to information and knowledge suddenly turning up in my memory but I was still at a loss as to how it happened.

The cloud soon passed and the sun was out again in full force. Since the long grass in the churchyard was wet dad said he'd seen enough and that we should head back via the main road till we got home. The rain had made the air smell lovely and fresh and even the birds seem to say so with their singing. We got to the road leading off to the right just before Aberporth village. The road sign said Heol Y Graig and it led towards the coast and directly to Uncle Ron's B&B. It took us just ten minutes to get there. Aunty Brenda asked if we had got caught in the rain and to come and have a nice hot cup of tea. Katy and I had hot chocolate instead. Aunty Brenda knew how I liked my chocolate so she put an extra half spoon of sugar for me.

That evening two new guests arrived. They didn't speak English very well and kept reverting to their own language. Aunty Brenda had to ask Uncle Ron to deal with them. Apparently, they had been sent to Aberporth by the London immigration service because they were plumbers from Poland and wanted to set up their own business in a small coastal town. They had been given hotel vouchers to cover a two week period only. They had given these to Uncle Ron who had confirmed that they were redeemable. A new development in my life was about to unfold.

That evening when mom, dad, Katy and I came down for our evening meal, we happened to be seated at a table next to the one with the two Polish gentlemen. Katy had her back to them as did I sitting next to her at a table for four. There was a general buzz of conversation in the dining room which must have held about twenty people, since the B&B was now full. Dad was telling us that we should begin packing our things for our trip home tomorrow. Just then one of the Polish gentlemen laughed and said something in Polish. I was dumbstruck for all of an instant. I understood every word he had said. Not only that but I also knew their names and the town they had come from in Poland. They had lived in Radom. Jan Bogdan had lived with his parents on Mikoiaja Reja and Sarul Kwaitkowski had lived in a flat on Gabriela Narutowicza. They had both gone to the same school on Struga a couple of miles from where they lived. They had both been apprenticed to a large factory making a variety of components for industrial machines. Having completed their five year training Jan had been kept on as a plumber in their maintenance section but Sarul had to find work elsewhere. In this he was unsuccessful and instead had advertised his services as a plumber in the local paper. He knew he was good at his job and soon the odd job requests came his way. He and Jan remained good friends but he was having difficulty keeping up with the rent on his flat, not having a regular income. Jan's parents had a spare small bedroom and Sarul was persuaded to move in there and pay what he could when he could. The advantage in this was that there was a phone in the house and Jan's father Janek let him quote the number in his weekly newspaper advertisements. The job requests became more frequent and on many occasions Jan had to go to jobs that Sarul was unable to attend. It became clear to Jan that the business was taking off and he could earn better money as a self employed plumber. So he gave up his job at the factory to work full time with Sarul.

When Poland joined the European Common Market Jan's father saw an advert for plumbers to work in England. Since none of them spoke any English, they didn't give it any consideration at all. However, one day they did a job in one of their old Struga school teacher's houses who still taught there. He was a short stocky man with a balding head and a very bushy but neatly cropped beard. What he lacked on top he made up for around his mouth. He taught English as a second language. He told them that they could earn ten times what he had paid them for the same job if they were in England. But they would have to learn to speak, read and write English. And he could teach them enough to get by in one year of tuition, for a fee of course.

Mr Barculek was a good teacher and had a few other pupils as well. He grouped them together on three nights a week and after a month insisted that no Polish be spoken at the class without first asking permission. At the end of each session he would tell them a joke in English, some of them quite rude. He said it was important to develop an English sense of humour if they wanted to get on in England. Jan was the quicker learner of the two but soon they were both reading children's story books borrowed from Mr Barculek and from their local library.

Jan's father was proud of his son and listened with pride when Jan and Sarul spoke to one another in English, even though he couldn't understand a word.

The plumbing business had its ups and downs but things came to a head when Jan's father was made redundant from his factory work due to cutbacks following a new quota system; from a new EEC Directive on selective output. Jan was a dutiful son and knew his responsibilities towards his family. And so it was decided after much consideration that Jan travel to England and set up business there. Sarul said he would also go as the two of them would have a better chance of making a success of setting up their plumbing business.

And so here they were sitting with their backs to me in the dining room at Uncle Ron's B&B in Aberporth. They had arrived two weeks ago on a Dover ferry and had been accepted into the country as EEC immigrant workers. They had signed on with the local unemployment office and been given National Insurance numbers and Benefits Claim forms. The hotel voucher scheme was a recent innovation at the unemployment office to get people out into the country and away from London.

How I got to know all of this I do not know but I felt exhilarated that I did. I had knowledge of Poland and Polish ways as though I had lived there all my life. My goodness, I suddenly felt as if I was a Polish gentleman in my forties. I felt I had travelled around Poland quite a bit and lived for a while in Warsaw. But I was a boy of eight years who had never actually travelled outside England. I knew that as soon as I thought of something new a whole raft of information entered my brain, like the Lych-gate history. But to suddenly acquire a whole new language and cultural understanding with no loss of my own was awesome. I had to tell dad and mom of this new development.

Dad was astonished when I told him and wondered what else I might be capable of. I asked if I should talk to the two Polish men and let them know that I could speak their language. Dad thought it could do no harm to just make conversation but that was as far as it should go. It would make matters too complicated for them to understand if I were to let on that I knew their whole life's background. Dad would ask Uncle Ron to have a word with them about me practicing my Polish on them and so introduce me to them later on this evening.

And so it was that Uncle Ron took me in tow into the music lounge after dinner. The two Polish men came in shortly after and went to the bar and ordered themselves a beer. They stood at the bar for a while and looking round the room spotted Uncle Ron and nodded to him. Uncle Ron signalled for them to come and join us at our square of settees and they smiled and came over.

'Hello gentleman,' said Uncle Ron, 'I hope you are enjoying your stay with us. Please let me introduce you to my nephew Ashley. He heard you talking in the dining room and would like to practice his Polish and wondered if you wouldn't mind talking to him for a while. He may look young but is very mature for his eight years.'

Jan smiled and said that they would be delighted. Then they spoke to me in Polish slowly and with a lot of pronunciation asking for how long I had been learning the language. I told him that when I was in Radom as a five year old on holiday I found that I had a natural love and affinity for the Polish language. And since I have a very good memory I had learned to speak it with the friends I made there inside a month. I even spent a few weeks at the Struga School and had gotten friendly with one of the teachers there. I think his name was Barculek.

'Tell me,' said Jan in Polish 'was he short and fat and bald?'

'O yes,' I said laughing a bit, 'and the problem I had at first was that I never saw his lips move because of his thick beard. I always like to look at peoples lips when they are talking. But he had a good sense of humour and I liked him.'

We all laughed at that and they told me that Mr Barculek had in fact been their own private English language tutor and if it hadn't been for him they would not be here today.

Uncle Ron said that as we seemed to be getting on famously and since he couldn't understand a word we were saying he'd leave us to talk as he had some accounts work to get on with.

From then on we spoke in Polish as though we were all natives. Sarul also joined in and asked where I had stayed. I said it was a hotel on Mikoiaja Reja not far from the crossroads. They asked me again how old I was and were astonished when I told them. They thought the English were very clever indeed. I just said that some of us were more than others. They asked if I could speak any other foreign languages and I said so far only Polish but that I knew I could learn another quite quickly when I got the chance. Every language had a key I told them and once I had found that key code I could learn the language easily. Of course this was just a lie to cover up my real abilities.

We talked about England and how they hoped to set up a plumbing business in a small town where there was less competition. I said I'd ask my Uncle to give them advice. They were a bit saddened when I said I had to go home to Birmingham with my mother and father the next day. We were to leave after lunch as it was a three hour drive but we could talk again in the morning.

I saw mom come into the room obviously looking for me. I stood up and said my mother was here and when mom came over I introduced her to Jan and Sarul. They said hello in Polish but I told them mom didn't speak it at all and they said 'how do you do' in their most polite English. Mom said how nice it was to meet them but she must take me off as it was after ten o'clock and past my bedtime. They told my mom that I was like one of their own and they wished I could stay on a few days longer. Mom said that I couldn't miss school on Monday but that they could visit us in Birmingham any weekend they wished.

'Perhaps when we begin our business we will have a little holiday in Birmingham,' said Jan.

We then shook hands, said goodnight and we left with smiles all around.

Next morning when we came down to breakfast Jan and Sarul were already nearly finished. They both stood up and wished us a very good morning in both Polish and in English. They asked if I could please have breakfast at their table so they could continue our conversation from the night before. Dad said it was okay by him if I didn't mind. I introduced my dad to them by name and they came and shook his hand vigorously and said how pleased they were to meet the father of Ashley.

Since I am not a big eater and have only cereal and toast for breakfast we had plenty of time to chat. They gave me their life history, which I already knew. I then nearly let slip about Jan's father.

'If your name is Jan is your father's name Janek?' I asked, 'I hope he is well.'

A moments silence then Jan asked me if I knew his father.

No, I said, I just guessed that he might be named after his father since Jan was quite a common name not only in Poland but in other EEC countries as well. Yes, Jan said, so it was, and yes, his father was well but now out of work. Jan had come to England so as to be able to send money home to him in Radom to help out. Therefore it was essential they advertise their plumbing skills. They said they were very good at their job but needed to buy or rent the tools and accessories they needed for their trade.

Later when I had said goodbye to them I said I would ask my Uncle Ron to talk with them and advise them about their work. And so he did but it was about six months before their business grant finally came through and their business was firmly established. I got regular letters from them in Polish and of course I replied in kind. We visited Aberporth again in the October half term and I met my Polish friends again. We were pleased to see each other and a firm friendship developed. I had taught mom and dad a little Polish so they could understand just a bit of what was said. The plumbing jobs started to come in and people seemed to be pleased at the standard of their work. But it wasn't till the following February and the big freeze that business really took off. They had bought an old post office van for £200 and named their business J & S Plumbers and had their advertising slips in a lot of newsagent's windows. Yet they were always grateful to Uncle Ron for his advice in pointing them in the right direction and helping with the form filling for their grants.

Uncle Ron told them that they should really think about moving to the bigger town of Cardigan if they wanted to expand their business but they said they preferred Aberporth. Besides, Cardigan was only five miles away and within easy travelling distance. Also, they had made a lot of friends here and the accommodation was nicer. They preferred to be beside the open sea; it seemed to have a magical effect. They said that this would be their new home from home.

CHAPTER 3

The Sportsman

1994

Ashley Bonner was now thirteen years of age and in the Second Form at Bishop Vesey Grammar Secondary School on Lichfield Road in Sutton Coldfield. Since meeting the Polish plumbers four years ago, Ashley had met quite a number of people from other countries of the European Union and the world. Consequently, he was now not only fluent in a dozen different languages but had acquired those people's memories as well. It was as though someone else's growing up memory had been implanted into him. And for some reason he knew that there was a whole lot more to be absorbed in the days and years ahead. Similarly, learning new facts and histories of knowledge came to him automatically as had the facts of the Lych-gate all those years ago. There seemed to be no limit to his capacity for absorption of knowledge; as an inner voice kept reminding him. This inner voice was a more recent asset that seemed to come at random. Ashley knew (or was told) to keep his talents secret from all but his immediate family. So, although he could excel at his school work, he made sure that intentional errors were always included in any work he submitted. In class he would often put his hand up to answer a question and then give an incomplete or erroneous response.

One of his friends was Jimmy Marshall from his primary school days. Although Jimmy had been a bit of a bully at first, he had seen the error of his ways when Ashley tricked him to see the school nurse which got him into trouble. He had then become firm friends with Ashley, David Matthews and Rory Jacobs. David and Rory had gone to different secondary schools although they all still met up occasionally. For some reason Jimmy now looked up to Ashley and was happy to follow any advice he was given. Perhaps it was because Ashley had been given the nickname of 'Slogger Bonner'.

When Ashley had started at Bishop Vesey the previous year aged twelve, he had been slotted into Blue House in the junior section. He had also been 'tried out' for the cricket second eleven or '2XI'. Ashley had watched cricket matches on the telly with his dad and so knew the game even though he had never actually played in any matches. But holding the bat or bowling the ball was another matter. However he soon got the hang of it and when batting, managed to hit nearly every ball to the boundary. Because he didn't play with the style of the other players he was usually put in at the lower end of the batting order when he did play. They thought he had a special eye for the ball no matter how fast it came at him. Ashley didn't think it was cheating to go slightly 'pink' just before he hit the ball since he made sure that he also missed a few of them. He even allowed himself to be bowled out for a duck occasionally.

Robert Black didn't like Ashley from the moment they met in the practice nets when Ashley was first tried out. Robert was a 'speed merchant' bowler and had a reputation for taking wickets and for physically knocking batsmen unconscious with his dizzy 'bouncers'. David Carter was cricket captain of the 1XI and also acted as coach to the 2XI team members. David was a known 'all rounder' and very much admired and liked by all the younger boys. He was also a great swimmer and his Swallow dives were the talk of the school and a 'beauty' to see. So when David helped Ashley to get padded up and showed him how to mark up crease for left stump position, Robert Black watched with a wry smile on his face. While David was explaining to Ashley the things he should watch for in the ball that would be sent flying at his stumps, the usual group of young girls from the neighbouring school had assembled behind and to one side of the nets. Among them was Victoria Chambers. She was nearly thirteen years old and was quite a 'looker'. Robert always showed off when he had an audience especially if they included 'Vicky'. Robert was also nearly thirteen and had been trying to ask Vicky out but had never quite got up the courage to actually talk to her. So the next best thing he felt was to impress her with his cricketing skills.

David Carter then came over to Robert and told him to first bowl a slower 'off break' at Ashley's wicket and then to gradually speed up with successive balls. Robert usually made a run up of about twenty paces when bowling in matches. However, for his first ball to Ashley he only made a run up of about six paces and that too was hardly a run. The ball lobbed outside the off stump and then cut sharply in towards centre stump. It was a perfect delivery that was bound to be missed and which would normally take out most batsmen's centre stump. Robert was pleased with the delivery. However Ashley went slightly 'pink' and watched the ball come towards him in slow motion. He put his bat in the path of the ball and nudged it away with a slight push. He'd forgotten that he was still in 'pink' mode and so when he returned 'out of pink' he saw the ball go whistling into the side netting.

'Well done' shouted David. Then to Robert he said 'Beginner's luck Robert, try a faster one this time.'

So this time Robert made his run up from about fifteen paces back and sent a sizzler straight at Ashley's leg stump. Once again Ashley went 'pink' and this time simply placed his bat in front of the approaching ball in a blocking action. The next ball was a sort of a bouncer and Ashley in 'pink' could see that it would fly over the stumps by quite a fair bit. So he fell flat on the ground in front of the crease and put his hands on the top of his head as if to protect himself. When he stood up again and retrieved his bat he still kept one hand on top of his head and played the clown by looking up at the sky. There was a round of laughter from the watchers and claps from a few. Vicky was one of those smiling and clapping and shouted 'Well played' for all to hear. Robert felt a jealous pang when he saw Vicky's response to Ashley's batting. He didn't like this new upstart at all. Yet he could see that Ashley appeared to have a natural eye for the ball and this made him like Ashley even less. For his next ball he made a full run up and sent the ball at Ashley at his fastest speed. This time Ashley thought it time to take a gentle swing at the ball in the 'pink'. It looked to everyone like a beautifully timed stroke and the ball went flying high over the bowler's head and landed outside the field and bounced on the road to the other side. It was definitely a 'six' at the very least. There was clapping and cheers from the crowd around the nets. Robert was not amused at all and gave Ashley a really nasty look. Ashley saw and understood so he quickly dropped his bat, sat down on his haunches and held his right wrist with his left hand while screwing up his face in an act of pain.

'My wrist hurts terribly' said Ashley to the other players who had come to see what was the matter, 'I think that ball was too fast and I've jarred my wrist. My hand is stinging as well'.

One of those showing concern was Vicky who came up to Ashley and asked if he was all right. She seemed a bit concerned but then said 'That was a beauty', referring of course to the boundary shot.

David Carter helped Ashley to the benches behind the nets and checked out his wrist and not seeing any swelling told him that he thought it would be all right after a bit of a rest. But to be on the safe side told Ashley to see the school nurse next morning if it didn't feel any better. He also suggested an ice pack if there was any swelling later on.

Robert came up to Ashley and pretended to show a bit of concern. Then he whispered so only Ashley could hear, 'I know you're shamming this; what are you trying to prove? And don't get any ideas about Vicky either. She's not for you, okay?'

Ashley knew then that Robert and he would probably never become real friends unless of course he did something about it.

And so he did.

The first thing that Ashley did was to find out what made Robert tick. He acquired Robert's thoughts and life history. There had been a tragedy in the family. Robert's older sister Elaine had become ill about six years earlier. He had idolised her as she had been such fun to be with. She was three years older than Robert. Then she became ill. They said it was leukaemia but that it was the curable kind. The next three years were endless bouts of to and from the hospitals. Elaine lost weight and interest in life and Robert had this terrible dread of losing her. His mum and dad also changed. They seldom laughed and just sat quietly at meal times. The tension in the house was terrible. At one time when Elaine seemed to be getting better there was a return of the old happy relationship between them all. But barely a month later Elaine collapsed and was rushed to hospital by ambulance. She died the next day.

Robert cried for a whole week. At the funeral everyone wondered at how well he bore up to this tragedy. Robert simply had no more tears left to shed. He was totally dried up. His dad kept a poker face but his mum was inconsolable. Everyone was very kind and that was when Robert first saw Vicky Chambers. She had come with her mum to the reception at the Navigation Pub after the funeral. Her mum Mavis was an old school friend of Robert's mum Ivy and they sat together for a while and chatted. Victoria sat next to her mum but never said a word. On a couple of occasions she looked up at Robert and smiled as if to say she was sorry. Robert smiled back.

Robert's dad stayed at the bar and got quite drunk. Everyone said he had a right to, but some thought he should have stayed beside his wife to give her his love and support. He never did. Not then, not ever. For a year and a half he lived in the same house but hardly spoke to either his wife or his son. He was never rude or angry; he just brooded and kept to himself. His responses to enquiries were simply grunts of yes or no. He went to the pub every evening but didn't ever stay very long.

And then he left. He said he was leaving and that he was going to find Elaine. She should have been home by now. He thought he knew where she might be and wouldn't return until he found her. Mum asked him to phone every week at least to let her know he was alright. He promised and kept his word. At first he did but after a few months he said he was going abroad and was coming home to collect his passport. He never did and that was the last they heard from him. Robert's mum went to the police with all the details and a photo of his dad but they said he wasn't classed as a missing person as he had left home voluntarily. They were sorry but said that this was not an uncommon occurrence.

Robert and his mum Ivy in the meantime had finally got partly back to a normal life and often sat and looked through the photo albums of when Elaine was fit and well. Gradually their smiles returned. And then they found an early video of Elaine when she was five. It was her birthday party and she looked so happy. They heard her laugh and even talk with her usual lisp as she said thank you to everyone for her lovely presents. At first the tears came flooding back. But after they watched her for the third time they couldn't help smile a little. His dad was on there too as his former happy self.

When Robert came to Bishop Vesey a year later he appeared quite normal. And indeed he was. The tragedy of losing his sister had made him a stronger character. But he never spoke about it. He loved cricket and found that he was a natural fast bowler. At first his accuracy was suspect but with practice this improved. Secretly he craved the limelight, and that only seemed to come to batsmen who scored centuries. But his batting skills were poor as he could never quite judge the spin of the ball. He wanted to impress Vicky who came regularly to all the matches.

Vicky and her mum Mavis had visited their home often and the two mums had renewed their schooldays friendship. Vicky and Robert had also become friends and played cards during the visits. They laughed and chatted as friends. Gradually, Robert developed a crush on Vicky but this was not visibly returned. They kept their feelings secret.

This was the picture that Ashley received. And so he considered his options and decided that the best way forward was for him to help Robert improve his chances with Vicky. This wouldn't be difficult since he knew that Vicky was also partial towards Robert. Ashley had also read her mind earlier as he had read Robert's.

The thing for Ashley to do now was to find out what made a good batsman.

In the First XI was their star batsman named Brian Felts. Everyone called him 'Feeler' and he didn't mind that at all. Feeler had scored a few centuries and umpteen fifties. He didn't have a single duck against any of his innings. His lowest score was twenty two when he was caught on the boundary. Another batsman nearly as good was Kenny Wells also in the First XI.

Bishop Vesey had a monthly magazine and the team though short staffed did a magnificent job. They were happy when Ashley asked to join as a cub reporter and they welcomed him with open arms. And so it was that Ashley managed to wangle interviews with both Brian Felts and Kenny Wells, separately of course. Ashley's topic was 'What makes a good Batsman?'

The article was received with much acclaim since Ashley recommended a way of producing better batsmen. Brian 'Feeler' Felts had hit the nail on the head. He said a good batsman needed lots of practice with good bowlers. Unfortunately there were not enough of these. One needed to learn to cope with each different kind of ball but these never came in consistently. The other thing was to watch the hand of the bowler as he released the ball and play accordingly. Too many players waited to see where the ball landed before offering a stroke. That was too little and too late.

The conclusion at the end of the article was that for good batting practice the balls needed to be sent at the batsman in a varied but consistent manner so that the batsman could develop a practised eye for the ball. Balls need not necessarily be pitched by a bowler. Ashley suggested that this could be achieved in the manner used by a Baseball Pitcher in the American Baseball game. Anyone could throw a ball so why not in the practice nets? There was some talk that this could lead to 'chuckers' entering the game. But the rules were strict and this could never filter into matches.

It was during one of their practice sessions that Ashley 'chucked' a ball so fast that it clean bowled their 2XI captain and star batsman Roger Carey. Roger asked Ashley to 'chuck' another similar ball and this time he just managed to block it. After that Roger always asked Ashley to pitch for him. He reckoned this was the best practice he could get. But Ashley needed to vary his pitches with some spin. For this he went to Robert. And so began an association between them in the practice nets and on the cricket pitch. It was not long before Ashley was regularly throwing the ball at Robert's stumps in the practice nets. They became more than just colleagues on the cricket pitch, they became friends.

Gradually Robert developed a batting style that became the talk of the teachers. Even the Head Master got to hear about Robert. He still hadn't scored more than thirty runs in a match but by golly he did it in style. And he reckoned it was all due to his daily practice sessions with Ashley.

Robert was not the least bit envious when his friend Ashley slogged his way to a century before him. Everyone said it was the worst bit of batting they had ever seen and that Ashley had been lucky not to have been out sooner. He had slashed at the ball in the most ungainly of fashions, using a cross bat stance on many occasions. Of course we know that Ashley went 'pink' before hitting the balls and so it was that he got the name of 'Slogger Bonner'. In order to maintain his reputation, Ashley allowed himself to be bowled out for much smaller scores. He would take a tremendous swipe at the ball and purposely miss on the occasions when he knew the ball would just miss the stumps, to a huge 'oooooh' from the fielders. On other occasions he would let himself be bowled out or caught when he snicked the ball high into the air.

Through all of this Robert and Ashley became very good friends and they could often be seen chatting in the school corridors. The other one in the group was of course Jimmy Marshall who had been Ashley's friend from junior school.

After school, cricket practice was carried out at the playing field site in Holly Lane a few roads away. There were six practice nets, three for each team. Before Ashley's time the 2XI always practiced in their allotted nets and never ever mixed in with the senior team. But ever since Ashley had started 'chucking' for Roger Carey the 2XI star who also occasionally played for 1XI, the rules were relaxed and an atmosphere of camaraderie existed between both teams. And so it was that Ashley was also 'chucking' in the 1XI nets on a fairly regular basis. Brian Felts and Kenny Wells became quite protective of 'Slogger Bonner' and considered him the best of all the 'chuckers'. And this they reckoned was very good practice for budding batsmen.

One day Ashley happened to remark to David Carter about a friendly match between the two teams. David thought this a good idea but needed to clear it with the Headmaster Mr Haddon. Ashley suggested a one day 50-overs match. The other players all thought it a jolly good idea although one or two said 2XI would get a trouncing.

Headmaster Haddon agreed that it should be a special affair with the whole school watching. Parents were to be invited and for a 'Tea and Refreshments' marquee also to be set up. The date finally arranged was the Friday before the half term break in May which was nearly two months away. This gave plenty of time for organisation and more important for 'net practice' for 2XI. Above all it was to be considered as a game between friends. There was no winning trophy at stake, just the pride of 2XI.

When Ashley told his mum and dad they just smiled and said, 'Don't overdo it son'.

Ashley knew exactly what they meant.

CHAPTER 4

A Cricket Match

Summer 1995

The Friday before half term started as a bright sunny morning though a bit breezy. I remembered dad's advice not to overdo it. By this he meant that I shouldn't use my gift to take too much of an advantage by scoring a huge number of runs to win the match. So I considered that if I let myself be bowled out or caught after scoring about thirty or so runs, that should be reasonable.

Mrs Jarvis the canteen manageress was in the refreshment marquee organising things for the mid-morning break just before the match was to start. This was to welcome all the parents and guests with a nice cuppa about 10:30 in the morning, and the match was to commence hopefully by eleven o'clock. Headmaster Haddon and most of the school staff would be in the marquee as well. It was to be an informal affair with no speeches of any kind. Of course the donation boxes were ever present near the entrances to the marquee.

School started as a normal day at 9:00am and there was a special assembly at 9:15 when Mr Haddon reminded everyone to be on their best behaviour and to be polite and helpful to any of the guests they came across in the course of the day. There was a general mood of excitement all around and before we knew it the headmaster announced the time of the match and that the school would close 'to all lessons for the rest of the term'; to the accompaniment of cheers and clapping.

Apart from Roger Carey, 2XI's captain and star batsman, we had Robert Black, Tim Brooks and Brian Martin who could be guaranteed to score runs. Not to mention myself as the 'Slogger'. There were just the two fast bowlers in Robert Black and Robin Nesters. The rest could all bowl spin of one sort or another. Rajiv Patel was considered our best spinner. He and Charlie Pyke our googly man were our best hope to slow down the opposition's run rate when needed.

The cricket pitch had been prepared near the centre of the ground so that there was more or less an equal distance to the boundary on all sides. Games master Frank Peers had done all the preparation work along with his second in command Tony Morelle. They would also act as the game's umpires. Old Javed Hussein the school super would keep score as usual. He was in his late 50s and had played as a professional in the counties umpteen years ago. There was a rumour that he had a double century to his credit. He got on well with everyone and was well liked. Unfortunately, he refused to become involved in any form of coaching since he said his cricketing ways were old fashioned and he had put them behind him. Yet he could often be seen shaking his head at a batsman's controversial stroke.

I had invited mum and my pretty ten years old sister Katy to the match and they were keen to attend. Katy's primary school had closed yesterday. Dad couldn't make it because of his work. Fridays were especially busy with progress and planning meetings at dad's place even though at three o'clock it was an early closing day. Dad said he expected mum to text him with a progress report of the match at midday and hourly thereafter. He said he hoped the 1XI would just manage to win to keep the morale of the team. He also said he hoped this didn't become an ongoing contest like the Harrow versus Eton cricketing contest. Apparently this was the longest-running regular fixture in the sport. The annual Eton College vs. Harrow School match at Lord's dated back over some 201 years to the Battle of Trafalgar. The contest was the highlight of both schools' sporting calendars and over the years both had impressive wins to their credit.

Our match was to be different. It was made clear that this was not an inter house match but just two parts of the same cricket team having a practice match. It was partly for entertainment and partly to test one another's strengths. It had been put forward by the headmaster that good sportsmanship was to be the prime factor dictating behaviour on the field. Yet it was 2XI who were taking a more serious attitude towards this match. To the rest of the school it was obvious that 1XI was the stronger team since its boys were not only older and bigger but also had the greater cricketing experience. So they were bound to win. However, 2XI put it about that this was to be a contest similar to that in the story of the race between the hare and the tortoise. There could be a surprise ending. When this story reached the ears of the headmaster he smiled and was heard to remark that he was pleased by the optimism of the second team members and expected a lively game.

Soon the guests began to arrive. I was pleased to see that mom and Katy had brought Vicky and her mom Mavis Chambers with them. At the time I was discussing my own batting order with Roger Carey our team captain when I saw mom arrive. I introduced Roger to mom and Katy but he already knew Vicky and her mom Mavis. I think he had met them as visitors to our net practice sessions. Of course it wasn't long before Robert joined us too. Vicky smiled at him and said she hoped we did well against David Carter's team as we strolled towards the refreshment marquee.

Headmaster Haddon came over to us as we approached and said to mom and Mavis how pleased he was that they could be here to attend the match and hoped they would find it entertaining.

I then took my little ten year old sister – going on fifteen of course – and showed her off to the other team members. I noticed Robin Nesters expressing a keen interest in Katy and she like the little charmer she was immediately noticed and preened herself for his benefit. Katy was tall for her age, nearly my height at five feet. However, I noticed she had on slightly higher heeled shoes which gave an added height impression. She had on a new floral patterned dress and I think mom had let her put on the palest of lip colouring not to mention a touch of blusher. Quite simply my little sister looked all grown up and beautiful. She had her hair done up in a girlish pony tail; I suppose to show off the pearl earrings mom had lent her. And suddenly, I in turn felt that I would like her to be proud of her big brother's cricket team, perhaps the winning team. For a brief moment I forgot all about dad's advice about not overdoing it. I needn't have worried as the whole team were quite exuberant about starting the match.

Back in the marquee Mrs Jarvis and her staff were busy serving up cups of tea and coffee and offering plates of biscuits to all the guests. There was a large tea urn steaming away in one corner. When I brought Katy back, mom and Mavis were talking to some of the other parents. The few dads who could make it were in the minority. Vicky then came and took Katy under her wing so that Robert and I could return to the makeshift tented pavilion that Frank had set up for the two teams. Our respective piles of equipment cluttered opposite ends of the pavilion. Old Javed Hussein sat at a table near the centre with his score sheets spread out in front of him.

Then the final moment arrived. Frank Peers called to the two team captains David Carter and Roger Carey and along with second umpire Tony Morelle the four of them walked towards the pitch at the centre of the field. David won the toss and elected to bat first. This was as I had hoped since now I could gauge my play in batting to approach the target score more closely. I might even gauge it to a nail-biting finish. Within minutes 2XI were spread out on the field and had been given the new shiny red ball. After a brief conference Roger gave the ball to Robert to open the bowling. The field was well spread out but there were a few slips on both the leg side and off positions. I was near the silly mid-on position but a few paces further back which I quite favoured. With my talents I could catch anything that came at me with force. Our plan was to limit 1XI's score to about 150 runs. Our tactic was to use a lot of spin for which we had Rajiv and Charlie.

The field was in place when the two opening batsmen walked onto the field. They were Brian Felts and Kenny Wells, two of their star batsmen. If we could get either of these out early on then that would be a big gain for us. There were cheers from all around the ground as the batsmen came on and the fielding side gave them a clap as well. Brian Felts was to face the first ball off Robert and umpire Frank gave the batsman his leg position which he marked on the crease. Andrew Payne was our wicket keeper and had a habit of mumbling to himself under his breath while behind the wicket. I think he did this to annoy the batsman to put him off his concentration. He'd mumble things like, 'Come on Robert ole chap let's have a ball that goes through his legs and smashes his wicket,' or 'okay Kenny, this one you're going to snick for a catch right into my gloves,' or 'hit this one for a six but straight to Charlie for a catch on the boundary.' Some of his other remarks brought smiles from the slip fielders as they were a bit on the funny though rude side.

Robert's first ball was a bit wide on the off side and Brian Felts lifted his bat in the air and let it go through to the wicket keeper. The next ball went for four runs all the way to the leg boundary. There were shouts of 'well done' from some of the spectators as Brian was quite a fancy stroke player too.

And so the game progressed and the score reached 25 without loss by the fifth over. There had been a close call for Kenny Wells in the third over when a strong appeal for lbw had been made. A ball from Robert Black had swung in from the off side and whacked Kenny low on the pad. Umpire Frank had hesitated for a long moment before shaking his head for a not out decision. The fourth over had been a maiden over from Robin Nesters.

At the sixth Roger brought on the spin bowlers and passed the ball to Rajiv Patel, a left hander. Rajiv bowled around the wicket and his very first ball turned in sharply and smacked Brian on the pads about knee high.

'How's that,' shouted Rajiv, and after a moments hesitation Frank raised a finger, to cheers from the team who ran up to Rajiv and smacked hands and patted backs. Brian had scored 15 runs but kept shaking his head as he walked back to the pavilion tent. The next batsman was David Carter their captain and all rounder. David was given centre stump position by umpire Frank and he marked his crease accordingly.

Rajiv took a short run and sent a flighty ball towards David that seemed well outside off stump. David raised his bat to let the ball pass wide, but then the ball cut in sharply and just clipped the off stump to knock off one bail. Rajiv jumped high in the air with glee while David just stood surprised. I was surprised myself as I was only a few feet away. I ran up to Rajiv and we smacked raised palms together. Then the whole team came up to Rajiv and patted him on the back with everyone in a jolly mood. Poor David was out for a duck and a captain's duck at that. Before he walked off he went to where the ball had pitched and tapped the ground with his bat to indicate that the ball must have landed on an uneven patch to come in so sharp. He then turned to Rajiv and gave him a little clap as if to say 'well bowled.' What a fine sportsman.

The next man in was Mickey Kane who was not only a good bat but also 1XI's wicket keeper. He too squared up and umpire Frank gave him his leg position which was duly scratched into the crease.

'Come on Rajiv,' shouted our Captain Roger, 'give us a hat-trick.'

The next ball was played defensively but pushed towards point which gave the batsmen ample time to run a single. Kenny Wells was now to take strike and had already scored ten runs. The next ball was smashed to the long leg boundary for four runs; as was the next past mid-on to the long-on boundary for another four. There was a smile on Kenny's face as he liked the slower pace of spin bowlers.

The next ball was a good flighty ball but Kenny ran out of his crease and whacked the ball on the full toss with tremendous force. The ball hissed straight at me and I had no time to react at all. It was at my chest in the fraction of a second but then the strangest thing happened. The world went rosy pink and misty without my willing it. I had nothing to do with this happening at all. It suddenly dawned on me that I was automatically protected from all harm by any form of projectile hitting my body. This must be another facet of my 'pink' gift. The ball was about an inch from my upper chest and moving as if in a slow motion. I reached up and cupped the ball in both hands and suddenly the world went back to normal and I could feel the momentum of the ball pushing me backwards. I held the ball tight to my chest and allowed myself to fall on my back onto the grassy pitch. I just lay there for a second and then held the ball up in my right hand. Rajiv ran up to me and helped me up and asked if I was okay. Then the whole team were around me patting me on the back and jumping up and down in elation that the big batsman had been taken down. And Rajiv had his near hat-trick.

Kenny looked stunned. He just stood there at his crease for a long moment; then whacked the ground hard with his bat and turned around to slowly walk back towards the pavilion, all the while shaking his head. The three main batsmen of the first team were out and we should be able to limit the runs the remaining batsmen could score. We didn't count on Andy Brew the batsman who came in next.

And I had just made a new discovery. The information that nothing could strike me hurtfully suddenly dawned upon my conscience. A whole catalogue of potential incidents came into focus and told me that none of them could do me harm. I was protected for a purpose of which I was as yet unaware. I must talk this over with mom and dad later today.

The game settled down to a slower pace of runs scored but at a regular rate of two, three or four an over. There were the occasional boundaries too but not very many. Roger had placed a man at each of the long boundary positions and these helped reduce quite a few fours to just one or two runs instead. The score sheet stood at eighty three for four when half of the 50 Overs had been bowled and with the time approaching one o'clock the umpires called for the lunch break. It was quite a warm day and we were glad for some liquid refreshments.

Mum and Katy came over to me and said how much they were enjoying the game. Headmaster Haddon also came over and said what a very good show the 2XI team was putting on.

'That was a brilliant catch Bonner' he said. 'I hope you didn't do yourself a mischief. Well done to both teams for some excellent entertainment. The school is proud to have such outstanding players. Keep up the good work.'

There were refreshments and snacks for visitors in the refreshment marquee but mum had brought along packed lunches for us. Mum had the car as dad and another colleague shared their journeys to work. So mum got the goodies from the car and we all sat under an old oak by the edge of the field. The other 2XI team members soon joined us when they had finished up in the canteen. Robert sat down next to Vicky and chatted to her. Robin Nesters stood near Katy and laughed at everything she said. Katy noticed his presence and I think she especially played up to him, never having received such admiration from anyone before.

Mom looked at me and said, 'That was a good catch son, I hope you didn't overdo it.'

I knew what she meant. 'I'll tell you and dad about it later. And didn't you promise to ring dad with the latest score?' I said.

'I'll do it as soon as you resume play,' said mom.

We all got back on the field at 2 o'clock and nothing dramatic happened. Andy Brew batted solidly and scored forty runs in all. At the end of the 50th over 1XI had scored 168 for the loss of six wickets. Mickey Kane had been run out after a misunderstanding when both batsmen were caught short at the same end. And Josh Rabinda had got out in a simple caught and bowled action by a 'flighted' ball from Charlie Pyke. Ronnie Michaels the fast bowler had come in and tried to bash every ball to the boundary but without much success. But he had been lucky not to have been caught out at least three times. At the end of play he had scored an unbeaten 16 runs. The time was just after half past three and it was decided that 2XI could begin their innings at a quarter to four.

In the pavilion Captain Roger gave his pep talk and said that we had a big task ahead of us to match this score, but that we could do it. He said to take a few risks if we judged the situation right. We must keep scoring runs even if it was just to take singles. That should be our target to try to score a run for every ball. Little pushes to unoccupied positions should do the trick. The other trick was not to get out. Tim Brooks and Brian Martin were our opening batsmen and were soon padded up and ready.

The umpires were already out on site when 1XI took to the field. They were soon followed by our two batsmen. Brian was to take first strike and soon marked his centre wicket position. Ronny Michaels would be bowling the first over. Ronny was known for his 'bouncers' and umpire Frank had a quick word about this before he started his run. And so the junior innings began.

The first ball was very wide and umpire Frank signalled an extra. The second ball was a no-ball and Brian took an almighty swipe at it but missed. The third ball took his centre stump clean out of the ground. It was a rare 'Yorker' beauty and whizzed right under Brian's bat. There was a roar from the field and a rush up to congratulate Ronny. Poor old Brian was out for a duck but to an exceptional ball. As he walked passed Ronny he gave him a little clap.

'Good ball Ron,' he said, 'bet you couldn't bowl another one like that if you tried.'

Captain Roger was in next and squared up to the bowler. This one was pitched short and Roger smashed it for four runs all the way passed cover. On the next they took a single, as they did for the next few balls. Tim and Roger seemed to have an understanding and each would start their run towards the batter as soon as the ball had been bowled. The strategy seemed to be working and after five overs the score was a healthy 27 runs. And then Tim got run out. Brian had nudged the ball passed silly mid on and then yelled a loud 'No' to Tim. But Tim was already halfway towards him and desperately reversing back to his crease. Josh Rabinda was at mid-wicket, ran and picked up the ball and flung it at the bowler's end stumps in one smooth fluid motion and hit them bang on before Tim was even near his crease. Tim didn't break stride and just kept walking on towards the pavilion. At least he had scored ten runs.

Robert Black was our next batsman in and he looked menacing as he walked to the crease at the bowler's end making practice swings with his bat. Roger held up his bat and walked across to him and they had a short confab. I don't know what was said but Roger seemed to nod agreement.

In the next three overs the batsmen ran singles like there was no tomorrow and the score went passed the fifty runs mark. At this rate of scoring a win was on the cards if only the batsmen didn't get out.

Then David Carter brought on his spin attack in Mickey Finn and Ray Raggi. They played havoc with our batsmen. In the next few overs there was a batting collapse. From a score card of 52 for two we slumped to 63 for six. Roger had been caught behind when he got a fine edge to the ball. Tich Marsh and Jay Misra each went for an lbw when they had barely got off the mark. Andrew Payne our wicket keeper smashed his first ball to the long-off boundary and then lofted a beauty for a near six towards the long-on boundary but unfortunately it didn't quite make it over and Andy Brew took a magnificent catch.

I was next in the batting line up and had just padded up when Andy got out. As we were about to walk passed each other on the outfield Andy stopped me to say for me to watch out for the googlies. I came to my crease and made a show of looking around at the field. I decided to block all the balls of my first over. Of course I did go to 'pink' each time as I wasn't much of a batsman otherwise. Robert also played carefully and at the end of the 20th over we had scored another five runs to reach 68 for six. 2XI had been batting for an hour and a half and I reckoned that 1XI thought that the end was in sight and they would win easily.

It was then that Robert got hit a glancing blow on the head by a bouncer and had to receive a spot of attention in the form of a wet compress to the injured area. Captain Roger also came to see how he was and in the process told us to play as we felt best.

He looked at me and said, 'Hey Bonner, why don't you just slog yourself to a century.'

So Robert and I began to hit boundaries to left, right and centre. I kept my scoring rate behind that of Robert and the innings soon reached 100 runs by the end of the 30th over. By the 35th over Robert reached his first half century and got a big cheer from the pavilion. And then he took a low swipe at a fast ball on the leg side and his bat hit his leg stump. Robert Black, hit wicket, out for 53 runs. He was cross with himself for his stupid mistake. Scorecard was now 123 for seven with fifteen and a bit overs remaining. The fast bowlers were back in action.

Rajiv Patel came in next and was clean bowled first ball and we were 123 for eight.

He was followed by Charlie Pyke who fortunately didn't have to take strike as the 35th over had finished.

I now faced fast bowler Ronny Michaels. The first three balls were bouncers which I just ducked under. The next I went 'pink' and hit for a six to the mid-wicket boundary. I hit the next two balls to the boundary for four runs each. But I should have hit a single to keep the bowling but forgot to keep track of the number of balls bowled.

Charlie Pyke was an excellent spin bowler but no batsman. Asif Din sent in a fast short-length delivery that came in to the batsman at about waist height. Charlie tried to block it with a straight bat but the ball hit him on his glove and first slip took an easy catch. We were now 137 for nine and the time was a quarter to six. The sun was still high in the semi cloudy sky and it looked as if we were about to lose the match. If only Robin Nesters our next man in could last the over.

I had a quick word with Robin when he came in and said if only he could get me on to strike we might win the game. Robin said he'd try his best. For the rest of Asif's over he managed to survive, though only just. He snicked a ball to first slip but it didn't carry far enough for a catch.

And so I was to face speedy Ronny Michaels. I had my plan laid out to score the remaining runs and I had 12 overs in which to do it. I remember dad saying that I shouldn't overdo it. And I won't, but I did want to make this game a memorable one for the history of the school. In that over I scored a single off the last ball and so kept strike. I had played defensively to all of Ronny's balls and he seemed quite pleased to have kept the runs down. I did the same for the next overs from Asif Din except that we also ran two runs on the third ball when we could have run three.

We were now on 141 with ten overs remaining.

David Carter now brought the spin bowlers back on and I was to face Ray Raggi. Again we ran two runs on the third ball and a single on the last. I now decided to step up the action and when Ronny sent me a flighty ball I sliced it through gully to the boundary. The next ball I hit to the long-leg boundary for another four runs. I decided that the last ball of the over would also be my last so I whacked the ball for an almighty six. This brought our score to 155 runs and just 13 runs short of 1XI's total. During the bowling change-over I had a word with Robin.

'Go for it Robin,' I said. 'Just take a swipe at every ball and run when you can. I'm giving you the chance to score the winning runs. Even if you get out before we reach their score we'd have given them a few anxious moments.'

'Thanks Ashley,' he said. 'I won't let you down. I'll give it my best shot.'

And so when Mickey Finn sent his spinners at Robin he was surprised at the response. Robin missed the first ball and the next. But he connected with the third ball and sent it to the square-leg boundary for four runs. Robin was off the mark and quite pleased. The next ball came in sharpish and hit him low on his pad. There was a shout for lbw but Frank just shook his head. From where I was standing I reckon it would have gone wide of leg stump. I think Frank saw it the same. We nearly ran a single but Andy Brew fielded the ball at extra-cover and was ready to throw it at the bowler's end stumps. We needed ten runs to win and I was on strike to Ray Raggi's googlies. I pushed the first ball between gully and point and we ran a single. Nine runs to win. Robin tried a swipe at the next but missed by a mile. The ball cut away from him quite sharply. The bowling was very tight and Robin couldn't see where the ball was twisting to next. And so the over ended and it was my turn on strike. Here too I blocked all the balls without a run being scored and Mickey was pleased with his maiden over.

David Carter saw his chance to end our game and brought on his fast bowlers again. Asif Din was to bowl to Robin.

The first ball whizzed passed the off stump by a fraction of an inch. Robin had taken a swipe at the ball but was too slow as the ball had already gone passed him. Robin got a fine edge to the next ball and it flew between first and second slip and went for four runs all the way to the boundary as there was no one at the third man position. Five runs to win and it was now all up to Robin. The next ball was a no-ball and a gift from heaven. Four runs to win. Asif's next ball was pitched well up and smacked into Robin's pad just below the knee. I think Asif's 'howzat' appeal must have been heard in Timbuktu. Umpire Frank leaned forward and stared down the wicket and then very slowly raised his right hand with the index finger pointing skyward. Robin was out lbw and 2XI had lost the match by just three runs. All the fielders ran up to Asif and clapped him on the back with smiles and cheers. He had saved 1XI's reputation. I think they must have all been in a bit of a sweat towards the end. I think dad would be pleased at the final result.

Later in the pavilion the headmaster came to give both teams his congratulations and to say what a thrilling game it was.

'Do you know lads,' he said, 'I have not enjoyed such an exciting game of cricket in a very long time. You had us on the edge of our seats with suspense. I look forward to your next match if you decide to have one. Both captains are to be congratulated for their strategy and sportsmanship.'

Then he turned to old Javed Hussein and said, 'What did you think of the game Mr Hussein? Was it as good as some of your county stuff?'

'Why sir,' said old man Hussein, 'I think it was absolutely thrilling. I like a happy ending. I also feel confident that the Vesey cricket team has a very good future with so many talented players in the younger group. I would like to see more matches like this one.'

I think he meant that he was glad that 1XI had won the match but also glad that 2XI had made such a good showing in scaring the living daylights out of the First Team.

After stashing our kit away we all went to the refreshment marquee for an orange squash and a biscuit and to say hello to some of the spectators and parents. I noticed that Robin was especially chatty and at my side when we got to mum and Katy. As was Robert who also joined our little group and got talking to Vicky and her mum. However, it wasn't long before we all decided to call it a day and head for home. Most of the lads had to catch buses but I got a ride with mum and Katy. Robin walked with us to the car and waved us goodbye. Katy was glowing and mum smiled at me and raised an eyebrow. Katy was ten years old and already interested in boys.

Later that evening, after we'd had our dinner and I was alone with mum and dad I mentioned my latest discovery. I told them how the ball had come whizzing at my chest and before I had time to react, that the world had gone 'pink' and slowed the ball as it was about to strike me. It had stopped a fraction of an inch from my chest and I was then able to do something about it. The thing about the event was the realisation and knowledge that I was somehow automatically protected from fast moving objects. I told mum and dad that I believed that even a bullet from a gun would behave in a similar fashion.

'We can try out your theory tomorrow,' said dad. 'I shall ask your granddad Eric to come over with that old Webley air pistol he's got in a drawer somewhere and we can conduct a few experiments.'

So next morning granddad Eric came over with his Webley and we all had a few practice shots at a wooden board suitably marked up as a target. Katy had a few shots but soon got bored and went to visit her friend Rehana next door. We still kept all my gifts secret from her.

Mum was concerned that I might get hurt in the experiment and so made me wear a padded apron. When dad fired the slug pellet at my midriff it just hit the apron hard but I didn't feel it much. And there was no special effect in time slowing down as it had done with the cricket ball. I said this. I then removed the apron and told dad to try again. I could see that mum had her hand up against her cheek and a worried expression. So I put my hand out to one side with open palm facing dad.

'Fire at my palm dad,' I said, 'I think it only works if I am put in danger. I think you ought to come closer too.'

So dad came within six feet, aimed at my palm and fired. Whoosh, the sky turned misty and a rosy red and I could see the pellet up against my palm but nearly stationary. I simply closed my fist over the slug and lowered my hand. It all then returned to normal colouring and time continued as before. When I showed them the slug and told them that it had worked they were amazed. I could see that mum was relieved too. After quite a few more trials I suddenly had a thought. What if my back was turned and I was not aware of any danger, would it still work? I said this and told dad to fire at the back of my head as I was walking away. Mum vetoed this idea and instead told me to remove my shirt so that my back was the target. I did and the experiment again worked as before. The world turned pink as I heard the airgun fire and I turned round and picked out the semi-floating pellet and held it between finger and thumb. I took it across to mum to show her so that she need never worry about me getting hurt.

'I'd like to try this with a real bullet, dad,' I said. But mum gave an emphatic 'no' to the idea.

I decided to let it go at that. I already had my confirmation and just knew that not even a canon ball could hurt me. And then it suddenly became clear that it didn't matter whether the motion was on the part of the striking object or whether I was doing the travelling towards it. It was the relative motion or speed that mattered. So if I ran towards a lamp post or a tree then I would be prevented from colliding with it by the automatic 'pink' factor. Or even if I tried to bang my head against a wall or to punch at it with my fist I would be prevented from hurting myself.

We went in for a cup of tea and I discussed the issue with mum and dad. It was granddad Eric who then said that the same should apply if I jumped out of a first floor window. And I instantly knew he was right. The same would be true if I happened to be travelling in a car or a train or even an aeroplane and it crashed. At the instant before impact 'Time' would freeze. The voice that I often heard also said this was true but I mustn't be seen doing this as it would draw attention to my gift. But I knew that I must conduct at least one jump experiment for the sake of curiosity. I kept this to myself. I would attempt it on a dark night.

Unfortunately we were in the middle of summer and it didn't get dark till about 11:00 pm. Even then there was always a pale blue lightness in the northern sky. So it would have to be done on a dark cloudy night. I began to take an interest in weather forecasts at the end of the evening news and it was about a fortnight later that heavy rains were predicted for the next day and night.

In the morning I awoke to blustery rain and dark grey skies. At the school we had to spend our lunch break indoors because of the torrential rain. However, by evening it seemed to clear and by the time I got home there were bright blue skies overhead. And it wasn't until a week later that the conditions were right for my experiment. There was a light drizzle from a dark threatening sky one evening and the weatherman for the Midlands said the cloud cover would persist well into the next day. And so at about midnight I went 'pink' and left the house via the back sliding patio door which I left unlocked. I made my way to a 3-storey block of flats on Kingsbury Road that had a fire escape at the rear of the building. The metal stairway went all the way to its roof and I stood there looking around. It was by no means as dark as I would have liked since there were quite a few street lights at the front of the building. However there was one spot where the side of the building seemed in comparative darkness. I chose this for my experiment. It now began to rain rather heavily and I thought this was perfect. I didn't want to chance being seen standing at the edge so I stooped low and just threw myself forward off the building. I fell down towards the darkness rather quickly and I didn't quite know at what instant I touched the ground. There was only a brief instant of 'rosy colour' and then I found myself lying in a puddle of rain face down. I was not hurt at all but I seemed to have missed the experience. So I decided to try again but this time where I could see what was happening. I repeated the experiment in my wet clothes but from the side of the building that wasn't in shadow. This time I saw myself approach the ground under normal gravity conditions. I seemed to be heading for total disaster and I shut my eyes automatically as I was about to impact the ground. Again I found myself lying face down on a wet concrete floor yet quite unhurt.

I knew I would have to try this again so I went up to the roof again. I had a good look around to make sure the place was deserted as before and then threw myself backwards off the roof. I couldn't see the ground approach so I was quite aware of every aspect of the fall. There was a sudden rosy tint to everything but only for an instant and then I felt my head and then my body gently touch the ground. Again I was totally unhurt but very wet. So now I knew how it happened and I had no control over the procedure. However I had other thoughts on how I could change that but that would be another experiment on another day. For now I walked back home and slipped in as before in the 'pink' and once in my room changed out of my wet clothes. I didn't speak to anyone about my little adventure.

Chapter 5

A Lesson for a Bully

1996

Ashley Bonner was fifteen years of age and in the Fourth Form at Bishop Vesey School. He was now nearly five feet six in height but still quite skinny. He was also in the first eleven cricket team along with most of his former 2XI team mates. There had never been another game like the first one two years ago. The match last year had been a disappointment in that the match had lasted hardly three hours and in which 2XI had been bowled out for 55 runs in just 16 overs. Ashley had been caught on the boundary when he tried to loft a ball for six in his first over. Robert Black had been unavailable to play because of a stiff neck problem from probably having slept awkwardly. This score was easily reached by the 1XI opening pair in just 13 overs, a ten wicket win. There had still been plenty of fun and joviality on the field but never any excitement within the game itself. That first match was simply a one-off wonder. It was then decided to discontinue the event as a feature of the sporting calendar except on special request from the prevailing 2XI team.

David Carter and most of the former 1XI team had left school to follow their careers in either jobs or further education, though some made an occasional visit to their old school. The Staff members were unchanged and Mr Haddon was still the Headmaster. Old Javed Hussein was thinking about an early retirement but Frank Peers talked him out of it, at least for another year or so. It was obvious that Frank and Javed were good friends and liked one another's company. They each had a rich field of experience with much in common.

Ashley had his little band of merry men. Jimmy Marshall was always near at hand and had developed an open personality and a crude sense of humour. He was very fond of Ashley and made an open boast that if anyone tried to hurt Ashley, physically or otherwise, they would have him to contend with. Robert Black and Robin Nesters were the other members of this group. Robin had initially been like a shadow to the group but then Ashley had gradually drawn him in. He seemed to blush a bright red whenever Ashley told something funny about the antics of Katy at home.

Bishop Vesey had open-day functions in the school grounds about three times each year and Lillian Bonner was a frequent visitor along with her daughter Katy. Since these visits were always timed for a Friday afternoon, Katy usually managed to get a leave of absence from her school teacher to attend. Ashley and his friends would be there to greet them and Robin made sure he was dressed in a clean and freshly pressed uniform.

There had been an incident of bullying by some of the Second Form chaps. It was Jimmy Marshall who heard about it from a cousin of his who had just started in the First Form. Apparently there was a little guy in his cousin's class who wore specs, had a strong Welsh accent and had an occasional stammer when excited. His name was Adrian Jones and he was from Swansea in South Wales. The family had moved to Birmingham when his father had relocated after having been made redundant from his works there.

The Second Form boys who had picked on Adrian were all from well off families and they tended to look down on the poorer lads. The ring leader was a chap called Brian Charles as he was the one always doing the talking. The other two were Lesley Carleton and Morris Cooney. They were all a bit overweight but otherwise quite smart in appearance. They also knew how to play the system. Any physical retaliation to their verbal bullying tactics would get that person into serious trouble. There were two CCTV cameras covering the playground and one in the dining hall. A reported incident could thus be checked on the recordings. Brian Charles ensured that his back was to one of the cameras and that his partners shielded him from the other one in the playground before he pushed or pinched his victim.

Mrs Jones came in to the school one day in January to speak to the Headmaster about her son Adrian. She said that her son had changed from a happy personality to a quiet and worried looking boy. He never laughed anymore and didn't join in family conversations like he used to. It all seemed to have begun about a month after he started at Bishop Vesey in September. He had said on several occasions that he didn't like this school; it was not nice like his previous Primary in Hodge Hill. Mrs Jones had another child, a daughter who was a few years younger than Adrian and who was at the same Primary school. Young Lisa had complained about Adrian not wanting to play with her anymore. They had always played together so lovingly.

32

Mr Haddon told Mrs Jones that it was always a big step when children moved into a Secondary school. They tended to find it a strange place after having left all their previous friends and familiar surroundings behind. As soon as he made some friends here he was sure Adrian would settle down back into the happy lad he really was. He said he would have a word with Miss Atkins his form teacher. He would also ask one of the class lads to keep an eye on Adrian. He asked her if Adrian liked to play any sport like football, rugby or cricket. She said that they did have a bat and ball at home but Adrian hadn't shown any special skill at hitting the ball. Mr Haddon then suggested to Mrs Jones that she had a word with Adrian at home about volunteering to join the Second Eleven cricket team at the practice nets after school. He might enjoy the company and even turn out to be one of their better batsmen.

At the next weekly staff meeting the subject of Adrian was mentioned but Miss Atkins said he was just a quiet child and did excellent class work. He was a loner and she couldn't remember seeing him chatting to anyone in particular, even at playtimes. But she would keep a special eye out for anything unusual in case someone was teasing him or picking on him. There was a strict policy in the school on the aspect of bullying. Anyone seen to be picking on another child would be severely dealt with. But it was an extremely difficult thing to pick out. There was another quiet child in the class and she would try and pair the two in the hope they made friends with each other.

It just so happened that the child Miss Atkins had in mind was no other than Jimmy Marshall's cousin Tim Richards. At first there seemed to be no inclination for friendship. They did speak when they had to, but it was only when they worked together on a class project that a gradual companionship developed. They also began to spend their recess times together on the playground. It was then that Adrian mentioned to Tim to beware of Brian Charles and his bullying gang. They were outwardly pleasant on the playground but it was in the dining hall and the corridors that one had to be careful.

One of the things the gang did in the dining hall was to get up from the table they were initially at and bring their food trays over to yours and squeeze onto the bench either side of you. It became very tense and if you tried to get up they would try and prevent it by leaning against you from both sides. And if you did manage to move to another place they soon followed after a bit. And while hemmed in you often got a hard nudge by an elbow just as you were forking food into your mouth. This caused the fork to jab you in the chin, lips or even your gums, which was very painful. Of course it wasn't you everyday, as they picked on a couple of other juniors as well. But no one reported them as it was just not the thing that was done by boys. There was a code of silence and stiff upper lip, and besides there was never any real proof.

When Tim became friends with Adrian they began to sit together at dinner times. For a while Adrian was left alone and he thought that being with Tim had altered matters. But then one day just after the Easter-break Brian Charles came over with his tray and sat down beside Adrian.

'Hello Adrian,' he said, 'I see you have made a friend, how nice for you.'

Then to Tim he said, 'I know who you are Tim, be sure to go and tale tattle back to your big cousin Jimmy. Tell him that I am going to get him expelled if he picks on me. And that is a promise. Now move yourself to another table as I want to have a private talk with my little welsh four-eyes here.'

But Tim just stared down at his plate and carried on eating his dinner pretending he'd not heard what Brian had just said. By now the other two, Lesley and Morris had also arrived with their trays and sat one beside Adrian and the other beside Tim. After a tense minute Brian Charles gave a great big sneeze and as he did so he pushed his tray hard against Tim's and knocked it flying into his lap. Poor Tim had dinner and gravy all over his shirt and trousers. Morris Cooney got splashed a bit as well and made a big noise about it by blaming Tim for his clumsiness.

'Look what you have done you clumsy clot,' said Brian. 'Get off with you and get yourself cleaned up. You had better go too Morris as there's some gravy splashed on your shirt. See that Tim makes a good job of it.'

Poor Tim was close to tears. He got up for some paper napkins which the dinner supervisor gave him and cleaned his shirt and trousers of excess food and gravy as best he could. When she asked him what had happened he just mumbled that it was not his fault but she couldn't make out what he said.

'Well, whatever happened there is no second dinner for you so you'd better make the best of it and go get yourself properly cleaned up. Look at the state of you. You had better get permission to go home and get changed. At least get a clean shirt.'

Luckily Tim had eaten nearly half his dinner already so he wasn't hungry anymore. He was angry.

He went alone to the toilets and leaning over the wash basin managed to get his shirt reasonably clean. He tapped the wet area with paper towels and got it reasonably dry too. The weather was mild so he didn't mind the dampness. The trousers also cleaned up a treat and Tim then walked around the playground facing into the slight westerly April breeze and wondering how Adrian was faring in the dining hall.

Back there Adrian began to stammer. 'P-p-p-please l-l-l-leave me al-l-lone,' he said.

But Brian just elbowed him in the ribs and hissed, 'Shut up wimp,' in a whispered tone.

When Adrian tried to get out of his seat Brian and Lesley forced him down again with a pretended affectionate arm around his shoulders. They then began eating their own dinners and made exaggerated elbow movements as they forked their dinner into their mouths, jabbing at Adrian's arm with each movement.

Adrian's eyes filled with tears but at the same time he was gritting his teeth in frustrated anger. There was nothing he could do.

'O look,' said Morris Cooney who still had a splash on his shirt, 'the little fellow is blubbing. What shall we do with him?'

The bullies realised that this could draw attention to them so they decided to get rid of Adrian from the dining hall. They let him out of his seat and told him to go and join his friend outside and warned him about blabbing to anyone.

Outside Adrian met up with Tim and it was while they were walking around the nearly empty playground that they came across another little group of Fourth Form lads. And that was when Adrian met Ashley Bonner. The fun was about to begin.

Jimmy Marshal asked his cousin Tim why he was out of the dinner hall so early. Tim mumbled that his dinner tray had fallen onto his lap accidentally. But Jimmy straight away knew something was not right and said so. But Tim wouldn't say any more. He remembered that Brian Charles wanted Jimmy to come at him for a fight, let himself get hit and so get Jimmy expelled.

It was then that Ashley read their minds and knew all that had taken place.

'Has that bully Brian Charles and his gang from Form Two been bothering you as well?' he said to Adrian.

'H-h-how d-d-did you k-k-know?' said Adrian.

'Don't worry,' said Ashley, 'we know bullies when we see them. I always knew him and the other two were up to something rotten. I think we had better do something about converting them into good lads again.'

It was then that Jimmy noticed the slightly discoloured and damp patch on Tim's shirt and trousers.

Angrily he said, 'Did Brian do that to you Tim? I think I shall go over to him and clip him round the ear hole.'

'O, don't do that,' said Tim. 'He said he wants you to fight him so he can get you expelled. He said he was not afraid of you.'

It all came out then.

Jimmy asked to be told all and it was Adrian who told the whole story. He said how he had been picked on ever since he had started school in the September Term. He said he wished he had never come to this school. He was not happy here at all. He had no friends except Tim. And with that the tears started pouring down his face.

Ashley put his arm on Adrian's shoulders and telepathically painted a complete scenario of how the bullies would be taught a lesson and how they would become a good bunch of lads again and be best of friends with everyone.

Ashley then verbally told the lads not to worry and that it would all be taken care of. And with that they left Tim and Adrian and walked to one of the benches at the far end of the playground.

Ashley knew that he couldn't let Jimmy or the other two into his own plans, for that would give the secret of his gifted powers away. Robert Black and Robin Nesters suggested doing a bit of surreptitious bullying of their own on the Form two bullies, but Ashley said that this would only make matters worse. No, what was needed was something secret so that they didn't know where it came from. Something ghostly-like to make them become superstitious about what they were doing. The thing was to get them worried that their bullying actions had caused some ghostly goings on against them.

Ashley said he had a plan.

They would ask Tim and Adrian to wait near the end of the dinner queue making sure that Brian Charles and his gang were served and seated before them. They must then go and also sit at the same table and as close to them as possible. They must start to eat but then both stop and look behind Brian and ask him who the old man was standing right behind him. Brian would of course look behind and see nothing. They must keep up this charade as best as possible, even to giving a pretend description of the smiling old man.

Then Ashley and the three others would walk into the hall and pretend to be looking for a lost something like a notebook or cap. When they were near the bullies they would pretend to hold a conversation with the smiling old man behind Brian and ask him if he had seen their notebook or cap. They would then thank him and leave the dining hall.

Of course Ashley had a bit more to his plan but he didn't tell the others for obvious reasons. No one should know that he could make time slow for everything except himself. There was an unspoken code to use it for good and not to harm anyone, though an initial punishing lesson was not out of the question.

Since Ashley did not want the bullies to see any connection between Adrian and themselves he asked Jimmy to meet up with his cousin Tim after school and tell him about the plan. Tim could then pass the details on to Adrian.

Little did Ashley know that events were to take an unbelievable turn even for him?

When he went home he confided to his mum and dad and said that the idea of the plan seemed to enter his head as if someone had telepathically placed it there. He knew that if he had to ask himself a question about a facet of history or science then the answer simply just popped up from nowhere. There were some things Ashley knew about that weren't even in the history books.

That evening while the Bonner family were sitting in the living room watching a program on TV everything seemed very peaceful. But Alex could see that his son was somewhat ill at ease. When the program ended the TV was switched off and Katy went up to her room to do her homework. Lillian went into the kitchen to do a bit of tidying up and Alex turned to his son.

'What's on your mind, son?' he said. 'There's something bothering you, isn't there?'

There was a moment of silence before Ashley communicated all his thoughts to both his mum and his dad telepathically. He found it easier to do this as it not only saved time but also painted a complete picture. Lillian came back into the room and sat in her usual chair.

'This voice that you think you hear speaking to you, do you think it is a real person?' she asked.

'Yes,' said Ashley. 'But it's not a verbal voice; it's more like a complete block of information that suddenly appears in my head. I know it is being put there telepathically, and I have begun to recognise characteristics in its quality that it makes me wonder about the sender. But when I try to communicate in return I find my thoughts being blocked in some mysterious way.'

It was Alex who suggested that perhaps the whole purpose behind Ashley's gift was a gradual grooming towards some intended objective. Perhaps this person or being also had a gift similar to Ashley's but of a much longer standing. After all Ashley was only fifteen and had a lot more to learn and discover.

'This gift could be extremely dangerous in the wrong hands', said Alex, 'so perhaps this person is a sort of tutor to make sure you develop the correct frame of mind for whatever task is before you.'

'You know son,' said Lillian, 'there was a time years ago when you were six that I worried about where all this was leading. But now I feel a confidence in your ability to take care of yourself. I feel proud that you have been chosen for something special.'

'Thanks mum and dad,' said Ashley, 'I know you are right, but I'm impatient to find out the why of it all if you know what I mean. I hope I'm doing the right thing in trying to teach those bullies a lesson.'

Lillian said that as long as Ashley didn't physically hurt them it might bring them back to being decent human beings again. Anyway said Lillian it couldn't hurt to try.

There was a sudden flood of emotion in the room as Ashley conveyed the abundance of his love for his parents. He got the same in return and the three of them stood up and came together in a huddle of love.

Just then a fourth person joined them. It was Katy.

'I heard you in my room,' she said, 'so I've come down to join the cuddle.'

Lillian was concerned when she asked Katy what she had heard.

'O, nothing,' said Katy, 'I could hear your thoughts and how much we all loved each other. Before that Ashley spoke to me in my mind about being worried about something. Don't worry, I have known about Ashley's gift of reading minds for some time now. I wish I could read minds too, and then I could play tricks on Rehana.'

'You mustn't tell anyone about this,' said Alex. 'It's important that we keep this in the family or they might think Ashley is odd. What else do you think Ashley can do?'

'O, he can also talk to you with his mind,' said Katy. 'I think that is so cool.'

'Anything else?' asked Lillian with a worried expression on her face.

'No mummy,' said Katy, 'not that I know of. Except of course that Ashley never gets angry or annoyed even when I play tricks on him. And his room is always so tidy, so unlike mine. We are a loving family, aren't we mummy?'

Alex let out a sigh and came and gave his daughter another big hug. Soon they were a cuddling foursome again.

The next morning Ashley was his usual carefree self and looking forward to putting the plan into action in the school dining hall. Before setting off for school he asked his mum if he could borrow her full length blue cagoule. This had a nice big hood and Ashley had worn it a number of times when they went for walks in Sutton Park. It could be rolled up into a tight little ball and kept hidden in his school bag. It was to be an essential part of the plan which he had kept secret from everyone else.

In another part of Birmingham, Mrs Jones was pleasantly surprised to see her son Adrian all up and ready for school well before his usual time. He seemed his old cheerful self again after such a long time too. He even wished his mum a very good morning with a big bright smile. When Lisa came down to the breakfast table he chatted to her like his old self and Mrs Jones was pleased to hear them laugh together at something Lisa had said.

'I'm meeting Tim Richards in the playground mum,' said Adrian, 'so I don't want to be late.'

And off he went to catch his bus. And it was only eight o'clock. Adrian had already been briefed about the plan and he was impatient to get to school. It felt like a new phase of his life was about to begin and he was quite excited about it. Just like waiting for the taxi to take you to the airport at the start of a holiday abroad.

The school day went as normal and it wasn't long before the dinner break was upon them. Both Adrian and Tim stayed behind in class pretending to finish some work they were doing. They delayed going to the dining hall by about five minutes as planned. And then they strolled slowly and joined the back end of the queue to the serving hatches. They could see that the three bullies had already been served and were walking to one of the tables. They also knew that no one would choose to sit near them if a place could be found at another table. And so it was that Adrian and Tim carried their trays across and sat down at the bullies' table. Adrian sat next to a surprised Brian Charles while Tim settled down opposite and alongside Morris Cooney.

'We thought we'd save you the trouble of getting up by coming to sit at your table' said Tim. 'Please, we don't want any trouble like yesterday. We just want to be left alone.'

Brian Charles smiled at them and also at his cronies and said, 'Just so long as you do exactly as we say like the good boys you are you can sit at our table. Now be so good as to keep silent while we finish our dinner.'

And with that he gave Tim a vicious kick under the table. Tim's 'Oow' was heard around the room and Mrs Jarvis the canteen manageress who happened to be standing a few tables away, came over and asked if everything was okay.

'Yes thank you Mrs Jarvis,' said Brian, 'I think I accidentally kicked Tim's foot under the table as I was settling myself.'

She told him to be more careful as the tables were quite narrow and leg room was limited.

'Sorry Tim,' said Brian in a loud enough voice for Mrs Jarvis to hear and at the same time giving Adrian a dig in the ribs with his elbow.

The dinner breaks were staggered for the upper school by half an hour. Forms three and four began their canteen attendance while the lower school were still at table. Although there was enough room for the whole school in the dining hall the serving had to be staggered to ease queuing at the serving area.

Ashley, Jimmy, Robert and Robin brought their own packed lunches so didn't need to enter the canteen for lunch, which was how they had met Tim and Adrian in the playground the previous day. There was no rule that said they couldn't enter to buy a snack from the vending machines placed near the entrance.

And so it was that Jimmy and Robin entered the dining hall as part of Ashley's plan. While Robin pretended to be selecting an item at the vending machine, Jimmy walked over to Adrian and said 'Hello.' He then walked back to where Robin waited and the two of them then left the hall.

Tim now looked up from his tray, and looking over Brian's head he said 'Hello sir' as if to someone standing right behind him.

With a quick look behind him Brian said, 'Who are you talking to, there's no one there? You must be seeing things'.

'I thought for a second there was an old man standing behind you looking over your shoulder,' said Tim.

'Rubbish,' said Morris Cooney. 'I didn't see anyone, and I'm sitting right next to you.'

This time it was Adrian who jerked upright and also looked quickly behind him.

'Some one just touched me on the shoulder,' he said, 'but there's no one there now.'

'This is some sort of a lark the two of you have hatched up,' said Brian with a smile on his face. 'I dare say your cousin Jimmy has put you up to this.' And with that he gave Tim another hard kick under the table.

It was now Ashley's turn.

He was standing outside the entrance to the dining hall when he made the world turn a rosy pink. While everyone seemed frozen, he put on his blue cagoule with hood up partially hiding his face and walked into the hall stopping behind Brian. Then he came out of pink mode and with a stooped posture leaned forward and touched Brian very lightly on his right shoulder.

Morris Cooney was staring at this figure with his mouth gaping open unable to utter a word. Slowly his hand came up and he pointed at Brian. But suddenly there was nothing there. Ashley had gone pink again and walked back out.

Brian had stiffened at the touch and whirled around but all he saw was a blur of something like a mist. There was nothing there.

It was Morris who finally found his tongue and said, 'I saw it, I saw it.'

Brian seemed slightly unsettled. He reckoned that Adrian had somehow reached around and touched his shoulder. After all he had been looking over to where Mrs Jarvis was standing before he planned another dig at Adrian with his elbow.

He looked at Adrian at his side and said, 'You think that's very funny do you? You can't fool me with your tricks you wimp.'

Then to Morris he said, 'What's the matter with you Morris. You look as if you have seen a ghost.'

But all Morris could still say was, 'I saw it, I saw it.'

'Saw what you idiot?' said Brian.

'T-t-there was a hooded man standing behind you Brian,' stammered Morris. 'I swear there was an old man standing right behind you. I swear it, I swear it Brian. And he reached out and touched your shoulder. I swear I saw it Brian.'

'Well where is he,' said Brian. 'I don't see anyone now, do you? Did you see anything Lesley?'

Both Lesley Carleton and Morris Cooney were a bit afraid of Brian who could be quite bossy towards them at times.

'No Brian,' said Lesley, 'I didn't see anything at all.'

'Well I did,' said Tim. 'He looked a pleasant old man. I saw him twice. The first time I said hello to him and he smiled back at me. But you didn't believe me. This time I saw him again as did Morris. And yes, he did touch you on the shoulder. I think he knows what a bully you are and has come to teach you a lesson. Oooooh ouch.'

Tim received a vicious kick under the table when he'd had his say. All was going according to plan though the old man appearing was a surprise turn of events. And what happened next was an even greater surprise for all.

One moment Brian was eating his dinner and the next instant his plate was upside down on his lap. Brian always put extra gravy on his mash and now this was running all down his trousers.

When Brian saw the plate on his lap he clearly thought that Adrian or Tim was responsible, even though he hadn't seen them do it. He was furious that someone could do this to him. His temper got the better of him and being the bully he was he lashed out at the nearest person. And that person just happened to be Adrian Jones. Brian twisted on his seat and hit Adrian smack on the cheek with his bunched up right fist. Adrian went flying over backwards off his seat and down onto the dining hall floor. He was knocked dizzy when his head hit the floor and he just lay there for the next few seconds.

Two of the dinner staff rushed over to him and helped him to his feet. Mrs Jarvis also came over to them and stared at Adrian.

'What do you think you are doing young man?' she said.

'I don't know what you mean miss,' said Adrian, 'I was just eating my dinner when he hit me.'

'Who hit you?' asked Mrs Jarvis.

'He did,' said Adrian pointing at Brian.

'Well mister,' said Mrs Jarvis to Brian, 'is that right, did you hit this boy?'

'No miss,' said Brian, 'I just pushed him because look what he did. He pushed my dinner onto my lap. I'm all covered in gravy and things. He started it.'

'Well,' said Mrs Jarvis, 'I'm reporting you both to the headmaster for fighting. You are both to report to his office immediately; right this minute; at once. Do you understand? I'll be along shortly.'

Mrs Jarvis could be fierce when she was annoyed. She didn't like boys who misbehaved.

And so Adrian and Brian found themselves outside Mr Haddon's office. Brian hadn't even tried to wipe himself down. They tapped on the door and were told to enter.

'What is it?' said Mr Haddon. And then he saw the state of Brian's trouser front.

'Well, well, well,' he said, 'I wonder what you have been up to.'

And before they could reply, Mrs Jarvis came thundering in.

'These two boys have been fighting in my dinner hall,' she said. 'This boy pushed this boy's dinner plate onto his lap and then this boy retaliated and pushed him onto the dining hall floor.' She gesticulated at each boy as she spoke.

'Did you actually see all of this Mrs Jarvis?' asked Mr Haddon in a quiet voice.

'Well not directly,' said the canteen manageress, 'but I saw this boy lying on the floor and the dinner plate upside down on this other boy's lap.'

'Thank you Mrs Jarvis,' said the headmaster, 'perhaps you would be so good as to return to the diners and find out if there were any other witnesses and get statements from them, especially from those at the same table. I'll be along as soon as I have had a word with these two.'

Then to Brian and Adrian he said, 'I'm going to ask each of you in turn for your side of the incident. And while I'm talking to the one the other will not interrupt. Is that understood?'

'Yes sir,' they said in unison.

Mr Haddon asked Brian to speak first.

'Well sir,' said Brian, 'I was sitting there eating my dinner when Adrian who was sitting on my left suddenly reached across and pushed my plate onto my lap. Sir, look at my trousers, I'm all covered in gravy and things. I was so shocked that my left arm went backwards on reflex and caught Adrian across the face and knocked him backwards. He fell off his seat onto the floor and the dinner staff came and helped him up. We weren't fighting sir, but it was his entire fault. He tipped my dinner over me.'

'And why do you think he would do a thing like that? He is much smaller than you.'

I don't know sir, but he just did,' said Brian.

'Okay young man,' to Adrian, 'perhaps you would tell me your side of the incident.'

'I don't know anything about how the dinner got onto Brian's lap sir,' said Adrian without a hint of a stammer, 'I didn't do it and don't know who did. But the next thing I knew was when Brian punched me with his fist and knocked me to the floor.'

Adrian's right cheek was very red and slightly swollen and the headmaster could clearly see this.

'Well boys, let us go back to the dinner hall and see if we have any witnesses to back up your stories,' he said.

And with that he stood up and the two boys followed him back to the dinner hall.

Mrs Jarvis who was talking to the three boys at Brian's table came over and spoke quietly to Mr Haddon. There was a hush in the hall.

'I see,' said Mr Haddon. 'Very well, I'll speak to him first.' He had pointed at Tim.

And so Tim was called into Mrs Jarvis' office and confronted by the headmaster.

They were in there about five minutes and in that time Tim told all he knew about the bullying of Adrian by Brian and his gang of two, Morris Cooney and Lesley Carleton. He mentioned about the incident the day before when Brian had pushed Adrian's plate across the table and onto his lap. Tim also said how Brian had been picking on Adrian since way back at the start of the September term.

Mr Haddon now recalled the visit by Mrs Jones last term and it all seemed to fit a pattern.

He then asked Tim why he had not reported any of this earlier. Tim said that he had been afraid to but that he had mentioned it to his cousin Jimmy Marshall in Form Four. He then recounted the threat Brian had made about getting Jimmy expelled if he tried to settle scores personally.

Mr Haddon looked extremely thoughtful.

'Thank you Tim for being so forthcoming. I shall now speak to Morris and Lesley in turn. Can you please ask them to come in together?'

When they were seated Mr Haddon looked at them in his sternest manner and asked each of them in turn to say exactly what they had seen.

Neither of them had seen Adrian push Brian's plate. Nor had they seen Brian hit Adrian. All they had seen was when Adrian had fallen backwards onto the floor.

It was Morris who then said that he had seen a strange hooded figure standing behind Brian and reaching out to touch him on the shoulder. Perhaps this person had done it. Perhaps it had caused Brian's dinner plate to drop into his lap.

'What hooded figure' said Mr Haddon sharply?

'Sir,' said Morris, 'I only saw him for an instant. One second he was there behind Brian and the next he was gone. Tim saw something as well because he seemed to say hello to him when he first came to sit beside me with his dinner tray.'

'Well, well, well,' said Mr Haddon, 'so now we have a phantom in our midst. And I suppose you are going to tell me that this phantom is the cause behind all the bullying that has been going on in the school. O yes, I do know what has been going on and I intend to put a stop to it.'

Both Morris and Lesley went a shade of pale.

Then the headmaster asked Lesley Carleton to say what he had seen but there was nothing he could add. He had been sitting on Brian's right side away from Adrian and didn't see anything till after Adrian had hit the floor.

'I shall want to speak to you two again as soon as I have had a chance to look at the CCTV recordings tonight,' said Mr Haddon.

He could see the worried expressions on their faces. They certainly looked guilty.

Then he said in his sternest voice, 'I'd be careful of the company I keep. It could get you into serious trouble.'

Both Morris and Lesley knew exactly whom he meant.

Matters had taken a twist that Ashley had not foreseen. The violent reaction by Brian Charles had been unexpected and had upset his plans but to a certain degree only. The plan for the next day would continue as before.

Adrian was sent in to see the school nurse about his slightly red and puffy right cheek. She made him sit on a stool and applied an ice pack to the cheek in question. She told him to hold it there for as long as possible. She had been told about his fall and checked him for any signs of concussion. There was no nausea or dizziness, and Adrian's eyes seemed to focus quite normally. Apparently he had no ill effects from his contact with the dining hall floor.

The nurse kept Adrian in the sick room for nearly an hour. The cold compress seemed to have worked for his cheek looked quite normal again. She then told Adrian that the headmaster wanted to see him before he went home.

In the office Mr Haddon told Adrian that he had a letter for his parents explaining the events of the day and the continuing action that was being taken. A full report would be sent by the end of the week.

'I see that the swelling on your face has gone down,' he said, 'I will not tolerate bullying in my school at any level whatsoever. Tim Richards has already told me that you have been picked on by these persons since you started here in September. Is this true and are the culprits the same Brian Charles, Lesley Carleton and Morris Cooney?'

'Yes sir,' replied Adrian and then looked down at the floor in embarrassment.

'I realise there is a code among boys against reporting other boys' behaviour to staff. And I have to tell you that your mother came to see me last term and she suspected that something was not right. I realise now that she had just cause to be concerned then and that this same bullying was the issue. I'm sorry to have failed you then. I shall remedy the matter from now on. Thank you Adrian, that will be all for now. You may report our discussion to your parents.'

As Adrian left the office he walked past a very worried looking Brian Charles waiting for his turn with the Headmaster.

By now it was the end of the school day and the more senior boys were already out on the grounds. Adrian was immediately met by Ashley, Jimmy, Robert and Robin to ask what had transpired in the Headmaster's office. Adrian gave them the whole story and they could see that his right cheek was now nearly back to normal. They could also see that Adrian was not in the least bit concerned or worried. In fact he seemed to be quite excited by what he could only describe as an adventure.

Adrian mentioned that he had seen Brian Charles waiting outside the Headmaster's office and that he had definitely looked worried. He also said that Mr Haddon intended to look at the CCTV footage that night to ascertain the truth of the incident.

Ashley suddenly realised that he had quite forgotten about the camera in the dining hall. It was located high up above the entrance to Mrs Jarvis' office for maximum coverage. Fortunately Ashley had kept the cagoule hood well up when he had been in a position to be seen by the camera. So at worst he might be seen on the CCTV recording but without being recognised. He hoped.

This new gang of four then discussed their plan for the next day and Ashley said in view of the unexpected events of the day they should do nothing. Tim and Adrian should sit at their own table away from the Brian Charles gang. Ashley already had his own plan in mind but he couldn't let on about it because it involved his action in 'pink' mode. They all then walked out of school to the bus stop to await their respective buses.

Meanwhile Mr Haddon had Brian Charles in his office and was spelling out to him the consequences of any evidence of bullying in the school. He then let him go home with the knowledge that a detailed investigation into the days events would be started and would include all matters leading up to it, even if it required going back to the start of the school year.

That evening Mr Haddon replaced the tape in the CCTV setup and sat down to view the lunchtime recorded footage. There were four cameras around the school and the monitor in the secretary's office switched to each in turn every seven seconds. The recordings covered the whole school but with gaps of 21 seconds for each designated area. This system had been approved by the contracted security firm as sufficient for their needs relating to break-ins and acts of vandalism.

However when Mr Haddon viewed the period in question the only bit on view was when Mrs Jarvis was talking to Brian Charles with Adrian and two dinner staff standing by. He went over it again from the start of the dinner hour but could see nothing unusual that he didn't already know about. Fortunately for Ashley the incident of his tapping Brian on the shoulder had been missed by the recorder.

The only evidence Mr Haddon had to go on was Tim's verbal report about the bullying. He also had Adrian's admission that this was true. It was really a matter of one boy's word against another. It was enough for him to put in a course of corrective action, but not enough to punish the accused. However he would ensure that he put a stop to any form of bullying in his school. So at least today's incident had brought this issue to his attention.

And so the next morning he phoned Brian Charles' home and spoke to his mother. She agreed to see him later that morning. He also phoned Mrs Jones and she too agreed to come in to see him but later in the afternoon.

Mrs Charles did not like what she heard. She was not pleased that her son had been accused of bullying of a much younger boy. Not Brian her only child? Surely it couldn't be true.

'And you say that this bullying of the younger boy has been going on since the beginning of the previous term?' asked Mrs Charles.

'That is what I am led to believe,' said Mr Haddon, 'I have not seen any direct evidence of it but I have to take the matter seriously once it has been reported. I cannot take any action against anyone at the moment as it is a matter of one boy's word against another. I shall continue my investigations to establish the truth and I thought it right that you should be brought into the picture, so to speak.'

Mrs Charles was concerned. If this was true, and of course boys will be boys, then she would conduct her own observations on her son's behaviour at home. She thanked the headmaster for his prudent handling of the issue and would be obliged if he could keep her informed of any developments. She would discuss the matter with her husband this evening.

Mrs Jones came in at 2:30pm and quietly listened to a very apologetic headmaster. She said that she was glad that the bullying matter had been exposed but that she had no further concerns for her son's welfare at school. He had formed a friendship with a group of boys and was back to his cheery disposition.

'Ever since Adrian became friends with Tim Richards, he has gradually reverted to his previous happy self,' said Mrs Jones. 'His friend Tim has an older cousin in the Fourth Form, I think his name is Jimmy Marshall, and Adrian speaks well of him. It seems to have made a big difference in his attitude towards your school, thank goodness. I feel that now that the bullying aspect has come out into the open, it may stop of its own accord. Don't you think so Mr Haddon?'

'Perhaps,' said Mr Haddon.

He then thanked her for her understanding. He hadn't told her the name of the alleged bully but only that he had also spoken to the parent in question. He assured her that he would keep a close watch on the boys from now on. He could take no punitive action as there was no hard evidence to go on. He said he had interviewed several other boys but had not learned anything new.

And so the matter gradually faded into the background of school life.

For a while Brian and his gang stayed away from Adrian and Tim in the dining hall. But this was not to last. It was now more than a week since the incident. And then it started again with the three bullies coming over to sit beside Adrian and Tim as they used to do.

'Hello Adrian how is your jaw?' said Brian giving him a sharp dig in the ribs.

'Very well thank you,' said a bold Adrian, 'and would you like some more gravy?'

Brian got all red in the face. He was especially annoyed because his dad had been on at him all week about how he must always play fair with other boys, especially those poorer and younger than him. There had been lectures and lectures and funny looks from both his parents till he wanted to swear at them. He'd had enough. He was sure this wimp was the cause of it all. He had blabbed to the headmaster and so would be taught a lesson. But not today as Mrs Jarvis seemed to be constantly watching him. But that didn't prevent him from stamping hard on Adrian's foot under the table.

After dinner Adrian and Tim met up with Ashley and the others in the playground and mentioned that Brian was up to his old bullying tricks again. Ashley just smiled.

It was time to put phase two of his plan into action. He had hoped that the events of the previous week plus one might have changed Brian's attitude and made the plan unnecessary. But no such luck.

Jimmy Marshall was all for going over and sorting it out with Brian, but Tim reminded his cousin that this would get him expelled.

Ashley instructed Tim and Adrian to sit as close to the serving counter as possible when they were in the dining hall. This might stop the harassment by Brian and his gang for now. Ashley then told them that he had a plan but he needed to talk to one of his dad's friends who earned a living as an entertainment magician. He'd see if he could get hold of a prop or two for some simple magic.

And so it was that a few days later weird happenings began to occur at the dinner table where Brian, Lesley and Morris took their meals.

Ashley would go 'pink' and then come into the dining hall and apply a gentle pressure to the shoulder of one of the three bullies and also move their tray around and then leave the hall before returning back to normal. No one ever saw him. And twenty minutes later Ashley would repeat this but to another one of the three.

At first none of them said anything but after a few days of this Lesley finally exclaimed that he thought the dining hall was haunted.

'It's that hooded figure I saw behind you Brian that day you hit Adrian,' said Lesley, 'I felt a hand on my shoulder and my tray was moved just now.'

'I felt it too,' said Morris, 'something's wrong. Lesley could be right in saying this room is haunted.'

'Don't be silly,' said Brian, 'I don't think......'

But then he stopped as he had just felt a hand on his shoulder and this time it had squeezed quite hard.

Brian's face turned quite pale for the next moment his dinner plate was upside down on his lap and there was gravy all down his trousers again. There was no one anywhere near him that he could blame.

Lesley and Morris looked on in horror. All school boys love telling ghost stories to one another and most are superstitious to some extent. But when something like this actually happens to them they do get scared. It makes them believe in the supernatural.

One of the dinner staff came over to Brian and said what a mess he had made and for him to go at once to the washrooms and get cleaned up. Brian was not a happy person at all. In fact he was also quite worried if not a bit scared.

It was then that Ashley sent out a telepathic message. It said 'You have only yourself to blame.' Nearly everyone in the dining hall must have heard this but to most it would have had no meaning. Of course, if you had something to feel guilty about or something odd had happened to you like a plate falling onto your lap, then the words would have a terrible impact. So Brian, Lesley and Morris looked at each other in surprise. Brian then stood up and left the hall for the washrooms where he wiped himself down as best as he could.

Mrs Jarvis was away that day so it was up to the senior-most dinner staff to report this incident. But the matter was considered trivial so no report was made.

Lesley and Morris sat expectantly for something else to happen but nothing did. It seemed that with Brian out of the hall all calm had been restored.

The next day Ashley repeated his 'pink' intrusions into the dining hall touching their shoulders as before. But this time he flipped Lesley's dinner plate upside down on his tray. Lesley could take this no longer and hastily stood up and left the hall.

Ashley then went into temporary 'pink' mode and went up behind Lesley and whispered, 'stay away from Brian.' Lesley spun around to see who was there but of course Ashley had gone 'pink' again and walked well away around a corner.

It was from there that Ashley tried to read Lesley's mind to see what he intended to do about Brian. It was then that he registered the uniqueness in Lesley's brainwave pattern. It suddenly dawned on Ashley like a new found knowledge, that everyone had a unique brain pattern just like everyone had a unique set of finger prints. This knowledge came to Ashley just like all the other bits of knowledge that appeared the moment he queried some fact. Just like the Lych-gate of so long ago.

Ashley now knew that he would be able to communicate telepathically on a strictly one to one selective basis once he had registered the person's unique thought fingerprint. But he knew it would require a little practice for his own brain to transmit in the exact same fingerprint pattern.

Ashley decided to first talk to his mom and dad about this latest discovery.

Where was this knowledge and skill coming from? And why had he only just become aware of it and not years ago in Aberporth when he first found out about his telepathic abilities?

Alex had said that he thought there must be a purpose to Ashley's gifts. And also that it must be intended that he learn things about his gifts in a gradual and progressive manner. It was as though Ashley's brain was meant to grow and develop together and that he was only granted new knowledge and abilities as he became able to cope fully with them. Lillian had come to terms with where all of this might be taking her son. Initially she had been ever so concerned of what might become of Ashley. She had feared for his well being and safety. She thought she was going to lose her son. But now she could see a loving and caring boy growing up to be a wonderful and considerate human being who wouldn't hurt a fly. And a bond had developed between them that went far beyond that between parent and child. They were like co-conspirators on some great mission. It was a lovely feeling. And both Lillian and Alex were extremely proud of their son. And not only that, they felt proud and privileged that they must have been chosen for Ashley to be theirs. Ashley had his gifts but they had theirs as well. They had their mutual gift of love which they deemed to be the greatest gift of all.

And so it was time for the family to conduct another experiment at Ashley's request. He wanted to see if he could communicate with each of them in turn on a selective basis. Ashley knew without a doubt that this new ability had already been programmed into his brain but he needed to reassure himself that he could do it. He also felt he needed to practice any newly acquired skill so that it could be honed to perfection. But most of all he was just curious to see how it worked.

And so Ashley first read his dad's thoughts, let his mind identify its unique thought-wave pattern and then he communicated a thought in return. His dad laughed out aloud at the message he received. It was so much easier to tell a joke telepathically. Verbally, the joke would have taken minutes to relate but here it came across in an instant.

Lillian looked her husband and smiled in a puzzled sort of a way. She hadn't received anything from Ashley.

'Well son,' laughed Alex, 'I got that loud and clear, but obviously your mom did not.'

Ashley then repeated the experiment with his mom and she definitely heard him and also laughed at the same joke he had sent his dad.

'I didn't receive anything that time,' said Alex, 'it looks to me that you have another skill in your arsenal. However, can you still communicate in the general way you did before?'

'I love you both mom and dad. You are my very best friends,' was the communication that Ashley sent out to them simultaneously.

'Yes I love you too son,' said Alex.

'And so do I,' said Lillian.

So they had both received Ashley's message together. Ashley didn't need to put any effort into doing any of these tasks. It was like going 'pink'. He just had to think about it and it happened.

The realisation came to Ashley quite suddenly that this gift would prove to be a very important one – in view of what he would be required to do.

Wham! There it was again!

Someone or something was communicating this information to him. Who was this being?

If there was one quality that Ashley possessed it was patience. He just knew that in time all would eventually be revealed to him. It was as if this also had been intimated to him. Ever since he was a child and been aware of his gifts he had known that things would just work out. He was quite happy to let events continue and to develop over time as he grew older. He did enjoy life to the full perhaps more so than most and was keen to see what the next day would bring. He loved his family and his friends and allowed himself to trust in the wisdom and experience of the voice that he kept hearing.

As far as the bully boys were concerned Ashley decided to leave them alone for a week or two. He noticed that Lesley Carleton was not always in the company of Brian and Morris, at least not as often as he used to be. He seemed to have made another friend in Jerry Mahawa, a boy from his gym class and was often seen with him on the playground.

Ashley thought this a good sign that his whisper to Lesley to keep away from Brian had worked. He could now try the same thing on Morris but this time he would use his new found one-to-one telepathy skill. After some careful consideration Ashley decided that he ought to make it seem to Morris as if it was his own conscience talking to him. And so it was that a week later he sent across to Morris the thought, 'I am not a bully like Brian and I don't want to become one. But if I stay friends with Brian I might become like him'. Hopefully this thought would repeat itself again and again in Morris's mind and result in the break-up of their friendship.

It was about a another week later that Adrian saw Brian sitting at the dining table on his own while Morris and Lesley were with Jerry at another table. Jerry came from an Indian background but had been born in Birmingham and was as Brummie as they came. He was a jolly sort of a chap and also a born mimic. He had the boys in splits when he mimicked some of the teachers. He was also in the 2XI cricket team. And it was not long before Lesley and Morris joined him at the practice nets after school. Even though they had no idea how to bowl or bat Jerry told them to just throw the ball at his stumps as best they could to give him batting practice.

Both Lesley and Morris got into the game and quite liked it. Lesley soon picked up the knack of batting from watching the other boys and showed promise as an opening batsman. Morris was a left hander and was much slower to develop. He decided he would stick with 'chucking' during net practice. Robert Black however saw potential in his left handedness and decided to personally coach him to bowl. Left handed bowlers were a particular asset to any bowling side. And so Morris found himself the centre of attention for the first time in his life and he quite enjoyed it. He felt he had missed so much by keeping company with Brian Charles. He regretted all the things he had let Brian drag him into. He never wanted to be classed as a bully boy ever again. There was so much more to life. There was cricket.

Lesley, Morris and Jerry became good friends and were always together in the playground. And as they tended to move around they made occasional contact with Ashley, Jimmy and Robin. It was on the one occasion when Adrian and Tim met with Ashley and his friends that Lesley and Morris joined up with them. Both seemed quite embarrassed. But Ashley immediately said that they should let bygones be bygones and there was no need for apologies. The important thing was that they had made things right.

But finally it was Morris who said to Adrian that both he and Lesley were sorry. Sorry for being such stupid fools and sorry for being part of Brian's bullying. Adrian said that being friends now was more important than anything that had been done in the past. And with that he came forward and shook hands with both Lesley and Morris.

And Ashley had the biggest smile of all of them. This was satisfaction in the extreme.

It was on a Saturday that Lillian had invited her friend Mavis Chambers and her daughter Vicky to tea and a chat. They often met at each others homes and both families had become close friends too. Ashley was home and playing cards with Katy at the dining table. Katy had learned a few card tricks from her friend Rehana who had been shown them by her dad. Vicky had mentioned it to Robert Black during a phone call that she and her mum were visiting Lillian that day, and before you knew it Ashley's little gang also turned up with Robert. Robin and Jimmy just couldn't keep away from the Ashley residence either. Robin Nesters was a bit taller than Ashley and also a bit of a pretty boy with rosy cheeks; which turned an even deeper shade of red when he happened to talk to Katy.

It was not long before Vicky had joined Katy and the boys for a game of 'Sly Donkey'. The laughter noise this caused could be heard halfway down the Close. The 'ready-to-pass-pass' phase of the game seemed to get quicker and quicker till they would all have to slam their cards face down on the table. The last person judged down was 'it' and given one letter from the word 'donkey'. The final loser was the first one to acquire all six letters and had to walk around the room making an animal noise. Katy liked to lose just so she could make her favourite animal noise. I sometimes wondered if she lost purposely whenever Robin was around. There did seem to be the odd look that passed between them. It was all good innocent fun.

While they were all enjoying tea and biscuits afterwards someone just happened to mention Brian Charles. They talked about how his bullying behaviour had simply evaporated now that he was without Morris and Lesley. He had no one to pick on anymore. In fact he looked quite pitiful. Ashley suggested that Brian be roped into one of the sports teams. Since Lesley and Morris were now playing at cricket Jimmy thought it best not to bring them back together in the same game. It would probably be embarrassing for them. Since Brian was quite a big-made fellow Robert thought he might be an asset in the rugby team. That is, if he had the energy. He knew that Frank Peers the games master was always on the lookout for suitable boys for the rugby team. He would definitely give Brian a practice session at the very least. Perhaps rugby was just the right outlet for Brian's aggressive nature. He could run himself ragged on the often soggy rugby pitch. Robert said he would talk to Brian with the suggestion.

But before Robert could approach him I had made a telepathic suggestion to Brian on the Monday to go and watch rugby practice that evening. He seemed to become quite interested in the physical side of the game and soon caught the watchful eye of Frank Peers who strolled across to him.

'Are you interested in having a go, lad', he said. 'We could use someone as big as you in the scrums. Care to give it a try. We might have some spare kit if you'd care to go and see my assistant Tony Morelle in the gym'.

Brian turned out to be a natural pusher in the scrums and Frank found him quite an asset. Over the weeks Brian also improved his running and passing skills to the extent that he was regularly put in to play by Frank. Ashley made it a point to attend some of the early games and on a couple of occasions sent telepathic suggestions to Brian for a particular pass or directional run for a try.

It was after one such winning game when Ashley and friends were grouped together near the centre line that they witnessed something unexpected and wonderful. Adrian and Tim were also spectators and were standing a few yards away. Brian Charles, all covered in wet mud from the game, was limping off the field towards the changing rooms in the school when he suddenly stopped and turned. He then made his way slowly towards the spectators on the opposite side of the field. He was making a path straight towards Adrian and Tim. When he got up to them he seemed to hesitate, looked around sheepishly and then began to say something to Adrian. Then he reached out his hand and Adrian also reached out and they shook hands warmly. He repeated the same with Tim. He then turned and began his slow limping walk back across the pitch. Halfway across he stopped, turned and gave a thumbs up sign to Adrian and Tim before carrying on into the school building.

Ashley and his group of friends saw all this with big smiles on their faces. All their scheming efforts had finally paid off. This was the best result anyone could have expected.

This had also been secretly observed by a figure standing looking out from a first floor window of the Admin building. Mr Haddon often watched rugby practice from this room, his second and more private study. It was where he came to concentrate away from the daily school business and where he did most of his thoughtful planning prior to implementation. Now a satisfied look appeared on his face. It had been nearly three months since the bullying allegations had been brought to his attention by Tim Richards and in that time he had kept a close watch on this particular lad.

He had seen the gradual isolation and change in attitude of Brian Charles and now he had just witnessed the final transformation of the bully into the sportsman. And so it was now time for him to once again speak to Brian's parents. And this time he would find it a very pleasant part of his duties. Of course he would insist that he see both parents together. Better still he would arrange to visit them at home one evening. He would have his thrill and not let on what it was he wanted to speak to them about. Watching their faces when he gave them the news would be worth every waiting moment.

It was bad news in his office and good news in their homes.

And so a few days later Mr Haddon was at the Charles' front door.

'Please come in Headmaster,' said a wary Mr Charles as he opened the hall door and led the way into a beautiful and tastefully decorated blue toned living room. Mrs Charles was standing just inside and came forward to also shake hands as a welcoming gesture.

'My wife Audrey, Headmaster,' said Mr Charles, 'but you have met before. I'm Frank and very pleased to meet you Mr Haddon. Do sit down please.'

They hadn't a clue as to the reason for this visit but assumed it must be something to do with Brian. Was he in trouble again? Was their son about to be expelled or excluded from school? Although they could keep an eye on their son at home they had no control over what went on at school. They did ask Brian about his day but apart from the usual 'fine' response he didn't say much.

Recently Brian seemed to have changed towards a more pleasant personality. He was quite talkative at the dinner table and laughed occasionally. Most of all he went on and on about the game of rugby. He talked about the school rugby team and some of the tries they made. He often came home with a limp or a nasty bruise on his face but always joked about 'You should see the other chap'. Of course if there was a rugby match on the telly Brian just had to sit and watch it all the way to the end. The only thing that worried Audrey and Frank was that Brian didn't seem to have any close friends. He never mentioned any names of boys at school in his class.

And now here was the headmaster about to give them some bad news. It had to be bad news or why else would he have stressed that he wanted to speak to both parents together?

Mr Haddon had remained standing and started with, 'So good of you to let me visit you at home. And you do have a lovely home.' Then he went on to say what a pleasure it was to bring them good news.

There was an exhaling of breaths from both parents as they visibly relaxed. Both were now smiling back at Mr Haddon just as he was smiling at them.

'Do please sit down Headmaster,' said Mrs Charles, 'and do let me make you a nice cup of tea.'

'Thank you very much, but let me first finish what I have come to tell you.'

'Please do,' said Mr Charles.

'Well as you know it is nearly three months since I last saw you Mrs Charles when certain allegations were brought against your son Brian regarding the aspect of bullying on the school premises. I do believe there may have been some substance in the accusations at the time and our staff had since made an extra effort to observe all such goings on at the school. Unfortunately there was nothing we could do other than try to intervene in any suspected case,'

Mr Haddon paused for a moment before he continued.

'The group of three boys of which your son was a member split up after the accusations and for a while Brian was on his own. As you know Brian has the physique of a rugby player and our games master invited him to join the team. I believe Brian has an aggressive streak and this proved an advantage in a game of rough and tumble. Within a few weeks it became obvious that Brian not only enjoyed the game but was actually quite good at it. Brian needed a contact sport to vent some of his physical energy and that I do believe has proved to be the case. Brian has become a key member of our rugby team. The other two boys joined the cricketing group and regularly attend practice in the nets after school. All three of them have found new avenues of adventure and I have not as yet seen any aggressiveness from them towards other junior pupils.'

Mr Haddon paused again and smiled an even bigger smile.

'However,' he said, 'however, the other day I witnessed something on the rugby pitch that truly gave me immense pleasure.' There was another pause.

'At the end of a rugby practice game I saw your son do something very brave and commendable. He walked over to where two junior boys were standing watching the game. These were the same two boys that your son had earlier been accused of bullying. As I watched from my study window I saw your son speak to them and then shake each boys hand in turn. I do believe your son took the first step and apologised to the other lads, a very commendable action on his part. I would think that this must have been witnessed by many of the other boys and is bound to change their perception of Brian.'

Mr Haddon paused again as he could see tears streaming down Mrs Charles' cheeks. There was a box of tissues on a table near her and she took one and dabbed delicately below her eyes.

Mr Charles put his arm around his wife and smiled proudly.

'Mr Haddon,' he said, 'thanks for bringing us this piece of good news. We love our son dearly but when those accusations were raised, and they were possibly true, our son was badly in need of guidance. I just didn't know if anything could be done. Apparently the environment in your school has taken care of that. I was concerned for his behaviour and worried about the type of person he was growing into. I do believe that he has changed his ways and I now know he will be alright. Thanks go to you and your school.'

Mr Haddon smiled at this and replied, 'Boys will be boys and some need their energies channelled in certain directions.'

And as an after thought he added, 'There is a group of fellows led by a very pleasant chap in the Fourth form. His name is Ashley. I don't know how but I somehow feel this group of boys played a significant role in your son's transformation. I feel he would benefit from getting to know these boys a bit more. Next time you are at one of our open days I shall introduce you to Ashley and his mother. The father is with the MoD and finds it difficult to attend. There is an aura of confidence in the boy that I find unique in one so young.'

Mr Haddon stayed another twenty minutes chatting pleasantly about non school matters over a cup of tea before he left. He was very pleased with himself and just wished there could be more occasions like this. It was a very satisfied outcome indeed, for him and for the school.

CHAPTER 6

Discoveries

1999

How the years have flown. I am now in the 6ᵗʰ Form and was 17 on my last birthday. I am 5 feet 9 inches tall and mom and dad refer to me as their bean-pole son since I am quite thin. I have lost count of all the languages I know but this is irrelevant since I can acquire instant communication with anyone on this planet. Not only that but I can acquire a complete lifestyle memory of anyone I wish. You do get to know a person really well from understanding their thought pattern.

Since those early days in Aberporth I have acquired a confidence in myself that I did not know I possessed. Then there is my 'instructor' who keeps telling me things and giving me instant knowledge of the item I might be querying at the time. Just who or what this person is still eludes me even though I have asked questions time and time again. All I get is that it will be revealed. So I just have to trust my instincts and leave it at that.

The history of things began to grab my interest during last summer when we spent a few days with Uncle Ron and Aunt Brenda in Aberporth. There was a car boot sale in a nearby field and we all thought it might be interesting to see what we could find. It was only when I picked up an item that I realised I had its history in my grasp. Not only that but I knew also what it would be worth in money terms if it was sent to an auction house in London. Not that there was anything of very great value at this car boot sale but an interest had been struck deep within me. There was one item that dated back to the mid-18ᵗʰ century but it was in a very poor state. This was a Chelsea porcelain jar but there was no lid to it. There was a large chip on the rim and a nasty crack down one side. It was in a grimy state though someone had tried half-heartedly to clean it up. The factory mark, a raised anchor on an oval medallion, was clearly visible on the underside.

The Chelsea Porcelain factory was started up in 1745 by Nick Sprimont a silver-smith. This particular jar was made, painted and fired in the April of 1752 just after the Easter celebrations by a 36 year old employee called Jimmy Mann at the Bow factory in Essex. He then lived in a semi-derelict mud-hut nearby with his wife and three children; two boys aged 9 and 11 and a girl of 13. His wife Mona was sickly and Nancy took over a lot of the housework her mum couldn't manage. Images of Jimmy Mann were also quite clear in my mind. He was a short skinny bald man and his face lined face made him look ten years older than his 36 years. Large nose and ears and piercing eyes gave him a hawkish look.

I found it fascinating that I could know so much from an item that I had just touched. That such and such a pot or glass item was made ages ago by a particular craftsman who could barely earn enough to feed his family. I even knew that if the item was very much older I would still get the same detailed images of its manufacture.

I bought the Chelsea porcelain piece for just 50 pence. And I decided then and there that I could make a living buying and selling antiques. When we got back to the house and I showed the piece to Uncle Ron he said I had been robbed. The item looked like a piece of junk he said but then when he looked at my smiling face he asked me to explain what exactly it was that I had found.

'Uncle Ron,' I said, 'I have just discovered another facet to my gifts.'

So we all sat around a table and I explained what I had discovered about myself and about the piece. Had the Chelsea porcelain jar been in mint condition and with its lid it would have fetched about £500 - £800 at auction. In its present condition it was worth about £10 - £20. But if I cleaned it up really well and attached a full printed history of its manufacture then it might make close to £50.

I told mom and dad that I had no intention of opening an antiques shop or anything of that sort but intended to work as a free-lance collector and to then offer my pieces to a dealer or auctioneer. The voice in my head told me that this would leave me free to travel all over the world in a legitimate way. Whatever was planned for me would best be served with this type of freedom.

'In that case son,' said dad, 'we had better get you started on some driving lessons. If you are to travel the country looking for antiques you will definitely need some transport of your own. I suppose an old banger would do to start with.'

'Thanks dad but there is no hurry at the moment. I'll probably only need a couple of lessons before my practical test. I'd like to finish with the sixth form exams first before I get serious on the antiques business. Perhaps Mr Ricardo our sixth form tutor might have a suggestion or two in that direction.'

Dad however persuaded me to apply for my provisional driving licence and to book some lessons with The AA School of Motoring since the charges for students were currently at half the normal rate. I was in for a surprise when I went for my first lesson just after Easter.

My mind reading gift had let me pick up all the information I needed so it was a nasty surprise when I found I did not have the manual skills needed to drive on the road. My coordination was poor and my steering ability was jerky. I completely failed to check my mirrors time and time again and at one point nearly went through a red light. I only started to improve on my fourth lesson. After my eighth the instructor said he would put me in for my practical test which would probably be in about a month's time when I should certainly be ready.

I sat the theory tests and passed with flying colours since I knew all the answers by using my gift of course. My driving test was set for a day in May but was cancelled due to the extreme weather conditions. There was heavy rain and strong winds all day. So I had to wait for a rescheduling of the test. This came through for the first week in June. By now I'd had twelve lessons and was fairly confident that I would pass. I didn't. The reason given was that I didn't check the nearside mirror every time I exited a roundabout. However the examiner had a little discussion with me and said the real reason he had failed me was that I lacked the necessary driving confidence on the road and my approach to driving hesitant and over cautious at junctions. Practice would cure this he said. He suggested I ride my bike a lot more to get a good feel for the traffic conditions.

All this had brought me down to earth with a bang. I realised now that although I had been given a very powerful gift it could be useless if I didn't get training and practice in its proper use. I also realised that I had never tried to do anything practical. My DIY skills were non-existent.

I resolved to correct this by visiting the carpentry shop at school and setting myself a project to make something. Mr Seers was very understanding and warned me that some people were just awkward and might never be able to acquire manual dexterity. He gave me a piece of soft white wood 3 inches by 2 inches and 4 feet long. He showed me how to mark off a piece from one end using a try-square, to hold it in a vice grip and to then saw the piece off using a flat handsaw. The purpose was to make a square cut and to test that it was so using the try-square. It looked so simple when he cut off the first piece that I thought it would be easy for me too. I was so wrong. Firstly, I got the marking crooked and had several goes before getting it right. Then putting the length of wood in the vice was not easy either. First time I didn't tighten the vice enough and the wood slipped as I began sawing. Then I got it in too tight and marked the wood. Then it was tilted downwards. Finally I got it right but the saw would not cut smoothly. Mr Seers said I was putting too much pressure on the saw. He said to let the saw do the cutting while I made the strokes. When I did get the hang of this I found I couldn't get a straight cut. After cutting six crooked pieces I decided to have a rest. My right shoulder was tired and a bit sore. This made me realise that I was not fit for purpose. So now I also needed to get fit by some sort of a keep-fit course. I needed to join a gym. Here I was nearly eighteen years old and suddenly discovering that I had so much more to learn.

And there was that inner voice again telling me that all this was not only important but absolutely essential to my objective. What objective I asked? Patience I am told, just have patience. And yet I knew that I would eventually be well prepared to achieve my goal whatever it was.

I remember dad telling me that anything that came too easily was never a lesson learned. At the time it meant nothing to me but today I feel so differently about that remark. It has a wider implication for all we do in this world. Something tells me that this will have a strong bearing on the way I will need to conduct my actions. As yet I don't know why but I shall keep it in my memory.

Incidentally I have noticed that my memory is extraordinarily clear all the way back to my childhood at age four and even a bit before. And I have noticed that my mind seems to be playing tricks on me when I read my history books. I feel as if I had been alive at the time and a déjà vu sensation comes over me briefly. But then it is gone and leaves me quite puzzled since I cannot recall any details. This is puzzling and mysterious to say the least if not enigmatic. Patience is certainly a virtue.

Another of the manual things that my carpentry tutor had me do was to hammer nails into a piece of pine wood. After a disastrous start when every nail got bent over, I finally managed to get it right nearly every time. When I mentioned all this to dad he suggested that I take up the game of darts and snooker to further my manual skills. Dad said that I could practice my darts game with him at our local pub The Navigation. I had no problem getting to know the rules of any game along with the best tips on play skills by simply acquiring the thought pattern of a champ.

I found that I quite enjoyed darts and once I got used to the flights I became very good at putting the tip exactly where I willed it. Dad said that I seemed to have an uncanny knack for it. But snooker was a very different matter. I found that although I had learned everything possible from my 'expert', the practice did not match the theory. I just could not seem to plan for my next shot or screw left or right as necessary. Someone remarked that my elbow was not made for snooker and I suppose he was right. Every time I went to make a shot the queue ball just did not go where I intended it to go. I even managed to scratch the green baize or as they said 'to field the cue'. Practice though I might I did not get anywhere with acquiring snooker skills and got no thrill from playing the game. Watching it was another matter. I just loved to watch the 'Pot Black' championships on the tele. I was fascinated by the game and the skills displayed by the young players. Apparently they practiced for hours every day and thought of nothing else. They ate, breathed and slept snooker. I guess one needed to be totally dedicated to the game to get where they were today.

Football was an exception for me. Here I found that by going slightly 'pink' at the right moment I could see exactly what my opponent was about to do. I could then push the ball gently in a direction away from him. I often got a 'wow' from spectators when I did this because it seemed that I had a fantastic dribbling skill. But I knew different and got no satisfaction from the game. I had been playing in a junior league team and had become the highest scorer. I could see that whenever I scored a goal everyone clapped except dad. He just looked on with a smile on his face. We talked about the football and it was only when he asked me if I had used my special gift during the game that I realised that I knew it was unfair on the others and that I was in fact cheating. So I decided to feign a calf injury and finally give up playing in the Junior League.

The sixth form exams were easy and I decided to go for high marks. I had to be careful to use my own words in my answers as it was easy for me to use my photographic memory to quote word for word from the texts that I had read. An examiner could so easily think I had cheated since he would assume I had somehow managed to sneak a text book or a set of notes into the exam room. And so my days at school ended once I had finished these exams. Whatever lay ahead for me would develop in time but for now I had chosen a career for myself in the free-lance antiques business.

I had been to a few more car boot sales but had not found anything of value. Dad had suggested I try some of the advertised house clearance sales in future. I also visited some of the smaller antiques shops scattered about the city and spent many a pleasant afternoon browsing inside their gloomy rooms. I did see some very interesting pieces but nothing that I could sell on at a profit.

Dad suggested that I take a year's sabbatical and just enjoy life at home. He said I might find myself attracted to something besides antiques. With my gifts I could become a very rich man but somehow I felt that was not what I really wanted. There was a purpose to all of this and I was curious, though not impatient to discover what that was to be.

Reading the daily papers often made me pause and think what I could do to help fight crime in the country or for that matter in the world. I did not get emotional one way or another when I read about a particularly nasty bit of vandalism or a horrific murder; I just accepted it as another event that fills our world. The inner voice seemed to caution me against any interference since it would do nothing to help the long term conditions. It was all part of the social evolutionary process that would eventually take us into a much better society. However, I knew that were I to witness a crime or an act of aggressive behaviour then I would act against it using my gifts of course. And such was to prove the case time and time again.

When the A-Level results came out I was placed third overall in the markings and received A-stars in each of my subjects. I had already decided not to attend university since I could learn nothing new there. I believed that I could learn far more from a form of meditation with my inner self and that inner voice that told me things. I was continually acquiring detailed specialised knowledge from my skill of reading people's minds. I already had the knowledge of a doctor of medicine, a chemist, a politician, a historian, a plumber and a carpenter, not to mention a linguist fluent in seven languages, the list was endless.

The headmaster Mr Haddon visited mom and dad at home one evening when I was out and tried to get their assistance in persuading me to attend university. He said he was saddened that his most popular student had decided to follow a non-academic career. Little did he know the career path that had been chosen for me? And for that matter neither did I, nor did mom or dad!

My driving test came through again a few weeks after the cancellation and this time I passed easily. It was the same examiner too. He said I was now a much better driver and that I should keep trying to improve as I went along. He warned me about the ease with which I could pick up bad practices such as speeding and driving without due care.

Dad took me for my first pub drink on my eighteenth birthday. I threw a few darts there and after a while a huge chap with a massive beer belly came over to where dad was and said I was good. He said I had a natural and steady throw. Dad smiled back at him and said that I was his son and today was my eighteenth birthday. So, he said, could he buy us a drink then? Dad said no thanks for himself but the birthday boy could do with a fill up. I had another half Bitter Shandy and after a few more throws I went with dad to join a small group at a table with the big guy.

'My name is Jim,' said the big guy to me, 'and these here fellows are our local darts team. That's Len, Ron, Malachi and Billy but we all call him Tich,' pointing to each in turn. They all had pints of beer on the table and each reached across to shake hands with us, and a firm handshake it was too.

Dad introduced us to them and offered to buy a round but they each said they were alright for the moment. Jim then mentioned that they had watched me at the darts and wondered if I would consider joining the darts team as they were a man short. I said I wasn't much of a beer drinker. They all laughed.

'I'm not asking you to throw mugs of beer lad, just the darts. This here belly is not from the beer but all the fish and chips and curry I shove down my neck. We've got a match with the Berries on the Friday middle of next month and it's our turn to host in the room back of the pub. We'd like you to play for us in the team. They call us the Gunners. They beat us last time and the time afore. What do say you lad?' said Jim.

'Why thank you sir,' I said, 'I'll be glad to play, I'll do my best.'

'Good,' said Jim, 'match begins when everybody is here but we try for seven. I'm the captain of the Gunners and not a sir just yet, so plain Jim will do me fine Ashley'.

'Thanks Jim,' was all I could say.

It was Tich who asked me if I would care for a practice game and I said okay. The board was free and Tich let me throw first. He said he would keep the count. He said we'd play a game of 501 which was the usual. The other games were to a score of 301 and 1001 but these were played under special conditions of championship deciders.

I threw treble twenty with each of my three darts. And Tich did the same. So it was 180 maximum points to both of us. But I had the advantage since I threw first. I then got a treble twenty twice and then just an eleven single.

'Bad luck,' said Tich who then threw and got the maximum 180 points again.

But I knew what I was doing. I then threw and also got the maximum 180 points. Now all I needed was a double five to win and I had three throws to get it. A groan went up from Tich who for a moment thought that he had lost. Whatever he did his next three darts had got to win him the game. If he had thrown first of course he would have been in with a better chance. As it was he seemed lost in concentration for a moment calculating his strategy, and then threw a treble twenty, a treble nineteen and finished with a double twelve to win the game in three throws. I know that I can put a dart accurately wherever I aim but my strategy in reaching a 501 score was yet to be perfected. And now it was.

'Bad luck kid,' said Tich. 'I'm in good form today but it's not always like this. I get some terrible days when I can hardly get a treble at all. You are good though, I can see it by the way you throw. The dart seems to float out of your hand. Glad to have you on our team.'

Tich offered to buy me another Shandy but I declined. Two halves were enough for me for one evening. The voice in my head made me feel uneasy with alcohol. It seemed to warn me that I could be a danger to others were I ever to get over the limit, so to speak. I therefore decided that I would just have the occasional Shandy or half glass of wine.

Dad and I then played a 501and I won quite easily. I followed in the strategic footsteps of Tich and applied his treble nineteen formulas to finish in three turns while dad was still in the hundreds.

'Guess we'll thrash the Berries this time, eh lads,' said Jim.

Then to me he said, 'You be a natural lad, see you on the Friday next month.'

When dad and I got home about 10 o'clock we sat in the kitchen and had a nice mug of tea. We both took one sugar and plenty of milk so it was easy to make. For some reason neither dad nor I drank coffee. There was a look on dad's face that made me think he was about to have a word with me regarding something. I didn't read his mind but I just knew it had to do with my darts throwing. But then he shook his head and said he'd talk to me in the morning about a minor matter that was puzzling him.

And I think I knew what it was. My accuracy with the darts was just too good. I realised then that when I threw a dart I was fiercely concentrating on the spot where I wanted it to go. Was I moving the dart with a form of telekinesis?

The next morning was Saturday and I was the last up. Katy and Robin Nesters had gone with Robert Black and Vicky to the motor show at the National Exhibition Centre. Robin was employed as a junior with Lloyds TSB bank in Erdington village and he drove an old Ford Fiesta. He was always studying and sitting exam after exam and had ambitions to one day become manager of a small branch. I could see that Vicky was quite happy in Robert's company. My little sister was not so little anymore. At fifteen she looked and behaved like a young and beautiful magazine model. She had a lot of mum's mannerisms and both mum and dad were very proud of her. Above all Katy was sensible and had her head screwed on firmly. She had a deep throaty sort of laugh which you heard before you saw her come round a corner. I could see that Robin was still struck on her ever since he first saw her at our cricket matches all those years ago. But Katy was not committing herself to anyone just yet. She and mum had become thick as thieves and had long head to head conversations. I loved to see them like that together and I think she was a good companion to mum. She even got on well with Vicky's mum Mavis and the three of them chatted away like old mates. Sometimes Vicky came with her mother but was then rather quiet and just liked to listen to the chatter from the other three. When she was with Robert it was another matter, you couldn't get her to stop chattering. For some reason I was a bit shy of Vicky and got a bit tongue tied when she was near. I sometimes read her thoughts and frankly I felt a bit embarrassed by them.

My own feeling towards girls in general was one of just mild admiration. I did like to see a good figure under a pretty face but I had yet to meet one I was attracted to. Something told me, that inner voice again, that I was destined to a full life with someone special. I still had to find out why these gifts had been given to me and I felt that the time for answers was not far away.

Dad came down just before they went out to do a bit of shopping. So we were alone in the house and at the breakfast table. Dad made himself some toast and after buttering it and spreading some marmalade on top he looked at me in a soft kindly way.

'Do you have any idea why it is that you are so good at the darts son?' he said.

'Not really dad,' I said, 'I just will it to hit the spot I'm looking at after I throw.'

Dad was quiet for a bit while he chewed on his toast. He took a sip from his mug of tea and then looked straight at me.

'I think you have another talent,' he said, 'I think you can actually make the dart go to the position you are looking at even though your throw may have been off a bit. I was standing behind you and I could swear that I saw a slight shift in the flight of the dart. What do you say we do a little experiment to see if this is really the case?'

'What do you suggest dad?' I asked.

'Well,' said dad, 'let us finish breakfast first and then we can have a game of speciality darts. I thought about this while I was in bed last night. You aim the dart at the bull each time but I will then shout out a number position just after you have thrown. I want to see if you can get the dart to change direction towards the new position. Go always for the double position of the number I give.'

'That sounds great dad,' I said. 'Last night I did have the feeling that there was a bit more to my darts technique than just the skill in my throw.'

And so we went into the garage where the dart board was set up on the far wall.

I picked up a dart and threw at the bull and that is where it hit. The next time I threw dad called out twenty but the dart went only part way to the double top position. The same happened with the other numbers he called, but I did seem to be getting the dart closer to the double each time.

And then it happened. I still don't know how but as I held the dart in front of me while I was aiming for the bull dad called out another number and the dart just flew out of my fingers and straight into the double position. Dad was as surprised as I was. And my hand was still in the ready to throw position. During all this time dad had been standing to one side of the dart board. Now he came and stood beside me and a bit behind.

'Wow,' I said, 'did you see that dad? It just flew right out of my hand by itself.'

'That was quite a surprise son,' said dad. 'Now try it again but this time just place the dart on the flat of your palm and stretch your arm out in front of you towards the dart board. Aim for any position you like when I clap my hands.'

I decided I'd go for the treble twenty. Dad clapped his hands and the dart flew off by itself and straight into the treble twenty spot. It went like a bullet and buried the point fully in the board. Dad had to pull and twist for a whole minute to get it free.

'That was fine,' said dad, 'but perhaps you need to practice a bit on the strength at which you get the dart to hit the board.'

'Okay dad,' I said, 'I think I should go a bit further back from the board.'

'No,' said dad, 'just stay there and try it again but with less intensity.'

And so I did. But this time the dart didn't even get to the dartboard. It slipped off my hand and sort of fell to the floor in front of it. Dad and I both laughed. This happened again and again but it seemed to be getting slightly better each time.

I was getting a little impatient with myself so my next shot went just like my first and the point buried itself again deep in the board.

Dad put his arm around my shoulders and said for me to have a rest. He said I must be patient with myself and that we could practice some more a bit later. So we went back into the house and dad made us both a mug of tea. I still have one sugar in mine.

I was a bit annoyed at myself for being impatient, but then I heard that inner voice telling me it could take a year to get to perfection. The voice was gentle and calming and I began to get a feeling of recognition for the person behind it. There was a nagging in my subconscious thoughts that I actually knew the owner but from a different time and era. I was getting these déjà vu feelings quite frequently of late and I had this strong expectation that I was about to discover what this was all about. Mum and dad had both said that I must have been given these extraordinary gifts for a definite purpose and I felt a revelation was not far off. The conviction was strong enough to give me a powerful confidence in myself and a willingness to fulfil the task that would be put before me. I just prayed that I could conduct myself wisely and with good judgement. Solomon asked for wisdom and I would ask for the same.

It is hard not to be religious in any one particular direction when one has acquired the personalities of so many differing people and their sectarian beliefs. Each person had a strong religious conviction from their childhood upbringing which was therefore set in their roots. Having acquired the same understanding through that person's memories I too could relate to it with the same conviction. I can happily say that I go along with the teachings of all the major religions and can tag each with a similar origin. The styles, rites and formalities may be different but the focal point of worship is the same for all. It is the same God, albeit by a different name, who is venerated as the creator of the world and benefactor of us all and to whom we all direct our prayers, pleas and worship. In essence we Earthlings have the same basic religious ideals and so are all really under the same fraternity. Perhaps it is to be my task to instil this same conviction into the hearts and minds of our disparate nationalities and religious leaders. How am I to achieve this goal? Is this the task set before me? Or is it something completely different? I don't know.

There is one conviction that I do have and that is that mankind will evolve towards a better society only by learning from its tragedies and mistakes. It is by seeing the pitfalls that one is able to steer a path to avoid them. A wise man is depicted as progressing forwards by looking to the past to gauge his course. I believe that sometime in the distant future we shall certainly approach a form of utopia but the path towards it will be a long and bloody one. The hair on our heads needs to be clipped and trimmed occasionally for it to be maintained in the style we desire. As an analogy is this not what happens in the world today? Tragedies may be hard to understand but perhaps it is the only kind of lesson that we humans are compelled to learn from. Perhaps my philosophy is naïve and will change as I grow to maturity. Perhaps then I shall also understand the role my powers are to play in bringing about change.

'A penny for your thoughts Ashley,' said dad as we sat together in the kitchen with our mugs of tea.

'Just thinking where all this is leading dad. If there is a grand scheme of things then where do I fit in? I hear this distant voice occasionally telling me to be patient yet I don't have any idea to whom or what the voice belongs. I'm sure that eventually all will be revealed to me but when that will be I have no idea.'

'I've been thinking that there is a way to help you control the power in your throw. If we could rig up something suspended on a wire or rope then you could practice on that by trying to push it by a certain amount. That way you will be able to visibly gauge the power you apply. What say you son?'

'Sounds like an excellent idea dad. Let's do it.'

Dad found an old canvas bag and put about two small shovels full of builders sand into it and tied some good cord firmly around its neck to form a tight little bag. He then suspended this from a beam in the garage ceiling so that it was about head height above ground. He then smiled at me and stood back admiring his handiwork.

'That'll do nicely I think,' he said as he came to stand beside me.

I think it is so nice to have the benefit of a family behind you helping you to cope with the burden placed upon you. I don't think I could have become so complacent about all of this if I had been alone with it. Mum and dad have made me feel quite normal with regard to my gifts and have shown me how to keep it all in perspective. And I can't forget the support I get from that other person who seems to whisper encouragement. I know he or she is real and that one day perhaps we shall meet. But for the present mum and dad are all the encouragement I need. And dad is like my very own personal trainer.

'There you go son,' said dad when the bag had stopped swinging. 'Try and move that about a foot away from you and hold it there if you can.'

Okay I thought, here goes. I stared at the bag and in my mind I aimed it at the far wall just as if it were a dart. And the bag swung out all the way and banged up against the garage roof. Too hard I thought. As it swung back I stared again and made it stop swinging as it came down again to the hanging position.

'I'll leave you to it son,' said dad, 'just keep practicing and I'm sure you'll get it right in your own time. There's something I have to do regarding the office. See you in a bit.'

I kept it up for about an hour trying to get the bag to stay at an angle of about 45 degrees but it kept swinging out too far. I even tried retreating to a spot farther back but with the same result. There wasn't any problem with the telekinesis because that worked every time. But I couldn't get the power applied just as I needed. It was mostly too much. I then came into the house and dad raised an eyebrow in an enquiring manner but I just shook my head and flopped onto a chair at the kitchen table.

'I'll have another practice session later on dad,' I said. 'I feel tired and a bit disappointed. I think it might take a while before I get it sorted.'

I didn't tell dad that it took 'somebody else' nearly a year.

And that is what it took for me as well. I went into the garage at every opportunity to practice. Sometimes if I couldn't sleep I'd wander down and spend about an hour swinging the sand bag to and fro. I did notice that I could only move the bag in a direction away from me. Never towards me even though I did concentrate and try.

It was when we were visiting Aberporth one weekend that I made a minor discovery. I was on my own walking along a stretch of beach and I happened to push one of the many rounded large stones out in front of me. I kept doing this for a bit until I noticed that I had been doing it through telekinesis without actually thinking consciously about it. So every time I came within a few feet of it I made it roll forward about ten feet from me. After a while I began to get the stone to roll different distances depending on what I wanted it to do. I seemed to have a perfect control on the pebble. And there was no conscious effort. Maybe this is what I should have been doing with the sand bag back in Birmingham.

Suddenly a weight had been lifted and I felt quite pleased with myself. I told Aunt Brenda and Uncle Ron when I got back to the B&B. They knew about everything that I could do at every stage of my progress to whatever it was that was planned for me. They offered encouragement too. I do love them both very much.

It was sad when they lost little Barclay through old age and they vowed never to get another dog. They said the heartbreak was too terrible. I used to enjoy my walks along the cliff path with him. It is a great pity that man's best friend should have such a short span of life compared to us humans. A dog bubbles with love and affection and its only aim is to please its master. I could swear that Barclay thought he was human. He didn't like or care for the company of other dogs and if we met any on our walks he would drop his banner of a tail and come to heel till the 'stranger' had passed us by. I like to think that there is a dog heaven and that he is there now running beside his new master.

The plumbers Jan Bogdan and Sarul Kwaitkowski had moved to the big city of Cardigan to expand their business. I hoped to go down there one day to renew our friendship. Aunt Brenda said that Jan had been up to visit them and had asked about me. He also said that his father had passed away and that he was planning to make a visit to Poland sometime soon. But that was last year. How time flies.

When we got back home I was able to exert a much better control on the hanging sand bag but still not to perfection. But I had brought a fist sized round stone back from the beach at Aberporth and I walked around our garden rolling it in front of me. I seemed to control this large pebble with surprising ease and yet not the sand bag. This was most curious. There must be a reason behind this and I was determined to find out why.

That night it suddenly struck me that if I put the pebble in the bag instead of sand maybe I might be able to exert a better control. I spoke to dad in the morning as he was preparing to go off to work. He smiled at me and said to go ahead and change over to stones instead of sand and good luck.

But I didn't want lots of stones I just wanted one large one. I thought of the large ornamental stones at the garden centres and asked dad if we could fetch one in the car when he came home again. But he said he might be late and why didn't we go on the Saturday instead.

'And don't forget you have the darts match this Friday. You're playing for Jim and his team.' said dad. 'I think they call themselves the Gunners and are playing against the Berries, the team that keeps beating them.'

'Gosh dad,' I said, 'I clean forgot about that. But do you think it fair that I should play, what with my gift and all?'

'Of course you should son,' said dad. 'You could win your round every time and yet probably make no difference to the result. Besides you have a gift and should make good use of it. For why else would you have been given it in the first instance? Until you are told what to do with it I think you should use it as you see fit. And by the way I think your granddad Eric will be there. He's much better now. I think the flu jab knocked him for six again. Do you know he will be 75 this summer? We should do a party for him.'

So for the time being I continued to practice my telekinetic gift on the bag of sand in the garage. There were one or two occasions when I actually held the bag at a good slant for a couple of seconds. But mostly it moved with too much violence for my liking. Consequently I tended to roll my large pebble around the garden much more frequently by choice than work on the sand bag. I think that once I get the large stone from the garden centre it might be a different story.

I decided to forgo any further 'bag practice' till Saturday and after the garden centre visit. But for now I thought I needed to get my hand in and practice my darts just a bit, which I did.

The match between the two teams would be between six pairs of players dad told me. Each pair of throwers would play a set of three games of 501points. The winner of each set would score a point for his team. The team with 4 points would be the winner. If it came out even then each team selected a 'Goliath' in a final set playoff to determine a winner. The Berries had a better record and were easy majority winners on the previous three meets. Teams must have specified their 'Goliath' choice at the outset if it came to a playoff.

I decided that I would win my own match on a 2-1 basis. I'd give my opponent the chance to win the second game by extending my throws by three.

On Friday mum rang granddad and he agreed to come over for lunch. Dad had already given him the latest update of my progress and I always looked forward to his visits. We seem to have a special bond, a special affection for one another. He had such a gentle and loving look that one couldn't help not liking him. I also thought that granddad Eric was very proud of me with my gifts and all. I think he approved of the way that mum and dad had handled the situation and coped so well. He was also very pleased to be in the 'inner circle' of seven, along with my grandparents Beryl and David and Uncle Ron and Aunt Brenda. And I too was very lucky to be able to share all this with them. I dreaded to think how I would have coped on my own. It just doesn't bear thinking about. Although my grandparents from Aberdare didn't travel about often mom kept them informed of my progress. They were both on prescribed medication and so tended to stay at home most of the time. Mom rang them nearly every weekend to see how they were and sometimes they would ask to talk to me as well. I found it easy talking to them but I wish they lived closer and visited more often so I could actually demonstrate what I could do. It might be an idea for me to visit them instead.

When granddad Eric arrived just after twelve we had a big hug as usual. When I was little he would kiss me on the top of my head, but now that we are nearly the same height we just gave each other a manly hug. I do love him very much and just can't wait to tell him everything. So the first thing I did was to drag him off into the garage, with a mug of tea of course, and show him my 'problem bag'. I told him what I was trying to do but that I still hadn't got complete control.

'Show me what you are doing Ash', he said.

Granddad Eric was the only person who called me by Ash instead of Ashley.

I looked at the bag and it gradually swung to a 45 degree angle and stayed there. I was so surprised to have achieved this that I yipped with glee. And the bag still stayed in the same position.

'So what is the problem Ash,' said granddad. 'It seems to me that you have the bag exactly where you want it.'

'But granddad, this is the first time I have done it perfectly. Every other time the bag has swung too far with too much force.'

'So what's different today,' he said.

'I don't know. Perhaps I was thinking of you more than I was of the bag. Maybe I was concentrating too much before.'

'Well,' said granddad Eric, 'the bag is still in the position you put it and hasn't moved at all even though you've been talking to me. Perhaps this is a subconscious thing performed in an involuntary manner. So why don't you go back into the house and bring me out another mug of tea but keep your mind on the bag and will it to stay as it is now.'

When I came back with the mug of tea the bag was still nearly as I had left it and granddad Eric had a big smile on his face. I put the mug of tea on the bench and went up to him and we put our arms around each other. And I couldn't stop the tears, I was so pleased.

He patted me on the back and said that I should look at the bag. I did and noticed that it was still out at a 45 degree angle but now it had rotated to a position directly away from where I was standing.

'Walk around the bag Ash and see what it does,' said granddad.

I did and saw that as I walked to one side or the other the bag went into a position directly opposite to where I was. My thoughts went into overdrive and I knew exactly the nature of my latest gift. It was a push force that I could exert on any object and from a distance too. What that distance was I was to find out eventually. But for the moment I was to accept that no distance would be too great.

I now willed the bag down and down it came. I willed it up and up it went again but always into a position away from me. I tried to get it to come towards me but could get no response at all.

'Granddad.' I said, 'I think I know what is different from before. Up till now I have been concentrating too hard in trying to push the bag out to a set position and it would just react to a sort of impact blow from me. But now I am just willing it to do what I want and it seems to respond to something my brain does automatically. I don't have to really try, I just have to command in my mind what I want it to do and it happens.'

Mum called us for lunch and as there were just the three of us at the table we could freely discuss my latest discovery. Mum knew that I was having a little difficulty from what dad must have said, and now she was pleased that I had harnessed the issue. Granddad Eric went through in detail what had just transpired in the garage and mum listened to it all. She was looking at me with such a loving expression and so full of pride that I couldn't help looking back at her. I then put my hand up to my lips and blew her a kiss with a big smile on my face. There was so much love at that table that watery eyes were inevitable.

'Your dad will be pleased when he comes home,' said mum. 'He told me that you were quite upset at not being able to control this latest gift. And he was upset because you were upset.'

Dad had made it a rule that we never discuss my gifts over the phone. So when mum rang Aunt Brenda in Aberporth she would use code words that they had agreed beforehand. In this instance mum asked her sister over to discuss the latest on 'Ashley's driving situation'. Mum said that my driving had been too fast but she had spoken to me and it was under control now. Aunty Brenda said she and Uncle Ron would visit next weekend.

We then discussed the darts tournament at the Navigation pub that evening. Mum said that dad had seen Jim a couple of days ago and had said that I was definitely playing and that a full contingent of the Bonners would be in attendance. I think that Katy and all her friends would be there as well including Vicky and her mum Mavis. Of course Robert Black would not be far away either nor would Robin Nesters. I think it was going to be quite an evening with all of us together.

The match was to be in the back room of the pub and it would be like a private party.

I wasn't sure if I would be selected as one of the team as Jim had about eight to choose from. But Jim said he had already chosen his six and I was to be one of them. There was myself, Len, Ron, Malachi and Billy also known as 'Tich' to whom I had lost so dramatically when I was first introduced to Jim last month. And of course there was Jim as captain of the Gunners team.

The Berries team captain was another big chap called Mike, and he and Jim seemed to be on really friendly terms. There was also a sort of camaraderie spirit between all the team's members of both sides. They greeted each other like old mates as they arrived and there seemed to be plenty of fun and laughter amongst them. The meeting point was generally at the main bar and it wasn't long before most had arrived.

It was about ten past seven that Mike got a call on his mobile that one of his team, a fellow called Jerry Marsh had been slightly delayed but was on his way now. He was bringing his family with him and for us to make a start and fit him in for later in the order of the play.

In the meantime mum, dad, granddad Eric and our crowd of myself, Katy, Vicky and her mum Mavis, Robert and Robin had got ourselves a nice table in a cosy corner of the pub lounge from where we watched the goings on at the bar. Dad had bought us the first round of drinks – mostly cokes and orange Britvics with a couple of pints for himself and Robert, and a gin and tonic for Mavis. We had got there about a quarter to seven after everyone had assembled at our place first for an early supper/tea that mum had served at five thirty. The pub was getting busier by the minute but with a pleasant atmosphere as music played in the background.

Mum and Mavis were all dressed up and looked posh in their prim outfits and makeup though everyone else had come casual. It was still quite mild even though it was the middle of October.

Big Jim came over to us with a pint in his hand and said hello to us men and a 'Good evening ladies' to the girls and said he hoped we were enjoying ourselves.

'I feel we are going to win this time,' he said. 'I just feel lucky today.'

He then suggested we move into the back room where the match was to be played. So we all picked up our drinks and strolled down a couple of steps and in through a set of double doors to a fair sized room. Again dad selected a set of tables at one side of the room and from where the match platform and dart board were clearly visible.

Then the draw for match pairing began. Jim and Mike placed a small table on the platform and placed two old ice cream tubs on it into which the six names of each team member had been placed on pieces of folded paper. They stood side by side facing the room and each in turn drew a name from the opposite teams box.

There were the usual ribald remarks by rival team members as each name was announced. Either a 'Oh no, not him,' or 'Oh yeh, I'll take him on easy,' followed by general laughter. I could see that although they were on separate teams there was a general friendliness between them that must have gone back many years. And all were on first name terms including some who had brought their families as we had.

My name came up against a chap called Ricky Parkes. There was a hushed moment before Jim called out, 'Don't worry Ashley, Ricky doesn't know the front end of a dart from its backend,' and everyone laughed. Later on Jim whispered that Ricky was their star player and if I won against him then the match might be ours. So beat him I would as dad had said it was up to the whole team of six to win the match.

The match was to be played to the 501 points system and in the order it was drawn except for Jerry Marsh who was still on his way. However he was drawn to play the fourth set against Jim so it might still go as scheduled. I was to play Ricky in the third match while Mike and Ron were to play the second. Billy alias 'Tich' would open the match against a chap called Manny. Our Malachi was pitched against a fellow called Wendell at fifth while our team's Len had another big chap named Sean in the last game. The winner of each pairing scored a point for his team. The first team to reach four points would be declared champions. It had been decided that if after the six pairs of matches there was a tie of three all, then a playoff between the two captains would decide the match.

'Ashley, aren't you nervous?' whispered Katy to me as I sipped my coke at our group table.

She still knew nothing of my other extraordinary gifts but I think her woman's intuition made her suspect that I had hidden talents. She never forgot the way I used to catch birds for her and put them in 'our' cage for short durations all those years ago. We were then and still are very close as brother and sister and I could see she considered me a sort of 'hero' in her world. I love her dearly and am so proud of the way she is growing up. She is so much like mum but with a beauty of mind and body that is all her own. There is such fun and laughter bursting from inside her that whenever she enters a room full of people her cheeriness affects everyone around her. You just couldn't help wanting to be in her company. She even smiled as she talked. And she did talk a lot. I could see why Robin was so taken with her.

'Not really sis,' I said in reply to her question. 'It's only a game of darts and it's not as if my reputation is at stake. To them I'm just a beginner, but I shall do my best of course.'

The match started with the first pair, Tich and Manny bowing to the crowd from the platform.

Tich threw first but it must have been one of his 'off' days and lost the first game by a mile. He recovered to win the second game but then lost the third by a throw. So it was one point to the Berries.

Next to play was our Ron against team captain Mike. Mike was in class form and we lost both games straight off. So it was another point to the Berries. We were two points down. It looked bad for the Gunners.

I was next so I walked up to the platform. I had decided that I would let Ricky win the first game but only if he took the chance I gave him. I'd see how he played. Since the Berries had won the last set it was their privilege to have first throw.

Ricky threw his darts and scored 100. I followed with the same score. We were even. Then Ricky threw a 60. I followed with a 60 as well. He then threw two twenties and a treble one, a score of 43 only. I followed with another 60. Ricky countered this with a 100. I then threw a treble five, a treble twenty and a twenty to score. At his next turn he just missed a 180 and got 135 instead. He needed 63 to finish at his next turn. So all he needed was a treble thirteen and then a double twelve to win and he had his next set of three darts to do it.

I then threw and scored the maximum 180 which left me with a double three to finish. But Ricky had his turn next and I had to wait to see if he messed up.

Ricky threw and got his dart in the treble thirteen. A groan went up from the Gunners. So now Ricky needed a double twelve to win. This is right near the top of the circle and an easy shot. His next dart was a fraction high and outside the ring. No score. There was a groan from the Berries. So it was all up to his last dart. And he knew that if he missed I'd have no trouble getting the double three. So he took his time....and won it. Double twelve it was and the Berries gave a loud cheer not to mention a sigh of relief.

Ricky was generous enough to let me have first turn in the next game. So I won it at my third turn of throws by following what Tich had done when we first played here a month ago. Ricky never had a chance of winning this one. Ricky and I had both scored 180 with each of our first two turns. On my third turn I finished the game by throwing a treble twenty, a treble nineteen and finally a double twelve. It was one game all and a loud cheer from the Gunners.

'I should never have let thee have first throw,' said Ricky. 'I underestimated thee lad and never will again.'

But he didn't seem annoyed or upset. He just eyed me and said would I return the favour and let him have first throw in the last game. Custom was for the winner of the preceding game to have the advantage of the first throw. I could see Jim shaking his head in the background, but I stepped back and said to Ricky to be my guest.

We each scored 100 with our first turn. Then on his second turn Ricky got only 58, two nineteens and a twenty. I then got the maximum 180. He got a treble twenty, but followed with two fives and shook his head in disappointment. So I thought I'd have a bit of fun and scored a bull and two twenties for a score of 90. I needed 131 to finish. Ricky got 180 with his next turn and so needed 93 to finish. I then got 91 to leave me a double twenty to win at my next turn. Ricky then threw a 60 and then a thirteen. This left him needing a double ten to win and he had one dart left in this turn. Cheers of encouragement went up from the Berries who sensed a win.

I'm afraid I have to confess to cheating a bit here. As Ricky threw his last dart I stared at a spot just inside the double ten wire. And that is where his dart went. It was right up against the wire and a cheer went up from the Berries who thought they had won. But it was the wrong side of the wire and was therefore a single ten. Ricky needed a double five but that would be on his next turn if there was one. There wasn't, as I had no trouble at all winning the game as I had the previous one. But I spaced out the suspense by sending the first two darts just outside the double twenty position. At my third throw I got the double twenty and a cheer went up from the Gunners followed by a groan from the Berries. It was 2 – 1 against the Gunners at the halfway stage. Ricky came over to me and I was surprised at the smile on his face.

'You're good lad,' he said. 'Very good by gum, and you'll make champion one day if you keep it up. Here come on let me buy thee a drink, what'll it be?'

'Thanks Ricky,' I said and smiled back at him. 'Just a small coke if you don't mind.'

'Aw come on,' he said, 'at least have a Shandy to put some hair on your chest.'

'Okay then,' I said, 'but just a half please.'

And a half it was as we stood at the bar in the private room. He was really friendly and chatty so I took him over to our table and introduced him to our group. I try not to read peoples minds as I find it so much more interesting to hear them talk about themselves. It is easier to gauge a person from how he speaks and what he says about himself than just picking up his past from his thoughts. When people try to hide things or keep their past a secret then that becomes obvious and indicates a complicated personality. But Ricky was quite open in answering questions and about his job as a postman. He said he loved his job even though he was up at five every morning. He spent a lot of time outdoors and walked miles everyday delivering his rounds. The best part was that his evenings were free to do as he pleased. His wife was a shop assistant in a posh big store in town and also loved her work. Unfortunately they couldn't have children and had given up after years of trying. Their consolation was their dog Bessie, a beautiful golden Labrador. They'd had her when she was just eight weeks old and fell in love with her from the start. They had a nice semi in Great Barr and there was the park quite near them just a short walk away along a narrow lane.

Dad and Ricky seemed to be getting on well so I turned my attention back to the darts tournament.

Jerry Marsh had arrived with his wife and teenage daughter soon after the second match had got going, so our captain Mike and he were up for the fourth encounter.

The set of darts that Jerry was using had to be replaced after the first game, which he lost, because one of the flights kept coming loose. But this must have unsettled him since he lost the next game as well. So now it was two points to each team. We were level with the Berries.

Then Malachi won his match against a tall thin fellow named Wendell making it three sets to two in favour of the Gunners. We could be in for a win with the next game. But Len was no match for a ginger haired fellow called Sean and lost two games to nil. So now it was a draw at three points each. It was up to the captains to decide the contest.

I decided that I wouldn't watch the throws in case I might subconsciously influence the flight of each dart as it was sent on its way. I told dad this and he agreed with that. So I went into the main bar area and got myself another coke. Dad came out and said that Jim had won the first game. We stayed together and just chatted about things in general. Dad said that mum had gone across to Jerry Marsh's wife and daughter and had invited them to join our group. They seemed very nice and sociable and the girl Tania had got on famously with Katy. Apparently Tania was just two years younger than Katy. They lived in Dudley not far from the zoo which is why they were late in getting to the match.

Dad went out and came back with the news that it was now one game all. The third game would be the decider. Then he said something that quite surprised me. He said that it only seemed fair for the Gunners to win the tournament seeing that it was such a close run contest and their having lost the previous two contests. He said that we should see how things were going in the final game and to give Jim a slight advantage if necessary. So we went back in to see the deciding game.

Mike threw first as he had won the last game. He scored 140. Then Jim threw and scored only 60 to a groan from our team. Mike then scored 100 followed by a 97 from Jim. Another groan went up from the Gunners. But then Mike got just 45 followed by a 180 maximum score by Jim. Cheers this time. At their next turn each scored 100. This left Mike needing 116 and Jim needing just 64 to win. And it was Mike's turn next. He could win with a treble twenty, a twenty and finish on a double eighteen.

Dad looked at me and gave me a shrug of the shoulders and raised both eyebrows. I knew what he wanted me to do.

Mike was on his third throw and just needed that double eighteen to win. So as he was preparing to throw I stared intensely at the inner wire demarcating the double eighteen zone. Mike's dart flew straight and true and bounced off the boundary wire and fell to the platform floor. A miss! A groan went up from the Berries and a cheer from the Gunners.

Jim then followed and got a sixteen, an eight which left him needing just a double twenty to win with his last dart. So I just stared at the middle of that zone as Jim prepared to throw. And that is where his final dart went straight into double twenty. A cheer went up from the Gunner's team who had finally won. I felt a tiny bit of guilt for my role in the win but this was allayed by what happened next.

Mike went over to Jim and congratulated him on a great win. And then all the Berries team stood up with raised glasses and said 'Well done Gunners.'

Mike stood up on the platform and said that he was pleased, nay relieved that the Gunners had finally won because they were all good friends and it would have been a shame to have thrashed them three times in a row, which they nearly did. There were so many smiling faces in this group that you wouldn't think that amongst them was a team that had lost.

Mum looked at me and raised her glass of coke towards me and then took a sip and ever so slightly nodded her head. I knew that she had spoken to dad before he had approached me. Then granddad came over to me and put his arm around my waist and gave me a gentle hug.

'That was a good result among friends,' he said, 'very well done Ash, I'm proud of you.'

Mum called me over and introduced me to Jerry Marsh's wife Milly and daughter Tania. For a very brief moment I had the weirdest sensation as though I was about to receive a message of some sort. Nothing happened and the moment passed without incident. I was to recall this moment years later as a rather fateful one. Something about this 13 year old went to the very core of my being. It was as though I was looking into the future.

Mum and the Marshes seemed to be getting on famously and it was not long before arrangements were made for an exchange of visits. It was just as we were all ready to leave about 10:30 pm that mum noticed her handbag seemed to have been moved from where she had left it on the floor. Perhaps someone had inadvertently moved it with their feet. But it was much too far across? Mum got suspicious, picked it up and opened it to check.

'My wallet is gone,' she said in alarm. 'I had all my credit cards in it too. Someone has been through it all right.'

It was then that Mavis Chambers, who had been with mum all evening, also stood up in alarm.

'I had some money in my purse and it seems to have gone,' she said, 'someone has been at my bag too'.

Dad looked angry and then walked to the bar. I could see him in earnest conversation with the barman who then walked away and returned shortly with a man I recognised as Harry the pub landlord. Harry listened to dad and kept looking across at our little group. He then shook his head and I knew exactly what he was saying. No, he hadn't seen anyone go to our tables apart from the lads who helped collect up the empty glasses.

'Wait a minute,' he said, 'we only have one lad collecting the empties. Let me ask Joe if he brought someone else along today.'

Joe was walking across the room with his hands full when Harry called him over. By now mum and I had joined dad at the bar.

'Hey Joe,' said Harry, 'who was that other bloke with you earlier helping collect the empties?'

'Dunno,' said Joe, 'he just upped and said he'd give me a hand and followed me around collecting empties. I thought you had got an extra hand to help and I was grateful. He was a pleasant bloke and quite chatty. Said his name was Andy. He helped for about an hour before he said he had to go home to his sick mum.'

'O god,' said Harry, 'I think we've been done over by a professional thief.'

Then he stood up on a chair and called loudly for silence.

'Ladies and gents,' he said in a loud voice, 'I'm your landlord Harry and I think we may have been visited this evening by a professional pickpocket. Would you all please check if any of your personal items such as watches, wallets or cash are missing? Some ladies here have had their purses taken from their handbags so I'm calling for the police.'

I could see he was worried as he dialled the local police number and spoke to the chap on duty. Harry had rung this number often but only if someone was making trouble or was drunk and wouldn't leave. It was not very long before two police officers in uniform came in through the doors. They knew Harry well and went straight up to him.

'Hello Harry,' said constable Rod Jenkins, 'what seems to be the trouble?'

By now of course people had started to discover what they were missing from their pockets and purses. Most people came in to the pub and took off their coats as a matter of course since it was quite warm in there. They either hung their coats on the pegs by the bar or more often just draped them across the backs of their chairs as had been the case at our table.

It was the men's coat pockets that act as their bags and contain items like mobile phones and wallets deemed too bulky to cart around while elbowing their pints. Rich pickings for the light fingered indeed and so it proved to be the case today when people checked. There was a rising murmur of voices as discoveries were made. More and more folk gathered around the two constables and began to call out their missing items. And there were quite a few.

'My wallet and mobile are gone.'

'I had twenty quid in my coat and it's gone.'

'My cards are missing.'

'I can't find my wallet.'

And so it went on. The thief or thieves seemed to have made quite a haul.

Harry explained what he thought had happened. He got Joe over to also give his report about the mysterious helper. It seemed obvious what had happened and the constables recognised the old familiar pub routine done over by professional thieves.

'Well,' said constable Rod Jenkins, 'we'd better make a start and get some statements. No point rushing out and chasing something that's not there any more. They are long gone but we are bound to hear something from our sources soon. Those of you who are missing credit cards had better phone in to your particular bank number to report the loss.

By now it was near midnight and I could see that the long arm of the law was also an exceedingly slow one. I don't know how it came about but it suddenly appeared to me like a shining light what it was that I should do. So I followed what to me were clear instructions and went and sat down by myself on the bench seat in the corner where our group had been seated earlier. Mum saw me and touched dad's arm and whispered something. They both began to walk slowly towards me – and they got slower and slower. The room turned a rosy pink as I then shut my eyes and concentrated my thoughts on the spot where mum's handbag had lain.

It all happened as if in a dream. The room was as it had been earlier in the evening and people were at the bar and sitting around the room. Joe was collecting the empties from the tables but there was also someone else following him and doing the same. Nothing was hidden from me in this dream world and I knew the other person to be a petty thief named Quigley Thorn. His thoughts were open to me and I could see that he had an accomplice hiding away out of sight in the toilets. His name was Johnny Price and he was waiting to receive anything that Quigley might pass to him.

Quigley came to our table and checked for any empties. There was one empty wine glass and while he picked this up he also reached down with the other hand and opened mum's handbag and slipped her wallet up into his coat sleeve. He was very good. He then did the same to Mavis's bag and as he strolled away his foot caught mum's bag and pushed it across under the next chair. He then went to the next table picked up a couple of empties and went across into the kitchen with them and thence to his mate in the toilets. Vicky, Katy, Robert and Robin were at our table at the time but were chattering away and didn't notice anything unusual. Not that they would have anyway.

After each haul one of the thieves went outside to an old white van in the pub car park and deposited their takings in the back. Finally after about an hours work they drove off to an address about two miles away. All this came across to me in less than a minute and I could see the name of the street and house number they had driven to. There was a quadrangle of garages situated around a central plinth which was planted with a lot of shrubs that had seen better days. Beside each garage was a door that led to an upstairs flat. They opened the door marked with the number 9 and climbed the stairs to the flat above. They had a single bulging holdall which they carried up with them.

I opened my eyes and the room was back to normal and mum and dad were still walking across the room towards me. They sat down in the chairs in front of me and looked at me with a bit of worry in their expressions.

'What is it son?' said mum after a while and in a quiet voice.

I was still in a bit of a surprised state at what I had been able to do and see. But mum and dad were even more surprised when I told them what had just happened. I said that I knew who the thieves were and where they lived. I also told them that all the stolen things were still at this address in the Vale estate. I gave dad the address as flat number 9 in Chevy Close off the Farnborough Road.

Dad said to mum, 'Stay here Lil,' and to me he said, 'come with me son,' and we walked up to the bar where Jim and Mike were in conversation.

Constables Rod and Ian were seated at separate tables and busy taking statements left, right and centre. Dad had a quiet word with the darts' captains and they rounded up another couple of big lads and we all walked out to the car park. We got into two cars and drove down the Tyburn road towards the Vale. It only took us about ten minutes to get to the address in question but we parked a bit away from the number 9 door. Mike said for dad and me to wait in the car while they sorted out the thieves but dad said we were coming along and wouldn't miss the excitement for the entire world.

We assembled quietly in front of the door marked with a 9 beside a garage door badly in need of a coat of paint. There was a light on in the room above and I nodded to dad that they were still home. I could hear their thoughts quite clearly.

Mike was all for smashing the door down but dad said he had a better idea. He took out a credit card and tried to push it into the gap near the lock and looked across at me. His thoughts said he wanted me to open the door by pushing the catch inwards. So I walked to a position opposite him the other side of the door and visualised the catch and mentally pushed as I had the sand bag in our garage back home. The door clicked open. Mike put his fingers to his lips and whispered a 'shush' and pointed to the stairs. Mike and Jim led the way but the stairs were creaky and would have warned the thieves had it not been for a radio playing some beat music in their room. There was a small landing in front of their door. This opened easily when Mike turned the door handle. It had not been locked. He entered the room but it was empty. He ushered us all in and we could hear low voices from the next room. The beat sounds came from a battered old music centre at the other end of the room we were in. Jim walked across and turned it off.

'Hey,' said a voice, 'what happened to the damned music?'

'I dunno Johnny,' said the other voice of Quigley, 'why don't you go and fix it. The thing's probably finally given up it's so old.'

But before Johnny could do anything, Jim and Mike walked into the next room and confronted the alarmed thieves. They are even more alarmed when the rest of us came up behind.

'Good evening gents,' said Jim, 'I hope you've saved us our share of your loot.'

At the same time Mike went forward, grabbed a tiny looking Quigley by his shirt front and pushed him backwards against the bedroom wall. The rest of the group were now fully in the room and we must have all looked rather sinister. The two thieves looked at us and just caved in.

There were two single beds in this medium sized room and one of them was laden with wallets, purses, watches and other bits and pieces.

'I believe all this stuff is what you've had off the people in the Navi pub this evening,' said Jim, 'unless you have done another place as well.'

I looked at dad and shook my head. I had read their minds and knew that they tended to do only one place on any one day. They were small time crooks and worked for themselves only. Neither of them was into drugs but both were heavy smokers and drinkers.

Dad looked at Jim and said, 'I reckon that all this is just from tonight's work.'

'Who are you,' said Quigley, who was probably the leader of this duo, 'what do you want with us?'

'Never you mind who we are,' said Jim, 'we're taking all this lot back to the pub including you. There's a couple of coppers there waiting for you.'

Then to one of his lads he said, 'Hey Len, can you give Harry at the Navi a buzz on your mobile and tell him we've got the crooks and all the loot and will be there in a bit.'

'Just hold on a minute Len,' said dad. 'We had better think this out. If we take these chaps back to the pub with us then to make a case against them the police will need to hang on to the evidence. That won't be any good to our lads at the pub. So why don't we just,' and here dad winked at the rest of us, 'return the stolen goods to their rightful owners and dump these two in the river Tame with their hands tied behind their backs.'

'No,' said Jim, 'that would be murder. But I have a better idea. Why don't we take these chaps back as planned but no one file a complaint or charge? There is no case to answer then and no evidence to hold. Case closed so to speak except for these two. How about if we make them do a months work in the Navi so as to keep an eye on them. That's about all the punishment they'll get from a judge anyway.'

'Sounds good to me,' said Mike, 'let's do it then.'

So Len rang Harry at the pub and told him the story and for no one to do anything like cancelling their credit cards and all. We put all the stolen stuff in the thieves own holdall, marched them ahead of us and made our way back to the Navigation pub.

Harry was waiting for us as were all the others including the two constables. We took the holdall into the pub and spread everything on the tables that some one had pulled together.

'Wait a minute,' said PC Rod, 'all this is evidence against these two if we are to make a case against them.'

'What case,' said Jim? 'No one is making a complaint so there is no case to answer. Besides these two have volunteered to do community service by working here in this pub and doing whatever Harry asks them to do for a whole month. Isn't that so lads.' He said this as he looked at the two thieves.

They vigorously nodded their agreement.

I think the two constables were relieved that they wouldn't have to fill out all that paperwork. But you could see that they were curious to know how we had caught these two so quickly. Dad anticipated their questions and said that there was someone in the pub who had recognised Quigley Thorn and knew where he lived. This person wished to remain anonymous as he or she had themselves been in a spot of trouble with the law.

It was now after midnight and everyone seemed to have retrieved their stuff off the tables. Except there was a scruffy black plastic wallet on the table still waiting to be collected? It seemed to have quite a bit of cash in it. Mike checked it out and reckoned there was at least a couple of hundred pounds cash in it. He held it up and asked who it belonged to.

'That's mine,' said a voice near the bar. It was Quigley Thorn. 'I left it on the bed and it has all my social security money in it that I collected yesterday.'

'Well then,' said Mike, 'you'd better come and collect it hadn't you. And what are you going to do to make it up to these good people that you robbed and nearly got away with?'

Quigley walked up to Mike and took hold of his wallet, but Mike didn't let go of it.

'I think the least you could do is buy everyone here a round,' said Mike. 'I think a hundred smackers should just about do it wouldn't you think.'

And with that he took about a hundred pounds out of the wallet before handing it to a demure Quigley.

'Ladies and gents,' said Harry the landlord, 'the bar will close at midnight so please get your drinks before then. I think the bar clock is twenty minutes fast so please be quick. Thank you.'

Unfortunately some people had already phoned their banks to cancel their credit cards. They would have to go through the inconvenience of waiting for a new one. Apart from that everyone seemed pleased that the evening had ended on a pleasant note.

Granddad Eric was beside me and I could see that he was proud of my part in all this. He said he could also see a future for these skills and gifts. He added that more people with similar gifts could make this world a much better place. Granddad and I had built a special bond right from the beginning when we first played at catching the ball.

I noticed big Jim coming in my direction. He asked if he could have a private word so I excused myself from granddad and walked with Jim to the middle of the room.

Jim looked at me for a moment before he said, 'I think you be special lad. I won't ask any questions since I promised your dad I wouldn't. But I know you had summat to do with this evening's good turnout. And it wouldn't be fair to keep you on in the darts team. Not fair to the other team because I reckon we'd win every time. So you're sacked as of now. But keep in touch and come and see our next match.' And with that he reached across and shook my hand for all it was worth.

As for Quigley Thorn and Johnny Price they came in and reported to Harry every day. Harry was fair and gave them the odd day off but never together. At first they never spoke to anyone but gradually they seemed to thaw and make a few friends. It was only when some people asked Quigley to demonstrate his light fingered skills that his popularity raised to that of an entertainer. He could remove your wrist watch without you being aware. Wallets just jumped out of peoples pockets or so he said.

Among other things Quigley also knew quite a few card tricks. He seemed to have a photographic memory and could easily remember the exact sequence of about twenty cards at the top or bottom of a deck. It was this knack that led to one of his most popular card tricks. He would shuffle the pack, spread it open and then ask you to simply take one card, look at it and put it back anywhere in the pack. He would then shuffle the pack again and ask someone else to take another card. Invariably it turned out to be the same card the first person had picked. Of course he kept up a patter of talk throughout the trick along with funny quips and jokes.

It was not long before Harry recognised that Quigley had potential as a pub entertainer and offered him a slot in his pub three evenings a week at fifty quid a time. Quigley said seventy five and they settled on seventy.

Unfortunately Johnny Price seemed to disappear after his month's servitude in the pub was up. He and Quigley had just drifted apart when their thievery ended so dramatically. It was generally thought that he had reverted to his old ways simply because he had no other skills. Quigley said that Johnny needed a leader as he could not think for himself. He required someone else to tell him what to do as far as making money was concerned. He'd probably end up in the nick sooner or later. Someone said they thought he had moved to Manchester where his sister lived but this was never confirmed. And we never did find out one way or the other, not that anyone cared.

Here at home I found that the control I developed over my telekinetic gift improved continually with practice. I could make the suspended sandbag move just as I wished. I only had to look at it and think how I wanted it to move and it happened. I could move the bag out a few degrees or to its maximum 90 degree suspended angle position up against the garage ceiling. I could do all of this by simply thinking it even if my back was towards the sandbag. I could even pinpoint where I wanted the push force to occur. And so by focussing on one side of the sandbag I could make it spin on its rope. At first it was all like a game to me. The force I applied was always directly away from me. No matter how hard I tried I could not make an object move towards me. But I did not give up. Since the age of six I had progressively discovered one gift after another, some quite by accident like when the cricket ball smacked into my chest or when I had heard the Polish plumbers speak. Why I had been blest in this way I did not know, at least not yet. But I knew beyond a doubt that all would be made clear one day soon. I was eighteen years old and still had a lot to learn. There was a reason behind all of this and I was happy that I had been chosen for the 'task' whatever it might be.

And so I decided to carry out some further telekinetic practice. I remembered how I had first managed to push that stone on the beach at Aberporth and had had such fun doing it. That was when I had finally got a better control of my telekinetic gift. It was at one of our family conferences when we were discussing this aspect that granddad Eric suggested I try moving bowling balls around in the garden. Dad said that these tended to be oval and might not be suitable. He wondered if we could get some round ones from the sports shop. Ones that were used for ten pin bowling matches in pubs. Granddad Eric said he would pick me up tomorrow and we could hunt around the sports shops. In fact when we were in the sports store we found something much better. It was an alley bowling ball but without the finger grip holes. They were perfectly round, much smaller and were meant for school age children. They were about six inches in diameter and in various colours. Granddad thought four should be enough for what we had in mind. When we got back home mum thought they were perfect, as did dad when he came home from work.

I started by walking all four balls around the garden. Of course I stayed a bit behind and pushed one ball at a time into a more forward position. I didn't think I could move all four balls simultaneously but I had a try anyway. I tried looking at the balls as a group and willed them to move. After a good few minutes of futile effort I gave up. But then I had a sudden thought. What if I went 'pink' then I could give each ball a push in turn before returning to normal. I tried this and was surprised at the outcome.

In the pink zone I had given each ball what I considered a gentle normal push. But as soon as I came out of 'pink' and back to normal all four balls went hissing across the grass and crashed into the wall at the end of our garden and rebounded back towards us. I immediately went pink again before they could hit mum and granddad and put a stop to their momentum.

'Phew,' said mum with concern in her voice, 'what was that all about?'

'Sorry mum,' I said, 'I was trying out a sudden idea I had for moving all four balls together.'

I then explained exactly what I had done. And it was granddad Eric who came to the conclusion that my power to move objects away from me was considerably magnified if I was in the pink zone. When I said that I had only applied what I had thought was a slight 'push' both mum and granddad said they wondered what would be the result if I applied a really good hard push in the 'pink.'

'It would probably be like firing an artillery shell from a modern field gun,' said granddad Eric. 'If you do want to try it out then we need to go somewhere where it can do no damage; perhaps something like a firing range or even the seaside. We could try it the next time we visit Ron and Brenda.'

'We are due there in a fortnight's time to drop off our Christmas presents,' said mum, 'you could do it then. We shall only stay the night but that should give us plenty of time. You must come with us Eric as I'm sure Ashley would want you to see the result. I shall also ring mother and dad and see if they can get up to Brenda's place as well. They haven't seen Ashley in action and this would be a good opportunity for them.'

'I wouldn't miss it for a world full of Christmas puddings,' said granddad Eric. He did come up with some funny expressions.

So in the meantime I did 'walkies' around the garden with my four trusted ball-buddies. Although I didn't go pink again I did vary the 'push' that I applied to each ball. I could nudge a ball to roll just a few inches or I could make it whiz along the grass and rebound off the garden wall nearly as hard as it had done when I did my 'pink' trial.

When we are in Aberporth I shall get a large round stone to roll into the sea with my best 'pink' push and see how far it goes. Then I shall ask dad or mum to throw a stone into the air, go 'pink' and then apply another big 'pink' push and see what happens. I wonder if the stone would fly into space if I really kept pushing on it. Now that is an interesting prospect.

And so it was one Friday afternoon early in December that mum, dad, granddad and I drove to Uncle Ron and Aunt Brenda's B&B. Katy didn't come as she was going out that weekend with her usual crowd and would spend the night at Vicky's. It was dark when we got to Aberporth and Aunt Brenda had a nice tea ready for us. Granddad David and grandma Beryl were already there and along with Uncle Ron and Aunt Brenda were keen to hear the latest development; and mum and dad – not to mention granddad – were eager to tell all. I had brought along one of the bowling balls and when the dining room was empty of guests and the one waitress and cook had gone home I did a little demonstration of 'walking' the ball around the room. Aunty Brenda asked why I had to walk behind the ball and I then explained that I could only push the ball in a direction that was directly away from where I stood.

'What about if you focussed the push slightly off centre,' asked granddad David, 'wouldn't that make the ball move to one side just like in snooker?'

'I've tried that,' I said, 'but the ball still goes in a straight line away from me even though it does go into a bit of a spin. The same thing happens in snooker when the cue gives the cue-ball a top or a side spin. It is what happens after the cue-ball strikes a red or a colour that is important. That is when the desired change of direction occurs and the cue-ball comes to rest in an intended position.'

We sat around till nearly midnight chatting about Christmas and what we planned afterwards. Uncle Ron invited us to come again about the end of January for a long weekend and dad said okay straight off. I think dad and Ron get along very well and Aberporth is a favourite with dad. Before we went to bed it was decided that we all met up on the far side of the 'pet's beach at 11 o'clock in the morning.

That night I had a weird dream. But it felt so real even though it only lasted a few seconds. There was someone talking to me but I couldn't make out what was being said. It was a man, a very old man, and he seemed to be smiling at me. In the dream I think he realised that I couldn't hear him so he made a hand gesture as if to say 'never mind,' then turned around and walked away. I woke up and puzzled over this for over an hour until I finally went back to sleep. I can't be sure but I think I may have had a similar dream when I was about four or five years old. It was all a bit vague.

Next morning after breakfast we went down to the beach and gradually made our way across to just beyond the pet beach area. There is a secluded spot just under the cliff wall which is where we were headed. Aunt Brenda and mom walked with their parents and made sure they walked on the easy path. They were not as fit as granddad Eric but were all keen to watch the experiments. As we walked along dad spotted some nice clean round fist sized stones and picked up a couple as did Uncle Ron also.

Dad remembered what had happened in our garden and how the balls went crashing into the back wall, so he suggested they all stand well back against the cliff face. He then went forward and placed one of the rounded stones on the sandy area between us and the sea. He then came and stood with the others.

'Okay son,' dad said, 'you can go ahead and do your stuff now. I think we ought to be safe back here.'

Because the sand was soft I decided to get as low as possible before applying my 'pink' push. I was halfway between the group and the stone so I sat down low. I then went into 'rosy pink' mode and pushed the stone as hard as I could think. I could see the stone begin to move slowly towards the sea. Everything else was practically stationary. I then returned to normal mode and even I was surprised at what happened next.

The stone hissed with astonishing speed down the beach gouging out a deep furrow in the sand and then hitting the surf. It partly skimmed over the sea while crashing through the crests of the waves it encountered. It kept doing this as it sped far out to sea. It must have gone out about a mile or more before finally slowing down and sinking beneath the waves. I realised that while all this had been happening the image of the stone was still clear in my minds eye as when it had been sitting on the sand before my push. So if I had wished I could have applied further pressure to the stone while it was crashing through the sea. This was another development. As long as I had a visual of the object in my mind then I could apply a force to it. I should have realised this when I was working on the sandbag in our garage. For when I had left to make some tea the sandbag had remained where I had positioned it. This was why I could also apply a push when my back was turned to it. I mentioned all this to my family group and included my thought about the possibility of the stone flying out into space if I continually applied a push to it.

'Well let's give it a try,' said dad. 'If I throw the stone up as high as I can then you can freeze it there before giving it the works.'

I liked the way dad phrased it and I was immensely glad that I was not alone in all of this. Also I was happy that I didn't have to keep all of this as a secret from my family. One day we shall have to bring Katy into the inner circle, but not just yet; perhaps when she was older. I do however think she suspects something already. She often asked me how I managed to catch those birds for our cage so easily and was never quite convinced at my replies.

So now dad stood to my left and after shouting 'ready' threw the stone high up above and in front of my position. I immediately went very rosy pink, stared up at the stone semi stationary above me and applied all the push I could muster to it. I found I was clenching my teeth as I did so. What happened next when I came back to normal mode was even more spectacular than the previous stone crashing through the waves.

There was a tremendous bang as the stone shot up into the sky. The stone was also enveloped in a foggy mist that formed a trail behind it. I kept applying pressure to it as it climbed high above us. Then I saw the stone begin to glow a cherry red and a smoke trail developed behind it. It was like a meteorite in reverse with an upward trail of sparks. The stone must have been several miles up in the sky when it suddenly exploded into a cloud of dust. The heat inside the stone from all the air friction must have been too much for it and had caused it to burst. Uncle Ron said that the initial bang must have been the stone going through the sound barrier as it started to speed upwards. This was the first time that grandparents Beryl and David had witnessed me in dramatic action and they just stood there speechless. The others stood silently amazed.

All mum could say was 'Wow' and I noticed then that there were tears in her eyes. I went up to her and we had a big silent hug. Aunt Brenda then came and put her arms around the both of us. I could hear mum saying 'Ashley my baby' over and over again. I couldn't help the tears that came into my own eyes. Dad then came over to us patted mum and suggested we call it a day and why didn't we all pop across to the café on the promenade for a nice cream tea. That perked the ladies up a bit and Aunt Brenda said 'Oh yes, let's.'

Mum and I walked back together holding hands. This was something we had done since I was little; me on one side and Katy on the other. Today was just like old times except this time dad was on the other side of mum. I could see that he had reached down and taken her hand in his. This felt very nice. Aunt Brenda and Uncle Ron walked in front with the three grandparents and they were all chatting away quite excitedly. A quick mental probe told me the topic was me and what I had just done. Granddad Eric had always taken a special interest in my progress ever since that time when I was six years old and we played catching the ball in our back garden and he had first noticed my gift. Now that my other grandparents had seen me in action I could see a change in their attitude towards me. I could sense the pride they had for their grandson along with a sort of possessiveness for one of their own. A new love for me was born within their hearts.

It was a nice sunny though cold morning so we sat indoors at the café. The scones and the jams were all homemade and were delicious with the clotted cream. There were two steaming scones to a portion and mum said she could only manage one. But after polishing off the first one she said she might just manage the second. We all laughed when granddad said that dad was disappointed since he thought he'd get the extra one off mum.

I hadn't told any one about my weird little dream but it suddenly seemed to come to the forefront of my thoughts. My expression must have alerted mum because she asked me what the matter was. At first I was tempted to deny that anything was the matter but thought better of it.

'Oh, it's just this weird dream I had last night,' I said. 'There was this very old chap trying to say something to me but I couldn't hear a word he said. He then motioned with his hand as if to say 'never mind', turned around and walked away. The dream only lasted a few seconds but I can't seem to get it out of my head. Something tells me that this dream is to be of great significance. But what that is I do not know.'

After a moment of silence it was Aunt Brenda who said that if this old fellow had a message for me then he was bound to repeat his effort. And then again it could be just an unrelated event. Mum agreed and said that I ought to keep an open mind and just wait to be contacted if that is what it was. Dad then came in with a sudden thought.

'What if this is the person whose voice you keep on hearing telling you things Ash,' he said. 'Your mum's right, don't worry over it. If there is a message for you in this then perhaps the next dream will reveal it.'

Grandparents David and Beryl had heard mom mention my hidden voice mentor but it all seemed to take on a new realism as this was talked about in the present tense.

I am glad I mentioned it because I don't like keeping secrets from mum and dad. It also helps to reduce any personal stress or worry that might build up. Had I not been able to share my experiences with members of my family I think I would have found it very difficult coping on my own. As it is I have had nothing but selfless support from them all and I don't feel in the least alone or strange about having these gifts. I should like so much to include Katy into this circle at some time in the future. At the moment she was still a bit young and impressionable and knowledge that her brother was a sort of superman might go to her head. I think it best to wait a few years perhaps till she was in her early-twenties.

Brenda had invited her parents to spend Christmas with them but they said they would like to be in their own home. They would however stay another time. Mom had already asked them if they would like to come to Birmingham but they had similarly declined. Perhaps next year they said.

We left for home in the afternoon as mum was driving and she didn't like driving in the dark. Mum and dad often shared the driving and sometimes I also had a turn. We drove up the coast road towards Aberystwyth and then across through Newtown and Welshpool to the M54, the route we usually took to and from Aberporth. It was quite dark by the time we got home. Granddad Eric had a mug of tea with us before driving himself home. Mum rang Mavis to say we were home and they offered to drop Katy over in their Fiat. Mavis is mum's best friend and they are frequent visitors in each other's houses.

Next morning after dad had gone off to the MoD mum got a phone call from Milly Marsh. She and her young daughter Tania were doing a bit of shopping in town and would like to pop over afterwards. Mum said that was fine and why didn't they stay to tea. But they said perhaps another time as Jerry was getting home early. It was not long to Christmas and there was a lot to do. They had still to put up the tree. And for that matter so had we.

We had a lovely Christmas. After coming back from the midnight service we all had some mince pies and a glass of Port wine. It was nice sitting around chatting; with Katy asleep on the settee. Mum went into the kitchen and got the turkey ready for the oven. She called dad to help her place it in. We finally all went to bed about 3. am.

In the morning dad did us all a nice fry up breakfast with all the usual trimmings. We had tomato, sausage, baked beans, mushrooms and bacon with plenty of toast. Mum said Christmas dinner would be served late so to have a good scoff now. After breakfast we all went for a walk in Sutton Park. It was great as there were lots of other people walking their dogs and we all said 'Hello' as we passed them by. This Christmas day was mild and bright with just a trace of clouds. We met some people mum knew but we didn't stop and chat apart from the usual greetings. After about an hour mum said we ought to get back as she needed to check on the turkey and prepare the rest of the items for the dinner.

We handed out our presents to each other just before dinner. We had kept to small gifts and mainly items of clothing. Of course it had all been a stage secret so it was with exclamations of feigned surprise that we opened each gift. I gave dad a silk tie and mum a silky scarf. But it was the actual opening of the presents that was the real thrill. In return I received a lovely hefty edition of an Antique's price guide from mum and dad. I couldn't resist opening it up and browsing its contents. I found a beautiful illustration of my cracked 1751 Chelsea porcelain jar which I proudly showed to everyone.

In the evening as arranged we were visited by Mavis and Vicky, and the Marsh family. Robert and Robin also turned up a bit later to add to the noisy chatter. Mum welcomed them all even though she looked quite tired. Dad

63

said for mum to sit down and enjoy their guests while he looked after the nibbles and drinks himself. It was a most enjoyable Christmas and just seemed better than ever before. Again I had the oddest sensation when I was chatting to the Marshes. Tania was thirteen years old and quite tall. She and Katy who was two years older had become good friends. I made it a rule not to read my friends' thoughts but I was sorely tempted with regard to Tania. I felt unsettled when I was in her company and I didn't know why. She had reddish brown hair and those hazel eyes of hers seemed to look right through me. I wondered for a moment if she had the ability to read minds like I did but then I discarded the idea and gave it no more thought; until the next time I suppose.

And so Christmas passed and we were well into the New Year when the phone rang and Jerry asked to talk to me.

'Hello Ashley,' he said, 'are you still interested in getting into the antiques business?'

I said I was but that my current collection of antique items did not amount to much as yet so I could hardly think about setting up my own business.

'Not to worry,' said Jerry, 'there is a shop here in Dudley on King Street near to where it joins High Street called McGill's Antiques. I'm quite friendly with the owner a chap called Philip. He is in his seventies now and has no family that I know of. I pop into the shop quite often. I was talking to him the other day and in casual conversation asked him if he was at all thinking of retiring from the business. Poor fellow nearly had a fit. What was he to do with all his collection? He couldn't just chuck it all away. No, no, he said what he really needed was for someone to buy up all his treasures. I then mentioned about having an assistant, someone who had an interest in antiques but was too young and inexperienced to start a business of his own.'

'No such person,' he had said to me, 'and besides I couldn't afford to pay him anything. I hardly sell anything as it is. I could give him a commission I suppose. And he would be company as well.'

'I could see that he was thinking about what I had said because he then asked me if I had someone in mind. I then told him about you Ashley. And he asked me a lot about you and what you were like. I told him the truth and I could see he was thinking about it seriously. I could tell because he squinted, cocked his head to one side and then stared up at the ceiling. I've seen him do this when he was bargaining with a customer and coming to a decision on the price of an item.

'Tell him to come and see me,' he then said.

'So Ashley,' said Jerry, 'what do you think? Would you like to come and see the old gent here in Dudley?'

'Of course I will Jerry,' I said my heart racing. 'Tell Mr McGill I'll be down on the bus tomorrow. I should get there about eleven o'clock.'

There was silence on the line for a brief moment.

Then Jerry said, 'You know Ashley, I've known Philip for a few years now and never thought to ask if he was the McGill of McGill's Antiques. Perhaps he is. Anyway I'll give him a buzz and tell him you'll be there tomorrow.'

Gosh that was an exciting phone call. When I told mum and dad they seemed pleased and said this could be a foot in the door to entering the antiques profession. We had discussed this earlier last year when I first thought about it. I had got hooked on antiques after that fateful car boot sale when I picked up the cracked Chelsea porcelain jar for 50p. Dad had then said that it would be the perfect cover for me when I began to make use of my gifts for the 'purpose' that was marked out for me. Dad firmly believed that I was to fulfil a mission of some sort and that it was essential that my identity be kept a secret.

Now that was one antique shop I had not seen. Whenever we drove through a town or village on our travels and I noticed a curio or antiques shop I'd make mum or dad stop the car so that I could have a quick look inside. I only stayed a few minutes as I could instantly sense if there was anything unusual or of exceptional charm inside. And if there was I'd be drawn straight to it. By simply touching the item I received its complete history. It is a lovely feeling to be able to travel into past times. Antiques are a history unto themselves and if that can be savoured for its sights, sounds and smells then who can blame anyone for wanting to become such a time traveller. Most antique shops appear as small dark crowded rooms stuffed with small objects but to the expert they are rooms lit up by diamonds that are bright and dazzling.

When I walked into McGill's Antiques shop it seemed deserted. The room I entered was quite large being about twelve feet wide and thirty to thirty-five feet long. There were wide shelves on each side down the length of the room from floor to halfway up the wall separated about two feet apart upon which the antique items sat. There was strip lighting along the centre of the ceiling down the length of the room. One of these was making a slight buzzing noise somewhere at the far end. The room was fairly well lit up except when I leaned forward for a closer look at any one of the items my own shadow would partially cover it. There was dustiness about the place which was quite noticeable especially to the nose. The closed door at the far end of the room indicated that there was more to the premises. In front of this door was a desk with a straight backed chair behind it. An old cash register rested on the desk among a few papers and a box of pens. The desk was centrally located at the far end so that there was space to walk either side of it since the shelves continued to the end of the room. The antique pieces were placed randomly on the shelves though the heavier pieces were all on the lowest shelf that actually rested on the floor. There were no labels either describing the item or stating a price.

There was one piece that I was drawn to. It was near the end of the room to the right of the desk on a middle shelf. A large number of the pieces on display in this area were porcelain or pottery. But the piece in question was a white glazed tawny owl. When I picked it up to examine it I noticed a small piece had broken off the rocky mound base. Turning it over I saw the raised anchor on applied oval medallion. It was definitely a Chelsea factory production. Holding it in my hand also told me so much more. Craftsman Rolly Hopkins made it in the winter of early 1751. He was then 45 years old, a bachelor who lived in one of the tied cottages up the hill a mile or so away. This was his second owl firing; the first had a crack in the base and had to be crushed. At about eight inches the piece must have been one of the more difficult ones to fire. It was made about the same time as my prized and lidless cracked porcelain jar that I had picked up for fifty pence at my first car boot sale.

The tawny owl was in a rather battered state though I could see that an attempt had been made to clean the ingrained dirt. I still reckoned its value in the thousands of pounds; perhaps three or four. When I put it back on the shelf I saw the old gentleman standing behind the desk. He must have come into the room while I was engrossed in the owl. For a moment I had a déjà vu experience; as if I had seen the old man somewhere before. No, I thought, I must be mistaken.

'Good morning Mr McGill,' I said assuming that he was the person in question. 'I'm Ashley Bonner. Jerry Marsh said to come and see you.'

He stared at me for a moment then smiled, held out his hand and gave me a firm handshake. I think I liked him right away. He was shorter than me and a bit on the stout side. He didn't look as old as Jerry had made out; more sixty-ish than seventy-ish with plenty of crow's feet either side of his eyes.

'Hello Ashley,' he said, 'I see you like my tawny owl. What do you think of it? I reckon it is worth about three thousand today. Do you think it's worth that?'

'Well sir,' I began and I wanted to impress him. 'It is obviously Chelsea porcelain and its quality tells me it was made in a very cold winter. That would be in the January or February of 1751. The craftsman who made it was one Rolly Hopkins, a bachelor who lived in a tied cottage up a hill about a mile and a half from the factory itself. This was his second firing as the first had to be crushed down because of a crack in the base. This one has lain hidden in the earth somewhere before it was finally rediscovered. The small chip off the base is probably where the spade glanced off it when it was found. I think with a bit more of a specialist clean and a card giving its full history and the site where it had lain buried could make it worth between three and four thousand pounds to the right collector. These white glazed porcelain owls are quite rare.'

I could see the old man was impressed. He came over to the piece and picked it up and held it close to his right eye. He slowly rotated the owl in his hand all the while examining it closely. He then nodded and put the piece back in its place.

'I'm Philip Stevens,' he said. 'I took over the shop from my sister and her husband. They were the McGills who gave the shop its name. They are both long gone now but I kept the name in their memory. They were my only family. You seem to know your stuff young man; so from what you see how would you run this shop if you had a free hand?'

I was completely taken aback by this.

'I'm s-sorry sir I don't know what you mean,' I stammered. I don't usually stammer but I was rather taken aback at the question. I didn't know what to say.

'Call me Philip,' he said nodding his head. 'You know antiques and Jerry said that you were looking to have your own shop one day. Well, here's you chance. I'll make you an offer Ashley. You run this shop as you see fit and after a year if you can make it profitable I shall make you an equal partner.'

'B-but you don't know me at all sir,' I stammered again. 'I'm really a complete stranger to you.'

'Not quite Ashley,' he said. 'I like what I see in you and besides Jerry is a good friend and speaks highly of you and your family. There's something special about you that I can sense and I'm not one to beat about the bush. I was hoping that someone suitable would come along and I believe you are that person. I believe you are psychic to a degree for knowing the name of the Chelsea craftsman that made that owl. I didn't know that but I don't doubt for one moment that you are right. So what say you young man?'

'Why sir,' I said without any hesitation, 'I accept. I hope I can live up to your expectations.'

'I'm sure you will Ashley. And do call me Philip if you will, I'm much more comfortable with it. There are rooms upstairs that reflect the size down here so you could live on site during the week if you wished. It would save you all that travelling everyday. It's not been used much since I have my own place not far from here, just a short bus ride away. You will need to do it up a bit to make it homely for yourself. Perhaps your mum and dad might give you a hand in sprucing the place up a bit.'

'That would be great,' I said. 'I've been storing some things in my dad's garage that I've picked up at car boot sales and the like so I could bring those here as well.'

'Do you have a car to get around?' he asked.

I shook my head.

'Well, I have an old Morris 1000 in my garage that hasn't been out for years. It must be about twenty years old but I believe it to be in excellent condition. It has done only about fifteen thousand miles since I had it from new. It is grey in colour but I'm sure you won't mind that. I will need to get it serviced and taxed and MOT certified. And you will need to get your own insurance of course. You do have a driving licence I presume.'

'Yes I do,' I said. 'I drive my dad's car when he lets me.'

'That's fine,' he said. 'Come on then and I'll show you the upstairs.'

We walked through the door at the back and came upon the stairs. Beyond was another door and we had a quick look in there. Another good sized square room which I could see had kitchen units in the left hand corner with a cooker range and a small fridge. There was also a small square table in the centre with two straight-backed chairs. We went up the stairs and I saw two really good sized rooms. There was a bathroom the other side of the stairwell. Philip had said the upstairs mirrored the lower floor capacity for space. There were no shelves on these walls so the rooms looked decidedly larger but were definitely in need of fresh wall paper. The woodwork could also do with a lick of fresh paint. I think mum would have a field day with this place. I'd let her decide on the colour scheme etc, as I had no artistic sense in that direction. There was no cooking facility up here as the kitchen was all downstairs in the back room. However I could see potential for some changes.

Philip seemed to be having fun. I could see a bit of a twinkle in his eyes as he showed me around. I sat at the kitchen table while he made us mugs of tea. I told him I didn't drink coffee as I had just never liked the taste. There was a carton of fresh milk in the fridge which Philip used to whiten my tea. He drank his black without sugar or sweetener. I usually have one sugar in my tea but as Philip said there was none I managed without. The mugs had seen better and cleaner days but the tea tasted okay. We chatted for a bit on this and that. He was a genuinely interesting guy and I was beginning to like him. He had a lot of dad's easy going ways.

We moved back to the front room or 'the museum' as Philip called it and he opened a desk drawer and gave me a large key on a ring with two other much smaller keys. The large key he said was to the mortise lock in the front door. There was also a Yale lock on the front door so the second key was for that. The third key was to the two locking features on either side of the roller shutter doors that secured the place at night. Philip said that the front door was reinforced internally with steel and had cost him a fortune to install. He had a spare set of keys at home just in case these were lost.

There was a burglar alarm installed which operated downstairs only and had a four digit number code system.

He said he had the car registration document at home and would dig it out so that I could get insurance on it. He said the car was a 'Y' registration with the 'Y' at the end of the number plate. That would make it a 1983 model. He also wrote down his home phone number on a sheet from the shop's official headed note paper. He didn't possess a mobile phone and I said it might be useful to get one. I told him I had one and gave him the number which he wrote down in a little book he kept in the breast pocket of his coat. I said I had my dad's old pay-as-you-go mobile phone at home and I would bring it along tomorrow. It still had about £15 on the Orange SIM card. Dad had been given a new one that was supplied by his office and it cost him nothing to use. I said I'd be here at the same time tomorrow. As I left I again had that déjá vu feeling that Philip reminded me of someone; but of whom and when and where? I shook my head unable to make any connection.

Mum and dad were quite pleased when I gave them my news. I told them in detail all that had happened and there was the very strong possibility that I was about to achieve my goal of starting my very own antiques business. I said I would like them to meet Philip Stevens and they were more than keen to do so. Dad said he had a few days leave coming to him so we could all visit the place tomorrow. He would like to meet my new boss and personally thank him. Mum was more interested in looking over the place to see what needed doing.

'What colour are the curtains,' was her first question. And then 'You'll need a bed and some furniture as well.'

I could see that I would have no problems settling into my new home.

CHAPTER 7

Changes

2001

It was over two years since Ashley began running McGill's Antiques for Philip Stevens and a year since becoming a full partner in the business. In that time the shop had flourished and profits had risen considerably. Ashley had diversified into nostalgic items to cater to what he saw as an affordable interest among the older middle class generation. And because space was limited downstairs the expansion had spread upwards into the upper rooms. This meant that Ashley needed to vacate and find somewhere else to live. Although Philip offered a room in his house Ashley decided that it was time he got a place of his own. He needed to get onto the property ladder sooner rather than later. He had enough for a sizable deposit and the business was doing extremely well. After looking at several properties close by, Ashley finally settled upon a three bedroom semi-detached house near the central part of Paganel Drive adjacent to Priory Park. He liked the view of the castle atop the hill from his front bedroom and fancied the distant animal sounds from the zoo. Not that he could hear them but it was nice to imagine them nearby. The back garden bordered onto Priory Park which gave it an open aspect. The process with the conveyance was long and protracted due to there being three properties in the chain. Finally after about six months the deeds were all signed on a Tuesday and the following Friday in June 2001 Ashley collected the keys to his very own home which he called his little plot of English soil. And he was very proud of it.

The house itself needed a bit of redecorating but the garden had been well maintained and was in colourful array. The previous occupant Mrs Jenkins, a widow, had been an avid gardener and had planted by the book. There were neat rows of flowering shrubs along each side of the rear west facing lawn. The garden was about fifty feet in length and the right hand bed was stuffed with Dahlias of all colours in full bloom. There was a rather dilapidated shed and green house at the bottom of the garden which dad Alex said had potential for replacement by a garden house with full length verandah. The grass on the lawn needed cutting and Alex said he'd bring his mower over during the week.

Since Ashley didn't have a lot of stuff in the shop he allowed himself a week to get gradually settled in. The main item was the bed which was a pine one and could be dismantled and then re-assembled. Everything else would have to be either bought or borrowed. When the Marshes came to visit they brought along a folding table and a couple of chairs which they said were surplus to their needs and could be dumped when Ashley got something new. Mrs Jenkins had left her old sofa set for Ashley so there was somewhere for people to sit when they came to visit. But it was very old and grubby looking so mum Lillian draped some of her heavy candlewick bedspreads over them and neatly tucked it into the sofa gaps wherever possible. The curtains had also all been left behind but Lillian said she despaired of them and was already measuring up for new ones. Ashley said he was relying on help from both family and friends to help him settle in. He said he was not too proud to accept help or charity and thanked Jerry, Milly and Tania for the very welcome 'dining table and chairs'. However the kitchen was the 'piece de resistance', the showcase of the house. It had been completely re-done about three years before and was in superb condition. It and the garden had been the main things that had impressed Ashley when he'd come to view the house for the first time. It even had a little breakfast bar to one side. It included a washing-machine, dishwasher and fridge/freezer left behind by Mrs Jenkins as these were built-in under the worktops and would have been difficult to remove; a real bonus for Ashley.

Katy and Tania went all over the house looking into all the cupboards and corners hoping to find something unusual. But Mrs Jenkins had done a through job of emptying all her things and cleaning up afterwards as well. But they did find lots of things in the garden shed. There were hair dryers and old irons galore. And there were two old ironing boards too. Lots of old rusting pots and pans and some things Katy and Tania didn't recognise. Apparently Mrs Jenkins had used the shed as a sort of dumping ground for discarded items. There was some rusting garden equipment and even a corroded and broken push type lawn mower. But it was interesting for the two girls as they wondered what things they might discover next. Tania seemed especially interested in the place and said she wouldn't mind living there herself. Prophetic words indeed.

It was by the middle of August when things took on a more settled-in look and the downstairs rooms were finally decorated and looked presentable. Ashley had done a lot of the work but without help from family and friends it would have taken much longer. Tania often came on her own in her grubbiest clothes when the walls were being painted with silk-finish emulsions. The ceilings were more difficult to paint as the rollers tended to sprinkle the person below with a fine spray of emulsion liquid. With the painting done and new curtains put up Ashley finally decided to go shopping for furniture. Philip said that it was only right that the business pay for part of Ashley's moving costs. As such the beautiful leather suite, the dining table with eight chairs and bedroom dresser were paid for from the McGill's business account. So at the end of August on the Bank Holiday weekend Ashley had his house warming party.

It was a beautiful warm weekend and everyone was out in the garden enjoying the picnic style party that Lillian and Alex had helped set up for Ashley their son. They knew what he was capable of and yet he never so much as showed off about it. There was a powerful though quiet presence of confidence around him that impressed and drew people to him. Ashley had been 'chosen' and bestowed with these gifts and his parents were very proud of the fact. But they still did not know the full purpose behind it all. What did the future hold for Ashley who seemed not to have a care in the world? Lillian was extremely optimistic about the future since she knew that nothing could physically harm her son. She just wished that he would have a normal life with a family of his own.

Lillian had secret hopes that Ashley and Tania might hit it off. She knew that Robin Nesters was all for Katy and had been so for years ever since he had seen her at the Bishop Vesey cricket matches. Robin had a steady job in a bank and was therefore a good prospect. Robert Black and Vicky were also together but something gave Lillian doubts about their relationship. It was the way that Vicky sometimes looked towards Ashley. Mothers saw things that others missed.

After everyone had finally left and Ashley was on his own he sat down and just relaxed in front of his television. He was content. He had a house of his own and an enlarged family of people that he loved and who loved him. He looked at the TV on/off power button and gave it a mental push and the television came on. But Ashley had to use the remote to change to the news channel. It was mostly gloom and doom. Two more soldiers had been killed in Afghanistan. War in Iraq was imminent. India and Pakistan had demonstrated that they possessed nuclear weapons. Iran was processing Plutonium from its nuclear plants. North Korea was threatening the South. A Russian dissident had been murdered in London. A teacher was critical in hospital after being knifed by an angry parent. A case had come to court accusing two youths of kicking a father of two to death outside his house when he found them vandalising his wife's car in broad daylight. There were witnesses who said the boys were either drunk or under the influence of drugs. A government minister had received donations towards his unsuccessful campaign for deputy leadership that hadn't been declared to the House. Rail prices were going up again more than the rate of inflation. Oil prices had reached $80 a barrel an increase of 100% from two years ago. Petrol prices were now over £4 a gallon. Policemen wanted the right to strike. Showery weather was expected over England for the next few days but the long range forecast for September was drier and warmer than average. Ashley didn't hear half of all this as he had put his head back and dozed off into a peaceful relaxed sleep. The TV seemed to have a somewhat soporific effect.

The next day Ashley got to the shop early. He opened up and knew he had a good two hours before Philip arrived. He had suggested employing an assistant but so far they hadn't done anything about it apart from putting a notice in the window. Tania had offered her services but Philip said a more formal arrangement was needed. Preferably someone a bit more mature and who had already worked in sales. But Tania came to help anyway whenever she could and very welcome it was too. It was company for Philip when Ashley was away on his hunting expeditions. That was going around the country hunting for antiques.

By studying the papers and country life magazines Ashley searched out where the contents of manor houses were to be sold or auctioned and it was extremely rare for Ashley not to find some object of interest or an antique of value on these trips. On one occasion an old lady in Wakefield had been taken into a residential care home and the family had put the contents of her house up for sale. There were some beautiful pieces of furniture which Ashley could not accommodate in the shop but he did advise the family to put these items for sale at a recognised auctioneers. Ashley gave them a few contact phone numbers and they were ever so grateful. There was a set of six bow-back Windsor side-chairs with bowed crests which Ashley valued at about £6000. Ashley told them not to try to clean them up as this would devalue them. Only a professional restorer could bring their value up another £2000 or so. They were astounded and quite pleased. There was also a very rough looking but recognisable George-III oak dresser with moulded cornice over three drawers flanked by reeded sides. As it was it would probably fetch about £1000, but if fully restored could achieve its full value of £5000 to £6000. Apparently the old lady or her late husband had been keen collectors of early nineteenth century furniture. There were a few other items that Ashley advised them on and they asked how they might repay his kindness. Would he care to look for something of interest to him and have it with their 'very best compliments?' But there wasn't anything else of great value and Ashley said so. Just then one of the family members came in carrying a pair of shiny brass candlesticks with the remark, 'Dad, look what I found at the bottom of the cupboard in the bathroom.'

'What about these,' said the dad, 'would you accept these as a gift?'

'You wouldn't want to give those away, sir,' said Ashley, 'do you know what they are worth?'

'No.' said the dad rather hesitantly. 'What are they worth?'

'Well they are early nineteenth century George-III brass candlesticks and worth a few hundred pounds at least,' said Ashley.

Just then a rather scruffy man came up to them and looking at the dad asked if he was the owner of the property. When given the affirmative he said he was a farmer and liked the set of six bow-backed chairs as they would do nicely for the kids to play with in the barn.

'I'm offering you £100 for them in the state they are in,' he said.

The dad looked towards Ashley and said, 'but this gentleman has already offered me £50 a chair.'

'In that case sir,' he said, 'let me increase my offer to double his.'

'I'm sorry sir but I couldn't do that. I've already accepted his offer and I have his cheque for the full amount. He is coming back tomorrow to collect them,' the dad said winking at Ashley.

'Well sir let me say that this man is a cheat and a swindler and has conned you into parting with something that is worth at least £2000. All I can say is you should tear up his cheque and put the chairs to auction.' And with that he turned and walked away.

The dad and Ashley looked at one another and burst out laughing. The dad then handed Ashley the two brass candlesticks.

'I don't care how much these are worth,' he said, 'I consider you a friend and we would like you to accept these as a gift. I don't for one moment think that was a real farmer but it was worth seeing the look on his face when I told him you had bought the chairs at that price.'

Ashley accepted the gift but only on the condition that the family visit the McGill's shop in Dudley when they were next travelling that way. He gave them his business card by way of introduction.

The man then introduced himself as Gary Prior and his wife Jill. Their three children were Malcolm who was twelve, Mary ten and Maura seven. They lived in Mansfield which was an hour's drive away from Birmingham and they would be very pleased to visit. Ashley told them to check the stock of books for any First Editions and also the old lady's jewellery as these could be quite valuable. Little did Ashley know of the relationship that was to develop with the Prior family? They all came out and waved him goodbye when he got in his car to finally leave.

The Morris Minor car had done very well for a couple of years but then Ashley found it lacked the comfort and speed of a more modern car. He part-exchanged it at a motor dealer for a one year old Toyota Avensis with a large boot area. It had all the mod-cons including power steering, electric windows, air conditioning and a CD player and came with a two year warrantee. And it was not grey. It was bright red and ran beautifully. Ashley favoured country and western style music and had a fair selection of CDs in the car storage compartment under the driver's left arm rest.

When Ashley first started bringing in old toys Philip was a bit sceptical of the idea. But when these were displayed on the newly erected shelves in the upstairs rooms they looked so good that Philip changed his opinion. Because Ashley wanted people in the shop he got Philip to agree to add the words 'and Museum' to the existing shop sign. So it became 'McGill's Antiques & Museum'. The museum was the upstairs part even though everything was for sale and was clearly marked. The 'museum' word attracted a larger clientele and most just came to look around and admire the old toys and gadgets on display. Ashley had added a short history to each of the antique items which seemed to remove some of their mystique in the public's eye. Word got around to the other Antiques dealers which incited their curiosity such that some came to see for themselves. Some even requested a visit to the 'back room' where items were stored prior to display. This was also where an offer might be made to purchase a particular item. Ashley would state a price and then reduce it by ten percent for a fellow dealer. McGill's Antiques & Museum subsequently acquired a reputation for fairness and value for money. Business was booming and the partners discussed expanding to larger premises but decided to postpone the decision for a year or so until suitable premises became available nearby. The ideal would be to expand into an adjacent property if or when it became available.

Ever since the Merry Hill shopping complex had opened some years ago there had been a steady decline of the shops in the main Dudley Town area. There were a number of vacant business properties still up for the taking but the shops either side of McGill's was not one of them.

There was a great mutual respect between Ashley and Philip and you could see that they had a great affection for each other. It was an uncle and nephew sort of relationship. Ashley found happiness and contentment in his role as 'chief executive' of the business and Philip went along with most of Ashley's decisions. If there was an idea that Philip found dubious he would suggest that it might be worth reconsidering the implications on the business's profitability. Philip had a quiet manner that Ashley found particularly reassuring. They went to a buffet restaurant at least one evening a week and many good business ideas were discussed there. There was one area that both thought very important and that was the raising of the McGill's image and the awareness of antiques in the public view.

No one could fault Ashley's little description cards placed alongside each displayed item. On more than one occasion tabloid reporters had investigated a few of these cards and actually authenticated the information to the extent of tracing the craftsman named in the church records listing baptisms and marriages. In a few cases where a factory's labour record was found the craftsman's name was traced and dated. There were a few cases where records did not exist but this didn't mean that the information was false. The reputation of the business spread on account of this and the McGill's name became well known and a byword for reputable antiques.

Although not directly on the High Street in Dudley Town, the shop was well known to the locals and anyone asking directions had only to mention the McGill's name to be directed straight there. There were of course the 'regulars'. These were locals who had an interest in antiques but didn't really have the ability to purchase. The fact that the shop also doubled as a free museum allowed them to wander around and admire their favourite items whenever they chose. They brought their friends and sometimes their children along to show them the 'stuff' upstairs which got to be known as 'the nostalgic room'. The old wind-up toys were of special interest to dads who would say they could actually remember owning some of them. One of the corners upstairs was devoted to Victorian era kitchen implements. There were even several old recipe books on display that Philip had inherited from his sister Grace. There were also a few early gardening tools and carpentry gadgets. All in all 'McGill's Antiques & Museum' became renowned as a place to spend a pleasant hour, especially on a cold or rainy afternoon.

Milly and Tania often came into the shop and would be made especially welcome. The Marshes had been good friends of Philip for many years and Milly could even remember having briefly met his sister Grace and her ailing husband David. Philip always invited them into the kitchen area and they would sit around the table chatting with their hands wrapped around mugs of hot tea. The rooms were kept cool rather than warm for the benefit of the items on the shelves. And so when you walked off the street the difference in temperature was minimal and visitors tended to keep their hats on and coats buttoned.

Tania was a young lady of sixteen and quite confident in her manner. She was four years younger than Ashley and chatted easily and seemed quite interested in the displayed antiques. Philip sensed her disappointment when Ashley was out on his many country-wide searches and he discerned a mood about her when she didn't get to see him. Ashley, on the other hand, was quite oblivious of Tania's charms and treated her as a very good friend. She was like a sister to him and he would often discuss with her the best place to display a particular item. They laughed and joked together like the very good friends they were and always kissed each other on the cheek when saying 'hello' and again when saying 'goodbye'.

On occasion Jerry also came in if he had a day off and then it was like a family reunion for Philip.

Philip thought about how his whole life had been uplifted by Ashley joining forces with him. Although Jerry had introduced Ashley to the business it had been Philip who had actually taken it up and so the credit was entirely his. The relationship between the business partners had taken off from there basically because they were so compatible. Philip looked upon Ashley with a mutual respect and in his heart a great admiration and affection had blossomed shortly after Ashley had joined the shop. Thereafter this had grown into a sort of parental affection. Ashley was the son he would have liked to have had if he had ever married. Grace and David McGill had no children of their own and so the shop had passed to Philip after they died. He would have so liked his sister to have met Ashley.

The thing with Ashley was that he drew people to him without even trying. A halo of invisible confidence surrounded him yet his manner in company and in business was gentle and caring. This made the people he was dealing with admire him. And as they got to know him better they developed a liking for this 'man of goodness'. Never a harsh word escaped his lips or even a reprimanding look. And whenever Ashley spoke he smiled with a wide genuine smile. It was as though he was in love with life and life was in love with him. He always made the person he was talking to feel important. He listened with due attention and a smile, always a smile. Of course his family who knew of his gifts understood the fact behind Ashley's good nature. But what was the greatest joy to them was that Ashley never ever showed off his skills or said anything to indicate or brag about the powers that had been granted him. The only times he ever made reference to it was during their regular family conferences. Ashley often referred to the fact he still had no idea what he was meant to do with these gifts; he was hoping that the hidden voice would one day reveal all. That voice had been strangely silent of late.

Ashley's attitude to other people was always an understanding one and this was perhaps because he understood the thoughts in the minds of the other person. Whether or not he wished to do so it seemed automatic that Ashley knew exactly what their thoughts were. Subconsciously he read their thoughts and knew what they really meant when they said something. Not everyone can correctly phrase what they mean when they express themselves. And so some people can be misunderstood if the wrong words are heard.

There was an occasion during a house sale when Ashley made an offer for a pair of eight inch George Jones Majolica plates moulded with strawberry blossoms on a light blue background. The plates were rather scuffed but otherwise unmarked. The lady of the house thought they were worth more. Her thoughts to

Ashley came across as someone who was in a great deal of financial difficulty and she was being forced to sell items that she had lovingly collected. These plates happened to be one of her favourite pieces and she associated them with memories of someone dear to her and who had been with her when she had purchased the pieces so many years ago.

Ashley gave her his best smile and then went on to give her the background history of the pieces.

'Well I can tell you that these were made in 1875 at George Jones Stoke on Trent manufactory by one of his older craftsmen named Joshua Gibson. I dare say his descendants may be around somewhere and traceable today. About forty of these plates were fired but only half came out well. These are very collectable provided they are in mint condition. However with frequent use on the dining table the majolica can scuff and the scratch marks become quite noticeable. At auction on a good day a pair in mint condition could fetch £400 to £600. These, in their present condition about half that. So I can only offer you that amount and hope to sell it on at a slight profit for my business. If I was a collector I would offer you more depending on how desirable they were to me.'

The lady seemed a bit disappointed but at the same time impressed at Ashley's knowledge and expertise. She was especially impressed that Ashley hadn't tried to argue over price and had instead armed her with further knowledge about the pieces. The fact that Ashley knew the name of the man who had crafted the plates was to her the most impressive fact of all. She said she would think about Ashley's offer and let him know in a day or two if Ashley would leave his contact number. So Ashley gave her his business card and wished her well in the sale of the other items as well.

And it was the very next day that she phoned to say she had decided to accept the price offer Ashley had made. She also said she was coming in to Birmingham the following week and would bring the pieces directly to the shop. She said that she had subsequently heard about McGill's Antiques and Museum shop from a friend and was keen to give it the once over.

That was in the summer. It was now December and a week before Christmas. McGills Antiques and Museum had festive lights on its frontage and the display window had been done up beautifully by Lillian, Milly, Tania and of course Ashley and Philip. They had managed to collect a variety of Santa Claus figures, all between one and two feet tall, and arranged them in the display. Some were electrically operated and some were not. But they all looked grand. Inside the shop there were tinsel strings laid out on the shelves and made to zigzag between the items but not so as to detract from their own display features. The tinsel was in gold, silver, green and red and it made the shop look very festive. This was something that Ashley had instituted with whole hearted approval from Philip who simply requested not to be asked to help when the time came to take everything down. Ashley had thought about a Christmas tree but that turned out to be impractical on account of the space it would take up in the shop. However instead Ashley had bought about twenty small one foot tall Christmas trees from the £1 store and placed them on the shelves around the shop on both floors. Philip hadn't agreed to all this at first since the shop was usually shut over the Christmas period. But because of its popularity after its first year with Ashley in charge they decided to close for only three days at Christmas and two days for the New Year. It was surprising how much business was done over the four days in between. Ashley had spent Christmas Eve, Christmas Day and Boxing Day at his parent's house in Erdington those first years just as he had brought in the New Year with them as well.

That first year when Ashley joined Philip in the shop he hadn't quite settled into the rooms upstairs and so had returned home for the full Christmas period. When he returned to the shop in the New Year he had noticed how drab and plain the shop had looked compared to others on the same street. He decided then and there to make some drastic changes to the shop's Christmas image. He also made sure that Philip did not ever again spend Christmas on his own. And so the Bonner household had one extra house guest for two nights either side of Christmas day.

This year it had been an especially joyous occasion. Philip had accompanied Ashley and all his family to the Sutton Town Hall for the Christmas carol concert on the Sunday a week before Christmas. Granddad Eric was also there with his walking cane which he now always took around with him. Just a status sign of his old age he said. Ashley had attended this concert every year since the age of six. This year they had all gone as a larger group with the Chambers and the Marshes. Robert Black and Robin Nesters were always around and were considered part of the larger family of friends as was Philip Stevens now as well.

The concert was very good again this year and the complementary mince pies during the interval were quite a treat. Afterwards everyone went to their own homes as it was quite late and the cars were covered in a light frost. Ashley drove back to Dudley with Philip and dropped him off home before returning to his own place in Paganel Drive. It was near midnight when he got in the door. The Christmas period was a busy one and McGill's Antiques did a good business mainly on the nostalgic items. Ashley made sure they had a good stock of these.

Christmas Eve was a wet day but the night turned out clear and cold. Quite a few of the group came back to the Bonner house after the midnight church service for a treat of pork pies and Port wine. There was lots of laughter and 'Merry Christmas' greetings were passed around; after all it was Christmas Day. Lillian dressed the turkey as usual and put it in the oven at 3 o'clock when everyone had gone to their own homes. They were invited to return later that evening at 6 o'clock for teatime snacks.

Christmas dinner was mainly a family affair in one's own home. For the past two years Philip had become a part of the Bonner family at Ashley's insistence and had become a favourite with both Lillian and Alex. Philip had a gentle manner and smiled when he spoke, just like Ashley did. With six at the table for Christmas dinner there was plenty of interesting conversation not to mention some cracked singing. Eric had brought along his Max Bygraves Christmas sing-along CD and it was played more than once that day. For some reason it got misplaced to Lillian's delight.

Eric and Philip gravitated towards talking about old times just after the war and food rationing and how there were hardly any cars on the roads and traffic was not a problem. They had both done National Service in places like Aden and Cyprus in the 50s but at different times. Apparently they had missed each other in Cyprus by only a few months. Ashley and Katy listened with interest to some of the very funny army episodes they came out with.

There was the incident with the corporal who had been cleaning his supposedly empty rifle in the barracks when it suddenly went off. No one was hurt and they began to wonder where the bullet had gone. At the far end of the barracks was a large metal cupboard with a lock on it. There was a neat hole through the side. It belonged to the staff sergeant and had his civvies stored away in it. He only opened it up just before going on leave and this wasn't due for another few weeks. In the meantime one of the men quickly stuck a pin-up poster to cover the hole and very soon no one gave it a second thought.

Weeks later there was a huge shout when Staff Sergeant Billy opened the cupboard and discovered a neat hole in nearly every item hanging up. His best jackets and trousers and even his dark suit had a hole in each of them. It was really odd how the bullet had found its way through the very centre of everything hanging up. Of course no one owned up and the whole squad was put on fatigue duty for a week. However word finally got around to Sergeant Billy that it had been an accident when someone was cleaning his rifle and it was just good luck that no one was shot. After that all rifle cleaning had to be done outside the barracks room no matter what the weather.

With the dinner over and the Christmas pudding sampled everyone trooped into the living room to listen to the Queen's speech at 3 o'clock. The telly stayed on and the men settled down to watch one of the old films. There were a few snores as was usual after a big meal. Lillian remarked that if she were to switch off the TV they would all wake up and remonstrate that they had been actually watching the film.

Katy and Lillian tidied up and loaded up the dishwasher in the kitchen. The bigger pots and pans had to be washed by hand in the kitchen sink. Lillian washed and Katy dried while chattering away to her mum as usual. When they had finished they came and sat down with the men folk and smiled at the occasional snores from Eric and Philip. Alex was awake now and got up to make tea for everyone. Philip was always apologetic when he awoke after a short doze. He and Eric were both in their mid 70s and it was quite acceptable to all that they should drop off occasionally. And Lillian always remarked that she considered it a compliment to her cooking that they did.

The rest of the friends had been invited for 6 o'clock so Lillian had a while to relax before they arrived. She would lay on a supper of cold foods for about 8 o'clock and everyone would be expected to help themselves buffet style as and when they felt like a nibble.

When they did arrive it seemed like a stampede and war zone all in one. The hugs and greetings were genuine and Tania blushed after giving Ashley his share of her welcome. Lillian was pleased that her closest friends Mavis and Milly were able to come and she said as much. The three of them retreated to the kitchen for a chat and then to begin preparations for the buffet. Jerry was always pleased to see Philip and they had plenty to say to one another. Jerry also complimented Alex on the way the Christmas cards were stuck to the picture frames around the room. He said they added to the decorations perfectly along with all the tinsel. The tree in the alcove was done up well and the best he had seen this year. Lillian was the architect and Alex said so. Jerry was always a smooth talker and Alex told him so but with laughter in his voice.

The younger generation retreated to the dining table and sat around it gossiping. Robert Black and Robin Nesters were in terrific form and had the girls Vicky, Tania and Katy in splits of laughter. It was a lovely easy relationship that they all seemed to have and one would never have guessed that Robert was nuts about Vicky and Robin about Katy. And of course the secret attachment Tania had for Ashley. They were all quite content to let the present friendliness continue without complicating the issue before their time.

Lillian and Katy talked a lot and discussed most things quite openly. Katy liked Robin as a good friend and she didn't want to get committed in any way. Lillian thought that one day they might tie the knot just as Robert and Vicky might. With regard to Ashley, Lillian knew her son and all that he was capable of. She understood that Ashley had as yet to find out the purpose behind his gifts before he committed himself to a family of his own. It was sad but Lillian reckoned that Tania was in for a very long wait if not a disappointment. Alex, Lillian and Eric had no inkling of the direction Ashley's life would take or the tasks he might be called upon to undertake. Nor for that matter did Ron and Brenda who were kept up to date with Ashley's progress. But if anything the family trait was one of patience and they were all happy to let things go along as they were. They were the only ones who knew of Ashley's gifts as far as they knew and never once had they asked Ashley to demonstrate any part of his powers. Of course Ashley still practiced pushing the sandbag in the garage and going pink every now and then. However there was one aspect that the family did use and that was to converse telepathically with Ashley. They could mind-talk to Ashley and he also to them but they could not converse with one another. And so it was that Ashley got Lillian's message that she was ready to start laying the dining table. So he said to the young group that they had better vacate the dining table to let the ladies set out the things for tea.

'You know Ashley,' said Tania, 'I sometimes think that you can read peoples thoughts. I know you pick up on things that I have just thought about and I think it's because we're so alike. I bet your mum in the kitchen thought it was time to lay the table and you picked up her thought waves from here. I'm right aren't I?'

'Absolutely right Tania,' said Ashley. 'Mum said she wanted to lay out the buffet things at seven thirty and guess what time it is now?'

They all looked at the wall clock and burst out laughing when Katy said 'Elementary my dear Watson.' Tania gave Ashley an impish look and poked her tongue out at him.

Then Katy added, 'I do wish we could stay like this forever. It's just so right.'

Since they all had a drink of sorts they stood up, raised their glasses and said, 'Amen to that.'

They all then walked into the living room and sat around but mostly on the floor. Katy went in to the kitchen and offered to help but Lillian said she had plenty of help with Mavis and Milly. And so the evening wore on.

There was a call from Ron and Brenda who wished everyone in turn for Christmas. Ron was on the upstairs extension so that they could both talk and not miss anyone. They said business was good and they had quite a few guests over the festive period otherwise they'd have loved to be down with the rest of the family as well. But they said that every year. They had also organised a New Years Eve party so would not be bringing it in alone. In fact they would be ever so busy. When Ashley was given the phone he spoke to them telepathically and gave them a visual of all that was happening in the house. But Ashley couldn't read their thoughts at this distance and said so.

'O Ashley,' said Brenda, 'thank you ever so much for that. We feel we are practically down there with you.'

'Merry Christmas Ashley,' said Ron, 'I got the message as well. Congratulations. We shall be down one weekend near the end of January and you can fill us in with the new developments. Love and God bless to all.'

Brenda repeated Ron's message before they rang off.

Ashley had never tried this form of telepathic communication before. The normal distance was too great. Perhaps the phone line had helped to concentrate the telepathic waves towards the persons on the line. Or perhaps this was another phase in the advancement of his gifts.

Tania then came into the room from the hall. She had been upstairs in the bathroom when the phone had rung. But she had a funny expression on her face when she entered the room and looked at Ashley. And Ashley knew straight away that Tania had been listening on the phone extension upstairs. What had she concluded from the conversation with Ron and Brenda? Had she received Ashley's telepathic detailed description of the festive goings on? Nothing had been said and so Tania would have a confused impression only. Ashley probed her thoughts and ascertained that she didn't suspect anything of Ashley's ability in telepathy. But she was confused as to why she had suddenly recalled this day's events in such detail. She even saw the Bonners having their Christmas dinner and the Max Bygraves sing-along music. She felt she had been there the whole day. Perhaps her mind was playing tricks with her. Ashley decided to remain silent and feign complete ignorance and let Tania sort out her thoughts regarding this matter on her own.

Lillian then rang her parents in Aberdare to also wish them a Merry Christmas. Beryl came on the line and they talked for a few minutes. David also came on the line when Beryl gave him the phone. David spoke slowly and had done so for the past two years since he'd had that minor stroke.

He had been at dinner one evening when Beryl had noticed a slight distortion to the left side of his face. She had told him about it but he said she must be imagining things. But when he had trouble pronouncing some words she straightaway new that something was seriously wrong. She rang NHS Direct and after listening to the symptoms they said to ring for an ambulance as they suspected David might be having a stroke. At the hospital the doctors confirmed this and had kept David in for a few days to monitor his condition. They also put him on a different medication and blood thinning tablets. Beryl had rung Lillian and Brenda from the hospital as soon as the stroke had been confirmed. Lillian drove down right away and Ashley went with her. They went straight to the house in Clifton Street having phoned from the car to make sure Beryl was home. She told them that David was fine except for the left side of his face being slightly drooped. He also had to be careful while eating and drinking as he tended to dribble a bit from that side of his mouth. Otherwise he was quite alert and appeared normal. Brenda and Ron had come down the next day.

Since then Beryl and David didn't travel to see their daughters anymore but relied on visits from them instead. Beryl didn't let David do any heavy work and when Ashley last saw his granddad a few weeks ago on one of his antique jaunts he noticed a thinner man who tended to nod off to sleep in front of the TV. He could see his granddad David going rapidly into advanced old age. The doctors had told Beryl at one the regular hospital checkups that David might have had a succession of very minor strokes since the first one the previous year. However they said the medication was helping and David's speech and facial muscles had all nearly returned to normal.

David always asked how his grandson was progressing and insisted they visit and give him a face to face update. Eric usually went down with Ashley at the planned weekends as with Katy coming along it would have been a bit of a squeeze for them all to fit in the one car. Sometimes Ron and Brenda also managed to visit at the same time if business at the B&B permitted. Katy wasn't one for grownup talk and usually left the room to do other more interesting things; thus leaving them free to discuss Ashley's latest gift. She had made friends with a brother and sister a few doors from her grandparents' house and usually popped round to say hello. Quite often they would simply go for a stroll around the streets of Aberdare.

At one of these meetings Ashley had expressed a wish to bring Katy into the fold of knowledge but both Lillian and Alex had considered it unwise. Katy was too bubbly and might not be able to keep the secret. They thought perhaps when she was older and more settled. The same could be said for Ashley's friends. As for Philip they thought that was out of the question even though he was such a lovable man. Philip was very religious and might not understand just as Lillian's parents Beryl and David Jones hadn't understood way back when Ashley was six years old. They had then been a bit horrified by what they had been told and thought it just a growing up passing phase.

Lillian's evening buffet had loads of different things. There was sliced ham, a plate of turkey meat left over from dinner, cocktail sausages, mini pork pies, scotch eggs, mince pies, an assortment of cheeses, cracker biscuits, coleslaw and cottage cheese, pickles and dips, a bowl of green salad and another of fruit salad. A large bloomer of bread had been neatly sliced by Alex with the electric carving knife and was placed neatly in the centre of the table. There was a jar of pickled onions and another of whole mini beetroots. There was margarine and spreadable butter and a jar of spreadable cheddar cheese. There was French and English mustard in their jars. There were slices of hot pizza which Lillian brought last to the table straight from the oven. And for dessert Mavis and Vicky had made a beautiful strawberry trifle in a large dish which they had brought with them from home. Lillian had also bought a 24 slice Black Forrest Gateau just so that people had a choice. There was a jug full of pouring low fat cream to go with it.

Everyone helped themselves. Some sat at the table while others took their plates and sat in the lounge with plates on their laps.

Philip sat next to Lillian at the dining table and said how much he had enjoyed this Christmas.

'I feel so comfortable here and so at home,' he said. 'And it's not just your home I care for but your family and all your friends. I think I take advantage of your hospitality and I know it must be a lot of extra work for you. But what I want to say most of all is thank you for Ashley. He has transformed McGill's into a thriving business. He has an extraordinary talent for the antiques business and I feel I'm holding him back. So from now on I shall take a back seat and give him full executive powers to do with the business as he feels fit. I know he wishes to expand to a larger premises and I am happy to go along with that. I only hope I'm not putting too much of a workload on him and taking him away from family commitments as such.'

'My dear Philip,' said Lillian putting her hand on his arm, 'please don't worry about Ashley in the least because I don't. He will always be close to us no matter how far away he may be. We have a secret connection for which I thank God. Ashley is special in a way you can never understand but one day I hope to be able to share that with you. I don't worry about him anymore as I know he will always be safe. He is a wonderful son and I know he also has a great affection for you Philip. I can see that and that is because you are what you are. And we share that affection because we have come to know you and like you over the past few years just as Jerry and Milly do as well.'

Eric was on the other side of Lillian and had been listening to what was being said.

'My dear Philip.' he said, 'I count you as a good friend. You are a part of us whether you like it or not and you have been sentenced for life to this family and all its friends. There's no getting out of it old chap. It is really quite terrible when you consider how many birthdays and anniversaries you will have to remember not to mention getting all those Christmas presents as well.'

Everyone laughed at this.

Then someone said, 'Why do we have to buy Christmas presents at all? Why not just give some money so that everyone can buy what they really want.'

Someone else said, 'Why don't we just give money to a charity instead.'

It was Philip who said in his quiet way that Christmas was all about celebrating the birth of Christ with one's family and friends and imitating the three wise men by giving out gifts. Gifts are important because there is joy in giving and joy in receiving and it expresses our love for each other. Even sending out Christmas cards simply tells the person that you are thinking of them with affection.

After a thoughtful pause Philip added that Christmas had become a universal event for non-Christians as well. It was the children who looked forward to their 'Christmas presents' and expected Father Christmas to visit them as well. Practically every home put up some form of celebratory decoration if not an actual tree in the living room. The children's excited and expectant faces were a joy to their parents and this joyousness was what would perpetuate the Christmas celebration as a worldwide event – even if its true meaning had become hidden.

Philip,' said Lillian, 'I didn't know that you were a philosopher and a religious, but you expressed that all so well. I certainly agree with everything you say and I'm sure that everyone here does as well.'

There were nods all around the room and a 'Hear, hear' from Eric.

It was not long before they had finished at the table and Lillian and the ladies began to clear away. Everyone picked up a plate and took it into the kitchen. There was so much food left that Lillian had to find containers to store it away in the fridge. Luckily the fridge had been nearly empty so there was plenty of space. One thing Lillian had was plenty of help.

Robert Black organised the party games but it was charades that they all opted for. The rule was for every one to have a turn and they were free to choose what they wished provided it was well known and restricted to a book, a play, a song or a film. No points were to be scored as it would all be just for fun.

There was much laughter and ribbing not to mention the occasional booing when something couldn't be guessed or an enactment was puzzling. Everyone had a turn even Philip and Eric the two most senior people in the room. Philip made a right mess of his choice of film 'The Sound of Music'. He kept ringing his ear as a clue for the second word but everyone kept repeating 'Sounds like' and then asking him 'sounds like what'. In the end Lillian and Mavis both guessed it simultaneously. Philip said that was the most exhausting and frustrating few minutes of his life.

This went on till about 11 o'clock when Katy brought out the Trivial Pursuit game. She said she would just ask questions off the cards and anyone could answer. This was one of Katy's favourite party fillers. It allowed people to take part or just sit and listen. There was an argument over one that asked which bird had the largest wingspan. Eric said the South American Condor but the listed answer on the card was the Albatross.

'That's wrong,' said Eric, 'because I know the Condor is so large that it can carry away a sheep. Some have even been known to pick up a small child. I never heard of an albatross doing that.'

'Actually,' said Philip, 'the albatross has a wider span but the wings are quite slim. The condor on the other hand has a much broader wing and nearly as large a wingspan so has many times the wing area of the albatross in comparison. Also weight for weight the Condor is by far the heavier bird. Did you know that the albatross can stay aloft for weeks or even months and travel thousands of miles at a time?'

'But surely it has to eat in between which it can't do if it keeps flying for months and months,' said Ashley.

'Well now,' said Philip with a mischievous grin, 'didn't you know that the albatross has a built-in mobile phone system so that whenever it feels like a bite to eat it calls up room service and presto another albatross brings it a fish.'

There was booing all around the room.

'That was terrible, Philip,' said Eric. He then said he was bushed and was going to call it a day and scoot off home. Philip also said it was way past his usual bedtime so he'd head for his bed as well.

Eric always went home as he preferred his own bed and pillows. Philip had the spare bedroom upstairs that used to be Ashley's.

It was not long after the two had said their goodnights that the rest of the friends also decided to leave for home. Ashley would stay and sleep downstairs on the blow-up bed.

The farewells took ages with everyone chattering as they put their coats on. The ladies made their round of kissing everyone goodbye and when Tania came to Ashley she reached forward to kiss him on the cheek. Just then Robert said something and Ashley turned his head towards him and Tania's intended kiss ended up partway on Ashley's lips which made Tania blush.

'Ooo Tania,' exclaimed a laughing Ashley, 'that was nice. You'll have to do it more often.'

'Get lost Ashley,' she said still all flushed, 'you'll have to wait till next Christmas for the next one. You moved your head purposely you …you…' and she couldn't find the right word and left it at that.

Only Robert had seen the half kiss and he laughed out loud and in turn got a glare from Tania.

The goodbyes were finally said and all drove off.

Alex and Ashley set up the blow-up bed downstairs in the living room while Lillian and Katy tidied and washed up. It was nearly 2 am when they too went off to bed.

Lillian said to Alex what a lovely Christmas she'd had and thanked him for all his help in the kitchen and with the guests.

Just before slipping off to sleep Lillian said she thought Tania would be good for Ashley.

Alex had been about to drop off to sleep himself when suddenly he was wide awake. He couldn't help puzzling over Lillian's remark. He hadn't noticed anything out of the ordinary between Tania and his son, but then he'd always relied on Lillian to keep him abreast of things. Lillian was the observant one so he'd ask her what she had meant tomorrow. It took Alex over an hour of this before he finally dropped off to sleep. In the morning he couldn't remember too much about the previous night's events and so quite forgot about Lillian's bedroom remark.

It was a lazy Boxing morning but not for Ashley who was up first. He collapsed the air bed and folded up the bed linen neatly and put it all to one side. He then made himself a mug of tea and thought about yesterday's events. Life was good and he was lucky to have such friends. Ashley knew exactly what he was doing as far as Tania was concerned. She was nice and he had a genuine affection for her. She was like a sister to him and he looked forward to her company. Except if she wasn't there with the others he missed her just that little bit more with a tinge of disappointment squeezed in. Ashley had no plans for a family and had never actually thought about one until now when he was thinking about it in a negative way. That partial kiss from Tania had been quite pleasant and he wondered what a proper one might be like. Then he began wondering about his mental gifts and whether she had guessed something from his telepathic revelations to Ron and Brenda. He knew that one day Katy would have to be brought into the family circle of understanding but it would be impossible to ask anyone else to keep such a secret. There was that voice again cautioning him that the secret must be kept if he was to fulfil his mission. But Ashley said he didn't know what that mission or task was.

'All in good time,' was the reply, 'one must learn to walk first before venturing on the journey.'

Again Ashley began to wonder at his tutor. Ever since he could remember, this hidden voice had been with him giving him information and guidance whenever needed. Questions seemed to get a reply in an instant. But there were no answers to some questions on decision making. And so Tania for the moment was not to be allowed into Ashley's life. Not as a companion anyway. But he would nevertheless keep her in his affections as a very dear friend. Also his dream about the old man still puzzled him. That déjà vu feeling seemed stronger than ever but remained undefined.

Breakfast was a couple of toasts with marmalade and slices of cheese when the others came down. Lillian did a light lunch in the early afternoon after which Ashley and Philip returned to Dudley to check up on the shop. Everything was normal and they sat around for about an hour before shutting up again. Ashley dropped Philip home and checked that he got in the door okay. He then got home and found the house was cold from having turned the room thermostat to a low temperature when he'd left on Christmas Eve. He turned it up again and then sat down to watch the news on the telly. It was the usual gloom and doom scenario of accidents in fog on the motorway, drunken brawls in certain areas and a special feature advising on burglaries over the festive period. Drink drivers were down on the previous year but by only a few percent. But binge drinking and drug taking by the younger generation was the worst ever. One teenager was in a coma from having taken Ecstasy tablets for the first time when celebrating her sixteenth birthday.

Philip and Ashley spent all next day in the shop. Some of their usual customers came in to wish them for the season and it was nice having the company. But no business was conducted. The same was the situation for the following day so in the afternoon Philip suggested they close up for the rest of the day and year and reopen on January Second. They went to a pub for dinner and spent a pleasant evening. Philip then told Ashley of his decision to give him full executive powers in the business. He told Ashley to run the business as he saw fit and that he would give his full support.

'The shop has gone from strength to strength over these last few years Ashley and that has been solely due to your vision and ability. You can continue your plans now and I shall look forward to seeing McGill's Antiques getting bigger and better as the years go by. I only ask that you keep the name. As a full partnership everything in the business automatically reverts to the surviving partner should anything befall either one of them. I have no other family and as I said to your mother you have brought a zest and a cheer into my life that I had not expected and for which I must thank you. I also thank God for sending you to me. Grace and David must surely be looking down on us and smiling. Their shop prospers as never before and they must feel good about it. So as I step down into retirement in my role as a sleeping partner let me congratulate you as McGill's new managing director and chief executive. Had I ever had a family of my own I would have wished for a son just like you Ashley. May God bless you and keep you in his care always.'

When he had finished there were tears in the corners of Philip's eyes.

All Ashley could do was nod and smile. There were no words to express how he felt but he also had a degree of moistness in his eyes. So they smiled at each other and then Ashley reached across the table for a handshake. Philip grasped Ashley's with both his hands and it ended as a two handed firm handshake for both of them.

'Thank you Philip,' said Ashley, 'thank you very much. And I love you like a second father and that is the truth. I do so enjoy your company and hope we have a long time together. Let's drink a toast to that.'

So they raised their glasses 'To a long and happy friendship.'

When Ashley dropped Philip back to his house on Griffin Street there was quite a gathering of youths of all sorts at the end of the street. They seemed to be having a good time talking and laughing rather loudly. Philip said that this had been going on for about a week now but they dispersed when the pub around the corner emptied near midnight. But it was very intimidating for people walking by especially the elderly. Ashley thought about asking them to disperse but thought it best to wait and see. But he did send a telepathic piece of information to the group that the police were patrolling in a car just in the next street and were about to reach them in a few minutes. And with that Ashley went in with Philip and stayed for a cup of tea. They phoned Jerry and arranged to meet up the next day in the afternoon. Milly invited them to stay for supper as well.

When Ashley left about an hour later the street was deserted. Ashley felt quite proud of himself as this was the first bit of law enforcement that he had ever undertaken.

And so the next day when they arrived at the Marsh's they were surprised that a few from the darts team were also there with their wives and children. Philip knew them all and it was like a reunion for him. Ashley had met them a couple of times and Big Jim was as jolly as ever. They talked about their recent match against the Berries which they had won by a good margin. The day was a wet one so the kids couldn't go out in the garden and became quite restless. Tania was not home and was spending the night out with one of her local friends. The Marsh's had a big house with a huge garden covering nearly half an acre. Jerry had been born in this house and was an only child. His father died when Jerry was twenty two and his mother had only recently passed away. Milly had helped look after Winnie through her many illnesses. If it wasn't one thing it was another till finally she had gone to hospital last winter with a chest infection, caught the MRSA super bug and despite the doctors' best efforts could not be saved.

When the darts group left there was a visible sigh of relief from all concerned. The kids had been getting more and more fractious and kept asking when they were going home. Apparently their parents had dragged them away from their new playstation-3 games consoles and they were all keen to get back at the next game level.

Jerry asked Ashley and Philip their plans for bringing in the New Year. Would they care to bring it in here with them? They could have a get together here just like they'd had at Christmas at Lillian and Alex's. So Milly rang around and invited everyone to bring in the New Year with them. They were to meet here at 9 o'clock for snacks and drinks on the 31st evening. Ashley said he looked forward to it.

When Ashley dropped Philip off that night the street was quiet. They had decided to open up the shop for the next two days, the last days of the year and would meet next morning at about ten o'clock.

With the local post Christmas sales on people who'd bought their bargains popped in to McGill's to see what else they might pick up. It was a particularly sunny day and that helped put people in the shopping mood. It seemed very busy in the shop but it was more of a browsing crowd than a buying one. Most considered this a very pleasant shop to spend an hour or so and look at the museum side for a bit of entertainment. But a few antique items were sold and that was enough justification for the decision to have opened.

Just before they were due to close Tania and two friends dropped in. They had been on their way back to her house when they saw the shop open. Tania said how sorry she was that she had missed them yesterday but she'd already made prior plans with Mich and Bev. She introduced them and said they couldn't stay more than a few minutes. It was half an hour later when they left. Tania gave Philip a peck on the cheek. Looking at an expectant Ashley she said 'You'll have to wait till next Christmas,' and screwed up her face and poked the tip of her tongue out at him. Ashley poked an even bigger tongue back at her. Mich and Bev said goodbye very sedately and all waved from the doorway laughing.

'Be wary of that one Ashley,' said Philip, 'she's got you written down in her book.'

Ashley knew exactly what Philip meant.

The last day of the year proved a duller day both for business and the weather. It was bitterly cold and the evidence of an earlier flurry of snow stayed on parked cars and the sheltered parts of the pavement. Later in the evening a light drizzle of rain commenced which cleared any remaining snow and made for slippery surfaces. Further north and on the motorways the conditions had been far worse when blizzards raged and snowdrifts closed roads over the Pennines. By 3 o'clock Philip suggested they close up and get home to some rest and freshen up before going to the night's festivities at the Marsh's house. And that is exactly what they did.

The New Year's Eve party at the Marsh's house was great with all the friends together again. Christmas seemed a long way in the past yet only a week had elapsed. Ashley didn't get to chat to Tania very much as she was busy helping her mum being hostess. The food was set on the dining table for people to help themselves as and whenever they felt like it.

Just before midnight the large telly was turned on and the countdown to the New Year began. Everyone was given a part filled glass of bubbly champagne and all crowded into the living room.

When Big Ben began to strike the strokes to midnight they all counted down to one followed by raised glasses and shouts of 'Happy New Year'. After placing the glasses carefully to one side everyone just milled around wishing one another with hugs and kisses. Tania gave Ashley a hug and a carefully planted kiss on the cheek just as she did to everyone else. No blushes this time. Ashley wondered what this year was likely to uncover for him and his gifts.

Then Philip mentioned that there was to be a huge firework display around the London Eye on the Thames to be also broadcast on BBC1. So everyone found a seat and watched the TV. The display had already started and lasted a fabulous ten minutes. In that time thousands upon thousands of colourful explosions erupted upwards and the crowds that were gathered on the opposite bank could be seen staring in wonderment at the sight before them. When it was all over Jerry distributed his own party poppers and everyone took a couple. There were strings of exploding colour everywhere. And it was lots of fun. Then someone suggested 'Auld Lang Syne' so a large circle was formed holding hands in crossed formation. As everyone sang, the crossed arms were waved up and down in time with the singing. Since no one knew all the words the same verse was sung twice and then all found their glasses again and drank a toast to the year 2002.

The telly was switched off after the fireworks and the friends sat around chatting and laughing. Some sat at the table for a snack while others remained in the living room. Robert suggested playing charades but the idea was vetoed by Vicky, Tania and Katy who said they were too tired and just wanted to sit and chat. Katy came and sat at the feet of her brother with her back against the settee. And Tania came and sat next to her followed by Vicky. Katy had some popper string on her head and Ashley reached out and picked it off.

'Gosh Tania,' said Ashley, 'you're going to have a job tomorrow cleaning up all this stuff.'

Ashley was making small talk and Tania knew that so she just smiled back at him.

Then she did the same by asking when he was going to take down all the shop decorations and she offered to come and give a hand. Ashley said that would be lovely. Lillian had always said to be gracious whenever someone offered help but so far as Tania was concerned he always welcomed her offers of help in the shop.

Katy and Vicky were into a conversation of their own until Robert and Robin came and sat on the floor opposite them. Then all started talking about the fireworks and how much they must have cost.

'Why didn't they do something like this for 2000 to bring in the millennium? Compared to all the other countries ours was the worst, if you remember,' said Vicky. 'I think something must have gone wrong when the river of fire on the Thames didn't happen. Even Scotland was better than us.'

'Well anyway,' said Robin, 'I think that this year they've made up for it, don't you think?'

Robin always had a way of ending his sentences with a question. But everyone agreed with him on this one. Philip was on the settee as well and had been listening to the conversation. He said that in the previous years the Londoners had tried to do it themselves and had failed miserably just like the Dome fiasco. But this year for the first time they had given it over to specialist firework contractors who regularly organised public displays on a grand scale.

'I think I read somewhere that it was costing around one and a half million this time,' said Philip.

'But I think it has been well worth the money spent. It was nice to let the nation see it all on telly as well. Mind you it would have been even better to have seen it right there on the banks of the Thames even if it was a bit cold and wet.'

'I'd much rather bring in the New Year as we have today,' said Milly who had also been listening. 'It's so much cosier for us older ones in the comfort of our homes than to be out somewhere in the freezing cold and wet. Then don't forget you have to get home as well through all those crowds.'

'Yes I suppose you're absolutely right.' said Jerry. 'But I did go down to London one year and join the crowds at Trafalgar Square; I think I was twenty-something then. I was staying with Joe and Ellen off the Bayswater road. Gosh I think I got back to their place about four in the morning.'

'They don't allow the Trafalgar thing any more, do they?' said Robin. 'There was too much trouble with the rowdies and hooligans and the police always had to be present. I think it's banned just like they don't have it here in Centenary Square any more. I think they have something at millennium point instead, don't they?'

The conversation moved around to various frivolous topics till finally Eric said he was tired out and it was time for his bed it being nearly two thirty in the morning. Although Milly and Jerry had offered him a bed for the night, Eric said he'd rather go home to his own pillow and bed. Besides, he hadn't brought all his pills for the morning. He also made the excuse that he could sleep all morning and into the afternoon if he wished. Lillian, Alex and Katy were staying the night but Ashley only lived nearby and so decided to go home taking Philip with him to spend the night.

'Ashley, why don't you and Philip come back here for a late breakfast or brunch whenever you are ready,' said Jerry, 'and Philip can stay with us when you go back to your mum and dad's; we'll take Philip home later in the evening.'

Ashley said they might sleep late and have lunch somewhere before he dropped Philip over to them. He had planned to spend the day at his Erdington home after dropping Philip to his own house. He felt bad about leaving Philip alone for the rest of the day and it was nice of Jerry and Milly to take him over. They were Philip's oldest friends and he could spend a nice day alone with them.

Ashley worried about Philip living on his own and tried to make sure he was always alright. Philip had not used the old Morris Minor before giving it to Ashley and had much preferred to make the short bus ride from house to shop everyday. When Ashley had first got the car back on the road he would pick Philip up from home and they would drive together to the shop. But when Ashley moved in to the upper rooms the car would be left at Philip's house as there was no room outside the shop for parking overnight. Eventually Philip had discovered that a lockup garage had become available for rent nearby and had snapped it up. It was a good long garage and they used it as storage temporarily when Ashley brought items back from one of his expeditions into the country. Ashley didn't care for the fact that Philip was living alone but Philip said he had too many memories tied up in his present place. Times were changing and Ashley worried about the rowdy youths who often congregated at the end of Philip's road. Philip said it didn't bother him.

As they were driving to Ashley's house on this New Year's dark morning they were each engrossed in the silence of their own thoughts.

Just before Ashley parked on his drive Philip said, 'Ashley, thank you for your care. You watch over me like a son. I'm lucky to have such good friends. You are all so kind.' And he meant every word.

They went into the house and each to his room but it was a long time before either of them slept.

In the morning although Ashley awoke after only a few hours of sleep he felt quite refreshed and keen. He came down and made himself a mug of tea. He was only partway through drinking it when Philip also came down and joined him. Both were still dressed in their pyjamas and sat chatting.

'I feel quite refreshed,' said Philip, 'it is nice and quiet here. I thought I could hear some sounds from the zoo earlier but I couldn't be sure.'

'That would be the morning feeding time,' said Ashley. 'I think they feed the animals around about nine or ten o'clock and the animals certainly don't let them forget it.'

'Do you know I haven't been in there since I was about twelve years old? Mum took Grace and me one lovely summer afternoon. I can't remember what dad was doing but he gave me a shilling pocket money that day. I remember him telling me to spend it carefully. And I did too. Grace was only five but she was really excited when told where we were going. Those were lovely times and before mum took ill.' Philip looked away so I wouldn't see the moistness of memories in his eyes.

Ashley had a sudden thought. 'Why don't we see if it is open today and pop in? It is years since I've been and there's talk of moving some of the bigger animals to London zoo. We don't need to spend too long in there. We can have a meal at the buffet restaurant and I can drop you to Jerry's afterwards.'

Philip agreed and showed his delight at the idea. So Ashley phoned and immediately got an answering service giving the times of opening. They were open everyday except Christmas Day. Closing times in winter were 4:00pm and in summer 6:00pm. The message continued to specify winter and summer periods but Ashley hung up before the end.

After they got dressed they had a breakfast of toast and marmalade and another mug of tea. Philip had his coffee fix as he called it. They wrapped up against the cold and made the short drive to the zoo car park and walked around to the entrance. As a Senior citizen Philip paid a reduced entrance charge.

They walked past the flamingo pond and up towards the elephant stand. It was a bit of a climb as the castle and zoo were on a hill but they took it slow for Philip's benefit. Philip kept saying that it seemed very much the same and that he remembered this or that feature. When they walked into the castle ruins area itself Philip led the way to one of the alcoves and sat on the plinth there.

'This is where mum, Grace and I came and had our packed lunches,' said Philip smiling sadly. 'It seems like only yesterday and it is all so vivid in my memory. It is all just as it was then.'

They sat in silence while Philip took in the surroundings as if seeing them for the first time.

'You are kind to bring me here Ashley,' he said. He looked at Ashley before turning away so Ashley wouldn't see the emotion on his face.

They spent another hour wandering around the animal enclosures before returning home to Ashley's. After freshening up they drove to the buffet restaurant for their meal. They had barely sat down when Tania came and said hello. She said they too had decided to have lunch out. Then Jerry and Millie also came over and said hello and why didn't they all sit together. No arguments it was to be his treat. So they all moved to a table for six as the place was only part full.

When Tania heard that Ashley and Philip had visited the zoo she exclaimed that she would have liked to have come too. It was at least ten years since she had been in there. They talked about the various enclosures and animals right through the meal. Tania made Ashley promise to go with her one day soon.

Jerry asked Ashley about his plans were for the rest of the day.

'Well I had planned on dropping Philip to your house and then going on home to visit mum and dad and spend the night,' said Ashley thinking that he needed to discuss the repercussion of Tania listening in to his conversation with Uncle Ron and Aunt Brenda on Christmas Day.

'In that case,' said Jerry to Philip, 'you can come with us from here and let Ashley go straight to his mum and dad's. We'll take you home later or whenever you are ready.'

'That'll be lovely,' said Philip. 'Perhaps if I could get back about six o'clock, after all we reopen again tomorrow. I'm glad the hectic season is over and I can get back to my old routine. Not that I haven't enjoyed the company of all my friends but I'm not used to so much eating and such late nights. Shall I see you about ten in the morning Ashley?'

'I hope to be there before then,' said Ashley. 'I think I'll say goodbye for now and thanks for the lunch. Next time it's my treat.'

Ashley kissed the ladies and shook hands with the men and again waved from the door as he left.

Lillian and Alex were pleased that Ashley had come to spend the night. As soon as Ashley got there Lillian made the three of them some tea and they sat down to talk. Katy had gone out with Robin and Robert to a football match. Vicky hadn't gone with them as she said she didn't see the point of kicking a ball around a field with other men especially in the cold and the rain.

Ashley said that Tania had been puzzled that she had received such vivid images of their Christmas morning festivities when she wasn't even there. She had partly put it down to a sort of déjà vu of a previous celebration or just something that she had imagined as it might have been. But Ashley had read her mind and knew she suspected that he had something to do with it. She already had a suspicion that Ashley could read her mind. She just sensed it and had even asked Ashley about it. Of course Ashley had feigned complete ignorance and had just not said anything.

Alex and Lillian both agreed that their son had done the right thing. Tania was a sensible girl and would keep her suspicions to herself. Whatever was planned for Ashley by the powers-that-be they agreed that it was imperative that his gifts be kept secret. Lillian said that she felt sad that Katy was not in the loop but the fewer who knew of Ashley's gifts the safer the secret. Perhaps it would do no good to bring Katy in at this late stage. Perhaps it would just confuse her and change the way she saw her brother. She might expect miracles when none were forthcoming. So far even Ashley had no idea as to the purpose behind all these powers. He knew with a certainty beyond all doubt that he had been chosen to do something special. He knew it was no freak of nature to have been given these gifts and he knew that whatever he did it would be for the general good.

Discussions stopped when Katy and the two boys came home. They all had mugs of tea or coffee as it had been quite cold out on the terraces. Katy was pleased to see Ashley again and gave him a big hug. Brother and sister were very close and Ashley would like to tell her all about himself. Perhaps he would make that decision as soon as he knew what it was that he was meant to do. After all Katy was eighteen and very mature for her age.

Robin and Robert left as soon as they finished their coffee and the family were left on their own.

'I miss you Ashley,' said Katy. 'You are the businessman now and I love the shop. Perhaps when I finish my A-levels I'll come and work for you. In fact we could all come and work for you because I know you are going to be very rich; and famous too. Everyone knows about McGill's Antiques.'

'Young lady,' said Lillian, 'you are going to university and have a career of your own.'

Katy had a provisional place at a teaching college provided she got the necessary grades in her A-levels. She admired her mother and had always said she would also like to teach. But she did not want to teach in a secondary school; she preferred the primary age groups.

'Perhaps when Ashley gets too old I can take over the shop. But I'll be old then too,' said a shocked Katy.

They all laughed. It was nice to be a family again.

And again Katy remarked that why couldn't they be like this forever.

The next morning Ashley got to the shop at nine thirty. He let the shop air by opening a back door to let in a flow of air. He checked upstairs and everything looked normal. He opened a couple of windows just a crack to allow a little circulation of fresh air. It was a nice bright sunny morning and Philip must be on his way. He would probably walk the distance instead of using the bus. Ashley rang the house as an alarm call just in case he might have overslept. He didn't know what time the Marsh's had dropped him home. There was no reply so Ashley assumed Philip was on his way.

By ten thirty Philip had still not turned up so Ashley rang the house again. The phone rang for a good while and there was still no answer. Ashley rang the Marsh house and Milly answered. They had dropped Philip home at seven o'clock last night and seen him get inside his front door. Jerry was at work but she and Tania would come over to shop sit while Ashley went to investigate. Perhaps Philip was ill or something.

They arrived in minutes and by now Ashley was thinking terrible things. What if Philip had been mugged by the crowd of youths on his street? What if he'd had a stroke or a heart attack and was unconscious in his own house? Philip had been hale and hearty yesterday surely nothing could be the matter. Perhaps he was helping someone who had fallen on the street and he was waiting with them while an ambulance arrived. Ashley tried to contact Philip telepathically but got no connection at all.

Ashley had tried to get Philip to own a mobile phone but he said he could never get used to one. He said these gadgets were for the young ones and not for him. Ashley even bought him a pay-as-you-go phone but Philip hardly ever charged it up when it ran down; or more often than not forgot to switch it on. He said the keys were much too tiny for his fat fingers. That was a year ago and Ashley had finally given up trying to convince Philip of its usefulness.

'You look very worried Ashley,' said Milly. 'I'm sure everything is alright but you go and check the house. We'll wait here for you.'

'Please let me come with you Ashley,' said Tania. 'Two pairs of eyes are better than one. We might see him walking along the road.'

'Thank you Tania that would be most welcome. I don't know why but I have this feeling that something is definitely not right. Mrs Marsh, will you be okay on your own? We will be back as soon as we find Philip.' Ashley had never felt so panic-stricken in all his life. An inner voice said to get to Philip's house as soon as he could. Ashley just knew that something terrible had happened.

The drive to Philip's house took just ten minutes most of which was taken up waiting at traffic lights. Ashley tried to will them to change but that was one area over which he had no control.

The front door was locked when they got to Philip's house so Ashley used his own key to enter. As partners in business they each had a key to the other's front door since that time when a key had been misplaced by Philip. Ashley entered first with Tania following close behind. The house was quiet except for the central heating pump that could be heard rumbling in the airing cupboard upstairs. The house was nice and warm but there was no response to Ashley's call to Philip.

'Oh, Ashley,' said Tania noticing some broken glass in the hallway, 'something's terribly wrong.'

They went into the living room and the place was quite untidy with a couple of items on the floor. Things were definitely not where Ashley had last seen them. The dining room and kitchen were the same except the kitchen drawers were all open.

Ashley and Tania both knew straight away that Philip had been burgled. It couldn't have been while Philip was away because he would have noticed it the moment he got in the front door yesterday and phoned his friends. So it must have been sometime last night when Philip was in the house alone.

Ashley rushed up the stairs two at a time in a panic.

Philip was lying on his bed with his feet and hands tied with plastic cable ties. He was not moving. His face was all bruised and there was a trace of dried blood around his nose. He was still breathing but ever so lightly. His lips were apart and they were caked with dried blood.

Ashley went pink and ripped the ties off Philip's hands and feet. He didn't care that Tania could see him in action. He then told her to ring for both the police and an ambulance.

Tania told the police that there had been an attempted murder in the house and that the person was near death. Of course she had to spend time giving her own name and address and then Philip's name and address as well. But both police and ambulance were there in ten minutes. The paramedics did a quick check on Philip and then stretchered him down the stairs and into the waiting ambulance. They told Ashley that they were taking their patient to the A&E at Russells Hall hospital. The street was crowded with the neighbours looking to see what had happened but they made way as the ambulance sped away with its siren blaring.

Ashley knew most of the immediate neighbours and so when one of them asked what had happened he just said that Philip had collapsed overnight. He didn't say anything about Philip's injuries or the break in. The police were there as a matter of routine he said.

Tania rang her mum and gave her the details of what had happened to Philip. She also asked her to ring all their friends and tell them what had happened.

More police arrived and the whole house was checked for finger prints. They took Ashley and Tania's prints as well so that they could rule them out from those that they would find.

Some police had gone out to the neighbouring houses, especially the ones across the street, and began asking if any one had seen or heard anything unusual the previous evening or during the night. They were told there had been a burglary with violence and it was essential to find out all they could. Had anyone seen someone unknown entering or leaving the house?

As a matter of course both Tania and Ashley gave separate statements to the police. Tania told them the time that she and her parents had dropped Philip home last night. Ashley was still in a daze but he felt no anger which puzzled him a bit. Surely he should be angry that someone could do such a thing to an old man. There shouldn't have been any need to beat him up the way they did, what resistance could he have offered? But all Ashley could feel was an extreme sadness for his dear friend and partner.

The police told Ashley and Tania that they could leave and that they would shut the front door when they had finished in about an hour. They would contact Ashley as soon as they found out anything.

Ashley and Tania then went back to the shop and Milly gave Ashley a tearful hug and said how terrible it was that Philip should be attacked in such a manner. Ashley locked up the shop and they went to the hospital in their own cars. Milly told Ashley that she had phoned everyone she could think of and that they all said they would get to the hospital as soon as possible.

When they got to the reception in the hospital Lillian, Alex and Katy were already there. They said that they had been told to wait in the reception area and a doctor would be out to give them information about Philip as soon as they could. About a half hour later Jerry and Eric also arrived separately though only a couple of minutes apart.

Ashley sat near the end of a row of seats with his feet together and hands clasped tightly. He was staring in a fixed manner at the far wall and his eyes were moist. He was thinking that he should have been more firm regarding his suggestion that Philip move in with him. Philip was in his mid-seventies and was a relatively fit and well person. Or at least he had been until today. Tania and Katy came and sat either side of Ashley and they sidled close so that their shoulders touched. Ashley smiled and felt the comfort of their nearness. Then a young man in a white coat came towards them.

'Philip Stevens?' he questioned looking around at them.

'I'm Ashley Bonner, Philip's business partner. These people are my parents and Philip's friends. He has no living relative. We are his only family and he spent the whole of the Christmas season with us. Mr and Mrs Marsh here are his oldest and dearest friends. How is Philip doctor?'

The young doctor looked at them and hesitated. Then he said to follow him and led the way into a medium sized waiting room and asked them to be seated.

'Hello, I'm Doctor Clifford. I'm the junior registrar here. Normally we only give information on our patients to direct relatives. Seeing as Mr Stevens is elderly and has no one else then I suppose it is alright to speak to his closest friends. I'm sorry to have to tell you that Mr Stevens is an extremely sick man. We have placed him in intensive care but he is currently in an unconscious state. That is to say he is comatose. There has been bleeding from the orifices of ear, nose and mouth but these have ceased which may be a good sign. We believe he has had a concussion to the head which may be the reason for his current state. We need to carry out a scan but that will be done as soon as an assessment of his condition is performed; perhaps in an hour or so. We will know more then. We cannot give information over the phone so one of you will have to come to reception and enquire. One of my colleagues will be here to brief you. Perhaps if you could nominate one of your number by name I shall make sure that person is treated as a relative.'

Ashley stood up and said, 'I'd like to be that person please. My name is Ashley Bonner. Philip and I are in business together and we have an antique shop in Dudley called McGill's Antiques. You may have heard of it. I shall be here as much as I can until I know how Philip is. He was like a second father to me.'

'Very well, Ashley Bonner it shall be,' said the doctor. 'I shall list you as Mr Steven's nephew, if that's okay with you?'

Everyone nodded their agreement.

'You may as well all go home now,' said Dr. Clifford. 'We won't know much more till this evening when the results of the tests come through.'

'Thank you doctor,' said Ashley. 'I shall return here this evening.'

They all walked to the car park in the silence of their own thoughts.

Jerry asked if they would like to come back to their place for a hot drink. All agreed except Ashley.

He said he wanted to go back to Philip's place to see if the police had finished with it and to check up on something. Tania and Katy said they'd come with him and help tidy up the place. Tania had told them what she had seen when she first went in that morning. Subsequently the whole group decided to go there first and then to Milly and Jerry's.

The police were just leaving when they got there and the detective in charge said they had got all they needed and it was alright for them to tidy up. Alex asked if they had any idea who could have done this and if there was any hope of finding the culprits.

'We shall do our very best,' said the detective, 'but at the moment we haven't much to go on. There were a few smudged prints but a lot of the stuff seems to have been wiped over. These chaps knew how to be careful. We hope some one around here saw something or someone. We do rely on the public for our leads but so far we don't have anything. I'm sorry but a lot of these burglaries go unsolved unless we get lucky.'

The women went around tidying up the place. Ashley went upstairs and found Philip's wallet on the bedroom floor and noticed it was intact but empty of any cash. Ashley was alone now so he decided to repeat what he had been shown to do when he traced the thievery of Quigley Thorn and Johnny Price in Harry's pub the night of the darts match.

Ashley went and sat on the end of Philip's bed and held on to the wallet. The room turned rosy pink and he shut his eyes tight and concentrated on the bed where Philip had lain unconscious when they had found him.

Ashley saw Philip come in the door and then turn around and wave to the Marsh's in their car. It was just after seven o'clock and dark outside except for the street lighting. It was the evening of the previous day.

He locked the door and then went into the kitchen, filled the kettle and switched it on. When the water had boiled he made himself a mug of tea and then sat down to watch the news on TV. It wasn't long before Philip shut his eyes and dozed off. The telly had that effect on him.

The door bell rang twice and gradually Philip came awake. At first he thought it was something on the telly but it rang again a number of times. He realised it was the front door. He thought in his dazed mind that the Marsh's had returned to check on him. Without thinking he went to the front door and opened it. There were two young men standing there smiling.

'Hello granddad,' the taller one of them said pushing his way into the hall, 'we've come to read your gas meter.'

They had glazed eyes and appeared as if they had been drinking. They pushed Philip backwards quite roughly causing him to fall over onto the floor. The shorter one stepped forward and kicked Philip in the head with the toe of his boot. Philip lay still where he had fallen.

'You fool Andy,' said the tall one, 'you've killed him. We needed him to tell us where his cash and all are.'

Just then there was a groan from Philip and he tried to sit up. They quickly grabbed him and asked him where he hid his money. Philip was still in a semi-daze and drunkenly pointed up the stairs. They half dragged, half carried him up the stairs and dumped him on his bed. They saw Philip's wallet on the bedside table and quickly emptied it of its cash.

'There's only two hundred quid here,' said the tall youth. 'Look around Andy there's bound to be some more stuff hidden about.'

The one called Andy then sat on the bed and punched Philip in the face twice.

'Where is the rest of the stuff granddad?' he said.

But Philip had passed out again and Andy punched him again thinking he was refusing to answer.

Philip's head was knocked sideways and a trickle of blood appeared at the corner of his mouth.

'Tie him up,' said the taller one, 'then we can search the place in peace.'

Andy gave Philip another punch in the face, then took white plastic cable ties from his coat pocket and wrapped one around Philips wrists and pulled tight. He did the same to Philip's two feet at the ankles. Philip hadn't moved but now there was also a trickle of blood from his nose.

They systematically searched through the bedroom dresser drawers and took whatever they thought valuable. They found and took Philip's gold ring and Omega watch which were in the top drawer and some of Grace's imitation jewellery that Philip had kept for sentimental reasons. By now Ashley knew that the taller one was Mark Tamper and the violent one who had done the kicking and punching was Andy Braid. Mark Tamper lived by himself in a flat but Andy Braid still lived at home with both his parents. He was an only child. Both were on the dole and lived quite close to each other and not far from the Black Swan pub at the end of the street. Just like before in the Navigation pub case Ashley knew exactly where these two also lived. Mark lived at 216A Hockley Lane while Andy Braid lived at 57 Yew Tree Crescent.

They systematically searched the house room by room all the time talking and joking with one another. They didn't give Philip another thought. There were a few of Philip's favourite antique items on the fireplace mantel in the living room but they never gave them a second glance. They found some loose change in a bowl in the kitchen that amounted to just a few pounds and which Andy Braid pocketed.

'Let's get out of here. I think we've got everything,' said Mark who was clearly the leader. 'Just let me wipe down our fingerprints.'

He then went around wiping everything that they might have touched with a kitchen cloth. But he didn't seem to be in any sort of a hurry. Nor did they seem to be bothered about Philip's condition.

They left by the front door and shut it behind them with a loud click of the latch. They had been in the house about twenty minutes and it was then about eight thirty in the evening. They then went into the pub at the end of the road and had a few pints to add to the ones they'd had earlier. They then went to Mark's flat and divided up the money. Mark said he'd see what he could get for the other items tomorrow. But he fancied the gold ring and omega watch for himself.

Ashley had seen it all and returned to normal mode. Only seconds had passed since he had come into Philip's bedroom. He would deal with the crooks later but only after discussing the matter with his mum, dad and Eric.

Alex came into the room and looked at his son in a questioning way eyebrows raised. Ashley looked up at his dad, shut his eyes briefly and nodded. Alex nodded back and knew that Ashley had seen it all in his mind just like he had done for Quigley Thorn and Johnny Price back on the night of the darts match in the Navigation pub. He also knew that Ashley would want a family gathering to discuss the action that needed to be taken.

Alex helped Ashley tidy up the bedroom as best they could. There were one or two items on the floor that they picked up. They smoothed the bedspread and then did the same for the other rooms upstairs. When they went down the others had also finished and were sitting in the living room. Lillian then went into the kitchen and put the kettle on to make them all some tea. They all sat quietly for a while thinking their own sad thoughts and worries.

'I hope Philip gets better,' said Katy to no one in particular.

'Yes, he is in the best place and getting the best care,' said Tania continuing the small talk.

'We should really all go back home now,' said Ashley. 'I shall get back to the hospital again about seven and see what the latest is on Philip.'

After another look around Philip's house they all left and headed back to their own homes; except for Katy who went with Tania to her place at Tania's request which Lillian thought was a good idea. This suited Ashley and Eric who went in their own cars to the Bonner house to discuss what Ashley had found out.

When they settled down in his parent's living room Ashley lost no time in conveying to them the full details of the attack on Philip. He did this telepathically as it was the only way to give a complete picture of what had happened. Seeing it all happen as if they had been right there was quite shocking and dreadful for them.

'That Andy Braid is a nasty, wicked person and should be taught a lesson,' said Lillian with tears in her eyes, 'what he did to Philip was cruel and unnecessary.'

'There's nothing we can do about that at the moment,' said Alex. 'Our chief concern is for Philip to get well again. I suppose we could always tip off the police about those two; like send them an anonymous note or something. What do you think Ashley?'

Ashley told them what he had in mind. Again he did this telepathically so that they got a complete picture of his plan.

When Ashley went to the hospital again later that evening he waited an hour before deciding to ask reception to make enquiries about Philip's condition. Visiting hours were nearly at an end but still no one could be found to give Ashley an update on Philip's condition or even where he had been taken. Ashley decided to take the matter into his own hands. He went around to the Accident and Emergency area and read the minds of the registering nurses behind the counter. From them he learned of the configuration of the entire hospital. He then walked to the intensive care unit ward. He asked the nurse sitting behind a desk where he might find Philip Stevens. She looked at a clipboard and said that he had been moved to a special high dependency room but she was not able to give any further information on his condition. Ashley probed her mind to discover that Philip was in the room to the right of the ICU. He also learned of an extreme concern on her part for Philip's state.

'Please nurse,' said Ashley, 'I am Philip Steven's nephew. I was told by Dr Clifford this morning that I would be kept informed of his progress by the doctor on duty. Could you please contact him and ask him and tell him that Ashley Bonner is here.'

The nurse said the doctor was extremely busy attending patients and was not available to see anyone. She was quite brusque in her manner. But Ashley had already ascertained that there were two doctors on duty and at the moment both were in the HDU with Philip. So Ashley turned around and walked towards the exit and stopped. He looked back and the nurse had stood up and was studying her clipboard. Ashley went 'pink' and then just walked to the room that Philip was in.

There were two doctors and a nurse there. One doctor was leaning over the bed Philip was in and appeared to be making an adjustment to one of the tubes entering Philip's nose. Ashley returned to normal and immediately read the minds of both doctors. He picked up the entire combined knowledge regarding their experience in medicine. Every aspect of their medical skill was now in Ashley's mind as well. He also knew of their family life and who their friends were.

Dr Ainslie Richards was twenty six and was single but was very friendly with a nurse called Wendy. Dr Mario Gonzalez was thirty three and had a wife Marcia and two daughters, Maria aged six and Rosita aged four. Dr Ainslie had qualified in London while Dr Mario had practised in Madrid before coming to his current job two years ago. Dr Mario was a specialist in trauma to the brain. It was his diagnosis of Philip's condition that worried Ashley.

When they saw Ashley they were about to raise an objection to his presence but stopped when Ashley telepathically conveyed into their minds that he was a colleague and friend of Dr Robin Clifford and that he was an MD. He gave them to understand that since he was also the patient's nephew, Dr Robin had given him permission to enquire at all hours regarding Philip's status.

As such they allowed Ashley to come up to the bed and look down at Philip. Philip had severe discolouration to his face but there was also a nasty red swelling just behind his left ear. Dr Mario's diagnosis had been partly based on the results of the CT scan which showed two things of concern. One was a large dark patch which Mario diagnosed as a subdural haematoma or clot of blood on the inside of the dura mater. A second scan would need to be done to ascertain if the dark patch had increased in volume. The major worry was that the entire dura mater lining around Philip's brain seemed to have been displaced ever so slightly towards the right side of his head causing severe trauma to the brain as a whole.

Ashley then spoke to Dr Mario in his native Madrid dialect of Spanish. By this time Ashley was fluent in about fifty language dialects. But before he could acquire a dialect he had to have met a person who spoke it. There were approximately twenty three different styles of Spanish spoken across Spain which made it possible to recognise were a person's origin's lay. Dr Mario had been born in Madrid and had grown up there and married there. And his children had also been born there. It had been a big decision for him to move to England but so far he had not regretted it. Both his and his wife's parents were alive and well and still lived in the same houses that had been the birth places of Mario and Marcia. Mario took his family home twice a year to visit, once at Christmas and again in the summer, and usually for a period of three weeks each time. Both parents also came to visit them when they had a yen to see their grandchildren, which was quite often.

Mario and Marcia made sure their children were bilingual; Spanish was always spoken at home and English at school and all other times.

Mario was surprised at Ashley's skill and fluency and they talked about Madrid and the places they used to frequent as young men. Ashley conveyed to Mario a telepathic memory of their having met on several occasions when they were teenagers. Ashley also let Mario believe that he was only a few years younger and that they had first met in a bar at a faculty of medicine social event. Mario now had Ashley imprinted in his memory as someone from his past. A lot of what Ashley imprinted into Mario's mind was what he had already read there, reformatted it with his own self inserted and transferred back. It was an art Ashley had developed some years back when he was introducing himself to specific art dealers who tended to be standoffish. Attitudes changed amazingly when Ashley was recognised as a previous school acquaintance.

Ashley knew all the streets and bars of Mario's memory so they had a brief discussion on the places they visited. It was like old school friends meeting up after a gap of ten or more years.

But now Ashley told Mario of his worry about Philip. So Mario gave Ashley a verbal picture of Philip's medical situation in the gravest medical terms.

The subarachnoid space of the lining around Philip's brain containing essential cerebro-spinal fluid or CSF was marginally thinner on the right side of the brain and was pushing on the meningeal dura mater there. The stress of this shift must have been the result of a tremendous external trauma or blow to the side of the head. The shock wave in the CSF would have reverberated through to the central region of the brain containing the Thalamus, Hypothalamus, Corpus callosum and Cerebral aqueduct and down into the Pons and so to the spinal cord. The shock wave may have caused a fracture of the pia mater covering the medial surface of the cerebrum allowing cerebro-spinal fluid to enter the soft lobes. The shock wave would have been magnified as it travelled into dead ended pathways and especially into the sheath of the spinal cord.

The shock to Philip's brain alone would have been extreme and caused its defensive system to activate a partial shutdown of all cognitive functions. This was a possible reason for his comatose status.

Dr Mario paused before he continued his report to Ashley. There was another factor he said. There was some capillary bruising which had caused some bleeding within the right cerebral cortex. However this should have stemmed itself through coagulation and should dissolve with time though a second scan was needed within twenty-four hours to ensure the bleed zone had not enlarged.

The first scan showed up a hair-line anomaly at the position of the central sagittal suture. This was not a real fracture but more of a re-opening of cranial bone structure that had fused together at infancy. Yet said Dr Mario it was quite worrying since it might not heal normally through the usual process of calcification. It also showed how great the trauma to the head had been.

Dr Mario then took Ashley to a recorder on a table beside Philip's bed. He showed Ashley the pads on Philip's head with wires leading to the recorder. He said that the sensitive electrodes attached to Philip's skull would pick up the electrical activity in the cortex of the cerebrum and record the pattern on the recorder chart. This was called an electroencephalogram or EEG. Ashley knew all this but let Mario continue. He knew that Mario was actually using all this explanation as a recap of Philip's condition and that very often a diagnostic thought might emerge to resolve a question.

Mario said that the EEG pattern at the moment was somewhere between deep sleep and comatose. But there had been blips on several occasions when a completely strange trace had appeared; one that he had not ever seen before in his experience. For some strange reason Ashley thought he knew what that pattern might indicate but he kept it to himself. Was Philip trying to communicate to someone? This gave Ashley hope for Philip's recovery. It was that old familiar voice again telling Ashley not to worry and that all was as it should be.

Dr Mario's voice brought Ashley back to the present. Mario said that perhaps the brain was trying to reset itself like the complex computer that it resembled; he didn't know. Mario said there was a danger that Philip's involuntary brain function might then also shut down temporarily on such occasions causing his breathing function to stop. If and when this occurred then Philip would have to be placed on artificial life support.

Mario told Ashley that another concern was the lack of any thalmo cortical response to any incoming sensory information. Tickling the soles of Philip's feet had not produced any alteration to the prevailing EEG pattern.

'There is one thing I am sure of,' said Mario, 'and that is that the human brain has evolved into an extremely complex organ and there is a lot of its function and power that we don't know much about. But given time it has a tremendous ability to heal itself. I only hope the trauma is not too severe for this to happen. Come back tomorrow and I shall have more to tell you.'

Ashley needed to be alone with Philip so he asked if he could come and sit by Philip through the day and perhaps talk to him. A familiar voice might stimulate a quicker recovery.

Dr Mario thought that a good idea and it had been proven in other cases. A familiar voice or some favourite music could only be beneficial. Ashley asked if he could have five minutes now. He would sit quietly beside Philip and not say a word but just let him feel a friendly presence. But Mario in a very polite way suggested Ashley himself looked quite tired and it might be better if he went home and returned tomorrow in the afternoon. There were some things the nurses needed to attend to with regard to Philip's hygiene. Also Mario needed to write some instructions on Philip's bedside chart. However he said Ashley could stay another couple of minutes beside the bed.

So Ashley stood looking down at Philip. He tried to read Philip's mind but could not get anything at all. After a few minutes Ashley turned around and without thinking sent Philip a telepathic thought that he'd be back tomorrow.

'Alright Ashley,' came back an instant telepathic response. Ashley could not recognise this since no one had ever communicated telepathically with him before; apart from that old familiar inner voice that he kept hearing on occasion. Ashley looked at Mario and then back at Philip. Nothing seemed to have changed. Ashley was in shocked surprise.

There was a hand on Ashley's shoulder and Mario gently steered Ashley towards the exit.

'Get a good night's rest,' he said in Spanish, 'we will give him the best of care.'

As Ashley walked past the recorder he glanced at the trace but there had been no change in pattern. So it couldn't have been Philip who expressed that thought. So then where had it come from? Was that inner voice of his playing games with him? After all it did sound the same to some extent. Ashley was confused and couldn't get it out of his mind as he drove home to his mum's house. He went there because he wanted to give them the latest on Philip. But he also needed their company.

As Katy and Vicky were also there Ashley gave a longwinded verbal report on Philip's current condition. He told them about Dr Mario and how caring he had been. A second scan was scheduled in the morning and hopefully that would show that the bleeding within the right cerebral cortex had been checked. If not then a decision would have to be taken regarding some sort of corrective procedure. It was all extremely worrying.

Ashley had never before been so powerless. There was nothing he could do for Philip; which made him feel utterly useless. It was a new experience for him and this feeling of sadness and sorrow was an emotion he had never had to deal with before. His sadness was that he was so impotent and the sorrow was for the very real fear that Philip might not survive. To lose a loved one or friend had never been considered. Of course Ashley had thought that one day he would have to say goodbye to members of his family as they aged. But all that was in the far distant future. This was now. Tomorrow Philip might be dead; or on the next day or the day after that.

Ashley felt lucky that he had his mum and dad for constant support; and also his granddad and aunt and uncle. They had been there from the very beginning when Ashley had first discovered his gifts. He didn't know how he could have coped if they hadn't been there to listen and advise. Ashley felt that being able to share his experiences with his adult family had been the one most important factor in helping him to accept the gifts he had been given. His only regret was that he had not brought Katy into this loop. After all she was very close to him and must have suspected something about his abilities when he used to catch birds for her when they were both children. This made Ashley wonder at the fact that Katy was never curious about the things he had done. She must have heard his childish chatter to his mum about the sky being sometimes pink. Yet she never questioned him about those past events and conversations. Ashley once thought that Katy might have some gifts of her own but he never ever saw evidence to that effect. Besides she became frozen in time just like everyone else whenever he went into pink mode.

When Ashley was fifteen he would experiment whenever he was in town among the crowds. He would go pink and then look around at all the people to see if anyone was still moving. He half hoped that someone would be unaffected, but no one ever was. Yet it was a habit that he still indulged in. That inner voice must be from someone out there. Would they meet one day?

Ashley felt guilty that he had not mentioned the telepathic message he had received when he was about to leave Philip. Until he could sort that out in his mind and be certain where it came from he felt he must keep it as his secret. He went to bed that night with those two words spinning in ever tighter circles inside his head. 'Alright Ashley' repeated itself again and again and again. But how could it be Philip? The EEG recorder pattern definitely hadn't altered. So where did the message come from? Finally Ashley fell into a fitful sleep where even his dreams seemed to recur around another theme. There was a knocking on the front door and when he opened it two men rushed in and started beating him around the head. It was Andy Braid and Mark Tamper the muggers who had attacked Philip. But this time they were beating Ashley and he had no gifts to defend himself. The pain in his head got worse as they continued to pummel him and he began to call out for help. Then he fell, but he fell on top of another body. It was Philip lying on the floor but just like he had been in the hospital with all those sensor pads on his head. Ashley woke with a start and there was his mum sitting on the side of his bed and running her fingers through his hair and whispering sweet nothings; just like that night when he was a child and had got scared by another dream. Ashley sat up and put his arms around his mum and hugged her tight. Not a word was said but both of their eyes were sparkling with bright wetness in the light of the bedside lamp.

When Ashley let go and sank back onto his pillow he told his mum of his dream and his fears for Philip.

'I don't think Philip will ever be right again mum,' he said. 'I think those two have done him in.'

Then he told his mum about the two telepathic words as he was leaving Philip last night. Ashley said he was certain Philip did not have the gift of telepathy. So where had those words come from?

Lillian said she didn't know the answer to that but it could be the same voice that had been guiding him all these years. Then Lillian said something prophetic.

'It may be you have a guardian angel my son,' she said. 'I believe we all have guardian angels but I think yours may be someone special that is able to talk to you. I know you are safe from physical harm Ashley but this anguish for Philip is another aspect so very different that we must all stick together for strength in order to see it through. One way or another Philip has had a good life and I think he was specially blessed to have you as a partner. He saw you as a son and often told us how proud he was for having you in his life.'

'And Ashley you have another special gift. You are like a puppy dog full of love for everyone you meet. The outpouring of your love and goodwill surrounds all those you meet and then stays with them. I feel sorry for the young girls you meet for they must get instantly attracted to you. Poor Tania is one of those and I hope one day you will give her just a little bit more of your attention. I worry about Vicky though as I have often seen her looking in your direction even when she is with Robert. We of your family get the bulk of your love. Your Aunt Brenda loves you like her own and your granddad Eric only lives for you and Katy. By the way he's not been too well with his arthritis flaring up with all that Christmas celebrating.'

Ashley looked at his bedside clock and it showed near to 4:00am. Their little chat must have taken about ten or fifteen minutes and Lillian then leaned forward and kissed her son on the cheek and whispered that they should get a bit more sleep tonight. She pulled his covering up under his chin and tucked it around his shoulders, touched her son's cheek affectionately, whispered goodnight and turned off the bedside light. She shut the door quietly as she left the room. Ashley heard its gentle click as he was drifting off into sleep.

Next morning Ashley went to the shop to start another day. Philip would have wanted it that way. At the front door was a sheath of flowers on its own. There was a hand written card attached to the outside wishing Philip a speedy recovery from his injuries. It was from the girls at the bakery across the road. News travelled fast. As Ashley looked across to their shop he could see they were already busy. Work for them began at 6:30 each morning. The first batches of baking had to ready and on display by nine o'clock. Ashley knew them by sight but not by name so he went across to thank them and also to give them the latest on Philip's condition. One of the ladies had seen Ashley crossing the road and opened the front door for him. Ashley thanked them for the flowers and told them about Philip. The manager was a pleasant grey haired lady called Loraine and she told all the girls who had crowded around Ashley to get back to their jobs. But she herself enquired after Philip and Ashley gave her a fuller picture. He said he was going back to see Philip in the afternoon.

She then handed Ashley a bag marked 'Cookies' from under the glass display counter and said it was with all their good wishes. Ashley knew they were all extremely busy so he thanked Loraine and turned to leave. But she reached up and gave Ashley a kiss on his cheek and said that was a get well kiss for Philip and to please tell him they were all thinking of him and for him to get well soon.

Ashley walked back across the road and opened up the shop. Before he went in he stepped back and looked up at the McGill's sign. It should have read 'Philip Steven's Antiques and Museum' but Philip had kept the McGill's name in memory of his sister whose shop it was before him. Inside Ashley went quickly to the alarm pad and keyed in the four digit security code. It was only yesterday that he had opened the shop and not suspected anything wrong. And yet Philip had been lying injured barely a mile and a half away. So Ashley knew that his gifts did not extend into that region of possessing a sixth sense or premonition of things to come. In a way this was a relief for him as it would have meant just one more factor to contend with; one more complication.

Being in the shop alone was a relief and it gave Ashley time to think about the future; his future and also that of the shop. If Philip did recover it was unlikely that he would be able to return to the shop for many months. So Ashley knew he had to make some provision for an assistant. He would think about it, sleep on it and then decide. That is what Philip had always advised.

At about eleven o'clock Tania walked in. Ashley was pleased to see her and said so. She was two years younger than Katy who would be nineteen this Easter. But Tania was the taller by a couple of inches. Today she had little make up on and her dark reddish brown hair was tied back in a pony tail that made her face look small and neat. She had a fresh faced appearance and a smile that showed an upper side tooth not quite in line with the rest. It gave her her own distinctive cheeky look.

Since his mum's words to him early this morning Ashley saw a different Tania. And Tania sensed a difference in Ashley's attitude towards her and she flushed ever so slightly. In fact she glowed. And still only sixteen as of last September. She had been born on the autumn equinox of '85 with her birthday celebration being a couple of weeks after Ashley's.

But girls play with dolls from the moment they can walk and have aspirations of running their own homes from the age of five. Somehow girls seemed to want to run the world when they are very young and as such viewed marriage and babies as their natural destiny. At least both Katy and Tania did.

Ashley on the other hand had never contemplated settling down. He knew there was a special purpose for his gifts and this took up all his thoughts and energy. He was twenty years old and had begun a promising career in antiques which he enjoyed immensely. He liked Tania a lot but like a very good friend. It was only his mum's words that had made him think that perhaps one day many years from now he and Tania might have more of a relationship. He would need to like her a lot more than he did now. He would want to be crazily in love with the woman that he asked to be his lifelong companion. And that was also dependant on what he discovered about himself and the tasks planned for him. So far that voice had been silent with regard to his future even though he had put the question again and again. From this he inferred that perhaps knowing the future was disallowed. He was left to speculate about that when it suddenly occurred to him that perhaps there was no future; it hadn't been created as yet. There was only the past which was definite and was unchangeable. At least that is what Ashley now believed.

'Would you like me to look after the shop when you go to the hospital Ashley,' said Tania bringing Ashley back to the present.

'There's no need as I shall stay on and close at normal time about five,' said Ashley with a smile, 'but you can keep me company till then if you like.'

'I like,' replied Tania. 'Is there something I could do perhaps? I could at least make some tea. It's still cold in here and I for one could do with a nice hot mug, wouldn't you?'

'That'd be great, thanks.'

When Tania came back with two mugs of hot tea, both made the same way with one sugar and plenty of skimmed milk, she asked what time Ashley was returning to see Philip.

'Oh, I think about seven when normal visiting time starts.'

'Can I come with you as well please Ashley,' asked Tania rather hesitatingly. 'I'd just like to be there even if I'm not allowed in to see him.'

'Of course you can,' said Ashley, 'provided you tell your mum and dad. You can go home first and have something to eat and I could pick you up from there about six thirty. By the way here's a bag of cookies the bakery girls gave me this morning. Would you like to try one, I suddenly feel rather peckish.'

There were lovely crumbly gingers in the bag and some rock cakes so they had one of each. Ashley made a face when he saw Tania dip hers in her tea. But Tania just took no notice and said he shouldn't mock it until he had tried it. He still made a face and they both laughed.

At the hospital Dr Mario was on duty and took both Ashley and Tania in to see Philip. Tania stayed a few minutes looking down at Philip and then said she would wait in reception. She kept her face averted as she left and Ashley knew she had got very upset at the sight of Philip all wired up and just lying so still. Ashley followed her to make sure she was okay. He caught up with her and took her hand in his and gave it a squeeze. And he got a squeeze back. They walked in silence to reception and were met there by their entire families.

Tania ran to her mum and burst into tears.

'O mum, he looks terrible,' she sobbed, 'there are wires all over him and he's hardly breathing.'

Milly just hugged her daughter tight and rocked her gently from side to side.

Ashley went back and asked Dr Mario if the group could see Philip for a few moments. Mario said they could but only two at a time and that for a couple of minutes only per visit.

They were all done in just fifteen minutes and sat in reception talking in hushed tones about Philip's condition. Katy and Tania sat together talking quietly. Both were very upset by what they had seen. When they all decided to leave Ashley said he would stay a while longer. He told them that Dr Mario had asked him to sit alone with Philip and talk to him. He hoped this might stimulate a recovery of sorts.

Ashley went back to Philip's bedside and looking down at him noticed that the colour of his face was much paler than before. He sensed Dr Mario's presence beside him and turned to face him. Dr Mario gestured for Ashley to come out to the adjoining room. He then told Ashley that the CT scan had shown up his worst fears. He spoke quietly in Spanish and said that the capillary bruising which had caused the bleeding within the right cerebral cortex had not abated. In fact it had doubled in size. Basically Mario explained that Philip was also having a stroke. The other thing was that the pressure of the cerebro-spinal fluid around the brain and in the spine had increased considerably and was exacerbating the trauma to Philip's brain function. It was a good thing that he was unconscious as he must have a tremendous pain inside his head.

'We have attached an intravenous saline drip and have given the appropriate dosage of the new drug Melanopane to help drain the sinuses of CSF,' said Mario, 'but we cannot attack the bleed until we know that the Melanopane has worked. The EEG pattern will give us that indication hopefully in about an hour.'

Ashley was shocked at this disastrous news and asked what it meant. But he already knew when he looked into Mario's thoughts. Philip could be in a coma for a very long time. That is if the brain survived the trauma.

'Not good I'm afraid. But give us time and something will work out,' said the doctor. 'Go sit with him and talk to him it might help.'

Ashley picked up one of the padded metal arm chairs and took it beside Philip's bed and sat facing him. He wasn't sure where or how to start a conversation with an unconscious person. He sent Philip a passionate appeal to please get well again.

'O Philip please, please you must try to get well again. We are all so worried for you. All of your friends have been to see you just now and all wish you to get better.' Ashley didn't realise that he hadn't uttered a word but had subconsciously conveyed all this telepathically. Ashley nearly jumped up out of his seat at what happened next.

'Don't worry Ashley,' came back the telepathic reply.

Ashley was puzzled. This was similar to the pattern and style of the voice that had talked to him so often before. Perhaps this wasn't Philip after all.

'Is that you Philip?' asked Ashley without speaking.

'Yes,' came back the response.

'But how can this be? Aren't you in pain? The doctor said it's lucky you were unconscious.'

'It is peaceful here. In fact I am even now looking down at you from up here near the ceiling. Communication is however restricted between us.'

Ashley had heard of out-of-body experiences and thought that perhaps Philip was currently going through the same. But not one in which communication took place. Suddenly a complete scenario was imprinted into Ashley's thoughts in the same manner that Ashley had used to convey the Christmas festivities to Aunt Brenda and Uncle Ron over the telephone and at which Tania had listened in.

The thoughts from Philip to Ashley came instantaneously that it left Ashley in a daze of confusion. Much he didn't understand though he glowed with pride at the big task role he must play sometime in the future. But his consolation was in the fact that someone would always be there to guide and advise him. It had been so from the beginning. The voice Ashley now heard had been the inner voice in his head. And the inner voice would continue to remain his gift.

The soul was a being of pure thought and as such could wander through time and space in an instant. Such a being had been allocated to watch over Ashley from the day he was born. The Lych Gate experience had been one of the earliest thought contacts that Ashley had received.

When Ashley had come to McGill's Antiques Philip did not have any recognition of the boy. Ashley now realised that the sixth sense that a lot of people experienced could in fact be their own guardian's thought communication with them. Ashley felt real peace at last after the worry of the last two days.

He looked down at Philip on the bed and there was a serene appearance and a hint of a smile on his face. Just then there was a loud beep from the EEG recorder and a continuous high pitched tone from the heart monitor. Dr Mario rushed in and looked at the traces on them and then at Philip. Ashley knew what he could see; a straight and unwavering line in both cases. Ashley stood up and stepped back as Mario went to Philip and felt for a pulse. There was none. He was about to call for the emergency staff to fetch the defibrillator to jolt the heart back to action when Ashley conveyed a telepathic intuitive thought that perhaps it was best to let Philip go in peace. Dr Mario looked at Ashley and Ashley looked back at him and there was complete understanding. Dr Mario nodded his agreement. There were too many complications in the brain trauma for any chance of Philip's recovery to be even marginally satisfactory.

Dr Mario got the nurses in and together they removed all the pads from Philip's head and chest and then the intravenous feeds and nasal oxygen tube. Ashley stood back as the nurses drew the top sheet up and covered Philip completely. Dr Mario put his arm across Ashley's shoulder and together they walked out of the room. The nurses followed shutting the door behind them. Mario said he would have to fill out the necessary forms and then also inform the police of Philip's death. They would now probably upgrade the case to a murder inquiry which might result in a delay to the body being released for burial.

Throughout all of this Ashley felt Philip's presence near. Then it was indicated that Philip must leave. He was not allowed to stay in this earthly domain any longer. This was not a direct communication but rather just knowledge imparted of what must be. It was the order of things; things of a heavenly nature. But Ashley's inner voice would remain as a one way communication just as before. In Ashley's mind Philip was not dead but living in another dimension. It was what religious belief was all about. No one knew for certain but now Ashley did and he would convey his knowledge to his family.

Ashley then drove straight to his parent's house after phoning them that he was coming over to stay for the night. They themselves had only arrived back a short while ago having first gone back to Jerry and Milly's for a cup of tea. Ashley said that he would come and tell them all that had happened. Could they phone granddad Eric and ask him to come over as it was quite important. And also to contact Aunt Brenda and Uncle Ron for them to be available at home. Lillian told Ashley that his granddad was there with them and had just been about to leave but would now stay till he arrived. Oh yes, and could mum please put the kettle on as he was desperate for a nice hot mug of her tea. Lillian smiled as she sensed that Ashley was a 'happy bunny' which was an expression she often used to describe a jolly person. Something her own mum Beryl had passed on to her as a child.

When Ashley came in the door they noticed that he had a flushed appearance about him which could also be described as a radiant glow. They sensed a change in his attitude. Lillian saw that Ashley was no longer her little boy wanting encouragement but had become a man. He looked so much like Alex had when she had first gone out with him. Her son was a man with a purpose and full of confidence and relish for the life ahead.

Ashley gave his dad and granddad a hug and then another big hug and kiss for his mum. Lillian brought in a tray with four mugs of tea and a few biscuits on a plate and they all sat down and waited for Ashley to begin. Katy had stayed behind at Tania's for the night which was most convenient for this meeting.

'Well, firstly I have to tell you that I have spoken to Philip and he has spoken to me,' said Ashley smiling. 'He has asked me to tell you everything. But he stressed that only those already in the know can be told and for now no one else must enter this circle of confidence. Later circumstances might warrant a change. But he did say that Katy had already guessed a lot so must eventually be brought into the inner circle. I'm very pleased about that as we shall then have everyone in the family in the know. So if you are ready here is the whole picture.'

The thoughts of the past few hours then flowed telepathically from Ashley's mind to theirs with all the detail that Philip had passed to Ashley earlier. It was just as if they could hear Philip's voice right here with them. Lillian glowed with the pride that only a mother could feel for a victorious son. Ashley her son had been chosen to play a role for the future of mankind. Philip may have been the voice in Ashley's head giving him the answers to all those subconsciously asked questions and providing him with all that wide ranging general information. But Ashley was not certain of this. Philip's physical body was lifeless but his spiritual self was alive out there somewhere. He was now gone from any earthly contact but Ashley's inner voice would remain a gift as before.

All of this only lasted a moment in time. Verbal communication took a great deal of time and energy whereas telepathy communicated in pictures and complete scenarios in an instant.

They were all silent for quite a while but all had a pleased expression on their faces and then looked around at each other and smiled.

Then Lillian picked up the phone and said that Ron and Brenda were waiting for their call. She dialled and they picked up after the first ring. After saying hello she asked if they were ready for some wonderful news. Ron said he was on the extension upstairs and was impatient for Ashley to come on the line. He remembered their Christmas phone call and how Ashley had communicated so completely all the events of the day.

'Hello Uncle Ron and Aunt Brenda I have some good news. I have spoken to Philip and he has spoken to me and he has asked me to tell you everything.' repeated Ashley. 'But he has stressed that only those of us already in the know should be told and for now no one else must know. But I shall be including Katy as well very soon. So if you are ready here is the whole picture.'

So once again Ashley sent his thought images racing down the line to Aberporth and straight into the minds of his uncle and aunt. The thoughts flowed telepathically from Ashley's mind to theirs with all the detail of everything that had happened. Ashley also included the details of the attack on Philip by the two thugs Andy Braid and Mark Tamper and of his plan to deal with them.

Again all of this lasted only for a moment in time. There was silence on the phone from both Ron and Brenda as had been the case with his folks here.

'Let us know when the funeral is planned and we shall come down for it,' said Ron. 'We'll talk more then Ashley. I'm very proud of you. In fact we shall try to come down to you this weekend.'

'And I am proud of you too,' said Brenda. 'God bless you till we meet soon.'

Just then Ashley received the following in his head which he recognised as his inner voice.

'Forgiveness is greater than vengeance; Compassion is more powerful than anger; Mercy and Justice go hand in hand.'

Ashley knew this was a reference to the two muggers. They would escape justice if Ashley did not do something to give the police a lead. After putting the phone down there was a moment of silence before anyone spoke. Somehow they too had received the message. But how thought Ashley? Perhaps his mind had subconsciously conveyed it to them. And he was glad that it had.

Lillian asked Ashley if they ought to ring her parents in Aberdare. But Ashley got a voice prompt saying that it would be best not to burden them with unnecessary details. Just let them know that Ashley's employer had passed away. So that is what they did as it would have been too much for them to cope with the full details. Beryl and David had never really met Philip and so offered their condolences and said that they would not be able to come to the funeral. David was still not fully recovered.

Alex then said that the first order of the day was to arrange Philip's funeral. Since they were his only family they would take on that responsibility. Ashley knew that Philip had left a Will and that everything he owned had been made over to him. All this would take time of course. Ashley said he would close the shop till after the funeral which would probably be sometime next week or when the police gave permission for burial. Philip had expressed a wish to be buried near his sister Grace and her husband David.

Lillian and Alex then got on the phone and rang around to the others to inform them of the tragic news of Philip's passing. Everyone was very upset as it had been such a lovely Christmas and New Year celebration together. They all said they'd come over to the house on the morrow but for Lillian not to cook anything as they could order a take-away.

Eric then said he'd go home now and return in the morning. He needed to take his medication which he'd not had as yet this evening. Ashley made plans to visit the shop in the morning and to inform the staff at the bakery and the other neighbouring shops about Philip. He would also put a large notice in the shop window announcing Philip's death and that the shop would be closed for a week as a mark of respect. But when Ashley mentioned his intention of putting his plan against the two muggers into action his dad suggested that perhaps it might be prudent to wait till after the funeral had been concluded. The police were less likely to place any objections to releasing the body if there was no suspect in the case. Ashley agreed.

The next morning Ashley went early to the shop. The news of Philip's death had been on the local news last night and there were dozens of bouquets of flowers on the pavement outside the shop. Philip had lived in the area all his life and was well known by all around. Ashley went from bouquet to bouquet and read the notelet pinned to each. Some names he had not heard of before but when he concentrated a recognisable face appeared and exactly who they were; just like picking up information on his antique pieces. He was partway through reading when Lorraine from the bakery came over and said how sorry they all were about Philip.

'He was a good friend,' she said, 'and we shall all miss him very much.'

Ashley thanked her and asked her to thank her staff as well. He said he planned to keep the shop closed till after the funeral which had not been arranged as yet. He said he would leave a notice in the window thanking everyone for the flowers and their good wishes. As soon as he knew he would post details of the funeral in the window as well.

'Mrs Hollings, I wonder if you could do me a big favour,' asked Ashley.

'Oh please, it's just Lorraine. And I'd be happy to help in any way,' she said.

'Well, it's just that these are such lovely flowers and if they stay here the frost tonight will ruin them. I shall keep all the notelets of course but could you please ask your staff to take them home or give some to their friends to put in water and just enjoy them. Perhaps some of our shop neighbours could have some and display them in vases in their windows as well. They'll last much longer that way,' said Ashley.

'Of course, don't you worry about a thing,' said Lorraine. 'Just leave it all to me.'

She stayed for a while and they went around reading the words on the notes and remarking about how nice that one was or 'That's nice of them' and so on. Finally Ashley had read them all and took one of the larger bouquets into the shop with him. Lorraine went in with him and asked if he had a vase for them.

'Oh, I shall use one of Philip's favourite antique vases to put them in. It is currently on display for sale but I don't suppose Philip will mind. At about a thousand pounds I suppose I could put it in the window and it will look quite nice. We have plenty of others too if I happen to need them,' said Ashley smiling sadly.

Lorraine laughed and then said goodbye and repeated that Ashley was not to worry about the flowers outside. She'd sort out a distribution.

Ashley put a detailed notice in the display window and then locked up and left. He first went to Philip's house and made sure it was locked front and back and then went to the hospital to see if Mario could speed things up. A death certificate was needed before any funeral arrangements could be made.

Dr Mario was out so Ashley saw Dr Robin Clifford the junior registrar. The police had been informed and Philip's body placed in the hospital mortuary. They had said it might be a week to ten days for the death certificate as the coroner was involved due to violence prior to death. An autopsy would have to be carried out to determine actual cause of death; a necessary formality.

Ashley then went to see Philip's solicitor whom he had met several times before; an elderly Mrs Anna Greig. Yes, they had heard the news of Philip's passing away but could not proceed without a death certificate. She then mentioned kindly to Ashley how sorry she was and how well liked Philip had been.

'We saw him last summer when he drew up his latest Will and Testament and may I say I never saw him happier,' she said. 'Ever since you became his partner he acquired a new lease of life. Please don't worry about a thing Mr Bonner, as soon as I have a copy of the coroner's certificate we shall put the wheels in motion and get probate initiated. It's all straightforward and I don't see any problems; though it is a lengthy and time consuming process and will probably take a few months. Let us have your address and phone number and we shall keep you informed.'

Ashley then went back to his house behind the zoo and sorted through a few things. The heating was on a timer though the central heating was set to constant 'on' with the thermostat on a reduced temperature setting. The hot water had been turned to 'off' as Ashley usually only used the high powered electric shower. After a shower and a change of clothes Ashley returned to Erdington to his parent's house.

It was now about one o'clock and the house was full of their friends. Tania and Katy both came to the door and gave him a hug and then burst into tears. It was only Tania who noticed that Ashley had not an ounce of sadness in his demeanour the same as Lillian, Alex and Eric. She puzzled over this for a very long time. And it was many years later that Ashley would be forced to confirm what she had already partially guessed for herself; a women's intuition was far beyond a man's reckoning or understanding. As the saying goes, never underestimate a woman for she may know exactly what you are thinking, even if you yourself don't.

In the house it seemed like a party was going on though with a hint of sadness. It was as if someone they loved had gone away on a long journey to a distant part of the world. Parting between friends had a sadness of its own.

They were in the process of deciding what food to order. Alex had a stack of take-away menus that were regularly posted through his letter flap. Lillian had wanted to dump them as junk mail but Alex said they might come in handy one day. They decided on Chinese.

It took about an hour for the order to be delivered and then everyone had a bit of this and a bit of that; a general free for all no matter what you had originally chosen. During the meal Ashley told them all what he had done during the morning. He had brought the notelets off the flower bouquets back here for everyone to read. He mentioned how he had requested Loraine Hollings the bakery shop manager to take care of the flowers by distributing them amongst her staff. They wouldn't have lasted in the frost overnight. Ashley said he had placed a lovely bunch in one of the antique vases and placed it in the display window and had brought another bunch home for over here. It was still in the boot of the car; he'd bring it in when they finished eating.

Alex said he had some contacts in the MoD and would ask for the coroner to hurry things along. Ashley was not to worry about that aspect any further. Alex said he would also approach a funeral parlour to begin arrangements. Everyone then said they would like to share in the expenses but Ashley said that Philip had made arrangements long ago on a burial policy with the Co-op. He only had to inform them and they would begin arrangements. Ashley said that the policy was in one of the files either in the shop or at Philip's house. He would go back in the morning and look for it. But even if he couldn't find it, the Co-op was very good and would have a copy on file. It would just need the death certificate to initiate the formalities.

After the meal everyone sat around drinking mugs of tea or coffee. Ashley raised his mug and said, 'Here's to the memory of Philip, a very good friend. We shall miss you Philip and will always remember your kindness and love. God bless you and cheers old mate.'

'Cheers,' was repeated by all.

At 9 o'clock Lillian, Milly and Mavis went into the kitchen and together laid out snacks for everyone on the dining table. Lillian had done a small shop early in the morning after Ashley had left and got in a few things for the evening.

Lillian looked around at the group and thought how they had gradually grown into one big family of friends. They were all here including her children's friends. Robin was never far from Katy; nor Robert from Vicky. And Tania only had eyes for Ashley. Lillian lived in hope but Tania was still only sixteen. And Philip was here too in spirit of course. His communication with Ashley had buoyed them up. Lillian was a religious person and although her faith was strong it was not so strong that little doubts had not remained. None who had died had ever contacted the living. Yet there were stories from those who'd had near-death experiences; of them floating towards a distant shining light amid a feeling of great love and serenity. But now Lillian was sure from what Ashley had told them and her faith became as concrete without a shadow of any doubt. It was like a new beginning and she felt compelled to share this miracle of rebirth with all her church friends. She felt so wonderful and full of love for the world that she would try to show this in the way she behaved and lived.

Katy came and sat beside her mum and gave her a tissue to wipe her eyes. Lillian hadn't noticed that in her thoughtful moment the tears had welled up in her eyes. They were not tears of sadness but more like tears of joy and fulfilment. She put her arm around Katy, smiled at her and gave her a snuggle-up type of hug.

Eric was the first to leave just before midnight and the rest gradually followed over the next hour or so. It was Saturday next morning and Ron and Brenda were due to arrive at about one in the afternoon. They would have to be circumspect in how they talked as Katy and Tania would also be in all day. Robin and Robert would probably turn up and they usually tended to stay in unless it was a beautiful warm sunny day, in which case they might decide to take a stroll in the park nearby. But it was early January and cold and miserable outside; so there was little chance of that.

Next morning Alex and Ashley went to Dudley to the shop. There were two new bouquets propped up against the wall beneath the display window. They were from a couple of their regular customers which Ashley thought a wonderful gesture from strangers. Ashley and Alex carried them into the shop and put them in a bucket of water. They would drop one off at the Marsh's house on the way back and perhaps offer the other to Mavis and Vicky. There was quite a bit of post. Most had been hand delivered with blank envelopes and Ashley guessed these were condolence cards from other customers who had come by the shop and seen the notice. People were wonderful.

Ashley looked in the filing cabinet in the section labelled 'insurance' and found the Co-op policy straight away. The other papers in the section dealt with the building and contents insurance for the shop and a separate one on Philip's house; and valuation based insurances for two or three high value antique items. Philip had always been extremely organised in his business ways.

The Co-op man said they were there to help bereaved families and once they had been informed would do everything from then on. It was the nature of their business. Complete details for the funeral had been chosen when the policy was taken out many years ago and that would be rigidly adhered to. They would deal with the coroner and if necessary the police as well. Once the death certificate was issued they would announce a burial date. They understood the nature of Philip's passing and estimated about a week at least. It was usually left to the family to make arrangements with their church minister for the funeral service and for the reception afterwards.

Since there was nothing more they could do Alex suggested that Ashley change his mind and reopen the shop on Monday. Ashley thought this a good idea and agreed. He subsequently removed the notice he had placed in the window.

They then went to the Marsh's house but no one was in. Milly and Jerry must have gone out shopping so they left one of the bouquets propped up against their front door. Ashley left a note with it saying 'Please put me in water, love Ashley'. They then drove back home and went via Mavis's place. She and Vicky were in and were happy to have Philip's flowers. Alex said they couldn't stay as Ron and Brenda were due any time now.

When they got home Ron and Brenda had already arrived. And it was just gone midday but Lillian was pleased to see her sister. There was no sadness in the meeting and Katy and Tania were a bit puzzled by the fact that they hadn't even condoled with each other about Philip. In fact they overheard Brenda remark to her sister about the 'wonderful' news; which confused them even more. They could only conclude that these grown-ups certainly grieved in a peculiar manner. Perhaps they hadn't really cared for Philip that much, him not being real family and all.

Ashley sensed their confusion and had a quick word with his dad. This was passed on to the others and subsequently the appropriate expressions of grief and sadness were uttered. But Katy and Tania were already discussing what they had observed. Perhaps Philip wasn't really dead and it was just a cover-up to root out the muggers. Then Tania related the incident of the phone call to Aberporth on Christmas day. Katy was quiet for a bit and then began to tell Tania of her childhood and how Ashley used to catch birds in his bare hands for her cage. She never found out how he did that but then she was only five. But she did remember when Ashley was playing catch-the-ball with their granddad Eric in the back garden. Eric would throw the ball in every direction but the next instant it would be in Ashley's hands in another part of the garden. She thought it quite funny at the time but now it seemed quite puzzling. Tania asked if there was anything else that she could remember from then.

'No, not really,' said Katy pensively, 'except that sometimes long ago I used to hear Ashley's voice in my head when I was upstairs and he was downstairs talking to mum and dad. But I don't hear him any more.'

'That's funny,' said Tania, 'because that is exactly what I thought I heard when Ashley was on the phone at Christmas. Don't say a word to anyone about all this Katy but keep a close eye on your brother. There's something he's not telling us.'

'Oh yes, there's another thing Tania,' said Katy, 'Ashley can speak lots of languages fluently but I never see him learning them from a book or anything. We were in a Chinese restaurant before Christmas and the waiters were talking to one another and I could see that Ashley understood what they were saying from his smile at something they said.'

'Curiouser and curiouser,' said Tania.

They were both puzzled but this conspiracy of sorts brought them closer as friends. They agreed to keep silent as they watched. They were like mice nibbling at a piece of cheese. They couldn't stop themselves.

Ashley picked up their conspiracy thoughts but had no idea what to do about it. They were not supposed to know about Ashley's gifts but it seemed that they were about to find out about some of it for themselves. Katy lived in the same house with her brother and was therefore bound to notice things. Ashley wanted his sister in on his secret but the others had suggested putting it off for a few years. It was time for another conference.

It was Lillian who suggested that Katy be told everything but with an added lie. They would tell her that one such person had always existed to help save the earth from a potential disaster. It was simply that Ashley had been chosen as that person for the time being. If the truth were widely known then this would defeat the purpose and the gifts given might even be withdrawn and passed to another. The secret must lie within the family. Tania must not be allowed to find out the truth. Not yet anyway. Perhaps a bit of ridiculous exaggeration of some wild imaginings of Ashley's powers could be related by Katy to Tania might make Tania discount some of the things Katy had said. But Tania was no fool and would always remain suspicious and on the prowl for facts.

But things came to a head and Ashley received a prompt from his inner voice that Katy needed to be brought into the family circle of understanding before she could conspire further with Tania. Ashley told his mum and dad about what he had received. Lillian said she was pleased and would arrange a meeting tonight. Eric said he would stay till after the meeting as he didn't want to miss his granddaughter's expression. Besides he wanted to be here to welcome her into the inner circle. And so it was that around midnight when all the guests had gone and they were alone that Lillian went up to Katy's bedroom and woke her up. She had only just put her book down and dozed off. But something in her mother's expression brought her wide awake and she came downstairs in her night gown expectantly. Her intuition told her this would be the most important day in her life. And so it turned out to be. Her entire family were there apart from her mother's parents.

'Katy we have something extremely important to tell you,' said Lillian. 'And I'm sorry we haven't told you sooner.'

'It's alright mum, I think I already know. It's about Ashley isn't it?' said Katy.

'Yes it is my darling, but it is far greater than you can even imagine,' said Lillian. 'We know that you and Tania have been guessing about Ashley and that must stop. We need to keep everything about Ashley a secret from the rest of the world; at least for now. We must keep this in the family, so no one else can know or suspect. We know that Tania suspects something after listening in to Ashley's conversation with your aunt and uncle but that is as far as it must go. My darling, forgive me for not telling you sooner but we agreed to wait till you were older. Philip's accident and death has brought this all to a head. So far it's just us and your Aberdare grandparents who have been kept in the know.'

Lillian paused as she watched Katy's expectant expression. There was no annoyance or disapproving expression on Katy's face.

'I think I know a little bit, mom,' she said. 'It's about Ashley having the power to read peoples' thoughts and also to communicate telepathically in return, isn't it?'

'Yes that is a part of it but there is a lot more. Ever since Ashley was four or five he told us that sometimes the sky became pink,' said Lillian. 'But it is a long story and I think I'll let Ashley fill you in with the whole picture. You mustn't be surprised or scared my darling as we are all in this together and I'm so pleased that I shall be able to share all my hopes, fears and joys with you.'

The thoughts of the past years then flowed telepathically from Ashley's mind to Katy's and this included those of the last few hours and the short contact with Philip. The volume of facts and answers to all Katy's questions left her in a daze of wonder. Ashley her brother had somehow been chosen to play a role in the world and an inner voice was to be his mentor and guardian; as it had been since Ashley was a child.

Philip's physical body was dead but his spirit had communicated with Ashley shortly afterwards before he had been pulled away by some greater power.

Within moments Katy had the complete picture. Verbal communication took time and energy whereas telepathy communicated in pictures and complete scenarios in an instant. Ashley had not restricted his communication but had kept it wide for all in the room to feel.

Everyone was silent for quite a while but Katy had a glowing though curious expression on her face. Her mother came and put her arms around her daughter and the tears finally appeared but they were tears of joy. She had a smile for everyone. And everyone smiled back. Katy was in the fold at last.

'O God, mum,' said Katy, 'I think I said too much to Tania. What are we going to do?'

'Don't worry,' said Ashley to only Katy telepathically, 'she only suspects and I shall let her think I can read peoples minds. I have read her mind and yours and I know exactly what was discussed. She is just puzzled at the moment and if you say nothing further it will fade. Mum likes Tania and so do I so one day you never know…..'

Ashley left the rest unsaid but Katy smiled conspiratorially back at him. She liked Tania too.

A thought entered his head with regard to the skill of telepathy and how this could be generally learnt. But it was gone before he could analyse it. Somehow Ashley knew the thought hadn't come from his inner voice. It would be nice if others in the family could also communicate telepathically with him. Sometimes Ashley felt that his thoughts were being monitored; but how and by whom? Thankfully the thought only came occasionally.

Brenda asked what the two of them were talking about as no one else had heard their telepathic communication. But Katy just smiled and said it was something special between brother and sister. And with that Katy went and gave Ashley a real big tight hug. They all sat around talking and it was about four in the morning that they finally went to bed. Lillian said it was too late for Eric to go home so she got the blow-up bed and made it up for him down there.

Lillian went into her daughter's room expecting to find her tired and ready for sleep. Neither of them felt sleepy. They were both so exhilarated by this newfound closeness that they talked softly till the sky started to lighten with the dawn. Then they decided to try for a few hours sleep which came quickly to both.

It was a week later that the coroner concluded his report and allowed the burial to go ahead. The Co-op did a magnificent job in arranging all the details and the funeral was set for the following Thursday at 11:00 am at St Barnabas' church on the High street. Lillian and Alex rang everyone they could think of and Ashley put a notice in the shop window. Ron and Brenda said they would be down the night before and stay over the weekend and return Sunday evening.

Thursday started wet but the rain stopped while everyone was inside the church. It was a simple ceremony and Ashley spoke for five minutes about Philip and the person everyone had got to like. Ashley ended with a quote from Hamlet in which Horatio bids his dying friend goodbye.

"Goodnight sweet prince and flights of angels sing thee to thy rest"

'And from all of us here Philip we bid you the same, you will always be in our hearts,' added Ashley.

For the Bonner family this was truly meant and in a literal sense too. Philip would certainly be in their hearts and minds; memories have a knack of persisting and springing up at odd moments. There was still some sadness among the Bonners as they wouldn't be seeing Philip any more; not to sit and laugh with as they had this last Christmas.

The journey to the cemetery was a slow one and took nearly half an hour. Afterwards a lot of friends went back to the Navigation pub where the reception was being held. The place had its regulars but the reception was in the private rooms at the rear. There was a blazing log fire and people picked a spot near it. The rain had returned along with a bit of sleet and an icy wind. There were sandwiches and other buffet style eats but most welcome was the hot tea and coffee in flasks on a long table near a window.

Later, all the friends gathered at Alex and Lillian's place and it was then that Eric went over to his grandson and made a suggestion.

'Ash, I'd like to propose something to you,' said Eric. 'Now that you don't have a partner or an assistant to help run McGill's, and until you find someone to assist, I'd like to help in the shop. We'd be doing each other a favour. I have lots of spare time and you need someone in the shop when you are out on your trips looking for antiques. And besides you may have other tasks to perform as well.'

Eric was referring to Ashley's plan against Andy Braid and Mark Tamper, the muggers who had been responsible for Philip's death.

Ashley hadn't given the shop much thought and was happy to accept his granddad's offer. Looking at Tania he said that Tania had offered but he had turned her down because she was due to start her A-Levels at college. Besides she was below the legal age limit to be formally employed. Ashley said she could come to the shop at anytime to help when someone else was also there. Eric's offer was most welcome as Ashley hadn't thought about an assistant at all. The company bank account was healthy and Ashley told his granddad that he insisted that he become a proper salaried employee of McGill's Antiques and Museum/shop, so that the insurance conditions were fulfilled of course.

Ashley added that Eric was the ideal person for the job since their customers were used to seeing an elderly Philip behind the desk.

'I shall be there to help you Eric as often as I can,' said Tania.

And everyone agreed that it was an excellent idea.

Afterwards when all the friends had left and it was just the Bonner family present Ashley said he would pass on to Eric all the necessary knowledge about the antiques in the shop in a series of telepathic lessons. He told his granddad that it would have to be done that way so as not to overload his brain with too much information in one go. Ashley had never done this sort of tutoring before and must therefore tread carefully.

'Perhaps you could take me around to each of the items in turn and relay the necessary information that way,' said Eric.

'That would be much easier granddad,' said Ashley. 'Yes, I think we'll do it that way.'

Then Katy had an idea. Would Ashley please do the same for her and help her learn her Spanish. She was having real difficulty in her oral class. Ashley promised her that he would. He reckoned that her brain was younger and could probably absorb a greater instant load. But he would still play it safe and pass on his Madrid Spanish picked up from Dr Mario at the hospital in phases. The voice in Ashley's head interrupted and said that it would be safe to do it all for Katy in a single session.

Although Ashley now thought that it was Philip who was guiding him, there was quite an impersonal manner in this communication. The thoughts put into Ashley's head came through as if they were a conclusion that Ashley himself had arrived at. This was more like what Ashley referred to as 'the Lych-gate phenomena' when he had first realised he came to know about things by simply enquiring about them. His in-depth knowledge of each antique that he looked at came to him in this way. And so Ashley knew that it would be safe to pass on to Katy a full and fluent knowledge of his Madrid Spanish at one session. And that is exactly what he did.

Before Katy realised it she found she was thinking in Spanish. She also knew the city of Madrid as if she had lived there all her life. It had only taken a moment for Ashley to telepathically feed Katy with Dr Mario's memories but without the medical knowledge part. Ashley found he could filter information that he had absorbed from others so that only parts were transferred telepathically as he desired.

Katy ran up to her brother and hugged him. Then she stepped back and kissed him on both cheeks again and again. She was laughing and crying at the same time. Then she hugged him again and kept repeating 'Thank you, thank you dear, darling Ashley' in fluent Spanish of course.

For a moment her parents, aunt, uncle and granddad were puzzled by what was going on till they realised that the words Katy was uttering was in Spanish. Then they suddenly knew that Katy had expressed a wish and Ashley had instantly fulfilled that wish.

'Mum,' said Katy, 'it's like a miracle. I can speak and think Spanish like I grew up with it. It's like I had another life in Madrid. I know the city like I do Birmingham. I shall 'wow' my Spanish teacher when I see her. I feel I must travel to Madrid one day to visit the places that are now in my memory.'

But Lillian and the others told Katy not to divulge how she had so suddenly become fluent in a language she had previously been having difficulty with. They advised her to show a gradual progress especially where Tania was concerned. They couldn't have Tania getting any more suspicions than she already had. Katy must pretend to be swatting her Spanish from her text books at every opportunity that she was with Tania and begin gradually to improve her oral skills with her Spanish teacher Mrs Rima Vigon. So over the next year that is what Katy did.

On the Monday morning Ashley reopened the shop at 9:30am as normal. Granddad Eric also turned up to start his new job as agreed. And it wasn't long before Eric had a full understanding of the antiques on the shelves and also those in the back storeroom. Later they sat together at the kitchen table and drank their tea. Ashley thought of Philip as this had been the routine between them. And it was good to have it continued with someone just as nice. Eric understood how Ashley felt and so raised his mug of tea.

'Here's to you Philip,' he said. 'I hope I can do you proud in this job.'

Eric half expected a response from the spirit world but there was only silence. But there was a faint smile on Ashley's face.

In the afternoon Ashley rang the local police station and said who he was; and asked if they had made any progress in finding out more about Philip's attackers. Regretfully they had no leads whatsoever.

Ashley decided that it was time for his plan to be put into action.

CHAPTER 8

Adventures

2002

I've been back at the shop for a week now and have been talking to the family about how best to proceed with the plan to bring Philip's muggers to justice. I keep thinking of the quote from Shakespeare's Merchant of Venice in which Portia talks about the quality of mercy. The bit that gets to me is where she says that 'mercy seasons justice'. However, Andy Braid and Mark Tamper must be punished for their crime and brought before a court of law. They would be my first case after the pub thieves and I must use my special gifts to make them see the error of their ways. I am in fact quite looking forward to converting them into law abiding citizens. I do hope they are superstitious and believe in things that go bump in the night. We shall see. I shall try to make believers out of them.

I remembered that the taller one was Mark Tamper and he was 23. The other one was Andy Braid and he was the one who had done all the violence against Philip. It was his kick to Philip's head that had been responsible for Philip's death. He was 19 years old and lived at home with both his parents not far from the Black Swan pub at the end of Philip's street. Mark Tamper lived not much farther away in a council flat and on his own.

I told granddad Eric that I needed to visit the Black Swan just to get a feel for the place. After all getting to know the regulars was part of my plan. So we decided that we get ourselves a pint that evening after closing up the shop. It was a Friday after all.

It was a small pub directly off the main road. There was a smallish room as you entered and there were seats and small circular tables along the walls to the right of the entrance. The small bar began on the left side and then continued into the next room directly ahead. It also had seating along the walls and it was there that we settled ourselves at a small table after getting pints of shandy at the bar. The smartly dressed barman who served us was also the manager and he seemed quite pleasant. There was another long room beyond this one and I could see it was set up with a table the length of the room and set up for a party of about twenty people. The two pub rooms were quite full of well dressed couples and I think they were the party and just having a drink while waiting for the others to arrive.

A lady came in from the long room and announced that their table was ready and would the party like to come through. This left us and another group of three men in the front room. There was a homely atmosphere to the pub and I wondered if Philip and his sister Grace and David ever came in here.

Couples gradually came in and took up some of the seating and a few men also stood at the bar. There was quite a buzz of conversation in the place but most of the noise was from the laughter in the party room.

Granddad and I decided to get ourselves another half to give us some more time in the place. Granddad asked the barman who was also the manager if he had known Philip Stevens who had lived just up the road and if he had ever came in here.

'O yes I knew Philip. A lovely old gent,' said the manager. 'He usually came in on a Saturday night for a half. I think his thing was lager with a dash of lime. It's sad about the break in and his passing. Were you close friends? I'm Reggie, by the way.'

'This is my grandson Ashley,' said granddad. 'He and Philip were in partnership running the McGill's Antiques shop just off the High street. But Philip was like family and we were sorry to lose him. We thought we'd come in to what must surely have been his local. During Christmas we noticed groups of youths gathering near here. Do you get much trouble from that lot?'

'No, not really,' he said. 'I think that at Christmas the kids were looking to enjoy themselves more than usual and were a bit of a nuisance, but they keep it all outside. I couldn't have them upsetting my customers now could I? There's the Black Dog pub up the road a ways and they have a much bigger premises including a heated terrace. It's a favourite with the youngsters. But my regulars prefer the Black Swan and I'm glad they do.'

We stayed at the bar and talked pleasantly to Reggie whenever he was not serving. He had been the landlord here for 25 years now and had seen a lot of changes. He even remembered Grace and David coming in occasionally with Philip. Those were nice times when things were reasonable and cheap. The place got quite crowded as the night progressed and we decided to call it a night at about 10 o'clock.

Next morning at the shop we thought we'd try the Black Dog that evening and see what or who we found. We might even see the two muggers in there. Tania came in and spent the morning with us. She was very pleasant and there was not an ounce of conspiratorial attitude in her manner. I had expected her to be a bit of a Sherlock Holmes after her earlier conversations with Katy. I read her thoughts and she seemed to be content just to be in our company. I knew then that she and Katy had talked again and that whatever had been said had allayed most or all of her earlier suspicions. I liked her attitude of knowing that to continue with any suspicions might soil her relationship with me and my family. In her mind the matter of the telepathic phone call was simply an oddity that really must have a simple explanation. For sixteen, Tania was very mature and I liked that in her. It is three years since we first met at that darts match and I remember I had the oddest feeling about her then. She has since grown to be a familiar face and a good friend.

Saturday was a good day for business and for visitors to the museum. Granddad had rearranged the old antiques upstairs and had added a few of his own from home. He thought we ought to add items from other walks of life so I told him he had a free hand to do things any way he liked. I think that two heads were definitely better than one when running a business. He said that there was a car boot sale in the field near Dunton Island just off the M42 and that he planned on going to it mainly in search of old toy cars and the like. I said I'd come with him as I did enjoy browsing through all the nick knacks especially with my gift of picking up information on the history of the items that I touched. Philip had been running the shop on his own for so long that new ideas had just run out of steam. Then I had come along and put new life into the business and Philip had been impressed. Now it was my turn to be impressed at granddad's input with new energy and ideas.

Granddad had been a sheet metal worker at a car factory in Longbridge and had taken redundancy and early retirement when the opportunity came along in the spring of 1983. He'd had a good deal and a reasonable pension and had not worked since. He was now 77 years of age and as keen as when he started work at fifteen. I honestly think granddad feels like he has had a new lease in life and I am pleased for him; and for the shop. I don't think that I shall miss Philip's presence in the shop as much as I had first feared. Granddad was ideal as a successor to Philip.

That evening we went in to the Black Dog pub. It can only be described as a working man's pub. There was a dusty atmosphere about the place albeit not unpleasant. There was quite an early crowd compared to the Black Swan of the previous evening. The bar was a large rectangular affair near the centre of a huge room. There were tables with chairs spread around in a sort of random pattern on all sides. There was also plenty of room to stand at the bar and there were three serving, a man and two women. Pubs were usually a family run affair and you could see that the people behind the bar were a husband, wife and daughter team. There were simple menu cards pasted on the bar top for the benefit of anyone who wished for a snack. By the look of things not many did. Perhaps lunch times were different when people came in during their work break. Along the wall on either side of the door through which we entered were located about a dozen slot machines but at the moment these were all vacant.

We bought our shandy halves and had a choice of place to sit. Granddad chose a place on the far side of the bar from which we could see the main entrance. There was a trickle of people coming in and the pub gradually filled up. A family of four turned up with two youngish children and they went around to the family area allocated in a far corner of the pub and separated by a low metal patterned railing. The atmosphere in the pub gradually changed to one of a buzzing noise of people talking and laughing. The children added a higher pitch to the background sounds.

It was about halfway though our vigil that the pair entered. Granddad recognised them straight away and whispered that they were here. They were a suspicious pair and looked around the room to see who was there. They stared at us for a long while as they awaited their turn at the bar. They looked different from the time I had seen them in my mental scan of events in Philip's house the morning after they attacked him. For a start they were both dressed in smarter clothes and both were clean shaven. The taller one named Mark Tamper stared in our direction again and whispered something to his shorter companion Andy Braid. I decided that I must know what they were thinking so I concentrated on Mark's thoughts and saw that he had recognised me from the shop. They had originally thought of raiding the till in the shop and had observed the goings on over a few days. The place was open to the public and they had walked around the shop and viewed the items as though they were interested customers. I would occasionally read the mind of a prospective customer to determine what kind of curio he might actually be interested in, but I had missed these two. Philip always carried a briefcase and took it home with him with the day's takings for banking the next morning on his way to the shop. These two crooks had done a complete observation of Philip's routine and had finally decided to raid him at his house when he was alone one night. I passed this information over to granddad. They had recognised me but weren't sure if I had recognised them. Granddad and I then turned away from them and pretended to carry on a conversation of our own.

They were obviously regulars here for when the barman came to serve them he asked if it was to be the usual. 'Yes please,' said the tall Mark Tamper, 'and have one yourself, Bill.'

'Why thank you sir,' said Bill, 'I'll just have a small whiskey if you don't mind.'

Not that Bill would drink the whiskey, he'd just add it to their bill when they paid and accept it as a tip. It was the usual way apart from the occasional 'Keep the change' remark when handing over payment for one's drinks.

I watched them from the corner of my eye and waited for Bill to place their two pints on top of the spill tray on the bar. I saw the shorter Andy Braid reach to pick up his pint and I then focussed on the top of the glass and gave it a little push. As Andy touched the glass it tipped over and spilled its contents all over the bar and dripped down the front and the back. I then transferred the thought that the barman had placed his pint on the edge of the spill tray which had caused it to fall over at the lightest touch.

Andy Braid had a very short and violent temper and swore loudly using the F-word. The barman and a lot of the customers heard this swearing and were quite shocked.

'I'm sorry about that sir,' said Bill the barman, 'I'll pour you another pint just as soon as I have mopped up the spill. I'll only be a moment.'

He then called to Madge his wife to fetch a mop and clean up the outside of the bar while he did the inside.

Some of the spill had wet a bit of Andy's left trouser leg and he again used the F-word in referring to his wet clothes.

I smiled as I looked at granddad and he smiled back. I was really getting a lot of satisfaction from this. It was time to start the next phase of the plan.

There was a middle aged couple sitting to our left and a bit towards the middle of the area in front of the bar section where the spillage had occurred. I could see that they were annoyed by Andy Braid's swearing. I chose them as my unknowing assistants.

I conveyed into both of their minds the images of the events of the evening when the two thugs had entered Philip's house and violently ransacked it. It was all so vivid in my own memory and I passed all this on to them. The couple were Brian and Ruby Griffiths and they lived on Church Road which was next to Griffin Street on which Philip lived; and so they knew all about the burglary and its tragic consequences. In fact Ruby was quite friendly with Sarah Winfield one of Philip's neighbours and so had been given a first hand account of what had happened there. I also passed into their thoughts that both of them had been specially chosen to receive this revelation by the powers that be in order that justice might be done. Both were church people and therefore believed that this was part of a divine intervention in earthly matters. Ruby knew that her mother was psychic and often wondered if this could have been passed on to her as well. So far she'd had only premonitions and dreams but never anything like this. I gleaned all this as I was reading her thoughts.

Brian asked his wife if she had the police contact number or the incident room phone number for this crime. He could remember that it had been advertised at the bottom of the TV screen when the report had first been made. Ruby couldn't remember the phone number either but she knew that Sarah her friend would know. She had been interviewed by the police on two occasions. Once shortly after the burglary and then again when it became a murder inquiry. They had asked her to ring them if she remembered anything at all later on. The police relied on the public to remember trivia which could put them onto something important. And it was usually something that was trivial in the mind of the witness as to seem unimportant that was often the key to solving the crime. Ruby used her mobile to ring Sarah her friend and I could see her hold the line and then ask Brian for his pen. She scribbled something on a beer mat which I presume was the police number Sarah gave her. She then phoned and I could see that she was getting impatient with whoever was on the other end of the line. She then nodded and said okay and ended the call. I read her thoughts and knew that she had been asked to visit the police station on Hill Street by Hillcrest School with her information on Monday morning about 11 o'clock. Tomorrow being Sunday the station was shut. She then rang her friend again, spoke a few words and ended the call. I knew she and her husband were going to pay Sarah a visit straight from here which was only just around the corner.

I conveyed all this to granddad Eric and he responded by saying well done. We often communicated telepathically; at least I did and then read his thoughts in return. I had begun to do the same with the other members of my family. I found it so much more convenient than lengthy conversations. We decided to call it an evening and see where the events would lead in the days ahead.

It was still early so I thought I might drive home to see mum and dad and spend the night there. Granddad thought it a good idea and that way we could pass on the events of the day not to mention getting a free dinner. He said that Lillian always had something she could quickly and easily prepare for her unexpected guests. I gave mum a quick ring to say granddad and I were coming over right away. It would take us about half an hour to get there at least. Mum sounded pleased.

When we got there Katy was also home and it took me only an instant to zap them with all the latest events of the day. Later granddad went home for a quiet Sunday while I stayed on like old times.

On Monday morning I left granddad to look after the shop while I drove down to check up on Philip's house in Griffin Street. I didn't feel like putting the house on the market and was actually waiting to see if my 'inner voice' had anything to say. Nothing. I locked up the house again and drove around to number 32 Church Road and parked on the opposite side of the road. Brian and Ruby Griffiths lived here and I waited for them to begin their trip to the police station. I didn't have long to wait. They came out together and got into a blue Renault hatchback and drove off. Ruby was driving. I didn't follow but took a shortcut to the police station and parked a short distance away. I then walked into the station and went to the enquiry desk area. The Griffiths hadn't arrived as yet so I sat down in one of the chairs against the wall.

When the desk was free I asked the duty sergeant if anyone had handed in a dark brown leather wallet. It had all my details in it plus about £100 of my hard earned money. I said I last had it in the High Street about two hours ago. I half suspected that I might have been the victim of a gang of pickpockets. There were plenty of those about. After the usual questions he gave me a report form to fill out and said there was a spot further along the counter for me to write on. As I moved aside I saw the Griffiths arrive and talk to the sergeant. When they said who they were he looked at his notepad and asked them to take a seat and someone would come for them shortly. He picked up his phone said a few words and then put it down again. He told the Griffiths that detective sergeant Mark Solomon would be there to call for them shortly. It was only a few minutes later when a medium height stocky civilian looking chap came through a door from one of the inner rooms and asked Mr and Mrs Griffiths to please follow him. He held the door open for them. I went pink and walked through first past the frozen-in-time sergeant and found a place to hide myself before returning to normal again. It was a room with plenty of office equipment and storage cupboards and the like where someone as thin as I could easily be hidden momentarily.

DS Solomon opened another door which led into an interview room which had a table and chairs. I could see that there was nowhere for me to hide in there so I would have to make do with working my plan from this room. This was not a problem since people's thoughts mirror what they say.

I could listen in to all that was said in there and could also contact them telepathically when the time came. I just hoped that no one came in here in the next few minutes.

'Right, please do sit down. What is it that you can tell me about the violent burglary at the Steven's house in Griffin Street?' asked detective Mark Solomon.

'I'd like you to listen to my version of the events as I, as we saw them,' said Ruby. 'Please don't interrupt until I have finished. I will then tell you how I came to see it all.'

'Fine,' said the detective, 'please go ahead, I'm listening. I'm also switching on the voice recorder so I can go over everything you tell me, if that is alright with you.'

Both Brian and Ruby said it was okay. Ruby then recited the events of the evening of January 1st exactly as Ashley had seen it and passed on to her starting with the moment that the Marsh's had dropped Philip home. She described how she saw Philip come in the door, then turn around and wave to the Marsh's in their car. It was just after seven o'clock and dark outside except for the street lighting. He locked the door and then went into the kitchen, filled the kettle and switched it on. When the water had boiled he made himself a mug of tea and then sat down to watch the news on TV. It wasn't long before Philip shut his eyes and dozed off. The door bell rang twice and gradually Philip came awake. It rang again a number of times and he realised it was the front door. Without thinking he went to the front door and opened it. There were two young men standing there smiling.

'Hello granddad,' the taller one of them said pushing his way into the hall, 'we've come to read your gas meter.'

They had glazed eyes and appeared as if they had been drinking. They pushed Philip backwards quite roughly causing him to fall over onto the floor. The shorter one stepped forward and kicked Philip in the head with the toe of his boot. Philip lay still where he had fallen.

'You fool Andy,' said the tall one, 'you've killed him. We needed him to tell us where his cash and all are.'

Then there was a groan from Philip and he tried to sit up so they grabbed him and asked him where his money was. Philip was in a semi-daze and drunkenly pointed up the stairs. They half dragged, half carried him up the stairs and dumped him on his bed. They saw Philip's wallet on the bedside table and quickly emptied it of its cash.

'There's only two hundred quid here,' said the tall youth. 'Look around Andy there's bound to be some more stuff hidden about.'

The one called Andy then sat on the bed and punched Philip in the face.

'Where is the rest of the stuff granddad?' he said.

But Philip had passed out again and Andy punched him again.

Philip's head was knocked sideways and a trickle of blood appeared at the corner of his mouth.

'Tie him up,' said the taller one, 'then we can search the place in peace.'

Andy gave Philip another punch and then took a white plastic cable tie from his coat pocket and wrapped it around Philips wrists and pulled tight. He did the same to Philip's feet at the ankles. Philip hadn't moved but now there was also a trickle of blood from his nose.

They systematically searched through the bedroom dresser drawers and took whatever they thought valuable. They found and took Philip's gold ring and Omega watch which were in the top drawer and some imitation jewellery that Philip had kept for sentimental reasons. The taller one was Mark Tamper and the violent one who had done the kicking and punching was Andy Braid. Mark Tamper lives by himself in a flat but Andy Braid still lives at home with both his parents. Both are on the dole and live close to each other. Mark lives alone at 216A Hockley Lane while Andy Braid lives at 57 Yew Tree Crescent.

They systematically searched the house room by room and didn't give Philip another thought. They found some loose change that amounted to just a few pounds which Andy Braid pocketed.

'Let's get out of here. I think we've got everything,' said Mark. 'Just let me wipe down our fingerprints.'

He then went around wiping everything that they might have touched. They left by the front door and shut it behind them. They had been in the house about twenty minutes and it was then about eight thirty in the evening. They then went into the Black Dog pub and had a few pints to add to the ones they'd had earlier. They finally went to Mark's flat and divided up the money. Mark said he'd see what he could get for the other items tomorrow. But he kept the gold ring and omega watch for himself.

'If you arrest them you will find the gold ring and the watch on Mark Tamper,' added Ruby. 'You may ask how I know all this and I shall tell you. Brian and I were having a quiet drink in the Black Dog last evening when these two came in for a pint. Andy Braid spilled his drink all over the bar and then showed what an evil man he was by swearing loudly at the barman. He used very foul language and suddenly as if by magic both Brian and I saw what I have just told you. I believe it to be the truth and that these two men are responsible for Mr Philip Steven's death. If I had been the only one to have had this vision, call it that if you like, then I may have had my doubts. But for both of us to have seen it at the same time made me believe it to be true.'

There was a silent moment from detective Mark Solomon and I could read the scepticism in his mind that here was another of those crackpots; only these seemed to have worked out their story in greater detail. This was the moment I had been waiting for and quickly I conveyed into the detective's mind the images of the events of the evening when the two thugs had entered Philip's house and as Ruby had tried to describe.

'My God,' exclaimed the detective as he too saw it all. But he didn't say anything more to the Griffiths except to thank them for their information and that he would be in touch. He had to decide what he must do now.

I went pink and went back into the reception area to the spot where I had to fill in my form. I told the duty officer that I didn't see the necessity for form filling and that if my wallet was handed in my name and address was in it and they could phone me. He seemed pleased with that and said that would be fine. I left knowing that Philip's case was now in good hands and that the two thugs would be pursued by the law. But I would still follow the case closely. Mark Solomon was a dedicated policeman and would follow up his 'revelation' to its utmost. I felt pleased with myself. I also knew that Brian and Ruby would spread their story to their friend Sarah and she in turn would also pass it on.

I returned to the shop and telepathically told granddad all that had transpired and how pleased I was with the way it had gone. He seemed pleased as well except for the fact that he would miss out on any arrests. I let granddad know that I hadn't finished with these two just yet. There was more to be done. Andy Braid lived at home with his parents and they were about to find out what their son had been up to. When I mentioned this to granddad he seemed pleased.

I had a ham sandwich, a banana and a yogurt at the back of the shop for my lunch and then drove to Yew Tree Crescent to Andy Braid's house. I had removed my jacket, rolled up my shirt sleeves and pulled the shirt tails half out of my trousers. I had also roughed up my hair. I knocked on the door and a rather well dressed middle aged man came to the door. I didn't give my name but asked if young Mr Andy Braid was in.

'No, I'm afraid he's out at the moment. I'm his dad, can I help,' he said looking me up and down in a disapproving manner.

I hesitated a bit, looked shiftily down the street and said, 'Just tell him Billy called and that someone has ratted on him. The cops are on to him.'

With that I turned around and walked down the street looking from side to side. I could feel the old man looking at me as I kept walking. I stopped, turned around and looked straight at him and quickly conveyed into the old man's mind the images of the evening of Philip's mugging. I then went pink and walked to the end of the street and around the corner before returning to normal. As far as the old man was concerned I had literally disappeared before his very eyes.

I made myself presentable again and walked back to the car. I wasn't sure what Mr Braid senior would do so I drove up to the house and parked on the opposite side of the road under a tree. From here I could read the thoughts issuing from inside the house. Mr Braid senior was telling his wife that he had just been visited by an avenging angel and that their son had been responsible for the mugging and murder of the antiques fellow that was reported in the papers a couple of weeks ago. She said she couldn't believe it, not her Andy. So I buzzed her with the same information I had given her old man. Even in the car I heard the scream followed by a wailing cry. I felt sorry for them but it had to be done. When Andy returned home later that evening he would have a surprise waiting for him.

I returned to the shop and felt rather tired. I told granddad what I had done and he noticed the tiredness in my eyes. I could hardly keep awake. The inner voice conveyed to me that the extensive use of telepathy was tiring on the human brain and I should in future ration myself to less frequent usage. In time I would find it easier. Someone was looking after me.

I think granddad understood and suggested I get some sleep in the armchair in the back room. Or better still to have the day off and go home for a proper kip in bed. I said I daren't drive so I'd settle for the armchair. I had barely got myself positioned comfortably than I dozed off. It was dark when granddad shook me awake. It was six o'clock and granddad had closed the shop at five. I had been asleep for nearly four hours. However I now felt quite refreshed and the tiredness had gone. I explained all this verbally to granddad and said that from now on I would return to the old form of verbal communication. I wondered what had been happening in the world of Andy Braid and Mark Tamper in the four hours I had been asleep. I decided to find out tomorrow.

Next morning granddad phoned me at home to say he wasn't feeling too good so he wouldn't be at work today. At about ten o'clock I got a call from detective sergeant Mark Solomon asking me to come to the Hill Street police station when I could. I told him I couldn't leave the shop without closing up. The earliest I could get there would be about five o'clock.

'I need to talk to you urgently,' he said. 'It's about Mr Steven's case. I'd like to personally brief you on the findings so far, and it shouldn't take too long. Also, do you think we could borrow a key to Mr Steven's property in Griffin Street? We would like to go over it again if that's alright with you.'

'No problem at all, officer,' I said. 'I'll see you in about an hour.'

I rang Milly at home but she was out, so I rang her mobile.

'Hello Ashley,' she said, 'what can I do for you?'

I explained that granddad was ill and that I needed someone to mind the shop for about an hour as I was wanted at the police station for a briefing. She said that Tania was with her and they were doing a bit of shopping on the High Street just around the corner and had thought of popping in when they finished. They would be around in five or ten minutes. I thanked her and ended the call.

Tania came in the door in five minutes flat. She gave me a hug and a kiss on the cheek with a mischievous expression on her face.

'Mum said you had to go to the police station,' she said smilingly. 'Are you under suspicion or something? Tell me the truth. Confess immediately what dastardly deed have you done? Tell me before mum comes in and I won't tell a soul. It'll be our secret.'

I had to laugh at this sixteen-year-olds propensity for adventure.

'Detective Mark Solomon wants to brief me on the latest developments,' I said. 'He also wants a key to Philip's house so they can go over it again for evidence. I don't suppose they know any more than before but it must be routine to keep the nearest and dearest informed of progress or the lack of it. I expect I'll not be gone long, probably less than an hour. I'll tell you everything he says. Okay?'

Tania sat at the desk across from me and smiled.

'Mum will be about another ten minutes or so as she's seen a nice dress in Littlewoods shop,' said this little tease. But I did enjoy her company. There was no pretend on her part and she clearly showed her affection for me. She was too young at sixteen but I could take her seriously in a few years' time. And my mum thought she was okay and had hinted strongly in that direction.

'Would you like a cup of tea now or will you wait for your mum?' I asked.

'Don't worry I'll make it Ashley, and I'll make one for mum when she comes in; she could be ages.'

'Don't expect to get paid for any work you do in here,' I said jokingly.

She poked her tongue out at me before going through to the back room and kitchen just as a customer walked in the front door.

I have never gone up to my customers and asked them if they needed help. I might just as well go up to them and ask them if they needed help in thinking. Or could I offer them a new brain or something. No, I just gave an acknowledgement nod and let them wander around the shop or the sign-posted museum upstairs if they wished. If they had an enquiry then they could come and ask. There had never been a case of theft so far. And if there had been I could recover the item soon enough.

Tania came out with two mugs of tea just as her mum walk into the shop.

'Is one of those mugs for me?' she smiled and gave me a hello kiss.

'Not unless you've started taking one sugar in your tea mum,' said Tania laughing. 'The kettle's boiled so I'll pour yours in a jiff.'

Tania and I both had one teaspoon of sugar in our tea.

I told Milly what it was about and how I appreciated her sitting in at such short notice. I was in no hurry so we chatted around the desk for a good few minutes while we drank our tea.

I had a spare key to Philips house and put it in my coat pocket before leaving for the police station. I promised to phone when I was leaving there.

It didn't take me long to find detective Mark Solomon and we went in to one of the back rooms at the station. I had to wear a visitor's badge as a matter of routine.

'We have made some progress and have two suspects in custody who are helping us with our enquiries,' said the detective.

'This has developed in a most curious fashion,' he continued. 'It would seem that a sort of divine intervention has come about.'

He seemed a bit embarrassed as he gave me details of what I already knew. He explained about Brian and Ruby having a quiet drink at the Black Dog pub and how one of the suspects had sworn at the landlord when a drink had been spilled. It was then that the two witnesses had received their vision of all the events inside Philip's house when he was mugged and burgled. They had then reported this to the station and had been interviewed the next morning.

'The surprising thing is that as they were giving me their story I seemed to get the same images from them that they had been given. I can see it all as though I was in the room while it was all taking place,' said Mark.

I then let him give me the whole episode in his own words. He went on to say that he had obtained a search warrant for two premises and had recovered an omega watch and a gold ring from one of them. Both had an engraving on them.

He opened a drawer in the desk and took out a folder which he opened. He showed me two photos which I instantly recognised as Andy Braid and Mark Tamper but I pretended not to know them.

'These are the two suspects,' he said. 'They have been in trouble with us before but only for petty things like breaking into cars and pickpocket thievery. I believe this case might have become just another one of their thieving adventures but for the fact that one of them kicked Mr Stevens in the head so viciously causing his death. I know they are guilty as do my two witnesses Brian and Ruby. And unless I can get them to confess to their crime I will need to gather evidence that will stand up in a court of law. Do you by any chance recognise the watch and the ring?'

I picked up the watch which I had seen Mark Tamper take possession of and turned it over. On the back was a neatly engraved 'D McGill' in straight print. The gold ring was a size L and had a date engraved on the inside. The date was 27.8.27 which I instantly knew to be the date that Grace and David had been married. It had been a Saturday and they had been married at 2 o'clock in the Dudley church of St Anne's. Although Philip had never mentioned or shown me the watch or ring I knew that Grace had given the watch to Philip when David had passed away. Years later when Grace had taken ill she had given the ring off her finger to Philip for him to keep for her for when she came out of the hospital. She had lost so much weight that the ring had become quite loose and she feared losing it. She never recovered and Philip kept the ring in memory of his beloved sister.

I told detective Solomon all of this and he wrote out a statement for me to sign. I think he just wanted confirmation from a witness that the items belonged to Philip. He had already seen the items being taken in his vision of the crime and knew they had come from the house.

I then handed over the front door key to Philip's house and I knew that he would get the crime people to concentrate in particular areas according to the facts as he could see them. I asked what was to happen with the two suspects.

'Well,' he said, 'I now have the proof I need that they were at the crime scene. I shall have a word with the super and if he gives the okay, which I am sure he will, I shall charge these two with criminal damage to property and involuntary manslaughter. I don't think they intended to murder Mr Stevens when they entered the house but since that is what resulted then they must bear responsibility for it.'

'Will the case go before a judge and jury?' I asked.

'It's too early to say,' said Mark. 'Firstly we need to charge them. Then they will need to get a solicitor to represent them. And if we can show them enough evidence they might just lodge a guilty plea. They will then need to be presented before a judge for sentencing. This could all take upto a year and in the meantime they might even get bail if their solicitor knows his stuff. Even then for a charge of manslaughter and the fact that they have saved the court's time if they plead guilty, they might get maybe two to four years in prison. This means that they could be out in a little over a year. Those are the facts young man and there is nothing we can do about it.'

I said nothing but the detective could read the stunned expression on my face. I wonder what Philip would have thought about it all. And then my inner voice came through. It said it really was an accident and to let it go.

Nothing could change that. There was a great task ahead but that was many years away. I must focus upon that and develop accordingly.

I asked detective Mark Solomon when the watch and ring would be returned. He said they would be retained as evidence so long as the case was in hand. After that they would be returned to the estate of Mr Stevens. He then stood up and put his hand out towards me and thanked me for coming in so promptly. He said he hoped to get the house key returned to me within the week. If they could get some DNA evidence then the case could be wrapped up quite quickly. I shook his hand and he led the way to the front door of the station. Once again he said thanks and turned around and went back inside.

Back at the shop Milly was quite excited. She had made a big sale. I looked around and straight away noticed that the Chelsea factory white glazed tawny owl was not in its usual spot. It had been here since I first joined Philip and although I thought it might fetch about £3000 on a good day at auction I had marked it down at £1950. I felt it was time we parted with it.

'This chap came in just after you had left, Ashley,' said Milly. 'I'd say he was in his fifties and ever so well dressed and spoken. I said I was minding the shop for the owner and he had a wander around for a bit. He gave a big 'Aargh' when he saw the chipped owl thing and came round to examine it. He asked if he could handle it and I said it was okay. He seemed to be in some ecstasy as he was turning it over and over in his hands. He asked how much we were asking for it and I pointed to the description card. He read the card twice over and I heard him give a sort of a whistle as he read the price.'

I knew that the card read that craftsman Rolly Hopkins had made it in the winter of early 1751. He was then 45 years old, a bachelor who lived in one of the tied cottages up the hill a mile or so away from the Chelsea factory. The card also said that a small piece had broken off the rocky mound base.

Milly went on. 'He said was I sure that this was the price. I saw what it said and thought it a bit high but then I don't know anything about antiques do I? So I said everything was as marked and he said fine. He then asked if I preferred a cheque or credit card payment. I said cheque as I'm not too familiar with these credit card contraptions.'

Milly opened the desk drawer and gave me the cheque and a business card of a Mr. Clive Davidson, a stockbroker at the London Exchange.

'He said he was just passing through from Mansfield where he had been visiting friends. They said they'd had dealings with you and recommended a visit to the shop,' she said.

'I think it must have been the Priors,' I said. 'I remember a couple of years ago their mother or aunt had gone into residential care and they were selling off the contents of her house. I advised them on the real price of some of their items. There were some Windsor bow backed chairs and an oak dresser that were quite valuable. I remember they gave me a gift in return, a pair of brass George III candlesticks. I made them promise to visit me here at McGill's and they did visit a few months later. They have three children, two girls and a boy with names all starting with M. I remember now it was Gary Prior and wife Jill and children Malcolm, Mary and Maura. Goodness what a small world.'

I then thanked Milly for helping out and especially for making the sale. I said if she worked here she would be entitled to a commission on all the sales she made as part of her employment contract.

Tania said, 'Mum was really good. She and this chap were chatting away like old friends. I wish I could talk to strangers like that. By the way who's for a cup of tea?'

'Yes please,' came in unison from Milly and me.

While we were sipping our tea I read Milly's thoughts that she was seriously considering my partial job offer. I'd bring it up again later on. She might want to think longer on it.

'How's your Eric?' asked Milly.

'Well he is going to be 78 this year and I think he tires easily,' I said. 'He's only helping out because I need him to until I can get a proper assistant. Philip and granddad were about the same age and both were getting on a bit. Philip often had his forty winks in the armchair in the back room. I had to do the same the other day after a day of driving around sorting things out. But I do need someone and quite soon too.'

I decided to jump in with both feet and ask Milly if she would step in for a while. I had the oddest feeling that mother and daughter both knew what I was about to propose.

'May I ask you something Milly?' I said.

'If it's about me working here then the answer is yes,' she said with a big smile. 'I was wondering when you were going to ask me. Only the other day Jerry and I had been discussing this very issue. Tania has wanted to come here every day and we have had to stop her from disturbing you. She just wants to chat and we can't have that. I told Jerry that if you offered me a job I'd take it. I wasn't sure how I'd like it but then a job is a job and I'd also be helping a friend. And today when I sold that tatty old white owl I got a real buzz from the experience. I know I'm going to like doing this.'

'Do you know Milly,' I said 'this is the oddest thing. When I first came to the shop to meet Philip, that white owl was the first thing I picked up and Philip asked if I liked it. It was his favourite piece then. We discussed its origins and it was on the basis of that discussion that he offered me a position. That owl has a lot to answer for. And I will make you the same offer that Philip made to me. I remember his words well. He said, 'You run this shop as you see fit and after a year if you can make it profitable I shall make you an equal partner.'

'That doesn't quite apply now but the principle is the same. I don't need just an assistant; I need a partner and confederate. So I'll make you a similar offer. If you like running the shop then you will be an equal partner after a year. And thank you Milly for saying yes. But what do we do about the brat?'

'Less of the 'brat' sir or I shan't make you another cup of tea,' laughed Tania, 'and then again I might just put rat poison in it.'

She then came up to me and gave me a big hug and a wet kiss on my left cheek. I think I was blushing when Milly came and did the same. It all felt like one big happy family. I had a warm feeling in my chest from the affection I felt for these two.

'Don't worry about Tania,' said Milly. 'She has college to go to and Jerry and I both insist she get a degree before she starts any kind of a job. Of course I shall be glad of her presence here whenever she can find time. I know you need to travel around a lot all over the country collecting antiques and that is at it should be. I shall be here every day from now on so you needn't worry any more.'

I said thanks again and we talked about her salary being on a commission basis just as mine had been with Philip.

'But what happened at the police station?' asked Tania. 'Tell us all.'

So I gave a detailed account of everything detective Mark Solomon said and the names and description of the two suspects. In the next instant Tania was her bubbly self again and listened eagerly to everything I had to say.

I told them all that had occurred at the police station and of the two suspects Andy Braid and Mark Tamper who had been arrested. I said that the police had retrieved Philip's omega watch and a wedding ring that belonged to his sister Grace from the house of the suspect Mark Tamper. I mentioned the part that Brian and Ruby had played in the arrest and that detective Mark Solomon thought they had a very good case. Tania gave me a very funny look when I mentioned how the two witnesses Brian and Ruby had received their visions in the Black Dog pub. I tried to read her thoughts but that inner voice of mine said not to.

I said that the police had asked for a key to Philip's house as they now knew what to look for. They hoped to get additional forensic evidence to build a water tight case against the two suspects. All we could do was await the results and hope that justice would be served as best as possible.

When I mentioned that the two muggers could be out on the streets again in just over a year after conviction, both Milly and Tania said what a rotten system we had in this country. In the eyes of the law it was after all just a burglary that had gone terribly wrong.

But I had my own plans for Andy Braid and Mark Tamper which I hoped to initiate as soon as they were out on police bail which I was sure would happen in the next week or two. Cases seldom came to court inside a year and there wasn't room to hold every suspect in a police cell. But this plan was known to my immediate family only. I could not as yet include Milly or Tania in that confidence.

The weeks went by and I stayed with Milly in the shop coaching her generally with regard to the antiques on the shelves. I gave her little bits of detail about the pieces telepathically and buoyed her interest on a wider scale as well. Although Milly had developed a keen interest in the pieces themselves she came to love the knowledge that grew with it. This only made her keen to learn more and I helped by implanting additional bits of information in her brain without her guessing what was happening. And I also quite enjoyed my own part in her development. I enjoyed it the more when I sensed that Philip would have been pleased at what I was doing.

Although Philip was not present physically I sensed his presence and was keen for his approval. I knew that no matter what I did with regard to Andy Braid or Mark Tamper he would not have berated me for my actions. I couldn't help remembering those remarks about compassion and justice. Forgiveness was greater than vengeance and that mercy and justice went hand in hand. But I'm afraid that although I felt no anger against the two muggers I felt no compassion for them either. For the moment however justice must be served. I hoped to do it in a way that would not only teach them a lesson but might also convert them to better ways. I remembered the bullies at school and how their energies had been channelled away from their bullying ways. Perhaps I could achieve something similar with these two. I would certainly try my best. A bit of fear and a bit of superstition just might work.

Granddad was still not well when I went to see him. And when I gave him the news that Milly was doing very well and how I had been coaching her he said he was pleased and relieved. But he said he quite enjoyed the time he had spent with me in the shop. Then he asked how Tania was and I could see a twinkle in his eye.

'I like her very much granddad,' I said, 'but she is only sixteen and I don't think I quite feel that way towards her just yet. I like her company but she can't half carry on. I just saw a humorous card in a shop that made me laugh. It said women talk even when no one is listening and men talk even though they have nothing to say.'

We both laughed at that.

But I suddenly got my inner voice telling me that granddad was more ill than we imagined. And that he should go into hospital and get his chest x-rayed. The diagnosis that came at me was that granddad had a touch of pneumonia in one of the lobes of his left lung. There was also some fibrous tissue in this same lung.

Somehow I knew that all would be well and that Eric would be back to his normal old self. He had a good few years ahead of him.

And so granddad went into hospital for treatment. He was two weeks in an isolated ward. After the first lot of antibiotics there was considerable improvement and when he was discharged it was on the condition that he didn't live alone for the next six weeks. Pneumonia takes longer to heal when you are 77 years old. Mum took over and gave granddad my room for the duration. The hospital made an appointment to see granddad in three months time. As far as the fibrous tissue was concerned there was nothing that could be done about that. It was a small area but needed watching. It had probably been caused by breathing welding fumes and dust during granddad's sheet metal working days.

We all took it in turns to visit when granddad was in hospital. I went every other day. I tried communicating long range from Dudley but without success. However mum rang me after her visits to say he was fine. Once he was home with mum and dad I went every evening which also gave me the chance of seeing my parents and Katy. I think mum would always remember me as her little boy who was now all grown up. I didn't mind in the least when she cupped my face in her warm gentle palms before kissing me on both cheeks every time. I missed her in my busy life.

It was while granddad was in hospital that I received news from Detective sergeant Mark Solomon that Andy Braid and Mark Tamper had both been released on police bail with conditions. They had to report once a week to the Hill Street police station and were not allowed to travel outside the county. One missed attendance and they would both be remanded back into custody. If they found employment then their employer could phone in on their behalf every week and attendance by them personally would be reduced to once a month.

I decided to begin with Andy Braid who lived with his parents. I suspected that he was getting the cold shoulder treatment from them ever since I had transmitted those images of their son's role in Philip's mugging into their minds. But before I could put my plan into action I had to see inside the house and get a firm visual of where everything was. And so early one morning I parked in Yew Tree Crescent a few doors away from number 57 and waited. I could have gone pink and just entered but things tended to become rather misty in pink mode and I wanted a clear sense of the interior. The first to leave was the father, Keith. He worked as a shop assistant at W H Smith and had to be on duty at 9:00am. The mother, Heather was a housewife and left the house about an hour later trailing a shopping bag on wheels beside her. She looked back up at the upstairs window and shook her head in disgust. I imagined that her layabout Andy was still in bed and probably fast asleep.

I decided not to wait any longer and with my usual skill pushed the lock open and entered the house. It had a small hallway with little waist high cupboards either side of the door. I imagined these housed the electric and gas meters. There was a telephone sitting on the right cupboard top with a few pens and a note pad. I was looking for items I could move easily without injuring anyone. The stairs were on the left and led to three bedrooms. On the right was a door which led into the front living room. It was very neat and tidy; obviously Heather was very house proud. Opposite the door was a fireplace with a neat mantel above it. This was crowded with lots of ornaments and a couple of tall brass vases. It would be a shame to knock them over onto the marble plinth below. A set three-piece furniture suite comprised the rest of the room with a standard lamp and large old TV set in one corner. There were three framed photos sitting on top of the TV and if knocked over would simply fall onto the thick lush carpet below.

The back room was the dining area with a three pronged brass candle holder in the centre of the dining table. There were four chairs tucked in close to the table. There was a long low sideboard along one wall on which were placed pictures and trays and two empty trumpet shaped brass vases. I noticed that someone was fond of their brasses as all had a high degree of polish to them. There was plenty here for me to knock over when the time came.

The kitchen was next and I noted that most items and been put away into cupboards and drawers. But the window shelf did have a few ornaments not to mention two small brass single candle holders. The top drawer was the cutlery drawer and I noticed that they were loosely placed in a wooden cutlery tidy. I shut the drawer and gave little pushes with my mind. The cutlery rattled inside the drawer and I got the impression that a mouse might be running around in there. Excellent I thought.

Then went pink and walked up the misty stairs as I didn't want any creaking to wake the sleeper.

I had a quick misty look in the bathroom and then went into the back bedroom. Still in pink mode I went into the front bedroom where the sleeping Andy lay. I came out of pink and stood very still and looked around the room.

It was an untidy mess but I noted where all the moveable items were. Of main note was the push button HiFi unit on the dresser. I made a note of each button so that I could operate it by 'remote control' so to speak when the time came.

I had seen enough and decided to begin by waking up this lazy thief. I went pink again and took hold underneath the base of the bed and gave a quick flick upwards. As I watched, the bed seemed to rotate upwards in very slow motion. I made a quick retreat out of the house and back to the car before I returned to normal. I heard the crash and a yell of surprise from the house and I smiled with satisfaction. I got in the car and drove to the shop.

Milly was there alone and pleased to see me. She asked after my granddad Eric. I then told her about the two muggers being on police bail. Milly said that Loraine Hollings, the bakery manager had been across and had given her the news. She had also brought a bag of doughnuts and had sat and chatted over a cup of tea. Milly said she seemed really nice and friendly and was surprised that they had not met before this. I told Milly that Lorraine had been a special friend to Philip over many years and had even known the original McGills couple, Grace and David. I said I would be in for the rest of the day and what would she like to learn about next. But just then about ten school girls, all in their early teens came in with a youngish looking male teacher. They asked if they could visit the museum part of the shop upstairs. Milly said they were welcome and she would be happy to answer any questions about the items up there. Everything was properly labelled and I was sure they'd have no trouble. Their teacher said they were from Hillcrest School on Simms Lane and had heard about this place being part museum as it was just around the corner from them. The students often spent their free time around here he said as this was a popular part of Dudley. He introduced himself as Noor Mahsud and when I looked puzzled he said his mother was English and father Egyptian. I was tempted to read his mind and acquire his history but thought better of it. I watched as they trooped up the stairs.

'Let's have a cup of tea and some of those doughnuts,' said Milly which I thought was a great idea as I was rather famished. I had noticed that whenever I use my gifts I tended to feel either hungry or sleepy. I think I must use up tremendous amounts of energy in the process. I wonder what it would be like when that really big task that my inner voice mentioned comes along. I hope I'm prepared for it whenever that is.

'Yes please,' I said to Milly, 'I think I could eat at least three or four.'

She laughed as Tania walked in the door.

'That child can smell doughnuts from a mile away,' laughed Milly. 'But I think we have enough here. That Lorraine is generous with her baking.'

I got my usual hug and two kisses and a questioning look.

'Where were you this morning Ashley? Mum had to open up all by herself,' asked Tania.

'O there was something I had to attend to,' I said.

I then told Tania that I had been curious about the two muggers being released on police bail and I had wanted to get a look at them. I told her I had seen Andy Braid walking from his house on Yew tree Crescent and that tomorrow I hoped to get a look at the other one. It was all just curiosity I said. I wasn't going to do anything foolish I assured her.

I felt easy that what I told her was at least partly true. I felt that there was more to Tania than was apparent. I would have thought that after her conversation with Katy about what I had done in my childhood regarding catching birds and all, and then with Tania listening in to my Christmas conversation with Aunt Brenda that she would begin to ask embarrassing questions about my talents. But it seems as though she has either put it out of her mind as ridiculous or has just forgotten it all as an imagined event. I personally think that she didn't want any blemish on our relationship and expects me to confess all at the appropriate time. That might well be the scenario that eventually develops. One must live for the present and not worry about what might or might not occur in the future. If we knew the future then that would just ruin the present. At least that is how I view it.

The doughnuts really were delicious and I had the prescribed three. Tania made a second round of tea and we passed the time pleasantly.

The Hillcrest students spent about three quarters of an hour upstairs in the museum and one of them wished to make a purchase. It was a little Dinky Toy model of a pale blue 1948 Austin A40 Dorset and still in its original box. The girl said her name was Vanesh Patel and that her father often talked about the Austin A40 car he'd had in India before he came here. They had a framed photo of it on their mantel and although it was a black and white print she had heard her father mention the colour as being sky blue. The price marked for it was £25 and the girl said she didn't have that much on her.

I felt a great deal of sympathy for the girl but we are a business and I said so. But I also said for her to speak to the lady manageress and see what accommodation could be arranged. I winked at Milly and withdrew to the back room. I was happy for Milly to deal with the sale in any way she felt proper. Five minutes later a quiet developed in the front room as all the Hillcrest students left and Milly walked in flushed and smiling.

'Another one bites the dust,' she said jubilantly. And she put a pile of coins and a £10 note on the table.

'There should be exactly £25 there,' she said. 'Her friends all chipped in to lend her the money. And the teacher added the rest and said he would make sure Vanesh paid everyone back. The £10 note was from him. I think she must be a popular girl as everyone was quite happy to give everything they had. I was going to ask her for a deposit or even an IOU note but it never came to that. I'm pleased for her sake and I'd love to see the look on her dad's face when she gives him the box with the car in it. I bet he puts it next to the photo on the mantel at home. I feel better about this sale than I did about the owl.'

I knew exactly how Milly felt and gave her my congratulations on a good sale. Today had been a good day for business. Since all items are clearly marked up for history as well as price, many purchases are made with the item being handed over for wrapping and a credit card presented for payment. Pin numbers are entered and the transaction goes through. Everyone is happy with the fair exchange. And it was my task to ensure that the shelves were adequately stocked with lots of interesting items.

There was to be a large fair at Trentham House and Garden next month and I thought it might be a good idea to make a picnic of the day with all our friends and go there. We might pick up something for the museum or even a genuine antique or two. There had been a couple of house clearances that I had missed because of my preoccupation with the two muggers. I now needed to get around again and collect a few bargains. There was always the Gloucester Docks and the six storey antiques and curios place there for picking up items of nostalgic interest. Perhaps Milly might like to do that trip on her own or with Tania.

'How would you and Tania like a day out shopping?' I suggested to Milly.

I was confident in her ability to recognise an antique bargain and some things of interest for the museum upstairs. Of course I'd first have to get her a charge card in her own name on the business account. That would be one of my tasks for tomorrow.

'That would be nice. I could do with a nice new pair of black courts,' she said jokingly. 'Please explain what it is you have in mind.'

'Gloucester Docks,' I said. 'There are a few curio places there and perhaps you and Tania could drive down for the day and see what you can pick up. But first I need to get you a debit card on the business. You will also need a few of your own introductory business cards. There's a machine in the market precinct that makes them quite well. You can put 'associate partner' for your descriptive title. You could plan the visit for mid-week in a fortnight's time?'

Tania came out of the kitchen and said, 'What's happened?' in a concerned voice when she saw her mum standing open-mouthed and staring aghast at Ashley.

Milly then turned around and looked at her daughter. She was blinking back the wetness that had appeared in the corners of her eyes but she had a smile that stretched from ear to ear.

'Ashley has just suggested we go shopping; a buying trip for the shop, just you and me Tania. What do you say to that?' said Milly in a husky voice.

'That would be great mum,' she said. 'But I don't know anything about antiques. I suppose I could learn as I go along. I hope it's a nice sunny day when we go.'

It was the middle of March and the days were improving rapidly. The clocks would go forward in a fortnight and then there would be Easter. Spring had come early this year and the countryside was a riot of yellow Daffodils. The grass verges beside most roads were packed tight with Wordsworth's 'host of golden daffodils'. Someone had even planted a few on the motorway embankments.

'I'm sure you can choose a day that's sunny and nice,' I said. 'And don't forget that for anything that is fragile you can arrange to have delivered on their insurance.'

Tania looked at me and then said in a low voice, 'Ashley, you are a nice man, isn't he mum? I think I'd like another cup of tea, anybody else for one?'

Milly and I both said yes.

And I felt quite pleased how things had gone today.

When we closed up shop later I said I'd be in as usual tomorrow.

Granddad was not coughing as much this evening and we sat watching the football on the telly together and passing the usual derogatory remarks at the mistakes being made by both players and referee. Mum stood watching us before calling us in to the dining room. Granddad was an easy person to get along with and I think mum was enjoying herself in looking after his needs. I had been coming over every day and had not seen so much telly in a long time. Granddad was however getting restless and talked about returning to his own place next week. I think he'd be happier there and not have to be on his best social behaviour, if you know what I mean!

Next morning I got to the shop well before nine but Milly was already there and going around giving the place a light dusting with her feather duster. I wanted to visit Mark Tamper's flat in Hockley Lane about midday. I was hoping that he would have gone out so I could go into the flat at my leisure.

Milly and I spent a pleasant morning and we were asked for a descriptive tour of the museum by another group of young children from the same Hillcrest School. I let Milly do the honours and it didn't take long as she was down again in fifteen minutes.

'I showed them around and explained where everything was and that all items had a detailed description. I said for them to take their time and enjoy themselves. I think they have been set a project about inventions or toys of the past or something of the sort,' she said.

I said I was going to pop in to the bank to arrange her charge card and maybe bring back a form for her to sign. At the bank the lady at the desk gave me the procedure and a large folded form for Milly and myself to sign. They asked if Milly had an account with this bank because if she didn't then that made it more complicated. However both needed to be at the bank together to sign the computer screen face-sheet in the presence of a bank official.

Back at the shop we both filled in and signed the form. Milly did have an account there so that made matters simple. Since the bank was literally around the corner on High Street we waited until there was a lull in visitors and locked the front door to the shop with a note saying 'Back in 20 minutes'.

In fact we were back in just a bit over but the business had been concluded satisfactorily and Milly should get her card in a week to ten days.

And no guesses for who was waiting at the front door when we got back.

'Where have you two been?' smiled Tania. 'Up to no good if I'm not surprised.'

I just smiled at her and said, 'Curb your imagination miss nosey, we've been to the bank for your mum's business card. What did you think? If you'd been here a minute earlier we could have left the shop open. And why aren't you at college miss truant?'

'That's two names you've called me, Ashley Bonner,' said a smiling Tania, 'I'll not forgive you for that. Besides today is my tutorial day and I do not have to see old Miss Maltby till two o'clock this afternoon? Anyway I came to see how you were doing and I find you both out gallivanting. But I'll forgive you if you get some of Mrs. Hollings' doughnuts while I make the mugs of tea.'

At about noon I left mother and daughter and drove to 216A Hockley Lane. I listened telepathically and noted that Mark Tamper's flat was empty. I went in through the front door in pink mode as I didn't want anyone to see me enter. Once inside I returned to normal and spent a few minutes checking the layout. The place was a mess of untidiness in every corner. Obviously Mark was not a fanatic for neatness. I left the flat and as I was returning to the car I had an idea. So I went back into the flat and did a job of tidying the place up. But I rearranged where everything had been. I moved the bed to a spot on the other side of the room and so on. In the kitchen cum diner I repositioned the table into a corner and switched around whatever there was in the cupboards. I also moved things around in the fridge. Items that were on the top shelf I put in a lower one and vice versa. There was a large portable style HiFi unit on the worktop and I noted that it had the old type round control knobs. The on/off knob worked clockwise for on and volume control. I found I could turn it on telekinetically by concentrating a push on the lower half of the knob. Similarly I could turn it off by pushing on the upper half.

There was a small bathroom with a half sized bathtub and hand held shower. I decided to leave a message on the bath mirror. I rubbed my fingers in my hair and wrote 'Boo' on it. Only nothing was visible now but would be when the mirror steamed up, except for where the word was written with my slightly oily finger.

I was pleased by the time I left the flat. The first phase was in place.

On returning to the shop I found Milly on her own. Tania had gone off to college for her tutorial class. It had been a good day for the sale of both antiques from down here as well as from the museum upstairs. We definitely needed to add to our stock. We should pick up a fair bit from both Trentham and Gloucester Docks within the next month. I might even make a trip to the continent next month. There were Fairs held in all the major towns in Holland during the spring when people tended to have a clear-out of old items during a general house tidying process.

That evening I went into the Black Swan and sat in a corner nursing a lone shandy and today's Daily Mail. I was ready to leave after nearly two hours when the pair walked in. They were in a heated discussion over something. Andy was insisting that forces unknown had tipped him out of his bed the other morning and had told his mum everything that had occurred the night they burgled that old geezer's place in Griffin Street.

'Rubbish,' I heard Mark say, 'there's no such thing. It's all in your imagination Andy. Don't worry it won't happen again, you'll see.'

It was obvious that Mark had not been back to the flat since my visit of the afternoon.

You should have seen the expression on their faces when they both heard my telepathic message that said, 'Just wait and you will see my dear chaps, just you wait and see. I'll not leave you alone until I see some remorse.' And I followed this with a bit of telepathic hollow laughter.

Mark shook his head as if to say someone was playing tricks. But Andy definitely looked worried.

They bought their pints and sat at a table for four to one side of the room against the inner wall away from the windows with their backs to me. I wanted to move their glasses but couldn't risk any telekinetic action as I might apply too much force. So I went pink, walked to their table and physically picked up both glasses and placed them at the far end of the rectangular table. I then returned to my table and back to normal mode.

'F--ken hell,' said Andy loudly in a panic, 'did you see who moved our glasses Mark? It's that thing that just spoke to us. I'm not staying in here; I'm off home and having a word with mum and dad about this. It's absolutely weird.'

And with that he got up and left the Black Swan. Mark stayed and finished his drink before also leaving about twenty minutes later. When he got to his flat he was in for a surprise.

I decided to call it a day and went home. I made myself a snack dinner and after an hour of telly I went to bed. I had a lovely dream too. I dreamt of all our family and friends and it was Christmas again and we were all chattering and laughing. And the best part was that Philip was there as well telling one of his national service yarns and having everyone in splits of laughter. I woke in the middle of the night to use the bathroom and when I got back into bed I tried to get the dream to continue but of course that was quite impossible. I lay awake for a long time before returning to a dreamless sleep. When I awoke it was light and somehow my pillow seemed damp. I remember that just before I dropped off again last night I'd been thinking how I missed Philip's presence and the way he gazed at you over the rim of his specs with that twisted smile. I remember my eyes welling up just before I must have gone to sleep. The thoughts and tears must have continued as I slept.

On my way to the shop I went via 216A Hockley Lane and 57 Yew Tree Crescent. It was not quite half past eight in the morning and I knew it was far too early for both Andy and Mark. I stopped the car opposite each of their houses in turn and turned on their radios at a good volume. I didn't wait to see or hear their reactions and went straight to my usual parking spot near the shop.

Milly was just opening up when I arrived and we went in together after first waving to Loraine Hollings who was standing outside the Bakery window checking her display. We had a surprising call from Gary Prior in Mansfield. We had a nice chat and during the conversation he mentioned Mr. Clive Davidson, a stockbroker at the London Exchange who had visited recently and made a purchase of a white glazed tawny owl. I remembered it well and asked Gary if there had been a complaint.

'To the contrary,' he said. 'Clive was extremely pleased with his purchase and has made a tidy profit from its sale at Sotheby's. There was great interest in the owl and it finally went for nearly £3000. Your descriptive plaque was part of the sale and there was some talk that it might have been invented, but no one had a care to say so. Anyway Clive said he'd like to visit you again and take you out to dinner. What should I tell him?'

'Please tell him he'd be very welcome as always and thanks for the generous offer of dinner. That would be great. And when shall I see you and your lovely family again Gary?' I said.

'Why don't you come and see us when you are on one of your antiques forays. There's a big car boot sale in a field near us come Sunday fortnight. Come up and spend Saturday night with us and we can go there together in the morning.'

I said that was very kind and I'd be happy to accept. I'd see him on Saturday fortnight.

When I told Milly about the owl she gave a whistle and seemed ever so pleased.

'And there I thought he was paying too much for it,' said Milly smiling. 'I think I'm beginning to like this antiques business more and more.'

Milly was perfect for this job and it was growing on her. I think she was beginning to like it and her enthusiasm was rubbing off on Tania as well.

Over the next few days I repeated my visits to Hockley Lane and Yew Tree Crescent; sometimes twice a day and even late at night on two occasions. I turned their radios on and got them to play at high volume. I tended to concentrate a bit more on Andy as I reckoned that he was quite on the edge. I knocked the tall brass vases off the mantel in the front living room which caused them to make an awful racket on the marble plinth below. I also rattled the cutlery in the kitchen drawer repeatedly which quite upset the mother who would yell at Andy that this was entirely his fault for kicking that poor man in the head. I knew when they were watching TV from the flashing tones of light through the curtains and caused the three photo frames to topple onto the carpet one by one. I did the same to the vases and pictures on the low sideboard in the dining room in a random manner.

I think the parents were exerting their high morals influence on Andy and there was nothing he could do but listen. And gradually it all started to make sense.

Andy went to the local Job Centre but had no qualifications or skills and therefore couldn't apply for any of the jobs on the board. However when he expressed a serious desire to work, egged on by his father Keith, he was sent on a government scheme to train as a brick layer. He also stopped meeting up with Mark Tamper in the evenings.

After a fortnight of supposedly ghostly goings on in the Braid household all became quiet when I stopped my visits there. I had noticed that on Sunday morning the Braid family went out at about ten o'clock all dressed in their best. I guessed that Heather and Keith were taking their son with them to their church service in a further bid to reform him. I decided I'd leave Andy alone from now on. I trusted his parents to continue to exert their good influence on their twenty year old son. They knew exactly what he had done that night to Philip.

Mark Tamper was a harder nut to crack. Whatever I did he seemed to take it in his stride. I couldn't switch on his radio any more as he unplugged it from the mains when it wasn't in use. When I caused things to fall to the floor he let them lie there and just pushed them to one side. He had thought nothing of all that tidying and shifting around that I had done. Frankly I was stumped what to do about him. He was twenty six years old and had never done a days work since leaving school at fifteen. Reading his mind I found that he had two older sisters but had lost touch with them early on. The father was a truck driver and often beat his wife who was part Spanish. And occasionally he beat them as well if the mood took him. He never held a job for long on account of his drinking and turning up for work much the worse for it. He would be fine when he started a new job and impressed his employers with his on time deliveries. But he reverted gradually to his old ways as the job lost its initial fascination. It all ended in a dense fog pile-up on the M6 one winter's night. It was not his fault and his was the sixth or seventh vehicle to plough into the tangle of wreckage. Five drivers lost their lives that night and he was one of them. Mark was fourteen then and his eldest sister Janet had left home and was working as a holiday rep for Thomson's in Rome. She didn't come home for the funeral but phoned her mum and had a long loving chat instead. Both sisters were good at learning languages and spoke fluent Italian and Spanish. Both were unmarried though they had lived with men friends on occasion. Mark also spoke a bit of Spanish but not having spoken to his mother for so long he had lost a lot of it. The other sister had been a rep but got bored with the same company and turned to free-lance. She lived in Dublin and was in great demand by the holiday companies organising coach tours and the like, especially around the Emerald Isle.

Mark had at first been proud of his sisters in their successful lives. But this had turned to sour grapes when he found he couldn't find employment of a comparable sort. This turned to envy and finally hatred toward his sisters for their achievement and success. Mark then became bitter and vowed to get back at the system that gave him nothing.

I was quite puzzled as to how I should go about his conversion.

Granddad had gone back to his own place at the start of this week so I went to see how he was getting along. It was quite late by the time I got there and mum, dad and Katy were also visiting. It was a pleasant get together and we chatted about things in general. Granddad looked quite well and he had his usual easy manner and humour.

'So what's bothering you Ash,' said granddad. He seemed to be able to read my moods, and I was rather preoccupied with this Mark business.

To save time I telepathically conveyed all that had gone on in the last fortnight to all in the room; my success with Andy Braid, the shop business and Milly's keen attitude and then my failure with Mark. I included his family history too.

'He's had a rotten childhood so who can blame him for the way he has turned out,' said mum. 'But then his sisters are doing quite well so it must be something in his genes.'

Mum had always said people were as they are from before they were born. She firmly believed that you were what your genes dictated. Your likes, dislikes, moods and orientation towards the arts or crime were governed by your gene profile. She said that some people had the wrong genes for their sex. A man could have a female's genes and vice versa. As such mum tended to accept people as they were and understood why they behaved in the way they did. I suppose it was one way of looking at the world. I thought it a very understanding perspective.

It was a good discussion that followed but none of us could see how we could get Mark to change his ways. It was Katy who said something that made me think of a way. So far I had been trying to scare him into a frightened submission and conversion to decent ways. And it hadn't worked at all.

'Why don't you get him to re-learn his Spanish, and it shouldn't be too difficult for him since he did speak it as a child with his mum at home. Then he could also become a holiday Rep just like his sisters,' said Katy.

Now there might be a solution to the problem. A lot of his anger had started with his feeling of inferiority when he saw how well his sisters had done. If he were to do the same then perhaps it would go a long way to rectifying his criminal intent. The question was how to go about it and at the same time get him to feel remorse at Philip's death.

Again it was Katy who came up with a suggestion.

'Ashley,' she said, 'why don't you and I pretend to be from Madrid since we know so much about it, and start talking in Spanish within ear-shot of this Mark. We could verbally run down some fictitious holiday rep, say Julie something or other, and say what rubbish she was and they should get a proper tour guide instead. Someone who knew what they were talking about and who actually knew Madrid inside and out. Perhaps you could implant Madrid and Spanish in Mark's mind like you did with me.'

I thought about this but I didn't quite like the idea of rewarding someone like this thief when he hadn't shown any remorse with regards to Philip's death. I had read his mind and all that he felt was that it had happened and that it had simply been an unfortunate accident. As far as he was concerned all that they had gone out to do was a burglary and it was Andy who had been vicious and had beaten up the old man. Mark judged himself innocent since he did not class thievery as a serious crime.

I said all this to our little family group and received a general nod. Katy accepted that she was being over generous towards someone who had played a part in Philip's death but then she had another idea.

'I think he needs to be punished and I don't mean prison,' she said. 'I think I am suggesting that you inflict some sort of physical pain on him. Like pinch his ear or hit his shins or something. And at the same time make him realise that this is happening to him because of what happened to Philip. Maybe this is the way for you to sort out some of the other general violent trends that we see so much of in and around the city. You could sort out vandalism and things like that. Goodness Ashley, maybe this is how you should be using your gifts. You could gradually instil a guilty conscience type of thing into the criminal's mind and stop them doing bad things.'

I thought about this and instinctively felt that what Katy had said was extremely relevant. It would be like saying no to a naughty child and then following it up with a smack if it didn't listen. A connection had to be made between bad behaviour and a slight amount of physical pain.

'I think Katy has made a very good suggestion Ashley,' said mum. 'It is about time you began a mission of some sort and helped to point some of these youngsters in a proper direction. Do you know I'm half afraid to walk past a group of youths on the street when I'm on my own? And on the buses sometimes they misbehave so badly that I'm afraid to say anything in case they turn their anger on me. I know others on the buses feel the same way. You don't know if they are on drugs or something but we could certainly do with you in a situation like that. I know that children in general have loads of energy to let off but we never behaved like this when we were young.'

Both dad and granddad said they agreed with what mum had just said. And I couldn't help but see that mum was right and I could do something that might gradually alter this little bit of anarchy that seems to have crept into our society. Perhaps I didn't agree with the principle of physical punishment for children in schools but I had come to realise that a total sparing of the rod had resulted in the spoiling of the child to the extent that the quality of respect and discipline had declined considerably. Smacking of a recalcitrant child by a parent was still permitted and tolerated but less and less of parents resorted to it. All parents naturally love their children so an occasional smack is usually the last resort in a catalogue of misbehaviour. Enid Blyton's stories in her Book of Naughty Children always had a happy end result for the child in question. The bully didn't like it when he himself was bullied. The boy who pulled the tails of cats and dogs didn't like it when he himself magically grew a tail and got it pulled by all the boys and girls at school. And the two rough children who slapped and pushed and pulled other children's hair were taught a lesson when they were invited to a fairy party and were themselves treated to rough treatment as part of the party games. And there was the boy who threw stones and learnt his lesson when the animals he hit threw stones back at him. The moral behind these stories was that the children hadn't realised what they were doing until it was done back to them. The hurt they caused only became apparent to them when they themselves were at the receiving end.

And that is how I would conduct my own mission.

Next morning I went to the shop first and helped Milly reorganise some of the shelves. I knew that there were some items still stored away in the back bedroom at Philip's house. Milly and I discussed what we should do and we agreed to bring all of it here to the shop. If there was too much then I could store some at my place and Milly said she could do the same at hers.

I rang Hill Street police station and asked to speak to detective sergeant Mark Solomon. He came on the line immediately and when I enquired if he had finished with Philip's house and had they found anything he said yes and no. Yes they had finished with the house and I could have the keys back and no they had not been able to find anything more. No DNA, no other fingerprints, no nothing. In fact their case was not strong apart from the fact that they had retrieved the ring and watch from Mark Tamper's flat. His story was that he had bought them off this unknown guy in the pub.

I asked if it was alright for me to pick up some things from the house and he said they had finished with it as far as he could see. I mentioned that I intended to put the house up for sale as soon as probate had been finalised and he said that would be fine too as they had nothing further to investigate with regard to the house. I said I would drop by in ten minutes for the key if that was okay.

I picked up the key and DS Solomon walked with me to the door saying how sorry he was that no further progress had been made with regard to Andy and Mark.

'You and I know of their guilt,' he said. 'Unfortunately in the eyes of the law they have to be proved guilty beyond a shadow of a doubt. The evidence thus far would not carry much weight in court and a good lawyer would tear our case to shreds in minutes. I can see those two getting off unless for some reason they pleaded guilty of course.'

I then went to the house in Griffin Street and entered the house. I stood in the hallway for a few moments thinking how often Philip must have walked in the same door and stood just like this deciding whether to put the kettle on first or change into something more comfortable. There were so many memories in houses where people had come and gone over the years. I wondered what attachment a departed soul might hold for their old place of residence. Perhaps it didn't matter much about the house. The memories of the living times were probably the important thing. Perhaps the soul-of-pure-thought had other more important things to contend with.

I went from room to room thinking similar thoughts. There was more in the back bedroom than I had expected. The two wardrobes were quite full of antique knick-knacks; nothing priceless but all of value. In fact I could remember buying most of them on my journeys around the country. There had not been room at the shop so Philip and I had ferried them here. I had left them downstairs on the floor and Philip had said he'd find somewhere to store them later on. I'd have to make at least three trips in the car to get them all back to the shop. I could do this over three days as I liked coming into Philip's house. At the moment there was a cold feel to the place so I turned the central heating thermostat up to a setting of 20 centigrade. I also turned the hot water setting to constant.

I loaded up the car and Sarah Winfield from two doors down came over and asked how I was doing. She said she hadn't heard from the police at all recently and wondered how the case was going. She seemed keen to hear all the news so I invited her in for a cup of tea and then gave her all the latest details. She was angered that the two might get off but then again perhaps the police had the wrong men. The central heating had warmed the house up a treat so I turned the setting back down to fifteen. Sarah couldn't wait to get away as I'm sure she wanted to pass on her privileged information to all her friends. It was her little news scoop of the day.

Back at the shop Milly was quite taken with everything I'd brought back and amazed that even more had been left behind. She was all for going back right away to retrieve it all but I said I'd bring the rest back over the next two days. We needed to draw up descriptive cards for this lot in the first instance. Philip also had a good library of books on antiques in his house and I suggested we relocate them; some here and some in our respective houses.

That evening I returned to visit granddad. He was on his own this time and I didn't like the way he looked. He appeared tired and listless. I sat with him and watched TV while he dozed on and off. I made us mugs of tea but he only sipped his a few times before putting it to one side. Something was not quite right. I phoned mum and told her that granddad was poorly.

Mum and dad came over right away and the first thing mum did was to check his medication bottles and packets; all six of them. Mum said she didn't care for all the medication that had been prescribed while granddad had been in hospital and she was sure some of it was unnecessary.

'I think all these pills are counterproductive and have caused him to lose his appetite. I noticed he was gradually eating less and less at our place. I'm going to ring the doctor right this minute.'

Mum rang and the doctor said he'd come over right away. When he came he made an instant diagnosis that granddad was on a drug high. He knew the case well and granddad had been up to see him earlier in the week. He said that sometimes a drug might result in a delayed reaction and this is what he feels may have happened here.

'I think Eric has progressed very well and quite recovered from the pneumonia,' he said. 'I'm taking him off these three tablets especially this one.' And he held up a bottle with large blue and white coloured capsules. 'This one shouldn't be taken over any prolonged duration as it does have a side effect for some that can cause the symptoms that Eric seems to be suffering from. I also don't think he could have had much in the way of food and drink so it might be good if you can get him to eat something. And discontinue any of the other tablets till he is back to his normal self. He should be better by the morning.'

Mum said she'd stay and make sure Eric ate and drank something even if it was in dribs and drabs. The doctor said that would be great and left.

When mum made granddad a mug of tea he drank it down double quick. Mum winked at me and said she had made it with two sugars instead of the half that granddad usually had. Mum also brought out some jam biscuits and put them beside granddad. He seemed a bit better and offered them to us as well. We all joined in with mugs of tea.

Mum asked if I had eaten and when I said no she went into the kitchen and cooked up quite a bit of mince with curry spice added and boiled rice enough for four. I knew granddad liked his food Indian style as we'd often been out to the Balti places together ever since I can remember. We all sat at the table and I think granddad and I had the largest servings. Mum and dad I believe only kept us company to ensure granddad ate well. They had already had their tea before I'd rung.

I left for Dudley around midnight and by this time granddad was chatting more like his usual self. Mum said she'd stay the night in the other bedroom but she'd like granddad to move back to theirs for a few days at least. And so it was decided and accepted by granddad with a sheepish smile on his face.

'I thought I was a goner for a bit back there,' he said. 'I felt I was floating around in a mist and wasn't sure what was happening. Thanks Ash, I believe you came to my rescue. How's Milly doing?'

'She's fine granddad,' I said. 'She's taken to the antique business like a duck to water.'

I had already told him that but no harm in repeating it all again. Granddad often repeated many of his stories and I never let on that I had heard them before. But I was relieved that he was feeling better and even more that he looked better. Here was an area that I had no control over although my knowledge of medicine was the same as that I had acquired from Dr Mario Gonzalez's mind when he was caring for Philip. But I hadn't the practice or experience of it.

Next morning I phoned from the shop as Milly urged me to do and there was no reply from granddad's house so I rang mum on her mobile which didn't answer either. But Katy picked up when I rang the house and said mum had gone out to do a bit of a shop and that granddad was here with them and watching telly and doing fine. All this was in Spanish because Katy just loved practising whenever she had the opportunity. I said not to disturb him and to give him my love and I hung up.

I then told Milly I was off to bring back some more of Philip's treasures and took the opportunity to stop off at 216A Hockley Lane. I had decided to pay Mark Tamper a long overdue visit.

I entered the flat in my usual fashion and looked in to find Mark wet-shaving in the bathroom. As I was in pink mode all was very still and a bit misty. I took his left ear lobe between my thumb and index finger and gave it a slight pinch. Then again using thumb as anchor I lightly flicked my middle finger against his forehead. I did the same to both his shins but with a little more pressure. I also squeezed both his ankles lightly. I thought that should be enough for the first day. I would see what effect all this had with regards to the pain factor and raise or lower it on the next occasion. I left the flat and returned to the car and back to normal mode. I then sent out a telepathic message into Mark's consciousness to make him realise that the pain he felt was only a beginning as punishment for his complicity in Philip's death. I hoped to instil in his mind a feeling of superstitious guilt for behaviour that was considered as criminal.

I heard a faint but distinct pitiful yell from the flat that sounded like some zoo animal in a losing fight. I felt satisfied with the action I had finally taken.

Back at the shop Milly again helped me unload the antiques I had picked up from Philip's house and the rest of the day was spent writing out descriptive cards. Milly often asked me how I knew the history of every piece I picked up and all I said was that I must be psychic because it just all appeared in my mind as if by magic. She took a ring off her finger and asked what I thought of it.

It was an emerald and diamond ring with one missing diamond. The emerald was quite small as were the diamonds which were set in a cluster around it. All of these gave it a very neat and beautifully delicate appearance. It was made by a Matt Cockerill then aged fifty two in 1857 in the jewellery quarter in Hockley, Birmingham. It was retailed for the sum of three pounds ten and sixpence to a tea trader Matthew Phelps aged 41 as an engagement ring for his bride to be a Miss Helen Davis aged 19 the daughter of Roland Davis the butcher. The engagement was to last a year but they never did marry on account of the passing of Mr Phelps from a heart seizure. Miss Davis went on to marry her childhood sweetheart a young Mr Peter Oakhurst, a farm labourer. In subsequent years they had five robust children. The elder girl Emily inherited the ring and passed it on to her eldest daughter Mavis in 1909. Each time it went to a different surname through marriage until finally it came onto the finger of Millicent Thomas in 1978 when she became engaged to her very young and handsome sweetheart Jerry Marsh. The ring could be valued between £600 and £800 today.

'Please write all that down for me Ashley,' said Milly when I gave her the ring's history. 'That is absolutely fascinating. Tania will be quite taken by this since she will one day wear the ring too.'

Just then Tania walked into the shop and asked what we were talking about as she had heard her name mentioned.

'Ashley has just given me the history of this ring,' said Milly with glistening eyes. 'I'm going to have to begin a trace of our ancestry. I'm absolutely intrigued and can't wait to find out more about my great grandma and all.'

I was a bit embarrassed by all this so asked if anyone would like a mug of tea. Tania said she'd make it as usual after all that was all she was allowed to do. I had a sudden strong moment of regard for this girl; she never seemed to take offence at anything. She grew in my affection everyday. And I knew what Milly was thinking when she mentioned that the ring would pass to Tania. I was just as much in her thoughts then. Who knows how the future will unfold.

That evening I went home first and spoke to granddad over the phone. I gave him a complete rundown of the day's events telepathically which cheered him up no end with regard to the Mark Tamper business. Granddad was back to normal again but had decided stay on at his son's for another week just to ease their worries concerning his wellbeing. Granddad then passed the phone to mum and she reassured me that granddad was much improved but still not 100 percent. She was going to have to supervise him a bit more from now on when he returned to his home again.

After making myself a dinner of mince and pasta I went to the Black Dog pub in the hope of seeing Mark Tamper. I spent an hour there sipping half a shandy but he didn't appear. I finally gave up and returned home and to an early night. I'd repeat my social visits to the pub each evening.

It was two evenings later that we finally met again. He had a walking stick and was hobbling along. He got himself a pint and stood at the bar sipping it. I also noticed the dark discolouration on his forehead.

'What've you done to yourself mate?' enquired the barman.

'I dunno,' said Mark Tamper. 'It just happened the other morning. Must have passed out or something 'cos when I came to I had all these pains. The quack at the A & E said it could be arthritis. My ankles are both swollen and painful, the right one is worse so he got me this stick.'

'Looks like you bumped your head as well when you fell,' said the barman pointing to the bruise on Mark's forehead.

I read Mark's mind and realised I had overdone the pressure on his right ankle. And his head still had a dull ache from my treatment. He was not a very happy person at the moment. I decided on one other degradation to his reputation here in his local. The pub was reasonably full and I thought it was time that all regulars got to know the kind of criminal act that Mark had committed; to have been arrested and then bailed by the police.

I shut my eyes and aimed my telepathic thoughts of the night of Philip's mugging at every mind in the room. It only took a second but suddenly there was a hush and all eyes were turned on Mark at the bar. They had all read the account of the break-in in the local papers but that was old news now and memory of it was fading. Suddenly they were all direct witnesses to the horror of the vicious beating that Philip had undergone at the hands of Andy Braid. And this man Mark had done nothing to stop him. No one could understand how they had come to see all this but to them they couldn't doubt the authenticity of the supposed mysterious vision they had just received. Most never went near a church or religious place of worship but all had some form of belief in the Unknown. And of course the spirit world was not far from their thoughts. Some thought it was the spirit of the dead man that had given them this picture of the events of that night and was seeking revenge.

I then concentrated on Mark's mind and sent him a repeated picture of Andy Braid kicking and punching Philip. I wanted this to remain fresh in his mind like a tune that sticks in your head and just keeps repeating itself over and over. Perhaps this and the pains in his body might make Mark finally realise the enormity of his criminal behaviour. Before I left the pub I went pink and repeated the pinch to each ear lobe and a slightly harder flick to both of Mark's shins. I wanted the shin bone to undergo a sort of bony injury that would cause pain for at least a week or two. The medical knowledge I had acquired from Dr Mario did have its uses.

Back at the shop the next morning Milly asked me what I had planned for the weekend. When I said nothing in particular she said to look in the diary. It was the weekend I had promised to visit

Gary Prior and his wife Jill in Mansfield for the car boot sale near them on the Sunday. I needed to get some presents to take with me for their boy and two girls. Malcolm was twelve, Mary ten and Maura seven years old.

I rang mum and told her about my weekend trip and the kid's ages and that they were all average in build. I said I had been thinking of something in the T-shirt area for them. Mum said not to worry; she would pop down to the Fort and Asda and pick up something trendy for the girls and a macho T-shirt for the boy. And of course she said that I should pick up a nice bunch of flowers for my friends. I told mum I'd be over shortly and we could get it done right away if she was free.

That evening I wrapped and labelled the gifts and put them in the hallway ready for me to pick up on my way out on Saturday afternoon. The drive would only take an hour or so to their house in Mansfield. I had printed off the directions from the Multimap program on my PC but I also had my Garmin Sat-Nav for when I was in the town itself.

In the shop Milly and I had prepared and printed off most of the descriptive histories for the items I had brought over from Philip's house. Milly had typed them out on our laptop and I had printed them out at home on 6" x 4" premium photo paper. I had included a miniature picture of the item itself that we had taken on my Nikon digital camera in one corner of the card. Tania had been keen to help and we were pleased to let her. She is one of the most pleasant young ladies of my acquaintance. In some ways she reminded me of my Aunt Brenda's Barclay. He had always a wag on his tail and had so much affection to give all and sundry. He was so full of the zest of life. I often think of him with great love and find it such a shame that 'man's best friend' should have been prescribed such a relatively short life-span. I was a great fan of the James Herriot books and his 'Dog Stories' had often brought a tear to my eyes. Tania will kill me if she could read my thoughts. And I half suspected that she often guessed what I was thinking. I looked up and found her looking at me in a wistful manner.

'What?' I said, thinking the worst as I stared at her.

She looked away and said, 'Nothing really Ashley, it's just you were miles away just now. What were you dreaming about?'

'I was actually thinking of my Aunt Brenda and the King Charles Cavalier spaniel she used to have. He was such a lovely little fellow. I was thinking of how full of love and affection dogs are and that it's a pity they are given such a short life compared to ours.' I didn't add the other bit.

This sixteen year old looked at me as if I were younger than her. She looked at me for about three seconds, smiled and then carried on helping her mother arrange the cards in front of the displayed items. I was sure she could read my mind and I felt a bit guilty with regard to those thoughts.

Saturday was nice and sunny and I was cruising along comfortably up the A38. I had picked up a nice bunch of flowers at Asda and kept them on the floor of the back seat. The presents were in the boot and I was pleased I had not left them behind. There was that occasion a few years ago when I had gone to a birthday bash and had left the gift wrapped present at home.

I had gone around and past Derby when I seemed to hear a voice in my head telling me to slow down. I came to a road sign for Little Eaton to the left and just ahead was a patch of dusty open ground alongside the road about a hundred feet long and fifty feet wide. On it were parked a large white van and ahead of it by a few yards was a small blue family car. I drove slowly past and pulled in and parked just in front of it. There was a young woman sitting in the front seat and she seemed to be in tears. There were also two young children strapped into their safety seats in the back. I came up to her window and tapped on it. She wound the window down and looked pleadingly at me.

'I only stopped for a minute because Jimmy needed a wee. We went to that tree over there and when we got back this van had pulled up and they put a clamp on that wheel,' and she pointed to the left front of the car. 'They said this was private land and not a lay-by and they wanted eighty quid to free the car. They said they wanted the cash now and if they had to wait longer it would double. I don't have money on me only my credit cards but they won't accept that. We've been here an hour and I can't get my dad on my mobile.' The tears were flowing freely now.

'Let me have a word with them and I'm sure everything will be alright,' I said. I looked at her kids and they didn't seem to have a worry in the world. They were both fast asleep.

I put on my most official look and walked up to the van. There were two scruffy chaps in the front seat puffing on their smokes. I walked past and made a show of looking for something. There was not a sign in sight warning that wheel clamping was in force here.

I then tapped on the driver's window and before I could say anything this big burly farmer type got out and told me to get lost.

'Bugger off you before we clamp you as well. This is private land attached to my farm and no one has any business stopping on it.' He glowered down at me from his six inch height advantage.

I just smiled back at him. Reading his mind told me his name was Trevor Packwood and he had a wife and one son aged six. He lived in Derby in a council semi and had worked on the farm as a general hand these last seven years. These two had levelled this strip of lay-by with the intention of catching the weak and innocent. So far they had got away with it and no one had dared report them. Today was going to be their unlucky day.

'Well, well, well,' I said, 'if it isn't old Trevor up to his old tricks again. You were a bully at school and you're a bully now. And you don't own any farm you just work there. And you call this working. Remember me we were in class together at Christ Church secondary? So you married Abigail Ball or so I heard. I hope you don't bully her as well. I remember you beat me up because I was talking to Abi one lunch time. You know I still get nose bleeds from time to time. It's Phil Egan if you haven't recognised me as yet.' I had all his memories in my head as well.

'I remember you, you runt,' he said, 'I told you this is none of your business so piss off and let the nice lady pay her dues.'

'Sorry Trev,' I said, 'I can't let you off this time. This van belongs to your employer and if anything happens to it you're out of a job. So I'm giving you five minutes to think it over. I'll be in my car over there and waiting. Remove the clamp and drive away or your van will be a write off.'

'What are you gonna do?' said Trevor, 'roll the van over on its side with your bare hands? We have a full load inside mate you'll need a crane or something. Your five minutes be damned. I'm telling you now Egan you runt if you're not gone in two minutes there'll be a clamp on your wheel as well.'

I turned around, walked to the blue car and told the lady to start her car and drive away. I said that these were con merchants and the wheel clamp was only imitation and would fall off as soon as she drove away.

'But I tried getting it off,' she said, 'and I couldn't move it at all. I don't want to damage the car. Jack will be furious if I do.'

I went pink and walked round to the clamped wheel. Carefully I peeled the clamp clear of the tyre and brought it round to the front window.

Back in normal mode I showed her the clamp and said, 'There you are madam it's off now, there's a knack to it when you know how. You can drive off safely. Give my regards to Jack. Tell him he has two lovely kids.' The kids were still asleep.

I stood watching and smiling as she drove away. I was going to enjoy this next bit.

When I turned around both men had got out of the van and Trevor had a wheel brace in his right hand. They were walking slowly towards me.

I held up the bright yellow wheel clamp and said, 'You forgot to lock it in place Trev so I just took it off.'

Trevor was swearing something horrible calling me everything under the sun, some of which I had never heard in all my school life. You must certainly learn things on a farm. Trevor was close to me now while the other chap had stopped a few paces back. He thought Trevor could handle me on his own, which he probably could in normal circumstances.

'Bastard,' said Trevor and raised the wheel brace and began his swing down at me.

I let it come and as it touched my neck everything went pink and the brace bounced slowly back. Nothing could hurt me but I pretended I was hurt and dropped to the dusty ground.

'That should teach him,' said Trevor and went to plant a kick to my head.

I decided to finish this off and be on my way. I went rosy pink, got up, moulded the bright yellow wheel clamp into a small ball as if it were putty and threw it at the van. While it was on its way I took the brace out of Trevor's hand and also bent it into a sort of a knot and threw it at the front of the van. I lay back on the ground and went normal again. The crash of the two items hitting the van made the two men swing about. Then I went rosy pink again and went to one side and pushed hard on the side of the van with my telekinetic gift. When I returned to normal the van not only skidded across the flat lay-by but also rolled over a good few times when it hit the farm ditch. It ended up some distance in the farmer's field on its back.

I dusted myself down and walked slowly between the two gaping and dumbstruck men until I got to my car. As I opened the door to get in I looked back at the two fellows. They were still standing stock still and their mouths were trying to utter something but I could not hear a sound. I got in the car, started it up, tooted the horn twice as a goodbye and drove off. When I looked in the rear view mirror I could still see two figures standing in the farmer's lay-by. I felt I had done a good deed today and taught some bullies a lesson. The voice in my head seemed to agree and I smiled at that. I think Philip would have approved.

When I arrived at Gary and Jill's house in Shelton Close near the Forrest Town area of Mansfield it had clouded over quite a bit. The family were all at home and greeted me with genuine affection. I had last seen them when they had come to the shop in Dudley and we had all gone out for a buffet meal. Philip had joined us then and got on well with Gary. The Prior's had then travelled on to spend time with a relative in Worcester.

Jill made us some tea and while she was busy at it I popped to the car and brought in the flowers and the wrapped gifts for the kids.

'I hope they fit okay,' I said. 'My mum helped me choose for the girls but I picked out Malcolm's T-shirt myself. The T-shirt said "Don't Muck with Me" on both front and back and had a print that looked as if it had been in a mud fight. The girls both had High School Musical tops in red and white.

Malcolm was nearly my height and came to say thanks. He hesitated on what to call me so I said to call me by my name.

'Mum said I should call you Uncle Ashley,' he said.

'Don't you dare call me Uncle? That would make me feel old. I'm only 21 you know. You can call me 'Your Excellency' though if you wish,' I said jokingly, 'but I would much prefer just plain Ashley.'

'Thanks for the shirt Ashley,' said Malcolm smiling, 'its real cool. My friends will love it.'

Mary and Maura were a bit on the shy side when they came to give their thanks too and slinked upstairs to try on their tops. Mum had chosen well with the High School Musical stuff. Apparently it was all the current rage with young girls.

I saw Jill looking at my shirt front before quickly looking away. I hadn't quite dusted off when I had dropped down for Trevor in the lay-by. I did so now but still a spot remained.

'The car picked up a plastic carrier bag somewhere underneath while I was driving down and the scuffing noise got so annoying that I stopped in a lay-by just passed Derby to free it,' I explained. 'I slipped and fell flat on my face while reaching under the car. I suppose I had better get cleaned up and put on a fresh shirt.'

Gary showed me up to my room and I took a shirt from my overnight bag and went into the bathroom for a quick cleanup.

I was down in ten minutes and Jill had the tea ready.

'One sugar for me please, Jill,' I said.

'I wish Malcolm would reduce his,' said Jill. 'He puts four in his mug and half of it remains at the bottom when he's finished. He used to put five last year.'

'Well I've come down from two,' I said. 'I tried reducing to half a spoon but couldn't really enjoy the tea then, so I went back to the one.'

'Have you tried a sweetener?' asked Gary. 'The Splenda doesn't have an after taste and is supposed to be better for you than sugar.'

'My mum uses a sweetener but I didn't like it when I had hers by accident once,' I said. 'Yet I've had tea on occasion without anything at all and quite enjoyed the taste.'

We spent a very pleasant afternoon chatting generally. After a while the young girls came down wearing their new tops and sat and listened to the chatter. I mentioned Philip and both Jill and Gary became serious and said how sorry they were at the manner of his passing. The kids didn't know quite what to say as they had only seen him briefly so I told them some of Philip's National Service stories. They laughed at the one when the rifle had accidentally gone off inside the barracks and made a hole through the sergeant's metal cupboard housing all his uniforms and suits.

That evening we all went out to a pub and had a lovely meal followed by a delicious sticky toffee pudding. We went in two cars and I sat with Gary and Malcolm. Jill followed with the girls in her little Fiesta. I convinced them to let me pay for the meal as I could claim it on expenses. After all this was an antiques foray that I was really on. As we drove back into the close I noticed quite a large group of youths assembled and mucking about at the entrance. One of them actually threw a bit of grit at the car. I had come across this sort of behaviour before. It was peer pressure among the group that usually caused individuals to do things as a dare.

Gary said that he had rung the police often enough but apart from causing a general nuisance the kids couldn't be charged with anything. He said he didn't like the girls going to their friends in the next Close and coming back late as these youths seemed to stay there half the night. So far they had just passed insulting remarks but one day they might go further. Gary said this had been going on for over a year and when he walked down to talk to them they gave him a mouthful of abuse.

'You can't touch us mister,' they had said. 'Lay a finger on one of us and the cops will have ya.'

And they were right too. Kids today seem to know their rights and play it to the full.

After a cup of tea in the house I said I was thinking about a stroll down the road to help digest some of that sticky toffee pudding I had enjoyed so much.

'I'll come with you,' said Gary, 'those kids won't try anything funny when they see two of us.'

But I convinced Gary to let me go on my own and I patted my belly and feign a burp at the same time. I gave him a wink and I think he understood about my need to be on my own. It's the same reason granddad had wanted to be back in his own house where his digestive functions didn't need to be politely held in check.

The group of youths had swollen in numbers when I walked towards them. I counted at least a dozen and all were about my height. They stood around the street lamp at the start of the Close that lit them all in an orange glow. I could see some had turned towards me and defiantly expected me to cross over to the other side of the road to avoid them. I kept walking towards them. They blocked the pavement completely and some even stood in the road. I had to stop or push my way through them. There were two girls among them.

'Come on lads,' I said quietly, 'let me pass.'

'Say pretty please mister,' said one of the girls.

'Okay then,' I said, 'please let me pass if you don't mind.'

'Who do you think you are mister? You don't own the road. Go around.'

'Say pretty please and I will go around,' I said to the chap who had just spoken.

'Ooo,' said the girl again. 'Look who's being all high and mighty. I think this one needs to be taught some manners guys.'

I then decided that a lesson definitely needed to be taught here.

'I think you all need to go home now,' I said. 'That big chap standing there in the middle of the crossroads looks as if he has his eye on you lot. I'd be worried if I was you, he's carrying something nasty under his arm.'

They all looked in the direction of the crossroads and then turned back to me.

'There 'aint anyone there, you having us on or something?' said one of the group loudly.

'Go home or you'll regret it,' I said equally as loudly.

'So what you gonna do mister,' said the tall one coming up to me and staring down.

'Nothing,' I said pointing to the crossroads again, 'he's going to do it for me.'

'We're going to stay here all night,' said the tall one giving me an aggressive nudge.

'Suit yourself,' I said stepping off the pavement and walking around the group and over the crossroads to the other side and pretending to avoid something in the middle. I carried on for a short distance and then stopped behind a tree about fifty feet away.

I stared at the group and began to apply a telekinetic force on all of them as a blanket pressure.

'Hey, stop pushing me,' I heard one of them shout.

I applied a bit more force and the group began a shuffling movement deeper into the Close.

I then sent a telepathic thought to all of their minds. I said that their wish to stay in Shelton Close would be granted and they would be locked here for all time. I ended the thought with a sort of mental laughter.

'This is too creepy,' said one of the girls, 'I'm going home.'

She got to the front of the group and tried to cross the road but I pushed her back and back and back till she was the furthest into the close. She then sat down and began to cry. A puddle appeared underneath her from the fear she felt. I was sorry for her but they all had a lesson to learn; a lesson that they could never be allowed to forget.

They were now all a few paces away from where the street lamp stood in the pavement. It was time for some dramatics. I concentrated on the lamp holder and the glass cover fell with a crash onto the roadway below. I then pushed on the bulb itself till it exploded under the pressure. All was suddenly dark here though there was another street light further into the Close.

I then went into pink mode and did to each of them what I had done to Mark Tamper that morning in his flat while he had been shaving in his bathroom. I returned to my hiding position again before returning to normal.

There then came a variety of yells and screams from the group. They had all fallen to the ground and were holding onto different areas of their bodies.

'O my God, O my God, O my God,' came from the girl who had first spoken and asked me to say "pretty please".

Gradually they seemed to quieten down. Then a dissention began to arise among them as they started to blame one another for their predicament. There is always a ring leader or two in every group and after a while I established them to be the two brothers Adam and Stuart Abbot who lived half a mile away on Throneby Road.

I came out of hiding and walked to the group.

'O dear,' I said, 'what's the matter with you lot? Bedding down for the night? I thought you'd be home by now.'

I then turned around and walked out of the Close again. They could see that nothing stopped me and some of them got up and began a limping walk towards the crossroads.

I waited until they had reached the darkened street lamp and then pushed them backwards again but with a bit more force this time.

'We can't get out of this damned Close,' said the tall one of them still being aggressive.

It was now nearly eleven o'clock and I was thinking about the Prior's and my own comfortable bed.

So I decided for one last bit of action before I left this group to their own devices.

I went pink again and this time I shredded the jackets and shirts off all the men and left them in a ragged pile in the road. I just took the coats off the two girls and ripped them down the middle and deposited them on the pile in the road. The Abbot brothers would not be very popular after this.

I then walked up the Close and entered Gary and Jill's front porch.

Jill offered me a cup of tea and I gratefully accepted. It was just what I needed after a good days work.

'Did you get any bother from that lot at the end of the Close?' asked Jill.

'No nothing at all,' I said. 'There was a panda car cruising around and it stopped to have a word with the lads. I think they had all gone home when I returned from the walk. You've probably seen the last of them, for a while anyway.'

We sat up talking till about midnight before finally saying goodnight. I thought I might be tired out after all that telekinetic effort but I wasn't. In fact I felt quite exhilarated by it all. Perhaps my system was getting into a sort of a higher gear in preparation for that big event that Philip had indicated. I went to sleep thinking about Philip and his favourite tawny owl.

We all had an early breakfast in the morning and Gary suggested we drive there even though it was barely a mile away. We went in both cars and Jill rode with me to show me the way.

'Just in case we find something of interest we may want to dump it in one of the cars rather than be lugging it around all day', said Gary. 'It will be just like when we go Christmas shopping. We keep going back to the car to drop off what we have bought.'

'Sounds a very good idea Gary,' I said. 'I'm sure I'll find something I like.'

'Can we buy something as well dad,' said Malcolm, Mary and Maura in unison.

'Of course you can,' said Gary, 'provided it's not just some bit of tat. You had better ask your mum before you hand over any of your good money.'

I think Jill had given them five pounds each in change just for this occasion. She'd said the money was theirs whether they spent any of it or not. I added a couple of pounds to each of their kitty and they were all smiles. I always carry those little bank plastic coin pouches and gave them one each for their coins. I said it helped to protect the lining of their pockets from the wear and tear of jingling loose change. They were also less likely to lose coins while paying out.

There was already a queue of traffic heading towards the field and we just crawled along till we were directed to a parking spot having paid the two pounds per car entrance fee. I had managed to stay right behind Gary and so was parked right next to him. There was a light cloud cover but the forecast on the telly last night had been for a dry day.

We started wandering among the stalls and tables together at first but then the kids said they wanted to see some of the things at the far end. They had obviously been here before and knew where their interests were stocked. Gary told them to stay together and to meet at the cars at about one o'clock for the lunch that Jill had put together. I suggested that I would do the same as I had a purpose to fulfil.

As I wandered among the tables I saw a lot of household items that people were essentially trying to get rid of and earn a bit of cash at the same time. I could see the regulars though because they had better quality items and there was usually a white van parked alongside their marquee covered tables. It was to one of these that I was attracted to after having wandered around for nearly an hour. It had two long trestle tables on which were placed a collection of mugs and jugs that must have numbered in the hundreds. There were even some placed on the grass below the tables. Someone had had a hobby collecting these and was now getting rid of them. It was a smiling middle aged couple who were the sellers apparently. I stopped to look at this wonderful display and gave a low whistle of wonder. They read my mind and the lady explained.

'It were me ma's hobby collecting this lot,' she said in a very Newcastle accent. 'She be gone this past year now and we be trying to see what this lots worth.'

'Well my dear,' I said, 'my compliments to your mother she must have been a fine lady to have collected all these. I'm sorry that she is not with you anymore I would have loved to have met her. I can see she had a good eye because some of these are very good and probably worth a bit.'

'Aye, I wish they was,' she replied, 'but there aint be nothing over a tenner here. Take your time mister and us hopes you finds yourself something you likes.'

The man was quiet all the while but kept a smile on his face. They both looked very pleasant so I took my time looking over the items on the tables. I took a quick look at the mugs on the grass and my heart skipped a beat at something I saw. It never failed to surprise me what you found at these car boot sales. I reached down and picked up an orange coloured pottery mug with a three-masted sailing ship printed in black with a faded green as the sea. It had a slight chip at the lip but otherwise was in reasonably good condition. There was a brown painted moulded frog on the inside. I turned it around and expected to see some printed wording but there was only a very faded effort at some sort of illegible script. This was made at the Staffordshire potteries to the northwest of Birmingham in the mid 1890s and they'd had a lot of start up problems in firing transfers on items. If the transfers weren't properly coated they got lost in the firing heat. That is what must have happened here. I'm surprised that this survived destruction as a faulty piece. In fact this made it more valuable than the good ones because of its rarity. I wasn't about to give the couple a lesson in antique valuations as they had been at this car boot game for some time now. I would put this item in the shop for sale at about a hundred pounds along with its history card.

I also picked up two Wedgwood pottery mugs with an inscription commemorating the coronation of Her Majesty Queen Elizabeth II in 1953. They were in good condition too and were designed by Eric Ravilious. These were in a pink tone so I looked carefully for any that had a blue colouring, which would have been ones from a much earlier coronation. Sadly they were not to be seen among this lot. As a pair I'd display these for about two hundred pounds back in the shop.

This was a rewarding day for me and I was well pleased with myself. I paid for the three items and the couple kindly produced a carrier bag with some bubble-wrap which they used to protect my wares. I wandered back to the car, placed my goodies in the boot and strolled back to the stalls and tables.

I met up with Gary and Jill and told them of the bargains I had bought. When I mentioned the mugs they said they had seen a nice one on a table a few rows down and offered to take me there. When I saw it I agreed it was nice but only worth about twenty or thirty pounds. Still at its two quid asking price it was a bargain so I had it. It was a pearl-ware mug six inches high decorated with a blue and white transfer print of a pavilion scene and it had a nice large loop handle. It was made in the late 19th century and had a small chip on the inner lip. It would make a nice ornament on someone's living room mantel. I thought it was also about the right size for a beer mug. Jill was pleased that they had managed to spot something for me and I think that she herself could get quite into the buying and selling of antiques. And so it was another short trip back to the car.

I managed to pick up a few other items before lunch. There was a brass signal canon on a wooden carriage. The original would have been made mid 19th century and worth close to two grand; but this was a very good replica and in far too good a condition to be an antique. Still it was a pretty piece and at a tenner would look good on a shelf in the shop. As would the 4½ inch long Tri-Ang Spot-On LWB Land Rover finished in grey with white roof and interior with spare wheels mounted on bonnet and rear door. There was some minor wear but it came with the original slightly faded box. The asking price was twenty quid and we settled at fifteen. I couldn't resist the red Dinky Royal Mail Van and the two tone Dinky 161 Austin Somerset saloon car both at about 3½ inches size. Here again we settled at fifteen for each. The Austin car would be a good replacement for the Dorset A40 that the Hillcrest School girl had bought for her dad from the shop. The Somerset looked quite fetching in its cream top and black body colouring. The cream hubs added a nice touch too. So it was back to the car with this lot and it also happened to be time for the lunch that Jill promised.

Gary and Jill were already there and had brought along a three foot diameter picnic table with push-in legs and six folding chairs. How they got this lot into their boot I don't know along with the two large cool boxes. When Jill placed the bread, salad and sliced cold meats on the table she had a pleased smile on her face. Gary laughed at my surprise and said that picnics were Jill's specialty and was always done in style. When the glass tumblers and bottle of sparkling white Shloer was placed on the table I had to join in the laughter.

'I don't suppose that you've got strawberries and cream for dessert,' I said jokingly not believing for one moment that there was the least likelihood of its being true.

There was a moment of hush before a volcano of laughter erupted from both parents and children.

'O Ashley, you say the nicest things,' said Jill. 'And if you are a good boy and eat all your lunch we just might have some.'

We had a lovely lunch and I wondered how I was going to keep awake after this.

'That was excellent Jill,' I said. 'I don't think I could eat another mouthful. I think I could do with forty winks right here and now and not bother with the stalls anymore.'

'O no you don't,' she said, 'don't forget your strawberries and cream sir.'

And with a flourish she returned from the open boot with a large bowl of fresh strawberries covered in cling wrap. This was followed by a carton of fresh single cream and a shaker of sprinkling sugar. And the cutlery was all proper dining room stuff too.

I just couldn't resist clapping my hands in appreciation at Jill's organization. This was really heaven and I said so. Gary said that the real icing on the cake for Jill had been when I had joked about the dessert.

'The way you said that about the strawberries and cream and the surprise on your face when Jill actually produced it has made her day, believe you me Ashley,' said Gary with one of the biggest smiles on his face that I had ever seen. The kids were smiling too.

What a lovely family, I shall have to tell mum and dad about this day; especially about the comfort of the picnic table and chairs. Granddad would have loved this. I couldn't help thinking of Tania and wondering if one day she might be doing this too with her family. I felt a pang at the thought. I looked forward to seeing her and Milly at the shop tomorrow.

There was another adventure in store and that happened at one of the far end stalls. It was nearly four o'clock and we were all together thinking about calling it a day and heading back to the house for a nice cup of hot tea. Malcolm had wandered over to a table on our left and was staring at some ornaments displayed. He came back to us and said that he had seen one of the ugliest vases ever. We all strolled to where he pointed and there in the middle of the table was something that caused my heart to skip a few beats. There sat the bottom half of an early 1880s Martin Brothers stoneware Bird Jar. This was an early design by Robert Wallace Martin and was extremely grim in its makeup. It had large grotesque webbed claws for feet and was on a dark grey-green integral circular plinth. The stall holder obviously didn't think it looked pretty either and had placed a few short stemmed plastic flowers in it. I looked around the table and couldn't spot the cover anywhere. This one should have the head of a bird with very large hideous beak pointing downwards as the jar's cover. The bird was a Martin Brothers creation and had been named as a Wally bird. I removed the flowers and turned the piece over and saw 'R.W. Martin & Bros, London & Southall' incised on the bottom just as I had expected.

'Ye can have that for a fiver mister,' said the stall holder who looked like the middle aged farmer that he was. 'I found that in me barn about ten year ago. I reckon it were made faulty and got throwed away. Ugly beggar that but I been using it as a flower holder ever since. Kinda got attached to it somehow and kept it. Didn't suppose anyone would want to pay good money for it. But as I said ye can have it for a fiver, it'd make a good paper weight.'

The head and neck of early Martin Brother's Wally birds fitted together in only one position as did this one. Later Wally birds had a simpler fitting that allowed the heads to rotate.

I asked Jill if she had a piece of paper and she produced a small notepad from her hand bag. I'm always amazed at what ladies carry in their handbags in addition to their cosmetics. She also handed me a pen. I then began to sketch the piece and then added from memory what the head cover should look like. I showed it to Gary and Jill and they shuddered at the ugliness of the complete bird. I then showed it to the farmer stall holder.

'Now that's an ugly critter,' he said, 'what exactly is it?'

'That, my dear sir is a Wally bird,' I said. 'It is a Martin Brothers' stoneware bird jar with cover worth about forty thousand pounds if complete.'

It was my turn to see surprise written on the faces of all those around me. I heard a 'Wow' from some of the passers-by who had stopped to see what I was drawing. The farmer gave a low whistle.

'Ye not be kidding me are ye sir,' he said. He swallowed noisily.

'He has his own antiques shop in Birmingham,' said Gary to the farmer. 'I had some stuff to get rid of and Ashley put me right as to the true price otherwise I would have been ripped off. He knows his stuff alright.'

The farmer looked at Ashley and said, 'You could have had it for a fiver and I'd ha been none the wiser. Ye be an honest gent mister, so what's it be worth as it is.'

'Without the head cover I'd say maybe a hundred quid or two to an interested collector at auction. Here at the car boot I'd say it's worth maybe ten or twenty to the ordinary bloke looking for an ugly paper weight,' I said.

Someone laughed out aloud at the back of the quite large group that had gathered around the stall. People can somehow sense when a drama is unfolding. I think the person laughed at my use of the 'ugly paper weight' phrase.

As an after thought I said for the farmer to give me his address and I'd post him a photo print from an antiques book and he could tell all his friends that he nearly had forty thousand smackers. And then again if he looked carefully in that barn of his he just might find the missing cover piece.

'Na, 'he said, 'that thar barns been long gone now and another built in its place with concrete floor. No chance of finding nowt now. Aw well, I'll just have to make best of it, no use crying over spilt milk. But I'll no sell the bird now I know what tis and I can tell me tale to the family not that they'll believe anything I say. Thank ye mister, if I can keep yon drawing on paper no need to send me picture in post. Wally bird you say eh?' And with that he picked up the bird jar less cover and put it beside his stool on the floor.

I gave him the sketch and then he came round the table and gave me a two handed handshake. He nodded to me and went back around to his side of the table. I think the emotion of the moment had rendered him temporarily speechless.

'Ye can have the pick of anything ye fancy on the table mister and I thank ye for what ye have done,' he said after a moment, 'I'll not forget ye mister as long as I live. Not many like ye around these days.'

There was nothing I felt worth having and it was Malcolm who came to my rescue.

'Can I choose something Ashley,' he said, 'then whenever you see it you can remember today.'

'Yes of course Malcolm, please go ahead and choose,' I replied.

I was surprised that I had missed the item that Malcolm chose. It had lain on its side behind an old table lamp at the far edge of the table. It was a Staffordshire pottery model of a seated spaniel with a yellow glaze. There was a small chip at the base but this was on the back face of the piece. It was a mid to late nineteenth century piece that might be worth around twenty pounds at auction. I told the farmer its worth and he said he was glad it was worth something and I should have it with his compliments. He was holding the bird jar base up to the light and saying something about it being a sly old fox. I imagine it will be at the centre of all the conversations he has from now on. There was no regret at all in his demeanor at the amount of money that might have been. He had just found a new toy.

Back at the house over a nice mug of tea the talk was all about the bird jar and where the head cover could have got to. I simply said that one day perhaps we just might see the other half turn up on its own at another car boot sale and with no one being any the wiser. I said that I had to say that so far as I was concerned it had been a very good day, especially with the strawberries and cream affair; at which we all laughed.

I said my goodbyes to Gary, Jill and the kids. I gave the yellow pottery spaniel to Malcolm to keep for the whole family in memory of today and the episode of the farmer's topless bird jar.

'Jill,' I said, 'I have an important job to do when I get back home. And that is to tell my granddad all about our picnic lunch and especially how you so magically produced the strawberries and cream. He is going to be so keen for me to do the same; and I will at the first opportunity. Mum and dad will hear of the picnic too. Thank you far a lovely time here I'm so glad I came. God bless you all.'

I received a hug and a kiss from Jill and handshakes from Gary and the kids before I got into the car and drove off. I was nearing the point on the A38 just before Derby where a sign pointed to Little Eaton to the right. I slowed and drove into the makeshift lay-by where the clamping episode had occurred. I looked around and there was no one in sight. The van that I had pushed into the field was not there either so I imagine Trevor Packwood and his mate must have righted it and got it towed out of the field and to a secret repair yard. There were deep track marks in the field that gave evidence to this. I smiled to myself as I continued my journey home.

Next morning Milly was pleased when I presented my purchases from Mansfield. She was ever so interested when I told her about the farmer's bird jar with the missing top. She pulled out one of our antique price guide books and searched for the Martin Brothers pottery section. She found the bird in question and whistled at its price.

'My goodness,' she said, 'it certainly is an ugly piece. Why would anyone want to own such a thing?'

'Beauty has nothing to do with it,' I said. 'It's the history behind it and who made it that matters most. Actually I would call the piece sad rather than ugly. As you can see the later bird jars are much more interesting – if that is a suitable descriptive term. This early one didn't have a head that could rotate and so can be considered as the grandmother of the later birds.'

I remembered the story of the mother who told her errant young son that the bird was watching him and would tell on him if he were naughty. And whenever she walked near it she would rotate the head to a different direction. Her son would always walk by it slowly and at his best behavior just in case. The fact that the bird's head was always pointed in a different direction whenever he saw it made him feel that the bird was indeed watching him. Even in later years he never quite got rid of the notion that he was being watched by it.

Milly laughed when I related this tale to her. She laughed even more when I told her of the style of the picnic that Gary and Jill had laid on for me and how the strawberries and cream had been presented after my sarcastic 'I suppose' remark. I don't know why but I was a bit disappointed that Tania wasn't here to listen to all of this. I suppose Milly will tell her all about my trip when they meet back in their own home.

Later in the morning I drove to Mark Tamper's house in Hockley lane to mete out a repeat dose of the earlier punishment. He was not in and there was evidence in his flat that he had left for parts unknown. All his clothes were gone and when I walked through the flat a spider's web strand brushed across my face and again in the bathroom doorway. I felt I needed to know and so went and sat on the end of Mark's bed. The room turned rosy pink and I shut my eyes tight and concentrated on the bed where Mark usually slept. I saw Mark limping around the room and putting things into a good size rucksack. He was sniffing and swearing and seemed on edge. He kept looking over his shoulder as if wary of someone or something. He then went to a drawer and took out a passport and a lot of other papers and stuffed them into a side pocket of the rucksack. He took one last look around the room and left the flat carrying the rucksack. I didn't need to follow him as I knew where he was going. He intended to lose himself in the crowded city of London with a change of identity. So far as I was concerned I didn't care what he did with himself. I felt that his exile from here was punishment enough for his life of crime and his complicity in Philip's death. I had successfully dealt with Andy Braid and Mark Tamper in a way that had taught them both that their crimes would not go unpunished. In essence they were now wholly superstitious and believed that they were under some sort of constant supernatural supervision. I was happy to let the matter rest there. As such I considered the matter as now closed.

That evening I went to visit mum and dad. Katy was pleased to see her big brother and I gathered she was keen to hear of my latest adventures. She now saw me in a very different light to that when we were children together. Katy was obviously in with mum and I was glad that they could discuss me between themselves. Mum had had to keep everything regarding my gifts to herself before, but now with Katy a grown woman of eighteen and in the know too she had a companion to talk to quite freely.

I had phoned granddad earlier in the day and had conveyed all my weekend's events to him telepathically. I could hear him laugh over the phone and thinking back I couldn't help a smile of my own. He said I must come over and repeat it all verbally as he liked it better face to face. Granddad liked to read your expression while you talked and I must say there is a lot to be said for that mode of communication.

Mum made us a lovely mug of char and she asked if I had eaten. When I said I wasn't hungry she knew instantly that I hadn't. Mum said she had cooked extra and was about to freeze the leftovers for another day. So in a matter of minutes she'd prepared me a tray with a lovely plate of steaming Shepherds Pie. I had to blow on the spoon to cool it as I ate. We had moved to the dining table and mum, dad and Katy sat around it listening to me reciting my adventures starting with the clamping episode.

'Serves them right,' said mum when I told how I had sent the van crashing out into the field. 'No one was hurt and they will know better than to harass innocent women and children. I have a thought Ashley but I'll wait till you've finished telling us about your weekend with your friends.'

'If you don't mind mum, dad and sis,' I said, 'I'd like to give you all of it telepathically so you get the full picture. Mum you are going to love this bit about Jill's picnic style.'

So I conveyed everything telepathically and mum laughed till the tears streamed down her cheeks. I guessed it was the strawberries and cream part that tickled her the most.

'I'd love to meet Gary, Jill and the kids,' said mum. 'They sound really nice. That's the good thing about you communicating this way Ashley we get to really know your friends. I would love to meet them. And also to go on one of those picnics.'

'What you did to that group of youths at the end of Shelton Close was great Ash,' said Katy. 'I'm always afraid to walk near such groups because they tend to egg each other on and then act so silly. And I'm sure some of them carry knives too just to show how macho they are.'

Dad said he had the utmost admiration for the farmer in the bird jar episode. Some people would go crackers just thinking about that amount of money being lost to them. And I just had the thought that I knew nothing about the man. I had been so wrapped up in the bird jar itself that I had neither read the farmer's mind nor had I asked his name or farm address.

I told them how pleased Milly was with the items I had brought back from the car boot sale. She was now beginning to put her own price evaluations on many of those that had been stored at Philip's house. I then added that I had closed the book on the two muggers Mark Tamper and Andy Braid. I said that they had both learned a hard lesson through my actions. The one Andy had had quite a change of heart for which his parents could be thanked; while the other was near to a nervous breakdown and had left to fend for himself in the City of London. The police would probably trace him to wherever he went, unless of course he changed to a new identity.

I finished eating and declined mum's offer of some ice cream for dessert. I opted for another mug of tea instead for which we moved back to the comfort of the living room. Mum quickly cleared up, stacked everything in the dishwasher, boiled the kettle and brought mugs of tea for all.

'Well Ashley I've been thinking,' she said sitting across from me with a serious look on her face. 'Everything you said about teaching these people a lesson in good behaviour has given me an idea. So far you have taken corrective action when you have come into actual contact with criminal elements. But if you read the papers there are similar cases all over Birmingham. In fact crime seems to be on the increase all over the country. Perhaps it was time you used your gifts in the same way that you have exercised so far on some of these others. This is where we as a family come into the picture. There are now six of us in the know and we are all one family. If we all keep our eyes and ears open we could establish where the trouble spots are and then jointly decide which ones you could tackle and so on. The local papers report a lot on the vandalism that is so rife. O Ashley, you have been given such a wonderful gift that it would be a shame not to put it to useful purpose. Let's all go up to Aunt Brenda's this week end and discuss this together. There is a lot to think about.'

Katy was immediately enthusiastic but dad said this was a serious matter and needed to be thought through more carefully.

'We are asking Ashley to take the law into his own hands,' said dad. 'That is a very big step to take and we must tread carefully. But I agree that some of these 'naughty fellas' do need to be taught a lesson. We need to establish a code for the type and severity of the punishment handed out. Everything you have done so far Ashley I have whole heartedly agreed with but we must ensure that it can never ever get out of hand.'

I then explained that everything I had done was to create an impression of the supernatural in the minds of my victims. This had the effect of instilling a fear of the unknown and was more likely to remain a deterrent to any future bad behaviour. And that is how I intended to continue. Of course there would have to be a proportion of the pain factor in the treatment but this was like a slap on the wrist for a naughty child. In the Shelton Close case the biggest factor there was when I kept pushing them back from the entrance and not letting them leave the area. This had been the ultimate horror for them and destroyed the credibility of the group leaders. I believe that that gang of youths had been broken up in mind and in spirit on a permanent basis. I should probably hear from Gary and Jill that they have peace at last from those rowdies. Word would also have spread of the strange goings on at that location and rumour would probably abound that the spot was haunted.

'I wonder what it feels like to feel something invisible pushing you,' said Katy. 'It must be a really scary feeling especially in the dark of the night with that street lamp knocked out.'

'Let's not decide anything now,' said mum. 'Let us all put on our thinking caps and I'll phone Brenda about this weekend.'

I said that with granddad's recent bout perhaps it was better if he didn't travel all the way to Aberporth. I suggested we could meet at granddad's place later in the week and see what he thought about it all. The problem was of course that granddad didn't like missing out on any excitement. He would want to be in the thick of any decision making. Granddad and I had a special bonding for each other and he looked on me as his protégé. It was granddad who had first noticed my gifts when we were playing at catching the ball in our back garden nearly fifteen years ago. How things had progressed since then.

I also knew that I could never become angered at the bad or nasty behaviour that I saw and read about. My gifts put me above that and gave me an understanding of what drove people to do or say such things. I intended to make them realise through my actions that it must never to be done again. If there was a case where I was unsuccessful in my purpose then I would just leave it alone and hope for the best for that person in the longer term. Some trees take longer to bear fruit.

The next morning I mentioned to Milly that I intended to spend longer out on the road and suggested she think about employing an assistant. She said that she had been considering it for a while now and had the ideal person for the job. He was family and was Jerry's maternal uncle Robin Morris. He was in his late sixties and had been retired from teaching for several years now.

He was currently involved with the National Trust as a volunteer guide at Packwood House in Lapworth just south of Birmingham. Uncle Robin lived in Solihull and it was a short drive for his three days of work there. He was occasionally asked to work at nearby Baddesley Clinton instead. As a consequence he had become intrigued by the history of these old houses and from this had developed an interest in their contents and of course antiques.

He seemed ideal for the job so I told Milly to offer it to him. Again the position would be of associate partner after a year. It would be nice to have a senior citizen once again in the shop. The memory of Philip sitting behind that desk three years ago was still fresh in my mind.

That weekend we all went up to Aberporth for our conference including granddad who insisted on coming along. It was a lovely weekend with bright warm weather. It didn't take very long to brief Aunt Brenda and Uncle Ron on the proposed plan of action and get their opinion. They agreed that something had to be done and that I was the perfect crusader for the task. They would let me know of any incidents they read about in their local paper which I might do something about.

We decided not to mention any of this to grandparents Beryl and David Jones in Aberdare as they would just worry unnecessarily. Besides grandpa David's memory had been on the decline for sometime now and he often forgot what you had told him the day before.

After a lovely tea we all went for a walk along the coastal path and memories of our walks so long ago with that lovely little dog Barclay came to mind. I remember surprising mum and dad when I caught those butterflies to show to them before letting them fly off. I thought about Tania and Milly and thought that one day I'd bring them here and take them on this same walk. It's a shame that one of my gifts was not where I could look into the future. Perhaps it was a good thing that I couldn't. My mind wandered towards what lay in store for me. Not that I had any worries; I was just keen to know what I had to do and how it would affect the world and mankind in general. It was only through me and my gifts that action could be effected. We were a partnership that had been bestowed upon us by a Supreme Power and for a special purpose. I had known Philip in life and I had loved him like a father. Now that Philip was in the next world I still had the same love for him. Only now that love seemed to extend beyond and towards that Supreme Being behind it all. I suppose I had come to love this Being for the goodness shown to me. At the same time I was a bit afraid that any displeasure in what I did could result in a rescinding of the gifts that had been bestowed upon me. Therefore my feelings were one of love and respect and a desire to please. Not to mention a little fear as well!

'A penny for your thoughts Ashley,' said Katy as she walked alongside me. 'You seemed to have been miles away, what were you thinking?'

I didn't answer her verbally but just transferred all my recent thoughts telepathically. At which point Katy looked at me and I could feel the love she threw at me in that moment. Love and pride in her magically gifted brother. She then linked her arm through mine, gave a tremendous squeeze and so holding on walked along the path with me. I did notice a slight shine of moistness in her eyes.

Mum and dad looked back at us and smiled.

CHAPTER 9

A Crusade Begins

2003

When the case against the two muggers of Philip Stevens came to court only circumstantial evidence was presented by the prosecution. Both Mark Tamper and Andy Braid had pleaded guilty to common burglary. They were represented in court by their legal aid barrister who said that there had been no intention on their part for any violence against the old gentleman. That had been accidental he said and they were extremely sorry for it. The one called Andy Braid was now a regular church goer and had renounced his path of crime and was under strict supervision by his mother and father with whom he lived. The other, Mark Tamper, had moved down to London and had there suffered bouts of nervous depression and was diagnosed as suicidal. He was currently under medical supervision in a secure psychiatric institution and so could not be present. The outcome was that they both received a one year suspended prison sentence. A monthly report was to be filed with the court at the end of each period.

Ashley read this in the local newspaper even though Detective sergeant Mark Solomon of the Hill Street police station had phoned to predict the likely outcome. Ashley was not disappointed at the result since he felt that the two had been adequately punished. And that so far as he was concerned it was an end to the matter.

Ashley got on well with Jerry's maternal uncle Robin Morris. He was in his late sixties and had grabbed at the opportunity to work full time at the McGill's Antiques and Museum shop in Dudley. Although he said he'd quite enjoyed his time as a volunteer at the National Trust's Packwood House in Lapworth. He considered though that it had been getting to be a bit of a set routine. McGill's was a fresh challenge for him despite his sixty eight years.

Robin had a slight stoop in his posture and he had a way of looking sideways at you when he talked. He was shorter than Ashley but that was probably because he had shrunk with age. It was a long drive from Solihull and Ashley let him start anytime before ten o'clock. He was pleasant in his manner and had a wonderful way with the customers, not to mention Loraine Hollings the bakery manager and all her staff. Jokingly, Robin said he was just making sure that his buns and doughnuts always came fresh. So when it was time for a cup of tea Robin would dash across to the bakery and return with a bag of something or other. And there was also many a time when either Lorraine or one of her staff would pop over with a bag of 'leftovers' as they called it for Robin.

Robin said he liked the Dudley area and was considering moving there as the daily journey time was over an hour long each way. Although both Ashley and Milly had offered Robin a room if he wished an overnight stay it was kindly refused. Philip's house in Griffin Street had been sold so that was not an option. It was Lorraine who provided the ideal solution to Robin's accommodation needs in Dudley. A ground floor maisonette in her block had become available for sale or rent and Robin had been accepted as a tenant buyer. He could take immediate possession at a nominal rent and complete the purchase within one year. After that the rent would double if the purchase had not been completed.

Milly subsequently teased her uncle to beware of Loraine Hollings as she was half his age.

'No she is not,' came the reply, 'she'll be forty five next September and I'm not quite ninety yet.' There was a twinkle in Robin's eye followed by a wink when he said it.

Tania had met Robin on occasion only and had always been quiet in his presence. She had known of him mainly as a name mentioned now and again. Apparently Robin looked a lot like his late sister Agnes who was Jerry's mother. Tania could remember her gran and had been spoilt rotten every time she had visited from Sheffield. She had died when Tania was eleven and Tania could remember crying at the funeral. Robin was so much like his older sister in both gentle manner and looks that a mutual affection was instantly kindled on their first day together at the shop. And when Katy came to meet him she also got to like him right away. In fact he had so many stories and anecdotes in his repertoire that both young ladies were quite enthralled.

Within six months he had met all of Ashley's family members not to mention their friends Mavis, Vicky, Robert Black and Robin Nesters. Without exception Robin was accepted as a trusted friend. Though more than anyone else Robin and Ashley's granddad Eric really hit it off. Both had done their two years of national service and although it had been at different times and places they had a lot in common.

Robin would visit Eric nearly every weekend and when Ashley was there all he heard was 'remember this' and 'remember we had to do that.' But there were quite a few new interesting stories too that came out and made them laugh.

But Robin was excellent in the shop too and picked up the antiques business rapidly and with great skill. He had a phenomenal memory and once he read an items' descriptive card he never needed to view it again. The words were indelibly imprinted in his memory. Milly reckoned that uncle Robin was blessed with a photographic memory.

Milly and Tania had been to the Gloucester Docks area and spent a whole day browsing the antiques shops there. They had returned with some very interesting purchases.

'Ashley,' Milly said on return, 'you have been holding out on me. I thought selling antiques was great but now I know it is nothing compared to the joy of finding and buying the things themselves.'

Ashley knew then that Milly had been well and truly smitten with the antiques bug. It was in her blood now and the thrill of a prospective find would always course through her veins. Since mother and daughter had long discussions on all matters it was soon evident that Tania also thrilled whenever she heard her mother carry on about such and such a piece so enthusiastically.

Tania had her college work to contend with and so was not able to go out on many of these foraging expeditions. Milly began checking the papers every week to note where house sales or car boot sales were being held. And she would often go on her own to these. The Mansfield one was a regular affair and Ashley arranged with Gary and Jill for Milly to meet them on her own one weekend and to visit the car boot field on the Sunday.

When Milly returned she was full of praise for the Priors. However she had a sad tale to tell. She had met the farmer at his usual stand and had hoped to see the bottom half of the Wally bird jar that Ashley had encountered on his visit all those weeks ago. The story had been reported in the local paper and farmer Jake Pelling, for that was his name, had had his brief claim to fame. He had brought it to his stand every other Sunday and had refused offers of well over a thousand pounds for it. Sadly about a month ago it suddenly went missing from the table at his stand. He reckoned someone with very light fingers had taken it while he was looking in another direction. Yet he didn't seem upset at the loss.

'Tain't no loss to me,' he'd said. 'Never knew nothin' till young city chappie told of value with top on. I liked telling the yarn though. Well tis gone now and I got me shillins worth of fun off it.'

When Ashley heard about the theft he decided to start his crusade against crime by making this his first case, so to speak. He thought it was sad that someone would want something that was practically worthless without the top. Ashley thought he'd have to visit the site of the theft – farmer Jake Pelling's stand – to view the actual theft event just like the Quigley Thorn affair and the mugging of Philip. But that inner voice said this was not necessary since he had already been there. All Ashley had to do was concentrate on the visual image of farmer Jake's car boot stand and the bird jar base.

The room turned rosy pink and Ashley shut his eyes tight and concentrated on the field in Mansfield and Farmer Jake Pelling's stand at the far end. Ashley wasn't sure if this was the wrong day for viewing the theft in question. He looked closely at the table and there stood the bird jar base with the plastic flowers still displayed. Ashley now thought about the theft and there then occurred a blurring of the picture for a few seconds before a return to a good image. Two tall young men walked up to the table and one spoke to the farmer and pointed to an item at the opposite end of the table. Farmer Jake got up slowly and walked to the item and as he did so the other man reached across and picked up the bird jar, removed the flowers and turned around as if inspecting the jar in a better light. He then began to stroll slowly away from the table with the jar now held close to his chest. The other man meanwhile paid for the item and farmer Jack had to get some change from the small tin box behind him. The man seemed in no hurry and walked slowly to the next table, looked at the items displayed there and then gradually moved away towards the car park area. He got into an old faded green Vauxhall Astra and smiled at his partner who held up the jar base.

'That was as easy as taking candy from a kid,' he said.

Farmer Jake didn't miss his precious jar till the evening when he went to pack things away.

Ashley now concentrated on the two men. They were brothers and looked very much alike. The elder one who had lifted the piece was Derek Williams and his younger brother was Alan. They lived in Worksop just a dozen miles to the north of Mansfield and the story of the bird jar had carried to all the nearby local papers. Farmer Jake was a topic of conversation in all the area's pubs for several weeks.

These two lads had at first talked about the bird jar from a point of interest only. But gradually the idea of owning it grew in their minds. They lived in the Kilton area of Worksop in rented accommodation in a block of council flats at number 23 Keats Crescent. They were both unemployed and had no intention of finding work. Both were happy to claim on the dole and between them they received enough supplementary benefit to keep them well supplied with cigarettes and beer. As brothers they had grown up together in social services' care homes after their parents had split up. Although separated for a few years they had been placed in the same school and grew up knowing each other. After finishing school without any GCSEs whatsoever they had signed on the dole and now seven years later had decided they were quite happy with their lot. They had no ambitions towards anything grander than what they currently had.

The idea of possessing the bird jar had been Alan's idea but Derek had been as enthusiastic after reading the story in the local paper again. They had done a survey of the car boot sale the previous week and checked the layout and conditions. This was their first conspiracy at theft and both were rather nervous. During the following week they had very nearly called off their little scheme having been quite unimpressed at the sight of the ugly jar base. But they went ahead anyway and so there it sat on the mantel of their living room.

Ashley came out of this vision experience and thought about the best course of action. Derek and Alan Williams were not criminals as yet and this had been their first foray into crime. However once they felt they had got away with it they might venture on another escapade just for the fun of it. And so it might go on till eventually they would begin a life of serious crime for profit.

Ashley decided to travel up early the next morning and be at their flat about nine o'clock and hope to catch them at home. In fact it was just after 8:30 the next morning when Ashley drove into Worksop. His Garmin Sat-nav then directed him north up Blyth Road, left along Shepherds Avenue, then across Kilton Hill and into Keats Crescent. Ashley parked on the other side of the road and looked across at the flat marked with a hand painted large numeric 23. These were all single storey two up two down affairs and the outside had not seen a lick of paint in years. The small front gardens were untended and the grass needed cutting in most of them. The impression the area gave was one of poverty.

Ashley thought about just taking the bird jar base and leaving the brothers alone. But then he thought that they had performed a criminal act and should be taught a lesson. So he went pink and entered the house and walked around the rooms. Derek was downstairs in the kitchen making a mug of tea while Alan was upstairs sitting on the toilet reading a magazine.

Ashley noted where all the moveable items were and went down the stairs. He picked up the bird jar base off the mantel and went back to his car.

Ashley then closed his eyes and visualised the layout of the rooms and began to systematically and forcefully send items crashing down. There were shouts of alarm from within the house and after a few minutes the front door opened and two half dressed young men rushed out. They went as far as the pavement and stood there staring back at the house. Ashley continued his telekinetic action and gradually some of the neighbours came out to see what the crashing noises were all about. There was an extra loud crash when the electric kettle fell and more neighbours came out. There were about ten people outside now and Ashley decided a message was due. He telepathically communicated to all those standing around the full visual events of the theft of the bird jar base from the farmer Jake's table at the car boot sale and exactly as Ashley had seen it. Ashley also added that the bird jar base was cursed and was being returned to its rightful owner by the powers that be. He left all this a bit vague but could see that the message had got through.

The neighbours now knew who had stolen the item they had read about in the local papers and looked with disgust at the two Williams brothers. There were even low voiced accusations against the two naming them as thieves and crooks before they all returned to their own properties.

Ashley sent a last few items crashing down before sending the brothers another message. He said every item in the house would be systematically destroyed unless the brothers confessed to the police and to farmer Jake as well within the week. The bird jar base had now been returned to its rightful owner but the curse had not been lifted. Ashley waited till the brothers had re-entered their home before slowly driving away.

Ashley knew the cottage where farmer Jake lived and drove to it. He checked for thoughts and sensed the farmer was in. Ashley then drove about a hundred yards further down the lane and stopped. He walked back to farmer Jake's front door and rang the bell. He then placed the bird jar base on the welcome mat and retreated out of view to one side.

The door opened and farmer Jake looked around and said a puzzled 'Hello, who's there?'

He then saw the item on the mat and gave an exclamation of delight.

'Well, well, well,' he said with a smile, 'sooo, yer've come back home 'ave ye. Finished with yer wanderins then? Well ye'd best be inside where ye belong me ugly beauty.' And picking up the jar base farmer Jake went in and shut the door behind him.

Ashley had a satisfied smile on his face as he walked back to the car. The pleasant thoughts and smile remained with Ashley on the hour and a half drive back to Dudley. He phoned Robin that he would be along later and to please get some doughnuts from his lovely Lorraine Hollings as he'd missed his breakfast.

Robin was on his own when Ashley walked into the shop just after eleven o'clock. There were doughnuts and croissants in their bakery paper bags on the kitchen table. The kettle had been on the boil before and Robin switched it on again for a quick heat up. Ashley had already tucked into his first croissant and had reached for a doughnut when two mugs of tea were brought to the table. Ashley was on his second doughnut when Milly walked in followed by Tania.

'Look mum,' said Tania laughing, 'we've caught the boys with their hands in the cookie jar.'

Ashley just looked and smiled at them with his lips all covered in the sugar frosting from the doughnut he was eating. Tania was nearly eighteen and prettier than ever and very much like her mum in poise and bearing. She was allowed make-up now and Milly had been teaching her to drive these last eight months. They went out everyday for practice and Tania was due to take her test next week again. She had been failed last month for not checking her mirrors properly and for crossing her hands while steering round a corner. She also had her A-Levels exams next month and hoped to go to Teacher Training College in the autumn.

Ashley finally finished eating, wiped his mouth and said hello to the pair and offered them the bakery bags of goodies. They refused but said a mug of tea would be nice.

'There's a disco and entertainment evening on Friday at the college,' said Tania, 'and mum and dad are coming. Please come Ashley and we can have a dance or two. It's for charity and I have some reserved tickets. There's to be a magician or a hypnotist or something and I'm sure it will be good fun. Mich and Bev said they were going as well so we could all sit together. It's only £3 a ticket.'

There was no way Ashley could refuse as he could see Milly looking on keenly as well. He would visit his parents this evening and fill them in on the day's events. This was something he did on a regular basis as a matter of course. Ashley felt he had to report to his family just so that they were kept abreast of everything he did. He always appreciated their comments and advice.

'Why thank you Tania,' said Ashley smiling gracefully, 'that's very nice of you to invite me, I'd be delighted to attend.'

Milly turned away smiling; she could read Ashley like a book and knew that he spoke in this formal manner whenever he was pushed into a corner. Now that Tania had an escort maybe she and Jerry could extricate themselves from their commitment to attend.

'Why don't you ask Katy and some of her friends if they'd like to go as well,' said Milly to her daughter. 'Daddy and I would rather stay home for a quiet evening after a busy day; after all it is a young persons disco. And the music is always a bit on the loud side.'

So that evening when Ashley had telepathically given his parents the saga of his early trip to Worksop and the recovery of farmer Jake's bird jar and his treatment of the two novice thieves he mentioned the college disco to Katy. She was quite enthusiastic and said the more the merrier and straightaway got out her mobile phone and sent text messages to Robin Nesters, Robert Black and Vicky. Within a matter of minutes their replies came back in the affirmative. She then sent a text message to Tania to get them the necessary tickets. Again an immediate okay reply came back.

Katy and her friends often formed a foursome and so on Friday evening travelled to the college together in Robert's car. Ashley and Tania were already there and had commandeered a table at the lower end of the large hall. Tania's friends Mich and Bev were there with a group of their own and seated quite near them. The hall was buzzing with student chatter and the DJ completed the setting up of his equipment and did the usual sound testing one - two, one - two. He then put on some soft music and adjusted the volume to a low level. The Principal then welcomed everyone to the disco and hoped they would have an enjoyable evening. He said a few words about the charity and the good that they did but the buzz of chatter returned and his words were drowned out by the time they reached the back end of the hall. He handed the microphone back to the DJ who immediately upped the sound on his first selection. It was the Abba song 'Dancing Queen' that always got people up and dancing. The first few pieces were other Abba songs as well and the floor was full of people dancing in little groups and waving their arms in the air.

Tania had got the whole table to get up to dance and they formed their own circle of wriggling bodies. There was a lot of smiling and laughter and nodding of heads when people tried talking while dancing. The DJ played all the right stuff and the dance floor was packed every time. Ashley was not much of a dancer and eventually after about thirty minutes of gyrating went to the makeshift bar to buy his round of cokes and shandies. When he brought the loaded tray back to the table the others of his group had also returned and were gratefully resting and mopping their sweaty foreheads.

And so the evening wore on till eventually it was time for the cabaret act. The Principal took to the microphone again and announced that it was to be a hypnotist who would entertain them for a good hour after which the DJ would carry on playing their favourite music till after midnight.

Six straight backed chairs were then placed in a line in front of the stage at the edge of the dance floor under the direction of a man in a long black coat.

'Good evening ladies and gentlemen,' he said. 'I'm Marvin Hayes and I am your hypnotist for the evening and hope to get some volunteers from among you to entertain you. If for any reason you do not wish to be a volunteer for hypnotism then do not follow any of the instructions I am just about to give you.'

He didn't use a microphone but talked as he stood in the centre of the dance floor. He was of medium height, broad shouldered and clean shaven and waved his hands around gesturing as he spoke.

'Now I'd like all of you who are willing to please raise your hands in front of you,' he said in a slow husky voice. 'That's right missus just like that. Now lace the fingers of one hand with those of the other and close your hands and clasp them together tightly. As tightly as you can and now close your eyes and think of being fast asleep. Everyone please. Thank you.'

He then walked around touching some of the clasped hands and saying 'Good' each time.

'Now, ladies and gentlemen,' he said, 'I have a little confession to make. Just before you clasped your hands I put a drop of superglue on the palm of each hand. So now your hands are stuck fast together and you will not be able to open them until I and only I pull them apart with my hands and say the magic word 'abracadabra' followed by the word 'open'. Is that understood?'

A lot of people nodded but most smiled and had their eyes open to see what was going on with the others. At Ashley's table they had all opened their eyes and their hands except for Tania. She still had her hands tightly clasped and eyes shut.

Marvin then said that everyone could return to normal again if they wished. He then came around checking for the ones who still had their hands and eyes shut tight. He told these ones to stand up. There were about eight people now standing and one by one he led them to the chairs placed on the front of the dance floor. Tania was one of those chosen.

'Right ladies and gentlemen,' he said, 'I have my volunteers so the rest of you can relax I shall not be asking anything of you. Not everyone can be hypnotised so I needed to find those who could. I shall now bring these eight good people out of their trance.'

He then stood in front of the eight and loudly said, 'I am going to release your hands now with my special words at the count of three and you will awake at the same time so listen carefully; one, two, three, abracadabra and open.' The five men and three women lowered their arms and opened their eyes and looked around them with smiles on their faces, Tania among them. Two more chairs were brought and Marvin had his subjects sit down.

'Ladies and gentlemen,' Marvin said, 'these are my subjects for the evening. They are all still in a hypnotic trance and will be until I release them. They will believe everything I tell them and do everything I ask of them that is reasonable to them. I cannot make them do something they would not normally wish to do, like go and rob a bank or something. Think how rich I would be if I could get them to do that.'

He then went to a tall thin chap sitting at the left end of his subjects and tapped him on the shoulder.

'And what might your name be young man,' he asked.

'I'm Nigel,' replied the young man.

'Well Nigel, thank you for being such a lovely volunteer this evening. There are eight of you and I only need seven so you may get up and return to your friends and enjoy the rest of the evening.'

Nigel stood up and took a step forward when the hypnotist stopped him.

'There's just one more thing Nigel,' he said. 'Anytime during the next hour when you hear the word 'jungle' you will do a Tarzan victory call. You know what I mean don't you. You stand up, beat your chest with your fists and do that yodelling cry from the Tarzan films.'

He then shook Nigel's hand and let him return to his friends.

'Now then,' said Marvin to the others seated in front of him, 'you are the lucky seven. Will you all now please cover your eyes with your hands? That's it, thank you very much.'

Then he turned to the hall and asked why every one had removed their clothes. He turned again to his seven volunteers and told them that the entire audience had removed their clothes and all were sitting around buff naked. He said he was so glad he had asked them to cover their eyes because it certainly wasn't a pretty sight.

'I can see that you don't believe me so why don't you have a peek for yourselves?'

The seven then took their hands away from their eyes and with a gasp the three girls quickly covered their faces again. The lads looked around and smiled sheepishly and looked down at the floor or up at the ceiling only to look at the audience again and this time with mouths wide open. The girls slowly uncovered their eyes and like the boys had their mouths saying a silent 'aaahhh' while trying to look everywhere except at the supposedly naked people in the audience. And then one of the girls began to giggle with her hand up to her mouth as if she had just heard a very funny joke. Soon they were all laughing and the whole hall joined in.

After a few moments Marvin clapped his hands and told his seven volunteers to close their eyes.

'Right my friends,' he said to them. 'The audience are all nicely dressed again and looking decent so you may once again open your eyes and you will remember nothing of what you just thought you saw.'

The seven opened their eyes and sat looking around and at each other as if nothing had happened and wondering what the hypnotist was going to say or do next.

'Now aren't you a wonderful audience,' he said to them. 'I wonder if any of you have ever been on a safari to Africa. I have and let me tell you that it's a wonderful experience. But you have to be ever so careful as there are so many wild animals in the 'jungle'.

At that instant Nigel who was enjoying himself back with his friends stood up, beat his chest with his fists and gave a loud Tarzan yodelling cry and then sat down again as if nothing had happened.

The hall erupted in laughter but poor old Nigel hadn't a clue why everyone was laughing.

He looked around at his friends and kept repeating 'what, what, what?'

Marvin turned once again to his seven and asked them to stand up. He then told them that for some unknown reason the chairs that they had been sitting on had suddenly become very very hot. So hot in fact, that you couldn't sit on them without getting burned. He then asked them to sit down again. But each time their bottoms touched the seats they would shoot up in pain. They all tried sitting a few times and then gave up. Some even tentatively touched the seats with their hands but quickly withdrew them, blew on them and rubbed them together while shaking their heads.

The hall was in fits of laughter as the seven continued to test their hot seats.

Marvin then clapped his hands again and said that the seats had finally cooled down and it was now okay to sit on them again. The seven sat down but very gingerly while looking from side to side as they did so. Ashley was mesmerised by the look and manner of Tania. It was like seeing a very mature side of her and he realised what a beautiful woman she was. Something sparked in his breast and caused a warm glow to commence. And he liked what he felt. Yes he certainly liked this woman and in a wholly new perspective. He now saw what the others in his family had seen all along.

Marvin then told his subjects that they were all new recruits in the army and were on parade in front of their barracks. They must all now behave as if they were listening to their sergeant major and stand to attention and then follow his parade instructions whatever they might be.

The seven immediately stood to stiff attention for a moment and then began marching with swinging arms around the dance floor. All were doing their own thing. Tania was marching as if she had a sergeant major's baton under one arm.

Marvin again clapped his hands and the seven stopped in their tracks.

'Thank you my wonderful recruits,' he said. 'You have all done excellently and have passed your training with flying colours. You are now quite ready for your next exercise in the 'jungle'.

Once again Nigel stood up, beat his chest with his fists and gave another loud Tarzan yodelling cry and then sat down again as if nothing had happened. As before the hall erupted again in laughter while Nigel once again remained puzzled as to why everyone was looking at him and laughing.

Marvin next went up to three of the lads and two of the girls and thanked them for their participation as volunteers and that he now released them to return to their friends. They seemed to awaken as from a daze and walked back to their tables to a big round of applause. But Tania was not among them. She was still up there with another blond haired young fellow. Marvin told them to stand again and asked them their names.

'Ladies and gentlemen we now come to our final act of the evening. Our last two volunteers Tania and Barry are going to perform a cabaret for our entertainment. I don't know what they intend doing but perhaps this will give you a clue.' Marvin then pointed to the DJ and immediately music began to play that was commonly associated with the stripper's dance and the hall erupted in laughter; except for Tania and Barry who began to dance seductively about the floor. Barry began to very slowly undo the buttons on his shirt while Tania began to slowly unroll imaginary full length gloves down her arms. Then she sat on one of the chairs and began to unroll an imaginary stocking off her outstretched leg, all the while gently swaying to the music. The audience had begun a slow clap and were chanting 'off, off, off,' to the rhythm of the music.

By now Barry had removed his shirt and was twirling it around above his head before releasing it at the audience. He then reached down and went to open his trouser belt when Marvin signalled to the DJ and the music stopped. Barry looked at his bare chest and quickly grabbed up his shirt and put it on again looking quite embarrassed. Tania looked around too but fortunately hadn't removed anything though she did look uncomfortable.

'Ladies and gentlemen,' said Marvin the hypnotist. 'Please give a big round of applause to our two lovely entertainers Barry and Tania. Weren't they just wonderful? And to show my thanks I have a big juicy apple for each of them.'

131

He went to a box on the stage behind him and brought out two large Spanish onions and showed them to the hall by walking to the front of the dance floor. He then went back and gave one each to Tania and Barry and told them to enjoy the juicy apples. He asked if they were sweet and so each took a big bite. As they chewed they nodded to Marvin.

'Right Tania and Barry,' he said, 'do enjoy your apples and thank you for your assistance. You may now wake up and return to your friends.' And with that he clapped his hands.

Both Tania and Barry looked in disgust at the onions in their hands and Marvin quickly produced the box they had been in. The onions were dropped in along with mouthfuls of partly chewed onion that Barry and Tania had spat out into their hands. He then produced bottles of ice cold coke and gave one to each of them.

'Ooo,' said Tania, 'my mouth tastes awful.'

She drank the coke all the while swilling it around in her mouth before swallowing. Barry did the same as they walked back to their respective tables.

'A big round of applause for Tania and Barry please,' said Marvin.

'Ladies and Gentlemen, thank you for being such a wonderful audience. And thank you also to our charming and willing volunteers. Goodnight and drive home safely to your own 'jungle'.

Once again, Nigel who was still enjoying himself with his friends stood up beat his chest with his fists and gave a loud Tarzan yodelling cry and then sat down again as if nothing had happened. There were hoots of laughter from everyone.

Marvin now came over to where Nigel was sitting and said that his one hour was up and he was not Tarzan anymore. He then clapped his hands and reached across and shook Nigel by the hand and thanked him before returning to the stage. Ashley was at the next table and had been most impressed by the hypnotist's performance. It had given him an idea for his crusade against crime. So he read Marvin's mind and hoped to learn the art of hypnotism at a distance as he had witnessed this evening.

The facts as Ashley saw them were that Marvin had been born in India and had lived in Delhi where his parents ran a staffing agency supplying the requirements of the growing technological industry. They advertised locally and internationally and recruited according to the skills that were in demand. Marvin had had his early education in a British run school in Delhi but had been sent to London to live with an aunt when he was nine to complete his education in the intended 'proper fashion'. He returned to India twice each year; once in the summer holidays for two months and then again for a shorter duration at Christmas. He loved India and visited whenever he could.

His choice of vocation came to him at a college function in London where an aging magician and hypnotist had performed. He had been so taken by the skill of the act that he begged the man who called himself Wallace Williamson to recruit him as an assistant. Marvin's parents had been in England at the time and though a bit disappointed at his choice of vocation had gone along with their only son's wish and had said they would continue to provide him with his generous allowance. Having lived in India for so long Mr and Mrs Hayes believed in the Hindu philosophy of Karma and that one's 'Destiny' was pre-ordained as God's will. It was all written in the Book of Fate according to some divine plan and far be it for parents to try and change their son's choice of vocation. If Marvin was happy then they were pleased for him.

And so Marvin began a new kind of life touring the country with his new master and tutor who was quite willing to share his secrets with his unpaid apprentice. Gradually Marvin began to acquire skills that even Wallace found impressive. And they grew to respect and like each other. Eventually after several years age got the better of Wallace and he didn't go out touring anymore. Marvin ran the business on his own after Wallace voluntarily handed him the reins.

When Ashley looked deeply into Marvin's memories he found that his phenomenal hypnotism skills were partly dependant upon a very primitive form of telepathy. Though not exactly conversational in form Marvin could subconsciously will his subjects to sense or feel what it was that he was saying to them. Ashley got the principle of the skill and knew that he could do better with his advanced telepathic skills. This would be an important tool in helping to reform the criminal mind on a more or less long term basis. Many ideas came into Ashley's thoughts and chief among them was that he may not need to apply the physical pain aspect on his victim.

'Ashley,' said Tania breaking into his thoughts, 'my mouth feels terrible. I can still taste that beastly onion. You should have stopped it then. Please get me something to take away this horrible onion taste that I have in my mouth. Maybe something that is sweet and gooey.'

Ashley couldn't help laughing as he said, 'I think I had better get some fresh-mint chewing gum as well while I'm at it for all our sakes. Your breath smells of that onion and I bet it will for quite some time. You had better come with me and choose for yourself.'

Ashley walked around the table to Tania and offered his hand to help her up. She took it but kept hold of it as they walked to the bar area the other side of the hall. Ashley looked down at her as they walked and he made a big pretence of fanning his face and then pinching the end of his nose. They both laughed and Tania pretended to punch him with her free hand. The others watched them from the table and smiled at each other knowingly. Vicky had a wistful look on her face and Katy noticed this immediately with her keen eye and was rather surprised. Vicky had a thing going with Robert and yet she had an eye for Ashley as well. When she was with Robert she looked totally happy and in love with him; it was clear for all of them to see. So this wistfulness in Ashley's direction was a bit of a puzzle for Katy. And she wasn't happy with it. Ashley could read peoples' minds and Katy decided to get to the bottom of this by asking Ashley to look into Vicky's. Tania and Katy were like sisters and Tania had confessed that there was only one man for her and that was her brother. Katy also knew that Ashley was extremely fond of Tania but had to hold back because of not knowing what the purpose was behind him being given his gifts. Now that Katy was part of the inner family circle she understood that Ashley could not commit himself to anyone until he knew more. But Tania had patience and had told Katy that she would wait for Ashley forever no matter what; which made Katy love her all the more.

Katy watched as her brother and Tania walked back towards their table. Tania had a schooner of sherry in one hand and a bag of sweets or toffees in the other. Ashley had his hand lightly across her shoulders as he strolled beside her and being a few inches taller occasionally looked down at her reddish brown head. Only Katy noticed that look and gave a pleased little smile.

Tania set her glass down on the table and silently offered her bag to the others. She seemed to have her mouth full of liquid and was swilling it from side to side before swallowing with a big gulp.

'Sorry folks,' she said, 'I'm just trying to get the taste of that bloody onion, pardon the French, out of my mouth. Please have a piece of fudge it really is quite nice though a bit on the sweet side. I've already had two but felt I had to swill some strong sherry around the molars to get rid of that beastly onion taste.'

Ashley sat down beside Katy and smiled at his sister. She faced him but with her eyes shut before looking away which was their code that she wanted him to read her mind. Ashley did so and received her message that she was puzzled and worried about the way Vicky looked at him. Katy's visual image of seeing Vicky's wistful look was also picked up by Ashley.

'I've picked up Vicky's thoughts once before and I didn't approve of them then,' conveyed Ashley 'and I can't do anything about it. But I have read her mind and she does genuinely care for Robert. It could be that I appeal to her from a curiosity point of view. I really loved Aunt Brenda's Barclay more than I thought I loved mum and dad and you, at the time; and I think you did too. So it might all be relative. Let's just ignore it and hope nothing comes of it'.

Katy reached across and squeezed Ashley's hand and smiled and Ashley smiled back as he read her thought.

'What are you two hatching up,' asked Robin. 'Any one for another shandy it's my round so speak now or forever hold your peace.'

'I'll come and give you a hand Robin,' said Katy. And after receiving everyone's order they walked across to the bar together with their index fingers linked loosely and looking at ease with each other. This time it was Ashley's turn to smile his approval. For Robin Nesters there was only one person in the whole world who mattered to him and that was Katy, and it had been so ever since he'd first laid eyes on her. He was consistent and very patient. He was happy just to be in Katy's company and was wise enough to know that it was all up to the lady to choose. And of course he hoped to be in that line-up of choice. He had mentioned this as an opinion in a general discussion one evening long ago and Katy had never forgotten it. And it endeared Robin to her just that little bit more.

But her life had changed ever since she had been drawn into the family circle of knowledge with regard to Ashley, and like Ashley she had decided to put her future on hold. The knowledge that someone was out there to mentally help and advise her brother in his future task, - whatever it might be, - made Katy's religious beliefs turn into home truths. She went to church and read her Bible more often and felt she had become a better person in mind and in character. She showed more in the way of affection and care and was much more forgiving than she had been before. She rationalised all this change on the fact that she knew she was not on her own.

'Come on Tania,' said Vicky, 'tell us, did you really think you were eating a juicy apple up there?'

'You may not believe this but I can still remember biting into that beastly onion and thinking what a delicious tasting apple it was,' replied Tania. 'I actually believed everything that fellow said.'

'But that bit when the stripper tune was playing,' asked Ashley seriously, 'would you have gone all the way if he hadn't stopped the music?'

'I don't know but I think I might have and I'll tell you for why,' said Tania. 'I imagined I was back in my bedroom getting ready for bed. Since I only wear a nightie to bed then of course everything else would have had to come off first. So I'm glad the music stopped when it did.'

This became a joke with her college friends at the other tables who ribbed Tania as they walked past saying that she could always fall back to being a stripper if she failed her exams. Some of the lads whistled at her and said what a shame the music had stopped. They would have liked to have seen the mole on her bottom.

Tania turned a bright red at this remark. Years ago when she was a little girl in primary school the other girls had seen the birthmark on her left upper thigh when changing for PE and of course had talked about it. Some of those girls were here today with their boyfriends.

'It's not a mole,' said Tania to Ashley and Katy. 'It's a birthmark. And mum has one in exactly the same spot, so it must be hereditary. Probably from a royal ancestor or even a king,'

Everyone laughed and said they too wished they had something distinguishing like that. People today had tattoos done in the funniest of places. This gave Tania an idea. She walked to the table where one of the lads was sitting with some of the girls in Tania's class.

'Hey Lizzie ask him to show you the tattoo on his…,' said Tania pointing to the lad's lower zone.

She then slowly winked at the girls and walked back to her own table.

Of course there was no tattoo but the girls wouldn't believe him and kept teasing to be told what it was and to please 'show us your tattoo Larry'. Before he knew it the chant was picked up by other tables and a chorus of 'show us your tattoo Larry' was being repeated to an impromptu tune.

The DJ started playing again and with the fun atmosphere in the hall nearly everyone got up to dance. Ashley was very glad that he had accepted Tania's invitation yesterday and told Tania as much. The bar closed at eleven thirty and the DJ stopped playing just after midnight. The last tune was a slow number sung by Englebert Humperdink called 'The Last Waltz' and among the couples on the dance floor were Vicky and Robert from their table. Katy thought Vicky was making a statement.

Ashley dropped Tania home before continuing to his place. He had a lot to think about especially with regard to his newfound awareness with regard to his feelings for Tania.

He must also discuss this exciting new hypnosis skill with the family tomorrow. He needed to first practice what he had acquired in theory from Marvin Hayes before becoming a confident practicing hypnotist. Maybe dad or granddad would have some ideas.

Ashley had been up for an hour when the phone rang at nine. It was Milly and she sounded very excited about something.

'Ashley,' she said, 'did you know about the auction up at Charlford House in Four Oaks Sutton Coldfield. It's today and starts at eleven o'clock. I've only just seen it by chance in last weeks paper that I was about to throw into the recycling bin. There's a detailed article about how the trustees of the house are throwing open the doors to the public for the first time ever and are auctioning its entire contents in the grounds itself. The article says that the place is steeped in perfectly preserved Victorian history and has heaps of antiques and trinkets and is a treasure trove of that period. It says that the owner died a few years ago, someone called Herbert Smith who was once the Mayor of Walsall, and everything must go prior to putting the house up for sale. I think we need to attend and see what we can pick up.'

'Gosh Milly,' said Ashley, 'that's great. I've had my mind on other things and must have missed it; and so local too. I hope you don't mind if I make a suggestion. Why don't you and Tania go as soon as possible? I'll try and catch you up later as I have something I need to attend to first. Take your business card with you and good luck with anything you find. Here's a tip; wait till the bidding is slowing on the item you want and only come in then. And look to see who is bidding against you. If it is an old person and he ups your bid more than three times then you should give up. He's a personal collector and really wants the item at any cost. If it's a phone bidder the same applies but you can keep bidding a bit longer. Try and get there as soon as you can to look around and inspect the items. Take pen and paper and note down the lot numbers that interest you. Sorry to leave you on your own but I'm sure you'll enjoy the experience. It gives one quite a buzz and you'll be impatiently looking out for your next auction. I think Robin still does a stint at Packwood House on weekends so he's not available.'

'That's fine Ashley,' said Milly. 'I've spoken to Jerry and he said he'd come along to help. We'd best be off now as it'll take us nearly an hour to get there. I'll ring your mobile if I have a query. Bye for now.'

'Bye, and thanks Milly,' said Ashley and hung up.

Ashley thought about it and decided he'd let Milly have all the fun of the auction. If he went later she'd only step back and let him take over. Ashley wanted Milly to not only get the experience of her first house auction but also to get the confidence of having done it on her own. Ashley knew that in the near future the shop would be Milly's to do as she pleased while he was engaged on the other matter that Philip had hinted at. Robin was a great help to Milly and could be trusted one hundred percent but Milly also needed another younger female to keep her company. Tania was filling that role at the moment but Ashley could see that the antiques business was not quite Tania's thing. She was interested in the shop but only because Ashley was there and to help her mum. There was much to think about and another item to discuss with the family.

Ashley rang his mum and said he was coming over. Lillian was pleased and said that Katy had told her all about last night and the lovely time they had had. Ashley said he had made another discovery which he wanted to add to their plan of action. Lillian said they were having snacks for lunch and going out for a carvery in the evening and would Ashley stay and join them. Ashley said yes and he'd like granddad to be there as well for a family confab.

Ashley spent a good day at home with his family. Katy stayed home too though she usually went out to town with her friends on Saturdays. Granddad Eric rang and asked to be picked up as his car was in for a service, which Ashley did. Being a nice sunny day they all sat in the back garden and had Lillian's snacks in picnic fashion. The discussion was about Ashley's plan and the new discovery of hypnotism. Ashley said it would make the task easier in that he could create illusions in the minds of the criminals. He said that the Tarzan response by the fellow Nigel to the word 'jungle' was a great way of reforming someone. Perhaps Ashley could induce a reaction in the person to one of their own thoughts, such as a thought of violence or anger.

It was Lillian who suggested that Ashley needed to practice his hypnotism skills before he ventured out against any quarry. Katy agreed to be a guinea pig and suggested he try the locked hand bit first. But Ashley was one step ahead of her. He had all of Marvin's skill and telepathically made Katy believe that whenever she heard the word 'holiday' she would develop an itch in her hair above her left ear and would need to scratch it for ten seconds. Ashley then told the others what he had done.

'I wonder where we should go for our holiday this year,' said Ashley to his mum and dad.

And there was Katy immediately scratching her head. She didn't realise she had done it and asked Ashley why he had changed the subject from what they had just been discussing.

'What subject,' asked Ashley?

'You just asked where we should go for our holiday this year,' said Katy and once again she gave her head a scratch above her left ear.

They all laughed and then Ashley clapped his hand lightly and telepathically told Katy that she didn't have an itch above her ear anymore.

'Why,' said Ashley, 'we could go on a one week holiday to Madrid where you could show off your Spanish skills.'

This time Katy didn't scratch at all.

Ashley then explained to Katy what he had just done and this time it was her turn to be amused.

'I think you are ready,' said Alex to his son, 'but I also think you need to plan ahead what it is you are going to suggest to your victims. Perhaps you should think out several plans of action and then choose the one you feel is the most appropriate at the time. Why don't you travel the buses on the upper deck and practice a bit on any unsavoury characters you come across.'

'Thanks dad.' said Ashley. 'I think I'll do just that but I'll start on Monday.'

Just then the phone rang. It was Milly on her mobile and she had a query. There were several mid-Victorian silver wall plaques being sold individually even though some were definitely matching pairs. They were all hallmarked and Milly said she thought they would be a good buy. How much did Ashley think they were worth?

Ashley said that they'd probably be okay at about fifty to eighty for the first one. And if she got it then for the matching one she could bid a bit higher to over one hundred. A matching pair would be worth at least several hundred to a collector. But Ashley felt there was something not quite right here and he told Milly that it might be a set-up by the auctioneer for a partner. So even if Milly won on the bidding she might not get the prize when the auction was over on the claim that a mistake had been made as an oversight by the lot manager for not pairing them up correctly. Ashley suggested she go along with the bidding but should not to be disappointed at the outcome.

'Thanks Ashley,' said Milly, 'you are a gem. I'll let you know how we get on.'

'Good luck,' said Ashley and ended the call.

Ashley spent a pleasant weekend with his family but was a bit concerned that his granddad didn't look quite a hundred percent. He was still on a lot of medication but had lost his usual sparkle and energy. Ashley asked how he felt in himself.

'I'm not too bad Ash,' he said, 'it's getting up in the morning now that is a bit of a chore. It takes me a while to get the stiffness out of my bones. But the thought of that first cup of tea does the trick for me. You know, Ash, tea must be the most addictive drink in the world. I just don't know what I would do without it. I was reading an article that tea alone is responsible for a third of the world's population today. If it hadn't been for the fact that tea must be made from boiling water there would have been more epidemics and a lot of people would have died from drinking the water from wells in the old days. I suppose coffee is the same except I'm not particularly fond of the stuff.'

And so the conversation went on to many other subjects in turn. The voice in Ashley's head said that Eric still had many years ahead of him and would live well into his nineties.

Tania rang Ashley in the evening from home and gave him a full account of the day's events at the auction. She said how embarrassed she had been when her mum had interrupted the bidding for the second matching wall plaque to ask why they were being sold off separately and not in pairs. The hesitant reply had been that everything must go and it had been decided to sell items individually so they were more affordable to the public. And so the shop could now boast two matching pairs of hall marked silver Victorian wall plaques. There was a lot of furniture and other biggish items which of course weren't suitable for McGill's shop but Milly did pick up a small oil painting in a gilded frame for literally pennies.

'Mum said she thought you'd maybe know more about it when you saw it. It looks like a Constable but only it isn't as it has an unknown signature in a top corner. Anyway she'll bring everything to the shop on Monday and you can see for yourself.'

On Sunday morning Ashley walked down to the corner shop Spa to pick up a Sunday newspaper. He noticed that they also sold Travel Cards and on the spur of the moment bought one to cover the entire West Midlands area for a full month. It had been a few years since he'd last rode the buses and thought it would fit in with his plan for meeting up with any unsavoury characters on the upper decks. Ashley wondered whether he should induce a vision of huge snakes crawling around or make them feel they were quite naked. Then again he could make them see the other passengers as great big vicious growling gorillas. Ashley would decide on the spur of the moment what he would do.

Just then there came a loud crash bang noise from outside the newsagents shop. The lady serving Ashley said that they were having this every day. There were about three or four biggish lads who played football outside and used the roller shutter doors of the neighbouring vacant premises as the goal. There was another loud crash of sound.

'We've spoken to them about it but only get a mouthful of abuse in return,' she said. 'The police say there is nothing they can do either except talk to them. The kids seem to know their rights and even taunt us with 'touch me and we'll report you for assault'. I just hope that one day they'll grow up and get a job or something.'

Ashley said nothing as he walked out of the shop. He walked slowly in front of the roller shutter door that was serving as goal and pretended to read the back page. He stopped there for a minute till one of the lads got impatient and shouted for Ashley to 'get the f… out of the way'.

Ashley slowly turned around and spread his arms outwards. To passers by it looked an innocent gesture but to the four lads he was a ten foot angry gorilla coming to get them, a suggestion that Ashley had induced in their minds. He also made them understand that if they played around here again the gorilla would be watching and waiting. In addition it would be watching them wherever they were and if they swore and behaved badly to others it would come and get them. Ashley made this a permanent hypnotic suggestion in their minds hoping for a long term reformation of attitude and behaviour. Only time would tell but Ashley was confident it would work. That inner voice said that it was a job well done. Here was something he could probably use again and again.

In their hasty retreat from the scene the lads left their football behind. Ashley picked it up and took it in to the newsagents and asked the lady if she would look after it for the lads who had been called away on other important business. Ashley winked at her as he turned around and left the shop.

'I wish I had come with you Ash,' said Katy when Ashley recounted the event to them. 'I bet you scared the living daylights out of them. I'd have loved to see the expressions on their faces when they thought you were that monster. Do you think it will last?'

'I don't know,' said Ashley. 'I should imagine they won't ever forget what they think they saw today and they have been warned to mend their behaviour or else. The suggestion I put in their minds should last at least a week or so. I'm hoping it could be even longer. We'll just have to wait and see and hope for the best.'

Katy was looking at her brother with an expression of admiration and possessive pride. She had always looked up to Ashley ever since he used to catch birds for her cage when they were youngsters all those years ago. She had always thought he was special and now she knew how special he was and that the hand of God must be upon him. To what purpose none of them knew but Katy was confident that her brother and her family which included her had been specially chosen. She felt privileged. But Katy knew that she couldn't repeat any of these things to anyone. She had slipped up when she had told Tania about Ashley's skill at catching birds for her cage and they had conspired together after Tania thought she had heard Ashley's telepathic phone message to Aunt Brenda that Christmas before Philip died. Since then neither of them had spoken about that conversation. It seemed to be an understood and agreed silence and the matter was just not mentioned again. Katy felt that Tania knew more than she was letting on but this only made Katy realise that Tania also had a sort of protective feeling for Ashley. Perhaps one day things might change as surely she hoped they must. Seeing them together at the college disco was encouraging.

Back at the shop on Monday morning Milly showed Ashley the items she had managed to acquire at the Charlford House auction. The silver wall plaques could all do with a bit of cleaning. Someone had applied a thin coating of clear varnish to them which gave them a dull appearance. Ashley said he knew a restorer who could get them to their original unvarnished state.

'O Ashley, all you need is a bit of solvent to get rid of the varnish and Jerry will do that. He's quite good at DIY and this would be right up his street. Now a painting is definitely a restorer's job. What do you think of this?' and she held up the one foot square frame with the part faded country scene oil painting.

Ashley picked it up and instantly acquired its history. An apprentice painter by the name of Michael Loader went from London to Paris in the mid-eighteenth century to join the Notre Dame School of Art. He could only afford to study there for about a year before his money would run out. But he had confidence in his skill as an artist and had hopes of being apprenticed to a famous name. All paintings completed at the school by the apprentices could only be signed at the top right hand corner and were not allowed to be sold. Very often a part of the paintings had the masters' hand in its colours and composition and some were even part painted over by that artist as a means of showing the student what was needed. The school was quite well known and famous painters often came to it to see what talents the students possessed. This was really a means of poaching a talented youngster for their own apprenticeships. Of course the artist had to pay the school a release fee for any new arrangement to be made. Michael Loader was one such apprentice and within a few months had been taken on by a well known landscape artist by the name of Pierre-Henride Valenciennes. It was under the new direction that this picture was painted and Valenciennes' hand did much of the lower part of the composition if not the actual artistry.

In those days artists had to mix their own colours by going to the markets and picking up items with the required colours in them. Clay from the river bank was a favourite for the dull yellows in paintings. These had then to be ground into a fine paste and oils added. Different artists preferred different makes of oil though generally olive oil was favoured as being odour free. Often after a painting had been sold and the picture colours had begun to fade the picture would be returned for the artist to reapply fresh colours in part or whole. Alas many artists acquired a reputation for poor colour aging in their pictures and subsequently were unable to sell their paintings. However, oil paints soon became the domain of tradesmen and this no longer constituted a problem.

After about two years with Valenciennes, Michael Loader returned to London never having quite achieved the fame he'd wanted and just faded from view. He died penniless at the age of fifty and was buried in a pauper's grave. No other paintings with his name have appeared on the open market. This was a mid-eighteenth century painting so the age of it counted for something. With this history attached it could fetch a couple of hundred pounds to an interested party.

'How mush did you pay for it at the auction?' asked Ashley.

'Well,' said Milly, 'I bid at the starting price of fifteen pounds and no one else seemed interested. So that is the price I paid. Perhaps if I had waited the auctioneer may have lowered it to a tenner.'

'This one definitely needs a bit of colour restoration. Yet I feel its aged look gives it a bit of character.' said Ashley. 'Perhaps we'll leave it as it is; what do you think Milly?'

'I think you may be right,' said Milly. 'I'd leave it as it is. With the history added I quite fancy it myself.'

Milly then put a blue and white porcelain mug on the table. It was in mint condition and Ashley picked it up and looked at the under side. There was an imprinted crescent and a circle of blue dots under it. It was just over four inches high and was printed with Chinoiserie figures in a landscape scene on one full side.

'This is an imitation of an early Worcester blue and white mug which would have been from around the end of the eighteenth century,' said Ashley. 'However the circle of blue dots on the base shouldn't be there at all. So I would put this as a very good imitation made to order to match the original that might have been dropped and smashed beyond repair. The dots signify that this is a copy. It was made by a craftsman in the late nineteenth century for a rich client. He probably made more than just the one. If he had left the dots off the others they could have fetched a good price as fake originals. But I doubt if he would have been allowed to do so by the factory manager.'

'I would say,' continued Ashley, 'that as a very pretty copy this mug would be worth about fifty to a hundred pounds. So if you paid around a tenner for it then you got another pretty good bargain.'

'Well,' said Milly, 'actually I paid twenty as there was another bidder going for it. An old lady and she kept looking around to see who else was bidding. I wasn't going over the twenty and thought she'd go for it on her next bid. But she just upped and left the room after my last bid. I felt a bit sorry for her but didn't see her again. So there you are.'

'Well Mrs Marsh, I think we have done very well out of this trip,' said Ashley smiling. 'You and Tania can go out on your own anytime; my thanks to both of you and I'm sorry I wasn't able to join you there.'

Ashley decided to stay at the shop all day and help Milly set up the latest acquisitions. They still hadn't put out all the items that Ashley had brought over from Philip's house but then space was limited and crowded shelves wouldn't look presentable, according to Milly.

Ashley wrote out the descriptive cards in free hand which Milly would type up later at home. There just wasn't room on the desk or the kitchen table for a computer system at the shop and Milly preferred to do the cards at home anyway. Tania didn't come in at all that day as she had a full day at college and then a driving lesson. Her second test was in a couple of weeks and she hoped to pass this time. She was getting plenty of practice on her mum's car.

Ashley mentioned that he intended travelling on the buses just to get a feel for how most people travelled. He didn't say anything about hoping to meet the rowdies that people spoke so much about. So the next day Ashley got on bus number 283 outside his house and rode in to the High Street and walked to the shop. Later that afternoon he caught the first bus that come along and spent an hour on various routes. Ashley had a bus route map with him so knew where he planned to go.

When schools emptied at about three o'clock the buses filled with noisy kids full of energy and playful excitement. Ashley saw nothing in their behaviour that was rude or nasty. In fact he quite liked to listen to some of their chatter especially when they were talking about the quirks of one or another of their teachers and mimicked the way he or she spoke. On one occasion two lads got into an argument and nearly came to blows but their friends intervened and stopped it.

Ashley decided on random bus rides in the evenings and still didn't come across anything that could be construed as offensive. There were instances of people using their mobile phones and chattering away for long periods to the annoyance of other bus users but again this was just the way of the times and Ashley ignored it. On one occasion a group of Asian girls and boys sat upstairs at the very back and talked loudly and excitedly. They were showing off to the girls and playing tinny Indian music on their mobile phones. One lad even got up and did a bit of a dance in front of the group. But it was all innocent stuff and Ashley again put it down to the life style among today's youth.

It was in the third week of Ashley's bus journeys that an incident did happen. This was an occasion when he was using the bus to get back home from an evening out with Katy, Robin, Vicky and Robert at a Symphony Hall concert in Birmingham. Katy and the others had caught buses heading for Erdington after the show while Ashley had got on the number 74 bus for Dudley. He was on the upper deck and decided to rest his eyes for a bit. There were a few other young couples sitting near the middle and to the front. A strong odour of fish and chips pervaded the bus and glancing back Ashley noticed a single scruffy individual sitting right at the back eating out of a plain paper wrapper. He was unshaven and must have been in his mid thirties. He was quite light skinned but had a shock of tight black curls on his head. Ashley put him down as being of mixed race but it was the wide-eyed expression on his face that didn't seem right.

Ashley resumed his arms-folded, head-down, eyes-closed posture and thought nothing more of it. Until there was a giggle from the back and a chip hit the floor in front of Ashley. Then another chip struck one of the couples on the seat just ahead. The girl complained to her partner so he looked back with a frown to see who was throwing the chips.

'What you looking at you piece of shit?' said the fellow at the back and threw a chip at him.

Ashley was interested now and decided to read the fellow's mind. His name was Joshua Dray and he had been released a few days ago from a psychiatric unit after two years of treatment for schizophrenia. He had been finally assessed as not a threat to the public although he had a record for a series of violent assaults, one of which had been a near fatal stabbing. He had a weekly appointment at the unit to see Dr Amrit who had been treating him since he was admitted under a court order. He was under strict orders to take his medication morning and evening but had thrown them away the moment he'd left the unit. There had been one thing continually on his mind during the two years he had been in the secure unit. And that was an urge to push a knife into another human being's flesh. The last time he'd done it he just loved the sensation of the knife in his hand rippling as it entered his victim's belly. He still thrilled at the feel of the knife being gripped where it sat and the pressure he had to exert to pull it out for his next thrust and the sucking sound it made as it come clear. The second stab went into the man's uplifted arm and grated against bone. That is when he lost his grip on the knife handle as the victim twisted away. The next thing he noticed was the bloodied knife in the hand of his victim and pointed at him. He turned and ran and only then realised that his victim had been an Afro-Caribbean man of mammoth proportions. He would pick his future victims to be smaller in size. He had picked up the flick knife that he now carried in his jacket pocket from the Bull Ring market for a tenner which he thought was quite expensive. But it looked a good one and boasted a six inch blade when open. This was his third late night bus ride and tonight it seemed he might get his thrill. He'd wait until there was just the one couple left upstairs.

Ashley thought hard about what to do. Joshua Dray was bent on murder and even craved it. There was no doubt that he had to be stopped from his actions not only today but for all time. His craze to feel his knife inside human flesh was an addiction he could not control; and he never would.

The couple right in the front then got up and moved downstairs. The other couple, a girl named Jenny and her boyfriend of a few days called Dominic were in serious conversation and Ashley could see that the girl wanted to leave. But Dominic who was quite a big fellow said he wasn't going to be dictated to. He stood up and pointed at Joshua Dray and told him to pack it in or he'd sort him out. Another chip flew through the air and hit his girl friend on the back of her head.

'Right you bastard,' said Dominic taking a step towards the back, 'let's see how you like a bit of your own medicine.'

It all happened too quickly for Ashley to prevent. Joshua Dray was fast. There was a click as the flick knife opened and an 'Aargh' sound as Dominic felt the knife blade enter his belly. And then the world went misty pink as Ashley reacted.

Ashley stood up and went to the pair frozen in slow time and standing a few rows behind him. Dominic had both fists clenched and his right arm was extended over Joshua Dray's left shoulder as though he had just thrown a punch and missed. Joshua was in a semi crouched posture and the knife in his right hand was up against the loose cloth of Dominic's shirt near his lower belly and halfway into the flesh and creeping slowly deeper. Ashley gripped Joshua's knife hand and pulled the knife out. Looking at the blade the blood stain on it was about two inches long. From Dr Mario's medical memory this meant that most of the wound would be in the surface muscle of the abdomen with possible minor punctures to the small intestine and colon. It was very serious for infection but not immediately life threatening.

Ashley then folded the tip of the knife into a fish hook configuration and pinched the flat end bit into another point. He then slowly pushed the blade into Joshua Dray's thigh just above the knee scraping it against the bone and avoiding the Femoral artery and vein. Ashley then pulled it back slightly so that the fish hook point dug backwards into the bone. There was no chance of Joshua Dray pulling it out easily.

To deal with the future safety of the public against a neurotic killer Ashley had to consider several options. Ashley could use hypnotic suggestion but knew that this would not last more than a few weeks. Joshua's neurotic subconscious killing urges would always override all memory implants. Ashley finally decided that there was only one course of action for a permanent solution. A partially blind man could do no real harm. And so using Dr Mario's medical memory Ashley stared at Joshua Dray's head and exerted pressure on the optic nerve of both eyes at the points were they rested against the bone of the eye socket. Once damaged the optic nerve could not function again. Ashley exerted just enough pressure on both optic nerves to leave a few fibres intact and functional. This would allow a very small section of the retina to transmit its light impulses to the brain. Joshua Dray would probably be able to differentiate between light and dark and see shadowy movement. He would most likely gradually develop a keen hearing instinct as most blind people do. The misery of losing his clear vision would be paramount in his thoughts and might lead to a suppression of his neurotic thoughts and schizophrenia. In time Joshua Dray would reflect upon the actions of his life and his thoughts might even revert to some form of religious awakening.

There was nothing more to be done so Ashley went down the stairs of the bus, forced opened the scissor doors and stepped out into the street and onto the pavement before returning to normal mode. Ashley smiled as he heard muffled screams from inside the moving bus as it disappeared down the street. Ashley's inner voice said he had done well and that Joshua Dray would see the light of conversion to Buddhism and become an asset to the country wide young offenders' programme.

The next day there was a brief report in the local paper of an incident on a late night Dudley bus in which two young persons had been taken to hospital with stab wounds neither of which was considered as life threatening. The facts were vague except that one of the stab victims had only recently been released from a mental institution and was still under medication. Doctors had to operate on his leg to free a knife blade that had become lodged in the bone of his thigh. He had also suffered a mental trauma that had partially blanked out his vision. Doctors felt that this might be temporary since no other surface injuries were visible. The police were asking for any witnesses who had been on the bus at the time of the incident to contact their local police. They had yet to interview the two men with the knife injuries to establish further details. The girl friend of one of the men had given a statement to the police. Police were also studying the bus company's CCTV footage of the incident.

A week later it was reported that the police having viewed the CCTV pictures decided the incident had escalated from the playful throwing of chips by the person at the back of the bus into a fight resulting in the knife incident. However it was the person who had displayed the knife who was arrested for the possession of a prohibited weapon. He was also referred back to the psychiatric unit that had released him a few days previous. How the knife became lodged in his own leg could not be seen on the camera footage as it was obstructed by the body of the other person who had received the abdominal wound. No witnesses had come forward and in the interest of costs it was decided to issue a police caution to both men and not proceed further with the enquiry. The incident was soon forgotten by the general public and Ashley was pleased about that.

As usual Ashley visited his family over the weekend and ever since Katy had come into the inner circle she made sure she was home to see Ashley and hear about his latest escapade. Of course, Ashley didn't have to recite the events but simply to telepathically transmit them to their minds with the full background details. This made them see and understand everything through Ashley's mind as if they were viewing the whole incident from his position. They usually sat around the dining table during these chats and discussions.

'I think this Joshua Dray got what he deserved,' said Katy. 'People like that should not be allowed to roam free to murder and what not. I agree with everything you did Ashley.'

'Do you think he'll ever get his eye sight back?' asked Lillian.

'He might,' replied Ashley. 'But I believe that Joshua Dray will eventually see the light of conversion to Buddhism and become an asset to the country wide young offenders' programme. At least that is what I heard my inner voice say.'

'In that case,' said granddad Eric, 'you would have done a public service to the nation. I only wish you could be everywhere and deal with all crime in a similar manner.'

Ashley suddenly felt dizzy as if a great revelation was about to be revealed. He tried to stand but went all wobbly and his mum and dad rushed to his side and helped him to the settee and told him to lie back and close his eyes. Ashley did so and was instantly in another world and being shown a whole new scenario of his future.

'Let him sleep,' said a tearful Lillian to Katy who was sitting on the carpet beside the settee and gently stroking her brother's head. Her eyes were quite moist and she had a worried expression.

'What's happening to Ash, mum?' asked Katy. 'Is he going to be taken from us? He just went all funny so suddenly.'

Eric and Alex were standing looking at Ashley and noticed that there was an aura of calm and sereneness about him. Alex then touched Katy and Lillian on the arm and motioned for them to come with him back into the dining room.

'I think Ashley is having some form of vision or revelation,' explained Alex. 'You can see that from the calm expression on his face. I wonder if he's had these bouts before. I don't think there's anything to worry about just yet and I'm sure Ashley will tell us all in time. Let's just let him sleep on for as long as he needs to.'

'He looks like he did when he was a child all those years ago,' said Lillian.

Ashley slept for two hours and then lay awake thinking for another twenty minutes.

Katy couldn't stay away from her sleeping brother and had been popping in to look at him every fifteen minutes or so. When she saw him with his eyes open she let out a joyful cry and sat down beside him. Ashley smiled up at her and asked if he had been away long.

By now the rest of the family were around him smiling down at their miracle of a lad.

'Welcome back son,' said Lillian and Alex together. 'Let's all have a cup of tea.'

'Mum, dad, everybody; I think I was just given a message,' said Ashley. 'I don't know who it is from but it said for us not to worry, I'm going to be around a lot longer than you think. It showed me something happening far far away in space that I am expected to deal with when the time comes. I can't say any more because I myself am not sure what it is all about.'

Ashley stood up and gave his mum a big hug and a kiss on her forehead. Lillian looked at her son and saw a change in his manner. He appeared so grown up that there was an attitude of wisdom and responsibility about him. Katy noticed this too but he was still her brother and she loved him as much as ever. Or just a little bit more as she gave him a hug and a kiss.

No one asked any questions perhaps because there were none to ask. Ashley's family understood that his gifts were there for a purpose which would be revealed to Ashley when the time came. This vision of his may have simply been an introduction of sorts and was for him alone. And so nothing more was said while they drank their tea. Lillian always worried about her son and was quite relieved to see him back to his normal self after the trance like event.

Ashley didn't want to concern his family about what he had been shown as it would happen long after they had all passed into a ripe old age. Ashley himself would be very much older when he would be required to tackle the task that had been given him. His gifts would always be with him to be used in saving the Earth from some distant threat. Also revealed was the help he would receive from Earth's neighbour. At the moment none of this made any sense to Ashley so he just put it to the back of his mind. In the meantime he was to continue in dealing with criminal and delinquent behaviour as he saw fit. He mentioned this aspect only.

'Well son,' said Alex, 'there are two reports in the paper describing acts of vandalism by youngsters that happened last week. One is here in Sutton where the Hollyfield and Whitehouse Common Primary School children planted a dozen young lime trees in Rectory Park and a week later vandals had trashed them all. The trees were up to three inches thick at the base and a considerable amount of force must have been used to break four of these 15 to 18 feet tall trees, the report said. The other is in Castle Vale where a gang of hooligans has been terrorising several neighbourhoods. I cut out the articles and saved them for you to read. There's also another mystery in which someone is setting fire to dead trees in Sutton Park. So far there have been eight incidents and no one knows who the culprits are and where they will strike next.'

Ashley said he would get on to it right away and he did. He read the first article and was immediately shown the whole scenario including the three culprits and where they lived. Ashley didn't need to go to the site of the events anymore. Ashley said he had an idea but would need some assistance from a member of his family. He would also need a van or pickup truck to transport some heavy objects.

When he explained what he had in mind they all volunteered eagerly. However practicalities prevailed and Lillian and Katy were chosen. The ladies were least likely to raise suspicion as they drove into Sutton Park for the first part of Ashley's plan.

On Monday morning Ashley booked a self drive Toyota combo-van from the Senior Rental company on Factory Road in Tipton for collection the following morning and to be returned by six o'clock the next evening. He specified that it needed to carry two people in addition to the driver. Two days should be enough to deal with the tree vandals. Ashley rang his mum and told her to be ready with Katy in the morning. The plan was to go to Rectory Park and collect all the vandalised trees, all one dozen of them.

The destruction had been carried out by four boys aged around fifteen and a sixteen year old girl who had egged them on. These five made up a gang of their own and were often seen in the Town Centre in the evenings when businesses had closed. The ring leader was a biggish fellow who called himself Iggy as he didn't like his real name Ignatius and none of his friends knew he had such a name. The girl was Jan Maltby and she was exceedingly well developed and knew it too. She boasted about all the affairs she'd had and that she and Iggy were doing it every day. This made Iggy proud of her and made it known that she belonged to him and was under his protection. The other three lads Jimmy Lester, Tim Carroll and Scot Condi simply wanted something to do but couldn't think for themselves. They were just happy to follow the ample dimensions of Jan and admire the bits that she regularly and intentionally exposed for their admiration. The tops she wore were practically see through and often during the warmer days she just didn't bother with a bra either. It was on one of these evenings that they were strolling through Rectory Park drinking lager from cans when they spotted the straight row of freshly planted lime trees.

'Okay boys,' said Jan pointing to the row of saplings, 'let's see how strong you are. Who can break me the most trees in ten minutes? A special treat for the winner.'

They didn't have to guess what that treat might be. Only last month Jan had made Scot nearly faint from lack of breath during one of her rewarding kisses. Iggy had watched with pride as she let Scot fall to the floor of her flat afterwards and all laughed as they watched a groggy though smiling Scot recover his breath.

The four lads each lived with their parents in the Falcon Lodge estate but Jan was collecting dole money along with supplementary benefit to pay the rent for her council flat on Carhampton Road.

Iggy and Jimmy Lester lived on the crescent but at opposite ends while Scot and Tim were a few houses apart on Churchill road and quite near the shops.

Ashley had received all this as if he were a part of the group and without having to visit the scene of the vandalism. All Ashley had to do was to concentrate on the past event he wanted to view and all of it came into his brain. This art of regressing to view past events had first come to Ashley in the pub after the darts match. It was a development that had a good reason behind it. What was to affect the very existence of mankind on earth was out in the far reaches of space. To view that fatal scenario of disaster Ashley would have to rely on his senses conveying those images to him. But all that was in the distant future many centuries away though the future of earth would ultimately rest with the actions that Ashley would have to initiate. As yet he still had no idea what that was.

Ashley picked up the van just before ten o'clock on a bright though breezy morning and noticed that it had an automatic column shift and a driver's bench type seat. Katy could sit in the middle beside him. The vehicle was several years old and had seen plenty of rough use but ran quite well. Ashley noticed that the fuel gauge showed only a quarter full so he added some more just before he got into Erdington. Lillian and Katy had prepared some sandwiches to take with them but they all had a hot mug of tea before setting out. Alex was at work and Eric was back in his own house eagerly awaiting news of their adventures.

Ashley asked his mum to drive while he directed the way. They drove through Walmley village and out along the Walmley road and then turned left till they finally got to Rectory Park. The row of damaged and broken trees was clearly visible from the small car parking area and Ashley asked his mum to park facing outwards. They all then walked to examine the damaged trees. Four trees had been snapped a couple of feet above ground and were still lying where they had been left. The others had simply been vandalised by what seemed like a hammer or metal rod. After looking at this sad spectacle for a brief moment Ashley explained what he planned to do. It would be a little bit different from what they had decided at the weekend. Both Lillian and Katy liked the change of plan and then went to the van and opened the back doors wide to await the arrival of the trees.

Ashley looked around and saw that the park was quite empty of people. He then went into pink mode and began pinching off the damaged trees near their bases and laying them to one side. The broken ones he pinched off where they had broken and left their stumps as they were. When he had all twelve trees bundled them together in his arms and still in pink mode carried them easily to the rear of the van and placed them inside base first. He then returned to normal mode and both Lillian and Katy were surprised at how quickly Ashley had worked and completed the first phase even though they knew that he could slow time to a fraction of its normal rate. Some of the tops of the trees were sticking out of the van body area but Ashley curved these inward so that the doors could be shut.

Again Lillian drove while Ashley directed. They went first to the top end of Falcon Lodge Crescent to the house where Ignatius and his parents lived. Ashley checked and determined that the house was empty of humans. These were old houses and had been built solidly in the period between the two world wars. The floors were of timber beam and boards but the walls were of solid double brick construction without any cavity.

Ashley went pink again and carried three of the tallest thickest trees into the house. He would plant a tree in each of the two rooms downstairs and the third in Iggy's bedroom. The first spot Ashley chose was an inner wall of the living room near its base. Ashley went rosy pink and everything seemed to be in a sort of foggy atmosphere. Ashley pointed his fingers together and pushed them into the plasticized wall in a downward 45 degree angled direction. He went all the way up to his elbow and then bent his wrist and rotated it to make a wide flat circular base. It was a long time ago since he had done something similar when he had shown his mum the trees in Rookery Park where he'd made holes in tree trunks so that birds could nest in them. He must have been six or seven then.

Now Ashley took one of the trees and used his fingers to spread the base of the trunk into a cross like configuration. He then smoothed the base back straight and fed it into the hole in the wall. It was a good fit. When he felt he had reached the end he pushed a little bit harder to make the base spread out into the circular flat area he had formed. The tree was now sticking into the room at a 45 degree upward angle. The wall had ballooned slightly with Ashley's working the hole so now he pushed down quite firmly and squeezed the plasticized brickwork and plaster to firmly grip the trunk and base of the tree wood. There would be no easy way of extracting this tree trunk out of the wall. They would have to saw it off first but Ashley had a hypnotic something to delay that for a day or two.

Ashley then repeated all this in the dining room and then again in Iggy's bedroom upstairs. He had a quick look at his handiwork with approval before walking back to the van and returning to normal mode. Of course he telepathically conveyed all he had done to his mum and sis and both said it was a job well done.

Jan Maltby was next on Ashley's list for three trees after all it was at her instigation that the vandalism had been carried out. This was a two room flat with a kitchen and bathroom. Ashley put a tree base into each main room as before but he couldn't decide on where to put the third tree. When Ashley walked into the filthy bathroom he immediately saw the ideal spot. First he went to normal mode and flushed the toilet twice before going pink again. Ashley put his right hand under the base of the tree and with his left hand gradually fed it and his hand into the dry bowl. He then moulded the tree wood under and up the back of the U-bend. He kept his right hand in the bowl but continued moulding and pushing it till it could go no further. Ashley returned to normal mode and washed his hands in the sink and smiled as he viewed his handiwork. He gave the tree a tug but it didn't budge in the slightest.

Back at the van Lillian and Katy smiled when he conveyed what he had done. Ashley said he wished he'd done this in Iggy's house also. But it was not too late for the remaining trees. So a slight change of plan was made once again.

The next was Jimmy Lester's house and Ashley had to carry out his handiwork while both parents were in though sitting out on the patio. One tree went into the living room wall and the other one went deep into the upstairs toilet bowl. Fortunately for them they had a second loo downstairs.

Tim and Scot lived close to each other on Churchill road and both houses were empty this early in the day so Ashley repeated his task again and viewed his handiwork in normal mode after washing his hands which he hadn't done at the Lester house for fear of being heard by the couple on the patio. Although the first part of the plan had been carried out Ashley would need to return when the families were in to complete the plan. This was the hypnosis suggestion part of the plan.

On the off chance Ashley decided to drive back to the park to see if the five vandals might be there. But there was no sign of them anywhere so Lillian drove back home. It was now about one o'clock and Ashley said they could get on to the other job after a snack lunch. This would involve taking the van to Sutton Park to the place of the tree fires.

Ashley had already received images about who was responsible for the eight tree burnings. The culprits were three young lads from the Four Oaks area. Their parents were all well to do and all had large detached houses worth over a million each. John Crocker and his wife Corrine lived on Blackroot road with an acre of land for a garden. They had two children Helen and Clive. Helen was fifteen while Clive was twelve and big for his age. The two had nothing in common so Clive went out with his own friends. Mum and dad were accountants and led very busy lines. Consequently Clive was left to his own devices most evenings. Helen had a boyfriend and subsequently was also either out when mum and dad were out or she was closeted in her room on her mobile to her friends.

Clive often walked round to his friend Jeff who was also twelve years old and lived just around the corner on Beaconsfield Road. He was an only child and his parents William and Judy Tarp were both head teachers at different schools in the Sutton area. They came home late and after dinner tended to work well into the night planning school stuff for the next day. Jeff had been a late child and had not really come according to plan. The Tarps had gone on a Caribbean cruise to celebrate their tenth wedding anniversary when Jeff had been conceived. Judy couldn't understand what had gone wrong because she had always taken the same precautions, namely the pill. But they accepted what couldn't be helped and were quite taken with the idea of a child in the house. Life had been getting a bit dull lately and the expectancy of a baby brought about a certain amount of excitement.

Jeff was an easy birth and was a lovely blond haired baby who never gave an ounce of trouble. He slept through the night and was hardly ever ill. Judy stopped work for two years to care for her child and grew to love him dearly. But then she was head hunted for a Headship at a nearby primary school and it was too good a chance to miss. Once again work took priority over everything else and Jeff was given over to the care of a child minder and day nursery.

It was at the child minder's house that Jeff met Douglas Salt. Douglas lived with his father on Bracebridge Road in a huge mansion type house in six acres of land. His mother Julia had died of complications several months after giving birth and Percy Salt secretly blamed the birth of his son for the tragedy. Father and son had always had an uneasy relationship and Douglas got more affection from the cook and the house maid than he did from his father. Even Terry the gardener gave more of his time to Douglas when he was working near the house.

The three lads became friends and would often stroll into the adjacent Sutton Park for something to do. It was while they were on the opposite side of Blackroot pool that they came across a foot high flat table-top type tree stump on which someone had tried making a small campfire. The few bits of charred twigs had been left on the stump which had become blackened at its centre. One thing led to another and before long the trio decided to try setting fire to one of the many dead trees that were prevalent in the park.

For some reason the dead trees that they set alight burned quite well for the first few minutes but then died down to a smouldering hulk that gave off tonnes of white smoke visible for miles around. They ran off when they heard people approaching. Over the next few days the lads had tried this eight more times and on the last occasion the dead tree had continued burning furiously and had even set a few branches of an adjacent healthy tree alight. The smoke given off had been tremendous and the siren of a fire engine was soon to be heard in the distance.

The excitement of all this was beginning to grow on the lads and they were continually planning their next fire. They had thought about using some white spirit to help with the fires but didn't want to take the risk of being seen carrying it around. Clive suggested they put some in small coloured Fruit Shoot plastic bottles and no one would know the difference. They could throw the bottles into a hole in the dead tree once they had set it alight to help with the burning. All agreed to this and they would each bring a half filled bottle. But they had yet to carry out this plan when Ashley decided to take action against them.

Ashley conveyed all this to his mother and sister while they were downing the ham and cucumber sandwiches that Lillian had prepared. This was followed by small pots of strawberry flavoured yogurt and glasses of cool Ribena drink. At about 2 o'clock Ashley, Lillian and Katy drove up through Sutton and on towards Four Oaks. They turned left into Blackroot Road and stopped in the car park beside Blackroot Pool. It was then a short walk around to the other side of the pool which was a good sized lake of about twenty acres and to the first of the semi burnt trees. It was about a foot and a half in diameter though one face was half eaten away with age. Ashley explained that he would first push the tree flat onto the ground by slicing through its base with his hand while in pink mode, and then similarly crop it to about eight feet so that it fitted inside the van. And this is exactly what he did much to Katy's astonishment. One moment the burnt tree was standing uptight on the ground and the next it was top and tailed and lying at their feet just as Ashley had described.

'But how will you get it to the van?' asked Katy. 'We can't drive here the path isn't wide enough.'

'Not to worry sis,' said Ashley, 'I shall just carry it to the van.'

'But won't it a bit too big and heavy,' said Katy as Lillian smiled.

'Not when I'm in pink mode,' smiled Ashley. 'It's all easy-peasy for me then. Now let's walk on to the next spot and see what that one looks like. It's only a hundred yards or so up this way.'

This next tree was too wide and dumpy and they'd have trouble fitting it into the van. The tree was a hollow half moon shape and was about four feet wide at the base and quite rotten. Ashley said they'd give this one a miss. He shut his eyes and visualised where the next burnt tree was before leading the way to it. This one was okay and very much like the first one. Again the burnt tree lay on the ground at their feet and top and tailed to a size of about 8 feet.

Katy was looking at a spot on the burnt tree thinking of Ashley and his wonderful gifts when the tree suddenly disappeared.

'What happened to the tree?' asked Katy in astonishment.

'Oh, I just went pink and carried it to where the first tree lay,' said Ashley, 'and I came back again before returning to normal mode. I'm getting quite good at going in and out of pink mode now sis.'

'Well I'm not yet used to seeing things disappear,' smiled Katy, 'so could you please give me a bit of warning in future. It might be better for my blood pressure.'

Ashley and Lillian both laughed.

When they had selected the third tree which was a fatter one being about two feet in girth Ashley asked mother and sister to return to the van and to wait for him there. Ashley still spoke as though he would remain in a normal time frame and so take as long to walk the same distances. It took Lillian and Katy about twenty minutes to get back to the van and found that Ashley was already there and had loaded all three trees into the back of the van and shut the doors as well.

'We are a bit overloaded in the back,' said Ashley, 'but if we drive slowly we should be okay. I didn't realise how heavy those pieces of tree really are. We haven't far to go though, just halfway up Blackroot road for the Clive Crocker house.'

And so Ashley drove at about 10 mph up the park road and right onto Blackroot Road and stopped in front of the Crocker house. It was now 3 o'clock and the house was empty of people. Clive wouldn't return from school for another hour at least. Ashley then wrote a note on an envelope saying that the forest elves were angry that Clive and his two friends had been burning their homes in the dead trees. Next time they would do the same in return. Be warned. Ashley left the note unsigned.

Ashley got out of the van and opened the rear doors. He selected the fattest and heaviest of the three trees before going pink and picking it up. He then walked up the drive towards the front door but stopped about a few feet away. He stood the tree upright in front of the door and then stepped back several paces and mentally pushed hard on the front of the tree trunk with his telekinetic gift. When Ashley returned to normal mode there was a hissing sound as the tree crashed through the front door taking it off its hinges and ripping the frame into splinters of wood. The combination of door and tree trunk caromed down the hallway and smashed into the far wall going partly though it as well. Ashley thought that he ought to use a bit less force in future. He then walked in through the smashed doorway and found a telephone in the living room. He dialled 999 and reported a burglary in progress at number 43 Blackroot Road. He then pinned his note to the tree lying in the hallway. Ashley went pink again and returned to the van.

'That was an awfully loud crash Ashley,' said Lillian, 'the whole neighbourhood must have heard it.'

'Good,' said Ashley, 'the sooner someone gets curious the better. I rang 999 from the house phone reporting a burglary so I expect the police will be around soon too. The next house is just around the corner on Beaconsfield Road so we had better head there right away.'

Ashley did exactly the same and sent the tree smashing through the front door but with a little less telekinetic force this time. This house was different in design with a glass partition door at the end of the hall that led into the living room which was also smashed beyond recognition. Again Ashley rang 999 using the house phone and pinned his warning note from the forest elves onto the tree trunk; a lesson for Jeff Tarp to take heed.

Ashley next drove to the Salt mansion on Bracebridge Road and repeated his plan. The driveway was a bit longer but Ashley had no problem carrying the tree trunk to its required position in front of the huge arched oak doors. This time Ashley used a greater telekinetic push as he reckoned the oak doors would be much more resistant. He stood the tree upright in front but several feet away from the door and then stepped back several paces and pushed hard on the front of the tree trunk with his telekinetic gift. Ashley then returned to normal mode and again there was a loud hissing of wind as the tree flew forward and crashed through the front door. The doors had been locked but not bolted so they had simply crashed open. Ashley remembered now that there was the cook and housemaid always in during the day which was probably the reason for the door being as it was. It was just luck that neither of them had been near the door when it crashed open. Ashley reminded himself to be more careful in future.

Ashley returned to the van and saw two women and a man come out of the house and look at the smashed gaping front doors. Ashley at once conveyed to them the complete scenario of the three lads carrying out their tree burning antics in the park. He also conveyed a message that only three burnt trees had been delivered, one to each boy's home and through the front doors only. Another five trees still remained and these would be sent crashing through one of the upper windows if the boys weren't suitably dealt with by both parents and police.

Ashley knew that it would require four or five strong men to shift the tree trunks and it was unlikely to happen in a hurry. They would probably also want the insurance people to see the damage for themselves.

Ashley then drove back to the Crocker house and parked on the opposite side of the road but a few houses away. Two police cars were parked in front of the house. There were quite a few curious people, presumably neighbours, standing on the road and pavement in little groups discussing what was going on. Ashley, Lillian and Katy got out of the van and joined a group of four on the pavement in front of the house. Looking towards the house they could see four policemen looking at the smashed front door and then scratching their heads when they saw the burnt tree trunk embedded in the end wall. One of them walked in and came out with Ashley's note and showed it to the others.

It was then that Ashley decided to convey the complete scenario of the tree burning to everyone in the vicinity. He telepathically communicated to all those standing around including the police at the house the full visual events of the three boys carrying out their tree burning antics in the park. The neighbours now knew who the tree burning vandals were. But it was a mystery to them how the tree trunk had been thrown in through the front door with such force. Ashley then made a widespread telepathic suggestion that the burnt trees had been the homes of forest elves that were simply exacting revenge.

The police were busy on their radios and two of them returned to their car and drove around the corner to Beaconsfield Road. Some of the group of people followed and looking down from the junction saw people gathered in front of the third and fourth houses down. Ashley sent his telepathic messages to this group as well so that all would know the cause behind the ruckus.

'I think our job here is done,' said Ashley a bit wearily to Lillian and Katy. 'The neighbours will pass the word around about the three lads and the police also have their lead and are bound to interview the boys. I can't see them not confessing to everything. Let's go back home for some well earned tea and I can get back to the Falcon Lodge estate about six.'

They returned to the van and Lillian drove them home. Ashley was fast asleep with his head on Katy's shoulder before they had turned out of Blackroot Road. The day's work had exhausted him mentally and he needed a good sleep to recover. He was still in a deep sleep when they reached the house and Lillian got some big cushions from the house and placed them between Ashley and the van door. Katy then shifted Ashley's head to rest against these cushions so that she could ease herself out on the driver's side.

'Let Ashley sleep for as long as he needs to,' said Lillian looking at her son sleeping serenely in the van. 'I've noticed before that when he uses his gifts or powers a lot he gets quite drained and exhausted. The sleep seems to rejuvenate him though.'

Katy was a bit worried and kept returning to the van to look in on her brother. Ashley hadn't moved from the position they'd left him in. The sun had move around and was shining full on his face but that didn't seem to affect his sleep.

Alex came home at half five but had walked right past the van without noticing Ashley asleep inside. Lillian told him everything they had done that day and that Ashley had planned to return to the Falcon Lodge estate later in the evening to complete their plan. At this rate he might sleep till morning.

It was close to 7 o'clock when Ashley walked in the door and said he was famished. Lillian had expected this and so had prepared a nice big shepherds pie for dinner. Katy was curious and asked Ashley how he had felt just before he went to sleep.

'I don't quite know sis,' he said. 'I was fine when I was doing all that stuff moving those trees but right at the very end when we decided to leave, I suddenly felt drained of all my energy. I must have fallen asleep the moment I sat down beside you in the van. It's like my battery had run low and needed charging and my system shut down so I could recover. And I have too. After dinner I must pass on to the families on the Falcon Lodge estate the images of the lime tree vandals' activities and then head for home. Milly, Tania and Robin must think I've given up on the shop. I must spend more time with them.'

'I'd love to be a fly on the wall in those houses when you communicate your thoughts to them Ash,' said Katy. 'But what about the girl doesn't she live on her own?'

'I hadn't thought about that,' said Ashley. 'I suppose I had better go to the local pub when it's busy and pass on the same info to all of them. Word will spread from there.'

'It might be an idea to also pass on all the images about the vandalism to the local newspaper chaps,' said Alex. 'A very good idea dad,' said Ashley, 'I'll do that too.'

It was near 8 o'clock when Ashley drove off in the van. He'd return it sometime in the morning tomorrow. He went to each of the family houses where he'd planted those tree bases in the walls and toilets. Ashley went first to the Crescent and stopped the van in front of Ignatius' house and read the thoughts of all those in the house. There appeared to be an argument going on in which Iggy was claiming his innocence. When Ashley sent his telepathic images to Iggy's parents there was a sudden silence. Ashley had added the bit about the forest elves wanting protection for their tree houses or they would take out and plant all the damaged and broken trees into the walls of the culprits' homes.

Then a quiet voice began to admonish Iggy and the four other associates by name.

'I know exactly what you and your precious friends Jan Maltby, Jimmy Lester, Tim Carroll and Scot Condi have been doing. You should be ashamed of yourselves,' said Iggy's mum. 'I shall tell the primary schools that you are to blame for the destruction of their lime trees and you will come with me and say you're sorry. And we will also go to the police station and you will tell them what you did. Is that clear Ignatius? I'll not have my only son turning into a criminal. Look at these trees stuck in our wall. However are we going to clear up all this mess?'

Ashley then went to the other two family houses and conveyed the same images and fictitious message from the forest elves. Again there was righteous indignation from both sets of parents and a promise of similar action. However at the flat of Jan Maltby he gave her the message from the forest elves with a sinister threat that the other trees would fly through her bedroom window if she didn't control her behaviour. Ashley also implanted a hypnotic suggestion that the two trees in her flat were alive and had eyes that were looking out for her and that they could grab her and squeeze her with their branches.

Ashley's next stop was the Hen and Chickens pub on the parade which was quite crowded and perfect for Ashley's purpose. Here Ashley conveyed the images showing who was responsible for both the lime trees destruction and the park tree fires. There was a sudden hush across the pub and then comments of amazement at what they had just been shown.

Comments of 'Wow' and 'Did you get that also?' were heard and someone remarked that they should tell the newspapers about it too. With close to seventy people in the pub Ashley was sure that the story would get around and so he need do nothing further. The police and the primary schools would also get to hear it all.

Now there was just one topic of conversation in the pub. People who had been strangers previously were now talking to each other across the tables. The fact that they had all seen the same vision had an eerie spectre about it and the topic moved on to the paranormal. Several people began to tell of their own previous experiences.

The next day all the local papers carried the story and the culprits were named and shamed. The police took all the youngsters in for questioning and took statements and confessions. All the boys' parents accompanied their children and supported the police fully in everything they did. In the end the lads were let off with a caution in the care of their parents. But it didn't end there as each parent couple had already decided on their own course of punishment which would be to carry out some form of community work.

The lime tree vandals were to be given cleaning tasks in the school for the next six months and would be supervised by one or other of their parents and occasionally by the head teacher. They would also dig up the old lime tree stumps and plant fresh ones in the same spot.

The girl Jan Maltby who was the oldest was allocated a social worker to supervise the thousand hours of community work she had been given when she elected to go before a magistrate after refusing a police caution. She was given a street cleaner's duties Monday to Friday for six months and was required to wear a bright yellow overall.

In the meantime Ashley had returned to the shop to carry on working beside Milly and Robin and occasionally Tania. There had been a cancellation at the test centre and Tania had accepted a test the following week. Although a bit nervous she put on a brave face and confidently said she would pass this time.

Robin had given up his volunteering work with the National Trust as he felt he'd like to go out with Milly on some of her increasingly frequent antique forages. Robin had been to his first car boot sale a few weeks ago and had picked up a few bargains. When he showed these to Milly she had been most polite and let him down gently by saying that they'd look nice on a mantel shelf in someone's home but had no appeal or value as an antique. They were modern reproductions usually meant for the seaside holiday centres. Robin smiled and said that he had a lot to learn. He soon picked up a lot from simply talking to Ashley and Milly and began to frequent auctions just to get a feel for the items on offer. Ashley could see that Robin had been smitten by the antiques bug just as Milly had been earlier. Even Jerry came in to chat occasionally and talked about things that Milly must have mentioned at home. On one of his days off Jerry came and helped out at the shop for a full day. He had been curious about the history cards attached to each of the items on display and Milly dared for him to find an error on any of them. She told her husband that Ashley had a gift for seeing an item's history by simply touching it. Ashley had told Milly the origin of the emerald and diamond ring she wore which her mother had passed down to her. The emerald was in the centre and the diamonds were set in a cluster around it; one of which was missing. It had been made in 1857 in the jewellery quarter in Hockley. Milly said that Ashley even gave her the name of the craftsman who made it.

'Now that is something,' said Jerry. 'No wonder Ashley and the business are doing so well. If I were to buy something from this place I'd be buying it for the history card as much as for the item itself. It would feel as if I were buying a piece from a museum. Ashley is a shrewd and clever lad to have hit upon this sales angle.'

'Don't forget Jerry, we are a museum as well just as the sign outside says,' said Milly. 'That was another shrewd move by Ashley. This shop is going from strength to strength Jerry and I'm happy to be a part of it. Ashley is a good manager and doesn't interfere in anything I do. He is now encouraging Robin to get more involved as well and I think Robin has also got the antiques bug in his system. He says he's never enjoyed a job more. In fact he said that he felt he actually owned the shop. He said it was the way Ashley just let him do things using his own judgement. But I've let Robin know that I have my eye on him.'

'And what about Tania?' asked Jerry.

'What do you mean Jerry?'

'I mean what's the situation with her and Ashley?'

'Nothing,' said Milly, 'they're good friends and 'slow and steady' is my motto. Tania's only seventeen and there's plenty of time for romance in their lives. Tania has a new confidant in Katy, so if you want to know anything in that area you'd better ask her. But just for the record I feel that Ashley and Tania are destined for one another.'

I know Lillian thinks so too. I can see it in the way they talk and look at each other and the way they avoid saying anything complimentary. Tania if anything is exceedingly patient and I do believe she is just happy to be in Ashley's company for as long as it takes. I only hope a third-party distraction for either of them does not suddenly appear.'

So far husband and wife had been alone in the shop kitchen discussing their daughter's future. Robin was upstairs in the museum section doing a bit of rearranging on the shelves. He liked moving things to different locations so that a different angle was presented to the public each week. Sometimes Tania helped him but he usually came back up when she'd gone and put things in the positions that he had originally wanted. And each time Ashley had noticed the changes and said how good the new layout looked. Robin had developed a great admiration and respect for Ashley and this had also grown into a feeling of affection for his boss.

Ashley had forgotten about the Castle Vale estate rowdies in all the excitement of his dealing with the tree vandals. He was at the barber shop awaiting his turn and looking through the daily papers. There was an article about a group of three hooligans terrorising the homes in a cul-de-sac in the New Town area of Brown Hills just north of Birmingham. They had been making a nuisance of themselves generally by dropping stuff in front gardens and throwing pebbles at some of the houses. One of the homes belonged to an ex-soldier named Keith Tibble. He went out and challenged the young lads and told them to stop behaving badly and to leave the Close or he'd ring the police. Keith was a big man and got no argument and the hooligans slunk off.

But the next day they came back and when Keith returned from work he found his wife in tears. She told him that the three kids had been throwing things at the house all afternoon and shouting abuse at the house. She had phoned the police on the anti-social behaviour hotline they had been given as part of the neighbourhood watch scheme but got no answer. The lads were not there when Keith came home. This continued all week and even when they rang 999 no one turned up.

So they were at their wits end and didn't quite know what to do. When Keith finally did see them he grabbed one of the louts and said he was making a citizens arrest. He demanded the boys name and his mother and father's phone number. While Keith was dialling the mother of the boy there was a knock on the door and the father turned up with some police and demanded that Keith be arrested for kidnapping. Keith in turn made a complaint that this and two other boys had damaged his property and showed the police the cracked window and the mess of bottles and cans on his front lawn. But the police were intimidated by Keith's sheer size and gruffness and arrested him on suspicion of kidnapping.

He remained on police bail for two months when the police said they would give him a caution to drop the matter. But Keith refused to accept this because to do so would be an admission of guilt. So he was charged with assault and a trial date set. But the case was dropped when all the neighbours petitioned their MP Linda Fields who took up the matter with the police. The three lads still pestered the neighbourhood and the residents were just too afraid to make a complaint because of the lack of response by the police.

Ashley read this and thought that something needed to be done to put some fear into the trouble makers. Because the youngsters knew that they could not be touched physically by anyone they did as they pleased without consideration for the feelings of others. An idea had come to Ashley as he was having his trim in the barber's chair. He would apply the same treatment to the Vale estate rowdies as well, but not until next week. There was work to be done in the shop and a couple of house auctions to attend. Ashley had promised Robin that he would show him how to choose an item of value and the need to set a limit on their bids.

It was the following Tuesday afternoon when Tania came breezing into the shop waving a piece of yellow coloured paper. She shouted that she had passed her driving test and ran and gave her mum a big hug. Robin also received the same and both gave her their congratulations. Tania was flushed with excitement and looked around her. Milly knew that glance and pointed upwards towards the museum rooms and silently mouthed Ashley's name.

Tania climbed the stairs two at a time to give Ashley her exciting news. Ashley was at the opposite end of the room and turned around at the sound of Tania's entrance. He had been studying the profile of one of the china dolls and was still holding it when Tania waved the yellow paper and blurted out that she had passed her driving test. She ran up to Ashley and threw both arms around his neck and gave him a quick kiss on his lips.

'There,' she said, 'that's my reward from you for my pass. Oh Ashley I'm so excited. I finally passed even though I made a few mistakes during the test.'

'Well then congratulations to you my dear you've done very well,' said Ashley putting the china doll back on the shelf, 'but come here and let me see that paper.'

Tania came forward again and handed Ashley the pass paper. Ashley took the paper and without reading it placed it on the shelf beside the doll. He then reached out and put his arms around Tania's waist and drew her gently to him.

He kissed her on the forehead. Tania sighed and leaned her head back further hoping for something better. Ashley looked straight into her wide open hazel eyes and smiled. He then rubbed the tip of his nose against the tip of hers before giving her a light kiss on her lips. Ashley pulled his head back to see a beaming smiling Tania still holding him tightly. Ashley returned the smile and then Tania started to giggle. Ashley couldn't help following suit and soon they were both laughing together for no apparent reason. They went into a cheek to cheek hug and gently swayed as they laughed. It was how Milly saw them when she came up to investigate. Robin was not far behind and both smiled conspiratorially.

Ashley and Tania let go of each other and turned to face the new arrivals. For a moment the laughter subsided but then exploded again when they saw the expressions on the faces of Robin and Milly. Their laughter was infectious and in seconds all were laughing together.

'What am I laughing about?' blurted Robin with difficulty in between breaths and laughter.

At which the laughter increased even further. Finally it all ceased and they started for the stairs. Tania and her mum now walked arm in arm as they went down the stairs and Tania said she would make them all some tea to celebrate.

'Perhaps Uncle Robin can scrounge some hot doughnuts from Mrs Hollings to celebrate my pass,' said Tania mischievously winking at her mum, 'while I put the kettle on.'

Tania was still quite flushed in the face and this time it was not from the excitement of her test pass. It was remembering the gentle embrace and kiss she'd had off Ashley that would linger in her mind. So Ashley did care for her or he would not have responded as he did. Tania was happy about that now. She always knew that they were good friends but now she was just that bit more sure. It was their first real embrace though definitely not a passionate one. But there was hope that she and Ashley would be much more than just good friends. Yes, Tania was definitely in a happy mood.

Ashley on the other hand was in a bit of a quandary. Although he was pleased about that kiss, he partially regretted that he had let his feelings for Tania come out as they did. He should not let that happen again, at least until a little problem could get sorted in his mind. The problem was whether or not to bring Tania into his family circle of knowledge regarding his unique assortment of gifts. His inner voice told Ashley that he was destined to be with Tania for a very long time and as such she would definitely become a part of his intimate family. So if he revealed his secrets to Tania would she be willing to keep it secret from her own family. This was something Ashley would have to resolve first. Ashley knew that it was important that knowledge of his gifts be revealed to as few people as possible. At the moment it was only his own family who were in the know. But if Tania became part of that family what was he to do?

Milly, Jerry, Tania and Robin all knew of Ashley's gift of instantly discovering the history of any object that he touched. It was through this gift that the history card for each antique was made and upon which rested the unique prosperity of McGill's Antiques shop. If Ashley and Tania became an item then he was duty bound to reveal all to her. But how would she feel about keeping secrets from her parents?

No, Ashley thought, his secret for the moment must be kept as it was to just his own family of six. He and Tania would just have to continue as they always had been as very good friends; at least for now. Ashley knew that he must wait for his future to be revealed to him. And until he knew what it was that was required of him he had no real right to a partner in life. Yet if he was to choose someone then it would definitely be Tania; but not just yet. Ashley decided to raise the issue with his mum and dad and see what they thought. Perhaps a partial revelation of one of his other gifts might be a viable solution. Ashley's inner voice was suggesting possibilities and alternatives and this raised his spirits a little.

However, in the meantime Ashley remembered that he had a couple of chores to sort out. And those were to teach a lesson to two groups of rowdies who had been upsetting people's lives. The first was of a group of youths making a nuisance and upsetting the residents in the Castle Vale estate. The other was the one Ashley had read about at the hair dressers of a similar occurrence in the New Town area of Brownhills.

Ashley thought long and hard about the kind of treatment he ought to mete out to teach these hooligans a lesson. He wanted something akin to an allergic reaction to occur in the physical makeup of the trouble makers for them to realise the error of their ways. They must be made to understand that whenever they behaved badly or viciously towards other people they would feel some small pain. And so Ashley decided to implant the hypnotic suggestion in their minds that whenever they threw a stone or hurled abuse at someone or simply behaved in a bullying aggressive manner they would suffer painful stomach cramp. This would last about a day and the remedy would be a minimum of two quiet hours lying on a bed at home.

Thinking about this Ashley heard the suggestion in his mind, that a similar hypnotic suggestion could be implanted in a general way in pubs, schools and colleges to nip in the bud any future hooliganism or unsocial behaviour on a wider scale. The task would be huge and Ashley would require help from more than just his family to organise such an undertaking. The thought then came to him that Tania and her family could be brought in to help. After all it would only involve letting them know that he had the gift of telepathy. This would come as no surprise to them since they already knew of his gift to see the history of objects. Here was a solution to his dilemma regarding Tania entering his inner circle and Ashley felt an instant relief at this development.

The pubs, schools and colleges thing was a non starter but the thought had revealed another solution. Tania was dear to Ashley and until now he had been unable to reconcile his thoughts to the fact of his keeping all his abilities secret from her. Their closeness when they had kissed made Ashley realise exactly what it was that he wanted. Although his ultimate mission in life had not been revealed to him it did not mean that Ashley should not get on with his personal life. And that life must include Tania. He had already decided to discuss this with his mum, dad and Katy although he knew what it was that he intended to do. Nevertheless he did want the approval of his family before he went ahead with it. Since it all centred on Tania, Ashley had little doubt that both families would be pleased. The hints had been broad for quite some time.

The next evening Ashley drove to the area of Castle Vale that had been reported as a trouble spot and parked on a side road just off Yatesbury Avenue and near to the main shops. It was here that the youths tended to assemble before beginning their roaming activities.

Ashley shut his eyes and concentrated on the report his dad had given him.

The main culprits were three girls all aged fifteen and a lad of fourteen. The ring leader was a girl named Josey Faith and she was supported by her best friends Pippa Riggs and Sheena Canwell. The boy was Ned Arnold and he was nearly six feet tall and still growing. Sheena was the girl from next door in Geeson Close and Ned had liked her when they were little. Their mums were friends and both Sheena and Ned were the only children in each family. Sheena had let Ned hold her hand when they were out together and recently had shown him how to kiss properly with their mouths open and tongues touching. Ned adored her and did whatever she asked and eventually joined the group with Josey Faith. Josey was of mixed race and extremely pretty. She was the tallest of the three girls and was currently eyeing Ned with interest. She was the youngest in her family of six; the only girl with five much older brothers. All had left home except for Dillon who had turned twenty one last birthday and was currently 'in between jobs'.

Pippa Riggs was the smallest of the group and lived with foster parents. She had been long term with the current elderly couple and had grown quite fond of them. They treated her like an adult and never checked her although Pippa was out late quite frequently. And on these occasions they waited up for her and usually had a little supper ready even if it was a bit past midnight. Subconsciously Pippa made a note to try and get home a little earlier. She told Josey she liked looking after her 'mum and dad' and didn't want them staying up too late for her. However Pippa was prone to 'moods' and occasional fits of temper which the old couple had discussed with their social worker. It was noted in Pippa's file but nothing was recommended. The social worker put it down to a growing-up phase.

Ashley watched them in his mind as they walked around the Vale intimidating the people they passed and quite often hurling little bits of road grit at the front doors of houses. They sat on people's garden walls and picked the heads off the carefully tended flowers and hurled filthy abuse at anyone bold enough to come out and check them. If they came to a car parked on the grass verge they thought nothing of giving it a few scratches with a key or a coin, on the hidden side of course. They discarded their fish and chip wrappers and drink cans on front lawns wherever they might happen to be. On occasions they took bikes off little kids and then left the bikes on another street. They thought this great fun when an irate parent came at them demanding the return of the bike and they just shrugged off any knowledge of the bike or its whereabouts. The police were called on several occasions but nothing could be proved. Josey knew her 'rights' and with bravado told the police to 'piss off' and to go catch some real criminals instead of picking on kids. The police subsequently left them alone despite the increasing number of complaints.

Ashley got out of his car and walked towards their usual meeting point outside the supermarket. He went inside and saw Pippa Riggs at the checkout putting a few drink cans and packets of crisps into a plastic carrier bag. There was no sign of the others so Ashley went back outside and decided to wait. Pippa came out shortly and strode purposefully towards the top end of the car park. Ashley followed slowly and soon saw the others waiting there. There were two other girls with them and Ashley guessed that the group was about to expand. There was some hilarity among them and Ned appeared to be a bit embarrassed by the talk. It was obviously girl talk and probably highly sensitive and new to Ned.

Ashley read the minds of the newcomers and got their names as Emma and Rachel Tilsley. They were twin sisters and looked a scruffy pair. They lived on Hansons Bridge Road and had met Josey in Pype Hayes Park in the play area behind the Hall. They were not quite fifteen years old but looked older because of their protruding chins and high cheek bones which incidentally gave them an aggressive appearance. They looked bored and seemed ready to follow any excitement that Josey Faith might devise.

Ashley thought it was time to nip their activities in the bud and so sent out a strong telepathic command to the whole group. Ashley implanted the hypnotic suggestion in their minds that whenever they threw a stone or hurled abuse at someone or simply behaved in a bullying aggressive manner they would suffer painful stomach cramps.

This would last about a day and the only remedy would be to lie down on a bed at home for a few hours. At the very last moment Ashley decided to add another proviso to split up the group. And that was if they happened to see any member of their group then a sharp pain would develop in their right ear lobe. Ashley added the suggestion that the pain would cease on closing both eyes so as not to view their companions. The longer they remained together the greater the pain would become. Ashley excluded Emma and Rachel from viewing one another since they obviously were a family. This earache hypnotic suggestion would last one year but the stomach cramp pain would be there for always in response to any violent or unsocial behaviour on their part. The pain would of course be a perceived pain only and would have no physical connection within their bodies whatsoever.

As Ashley turned to walk back to his car he heard loud complaints from the group.

'My ear hurts,' said one.

'So does mine,' said another.

'Oow,' said a third.

'Shut your eyes and the pain goes away,' said Josey.

'How do you know that?' asked Ned.

'I just do,' replied Josey, 'so bloody well just do as I tell you.'

'She's right,' came from Pippa.

'How am I to get home then?' asked Sheena.

'Oow, it's come back,' Emma cried.

'I don't like what's happening and I don't want to be with you lot,' said Rachel angrily. 'I'm going back home. Come on Emma lets get out of here. We should never have come in the first place.'

'So then bugger off you idiots,' shouted Josey, 'and don't come crawling back when you just feel like it.'

She then spat at Rachel and within seconds she screamed and doubled up clasping her belly.

'What's the matter Josey?' said Sheena opening her eyes to see what was going on and to instant ear pain.

'Oow,' yelled Sheena and she turned around and ran towards her home. Within moments the pain had subsided and she slowed to a more leisurely walk. She turned to see what the others were doing and the sharp pain returned but disappeared as she faced away again. She realised that looking at any one of the others brought the pain back. She resolved never to see them again.

The others came to a similar conclusion and also made off for their own homes but each by a separate route out of sight of any of their group members.

Josey found herself on her own. Her stomach hurt terribly. It felt like a cramp so she headed for her own home as well. Somehow she knew that if she lay down on her bed for a while the pain would ease. She realised that it had begun the instant she had spat at Rachel and sworn rudely at her. Her subconscious warned her that the stomach pains would get worse every time she behaved in a nasty and bullying manner towards others. This made her think long and hard about her future behaviour. It was as if something supernatural had a hand in trying to teach her a lesson. She then realised that there was no escaping punishment if she behaved badly.

Ashley went back to his car and drove to his parent's house. He knew that over the coming weeks each member of this group would do something to warrant a stomach cramp symptom and finally realise the cause just as Josey had. Ashley was pleased that they would all eventually be reformed characters and the Vale would be a better place for it.

Ashley relayed everything telepathically to his mum and dad and then again later to Katy when she came home. Katy said she approved of everything that Ashley had done and would have so liked to have been there to see it all actually unfold. And when Ashley mentioned meting out the same treatment to the hooligans on the New Town Brownhills estate the next evening she said she was definitely coming with him. It would be too good to miss.

Ashley mentioned to them about bringing Tania into the knowledge circle regarding his telepathic gift. He said he had given a lot of thought to dealing with unsocial behaviour around the country and felt that it would help if he got the support of Milly, Jerry and Tania. They already knew of his ability to trace the history of antiques or for that matter any object that Ashley touched. Now Ashley wanted to tell them about his telepathic skills. He could then let them know what he had done with regard to the Vale estate hooligans to inflict pain through telepathic hypnosis and his plans to extend his sphere of action.

'I shall need to spend a lot of time away from the shop and I would like for Milly to understand the reason for it,' said Ashley. 'I believe also that Milly, Jerry and Tania could contribute to our pool of thought with regard to any long term strategy of action.'

'If you are sure about this Ashley,' said Lillian, 'then I shall invite them to an evening meal this Saturday and we could tell them then.'

'I don't think that Robin can keep something like this under his hat,' said Ashley. 'He's very fond of me and takes a great interest in everything I do or say. But he is more than likely to blurt out in a proud bragging sort of a way about what his boss is able to do, especially after a drink or two at the pub. So I think it best to leave him out of it for now at least.'

Although Ashley didn't mention anything about his strong feelings for Tania, Lillian and Alex already knew from frequent talks with Milly over the phone. Also Katy had begun to talk to her mum about some of the things she discussed with Tania with regard to Ashley.

So secretly Lillian was pleased that Ashley wanted to bring Tania and her parents into their circle of knowledge. She could read between the lines that Ashley was not telling them the whole reason for wanting them in. Lillian was certain in her mind that Tania came into the reasoning far more than he was letting on. Lillian was secretly pleased and happy for her son to want to reveal his secrets to the girl who would one day - Lillian hoped - become his partner in life.

'Tania is my best friend,' said Katy, 'and I'm glad she's to be included.'

Katy hadn't realised what she had said but they all knew what she meant. Prophetic words perhaps.

So quickly Katy added, 'What time are you picking me up tomorrow evening Ash?'

'Oh, I should say about six if that's alright with you sis,' said Ashley. 'It shouldn't take us more than thirty or forty minutes to get there if we go straight up the Chester Road. I expect the rush hour should have eased by then.'

'I'll ring Milly and Jerry now and invite them over for dinner on Saturday evening,' said Lillian. 'I can't wait to see the expressions on their faces when you tell them about your telepathic gift. You'll have to give them a demonstration Ashley.'

The next morning Ashley was at the shop as usual. Milly and Tania were already there and were all smiles.

'Your mum has invited us over for dinner on Saturday Ashley,' said Tania, 'she said it was a special occasion and we were to come prepared for some big news. What have you been up to Ashley?'

Ashley just smiled back, shrugged his shoulders and feigned ignorance.

Milly looked at the two of them and could see that something had changed in their relationship towards one another. It was a subtle change in the way that they passed by one other without saying a word as if to show the world that they meant nothing to each other. Seeing them hugging cheek to cheek and laughing yesterday spoke volumes and it had boosted Milly's hopes no end.

Milly had grown extremely fond of Ashley and had kept hoping that he and Tania would find happiness together. She needn't have been concerned and wondered if Lillian's invitation to dinner had anything to do with this. She'd just have to wait and see.

That evening Ashley went back to his mum's and they all had an early tea of cottage pie, a Lillian speciality. Alex wasn't home from the MoD and had phoned to say he'd be home later around seven, so it was just Katy and Ashley at the dining table with mother looking on. Lillian would eat when Alex came home.

In fact Alex drove up just as Ashley and Katy were reversing off the drive and waved to each other. A slight hold-up on the Chester road meant that they didn't get to the New Town Brownhills area till nearly seven o'clock. Being summer it was still bright and sunny. Ashley found his way to Parkview Drive and parked just inside the entrance to the Close.

It was a neat little cul-de-sac and all the front gardens were neat and in full bloom with a variety of flowers, shrubs and small ornamental trees. There were three young lads sitting on one of the low garden walls halfway down the Close and Ashley picked them out as the culprits from the newspaper article who had been pestering the neighbourhood. They were drinking something from cans and were talking and laughing quite loudly.

Ashley looked at Katy and nodded and then shut his eyes and concentrated once again on the newspaper report. Whatever Ashley saw then he communicated instantly to Katy telepathically.

Martin Whyte was twelve years old as was his friend Alan Reeve. Both were quite big for their age which gave them a certain proud image. Reg Bishop was younger by a year and much smaller. It was Reg who looked the scruffiest and was the first to throw his empty drink can into the garden behind them. The others did the same a while later and then began to pick the heads off flower heads and throw them at the houses. They used abusive language at random as they talked and laughed loudly. The F-word was used frequently.

They all went to Open-Hey Secondary school and lived within close proximity of each other on Vicarage Road and Poplar Avenue just off Great Charles Street. They frequented Holland Park and had come upon Parkview Drive one evening by chance. After an initial walk around they decided to have a bit of fun as the area looked so neat and upper class.

They returned the next day with a few eggs and tomatoes and threw them at random at the houses as they walked along. This was when they had been challenged by ex-soldier Keith Tibble and the trouble really began as reported in the papers. The police had been no help and Keith Tibble had tried a citizen's arrest and got into trouble himself by being accused of kidnapping. The three hooligans had brought their parents into the picture with wild accusations of assault by Mr Tibble and there the situation rested. The case against Keith Tibble had eventually been dropped but the three hooligans were a vindictive lot and continued to parade in front of his house. Keith, his wife and neighbours kept indoors and continued to phone the police who never turned up.

Ashley decided not only to apply his hypnosis treatment to this lot but to also scare them with the same treatment he had meted out to that large group who used to congregate at the entrance to Shelton Close where Gary Prior lived up in Mansfield. So first Ashley sent the three lads a telepathic message that since they were so fond of this cul-de-sac then their wish would be granted and they would be locked in here forever.

Ashley had already told Katy of his plan and she looked on keenly to see him in action again; the last time he was teaching the tree vandals a lesson. Katy thought her brother Ashley was amazing in what he could do and she clearly believed in teaching these hooligans a lesson with the aim of making them realise that their behaviour was criminal and not to be tolerated. Ashley's message created in their minds a superstition and fear of the unknown and a sense that they were being continually watched.

When Martin Whyte, Alan Reeve and Reg Bishop got Ashley's telepathic message they spun around to see who had spoken. They at first thought it was someone from one of the houses who had shouted at them.

'Who said that,' said Martin loudly, 'come out and show us your ugly face you bastard.'

There was a hint of nervousness in his voice.

'Martin,' said Reg Bishop, 'that voice was inside my head. Something is funny here, let's go home.' There was fear in his voice too.

'Rubbish,' said Martin Whyte as he picked up a large pebble and threw it with force at a window of the nearest house.

Ashley saw this and immediately went pink. The pebble froze in mid air as did everything else. Ashley then exerted a telekinetic push on the pebble before returning to normal. The pebble whizzed directly away from the house and upwards at a shallow angle making a whistling noise as it shot far out into the fields beyond.

'Wow,' said Katy, 'that's the first time I've seen you do that. It was fantastic bro.'

Martin Whyte was staring with mouth wide open at the house window that hadn't been broken. He had clearly seen the pebble fly off at a tangent with that eerie whistling noise. He was getting a bit scared now. Something was definitely not right.

Ashley then stared at the three boys and began to apply a gentle telekinetic force upon each of them as a blanket pressure.

'Something is pushing me,' said a scared Reg Bishop.

'And me,' said Alan Reeve.

'Yeh, and me too,' said Martin Whyte with a lot less confidence than before, 'let's get out of here.'

But it was no good. Try as they might there was an invisible barrier keeping them back.

Ashley applied a bit more force and the three boys began a slow shuffling backward motion as if they were being jostled in that direction by a large crowd. Ashley pushed them to the back part of the cul-de-sac and then sent them another telepathic message that he was the spiritual guardian of this area and that they were to be punished for desecrating an ancient graveyard. They would be locked here forever.

Ashley then also sent out his telepathic hypnotic suggestion that every time they behaved as hooligans or bullies they would get a severe pain in the abdomen area similar to a muscular cramp. Only lying on a bed for about two hours would relieve the pain.

By now Reg Bishop had started to cry and had flopped down onto the kerb where he sat with his head in his hands.

Ashley decided on a bit of physical punishment since in their current fearful state they were not likely to do anything nasty that would bring on the stomach pain. So he opened the car door and went pink again. This time he walked up to each of the lads and pinched their ear lobes and flicked his finger against their shins before returning to the car and then to normal mode.

'Oow,' came from Martin cupping his hands over his ears.

'Ouch,' from Alan, and 'ooo, ooo,' from Reg with two more pairs of hands going to their ears.

Then Ashley sent out a telepathic demonic laughter as a wicked message to the boys.

All three lads then lost control of their senses and wet themselves. Puddles appeared at the feet of each and Alan began to cry hysterically. A terrible premonition of disaster came over him.

'I want to go home,' he cried.

'I'm getting out of here,' said Martin Whyte again and this time Ashley let him walk up the cul-de-sac. Reg and Alan began to follow him. They got to within ten feet of Ashley and Katy when Ashley once again began to apply a sudden and fierce telekinetic push against them.

It was like a hurricane wind causing them to back peddle all the way back up the cul-de-sac and finally to crash down onto the pavement at the end.

By now quite a few of the neighbours had come out of their houses and were watching from their front gardens.

Ashley thought the boys had had enough of a fright and so sent them a new telepathic message that they would be allowed to return to their homes if they went to each house and said they were truly sorry especially to Keith Tibble.

The boys didn't move for a good ten minutes so Ashley gave them another sudden push that knocked them flat on their backs. The wet patches on their trousers were clearly visible. By now practically every resident was standing outside in their front garden looking at the sorry state of the lads.

One old lady took sympathy on them and went up to the boys and asked if they would like to come into her home and have a nice cup of tea. She wrinkled her nose at the strong urine odour coming from them.

'I'm Marge Jarvis,' she said, 'and you are the same age as my grandson Jeremy. I'm sure you didn't mean all that you did and are quite sorry for it now.'

'Yes miss,' said Alan Reeve. 'Thank you miss. I'm sorry about before, but can I just go home please.'

'I'm sorry too,' said Martin and Reg together.

And with that the three lads meekly stood up and began to walk slowly up the cul-de-sac mumbling sorry to all the people they passed.

Ashley let them go, after all the stomach cramp hypnosis command would remain firmly implanted in their minds forever. It would give them no hardship if they remained within the bounds of decent civilized behaviour. Ashley was sure that sooner or later they would associate the stomach cramp to their behaviour pattern.

When Ashley and Katy got back home Katy enthusiastically told her mum and dad everything in detail that Ashley had done.

'You know mum,' she added, 'I got a lot of satisfaction from actually seeing those nasty boys being made to apologise to the residents they had terrorised. They were so scared by what Ashley did that I don't think they'll ever bother anyone again.'

Ashley just sat there smiling at his sister and sipping his tea. For some reason he felt quite thirsty and rather hungry as well. It seemed to be the norm after a day of telepathic and telekinetic exertion. Well at least he wasn't tired or sleepy. Lillian brought out a tray of freshly made ham sandwiches which Ashley attacked with vigour.

Back at the shop the next day Tania was helping out by dusting the shelves with a slightly damp cloth. Her mum had said that using a feather duster just spread the dust around. Milly was at the desk busy with the accounts for it was still early for either customers or browsers. Ashley came in with a cheery 'Good Morning' and got two big smiles in reply. Milly continued with her accounts while Tania stood looking towards Ashley. He walked right up to her and with a serious expression looked directly at her and said she had a nice nose. Milly was looking at them and smiled when she saw Ashley briefly rub the tip of his nose against the tip of her daughter's.

'What do you mean by nice', said Tania giving a feigned frown and looking towards Milly. 'Mum says it's a lovely nose, don't you mum?'

Milly put her head back into her books smiling to herself and pretended not to hear.

'Just get on with your dusting missy,' smiled Ashley, 'and keep your nose to the grindstone. I'm going to make myself a cup of tea. Anyone else want one?'

Tania laughed at the pun and replied in similar fashion by telling him to keep his nose out of other people's business.

'I'll go and ask Robin if he wants one as well,' said Tania. 'He's upstairs doing his rearranging thing. He must have been thinking about it all night. He was waiting for us to open up and said something about a brilliant plan. We haven't seen him since.'

'It's alright,' said Ashley, 'I'll pop up and ask him. And he does have some very good ideas for the displays.'

'In that case,' said Tania, 'I think I had better make the tea. Fancy a cuppa mum?'

Ashley went up the stairs and saw Robin standing back looking at his handiwork with elbow cupped in one hand and chin cupped in the other. Ashley read his mind and knew exactly what Robin was trying to achieve but somehow wasn't getting there.

'I like it Robin,' said Ashley and then suggested a subtle change in the arrangement and the lighting.

'That's it,' smiled a relieved Robin, 'that was what was missing and I just couldn't put my finger on it. And here you walk in and the first thing you do is solve my little dilemma. Thanks boss.'

'It was all your idea and I must say it looks really good, even as it is now,' said Ashley. 'Tania's put the kettle on, do you want her to bring you a cuppa up here?'

'No thanks,' said Robin, 'I'd like to get this sorted first. I'll come down after that.'

So Ashley left him to it and walked down into the kitchen. Tania had made three mugs of tea with a fourth ready. As Ashley picked up his usual mug their hips touched. Tania didn't move and smiling up at Ashley she picked up a mug in each hand and slowly turned to face him. Ashley leaned down and placed his lips gently against hers in a light kiss. Milly noticed her daughters flushed face when she got her tea and smiled inwardly. Things were turning out just as she would have wished.

Saturday was not for another day and a half and Milly had hopes for an announcement regarding Ashley and Tania's future plans. Robin had not been invited and this gave her some doubts. But then Robin didn't socialise much and liked to keep to himself over weekends. It was all very secretive especially since he now lived in the same block of flats as Lorraine Hollings the bakery manager. And so business continued as usual to the end of the week.

The weekend began with a hazy and misty morning but this cleared up by midday. Milly, Jerry and Tania arrived at Lillian and Alex's place just after five o'clock and the summer sun was still high in the sky. Eric was already there but not looking at all well. He had been briefed by Lillian and the excitement showed on his face despite the pallor. He made sure he'd brought all his medication with him as he meant to enjoy the day. This was going to be memorable for him as he just couldn't wait to see the surprised and astonished expressions on the faces of his dearest friends when they heard the news. Eric saw this event as a twofold gift. The first was that Tania was to become a part of his dear grandson Ashley. What other reason could there be for bringing her into the family fold. Eric had known in his heart that Ashley and Tania had a special bond from the very start when he had seen Ashley's reaction to the 13 year old at that pub darts match so long ago. And the second was that Jerry and Milly were also to be included and drawn into the family fold as it were.

Eric had always looked at and admired Milly as a very attractive woman and he enjoyed her company enormously. Milly was managing McGill's more or less by herself now and Eric was pleased that it was she who had taken over from him after he fell ill. And Milly for her part looked on Eric not only as a father figure but also as a secret admirer. Every woman knows when an admiring look is cast in her direction and Milly was quite flattered by Eric's kindly gaze.

So when Eric stood up a bit unsteadily to greet the new arrivals she went straight to him and gave him a firm hug and kiss on both cheeks.

'Hello Eric,' she said still holding him around the waist, 'I'm so glad to see you up and about. Ashley wasn't sure if you'd be here today but I'm very glad that you are. I can't imagine what the occasion is but I have my hopes.'

'My dear dear Mrs Marsh,' said Eric teasingly with a twinkle in his eye, 'I'm here to see the surprised expressions on your faces when you hear what we have known for years. I won't say more than that – you'll just have to wait and see.'

If they had known whatever it was for years then perhaps it wasn't what she expected, thought Milly.

Jerry was welcomed in turn by Alex, Lillian and Ashley at the other end of the room. Tania and Katy had gone to one side and were chatting away merrily. Everyone was on informal terms and after pleasantries had been exchanged and all had been seated faces were turned towards Lillian and Alex expectantly.

'Would anyone like a cup of tea or a drink?' asked Alex.

'I think I'd like to hear your good news first please,' said Milly.

Tania looked across at Ashley with raised eyebrows as if to say 'What's all this about?'

Ashley had carefully prepared a section of his thoughts for Tania that would reveal to her his telepathic prowess and his ability to read peoples' minds and acquire all their knowledge, including their spoken language and life history. He looked directly at her across the room and sent her and only her all this information telepathically. He also gave her a complete knowledge of the Spanish language as he had acquired from Dr Mario and that he had previously passed on to Katy.

'Wow,' yelled Tania to everyone's surprise as she stood erect, walked slowly towards where Ashley sat and looked down at him with tears in her eyes. Very slowly she knelt down in front of him her hands down by her sides.

'Why have you told me this Ashley?' she whispered.

Ashley replied telepathically that he wanted her to be the first of her family to know. He conveyed all his feelings in his message and Tania now knew that Ashley loved her as much as she loved him and that they would be together always. She then stood up but bending down lightly rubbed the tip of her nose against his and then stood back.

It was at this moment that Ashley sent the same prepared telepathic message to everyone else in the room. He did this so his family would also know the exact moment that all had been revealed. However he did not include the Spanish lesson. Ashley also conveyed the fact that Tania was special to him and he wanted the two families to be as one.

There was a deep intake of breath from both Milly and Jerry but there were ecstatic smiles on all the other faces. Tania was now standing in front of a still seated Ashley. She reached down for his hand and pulled him to his feet and put her arms around him in a tight hug. They stood like this for just a few seconds but that was enough to get everyone else up and begin a general hugging session.

'I always knew there was something special and unique about you Ashley,' said Milly as she hugged him, 'ever since I saw you give the history of any item you touched or saw. Like my mother's ring, even I hadn't known its full history. I'm so glad we are now in the know.'

'Thanks Milly,' said Ashley and he kissed her on the top of her head, 'though I have a favour to ask of you.'

'Fire away and ask,' replied Milly.

'Would you mind taking on the full responsibility of running McGill's as its chief executive and managing director from now on,' said Ashley. 'I'll shall remain as partner of the business and still assist as always. I may be called to other matters the nature of which is yet obscure.'

There was a long pause before Milly gave her agreement to Ashley's proposal

Then out of the blue Ashley's inner voice indicated for Ashley to reveal all to this select group who would become his own family.

Ashley trusted his inner voice implicitly and was glad to conform. He walked to one end of the room and asked everyone to be seated. It took but a moment for Ashley to telepathically convey his full life history to all present. Ashley also conveyed the fact that his family had initially decided to reveal only a part of his gifts to the Marsh family and in a gradual manner. However his inner voice intervened a moment ago and asked that it be all done today in one go. After all, Ashley trusted his inner voice to guide him in all things and it had done so ever since he was a boy aged six.

There was astonished wonder from Milly, Jerry and Tania except Tania was the one with a big smile on her face; though all had eyes that glistened with wetness and this included the Bonners.

'It is a lot to take in, so I would suggest we have an early dinner and discuss Ashley's gifts and what it has meant for us as his parents. Katy only came into this knowledge recently and we wish we had done it sooner,' said Lillian smiling at Katy.

During dinner the 6.pm sun shone through the west side of the house and imparted a sense of heavenly glory to the atmosphere in the room. The summer sun didn't set till well after nine. There was much serious chatter about Ashley's gifts and it was Jerry who asked the crucial question.

'And what are you to use all these wonderful gifts for Ashley if I may ask?' he said.

Everyone paused with forks and knives half lifted and keenly waited for Ashley's answer.

'I honestly don't know as yet,' said Ashley, 'but it has something to do with saving the Earth. My inner voice will inform me when the time is right. But it was hinted that Earth's neighbour would assist me. I don't understand any of this but will be told when the time is right I suppose. In the meantime I think of this and that and try and correct some of the wrongs that are reported in the press. It would be impossible for me to spend all my time teaching some of these people a lesson as I have currently been doing. I've had a good go at vandalism and shall continue the same as and when the opportunity arises. I try not to hurt anyone physically and the hypnotic thing is a powerful tool in itself – but the world is a big place and much goes on that I can never know. Reading peoples minds lets me know if they are telling the truth or not, so I just might sit in at court cases and assist in that area. But really I'm just waiting for my inner voice to guide me to whatever is needed of me. I think that whatever this great task is I shall find out in due course when the time and conditions are deemed right for me.'

They were all listening to what Ashley had to say and Lillian thought of the little boy not too long ago telling her that the sky was also sometimes pink. She looked upon her son as a miracle with the pride only a mother can have for a deserving son. Milly was also thinking of the kindly youth who threw those darts with such accuracy at that match so long ago. But Tania had a quizzical look about her. She was wondering how this would affect her love for Ashley. Nothing had changed for him as far as he was concerned but for her the world had been turned upside down. Ashley was simply a tool in the hands of a Superior Being and Tania felt a slight jealousy at the fact she may not have a say in the matter when the day arrived that required him to submit to his destiny. But just like Lillian, Tania's love for Ashley was similarly tinged with a new found quantum of pride. It was like being in love with and being loved by a superhuman. The Ancients would have classed Ashley as one of their gods.

After dinner it was still bright and Ashley decided that a demonstration of his gifts would be quite in order. One by one he showed off his skills. He explained what they would see before he did each demonstration so that the Marshes wouldn't be too surprised at what they saw though their amazement was no less for it.

Ashley went pink and moved from one spot to another before returning to normal. It appeared as though he had dematerialised at one spot only to reappear at another. He then showed off his telekinetic ability by walking a bowling ball around the garden with the ball ten feet in front of him. Ashley took one of these balls and threw it up into the air above his head. He then went pink and applied a controlled telekinetic push on the ball before returning to normal. The ball went upwards with a slight hiss and continued going as Ashley stared upwards for a good minute. Ashley explained that the ball had disintegrated from overheating approximately ten miles up.

'I'm afraid I can only push things directly away from me. I cannot pull them towards me even though I have tried till my head hurts. Somehow I feel that this aspect will play a crucial role in whatever awaits me.'

Ashley went into the house and returned carrying a short thick iron bar and a half inch thick metal plate about six inches square. He then demonstrated what he could do to these. He first bent the bar double and then pinched it into two pieces just as if it were soft putty. Of course they didn't actually see this happening since Ashley was in pink mode each time. The metal plate suffered a similar fate and ended up with a hole through the centre. Both were quite hot to the touch after Ashley had completed his demonstrations.

'Gosh,' said Jerry. 'I can see why you were so good at that darts match when we first met. It's a good thing you don't have a criminal mind or the banks would be easy picking for you.'

'Jerry,' exclaimed Milly, 'trust you to come up with a thought like that.'

'Actually, the temptation has always been there, but only as a thought,' said Ashley. 'A part of the gifts handed me must include honesty and a respect for my fellow human beings. Besides I know that 'someone' is watching my every move and that helps keep me on the straight and narrow. So Jerry it is quite okay to mention it as you did.'

Ashley then remembered about his ability to see into past events and so explained how he had witnessed everything that the muggers Andy Braid & Mark Tamper had done to Philip that terrible night. He had first used this gift just after that pub darts match when the ladies' handbags had been pilfered. Ashley said he had received clear instructions on what to do – that inner voice again. He had concentrated his thoughts on the spot where his mum's handbag had lain. The room turned a rosy pink and it all happened as if in a dream. He saw Quigley Thorn & Johnny Price doing their thievery and then going off to where they lived. The rest was history and the items were recovered.

Lillian then remarked that assisting the courts might be a good idea especially since Ashley could convey a visual of the crime scene and what really had occurred in the entire court including the judge and jury.

'Yes,' said Ashley, 'I suppose I could sit in the public gallery and watch the proceedings. I'd like to see how the system works.'

'I think there is a listing of the day's business somewhere in the entrance hall of the Elizabeth Criminal Courts building,' said Katy, 'we could choose which one to attend.'

'I've never been inside a courtroom,' said Tania wistfully, 'I wonder what it must be like.'

'You can sit beside me and lean against me,' went the telepathic message from Ashley to Tania.

'I'd love that immensely,' thought Tania back and Ashley instantly picked this up.

No one else in the room was aware that these two had just held their first private telepathic conversation. Ashley could send out his thoughts to anyone he chose but he had to read the other person's mind to pick up their thoughts in return.

'My dear Tania I read you loud and clear.'

'Oh Ashley, this is just too fantastic. It is the ultimate form of communication for two people in love. And I do love you so very much Ashley.'

'And I love you too Tania. And I suppose this was fated from the very beginning when we first met at that darts match. Can you remember, you were only thirteen then but I had a weird premonition about you which I didn't understand at the time.'

'I've not mentioned this to anyone but from the first time that I saw you I thought you were the handsomest boy ever.'

Ashley laughed out aloud at this and reached out to give Tania's hand a squeeze.

And so for Tania and Ashley a new form of communication began that was unique and intimate. And unbeknownst to either of them was the fact that as Tania received Ashley's telepathic thoughts on a more frequent basis her own brain would unravel the mystery of telepathy and she herself would be able to communicate to others in a similar fashion. But that would not be for some time.

'Then why don't we go down on Monday morning and have a look around,' said Katy to Tania continuing the earlier theme, 'and we could do a bit of window shopping in the Bullring afterwards.'

Tania and Ashley's telepathic dialogue had only taken an instant so Tania had to jog her memory quickly back to the last bit of verbal conversation.

'That would be lovely. I could meet you outside the courts near the corner of Newton Street and Corporation Street. Shall we say about ten o'clock? I could ring your mobile if I get there first.'

'That sounds fine,' said an excited Katy. 'And then we could find out which cases would be ideal for Ashley's attention.'

Ashley just sat back and smiled as he listened to the pair making their plans. After a moment he went and sat beside his granddad. Milly also came over about the same time on the other side of Eric.

'And what do you think of our Ash?' Eric asked Milly. 'I'm so glad we don't have to keep it all a secret from you anymore.'

'You ought to come here and live with Alex and Lillian,' said Milly, 'they would see you okay and you'd have the company.'

'Maybe later,' said Eric, 'for now I'm quite happy in my own house. I suppose it's just the habit of living alone and doing as I please. Now tell me all about the shop. And how is that uncle of yours getting on with that bakery lady? I want to hear all the gossip.'

Ashley left them and went and sat beside his mum. She looked proudly and lovingly at her son and gently ran her hand over his head as though smoothing his hair into place.

'Happy,' she said smiling at him.

'Yes, very.'

'And Tania?'

'She's happy too, mum.'

'I'm glad. Can I ask when?'

Ashley knew exactly what his mother was referring to.

'Not for a year or two at least. But you and Milly can make all the plans you like. We shall leave it all to you. Happy mum?'

'Yes very. It is what Milly and I had hoped for,' said Lillian.

'That was obvious to the whole world,' said a smiling Alex who was seated the other side of his wife. 'These two women have been scheming their schemes for quite some time Ashley and I suppose they'll now be revelling on making plans for the big day. Anyhow, congratulations son, you and Tania were made for each other. She will be the ideal person at your side for whatever task lies ahead of you.'

Later after Lillian had made mugs of tea for everyone Jerry came up to Ashley and said how immensely privileged he was to be a part of this family.

'I can't help thinking about Philip's last message to you,' said Jerry. 'He said a great task lay ahead and that we should give you all the support we could. I have been thinking about that and think that for you to have been bestowed with such gifts must mean that the task ahead of you is equally immense. Can it be that our world is in grave peril at some future date? The last worldwide disaster occurred 65 million years ago when an asteroid collided with the earth and wiped out most life on the planet. Is something similar to threaten us again?'

Ashley was silent and thoughtful. Everyone had heard Jerry and now Milly came and stood beside her husband and put both her hands into his. She received a premonition that caused a cold feeling inside her and she gave a slight shiver. Jerry let go of her hands and put his arm around her shoulders and held her to him tight. He too had felt coldness at the thought of what he had just said and knew instantly that he may have guessed not a million miles from the truth.

Everyone in the room had gathered around Ashley and was patiently awaiting his response. Tania and Katy were either side of him and each had an arm around him. It was at least a minute before Ashley said anything.

'I honestly don't know but I do have a strong feeling that Jerry just might be on the right track,' he said.

'In that case perhaps there is something we can do to help,' said Alex.

It was then that Ashley's inner voice confirmed that a potential disaster was destined for the earth but was still over two millennia away and that he would need to do something about it in his lifetime to avert it from happening. But what that something was wasn't revealed to him.

Then a massive block of information powered itself into Ashley's brain and revealed to him the physical make-up of the universe. The surprise for Ashley was that it had all started in such a simplistic manner and had developed gradually by stages into what we behold today. Gravity, magnetism, light and even the pace of time were simply by-products from this structural evolution. The 'E' in Einstein's formula was the key to everything. The 'E' was meant to signify an *energy quantity* thing but could similarly represent all 'unseen' or 'dark matter'. Streaking into Ashley's thoughts were the laws that this 'subtle' medium obeyed for it to coalesce by stages into the sub-particles that made up the elements of our world today.

Just as Ashley had mentally regressed to witness the events of Philips mugging, so now too in a flash he saw an empty universe or 'realm of dark matter/energy quantity' careering through the infinite cosmos. The subsequent 'phasing without hindrance' with a myriad of other such realms resulted in 'concentrations of energy' or 'density intensities' that approached set 'critical' levels. This was the start of the physical structure to our universe when the first imploding '*mass-point*' crystallised to make its brief appearance. Although it had an exceedingly short lifespan, nevertheless the explosive return to its initial state resulted in an extremely high velocity for outward '*energy-medium-flows*' such that other *mass-points* instantly resulted. The multiplication of these mass-points was exponential to the degree that they began to congregate into clusters when a second higher critical *energy-medium-density* level was approached. There was still too much dark matter around and these 'congregations' grew ever larger. Their structures were concentrated into densely bound congregations that resembled the protons of today except infinitely larger to approach the size of our solar system in diameter; the largest single mass objects in the universe. Countless numbers of these were formed throughout the universe realm and each one to become the gravitational core of a future galaxy.

Ashley learned of the reduction of the dark matter intensity levels to just above the *first critical level* and the continuing formation of lesser mass-point clusters which gave us the protons of today. There was no light propagation throughout this period simply because it was not possible for the wave-front mechanism to remain in synchronism while the energy density levels were above the *first critical level*. Nor at this point was there a 'time' relationship in existence. Ashley saw the entire life cycle of our universe realm depicted graphically on a diagram of seven circles and was shown that today we were in the sixth circle phase. Gravity in this phase was explained as being linked to the decay of the proton in a gradient of 'energy medium density' spatial grid zones and that similarly the pace of 'time' was also linked to the average rate of diminishment of the mass of the proton, i.e., its decay process rate. Light waves propagated in a varied quantum step that was shorter in the higher 'energy density' zones. The *mass-point* cyclic period was a central functionary in all of this and was the basic yardstick for all 'duration' measurement i.e. 'Time' itself.

As this disclosure progressed into the complex functionality of individual aspects within the universe structure from varied wavelengths of light to the myriad of fine structure particles of mass Ashley began to see the purpose to the order of things. All of this took but an instant of time comparable to the flash of a camera recording a great outdoor panoramic scene. Then suddenly it was over and Ashley had to sit down on the floor and rest for he had never before absorbed so much information in one go. Apart from the wonder of it all there was a lot to take in.

'What's the matter son?' asked Lillian with concern when she noticed Ashley's flushed face.

Ashley held his head in both hands and just sat quietly for the moment.

Tania and Katy plonked down on either side of him and both put an arm around his back.

It was a very long minute for everyone in the room before Ashley looked up and smiled.

He then sent them all a telepathic picture of the essence of what had just happened to him without the intricate detail on the structure of the universe.

'I have an idea why all this has been revealed to me,' said Ashley. 'I believe it may have something to do with the task ahead and that an understanding of the vastness of the universe is a part of it.'

'It is all very complex and confusing for me,' said Katy, 'but how big is our universe Ashley, can you describe it in simple terms for me please.'

'Well,' said Ashley, 'let me see how best to describe it. I suppose it is comparable to a cloud in the sky. There are other clouds as well but they are quite separate from our cloud and don't really concern us at the moment. Except these clouds are really vast realms of the 'energy-medium' factor from Einstein's famous equation and are also existent in the infinite cosmos. I'll skip the bit about the formation of matter through the first five circle phases in the structural evolution and come straight to our present status in this part of the sixth circle phase.'

Ashley looked around the room and saw that he had everyone's full attention.

'A considerable period of 'event-duration' has elapsed since our realm entered the circle 6 phase and most of those proton giants that formed in the fourth circle phase have evolved into the galaxies we see today. The fact that there may be a few orphan proton giants lurking in the realm regions is no cause for concern as we just couldn't fall into one if we tried. Proton giants with or without their entourage of stars seem to be uniformly dispersed throughout the realm volume. Currently we see only a small part of the realm but I can give you an idea of this galaxy distribution in a pictorial example.'

'Consider our own Milky Way galaxy as the local centre of our realm area. In size it is like a disc approximately 100,000 light-years in diameter and contains billions of stars that make a complete revolution about its centre once every 200 million years. Now if we reduce our Milky Way galaxy to the size of a little round aspirin then the nearest galaxy which is Andromeda is only another aspirin 5 inches away. This plus a few other galaxies form our local group of galaxies. The next similar group of galaxies, the Sculptor group is then 2 feet away on this scale. The Virgo cluster, a huge collection of about 200 galaxies spread over the size of a football is only 10 feet away. The Virgo cluster is the centre of a loose swarm of galaxies called the local Super-cluster and of which the local group, us and the sculptor group are a part. On this scale just 65 feet away is another Super-cluster, the Coma cluster containing thousands of galaxies. Farther out there are even larger clusters of galaxies some 60 feet across. There are galaxies in clusters spread out in every direction from us and as far as we are able to view they are uniformly distributed across the sky. The brightest star or quasar in the night sky is, on this scale, only 420 feet distant. There are about 140 billion galaxies in the visible part of our realm. Everything we can see with the aid of the most powerful telescopes can be contained in a sphere roughly one mile across, on our aspirin scale of course. Beyond our vision zone on this scale the galaxies continue in the same uniform distribution for about half a million miles in every direction until a gradual lessening of content becomes apparent. Finally at a few more thousand miles on this pictorial scale the galaxies disappear altogether and a progressively lower intensity of the energy medium/dark matter is all that remains. There is no definitive end to our realm, just a gradual depletion of the energy density that fades away to become the cosmic void. So in reality it would take a beam of light approximately 40 million billion years to traverse from one side of our realm to the other.'

Ashley smiled at the room of intense faces.

'I can continue in the same vein by reducing our realm universe to the size of an aspirin and expanding the example again to give you the relative positions of other realm universes in the cosmic void,' said Ashley with a twinkle in his eye.

'Thank you Ash,' said Katy standing up, 'but that's quite enough for me. I think my brain is beginning to hurt with all this stuff going into it. I'm going to put the kettle on. Who's for another cuppa?'

Tania gave Ashley a sideways hug and then stood up and said she'd give Katy a hand with making the tea.

Ashley also stood up, stretched his arms up and outwards in slow motion and then said he was going for a stroll around the garden to clear his head and get some much needed fresh air.

Five minutes later the others followed with their mugs of tea and they saw Ashley staring at the half moon that was clearly visible high up in the sky.

'Here's a tea for you Ashley,' said Katy coming round and handing him his favourite mug.

'Thanks sis,' said Ashley taking a small sip and again looking up towards where the half moon hung motionless and mysterious.

It was a beautiful barmy summer afternoon and the sun was well across to the west and still above the line of trees lining the far side of the school playing field behind the house. The shadow of the high boundary hedge extended into the centre of the garden while the house was still in full sun. The shadow was however broken by squares of sunlight reflected off the glass panelled upstairs bedroom windows. This was one of the advantages of having a house that faced in an east-west direction.

'What is it son?' asked Lillian coming up beside Ashley. As a mother she had always sensed when there was uneasiness in his demeanour. Something was bothering him.

'I don't know mum,' replied Ashley loud enough for the others to hear. 'I've been puzzling over this task that Philip referred to. I don't know what it could be but I feel that it may have something to do with 'moving a mountain' as the saying goes. And I don't think I could extend to such a feat, at least not yet.'

'Or maybe a moon,' said Jerry without thinking.

Everyone looked at Jerry for further enlightenment but he just shrugged his shoulders with both palms extended and eyebrows raised.

'Thanks Jerry, that is exactly what I have been thinking,' said Ashley, 'except that I need a lot of practice on something first. I'm not sure if my gift as yet extends that far to allow me to move something that huge.'

It was Alex who then gave his fatherly advice.

'There's no need to speculate or worry about any of this,' he said with his hand on his son's shoulder, 'why not just leave it all to your inner voice. It knows the course that you will need to follow and I'm sure will guide you when the time is right.'

'You're absolutely right dad,' said Ashley aloud.

After several minutes of quiet reflection Jerry broke the silence by suggesting that Ashley should write a book about all that had been revealed to him about the origin and make-up of the universe.

'And please keep it simple for the ordinary lay person to understand. I had been taught that the universe started from nothing in a Big Bang from a single point in space,' said Jerry, 'and I believed it to be absolutely true; but not any more. I also believed that Black Holes would swallow up everything in the end; another fallacy. You must write all this down in an orderly fashion Ashley and get it published so as to put scientists back on the right track.'

'I'm afraid they wouldn't accept a simple account from an unknown especially without scientific experimental proof. To them it would simply be another outlandish theory. The energy medium or dark matter is extremely elusive and no instrument would ever be able to detect its existence. But I shall certainly make the attempt with the hope that someone somewhere will one day realise its truth and prove it by a related experiment when the technology allows,' said Ashley smiling.

'And you could give it an outlandish title too,' said an impish Katy, 'something that will shock.

You could call it The Real Story or The Cosmic Realm. What about The-Seven-Circle-Event?'

Ashley smiled at his excited sister's suggestions and thought back to the times when she was little and had pressed him to catch birds to put in her cage. He looked at her with pride and love now and noticed her as a charming and beautiful woman. Robin Nesters was lucky to have her love.

'Let me write the thing first,' said a grinning Ashley, 'I'm open to suggestions for the title and an author pseudonym. I'm certainly not putting my own name to it. I need to be well out of the public eye for obvious reasons.'

'I think a title that shocks a bit might be appropriate,' said Lillian who was the most scientifically qualified of the group with a degree in physics.

'Yes,' said granddad Eric from his position on a garden chair on the patio, 'something that cuts across the boundaries of good sense and shocks a bit and is controversial. What about 'Black Holes Repel' or 'Proton Giants in Space' for a title?'

Again Ashley gave a faint smile and said that he would think of something suitable.

And so the evening wore on and the conversation returned to more mundane everyday topics like the terrible state of the economy and the high crime rate.

'I think they ought to bring back some form of the caning principle in schools,' said Jerry. 'Today's youngsters are quite out of hand and that's because they're not taught discipline and respect for their elders when they are young. Verbal reasoning doesn't always work and that's where a sharp controlled whack on the back of the legs would speak a thousand words.'

'I don't believe that the school should be made responsible for a child's behaviour,' said Lillian. 'I think that it is the duty of the parents at home. A child is born with certain tendencies that especially become noticeable when they develop to the age of two. You've heard of the 'Terrible Twos' haven't you? That is simply when the child is trying to assert itself to the world and no one is taking them seriously. So it is up to the parents alone to channel that energy constructively and guide the child's impulses along with the setting of boundaries of behaviour. When those boundaries are not understood then a gruff voice can do just as much as your whack on the legs Jerry. I accept that there can be exceptions but I believe that in general smacking or the birch doesn't do any good.'

'Perhaps you're right Lillian,' said Jerry, 'but the very fact of the possibility of the cane could act as a deterrent to bad behaviour. I don't think I was ever caned when I was at school but I do remember being scared of it and perhaps my behaviour was all the better because of its existence.'

'And do you think that there is a link with later criminal behaviour and activity?' asked Alex.

'I think criminals are opportunists,' said Milly in a serious voice. 'And I'm not just referring to the petty thieves, burglars and muggers. There are corporate criminals too who defraud companies of millions of pounds or embezzle funds from unsuspecting clients or fiddle their expense accounts. Most of these are respected members of the community or are even in government. Their actions are just as criminal.'

Ashley listened to these arguments which took his mind off other more serious concerns and he even added his own views as well. He said he favoured his mum's opinion on corporal punishment and agreed with everything Milly had said.

'Yes,' said Ashley, 'like marrying a rich widow for her money and then leaving her penniless after a few years of profligate living.'

'There was never one around when some of us could have wished for one,' said Eric laughingly.

'Oh, by the way,' said Lillian, 'what news of Vicky and Robert? Mavis said that she'd thought they were heading towards setting a date but all has been put on hold because Robert is joining the police force and is due to start his three month residential training course in Burton next month.'

'I do believe that a policeman's wage starts in the mid-twenties and should make life a lot easier for a newly married couple,' said Eric. 'Mind you I somehow don't see them as a couple, they are such complete opposites.'

'How can you say such a thing Eric,' exclaimed Milly in horror at the suggestion.

'Well my dear, an old man notices little things and many of those are puzzling. Have you ever seen the two of them in secretive conversation – like those two over there?' said Eric pointing to where Ashley and Tania were seated together.

'That doesn't mean that they don't care for one another,' said Milly. 'Opposites often attract.'

'Yes, but will it make for a lasting relationship?' said Eric. 'Even if they get married, what happens when the fun and games runs out and they have to settle down to good old everyday conversation and companionship? Will they want to be in each other's company then, and will it be enough?'

Milly was thoughtful for a moment and then decided not to pursue her argument. She thought back to when she and Jerry had been fiercely in love. They had not a care in the world apart from the scarcity of money. The arguments had been minor and she had always won. Jerry was a coward when it came to dealing with tears and she loved him more for it. Gradually over the years that love had blossomed sideways into a very comfortable companionship and bond. Each had grown dependant on the company of the other even though no words might be exchanged. Just his presence in the house was sufficient to give her comfort. She listened to his breathing – and occasional snoring – and felt happy that he was there beside her. She tolerated his whims and idiosyncrasies because he was a man and therefore different. His forgetfulness could be irritating. Sometimes she berated him for his easygoing manner as a shortcoming but secretly was glad that he was so. It made her role just that bit easier. Jerry was a typical man and was happy for Milly to manage the house, the shopping, the laundry routine, etc. and Milly was quite happy to delegate some of those tasks to him as and when she felt it necessary. The garden was his domain as was the allotment. Jerry kept an easy garden with mostly hardy herbaceous shrubs that came up each spring and bloomed throughout the summer and Milly was often asked to examine the beds and give her desired praise. Yes, they were good for one another and she wished the same for Tania and Ashley.

'I see what you mean Eric,' said Milly, 'but I hope you are mistaken.'

Alex brought out some more folding garden chairs and they all sat around the table on the covered patio. The sun had travelled around to the north-west and was just touching the tops of the distant tree line so that there was still sunshine on their faces at eight o'clock. Lillian produced a large hedgehog bloomer of bread that had been neatly sliced by Alex using the electric knife and placed it at the centre of the table. Katy and Tania helped with bringing out the spreadable butter, sliced ham and cheeses to the table along with a large bowl of neatly arranged salad topped with slices of hard boiled eggs.

'I thought a light supper out here on the patio would be nice,' said Lillian, 'and there's tea and coffee in the kitchen. It's a shame that Ron and Brenda couldn't be here with us today. I'll ring her later and give her all the news.'

'How's the B&B doing up there?' asked Jerry. 'They must be quite busy in this weather.'

'Yes,' said Lillian, 'they are. I spoke to Brenda about our little get together and she said they were fully booked for the next month and just couldn't get away. I suppose they have their ups and downs but summer is always a busy period for them.'

'How long have they been at it?' Jerry asked again.

'Gosh,' said Lillian looking up at the patio canopy. 'They married in seventy five and must have moved up there not more than a year or two later. They started the business more or less straightaway. So that would make it about twenty five years now. And I think they still find it quite enjoyable though it is a lot of hard work.'

'It's nice to be your own boss I suppose,' said Alex, 'but then it is a twenty four hour job seven days a week. You tend not to mind when it's your own business.'

'Well I certainly wish them good luck in the business and hope it always stays busy,' said Jerry looking across at where Tania and Ashley were standing and talking near the ornamental pond at the far side of the garden. 'And I wish those two all the luck in the world. Ashley has some task ahead of him, and it must be a big one, and Tania will have to cope with that as well. I only hope it doesn't come between them and spoil their relationship.'

Lillian looked up and smiled and thought how there was not a chance of that happening. These two were meant for each other and nothing would come between them.

'What do you think Milly?' asked Lillian, 'do you think there is cause for concern?'

She smiled back.

'Those two are committed for life come hell or high water,' she said. 'I know my Tania and I have also come to understand and love Ashley. They are both genuine people and what they have is absolutely rock solid.'

Then Milly turned to her husband and said, 'I wish you weren't such a pessimist Jerry. Look at us. You were disappointed when we couldn't have any more children and so was I. But we muddled through that somehow and here we are with a brand new son in Ashley. What could be more wonderful than all the news we have had today?'

'I'm sorry,' said Jerry, 'I open my mouth too soon and just say what I'm thinking. I'm just an open book to read as you will.'

'And I love you for it darling,' said Milly making a face at him across the table.

'Now, now children behave yourselves,' chuckled Katy, and everyone laughed.

It was about ten o'clock and the sky was still quite light when the party broke up and everyone left to return to their homes. Granddad Eric was tired out and Alex dropped him home shortly after the others had left. But Ashley stayed the night with his family and they sat up talking till well past midnight.

Ashley decided to put the big mysterious task to the back of his thoughts and to once again concentrate on the affairs of the world around him. He thought Katy's idea of the criminal courts was worth pursuing and should prove rather interesting if not challenging. Ashley thought this could be quite exciting and would make a change from dealing with individuals. He was looking forward to the expressions of surprise on the faces in the courtroom when they received his telepathic revelations of the truth in the case. He would of course continue to try to deal with vandalism issues that came to light through the local press as he had done previously.

The next day being Sunday Ashley had arranged to spend the day out somewhere with Tania. For some reason Ashley asked her to bring along a spare pair of shoes. He had no idea why he had suggested this and Tania had been only too happy to oblige without question.

They drove through beautiful Henley in Arden with all its luxuriant flowering hanging baskets and through the curve of Wootton Wawen and on to Stratford on Avon. They spent an hour there and watched a beautifully painted forty foot canal boat manoeuvring through the lock. There seemed to be an unusually large number of white swans on the river and they were quite majestic in the way they moved effortless through the water.

They had been holding hands lightly as they strolled along and to onlookers they would seem not to be saying much to each other. In fact theirs was a unique form of communication being entirely telepathic. Had they been watched more closely someone would have observed the smiles they gave each other with the occasional raised eyebrow and accompanying chuckle. For some reason Tania was getting more proficient in getting some of her own messages across to Ashley without the need for him to actually read her mind. Ashley mentioned this, telepathically of course, and Tania replied that perhaps some of Ashley's ability was filtering through simply because of the practice she was getting in communicating with him so intensely. Perhaps she had developed a partial telepathic ability simply through her association with Ashley. In time she might become fully proficient. She mentioned that perhaps Ashley should start communicating telepathically with the rest of the family as well and then eventually they could all chat freely wherever they might be. Ashley agreed and would do so from now on. This would prove essential in the case of granddad Eric a few years down the line but Ashley was not as yet to know that.

They then drove on to The Three Ways Hotel in Mickleton for a lovely lunch at one o'clock. This was the home of the famous Pudding Club well known for it's weekly evening dinners that were followed by a sumptuous variety of puddings. You only got another pudding if you had finished the previous one. The pudding courses were small and ran to six or seven. After they'd had their lunch and as a matter of interest Tania enquired of Lisa who was one of the serving staff when an evening booking could be had.

'O miss,' said Lisa, 'I'm afraid it's fully booked right up to the middle of November. There are about forty Pudding Club members but not all can attend every week so the spare places are given to non members. You can put your name down if you wish and we will contact you nearer the time.'

'Oh that's alright,' said Tania, 'I was just curious that's all and thanks for a lovely meal. It was perfect.'

'Thank you, miss,' she said, 'have a lovely day.'

Hidcote Manor and Garden was just a few miles away at the top of a hill so Ashley and Tania spent the rest of the afternoon wandering through the grounds and admiring the pretty herbaceous border plants, shrubs and trees not to mention the sweeping views of the surrounding countryside.

This was a National Trust property and they had become Annual Members when they had visited Packwood House last year with Uncle Robin who had taken them there as a special treat. He had introduced them to a few of the other volunteers on the site and had got them special rates for their first year of membership of the Trust. They had also visited nearby Baddesley Clinton on the same day at Robin's insistence.

And so it was that as they strolled down some steps to the Dahlia Border the heel of Tania's left shoe just broke off. Tania lurched to her left and would have fallen but for Ashley going into pink mode, stepping around her and placing his arm firmly around her waist.

'My hero,' whispered Tania realising how Ashley had prevented her fall, 'thank you darling.'

There was a bench nearby and Tania walked to it with an exaggerated limp.

'What shall we do with this shoe?' said Tania just before suddenly remembering the spare pair that was in the car.

She looked at Ashley in wonder and telepathically asked how he knew in advance that this would happen. Could he now also anticipate future events before they happened? Was there no end to the surprises from this wonderful man? Tania's heart seemed to swell to near bursting with her love for Ashley and not caring who might see she reached around and kissed him firmly and quite fiercely on the lips.

'Excuse me miss,' said a smiling Ashley, 'have you no decorum on this busy street. Whatever will the neighbours think not to mention all these beautiful Dahlias?'

'Shut up and get my shoes out of the car,' said a taunting Tania and after a pause she added, 'please Ashley.'

This time Ashley leaned over and rubbed the tip of his nose against hers and then gave her a light kiss on the lips before standing up. He looked down at her and telepathically conveyed his feelings of love for her. Words cannot do justice in describing one's emotions it is only telepathy that does it perfectly. The emotion comes across strongly to leave a tight feeling in your chest.

Tania smiled up at Ashley and then closed her eyes and leaned her head back taking in a deep breath of complete satisfaction with life. No one could be happier than she was at this moment. She was happy and proud that this man was hers; hers for the rest of her life.

She opened her eyes expecting to see Ashley walking away, but there he was sitting beside her again holding her good pair of shoes in his hands.

'There's no point in having these gifts if I can't use them now and again for the benefit of a damsel in distress, now is there?' said a grinning Ashley.

This was all too much for Tania and the emotion of the moment got the better of her. She flung her arms around Ashley and sobbed her heart out. Ashley just held her tight; he understood perfectly and got a lump in his own throat as well. Love was a funny creature and came in many disguises.

They sat like that for quite a while silently exchanging thoughts of mutual affection and love when suddenly Tania began her usual giggling thing which escalated into a shaking fit of laughter. Ashley automatically followed suit and then several moments later both sat back side by side and just smiled at each other.

Ashley then held up the broken shoe and was about to ask what Tania wanted to do with it when they both once again broke into peels of laughter.

'Just,... just,' gasped Tania between deep inhalations and she pointed to the waste bin a few yards away indicating a simple disposal. But it was the way she pointed and then dipped her hand at the wrist that made Ashley mimic her action and raise his eyebrows in query while tilting his head sideways that sent Tania off once again into peals of laughter.

Other visitors smiled as they strolled past. It was a comforting sight for them to see a well dressed handsome young couple in such a happy mood.

Tania and Ashley finally went to the Barn Café near the car park and sampled a slice of carrot cake between them along with a hot drink for each. There were some interesting plants on sale there but nothing unusual that took their fancy.

The drive back to Dudley was a silent one with each immersed in their own private thoughts. Tania reclined her seat, gave Ashley's arm a squeeze and then shut her eyes for a peaceful doze. Ashley glanced down at her sleeping upturned face and thought how much he loved this woman.

'Keep your eyes on the road, boy,' she said smiling and without even opening her eyes. However she reached out again and gave his thigh a gentle pat and then telepathically said 'Thank you for a lovely day out.'

Ashley just smiled as he drove.

The next morning Tania and Katy met up as planned outside the Criminal Justice Courts. They were surprised how easily they got into the building after the briefest of handbag searches. They went to the information desk and said they were doing a college project about the justice system and would like to sit in on a couple of interesting trials with juries.

'Well then,' said the old chap behind the counter, 'there's a case that started last week in Courtroom Three but they only just managed to set up the jury. Go in through the Room 3 door and up the stairs on the left to the visitor gallery and you should find the case interesting. A mugging case in which the victim identified one of the culprits but it's her word against his and entirely up to the jury to decide who to believe. All in all an interesting case I should think.'

Tania and Katy thanked him and started to walk away when he called to them.

'Just one minute ladies,' he said, 'for your interest there's a murder case starting in courtroom four next week. These are very popular and you will need to get here early for a seat in the gallery. No standing is allowed.'

'Thank you,' said Katy, 'We'll be here nice and early. But won't they have to select the jury first. How long does that take?'

'Probably a day or so I should think. But it is an interesting procedure if you want to see how the entire system works.'

So off they went in through the Room 3 door and up into the gallery. There was a large seating area with pews like in a church but stepped like in a theatre. The place was near empty and they found seats near the front beside an elderly couple.

'Hello,' the lady said, 'I haven't seen you here before. Is this your first visit? You'll love it,' she continued when both Katy and Tania nodded, 'it's better than watching TV at home.'

'Thank you,' said Katy. 'We're doing a project and have just come to see how things work around here.'

'The chaps on the back row of seats are usually reporters so don't sit there,' said the man. 'They leave the room quite frequently to make calls on their mobiles. So don't sit there,' he repeated.

The jury were already seated in their pews to the right side of the courtroom when the girls had come in. They all had to stand up when the bewigged court clerk announced the entry of the judge.

He came in through a door in the panelled wall just behind the Judges Bench, which was a long table affair positioned on a foot high raised dais. There were three ornately carved throne-like seats behind it and the judge selected the centre one.

'The other seats are for when they have a panel of judges to sort out a case,' volunteered the old lady to Katy who was closest to her.

The barristers were called up to the judge's bench and for the next few minutes a silent conference ensued before the proceedings actually began with the court clerk reading out the title of the case. There were in fact two cases to be decided as each defendant would be judged independently even though they were jointly accused of the same crime. The cases of Crown vs. Craig Joyner and Crown vs. Adam Gow were to begin.

The prosecution attorney then made his opening statement in which he stated the case against the defendants.

Mrs Carol Vann-Smith a mother of two aged in her mid thirties was driving through the Falcon Lodge estate of Sutton Coldfield and stopped to check directions in her A-Z street map. A gang of youths then surrounded her car and the defendant Craig Joyner one of the gang smashed a back window, grabbed up her laptop computer off the back seat and ran down the street. Mrs Vann-Smith chased him but gave up when he threatened her with a short iron bar. She saw him clearly for several seconds as she backed off and returned to her car. There she saw another youth, the other defendant Adam Gow rifling through the glove box. She grabbed him and was face to face with him for about three seconds before another member of the same gang punched her to the ground breaking her nose.

Police later organised an identity parade and Mrs Vann-Smith positively picked out the two defendants. She said that there were at least six in the gang but couldn't be sure of their identities.

The prosecutor then told the court that both defendants were from the Falcon Lodge area and had already admitted to a separate conspiracy to burglary and were part of a gang involved in auto theft. However, they denied ever being involved in any way in the mugging of Mrs Vann-Smith.

Tania looked at Katy who nodded a reply. Tania had just used her rudimentary telepathic skills to suggest to Katy that they contact Ashley immediately and get him to come to the court and establish the truth.

Tania knew that Ashley would be at the shop all day so they went into the hallway downstairs and rang from there.

'Hi mum, it's me,' said Tania into her mobile phone, 'everything alright? Is Ashley there?'

'Yes darling, is everything alright?' asked Milly.

'Yes mum we're fine. Katy and I are here at the courts and there's a beauty of a case on trial and we thought Ashley ought to come over to help sort it out by getting the true facts using his you know what.'

'Just a minute darling and I'll get him for you.'

There were several seconds of silence before Ashley came on the line. Tania explained the case and asked Ashley if he could come over.

'Robin and I are just re-arranging the shelves upstairs but I could be with you in a couple of hours,' said Ashley. 'What about one o'clock?'

Tania sent her thoughts down the line pleased that she was getting better at this form of communication. Ashley in turn responded with a complete picture of his entire morning showing exactly what he and Robin were trying to achieve upstairs. After a brief intimate exchange Tania switched off and then tried to convey Ashley's thoughts to Katy.

'What was that,' exclaimed Katy confused at the jumble of images and sounds she received.

'Sorry,' said Tania, 'just practicing my telepathic skills. Ashley is teaching me this telepathy thing and I'm not very good at it as yet. I need to keep practicing though. Ashley wants us all to learn how to do it and said we could all eventually become quite good at it.'

'Well that first bit inside the courtroom was very good when you indicated we should phone Ashley. Keep at it Tania and I hope I can pick it up as well,' replied Katy.

They went back to the gallery and found the proceedings slow and monotonous.

Mrs Carol Vann-Smith was on the witness stand as the only prosecution witness and she related in a clear and precise manner all the events of that fateful day.

On cross-examination the defence attorney tried to get her to admit that she wasn't 100% certain of the identity of his clients but he couldn't dent her confidence in that area. He said she was too believable and that no one could be that sure of anything that happened over six months ago. He said her story was a fabrication and she had only picked out his clients because they were of a similar age and appearance to the mugger youths she saw that day.

The judge called a recess and said that the court would reconvene after lunch at 2 o'clock sharp.

The two girls then strolled across to the Minories Shopping Centre and bought blueberry muffins and hot drinks from the corner café. They then sauntered towards the Corporation Street bus stops in the hope of spotting Ashley. But he saw them first as he came down the ramp from the Palisades shops. He had come by train on the Wolverhampton line of the Centro system to New Street from Tipton. He called to them telepathically and they spotted him right away. A hug and kiss from both followed and then all three walked back to the Minories shops where Ashley bought a hot chocolate drink and a muffin. They sat on a bench outside and chatted away as Ashley peeled back the wrapping and bit into the muffin.

'Blueberries are supposed to be good for your memory,' said Katy, 'granddad told me that.'

'Excuse me,' mocked Ashley, 'what did you say your name was young lady?'

They all laughed.

'So tell me about the case,' said Ashley to Tania, 'and try telling it telepathically for practice.'

Tania closed her eyes and concentrated and then looked up at Ashley with an enquiring look.

Ashley smiled back and said, 'I received some of it but I had to read your mind to get the full picture. I hope you didn't mind. But you are getting better.'

Tania gave him a mischievous grin and said,' You can read my thoughts anytime Ashley.'

She looked across at Katy and jiggled her eyebrows up and down and they both burst out laughing. Ashley couldn't help a smile himself.

Back in the courtroom the proceedings continued with the defence putting Craig Joyner in the witness box. The first question was to ask Craig if he had ever seen Mrs Carol Vann-Smith before today.

'No sir,' he replied, 'I have not.'

Ashley had closed his eyes and was concentrating on Carol Vann-Smith and regressed to the events of six months ago.

A sort of a mistiness developed and he saw her drive up past some shops in the afternoon and turn up a road with a slight incline. She parked near the junction with Falcon Lodge Crescent and looked down at her street map. It was then that the six youths surrounded her car and stood around it laughing. They were Craig Joyner, Adam Gow, Jasper Nolan, Sam Maltby, Daniel Ash and Martin Hussein. They had all been in school together, were nineteen or twenty years of age and all keen on driving and crashing the cars they had stolen. They referred to themselves as joy riders. Three of these had been caught red handed in a stolen car and had admitted a guilty plea in another court. They were currently awaiting sentencing.

Craig noticed the laptop in the back of the car and smashed the window with a short iron bar he always carried. He grabbed hold of the case handle and walked briskly away up the crescent.

Carol got out of the car and shouted at him to give back the laptop as it had all her work information on it. But he just laughed and continued walking. Carol ran towards him. She was a biggish woman and was used to looking after herself.

Craig heard her coming and turned around to face her. He raised the iron bar in a threatening gesture and Carol stopped a few yards from him and hesitated about what to do. They stared at each other for several seconds and then he ran off down the crescent.

Carol went back to her car only to find one of the youths, Adam Gow, seated inside and going through the glove box. She rushed around and grabbed him and pulled him out of the car. She wasn't sure what to do next and just glared at him. Then suddenly she felt something smash into the side of her head and she fell to the ground in a daze. It was Daniel Ash who had come to his mates rescue by punching Carol with his fist. He kicked her in the face for good measure before they all ran off.

A car had stopped and the elderly driver tried to help Carol rise. When she finally stood up she had a bruised cheek and a bleeding nose. There was blood all down her front. She got some tissues out of the car and gently dabbed the blood off the front of her dress. But when she tried wiping the blood off her nose she found it very painful and realised it might be broken. She sat quietly in the car and sipped at the bottle of water she always carried.

The elderly gentleman, a man called Jim had phoned the police and when they arrived he simply told them he had seen the lady lying on the pavement and had stopped to help. No, he hadn't seen anyone else around. They took down his details and said he could leave.

For Carol it was all a blur. An ambulance took her to the Good Hope Hospital A&E department where she was treated after about an hours wait. Her nose was painfully straightened by the doctor and she was allowed to return home.

Carol rang her sister Mary and told her what had happened and could she please pick up the kids from school about now. A taxi took her back to her car and she drove home with the window still missing. She'd get Auto-glass out later to fix it.

Ashley saw all this and felt sorry for the woman. But it was her word against theirs and they would get the benefit of the doubt and go scot-free, he felt sure; unless of course he did something about it.

As the case was very likely to be concluded today, Ashley decided there was no time like the present to take action.

So first he sent out a strong telepathic command to the two defendants Craig and Adam. Ashley implanted a hypnotic suggestion deep in the subconscious part of their minds that whenever they acted in a bullying aggressive manner or told a lie they would develop severe cramping pains in their abdomen area. And also if each time they repeated the lie or actions the pain would become more severe and last for longer.

Next Ashley sent out a full telepathic pictorial account to every one in the courtroom of exactly what had taken place with regard to the mugging of Mrs Carol Vann-Smith. Ashley included the full names and addresses of all the six youths involved.

There was a loud audible gasp from all in the room including the judge who immediately called a half hour recess and for the prosecutor and defence attorneys to meet him in his chambers.

Of course the two defendants simply thought they'd had a mental flash back to the day of the mugging and were also completely unaware of Ashley's hypnotic implant in their minds. So when the court resumed and the defence attorney repeated his question of whether he had been involved in the mugging of Mrs Vann-Smith he again replied that he had not.

Almost immediately Craig Joyner felt a severe cramping pain in his abdomen. He doubled up clasping his stomach with folded arms and cried out with the pain.

Ashley then sent out another telepathic thought to the whole of the courtroom that each time the defendants told an untruth the hypnotic suggestion planted in their subconscious would result in an imagined sensation of severe abdominal pains.

There were smiles on many of the faces in the courtroom including the judge who was now quite unsympathetic towards the defendants.

'The defendant will stand up straight,' commanded the judge, 'and this time I ask you directly whether or not you smashed the window of Mrs Carol Vann-Smith's car and stole her laptop computer off the back seat?'

'I did not .....,' and before he could add to this he screamed with an even more severe pain. The pain shot up his chest and down to his groin bringing tears to his eyes.

'No, no, no,' he exclaimed again and then 'yes, yes I did it, I did it, me and the other guys.' And he pointed back at Adam Gow seated behind him.

At once the pain got considerably less and his brain made the connection with Ashley's last telepathic message about the pain getting worse with each lie he told. He now stood up straight with a sigh of relief.

The judge then called the attorneys to the bench and there was another whispered conference for several minutes. They discussed the truth of the case in view of the telepathic picture of the events that they had all received. The judge pointed out that he intended to suspend the trial and bring in the police to get fresh statements from not only the two defendants present today but also from the other four whose name and addresses had been revealed. The attorneys gave their agreement and returned to their respective places. The judge banged his gavel twice and the courtroom hushed.

'This court is now suspended in the light of what has just occurred. The defendants will remain in custody and I have asked that the police once more become involved and obtain fresh statements from not only the defendants here but from the other gang members as well. The police will be provided with all their names and addresses,' said the judge.

He then continued, 'Providence has intervened rather miraculously and I believe that the entire courtroom has been made aware of the truth in this case. The jury is dismissed as is the court.'

The judge then stood up and left the courtroom through the door in the panelled wall behind the bench.

There was a buzz in the courtroom. The defence team wandered over to the prosecutor's table and an earnest conversation seemed to be taking place until one of them laughed. They were on friendly terms and frequented the same club of an evening. That was when deals could be struck on the cases they happened to be dealing with at the time.

'I hope this doesn't happen often,' said the defence attorney, 'or else we should all be out of a job.'

The defendants were led away to the detention area and the police were called to interview them again and take fresh statements.

The jury seats were empty but there were still a few officials in the courtroom. The prosecutor's table was still occupied by both teams but they were engaged in pleasant light-hearted conversation mainly to do with the judge's remark about providence having intervened.

'Mrs Vann-Smith must have a guardian angel watching over her,' said the prosecutor. 'I really didn't hold out much hope of a conviction in this case. It was one person's word against another. We simply didn't have any hard evidence at all.'

Up in the visitor's gallery Katy, Tania and Ashley were the only ones still seated there.

'Well done Ashley,' said Katy. 'I enjoyed that immensely. Even more than the punishment and terror you handed out to that Brown Hills New Town mob.'

Tania looked at Ashley and smiled. She was glowing with pride for her man. And yet she had the oddest intuitive sensation that Ashley would be needed elsewhere and somewhere where she could not go. And so there was a hint of sadness mixed in with her joy.

Then turning to Katy she told her about the incident with the broken shoe at Hidcote Manor Gardens yesterday.

'I think Ashley has the gift to predict the future,' she said, 'or how could he have known that I would bust the heel off my shoe? He asked me to take along a spare pair when we set out in the morning and I just assumed he meant for me to take along a pair of comfortable walking shoes for something he had planned. Katy I think your brother is absolutely wonderful and I wonder what else we shall discover about him.'

'You're reading too much into this,' said Ashley. 'I haven't a clue why I asked you to bring along extra shoes. It was just something I said on the spur of the moment. You know about my inner voice and how it tells me things like knowing the history of an antique piece. Well it wasn't even that as I didn't hear anything at all. But never mind that now, what's the next case?'

'The chap at the information said there was a murder case starting next week in Courtroom 4,' said Katy.

'Perhaps with this case ending so soon they might bring another one forward,' said Ashley. 'Let's go and ask your friend at the information desk and see what's next.'

When they spoke to him he explained how the system worked. If a case took longer than expected then other cases might have to be put back to a later date. But cases could not be brought forward on account of all the preparation work involved and a barrister's other commitments. So Courtroom Three would remain unused for the two days that had been allotted to the mugging case.

'The murder case starts here next Monday in Courtroom Four,' he said. 'In the meantime why don't you go over to the Magistrate's Courts in Newton Street? They have some very interesting cases too, though mostly compensation cases against companies for injuries and the like. The magistrate judges the case on his own and makes the ruling and then allocates the compensation amount or not as the case may be. The poor chap makes all his own notes too throughout the proceedings. He has a very responsible task to fulfil. It's late now so you'd best come back tomorrow for the morning session. Most cases tend to only last the one day.'

So the trio left the building and made their way across to Newton Street to the Magistrate's Courts. Tania found the Notice Board near the entrance and read the listing of cases for the next day. There were eight courtrooms and each had a case listed. The one that caught Ashley's attention was an industrial injury compensation claim case. The others were mostly State vs. somebody's name. The injury case was listed as Thomas MacLean vs. T.I. Steels Co and had been allocated to Courtroom Six. They decided that this was the one to attend.

'Well, it's 3 o'clock now and I think I'll get back to the shop,' said Ashley. 'I promised Milly with a few more history cards.'

'I'll come too,' said Tania.

Then to Katy she said, 'You're meeting Robin later aren't you Katy, so I expect you'll be heading the other way.'

'Yes,' said Katy, 'Robin said he'd finish at the bank a bit earlier and pick me up from home. There's a show at the Alex he's got tickets for and I promised to go. Should we meet here in the morning tomorrow?'

They agreed to meet at ten o'clock in the morning outside Courtroom Six.

'I parked at Tipton station and caught the train,' said Ashley, 'so I need to get back on the train.'

'Oh, I came in on the bus,' said Tania, 'so I can come back with you on the train. Then we can go back to the shop together. Poor old mum all by her self. Uncle Robin always seems to be upstairs on his own tinkering about in the museum.'

They said their goodbyes and Katy caught the express service to Gravelly Hill while Ashley and Tania walked to New Street station. They held hands and communicated telepathically all the way there and during the train journey as well.

Back at the shop Milly was pleased to see them and straightway put the kettle on. Robin had been over to see his lady friend at the bakery over lunch and she had given him a bag of fresh doughnuts.

'I only had one so there are still a few in the bag for you,' smiled Milly. She was extremely proud of Ashley and had in her own mind become quite possessive of him. They were all one family now especially after the revealing of all his secret powers. She loved the boy and the man not only because of his pleasant nature but mainly because she could see how happy Tania was ever since they had first met.

'Would you like a mug of tea as well mum?' asked Tania telepathically of her mum.

For a moment Milly thought that Ashley had called her 'mum'. But the associated thoughts weren't his, they belonged to her daughter. Just like a voice being uniquely recognisable so too did a telepathic communication carry with it the thought imprint of the originating person.

Milly realised that Tania was staring at her and waiting for an answer.

'Was that you Tania?' she exclaimed. 'Goodness, has Ashley given you his telepathic ability?'

'No mum,' replied Tania telepathically again, 'Ashley and I have been communicating telepathically, he insisted upon it. At first he read my mind for my replies but gradually my brain picked up how to communicate back and I can now send a few simple sentences. Ashley said that with practice we should all become proficient. The more I talk to you in this way the quicker will you also be able to adapt to telepathy. Only I can't read thoughts like Ashley so for the moment you will have to reply verbally.'

'Wonderful,' said Milly. 'In that case, yes please I'd love a mug of tea.'

Robin came down when he heard their voices and joined the group around the kitchen table drinking tea and eating 'his' doughnuts.'

'I think I'll just have another one,' said Robin, 'and this time I'll try not to lick my lips as I'm eating it.'

It was Robin's favourite joke that no one could eat a sugar covered doughnut without licking their lips at some stage of the process. His other favourite one was that no one could lick their own elbow. And it was Milly's usual reply that why on earth should anyone want to lick their own elbow in the first instance. What a ghastly thought she would say.

Ashley had followed the others in addressing him as Uncle Robin and secretly Robin quite liked the attention and feigned prestige that such a title commanded. Ashley had always had a polite regard for Robin and calling him uncle extended that courtesy.

Robin liked to recount stories of his childhood, especially the one when he and Agnes had gone strawberry picking and had nothing to weigh because they had eaten the lot beforehand. He had been twelve and Agnes ten at the time. Agnes had felt ill in the car on the way home and when Robin had teasingly said there were worms in the strawberries she had promptly got sick over the back seat. His dad was quite annoyed at them and had to stop to clean out the car. Agnes had got sick again after a few miles because Robin had made a wiggly gesture with his index finger out of sight of his dad and mum.

Robin and Agnes were very close as brother and sister and he had been chief usher at her wedding to Jerry's dad. She had died of a sudden illness when her granddaughter Tania was ten years old and Robin was out of the country at the time. He had heard the news only when he returned a week after the funeral. It had devastated him.

Tania loved her uncle Robin because he so reminded her of granny Agnes in both looks and mannerisms. Which was also the reason he so enjoyed working in McGill's. He was close to the only family he had. Robin had never married although he'd always had an eye for the ladies. And to him Lorraine Hollings was no exception.

Next morning Tania and Ashley again went by train from Tipton station and met Katy inside the Magistrate's Courts. There was a group of people waiting outside Courtroom Six and Ashley knew these to be those involved in the case to be heard. There were curious looks in their direction.

One of the attorneys came up to them and asked which side they were for. Ashley replied that they were college students doing a project on the justice system. The word went around and thereafter they were ignored.

The doors opened at ten o'clock sharp and all went into the room. It was a medium sized room with several bench seats at the rear on either side of the entrance to the room. Tania, Katy and Ashley quietly seated themselves at the very back.

The magistrate came in through a door behind the large desk on a dais. It looked an informal affair as the attorneys and the magistrate were simply dressed in grey coloured lounge suits. The magistrate looked an ordinary elderly gentleman though his manner and moustache were rather imposing. All rose as he walked in and he settled down immediately and nodded to the court clerk.

The clerk who was also dressed smartly announced the case of Thomas MacLean vs. T. I. Steels Co. He then read out the details of the claimant's case for industrial compensation for the loss of two fingers on his left hand due to the negligence of his employers.

The case was a simple one. The two factory workers Thomas MacLean and Albert Poole were helping a team that was refurbishing the brick lining of a heat treatment furnace inside the factory of Messrs T.I. Steels Co. This was during the 2001 summer shutdown two years ago when the factory closed for a fortnight. Although normal production was at a standstill and the factory workers on the annual holiday, the maintenance teams were all in place carrying out essential maintenance and repairs. Thomas MacLean and Albert Poole had been delegated to carry old discarded bricks to an adjacent large metal skip. When the skip was deemed full an overhead travelling crane was signalled and a double-leg chain sling was attached to its main hook. The crane driver then positioned himself and the sling above the skip. One of the men on the ground then walked around and fitted the two sling hooks one at a time to each of the lifting lugs on the skip. There was a procedure to be followed and all men were trained accordingly.

In the present case Albert Poole fitted the sling hooks to the skip and then gave the crane driver Eddie Bellingham the hand signal to lift. The lift commenced and the skip was raised about two feet when Thomas MacLean rushed forward and frantically signalled the crane driver to lower the skip back down. Thomas had noticed that one of the sling hooks was incorrectly fitted to a skip lug. The sling hooks should always face outwards but in this case Albert Poole had fitted one side that was facing inwards.

As the skip settled back on the ground and the slings became slack, Thomas MacLean walked around and refitted the sling hook in question correctly. It was at this point that the crane driver once again began his lift and Thomas MacLean's fingers became trapped between the hook and the lug of the skip as the sling tightened. The index and middle fingers of his left hand were subsequently crushed and his scream alerted the crane driver who immediately reversed the lift and allowed the sling to slacken once again. Thomas MacLean was hospitalised and the crushed parts of both fingers had to be amputated.

Thomas MacLean claimed that the crane driver Eddie Bellingham was at fault as he had initiated the lift without any signal being given. On the other hand the crane driver Eddie Bellingham said that Thomas had clearly signalled with his free right hand for the lift to begin. Unfortunately there were no other witnesses apart from the three men on this job. Albert Poole said he was looking elsewhere when he heard the scream and did not see how the accident occurred. It was a case of Thomas' word against Eddie's.

Thomas MacLean's attorney outlined all of this and then put his client on the witness stand to confirm his statement through the questions his counsel would ask.

Ashley wondered whether he needed to interfere in the case but his curiosity got the better of him and he wished to know how the accident had actually happened. Who was telling the truth? Ashley only needed to see that part of the event when Thomas MacLean reconnected the sling hook the correct way round and just before his fingers became trapped.

Ashley closed his eyes and concentrated his thoughts on the witness. The incident went back two years and it took a while for the proper scenario to come into focus.

Ashley saw Albert Poole fit the central ring of the chain sling to the large crane hook and then the sling hooks to the skip. Yes, one of the hooks on the right hand side was fitted facing inwards. He saw Thomas MacLean rush forward and signal the crane driver to lower the skip back to the ground. Thomas walked around to the inward facing hook and removed it from the lug with his right hand. The skip was on his left side so he then transferred the hook to his left hand and refitted the hook to face outwards. It was while he was doing this that he decided to scratch an itch near his right temple using his free right hand. Eddie Bellingham the crane driver mistook this hand movement for a signal to lift and operated his controls accordingly. It was clear what had happened and both men were convinced that they were in the right.

Ashley decided that there was no right or wrong in this case as it was all due to a misunderstanding caused by a legitimate arm movement. Therefore all that Ashley decided to do was to give the magistrate a factual pictorial view of the events as just seen and so let him make his judgement. An injury had taken place on the employer's premises and as such the onus was on them to fulfil their duty of care to all their employees. Therefore some compensation was due to Thomas for the loss of his two fingers. Contributory factors might be taken into account to lessen or to increase the amount awarded. Ashley conveyed all this to Tania and Katy and indicated his opinion and what he planned to do.

'Poor chap,' whispered Katy to Tania, 'he was just unlucky. I feel sorry for the crane driver though. He must be going through hell mulling over it again and again in his mind and still thinking that a signal was given.'

Ashley then telepathically beamed his thoughts directly to the magistrate to show him the true sequence of events. The magistrate jerked upright momentarily before resuming his normal position. An expression of understanding beamed out from his face and it was clear that he intended to question both parties concerned.

When the cross examination of Thomas was completed and he was about to rise the magistrate raised his arm and said, 'Just a moment Mr MacLean, I have some questions.'

Thomas MacLean had partly risen off his chair but now sat down again and faced the magistrate expectantly.

'Firstly,' began the magistrate, 'which hand did you use to move the sling hook from its incorrect position to the correct one?'

There was a brief pause while Thomas thought.

'Well your honour,' he said, 'I used my right hand to first remove the sling hook from the skip lug. I then turned it around and transferred it to my left hand and so fitted it correctly to the skip lug.'

'Thank you Mr MacLean,' said the magistrate, 'that was very clearly stated.'

Thomas MacLean looked around at his attorney with a smile.

'And now Mr MacLean,' continued the magistrate, 'can you tell me which hand you would have used to signal the crane driver if everything had gone according to plan.'

Thomas MacLean looked down at his hands before he replied.

'I always signal with my right hand your honour. I'm right handed you see.'

Thomas MacLean had been primed by his attorney to always address the magistrate respectfully.

'Now tell me Mr MacLean,' asked the magistrate, 'what was your right hand doing during the time your left hand was actively engaged in positioning the sling hook to the skip lug?'

Another pause while Thomas thought hard about the question.

'I'm not sure your honour,' he said. 'It could have been resting at my side or on the rim of the skip. I just don't know.'

'I see,' replied the magistrate. Then after a brief pause while he made some notes he looked again towards Thomas.

'And what would you have done if a fly or a bee happened to wander near your face at the exact time you were fitting the sling hook to the skip?'

'Why I would have brushed it aside your honour,' said Thomas.

'And what if you had a sudden itch on your face Mr MacLean,' continued the magistrate, 'would you have rubbed or scratched it with your free hand?'

'I most certainly would have your honour,' said Thomas MacLean smiling at the court.

'Thank you Mr MacLean,' said the magistrate, 'you have been most helpful. You may leave the stand.'

Next the company's attorneys presented their defence and produced witnesses to vouch for the training systems that were in place. The Safety Adviser stated the company's safety record and detailed the checks that were in place to prevent accidents. Finally Eddie Bellingham came to the stand and gave answers to the questions put to him by his attorney. He was firm in his belief that a signal had been given by Thomas MacLean and to which he had responded. He repeated the same on cross examination.

Again just as he was about to step down the magistrate said he would like to clarify a couple of things.

'Mr Bellingham how long have you been driving this particular crane?' he asked.

'Your honour,' said Eddie,' I've been a crane driver with this company for thirty years. I'm also now a crane driving instructor and I've been on this crane for about ten years.'

'What exactly is the hand signal for a crane lift operation Mr Bellingham?' asked the magistrate.

'It is a hand pointing upwards about level with your head and rotated in a circular fashion,' said Eddie and he demonstrated this while he was speaking.

'And in your experience Mr Bellingham, does everyone employ this signal exactly as you have shown?'

'No your honour, there are slight variations. Some do it like this and others like this,' said Eddie giving hand demonstrations, 'but in general crane drivers will know exactly what is required of them.'

'Now Mr Bellingham I am coming to a very important question. First, how clear is your view from the crane cabin with regard to men signalling up at you from below?'

'Very clear your honour,' replied Eddie instantly.

'And when you are expecting a signal to lift and the man in question waves his hand to a colleague or tries to shoo away a bee or fly from near his face, could that be mistaken for a signal?'

Eddie was silent for a considerable length of time thinking back to the event of that day two years ago.

'I asked you a question Mr Bellingham,' repeated the magistrate quietly.

Katy whispered to Tania, 'I think this is the first time the poor fellow has had a doubt as to what he believes he saw. I feel sorry for him.'

'I don't know,' said Eddie in a low voice forgetting to say 'your honour'.

Then he suddenly sat bolt upright and exclaimed, 'Oh my God! Is that what he was doing? I felt certain it was a signal with his right hand. Did I get it wrong?'

'No, Mr Bellingham, please do not reproach your self,' said the magistrate in a kindly voice, 'I only asked a hypothetical question as to the probability for a false signal. Thank you, you may now step down.'

The magistrate looked at a paper on his table and then said, 'As there are no more witnesses the court will recess for lunch and reconvene at 2 o'clock. I will then give my ruling on the case.'

All rose as the magistrate left the court through the door behind the bench.

It was well after 12 o'clock and Ashley said there was nothing more for him to do here. There was work to do at the shop and he had told Milly he'd be back as soon as the case ended.

'But don't you want to see what the magistrate decides?' asked Katy. 'I know I do.'

'Well,' hesitated Ashley, 'I think the magistrate knows that neither party was really at fault. A simple mistake was made when Thomas MacLean raised his hand to scratch his head and Eddie Bellingham thought it was a hand signal. The magistrate will probably award Thomas a sum of money with costs simply because T. I. Metals Co has a duty of care to all the employees working on its premises and after all the injury did occur there.'

It was Tania who suggested they go to the Pizza Hut for lunch and return to see the case through. After all they had said they were doing a project on the justice system and wouldn't it look odd if they missed the ending.

'Actually, that is an excellent idea,' said Ashley who had missed out on breakfast and was feeling quite famished. 'We might as well stay on till the bitter end. By the way lunch is on me.'

'But of course it is,' said a smiling Katy. 'Besides, you eat the most anyway.'

It was a good walk to New Street and the place was not very full as yet. They shared a large pizza which they just about managed to finish, with Ashley having the last slice. They got back to the courts at a little after 2 o'clock.

The doors to the courtroom had not opened and all concerned were still milling around in groups just outside it. The doors opened suddenly then and they all made their way inside. It was about five minutes after they had settled down in their seats that they had to rise again for the magistrate's entrance.

He called the attorneys to the bench and a short whispered conference ensued. There was a nodding of heads by the attorneys and they returned to their own table positions.

The magistrate then gave a lengthy summation of the case and finally came to the essential part when the injury had occurred.

'It is my opinion that an honest mistake may have occurred,' he said. 'The question remains that at the crucial moment when Mr Thomas MacLean was refitting the sling hook to the skip, what was his right hand and arm doing? We do not exactly know. And yet Mr Eddie Bellingham the crane driver was positive in his view that he saw a movement in that arm that led him to believe a signal had been made. Between the two statements that I'm certain were both truthfully given I must conclude that some form of upward movement of Mr Thomas MacLean's right arm did occur. It may have been that Mr MacLean simply scratched the side of his face or even brushed aside a strand of his hair. We don't quite know. Viewed from overhead any such arm movement could have been misinterpreted by the crane driver Mr Eddie Bellingham as a signal to operate the crane. These are the extenuating circumstances that resulted in the incident causing Mr Thomas MacLean's fingers to become trapped and the injury sustained.'

The magistrate paused for a moment as he studied his notes before continuing.

'T. I. Metals Co is a long standing manufacturer of considerable reputation employing a large workforce. Under the Health and Safety at Work Act 1970 the company has a duty of care to all its employees and must ensure that the workplace is deemed a safe place to work. The fact of the matter is that an injury occurred to one of its employees on these premises during the course of normal working. As such the company failed in its duty of care to Mr Thomas MacLean and is therefore liable under the Act.'

'Mr Thomas MacLean has suffered considerably in losing two of the fingers in his left hand and there are psychological aspects also to be considered. It is fortunate that the injury did not occur to Mr MacLean's principal hand or this may have resulted in a greater degree of impairment to his activities and future job prospects which I should have had to take into consideration in connection with the compensation to be awarded.'

Once again the magistrate paused before making his final announcement.

'The decision of this court is that the claimant Mr Thomas MacLean be awarded the grand sum of twenty thousand pounds sterling and all costs to be paid by the employer T.I. Metals Co. This decision is binding on all parties concerned and the case is now closed and the court adjourned.'

The magistrate left the court through the door behind the bench and a buzz of conversation commenced the moment the door closed behind him.

Ashley, Tania and Katy joined the queue leaving the courtroom and when they reached outside Ashley expressed the opinion that he thought the judgement by the magistrate had been very fair.

'Well I don't think so,' said Katy. 'I think he got too much, after all he didn't have to go and change the hook around in the first place. And secondly he was careless with his right hand. That crane driver chap has been made to feel guilty about it all, poor chap.'

'It's a funny world,' said Ashley. 'It doesn't matter whose fault it is, it's the fact that it happened on the company's premises that makes it their liability. And that's the law Katy my dear. Besides, the company carries insurance for this sort of thing and so it doesn't cost them a penny. They've already paid it in premiums to the insurance company. Mind you their premium may go up next year because of this.'

'So are we meeting here again on Monday for the murder case?' asked Tania.

'I think Tuesday might be better,' said Katy. 'What do you think Ashley?'

'That's fine by me,' replied Ashley, 'hopefully the jury will be in place by then and the case proper would have begun.'

'I've never been to a murder case before,' said Katy. 'Will the murderer be in court?'

'Tut, tut Katy,' chuckled Ashley, 'the accused is innocent until proven guilty. Don't jump to conclusions girl.'

The trio parted company at the bus stop where Katy caught the 905 bus to Erdington while Tania and Ashley walked on to New Street station to catch the Central train to Dudley Port.

Once on the train Tania practiced her telepathy with Ashley and they conducted a most interesting conversation in silence. Ashley didn't like holding hands in public and Tania respected that, though she did sit up close so that their legs touched.

'We should communicate this way with all the members of our families,' indicated Tania, 'we should all be at ease with it.'

'Of course darling,' was the reply from Ashley.

'I'll begin using my telepathy skills with mum and dad and you can start with your folks too, that way we'll all get proficient quite quickly,' from Tania.

'I'll make a start this weekend,' conveyed Ashley with a smile.

Just then they heard raucous laughter from the front part of their carriage which somehow didn't seem pleasant. This was followed by a rude remark in a male voice that made the hairs on the back of Tania's neck stand on end. She remembered a similar remark being thrown at her once when she was still at school.

'Where are you going Chrissie?' bellowed the voice, 'come sit here with us.'

There were three of them and they were now standing in the isle and directing lewd remarks at a seated Chrissie who was out of Ashley and Tania's line of vision.

'Oow, leave my hair alone,' cried Chrissie standing up and moving away from the trio.

Ashley could see that Chrissie was a dark haired pretty Asian girl and she was trying to get past the scruffy young lads. They were all obviously from the same school and Ashley could imagine them making her life difficult with their bullying antics. Chrissie had long dark hair with artificial brownish streaks and Ashley could feel her annoyance. The lads were wearing a school uniform of sorts but with ties loosened and shirt tails outside their trousers. They gave a very scruffy appearance indeed.

'Do something Ashley,' whispered Tania forgetting her telepathy, 'I was in her situation once.'

'Mental or physical?' asked Ashley telepathically.

'Anything, both,' responded an agitated Tania, 'just teach them a lesson they won't forget.'

Ashley went into pink mode and walked to where the three lads stood partially frozen in time. He pinched each of their ear lobes, flicked his index finger against their foreheads and then gave a harder double flick against the shin bones of their legs. Ashley was about to return to his seat when he had a wicked humorous thought. He reached across to each of the lads and gently ripped open the zipped front of each of their trousers before walking back to his seat and resuming normal time mode.

The whole carriage was suddenly filled with screams of pain as the three lads didn't know which part hurt the most. Tania smiled at Ashley who had just informed her of what he had done.

'Ooo shit, my trousers,' came from one of them.

'Bloody hell,' swore another.

Ashley then stood up and stared across at the group of lads and telepathically conveyed to each of the lads the hypnotic suggestion that Chrissie had just turned into a great big dark haired tarantula spider with a bite that could maim in seconds. Ashley put the proviso in with the hypnosis that whenever they teased or bullied someone in a vicious or nasty way their subject would again become a similar nasty looking spider.

'Get out of here fast,' screamed the tallest lad grabbing hold of his trousers with one hand and school satchel in the other.

Tania stood up to get a look at the results of Ashley's actions and was just in time to see three extremely scared and panic stricken fourteen year olds hobbling down the isle towards her and then on towards the back of the carriage and through the connecting door. They all had tears in their eyes and one of them seemed to be actually crying with pain and fear.

'Oh, Ashley do you think we over-reacted,' telepathically from Tania.

'The pain will only last a few minutes,' responded Ashley, 'but it's their pride and image that has been hurt the most. I think this will put an end to their bullying ways.'

Tania decided to see how Chrissie was and went over to her.

'Are you alright?' asked Tania, 'what happened?'

The girl Chrissie was still standing and swaying gently with the movement of the train.

'I don't know,' replied Chrissie, 'Trevor and his mates have been a right pain this term. They wanted me to go out with them but I said not in a million years. Whatever happened to them just now I hope it lasts. They looked at me just now as if I was a monster. I would prefer it that way.'

Tania smiled at Chrissie and said, 'Perhaps all the trouble with these chaps is over. Good luck.'

Tania walked back to Ashley who had put his head back and closed his eyes. She looked down at him and conveyed her love to this boyish looking man. She then stooped down and planted a light and gentle kiss on his forehead.

Ashley's eyes remained firmly shut but a smile was now quite evident. Tania sat down beside him and pressed herself up against his side. She put her head back against the seat rest and also closed her eyes but couldn't get rid of her smiling expression. Nor could she stop the giggles that began silently as she thought of the three lads holding up their trousers as they ran past her. It was too much when she sensed Ashley shaking with laughter and her giggles just burst out loud. She put her hand over her mouth to stifle the sound and turned to face Ashley. He was laughing silently as only he could do but Tania could see the wetness in his eyes.

Oh how she loved this man, thought Tania and on impulse she leaned sideways and put a kiss on the corner of his mouth. It is very difficult to kiss and laugh at the same time and a renewed bout of laughter began. Chrissie who was still standing was looking back at them and smiling approvingly.

'Thank you Ashley,' from Tania and she conveyed all her love in her message when her giggles had finally ceased.

Ashley leaned across and gently rubbed his nose against hers before once again resuming his eyes closed posture.

They were silent for the rest of the journey immersed in their own peaceful thoughts.

The train slowed as it came into Dudley Port station where Ashley had parked this morning. Ashley and Tania joined the exodus of people towards the exit door and waited patiently till the train finally came to a stop at the platform.

The doors hissed open when the green indicator light appeared and someone pressed the button. People began stepping off the train into the crowd waiting to board. Tania stepped off and when Ashley followed his shoulder lightly bumped the arm of a great big fellow. Ashley looked up at the fellow who had boyish rosy cheeks in addition to his six feet four inches of height.

'Sorry,' said Ashley.

'No worries mate,' said the chap in a strong Australian accent and a smile.

There were still people getting off the train and the crowd of about twenty were getting impatient to board.

Ashley looked at the baby faced Ozzy giant again and suddenly out of the blue received a medical condition diagnosis on the man. Ashley was amazed and immediately conveyed this telepathically to Tania. She had been ahead of him in getting off the train but now immediately came back to his side.

'What's up Ash, another gift?' was her query

Ashley was as surprised as Tania was at this latest development. In reply he telepathically conveyed to Tania the entire diagnosis on the big Ozzie's medical condition that had just been revealed to him. He supposed that this occurrence was not all that different from his skill of knowing the detailed history of his antiques and which Milly had found so intriguing. Perhaps this was simply an extension of that gift.

However it was urgent that the big fellow be seen by a doctor as soon as possible. The tumour in his brain was currently the size of a pea but was growing at a phenomenal rate. It would double its size within six months. It was benign in nature but was generating a mass of blood vessels to supply its hungry growth. Although the tumour was reddish in colour it had a purplish tint on one side and was growing inside the partition zone between cerebral hemispheres in the region adjacent to the olfactory bulbs and tracts.

Ashley decided there was only one course of action and decided to go for it right away.

He went into pink mode and gave the chap a sharpish rap on his forehead just as if he was knocking on someone's front door. Ashley then used his finger nail to scrape the surface of the skin in that area before returning to normal mode.

The man just collapsed towards the platform floor but Ashley was ready and with Tania helping they lowered the Ozzie down.

The man whose name was Oliver Ramirez was just twenty two years of age and came originally from Perth in Western Australia. He was the baby of six grownup siblings and currently worked as a porter at the Guest Hospital on Tipton road. He'd had a work visa for one year but that had been extended to five years. He was currently living with his mother in the Acocks Green area of south Birmingham. She had been widowed recently and had returned to her place of birth.

All this had come automatically into Ashley's head and Ashley could immediately see the benefits to others from this gift. Visits to hospitals could become an essential item on his agenda.

'Someone please phone for an ambulance,' shouted Ashley loudly, 'I think this man has had a heart attack or a stroke.'

Tania was kneeling beside Ashley and knew exactly what Ashley had intended. Hospitals and A&Es do not send people for brain scans if they can help it and there needed to be a very good reason to use this limited and valuable hospital resource. But suspected strokes and serious head injuries were most definitely scanned.

Ashley took his jacket off and was just rolling it into a ball when the man Oliver opened his eyes and sat up.

'What happened? I feel a bit dizzy,' said Oliver Ramirez with both his hands at his temples.

'I think you have had some kind of a turn,' said Ashley. 'These are an indicator of something wrong inside your head. I think you ought to go to hospital and have a scan to make sure everything is okay.'

Two paramedics finally arrived and were hailed over by Ashley to the bench where they had seated Oliver after he sat up.

'What seems to be the matter?' asked one of them. He was another big fellow but in his forties.

'This man just collapsed as he was waiting for the train. He fell and banged his head on the platform floor when he fell,' said Tania. 'I saw it all.'

'Right young man,' said the big paramedic, 'let's have a look at you. That's quite a bump you have there and bruising to boot. We'd better clean that up as there might be grit from the platform in it.'

Ashley then went pink again and gave Oliver's forehead a lighter flick with his index finger before stepping back and a return to normal mode.

'Oow!' exclaimed Oliver swaying back on the bench and putting both hands to his head, 'my head hurts something awful.'

The big paramedic shone a pencil light into Oliver's eyes one at a time and then turned and had a whispered few words with his colleague.

Then to Oliver he said, 'I've asked Joe to get the wheelchair. I think you need to be seen by a doctor and have tests carried out. We'll take you to the A&E at Russells Hall hospital, its not far. Now can you walk up the stairs to the station concourse level? It'll save us having to carry you up, and you are a big fellow.'

'Yes I think I can. I'm alright now, only my head feels like it's been hit by a brick,' said Oliver.

'Right then,' said the paramedic, 'we'll just take it slow. Thanks folks, if you would all kindly give us some room we'll make our way to the stairs.'

The onlookers who were waiting for the next train quickly cleared a path for them.

'Can we help,' offered Ashley.

'Thank you, yes. If you come with us to the top of these stairs we can take it from there. I reckon Joe should be back by then with the chair.' The big man smiled as he spoke. It was all part of their training to reassure the sick and injured.

When they finally arrived at the top the other paramedic Joe was waiting for them with a shiny new black wheelchair. He looked relieved when he saw Oliver at the top.

'Phew Sid,' said Joe, 'I'm glad you managed to get up them stairs with the patient. I didn't fancy carrying him and the chair up that lot.'

'I can walk,' said Oliver.

'I'm sure you can lad,' said Sid, 'but lets get you to A&E in one piece, so its best if you just let us do it our way, okay? Now hop into the chair like a good lad and we'll be off.'

He turned to Ashley and Tania and smiled again.

'Okay, we'll take it from here. Thanks for staying with this chap Oliver till we arrived.'

As Sid was wheeling Oliver towards the waiting ambulance Ashley decided to plant a fixation in Oliver's subconscious that he had a tumour in his brain. Ashley also added that Oliver should ask for a second opinion if the first doctor didn't put him forward for an immediate head scan.

Tania was standing beside Ashley as they watched the wheelchair and paramedics disappearing round the corner and she put her arm around Ashley's waist and squeezed him to her. It was her way of showing him how much she appreciated what he had just done.

Her thoughts were milling around in confusion because she just couldn't fathom what it was that Ashley was meant to do with regard to the task that Philip had so briefly mentioned.

Ashley was elated at the prospect of finally doing something beneficial and worthwhile. He briefly wondered whether this could have anything to do with his future but then discarded the idea. This was just a facet of his development and he felt that if he had concentrated more on peoples' physical makeup perhaps this gift would have surfaced earlier.

Ashley and Tania had a telepathic discussion about this latest development and the best way to put it into action. Tania suggested that they discuss it with their families individually or at a joint conference before deciding; though it was her opinion that Ashley could begin by visiting hospital wards for a start. Her suggested plan was hazy but she felt Ashley could pretend to be an exchange program doctor from Spain or Portugal.

But Ashley thought this unsuitable for the simple reason that he felt he must keep his identity a secret. He rather fancied reviewing the medical condition of each patient and then attaching an official looking note to the bed clipboard with his diagnosis and prospective treatment. He could sign the note with an illegible signature.

They got back to the shop and Milly was keen to hear the latest development. Ashley conveyed everything telepathically and Milly said 'How wonderful' in a sort of rough telepathic reply.

'I find I get a bit of a dull headache when I try this telepathic lark,' said Milly aloud, 'but I suppose that's because I'm probably straining with the effort.'

'Actually, my dear future mother-in-law,' smiled Ashley, 'I should have spent more time with you the way I did with Tania. So try not to have a go with it just yet, I shall be in for the rest of the week and I'll practice it with you then. That way your brain will adapt gradually and it will become second nature to you in no time at all. It's getting late now so why don't you and Tania head off home and I will lock up. Where's Robin?'

'Oh I forgot to mention about the house clearance auction,' said Milly. 'There's one in Henley-in-Arden next week so I sent Robin down there to investigate and bring back a catalogue of what's up for sale. I'd like to get down there myself if you'll cover the shop.'

'What day is it mum,' said Tania, 'because there's a murder case on Tuesday and I want Ashley to be there.'

'Let me see,' said Milly picking up a newspaper clipping. 'Yes here it is. It's to be held on Monday at 9:30 am at the house itself. I'll take Robin with me. We'll have to make an early start to get there on time.'

For a brief moment Ashley received a vague feeling that an important phase of his life was about to begin. But it was gone in a flash and he thought nothing more of it.

'Will you be over later?' enquired Tania of Ashley.

Tania spoke verbally as she wished to include her mum in the conversation. She hadn't as yet learned to communicate telepathically with more than one person at a time.

'Actually I was thinking of visiting my folks this evening and the next few evenings as well,' said Ashley. 'I especially want to visit my granddad Eric to see how he's getting along. I'd like to do a diagnostic on him for a start just in case there's something the doctors might have missed.'

'Oh how silly of me to forget,' exclaimed Tania. 'Could you please do a diagnostic on mum right away? Please Ashley.'

'Why yes of course,' said Ashley looking at Milly, 'that is if Milly would like me to.'

'I don't mind at all,' said Milly smiling, 'nothing like a free medical check up.'

'Then take my hand and think of England,' joked Ashley.

Milly stepped forward as Ashley did the same and they came together with a gentle bump. So Ashley put his arms around her and placed his cheek against hers for a few seconds. He then stepped back and looked at Milly in his most serious manner.

'Now let me see,' he said, 'here we have a fine antique made in the mid-twentieth century in the Staffordshire area by a craftsman one Wilfred Thomas aged around thirty years. The product has worn well and apart from a few scratches at the base is in excellent condition.'

Milly and Tania both laughed. But then Milly kept on laughing till the tears rolled down her cheeks and she could hardly catch her breath.

'What is it mum?' came from a very concerned Tania.

But Milly just waved both arms to indicate there was nothing to worry about. Finally after several more seconds when Milly had caught her breath she explained.

'Oh Ashley that was so funny,' said Milly. 'It's the bit about the few scratches at the base remark that brought back memories. Let me explain.'

Milly paused for a moment before continuing with the broad smile still very much in evidence.

'When I was about ten years old I went with mum and dad on holiday to the peak district. We did a lot of walking up and down the hills and in the forests. It was lovely. Then on one of the days I had to go behind a bush so to speak when we were trekking up quite a steep hill. You know what I mean? Well the long and the short of it was that while I was in an uncompromising state my foot slipped and I went sliding downhill for several yards on my bare backside. Mum said she could hear my scream for days afterwards. I was in tears while mum and dad were in splits of laughter. I got a rash there and some terrible scratches not to mention a painful tailbone. So when you mentioned the few scratches on my base I finally saw mum and dad's viewpoint. Yes Tania, I still have the faint scars from that day.'

Ashley and Tania were smiling again and this time it was Tania who began her usual giggling. It only took a second before all three were in splits of laughter. Tania drew her mum towards her and Ashley joined them in a threesome hug.

'Actually, I drew a complete blank on any diagnosis for you Milly,' said Ashley, 'so I suppose that is good news really. And can I add that I had no message about your sliding experience either. My remark was just a humorous ad lib on my part. I put your father's name in just for effect.'

The phone then rang and it was Robin saying he was just about to make his way back from Henley in Arden. There were some very exciting items in the auction and he thought that Ashley ought to take a look at one of the items. Or rather one particular set of items and Robin sounded quite excited by this. Apparently the late deceased owner of the house had been a collector of time. In fact he must have had a crazed love for clocks. There were hundreds about the house. There were at least ten long-case grandfather clocks standing about in hallways and in corners. Then there were the Bracket clocks, Mantel clocks, Garnitures, Carriage clocks and even skeleton clocks, not to mention other more modern late nineteenth century wall clocks and pocket and wrist watches. The latter were arranged in a chest of thin flat drawers more reminiscent of a butterfly collection.

Robin said he had no idea what each could be worth and the local auctioneer had listed the collection in their groups although each item had been individually numbered. Apparently a cousin of the late gentleman was the sole beneficiary. The cousin was a semi-retired person in his late sixties and didn't share in his relative's passion for clocks. As such he was happy to let every item be sold. It was a big old rambling house on three floors and everything had been left in their last known positions. It was several months ago that the previous owner had passed away and so none of the clocks were actually operating.

'The house must have been alive with ticking clocks when the old man was living there,' said Robin.

Ashley looked at Milly and telepathically conveyed all that Robin had said.

'Oh dear,' said Milly, 'I'm not too up on clocks and watches at the moment. I shall have to read up on it. Perhaps you could come with me and let Robin look after the shop for the day.'

Over the last few years Ashley had systematically read the minds of all the antiques dealers and auctioneers he came across and so acquired all their knowledge. He now conveyed all of this telepathically into Milly's consciousness.

'Wow Ashley,' exclaimed Milly back pedalling towards a chair and sitting down. 'This is fantastic. I feel quite the expert antiques dealer now. Before this I was struggling to keep abreast of things and living on my wits. But why only now Ashley and not when I first took over the running of the shop?'

'The joys of discovery can never be equalled,' said Ashley seriously. 'You developed a love for the antiques business based on that joy. There's still a lot of stuff out there that even I don't know about. So I shall come with you to the auction and fill you in on the history of some of the more interesting items. I think we ought to bid for items that have an intriguing history and not just value. What do you think?'

'Oh yes please Ashley,' said Milly feeling quite relieved now that Ashley had agreed to come with her, 'yes that would be great. And thank you.'

'I'm coming with you,' said Tania. 'I need a day out after that stuffy courtroom.'

'Okay Miss Seventeen year old,' said Milly. 'But I'd like to see a bit more career mindedness from you. It's not too long to your A-Levels and you need good grades if you want to follow in Katy's footsteps and get into teacher training college next year.'

Tania looked at Ashley for support but Ashley was looking at the ceiling as if there was something of interest there. Tania pretended to pout but couldn't hide a smile. She went up to him and put her arms around his waist and her head on his chest and gave a great big stage sniff.

'Now, now, fair lady,' said Ashley giving her a great big squeeze in return and winking at Milly, 'thy mother is right and thou must do as thou art bid. After all how will you look after me when I'm out of a job? Seriously, I know you want to work with school kids and teacher training is the only way to get there. I'll help you with picking up ethnic languages if you wish.'

Tania then went over to her mum and gave her a hug and said, 'I'll start revising every evening mum, I promise.'

'About your new gift Ashley,' Milly said, 'Tania and I will discuss it with Jerry tonight and you can do the same with your folks when you see them. Perhaps together we can come up with a good way to use it.'

'Thanks Milly,' said Ashley.

They closed up the shop together and Milly smiled as she watched the two of them walking out holding finger tips only and swinging their arms together. Milly liked the way that they didn't over display their affection in public. Jerry and she had been like that too when they were courting.

'Gosh,' she suddenly thought, 'that was a long time ago.'

Ashley went to visit his grandfather first and spent over an hour with him. Eric would be eighty at the end of the year and Ashley could not see anything physically wrong with him. His arthritis worried him a bit especially after a glass of wine in the evening. Sour things like citrus fruits and juices were an absolute no go area as he had recently discovered. Eric was on blood thinning tablets since his last bout at the hospital plus some other pills that the doctors prescribed for his blood pressure and cholesterol. There was also a slight case of an age related sugar problem so Eric had to watch what he ate but as yet he was not on any pills for it. Lillian had suggested he eat little and often and this suited him perfectly since he got full very quickly. He used to say that one of the drawbacks in getting older was that he couldn't eat and drink as much as he used to. He reminisced that at one time he could eat all day meal after meal and never feel full up. As a young lad his mum used to refer to him as a caterpillar forever chewing on something or other.

Eric perked up no end when Ashley began to communicate with him telepathically as a silent two way conversation.

'Just think what you want to say granddad and I'll know it from reading your mind,' said Ashley.

Towards the end of Ashley's visit Eric had acquired a very small degree of telepathic skill.

'I do enjoy this way of talking,' communicated Eric, 'it's so much easier and less tiring. Who else have you taught this to?'

So then Ashley passed on everything he had done over the past week and Eric smiled and reached out from his easy recliner sofa armchair and squeezed Ashley's hand.

'I'm very proud of you Ash,' he said aloud. 'When I get really proficient at this telepathy talking I shall pass on all my National Service experiences. Those two years were very good for me. We had none of this yobbo business on the streets. I wish they'd kept it on, it was so good for character building and gave us discipline and a purpose not to mention a skill in one of the trades.'

'Times have changed granddad,' communicated Ashley. He kept to telepathy.

'Yes I suppose so,' came from Eric's thoughts. 'Still I have fond memories of my time in Cyprus with all my army mates.'

Ashley communicated his thoughts about his latest gift of diagnosing physical medical anomalies in people through personal contact. He had already given Eric a full rundown of the day's events and now asked his granddad what he thought about the way he had dealt with Oliver Ramirez.

Eric smiled at that and indicated his approval in thought of everything Ashley had done; especially the way Ashley had forced an issue to induce symptoms that otherwise could have been missed until it was too late for treatment. By exaggerating Oliver's pain symptom Ashley had influenced the opinions of the paramedics towards the trauma to the head diagnosis.

But Eric had no firm thoughts about how Ashley should best use this latest gift. He supported Tania's suggestion about visiting hospital wards but also agreed that Ashley keep his anonymity. Perhaps Lillian, Alex and Katy might have better ideas.

Ashley left his granddad in a cheerful frame of mind. Eric had a lot going wrong but it was a question of wear and tear brought on by his years. As it was Eric had the body of a man ten years older and Ashley could see old age getting the better of him. There was nothing Ashley could say or do to alleviate his granddad's condition and so decided not to say anything.

He did of course discuss all this with his parents and Katy after he had passed on the events of the day and his experience with Oliver Ramirez. Telepathy dominated the early part of the conversation and Ashley found that his mum was quickest at picking up the new skill, just like Milly had been too; though of course his dad and sister were not too far behind.

'I'd like to talk with my friends this way,' communicated Katy, 'but I suppose that's out of the question.'

'Well for a while yes,' came from Ashley, 'but I see no reason why it shouldn't be adopted universally in the near future. Perhaps we need to think about the implications before going public. It could be the new world language.'

'Oh Ashley,' said Katy aloud, 'I've just had a thought. When I finish my teacher training in another year or so I could be a telepathic tutor and run classes. I could be the first to make a career out of it.'

'Perhaps one day Katy,' said Alex, 'wait till you get as proficient as Ashley before you think along those lines.'

'Just think of all those deaf and dumb people who use sign language to talk to each other,' came back from Katy thoughts, 'I could teach them first.'

'Yes,' came from Lillian in agreement. She was frowning in concentration with the effort to communicate more. She looked at her son and raised a questioning eyebrow and Ashley read her thoughts.

'Mum says we should do nothing for at least a year by which time we should have thought this out more thoroughly,' communicated Ashley to the others.

'Thank you,' came from Lillian who was determined to master the art of telepathy.

'Ashley,' came from his dad so Ashley read his thoughts and smiled.

'Yes dad,' telepathically from Ashley to all in the room. 'That's an excellent idea to let the hospital diagnosis come from a doctor already there on the staff.'

Alex had proposed that Ashley communicate his patient diagnosis to a doctor doing his rounds on the ward and let it appear as a sudden inspirational revelation. It would seem as though the patients true condition had suddenly surfaced in the doctor's mind as a meditated perception from a previously thought hunch. Checks would then prove the diagnosis to be correct. No one could possibly suspect Ashley's part in it.

Ashley and Tania or Katy could also visit patients as part of a church or charity organisation. The A&E departments might be a good place to start though.

By the end of the evening Ashley was communicating with his family on an individual basis and receiving back a rudimentary form of telepathy. Sometimes he had to read the person's mind to make sense of the jumble of meaning that came across. The fact that their brains were actually sending basic telepathic transmissions was progress enough and Ashley smiled his approval and encouragement.

Ashley spent the night in his old room and stared at the ceiling patterns for ages before finally drifting off to a disturbed sleep. He kept dreaming of a large whitish glowing ball bouncing through his dad's garden shrubs and flowers and crushing everything in its path. The odd thing that Ashley noticed was that as the glowing ball approached, each shrub and flower seemed to bend towards the ball before being crushed by it. And this was a persistent dream that repeated itself after he had woken momentarily to use the bathroom. There was something about the ball that was rather puzzling too. It wasn't just the fact that it was ruining a perfectly lovely flower bed but that the flattened plants seemed to disappear from view altogether. Could there be a meaning somewhere in this dream?

Ashley was glad to wake up when his mum brought him a morning mug of tea but he still puzzled over its significance as he drove to the shop. Perhaps it was nothing at all but then again what could it mean. He mentioned the dream to Tania and she said it might be just a dream and may not mean anything other than that perhaps it reflected something he had been thinking about, like the mysterious great task to which Philip had made a vague reference.

'Maybe you should try stopping the ball by pushing it away Ash,' communicated Tania, 'that is if you can use your powers in a dream. You know I get this recurring dream about me running to catch this bus but I never seem to run fast enough. My feet seem to move in slow motion and the bus is always out of my reach. I think that one day I'm going to get on that bus. But I don't think it means anything except to remind me that perhaps some things in life are unattainable.'

The next few days passed without incident except that Ashley had contacted the Russells Hall A&E to enquire after Oliver Ramirez. All they would say was that he had been seen, tests carried out and discharged. No further information could be given. Ashley became concerned so got his home phone number from directory enquiries. His mother answered and Ashley introduced himself as the person who had assisted her son Oliver at the Centro station when he had collapsed on Tuesday evening.

'Oh yes,' said Mrs Ramirez, 'he was treated at the hospital and a head scan was done and he was then discharged. The doctor said there was nothing to worry about. Oliver feels fine and is back at work. Thank you so much for helping him at the station.'

'I think you should get a second opinion Mrs Ramirez,' said Ashley, 'I'm a medical student and I think for him to have fainted like that indicates something serious.'

Ashley then sent her a telepathic message over the phone with a picture of his true condition showing the tiny tumour that was breeding inside Oliver's brain and that in a year he could be dangerously ill.'

Ashley heard a gasp at the end of the line just before he said 'goodbye' and cut the connection. Ashley knew that she would pursue this with a mother's zeal and that Oliver Ramirez would survive the tumour.

Tania was the most fluent with her telepathy skills when the two families met at the weekend at Lillian and Alex's place. Eric had driven himself over too but said that he would not stay very late. He found he had a better nights rest if he went to bed that little bit earlier as opposed to midnight. He had found himself dozing off on his recliner and said he'd rather drop off to a proper sleep in his comfortable bed. He said he'd realised this when he woke himself up with a loud snoring grunt one evening while he had been watching TV. Eric said he'd probably leave a bit before ten o'clock if that was alright by everyone.

'Glad to have you here anytime dad,' said Alex, 'just suit yourself as best you please. Don't worry about the snoring as I drop off myself quite often now. It's these repeats on tele and nothing else to watch that does it I think. So don't worry dad just make yourself at home, glad you could make it here today.'

They had all managed to grasp the basics of telepathy and Ashley said it was a simple matter of practice for the brain to develop the patterned electrical impulses as and when required. Receiving these and interpreting them had always been a part of the brain's functioning so there was nothing new there. Animals were usually more attuned to interpreting such transmissions though this was usually to alert them when a predator or rival was near. It was noticed that pet dogs could sense what their owner was thinking and so were one step ahead in reading their master's thoughts. Think 'walkies' and see how your dog pricks up his ears with interest.

Jerry and Milly had some thoughts with regard to Ashley's diagnostic gift but these were on similar lines to what Alex had suggested. However Milly made the added suggestion that Ashley could very occasionally visit the waiting room of a doctor's surgery and so check out those waiting to be seen. Ashley very politely said he'd think about it but that he had doubts about this course of action.

'Let them come to you by chance,' said the voice in Ashley's head. His inner voice had spoken.

There was no great need or hurry for Ashley to know anything about the future awaiting him. He was to carry on quite normally and use his gifts as best as he thought with guidance from his family and friends. As for the dream he'd had Ashley decided to ignore it and put it to the back of his mind. It was just a dream, nothing more.

Lillian then mentioned to Ashley that she and Alex planned to visit Ron and Brenda next weekend and would he and Tania like to come as well. Brenda had especially expressed a wish to see them. The B&B was having a slack period and so there was ample accommodation for them all.

Ashley and Tania had a quick telepathic discussion before conveying their acceptance directly to Lillian.

'It will give us the opportunity to coach Ron and Brenda in telepathy skills just as we are doing with you,' communicated Ashley.

Later in the evening Lillian produced snacks and they just sat on the patio talking about inconsequent things. There were moments when they sat quietly and gazed at the beauty of the approaching sunset. Alex brought out his little basket shaped wood burner, a circular metal basket affair on short stubby legs, and lit it up for a bit of warmth on the patio. At first it gave off a lot of smoke before the cut log pieces caught fire to produce orange flames that gave out a welcome warmth to all around. Lillian put on a CD of her favourite country music inside the house which then produced a nice background of sound through the open patio doors.

Sometime later Eric wished everyone goodnight and remarked that it had been a lovely day but it was now way past his bedtime. There was still an orange glow in the western sky and Eric said he preferred not to drive in complete darkness. Eric had progressed well with his telepathy and impressed everyone there with his skill by saying a silent goodnight to all.

Ashley and Katy walked with their granddad to his car at the front of the house and waved as he drove away. They used the little gate at the side of the house to return to the warmth of the patio burner. It was well after midnight when the others also left for home.

Next morning Milly drove to Henley in Arden directed by her Garmin Sat-Nav. Tania sat in front alongside her mum while Ashley relaxed in the back enjoying the country views rolling by. Milly had only recently changed her old Viva for this six month old dealers demonstration model VW Golf with a bit less than seven thousand miles on the clock. They arrived at the address in Brook End Drive but had to park some distance away on Station Road.

There was an hour's delay to the start of the auction schedule which gave them time to browse around in the house. Every item was in its original setting and as they walked through each room Tania remarked that it felt a bit like visiting one of the National Trust manor houses. Although the colours had faded the furniture and décor were in good taste. The walls in all the rooms were covered with large portraitures and all were original oils. Much of the artwork was of a foreign origin indicating that the deceased must have travelled widely to have collected them. And of course there were clocks galore everywhere just as Robin had described.

Ashley established that the late owner was a gentleman named Andrew Pando and that he had remained a bachelor all his days. Perhaps he had been so involved with his collecting hobby to have ever considered involvement with the fairer sex. Andrew had been an only child and was raised by successive governesses employed by his widower father Lester. His mother had died shortly after Andrew was born. His father had been a keen collector of all sorts of things and this had been passed on to his son. Although father and son grew up liking each others' company, for they were brought together by their common interests, there was never any show of affection between them. They did however respect each other and when Andrew finished his schooling he joined his father's small business as an apprentice. It was a small manufacturing company employing twenty or so persons making a variety of children's toys. Most of the workers were men but quite a few had their wives working there as well mainly in the finishing and packing sections.

When his father died Andrew took over the business and continued to run it just as his father had done. Ten years later he sold the business to a rival company and retired to his collecting hobby as a very well off gentleman aged only fifty one.

Andrew had no relatives other than his Aunt May and her two sons Lester and Anthony Dutton. Richard Aloysius Dutton had been killed in a motorway pile-up on the way to work one cold winter morning when the boys were quite young. As a widow Aunt May had visited Andrew often and though much younger than her brother Lester, after whom she had named her eldest son; she was much the stronger one in character and purpose. Brother and sister had been close and Lester senior had been very flattered that May had named her first born after him and Andrew had grown up knowing and quite liking his two younger cousins. Both had eventually married and had had families and after their mother died had moved down to London. Andrew and his cousins however kept in regular contact and visited each other often. And so it was that when Andrew died at the ripe old age of eighty three this past year he had bequeathed everything to his nearly seventy year old cousin Lester Dutton; hence the auction.

All of this had come to Ashley from his contact with the house and he then telepathically conveyed it all on to Tania and Milly. Milly smiled her understanding while Tania reached for Ashley's hand and gave it a firm squeeze.

Suddenly Ashley received a danger signal of something portentous, possibly foreboding attached to the house. His inner voice indicated that here lay a mystery that would have a bearing on his future. The feeling of presentiment stayed with Ashley for several minutes before gradually fading to the back of his mind. Ashley knew it would resurrect again sometime.

Milly walked around noting down the lot numbers of the items she hoped to bid for; Ashley and Tania followed behind with Ashley giving her a quick history and evaluation of each.

There were several Mantel clocks Milly liked that she thought would make them a tidy profit at McGills. None of the clocks was actually working since there had been no one to wind the mechanisms. The auction booklet stated that no guarantee could be given as to workability of the clocks and that they were to be sold on an as seen basis only.

It was during one of her inspections of a particular clock that Milly bumped into a stocky well dressed gentleman of medium height. He was looking at the same clock with interest and before long they got talking and he introduced himself as Graham from Droitwich. He said he'd always had an interest in clocks especially antique ones and travelled to Europe on occasion to pick up a bargain or two at some of their Fairs. Milly introduced Tania and Ashley and they had a very pleasant conversation and eventually agreed not to bid against each other. He was a likeable chap and Ashley took to him instantly.

When Graham learned that Milly ran McGill's of Dudley he seemed quite impressed and said that he and his wife Anne would most certainly make a point of visiting them one day soon. He'd heard people talk about McGill's and how every item had a history attached. His wife ran a hair dressing shop while he himself served on the Droitwich town council. Milly said that McGill's was open every weekday and she looked forward to seeing him there.

'What a charming gentleman,' said Milly when they were alone again, 'I do hope we see him again. Do you know I never asked him his full name?'

As they continued on their round Milly said that she thought the tall grandfather clocks would be too big for the shop besides being rather expensive. However there was one housed in a black lacquered and chinoiserie case that she particularly found attractive. Ashley suggested she bid for it up to a maximum of £400. Milly was pleased at that and made a special note of its lot number.

Tania was rather taken by a green marble and bronze clock with marching twin vases. Ashley informed her that it was a 19th century St Etienne's clock and could be worth around a thousand pounds. It certainly was an attractive piece and Ashley said that it was a very collectable item. It would be a bargain at £400 and he suggested she bid up to that limit. He said that with so many clocks to be sold off she just might get it for less.

'But look out for that Graham fellow,' said Ashley, 'because Milly promised not to bid against him.'

There were a number of gentleman's pocket watches that Ashley found interesting and Milly made a note of the lot numbers.

Apparently Andrew Pando had had an eye for anything with a clocklike dial and so had also collected scientific instruments in the form of barometers, barographs and compasses. There was a Nagrette and Zambro barograph, seismograph, humidity dial, barograph clockwork mechanism and altimeter with combined thermometer and spirit level that caught Ashley's fancy. It would make a very good addition to the items upstairs in the museum section of McGill's. Ashley had Robin's interests at heart and this would be just the sort of thing to please him. Ashley had to smile when he thought how Robin would spend ages deciding on a location for it. So it went on Milly's list and she too smiled when he explained.

The auction began just after ten o'clock and there was plenty of interested bidding. The furniture items were the first to be offered up and these were followed up by the long case grandfather clocks. Milly got the black lacquered one for £320 and was pleased to have won it so easily. Tania however lost out on the green marble St Etienne clock which went past her limit very quickly and sold for a huge £650. Milly's friend Graham was standing quite near and made a bid for a Tiffany Furnaces house shaped gilt mantel clock but lost out to another keen bidder.

By the time the lunch break arrived at one o'clock McGill's Antiques had acquired six very interesting items. Ashley was wondering how they would transport the eighty inch high grandfather clock back to the shop when they were approached by a father and son duo who said they were in the business of removals. Would Ashley be interested in their transportation rate of £50 for a fifty mile radius plus an additional £2 per mile thereafter to be paid in advance? They left their card with Ashley before moving on to another bidder.

Ashley, Milly and Tania then strolled to the high street and found a little café restaurant and ordered sandwiches and tea. They chatted about the items they had bought and Tania said how sorry she was to have missed out on the St Etienne clock. She had really liked it.

The afternoon was much the same as the morning and Milly won another two items while Ashley picked up the barograph combination for just £120. The auction was adjourned at five o'clock and would recommence the next morning at nine o'clock sharp.

Most of the items Milly had listed had gone under the hammer and the next on offer would be the watches in the chest of drawers display and also the framed oils around the house.

It was while they were settling their account with the auctioneer's clerks that Milly again bumped into Graham. They exchanged polite information with regard to their purchases and how pleased they were with them and sorry to have missed out on some of their other bids.

'But then you can't win them all,' said Graham.

'No, I suppose not,' said Milly, 'after all this is rather a large collection isn't it?'

'This Andrew Pando chap was quite the collector wasn't he?' said Graham. 'In fact I've learned that in his later years he turned his interest to ancient history and archaeology. And yet there's nothing in the house to show for it.'

Ashley was intrigued by this and his inner voice started the alarm bells again in his head. That feeling of presentiment and futurity of something mysterious resurrected itself to prominence in his mind again. If the late Mr Pando had indeed been so interested then he would most certainly have travelled to the places of their origin and picked up some things of value.

Graham could see Ashley thinking about what he had just said and added that McGill's Antiques might be interested in contacting the present owner of the house Lester Dutton, cousin to the late Andrew Pando, and who now lived in the East End of London.

'He runs a small family business there,' said Graham, 'and his business address can be gotten from the auctioneer I'm sure. I wouldn't be surprised if he didn't have some archaeological artefacts stashed away somewhere.'

'This is most interesting indeed if correct,' said Ashley to Graham, 'I shall certainly follow up on what you have just said. This Lester must be in the phone book if he runs a business. Thank you Graham.'

Ashley would certainly follow up on Graham's suggestion. His inner voice indicated that that was where the answers lay.

'Let me know how you get on,' said Graham, 'here's my card though I shall probably see you at your shop one day soon. Goodbye for now it was a pleasure meeting you all.'

'Thank you,' said Ashley and gave him his McGill's Antiques business card in return, 'and please do come and visit us whenever you can.'

'I will,' said Graham smiling, 'and sooner than you think.'

They all shook hands and said goodbye.

The next day Ashley hired a small van and took Robin along to give him a hand with bringing all their auction items back to the shop. The black lacquered long-case clock at seven and a half feet long was quite awkward and heavy but they managed to fit it into the van. Ashley had first removed the pendulum so as not to damage the clock mechanism. It became Milly's pride and joy and she placed it near the front of the shop just inside the entrance.

Ashley had managed to speak to the auctioneer's office and was given Lester Dutton's business address in London. He ran a consultancy firm that helped promote efficiencies in manufacturing businesses. The consultancy was called 'Total Quality Principals' and Ashley suspected there was a double meaning in that last word. There was a web site and email listing but this was not known by the person Ashley spoke to. Ashley had decided to travel down to their offices sometime in the next week or so and hoped to meet with the man himself and learn what he could. Ashley knew exactly what he would do.

In the meantime Tania and Katy had gone as planned to the murder case being heard in the Queen Elisabeth Crown courts. Ashley had said that he would join them later as soon as he and Robin had retrieved all the items from Henley in Arden.

The jury selection had been complicated and had taken the best part of the morning. The preliminaries of the case had been introduced late in the afternoon but by then Katy and Tania were both quite bored and decided to leave early and come back with Ashley the next day. Tania phoned Ashley and told him about the progress of the case and not to bother about coming to the courts, and that she would see him back at the shop.

Next morning the court was quite full and the three of them just managed to find seats together. There were five youths in the dock all between nineteen and twenty years of age and were each accused of malicious assault resulting in the death of a thirty two year old family man named Daniel Johns. Ashley shut his eyes and concentrated hard on the events of the assault which took place on the night of April the sixteenth just over a year ago.

Ashley saw the lads Matthew Abbot, Rory Bergin, Darren Ward, John Barney and Vijay Romas standing outside a house in a residential district of Yardley Wood and each with a can of lager in their hands. They were under a street light and used it as their meeting point that night. They seemed to be in a jolly mood and were pleasantly teasing Vijay about his new girl friend. Rory was now sitting on the low garden wall opposite and drinking from his can. As the moments passed their raucous banter got louder. Vijay Romas had a carrier bag with another few cans in it and he went and sat on the garden wall beside Rory and placed the bag on the pavement at his feet.

It just so happened that the garden wall belonged to the house that Daniel Johns lived in with his wife Julie and two small daughters. It was the school holidays after Easter and the tired children had finally gone off to bed at nine o'clock which was quite late for them. The time was now about eleven o'clock and the noise from the lads outside could be clearly heard inside the house.

Daniel and Julie were watching a program on their TV but the sounds from outside were rather disturbing. One of their daughters slept in the small bedroom at the front of the house and they felt she might wake and be frightened at the noise. They were used to the noisy outbursts from people walking past the house from the local pub at the end of the road which was only about five minutes walk away. But this was different and after about twenty minutes Daniel decided to go outside and see what was going on.

'I'm going to have a look to see what the racket is all about,' said Daniel going to the front door and Julie followed close behind.

He stepped out and walked around his car parked on the short front drive and approached the five lads.

'Hi guys,' he said in a low voice, 'if you don't mind could you please keep the noise down. I've got two kids asleep upstairs and you might wake them up.'

Julie came and stood beside her husband and smiled nervously at the lads. She could see that they were a bit drunk by the way they stood and raised the cans to their mouths. There were two empty cans lying in their front garden and a third can flew through the air to land beside them.

'Piss off, bastard,' said one of them and the others all laughed. 'Just bug off back into your cosy house and leave us alone, shit face.'

'In that case I'm ringing the police to ask that you be moved along as you are making a nuisance here,' said Daniel turning around to walk back to his front door.

It was then that the burley Matthew Abbot stepped forward and grabbed Daniel by his shirt collar and jerked him backwards with tremendous force. Daniel was already unbalanced and tipped onto his back and smashed the back of his head on the drive flagstones. Julie screamed and called for help.

Matthew Abbot laughed and kicked the fallen man in the ribs. Rory Bergin and Darren Ward also step forward beside Matthew and laughing they administered a few of their own kicks to the body of the prone man.

They suddenly realised that Daniel Johns had not made a sound or movement since he went down and they all turned about and ran off down the road leaving the bag of cans on the pavement.

Julie sat down on the ground beside her husband and sobbingly called his name repeatedly. The neighbours by now were also outside and quickly came to Julie's assistance. They rang for the police and an ambulance which were both there in a matter of minutes. Daniel was diagnosed with severe concussion to the head and taken to hospital. He remained in a coma for two days and was then pronounced as brain dead and his life support machine was switched off.

The police launched a murder inquiry and retrieved all the beer cans left behind by the lads. The beer cans had plenty of clear finger prints and this helped the police identify the culprits.

Julie had got a good look at the lads and positively identified three of them. The other two were named in the confession statements given by the identified three.

Ashley conveyed all this to Katy and Tania and also the fact that this was a simple enough case for the jury to decide.

The five lads all pleaded not guilty to the death of Daniel Johns. However, their solicitors pleaded that all that they were guilty of was a bit of youthful rowdy horseplay gone wrong. There had been no intention to wilfully harm Daniel Johns. In the horseplay he had fallen and fatally cracked his head on his drive. It was not the lads' fault but simply an unfortunate accident.

'What would you like me to do?' Ashley conveyed his query telepathically to the two girls since he felt that this was a simple enough case for the jury to decide. They would get all the relevant facts from the witnesses.

Katy looked at her brother and conveyed that although she felt a certain amount of sympathy for the five lads they had done wrong and the jury might reach too lenient a verdict. They needed to see for themselves all the events of the evening exactly as they happened. They needed to see that Matthew Abbot was the main culprit who started the violence by pulling Daniel Johns to the ground and of him kicking him when he was down. And also the other two who joined in the assault on the fallen man.

Ashley thought about this for a moment and agreed with Katy. However he felt that the whole court needed to know the real facts especially all the news reporters that were present.

It took an instant for Ashley to telepathically convey his vision of the events of that fateful evening to the entire court. There were audible gasps from around the courtroom and the defence solicitor who had been in the middle of a statement just sat down in mid sentence.

The judge realised that everyone in the court had also seen the full pictorial events of the case as he had and so called for a short recess. He asked that barristers for both sides come to his chambers. The recess was then extended in order that the defence solicitors might confer with their clients.

It was during this recess that Ashley conveyed that he was leaving to return to the business of the shop. Both Katy and Tania responded that there was nothing more of interest to excite them and they would come back with him.

Robin was supposed to meet Katy later on in the evening so she phoned him at the bank and said she'd be at Tania's house and could he come there for her. He said he would and after a brief conversation hung up.

Back at the shop Ashley conveyed to Milly the facts of the case including his vision of the events as they had occurred that evening.

'These youngsters just don't think what the consequences can be from their supposedly playful actions,' said Milly heatedly and conveyed her own thoughts back that the death of a family man had been directly caused by the irresponsible actions of those five youths and that they should suffer the consequences. She hoped that they received suitable punishment; after all the wife of the dead man had received a life sentence of sorrow as did her fatherless children.

'Oh, by the way Ashley,' said Milly aloud, 'our friend Graham from the auction phoned to say he hoped to visit us here at the shop sometime in the afternoon this Friday. I told him we looked forward to seeing him again.'

Ashley didn't see Tania for the next few days but they were in continuous touch over the phone. Milly and Robin got most of the history cards sorted, printed and laminated. Computers were wonderful gadgets and Robin loved sitting at their new E-Machine and transcribing Ashley's scribbles into a sensible word document. Either Milly or Ashley usually checked the finished product before letting Robin laminate the lot.

By now Ashley and Milly could communicate telepathically on a regular basis and Milly thought to herself that there was never any misinterpretation of intent as was so often possible with verbal dialogue. They were both careful not to use telepathy when Robin was near as on a couple of occasions he had actually jerked his head up and asked Milly if she had said something. He'd obviously picked up one of her communications to Ashley.

On Friday afternoon the shop had several visitors. First Gary Prior popped in with his wife Jill and their youngest daughter Maura who was now ten and nearly as tall as her mum. They spent nearly an hour in the shop chatting as they walked around studying the items on display. Robin took Maura upstairs into the museum room and explained how some of the stuff was used in the 'old days'.

Gary told Ashley that they had left Mansfield that morning and that Malcolm and Mary were spending the night with Jill's mum. They had brought Maura to see her favourite girl band at the NEC Arena and would spend the night with friends in Sutton. They hoped to do a bit of shopping in Birmingham before returning to Mansfield later the next day.

It was while they were chatting merrily that another face popped in. It was Clive Davidson and he was pleasantly surprised to see Gary and Jill. And then in walked Graham. He went straight across to where Milly was seated and surprised her with his 'hello' greeting.

There was Ashley conversing with Gary, Jill and Clive, Milly showing Graham around the shop and Robin trying his best to entertain a young Maura. Gary kept staring across towards Milly and Graham and finally remarked that he was certain he had seen that gentleman somewhere before.

'I'm sure I know that chap,' said Gary to Ashley, 'but I just can't seem to remember from where.'

'Come over and I'll introduce you,' said Ashley.

So they walked over to where Milly and Graham stood.

'Hello Graham,' said a smiling Ashley, 'may I introduce my friends to you. This is Mr Gary Prior and his wife Jill. And this is another friend Mr Clive Davidson. Gary and Jill are from Mansfield while Clive is a Londoner. Gary thinks you two have met before but he can't remember where or when.'

Graham shook hands all around and looking at Gary he said, 'I never forget a face and yes I do seem to remember you. Wasn't it at the Clock Fair in Amsterdam last summer? You nearly bought that clock didn't you until I pointed out that it was a modern copy. The casing looked just too good to be true for its age if I remember correctly. It was a beautiful George III mantel clock in ebony that looked in exceptional condition but no serial number anywhere in sight. A tiny detail the fakers had overlooked.'

'Yes, that's right,' said Gary, 'now I remember. I was just about to agree a price when you happened to ask me whether the serial number of the clock was a two or a three digit number. What serial number I had asked and you had explained that all originals were limited editions with a serial number under the manufacturer's stamp. I remember the Dutch chap got quite annoyed at your interference.'

'Well it was a very good quality of fake and I hadn't meant for you to cancel your purchase,' said Graham. 'I thought you could perhaps bargain some more and bring the price down to about half what was on the tag. Anyway after our pleasant cup of tea at the tea stall and much later that same day I did go back to have another look at that clock but it had been sold. I was disappointed because it was a good looking piece and I could have made a tidy profit on it back in Droitwich.'

Gary laughed out loud and putting his hand on Graham's shoulder he said, 'My dear dear fellow, just fancy that. Do you know Graham, after we parted company I went straight back to the Dutchman and bought that clock at nearly half the original price though I did have to bargain quite a bit. I even pretended to walk away before he finally agreed the price. I still have it and its Jill's favourite piece on our living room mantel even though it keeps terrible time.'

'Yes, it was a beautiful looking piece and I'm glad you did buy it,' said Graham. 'It's in a good home.'

'Well then sir, why not come and see it for yourself one weekend,' said Gary. 'There is a pretty good car boot sale near us held on every last Sunday of the month. We usually attend as a family and Jill packs a fairly decent picnic basket as Ashley will testify.'

'Oh no,' exclaimed a laughing Ashley, 'not the strawberries and cream dessert.'

And they all laughed except Graham who appeared puzzled.

'Don't worry my friend,' said Gary smiling, 'it's our little joke and one day we shall tell you all about it.'

Clive chatted to Ashley and said that he was on his way to the Lake District to meet up with some friends for a week of sailing on Windermere as a break from the hustle and bustle of the London stock exchange. It was something he and his three mates did every year. A sort of four men in a boat thing except the boat happened to be a rented four berth luxury cruiser.

Jill insisted that Graham come up to visit them sometime soon so they got out their pocket diaries to settle on a date. Ashley left them to it as they seemed to be getting on famously.

Clive was the first to leave followed a bit later by Gary, Jill and Maura. Maura actually gave Robin a hug and a kiss on his cheek when saying goodbye. Robin had a way with the ladies that made them all like him. Even little babies in pushchairs seem to take to him from the start.

Graham stayed till closing time which was spent mostly on his own upstairs in the museum area. As they were walking out Milly invited Graham and Ashley over for dinner but Graham politely declined and said that he and his wife Anne were members of a 1940s revival club and had a do on that very same evening. All members dressed up in their uniforms and it was quite a grand spectacle. He and Anne wore their Home Guard outfits and Graham drove his vintage 1947 black Austin Eight saloon to the club hall.

'Does that mean dinner is off,' joked Ashley at Milly, 'or am I still invited?'

'Tania will have my guts for garters if you don't show your face,' said Milly. And then to Graham she jokingly stage whispered, 'Future son-in-law and all that it entails you know. I tolerate him for her sake.' And they all burst out laughing.

Graham took his leave of them then and gave Ashley a firm handshake with both hands and then Milly a kiss on both cheeks.

'Thanks for having me,' said Graham. 'I really have enjoyed my visit. You have a very interesting shop. That museum upstairs is a brilliant idea and so well displayed. I'll certainly bring Anne with me the next time I visit. Goodbye both.'

'What a nice man,' said Milly when they were alone. 'Now that is what I call a real gentleman. I wonder what this 40s revival club must be like.'

Ashley and Tania had decided to drive down to Aberporth on their own and take the scenic route via Aberystwyth and New Quay. If they left early they could ride the cliff railway in Aberystwyth and then watch the surfers in New Quay and still arrive at Aunt Brenda's in time for tea. So Ashley was at the Marsh's house for 8:30am as promised. Tania was dressed and ready and came out of the front door with her overnight case as Ashley got out of the car.

She came up to him and put her arms around his waist and looked up at him. Ashley lowered his head and kissed her gently on the lips. Tania responded a bit more firmly and all the time they were communicating loving thoughts to each other. Today Ashley conveyed how much he loved her and that she was the light of his life. 'The moment I met you I felt as if I had passed through an open door into a garden in spring that was so full of colour and song that I was overwhelmed by its beauty. And I still am my darling Tania and I always will be.'

'Oh Ashley I too have passed through that same door but I walked into a great blaze of light that dazzles and blinds me. Can we be like this forever?'

Ashley looked up and saw Milly with a smile on her face peering down at them from her bedroom window. Ashley waved to her and she blew him a kiss and a 'good morning' happy thought. Her emotion of wellbeing and kindliness also came through along with her love for this couple; this couple who had brought so much new joy into her life and rekindled her mood of romance. Milly felt a tender motherly love for Ashley, and not just because he was besotted with Tania. He had bewitched them all with his gentle and kindly nature. A thesaurus of kindly thought expressions passed through her mind when she thought about Ashley. She knew exactly how Lillian felt about her son.

The verb love means to care for and hold dear. To be tender towards and cherish, appreciate and value infinitely; to treasure and think the world of with the utmost regard. To respect, adore and idolise in a kind of gentle worship and want to bestow all favours upon. To spoil, pet and make much of and forever be a friend. Ashley smiled and sent his own kindly thoughts back to Milly.

Jerry came up beside his wife and looked down at the couple below. They all waved to each other in the beautiful morning sunshine as Ashley and Tania drove off.

The journey to Aberystwyth was a pleasant one with the bright sun at their backs. It was so much easier that way as one didn't have to squint into the brightness in front. Ashley drove on the M54 past Telford and Shrewsbury to Welshpool and on down to Newtown where they made a stop off at a little café for nice hot drinks. They finally arrived at the seaside town of Aberystwyth just before noon.

Ashley followed directions for the beach and drove onto Marine Terrace where there were plenty of free parking spaces. They walked along the promenade stopping occasionally to lean on the railings and stare out at the sea. Ashley read Tania's mind and so leaned across and kissed her on the top of her head. She turned towards him and responded with a kiss to his lips.

'Nice,' came Ashley's thoughts.

'What, only nice?' returned Tania.

'Very nice,' from Ashley.

'Mmmmm,' from Tania with eyebrows raised quizzically.

'Superb then, and sublime, gorgeous, splendid, dazzling and lovely. Also tender and soft and quite edible but not spongy, soggy, mushy or squishy. Rather velvety, silky and full of flavour.'

'Shut up Ashley Bonner,' said Tania as she laughed out loud.

They walked towards the north end of the promenade and turned right towards the station of the Cliff Railway which required a bit of an uphill climb to get to. Tania had read about the Aberystwyth Funicular Cliff Railway rising nearly 500 feet to the top of Constitution Hill and of the fantastic views on a clear day when nearly a dozen Welsh mountain peaks could be seen. Today was such a day so they paid the £3 fares and hopped onto 'Lord Marks' which was one of the twin carriages that would take them to the top. They were the only passengers on this trip up. Twin lines operated by a powerful electric motor hauled one carriage upwards at a speed of 4 mph while the sister carriage counterbalanced it by coming down the hill on the other set of railway track. Both were connected by a single thick steel cable.

They passed through a deep cutting in the mid section of the journey and it took just ten minutes to reach the top station. There were breathtaking views of Aberystwyth Town and the houses along the beach road. They could also see the beauty of the Welsh hills spread out inland as far as the eye could see.

Tania and Ashley walked around and just admired the view. Looking down at the town Tania pointed out where they had stood on the promenade and kissed.

'It looks so much like a model village from here, only there's real people moving around in it,' came from Tania effortlessly.

'Yes,' said Ashley in agreement.

It was rather windy on the hill so they went into the restaurant up there for a hot drink but changed their minds when they spotted the 'Lunch specials' board. Both chose the beef lasagne and a separate side salad to share to be followed by mugs of tea.

After lunch they walked up a path to the hut that housed the Camera Obscura but this was disappointing since the views were rather dull and indistinct as compared to their own outside view.

The trip back down was an anticlimax as the scenery disappeared with the tree tops that rose up to meet them. It was near 2 o'clock when they were back on the road to Aberporth.

'It'll be good to stop off at New Quay,' whispered Tania, 'and wet our feet in the sea, it's such a lovely day for it. Mum, dad and I went there on a few holidays when I was little. It's been years since I was last there and I wonder how much the place has changed.'

'I've never been there,' responded Ashley, 'so maybe you could give me the grand tour. It's only twenty minutes or so to Aunt Brenda's from there so we've plenty of time.'

Ashley felt it was good to also use verbal communication as voices were good to listen to. Sounds were important to the senses and added a musical note to the atmosphere between two people; especially for those in love.

'Oh goody,' said Tania who reached across and gave Ashley's thigh a quick squeeze.

They followed the signs for a pay-and-display car park and Ashley put money in for two hours just to be on the safe side. They had a bit of a walk down a steep footpath to the level of the beach and then a short stroll to the water's edge. The tide was only just beginning to ebb so the sea was still managing to surge quite far up the beach.

Tania took off her sandals and carried them by their heel straps, one in each hand, as she went to paddle in the sea. She only went in up to her ankles as she didn't want the hem of her floral summer dress getting wet. Ashley, on the other hand, had to remove his socks as well as roll up his trouser bottoms before gingerly entering the water and walking beside Tania. He just about got the odd wave to wash over his toes. The sea was icy cold and it took Ashley a while to get used to it; not quite his cup of tea.

Tania pointed out the large white building on the top of the adjacent hill and said that was the hotel they had stayed at.

'Isn't this lovely?' she said aloud. 'I feel like I'm a little girl all over again. I'll have to tell mum about this and that I saw the old hotel on the hill. I think it was called The Pentire Hotel if I remember correctly.'

'You'll like Aberporth too,' responded Ashley, 'especially the coastal path walks and the railway carriage houses on the hillside. Aunt Brenda used to have a lovely little dog but he's long gone now. It's such a shame that dogs have shorter lives than us. I think she had Barclay for about eleven years. Katy and I used to take him for runs on the doggie beach. Aberporth has two beaches you know and one of them completely floods at every tide so dogs are allowed on it. Their doggie doings get cleared twice a day by the tide; clever isn't it?'

They chatted verbally and telepathically as they walked along quite enjoying the fresh sea breeze blowing into their faces. When they reached the western end of the beach they turned around and retraced their steps. Ashley could see a large rock feature in the distance standing out from the rest of the hill of Newquay town. As they got closer he noticed a house on the top. It was quite a large house with a red roof and dormer windows.

'How do they get up there?' asked Ashley. 'That rock structure must be at least a hundred feet high.'

'Wait and see,' smiled Tania still splashing her feet in the sea.

It was only when Tania took Ashley around the other side of the rock that he saw the neat little suspension bridge connecting the house to the mainland. The gap must have been nearly a hundred feet across and the walls were sheer on both sides. It seemed as if someone had intentionally separated the rock from the mainland as if for a defensive measure.

There were sunbathers at the base of this rock hill which was quite sheltered from the sea breezes. There was also a dip in the rock base and someone had built a wall to create a natural looking rock pool to retain tide water for kids to paddle in. The wall also formed an artificial seating so Tania and Ashley sat on it and dangled their feet in the clear water. After a while they let their feet dry naturally on the rock wall before putting on their footwear and deciding they'd had enough of the sea for now. They headed back up to the town and the car park.

Lillian and Alex were already at the B&B when Tania and Ashley arrived at six o'clock.

'You're just in time for a cup of tea,' came to Ashley telepathically from his mum who was standing just inside the entrance with her sister Brenda.

'Hello Aunt,' responded Ashley, 'has mum been practicing her telepathic skills on you too?'

Ashley read her mind thoughts and smiled. 'Don't worry Aunt; we'll have you fluent in telepathic lingo in no time at all.'

They carried their overnight cases inside and Ron took Tania's off her as soon as they got in through the door. There were hugs, kisses and handshakes all around in the cramped doorway.

'Lovely to see you again Tania,' said Brenda, 'and so glad you could come. How are your mum and dad?'

'Thank you, they are both well and send their love. I suppose I had better call you Aunt Brenda from now on the same as Ashley does,' said Tania'

'Nonsense my dear, just plain Brenda will be fine. In fact I insist on it. That way you'll have one up on Ashley. Start the way you mean to carry on,' smiled Brenda as she put her arm around Tania.

They laughed and went into the hall.

'We've been paddling in the sea at New Quay and I think I still have sand between my toes,' said Ashley, 'I need to wash and dry my feet properly and put on a fresh pair of socks before I do anything else. I don't much like the sand as it gets everywhere.'

'Come along then,' said Ron, 'I'll take you to your rooms so you can freshen up.'

They walked up a creaking flight of stairs and then down a narrow corridor with Ron leading the way.

'Here you are,' said Ron to Tania, 'this one with the pink door is yours and the next one with the red door is Ashley's. There are no keys needed and the doors have bolts on the inside. Though they do have a mortise lock and a key can be provided on request. It's easier this way for access by Brenda and Julie for housemaid duties. Julie Griffiths is also our desk receptionist and a great help to us. Just come back down whenever you are ready, we'll be in the TV lounge. Ashley knows the way.'

Ron opened the door to Tania's room, placed her bag just inside the door and then smiled at her and left.

'Thanks Ron,' said Tania telepathically. She saw Ron jerk to a halt, turn around and smile again at her and then continue on his way. He remembered that Lillian had said that one of the purposes of this weekend was to get him and Brenda to practice the new form of communication. He was quite looking forward to it. Ashley would tutor them with lots of practice.

Twenty minutes later they were all sitting together in the TV lounge chatting merrily over cups of tea and coffee. Ashley telepathically conveyed all that he and Tania had done on the journey down in Aberystwyth and New Quay.

'I loved New Quay particularly because of my childhood memories,' said Tania aloud for everyone to hear as telepathic group communication was still not in her repertoire. 'It brought back all those happy and carefree childhood memories. And it still seems quite the same as what I remember of it.'

'I think these seaside towns tend to remain the same over the years,' said Ron. 'Take Barmouth for instance, nothing has changed there in twenty years as far as I can remember. Aberystwyth is much the same too. Except there they electrified the funicular in the early twenties. Mind you, keeping to the old ways does have a certain charm, don't you think so?'

Brenda changed the subject then and asked Ashley how long it would take for her and Ron to become proficient in telepathy.

'Well aunt,' said Ashley telepathically and included Ron in this message, 'let's start right now. Just think what you wish to say and I shall read your mind and pass it on. That way we can have a proper conversation right away.'

'How fascinating Ashley,' thought Brenda, 'but when can I begin sending out my own telepathic messages like the rest of you?'

'Once your mind gets used to receiving my telepathic signals, your brain will very gradually tune in and begin to respond by transmitting its own thoughts too. You might experience a dull head at first but that's because you're concentrating too much on sending out your thoughts. Relax and don't worry about whether your transmission has succeeded or not. If we spend a while at it on a regular basis I think you and Uncle Ron will both be telepathically communicating with one another quite comfortably by the time we leave you on Monday morning.'

'What distance does this telepathy work up to?' from Brenda.

'I'm not sure. So far I've only applied it to people I can see,' replied Ashley.

As the evening wore on Ashley also worked one to one with his Uncle Ron.

However, Ron was much quicker to learn than Brenda and was actually transmitting a few jumbled thoughts by the end of dinner. But both had developed a slight headache from their efforts and requested a stop for the time being.

'We'll communicate with you telepathically,' said Lillian aloud, 'and you can simply respond verbally if you like. That should make it a bit easier for you.'

'That's fine,' said Brenda. Then she added, 'Anyone for a stroll to the sea front? It's a lovely evening and it won't be dark for at least another hour and I certainly need to clear my head.'

'That would be lovely,' came telepathically from Alex who was smiling at Brenda as if to show her how easily it came to him.

Brenda poked her tongue out at him as her own response to him showing off his telepathic skill.

It was while they were standing at the railings overlooking the 'dry beach' that the conversation turned to UFOs.

Ron said that he had always treated the reports about sightings with a degree of scepticism. There was so much in science that we didn't know and he thought that what people reported seeing could simply be some unknown phenomenon of nature.

'Take for example the phenomenon of ball lightning,' he said. 'It's a ball of light that has been seen to float through the air and once occurred right inside a passenger jet flying high over the Atlantic Ocean. And most UFO sightings are of lights flying in some sort of a formation and then simply vanishing from sight as though speeding away.'

'I would like to believe in spacemen from other worlds,' said Alex, 'but I'm not sure one way or the other. Nearly everyone carries a digital camera or phone these days so why hasn't someone managed to get a clear photo or movie clip of any of their sightings. I find that strange, don't you?'

'Well,' said Ron, 'I have this friend Freddy in Perth who used to drive all the way across to Sydney on occasion. On one of his trips he said that a very bright light hovered just above his car for over an hour as he drove along. When he stopped, it also stopped. He said he never saw or heard anything apart from the bright light and said that he got quite scared and was very relieved when it finally disappeared.'

'It could have been a police helicopter,' said Tania.

'Freddy said there was no sound at all,' replied Ron.

'Yes,' said Alex, 'I have heard similar weird stories and I often wonder if people exaggerate some of their experiences. If there are spacemen out there then what are they waiting for? Why don't they just land and say 'we come in peace, take me to your leader' or something similar.'

Everyone laughed at that.

'You know,' said Ron, 'there was a lot of excitement back in the fifties when a lot of UFO sightings were reported. Then it sort of died down with just an occasional report. But do you know that reported sightings have once again picked up especially in the last five years. I read an article in the papers that said the sightings were up more than 30% above those at the peak phase of the fifties. Do you think that they've been back to their home planet to report their discovery of us and now a new and bigger expedition has been sent to investigate us even further?'

'I wonder what they look like,' said Lillian. 'Could they be like us in any way?'

No one replied to that as it was too vague a thought.

'It's getting a bit chilly,' said Brenda, 'lets head back and get ourselves a sherry or something. I'm ready to practice a bit more of this telepathic thing now that my head has cleared.'

'Incidentally Ashley,' asked Ron, 'what language is this telepathy in?'

'There is no language Uncle Ron, just thoughts of intentions and opinions. It's a sort of universal communication form.'

'So can you communicate with animals then?' said Ron.

'I suppose it should be possible if they had a thinking capability,' said Ashley, 'I've not tried it but maybe I could pass on a fear of attack or directions to food or something like that.'

Ron was deep in thought as they strolled back to the B&B. It was pleasant just sitting together and chatting. Ashley and Tania communicated silently with each other whenever there was a lull in the conversation. Lillian practiced her telepathic skill with Brenda and Alex did the same with Ron.

By the time they were ready for bed at 1:00am, Ron was actually having a rudimentary telepathic conversation with his wife. Brenda in her own way appeared a bit frustrated if she had to reply verbally. Once again she had a dull ache in her head and this time it was near her right temple.

'I'm going for a hot shower to clear my head and straight into bed,' said Brenda, 'so goodnight all and I'll see you at breakfast about 9 o'clock.'

'Goodnight Brenda,' came from everyone telepathically including Ron. Brenda smiled as she got up and walked away.

The next morning after a good English breakfast of eggs, bacon, baked beans, fried tomatoes, cheese, marmalade and toast they all went for a walk along the coastal path as they had done so often before. They used a mixture of verbal and telepathic communication but Ashley suggested that Brenda and Ron stick mainly to the latter. Brenda's brain must have adjusted while she slept since although her skills hadn't improved much she no longer got that dullness in her head, much to her relief.

On the walk Ashley demonstrated to Tania how he used to catch butterflies for Katy and then let them go again. It still surprised Tania when Ashley would suddenly move location as if by magic. Try as she might she could never sense anything untoward when Ashley went into pink mode. Everything just continued for her as normal.

Tania was curious about the quaint railway carriage houses on the hillsides and was keen to see inside one.

'Do you know,' came telepathically from Brenda, 'I have always been curious too but never had the gumption to walk up and knock on one of their doors?'

'Then why don't we call out to that one and request a visit,' said Lillian pointing, 'I'm sure they'd be pleased of the company, especially on a Sunday morning.'

'Oh yes, let's,' exclaimed Tania in excitement forgetting her telepathy.

Ron then made a portentous suggestion to Ashley and that was for him to send out a powerful telepathic message to the occupants of the carriage house that they had visitors outside their door who were old friends.

The house on the hill was a good hundred yards away but as soon as Ashley sent out his mind message the door at one side opened and an elderly man peered out.

'We're here,' telepathically from Ashley and he waved both arms at the man.

Ashley then read his thoughts even at this distance and acquired the man's life history. He was Peter Ellis and he lived with his wife Fiona. They had lived in the same street in Cardigan and their parents had been school friends. The Ellis's and Jones considered themselves as family and all were doubly pleased when the Ellis boy began courting the Jones girl. They were each an only child and the whole street had been invited to the wedding 45 years ago. They'd never had any children and had moved here from Cardigan twenty two years ago this autumn when the last of their parents had passed away. Peter had taken voluntary redundancy from his job in a bakery and Fiona had handed in her notice as shop assistant in Woolworths when they found this vacant hillside carriage 'bungalow' on a holiday. They immediately put in an offer and returned to sort out their own properties. They sold the Jones' house but rented out the Ellis property to the local city council.

Ashley conveyed all of this telepathically to the rest of the family group and they all waved up at Peter. There was a grassy path that led to the house and Peter came partway down it.

'What can I do for you folks?' he asked with a pleasant smile on his face.

It was Ashley who replied, 'Oh, my aunt and uncle here live in Aberporth and own that big B&B house on the hill. They've often seen you at The Royal Oak pub and even had a game of darts with you. Ron and Brenda Davies, ring any bells? They thought they'd come and say 'hello'.

Part of the thoughts that Ashley had picked up were that Peter enjoyed a pint and a game of darts and didn't mind whom he played against so long as it was a good contest.

'Why of course, you are very welcome, please come on up,' said Peter. 'The path starts there just a few yards on your right. Be careful mind you as it's rather steep to begin with.'

'Thank you very much,' said a smiling Tania in her most pleasant voice, 'you are most kind.'

As they were walking up to the house Ashley had the oddest sensation that an inner voice was trying to tell him something. It was as though the voice was muddled and distorted but was gone after a few seconds. Ashley would remember this moment in later days.

There was a small fenced garden area in front of the house that faced seaward. The carriage was bigger than it looked from the path and was about forty feet long. It had an awning stretching out over the garden with a hardwood bench underneath.

The inside of the carriage house was luxurious and looked nothing like the outside which needed a lick of paint. It was divided up into four sections. You entered the kitchen with its modern electric cooker and oven and beautifully arranged units. Peter introduced his wife Fiona who was a short tubby lady in a stained apron and slightly dishevelled hair.

'Please excuse the mess,' she smiled, 'we don't often entertain royalty this early on a Sunday morning.'

She had a sense of humour which Ashley found pleasing.

Peter took them around and showed them the dining cum lounge area which was separated from the kitchen by a part wood and part glazed small partition. A small table was placed against one side near a window facing seaward with two straight backed chairs neatly tucked under. There was luxurious thick pile carpeting covering the floor which gave the whole room a soft quiet feel. A low sideboard stood against the opposite wall and covered the bottom half of the window there. It was a long room and two sofa armchairs faced a small TV set on a wooden stand with a bookcase beside it. All the windows had pale green festooned curtains but they showed their age and were faded in places where the sun had got to them. All in all Ashley thought it a very cosy establishment and Lillian said so.

'The next is our bedroom and beyond is the bath but it's a bit of a mess at the moment and I'd rather you didn't see it today,' said Fiona apologetically.

'Oh, please don't worry about that. It is us who are intruding and you are very kind to let us into your lovely home. We are most impressed at how cosy and comfortable it is in here. You keep a lovely house. I wish mine was as nice,' said Lillian.

'We have electricity and water but no sewage connection,' said Peter, 'so I've had to have a septic tank installed just down from the garden. A chap comes to inspect it once a year.'

'Thank you for letting us see your beautiful home,' said Brenda, 'the next time you are at The Royal Oak please pop in to our B&B on the hill and we can get to know each other better, after all we are neighbours aren't we?'

'Oh, I'd offer you a cup of tea but we're a bit short of mugs at the moment. You are the first people to visit us here in ages,' said Fiona.

'Thank you my dear,' said Brenda, 'but please don't bother yourself. We've only just had a big breakfast and came out to walk some of it off when Tania here saw your beautiful place on the hillside.'

They all waved to each other as they walked back down to the coastal path and again just before they walked around the bend and out of view.

Ashley pointed out several other similar carriage cottages dotted on the hillside as they walked along. All had seaward facing gardens full of flowers and shrubs. Some looked really pretty with hanging baskets and added extensions. One even had a greenhouse on one side.

'They all face the sea in a north-west direction,' said Ron, 'so they get a lot of the summer sun from mid-afternoon onwards. And on a clear day they should be able to see the sun setting into the sea. But in the winter months they must hardly get any sun as it stays low and sets behind the hill over there.' Ron pointed back towards Aberporth.

'Still it must be nice living here looking out to sea from your bedroom window especially with a storm raging down there,' said Lillian. 'I suppose it's quite safe up here.'

There was a sloping drop of at least fifty feet from the coastal path to the sea level and there didn't seem to be any evidence of erosion of the coastline at all.

There was a large black cloud billowing in their direction from the seaward side and Brenda suggested aloud that they turn around and head back home before they got caught up in a freak cloudburst.

Ashley telepathically suggested to Brenda and Ron that they direct their thoughts to him and he would instantly pass these on to the others. He would do this to improve their telepathic skill and so the walk back to the B&B was full of silent conversation. Ron and Brenda found this most interesting and quite liked this mode of communication. It was as though they could see into each others minds. For another thing it didn't leave your mouth dry from too much talking. And there was never any misunderstanding as to what was meant. Brenda laughed out loud when she conveyed the thought that Ron couldn't claim not to have heard something she said. The habit of being conveniently deaf by some men would no linger apply.

They were back in the comfort of the B&B and sipping a hot drink when Ron conveyed through Ashley that Brenda had a lovely singing voice.

'I wonder whether she can convey her songs telepathically as well,' he added. 'And will they still sound as good?'

There was a moment of complete mental silence before Ashley gave his opinion. He conveyed to them that singing was like music which was a pleasure thing experienced through the ear just like the viewing of a beautiful painting or scenic panorama was enjoyed through the eyes. In the end it all ended up inside the head and was translated into appreciation or emotion by a section of the brain. Telepathy could never substitute for the sights, sounds or odours around them that give so much pleasure though it could convey a sense of it.

'And that reminds me about my sense of taste,' said Brenda aloud, 'can I convey to you telepathically how nice a slice of walnut cake tastes or would you rather find out for yourself in real life.'

Everyone laughed and said 'Yes please' in unison to receiving a slice of Brenda's famous Walnut and Date cake.

Lillian and Alex left for Birmingham just after teatime as Alex had work the next day. Tania and Ashley were to spend another night here and Tania said she would like to watch the sun setting over the sea.

'Plenty of time for that,' said Brenda to Ashley, 'the sun doesn't set till near nine o'clock. But you'll need to go up the hill to the viewpoint there. Unfortunately there always seems to be a few clouds on the distant horizon so it's seldom that you actually get to see the sun dipping into the sea. Most times it just fades into a sort of a misty haze that rests just above it. But it's lovely to watch anyway. Dinner will be ready at six thirty and then when you get back we can have a light supper about ten. How's that sound?'

'That'll be lovely aunt ..... I mean Brenda,' conveyed Tania with a smile.

'You two get down to the beach or wherever and be back in an hour,' communicated Brenda, 'Ron and I have things to do in the kitchen.'

It was a ten minute walk to the beach and Ashley and Tania sat on a bench facing out towards the sea. They sat close up against each other holding hands and just stared in silence at the lapping waves. The tide was coming in again and both watched the succession of waves creeping up the beach. It was hard to really judge if the tide was coming in as some waves advanced higher up the beach than others.

There was no communication between them verbal or otherwise, though occasionally they looked sideways at each other, smiled, gave a hand squeeze and then turned back to looking at the waves.

Finally Tania sighed, leaned across and kissed Ashley lightly on his cheek and whispered 'I do love you Ashley Bonner.'

Ashley released his left hand from hers and reached across and put it across her far shoulder and pulled her to him in a gentle hug. Tania jiggled her hips and got to move close up against Ashley. She then inclined her head and rested it against Ashley while her left hand then reached up and took hold of Ashley's that was on her shoulder.

A middle aged couple walking on the beach looked up at them and smiled as they walked past. The man then took the woman's hand in his and they walked on like that.

The sun sank behind the bluff to their left and after a bit Tania shivered in the cold breeze. Ashley noticed and suggested they return to the B&B; it was after six.

After a delicious dinner at a table for two served by Uncle Ron, Tania and Ashley walked up the hill to the viewpoint to watch the sunset. There were no benches but there were about six other people already looking out towards the sea. One was a family of four with two young girls. All stood at the waist high railings and chatted away merrily and turned and said hello when Ashley and Tania took a stand beside them.

The sun seemed to be racing towards the right while gradually getting closer to the horizon. The lower half gradually paled till finally the entire sun appeared as a dull glowing ball. It was still about a couple of its diameters above the horizon and looked like the full moon. Then it slowly faded as it lowered further and finally just disappeared from view altogether as it sank into the haze. Tania sighed and thought of all the sunsets she had seen this was quite the anti-climax. Ashley in turn shivered as he was reminded of his dream. For that brief moment the sun had appeared as a glowing ball and for some reason Ashley found it menacing.

Tania felt him shiver and sensed his unease for that brief moment and tried to look up at him. Ashley was standing snug behind her with his arms about her waist and hands entwined in hers.

'I was reminded of my dream with the glowing ball destroying all in its path,' conveyed Ashley.

Tania understood how he felt since telepathy conveyed emotions along with the expressed communication. And she knew it was his inner voice that indicated to him a sinister interpretation to that dream. Just as Lillian had worried about what the future might hold for her infant son all those years ago, so Tania now underwent a similar anxiety. This came with the knowledge that there must be a purpose behind Ashley being given such fantastic gifts. Or did she mean powers? The power to do what? Tania worried in her heart that Ashley might be taken from her in order to fulfil some destiny chalked out for him. And what had the glowing ball got to do with it? Why did it appear menacing to Ashley?

She instinctively turned around and putting her arm around Ashley's waist hugged him tight. She kept her head flat against him to hide the tears that welled up in her eyes which she tried to rapidly blink away.

When she finally looked up into his face she saw a faraway look in his glistening eyes and knew that he too had been thinking similar thoughts. She reached up and kissed him gently and conveyed that it was getting rather chilly and they ought to head back to the house. They were now the last on the hill and could see the others on the path leading downwards and back to the town.

'Yes love,' said Ashley in a husky voice, and together they began the walk back down still holding each other around the waist. When the path narrowed they had to go single file but only for a moment. Tania came back alongside Ashley and they continued the rest of the way holding hands.

When they walked in Ron and Brenda were relaxing in the living room with mugs of hot tea.

'Hello young lovers,' said Ron aloud, 'welcome back. How was the sunset?'

'Quite unspectacular,' conveyed Tania and Ron nodded when he received the full picture.

'Yes, there always seems to be a haze on the horizon which is such a let down. I prefer to see the sun set behind those distant hills as you can then actually see the sun slanting downwards. It also gives you an idea of the motion of the earth in its spin away from the sun,' he conveyed.

Ron was getting quite proficient at his telepathic skills. He hadn't yet perfected the knack of communicating with more than one person at a time so he spun his thoughts around to each person in turn. Telepathy only took an instant so it appeared to be more or less instantaneous in its effect.

Tania conveyed that she would make Ashley and herself mugs of tea and disappeared through the door to the kitchen. Ashley flopped down on the sofa beside his Aunt Brenda and conveyed his thoughts and those of his recurring dream. His concern that the dream implied something sinister was also conveyed in his communication.

Far, far above them a silver craft hovered noiselessly with its occupants concentrating intensely trying to pinpoint the source of the very faint telepathic images that they were picking up with increased frequency of late. Could it be possible that their long search might finally be at an end and the prediction fulfilled. The reception was much too faint to be certain. The human brain emitted thought signals quite naturally as did all animals too, and it was rather difficult to differentiate between the intentional and the involuntary patterns. But recently over the last several months a small group had been sending out controlled signals of which one was by far the strongest. As it got dark on the earth down below all signals tended to diminish as the Earth's inhabitants went to sleep. It was then possible to hover much lower down without detection. But they had to be extremely careful. Nothing was being picked up by the underground implants. In addition they were hampered by the electronic shielding around their own craft which was solely there to prevent those below from receiving their advanced telepathic thoughts. The search would continue.

Ashley, Tania, Ron and Brenda had gone to their rooms around midnight after a very pleasant evening of quite intense telepathic chatter.

Next morning after a satisfying English breakfast, Ashley and Tania said goodbye to their hosts and set off for the long drive back to Birmingham. They must have been a good mile or so travelling up the B4333 when Ashley suddenly stopped the car.

'We have to go back,' communicated Ashley, 'you've left your handbag on the sofa in the lounge.'

'Oh,' said Tania aloud, 'I could have sworn I put it on the back seat. How did you know?'

'I picked up Ron's telepathic message,' communicated Ashley. 'He's got a very good brain transmission you know. I've sent him a reply that we are on our way back.'

Ron was waiting for them by the front door with the handbag across his shoulder and hand on his hip in a humorous pose. They were already communicating as Ashley drove up and Tania indicated that the bag quite suited him but that he should get his own. Laughter doesn't quite come across telepathically, only the mood of pleasure and happiness. So Ron just gave a loud laugh.

'Here you are Miss,' he said out loud as they came abreast of him, 'it's a very nice handbag but doesn't do much for my image.'

Milly laughed too when Tania related all this to her back at the shop.

Ashley left for London early on Tuesday morning for his appointment with Lester Dutton at his offices. He had bought a day return trip with the National Express coach service from Wolverhampton to Victoria. He would then get the Underground Tube to the Oval in Kennington and walk across the park to the Commercial Centre. Ashley had a pretty good idea of where to go from the detailed instructions that Lester had given him when they had spoken at length over the phone. Although Ashley couldn't read Lester's mind then he did manage to implant a vagueness of a memory that they had perhaps met each other sometime previously in Birmingham. Ashley would of course develop this further when they were face to face.

Something about what Lester might tell him had Ashley's instincts prickling but his helpful inner voice was unusually silent which led to some doubts as to the productive outcome from this visit. Ashley would just have to wait and see. And why did he keep thinking back to his glowing ball dream? What connection did that have with reality?

When Ashley walked in through the front door of Dutton and Dutton Consultants at twelve thirty he was met by a smiling young face seated behind a counter which also doubled as an office desk. She was semi blonde and was without any make-up apart from a light lip colouring. Ashley instinctively did his usual mind scan and ascertained that her name was Margaret Dutton. She was 24 years of age and Lester's elder and unmarried daughter. She was a business graduate and a partner in the firm. She was not an exceptionally pretty woman but had a very pleasant personality with intensely confidant eyes.

'Hello sir,' she said, 'welcome to Dutton Consultants, you must be Mr Ashley Bonner who has come to see my dad Lester.'

'Yes, I am,' replied Ashley, 'I'm from Dudley near Birmingham and I arranged this visit last week. I own an antiques shop called McGill's Antiques and I made some interesting purchases at the house of his late cousin Andrew Pando in Henley in Arden.'

'Dad has been quite keen to meet you. He thinks he's been to your shop a very long time ago when his uncle took him there on one of his forays. Of course you wouldn't have been around then but dad seems to remember the trip.'

'That would have been in the time of David and Grace McGill who were the original founders of the antiques shop. I hope your dad enjoyed his visit then,' said Ashley smiling.

A tall grey haired elderly gentleman then came into the room from a door at the back and walked towards them. He turned and smiled at Ashley. These people knew how to make a person feel welcome thought Ashley. It must be important to their business to exhibit a pleasant manner. Ashley put this in his mental memo to mention this aspect to Milly and Robin.

'Dad, this is Mr Ashley Bonner from McGill's Antiques in Dudley near Birmingham,' said Margaret. 'He's here for his appointment with you and he's absolutely on time.' How pleasant of her to say that since Ashley knew he was about twenty minutes early.

'Oh yes of course. Pleased to meet you Mr Bonner,' said Lester putting his hand forward for a welcoming handshake. 'Do come in to my office and we can talk comfortably.'

He smiled at his daughter and then turned and led the way forward. He held the door open for Ashley to enter ahead of him.

Ashley took the opportunity to read his mind then and get all the necessary information about Lester and his family.

Lester Dutton was the older of two brothers. Anthony was four years his junior. Their mother May was very much younger than her brother Lester senior who was the late Andrew Pando's father. The Duttons and Pandos had got on very well together and Andrew and his younger cousin Lester had been very good friends even though there was a thirteen year age gap between them.

Anthony Dutton had been a bit of a loner and played for long periods on his own with his toy soldiers. Lester senior encouraged the boys in their interests and one Christmas when Anthony was fourteen he had received a beautiful BSA air rifle from his uncle.

After several broken window panes and the gun being quarantined for a week each time, Anthony learned to be more careful and shoot at paper targets with great accuracy. Unfortunately there was still the odd small bird on the rubbish heap that Anthony had targeted. Lester consoled his sister by simply saying 'boys will be boys' and that they needed to expend all that bottled up energy.

Lester Dutton was seventy years old when his cousin Andrew had died this past year. He was still active in the consultants firm that he had founded when he was thirty although his children thought that it was time he retired and took their mum on that long promised holiday. They were still young looking and active and Lester could pass off for a fifty five year old. His wife Mary who had just turned sixty could still turn heads on the main street. They had married late when Lester was nearly forty and had two boys and two girls at two and three year intervals who were all now a part of the consultancy firm.

Andrew at twenty nine was the eldest but his brother David at twenty seven was the real brains behind the company's recent success. Margaret the one behind the reception desk was twenty four while Geraldine the baby of the family at twenty one was away at university.

Lester and Mary had been keen ramblers and had belonged to a Ramblers Club. Their weekends were then often taken up driving to remote spots to join groups of club members for a five or six hour trek across fields and bridleways. They had both been extremely fit then and had enjoyed the open air, come rain or shine. But with age they'd had to settle for the more mundane forms of entertainment. Mary now enjoyed the coffee mornings with her friends.

Anthony Dutton, the younger brother had done his National Service and then joined Barclays Bank as a trainee clerk on his twentieth birthday which just happened to be a Monday. He had made several sideways career moves to different branches around London and had finally made assistant branch manager in Willesden Green quite near the General Hospital. He retired at sixty three after six years in this senior post. He and his wife Joan now lived a very comfortable life together in their cottage in Sunbury not far from the Hazelwood Golf Course, not that either of them were into golfing.

Early in their married life they had been blessed with a little girl who unfortunately was born with Downs's syndrome features and diagnosed accordingly. Joan gave up work to care for her baby. Little Jeanette was a beautiful and loving girl and quite playful in her manner and full of fun and laughter. Anthony simply doted on her and spent his evenings and weekends entertaining and playing with her. Jeanette tended to catch every bug that happened to be doing the rounds. She got on well with her teachers at school and was quite a clever little girl though not at the top of the class. She was an avid reader of the children's story books that her mum bought for her and used to tell her tales on to the other children in her class. She was not good at sports but took an interest in the games played by the other children and cheered them on whenever playing an outside team.

It was shortly after her twelfth birthday that she never woke from her sleep one rainy morning. Anthony and Joan had both been warned that such a scenario did exist for little Jeanette and although saddened by the sudden loss of their beautiful little girl they coped quite well, all things considered. They were grateful for the joy that she had brought into their lives and often looked through the many albums of photos of all the fun times that they had recorded. It was nice to remember the laughter and joy that their little girl had brought into their lives.

Although the brothers had drifted into their own busy lives there was one tradition that remained. When their mother had been alive she had insisted that the brothers meet up with her on her birthday in May.

And so it was that on the thirteenth day of May each year the two brothers would meet at an exclusive restaurant in Central London to remember their mother. Each found no special emotional attachment to this date but neither had the courage or desire to break the tradition. In fact in an abstract way each looked forward to their meeting. An unspoken code had been not to bring any children to this reunion.

Ashley smiled at these thoughts as he walked into Lester's office. He also learned that Lester had been summoned to the death bed of his cousin Andrew and been given a set of diaries covering his final three years. It was these records that Ashley was particularly interested in. Apparently Lester had not been the least interested in his cousin's writings and so had not even glanced at them since they had been given into his possession. As such Ashley had not been able to ascertain their contents from Lester's thoughts.

'So Mr Ashley Bonner of the famous McGill's Antiques you are very welcome here and I am pleased to meet you. However I am curious as to the nature of your visit and what it is that you wish to learn from me,' said Lester with his charming smile as he sat down behind a large ornate desk and gestured for Ashley to sit down opposite.

Ashley knew the nature of the consultancy from his research and of the good reports of its success in helping businesses increase their productivity and profits. Total Quality Management was a philosophy that was first used by the Japanese in the sixties to great advantage. It entailed a progression of involvement all the way down to the lowest worker on the shop floor in helping to solve manufacturing problems there and promoting ownership in the company no matter how basic.

Lester had developed this theme for application in the West and once he was contracted to a productive business he set about installing those Japanese principles. Andrew and David were both graduates from the London Business School and were designated with first contact by carrying out a thorough diagnostic investigation of the company. The report detailed how all levels of employee perceived the company's strengths and shortcomings.

Honesty was crucial in this phase of the play. The subsequent report was an open document for all to view and comment upon and Managers could then decide if they wanted to go to the next phase of the program.

The first step was to set up small cells of problem solving groups in every work area and to pick leaders to supervise them. The bigger task was for managers to delegate personnel from within the employee zone to be trained with the title of Facilitator. David and Andrew would then provide full training to these Facilitators to run two day and four day courses for giving every single employee a practical idea of the principles of Total Quality Management or TQM. Complete training manuals and course syndicate work would be provided by Dutton and Dutton Consultants for the length of the program. The whole theme was for the Company to adopt the new philosophy and then to effectively manage it on their own in the longer term without further assistance from Dutton and Dutton.

And they didn't come cheap. The diagnostic phase alone cost a one-off fee of £10k and the remaining package if taken up was a further £50k. The reputation established so far was a good one and they were in great demand.

'Oh please call me Ashley,' said Ashley, 'after all we both originate in the Midlands. I have heard good things about your consultancy and I believe you also are familiar with the name of McGill's Antiques up in Dudley. We pride ourselves in being able to deliver a history with all our items for sale as you probably are aware.'

'Yes that is true Ashley,' said Lester. 'I vaguely remember visiting McGill's Antiques shop when I was a teenager but I was not very interested in old stuff then. Though, I do remember the lady who gave me a bag with two fresh doughnuts; I polished them off in no time at all. Funny how some things stay in your memory despite the years.'

'Well sir,' said Ashley sticking to formality, 'the baker's shop is still across the road from McGill's and I can vouch for their excellent doughnuts. I promise you a taster when you come for a visit for which I extend an open invitation here and now. Come whenever you can or if you are passing that way.'

Ashley took an instant liking to Lester and knew that the success of his business had a lot to do with his pleasant and professional attitude. He gave Ashley a politeness and respect in a completely natural manner as though Ashley were the most important person in the world.

'So Ashley, let us get back to the purpose of this meeting. What exactly can I do for you?' asked Lester.

'Well sir,' said Ashley, 'I have been led to understand that the late Mr Andrew Pando widened his collecting interests and travelled abroad a lot in his last years. Yet there was nothing to show in the house sale of any items that he may have collected on those journeys. I wondered if you might be able to shed light on his last interests and if he in fact returned with any artefacts of note. On the other hand did he keep a record of any kind?'

'He did keep some diaries of his last years but how can that be of any interest to you. I haven't as yet had the opportunity to read them but as far as I understand they are just logs of his travels. I consider them as private and I can't imagine how they can be of interest to you. I don't mean to sound rude Ashley but I would like to preserve his privacy in the matter if you can understand what I mean,' said Lester in a rather serious manner.

'Mr Dutton sir,' said Ashley in his most formal and polite manner. 'I fear I have a confession to make. I have been blest with a unique gift which has stood me in good stead at McGill's. I'm not sure how it works but the moment I hold an item in my hand its complete history of origin and manufacture is revealed to me. So you see how all the items for sale at McGill's acquire their history cards. Many have been authenticated where records exist and others have not, though none has ever been disputed as erroneous. So you see I thought if I could touch something that Mr Pando had acquired abroad then I could establish its origin and satisfy a curiosity. When I was in his house during the auction I received a presentiment that there was something important attached to Mr Pando. And when I was told that many of his travels had been abroad that sense of futurity seemed to rise to prominence in my instinctive awareness. I sensed a danger signal of something portentous, possibly foreboding and ominous, attached to the house. I'm not particularly religious nor am I a spiritualist of any kind; nor do I believe that I am psychic. I only know that I have this God given talent that lets me trace the history of items that I touch or hold in the palm of my hand. Some people can sing or compose beautiful music and songs. Others can play a musical instrument to perfection. I am shown histories.'

There was a silence for a moment between the two men. Then Lester removed a gold signet ring from his left hand lazy finger and silently passed it to Ashley. It had a bright blue Lapis Lazuli flat disc stone inserted in the top.

Ashley took it in his right hand and held it up to the light between thumb and forefinger while admiring the blueness of its stone before passing it back. Lester put it back on his ring finger a cynical smile on his face with a hint of scepticism.

'That is a beautiful signet ring sir,' said Ashley slowly, knowing that he was being tested by Lester who just couldn't believe what Ashley had stated about his gift. Ashley didn't normally rise to the bait to prove himself to anyone least of all to someone he had never seen before. But this man had something in his possession that Ashley knew was important to his future. Something in those diaries was worth reading which was warranted by Andrew Pando setting an importance to them in as much as passing them to his cousin for safe-keeping. So Ashley paused a bit longer and Lester slowly began to rise from his seat obviously to end the meeting with this pretender.

'There is a lot of love in that ring,' said Ashley, 'and it was given to your father Richard Aloysius Dutton by your mother May Agnes Louise Mariner at the altar of St Luke's church in Birmingham on the thirteenth of May 1932 at approximately 1:20pm. It was a Friday and was a wet day, one of the wettest on record. It was also your mother's 25th birthday. They had met roughly eight months previous at a church bazaar at St. Luke's and had been smitten with each other. Your father had been taken by the slim girl in a blue dress serving at the second hand stall and she by the tall golden haired man with the Errol Flynn moustache.'

Ashley paused while Lester with mouth slightly open sat down again. Ashley smiled and continued.

'The ring was specially made to your mother's specification in the jewellery quarter of Birmingham by a young apprentice craftsman named Matthew Lloyd aged just twenty. Your father said he didn't want a simple wedding band but something he could show off and wear with pride. His favourite stone was Lapis Lazuli because he had always liked the colour blue.'

Ashley paused again before continuing in a sad tone.

'Sadly, your mother had it removed from your father's swollen finger after his accident and wore it on a chain around her neck. She wore it for nine years and then gave it to you on your twenty-first birthday. She said to you then that it was your father's ring and that you looked a lot like him and you were both the same in height and physique. The ring fitted you perfectly then as it does now. On the inside of the ring band is etched '*with love forever,*' followed by the date '*13.5.1932*'. Your mother never ever recovered from the death of her only true love even though she put on a brave face in front of her family. Every night she lit a candle in front of her Richard's framed portrait with tear filled eyes. And she then spoke to him as if he was still there.'

Ashley paused and looked away from Lester's admiring tear filled eyes. Very slowly Lester stood up blinking rapidly and walked to the door. Opening it he asked his daughter to come in for a moment.

'Margaret,' he said, 'I want you to meet a truly gifted man. He has told me all about my parents in such a way as to bring them fresh into my memory all over again. I'm sure he deserves an excellent cup of tea, and so would I after what I've just heard.'

Margaret smiled as she went to leave. 'Sure dad, I won't be two ticks,' she said.

After another moment of smiling silence Lester came around to Ashley and said, 'I would like to shake your hand Mr Ashley Bonner and thank you for what you have just revealed. This ring means a lot to me, always has, but now I value it even more. I shall tell the family and I shall hope to make a visit to St. Luke's in Birmingham. I'd like to see where mum and dad got married and exchanged those vows back in '32. Of course I shall hope to visit McGills on the same day and hold you to those doughnuts as promised. So now how can I help you resolve your sense of instinct with regard to my cousin Andrew?'

Ashley knew that he could now ask for the earth and if it were possible then Lester would deliver. As it was Ashley's only interest was in the diaries and notebooks that Andrew Pando had passed on to Lester at their last meeting. So Ashley explained his interest again and how he was curious to determine Mr Pando's late interest in archaeology or antiquity and anything he may have discovered in his travels.

'The curious thing for me,' said Ashley to Lester, 'is that despite Mr Pando's late fascination with antiquity, there was absolutely nothing in his house to reflect that interest. I find that curious and wonder if you can shed some light on the matter.'

'I can and I will,' smiled Lester. 'In fact I can do better that that. I shall let you borrow Cousin Andrew's diaries for as long as you like. There are two diaries and one rather grubby notebook and to tell the truth I haven't even looked at them. There is also one small tablet of sandstone about six inches square and about half an inch thick which has some blurred scratch marks on both sides. Andrew seemed extremely keen that I take great care of it and stressed that it was an important acquisition. He said something about a prediction but I honestly thought he was simply babbling on about some myth he had discovered. I have them in my safe at home so why don't you come to dinner this evening then you can meet the rest of the clan as well. I shall phone Mary to lay an extra place. Would 7 o'clock be okay with you?'

Ashley thought about what he'd have to do. Since he'd planned returning on the coach today he didn't have anything for an overnight stay. He could of course book into a hotel and then also hire a car for the return trip to Dudley. He mentioned as much to Lester.

'Do forgive me for presuming on your time,' said Lester. 'I don't like to upset people's plans and I seem to have jumped the gun here. Should we postpone dinner for when you come to return the items then? What time does your coach leave?'

'Oh, it's not till six this evening,' said Ashley. 'I had planned doing a bit of sight seeing around London when I left here.'

'In that case why don't you come to the house at about four thirty and I can give you the items Andrew left with me. Mary makes excellent scones and we could have a light tea before I drop you to your coach station. Here's my business card, it also has my home address. You will need to get a taxi as we are not near any of the tube stations.' Lester smiled again as he passed his card across to Ashley.

'Thank you,' said Ashley also smiling, 'I look forward to meeting you later.'

Margaret then came in with a tray on which were a teapot with cups, milk jug, sugar bowl and a large plate of biscuits.

'Shall I be mother?' she smiled at Ashley and immediately began pouring out the tea. 'Please help yourself to milk and sugar and do try a biscuit as well.' She picked up one of the biscuits as she turned and left the office.

Lester laughed and said that it was just like Margaret to be informal.

'She is really very professional when we are involved with a company on one of our consultancy instructional programs. We train them in the art of efficient management,' said Lester.

'Yes,' said Ashley. 'I did manage to brief myself about you and your TQM philosophy. I must say that I find it to be such good sense that I wonder how others don't adopt it as a matter of course.'

'I would hope not,' laughed Lester, 'or we should be without a job. Of course it's not just the philosophy of Total Quality that is important but the way that it is implemented throughout each level of the company. It's an ongoing fight and we stress that point. Quite often management changes take place and the impetus is lost. It is sad how soon they lose their TQM drive and revert to their old ways. But then we are happy to step in again and reintroduce our program and charge for the privilege of course.'

They talked generally about life in London as compared to that in Birmingham and Dudley. Ashley left when he'd had his tea and a biscuit and said that he hoped to get to see Buckingham Palace, Trafalgar Square and walk through Hyde Park at the very least before meeting Lester again at his house.

'I'm so glad we met,' said Lester, 'and Mary and I look forward to seeing you this evening.'

Ashley returned to the Underground Tube Station and was soon wandering around Trafalgar Square. He found a Garfunkal's restaurant on a side street nearby and had a veggie lasagne and a coke before walking the length of The Mall towards Buckingham Palace. He climbed the steps to the Queen Victoria Memorial and sat with the hoard of tourists there and just took in the view all around. It was a bright sunny day finally and everyone seemed to be enjoying themselves. From there it was a short stroll on the bridleway beside Constitution Hill to the Duke of Wellington roundabout and across it to Hyde Park Corner. The park was massive and stretched westwards from where Ashley was standing. There were people dotted about with many just relaxing in the late sunshine or walking purposefully across its criss-crossing tree-lined pedestrian ways.

After taking in the view Ashley decided to spend the next couple of hours at the Natural History museum so he took the short ride on the Piccadilly Line to South Kensington station. It was just over a hundred yards to the museum from there and Ashley stood admiring the size of the Tyrannosaurus Rex skeleton mounted just inside the museum entrance. It's a good thing these monsters died out 65 million years ago he thought, because he wouldn't care to meet up with one of them today.

Ashley blocked his mind to the histories that kept screaming out to him and just walked from one hall to the next admiring the way the exhibits were arranged. He thought it might be a good idea to suggest that Robin make a visit here or even to the V&A just around the corner. Robin never seemed to be satisfied with his upstairs layouts and was continually rearranging things.

Time just whizzed by and when Ashley next looked at his watch it was nearing four o'clock, and he hadn't seen even half of the museum. Perhaps he'd come back with Robin whenever that came to be.

Outside Ashley hailed a black cab and gave the address from Lester's card. So with a 'right you are gov,' he zoomed off in a westerly direction towards Ealing and a house on Mount View adjacent to the playing fields of Hanger Hill Park. It took nearly twenty minutes in heavy traffic for Ashley to get to Lester's little mansion and Ashley was impressed by the gated entrance and asked the taxi driver to stop just outside it. The front door was a good fifty yards or so from the road and opened as he approached. A portly grey haired lady stood just inside and welcomed him with a broad smile. She was dressed in a pale green day suit that fitted her well. A patterned broach of jade stones mounted in dull silver was prominent below her right shoulder.

'Hello Mr Bonner,' she said and stepped down to meet him. She gave him a kiss on the cheek and put her arm round his and walked back into the house with him. 'Lester has spoken to me of your wonderful gift and everything you told him about his parent's ring. I think it is absolutely wonderful that you should possess such a talent. I think we are going to become good friends and you will be so famous,' she added.

Ashley was not impressed by this and after reading her mind decided that Mary was a simple woman who craved to be with celebrities. She definitely thought of Ashley as one. She liked giving parties and was a bit of a snob. She admired her husband but was more in love with the large amounts in their joint bank accounts and investment portfolios. She was proud that her children were all doing well and was continually fussing over their needs even though Geraldine was still at university. She was not a conversationalist and didn't read much though she spent long hours watching soaps on TV. Basically Mary was a bored housewife who craved excitement of whatever sort could be conjured up. For the moment Ashley was that distraction. All in all Ashley decided that Mary was a simple well meaning woman and a good wife and mother.

'Thank you Mrs Dutton, you are very kind,' said Ashley in his most formal manner, 'I'm pleased to be here. You have a palace of a house or should I say mansion. I'm afraid my entire downstairs would easily fit into your hall. You must have a dozen bedrooms I'm sure.'

Mary was proud of her home and pleased by Ashley's remarks.

'Not quite a dozen, my dear,' she said with a gracious smile and didn't elaborate further. 'Come into the drawing room and I'll make some tea. Janice is just about to leave so we won't trouble her. Would you like to freshen up first?'

'No I'm fine thank you,' replied Ashley settling down into a very comfy overstuffed sofa. He had used the facilities at the museum just before he'd left. 'Is Janice another one of your family?' he asked knowing full well she was not.

'Oh dear me, no,' laughed Mary. 'Janice is our house maid and a companion to me during the day. Lester gave her to me to help with the housework and she has been with us for ages now. It must be ten years at least. Or is it eleven? I know that Geraldine was still in school then and Janice picked her up at three thirty when I was too unwell to do it. We have her four and a half days a week as she finishes early on a Friday. Nine to four mainly but she can have a day off anytime she wishes. Her husband Nicholas is much older than her and we have had him too these last five years since he retired from his work. I think he was in a factory of some sort but I can't remember doing what. I'm sure Janice has mentioned it. He tends the grounds for us but only does three mornings a week. I do like to hear his whistling when he's about the place; he's such a happy chap. Which reminds me that he mentioned that the mower needs fixing or did he say we needed a new one? I'll have to speak to Lester about that. Now do you take sugar or is it a sweetener you prefer?'

'Sugar will be fine, thank you. Just one please,' smiled Ashley. He was beginning to like this portly lady and her conversational style. Ashley knew she was dying to ask him about his talent regarding histories so he thought he'd reward her hospitality with a little example.

'I do love your jade broach, it compliments you perfectly,' he said. 'Would you like to know its history? No, please leave it on I don't need to actually touch it, just seeing it is enough.' Ashley knew Mary had specially dressed for him when her husband had phoned her earlier. She had worn the brooch because it had been given to her by her grandmother as a wedding gift, who in turn had said that her own grandmother had given it to her before that. She had hoped to ask Ashley to tell her its history but was not sure how to go about it without seeming rude or presumptuous. After all you didn't ask a guest in your house to perform tricks now did you?

Mary smiled widely at Ashley and kept her eyes on his as she passed him his cup of tea.

'Thank you Mr Bonner,' she replied, 'that would be wonderful. I'm simply dying to hear its full history. My grandmother Margaret gave it to me when I married Lester and mentioned that it had been in the family for generations. I'm afraid I don't have a recorded family tree much before grandma except that her grandma had given it to her before that. So I know it goes back at least four generations.'

'Well actually it goes back to one more generation before that,' said Ashley. 'And please call me Ashley as I do find the Mister a bit stuffy, don't you?'

'Of course Ashley my dear just as you wish. And we shall be Lester and Mary to you also,' replied Mary. 'I agree that the formal address is quite out of place between friends.' And she smiled hugely at Ashley as she said it. Ashley was quite won over and smiled back at her.

'I shall start at the beginning,' said Ashley. 'The brooch is a Star brooch made by one Joseph Elliot, a silver smith who had set up in business on Frederick Street in the Jewellery Quarter of Birmingham. He had an elder brother William in the same area but who was involved in the button making trade using a new industrial revolution machine in 1829. Young Joseph was twenty-three years old when he joined up with his brother a year later but his heart was not in it and in 1832 he branched out on his own making silver jewellery. He was self taught and acquired his skills and the new techniques of the trade from talking to the other jewellery makers around him. The jewellery quarter of Birmingham was by then the most advanced and renowned jewellery making centre in the world. Joseph was a one man business and remained single all of his seventy three years.

In the November of 1835 a new bright comet was seen to light up the night sky and much speculation abounded as to its significance. This was Halley's Comet and as you know it appears near Earth approximately once every seventy six years. Young Joseph decided to follow the trend of what the other jewellers around him were doing and decided to make pieces of the new fashioned Star Jewellery. Subsequently he personally designed and made this jade brooch in the December of 1835 a full month after Halley's Comet had passed its zenith and brightest moment. It was on display in his window for exactly two days. The morning sun made the jade stones in the six pointed star sparkle a brilliant green and this caught the eye of a passing gentleman by the name of Daniel Honnor.'

Ashley paused and sipped his tea before continuing. 'Daniel Honnor had married a lady named Catherine Alexander the previous year in 1834 and they were expecting their first child early in the New Year. Now green was Daniel's favourite colour and the bright green lustre emitted by the jade stones in the morning sunlight simply mesmerised him. He immediately walked into the shop and paid the asking price of three guineas and took it home all nicely gift wrapped. He then presented it to his pregnant wife Catherine as a Christmas gift and she just loved it. Catherine who was born in 1814 would be your great, great, great grandmother. Their beautiful daughter Marie was born in late January and although they were to have other children, Marie was to be their only daughter.

As Marie matured she and her mother became inseparable in both mind and dress. Then she was introduced to and fell in love with the handsome Justin Wolff and they were married in 1855. She was then just nineteen years of age. The Star Brooch was a wedding gift from mother to daughter and had by then become a symbol of good luck or so her mother said. The marriage was blest with three sons and the eldest David married a Miss Irene Hope in 1886. Irene was a gentle and plain looking lass and being of a shy disposition never really connected with her mother-in-law Marie. As such the brooch was not passed on to her. David and Irene had two daughters Margaret and Josephine, both of whom were adored by their grandma Marie.'

'In 1909 Margaret the elder daughter met and married a businessman named Roland Salt who was from Newcastle on Tyne. The Star Brooch was a wedding gift to Margaret from her grandmother Marie. They had two sons William and James. Sadly Margaret was abroad when her grandma Marie took ill suddenly and died. She missed the funeral by a week even though she began the journey home as soon as the news reached her.

William joined his father's business while James bought a commission in the army and went to service in India where he died of a fever after just six months. William Salt then met and married a Miss Heather Shaw, your mother. They were married in 1941 and Heather insisted on living in or near Birmingham where you were brought up. Your father William eventually set up his own business in Henley in Arden which was fortunate for you because it is where you met your husband Lester Dutton.

Unfortunately, your grandparents Margaret and Roland Salt continued to live in Newcastle and did not look favourably upon their daughter in law Heather. As such the Star Brooch stayed with Margaret.

Then in 1942 you were born and you became the proverbial apple of your grandmother's eye. You made frequent visits to Newcastle with your father and were visited frequently in turn by your grandmother Margaret. There was some magical connection between the two of you and your grandma was most happy to present you with the Star Brooch on your eighteenth birthday. And there you have it to this day.'

'I wonder how you can be told all of this,' said Mary, 'it is truly a gift from God and I must thank you from the bottom of my heart for sharing it with me. Lester will be pleased when I tell him all that you have just revealed about the brooch and how it got to me. He always said I had a fierce and unnatural attachment to it; now he will understand why. I had often wondered at its star design and which one it portrayed or represented.'

'Comets were thought of as great omens for princes and kings,' said Ashley, 'and Halley's Comet caused a great deal of speculation in 1835. The brooch is as beautiful as the day it was made and I'm sure Joseph Elliot would be pleased to know that one of his creations is still appreciated today.'

Just then Lester and Margaret walked in and asked what they were talking about.

'Oh hello dear,' said Mary, 'Ashley has just been telling me the history of my jade Star Brooch. Did you know that it dates back to when Halley's Comet appeared back in 1835 and was bought and presented that very year to my pregnant great, great, great grandmother Catherine as a Christmas present from her husband Daniel? It is so wonderful to finally know when it came into the family.'

Lester could see that his wife was in a happy mood and for this he knew he had to be thankful to Ashley. Mary was extremely impressionable and Ashley by his revelations had brought quite a bit of excitement into her day. Also to her Ashley was a celebrity and she would be anxious to boast about him to her charity set at the earliest opportunity.

'Sit down my dears,' continued Mary, 'and join us in a cup of tea. I shall make up a fresh pot. I'm quite thrilled with my bit of news. Isn't Ashley wonderful? I can't wait to tell Astrid and Jane.'

'I think my dearest that Ashley would like his history telling gift to be kept as a secret from all and sundry,' said Lester in a quiet voice. 'He fears being swamped by the press and others were it to be generally talked about. So I'm afraid you mustn't mention it to anyone outside our family, he has specially requested it of me and I gave my word. So we must respect his wishes mustn't we if you would like to keep him as a friend?'

Mary looked crestfallen but then smiled meekly at her husband and said, 'Yes of course I will my dear, just as you wish. I understand fully.' And she smiled widely at Ashley.

Ashley smiled back at her and induced a feeling into her mind of a very pleasurable sensation based on the keeping of this particular secret to herself. That pleasurable sensation would cease to be if she told anyone about Ashley.

Mary then suggested that they move out onto their west facing patio where Janice had prepared a lovely little buffet tea with sandwiches and rolls and slices of turkey and chicken along with a huge bowl of her speciality egg salad. There was even a trifle for a dessert. All covered in protective cling-film of course.

'Janice insisted she prepare all this before she went off home. She really is quite an angel. I think I'd be lost without her,' said Mary.

'These are lovely tasty sandwiches,' said Ashley when he had bitten into the first one. 'I just love cucumber and cress but there's something else in these. What is it?'

'Aha, now that is my secret recipe,' smiled Mary looking across at Lester who was also smiling. 'It is a sort of herbs mixture in paste form that my grandmother passed on to me when she gave me the brooch. It goes with nearly everything. I'm surprised you didn't include that into your history description.'

'I don't see all the minute details just the bare essentials,' said Ashley, 'so your recipe is still your very own secret.' And there were smiles all around.

Lester then disappeared briefly only to return with a scruffy notebook, two diaries and a greyish stone tablet about six inches square and half an inch thick with softened edges. He placed these on the table near Ashley and went and sat back in his place.

'As promised these are for you Ashley to keep for as long as you need to,' he said. 'Andrew entrusted them into my care and somehow must have known that I would meet someone like you who would know what to make of them. Frankly I was a bit embarrassed by his faith in me then but I'm certain I am doing the right thing in passing these on to you. Personally I was not the least bit interested in many of the things that Andrew mentioned. In fact I didn't even read his diaries nor that scruffy little note book. As for that stone tablet I haven't the foggiest as to what it is meant to be.'

All manner of emotions hit Ashley at that instant. There was a bit of anxiety emotion mixed in with a warning signal for him to be circumspect. Then a bright light filled Ashley's vision and that vague warning seemed to flash out at him again. A warning of what; and by whom? Certainly not his inner voice surely? And yet a mood of expectant adventure and joyous anticipation also came across into Ashley's mind. A new beginning in far away places was indicated but this confused him even further.

Ashley reached out slowly and pulled the stone tablet out from under the books. He held it up to the light and could see what looked like a criss-crossing of scratch marks on its shiny surface. He turned it over and saw that there were similar markings on the other side as well. Both surfaces were of a highly polished nature. Somehow it seemed to speak to him in his thoughts.

Ashley closed his eyes and very lightly ran the tip of his middle finger across each surface; but all he could feel was a perfect smoothness. He looked at each surface obliquely and in the surface shine there were no scratch marks to be seen at all. It was as though a fine glaze covered the stone tablet and that the scratch marks were underneath this.

Ashley looked up to see Lester and Mary looking expectantly at him.

'I'm afraid I'm not getting much of a history from this,' he said. 'However what I am being told is that there are literally hundreds of thousands of similar stone tablets all over the world. It's as though someone was advertising a product and trying to draw customers to their shop. I'm guessing here and don't really know what to think except that this is very very old. It is definitely artificial and made somewhere in the region of five or six thousand years ago. And yet it looks brand spanking new. Perhaps your cousin's notes and diaries might shed some light on the matter. I'll let you know when I've had a read.'

What Ashley did not let on was that the tablet was not made on this earth. It was of an alien nature and probably a very advanced piece of technology. But Ashley had no idea what function it actually performed.

'Take your time,' said Lester, 'I know Andrew would be quite happy that you have his stuff. I certainly had no use for it or any idea of its possible importance. Though I will say that you have aroused my curiosity a bit and I'm rather keen to know more about it.'

Margaret the elder of their two daughters then came into the room and smiled at Ashley. She knew about his history telling talent and also that this knowledge was to be kept a secret within the family. She looked at Ashley with a keen eye and guessed that there was a lot more to him than he had let on. She had never heard of anyone with a talent like he'd shown and she was certain that he had other skills that he had not told them about. But that was his business. Her own talent was reading into other peoples potential abilities and helping to draw them out, and she saw in Ashley someone with a powerful potential to do whatsoever he put his mind to. She saw in him a super human being and her affections poured out towards him. She felt a strong physical attraction for this tall thin gangly looking youthful man. Ashley sensed this immediately and telepathically introduced the thought into her mind that he was happily engaged elsewhere.

She looked at him for a moment and then quietly said, 'Ashley did you just implant a thought into my mind?'

'I'm sorry,' Ashley replied, 'I haven't a clue as to what you are talking about.' He would have to be extremely careful with this one he thought. She had a keen and instinctive awareness for everything that went on around her. 'What kind of a thought would that be Miss Margaret?' Ashley tried to keep it slightly formal.

Margaret shook her head then said, 'Never mind, I just had an instinctive thought and I wondered where it could have come from.'

'Perhaps Miss Dutton,' said Ashley with a bit more formality and feigning puzzlement, 'perhaps you have the talent to read peoples minds from their body language. It is an admirable skill and very important as a management tool. Reading minds is not uncommon between twins, or so I hear.'

Margaret smiled at Ashley but stayed silent. She had got his message loud and clear. Ashley smiled back. Here was someone he felt attracted to as a friend. In a few years time Ashley knew that telepathic communication would become an established skill among many. But it would have to appear as part of the natural evolution on the part of mankind. It must not be seen to have originated through the efforts of a single person. But that was still in the future.

The conversation turned to Ashley and his family and the shop. He spoke lovingly about his grandfather Eric and the sadness he felt as he saw his general decline through age related illnesses. Ashley briefly mentioned his mom, dad and sister Katy and what they were involved in. He then explained about Milly who was his business partner and who managed McGill's Antiques. She was also soon to become his mother in law when he and Tania got married sometime in the near future. Tania was still doing her A-Levels and hoped to go on to teacher training college and then teach in a primary school.

When the time approached Ashley graciously thanked each of his hosts for their generous hospitality and gave a special thanks to Lester for the loan of Andrew's notebook, diaries and mysterious stone tablet. He would take special care of them and return them as soon as he had sorted through them.

Mary fetched an old plain canvas shopping bag and put the books and tablet into it and handed the bag to Ashley.

'There,' she said with a smile, 'that should make it easier for you.' And she leaned forward and kissed him on the cheek. 'Lester has promised to drop you to the coach station I believe. Goodbye Ashley I do look forward to seeing you again, sometime soon I hope. Do take care of yourself.' And she stepped back.

'Goodbye Ashley,' said Margaret and she put out her hand which Ashley took in both of his.

'Goodbye Miss Dutton, Margaret,' said Ashley, 'it has been a pleasure.' And he leaned across and kissed her on the cheek though also caught her on the very corner of her lips, just as he had intended.

'Keep my secrets Margaret,' Ashley conveyed telepathically and she smiled like a Cheshire cat.

'I knew it,' she thought back which Ashley instantly picked up and acknowledged with a returned knowing smile.

On the coach ride back to Birmingham Ashley's thoughts dwelled considerably on Margaret and how she had managed to see into his potential. She must be quite an astute business manager with such a discerning talent. Lester was lucky to have her. Ashley could see Tania not quite getting on with Margaret. Tania was easy going while Margaret was extremely intense in whatever she did. After a while of comparing the two women Ashley dozed off to the drone of the coach wheels on the motorway tarmac though he still clutched Mary's canvas shopping bag firmly on his lap.

He lay awake for a long time once he was back home and in his own bed. He was reminded of the emotions that had been evoked in his mind suddenly and momentarily when Lester had brought Andrew Pando's books and stone tablet to the table. Yet it all seemed a distant event and Ashley had to remind himself that it did happen. The stone tablet repeatedly came into his mind as something very important from a far distant past. The fact that it was one of many hundreds of thousands on Earth added to its mystery. Could the scratch marks be a sort of ancient hieroglyphic text? As Ashley fell asleep a passing thought hinted that it might be some form of communicating or monitoring device.

The next morning Ashley awoke fresh with a feeling of optimism and instinctively realised that a new chapter in his life was just about to begin. On impulse he walked into the dining room and picked up the stone tablet and held it at arms length in front of him and peered at his reflection in its shiny dark grey surface. He then placed the tablet back on the table and studied the scratch marks for any system or pattern to them. It was as though it had been used as a chopping board before being preserved in its fused glaze of a coating. The opposite face was no better with similar erratic markings and Ashley stared at it for a full minute before finally giving up. He had totally forgotten about that passing thought just before he'd fallen asleep. The diaries and note book that Andrew Pando had kept came across as important via Ashley's inner voice which had once again responded to his questions. The answer was there but would need to be extracted from a confused man's garbled notes.

Later at the shop Ashley conveyed telepathically to Milly and Tania all that had happened on the previous day in London. Both were concerned at the warning sensation that he had received when first being confronted with the books and stone tablet. Tania's belief that Ashley's future was purpose built and linked to his super gifts was a constant concern and worry to her. Those gifts had a purpose she felt that would take him away from her eventually and her instincts in this respect were strong.

'What have you discovered from the books?' asked Tania.

'I haven't looked at them as yet,' said Ashley, 'so I don't know. This may sound funny but each time I think about them I get a queasiness in the pit of my stomach and I put off picking them up.'

There was a long silence when mother and daughter communicated silently with each other.

Then Milly said, 'Ashley we are all in this together since we are family and share your secret. Would it help if we all came over to you tonight and were there with you to start you off reading these diaries? I'll ring Lillian about it too. We could each have an early supper before we got to your place.'

'That is a lovely thought,' said Ashley, 'but would you mind very much if we left it till the weekend. You could all then look through the diaries and see what you make of them. Then if you find something that I have missed you could fill me in. I'd like to have a go on my own first.'

'Yes of course Ashley,' smiled Milly sounding a bit disappointed, 'the weekend should be fine.'

Tania then put her arm around Ashley's waist and began a telepathic communication.

'Is this Margaret very pretty?'

'Not particularly, but she has a keen brain.'

'How so?'

'She immediately sensed that I was hiding some of my potential.'

'Do you want to include her in your secret?'

'No I think not.'

'Why not?'

'She was interesting but I think she's very intense in all she does. She'd want to know the reason for this and for that. Also she is someone who needs to be in control and have all the answers.'

'Show me her face.'

Ashley smiled as he recalled the images of Mary, Lester and Margaret and conveyed them in movie form to Tania's mind. He included the image of Mary's Star Brooch and its history. He also included all the conversation that he'd had with each.

'Ashley I love you.'

'Yes I know and I love you.'

'What attracted you to her?'

'I'm more attracted to your mum.'

'Ass.'

'Pig.'

'Answer the question.'

'She was different.'

'Yes I know. Clever, intelligent etcetera, etcetera. Explain further.'

'You know, a person's mind is a funny thing; some things stick and some things don't. Memory is like a little child walking along a beach. You never know what small pebble it might pick up and store among its treasured things. I suppose Margaret stood out yesterday and I've saved her into my data-bank of a memory. You've no need to be jealous, I don't want to be with her at all like I want to be with you.'

'Am I a pebble?'

'A very nice one.'

'You're not supposed to say that.'

'Why not?'

'I don't know. I just wanted something nicer'

'Okay, you're not a pebble at all. But you are everything else to me Tania. Everything and more.'

'The perfect answer.'

'Thanks.'

'I liked the Star Brooch.'

'Do you want one?'

'When I'm a granny.'

They both laughed out loud and Milly turned to look at them arm in arm. She knew their bond had just grown that little bit stronger. She remembered when she and Jerry had been like that. The newness faded but the love remained. The excitement and passion became just a fond memory.

It was back to shop business when Robin came down and joined them. He wanted Ashley to come upstairs with him to give his opinion on something he had rearranged. Ashley remembered his thought about sending Robin down to London to look at the display styles in the Natural History Museum as well as in the V&A. He might want to treat his friend the bakery manager to a day out. Ashley could implant the thought in Robin's mind.

That evening after a light supper when he was finally alone in his home he settled down on the sofa with the books and tablet placed beside him. Milly and Tania had understood his need to be alone to tackle Andrew Pando's stuff. Ashley had conveyed his feelings with regard to being on his own while reading the books as he needed to also delve into their histories. If Andrew had done any extensive travelling he would need all his concentration powers to uncover any underlying truths. He could do this best when he was alone. Tania conveyed that she understood perfectly and wished him good luck as she kissed him before getting into her mum's car.

Their communication continued for quite some distance as Milly drove away. Ashley's telepathy skills had improved considerably and he could now communicate with Tania even when she was out of sight and about a mile away. But after that it was hit and miss and he was unable to receive any of her thoughts at all. Practice made perfect and they'd keep trying.

CHAPTER 10

A Revelation

2003

I felt sad that Andrew Pando was not around to answer some of the many questions I wanted to ask. I had read his extensive notes and both his diaries and had discussed them with Tania and both our families. His notes were mainly of his research into the mysteries surrounding the Dogon tribe of Mali in West Africa and how they came to possess advanced astronomical knowledge with regard to Sirius the brightest star in the sky.

The Dogon stated that Sirius was part of a triple star system even though the third member had not as yet been observed by western astronomers with their evermore powerful telescopes. Andrew's research and notes stated that it was believed that the information that the Dogon people had acquired could in fact be traced back to the ancient Egyptians - from whom they are believed to descend - and a suspected extraterrestrial source. The Dogon tribe had other information as well. They knew of the rings around Saturn and also of the four major moons that orbited Jupiter and which were only discovered when Galileo had invented his telescopes.

Andrew's notes were detailed and his interest appears to have been keen. But what had led him to follow this line of enquiry is what puzzled me. His diaries showed that he had followed up his findings by actually spending several months with the Dogon tribe in Mali during the seasonal September to May flooding of the Niger River in 1991.

Mum and dad suggested that perhaps Andrew had picked up a book detailing the worlds last mysteries and that this particular angle had caught his fancy. And the more he delved into it the more intrigued he had become and totally immersed himself into further research. Dad thought that Andrew must have initially intended to debunk the Dogon myths but had personally been caught up and drawn into their mystery.

But I felt there was much more to it than just an intense curiosity into a printed story. The question of why, why and why again had Andrew followed his instincts with such conviction? Was he just bored and looked to adventure? Or had he seen or heard of something to spur him on?

Andrew's notes stated that according to the Dogon legend and oral tradition a race of people from the Sirius star system called the Nommo had visited the earth thousands of years ago. The Nommo or Nommos were amphibious beings that resembled mermen and mermaids. His notes linked this to ancient Sumerian and Egyptian myths in which the goddess Isis is somehow connected to the star Sirius and sometimes depicted as a mermaid.

Andrew's notes continued with the Dogon legend that the Nommo landed on earth in an egg shaped ark that made a spinning descent with a great noise and wind. It was they who supposedly gave the Dogon their astronomical knowledge.

It was Katy who raised the question of how an advanced race could have communicated complex knowledge to a primitive people of limited vocabulary so effectively as to make their information understood and remembered. Katy said that the only effective way she could see for this to have been achieved was via direct mind to mind telepathy.

This was most interesting, and I said 'well done' to Katy. It was definitely a probability. I shall need to trace all of Andrew's information with this in mind. But the wheels were turning and I felt myself being caught up with Andrew's enthusiasm as much as perhaps he himself had been.

His notes also extended to the Sumerians who could be traced back far earlier than the Egyptians and all the way to about 5500 BC. However their record keeping and development of writing came 1500 years later. Andrew believed the Nommo must have also contacted these people and similarly imparted advanced knowledge to them which was eventually passed on to the Babylonians.

The Sumerians as researched in Andrew's notes had far more exact knowledge of the solar system and its place in the universe than their Babylonian heirs whom they predated. Their calendar that was devised as early as the third millennium BC was the model for today's calendar. And they also understood a number of more arcane astronomical matters. The Sumerians made star charts showing the distances between stars precisely. Andrew asked in his notes what possible use they could have found for these star maps which were clearly meant for space travellers.

The Sumerians had assigned twelve celestial bodies to our solar system; namely, the Sun, earth, moon and nine other planets. So far we account for eight of these 'other' planets. The Sumerian twelfth body has yet to be discovered somewhere beyond the orbit of Pluto. In 1972 a perturbation in the orbit of Halley's Comet could only be accounted for by the pull of a huge planet about the size of Jupiter and which orbited the sun approximately every 1800 years. Pluto's orbit around the sun was just 248 years in comparison.

The Sumerians also knew of the wobble of the earth's axis as it rotated and which caused a change of one degree of arc every 72 years in where the North Pole points. This is known as precession. The Sumerians calculated that a Great Year, which occurred when the precession went around full circle and the North Pole again returned to its original position, took 25,920 years. How could the Sumerians have known all this, Andrew asked, given the lengthy calculations involved and the lack of advanced instruments available to them? He suggested that here once again the Nommo might have had an influence.

Perhaps, I thought, that if Andrew's speculations had any foundation then it was quite possible that earth had been visited by beings from another planet.

If the Dogon accounts had some remnant of truth about a momentous landing on earth by beings from space then there should be comparable descriptions elsewhere in history too. Andrew did find this in the Babylonian records that beings they called the 'Oannes' were amphibious creatures who came to this planet for the welfare of the human race. Their vehicle was egg shaped and they landed in the Red Sea. They were dressed as fish but also had an appearance similar to a man. They communicated fluently with humans and gave them insight into writing and the sciences. In short, these 'Oannes' (Oh-anz) instructed humans in everything a civilized nation should know. When night came it was the custom of these beings to return to the sea.

Andrew found an account of the Oannes by the historian Hellandus who recounts the story of a man named 'Oe' who came out of the Red Sea having a fishlike appearance but the head, feet and arms of a man and taught the people astronomy and writing. As Katy suggested was this done via telepathy? If any of this was factual then most certainly I felt that telepathy would have been the only effective way of conveying all such information; and making it stick in the human mind.

Andrew's research indicated that the Dogon Nommo and the Babylonian Oannes were one and the same. He also found that the Dogon had not always lived in Mali but had migrated there from far to the northeast and may have originally been close enough to the Red Sea to have experienced a similar encounter with the Babylonian Oannes but whom they referred to as Nommo.

Once again Katy asked a keen question. Where are they now? And what about the stone tablet of which I had been given to understand from my inner voice that thousands upon thousands had been distributed across the surface of the earth. I replied that we'd just have to wait and see and I was sure the answers would be forthcoming in the not too distant future. I speculated that for all we knew they might be here on earth in a disguised capacity. They might even have integrated with the human race; after all we are quite a concoction of physical diverseness.

Andrew's research was very extensive and he included a section on ancient mythology in an attempt to correlate them with the Dogon myths in regard to the Nommo. There was serious historical evidence about creatures that were part man and part fish and who tried to lure ships and the minds of sailors in their direction and to destruction. The sailors referred to these creatures as Sirens and warned about the effects of their calls or beautiful singing voices. This was again in line with Katy's suggestion that the Sirens communicated telepathically over fairly large distances for how else would the sailors have reported hearing singing voices in their heads. I could not understand why the Sirens were considered bad since all previous evidence seemed to point towards a benevolent race that was keen to instruct us in civilized ways. Perhaps the sailors had primitive prejudices that had since distorted the truth. It is all very circumspect anyway.

Andrew speculated further that there must have been a continual contact with the Nommo such that the Babylonians worshipped a fish-god like image that they passed on to the Philistines as their sun god Dagon.

I tried over the next few days to establish from my inner voice the truth of all of this but my Lych-Gate assistance was not able to reach out that far into the past; or perhaps for some reason it would not. I had been given a complete view of the universe including its detailed functioning but this eluded me. Perhaps there was no fact in it at all. However I did view the Sirius star system with my universe knowledge and indeed there were three stars orbiting each other though one of them was an exceedingly small red dwarf completely invisible from earth. But nothing indicated that any planets existed within the system. Therefore it was not possible that any extraterrestrials could have come from there. The Sirius star was truly the brightest star in our night sky and I wondered if this was a factor in the Dogon mysteries.

Andrew had felt compelled to travel to the land of the Dogon and personally meet these people. A tourist trade had already been set up and Andrew made special arrangements to spend three months with the Dogon people near the city of Bandiagara during the time of the seasonal floods. An unusual feature of the Niger River is the Niger inner delta which forms where its gradient suddenly decreases. The result is a region of braided streams and lakes the size of Belgium.

Money talks was a reference made in one of Andrews diaries and a Dogon family were happy to take him into their home to live with them as one of them. Andrew learned their customs and tried to live as they did and did so with quite some degree of success. He wrote that his intended three months stay had not seemed enough so he had extended this by another two months. He wrote that those were the most peaceful and fulfilling months of his life. The Dogon were an extremely polite people orientated towards a life of complete harmony.

Andrew related examples of their rituals of greeting and appreciation. The women praised the men, the men thanked the women, the young expressed appreciation of the old and the old recognised the contribution of the young. Also, when Dogon met Dogon an elaborate greeting ritual was followed. Andrew wrote that he particularly liked this tradition.

In the ritual the visitor was asked a series of polite enquiring questions about his or her whole family. Invariably the answer was 'Sewa' which meant 'everything is fine'. Then the whole was repeated in reverse by the visitor enquiring politely after the other person's family also. Sewa was repeated so often that Andrew and others dubbed them as the 'Sewa people'.

I was impressed by what Andrew had written and thought this a wonderful custom. Perhaps I might adopt it into the repertoire of my own politeness towards the people I met. I mentioned this to Tania when she was with me one evening and she thought it an excellent idea.

'How are your mum and dad?' I asked her telepathically in a sort of practice run.

'You mean how my mother and father are? I think you need to be formal as well as polite,' from Tania. 'And perhaps individually rather than as a group, don't you think?'

'My dear Tania, how is your mother, is she well?'

'O yes thank you Ashley she is very well and everything is fine. Sewa.'

'Very good. And is your father well and does he prosper?'

'Yes thank you he is well. Sewa.'

'And is your Uncle Robin well?'

'Yes thank you, Uncle Robin is very well indeed, Sewa.' Tania started to giggle but I checked her with one of my imitation frowns. If she started I'd probably follow.

There was a brief pause as we composed ourselves and smiled at each other.

'O Ashley I do like this custom especially the way you look into my eyes when you ask the questions. It's my turn now,' said Tania aloud.

'Dear Ashley how is you mother?'

'My mother is very well thank you Tania. Everything is fine. Sewa.'

'Excellent. And how is your father, is he well?'

'Yes thank you he is well. Sewa.

'I'm very pleased. And is your sister Katy well?'

'Yes thank you my sister Katy is very well indeed. Sewa.'

'Very good I'm pleased to hear it. And are all her friends well?'

'Yes I believe they are all well. Sewa.'

'And is your pet rabbit….?'

We couldn't keep serious any longer and it was Tania who first went into a fit of giggles. Then we both burst into laughter and I stepped forward and drew her into my arms. We hugged and laughed and our passion kindled with the motion so that I bent my head down and kissed my love firmly on the lips. We stayed that way for a long moment feeling the warmth of our bodies. Tania ran a palm down my face before pulling away. We had learned to convey our emotions to each other in the same way that we had felt the overwhelming love around us.

It was a wonderful feeling of love that came across to me from Tania and I'm sure she felt the same from me. I think since my telepathic skills were the greater then the emotions I transmitted must be correspondingly more powerful. But Tania didn't seem to notice anything different. And when I looked into her eyes I saw nothing unusual either.

In his diaries Andrew wrote that he soon learned to speak the Dogon dialect and was subsequently permitted to attend some of their rituals not normally permitted to outsiders. He was befriended by the spiritual leader of the village called the Hogon. The Hogon was elected as Chief from the oldest men of the enlarged families of the village and the current one was an ancient called Ogemtali. According to their system of accounting Andrew was given to understand that Chief Ogemtali was well over a hundred years in age and could even have been as old as a hundred and thirty.

The first time that Andrew was called into his presence was after Andrew had been living with his Dogon family for three months and on the eve of a full moon. Andrew had been silently and unknowingly led by the elder of his host resident family, an old gentleman by the name of Otembalinish, to the hut of the Hogon chief and instructed to squat on the bare earth just outside the entrance. The elder Otembalinish had then just melted into the darkness.

Andrew wrote that he had sat there for hours on end and only when the full moon was at its zenith overhead had he received a call to enter the hut. He had been dozing at the time thinking what a way to spend the night. Yet later on reflection he wrote that he couldn't remember hearing any voice call to him, just that he knew with certainty that he was required to enter the hut.

An oil lamp was on the floor to one side and Chief Ogemtali was seated on the rush matting that covered most of the floor area of the fairly large hut. Ogemtali was required to live alone as was the custom for the Hogon. He'd had a wife and many children but that was all in the past. His wife was dead and the children were a part of the enlarged village family or 'guinna'. He was wearing a large red feathery bonnet and wore an ornate armband on his upper right arm. There was a large pearl mounted at its front which shone silvery in the lamplight. Otherwise his dress was just a white cloth tied around his waist.

It was only then that Chief Ogemtali spoke to Andrew and then in the ritual of Sewa. Andrew had responded politely in fluent Dogon and then repeated the ritual asking Ogemtali how he was and the welfare of his non-resident family. The responses of 'everything is fine' to all the enquiries were finally completed and Ogemtali reached behind him and brought forth a bowl of sweetened cereal balls. He placed these to one side between them. Ogemtali then took one of the balls and held it just in front of his lips and paused. Andrew knew of this custom and so also took a cereal ball and slowly moved it towards his lips. But first he sniffed it, nodded his pleasure with a smile and then bit into its softness. He chewed slowly, nodding and smiling all the while. The Hogon chief then followed suit also nodding and smiling. Andrew said it was only then that he noticed the small shiny stone tablet placed strategically on the mat floor between them. It was polite custom for a visitor to notice and enquire about anything nice that he observed in the hut of his host.

'What is this beautiful thing that sits on the mat between us?' Andrew politely enquired said his notes.
Ogemtali smiled his pleasure.

'This is the 'Thinking Stone'. It carries great wisdom,' said Ogemtali. 'You may inspect it.'

He then picked up the tablet and held it up in both hands and presented it for Andrew's inspection.

Andrew wrote in his notes that it was about six inches square in size and about half an inch in thickness and quite smooth in appearance with softened edges. The chief then brought the stone further forward towards Andrew indicating that he wished Andrew to hold it.

'You honour me greatly Chief Ogemtali,' responded Andrew reaching out and taking hold of the tablet in both hands. Andrew wrote that he made a great show of examining the tablet and feigning great wonder at it. He noticed that the tablet was exceedingly smooth and cold to the touch and he instantly felt intrigued by it.

'It is a thing of great beauty and you are fortunate to possess such an object,' said Andrew turning the tablet over and over in his hands.

'Then it is yours to keep and admire and it would honour me for you to possess it,' said Ogemtali. 'It will give you great wisdom and peace.'

'Thank you Chief Ogemtali,' said Andrew, 'this poor man accepts your gift with gratitude and thanks.' Andrew had become well versed in the harmonious traditions and rites of the Dogon people. The chief nodded his head repeatedly and smiled his pleasure at Andrew's proper responses.

Andrew wrote that he always wore a gold watch on his wrist and that it had often been remarked on as an ornament of beauty by the family he lived with. Here in the chief's hut he was reminded of the custom never to receive any gift without being able to give one in return. And he had noticed the chief eyes looking at the watch from time to time during their conversation. So Andrew slipped the watch with its flexi strap off his wrist and cupping it in his open palms reached forward in a presentation gesture towards Ogemtali.

'Please accept a humble gift from a poor man in token of the friendship between us,' said Andrew smiling and nodding as was the custom.

'This Hogon Chief accepts your honourable gift with great pleasure and may you have a long and fruitful life,' said Ogemtali and without further ado he picked up the watch and slipped it onto his wrist with a wide smile of pleasure on his cracked and lined old face.

Andrew had by now got used to the dim lighting in the interior of the hut and glancing politely around the room observed the lamp's light reflected on a number of other similar shiny stone tablets placed at several strategic positions. There must have been at least six that Andrew could see and Andrew wrote that he suspected that the chief had many more.

Seeing Andrew's look of enquiry the chief explained that his people had found many of these tablets littered around the country; and in their wanderings and ancient migrations they had managed to collect quite a few. Ogemtali said he believed that countless numbers of the tablets existed around the world and that the Nommo had placed them there.

'And why do you call these beautiful objects as 'thinking stones' my chief?' enquired Andrew smiling politely.

'The name was given by the Nommo,' replied Ogemtali. 'Perhaps the stone gives you something to think about. But I feel that it relaxes me if I place one against the side of my face, especially if I am troubled and can't sleep at night. The Nommo are a very wise and clever people even if they do prefer the sea to the land.'

I put down Andrew's diary and thought about what the chief had said. But I knew that there must be a great deal that Ogemtali did not divulge. I wondered then whether I should retrace Andrew Pando's footsteps and hopefully meet the Hogon. Whether Chief Ogemtali was still alive was doubtful since he was already a very old man in 1991. But I was sure tradition would have prevailed and any newly elected Hogon would have all the knowledge of his predecessor.

I looked at Tania and conveyed my thoughts to her but she could offer me no advice on the matter.

I then picked up the 'thinking stone' and once again tried to trace its historic origins but nothing came into my mind. This was most unusual. Perhaps it might be true that it was brought to earth thousands of years ago and had been placed around the world in their hundreds of thousands. But what would have been the purpose?

Tania was reading the second diary and looked up to see me staring at the stone I held in my hand.

'What is it Ashley?' she asked aloud with concern.

'Oh I don't know,' I replied slowly. 'I have been so used to getting my own way with the knowledge of things that I took it for granted that my inner voice would help me out and explain what this stone was all about. But I get nothing. It's an absolute blank. Why would an extraterrestrial people plant thousands of these tablets around the world at a time when we were all so very primitive? And how are these stones still around today and in such a pristine condition?'

Tania put down her diary and came and sat down beside me.

'I don't know either my love,' she said with her hand on my arm. 'Perhaps it's a sort of a trial or test. Or...' Tania stopped short in mid sentence and sat bolt upright.

I read her thoughts and conveyed back, '\That's a possibility.'

'Let's think about it, but let's get the whole family together Ashley and get a multiple opinion. How about this weekend at your mum's then Eric can also be there,' responded Tania.

'Sounds fine to me' I conveyed back telepathically and then I spun around and stared at the 'thinking stone' as did Tania. Then we stared at each other asking the same question.

'Did a sign of approval just come from the stone?' we both conveyed together.

And we both thought 'Impossible, we must have imagined it.'

Tania came and stood beside me and put her arm around my waist. I did the same while holding the stone in my free right hand. I held it up as though it was a mirror and stared at my own reflection in its shiny surface.

'Excuse me stone,' I asked of it telepathically, 'did you just convey an approval? Please repeat that if you will.' Nothing. Complete silence.

'I repeat myself to you the Dogon's thinking stone,' telepathically again from me. 'We definitely did receive something from you. Are you Nommo from the star system Sirius and messengers to the Dogon and Sumerians?' Nothing. Complete telepathic silence again.

Except I had a strong compulsion to do what the chief Ogemtali had said to Andrew about finding peace and relaxation which was to place the tablet against the side of his face. So I followed his example and placed it at the right side of my face.

I looked sideways down at Tania and sensed her love flow towards me and I responded in kind with all my own love for her. Then Tania without thinking came around to me and placed her face against the tablet so that it rested between us touching both our cheeks.

Nothing happened at first but then gradually a feeling of peace and calm came upon us and we both felt totally relaxed and at peace with the world.

On instinct I conveyed my life story to the thinking stone which took barely an instant. I don't know what made me do this but at that moment I felt it was the absolutely necessary thing to do. Somehow my inner voice also indicated that it had been the right thing to do and that I had conveyed a very important piece of long awaited information. But who or what was on the receiving end of my life story?

I believed that if Andrew's research with regard to the Dogon legend was true then according to Tania's sudden hunch these might very well all be listening devices planted on the earth by the extraterrestrials to monitor us humans. But was it a two way system and more important was it still active after so many millennia?

Again there was no telepathic response from the stone that I had half hoped for but did not really expect. Nothing at all; except now a feeling of euphoria and joy seemed to fill the room that even entered into our own minds. I don't know why but I also felt extremely happy.

I queried Tania's mind and asked if she felt what I was sensing.

'Yes Ashley I do, I do,' she conveyed telepathically while hugging me tighter. 'But what is it, I don't understand? Is it the stone, and is it really a thinking stone?'

I'm glad that I had my girl here with me at this moment as I might have been a bit nervous on my own. It was an eerie feeling that came across to me. It was like sensing a ghostly presence in the room. All sorts of thoughts raced through my mind with regard to the 'thinking stone'. All I was sure about at the moment was that it had conveyed its own mood to us in no uncertain manner. First it was peacefulness and then pure happiness.

Suddenly I felt a trebling of my love for Tania and an impulsive and spontaneous desire to hold her close. And I sensed the same emotion from Tania. There was excitability in the room that seemed to defy rational explanation. I began to kiss Tania and she responded with a fierceness that excited me beyond my wildest expectations. This normally sedate and rational person had been changed to one with a recklessness of desire and passion. It was beyond my understanding and I didn't seem to care. Our lips were clamped together in a firm actively engaged mouth-lock with our tongues probing forcefully. Our hands were similarly engaged and caressed where they willed. Our passions were running completely wild and against our normal moral code. This was reckless abandon of our emotions and my inner voice reined me in with the cautionary thought that this was a test of wills. I pulled myself back from the brink. My mind was open to Tania and my thoughts were conveyed instantly to her.

This really was a 'thinking stone'. It could induce peace and joyousness in our minds. Now it had shown that it could also induce hot-blooded physical passion too.

Tania and I looked at each other. We were still breathing heavily from our frenzied clinch exertion and now we just smiled at each other. We rubbed noses indicating to each other that we were back to normality again. The 'thinking stone' lay on the carpet where it had fallen. Tania smoothed out her dress and then reached down and picked up the tablet.

'Don't ever do that again whoever you are,' she said in a loud angry voice full of indignant emotion. 'That was an underhanded thing to do and not at all pleasant. Let me convey to you the emotion of shame which is what you should be feeling at this moment. Or are you shameless?'

Tania looked at me and shrugged her shoulders. 'It's like talking to a brick wall,' she conveyed as there was no response from the stone.

However there was a different mood in the room. It was a strong desire to visit and be with friends and family. What was the stone trying to tell us? The emotion was to go to a celebration of sorts with a firm desire to meet and make new friends. We were in party mood. Suddenly the whole scenario burst upon my consciousness as though a brilliant light had been turned on.

My telepathic skills were simply the conveying of my thoughts and intentions in a non-verbal manner into the mind of a recipient or recipients. But now I was made to feel that my telepathic skill was just a very basic and primitive form within the telepathic range. There had to be higher levels of mental contact similar to what we had just experienced.

I believe that telepathy in general would gradually evolve on Earth and I think that Tania and I had already taken it to another level. We could induce in each other a positive surrounding of emotional love. Tania must also have had the same thoughts and she conveyed these to me and I instantly concurred.

'Ashley,' she whispered aloud, 'who are these people that they can manipulate our minds so easily? Are they listening to our every thought?'

'It would appear so my love,' I replied. 'But I don't think we should do anything that they suggest. Let's just play a waiting game and see what transpires.'

I now sensed an emotion of sadness as though something of value had been lost. Like when friends have gone away and you know that you miss seeing and talking to them.

'Tania my darling,' I said in a loud affected voice, 'I don't think the 'thinking stone' can pick up our verbal communications. I think it is tuned to only pick up thought waves whenever we communicate telepathically. So let's revert to normal speech for the time being.'

'O Ashley,' said Tania laughing, 'that will be a relief because I was beginning to miss your dulcet tones.'

I couldn't help laughing at that and Tania joined in.

I put the stone tablet back on my bookshelf and we went to watch a program on TV. We sat together on the sofa in a sort of semi-cuddled up fashion more snug-as-a-bug-in-a-rug style than lovey-dovey.

'Ashley,' queried Tania, 'you know when we had that moment of passion and reckless abandon all I could think of at the time was that I wanted you to be a part of me more than anything else in the world. I still do but not like that. That was too full of wildness on both our parts and it scared me. It was not love but raw passion now that I can think back on it. These people must possess a great power to be able to induce such passions in the minds of ordinary humans. What worries me is that if they wished they could do the same with regard to the other emotions such as hate, jealousy, greed, a desire to destroy or kill and so on? They could literally make the unsuspecting person do as they wished.'

I was silent for a full minute. Somehow I didn't think that Tania's fears were a correct interpretation of what had occurred. My inner voice raised no alarms so I gave her my own thoughts on the matter.

'Perhaps and perhaps not,' I said aloud. 'I think that what we felt was an overflow of their emotional state. Don't forget that I had just responded to one of their induced telepathic queries which led me to reveal my life story to them. It was just after this that we sensed that tremendous feeling of euphoria and joy. For them a wonderful discovery had been made. And what do you do when you receive such exciting news? Why you just want to dance and laugh and hug the person closest to you. And that is exactly the emotion we sensed and very strongly too. It was because we love each other so much that we got caught up in the joy of the moment and got carried away. I don't think they intended anything sinister. But now I can imagine what it might be like on our honeymoon.' I was smirking as I said this.

'Ashley Bonner!' exclaimed Tania kicking my foot in the process but half smiling at the same time. 'I'll have you know that my parents brought me up as a decent girl to behave in a decent fashion. I'm not one of your run of the mill floozies to do with as you please, thank you very much. So mind your manners or you'll be sorry.' Tania was trying to make a frowning expression at me but not making a very good job of it. I just smiled and looked up at the ceiling before we both burst out laughing. I do love this girl.

'Seriously Ashley,' she continued, 'if you are right, and I do think you may be, then hearing about all your super gifts from the information you gave in your life story must have been the cause of their jubilation. So do you fit in with some special project of theirs and are you like a long awaited someone or something important to them?'

'You know my love,' I said, 'you could be right. It may also mean that the last emotion we felt of wanting to go and make a social visit and meet new friends was their own emotion of wanting to meet up with us.'

'So how to we go about arranging that?'

'Well I think we can leave it to them. They must know where we are surely. I'm presuming of course that they are somewhere on this planet or pretty close by. If not then we have a long wait.'

There was no point in speculating further so we decided to call it a day and go out. Since it was still early Tania suggested we eat out at the Kashmir Diner we had been to before which was not far from the shop. When we got there the place was rather full but when 'Charlie' the diminutive waiter spotted us he come over with a hello and a big smile. He said there'd be a table for us in about five or ten minutes if we didn't mind waiting where we were.

'Not at all Charlie,' said Tania smiling her best toothy smile and putting an arm around my waist. 'Just tell Yusaf to get my chicken tikka masala started, I'm starving.'

Just then a group of four began to make their way from the far end of the room. Charlie followed them and replied to something one of them said. They were all smiling and were in a happy mood and seemed to be regulars as they were talking to Charlie on familiar terms.

As regulars we all called him Charlie even though his real name was Tariq Rashid. Yusaf the chef was his brother as was the owner Riaz. Both Tania and I found this a very relaxed and friendly restaurant which was why it was such a popular place for us.

After the meal I drove Tania home and over a mug of hot chocolate conveyed to Milly and Jerry all that had happened with regard to the 'thinking stone' and our speculative thoughts about the possible extraterrestrial people from the Sirius star system. Jerry was quietly thoughtful and said that he'd like to experience the stone for himself.

'I'm planning a meeting of our group at mum's on Saturday lunch time,' I conveyed, 'and I'll be bringing the stone for all to see. You can feel it then to your hearts content. But I must warn you it employs a very advanced form of telepathy. So beware.'

'If someone is listening in to our thoughts through this stone device,' said Jerry aloud, 'then they can't be very far away. They have to be on the Earth or very close to it for thought waves like light waves take time to travel distances. And their response was fairly immediate from what you said so they have to be relatively near.'

Milly rang my mum and after a short chat passed the phone to me. I conveyed all the day's events telepathically down the line and mum was silent for a considerable time. I didn't know what she was thinking but I guessed that the events of the day had brought back the old concerns for my welfare. Mum used to worry about where all my gifts would take me and now it seemed that the big task that Philip had mentioned was about to become known. She knew about my recurring whitish glowing ball dream and had never taken that lightly. Mum also had a very strong intuition about things and I think she foresaw a potential danger and worried about it. I felt that her concerns were not unreasonable and in fact only reflected those of my own.

'Saturday lunch will be fine son. I'll tell your dad and Katy about it and make sure that your granddad is here also,' she said just before hanging up.

The next day was midweek and back at the shop everything was as usual though it was a good day for business with Robin making the most sales upstairs. Milly and I had given Robin complete control and responsibility for the museum section of McGill's and he revelled in it. He had his own sales counter and Cash Till with mobile card reader and had even had the place decorated in colour coordinated wallpapers. Robin had made it a cheery place though he did wish for a bigger space to display more of his 'toys'. When I suggested he put rummaging boxes in the corners of the room he had leaped at the idea with enthusiasm and put an additional two in the middle area as well. Robin had become an addict for the Sunday car boot sales and knew exactly where the one in the Midlands was always being held. I told him he could recover his petrol expenses from the petty cash at £20 a trip with no questions asked as was also the case for our tea and coffee makings. There was never a doughnut expense as Lorraine Hollings would often pop over for a tea and a chat and invariably bring a bag with her. Milly, Tania and I often discussed and wondered at the relationship between her and Robin and whether it might progress further. But they seemed content in their current routine and it was pleasant watching them enjoy each other's company. Robin had once hinted that they each preferred their own homes and he was quite happy with the status quo arrangement. Milly and Lorraine had formed a liking for each others company and Lorraine visited even when she knew that Robin was out at one of the home clearance auctions.

Tania was now at her teacher training course and quite liked it. As part of the environmental studies her course group was to spend a few days away in Salisbury on a study tour at the end of the following week.

It was late in the week when Katy rang me. She said she was at the Criminal Courts and would like me to come over tomorrow and help sort out a case as a special favour to her. She explained that it was a murder case before a jury and it was to go into its third day. Katy said that the prosecution had a police statement from the accused in which he is alleged to have confessed to the crime during the enquiries over a year ago.

'O Ashley,' said Katy, 'the defence lawyer maintains that the 26 year old man has a mental age of between six and ten and had no idea what the police were asking him at the time and simply agreed to everything they put to him. The man's name is Peter Hindle and he lives with his widowed elderly mother a woman named Moira Parkes. She reverted to her maiden name after her husband died several years ago.'

Katy gave me the rest of the case details as she had been at the case since the first day.

Another elderly lady of sixty-nine named Lucy Hambling was used to walking her Jack Russell dog in Sutton Park every evening. She lived on Monmouth Drive close to the park's Boldmere entrance. Peter was often seen in her company and they seemed to get on well together. He would wait near the park gate every evening and witnesses said that Lucy would wave to Peter when she saw him and they would walk into the park together and follow a path through the gorse bushes led by her dog Bluey.

Then one day both Lucy and Bluey were found dead between densely packed bushes. Both of their heads had been bashed once by a large blunt object but no such object had been found anywhere near the scene of the crime.

The police had spoken to several people who frequented the park and from them Peter Hindle's name had been obtained. The police were gruff in their approach to Peter who instantly broke down in tears and said how sorry he was that Lucy and her dog Bluey were dead. The police interpreted this as a sign of guilty remorse and took him in for further questioning and subsequently charged Peter with the murder of Lucy Hambling. Of course Peter had wanted to be helpful and said yes to everything the police suggested. And when he said he used to wait every evening for Lucy and Bluey to appear at the park entrance the police upped their charge to one of premeditated first degree murder.

Katy had got all this from the opening statements of both sets of lawyers but it was the defence counsel plea that the case be dropped on the grounds that the defendant had a mental age of a child and so could not have committed the murder let alone have planned it that got Katy interested.

'Oh Ashley,' Katy pleaded, 'you must come. Peter looks so lost and I know he couldn't have done it.'

'Okay sis,' I said, 'I'll be there in the morning.'

'Its Courtroom Three,' she added, 'but I'll wait for you at the entrance. And thanks bro.'

I spent the evening on my own as Tania was out with her college friends. After watching the news and 'The One Show' on TV I picked up the stone tablet and sat back down with it in my lap. I had forgotten to switch the TV off and there was some sort of a row being enacted on Eastenders. There was also a quite a bit of swearing involved and I thought how unreal it all was. I reached for the remote and just as I was about to press the off button I had a sudden desire to find out what happened next. I paused for just an instant before switching off the TV. I had never been interested in the program and was not about to start now. So now I knew a bit more about the 'thinking stone'. It could read the thoughts that came into my brain from me watching TV. In which case if I went for a walk and took the stone with me that all my experiences would also be received by my extraterrestrial friends. I felt that the thinking stone was simply a very advanced monitoring system and communication device. Who were these people and where had they really come from?

According to the Dogon legends these stones had been brought to Earth thousands of years ago. And yet my inner voice encyclopaedia indicated that the Sirius star system had no habitable planets whatsoever. My research also indicated that Mesopotamia was the cradle of Earth's civilization and it was the Sumerians who had first begun to develop socially in the late sixth millennium BC. What influence had caused this sudden spurt of development? I wondered if that was when the thinking stones were first brought to Earth. My 'Lych Gate' inner voice said yes, but I was still not certain.

Somehow I had expected that whenever I desired some information or a piece of knowledge that it would be revealed to me more or less instantly. I was being naïve to say the least. For instance I still didn't know of the big task that Philip had last referred to. However, I did know for a fact that a couple of hundred thousand of these 'thinking stones' had been distributed around the world. But by whom and how long ago was not revealed to me.

The Sumerians developed a complex system of metrology, a system for a scientific viewing of weights and measures around 4000 BC which then resulted in the creation of our mathematics, geometry and algebra. I would think that all this had to have originated from some form of masterly tuition. Could the 'thinking stone' have been instrumental in any of this?

The Babylonian astronomers knew a few thousand years before Copernicus that the Earth and other planets were spherical and that they revolved around the sun. Thus they could calculate and predict accurately lunar and solar eclipses. The motions of stars and planets were calculated according to complex equations inherited from the Sumerian civilization. But the Sumerians had even more exact knowledge of the solar system and its place in the universe than the Babylonians. Their annual calendar of around 3000 BC is the model for our calendar today.

Andrew Pando's research was very thorough and he listed all the phenomenal achievements and predictions the Sumerians made. I wonder if there was ever any visual contact between the people of our Earth and the supposed visitors from Sirius. So far I could find no direct reference to such meetings. Yet the Dogon myths according to Andrew did indicate that a benevolent half human half merman type of creature and called Nommo came to be seen occasionally. I very much doubt whether an alien being would present itself to primitive man who would have been full of prejudice and conceit. A meeting would then have been fruitless, unless they thought they had found someone or something of importance.

I guess that then points to me. Am I the one to finally meet and converse with them? That is if they even exist at all. But I feel it in my mind that they do exist and as Jerry said they must be reasonably close to be able to communicate through the thinking stone. I was back in my home now and still none the wiser.

'Get a TV of your own my friends from Sirius.' I communicated to the stone telepathically.

'Not Sirius,' somehow came through to me. Although this was not a telepathic communication nevertheless it was a loud and clear conclusion in my mind. I was shocked speechless, or should I say telepathically silent and aghast such that the stone slipped from my hand and fell to the carpeted floor. Slowly I picked it up again and stared at the reflections in its polished surface.

A feeling of good humour pervaded the room and I could sense that someone somewhere was in a jolly good humour; probably at the fact that I had gone blank with amazement.

'Excuse me!' was my shocked response. Then the humour of it all hit me and I began to laugh out loud. It was a laugh of exhilaration and discovery and I felt like yelling out the word 'Eureka!' The thought in my head was that perhaps I should have used the phrase of that famous meeting in the African jungle so long ago, 'Dr Livingstone I presume?' The more I thought about it the more I saw the funny side. I could sense the amusement within the stone that I was holding tightly in both my hands. I stared at it closely and received a very pleasant sensation of friendliness and welcome.

'Not Sirius,' came through into my mind again but this time it was accompanied by another name, that of 'Barnard's Star'. And I suddenly knew that our space visitors were from this new system and not Sirius as given in the Dogon legends. So I queried my mind about Barnard's Star and was immediately given a full analysis.

Barnard's Star is a low mass red dwarf star just over six light years from Earth in the constellation Ophiuchus. It intrudes into the zodiac between Scorpius and Sagittarius and is in the general direction towards the centre of our Milky Way galaxy as viewed from Earth. It has very low brightness luminosity and is not visible from Earth with the unaided eye. Sirius on the other hand is the brightest star in the night sky and was probably indicated to the Sumerians simply as a general example of where the 'extraterrestrials' had come from.

Barnard's star is about ten billion years old and considerably older than our own Sun's four billion year age. Barnard's star can be considered among some of the oldest stars known to astronomers. In size it is a fifth the size of our Sun and is heated by convection currents from within and so burns less furiously and is likely to last a trillion years in its current state. In contrast our Sun is likely to burn out in another five to eight billion years.

Barnard's star is one of the fastest moving stellar objects in the galaxy and has a true relative speed to the Sun of about 140 kilometres per second. The 10.3 seconds of arc it travels annually amounts to a quarter of a degree in a human lifetime, roughly half the angular diameter of the full moon. It is also tracking towards our Sun and in about ten thousand years will have approached to its closest distance of just under four light years; after which it will steadily recede.

It has the occasional stellar flare which reaches nearly twice the 3000 degree temperature of the star. This indicates that Barnard's star has a strong magnetic field which suppresses the internal plasma convection resulting in these sudden outbursts. There is plenty of life in the old star yet!

Its luminosity is low compared to our Sun and if it were the same distance as the sun is from the Earth then it would appear only a hundred times brighter than a full moon. However on a planet that is about a third of this distance at about thirty million miles Barnard's star would appear considerably brighter and hotter and have ideal conditions for life roughly similar to that which we have on Earth. And I can confirm that there is a near Earth-size planet within this zone. It is one of four.

I could understand how easier it may have been for the visitors from space to have pointed out the bright star Sirius as their home. It would have made it simpler for our primitive ancestors to understand.

There was no further communication through the stone tablet and I suddenly felt quite tired out so went to bed. I was meeting Katy in the morning at the Queen Elizabeth Criminal Courts and wondered what new adventures might unfold there.

I was a bit late getting there in the morning as there had been two train cancellations for some maintenance work on the Wolverhampton Line. The rail company apologised for any inconvenience caused over the Tannoy speaker system at Tipton station.

Katy was waiting outside the entrance impatiently though I had sent her a text message about being delayed. We managed to find a couple of seats in the very last row in the upstairs visitors' gallery and it looked as though the proceedings were nearing a conclusion with the prosecuting attorney presenting his summation speech.

I concentrated my thoughts on Peter Hindle who was sitting between two prison staff on a raised area on the left side of the courtroom and facing towards the jury seated opposite. I read his thoughts but they were a confused jumble of mixed emotions, though a visual image of the woman Lucy Hambling and her little dog Bluey were rather prominent. My mind raced back to the day of the killings and I could see Peter walking hurriedly down Boldmere Road towards the park entrance. He had been to the recycling bins to drop off an old pair of shoes his mother had given him and he had got a bit confused about which bin to use. Someone had shown him though and he was soon on his way to meet Lucy and Bluey. When he got there he could see them ahead and well inside the park. He ran up to them and said a pleasant hello. Bluey liked going down towards where the geese were near the North end of Powell's Pool just around from the children's play area. As usual Bluey broke left to yip at the geese but got hissed away by two rather vicious ones.

Peter and Lucy chatted away merrily as they walked a well worn grassy path towards the Longmoor Pool just ahead. It was some time later and well into their walk that Bluey ran between some gorse bushes and didn't return. Lucy called to him repeatedly but to no avail. They came upon him lying on the ground with blood pouring out of a head wound. He was still breathing but had his eyes closed and lying very still. Lucy looked around to see who could have done this while Peter sat down beside Bluey and began to cry while rubbing his hand down the furry little back.

My mind's eye then raced to a copse of trees about a fifty or sixty yards away and I could see a couple of thirteen year old boys Nigel King and Jimmy Clamp. They had fashioned a sling out of two lengths of clothes line cord attached to a makeshift canvas pouch. They were taking it in turns to see who could send a stone the farthest. This was not their first time with the sling and they were now quite proficient in sending quite large stones a fair distance but not necessarily in an accurate direction. However, they were both getting better at it. They had discovered that the larger and heavier the pebble shaped stone the easier it was to twirl and the farther it went; and there were plenty of these large round smooth stones lying around on the Bunter Pebble base of the park. Jimmy Clamp was nearly an inch taller than his friend Nigel King and he had a more natural style with the sling.

'Look at me,' said Jimmy as he twirled the sling round and round above his head. See that bush way over there near that dead tree, I bet I can sling this stone near it.'

And he did. Only, it was the stone that knocked out Bluey.

'Aw shucks,' said Nigel taking the sling from his friend, 'let me have a go, it's my turn.'

He picked up a nice big round stone and placing it in the sling pouch twirled it around his head and then let go a bit too early. The stone flew in a completely different direction to that intended and whacked a tree way to his left.

'You're useless Nige,' laughed Jimmy. 'Here, let me show you how it is done. This time I'll get it smack centre into that bush over there.'

Jimmy took the sling off Nigel. He carefully put his hand through the large slipknot and tightened it around his wrist with the cord passing over the palm of his hand. He put his middle finger through the smaller fixed loop of the other end and curled the finger to hold the loop in place. He then placed the near fist size smooth stone into the pouch and swung it back and forth like a pendulum to obtain a throwing rhythm. He then began the overhead twirl and fixed his gaze on the bush far ahead. With one last forceful twirl he released the loop off his middle finger. The stone flew with a hiss and arced high into the sky before dropping right near the bush in question.

It struck Lucy Hambling on the side of her head just above her ear and she was dead before she hit the ground. There was a bit of a slope there and the stone rolled away downhill for some distance before disappearing beneath one of the many gorse bushes. Seeing Lucy fall down and lie still Peter began to scream.

'O God,' said Nigel, 'you've hit somebody. Get down before we're seen.'

The two lads then moved back through the copse and then out of the park. They had no idea of the seriousness of what they had done.

Peter eventually stopped screaming and his mind went a complete blank with the shock of it all. He got up slowly and began the long walk back to his house. He went straight up to his room and got into bed fully dressed even with his shoes on. He covered his head with the duvet and that was how his mum found him later when it was time for his Ovaltine.

I saw all this in but an instant and conveyed it all to Katy.

'O Ashley,' she conveyed back, 'you must let the whole court also see what really happened. It was an accident but one that was just waiting to happen. Lucy and Bluey just happened to be in the wrong place at the wrong time. Thank you bro I knew I could count on you.'

I smiled back at my beautiful sis and conveyed the whole scenario to the judge, the jury, the lawyers and the police and in fact to the whole courtroom as I had done in all those other cases. However, I added the compulsory hypnotic suggestion to the judge that Peter was innocent of any wrong doing and should be released to his mother's care forthwith. A full apology must be demanded of the police for mishandling the case and a reprimand from the court was in order.

There was a complete hush in the courtroom for an instant and then many an intake of breath could be heard. Then there was a clambering of noisy voices and a general pandemonium of noise broke out.

Katy and I decided to leave it right there as there was nothing more I could do or say.

'What is it Ashley?' asked Katy when she saw me come to a dead stop at the top of the stairs.

'I don't know,' I replied, 'but I'm sure I got a sense of someone congratulating me on a job well done.'

'Your new friends?' queried Katy telepathically.

'Possibly,' I responded.

I was however thinking that these 'new friends' as Katy put it had a much stronger telepathic power than I had first thought. And then the answer came to me. With thousands of these 'thinking stones' put on the Earth all those eons ago they must be all over the place at locations perhaps covered by tons of Earth or even under stretches of water. The Dogon must have retrieved and held onto their little hoard from ancient times. The whole of the earth then was like one giant listening outpost for the visitors from the Barnard's Star system. I shook my head at this new discovery that perhaps we were being constantly monitored.

Rather than catch the train back to Tipton where I had parked my car I decided to go home with Katy and give mum a surprise. Mum was pleased to see me and I got a tremendous hug from her. I felt like the prodigal son who had returned after a long time. But it had only been a couple of days. She cupped my face in her palms and silently conveyed all her anxieties. Was I okay with the new development? Did I think they meant me any harm? Did I know any more about them?

'Stop mum,' I said aloud. 'They just listen and convey their feelings telepathically. They pick up our thoughts but not our words when we talk aloud.'

'O Ashley I'm just a mother who….' she started to say and then abruptly stopped in mid sentence.

'What is it mum?' Katy asked before I could.

Mum smiled back at us.

'It's quite alright,' she said, 'I just got a tremendous feeling of peace and affection and a reassurance sensation with regard to Ashley my son. I feel wonderful and calm about these new friends of ours whoever they may be. Didn't you sense it as well?' Mum was looking at Katy and me.

'No mum,' I said looking across at Katy who also shook her head, 'we didn't. It must have been beamed solely for your benefit. I suppose you can give them a reply telepathically now that you have been properly introduced.' I was smiling like a Cheshire cat and quite pleased that mum had been contacted.

And that is exactly what mum did. I could see the calm come to her face and something additional which I couldn't fathom until she explained.

'My darling children,' she said her face glowing; 'these people are a kind and gentle race. They feel that a long search is about to be ended and that you Ashley my son are to be the instrument in saving both our worlds. They say that no harm shall befall you or anyone on earth. O I do feel so proud. I only hope I don't get a swollen head.'

'O I forgot to mention but dad won't be home tonight,' said mum to Katy. 'One of his trips down south to Aldershot he said. That's why his car is still here.'

Just then the door bell rang and we all came back down to reality. Mum opened the door to Mavis and Vicky whom I hadn't seen for ages. There were hugs and kisses all around and I felt that Vicky's kiss lingered a fraction longer against my cheek and her hug was a little bit tighter. I knew Vicky's thoughts but now that I was secure in my connection to Tania I didn't mind in the least. Not after Margaret's admiring glances down in London. I quite appreciate the attention and the admiring looks I get from pretty women; it is rather a boost to my ego. I liked the feeling that came with it which I had communicated to Tania. I was happy in my love for Tania but that didn't mean that I couldn't admire or be admired by other pretty faces or figures.

So I smiled at Vicky and said she was looking really lovely.

'And how is my friend Robert?' I asked her.

'O Robert's fine. He's down in London on his police training course. He should be back before Christmas,' she replied.

I sensed that she and Robert were somehow stuck in their relationship. Vicky didn't have that glow when she spoke about Robert. Not like when Katy was talking about her Robin Nesters, her banker boyfriend. Now there was a relationship somewhat similar to Tania's and mine.

'How's the Spanish coming along Katy?' asked Vicky when Mavis and mum had gone into the kitchen.

'O Vicky, I'm quite good at it now. Ashley gave me a few tips. But I'd like to go to Madrid for some real conversation practice,' replied Katy. 'You do know that Tania started teacher training college this term? But tell me what you've been up to?'

I left them to it and went for a wander around the garden. The shrubs were in decline now though the Hostas still looked quite good; except their leaves were rather full of holes from the slug army. As I walked around looking at the individual plants my mind was wondering about our Barnard's Star friends. I sent out a general telepathic curiosity query as I believed that I had progressed to a more advanced non-articulate telepathic form of communication that I thought might be similar to their style.

I immediately knew I would be meeting our new acquaintances face to face quite soon and that I would be taken to their home on earth and all my questions answered. I knew also that it would be necessary for me to demonstrate my special gifts in a positive and unambiguous manner. Apparently there had been others before me who had appeared promising but lacked the essential endowment. To them I was another one who excited their expectations. But they had been disappointed before by apparent wonder workers who professed magical powers but could not deliver when asked to demonstrate. I looked forward to my own series of tests.

I conveyed my own mood of exhilaration and confidence at the prospect and knew I had nothing to worry about. My gifts were real and that was all there was to it. How and why I had been given these talents was a mystery to me but I felt that an answer was fairly imminent.

Again a mood of joy and exultation pervaded my mind and an expectation that millennia of waiting might be over. I expressed my own joy at their happiness and when I returned to the house Katy asked me what I appeared so happy about. I hadn't realised that I had walked into the room with a big smile on my face.

'Gosh Katy I just feel happy,' and I winked at her as I took a seat on the settee beside them. 'I suppose I'm happy to see Vicky and Mavis again. And pleased to be at home among such beautiful women.' I smiled my best cheesy grin.

Mum and Mavis were back in the room with the tea tray.

'Your grandfather Eric said he'd be here for the lunch get together on Saturday,' said mum. 'I only wish that Ron and Brenda could be here too. Do they know the latest about the shop and all that you have been doing?'

Mum's query was circumspect on account of the presence of Mavis and Vicky.

'Yes mum,' I replied, 'I spoke to Uncle Ron the other day and gave him all the news. In fact he said they might visit for a long weekend in about a fortnight's time if the bookings stayed as they were. Did you know they have a temporary assistant for Julie? Her name is Barbara Milosevic and she's a relative of Jan Bogdan the polish plumber we met there long ago. Her English is very good and they've taken her on for six months as a favour to the two plumbers and she is currently working as a volunteer on a bed and board basis only. I'm sure she gets something from social services though.

Her widowed mother had a small hotel in Radom and Barbara had helped while she was growing up. Unfortunately business was poor and the debts piled up and they were forced to sell. Her mother found a job in a factory while Barbara had long term plans for a business of her own. She hoped to learn about the B&B business here and to eventually get her mother and sisters to help run one of her own as a family business.

'I'll ring Bren later tonight and tie up details,' said mum.

I spent a very pleasant evening with mum and Katy after Mavis and Vicky left. They planned to visit my granddad Eric next and apparently they did so quite regularly. I know that Eric did have a soft spot for Mavis and I think Mavis knew this and quite enjoyed the attention.

As mum had said earlier dad was on one of his visits for the MoD down south sorting out something technical and would be back tomorrow. He'd left the car for mum as a hire car was always provided for his trips away.

It was quite late when I drove back home to Dudley. That night I slept soundly and couldn't remember when I'd last had such a peaceful night. No dreams, no concerns, no nothing whatsoever.

Saturday dawned bright and sunny for an October morning and I got to Erdington quite early. Granddad Eric was already there and was pleased to see me again after my midweek visit. He'd not been too well then but seemed quite perky today. He wasn't driving anymore and dad had fetched him when he had rung up to say he was ready. Dad made sure his aging father brought all his medication with him.

We sat and chatted while mum did her preparations for lunch. Dad had come home quite late yesterday and never talked about work and mum never asked even though there was all this trouble in Iraq and Afghanistan. We knew that dad had had a big promotion and was responsible for a large new project. I didn't mind-probe as my principles prevented that where my family was concerned. Besides I'd never had the desire to do so either. And they all knew it. The same was true with regard to my friends and acquaintances.

When the others had all arrived and Tania and I had rubbed noses to everyone's amusement, I went to the car and brought out the six inch square stone tablet. I passed it to dad to inspect and then to pass on to the others in our group.

I waited while everyone had a chance to examine the stone before I conveyed telepathically to them everything that had occurred since my return from London with Andrew Pando's notes and diaries. I placed the 'thinking stone' on the mantel and I expressed the wish for it to get to know my family who were also in the know of my gifts so to speak. This was my way of introducing all my family members to our new acquaintances from another star system, if indeed that was the case. I still had vague doubts about that.

I then specially conveyed that the thinking stone only picked up our thought waves and so understood everything we were thinking. However it was unable to interpret our spoken words and so if we required confidentiality from the stone then verbal communication was the way to do it. I also conveyed that I knew that the stone tablet was a form of communication device that relayed information to our Barnard's Star visitors and that any emotion they felt was also transmitted to us.

'As you will presently experience,' I said aloud.

'What do you think their appearance is like?' asked granddad Eric.

Again I reverted to telepathy in the hope that our visitors would listen and convey an impression.

'I really haven't the faintest idea,' I conveyed. 'But I do know that their sun is twice as old as ours and so their evolution must be eons more advanced. Eight millennia ago they were travelling between star systems for a certainty to have visited Earth and met our ancestors the Sumerians. Consider the diversity of life here on Earth and the changes that have taken place over time. So they can't be too unpleasantly different to us or else how could they have got on favourably with our fierce and primitive ancestors.'

It was Jerry who again brought us down to basics.

'If the old myths can be relied upon,' he said, 'then our friends may well be residents of the sea. The Dogon accounts of somewhat amphibious beings landing their egg shaped craft in the red sea indicate to me that they are very similar to us but with a fishlike orientation to their facial representation. From what you conveyed to us Ashley, the ancient historian Hellandus wrote an account of someone who came out of the sea with head, feet and arms of a man but with a fishlike body and who then taught astronomy and the art of writing to the people of the day.'

I said that we would know soon enough since I was sure that it would not be too long before a meeting between us took place.

'I do believe they are keen to meet up with me ever since I conveyed my life history to the stone.' I said. 'Apparently they have been looking out for someone like me and I got the distinct impression that what they found out was very pleasing to them. I must fit in with some future plan of theirs whatever that may be.'

'I only hope they don't take you somewhere far away to suit their own plans,' said mum. 'I do worry that you might be given some great responsibility that even you cannot fulfil. I know they gave me a feeling of peace and affection and a reassurance with regard to my son but that doesn't mean that the big task that Philip mentioned does not have a modicum of danger associated with it. It would be awful if it took Ashley away from us. Barnard's star is light years away and if Ashley were to be taken there we might not be alive when and if he returned.'

She bit her lip and I could see her just managing to hold back the tears though I could see a distinct shiny wetness there. I instinctively sent out a message of love to all in the room just like Tania and I have learned to do with each other. I went to mum and sat down beside her and putting my arm around her shoulders squeezed her to me. No matter what may occur in the future one thing would not change and that was our shared love.

Suddenly a much more powerful sense of belonging and security filled the room. An assurance came into our minds that nothing would change. We looked at each other and our concerns seemed to vanish. Only pleasant thoughts remained. What also came across strongly was that there was no urgency of purpose about doing anything. Whatever needed to be done in the future was important but would be fulfilled as and when it was most convenient for us all.

I could feel that the thinking stone had transmitted our concerns to their home base and it had been clearly understood by these people and an attempt was made to allay those fears in a positive manner.

A desire to meet with us came as a thought into our minds and we looked at each other with raised eyebrows and the big question of 'when' came to mind?

'Soon,' came the thought back to us in a form that was conveyed as a general mood of eager expectation that was about to be fulfilled.

I thought then that perhaps our Barnard's star visitors were having difficulty in lowering their communication format down to our level of telepathy. They could read our thoughts easily enough and they could convey their general intentions but we were not picking up the detail of anything that they were probably trying to communicate. I conveyed these thoughts to the others in the room and to the thinking stone as well.

The 'meetings' thought and mood remained strong in the room and suddenly the thought came through loud and clear that it was not that our extra terrestrial visitors were unable to communicate at our primitive telepathic level but rather that the thinking stone was not designed for that purpose. It was simply a monitoring device – literally a listening outpost to read human thoughts and to convey a basic emotion or direct a line of thought.

I could see how development had been induced in the human psyche over the years – thousands of years – to gradually bring it towards modernity. I wondered why more influence had not been brought to bear to prevent some of the gruesome events of our history. Perhaps it was not their plan to interfere in this area and that peace in society was better achieved through difficult times than by inducement; a sort of 'learning from our mistakes' philosophy. When I thought about it I concluded that this was perhaps a more permanent social evolutionary process for the longer term betterment of society.

I therefore suggested that we keep nothing from the thinking stone and to conduct all our communication in telepathic mode.

But Jerry disagreed with this and said that we should just continue as normal as possible. Why should we change our behaviour?

'If they are monitoring us then let them get us in a truthful manner,' he conveyed.

'How can we act normally when we know everything we think is being listened in to?' from Katy.

'We'll just have to get used to it and carry on as best as possible, I suppose,' said granddad Eric aloud. 'If, and I say if we are being monitored then surely they- whoever they are – must have a pretty good idea of how we think and behave. We'll have to grin and bear it, not that it bothers me. What can't be helped must be endured.'

'Then if they are listening to us,' replied dad, 'why don't we convey a code of behaviour we expect from them. Perhaps we ought to suggest or even push for a face to face meeting as soon as possible. Surely as an advanced society they would command a very high degree of social etiquette.'

I could see how useful our little group meeting was in getting a broader view of the situation. As always two heads were better than one especially in this instance. Poor old Andrew Pando had no one to consult or to share his thoughts with. Or perhaps he had not progressed as we had. So I now conveyed dad's thoughts to the 'stone' and requested that we should meet as soon as was convenient or possible for them.

'From the Dogon myths 'they' are amphibious beings,' I conveyed telepathically, 'so I wonder if they would expect us to be somewhere near the sea. Somewhere remote I would imagine, preserving a modicum of secrecy.'

'They do seem to have kept to themselves since I never heard of them before this,' said Milly.

'I wonder if that is because they still consider us too primitive to mix with,' said mum. 'And yet they are interested in our Ashley now that they have learned about his gifts. I only hope its not just curiosity that has prompted them to want a meeting.'

Then mum looked at me and said, 'Ashley, promise me that you will insist that we are all in this together. And that we stay together as a family. I don't want you going off on your own with them in order to undergo some form of testing or experimentation.' Mum smiled as she continued. 'I am your mother and I worry about you. I always have since I first knew that you possessed such wonderful power. I knew you were born to a purpose but I don't know where it will take you. I have lain awake many a night considering the matter but never got near to an understanding of its purpose. And your 'glowing ball' recurring dream does seem vaguely important somewhere in the overall picture and which is a further worry to me.'

Again a feeling of peace and security pervaded the room and was quite strongly felt. Were our fears being allayed? I think mum's emotional state of concern for me had filtered through to the 'stone' and they were attempting to calm her fears.

My inner voice then began talking to me. This was a relief as I had begun to think it had deserted me. It said that the Dogon custom of greeting or 'Sewa' had been something that had been handed down through the generations and had probably begun when they had met another race of people. Perhaps even by the Barnard's star visitors. And also this emotion of wanting to meet with us that had filtered through so strongly from the stone was simply an indication of something that was wished for but could not be fulfilled without an invitation from us. As a very advanced civilization our visitors were loath to impose themselves on anyone and were therefore waiting for a formal invitation before committing themselves to a visit.

I conveyed my thoughts to everyone in the room and got back a mixed response.

'I had assumed that they could do as they wished being so advanced and all,' said Jerry. 'Surely they know where we are and can come to us whenever they choose. I wonder if all those UFO sightings and activity that has been reported around the west coast of Wales especially near Aberporth was them picking up our telepathic conversations there and trying to pinpoint where the signals were coming from. But then there was never any direct telepathic contact with them as we have now through this stone. I think I'm beginning to take a shine to these chaps and their suspected polite ways. Yes Ashley, by all means let's invite them to come and visit with us but where?'

'I would think they'd need a private location where there was plenty of open space around such as a farm or the like. I'm assuming of course that they would land from the air,' said dad.

Granddad Eric then conveyed that if they had been here on earth for thousands of years surely they must have managed to do a little bit of integration and disguised their selves in order to move freely around among us.

'I know what I would have done in their situation,' he said, 'I would have made myself a face mask of sorts and a suitable body disguise and melted into the crowds. What do you think?'

'What about plastic surgery?' from Katy.

'No, I think they might be under some form of social restriction to keep themselves separate and apart,' said dad. 'After all with all those thinking stones all over the place they could learn everything they needed to know about us. No, I think they have been watching, listening and waiting for a moment such as this. They have been looking for something specific and in Ashley I do believe they think they may have found it. If they are too polite to force themselves on us then we must definitely extend an invitation for them to come to us.'

'I suppose we could invite them here,' said mum, 'but it is rather public and confined for space.' Mum smiled as she added, 'Whatever will the neighbours say if they saw a mysterious object landing on our front lawn.'

It was Jerry the sensible who summarised our thoughts.

'Okay,' he said, 'are we agreed then that we extend as a welcoming gesture an open invitation for them to come and visit us? How about if we ask that just two of them come to dinner on a specific date and at a specific address? The question is where should that location be?'

'Aberporth,' said Tania, 'why not at Aunt Brenda's B&B in Aberporth?'

I liked the idea immediately and saw great sense in it. Not only did they have an acre of back garden but also there was nothing beyond it other that a huge expanse of field that no one seemed to be doing anything with other than to graze a few sheep occasionally. Further back the ground sloped up gradually and eventually peaked in a low hill that was covered in forest. Although we had tended to take most of our walks along the coastal paths there were occasions when we went for a ramble up the hill. Unfortunately there was no scenic viewpoint at the top because of all the trees. But I can remember little Barclay quite enjoying the run up there.

Both mum and I said 'Excellent' at the same time. We looked at each other and smiled. I signalled for mum to go ahead with her say first.

'Yes Tania my dear,' she said, 'now why didn't I think of that before. There's plenty of open ground there and not many people about. That way we'd be including Ron and Brenda in our adventure. What do you think darling?' This last was directed at dad.

'Yes dear,' he smiled, 'that would be ideal. What does everyone think?'

'Seems like an excellent idea,' said Milly and Jerry nodded his agreement.

'Well done Tans,' teased Katy with a broad grin, 'brains before beauty eh?'

Tania poked her tongue out at Katy and said, 'Thanks Katy nice to be finally appreciated. If they do take us anywhere I'm sitting in front; or at least at a window seat. I'll tell you when to open your eyes.'

They both laughed as did mum and Milly looking conspiratorially at each other. It was a look that said volumes and I knew what they meant. They were pleased that Katy and Tania already acted like sisters.

I hadn't thought about being taken anywhere in any spacecraft until now. Perhaps my big task lay somewhere off this Earth. Perhaps an asteroid or something similar was threatening the Earth and my skills were needed to push it aside in a path correction. Well there was no point in speculating and my 'Lych Gate' intuition told me nothing either. Life wasn't so simple after all even for me who supposedly should have the answer to most things. My instincts however, told me that my whitish glowing ball dream might just be something out in space that could become a reality sometime in the distant future.

'So when should we all get up to Aberporth?' I asked.

'Well,' said mum, 'why don't we make it the weekend that Ron and Brenda had originally planned to visit here. Only now we would be going up there instead. Let's give them a ring right now. Ashley perhaps you could talk first and convey everything that's gone on here today and then pass the phone on to me. I can then tie up the details of our visit. Eric you'll come as well won't you?'

'I wouldn't miss it for the world,' he replied. 'Who knows they might even have something new to ease all my aches and pains.'

I picked up one of the cordless phones and dialled. Uncle Ron picked up on the second ring tone. I said hello and conveyed that I had information so could Aunt Brenda get on the extension as well.

'I'm already here Ashley,' came from Aunt Brenda, 'what is it? What has happened?

I then conveyed everything we'd done and discussed today over the line telepathically and got an 'Oh I see,' from Aunt Brenda. This must be what it was like for the listeners on the other end of the thinking stone. Information must come in fast and furious from all over the world but now they had probably decided to concentrate their efforts on me. I wondered if they had suspected anything at all before I'd received the thinking stone. I think it's probably a yes to that.

'Here's mum,' I said aloud, 'have a word with her. She'd like to talk about the arrangements for us all to come over one weekend.'

I handed the phone to mum and the two sisters had a little chat before mum got on to the purpose of the call. After several minutes mum put the phone down.

'It's all arranged for the second weekend in November. Brenda reckons the B&B has no bookings then and we can all stay in comfort,' said mum.

'So is that when we invite our spacemen for dinner?' asked Tania. 'I should be back from my field trip by then.'

'Okay then,' said Jerry, 'how do we do this?' He was referring to the mode of conveying the invitation to their newfound friends.

'I think I should do this,' I said, 'since I seem to be the focus of their interest. But then again since we are all telepathically proficient why don't we do it jointly?'

Tania suggested we place the 'thinking stone' in an upright position like a mirror and then we can all look towards it and convey our invitation together. And that is exactly what we did.

'You know what?' said Katy, 'with bonfire night being so close to that weekend anything unusual in the sky wouldn't be given a second thought. Even if some stroller did see something they'd think it was just a Guy Fawkes gimmick thing.'

There was a new emotion now coming across to us in the room. It was an emotion that reminded me of when I was a child and we were just about to go away on holiday to the seaside. It was a thrilling feeling of anticipation for the joy of being on holiday and swimming in the sea. It brought back memories of the joy of my new play tent and I couldn't wait to have it put up so that Katy and I could play in it. And the thrill of my first little umbrella and how impatient I had been for it to rain so I could finally try it out. Like when I had done my homework essay and couldn't wait to get to class next day to proudly hand it in to the teacher.

I also recognised my present emotion as one in which I was keenly looking forward to meeting these new people whom I felt I was getting to know with a slight degree of affection. A feeling of well being and confidence came over me and I then knew that their response to our invitation was a positive one, a definite yes. This emotion that we were all experiencing was really their own emotion transmitted to us through this marvellous 'thinking stone' piece of technology.

We all looked at one another and smiled great big Cheshire cat grins.

'Now that is the best invite acceptance ever,' said Tania squeezing my hand and looking into my eyes.

'O Ashley,' she conveyed telepathically, 'although the future is unknown there is one thing I do know and that is that I love you with all my being and strength and I always will. And I feel so good about all of this.'

I leaned across and rubbed my nose on hers as we smiled at each other.

There was a great atmosphere in the room and first one then another got up and eventually we formed a great big circle with our arms around each other in a big huddle. I was between mum on one side and Tania on the other and I felt tears well up in my eyes. I felt as though I was passing through a door and into a blaze of light so dazzling that I was blinded by it. And yet I was not afraid or even apprehensive and I conveyed this to all in the room and also to the 'thinking stone'. The future looked bright, as bright as that mysterious glowing ball of my dream.

Later, as we were sitting at the dining table enjoying mum's cooking, Katy asked me to solve a recent crime. The crime had been reported in all the papers today and Katy said she had been particularly horrified at its violence. It was a robbery at a high street post office in Kenilworth and three people were in hospital with serious stab wounds. I normally pick up the Daily Mail each morning but had not had the time for a read of it on account of coming here to mum's.

'It's all reported on page five in dad's paper so you can read it after dinner,' said Katy.

'What's that Katy?' asked Jerry who was sitting at the other end of the table.

'Oh, I just mentioned to Ashley about that nasty hold up in Kenilworth that was reported in today's papers,' said Katy.

'O yes, I read it too. It's also in the Express,' said Jerry. 'It's a real nasty one too. And yet when they are caught all that they'll get is some years in prison and then let out in half the time. I feel sorry for the victims. I believe one is critical in hospital and not expected to recover.'

'So what happened?' I asked.

Jerry looked at Katy but she signalled for him to continue. By now everyone else was also listening and a silence had descended in the room.

'Well apparently cash is delivered to the post office on a Friday morning but for some reason there had been a delay,' began Jerry. 'Then at about ten thirty in the morning when the high street was quite busy and the post office crowded, three hooded men had rushed in and demanded that the postmaster open the safe and hand over all the money inside. Two of the men were reported as carrying large hunting style knives while the third had an iron bar which he displayed very threateningly.'

Jerry paused and took a sip of his drink before continuing.

'There was a lot of shouting which caused the postmaster's wife and teenage son to come out from the back rooms where they all lived. They were immediately grabbed as hostages and the raiders threatened to kill the pair if the postmaster didn't hurry up with the money. The man with the iron bar stood near the door and prevented anyone leaving. The postmaster gave them all the money he had which was only a few hundred pounds. They demanded more and when the postmaster explained that the Securicor delivery was late the raiders went into a frustrated rage. The knifemen began stabbing their hostages in the arms and legs continually demanding more money. The man with the iron bar ripped the cash register off the shop counter, smashed it to the floor and began bashing it with the iron bar till the cash drawer flew open. Apparently there was nothing much in there either and in frustration he struck out and hit the shop assistant a violent blow on the side of her head. The knifemen finally released the wife and son but viciously stabbed each in the belly before running out of the shop. Police think a fourth accomplice was waiting in the getaway car, a black Toyota. Police have taken statements from all the witnesses but the raiders were too well hooded for any one to give a description except that one of them was thin and very tall. The security cameras recorded everything but again no faces could be seen,' concluded Jerry.

O dear,' said Milly, 'what a nasty crime. I suppose they'll eventually be caught, sent to prison and then be out again in a year or so.'

'And which one is the most seriously hurt of them all and not expected to live?' asked mum.

'It doesn't say in the report,' said Jerry, 'but I would think it was the shop assistant who was hit on the head with the iron bar. You can treat a stab wound more easily than you can a smashed skull. Poor thing.'

I could see that Katy was quite upset at what these raiders had done and I think she wanted me to find and teach them a lesson like when she had seen me deal with those hooligans on the Brownhills estate. I suppose I could do something similar to these three or should I say four, for the car driver was just as involved in the crime.

I tried to concentrate my mind on the crime but could find no connection. I told Katy that I would need to be at the post office location to mentally view a re-run of the crime.

'Well the post office shop won't be open till Monday,' said Katy, 'so I could come with you then.'

'I don't need to go into the post office Katy,' I said, 'I just need to be at the location of the crime so we could pop around tomorrow if that's okay with you. There'll be less traffic on the roads as well.'

'Actually I was meeting Robin tomorrow but not till evening,' she said, 'so I'll come if we can be back by mid afternoon.'

'I was thinking why don't we then just give all the information to the police and let them deal with it?' I said. I didn't really want to go around punishing thieves and robbers even if they might deserve it. There was far too much crime going on for me to get deeply involved in every case.

'O Ashley' said Katy reaching over and touching my arm. 'Do this one for me please. Plan it in a way that will make them want to go to the police and confess everything. I know you can, please.'

How could I refuse my little sister when she said her pleases so pleadingly. It was just like this all those years ago when she'd beg me to catch another bird for her cage.

'Yeh, okay Katy,' I replied with a big smile. 'And I suppose you want to be with me when I scare the living daylights out of them?'

I thought I might do something similar to the Derek and Alan Williams case up in Worksop for stealing farmer Jake Pelling's antique Bird Jar. But I sensed that Katy wanted them to be given a bit of their own medicine, pain. I'd think of something appropriate on the spot including a hypnotic suggestion implant to make a confession to the police.

I conveyed all my thoughts to all in the room and I could see that mum approved. Mum didn't like me to play judge and jury as she didn't think I had been given my gifts just to go around the country bringing criminals to their senses. I wondered what our friends behind the 'thinking stone' might be thinking as they listened to our discussions.

'Yes please,' said Katy, 'that should do it nicely. Who else wants to come along and see Ash in action?'

'I'd like to come,' said Tania, 'though college also beckons. We're on a field trip next Wednesday and there's a tutorial about it on Monday. But tomorrow should be fine, count me in Katy.'

Milly changed the subject by asking if the clocks went back tonight.

'No darling,' said Jerry, 'that's next Saturday. Officially it's supposed to be done at 2 am on the Sunday but everyone does it on Saturday night just before going to bed.'

'I'm never quite sure. I know it's sometime at the end of October about half term time,' said Milly. 'And I can never remember whether it's putting the clocks back or forward.'

'That's simple,' said Katy, 'just remember the expression, 'spring forward and fall back'.'

'How clever,' said Milly, 'I shall remember that, thank you very much Katy.'

Our enlarged family gathering was a very pleasant one and I think granddad Eric quite enjoyed flirting with Milly even with an amused Jerry and Tania looking on. It was all very innocent and just a bit of amusement fun for someone who always appreciated the looks of a pretty woman. I know that Milly was quite flattered by the attention, and I do believe she encouraged him a teeny weeny little bit. We were all pleased to see granddad in such perky form.

'You know,' said granddad Eric, 'I see Mavis and her pretty daughter quite often. They came and saw me only this past week. Mavis could do with a man about the house you know.'

'Are you offering yourself dad,' remarked dad laughing. 'Besides they've got Vicky's young man to fix things for them. He's to be a policeman now and is currently on a training course in Milton Keynes I think. He should do well in the force.'

And so the evening passed. Tania and I sat together for a while on the back patio but came in as it got dark and chilly. The nights were closing in as winter approached though it was still fairly mild for October and there hadn't been any frosts as yet. There were still lots of plants in bloom in the garden though the Hostas had mostly wilted to a pale colouring. The Dahlias were sagging from the recent rain but nevertheless put on a good show of bright colours. It was usually after the first frosts came that all these would wilt and need pruning to ground level. Dad left his Dahlia corms in the ground over winter though he applied plenty of mulch over the area.

Back in my own bedroom in Dudley I thought about Aberporth and Uncle Ron and Aunt Brenda and the approaching meeting with our Barnard's star visitors. And I did wonder a bit what their appearance might be like before I dropped off to sleep.

Sunday was just as it was meant to be sunny and bright. After an ample cereal breakfast I walked down to the local newsagent near the bottom of my road and picked up the Sunday paper and had a good read when I got back to my comfy sofa. Tania rang and we had a loving chat for about twenty minutes. I told her I was thinking of driving over to Kenilworth a bit later on so would pop over to pick her up then. Perhaps about midday I added? She said okay she'd be waiting.

Actually I got to her place slightly before and we sat out in the back for a bit in the bright sun and just enjoyed each other's company. Milly brought us a mug of tea each, mine with one sugar just as I liked it. I couldn't understand how all the women in our families drank theirs without. Perhaps it was a slimming thing?

'What a lovely feeling I get whenever I'm around you two,' said Milly as she stood looking down at us.

'That's because you've entered our little circle of loving,' I said. 'It's something we've learned to convey telepathically when we are together. Remember that feeling of love and peace? You should try it when you're around Jerry and see if he senses it too.'

'Hmm, I think I might try it too,' she said thoughtfully.

The drive to Kenilworth via mum's place to pick up Katy took nearly an hour. We went via the M5 and then the M6 to mum's place and then the M6 again and got off at Junction 4 and onto the A452 going south. Kenilworth is a pretty place and seemed quite busy for a Sunday afternoon. I parked the car on Whateleys Drive which was just off the main street that was Priory Road and we walked back towards the post office sign we had passed as we drove in. The post office itself was closed of course so I stood outside it on the pavement and concentrated my thoughts to the past few days.

In my mind I saw a black Toyota pull up on the road in front of the post office shop. It had been splattered with mud and dusty Earth especially over the number plates. A little corner window was smashed and this told me that the car had been stolen and probably off someone's front drive early that morning while they still slept. There were four in the car and I could see all their faces clearly. The driver was a big girl named Mary Webster. She was nineteen and had piercings all over her face. Her eyebrows, ears - four each side – nose, lip and tongue. She also had an emblem tattoo on the left side of her neck. Beside her sat Usain Madi aged twenty three and an immigrant from north east Africa. He was very tall and thin and of a shiny black colouring and I knew he was Mary's lover.

'Okay, let's do it,' said a dark haired Ben Kaiser from the back seat. He was twenty six and the recognised leader of this little group. Beside him sat Lance Stogl aged twenty three the same as Usain except he was very blond.

Each of the men pulled down on their balaclava caps and rolled them down over their faces. There were small holes for the eyes and mouth only. Usain leaned over and gave Mary a kiss before he got out. She'd had her hand on his thigh all along and now gave it a tight squeeze.

The three of them then raced forward and burst into the post office shop and shouted for everyone to stand to one side against the bookshelves wall. Ben and Lance had their ten inch hunting knives out and began waving them from side to side.

There was a sales counter near the entrance with an old fashioned cash register on one side of it. Usain stood near this with the 18 inch iron bar in his right hand and guarded the door. He smiled confidently through his mask but was not to know that no money had been delivered that morning.

The rest happened just as Jerry and the papers had described it and it was Ben who had decided to begin stabbing the post master's wife and son who were all Asian. The lady at the shop counter was Naveed the postmaster's sister. She lived nearby with her own family and came to help in the shop most days.

When Usain heard that the post office safe was near empty he went into a rage and grabbed the cash register and smashed it to the floor. He then struck at it repeatedly till the cash drawer flew open to reveal the few notes and coins. While he had been at this Naveed began shouting to him that he didn't need to smash up the till as it was open so he swiped at her with the iron bar and caught her a whacking blow on the side of her head. She dropped like a stone.

All three raiders had adrenalin racing in their veins and they reacted violently to anything that didn't go to plan. The stabbings had been their instinctive reaction to the disappointment that very little cash was to be had. Grabbing what they could they raced out of the shop and leapt into the black Toyota that Mary had kept ticking over. The raid had taken less than five minutes and Mary gunned the engine and carefully pulled out into the traffic before racing away at speed to where they'd left their own car.

There was blood on the knives and both Ben and Lance wiped them clean on the car seats as they got out. These were good sturdy knives and hadn't come cheap. They could use them again on their next job.

They then drove north to the Chelmsley Wood estate area and Mary parked the car outside her maisonette on Greenlands Road. All four went in and Mary put the kettle on to make them a hot drink. Ben emptied his swag bag onto the coffee table and counted their haul. They'd only got £310 when they had expected thousands. Ben divided it to £70 each and told Mary to put the remaining money towards the petrol for her car.

Later they each went to their own houses as they all lived nearby. Ben had a bed-sit in Marlene Croft while Lance was just around the corner in Marlene Crescent. Usain was a bit further away on York Minster Drive in a halfway house setup. All three men had served several stints in prison while Mary had been at a youth correction facility twice, the first time when she was just thirteen.

I conveyed all this telepathically to Tania and Katy and I could see the look of determination in Katy's expression when she said, 'Okay, so let's go sort them out now.'

'Alright,' I said, 'we'll go but only to see where they live and nothing more today. I'd like to think this one through,'

Tania didn't say anything but Katy looked a bit disappointed. I said that there should be no rush in meting out punishment after all we didn't want to do anything rash or illegal.

Katy conveyed that she had some thoughts for the iron bar and the knives. She'd like me to wrap the iron bar around the neck of the African Usain Madi so that he couldn't get it off without professional assistance. And that I should fish hook bend the tips of the knives and insert and lock the tips upwards into the thigh bones of both Lance Stogl and Ben Kaiser. It was what I had done to that schizophrenic Joshua Dray in the chip throwing incident. That would teach them a very painful lesson. Katy also conveyed that she'd like me to put a fear into their minds that would deter them from committing a crime ever again. She left that for me to plan and I said I would.

Tania had picked all this up as well and said she agreed with everything Katy had suggested.

We drove back along the A452 and into the Chelmsley Wood estate. Katy had my A–Z street map open on her lap and directed me to the address at 21A Marlene Croft. We stopped on the road just outside Ben's bed-sit and looked up at the first floor window facing us. There was no one in and I conveyed this to Tania and Katy.

'Let's go in and take a look around,' said Katy, but I responded that it would not be a good idea just at the moment. I'd rather he was in and on his own for me to do what I was planning. A rough idea of the punishments I'd administer was already forming in my head.

We then drove to Lance Stogl's flat at 63 Marlene Crescent which was just around the corner from Ben's bed-sit. This too was unoccupied at that moment. I sat looking at the upstairs window and here again I had the mental view of a bed-sit similar to Ben's.

Next and quite close by on Greenlands Road was the girl Mary's maisonette. This was on the ground floor and there were two largish ornamental pot plants of faded artificial roses on either side of the front door which had been painted a deep magenta colour. There was someone in the front room watching TV but it was not Mary. I needed to find out who this was so we all went to the door and rang the bell. The door was opened and a young teenager looked at us curiously and said 'Hello?' questioningly.

I read her mind and determined that this was Mary's young sister Veronica. She lived with her parents in a semi on Helmswood Drive which was a good ten minute walk away. She'd let herself in with the key that Mary kept under one of the pot plants after getting no answer to the door bell.

'Hello,' I said in return. 'You must be Veronica. Is Mary in?'

'No she's out,' she said impatient to get back to her TV program. 'Who shall I say called?'

It was Katy who jumped in quickly with a reply. 'O just tell her that Roger, Tess and Jane called about the puppy. We're from animal rescue and Mary was around last week and we were given to understand she'd like one of the little fellas as a pet. Just tell her to contact us again if she has decided, she's got our number. Come on Roger we've two more places to visit and I haven't had my dinner yet.'

I was smiling and so was Tania as we walked back to the car. I thought what a quick witted liar Katy was. I conveyed as much to Katy and she smiled back.

Tania looked at Katy with admiration and said, 'How did you think up those names on the spur of the moment Katy? And which one was me, Tess or Jane?'

'Why you've got to be Jane,' said Katy mischievously, 'as in Tarzan and Jane.'

I lightly beat my fists on my chest and made a crude yodelling sound and said, 'Me Roger.'

And we all burst out laughing as we got back in the car.

We then drove to York Minster Drive a bit further along and off the main Chelmsley Road to the halfway house of Usain Madi. It was a large four bedroom semi that had been converted into student type flats. All the bedrooms were on the first floor and Usain had a room with a wash basin plumbed in at one corner by the window. The other rooms were all occupied by other ex-prisoners who were all also of African origin. They shared the one bathroom which was also upstairs. A second toilet was downstairs beside the tiny cloakroom.

All four residents were in the common lounge downstairs and were watching the football on Sky TV. Mary was there too and was sitting snuggled up on Usain's lap.

I conveyed all this to Katy and Tania and indicated that I'd prefer to catch Usain when he was on his own. And I'd like to attack all four of the gang separately though on the same day. Katy suggested that in the early morning before they went out would be a good time. I agreed.

We drove back to mum and dad's place and stayed for mugs of tea. I conveyed the details regarding the post office raiders and again mum indicated that all the information should be passed to the police and for them to arrest the lot.

But Katy disagreed and said that they at least needed to be taught a lesson and feel a fear that would deter them from doing the same again. She said that criminals like these welcomed the notoriety of being arrested and sent to their mates in prison.

'Mum,' she said, 'I promise I won't ask Ash to do this ever again, but I do want these raiders well and truly punished for what they did.'

'Okay darling,' Lillian said, 'but do be careful. And Ashley take it nice and easy and don't be too harsh with them. It can be disastrous – for the criminals I mean.'

I could see what mum meant. Perhaps I should stick to the mental hypnotic suggestions of guilt and pain than physically stabbing the knives into them. I'd think about this. Yes I'd think about this a lot. After all there was the very real danger of them complicating the wounds by their own attempts at extracting the blades. They might even bleed to death. Alternative ideas came to mind for which I said 'Thanks mum'.

Monday morning was wet, cold and windy. Autumn leaves were blowing everywhere. For some reason they collected in piles at odd places in the open on drives and pavements. The leaves reminded me of penguins huddled together for protection from the polar winds – from the TV documentaries I'd seen of course.

I had picked up Tania and we drove in silence to gather up my aggressive sister. Tania reinforced mum's thoughts with regard to the raiders and I felt obliged to take that into account. Actually I felt better in myself because of it. But I obviously had to take some sort of action or Katy would never leave me in peace. It was now clear in my mind of the course of action I should take and I conveyed this to Tania. She smiled her thanks and reached over and squeezed my arm. I smiled back at her.

Katy was still in her aggressive mood though I sensed a mellowing of intent. Katy said that she and Robin had discussed the newspaper article about the post office raid last evening on their night out, and it had been a point of discussion in their party group. They had all expressed their indignation at how ineffective the law was in deterring criminals and how it was all weighted to protect the rights of the criminal. It was always a popular topic of discussion.

When Katy had expressed her opinion of a suitable punishment one of the group had said, 'Gosh Katy, that's a bit strong isn't it? Next you'll be advocating that their hands be cut off for theft and their 'thing-um-a-jigs' for rape.'

Katy conveyed that she hadn't quite meant that but just that she felt so frustrated that people like these raiders got away with the proverbial murder that she felt something more ought to be done to deter them.

Yes, I definitely felt that Katy had had time to think about it all and her attitude towards a suitable punishment in that direction was somewhat tempered.

'Perhaps we ought to rethink some of the things I suggested,' she said reaching forward from the back seat and touching my shoulder.

'I understand sis,' I said. 'Don't worry, I've decided to follow mum's advice and play it down a bit. There'll be no stabbings.'

'Thanks bro,' she said after I'd conveyed my full plan of action to her.

The first home we stopped at was where Usain Madi lived. I entered through the front door by pushing the spring catch open through my gift of telekinesis. I walked up the stairs and paused outside the door to the right. It was not locked so when I turned the handle it opened. I entered the room quietly and was lucky to find that Mary was also there and in the bed fast asleep. Usain was stripped to his boxer shorts and was leaning over the wash basin in the far corner of the room and cleaning his teeth. He turned to see me by the door whereupon I immediately read his mind and induced the hypnotic suggestion that he was totally blind. I added that his blindness would continue until he made a full confession to the police about the post office raid. He must include the names of his accomplices in that confession. After that his sight would return but only to be lost again if he even contemplated returning to a life of crime. I added the proviso that accompanying all phases of his induced blindness would be an excruciating arthritic like pain in all the fingers of his right hand. The hand he had used to wield the iron bar which had struck and nearly killed the shop assistant.

His cry of confusion and pain woke Mary and she sat up and looked at me. I immediately went into pink mode and walked across and pulled the covers back. She was completely naked. 'No violence' came as my 'reminder' so I re-covered her and then picked up the iron bar that was under the bed. It was the same bar that Usain had used in the post office raid. I bent it into a U-shape and then placing it around Mary's neck bent it further to form a loose but fitting ring around her neck. I then returned to normal mode and induced in her mind the hypnotic suggestion of a pain in her stomach whenever she was in viewing contact of any of her fellow raiders Usain Madi, Lance Stogl or Ben Kaiser.

Her immediate cry of pain was loud and shrill and I knew that one or other of the residents were bound to come to see what the noise was all about. She also began swearing at me something awful. All the while Usain Madi was moaning and squeezing his painful right hand with his left one.

I returned to pink mode and walked out of the room, down the stairs and back to the car before returning to normal mode. I opened the door and sat down behind the wheel and telepathically conveyed to Katy and Tania all that I had seen and done. We could hear the shouting and swearing coming from the house and we all smiled at each other in satisfaction.

'I like what you did with the iron bar,' said Tania.

'That came to me on the spur of the moment when I saw the bar under the bed,' I said. 'I had thought about trashing the place but that would have been puerile and quite pointless and could have created a sympathetic response from their fellow house mates.'

'I'm quite pleased at what you did bro,' said Katy. 'I actually feel better in my mind too that there has been no bloodshed or violence. The last thing I'd want is to start feeling sorry for them.'

'Shall we proceed to the next patient or should I say victim.' I smiled as I said it.

'That would be Marlene Crescent and Lance Stogl,' said Katy who had the A-Z street map book open on her lap. 'The other place is quite close too on Marlene Croft. Take your pick.'

'The first one will do,' I said impatiently, 'let's get this over with.' Suddenly I felt guilty about what I was doing. Did I really have the right to be judge and jury over my fellow man? But then I had also seen in my mind that these were definitely the perpetrators of the post office raid.

We stopped outside Lance's bed-sit and I listened with my mind for his thoughts. Yes, he was still in bed and thinking of getting up and making himself a mug of tea. He was unemployed but today he needed to collect his benefit money from the local post office. Somehow I didn't think he'd make the journey today.

I entered the building with ease and went up the stairs and knocked on his door.

'Who is it?' shouted the voice from inside.

I knocked again rather more insistently this time and added a muffled 'It's me' in a falsetto feminine voice hoping he'd think it was Mary.

'Just a sec,' was his reply and after a brief moment the door was opened wide by a smiling Lance who froze when he saw me.

It was a large untidy room with clothes on the floor and on the chair and corner table. And it wasn't clean either as the old carpet could have done with vacuuming. The bed was unmade and was in the corner well away from the window through which the early morning light filtered in. The overhead light had no lampshade just a naked low energy bulb in the holder. The net curtain across the window was quite grey but suited my purpose perfectly.

I went into pink mode and slipped past Lance and into the room. I walked across to the window and stepped behind the net curtain before returning to normal mode.

'Hello Lance,' I said in a bass voice, 'remember me from the post office? I've come for you to join me in my grave.'

He turned towards my voice and looked horrified at the shadowy mask like image profiled prominently by the grey white net curtains. I had to smile my satisfaction at his reaction.

Once again as in Usain's case I read the man's mind and induced the hypnotic suggestion that he was blind and would remain so until he confessed to the police about his part in the post office raid; and for stabbing the postmaster's son in the arms and legs and finally deep in the belly which killed him. Although the son was still alive in hospital I wanted Lance to think that he was in fact a murderer. He must also name all his accomplices. After that his sight would return but only to be lost again if he even contemplated any crime. I added the hypnotic suggestion that accompanying his blindness would be an excruciating arthritic like pain in the fingers of his right hand. The hand that had held the knife he had used to stab his victim.

There was a single loud exclamation of pain from Lance before he crumpled to his knees holding and squeezing his painful right hand with his left. He was moaning quietly while moving his head from side to side and squinting with his eyes as if trying to see. I suggested he dial the emergency services for help and tell them he was having a stroke and that he had suddenly gone blind.

I discovered through reading his mind that he kept his big hunting knife under the mattress of his bed at the pillow end. I walked over and got it out and for a moment wondered what I should do with it. The thought then came to me of an anklet for Lance so I went into pink mode again. I first ran my finger over the sharpened edge to blunt it and then I wrapped it tight around his right ankle. The ten inch blade and handle overlapped nicely and it would require professional help to cut it free. I returned to normal mode and quietly left the bed-sit, walked down the stairs and out to the car.

I conveyed the whole scene of events to Tania and Katy and was pleased to sense their relief and pleasure at the way I had handled the whole affair.

'I do like the ghostly image you portrayed Ashley,' said Tania. 'I wonder what effect that will have on him?'

'I don't hear any shouts or cries from the flat,' said Katy.

'Some people have a high threshold for pain and I think Lance is one of those. He's quite a stoic from what I read of his mind and not one to admit to pain. I just wonder if he will ring for help right away or delay it as much as he can. I expect the pain in his hand and the discomfort of the anklet will eventually tell.'

'One to go,' said Tania. 'I'm actually beginning to feel sorry for this lot even though I know I shouldn't.'

We drove around to Ben Kaiser's address on Marlene Croft which was barely a minute away in the car. The sun had come out from behind the scudding clouds and everything looked really bright.

Tania leaned across and gave me a light kiss and wished me good luck before I got out of the car.

'Good luck Ash,' said Katy too as she put a hand on my shoulder and squeezed lightly.

After entering the common front door I walked up the stairs to Ben's bed-sit. I had a very odd sensation of anxiety as I did so. Something had prompted an emotion and put me on my guard.

Could it be our Barnard's star friends telling me to be careful? I wasn't sure.

As I took the last step to the landing a figure rushed out at me and I could just see a glint of silver from the corner of my eye. A knife was thrust at my midriff and just as it touched my shirt the world turned a deep rosy pink and everything seemed to be shrouded in a thick fog. I could barely make out Ben Kaiser's contorted face with his snarl expression showing his gritted teeth. All was frozen in time and I easily moved away from the knife. I instantly knew what had happened. Mary Webster must have phoned Ben to warn him and put him on his guard.

The bed-sit door was open so I very carefully put my arms around his waist and picking him up carried him back into his room. I lay him on the single unmade bed and only then went into a lighter pink mode. For me it was like watching a slow motion film as I saw Ben gradually relax and sink onto the soft mattress. I took the knife from his loosened fingers and for a moment thought to give him similar treatment to the one meted out to Joshua Dray on the Midland bus. After all he had just tried to stick the knife into me. But I remembered mum and so just blunted the sharp end of the knife and carefully bent it around his neck. It didn't quite go all the way round and left a gap of about an inch between the tip and the base of the handle. He'd have a job getting it off.

I then returned to normal mode and putting my hand up to shield my face I induced the hypnotic suggestion that he was blind. This would be accompanied by a severe toothache in his upper left wisdom tooth. He could only expect relief from both these symptoms when he confessed all his crimes to the police. The suggestion included the fact that the blindness and toothache would return whenever he thought about or contemplated committing another crime or an act of violence.

Normally I would have thought that becoming blind and undergoing severe pain would have induced a feeling of fear but Ben was made of sterner stuff and I had to admire his grit.

He had one hand cupping his jaw and with the other he felt the air in front of him. He stood up and began walking towards me. I moved away towards the door and left the room for the landing. He knew I had gone.

'Bastard,' he shouted at me, 'you bloody bastard I'll kill you. I'll kill you. Come back here you bastard.'

I walked back into the room.

'I'm back,' I said before going into pink mode again.

I'd decided to reprimand Ben with further punishment for his unrepentant attitude. Mary must have primed him on what to expect so he had geared up his own mind to accept the blindness and some pain. Well he was in for a surprise as to the pain factor.

I pinched both ear lobes, flicked his forehead with my index finger, did the same to both shin bones and the lightly jabbed him in the belly. For good measure I gave him a light slap on his back before leaving the room a second time and returning to normal mode.

This time he gave a loud painful scream and I'm sure Tania and Katy must have heard it across the street.

I heard Ben fall to the floor and his repeated invocation to a deity as 'O my god, O my god, O my god' in a kind of half sobbing, half gasping exclamation.

'Ring the police and confess,' I shouted up at him as I walked down the stairs. I then left the building and walked out to the car.

Tania and Katy were smiling when I got behind the wheel but both felt concerned when I conveyed the whole series of events beginning with the knife attack.

'That was a quick reaction on your part,' said Katy referring to the knife thrust.

'No it wasn't,' I replied. 'It happened automatically. I remember the first time it occurred too. It was at that school cricket match between the first and second teams. I think I was about twelve then. I'm glad I said I was going up there on my own. He might have stabbed one of you before I'd have had the chance to react. Though I think someone tried to warn me of danger as I was climbing the stairs. I wonder if it was the thinking stone.'

I could see Tania's concern for me. She put her hand in mine and squeezed tight.

'O Ashley,' she said, 'it could have been the end of you if it wasn't for your super gifts. I worry that this big task of the future might be too much even for you. I'm not afraid to die, but I just don't want to. I want us to have a long and happy life together. Promise me you'll take extra care my darling, for all our sakes.'

I looked at her and conveyed all my love to the zone surrounding both her and Katy. They knew I would, as I was not going to lose any of this. I conveyed that my crime fighting days were over as of now. I would henceforth concentrate on our meeting with our Barnard's star visitors and prepare my mind for the big task ahead; whatever that might be.

We drove back to mum's place for a well earned breakfast. It was just after nine o'clock.

Mum was pleased that I had not been too physical when dealing with the post office raiders but wondered whether I also ought to convey their names and addresses to the police as well. I thought about it but then said I'd wait a day or so as I was sure that my hypnotic implants would do the trick. Besides, if they did in fact report their crimes to the authorities then that would be their first mental step to a conversion onto the straight and narrow, so to speak.

I was glad to have done this for Katy's sake but conveyed to her that it would be the last time I did it. Henceforth I'd rather not solve crimes or try to punish the criminal mind into gentler ways. Not that I was saying never again but simply that it had to be a very unusual circumstance of events to get me involved again. The solution had to come via an evolutionary process in the natural development of our society. Crime needed to become an inhibition within the mind as the person matured from infancy rather than through control after the fact. The majority of the population were decent law abiding people so I believed that society was not as bad as portrayed in reports in the newspapers. I do believe that the good will eventually influence the bad in the long term.

And yet street crime is not the only evil that occurs out there. There is after all corporate crime that occurs within the moneyed classes of our society all over the world and which goes by many different names. And it is all done for the same monetary gain in a pretentious civilized process. But then the human mind is complex and devious and a variety of passions are built into it. We shall never be rid of these for then we should lose all our character as a nation. But enough of my philosophising; mankind will eventually evolve towards a boring utopia – let us hope we never quite get there.

Back at the shop it was business as usual though Milly and I continually talked about our trip to Aberporth in a fortnight's time. Tania went off on her college field trip to Salisbury Plain and the time just flew by and it was the weekend again which I spent at mum and dad's place.

Tania had returned on the Monday and we spent a very pleasant evening together. I had missed her laughter and chatter and of just being with her and I conveyed as much to her. She laughed and said that her own days had been so full of new things to do that she had only thought of me when we had our conversations over the phone in the evenings. And then too she'd been quite exhausted from the day's tramping about that she would just get into bed soon after their evening meal.

There were six of them to a dormitory style accommodation and it was surprising how little chatter there was between the girls before they all dropped off to sleep once they'd snuggled into their beds. There was another similar field trip planned for sometime after Easter next year and this would take them up north around the Manchester area.

I spent the next few days in our McGill's shop with Milly and Robin and a few busy days they were too. There were visits from Hillcrest and other schools and Robin was in his element relating tales of 'the old days'. In many cases these were a bit fictional but nevertheless quite entertaining for the children.

Business was good as usual and both Milly and Robin expressed the view that we could do with a bit more room. I was loath to the idea of relocating to a different site as we were central to the town and very accessible where we were. I said if either of the adjoining shops became vacant we could grab the lease. Alternatively we could expand by simply extending the building rearwards for a longer room provided planning permission could be obtained.

'Would that include the upstairs?' asked Robin.

'Why of course Uncle Robin,' I replied, 'it's the upstairs I was chiefly thinking about.'

Milly smiled at that.

'And how soon will that be?' said a keen Robin.

I looked at Milly and conveyed my agreement telepathically along with a nod of the head.

'Well, Uncle Robin,' she said slowly, 'let me see now. First we'll have to get some plans drawn up and then have them submitted to the planning people. And if that meets with approval then we'd have to find a builder and agree a price and a start date. It all takes time but I expect it could all be done in about eighteen months or so from start to finish.'

Robin looked up at the ceiling and rolled his eyes in mocking fashion before shaking his head and heading back upstairs.

'Are we serious about extending?' queried Milly looking sideways at me in that way of hers that I came to recognise as her sceptical stance.

'Well why not?' I replied. 'It's worth thinking about. I'd rather extend than move from Kings Street to some strange posh estate. I think Philip would be of the same view, don't you? Besides we owe it to his sister Grace to keep to her original site for as long as possible.'

'I'm not sure,' said Milly slowly. 'Bigger is not necessarily better. But we certainly could do with a bit more space as we are a bit full up.'

'Have a word with Jerry and see what he thinks about the expansion,' I said.

I knew that Milly valued Jerry's opinion in all things as he was practical and down to Earth in his thinking. He'd point out the benefits and any shortcomings in the plan and probably come up with some practical suggestions of his own. There was no urgency for the idea which was at the present just a passing thought. But a favourable one that grew on me the more I thought about it.

I nodded to myself and thought, 'Yes, why not and maybe about time too,' and conveyed as much to Milly telepathically.

Time passed and the weekend approached. Each evening Tania and I sat and communicated silently and in our usual affectionate manner but now we also did our messaging for the benefit of the thinking stone which we placed at a strategic location nearby. We discussed the approaching meeting in Aberporth and expressed our keen anticipation of the prospect of coming face to face with people from another world.

I tried to visualise in my mind what they would look like but I received nothing from my mental library. Could the historian Hellandus have been writing about the same people when he described the appearance of a man named Oe who came out of the Red Sea having a fish-like body but the head, feet and arms of a man? Some accounts however stated that he was actually a man but only seemed fish-like because he was clothed in the skin of a sea creature. A similar description was made by the Babylonian priest Berossus in the third century BC whose writings had just about survived in fragments.

Tania and I tried to assemble a rough image from these stories yet all we could imagine was a man's face with minor variations. If the ancients considered them man-like and learned from them then they must be a very presentable looking race of people.

'Ashley,' conveyed Tania smiling, 'I feel like laughing yet I don't know why.'

I too smiled at the thought. The thinking stone was conveying the mood of our listeners at the other end and they appeared amused at our speculations. The feeling also came across that we would be pleasantly surprised at their appearance. A sense of keen anticipation filled the room along with an emotion of affection for a good friend. Tania and I both had a very strong sensation that we were going to like these people. I conveyed this to the 'stone' and an even stronger emotion returned to us to fill our minds with affection. This was certainly a positive beginning.

Friday finally arrived as a bright sunny morning and the sense of anticipation in the shop was noticeable. Robin even commented on it over the doughnuts we had with our eleven o'clock mugs of tea. Milly and Tania just smiled at him and said what a pretty place Aberporth was and a weekend of leisure there in the company of the Davies and Bonner families was certainly something to look forward to.

'The west coast is too windy for my liking,' said Robin, 'I prefer somewhere like Bournemouth or Poole. Now those are the places to go to even in the middle of winter. Christmas can be very festive there with all the lights and all.'

'So are you going to take your lady friend there one day?' I asked jokingly. I think I was teasing him.

'Nooo,' he replied wistfully, 'she's too prim and proper for that sort of thing. She's overly conscious of what the neighbours might say; which is rather a shame really.'

'Then why don't you make a decent woman of her Uncle Robin?' asked Tania quite seriously.

Robin smiled at that and said, 'That would be a step too far for us at our age. Besides we're good friends and we do enjoy one another's company so why change the status quo.'

Robin liked his little Latin quotes but often got them mixed with something else. Then he added, 'Are you really serious about the extension?'

'Of course Robin,' said Milly, 'but you must be patient as it won't happen overnight. It is a slow process but I will get started on it when I return from Aberporth on Monday.'

Robin had agreed to close up the shop at the usual time today as we had planned on leaving for the coast at about three. I had packed my overnight bag as had Tania, Milly and Jerry. We were all travelling together in the one car. Mum, dad, Katy and granddad had already set off sometime that morning. Both dad and Jerry had taken the whole day off from work.

There was not too much traffic or any hold-ups on the way so we arrived in good time albeit after dark about six o'clock. We had the B&B to ourselves by design as both assistants Julie Griffiths and Barbara Milosevic had been given the weekend off. A 'Full-Up' notice was clearly displayed below the B&B sign.

We all exhibited a keen sense of anticipation and Uncle Ron and Aunt Brenda were quite taken by the appearance of the thinking stone when I brought it to them in the lounge. I conveyed everything about the stone to them and suggested they give it a telepathic 'Hello' and then welcome it to their home and any other thoughts they might like to convey.

'I know that telepathy is a very efficient form of communication and we are now quite good at it,' said Aunt Brenda, 'but I do like to hear Ron's voice as he does mine. And the same goes for you all too my dears. So let's have a little bit of both please.'

'Here's something now for you Aunt,' I said and then filled the room with a feeling of love and affection for my family so that all could feel it positively and knowingly. I then conveyed that Tania and I had discovered this new skill by accident. At first Tania and I had just communicated our love to each other but then discovered that it gradually grew until it became a tangible cloud that surrounded us.

'When you love or like someone then this is a lovely way of conveying it,' I said. 'You should try it.'

'And it is also how the thinking stone has been communicating with us,' I continued. 'So far it has conveyed it's moods of joy and anticipation at meeting with us, a reassurance sensation of friendship, a sense of congratulations on a job well done, a feeling of joyous exultation in a new discovery, and a sense of curiosity about me and my gifts. O yes, passion and love also came across at one point but that was misread by us I think.'

Tania went a beetroot red at this last reference so I immediately conveyed as briefly as possible about us nearly getting carried away by our emotions of affection for each other and of Tania subsequently reprimanding the thinking stone about that and then receiving back a new mood of contrition and apology.

'I wonder how we are to communicate with these people when we are eventually face to face with them tomorrow,' said Jerry. 'That is if it actually does happen. I still cannot quite get to grips with this and I can hardly believe that we might be meeting people from another planet.'

'If Andrew Pando's research notes are correct then it would not be the first time that these people have met with humans,' I said. 'They came to Earth thousands of years ago and conversed or communicated with men and gave them an insight into letters and science and art. They then presumably taught man how to construct buildings and temples, to compile laws and explained to them the principles of geometrical knowledge, mathematics and astronomy. They must have communicated telepathically as this would have been the most efficient way of implanting all that information in man's then primitive mind. Compared to them I suppose we might still be considered primitive though perhaps a little less so.'

'Except for you Ashley,' said mum. 'I somehow know that you are the key to something extremely important to them for why else should they have been awaiting your arrival for so long. They do know all about you since you were induced to reveal all about yourself to this thinking stone.'

I could not help thinking about the 'big task' that lay ahead and which Philip had mentioned at our final communication. I was certainly getting all the support I needed from my family but I had no idea at all of where I was going or what I was supposed to do. I could only be certain that it was somehow intricately connected to the gifts I had been given from when I was a child. I had made progressive discoveries of each gift as I grew older and I wondered if there was more to be discovered. I had no inkling of the path ahead nor where it would lead but I firmly believed that the desire to fulfil my destiny and to achieve whatever was needed would be a satisfaction to all including myself.

My inner voice conveyed much that I had wanted to know of the future and I somehow came to realise that the fear I'd had that I might lose my family was unfounded. We would all stay together and just as I would have wished it. My destiny was connected to our Barnard's Star visitors but I would ensure that it was based upon my terms and my welfare at least in the short and medium term. What the very long term held is something I would deal with when the time came.

There was much discussion between us on these lines and it was way past midnight when we all finally decided to go to our rooms and to a welcoming bed. Tomorrow would begin a turning point in my life. At least that is what I believed.

Chapter 11

New Friends

November 2003

Saturday November 8th 2003 dawned clear and bright and quite mild for the start of winter. Aberporth was a sleepy little place on a weekend and Ashley's group all slept late. They had gone to bed in the early hours after much excited discussion at the prospect of the developments to come. Sleep had come only gradually to each after they had retired to their own rooms and their beds. Ashley didn't think he had really slept at all apart from a little doze in the early hours.

Ron and Brenda had to wake as usual when their radio alarm began playing shortly after seven o'clock. But they stayed in bed to savour the mugs of tea that Ron made for them and brought up. With no other guests to cater for they spent a rare relaxing morning in bed and talked about the expected 'visitors' that evening. There was no doubt in Brenda's mind that 'they' would most certainly turn up as the thinking stone had conveyed this quite clearly.

It wasn't till close to nine o'clock that they heard the house begin to creak awake as someone else began to move about. Yes, their guests were definitely stirring so the two of them decided to venture downstairs to the kitchen and boil some more water for tea. Brenda had shown everyone around the kitchen cupboards the night before in case anyone wanted to make themselves a hot drink during the night or early morning. So Brenda was not surprised to see her sister Lillian in there waiting for the kettle to boil and still in her night clothes though with an open silk dressing gown over the top. They spoke to each other quietly via telepathy and talked about things that sisters often do. Alex and Ron joined them and Brenda told them she would bring their mugs of tea to the lounge if they cared to go in there. All were in their night time pyjamas.

'Okay,' said Alex smiling, 'we'll let you carry on with your sisterly gossip. Come on Ron, we know when we're not wanted. Let's see what's on the news.'

Brenda made a face and poked her tongue out at her husband and said, 'Stay if you want but I know you'll only be embarrassed by our women talk.'

'No thanks,' said Ron, 'we'll go to the TV lounge. It should be quite sunny in there and it is just about time for the hourly news.'

Just then Katy and Tania entered the kitchen and said a good morning to everyone. Ron and Alex threw up their arms and with horrified expressions and feigned a hasty retreat smiling as they went. Ashley also in his night pyjamas joined them half an hour later when they were into their second mugs of tea. Tania told Ashley there was a recently made pot of tea in the kitchen when Eric appeared all dressed up ready for the day. Lillian told both men to get comfortable while she brought them their drinks. Ashley only drank tea but Eric liked his first cup to be coffee and he liked it black and with two sweeteners. Lillian knew all his habits and went into the kitchen and Tania followed her.

It was well after ten when they all went back to their rooms to wash and dress with the exception of Eric who sat watching the news on TV. Eric had a thing for the news channel and could happily watch it on the hour every hour. Alex said it was a thing his dad had about being the first to get to know of any spectacular news and so be the first to tell everyone about it.

After breakfast it was agreed to go for a stroll along the coastal path as it was such a lovely day. They waved hello to Peter Ellis and his wife as they passed by their hillside carriage cottage home which was now quite bare of its previous summer floral displays.

The day seemed to drag ever so slowly but that was only because Ashley and Co wanted the evening to arrive sooner for their expected historic meeting with the visitors from the Barnard's star system.

'I wonder how they'll arrive,' said Tania aloud as she squeezed the hand she held in hers. They were once again seated back in the B&B and the sun was low in the sky. No one answered as it was just a random thought expressed aloud but which had also been on everyone else's mind.

Lunch had been a proper dinner of stew and dumplings and Brenda had said she wanted it to be the main meal of the day since she couldn't be sure what time their visitors might arrive. There was apple pie with hot custard to follow though Eric said he preferred his plain. It was not that he didn't like the custard but he preferred to taste his apple pie unadulterated by any other tastes or flavours.

As the evening drew to a close and the sun drifted downwards and finally rested on the brow of the hill to the south west the group got more restless. The sun finally sank behind the hill and suddenly the sky seemed to glow a brighter shade of light blue. And as if finally seeing its chief competitor retreat the huge full moon began to make itself known; it peeped through the shadowy haze that marked the distance to the north-east. During each solstice the sun and moon traded places as if by agreement on who would occupy the higher position and where they rose and set. This November night the full moon would travel that great arc that the sun usually followed in the months of May or June. It was the perfect night for a streetlight approach for visitors arriving from the sky.

As the dark settled and a chill developed with the evening dew, Ron suggested they all return to the warmth of the TV lounge. Ron knew that soon the cold sea breeze would begin to penetrate their layers of clothes and chill their bones.

'Oh look,' shouted Katy pointing upwards into the western sky. 'What is it? Is it them?'

A very bright star was travelling slowly and was moving from the West to the East. It travelled slowly and majestically without a twinkle or sound. They all stared silently up at it as it serenely went across the heavens. Of course the same thought was in all their minds as it reached a point in the overhead sky. But it didn't stop or even slow down; it just continued onward quite unconcerned.

It was Jerry who began to chuckle and they all looked at him quizzically as if he were daft or something.

'Just because we're expecting visitors from space it doesn't mean that the first moving light we see in the sky has to be them. I've just realised that the star we can see is the sun reflecting off the International Space Station. It is the largest man-made object in space so it is also the brightest. It should disappear as soon it passes into Earth's shadow which should be about there,' said Jerry pointing to an area in the eastern sky.

The point of light travelled at its regular pace and soon reached the area that Jerry had indicated. But the moving light continued eastwards to a point further along before eventually disappearing. One moment it was there and the next it was not. Gone like when a light switch is turned off.

As they strolled into the warmth of the house a car approached slowly and after a brief hesitation drove into the B&B car park and stopped in a spot near its centre.

There were two occupants in the car and at first appeared to be rather small people or even two little ladies. They sat in the car for a good little while before finally opening the doors and getting out. The one nearest the B&B stood waiting while the other walked around the front of the car. Both were about the same height which was just about five feet. They wore long dark overcoats with collars turned up against the chill of the night and dark coloured Fedora type hats tight on their heads. Both then began a slow walk towards the well lit front porch of Ron and Brenda's B&B.

Ashley stood up in the lounge and cocking his head to one side said, 'They're here. They are in the car park and are walking towards the front porch door. There are just two of them.'

'Wait here,' said Ron smiling with pleasure, 'as their host it is my duty to welcome them and bring them in.'

Ron went to the front door and opening it showed himself clearly in the brightly lit hallway. The two visitors were just stepping up onto the raised plinth of the covered porch.

'Welcome my friends,' said Ron with an overly wide smile, 'please come in and make yourselves at home. We have all been eagerly awaiting your arrival.'

'Thank you,' came the reply from them telepathically along with a warm sensation of affection and calmness, 'we also have anticipated this moment for a very long time.'

'Please follow me and I will take you to meet all the family. If you care to take off your hats and coats, I can hang them up in the closet.'

'No thank you,' came their response. 'If you don't mind we would stay covered for now.'

'No problem,' replied Ron telepathically now, 'this way please,' and he led the way into the TV lounge.

An immense aura of peace and affection filled the room as they entered and for a moment Ashley thought that the 'thinking stone' was active again. But then he realised that this was the telepathic atmosphere created by the two visitors. What a lovely way to introduce yourself to a group of complete strangers.

The two short visitors stood side by side and slowly looked around the room at each person in turn before their gaze rested on Ashley. It was only then that they reached up and in perfect unison took off their hats and placed them carefully on a coffee table beside where they stood. They stood bare headed with perfectly normal human features and in fact were rather good looking or so the ladies thought. They did have the handsome looks of a recognisable film star except for the excessively luxuriant hairstyle that seemed a bit artificial and covered the sides of their faces.

'Please forgive our looks,' came from one of them, 'we must wear these guises when we are among you. But today we are with friends and so can uncover ourselves to show you our true appearance. We are different from you and would not wish to cause alarm.'

They then took off their overcoats and carefully folded and placed them on the back of a chair to the one side. Next they eased the elastic brown coloured braces off their shoulders and let their very loose fitting black trousers drop gently down to the floor. They then slowly and carefully stepped out of these and stooping down picked them up and then folding them along the front crease placed them with great care on top of their coats. The loose shirts came off next and the visitors then stood in their own usual attire for all in the room to see.

'How beautiful you are,' said Lillian smiling at them as she looked admiringly at their very slim figures? 'You have such perfect figures. And such handsome looks.'

They had a near perfect slim line human like body but more like that of a young boy aged about eleven or twelve. They both wore yellow tunics that covered them down from the shoulders to just below their hips. It seemed to be made of a plastic material with metal coloured oval patches that stood out just below each arm from armpit to waist. There was a two inch size recession or hole at the raised central high point of these as if something was meant to be attached there. The tunic had an inverted triangular pattern of holes in the centre of the chest area and just below the neck line. The base of this tunic had a curved hem and from there on exposed two beautifully shaped legs. These were covered in a smart pair of bright orange coloured segmented leggings that extended down to a very large and ungainly pair of black leather shoes.

They now carefully undid the laces of the shoes and removing them placed them under the chair holding their other clothes. This exposed the straps of the sandal like footwear that housed their hidden feet. The sandals were made of a plastic material with thick soles at the base.

The tunic extended out to the end of the shoulders only and left the arms uncovered. The arms themselves had a very pale pinkie red tint and Ashley realised that this was the natural colouring of their skin. The skin was smooth and hairless and gave the appearance of a synthetic material and the arms ended in small hands that were partly webbed between the thumb and three fingers. There was also a fin of stiff ribbing that extended from elbow to the back of the hands along the outer edge of the arm. These were coloured like a rainbow and had a fan like design and looked very decorative.

It was only when they turned to one side that another large stiff ribbing came into view and which extended down the centre of their back from the neck to waist position. This was similar in colouring to that on the arms except this was larger and curved at the top. It reminded Ashley of a butterfly's wing. It was also rainbow coloured and had a fan like appearance but had quite a different pattern for each of the visitors. Again it blended perfectly with the rest of the body.

The oddity was the face and head. They were too large in proportion to the slim body and were a completely different colouring from that of the arms. What happened next was a surprise to them all. One of the visitors turned his back to his companion, who then reached up and began to work on an invisible fold inside a section of the bushy hair. Gradually the one started pulling open two flaps inside the hairline and simply continued the peeling process outwards and forwards. There was a slight sucking sound as the entire face seemed to first sag and finally come away as a mask to reveal the true features of the visitor. The mask was carefully placed to one side.

The whole was repeated slowly and carefully for the other visitor until both stood there looking benignly at the surprised group in the room.

'Please may we have the use of some wet cloths to wipe the adhesive off our faces? The masks are a necessity when we travel among you but we find that they are extremely uncomfortable and leave one feeling unclean from the adhesive paste,' telepathically.

Brenda was out and back in seconds carrying a clean very wet hand towel in each hand which she presented to the two visitors. Brenda was five feet six inches in height and everyone noticed how little the two visitors were. Being so close to these citizens of another planet was thrilling for her because she was the first to do so knowingly. Their hands actually touched as they reached out and took the towels from Brenda and she noticed how smooth and silky they felt.

Having thoroughly wiped their faces they handed the towels back to Brenda who had stood close by them all along. She was impressed at what beautiful faces and bodies they possessed.

Ashley and the others now also looked at them and noted that they had a very pleasant aspect to their facial features and both could be deemed as a quite handsomely smart person. Ashley took an instant liking to the two visitors and was keen to get to know them better. He was certain in his mind that they would all eventually become good friends. Ashley liked what he saw and especially the fact that they were quietly and serenely waiting to be greeted as perhaps was their custom.

The two visitors had very humanlike general features of a rounded head with a hairless crown, two eyes, a central downward flowing ridge for a nose and a mouth with wide sensuous lips above a large protruding jaw line and a small pointy chin. The face was very smooth and unwrinkled. The eyes were large and rounded and very green. They were sunken slightly and positioned similarly to those of a human. Ashley thought they reminded him of a possum's large rounded eyes but with an emerald colouring. The face was the same pale pinkie reddish colour as their bare arms and they were completely without hair. The top of the head was smooth but with evenly spaced inverted ridge lines running from front to back that were patterned from two semi circular curves that arched over the eye sockets. The arcs were smooth and were similar in shape to the human eyebrow though much broader. The brow arcs met at the centre of the face and seemed to continue downwards as a narrow slightly raised ridge. This ridge was in the character of a human nose and was quite aesthetic. It ended with a slightly raised softly pointed peak that gave it a childish appearance. Underneath and part of the peak were two little round holes which Ashley took to be the breathing apertures similar to his own nostrils. Below this was a smooth area about an inch wide before the vermillion coloured lips of the wide mouth was reached. The mouth was very similar to the human mouth though the lips had a slight pout to them with the lower lip the more prominent. The corners of the mouth had a slight upward curve which gave the impression of a smile. The jaw line was long and placed their mouth and chin slightly ahead of their eyes so that the lower face protruded fractionally.

The head was supported on a rather thick neck structure that seemed muscular and firm and broadened as it entered the yellow tunic and joined the body.

They had no ears that could be compared to a human but instead had a near two inch wide ribbing similar to that which existed on their arms and which ran in a backward curve along each side of the face from outside of the eye arc and down to the pointy chin. This too had an iridescent rainbow colouring and Ashley was reminded of a Victorian gentleman's large lengthy sideburns. They cupped and shaped the face nicely as though it were colourfully framed. The general appearance was a lean excitable face with keen far apart eyes like those of a child with a frantic wondering look. Apart from this Ashley could discern very little expression in the face though this may have been because it was all new to his perception.

There didn't seem to be any apertures to indicate a hearing feature or earlike function.

'We can hear sounds just the same as you,' came telepathically from the visitors as though in direct response to Ashley's thoughts. 'We hope we are pleasing to you just as you are to us.'

'O yes,' said Ashley aloud, 'we are very pleasantly surprised at how beautiful you are and how similar you are to us.'

Ashley noticed that the two visitors each had a mannerism of every so often running the tip of a shell pink coloured tongue over the outside of their lips and then briefly compressing them together as if to moisturise them thoroughly.

However their eyes were their most striking feature. Not only were they the absolute jewels within their face but they seemed to draw you into them. Ashley was hypnotised by the beauty of their emerald colour. It was as though he were looking directly at the eyes of a tiger though a benign one at that. They drew you into their mystery and Ashley felt he was looking through to another part of the universe.

About once or twice every minute a semi opaque eyelid would flicker over the eyes briefly though not simultaneously. It gave a sort of a humorous winking aspect to their disposition and in time this would endear them to mankind as a whole.

It was Jerry who took the lead and broke the silence.

'I am very pleased and thrilled to meet you,' he said aloud not knowing what else to say.

'And we are as pleased to be meeting you,' came the telepathic response.

There was a lengthy pause and then a telepathic request came from them for a general introduction along with the family connection.

This time Jerry felt more confident and began to walk around the room stopping beside each person and introducing them just by their name. He left Ashley for the last and paused in front of him with a kind of proud flourish.

'And this, my friends, is Ashley Bonner the one person whom you have been most keen to meet for it is he who has the special gifts. He may look young but I assure you he is a giant among us all,' said Jerry. Then turning back to the others he provided the family relationships.

'And this is Lillian his mother, this is Alex his father and this beautiful young lady is Ashley's loving younger sister Katy. Eric here is Ashley's grandfather and father to Alex.' Jerry paused in order that they might appreciate Ashley's direct connections.

'And this is Brenda Davies who is Lillian's sister and Aunt to Ashley. This gentleman is Ron who is husband to Brenda and we are in their home and extremely thankful to them.' And again Jerry paused for effect before continuing with the introductions.

'And this beautiful lady is Milly my wife and partner in life and this is our only child and daughter Tania. She is engaged to wed Ashley and become his partner in life and Milly and I already look upon him as our son.' Jerry concluded. There was wetness in his eyes as he conveyed the last part with a degree of emotion.

Ashley could sense an understanding developing in the minds of the visitors and yet they seemed to expect something more. And then it suddenly dawned upon Ashley's consciousness that the Dogon's ritual of Sewa needed to be performed. So in telepathic mode Ashley welcomed them and requested them to inform the group of their needs. Also it would be kind if they could supply their own titles and connections.

'I am Brazjaf and I am of the male gender. My companion is Muznant. She is of the opposite gender and my partner in life just as some of you are. We are people of Nazmos a planet several light travel years distant from this place. A few of us have lived here on your planet Earth for many thousands of your years and are now citizens of Anztarza, a city beneath the sea but also on land. We are familiar with all your customs but have not been able to live freely among you though we would very much have liked to have done so. Muznant and I have no offspring of our own as yet but hope we shall have one or two one day soon.'

Brazjaf was rather thicker set than his partner Muznant though it was very difficult to differentiate between them. Perhaps later in time as Ashley got used to seeing them the little differences would become more apparent. It was like trying to tell twins apart when you first met them.

Muznant had brighter colours to her arm and facial webbed fins and the ribs in these were finer and more delicate in structure. There was a greater iridescence of colour with pink highlights in the webs as compared to the deeper reds and purples for Brazjaf.

Ashley thought it was now the right time for the ritual of Sewa – for politely enquiring after the well being of their visitors.

'And are you both well?' enquired Ashley telepathically.

'Yes thank you, everything is fine,' was the response.

'And are your family members well?'

'Yes thank you, our parents and relatives are all well.'

'And are your people at peace and do they prosper?'

'Yes thank you, everything is good and all prosper.' They were both definitely smiling now as their mouths widened in a closed lip smile expression.

'And are your homes comfortable and is your city safe?'

'Yes thank you everything is fine.' The perfect Sewa answers.

Ashley could not think of anything further to ask and so remained silent as was the custom with the Dogon people in order to give the guest the opportunity to carry out his part of the greeting ritual.

Ashley noticed a further widening of Brazjaf's smile and knew that he had been pleasantly surprised at Ashley's familiarity with their customs especially at the politeness of his questioning.

Brazjaf looked around at the whole room of people and asked Ashley if he was well and in good health.

'Yes thank you,' replied Ashley, 'everything is fine.'

And so the polite enquiries of Ashley's wellbeing continued till all forms of the Sewa ritual had been exhausted.

After a brief pause at the end of it all Brazjaf said telepathically to everyone in the room that he and Muznant were very honoured to be welcomed as guests in this house.

Brenda invited them to relax and to sit down and be comfortable as they must be tired from their journey here. The two visitors then moved to the vacant single seat sofa armchair and perched themselves lightly on each of the arm rests.

'We are quite comfortable this way as we do not wish our back appendage to become folded again'. This was in direct response to the mental thoughts of Ron and Brenda and of course referred to the large beautiful butterfly wing-like fin on their backs.

'It is customary here to offer a guest some light refreshment after their arrival from a journey. So may we get you something,' enquired Ashley. 'We can offer you a hot or a cold drink.'

It was Muznant who replied after first looking at her husband Brazjaf.

'Yes thank you Ashley,' she said, 'a measure of cold water with a light sweetening would suit us very well.' She conveyed exactly how the drinks should be prepared and in essence she had requested a light orange squash type drink.

All the while Brazjaf sat placidly on the arm of the sofa and gazed alternately at Ashley and the others in the room and at his partner Muznant. Ashley realised that these two had also been privately communicating with one another all along. Their telepathic skills were quite extraordinarily complex and beyond anything that Ashley could have anticipated.

Finally Brazjaf looked at his partner and when she nodded her approval he turned to all in the room and said aloud in a low timbre tone of voice, 'It is time for me to tell you about us. Yes we do have speech and we have been observing and listening to you for several thousand years. We are Oannes from Nazmos which is some six light years from Earth. Currently we live secretly here in a city called Anztarza. We have seen your progress through time and are familiar with how you live and think. Many of your customs for recreation and art have given us much joy and some of these we have included into our own ways. We have never interfered in your affairs though we may have prompted a thought or two. Your wars or battles of violence were your own to win or lose and we remained as observers only. Our distant history had similar episodes of strife and progressed to peace as we learned from those mistakes as surely you shall one day. But to give you our history in this manner would take overlong and so I shall revert to our preferred form of mental communication.'

Brazjaf looked at Ashley and nodded. He then inclined his head to one side. Closed his eyes and waited. Ashley understood immediately that this was an invitation for a mind read and that is exactly what he did.

In an instant Ashley learned everything there was to know about Brazjaf and literally all that was in that mind. Though Ashley also felt there were gaps in the memory sequences which he realised must be the bits that Brazjaf wanted to keep private and had blocked off. Nevertheless, Ashley received a complete understanding of Brazjaf's people's history and all their customs and planet details.

There was a lot of general information to absorb and Ashley understood why Brazjaf and Muznant had done it this way. It was because their mental communication style was so far advanced and complex that had they attempted to transfer all their information directly to the human mind there was the possibility that a lesser developed brain might not be able to accept such a rush of facts with impunity. There was that danger of an incompatible overload or even a wipe out of functioning in some sections of the human brain. Ashley received also a feeling of joy that for the first time a full communication between humans and Oannes had been accomplished with ease.

Ashley paused and smiled at Brazjaf and Muznant and conveyed that he would now relay all the received information to the rest of his family here in the room. It took but an instant for Ashley to convey this retrieved information to the others and a loud 'wow' came from Jerry at the end of it.

There was now a completely different atmosphere in the room. It was an atmosphere of friendliness and understanding and Ashley realised that Brazjaf had brilliantly drawn them all into his own domain. Suddenly it was as if they had all known one another for ages. Affection was born in that instant and any qualms that might have existed in anyone's mind were a distant memory.

The Oannes might be small and different yet they had a tremendous personality and were quite beautiful to behold. They had a welcoming presence despite their slightly marine appearance because they exuded pleasantness and smiles full of gentle warmth.

Brazjaf and Muznant lived in an underground city called Anztarza which was at a secret location beneath the landmass of Antarctica. Although deep underground yet it was still just at a sea level altitude. It was accessed from a portal that was 500 feet in diameter that began at a sea depth of 2000 feet and inclined upwards gently for a hundred miles till it reached a large circular shaped domed bay area at sea level. The dome was about a mile wide at its base and rose to a height of nearly 2000 feet. There was a wide shoreline with jetties and moorings for a variety of strange looking floating craft. These were clearly designed for underwater manoeuvres as well as aerial flight and space travel. The dome was lined with a specially strengthened material about ten feet thick although the underlying rock formation was self supporting. The structure was several thousand years old and the lining was an added safety feature and catered for any untoward rock structural movement or shifting. None had occurred so far.

There was a system of canals and roadways that went through the bay dome walls at ground level and out towards the main city areas. These were a succession of large domes similar in size to the entrance dome with each separated and connected by half mile long arched tunnels. These tunnels were about two hundred feet in height and 100 feet in width and were well lit by a system that made the walls glow bright. The same lighting was in every dome and the whole city was bathed in a perpetual light as for a normal Earth-like cloudy day.

The city of Anztarza comprised twenty three inhabitable domes and housed some ten thousand Oannes. The Oannes were the citizens of Nazmos which was a planet roughly the size of Earth that orbited their red dwarf star Raznat but which was known as Barnard's star in the constellation Ophiuchus by Earth's astronomers and was a little over six light years distant. Raznat was a fifth of the size of the Sun and Nazmos orbited it between the distances of 26 and 31 million miles and made a full cycle in 283 of its revolutions or days. For the planet Nazmos their star Raznat appeared as a glowing sun that was a thousand times brighter than that of the full moon as seen on Earth.

Nazmos was one of four planets orbiting Raznat but the only one to sustain life. It was two thirds sea and the land areas were too cold to support anything other than basic mosses and lichens.

Any animal life was in the seas which regularly acquired a thin layer of ice during the winter periods. Like Earth Nazmos rotated in the direction of its orbit and its axis was inclined at an angle of twenty degrees. Nazmos was near Earth size and just within the outer limits of the temperate inhabitable zone for a planet in relation to its star. A few million miles closer and a lesser eccentricity of orbit would have been more appropriate for sustaining flora and fauna.

The Oannes progressed from sea to the land based dwellings about a million years ago and flourished there under the houses and then domed structures as they developed technologically. But water living was always their preference. They remained amphibious creatures who were equally at ease on land as in the sea. The large iridescent brilliantly coloured webbed fin-like features on their arms, face and back were their underwater respiratory system and functioned by absorbing sufficient oxygen from the water for comfortable survival. Propulsion underwater was affected by means of two impulse motors which were plugged into the metal coloured circular shaped mounds on their tunics and just under each arm above their waist. The impulse motors were similar in principle to the larger versions that effortlessly powered their space cruisers. Basically these operated on the theory that two adjacent electromagnets could be synchronised at a designed extremely high operating alternating current frequency to produce a unilateral linear impulse. This principle had been fine tuned over thousands of years such that now tremendous powers and efficiencies were being achieved. The basic principles of this had been conveyed to several Earth scientists and the idea was currently under their innovative experimentation. It would be several decades before a linear impulse mechanism was realised.

Electric current was generated in a direct manner by stimulating the nuclei strings of protons inside the atom which resulted in the emission of those electrons that were normally reabsorbed within the nucleus confine. Currently on Earth this was effected by using a strong magnetic field to move through each atom nucleus to cause just a few of the I-proton released electrons to be emitted through one of the nuclei windows and so out of the atom confine; a rather inefficient and primitive way of producing electrical energy.

Anztarza was governed by a complex body of Oannes not dissimilar to Earth's own systems of good democracy. Their chief minister as head of government was not a single person but a body of three or more appointed members. The appointments were all made from the home planet and a rotation of appointments was effected every fifty years or so. They were a peace loving people and wars or battling for territory was quite extinct in their culture.

The Oannes lived to a good age and on rare occasion a few had attained 400 Earth years. But this was exceptional and a peak of just over 300 years was more the norm. Brazjaf was a hundred and twelve years of age and Muznant was nearing her first hundred. They tended to mature after reaching thirty.

All hoped one day to integrate with the Earth population and live beside the sea in the open air as they did on their home planet Nazmos. But this could only be achieved through acceptance by Earth's indigenous populations of humans. It was anathema to the Oannes' ideology to assume any rights that were not given freely. It was their code and had been for the thousands of years that they had been living secretly on Earth in Anztarza. It was a strict law in Anztarza and an edict from the Nazmos government that all contact with Earth's humans must be avoided until the time was right. That moment appeared to be fast approaching. Ashley was the exception because of his unique powers and also because it had been foretold in their faded distant mythology that one would arrive from 'another' planet and have the power to avert a great disaster.

Lillian now understood a little of what was expected of her son by these people. There was a wetness to her eyes and a lump in her throat as she remembered her thoughts of when Ashley was a boy running around catching birds for his sister and making holes in tree trunks. Philip had communicated a great task that was before Ashley and Lillian realised that although she did not quite know what that task was she realised it had to do with these people from Nazmos. What was the danger to them and how would it affect their lives? Lillian could never guess the half of it and yet it would make her the proudest mother alive. She looked at her husband and conveyed her thoughts and he came and put an arm around her and kissed her cheek.

Travel between Nazmos and Earth was on an annual basis and undertaken by a monstrous two mile long and quarter mile diameter space cruiser of unique design called a starship. It was a space bound vessel which could never land on a planet since it housed a dense proton/neutron structured shielding at its forward end. Travel between the two planets was at speeds approaching ten times light velocity and it was only the forward shield that kept the ship and its inhabitants safe from the intense energy medium flow that would otherwise have been destructively absorbed by them. The proton shield was made from neutron star material that covered the front shield surface of the spacecraft in a thin blanket. Nothing could pass through this ¾ mile diameter protective umbrella. It took a day in time to achieve maximum velocity and considerably less to slow down again when nearing destination. As such travel time between Nazmos and Earth took about seven months in real time duration. Time within the space cruiser remained at normal Earth event duration levels such that time frames on clocks were quite unaffected because of the shielding aspect. All the travellers only aged by the actual seven month journey duration. Gravity aboard the starship was the natural attraction towards the dense forward neutron shield. Each starship could stay in space indefinitely.

The Oannes had been space bound for some 20 thousand years in Earth time and early missions had been sent towards several star systems. A few had never returned to Nazmos and all communication with them had been lost. Earth was their only success story.

The lesser planet bound spaceships created their own gravity by keeping the craft at a continual level of acceleration between two points in space. As such the Oannes had all the comforts in space that they would normally have had on Nazmos. For them and their children space travel was a normal and easy experience.

An important feature of each spacecraft was the very powerful central polar magnet. This created an extensive Van Allen type magnetic field that deflected spatial radiation around and away from the ship and its inhabitants. The field belt usually extended some fifty or sixty miles around the ship depending upon its size.

The Oannes preferred to sleep and rest under water and as such all their above ground habitation also housed swimming pool style ornamental facilities called 'sleep tanks'. The Oannes were quite artistic and as such each sleep tank was individual in style and could be quite ornamental and decorative in design.

They lived here on Earth on a diet of foods grown in three food domes that was similar in a variety of ways to their home products. Essential supplements could be taken separately. Although their ancestors had hunted and eaten meat from their abundant supply of other sea animals, they had gradually been weaned off this practice on moral grounds when alternatives had been synthesized. They had noted with interest Earth's own development along similar lines with regard to the production of veggie burgers from Soya beans. Space travel created its own demands and some foods were grown on board.

The Oannes were a social gregarious society that engaged in a colourful life of self fulfilment in the fields of art, fashion, cuisine and general entertainment. Sport was a very minor part of their life style. Achievement of high degrees of adeptness in any field was acclaimed and had its own rewards and as such the Oannes had their own hierarchy of wealthy inhabitants. Each Oannes individual was free to pursue his or her own interests provided this did not adversely affect anyone else. Monetary gain was secondary to ethical values and crime was unimaginable. This was mainly the result of being a mind reading telepathic society where criminal imaginings or inclinations are quickly understood and overridden by their strong ethical codes. This does not mean to say that petty jealousies and dislikes did not arise. Of course they did, but they were easily suppressed and kept them from any direct action.

Ashley would encounter a great deal of suspicion in his early contacts with the Oannes people but much of this would vanish as he impressed them when he performed his impressive demonstrations. In fact one of his early opponents by the name of Puzlwat had started off a campaign against Ashley and warned the Chief Ministers of trickery on Ashley's part. It had been Puzlwat who had persuaded the Chief Minister Rymtakza to be suspicious of Ashley's intentions especially with regard to Ashley's professed abilities. It was all a sham according to Puzlwat and Ashley was just another Earth magician similar to the many who had professed the same in the past.

After the Asteroids event though, Nogozat who was Puzlwat's wife and partner had taken a shine to Ashley's gentle manner and persuaded her Oannes husband to mend his ways towards Ashley. And he soon did when he saw the result of Ashley's actions with respect to the Asteroids experiment. But more of that in its proper place.

For the moment the Oannes Brazjaf and his wife Muznant sat before them in Ron and Brenda's B&B lounge. The two visitors now stood up and walked to the centre of the large room and looked around at their human hosts.

'Please come forward that we may touch you,' said Muznant, 'and you may do the same to us.'

When she spoke her voice had a beautiful low timbre, soft and modulated and yet with ringing overtones. In comparison Brazjaf's voice though of a similar low timbre had a much heavier base resonance to it.

Ashley stood up first and taking Tania's hand he walked forward till he stood close up to Muznant. Tania still held tightly onto Ashley's hand and hesitantly looked down at Brazjaf who was a few inches shorter than her own five feet and four inches height.

'This is Tania who is to be my partner and wife,' said Ashley aloud. 'We love each other and always want to be near one another. She will share my happy moments as well as my sadder ones. It must be the same for you?'

'Yes it is,' said Brazjaf reaching up and putting his webbed hand on Tania's cheek. The hand was cool and smooth as it gently moved over Tania's face. He reached up with his other hand and cupped Tania's face in both his palms. After a moment he moved both hands slowly downwards onto her neck and then continued across to her shoulders and rested there. Then gradually he felt his way down her bare arms and finally held both her hands in his. He smiled up at Tania and raising her hands up to his own face he released them there sending her a telepathic message that she may do the same to him.

Ashley was experiencing the same with Muznant and when he passed his palms over her face she smiled her pleasure and lifted up her face to him. Ashley felt a great affection for this little person in front of him and after running his feeling hands down her neck and arms as she had done to him he instinctively let his arms encircle her waist and enfolded her in his arms. He then raised her up slightly and planted a gentle kiss on her broad smiling lips. She in turn had also got her little arms around Ashley as much as was possible and her squeeze was surprisingly firm. Ashley felt a moment of embarrassment at what he had done but Muznant quickly conveyed to his mind that she had willed him to do just that. Looking aside at Tania, Ashley saw that she was in a deep blush from having done the same with Brazjaf. They both released their partners in haste and stepped a couple of paces backwards. Ashley put his arm around Tania and hugged her to him.

'Please do not reproach yourselves for your kiss upon us. We also kiss after a fashion but not as you do. Living here on Earth we have seen much of your ways and how you live and behave towards one another through direct observation and from your films on TV. Over the years many of your ways and customs have found favour with us and we have adopted many. But this kissing was a curiosity and we wished to see for ourselves what pleasure there was in it. It is indeed a good custom and felt most pleasant and affectionate. We have tried it among ourselves but without feeling anything other than contact pleasure as in the touching of hands. Is there more to it than we have seen?' said Muznant.

It was Katy who smugly replied to Muznant but via telepathy and quite privately. Katy conveyed that kissing also involved the touching of tongues while the lips were locked together. Also the tongues could in turn enter the other person's mouth and roam around inside touching the ticklish areas of palate and gums. Muznant smiled and conveyed this to her partner Brazjaf. Katy quickly added that tongue kissing was only to be done between two people who loved each other intensely. Kisses between general friends and acquaintances were usually planted on the other's cheek only.

'Your lips are very much softer than ours as is the skin of your arms and face structure. So perhaps you have a better and more sensitive sensory perception than we have. Our skin layer is much thicker than yours because of our ability to live under the sea and as easily on the land,' said Muznant. 'Brazjaf and I will try out this tongue kissing when we are alone in Anztarza.'

Muznant then moved across to Alex and stopped in front of him and repeated everything that she had done with Ashley. Brazjaf did the same with Lillian. Alex noticed that Muznant's lips had a much firmer feel and a thicker skin structure than Lillian's. He also noticed the coolness of her face and arms and inferred that their body temperature was somewhat lower than for humans. At close range Alex noticed that their skin had a much thicker texture and no veins were visible on the arms and face. The webbed areas on their faces and arms pulsed with fine deep coloured capillaries as did the much larger butterfly wing on their backs. Alex no sooner puzzled over these features than the answer was given to him telepathically. The webbed areas were finely porous and designed for picking up oxygen when they lived in the sea and so functioned as very efficient underwater lungs. The Oannes were fully amphibious and could live in the sea indefinitely.

Eric was the last to be approached by Muznant and before he put his arms up to her face he asked her to open her mouth and show him her tongue. At first she was puzzled by this request but upon reading Eric's mind she readily obliged. She opened her mouth wide and moved her face from side to side so that all in the room could see her fine rows of tiny teeth. They were small pointy teeth set low in the gums of her pink mouth and were too many to count. She then poked out her tongue which was pink and narrow and came quite far out. Muznant smiled at Eric with a mischievous twinkle in her eye and slowly let the tip of her tongue extend upwards and just touch the tip of her quaint little nose. Her shoulders and chest shook with a sort of repetitive sucking in sound which was her laughter at seeing Eric's expression of surprise. The laughter was infectious and soon there was laughter all around the room. Brazjaf however was not of a disposition in which happiness overflowed in mirth and Ashley thought perhaps he hadn't seen the funny side of Muznant's display for he simply displayed a smile of amusement.

Ashley looked around and thought that this was the most perfect of beginnings for a meeting between peoples of two very different cultures and origins. All his concerns of the past weeks had evaporated and he now looked forward to his association with these Oannes people. They were pleasant and presentable physically and Ashley had taken to them with all his heart. And he knew that the others also felt the same.

When Eric had Muznant in his arms with everyone looking on he changed his mind about kissing her on the lips. Instead he planted light kisses on her forehead, her cheeks, the tip of her nose, her webbed facial fins and finally on her bottom lip. He conveyed to her and to Brazjaf that kissing among humans could be bestowed upon any part of the body and was a natural part of the act of love or foreplay prior to intimacy. Eric explained that a simple kiss on the cheeks was also a greeting custom when friends met or departed but not between the men. These either hugged and patted one another's backs or simply shook hands.

'You are beautiful Muznant,' said Eric aloud, 'your husband is lucky to have such a lovely wife. I wish you happiness in everything. I hope we can always be friends. This has truly been a good beginning don't you think?'

A feeling of peace and affection pervaded the room again.

'I think we are all ready for a nice hot cup of tea,' said Brenda, 'I'll just go and put the kettle on.'

She enquired of Muznant and Brazjaf if they too would like to try a cup of tea with the rest of them.

'It's a very refreshing but hot drink that we all love,' she added.

After a brief pause during which they read Brenda's mind as to what tea constituted they said, 'Yes please we will try some the same as you all.'

'I'll make yours just the same as Ashley's,' said Brenda. 'He has his with one sugar and plenty of milk.'

'I'll come and help,' said Lillian following Brenda into the kitchen.

In the kitchen Lillian looked at Brenda and both smiled at each other.

'Aren't they just gorgeous,' said Brenda. 'I find them so cute and polite and lovable. I know I shouldn't say this but I never felt like adopting anyone as I do these two. They are so charming and accommodating and I sense they are keen to learn our ways and customs better. You know what I mean.'

'Yes,' said Lillian, 'I do. And I feel most reassured by them. Bren, I can't believe how comfortable I feel about them. Somehow I know their dream of integrating with us on Earth is a far off thing. Perhaps when we develop socially into a unified peace loving race that dream may come true, but not for hundreds of years I fear. I know that they are chiefly interested in our Ashley. I know they will adopt him by cultivating his friendship and confidence. O Bren, he is the reason they have waited so long here on Earth and watched, listened and waited for his arrival. I know they are nice and friendly and I know they also have a purpose for Ashley's gifts and mean to take him away to fulfil this task that Philip had conveyed.'

There were tears in Lillian's eyes as she poured out her feelings to her sister.

'Ashley can look after himself Lil,' said Brenda, 'don't you worry yourself on that account. He knows what they are after so we must stress that wherever they wish him to go that we will go with him as a family. Where Ashley goes we all go too.'

'Yes I suppose so,' said Lillian.

Just then a clear thought entered their minds which they immediately interpreted as an advanced communication coming from their visitors. It was as though their every thought was known.

'Calm yourselves,' it conveyed, 'we desire nothing from Ashley that he will not volunteer freely. Yes, you may all come with us wherever he goes and that may be far out in space. And please know that there is no urgency in what he can do for us. So let us get to know and trust one another first and then we shall reveal all our secrets. Many years will pass before actions of any kind need to be taken.'

A mood of peace and calm accompanied this message and Lillian knew again that her motherly concerns were misguided. Yet she knew that those concerns would raise their heads repeatedly from time to time. But for now they were allayed.

Brazjaf and Muznant were polite in their appreciation of their mugs of tea and referred to them as interesting but that they were not used to ingesting hot liquids. However they said it was an educating experience of an Earth custom. They said that although they had been observing and listening in to the variety of customs and ways of peoples across the world it had been impossible to comprehend how we all related to one another. It was as though each race lived on another planet and communicated across their borders as befitted each.

When and if ever the Oannes were allowed to settle openly on the Earth as they hoped then they believed that they could become just such another indigenous race living among humans. In fact they would be unique in that they would be also classed as sea dwellers. But that of course was in the far distant future though this first contact would go a long way towards encouraging that hope.

It was Jerry who stood up and said that he had a query. He then walked to a bureau in the corner of the room and picked up the 'thinking stone' tablet that Ashley had placed there yesterday.

'This 'thinking stone' tablet was given to someone who visited the Dogon tribe in Africa,' said Jerry bringing the tablet close up to Brazjaf. 'In turn it was given to Ashley and we know that it is some sort of telepathic monitoring device because we have experienced its moods and received its communications. Could you tell us how many were placed on Earth and when and for what reason?'

It was Muznant who came forward and taking the tablet into her own delicate hands looked at it with interest.

'These are indeed communication devices,' she said in her low timbre soft melodic voice. 'I have never seen or for that matter held one before but I know of their history.'

She paused and then handed the tablet over to her husband Brazjaf who also looked keenly at it before passing it back to Jerry. Brazjaf now took up the tale.

'Our ancestors visited Earth for the first time about ten thousand years ago,' he said in a voice that was similar to his wife's but with a slightly lower pitch, 'and found a beautiful luxuriant Earth populated on land and in the seas by a great diversity of creatures. There was one on the land who most resembled us in manner but was quite primitive in habit. They possessed no social system or any technology then. Our ancestors recognised their potential and the similarity with our own very early history of some hundreds of thousands of years prior to our own development and decided to simply observe and not interfere or assist. There had been a brief moment of a thought towards colonising Earth for ourselves but this was against our moral and ethical code. We had been space bound for some twenty thousand years and it had taken one of our ordinary spacecraft fifteen years to travel from Nazmos to Earth. The return journey a year later had been as long again and the report back received with great interest. But sadly nearly eighty percent of the crew didn't make it back because of illnesses contracted on the Earth despite our best efforts and advanced medical technology. All the samples and specimens brought back were quarantined on the ship. This included the entire crew both living and dead. The sea water was especially vibrant with organisms and bacteria that were harmful to our system but we hoped could be overcome with research and of gradually acclimatising and adjusting ourselves to the new conditions.'

'General immunisation was affected and another expedition despatched to Earth after an interval of a hundred years and this time in a larger ship with full medical research teams and facilities. This time the Oannes stayed on Earth for seventy years during which time a great success in adjustment to the Earth conditions was achieved. At first our ancestors made their bases beside large rivers and lakes and as they adjusted to the environment progressed closer to the seas and oceans. Eventually ideal locations in the seas were found near both Polar Regions which had less concentrations of the earlier harmful organisms and recommendations were made for eventual settlements in these areas.

Communication with Nazmos was simply a question of relaying information and progress data. Replies to problems were not possible though general news was constantly relayed from the home planet. All news was of interest even if it was six years behind in date. Our ancestors had to rely on their own judgements and ethical code when crucial decisions had to be made.'

Brazjaf licked his lips and looked towards Muznant for her to continue in her melodic tone. Ashley knew why they were offering a verbal communication as opposed to telepathy. They still feared overloading the human brain structure if they transferred blocks of information in an incompatible format and too concentrated a mode. Ashley suspected that they had also grown to like the sounds they made with their voices resonating around the room and were quite enthralled by their speech vibrations. Perhaps they did not talk often and this was one of those rare opportunities for practice.

'It was also about then that we developed and achieved faster than light travel in space,' said Muznant. 'Many ships were lost prior to developing the proton shield since we already had the propulsion systems to approach and exceed light velocity. Space is filled with the consistent outflow of energy-medium that issues from every mass object of the universe. This is because all matter in the current phase of the universe cycle is in decay. That is mass reverting back to an energy medium. These outflows have a velocity relative to their origin that exceeds that of light by many factors and are collectively responsible for what can only be deemed as the structure of space. We refer to this invisible structuring as the Space Grid. Energy medium intensity levels vary across this Space Grid and subsequent gradients are what give rise to the gravity forces near all mass objects. The subsequent acceleration due to this gravity force is always in the direction of the increasing Space Grid gradient.'

'Spacecraft travelling through this space-grid would absorb into their atom structure some of this energy medium. Your scientists sometimes refer to this energy medium which is everywhere as Dark Matter. When below light speeds this absorption of energy medium is inconsequent and causes no detriment apart from a misconception in the elapsing of time which is really the measurement of event duration. Subsequently all clocks run slower as also does your physical atomic structure. However once you begin to exceed light velocity by a significant factor this space grid gets increasingly absorbed into the atoms of both spaceship and its occupants which ultimately results in a disintegration of atomic and molecular bonding. This is because the electron shell is stripped from around each and every atom and the entire structure collapses. We lost many spaceships in this way until the proton-shield was developed. This is simply a skin of neutron star material that is coated onto the forward facing surfaces of all faster-than-light craft. It adds considerable mass to the already bulky spaceship and provides a certain gravity condition to the living platform within.'

'We could subsequently journey between Nazmos and Earth in just seven months. The spaceship anchorage or port is located in a zone beyond your planetary zone in the direction of Sagittarius and quite invisible from Earth. We live in space under Nazmos gravity conditions which is achieved by continual acceleration of our spacecraft in a parking loop. We are also currently developing an artificial energy medium flow that should enable us to transmit basic messages at those velocities across the space grid. So far results have been encouraging.'

Muznant paused and Brazjaf took up the narrative in his low tone voice.

'Anztarza was built gradually dome by dome as the contingent on Earth was enlarged. At first about six thousand years ago it was only our experts in the science and medical fields who came and lived here. Then as conditions were proved safe and stable for the Oannes, many of the general public volunteered to spend time here. Their reactions and adaptation was studied thoroughly and all of them thought that Earth was a most suitable environment. There was envy at the beauty and diversity to be found on this planet and some dissention at not taking the planet for our own. However our code was strict and no exceptions were allowed. No contact was permitted with humans at any level. There were infringements in the early years but these were dealt with severely by returning all involved back to Nazmos and banishing them and their children both present and future from ever visiting Earth.'

'There was one exception in all of this and that was the 'thinking stone' tablet communication device. Some three hundred thousand of these were spread across the Earth at evenly spaced locations on land and sea by simply dropping them carefully from one of our low flying spacecraft. This was affected about four thousand years ago. The tablets are powered by a tiny internal electron generator that has an indefinite life. They can pick up thought patterns at distances of nearly a mile and each has a uniqueness of identity. Our ancestors listened to much of your culture and as societies developed we occasionally transmitted an idea or two into your thoughts for your future development. You had many good thinkers and philosophers in the sciences and when monitoring their thoughts we found that the tablets had inadvertently relayed some of our own thoughts to their minds. This set a precedent and our code was altered to allow this to happen.'

'Thoughts are relayed to a centre in Anztarza and the teams there have monitored this particular tablet 'thinking stone' over a very long time and sent across emotions of peace and tranquillity. After many centuries of this it was a great surprise when we began picking up telepathic communications from your area. At first the telepathic signals were of a random nature directed as a recognisable communication between persons and then you actually communicated directly with us through the tablet and we knew then that a new era was upon us. We are sorry but in our excitement we sent out a strong compulsive message as a demand to know all about you which resulted in Ashley giving us his full life story. Many of us believe that Ashley is gifted with the power of the universe and which is of a magnitude quite unimaginable even to us. But he is young and will not comprehend the awesome power at his disposal and how to channel it to best advantage. We may be able to guide him.'

While Brazjaf had been talking Muznant had reached into a pocket of her yellow tunic and brought out a number of small metallic looking shield shaped objects and placed then on the table beside her. So now when Brazjaf paused she took over the story.

'Our council of ministers has permitted us to present each of you with one of our latest communication devices. These were developed only a lifetime ago and can be looked upon as the equivalent of your mobile phone system. You have only to think a communication to one of you or as a group and it is done. You will notice that it is small and thin and may be concealed upon your person very easily. It has a range of anywhere on Earth and can never be lost. You will instantly be made aware of its location by thoughts from us should you enquire after it. We hope that you accept this and we request that you keep it with you at all times if that is agreeable to you,' said Muznant.

She then stepped forward and handed a coin-sized badge to each one of them in the room. Ashley examined his and saw that it was approximately in the shape of a shield about 1½ inch square with a curve to one side. It was about the thickness and weight of large coin, had rounded edges and was very similar in texture to the Dogon 'thinking stone' tablet.

As they held these in their hands they each received a personal telepathic communication of welcome and good intentions from the people of Anztarza. It also conveyed that Brazjaf and Muznant were highly placed and respected members of the Oannes community of Anztarza and that they were authorised to issue a general invitation for Ashley and all his family members to visit Anztarza when they wished. Special transportation arrangements and living accommodation had already been allocated for such a visit.

'All our people are keen to meet you,' said Brazjaf reverting to telepathy, 'ever since they knew of this planned visit. It would give us great satisfaction if you were to come and spend some time in Anztarza. You may discuss this among yourselves when we leave you and convey your wishes or plans to us later through these badges.'

It was Ashley who responded by thanking them for their kind invitation and conveyed that they would all be happy to accept. Perhaps they could visit in a month's time when they had discussed and made suitable arrangements for their businesses.

Jerry was curious about something and couldn't help enquiring after their travel arrangements today. Was their car a special car? And how would they get back to Anztarza tonight?

There came a tinkling melodious laughter sound from Muznant. 'No,' she said with a smile, 'this is one of your ordinary Earth vehicles. We purchased it at a used car lot just outside Cardigan. It is well used but runs conveniently and suited our disguised purpose perfectly. We have bank accounts in most countries with ample funds. In this case the car was purchased for cash and the dealer was happy to oblige us with a full tank of your fuel and all the documentation which is currently on the back seat of the car. We drove around slowly and parked at the headland view point just above this place. We have no further use for it and wish to leave it here with you for disposal as you see fit. The craft that brought us to Cardigan now rests on the sea floor a few miles out from here so when we leave we shall propel ourselves to it. The propulsion devices which we shall attach to our sides are in a sealed bag in the back of the car.'

Muznant indicated the two circular and slightly domed metallic looking structures moulded as part of their yellow tunics and located under each arm.

'Perhaps we could all walk together to the beach and say our farewells there,' said Muznant.

'It has been lovely meeting you both,' said Lillian, 'and we hope we meet you again soon. I speak for us all when I say that we are looking forward to visiting your city and we hope to make many friends there.'

'That you certainly shall,' said Muznant and Brazjaf together. 'Our people anxiously await your visit. They have enjoyed this visit too since all that has occurred here today has also been mentally witnessed by them. They are currently conveying their goodwill to you all.'

Muznant and Brazjaf then helped each other in putting their face masks back on though perhaps not as firmly as previously. Next came their over clothes, boots and hats. All communication was now telepathic and they conveyed that it had always been a part of their rules and code of conduct never to venture into the open spaces without their disguises firmly in place. They all then walked out to the car park and to the car parked near its centre. There was a shiny plastic looking bag in the back which Brazjaf took hold of and carried in both arms.

'These are our underwater propulsion units that we shall attach to ourselves when we are in the sea,' conveyed Muznant as she walked along slowly and carefully. The boots on their feet did not fit well since they were oversized and really only meant as a disguise and not for comfort.

It was now well past midnight and there was a slight fog and a frosty chill in the air. The beach was empty though the full moon beautifully exhibited a brilliant wide circle of a halo fringed with coloured edges. The visitors didn't seem to feel the cold at all and from having read Brazjaf's mind earlier Ashley knew that their home planet Nazmos was much cooler than Earth and they were used to the cold. They could probably live quite happily among the Eskimos for that matter.

They walked to the sheltered spot where Ashley had demonstrated his telekinetic gift to Ron and Brenda by sending those large stones zipping through the air and out to sea. With the cliffs at their backs in this secluded spot Muznant and Brazjaf once again began removing their disguises. They placed each item one by one on a large rock at the base of the cliff alongside the bag containing the propulsion units. With all their disguises removed Brazjaf then commenced to take the units out of the bag. They were cigar shaped and slender and just over a foot long. The first one he took out was red in colour and quite streamlined. This he attached to himself by fitting it to the socket of the circular metallic bulge on his tunic under his left arm. The next one was also red but with a hint of green in places. He handed this to Muznant who looked at it and clipped it into place under her right side. The next was also Muznant's and went into her left side while the last one Brazjaf attached to his right side. They stood balancing the propulsion units and looked up at their assembled hosts and smiled contentedly. A feeling of great affection spread outwards from them.

Then Muznant took hold of the empty bag and began carefully rolling their coats and placing them inside the bag. The hats and boots followed suit and then while Muznant held the bag firmly Brazjaf came across and pulled the zipper up tight. There was a carrying loop of a strap which Muznant put over her shoulder.

'Goodbye my friends,' said Brazjaf aloud in the chilly air, 'we shall meet again.'

They smiled their wide lipped smiles, turned around and walked to where the waves lapped at high tide. They waded casually into the sea and when the water came up just under their armpits they turned around to smile once again at the watching group and then dipped down and were gone.

The wonder and astonishment tinged with a hint of sadness was picked up by the underwater duo and Ashley thought he sensed Muznant's distinctive amused laughter emotion. Ashley and Tania were holding hands at the water's edge and all waited to see if something would rise up out of the sea. After several uneventful minutes the chill got to them and they decided to return to the comfort and warmth of the B&B lounge.

Brenda and Lillian made hot drinks for everyone and it was well after 3 o'clock before they all went to their rooms. The badge communication devices given to them by the visitors were most intriguing and would now become one of their most prized possessions. Alone in his room Ashley decided to test his.

'My dear friends Brazjaf and Muznant I hope you reached your craft safely,' he conveyed telepathically while holding the badge up in front of his face.

'Yes thank you Ashley,' replied Brazjaf loud and telepathically clear, 'we reached our ship just as you all decided to return to the warmth of the house. We shall travel at speed towards mid-ocean before rising upwards out of the water and looping across the sky towards Anztarza. We shall then re-enter the sea and be in the city portal within a few hours. You will like Anztarza when you visit as we did with our own visit to you today. Sleep well my friend.'

A feeling of peace and tranquillity accompanied this message and Ashley allowed his head to sink deeper into the pillow and closing his eyes sleep came gradually. His last thought was that he must return Andrew's tablet, notebook and diaries to Lester and Mary Dutton but without divulging any of their deep secrets. He also thought of Margaret briefly and wondered what she would have to say to him. Perhaps he might just mention the aspect in which the Dogon chief used the tablet as a form of mental relaxation by holding it against the side of the head. It would certainly help Mary to relax.

After having left their new friends on the shore Brazjaf and Muznant had made their way speedily underwater towards the waiting transport craft. This was sitting on the sea bed three miles out and 150 feet down. The moment they had dived downwards into the sea their propulsion devices had become active. These were thought controlled and pushed them firmly in the direction they wanted and at speeds that could be tolerated. Being in telepathic communication with the captain of the craft they gave their estimated arrival as five minutes when they could see the glow of underwater lights in the distance.

Muznant had led the way into the large water chamber near the forward side of the craft and the door closed with a hiss as soon as Brazjaf had entered. The water level had then dropped gradually and soon the chamber was quite empty. Another door then hissed open and two people entered and greeted the newcomers. One was the captain of the craft and the other was a senior crew member. Another crew member briefly appeared carrying delicate shoes made of tunic material. These were handed to Brazjaf and Muznant and had been omitted from the kit makeup for the visit to Ashley and family.

'Greetings Nazaztal and Byuzlit,' communicated Brazjaf, 'is all well with you? Thank you for receiving us.'

Nazaztal and Brazjaf were old friends and his wife Ribuzalt was very fond of Muznant. They lived in different though adjacent domes in Anztarza and paid frequent social visits to each other's apartments. Nazaztal was nearly 150 years of age and Ribuzalt was thirty years his junior. She was quite slim and slightly taller than her stocky husband and was quite pretty in a coarse sort of a way. This was because the webbing around her face was finer than usual which gave it a glow from the light passing through it. Also her nose was more aquiline and longer than the average. Both she and her husband were well liked in the community and they entertained frequently. Ribuzalt was an amateur artist and one of the very few in Anztarza. She had painted scenic views of the Earth from the image scans taken on her excursions while in disguise and had sold many to those who showed an interest in its beauty. She also painted scenes of Nazmos from memory especially those of her home town Wanzpan on the shores of the great sea Peruga. The setting of the glowing Raznat each evening was a particular favourite. Each apartment in Anztarza had at least one framed picture print of a Nazmos scene to remind them of home.

Byuzlit was the senior crew member in charge of the maintenance of the craft and he was approaching 150 years of age but looked barely 100. He was unmarried and made a trip every ten years or so to see his 230 year old mother back in Arznat a small town on the shores of Peruga the great sea of Nazmos.

'Greetings Brazjaf and Muznant,' communicated the captain, 'I see all went well with your visit. We listened to every word, thought and emotion of your time with Ashley and his family. We were pleased to make his acquaintance even if it was by proxy. I expect you would wish to remove the salt water traces off yourselves. Byuzlit will accompany you to your cabin where all facilities have been anticipated.'

It was usual for any of the Oannes who had been in the sea to clean themselves by showering and then immersing themselves in a tank of Nazmos composite water and afterwards donning a fresh tunic or other attire.

Brazjaf and Muznant conveyed their thanks with an emotion of affection for Nazaztal as they followed Byuzlit down the large corridor and into the heart of the craft. This was of average size and quite capable of spatial travel though not above 80% of light speed. It had a complement of 35 Oannes technical personnel who were mainly there in case of a breakdown or malfunction.

The craft was about 300 feet long, 150 feet wide and 50 feet in depth and had an oval flat shape. It possessed three deck levels but only the central deck had small circular outer viewing ports. The front of the craft housed the control room or bridge and was noticeable by its large viewing window panels. While under Earth's gravity the craft travelled in the direction of its length with the control room at the front. In space flight however the craft travelled upwards and perpendicular to its floor plan under an acceleration format to 90% of Earth gravity. This was to maintain a constant level of Nazmos gravity for its occupants and once cruise speed had been attained it flew in a closed loop pattern to continue that gravity effect.

The craft was simply known by a number and designated colour. This particular craft was 8962-Green and was quite a recent model. It had been manufactured on Nazmos about 500 years ago and had been ferried to Earth inside an FTL (Faster than Light) starship just 300 years later.

The heart of any ship was its Bio-computer which operated all its functions. The Bio-computer on this craft was Zanos-268 and was capable of limited self maintenance within its structure. Regular updates of information were fed to it telepathically from the base in Anztarza. As with all Oannes the computer was mind-linked to the delegated captain of the craft. Should the captain cease to exist on the craft for any reason then the mind-link was automatically transferred to the next designated senior authorised person.

Zanos simply operated the craft's every function and carried out the intentions of the captain as to mode of travel, direction and destination. No physical controls existed. Running vertically up the centre of each craft was its magnetic pole core which generated the intense magnetic field around the craft when in outer space. The power plant and impulse generators were housed within the top and the lower decks and were capable of accelerating the craft in any desired direction.

Brazjaf and Muznant entered their spacious cabin which was the same as before and fresh sets of clothes hung on pegs in the open closet. One corner of the room housed a clear-sided water tank which was about six feet high off the cabin floor and measured twelve feet into the corners with a curved front format. A set of steps existed along one cabin wall that led to the top of the tank. Near the foot of the steps was a showering cubical that was multi-functional and mind controlled as desired by the occupant. Again Zanos-268 was in control of all function aspects in the cabin as it was for the rest of the craft. Food and beverage however was delivered on request by the catering personnel via a special conveyor system.

It had been a long day for Brazjaf and Muznant and both were quite hungry. They collected their meal choice from the open collection-cubical and sat at the central table to carefully open the steaming boxes and take in the aromas within before placing the contents on pale green oval platters. There was a pause for a brief meditation and a communication of thanks was sent out before they tucked in with spoon-like cutlery. When they had completed the meal which had only taken a few minutes the empty plates and boxes went into a lid covered hole in the centre of the table.

Brazjaf and Muznant sat for a while communicating their thoughts to one another and then they commenced to undress. They removed their tunics and then their leggings to expose quite slim torsos which were without any hair whatsoever. The body skin was the same colouring as their arms though with slightly less of the pinkie reddishness. They were not self conscious about their nudity which was not very different from the human form. Outwardly the Oannes anatomy appeared similar to humans in basic structure but they were very different internally. They were amphibious creatures after all.

Brazjaf went into the shower cubical first and luxuriated in the coolness of the water jets and overhead spray. He then walked up the steps and stepped into the water tank via the steps within it. Muznant was not long behind. After a moment of intimacy they both relaxed in the cool water and both gradually fell asleep as they floated halfway down underwater.

Brazjaf felt refreshed and invigorated when he awoke about an hour and a half later. It was always so after a spell in the specially imported Nazmos sea water. He had never been one for long periods of sleep and now he looked at his wife and studied her beauty with loving eyes. The webs on her face and arms and the butterfly wing on her back all pulsated gently in time with her heartbeat and Brazjaf admired the calmness of expression as she slept with eyelids closed.

He remembered the first time he had seen her back on Nazmos all those twenty years ago. Or was it longer? It was the year after the big quake and the stormy seas had only just begun to calm down again a year later. Muznant and her friends had been visiting the capital city port of Wentazta and had seemed quite in awe of the magnificent colourful structural domes spread out before them. Muznant's own home was in the much smaller town of Latipuzan which was much farther inland and on the shores of the medium sized ice-water Lake Voolzort.

Brazjaf had been with his friend Grimztani as they did most evenings after work. Both were single and unattached and tended to meet up with a few other friends and acquaintances at the Silver Star Cafe on Lake Street to exchange stories and jokes. Wanzsogi had just met up with them and communicated for them not to look behind. Of course that was the last thing he should have said for the friends immediately spun around to look. And that was when Brazjaf saw Muznant for the first time. She was with two other girls and all seemed to be enjoying themselves laughing and turning this way and that as they took in and admired the views of the big city scenery.

Muznant was the smallest of the three and the prettiest. Brazjaf fell in love with her as he watched her walk by. His emotion of love and admiration was immediately sensed by Muznant and she stopped and turned to look at him. Yes, he was a good looking fellow and so were his two friends. Muznant was never one to be bashful or hesitant and both her friends Wigzolta and Partuzna agreed with her communication. Why not they thought?

There occurred then a full complex telepathic communication between the two groups and after enquiries of wellbeing in the Sewa tradition the three men offered to show the ladies the sights of their city. And so began a friendship that could have only one conclusion.

A year later Brazjaf and Muznant declared a legal partnership and began living together in Wentazta. Grimztani and Partuzna had continued seeing each other and remained good friends. But Grimztani was very independent and did not want to commit himself just yet and their relationship cooled. Partuzna eventually met someone else, a government chap called Ripozatan who was a work colleague of Brazjaf and settled down with him.

Muznant's other friend Wigzolta was tall and slim looking and Wanzsogi was quite in awe of her beautiful smile. But he was too timid to propose anything for fear of rejection.

Wigzolta however sensed his bashfulness and was not one to be denied an opportunity for her own happiness. She took matters into her own hands and proposed living together to the total surprise and delight of Wanzsogi. Thereafter communication between them was open and intimately frank such that Wanzsogi and Wigzolta were bound together legally a little less than a year after that of Muznant and Brazjaf's own marriage bond.

The two couples lived not far from each other and soon drew Partuzna and Ripozatan into their circle of friendship. Partuzna and Muznant had grown up together in the same Latipuzan neighbourhood and had always been close. Ripozatan was totally under Partuzna's spell and was the quiet one in the relationship and so fitted in well with the other two. He was a work colleague of Brazjaf and had often to be told to shut up about work. He would just laugh at this and say he was sorry. But they all knew he was a serious minded person and was a good worker and very conscientious about his job with the government.

Grimztani on the other hand remained single and became a crew member of an FTL starship. Brazjaf received news of him often and it was Grimztani at one of their get together meetings who had persuaded Brazjaf and Muznant to visit Earth's Anztarza. His descriptions of that planet's beauty and climate which far surpassed that of the relatively cool Nazmos filled Muznant with awe and a desire to see this beauty for her own self. She eventually persuaded her husband to pull the necessary strings and get permission for them to travel there on official tour business. Brazjaf was to report back on the morale and wellbeing of the long-term citizens of Anztarza while at the same time giving his own independent impressions of the thought structure among the Earth's own indigenous peoples. In other words it would be a contrived and paid for luxury holiday.

Brazjaf looked again at the sleeping Muznant and an emotion of love and caring filled the room. Muznant's eyelids flickered and one twitched very slightly and a dreamy smile appeared briefly on her lips. Slowly her body rolled over and she was now suspended face-down in the water with her arms spread slightly out from her sides and reaching downwards. A bubble of air escaped upwards from between her thighs and Brazjaf smiled and decided to let her sleep on while he got out and visited with captain Nazaztal.

Brazjaf moved to the side of the tank and climbed out and down the outer steps. He walked past the shower cubical and entered a door just beyond. Having completed his necessary body functions he entered the shower cubical for a quick spray followed by a prolonged blast of warm air till he was completely dry. He then went across the room to a closet and chose his attire for the day. He chose a silver and blue tunic with matching leggings and matching footlets which quite resembled ankle length moccasins. He was just getting a leg into the leggings when he glanced up and saw a smiling Muznant looking at him over the rim of the sleep tank. She conveyed that he should wear contrasting leggings and suggested the silver and black ones.

'Of course,' Brazjaf conveyed back, 'how misguided of me,' and he smiled at his admiring wife who now placed her chin on her folded arms that were resting on the soft rim of the tank. She continued to smile as she cast an admiring look over his nakedness while he got dressed.

'Hello my handsome husband,' she said aloud in her soft melodic low tone voice, 'and where are you off to without me?'

Brazjaf conveyed that he was going to the bridge to meet up with Captain Nazaztal at the control centre. They would soon be airborne and he always found it quite exhilarating to see and feel their swift climb up into space.

Muznant conveyed that she would rest a while longer before getting out of the tank to fulfil her morning ablutions. She also added how handsome he looked in that silver, blue and black combination just as he opened the outer door, smiled at her and exited backwards out into the corridor. Silently the door slid shut behind him.

Brazjaf knew the layout of the craft and was soon at the entrance of the control centre with its clear polycarbonate type doors. These didn't open for him until he had mentally requested permission to enter and conveyed his purpose. From inside Captain Nazaztal smiled at his friend's presence and immediately gave authorised entry. Brazjaf came up beside him and enquired as to their progress.

'We are in a remote area and are rising to the water's surface,' conveyed the captain, 'we should be in the Anztarza corridor in little over an hour.'

'I didn't want to miss our space hop,' Brazjaf responded, 'I do so love the exhilaration of the swift climb up into space.'

8962-Green quickly ascended and reached the surface of the Atlantic Ocean some 300 miles out from Aberporth. Silently and smoothly it continued to rise as Zanos momentarily set the ship into hover mode just above the choppy waves. Monitors indicated that there were no Earth vessels anywhere near and the craft rose swiftly upwards. The craft's shape and surface coating was such that it was invisible to any Earth radar and its colouring was such that it was not easily visible during daylight. The acceleration was barely noticeable apart from a slight feeling of increased weight as the craft broke through the Atlantic cloud cover and raced up through the stratosphere and to the edge of space. The craft had also acquired a forward momentum as it rose upwards and subsequently was well into its planned space hop as it levelled off at the 100 mile altitude. It would now fly level so that its occupants and contents would continue to be under Earth's gravity influence. The craft maintained a directly southward course and had already bypassed the Azores and the Canary Islands. Its passage was swift and at its maximum was travelling at close to 10,000 miles an hour.

Tennis ball sized beacons had been placed strategically at a vast number of locations around the Earth both on land and in the shallower areas of the seas and lakes. These functioned as a guidance system for craft anywhere above the Earth and allowed the Zanos controllers to navigate around; but especially back to Anztarza.

The night-time lights of the cities on the east coast of South America slowly moved by as they sped south towards the brilliantly white continent of Antarctica. Since it was summertime at the South Pole there was perpetual daylight there and this gradually became visible to Brazjaf as he peered out through the forward view port. The horizon ahead had a sunrise appearance about it for a while. Within moments though the craft was suddenly bathed in brilliant sunshine and the vast whiteness of Antarctica was spread out below them in all its dazzling glory. The scene below was not very much different from Nazmos in its winter zones and for a moment Brazjaf was reminded of his love for this planet and for the people he had just met. He could live here forever and now the chance for a limited form of integration had come just a little bit closer to reality; a truly beautiful thought.

It was not long before the craft had passed across much of this whiteness and began its descent towards its destination for sea re-entry at a point in the Davis Sea just beyond the Shackleton ice shelf.

The flight had been barely 50 minutes as the craft passed over the South Pole at an altitude of 60 miles and a speed that was continually slowing. It flew over Queen Mary Land at 2000 miles per hour at 20 miles up and in full daylight. The craft slowed considerably as it approached the sea beyond the ice shelf and eventually reached the ocean surface quite effortlessly. Without further delay it entered the water of the Davis Sea and sped downwards below the waves and headed around in a curved path for the Anztarza tunnel entrance 2000 feet down. Beacons had been placed around the entrance of the tunnel and also at regular intervals along its entire upward sloping 100 mile length.

This would be the slowest part of the journey and would take about two hours to complete. As there was nothing more for Brazjaf to see he decided to return to his cabin to determine what had become of Muznant. He hadn't received any communication from her in response to his enquiries so was not surprised to see her once again floating in the sleep tank fast asleep. He looked at her serene expression and decided to make a tour of the recreation area of the craft and so leave his wife to her well earned relaxation. He'd return just prior to when the craft was to dock in Anztarza Bay.

The recreation lounge was large and spacious and about half the crew were already there enjoying glasses of the cool drink Wazu. Little furry seeds floated in the glass and these were packed with protein energy. Wazu served not only as a refreshing drink but also as part of the Oannes essential diet. The seeds were cultivated on Nazmos on a large plateau island that was just twenty feet below the water surface of the Great Sea of Peruga. The underwater plateau was covered in thick rich sediment and was essential for growing most of the Nazmos food supply. Sometime ago an unwanted weed had grown up between the staple crops and attempts to prevent a recurrence had not been successful. Then some one had by accident discovered that the seeds within the pods below the dead weed flower when dried on land in sunlight contained a very high level of protein. But the tiny seeds were quite unsavoury and had a bitter after taste when chewed normally. However when these were added to the Wazu they not only gave the drink a decorative appearance but also added a perfumed flavour to it. Best of all the protein in the seed gave essential long lasting energy. It was not certain from where or how the weed now named Mizton had evolved but some suspected that it may have inadvertently been carried to Nazmos from Earth perhaps as long as ten thousand years ago on one of the very early expeditions. It must then have mutated in the Nazmos conditions and so evolved into this useful weed. The Anztarzans had tried cultivating it in one of their food domes but without success. Subsequently all supplies had to be imported from the home planet.

The general crew members of craft 8962-Green were not personally known to Brazjaf but they all knew of him as an important government person. They conveyed their good wishes to him and he acknowledged these in return. They were well aware of the Ashley mission and most looked forward to the day when a return visit by Ashley and his family would be made to their city.

However there were also doubters among the crew who knew of the failures of the past. They did acknowledge that all avenues for peaceful contact must be followed up especially since Ashley was the first example of an Earth creature with a self-taught telepathic ability. They would like to hope that he was the one.

Brazjaf finished his Wazu and then received a message from Nazaztal to come to the control centre as they were now only a few miles from docking in Anztarza Bay. Brazjaf relayed this onward to Muznant hoping that it would wake her from her relaxation sleep. Almost immediately he received her response to say that she was nearly ready and would meet him up at the control centre in a few minutes.

The Anztarza berthing was a textbook affair and as always performed to perfection by the onboard Zanos with guidance and instructions from the main Bio-controller of the Bay Dome. Nazaztal conveyed his final instructions to Byuzlit regarding the maintenance to be performed within the craft and handed control over to him. He then led Brazjaf and Muznant out of the control room and finally out onto the quay where a small group was assembled to greet them.

Ribuzalt came forward out of the group and met her captain husband with a smile as their foreheads touched in the public Oannes greeting between a husband and wife. Their communication was completed within seconds and Ribuzalt then smiled at her friends Brazjaf and Muznant and went through a mental 'Sewa' with them.

The group meeting them were the three Chief Ministers Rymtakza, Zarzint and Tzatzorf. And they were accompanied by some of Anztarza's leading citizens. Among these were Puzlwat and Mytanzto who from the outset had been against this excursion to meet Ashley and his family. They had argued that more research and more information were needed on this child of humans since they believed him to be too young to be of any consequence. All that Ashley had revealed about himself could be contrived and in fact they argued that most of it was quite unbelievable. Basically Puzlwat hinted that Ashley was just another upstart pretender claiming fantastic powers. His knowledge of Anztarza and its people would be a threat to their very existence should it become known among the general Earth population.

When all greetings were completed, Tzatzorf who was the most senior of the chief ministers led the way to the large deck transport that sat upon the flat beach area well back from the waters edge. This was a simple looking rectangular shaped open platform affair with railings all around its upper perimeter. The decking for passengers was four feet above ground level which was also the depth of the craft. It had a set of six small steps leading up through the back and up which the group climbed to get on top of the platform. The deck itself was covered in a soft blue carpet-like material. The decking was 25 feet long and 15 feet wide and all on board tended to stand near the perimeter railings. There was a slight bulge in the shape of the sides and it had rounded edges at its top and bottom. It was made of the same composite material as the spacecraft and was bright orange in colour with two yellow stripes halfway up from its base.

There had been one person standing beside the craft near the steps when the group boarded and he was the last to step aboard. He was the proud operator of Deck Transporter 536-Orange and was well known to the chief ministers and also to most of Anztarza's citizens. He was approaching 260 years of age and had been in Anztarza for nearly ninety years. He had served on several spacecraft prior to that and had many exciting tales to tell. All the children loved him for that. His name was Kazaztan and he lived in Dome-17 with his wife Zarpralt aged 220 years.

The onboard Zanos Bio-computer responded to Kazaztan's telepathic instruction and 536-Orange rose silently and smoothly upwards till it reached a height of about twenty feet. It then moved forward at a sedate 15 miles per hour towards one of two dome linking tunnels. It entered the tunnel on the left leading to Dome-2. Each connection tunnel was half a mile in length had a width of 100 feet and arched up to a height of 200 feet at its centre. The slight breeze on the deck was a welcome sensation and most on board faced into the direction of motion.

Muznant was one of the exceptions as she stood holding the deck railing and looked down at the passing scenery below. She loved being high up and this had always fascinated Brazjaf. She had told him that looking downwards was a completely different viewing sensation for the eyes and it gave her a kind of thrill. The light breeze caused by the craft movement caused the butterfly wing on her back to flutter slightly and this again had a pleasant tickling sensation.

The deck transport entered Dome-2 and Kazaztan directed it across this towards another connection tunnel on the left side. While in the dome area the transport had to rise to a height of 50 feet in order to avoid the tops of the accommodation structures. Each dome was about a mile in diameter and nearly 2000 feet high at its central point. Passing through the next connection tunnel the Transporter entered Dome-3 and then went straight on to the next tunnel leading to Dome-4. Although similar to the other domes this one had an amphitheatre near its centre. All domes had a clear central square area for the deck transporters to land on and 536-Orange headed straight for this and gently settled down at its centre. Kazaztan climbed down the steps onto the dome floor and stood to one side. It was impossible for the deck transporter to move if the designated operator was not aboard so the chief ministers and their entourage felt it safe to disembark. Each thanked Kazaztan for a pleasant journey and then headed for the waiting assembly. This was to be a momentous occasion as Brazjaf and Muznant were to report on the detail of their meeting with the Earth people, namely Ashley and his family.

All of Anztarza had already experienced the thoughts and spoken words of that meeting through their communication badges and there was generally a good feeling about everything that had taken place. There was a minority group of Anztarzans led by Puzlwat who had been against the Aberporth visit on the grounds that it was a rash move that would expose the knowledge of the secret existence of Anztarza to the general Earth population. Earthlings were currently considered too volatile in nature for any bringing together of their differing cultures.

Puzlwat argued that Ashley might just be a clever manipulator of the system and the art of telepathic communication with an ulterior motive. If he was what he claimed then he could threaten the very fabric of Anztarza.

However the majority had voted for the visit which had gone ahead as planned and Brazjaf and Muznant had been given the task of determining the truth of the inner emotions and intentions that lurked deep within Ashley's mind. For deep mind reading to occur Brazjaf or Muznant had to make a physical contact with the subject. And that is exactly what had been the purpose behind the touching and kissing episodes with Ashley and each of his family members.

The chief ministers and some of their selected entourage approached a prepared raised stage area. They climbed the three steps up to the platform and turned to face the gathered assembly of about a thousand of Oannes' officials many of whom were standing though some were also seated on backless padded stools.

Tzatzorf as the most senior chief minister conveyed that the assembly would commence with a communication from governmental aide Brazjaf and then from Muznant his wife who'd had the privilege of a deep mind probe with Ashley the one they were all talking about.

An emotion of peace and calm filled the amphitheatre as was usual prior to all meetings of this kind. Brazjaf then stood up and conveyed his impressions of the members of Ashley's family that he had met and with whom he'd made body contact. He conveyed how extremely well behaved and civilized they all were. He had felt a compatibility with these people and an emotion of affection had come at him from them. The family members were all very close to one another in affection and they all knew of Ashley's tremendous gifts and powers. They also knew that a great task lay ahead of him but were quite unaware of what that was or entailed. All had learned to communicate in a basic form of telepathy though they still preferred the sounds of their verbal language. Ashley's mother Lillian was extremely protective of her son and feared that the people of Anztarza might take him away or put him in terrible danger. Brazjaf conveyed that he had assured her that such was not the case and had informed her that wherever Ashley went she could always accompany him.

Brazjaf then communicated to all the assembled official class of the Oannes that he'd had direct body contact with each of Ashley's women relatives in turn. The image he conveyed was the kissing process that was such a favoured custom among the Earth people. By this means he had been able to affect a complete deep mind probe on each. Telepathic mind reading was one aspect but this physical contact probed into the deepest roots of their innermost emotions and ambitious cravings. In no case did Brazjaf find malicious intent of any kind. No deceptions were hidden nor were any found. All however harboured a concern for Ashley's welfare. His partner to be, the one named Tania, was especially worried for him. Within the space of the few hours that the visit had taken Brazjaf conveyed that affection had blossomed within his being for this family. He couldn't help but feel a kindness towards them. He was seldom mistaken.

'We have nothing to fear from this group of people,' he conveyed, 'and when you do meet them you will find them likeable and affectionate. I do not think we should extend contact with anyone else since we do not know of any similar situation. Ashley first made telepathic contact with us through the monitoring device which he referred to as his 'thinking stone' which then subsequently led us to seek him out. This was a unique situation and not likely to be repeated ever again or at least very unlikely. But at last we have a breakthrough in which we are finally in communication with a small group of Earth people. It is a beginning which could lead one day, perhaps in hundreds of years from now to the wish for a full integration of our two peoples. Do not throw away such an opportunity.'

Brazjaf then stepped backwards as Muznant took his place on the dais.

'I too had facial contact through the kiss custom,' communicated Muznant, 'and I can only concur with everything that my husband has indicated to you. There was only truth and affection directed at me and their innermost feelings and emotions had a calm and peaceful intent. They all conveyed goodwill and the senior most man in the group who is the grandfather of Ashley showed a great admiration for me similar to that which I get from my husband. This feeling a woman cannot mistake as you all know. But I cannot speak for the general population on Earth which as we all know are extremely diverse and in disharmony with one another. We do not have to deal with them. But I can vouch for this small group and family of Ashley that have an honourable and good intention towards us. No one outside this family knows of Ashley's unique gifts. It was good and very wise of Ashley's parents Alex and Lillian to have ensured that those qualities were kept secret from the rest of their people.'

Muznant paused to allow what she had conveyed to sink in. She knew that her audience was not just those in the amphitheatre area but the entire population of Anztarza. All were mentally tuned in to what was being communicated here today with a keen anticipation to know more about the wonder boy Ashley. Muznant continued.

'Now Ashley is what you all wish to hear about and I will tell you. When I made contact with him in the kiss process it seemed as though he drew me into his innermost thoughts. His gifts evolved gradually from when he was just five years old and he currently believes that there may yet be more for him to develop. I felt the power of the entire universe at his beckoning and I understand what he is capable of achieving. He can freeze Time itself to a near standstill at a mere thought but has never in all his years misused this gift for either amusement or self gain. He has the gift of telekinesis and as yet has not had the chance to test it to its fullest. He did not have to convey any of this to me. It was all there inside his mind for me to read. I not only read it all but it is now prominent in my mind as though Ashley is a part of my thoughts. And yet there is a mystery within. Someone called Philip. This person had a great love for Ashley as Ashley still has for him. The mystery is that this person Philip died two years ago violently during a burglary within his house. It was he who conveyed to Ashley that a big task lay ahead of him at a moment shortly after his death. Ashley feels that this Philip might be his mentor who will guide him. Ashley receives guidance from something or someone he calls his inner voice.'

Muznant paused again in her mind communication. She paused for some considerable time but the waiting Oannes knew instinctively that there was more to come.

'We Oannes live to years that are three times longer than the Earth people. But when we die we know that a completion has been made and only our thoughts are remembered. We do not believe as the Earth people do that there is another phase of life afterwards. We do not have the religion of the Earth people that a supreme being exists and was the architect in the construction of the universe. We believe in science and no matter how far back in time we go we find a cause and effect for everything that existed or came into existence. I have looked into the depths of Ashley's mind and have seen all his experiences and I know that this man Philip died. But his mind escaped from his dead body and was able to communicate fleetingly with Ashley before being pulled away as part of the rules that must be obeyed in that dimension which is without physical form.'

Muznant paused again to let what she had just revealed to sink in. She half hoped that this Philip person or whatever he was might somehow indicate his existence. Nothing occurred apart from an emotion of humour that seemed to pervade all their minds. Muznant thought that this came from Puzlwat and his group of dissenters. Let them laugh she thought, but she knew what she knew. Another thing that Muznant knew was that she herself was the first among the Oannes to begin to consider an Earth type religion; that the seed of creation was possibly the work of an invisible all powerful Supreme Entity. Of course Muznant could not convey this to her people just yet but she certainly could give her opinion of Ashley.

'Only I have been able to look into the depths of Ashley's mind,' she continued, 'and I know that he is the one that has been foretold in our mythology. There have been false leads over the millennia and many disappointments but with the disaster looming ever closer I believe that Ashley has been sent to us in this time of our need. Although this Philip person had communicated to Ashley that a great task lay ahead of him I do believe that Ashley can also assist us in our Nazmos dream. Once the big threat has been resolved I know that Ashley will be able to render Nazmos with an Earth like climate and appearance. But at the moment he is young and inexperienced and has not as yet realised the full extent of his power of telekinesis and so it will be up to us to nurture his gifts to bring them to their full potential. This will require many years and we can test and develop his skills far out in space in a safe and efficient manner. We have invited Ashley and his family to visit Anztarza sometime soon. This was based on the consensus conveyed to us when we were still in Aberporth.'

Muznant stood calmly facing the assembled dignitaries of Anztarza. She had one more surprise for them.

'Dear people of Anztarza,' she continued, 'there is one more gift that Ashley has been bestowed with and that is knowledge. We Oannes believe that over the years we have achieved a considerable knowledge of all things. And although we do understand that there are some things we still have to learn and discover in the main we feel we have reached close to the limits of all knowledge. Some have even claimed that our science is now complete and that there is nothing that we do not know or understand. My people I must inform you that we are grossly mistaken in our complaisance. Inside Ashley's mind is a seed that is blossoming. Since his very young days he has had the gift of knowing. Whenever a puzzle or question presented itself an inner voice gave him the correct solution. Wherever his thoughts might wander he would receive a clear answer to his unasked questions. Ashley can tell us more about the extent of the universe than we could ever hope to imagine. We can learn from him as though we were mere novices. He even understands the nature of the phenomena of time and how it relates to our basic atom structure. We understand the functioning of the attractive force of gravity but Ashley can tell you of its simplistic mechanical working within the invisible energy grid that exists throughout space. It was suggested to him by his family that he record all this in written form as a reference for future generations. We must give him time to do all this and I would advise that we do not rush him into any project or scheme. He must also be allowed to have a life of his own with his family. Let us nurture him as we would a child because when he is advanced in years he will give us everything.'

Muznant turned around and went to her adoring husband's side and sat down. He reached sideways and touched her hand and she smiled at him. He expressed that he was proud of her and she responded that she was proud of him. Their current mission was completed.

Tzatzorf looked at his fellow ministers and conveyed for Rymtakza to project his opinion. All knew of his affection for Brazjaf and Muznant and were therefore not surprised when he fully endorsed the planned visit by

Ashley and his family members. He added that they should be free to meet anyone and go anywhere in Anztarza. He recommended that a period of at least ten years be set aside for Ashley to be given suitable training with tests conducted in space before he be requested to undertake his first major project.

Rymtakza then looked across at his fellow chief ministers and conveyed an opinion that was given immediate agreement.

'I call upon Puzlwat and Mytanzto to join us here and face the people with their argument,' he conveyed. 'It is good that they have a differing opinion and it is important that we listen to what they have to say so that we can be made aware of any shortfalls we may not have considered.'

Puzlwat at 175 was nearly the same age as Rymtakza the youngest of the three chief ministers. He had only recently returned from a visit to Nazmos. And there too he had communicated his disagreement with regard to many issues that were being planned for the great city of Wentzata's further development. Puzlwat did not like change and conveyed that opinion at every opportunity. So now he walked up the dais steps along with Mytanzto and a few others for company. They gathered around him as he faced the assembly.

Politeness was essential with the Oannes so Puzlwat first thanked the chief ministers for letting him convey his own views to the people with regard to this disastrous decision.

'People of Anztarza,' he began and paused momentarily for effect, 'our people have lived here in peace for thousands of years. And that is because we have maintained secrecy of our existence here on this planet of Earth. We keep separate from these savage quarrelling Earth people because they are not civilized and are unfit as yet to mix with us Oannes. They kill each other in horrendous wars and commit murder among their own and are generally a very violent people. They are meat eaters and that according to our code makes them cannibals upon their own planet. We know of their history and we had all generally agreed that a thousand years must pass before any semblance of civilized harmony could be expected to develop within their society. There are many manipulators of chance and many opportunists among this race of people. There always have been and I say there always will be until they develop mentally like us. Now with this visit our peace has been put at risk. This contact is premature and no good can come of it. It is not too late to reverse the situation.'

After a brief pause to let what he had conveyed to sink in Puzlwat continued.

'We must not allow Ashley or his family to come to Anztarza. He may be unique among the Earth people but that may just be a trick on his part. His telepathic powers did not come from us and so may not be like ours. He has projected into our minds the hallucination of his possessing great power but that might be his demonic plan against us. I do not know what that plan might be but that makes it all the more suspect and dangerous. We have nothing to fear from the Earth people in general but this Ashley would bring a mental disruption to our peaceful existence and that would be most unwelcome. So I recommend that we cancel this visit and break contact with the communication badges so mistakenly distributed. Let us just continue to monitor this Ashley person and his family and see how they behave. If it is true that Ashley has all the powers he stated in his life story to us then let us observe him to see how those powers are used before we invite him here. We have always been careful in our dealings with these creatures so let us continue that cautious policy. It would be the prudent course to follow. Disaster is millennia and more away and as such we have no urgency for action. So why do our Chief Ministers believe that this Ashley is the solution simply because he conveys an unbelievable tale? I will tell you why. Because they are weak and so have grasped the first semblance of hope that has appeared. Muznant says that she had a contact reading of Ashley's mind and found only truth and sincerity there. That may well be true, but she did not say that she saw any evidence of these tremendous gifts that our Chief Ministers believe him to possess. Why was not Ashley asked to demonstrate all his powers to Brazjaf and Muznant before they invited him here? I find that extremely misjudged and careless of them. And if he does possess such a power then why has he not acquired fame and fortune among his own people. There are many ways he could have benefited but he has not. His thoughts convey that only his family members know of his gifts and they have advised him to keep it secret from the rest of their people. So why has he now told us his life story at the very first opportunity? I tell you my people to beware of this Ashley person. He is secretive and cunning and is intent upon some devious plan. I fear for our culture and peaceful way of life.'

Puzlwat paused while he gathered his thoughts before concluding his argument.

'I name Ashley as a liar, a cheat and an opportunist and we must break all contact with him and his family. Let us wait and secretly observe him before we ever contact him again. That would be the prudent course of action and not this sudden rash invitation to an unknown figure that promises much but has proved absolutely nothing. Thank you all for listening to me. We are few but we are the careful minority and have only the interests of Anztarza at heart. Let our principles prevail and persuade more of you to think carefully of what we are about to unleash. Because once we do so then there can be no going back. The path to disaster will have been set. So please say no to the recommendation of our Chief Ministers and get this visit stopped. Time is on our side if we do this. In ten, twenty or thirty years from now Ashley will still be there and if he proves to us that he is indeed whom he says he is then I will be the first to recommend him. For now though let us be circumspect in our approach to these people. We must take care of Anztarza's future and follow the course I have stated. That is all I ask.'

Puzlwat stood for several moments in silence. He was a good communicator and had been known to go on with a lot more in argument on government matters that he opposed. So it was a bit of a surprise to everyone when he turned around, nodded to the Chief Ministers and then walked back to his previous position among the gathered Oannes.

Zarzint who was the second most senior Chief Minister now came forward and gave his opinion.

'Anztarza has nothing to fear from these Earth people. Puzlwat and his friends are mistaken in their fear. Muznant has read Ashley true and knows what he is and has told us so. We gave her the authority for the visit to Ashley and we then gave our authority to invite him here after she had read his mind and found him of honourable intent. Muznant has never been mistaken before and is not so now. She has a special talent for reading inner minds as very few of us possess and therefore I say to Puzlwat that he is mistaken in his suspicions with regard to Ashley. But since he has been so eloquent in has argument let us see how many have been persuaded to his views. So please will all of Anztarza now state their opinion through their communication badge.'

Zarzint paused and mentally stated that he was in favour of the visit. All of Anztarza did likewise and gave their opinion. The result was instantaneous and was immediately conveyed to the mind of every Anztarzan citizen. It was 9973 for the visit to go ahead and 23 against.

'Thank you my fellow citizens of Anztarza,' communicated Zarzint, 'the visit will proceed as planned. I hope that Puzlwat and his fellow dissenters will be persuaded to our view once thy have met Ashley and his family here in Anztarza. All may now return to their businesses; this conference is completed.'

Brazjaf and Muznant smiled at each other and Mizpalto who was the wife of chief minister Rymtakza and their very close friend came up to them and they touched foreheads.

'Tell me about this Ashley,' she queried of Muznant, 'is he as handsome as you have conveyed? I look forward to meeting him.'

Muznant laughed. 'Are you intent on flirting with him?' she conveyed jokingly. 'Yes he is handsome and kind and honourable and very much in love with his partner-to-be Tania. She is very beautiful and as much in love with Ashley. But there is one among them who is as much a flirt as you are my dear Mizpalto. The one called Eric who is Ashley's grandfather and quite aged by Earth standards. He has no partner and has quite a roving eye for a pretty face. His health is weak but his mind is strong. He will accept your flirting with good humour.'

Brazjaf then conveyed that he would like to go to his house for a well earned rest. He had not had much sleep and was in need of relaxation in his own home. Mizpalto smiled and gave Muznant a special teasing look. They had been friends for a long time and were used to teasing one another over little things.

The deck Transporter 536-Orange had taken a position high up in the dome and at Brazjaf's thought request was brought down to floor level in front of the dais by Kazaztan its operator. Other deck transporters also floated down to the floor positions beside it. The Oannes were an orderly people and the decks of the Transporters were soon full. 536-Orange rose up and slowly moved to the central connection tunnel at the far end. This led to Dome-7 which was home to Muznant and Brazjaf.

The journey was a slow one but once inside the dome the Transporter went to the central square and settled down gently. About ten Oannes got off including Muznant and Brazjaf who walked slowly towards their street. This dome was also referred to as 7-Blue and had five parallel streets evenly spaced with block housing facing the walkway. There was one broader main street that ran at right angles to all the five streets and bisected them as it connected with the central square on either side. Brazjaf and Muznant were housed on the fifth street and quite close to the dome wall. They had a slightly larger space behind the house which gave them an extra area which Muznant used as an out of house sculpting studio. She had taken up sculpting about two years ago after watching an Earth TV programme showing various artists at work. She had been fascinated by the work and had decided to try it for herself. She found she liked it immensely. There were plenty of the right size rocks available from the new proposed food dome number twenty four which was currently being constructed.

Upon entering their rooms they removed all their garments and Muznant went up the steps to the next floor above which housed a large indoor water pool. The pool had one clear glass side which stretched right across the width of the house. The pool was just over six feet deep throughout. This floor covered the entire area of the house below and the pool occupied more than half of it. This made the pool about 40 feet by 30 feet in size which was about the same as in most of the dome houses. The open space in front of the glass panel was about 40 feet by 20 feet and housed a table and cushioned stools and a cool cupboard for the dispensing of drinks and food. The area was used for entertaining when desired and several more stools were lined up against a wall. Nudity in front of friends was not the custom so in company a basic lightweight tunic was always worn.

Steps led to the top of the pool-tank and also down on the inside. Muznant climbed these and when at the top simply dived headfirst into the cool clear Nazmos water. She was luxuriating in its cool wetness when Brazjaf came up with two large drink containers and placed them on the wide ledge that ran along the wall on each side of the pool. He then climbed up the pool steps and did not follow Muznant's example but simply and sedately walked down the steps on the inside. Muznant swam up to him and rubbed her body against his in a seductive manner and Brazjaf put his arms around her in a gentle embrace while touching heads. This was responded to eagerly and a period of intimacy followed. Later they had their Wazu drink in sips each time they swam an underwater circuit of the pool. Gradually tiredness overcame Brazjaf and he floated halfway down in the water and slept. An internal bladder system automatically kept his body at this position after he had willed it so. Brazjaf preferred to sleep face down with arms and legs outstretched.

Muznant on the other hand was wide awake and deciding to let Brazjaf have his rest so she climbed out and went down to the living area. The facilities here were similar to their accommodation on spacecraft 8962-Green but much more spacious. The décor had been tastefully done to Muznant's specifications and she now looked around at it with pleasure.

Night and day was relative and was simply a matter for the dome lighting being brightened or dimmed on a regular cycle. Although it never turned fully dark it nevertheless gave the Oannes a concept of the elapsing days, weeks and months. It also helped maintain their body clocks at a healthy level. Time in Anztarza was kept to the GMT status or zero meridian time.

Dome temperature and oxygen levels were constantly monitored and controlled by the central Bio-computer system. Food parcels could be delivered on request and were usually stored in cold storage cupboards fitted into the walls of the house. There were two large TV screens built into the décor of the walls which were normally quite invisible to the naked eye but which became apparent when activated. One was for terrestrial programs relayed from the Earth based satellite network and the other was for holographic projections of Anztarza's home news and entertainment programs.

The Oannes liked their wall ornaments and these were usually in the form of holographic scenes on nearly every wall giving the impression of open spaces. Forests were a favourite theme and since few existed on Nazmos most were of Earth's flora. The scenes were large and panoramic and gave window like scenic views.

The houses were constructed of the same synthetic material as the structure of the dome lining blocks. These were usually manufactured on the home planet and shipped out whenever required. Currently a new dome was under construction and when this was completed it would house the fourth food growing facility of Anztarza. These had twenty feet of Nazmos sea water in them that had thick rich sediment laid on its bed that came from the growing plateau of the Sea of Peruga. The base was shaped so that a gradually sloping shoreline extended centre wards from the dome wall. These were planted with Nazmos plants of varying produce for the nutrient needs of its people.

The crops were of Raizna a small potato, Starztal a flat pea-like vegetable, Yaztraka a fruit tree with long hanging fruit that was cooked into a mash, Mirzondip a bit like rhubarb, Lazzonta a sort of runner bean, Tartonta a pear like fruit and Yantza a root product to name a few.

The main oxygen supply for all of Anztarza came from the synthesis of sea water. The hydrogen by-product was compressed, liquefied and then returned by pipeline to a point deep into the ocean floor under the Davis Sea.

Each dome possessed a large food outlet bordering the central square and every family had the right to access and acquire its needs from this outlet. A mental monitoring was done by the dome bio-computer and information conveyed to the Anztarza central computer system. A system of credits was in force similar to that which existed on Nazmos but which had only been introduced in Anztarza when the population had risen above 5000 a few thousand years ago.

All Anztarzans had a work function whether it was manual or mental and were paid in credits accordingly. Pay was good and credit balances were healthy. Proportionate amounts could be transferred to Nazmos freely and as necessary.

The Oannes had lived on Earth a very long time and one of the first things they had wondered at was the richness of the vegetation as compared to Nazmos. They had found that many of their own crops were similar to the edible vegetables that humans cultivated. As such reliance on imported food from Nazmos became less urgent though always welcome. A favourite was the bread that was the product of wheat and monitoring its use by humans raised a curiosity that eventually led to its being adopted into the Oannes diet. Gradually other cereals got included also. But when milk products of butter and cheese were sampled they became an instant favourite with the Oannes people not only in Anztarza but also back home on Nazmos. An exception was sugar and sweet products. For some reason sugar if eaten in concentrated form led to a feeling of nausea especially in the young. Most spices had a similar effect except salt which could be harvested from the sea. Aromatic herbs were another favourite and mint was considered unique. It was grown in pots inside the dome houses. Apparently the Oannes had a strong sense of smell and the growing mint exuded a pleasant aroma for them. They had no taste for tea or coffee beverages and liked nothing that had to be drunk hot. They much preferred the cool drink Wazu with those furry seeds floating around lazily in it.

Procurement of Earth products was made on a bulk basis through agency offices set up in strategic areas and stored in warehouses specially constructed to permit their spacecraft easy access. Oannes disguised appropriately as humans operated in limited form and as was considered necessary. Swiss type bank accounts using a gold exchange had been set up and all transactions were correctly paid through the recent system of cashless transfers via Earth computers. Before that it was banker's cheques and preceding that by about a hundred years was the literal handing over of bags of gold coin. The Oannes were an honest race and stealing was never even remotely considered.

Brazjaf and Muznant were given the administration task of arranging housing for their guests when they arrived. Since Anztarza would be a strange environment with strange customs Muznant suggested that Ashley and his family members be lodged as guests with an Oannes family or person. Ashley and Eric lived on their own so Brazjaf considered it appropriate that they both be housed together with one family. The three Bonners, three Marshs and two Davis family members could be housed with three separate Oannes families. It would be nice if they were all on the same street and even better if they were put into four connecting houses. These thoughts were communicated to the Oannes population and offers of hospitality flooded in. Most were offers to house Ashley and his grandfather.

Brazjaf conveyed that the guest accommodation was mainly for sleeping arrangements and for getting ready for visits. Since Ashley and his family would be here on the specific invitation from Brazjaf and Muznant then Dome-7 would be the preferred base with accommodation on their street. Since the Oannes did not use beds for sleep but floated in their sleep tanks or pools then for the benefit of their guests new arrangements would have to be made or manufactured. Muznant did not envisage a problem.

In order to avoid any contentious issues the chief ministers jointly conveyed that Brazjaf and Muznant would have the honour of housing Ashley with his grandfather Eric. Theirs was the first of the row of houses and the rest of the family would be accommodated in houses alongside on Fifth Street. The entire street happened to house couples that were all in administrative functions and were all close friends of Muznant and Brazjaf.

The first neighbours were Laztraban and his wife Niktukaz. Laztraban was 196 years of age and his wife whom he lovingly called his Niktu was younger at 166. They originally hailed from a small town on a remote lake quite far from Wentazta and had no one left there now whom they cared to visit. They had lived in Anztarza for nearly half their lives and had been back to Nazmos only twice in that time. They had literally fallen in love with Earth at their first arrival and had been given permission to roam an uninhabited island forest off the west coast of a land mass in the far north of the northern hemisphere. They had to be in appropriate disguise of course. The island was approachable from the open sea and their travel craft had to be left on the ocean floor at least a couple of miles out from the shore. They also had a great affection and admiration for the majority of Earth's inhabitants mainly through the many factual TV programs they watched. They viewed the trees and vegetation with great curiosity and longing. The Oannes dream was that one day Nazmos would become similar to Earth in its richness. And that could all depend upon Ashley. Most Anztarzans thought the same which was why they looked forward to his visit. They considered themselves privileged to have been given the honour of housing Ashley's parents and sister.

The next house was that of a relatively younger couple Fruztriv aged 70 and his wife Rontuzaj who was ten years his junior. At the moment the house was unoccupied due to their being on a visit to the home planet to be with Rontuzaj's family. She was expecting their first child and it was usual for all children to be born on Nazmos in the family home. They would be gone about two years and would return without the child as was usual. No children under the age of nine were permitted to risk FTL travel. Or they might change their minds and decide not to return at all. In that case the property would become available for another couple when such a decision was brought back with the next contact. There were many such vacant houses in Anztarza and these were maintained in good order by the neighbours for any new comers from Nazmos.

The house was similar to Muznant's house and so had plenty of rooms to accommodate five people comfortably. So it was decided to place the Davis and Marsh families together and get Laztraban and Niktukaz to supervise their needs also. When the decision was conveyed to them they were quite pleased.

All this was communicated to the Oannes people and invitations were conveyed to Brazjaf for the visitors to take one of their meals in their house. One of the requests was for a banquet to be held in the central square of the dome which all the dome's residents could attend. This was immediately taken up with a similar request from all the other nineteen domes and Muznant replied that it would be considered but may not be possible. However, at least one visit to each dome would be made on a tour basis. It would be of great advantage for all of Anztarza's citizens to see and possibly meet these Earth people during their visit. For sleep purposes dome lighting may have to be adjusted even further for the visitor's benefit.

When all of this had been agreed and welcomed by the people of Anztarza, Muznant decided to convey the information on the arrangements to Ashley.

'Greetings Ashley and to all members of your family,' the communication went out to all the ten badges that Muznant had handed out at the B&B. 'Greetings from Anztarza and its entire people. There is great emotion of keen anticipation here of your expected visit. Our people are eager to meet you and talk with you.'

Muznant then conveyed all that had taken place since their return with special emphasis on the conference and all that had been stated including the doubts implied by Puzlwat. She then detailed the accommodation arrangements that had been made and hoped they would be comfortable.

Ashley was with Milly and Tania in the shop at the time when Muznant's message came through. They all smiled and Milly remarked at how quick they had been in Anztarza in making the arrangements for their visit. It was time to set the scene for their own getaway for the benefit of the locals and Robin.

'I think I need a nice long holiday,' said Milly in a contrived loud voice. 'Why don't we all go away on a relaxing cruise or something for a week or two? Somewhere nice and warm would be good.'

'An excellent idea,' said Ashley, 'but with Christmas coming up we'd have to wait till after. Perhaps about mid-January would be ideal.'

Ashley was thinking of the objectors little group in Anztarza. He felt it a healthy sign and very democratic that there be a voice of dissenters permitted to state their view openly. Ashley was sure he could get them to change their opinion of him once they actually met. He also had a little plan in mind for this purpose. He understood their concerns with regard to the fact that general knowledge of their presence on Earth could endanger their anonymity and security. The people of Earth were too diverse and prejudiced in outlook to adopt a friendly viewpoint. Puzlwat and his friends were perfectly justified in their doubt and Ashley conveyed his thoughts to the Oannes people through his communication badge. Their existence here in Anztarza must remain a closely guarded secret for as long as was necessary. It would be for the Oannes to decide when the moment was right for a harmonious general contact between the two races. Ashley could not see this happening for a very long time. Earth had a long period of development ahead of it before a civilized harmony of thought could be achieved that was anything nearly similar to that which existed among the Oannes people.

Ashley conveyed that their visit would hopefully be about the middle of January after Christmas had been celebrated.

'We should like to visit Anztarza sometime in January if that is convenient,' communicated Ashley. 'A period of about two weeks would be ideal. We have much to arrange and discuss between us so as not to arouse suspicion among our community and friends.'

'We understand,' came the reply from Muznant. 'January would be most suitable. Anytime would be suitable to us. In fact we feel you are already with us now. And we are keen that you should see Anztarza our city of which we are very proud. Incidentally our FTL interplanetary cruise ship is expected about then and it would be good for you to see it and how one day you may even travel in it to our home planet Nazmos.'

A pause and then Muznant conveyed a worrying question.

'There is something disturbing your thoughts Ashley. We can read it in your subconscious. Please consider it and then let us know what it is and we will try to help. We feel it concerns us in some way but you will need to clarify it for us to see it. There should be no hidden concerns to cause a conflict of opinion between us. There must be no doubts in our relationship. We are a transparent community and have been completely open with you. We have more to reveal but that will be done at the proper time.'

Ashley looked at Milly and Tania and shrugged his shoulders while raising his eyebrows in query. They in turn looked puzzled as they had also heard Muznant's communication and weren't quite sure either what she was referring to.

It was Tania who suddenly remembered something she'd mentioned earlier that had been a bit of a concern for her but which she had quite forgotten about.

'They seem to know all our thinking,' said Tania. 'I sometimes feel we have no privacy left. These badges are like mobile phones only they pick up everything we say or think.'

'That's it,' exclaimed Ashley. 'I knew there was something I was concerned about when we first came in contact with the 'thinking stone'. I remember thinking 'there goes our privacy'. Only, in the excitement of our discovery and the contact with our new friends Muznant and Brazjaf, I seem to have forgotten about that side of it. I know that I can read a persons mind at will but I don't go around reading every mind I meet. That would be too intrusive.'

Ashley paused and then conveyed these thoughts to his badge and so to Muznant, even though he was certain she had already picked up on their conversational thoughts. Yes she had.

'Yes Ashley we can see how that can be an intrusion and disturbing for you. We Oannes have developed the art of containing our thoughts and blocking general transmission to all but the one we are communicating with.

You obviously have not attained such a stage in your telepathy so the badges each of you were given had been programmed to respond to your wish to shutdown reception from you. You just have to mentally command it and it will respond to that shutdown wish. The badge will then cease to transmit any of your thoughts to us and we will receive nothing. However it will still allow us to contact you should we find it necessary. And again should you desire to return to communication mode then you simply have to will it and the badge will comply. You may also wish to communicate privately with a single person only then the badge will do that also. You may use this method to communicate with one another. I'm sorry I did not instruct you of this facility when I gave you the badges but you must understand that it was an exciting historic moment for us too and we are people just like you and are not infallible. Please excuse the omission. We all value our private thoughts and you must have yours. So until we communicate again my friends live well.'

Ashley thanked Muznant for the information and then shut down his badge. Milly and Tania did the same. Ashley had thought about phoning Ron and Brenda with this bit of information when he realised that he could use the badge as a communication device. This was a wonderful bit of Oannes technology. Ashley just thought of this intention and immediately he knew that he could communicate with his Aunt and Uncle in faraway Aberporth. How wonderful and easy.

'Hello Uncle Ron,' form Ashley.

'Why hello Ashley,' came back from Uncle Ron, 'this is nice to hear from you. How are you doing it? Is this another development of your skills? Brenda is here with me and can also hear you.'

Ashley then conveyed all that had just occurred and what Muznant had explained about the badges.

'These badges are under our complete thought control and it will only communicate as you wish,' conveyed Ashley. 'So we don't need to phone each other anymore when we wish to talk. Isn't that grand?'

Both Ron and Brenda conveyed that they'd had similar concerns for their privacy and had considered discarding the badges or even destroying them. Anything as invasive was not worth keeping. But this solved the problem.

'Thanks Ashley,' said Brenda, 'I'm glad that's been sorted. What did your mum say when you told her?'

'Oh, I haven't contacted her or dad yet,' replied Ashley, 'you were the first I communicated with after Muznant signed off. I'll get them on this system now. You can stay connected if you wish as I pass on Muznant's revelations.'

It was only in a matter of minutes that everyone had been informed. And they were all thrilled about it. Lillian could convey her thoughts to any of her family whenever she wished. It was just great. The sisters could discuss things at any time of day or night via telepathy even though they were in different parts of the country. This would bring the phone bills down laughed Brenda.

Jerry remarked that this was the ultimate in communications technology and wondered how many centuries or millennia the Oannes were ahead of the Earth. If they first went into space twenty thousand years ago then that is probably how far ahead in technical development they must be. But there was also the social side to consider and Jerry reckoned the gap there was even wider. It was something to wonder about.

Ashley had always been wary of sending his telepathic thoughts over the phone lines ever since that Christmas when Tania had inadvertently received the images of Ashley's phone communication with Ron and Brenda. That was before Tania had been brought into the inner circle regarding Ashley's gifts. She'd been ever so suspicious then and had connived with Katy to try to get to the bottom of the matter. Katy hadn't been in the loop then either. Ashley knew of Tania's tenacious approach and she would not have stopped her probing until she'd found out the facts. It was good they had no secrets from each other now. Ashley couldn't help wondering what the future held for him.

This big task that was so much on his mind remained a puzzle. He was sure that Muznant and Brazjaf knew what that was and in her communication report to the Oannes people in the amphitheatre she had referred to the fact that once the big threat had been resolved other benefits would follow. Muznant had then referred to Ashley's youth and inexperience and that they would need to nurture his gifts, especially in telekinesis, to bring them to their full potential. She had said that it might require many years for that and that they could practice his skills far out in space for full development before the big task was attempted. For Ashley the puzzle remained but without the worry. He had faith and trusted the genuineness of the Oannes people and knew that they would never engage in anything that was underhand or dangerous as far as he was concerned. The one clue in all this seemed to be the importance they placed upon his telekinetic gift. Was the big task to do with an asteroid type of danger to their planet? Or was it something larger? Ashley was sure he would find out soon enough. He conveyed all these thoughts not only to the family but to all of Anztarza as well. And then let it rest there for now.

The next few weeks were busy ones for McGill's Antiques as people frantically searched for ideas for Christmas presents for their loved ones. Robin's floor was particularly busy and profitable as many items were bought as mementos of the old days. Robin was constantly shuffling new items about on the shelves where gaps had appeared. A favourite present seemed to be models of cars of the 40s and 50s. A lot that wasn't displayed was left in the six open-top boxes that Robin had placed against the walls around the room and a favourite browsing spot for accompanied children.

Among those who visited were their old friends from Mansfield, Gary Prior and wife Jill. The children had not come since they preferred to stay with their neighbouring school friends. Gary asked about the clock chap Graham and Ashley said he'd visited the shop once after the Henley auction though another visit had been promised with his wife Anne. Gary said he would love to see him again as they had got on well the last time. Ashley offered them a bed at his house and they agreed to stay the night provided they could make an early start in the morning. They planned the early start so as to be at the Clock Fair in Elvaston in the grounds of the castle just a few miles southeast of Derby by 11 o'clock at the latest.

Ashley thought about joining them but decided against it and asked Robin if he wished a day out. But Robin declined on the grounds that he was far too busy with his floor's sales and besides prices at Christmas fairs were far too inflated anyway.

That evening they all went to the Kashmir Diner for a pleasant dinner. It was Tania's favourite curry house and was not far from the shop and Milly and Jerry were also invited. They were served by 'Charlie' the chatty diminutive waiter but Gary and Jill found the spiced dishes a bit on the fiery side. So to cool down they all had ice cream for dessert.

'Sorry Jill,' said Ashley laughing, 'I think I forgot the strawberries and cream.'

They all laughed at that. Milly and Jerry had heard the story of Jill's famous picnics from Ashley's first visit to Mansfield.

Afterwards they all went back to Ashley's house for tea and coffee but didn't stay up very late. Milly, Jerry and Tania left for home shortly after midnight and then Jill and Gary also decided to call it a night and settled into Ashley's spare bedroom for the night. In the morning they were all up quite early and after a light breakfast of tea, toast and marmalade Gary and Jill said their goodbyes and were on the road just after 9 o'clock.

Ashley had been thinking about Andrew Pando just before he'd dropped off to sleep that night and thought he should return the diaries and stone tablet to Lester Dutton now that there was no further need of them. Ashley wondered what Margaret would make of his reappearance at her office in Kennington. On impulse he made the decision to visit the Duttons unannounced and he would take Tania with him. It would be interesting to see how Margaret reacted to Tania's presence. It would certainly give her the right message – or so Ashley thought. In fact events were to take a turn that would see telepathic communication developing as a taught skill in the longer term.

'Do you fancy a day in London?' Ashley asked Tania. 'I thought we might drive down and return the diaries and stone tablet to Lester Dutton.'

'Will Margaret his daughter be there? I'd like to meet her to see what it is about her that so fascinates you,' conveyed Tania smiling though with a raised eyebrow.

Ashley just smiled back and said nothing for a while. He'd already explained about Margaret.

Then aloud he said, 'I thought about one day next week, perhaps on Wednesday. We'll drive down and just pop in to the offices unannounced. We could then take in the sights around London. Trafalgar Square, Buckingham Palace, etc; there's a Garfunkel's restaurant quite near Trafalgar Square where we could have lunch or dinner.'

'Sounds good,' replied Tania, 'but won't Lester want you to stay to dinner with his wife Mary? Mind you I wouldn't mind seeing her star brooch for myself if it is as beautiful as you described it. Perhaps we ought to go prepared to stay the night just in case.'

Tania knew the full details of Ashley's last visit and because she'd felt a pang of jealousy regarding Margaret, all was still vividly fresh in her memory. Ashley had telepathically conveyed all in describing his earlier trip.

When Tania revealed the plan to her mum she received an encouraging, 'Go and enjoy yourselves darling and bring back a few London souvenirs for Robin's displays.'

'We also need to discuss our visit to Anztarza,' conveyed Ashley to all the family through his badge and received an immediate response from everyone. 'Perhaps we could all think about a date and duration. Personally I think a fortnight should be good and sometime around mid-January. We could say we were going on a cruise to the Med or something.'

'It might be more plausible if we just said we were going on holiday to Tenerife for two weeks,' conveyed Milly. 'Jerry and I have been there with Tania when she was a toddler. It shouldn't stir any interest one way or another since everyone seems to go there in the winter. We could say we'd got a couple of large adjoining apartments.'

'That sounds fine,' responded Lillian. Brenda also conveyed her agreement as did all the others.

'I think the B&B would be the best place to be picked up by our friends,' conveyed Ashley. 'It will be familiar territory to them and also remote from prying eyes.'

'The seventeenth of January is a Saturday and that is a good date for us. It is then generally a quiet period at the B&B. Julie and Barbara should be able to cope well for the duration,' conveyed Brenda.

Eric's thoughts came in loud and clear. 'I can't think properly with this new fangled thought gadget,' he conveyed. 'I'd much rather discuss this face to face with you all. Why don't we have a lunch meeting as we normally do to discuss matters like this? Couldn't we all meet at Lillian and Alex's place? This Saturday would suit me fine.'

Milly agreed and added that she enjoyed the get-togethers at Lillian's, though it would be too cold for anything out of doors.

Ron and Brenda conveyed that they wouldn't be able to come to that but would listen in through their communication badges. And so it was agreed.

Later on when they were having a mug of tea in the shop Tania smiled at Ashley and winked.

'O yeh mum,' she said aloud, 'we know why you look forward to these meetings at Lillian's. You can't get enough of Eric's compliments. Mind you there's competition for you in Vicky's mum Mavis.'

'I don't know where you get these fantasy notions from Tania,' smiled Milly rolling her eyes upwards, 'I do enjoy Eric's company, a girl needs a bit of flattery now and again and goodness knows I don't get any here.'

Tania went across to her mum and gave her a pretend hug.

'O you poor thing,' she said with a feigned sad looking face, 'is it such a hard neglected life? Ashley quick your hanky please I fear a tear is on the way and a great big crocodile one too.'

'Get off with you,' said Milly and they all laughed. This time Tania gave her mum a genuine hug followed by a kiss on her cheek.

'O mum, I do love you. I think you're the best of all mums and I think you are really pretty,' said Tania, 'and clever too to be running the shop the way you do.' Then she added, 'You are the most perfect mum of all.' And this time there appeared a wet glistening in both of their eyes.

'I'm off,' said Ashley suddenly and walked towards the door.

'Where are you going?' asked Tania with a surprised concern in her voice.

'Why, across the road of course to Lorraine's for our morning doughnuts,' he smiled mischievously, 'isn't it that time again?'

They all laughed as Ashley went out of the door.

'I'd better put the kettle on and fetch Robin down,' said Milly with a happy look on her face.

Saturday started sunny and bright but cold. There had been a severe frost during the night and the cars were covered in the white stuff. The air was still and by mid-afternoon it had warmed a bit but not by much. It was nice in the sun and was especially warm inside the car but otherwise too cold to do anything out of doors.

The gathering at Ashley's parent's house was complete apart from Ron and Brenda and all were seated at the dining table. Lillian had cooked a roast with all the usual potatoes, vegetables, stuffing and plenty of gravy. Eric had a bottle of dark ale while everyone else had a glass of either red or white wine. Eric said that the wines set off his aches and pains even though he used to love a glass of the red. Telepathy had been practiced by all as often as was possible but most usually lapsed into the spoken word. It just felt so much nicer hearing the sound of the other person's voice. But now with the badges even the thoughts that were received were recognisable as that of a distinct person and each had a timbre quality similar to the voiced words.

Earlier in the lounge they had discussed the date and duration for their visit to Anztarza and it had been agreed as Ashley and Milly had suggested. A visit of a fortnight's duration from the middle of January would be fine by all. Ron and Brenda conveyed that they too agreed that a 'holiday in Tenerife' was certainly something to look forward to.

So it was agreed that Saturday the seventeenth of January 2004 would be the date for the start of their Anztarzan adventure. And the pickup or meeting point would be at Ron and Brenda's B&B at Aberporth.

Ashley wished for communication with Muznant and she was instantly on the thought line.

'Greetings Ashley,' she conveyed, 'it is nice to communicate again. And I send greetings to all your family. You have news?'

Everyone else had unlocked their badges for general communication and their emotions of affection flooded across to Anztarza. A return feeling of peace, love and caring filled Lillian's lounge and was pleasantly sensed by all. Ashley then conveyed that their visit date had been finalised and agreed by all.

'As a first visit we have decided to limit it to a stay of two weeks commencing on Saturday January the seventeenth,' he conveyed. 'We hope this is enough for you to show us your city and to meet your people. We shall all assemble at the Aberporth B&B where we met you on your visit to us. We hope that you will be able to pick us up from there.'

Muznant conveyed that arrangements for their visit had been completed some time ago and accommodation for them all had been reserved in adjacent dwellings to their own in Anztarza's Dome seven. A complete itinerary had also been planned.

Badges were then shutdown for privacy but Ashley decided to leave his open. He wanted Muznant, Brazjaf and all of Anztarza to follow the pattern of his thoughts and know what was going on with them. He conveyed his decision to the others and Tania and Eric followed suit. Later Ron and Alex also opened theirs. Jerry and the ladies said they'd keep their badges closed.

Back to the present Lillian served a hot apple pie with a choice of custard or ice cream. Eric had his just plain. And as usual he was seated beside Milly. He quite enjoyed his chats with her.

'Do you think they'll give us a ride up into space?' asked Jerry. 'They did convey the information that their ship from the home planet was due and that they'd like us to see it, did they not?'

'Yes,' said Ashley, 'and Muznant did indicate that one day I or we may travel in it to Nazmos. Gosh I sometimes think all this is a dream including all these gifts that I possess. I think to myself that I might suddenly wake up and find myself to be just an ordinary chap. I wonder if one day when all this is over and the big task has been completed and the purpose for my gifts ceases that they are taken away and I become an ordinary person like everyone else. In a strange way I look forward to such a time. And then again what else is waiting beyond that for me to do?'

'Something very special,' was a thought that raced through Ashley's mind. But he kept this to himself as he did not as yet understand what was implied.

There was a wistfulness tinged with sadness in Ashley's thoughts and they all picked up on it. And this got to Lillian and she put down her head and fought against the desire to cry out. She felt Ashley's reassuring hand on hers which he followed with a gentle squeeze. She looked sideways at her son and sheepishly smiled her thanks while blinking away the tears that had come to her eyes.

'I'm not sure about this space business,' conveyed Ron, 'I just don't know how I'd cope with being weightless for that long.'

'Actually I don't think you will be,' explained Ashley. 'The impulse from their magnetic motors will keep us at a constant Earth-like gravity through constant acceleration. When the desired velocity is attained the craft is maintained at that one-G condition by affecting a backwards and forwards travel loop. However I'm not sure how this applies when travelling between Earth and Nazmos. I expect we'll find out when we visit Anztarza or when they give us a tour of their starship.'

After a while the topic of discussion returned to the home front and what they had all planned for Christmas.

'Why don't we all spend this Christmas together?' conveyed Katy.

Tania gave a thrilled agreement to this. 'Yes,' she said, 'and perhaps Ron and Brenda will join us.'

'Sorry,' was the response from Brenda, 'I'm afraid Christmas is a very busy time for us here, but thanks for thinking of us. We will be with you in thought though now that we have these communication badges. Can you imagine what all of Earth would be like if everyone possessed one.'

'There'd be no secrets and no conniving for a start,' conveyed Jerry. 'Perhaps that might be the way to universal peace. I wonder if that is the secret ingredient.'

A thoughtful pause followed this.

'Last year we had Robin with us,' said Milly returning to Christmas, 'but he couldn't wait to get away after his pudding and the Queen's speech to visit Lorraine. I think they might be planning Christmas together this year. Isn't that nice?'

'I think I have a very good idea,' conveyed Jerry. 'Milly and I have thought about this, just this minute, and wondered if everyone would like to come to us in Dudley for a change.'

A pleasing emotion of agreement filled the room and Milly took this to mean a general 'yes'.

'Lillian,' she said, 'you, Alex, Katy and Eric could come over for one o'clock on Christmas day or sooner if you wished. It's Thursday this year and you could stay till late. You're all welcome to stay the night if you wish but I know how we all prefer our own beds. And since none of us drinks much driving shouldn't be a problem, should it? Besides we could all have a relaxing day next morning.'

'I think we should still ask Uncle Robin,' said Tania, 'even if he is planning to be elsewhere.'

There were chuckles and smiles all around.

'Would you mind if I brought along a small beef roast?' asked Lillian aloud. 'Eric doesn't care for turkey and I've always made one on the side for him, haven't I Eric?

Eric nodded his agreement.

'That would be excellent,' said Milly, 'and please feel free to bring anything else if you wish, but no wine please as we've got tons.'

Meanwhile Ashley and Tania had moved slightly apart from the others, had shut down their badges and were conducting a private telepathic conversation with one another.

'What are you thinking Ashley?'

'I was thinking what a cohesive family we have become.'

'What else?'
'You.'
'What about me.'
'You and me together.'
'So?'
'You and me together forever.'
'Hmmm, I like that.'
'And kids.'
'What about kids?'
'Will they have my gifts?'
'I don't know. Maybe not.'
'Why not?'
'I think you have to be specially chosen.'
'By whom.'
'I don't know. Divine intervention perhaps?'
'I still don't know why me?'
'Philip mentioned a Big Task?'
'Perhaps. But I still have no idea what that is.'
'You'll know one day.'
'I think the Oannes know.'
'Know what?'
'What this big task is all about.'
'Then you'll soon know when we visit them.'

The emotion of love enveloped Tania and she knew it came from Ashley. But it must have been too much to contain and so spread to the whole room for they all looked towards Ashley and Tania seated on their own. Subconsciously Tania had reached out and had Ashley's hand in hers. She lifted it to her cheek before lowering it again and continued to smile up at him. There was a visible degree of earnest admiration and love in her look which all in the room were happy to observe.

Milly looked at Lillian and both smiled with pleasure and there was love here too expressed by the glistening shine that appeared in their eyes. They both felt good about their children.

As Christmas approached they all found it hard to believe that this would be the second one without Philip. That Christmas of 2001 had been memorable but seemed to have taken place so long ago. So much had happened since then and so much had been achieved. They were now on the verge of something historic; a meeting with people from another world. A civilization that was so advanced that humans were primitives in comparison. But then Earth had been given Ashley Bonner, the son of Lillian and Alex Bonner, and to the Oannes peoples he was someone out of their mythology. Ashley by all indications was to be their saviour from some terrible impending catastrophe. The approaching disaster was of such stupendous proportions that even the Oannes with all their science and technological know-how were powerless against it. The disaster was not imminent, it was millennia away, and had been suspected since before they had even come to the Earth that first time. In fact their search for other worlds had been accelerated by the potential threat. Although the Earth was a pleasant surprise for them its discovery was not a solution. Earth and Nazmos were too close together and as such Earth came within the boundary of the same danger.

Prominent in the minds of the Oannes people was an ancient prophesy that had been considered a myth. It said that a person would be brought forward from a very green land who would be a key player in saving their world. When Ashley had involuntarily given his life history to the 'thinking stone', there had been surprise and suspicion in Anztarza. This had however created excitement among some elders and they had at once connected Ashley with the myth. An investigation was demanded and contact was agreed. Suspicion had remained until the moment that Muznant had touched Ashley with her hands and affected a deep mind read of all his subconscious desires and emotions.

It was then that the truth was revealed to her. Muznant was sure that Ashley did have the potential to fulfil that vague prophesy, but not yet. He was far too young and immature at the moment to do what was necessary. Ashley was looked upon as a lost hope until another better prospect could be unearthed. He was a straw to cling to in the fast approaching flood, metaphorically speaking. And Ashley was as yet quite unaware of any of this.

On the Tuesday after the get-together Ashley and Tania spent a whole day in the Merry Hill shopping centre buying presents for all the family members. They had decided to give out a joint present since they were now a couple. They planned a wedding when Tania finished her teacher training course in three years time. She would be twenty one in September 2006 and they could have the wedding about then.

Tania had a list of names which she ticked off for each gift bought. It was more of a leisurely stroll between shops than an arduous rush. In between the present buying they'd stop off for a hot drink and then later for a snack lunch in the food court at the appropriate time. There was plenty of variety and ample seating too. By five o'clock Tania's list was nearly completed and they decided to call it a day and head for home. All that was left was for them to buy gifts for each other. Tania suggested they each buy themselves something and that way they wouldn't worry about what to get. Tania said she fancied a pair of pink tinged opal earrings and Ashley said he'd like tickets to see a ballet or opera. They held hands as they walked out through Debenham's and down to where the car was parked.

Ashley was smiling and Tania couldn't help liking that and smiled too. But when Ashley gave a little chuckle she asked what was so funny. He told her telepathically and she laughed out loud, pulling her hand out of his and feigning annoyance.

'Is that what you think of us women Ashley Bonner; that we are all addicted shoppers?' said Tania with an amused expression on her face.

'No,' said Ashley, 'it's just what I heard on the radio this morning. My radio alarm comes on at seven and this morning they were talking about the secret for a long and happy marriage. People were phoning in their comments and this one made me laugh. I think people who invent jokes are very clever. When this chap said that holding hands was the secret of his 40 married years I thought how nice. And then when he added that it was to stop her from going shopping, I nearly spilt my cup of bedside tea with laughter. I believe he meant it as a joke. The simple ones are really the best.

'I shall report you to my mother Mr Ashley Bonner,' laughed Tania, 'and I shall always think of this when you hold my hand.' Tania had placed her hand back in Ashley's.

Ashley smiled and said nothing. Then he gently squeezed her hand before raising it up to his lips, planting a little peck on it and lowering it down again.

Tania looked up and smiled too. She thought that he had responded in the most perfect of ways by that simple gesture but more importantly by not saying anything.

'Ashley Bonner, you know what you are don't you?' she said. And after a pause she added, 'You're just perfect that's what you are.'

Again he looked at her and smiled. And this time he released her hand and moved his arm across her shoulders and gently pulled her to him as they strolled towards the parked car. Tania looked up at him and her eyes glowed bright as love enveloped them both like a mist surrounding a forest. For that brief moment they were in a world of their own.

Tania thought about that moment as they were driving down towards London the following day. Ashley had wrapped the diaries, notebook and the stone tablet in a brown wrapper and had taped it closed quite neatly. It was in a carry bag in the boot of the car.

The sun was shining and Tania looked sideways at Ashley as he concentrated on the driving. He sensed her gaze and gave her a quick look and smile before shifting his concentration back to the road ahead. There was a lot of traffic on the M40 especially the huge juggernauts. They seemed to travel in bunches and caused all traffic to slow down behind them when one was overtaking in the middle lane.

Ashley said he had no intention of driving into the congestion zone of inner London and would instead park way out at East Acton or similar. They could then catch the tube from there. Tania thought it a good idea as an all day pass would be ideal, especially for getting around and seeing the sights of London.

After a thirty minute stop at the Oxford Services on the M40 they continued on to London refreshed by the hot chocolate drinks. Ashley drove past Hanger Lane and then turned left off the A40 when they got to East Acton. There were plenty of pay and display parking spaces on Ercowald Street and Ashley found a space just beside the tube station and underneath the railway bridge. It was after midday so Ashley put in for six hours of parking. Parking was free after 6:00pm.

At the station which was a tiny one room affair with only one service window they purchased their all day tube tickets for zones 1 to 4 and climbed the steep stairs up to the eastbound platform. It was ten stops to Tottenham Court Road where they changed for the Northern Line. Here they caught the southbound train to the Oval stop just after Kennington. The Commercial Centre was just across the road from the tube station and Ashley led the way to Lester's consultancy offices.

Ashley opened the door and stood back to let Tania enter. As he followed her in new thoughts raced through his mind as though he had just been sent a telepathic message of sorts. He immediately conveyed this to Tania and she looked back at him with a smile and nodded. It would be a start of something new and they might as well begin somewhere; and what better place than a training establishment?

Ashley had the neatly wrapped package containing the diaries, notebook and stone tablet in his left hand down at his side. Margaret Dutton looked smart and pretty in her blue-green two tone outfit as she sat behind her reception table. Her semi-blonde hair had been cut short and made her face look rounder and younger than her 24 years. She now had the chubby faced appearance of a school girl and she smiled as she recognised Ashley.

'Hello Margaret, we've come to return the diaries and artefact that Lester loaned me,' conveyed Ashley telepathically. 'And I've brought my fiancée Tania to meet you. We've also brought you a gift.'

Margaret's smile vanished and in its place was an expression of astonishment and some confusion.

'I'm sorry,' she stammered, 'what is that you just said?'

This time it was Tania's turn to communicate with a big pleased grin on her face. She was enjoying this especially since it was Margaret she was dealing with.

'It's alright Margaret,' she conveyed, 'we have just used our skill of telepathy to communicate with you. We hope to teach you how it works and are sure you'll pick it up quite quickly. You already suspected as much the last time Ashley was here.'

Margaret was now standing fully upright behind her table and the confused expression was quickly fading for one of comprehension and understanding. But all she could utter were the words 'You too?'

'Yes,' conveyed Tania, 'and both our families are also good at telepathy. It is a most efficient way of communicating with each other. All you will need is practice with us and your brain will adapt to it once it has been triggered in that direction.'

'But this is wonderful,' exclaimed Margaret aloud. 'Your thoughts are so clear and instant.'

She then came around to them and gave each a welcoming kiss on the cheek.

Ashley gave her the package and she turned to place it on her table. She was smiling when she turned back and nodded her agreement. Ashley had just conveyed his plans to her in that instant and Margaret seemed pleased.

'Yes,' she said, 'we could add that to our portfolio of training. Gosh, dad will be surprised and pleased when I tell him. But how did this telepathy thing start? O don't tell me, its part of that history-thing gift you possess Ashley isn't it?'

'That's right,' Ashley conveyed and then added a bit of a lie that an ancient piece of a stone figurine object had seemed to communicate with him when he had held it in his hand. He had simply replied back in the same thought terms. Then before he knew it he realised that he could also communicate his thoughts to his mum and dad. Later he included the rest of his family which were his sister, granddad and Aunt and Uncle in Aberporth.

At first he didn't get anything back from them but after a few days he began to pick up bits and pieces of thoughts and then suddenly they were all communicating telepathically with one another in a rough hit and miss fashion. Over the following months this skill improved considerably and then Tania and her mum and dad were included as well. Ashley made all this sound matter of fact and very plausible. He was certainly good at telling tales.

He then conveyed to Margaret that he thought it was time to begin teaching others this telepathic skill which was latent in every human being. It just needed awakening and Ashley thought that Lester Consultants was a perfect vehicle from where a start could be made. It's what I came to speak to Lester about.

'Oh I'm sorry,' said a flustered Margaret, 'but dad is out on a factory job. He's currently doing a diagnostic on the company and is quite busy with it. He'll not be back till late but you could meet him at Mount View. I'm sure mom would be pleased to see you. You could stay to dinner.'

'Thank you but no,' conveyed Tania, 'but a cup of tea would be most welcome. I'm absolutely parched. Ashley intends to show me the sights of London.'

'Do forgive me,' said Margaret, 'this is so remiss of me. I'll put the kettle on right away. Please do come and sit here, its quite comfortable,' as she gestured towards the sofa armchairs.

As Margaret served them tea Ashley conveyed that he'd like to begin practicing with her the art of telepathic communication.

'Lesson number one Margaret,' conveyed Ashley, 'is that we must have no more verbal talk from you for the next few moments. Our telepathic skills allow us to pick up a person's thoughts in a general manner so just talk to me mentally and I will answer. If we spend about an hour with you it might just get you started, telepathically of course.'

Ashley didn't reveal that he could read her mind. That was not for her to know nor would Ashley reveal anything about his other special gifts. That was to remain a secret from the world, possibly forever.

Over an hour later they began to pick up a few independent telepathic transmissions from Margaret. And as her mind tried to adjust to the telepathic effort it made Margaret tired and sleepy with a bit of a headache, which was not unusual. The human brain is a complex organ and extremely resourceful in its adaptation but it is not a machine. So it gets tired out with extended effort. Sleep was the mechanism used to rejuvenate it. Sleep was also a healer when sickness threatened.

'We should stop this now,' said Ashley aloud. 'Awakening the brain to telepathy is quite stressful and my Aunt Brenda had a similar reaction. There too I think we were pushing too much too soon. So for now let us talk normally which should relax you. Would you like to lie down Margaret?

'I'll be alright in a moment,' she replied. 'I'll just sit here and shut my eyes for a bit while you talk. Tell me about the diaries and the tablet, did you find out anything from them?'

'Well, the diaries gave a good account of Mr Andrew Pando's travels generally though mainly to a tribe in West Africa,' said Ashley. 'Andrew spent about five months with the Dogon tribe and wrote that he enjoyed every moment of his time with them. You can read about this tribe in books and their weird knowledge about the stars which mainly concerns the Dog Star Sirius. It was the chief who gave the stone tablet to Andrew in exchange for Andrew's gold watch. The chief told Andrew that the stone had some magical influence and brought peace of mind if placed under your pillow at night. All your worries will melt away said the chief to Andrew. Maybe it's true but I found nothing extraordinary when I tried it. But I did think up a few good ideas for the business that night which turned out well. So please do thank Lester for lending me all this stuff, it was really appreciated.'

Ashley and Tania stayed for another half hour in which Tania made them some more tea. Margaret looked sufficiently recovered when they finally left.

'We'll pop in this evening again,' said Tania, 'after we have done a bit of sightseeing.'

'You could go around London on the Big Red Bus tour. It does a commentary through headphones as it travels around the city and is really informative,' suggested Margaret.

Ashley and Tania smiled at each other as they walked to the Oval underground tube station. It was not long before their train arrived. The train was nearly empty. They got off at Charing Cross and went up the escalators to the exit. They came out at the Strand and walked across the street to where Nelson's Column towered above them. Trafalgar Square was bustling with people strolling around and getting their photos taken in front of everything that looked mildly interesting. A favourite seemed to be in front of the reclining lions and the fountains. A large group of school children were being chaperoned by several teachers and were obviously on a school trip. They all had bits of paper on clipboards on which they scribbled their notes.

It was a lovely sunny day though a bit on the chilly side. The general atmosphere was a happy one and everyone seemed to be there to enjoy themselves and Tania and Ashley revelled in it. Laugh and the whole world will laugh with you. For brief moments they held hands but only when they were walking towards something or other. Tania had brought along her little digital camera and would rush off to one side or the other to take a photo. She would then bring it to 'view' and show Ashley what she'd taken. They also took pictures of each other and when a passer-by offered to take one of the two of them they posed with their arms around each other's waists.

It was now half past two and Ashley took Tania around the corner to a side street to Garfunkal's restaurant. They both had the Lasagne with salad and a Pepsi. The price was reasonable and the service was quick. It was just after three o'clock that they were out on the street again and strolling down The Mall and straight towards Buckingham Palace. Tania felt at peace until the thought of their visit to Anztarza came into her mind. She worried about what was expected of Ashley by the Oannes people and tried to rationalise that Ashley could look after himself.

But a little voice kept prompting doubts into her thoughts. She needed the walk to clear her head. They walked down Constitution Hill but kept to the Bridle Way just inside Green Park and came to the large traffic island which contained Wellington Arch. They crossed over towards Hyde Park Corner and then into the Park. The tree-lined avenues inside the park beckoned and they followed one to the Serpentine, a lake that curved around to the Bayswater Road. They found a bench overlooking the lake and settled down to enjoy the view. It was approaching dusk and the world was blanching towards the evening grey though the sky was still brilliantly tinted with a reddish hue. Winters had such short days especially around Christmas time.

Tania was at peace again and this time she leaned against Ashley as they sat closely together.

'I think I like London,' from Tania.

'Yes, so do I.'

'It's different though.'

'Yes.'

'It's very busy.'

'Yes, quite.'

'We could come here for a sightseeing holiday.'

'A week?'

'Yes, or even two.'

'Okay by me.'

'We could stay in a cheap hotel.'

'There are no cheap hotels in London.'

'Well reasonable then.'

'I suppose.' Ashley wasn't committing to anything.

'I'll look into it on the internet.'

'They have some good deals.'

'Maybe we could do a few long weekends now and then.'

'That sounds good.' Ashley was smiling.

'You mean more practical, don't you?'

'Yes.'

'O Ashley, what's going to happen?'

Tania conveyed all her sad thoughts and concerns to Ashley and he put his arm around her shoulders and hugged her to him. His own thoughts had no such concerns.

'I don't know exactly, my love. But I do have a good feeling about it all. They are a good and gentle race of people. They live an open style of life with nothing hidden. There is a threat somewhere that they feel I may be able to prevent. It may be a danger of some sort but I believe it is not an imminent one. There seems no urgency to it and I think we shall know soon enough.'

'Yes, but I can't help worrying.'

Ashley read her mind and understood the root of her concern. And that was being left alone without him.

'I'll not leave you on your own. Where I go you shall go. We must always do things together. Wherever this task takes me it takes you also. That is my promise to you Tania,' he said aloud.

They sat quietly on the park bench and Ashley brought his other hand around and entwined his fingers into hers. Tania also brought her free hand around and placed it on top of his. They sat like that for what seemed like ages. It was nearly 4 o'clock and the sun was just setting behind the skeletons of the trees in the distance. The chattering starlings were noisily jostling for their favourite places on the branches. A chill had developed in the air and Tania shivered.

'I think I've had enough of London for now,' said Tania aloud. 'Let's get back to Margaret as we promised.'

'I was just thinking of her,' conveyed Ashley. 'There's something about her that intrigues and puzzles me. She has a very strong intuitive sense and I'm sure she suspects that there is a great deal more than we are letting her know. Tania, we must be careful with that one or she might just guess at things I'd rather she did not know. And there's another thing that's been playing on my mind. When we planned on coming to London I'd not even considered revealing our telepathic skill. Yet as we approached the Dutton offices thoughts raced through my mind as though I had just been given a telepathic command of sorts. I believed it to be the start of something new and I'm now quite happy to let it continue. I think that this has been planned by Muznant and her crowd. They are looking into the far distant future when humans will approach the Oannes in telepathic skill. It is one way of creating harmony and peace on Earth between all nations. They will then achieve their aim of revealing themselves and moving around freely. It would be a nice state of affairs and so I'm happy to help Margaret start the ball rolling – so to speak.'

'That's very interesting,' responded Tania aloud, 'and I never even gave it a thought. I believed it was your idea and I trusted your judgement. Come on then, how do we get back to her?'

'We catch the tube to Leicester Square, change to the Northern Line and go south to the Oval. We leave the station, cross the road…'

'Shut up you idiot.'

They both laughed. An atmosphere of love and fun enveloped them. It was a pleasant sensation that seemed to remind them of Philip.

Margaret was at the glass paned door and saw them crossing the street.

'Hello you two,' came from her telepathically strong and clear.

'Hello back to you Margaret,' conveyed Tania. 'That was very clear.'

'Dad's here and quite excited. I practiced on him for a bit but I couldn't get anything in return.'

Ashley and Tania walked into the warm office and smiled at Margaret. It had turned really cold outside and it was nice to warm up again.

'Brr,' said Ashley aloud, 'by gum it's chilly out there!'

'Hello Ashley,' said Lester walking towards them from his office doorway. 'And hello Tania, I'm Lester, Margaret has told me all about you. I must say you are as lovely as she described.'

Ashley and Lester shook hands warmly and he bent down to give Tania a kiss on the cheek.

'My goodness,' he exclaimed, 'your cheeks are like ice. It is really cold out now. They have forecast quite a severe frost for tonight. Do come and sit down and we'll all have a nice hot cuppa. Margaret would you mind?'

'Not at all dad,' conveyed Margaret telepathically to her dad's surprise, 'the kettle is already on the boil.'

There was plenty of seating but Lester went into his office and came back with a straight backed padded chair. He placed this appropriately and sat facing his guests.

'Now tell me what you have been up to today,' he said.

Ashley thought this an opportune moment and so telepathically conveyed to both him and Margaret all the days events in vivid pictorial detail. It took but a moment and Ashley smiled as he finished. He had implanted into their minds the visions of the day according to Tania and Ashley in glorious colourama. Of course Ashley left out all their conversations. He explained that conversations between him and Tania were delicately private.

'Goodness me,' exclaimed Lester, 'I can see how much better telepathy is as compared to our verbal system. I just saw everything you did including that delicious lasagne you both had at Garfunkal's restaurant. I hope I can learn it myself. And what will Mary think, I wonder?'

He paused and Ashley read his thoughts and replied telepathically. Lester was thinking about asking Ashley and Tania to dinner at Mount View and hoped they could stay the night.

'We'd love to stay the night and hoped you would invite us. So in anticipation we packed an overnight case,' conveyed Ashley to the whole room.

'I didn't hear dad's side of it,' said Margaret, 'but it would be lovely to have you staying with us. If only you could stay for longer then we could spend more time practicing.'

'Oops nearly slipped up there,' thought Ashley, 'can't let on about my mind reading skills just yet.'

'I don't think his signal is very strong as I only got part of it and guessed the rest,' conveyed Ashley to Margaret.

'Thank you Mr Dutton,' said Tania aloud to be polite, 'that is very kind of you. We'd love to stay. I look forward to meeting Mrs Dutton and I hope to see her beautiful star brooch that Ashley talked about.'

'O please Tania,' Lester replied, 'do please call me Lester, I feel we're all friends already. Excuse me but I'll just ring Mary and give her the news. She loves having guests to stay over. I fear she finds my conversation a bit on the dull side.'

While Lester was out of the room Tania and Margaret had a short telepathic exchange. At one point they both laughed at something from Margaret even though her skill was still quite hesitant in its flow.

When Lester returned Ashley began a telepathic conversation with him. It was easy for Ashley since he could pick up Lester's mental efforts by simply reading his mind. But gradually after an hour and two mugs of tea, Lester's mind began to send out intermittent pulses of telepathic thoughts. Margaret laughed when she saw her dad looking extremely drowsy.

'I think dad's had enough lessons and practice for the moment,' she said aloud. 'His age probably doesn't take to telepathy that easily. Do you want to rest for a bit dad?'

'Actually I do feel a bit woozy,' said Lester, 'I think I'll just close my eyes for a while.'

He came and sat on the settee beside Tania.

Ashley stood up and walked over to Lester and touched his forehead with the back of his hand as though to check his temperature.

'He does feel a bit clammy,' he conveyed to Margaret, 'perhaps a cool glass of water might help.'

'Yes of course,' from Margaret as she got up and went to the back room and came out carrying a glass of water.

'Here dad,' she said, 'sip this, it'll make you feel better. The same happened to me too earlier today.'

'Thank you Margaret,' came from Lester.

'I got that dad,' exclaimed Margaret aloud. 'Gosh dad you have made quick progress. Just wait till we get mum trained up as well. She'll want to practice on all her coffee club friends.'

'Janice was working late and Mary has asked her to stay even later so she can cook up one of her specialities,' said Lester with his eyes resting shut. 'I'm glad you're here Tania,' he continued, 'you must be very proud of your Ashley with his wonderful gifts.'

Alarm bells went off in Ashley's brain and he quickly read Lester's mind to see exactly what he meant. But Lester was simply referring to Ashley's gift of reading the history of all the objects he touched along with this new telepathic skill. Ashley immediately conveyed this to Tania who had also raised her eyebrows in query.

While Lester rested, Ashley and Tania continued an intense telepathic conversation with Margaret, who was gradually getting quite proficient. She was a quick learner and both Ashley and Tania complimented her on the speed at which her brain had adapted. Ashley conveyed some suggestions for when Lester Consultants began their program in teaching telepathy to their course clientele. One of these was for the learner to use both verbal and thought communication in the early stages. Margaret responded with her appreciation of Ashley's suggestions and wondered if age should be taken into account during the training.

It was now quite dark outside and Margaret suggested they make their way home to Mount View where her mum and dinner awaited. Ashley used his badge to convey all of the day's proceedings to the rest of the family and the news that they would be staying overnight with the Duttons at their Mount View home. Tania smiled as she received a reply from her mum and they all had a pleasant conversation. Milly conveyed the news that she'd received a phone call from Graham to say he and his wife Anne would be visiting the shop the next day in the afternoon.

Ashley confirmed that he and Tania would leave London early and hoped to be there by midday at the latest. These badges were certainly useful. One could never feel alone anymore.

Ashley made the pretence of using the Dutton's landline phone to convey to his folks that they would be spending the night in London. Ashley had gone to Margaret's table, picked up her phone and dialled a number. He then seemed to pause before putting the phone down again and conveyed to Margaret that they were expecting a visitor at the shop the next day and so must leave sometime early in the morning.

'Gosh,' said Margaret, 'all that in a couple of seconds. I certainly see the advantage of this form of communication. I wonder what the downside is.'

Margaret drove them to their parked car making a detour to show them some of the festive illuminations put up by the borough council on many of the London streets. There were also private houses that were lit up with strings of multicoloured lights that twinkled pleasantly in the frosty night. A bit of a fog seemed to be descending now and Margaret said that she didn't think it would get any worse. They'd had it similar last night as well.

'I'd like to take you down Oxford Street as the council have done a really fantastic job there but it's much too congested with traffic,' said Margaret.

'We have a street in Stourbridge named Leonard Road in which all the houses are really done up well with thousands of lights,' said Tania. 'People come from all over to see it. It really is something spectacular and the residents take a collection for charity – usually to help leukaemia research.'

At East Acton Ashley retrieved his car and they then followed Margaret to Mount View.

Earlier, Lester Dutton had said that he needed to stay on at the office a bit longer to complete some paperwork. He said he should be home for 7 o'clock at the latest. He had tried conveying some of this information telepathically but had given up when no one responded. Ashley had thought it best at the time not to interfere and that Lester was given more time to adapt.

Mary was pleased to see Ashley again and gave Tania a joyous welcome and was wearing her star brooch especially for Tania's benefit.

'O Tania,' she said in her most welcoming voice, 'you are as young and beautiful as Margaret described you. And Lester said the same. Ashley is a lucky man.'

She gave Tania a kiss on both cheeks.

'I think I'm the lucky one,' said Tania smiling her best smile, 'Ashley is very special. And so is that star brooch you're wearing which I have heard so much about. Ashley told me its history and I believe it was made because Halley's Comet was quite spectacular that year in 1835.'

Mary took off the brooch and handed it over to Tania.

'Please put it on,' she said. 'I want to see how it looks on you. Wear it to dinner and you can return it to me after.'

'Oh I couldn't,' hesitated Tania looking at the brooch in her hand. She had never seen anything so sparklingly beautiful. Tania looked up at Mary and her big hazel eyes glistened with affection for this homely lovable woman.

'O nonsense my girl,' Mary said with an affectionate grin, 'it's only right that I see it adorning someone as pretty as you. Margaret wears it occasionally to please me. I see more of its beauty displayed that way. Here let me pin it on for you.'

She stood back when she was done and said, 'There, now isn't that just beautiful?'

Tania looked towards Ashley and he inclined his head and smilingly winked at her. He conveyed his love and admiration and unwittingly the whole room filled with the emotion. That was all Tania needed for her eyes to brim with tears.

'There, there my dear I know how you feel,' said Mary coming up and hugging Tania to her ample bosom and patting her gently on her back. 'I too get this way when I wear it after a long interval.'

Margaret was staring in Ashley's direction and Tania saw the look. She saw the look of admiration from Margaret and knew that she was taken with him; probably from when they last met. To Tania it seemed quite natural for people who got to meet Ashley to become enamoured by his boyish charm. Margaret was not the first nor would she be the last.

'One day,' Tania thought to herself, 'the whole world will admire and love this unique man.' But for now he was hers and vice versa and there was no room for jealousy or possessiveness in her emotions.

She wondered about their visit to Anztarza and at the kind of reception they would receive from its people. Muznant had already shown her admiration of Ashley at their meeting in Aberporth. But it was an innocent admiration filled with genuine affection. Perhaps the myth inspires an aspect of adoration of the expected one. The Oannes would initially adore Ashley as the promised saviour that was foretold in their myths who would avert disaster; if such a disaster was indeed impending.

Tania was brought back to the present when Margaret offered to show them to their rooms. And separate rooms it was though each was large enough for two; each had its own bathroom. Apart from overnight things neither Ashley nor Tania had brought along anything special to wear for the evening.

But Margaret understood their looks and assured them that dinner was a casual affair for everyone except her mum. Being home alone most days and apart from her coffee club she rarely went out. So of course she was always hoping for visitors and kept herself ready just in case. Their consultancy clients were often invited for the usual softening up process. As such Mary kept herself always dressed to the nines as though she expected the Queen of the Realm to drop in unannounced.

Lester was home earlier than he had thought and at dinner they all had a pleasant conversation.

'Do say something to me in this new form of talking,' said Mary. 'Margaret and Lester have told me about it but I confess I find it hard to comprehend.'

So Ashley conveyed to her all of the day's events just as he had done for Lester and Margaret back at the offices. It took but a moment and Ashley smiled at Mary's reaction and expression of wonder.

'How wonderful,' said Mary facing towards Ashley, 'I feel as though I've just had a vision? What an interesting day you have had. I feel as if I've been beside you all day.'

Margaret then conveyed to her mother the news that Dutton Consultants were to commence planning a program in teaching the art of telepathy and that she would personally coach her mother in the skill. Ashley then also added his opinion that Margaret must have something special to have picked up her telepathic skills so rapidly. It normally took several days of practicing with a proficient before the art was learned by the human brain. But Margaret had adapted within a few hours. There was still much for her brain to transmit but the essential basics were there.

'That was clever of you Margaret,' said Mary looking at her daughter. 'Goodness knows you'll be reading my mind next.'

'No mother,' said Margaret aloud, 'I can only receive what your brain sends out telepathically.'

'What's the world coming to when you don't need to talk to say something? O I shall miss listening to all my friends' voices. And what about music and singing; will we still have opera?' said Mary wistfully.

Lester looked at Margaret and rolled his eyes and tried to convey without much success that her mother loved the sound of her own voice and would probably not use telepathy very much.

Ashley conveyed a special little message to Margaret. Yes, she would be able to read peoples' minds after a fashion. The brain works on electrical impulses and so thought waves continually surround the vicinity of a person. A skilful telepath could tune in and interpret those weak transmissions and so know what a person was thinking. However at any larger distances the waves fade and become quite indecipherable. Margaret looked towards Ashley and conveyed her thanks.

Mary was not far from the truth in her opinion, at least with regard to Margaret in the future. Margaret, with her intuitive skill was already heading along that path. Margaret like Ashley would advance to reading other peoples minds eventually. But unlike Ashley or the Oannes she would not in her lifetime ever be able to look into a persons mind and learn all about them. Nor would she be able to implant a memory into another brain like Ashley had done to teach Katy her Spanish. Even the Oannes could not do that.

Dinner was filled with pleasant conversation, mostly verbal, and both Lester and Margaret said they must visit McGill's Antiques sometime soon. Perhaps they'd visit when it was warmer.

Ashley made a point of conversing telepathically with Lester and tried to include Mary as much as possible. Mary's replies were however all verbal. Ashley knew that even though her inclination towards telepathy was not great nevertheless she was intrigued by it. Eventually her brain would awaken to the technique and automatically begin to transmit her thoughts. With both Lester and Margaret to prompt her Ashley had no doubt her telepathic skill would improve.

On impulse Ashley opened communication with Muznant and conveyed all the days' events to her and inevitably to the Anztarza population. Muznant replied that it was part of their overall plan for human development and was a good step forward. When Ashley asked if she had prompted his thoughts in that direction he only received a laughter emotion as a response. Ashley knew then how things must have happened all those thousands of years ago with the Sumerians and Babylonians.

He subsequently requested that Muznant keep a watchful mind on the Duttons and perhaps assist them in their training task with ideas prompted through the 'thinking stone'.

Muznant conveyed to Ashley that progress would be monitored and she let Ashley know that even the Oannes children had to be prompted towards a telepathic awakening at the appropriate age. The techniques used with them however could never be used on humans due to the differences in brain makeup and capacity.

Ashley left his badge on open communication and Tania did the same. He considered that the Anztarzans had the right to know what his days and nights held. From now on only at moments of thought intimacy would he disconnect. He conveyed this to the family as well and received a favourable reply.

Perhaps the Oannes would like to hear more from the Duttons and so Ashley came up with an idea which he put to Lester.

'Do you know Lester that stone tablet you lent me along with Andrew's diaries and notebook made a terrific talking point at home when I placed it on my mantel shelf. Andrew's notes said that it was given to him by an African tribal chief who claimed it possessed mystical powers. Well I do believe that it does have something. It brought a peaceful atmosphere into the room and I found that simple problems that were bugging me got resolved by me the following day. Whether the stone had anything to do with it I don't know. But I did feel its presence was like a good luck charm. Give it a try and see for yourself. I'm keen to know if it has the same effect for you.'

Lester shook his head. 'I'm not sure Mary would like that at all,' he said. 'She is very particular about what goes on display in the house so I won't even try. But I shall place it on my desk in the office. I'll certainly let you know how it fares.'

Ashley was sure that all of Anztarza was listening to what he had just suggested.

After the dessert, coffee and tea were served at the dinner table which was all very civilized and cosy. Conversation was easy and relaxed and Mary said that Tania and Ashley would always be welcome in her house. Anytime they were in London they must visit and stay at least one night. She said that the star brooch seemed to shine ever so brightly on Tania and she herself was falling in love with it all over again. Daniel Honnor had done a great thing when he had presented it to his wife Catherine that Christmas in 1835. Mary called it her 'Comet brooch' to her coffee club friends and often repeated its history to them. They were all too polite to remind her that she had already repeated the story umpteen times.

Janice the maid had left shortly after serving dinner and it had been for Margaret to take over after that. She had brought the dessert to the table, a Crème Brûlée, one of Mary's favourites and which Janice had prepared that morning. Lester had his ice cream alternative instead. He was not an ardent Crème Brûlée fan. Both Tania and Ashley pleased Mary no end when they accepted a second helping.

It was past midnight when they all said goodnight. Tania took off the star brooch and handed it back to Mary and thanked her for allowing her to wear it. It was a joy to wear such a famous jewel Tania conveyed. Mary fondled it lovingly and Tania could see that she was glad to have it back in her possession.

Lester and Margaret said goodnight and goodbye since they planned leaving very early. Lester had a busy day and always made an early start. Ashley said he and Tania would like to start back towards Dudley by about 9 o'clock. Mary said she had a coffee morning for her ladies at ten and so would also be up in time to say goodbye to her guests. Janice usually arrived at eight and would serve up them a simple breakfast as they wished.

'Just a cup of tea is all I usually have in the mornings,' said Ashley, 'and Tania just has some toast and marmalade with her tea. It'll take us a little over two hours to get back so nine o'clock would be a good start.'

The next morning all went according to plan and after thanking Mary for a lovely stay they set off for the M40 and home. Tania looked sideways at Ashley as he drove and sensing her stares he glanced her way. Both smiled contentedly at each other.

'She was nice.'
'Who?'
'Margaret.'
'Hmm.'
'You know she's in love with you?'
'So are you.'
'How do you feel knowing she loves you?'
'She knows I love you.'
'So?'
'She knows I don't love her in the same way but it is a nice feeling to know you are admired. I feel a lot of peoples' love Tania and that in itself is a great emotion. It makes me want to smile at the world which is so full of beautiful people. I should of course say worlds. My badge remains open to listeners and Muznant and Brazjaf must be smiling at us and our thoughts this very minute.'

'Muznant sleeps,' was the message from Brazjaf.
'We look forward to meeting you again.'
'All are in anticipation of your visit.'

A view of Muznant sleeping facedown in her sleep tank was a wonderful sight. It was the perfect vision of underwater floating peacefulness. It looked the most comfortable of postures in which to rest. The emotion of deep affection crossed the telepathic airwaves in both directions.

'O Ashley, there you see two people who are content in their love for each other. I hope nothing changes for them as a result of this contact with us.'

'That is all the more reason for Anztarza to be kept secret from our world.'

'Yes it must, at least for the next thousand years.'

They didn't stop during the journey and Ashley reached the outskirts of Birmingham just inside the expected two hours. But it took another half hour to McGill's Antiques in Dudley. They were in constant contact through their badges and Milly conveyed that Graham was not expected till later in the afternoon. Tania suggested to Ashley that she be dropped home instead as she needed to freshen up first. She would find her way to McGill's later in time to meet Graham.

Ashley also went home to put on fresh clothes. He had showered at Mount View and put on clean underwear and socks but his shirt felt creased as did the trousers.

Milly was pleased to see him walk in and Ashley gave her a hug and a kiss on the cheek. Robin came in right behind Ashley carrying a paper bag of doughnuts from Lorraine's bakery. It was just gone midday and Ashley suddenly felt famished. Two doughnuts with as much tea did the trick though.

Graham and Anne arrived a little after 2 o'clock and both had big smiles when they saw Ashley and Milly. Tania was upstairs helping Robin and Milly used her badge to convey the news of their arrival and she came down immediately. Anne was slim and had on a blue and grey outfit which Tania said was stunning. After that a mutual admiration developed between them and Tania took Anne around the shop. Graham was taken in hand by Robin who showed off his favourite and latest acquisitions. Tania took Anne upstairs and explained how Robin was in charge here.

'This is so unlike any antique shop I've been to,' said Anne smiling pleasantly, 'it's so interesting and more like a themed museum.'

'It was Ashley's idea when the original owner was still alive,' said Tania. 'Philip gave him a free hand in running the business and in turn Ashley lets Robin do as he pleases up here. This is Robin's domain and he loves it. Ashley does make the odd suggestion or two if you know what I mean.'

'And how is business?' asked Anne.

'It must be good because Ashley takes me out to dinner quite often,' replied Tania laughing.

'I hear McGill's Antiques has quite a reputation from what Graham tells me,' said Anne. 'Every item has a history card especially the antiques in the room downstairs. How do you manage that?'

'I really don't know too much about that side of things,' said Tania, 'you'll have to get Ashley to answer that one yourself.' Tania didn't want to reveal anything about Ashley's gifts.

'And what are you ladies chatting about?' asked Ashley as he and Graham came up to them. Ashley stood beside Tania and placed his hand across her far shoulder.

'You do make a lovely couple,' said Anne, 'I wish both of you every happiness.'

And then she added, 'I was just asking Tania how you managed to get history cards made out for all your items. It makes your shop unique in that respect. Graham is always talking about it.'

'O it's just a gift I seem to have,' said Ashley. 'I only have to touch an object and it seems to talk to me. I really don't know how it works but it just does.'

'That is truly a tremendous gift,' said Anne. And then rather hesitantly she added, 'I have a confession to make. Or rather we have a confession to make. We'd like your advice on something along those lines.'

She paused for a while and was nervously twisting her fingers together in front of her. Ashley could see she was nervous about asking a favour such as this. He read her mind and knew exactly what the request was about.

'Well it's like this,' Anne said hesitantly. 'Graham is such a coward and has put me up to this. Well the long and the short of it is that he found this clock at one of these fairs he visits. It's a mantel clock and I think it quite an ugly thing with grotesque figures sculpted all around the dial. Graham says he was attracted to it for some odd reason. He's not sure if he can ever get it working but he says he is still fascinated by its appearance. Well we've brought it along and it's in the car outside. He'd like you to have a look at it and give us your opinion of it.' Graham was standing beside her and smiling his thanks.

Ashley winked at Tania and then shaking his head he smiled and looked Anne straight in the eyes.

'I'm so sorry,' he said trying to keep a straight face, 'but my gift seems to have just deserted me. But if you both join us for dinner I shall try my best to help.'

Anne and Graham both smiled at that.

'Why yes that would be lovely,' said Anne, 'we'd love that. Graham owes me a dinner outing so it would be nice to round the day off with a slap up meal.'

'I don't know if you like Indian food but there is a nice place near here called the Kashmir Diner which we go to quite often. We could eat there,' suggested Tania.

Graham's not much into curries and things are you darling?' said Anne, 'but I love them. Perhaps they have something a bit on the mild side?'

'Don't worry about me,' added a smiling Graham, 'I'll find something on the menu. I can always have ice cream for afters to cool my burning tongue.' They all laughed.

Milly had come up the stairs to see what the laughter was about.

'I've got the kettle on if you'd care for a cuppa,' she said, 'but you'd best come down for it when you've finished up here.'

'Mom,' said Tania, 'Ashley and I are thinking of taking Graham and Anne out to dinner. We thought about Charlie's place but Anne says Graham isn't really into curries. Do you have any suggestions?'

'Yes I do,' said Milly with a big grin on her face. 'I'm sure Jerry would like to meet our guests so why don't you all come to Mr and Mrs Marsh's resident hotel for dinner. Tania can act as serving maid for the evening.' Tania laughed at her mum's humour. 'It'll be simple fare,' continued Milly, 'but we can sit around in comfort afterwards and chat.'

'Thanks mom-in-law,' said a grinning Ashley, 'that would be perfect. I could then also look at Graham's clock after dinner.'

Tania looked a bit disappointed but only for an instant. She realised the benefits of her mom's suggestion especially since that way Graham and Anne would get to meet her dad.

'Thank you,' said Anne to Milly, 'this is very kind of you. But we won't stay very late as I have a kitty at home and she gets annoyed if we leave her alone for too long. She is quite a moody little thing.'

'Then we shall eat early,' said Milly. 'Do you like pasta?'

'O yes I certainly do,' said Anne, 'and so does Graham, don't you darling?'

'I love pasta,' agreed Graham. 'Anne calls me a lazy eater because my two favourite foods are pizza and pasta.'

'Come on then,' said Milly, 'we'll have this cup of tea and then we can leave early and relax at home. I'll get Jerry to come home early too. Tania and Ashley can then join us when they close up at 5 o'clock.' Then she added, 'We can chat in the kitchen while I cook.'

'Perhaps I can help,' said Anne. 'I'll feel more at home if I do.'

'Of course you can,' said Milly, 'you can do the salad if you like.'

'I like,' said Anne smiling.

'Mum,' said Tania, 'why don't we take Graham and Anne to Leonard Road afterwards?'

'Now that's an excellent idea,' said Milly, 'it'll be a lovely surprise.'

Then she asked Anne and Graham if either of them had seen the Christmas lights in Stourbridge's Leonard Road.

'No, I don't think I have,' replied Anne, 'what is it like?'

'Well all I can say is wait and see. We'll have to wrap up warm as we shall be walking the street,' said Milly. 'We go there every Christmastime.'

And so they did.

Dinner was a fine chatty affair and Ashley noticed that both Graham and Anne were very small eaters. Jerry seemed to get on well with Graham and this pleased both wives. The spirali pasta had been cooked to perfection in the boil for the twelve minutes allotted time and Milly had mixed in a little white sauce to prevent the pasta from becoming sticky. She served a meat balls dish made from one of her recipe books which had always been a favourite with Tania. It came in a tasty tomato sauce with parsley and garlic mixed in. And there was apple pie and hot custard for afters another general favourite. Milly didn't take risks with her menus.

It was when they were onto coffee in the lounge that Graham went to his car and brought in the old clock he had asked Ashley to have a look at.

'I think it's a nineteenth century French gilt bronze mantel clock,' said Graham, 'and its got this horrible looking decoration of cherubs and gargoyle figures on it. They are quite grotesque looking aren't they? But something doesn't seem quite right about the way it's all combined. The mechanism is not complete but I can remedy that.'

Ashley took the clock in his hand and looked at it. It had a white enamel clock face with Roman numerals. It was about ten inches high and about twelve inches wide at the base. The figurines were a mix of the cute and the ugly and something didn't quite gel in the overall design. Ashley sensed intent to deceive and so couldn't get a clear history of its manufacture. Many faces and facts flashed past his minds eye and it was when he looked more closely at the ornate embellishments that he notice the jigsaw effect to the assembly around the clock body. And when he turned it over to look underneath the metal base the initials JS were neatly engraved in the centre. The engraving was mechanical and not stamped and had been done very professionally but in a most modern way. This was not mid 19th century at all but more like mid 20th century.

'Jerry do you have a magnifying glass I could borrow for a moment please?' asked Ashley.

'Yes of course,' replied Jerry. 'Milly gave me a lovely one on my birthday some years ago. I'll just go and get it, I won't be a moment.'

It was a good sized three inch diameter glass with stainless steel ring and handle. Ashley looked closely at the ornate figurines and then said a single 'aha.' He put the clock on the table and placed the magnifying glass carefully beside it and smiled up at Graham.

'This is a lovely clock and I can see why you were taken with it,' said Ashley. 'It's been made to look that way especially by someone. I imagine that the original clock was a simple Victorian brass clock with the usual painted porcelain clock garniture probably about the 1880s. I'm getting too many names and faces for a clear picture of its manufacture. However I'm also getting a workmanship date of 1946 and a Scots named Julian Silverman from the Soho area of London. He owned a jewellers shop but professed an interest as a craftsman and learned the necessary skills through invention. He was clever and often made improvements to the embellishment on objects he came across. He thought this clock was too plain and so went about adding to it to make it more saleable.'

Ashley paused as he looked again at the clock on the table.

'Now if you look carefully you will see how cleverly the joining has been effected. Mr Silverman has used a modern chemical glue to fuse the cherubs and gargoyle figurines to the sides of the clock brass. The cherubs probably came off a large mirror frame and the gargoyle faces off some ornament complex. You will notice how he has tried to develop a waist in its appearance to give it its 19th century gilt brass look. And I think he has succeeded brilliantly except for the fact that there is oddness about the whole that doesn't quite gel to the eye of a professional.'

'Yes,' said Graham, 'something didn't seem right about it but I still liked it immensely. I never suspected that it might be a fake.'

'Oh.' said Ashley, 'I wouldn't say it was a fake at all. I don't think that was Mr Silverman's intention. I do believe he had a genuine interest in creating something new and beautiful and I think he has succeeded brilliantly. The initials engraved on the base are his and I dare say there might be other objects around with his initials on them as well. I wonder what his thinking was in mixing the cherubs with the gargoyles. Was he trying to express an opinion or a political statement? I wonder.'

'Well thank you very much Ashley,' said Graham smiling broadly. 'I'm absolutely amazed at everything you've said and discovered. I guess Anne here is even more gob smacked. I liked the clock by instinct when I first saw it but I like it even more now that I know some of its history and of Julian Silverman's creativity. I must admit that I admire the fellow for what he has done and I say 'well done' to him.'

'When did you get this gift?' asked Anne in admiration. 'I just think it is really wonderful. I was never fond of history in school with all those dates to remember but now I wish I had taken a greater interest. When I was reading your history cards in the shop I wondered if they were actually true. Now I know they are and I realise why McGill's has become so renowned. Business for you must be thriving.'

'Yes it is,' said Milly. 'At first many doubted their authenticity and made their own checks on the truth. But now every dealer accepts the cards as read. Yes I do think we are unique in that respect thanks to our Ashley.'

'Less of the jam and honey mum,' was the telepathic remark from Tania to her mum.

Milly gave her daughter an injured look followed by a wink which everyone noticed.

Ashley laughed out loud and said, 'Thanks Milly it's nice to be appreciated by the few. I think you're approved for the role of good mother-in-law.'

Jerry now also gave vent to a chuckle and said, 'You have her in the palm of your hand Ashley. Nothing you can do or say will ever change that. Eh Tania, what do you say to that?'

Tania gave her dad a frown and poked her tongue out at him. She always did so when he embarrassed her in front of people.

Dinner ended and after coffee and tea Jerry suggested they all drive down to Leonard Road to see the Christmas lights.

'It's not Blackpool or anything like that,' he said, 'but I like it better. We'll go in two cars, ours and Ashley's.'

'We'd better wrap up warmly against the cold since we'll be on foot to view the displays,' said Milly. 'And keep plenty of change at hand for all the collectors' boxes.'

It was a cloudy night and not too cold. The clear nights were the frosty ones. Jerry parked on Harmon Road when they arrived and Ashley pulled up close behind. This was a quiet road parallel to Leonard Road and had just one house done up with lights. The group stopped to talk with the owner a widower and put some silver in the charity box taped to his gatepost. He was a chatty bloke and explained that it had taken him a month to get all the lights up. When asked what he did with the lights for the rest of the year he said they were all carefully stored in one of his spare rooms upstairs.

Harmon Road looped around onto Francis Road where most of the houses had lighting displays that were quite good. But when they walked around onto Leonard Road both Graham and Anne 'oohed' and 'aahed' with delight at the spectacle spread down the road before them. Every house in the road was lit up with a variety of Christmas lighting displays from rooftop to ground level and from front door to garden fence such that the entire street was aglow with brilliance. There was every colour on display and the street was awash with groups of people some standing and staring while others walked about taking pictures with posh digital cameras that were setup for night photography.

'My goodness,' exclaimed Anne, 'this is truly wonderful. I never imagined it could be so lit up. Look Graham, every house is decorated differently with a different theme. These people must be great neighbours. How long does the display last?'

'O I think from early December to about the end of Jan,' said Jerry. 'And I believe that last year the collections reached nearly twenty thousand pounds for leukaemia research.'

They strolled slowly down the street stopping to admire each display.

The one that caught everyone's eye was the all white lights display. The entire house was lit with white lights in all shapes and sizes. The trees and bushes were similarly adorned not to mention the footpath, the grass lawn and the front fence. It gave the appearance of a fairy castle and Tania said that for her it was the best display in the road. The air above the house was just aglow with the brightness.

'Simple is best,' said Ashley reaching out and getting hold of Tania's hand. He smiled at her and repeated his words. Tania knew exactly what he meant.

Anne agreed with Tania and said that the 'Fairy Castle' was definitely her favourite too.

I'm glad we came,' said Graham to Jerry. 'Thanks ever so much for bringing us. I must tell the rest of my family about this place. I know Simon and Karen would simply love it. That's my son and his wife. I'll inform my Forties Club people as well.'

It was an hour later when they all finally got back to the cars and drove back to the house for a nice hot drink. Graham and Anne said their goodbyes finally and once again thanked Milly and Jerry for a lovely time.

'And Ashley I must thank you especially for enlightening me about my clock,' said Graham shaking Ashley by the hand. 'I hope to see you again sometime soon. You must come down to us too and have a look at my collection of clocks. They're all for sale you know. And goodbye Tania, good luck with everything,' he said turning to Tania and giving her a kiss on the cheek.

'And Merry Christmas to all of you,' he added.

'And a Merry Christmas to you too,' they all said in unison.

'Merry Christmas,' communicated Ashley and Tania telepathically as Anne was getting into the car. She hesitated in surprise before shaking her head in disbelief and closing the door. Perhaps the 'Merry Christmases' were just echoing around in her head she thought.

The next few days were quite hectic though pleasant both in the shop and in all their homes. Robin and Milly did all the decorations in the shop but avoided any electric festive lights. Robin thought them dangerous and a potential fire hazard and refused to have anything to do with them. He said he'd known of houses being burnt down because of faulty Christmas lights. Otherwise the shop looked very festive indeed and Tania said so.

Ashley picked up an eight foot tree and placed it in his front garden with coloured baubles and tinsel decorating it. It was nice to see and the neighbours and passers-by all smiled when they saw it. Ashley thought it better out there since it wouldn't shed its needles quite as quickly. Besides it was too big for his living room anyway. Whatever was he thinking when he bought it?

Ashley and the family had all kept their badges on open communication mode since they wanted to share the joyousness of Christmas with each other and with the people of Anztarza, especially Muznant and Brazjaf.

When it snowed a few days before Christmas Day Ashley conveyed the images to Muznant and received a pleasant thought in return. She communicated that it snowed regularly on Nazmos and that it came down for days on end. The best place away from the extreme cold was simply under the sea. Luckily in Anztarza the climate was an indoor one and remained pleasantly constant all the time. The Anztarzans were looking forward to when Ashley and his family made their visit which had not long to go. Much was planned for them including a trip out into space and Brazjaf hoped that the FTL interplanetary starship would have arrived in position by then. It would bring an added dimension to their visit. It was the only craft that possessed a unique gravity of its own while stationary in space. It tended to park well beyond the solar system but within an easy day's travel distance from the Earth.

As such the talk at the Marsh's Christmas dinner table was all about the coming visit to the city underneath Antarctica. Although visual images had been conveyed to them by Muznant it still intrigued them with a kind of mysteriousness. Especially with regard to the reception they would receive and the many people they would meet.

Lillian remarked how lovely Brazjaf and Muznant had been and how affectionate she felt towards them. She said she expected to make many more friends during their visit. This was immediately followed by a flood of affection and goodwill that filled the room and it seemed like they were being welcomed and enfolded in the arms of thousands of people. It was an indescribable feeling of belonging and peaceful loving. And Ashley knew then that the Anztarzans were desperately impatient for the day when they could all live together in harmony and peace on the Earth with their planetary neighbours. They saw the coming visit by ten Earth humans as an important first step towards that goal.

After dinner all gave each other presents and there was pleasant laughter as each opened theirs. They were mostly gimmicky toys, music CDs or clothes items. Milly gave Jerry an apron with a chef's hat. Only, the apron was flesh coloured and the upper part was that of a well endowed naked beauty. Lillian got a cardigan, a pair of opal earrings and a small box of chocolates among other things. It was a joy to receive and a joy to give and Ashley conveyed this to Muznant and the Anztarzans. It was just an Earth custom to celebrate an auspicious occasion by the exchange of token gifts.

Tania bought a toy battery operated miniature helicopter for Ashley and it took centre stage with the men for a great part of the evening. The saying that boys will be boys and so will some middle aged men was an apt description of the moment. It took only a few minutes for the battery to recharge so everyone had a go in turn. Katy was best at it from among the women. Tania said she had seen it demonstrated and had at once thought of it as a present for Ashley. And Ashley did enjoy seeing everyone having a go with his present. Tania looked at Ashley and her eyes glowed with love as she watched him seated back comfortably with a contented and relaxed look on his face.

'Merry Christmas darling,' conveyed Tania to Ashley.

'Merry Christmas and thanks for my lovely present. I just love watching these children at play,' responded a smiling Ashley.

Tania burst out laughing and she came over to Ashley and sat down beside him on the sofa. Everyone seemed to be enjoying themselves which was just as it should be at Christmas, a joyous and religious time of year. A time of Christ. A time for peace and love.

Later when all were relaxed and seated comfortably Milly brought out her Trivial Pursuit box to many a groan from the men.

'Don't worry,' she said to the groaners, 'it's not what you think. You can stay seated where you are and one of us will ask the questions from the cards in the box. Anyone can shout out the answer at will and it'll just be a bit of fun for us all. I'll start asking the questions and then someone else can take over after a bit.'

'That sounds a nice way to play,' said Eric. 'I think I can rest my eyes for a bit too.'

All knew exactly what he meant.

'We'll give you a nudge when you start to snore granddad,' said Ashley to general laughter.

Milly took out one of the boxes containing the colourful cards and placed them on the table in front of her. She picked one of the cards and read the first question.

'Okay, are you ready?' she said. 'Here goes. What colour was the hammer and sickle of the Russian Flag?'

'Black,' said Katy.'

'Nope.'

'Red,' said Jerry.

'Nope.' Milly was smiling.

Ashley laughed and said, 'Gold of course.'

'Yes,' said Milly, 'and you know I wouldn't have known it either. Ashley did you cheat?'

'I'm afraid I did,' he admitted. 'The answer just came to me the moment you asked it. I'll answer last in future.'

'I think Ashley should just listen to everyone else's answers instead,' said Tania. 'It is still fun.'

'Okay next question. What were the last words of Julius Caesar?'

'Et tu Bruté,' all shouted together and then burst out laughing.

'Here's my last one,' said Milly. 'What did the Romans call Scotland?'

'Scotlandia?' asked Lillian tentatively.

'Nope,' smiled Milly.

'Caledonia,' said Jerry proudly.

'Yep. Okay here's the box Jerry; you can ask the next few questions. Put the used cards in the back of the box please.'

Jerry took the box and pulled out a card and read what was on it. He shook his head and replaced the card at the back of the box and took another one from the front. He replaced two more before he said, 'aha.'

'Right,' he said, 'what mountain has the longest road tunnel in the world?'

'Everest,' said Katy jokingly to laughter all around.

'No,' said Jerry seriously. 'Not Everest. There are no roads there.'

'The Alps,' said Eric. 'A mountain in the Alps, mount what's-its-name.'

'The Matterhorn,' said Lillian and Eric nodded.

'Yes that's it.' he cried, 'The Matterhorn.'

'No but close,' said Jerry.

'The Mont Blanc,' the answer came telepathically to all of them.

'Who was that?' asked Jerry.

'It is us from Anztarza, Muznant and Brazjaf. We do enjoy your quiz games.'

'Happy to have you join us,' communicated Jerry. 'The more the merrier.'

'I had better make the questions more obscure for extra-terrestrials. So here's the next one. What country is home to Hamlet?' said Jerry aloud.

'Denmark,' was the multi-voiced shouted reply.

'Right here's the next question. What eagle is the USA's national bird?'

'The golden eagle,' said Katy.

'Nope.'

'The bald eagle,' said Eric.

'Yep, very good,' said Jerry. 'Okay last one from me. Who was the oldest member of the Beatles?'

Jerry looked around smiling.

'Lennon,' said Milly.

'No, one more answer only please after all there were only four of them,' said Jerry.

'The ugly one, what's his name,' said Eric.

'No I'm sorry,' said Jerry, 'you have to give a name. Some might say they were all ugly, what with those haircuts.'

'I know who granddad means,' said Katy hurriedly, 'it's Ringo the drummer.'

'Correct. Okay, someone else can take over now,' said Jerry putting the box on the table.

They played on pleasantly for another hour when all had a turn at the questions except Eric. He said that the print on the cards was too small for him to read easily. Ron and Brenda had also joined in the game with their answers telepathically conveyed through their badges when they had got their B&B guests settled in. The one question that no one could get was about how many plays Shakespeare had written. All were surprised when the answer was revealed as thirty seven, with an added 'Don't expect me to name them all,' which brought forth laughter and some attempts at naming a few.

It was well after midnight when all decided to call it a night and left in their cars for their own homes. Eric had a lift with Alex, Lillian and Katy. There was nothing like one's own bed said Eric and added that he might lie in till after eleven in the morning.

'Lazy beggar,' said Alex smiling, 'but that's not such a bad idea and I might just do the same.'

Ashley stayed on for another cup of tea and a cosy tête-à-tête with Tania before also saying goodnight and driving home to Paganel Drive. It had been another very pleasantly spent Christmas with all the family and Ashley wondered what surprise the next year might bring.

McGill's was not to open till Thursday and then it closed again for the long weekend and the New Year. But on Wednesday evening there was a heavy snowfall and Ashley didn't get to the shop till quite late on the following morning. Traffic was all snarled up because of the snow and the council was being blamed for not having gritted the roads enough. But by Friday nearly all the snow had disappeared with the coming of milder temperatures, though a drizzle of misty rain persisted throughout the day. Such were the vagaries of the English weather.

Ashley brought the New Year in with his mum and dad while Eric stayed in his warm home not wishing to venture out again. When he'd arrived home on Christmas night he'd been tired for the whole of the next day. Late nights were not his cup of tea anymore so he excused himself and said he'd rather get a good nights rest and be fresh for the New Year in the morning. Besides he was not alone he said. He had his badge to listen in on the entire goings on. It was wonderful how they could all communicate in thought with each other no matter how far apart they were. Even Ron and Brenda had taken part during the Trivial Pursuit quiz on Christmas day as had Muznant and Brazjaf.

Katy and Robin were out with their friends at a bar in town and Robert and Vicky had accompanied them. Robert was home from the police academy on a break of two weeks. Katy thought he looked changed and had a more formal attitude in his manner towards her. Although he still gave her a hug and a kiss when they met, she noticed he didn't joke or laugh as he used to. Perhaps he planned on becoming a strict copper when he passed out in a couple of months she thought. He seemed to revert to his old jolly self as the night progressed and as midnight drew near. He'd also had more than his usual number of drinks. Since the bar was adjacent to Centenary Square they all decided to brave the cold and venture in amongst the crowds gathered there to bring in the New Year.

Music was blaring from a makeshift pavilion and a BRMB DJ was announcing what everyone was to do. Each person was asked to join hands with the person nearest them as the clock chimed midnight. Then Auld Lang Syne would be played by the band and all were to join in the singing and swaying. Then shortly after this there would be a firework display for all to enjoy.

But at 15 minutes before midnight the crush got quite fierce and twice Katy had her foot stamped on.

'Robin,' she moaned, 'I'm not enjoying this. It's too crowded and I'm freezing. I'd like to go back to the bar if you don't mind.'

Vicky was like minded but Robert said he wanted to stay on a bit longer as he was enjoying this.

'I'm going with Katy and Robin to the bar,' she shouted above the din to Robert, 'I'll see you there when you've had enough here.'

'Okay,' said Robert without looking back at her and he began worming his way through the crowd in the direction of the pavilion.

When they got into the bar the place was packed tight with hardly any room to move let alone get served at the bar.

'This is not my idea of fun,' shouted Katy to Robin and pointed to the exit. He nodded and grabbing Vicky by the wrist pulled her along towards the door. It was ten minutes to midnight and they walked to where Robin had parked his car early that evening. Five minutes later they were travelling down the Expressway with the car heater making a feeble attempt at heating the interior.

Robin had the radio tuned to BBC Radio 2 and they heard the chimes of Big Ben ring out just as they drove up Gravelly Hill.

Katy reached across and touched Robin's arm and said, 'Happy New Year Robin. And you too Vicky, Happy New Year.'

Robin and Vicky both said Happy New Year to Katy and then they all accompanied the radio in the singing of Auld Lang Syne as loudly as was possible. Robin said he hoped no police were around to hear them or they might think they'd had too much to drink.

They parked on the drive behind Ashley's car and Katy used her keys to let them into the house.

'Hi, I'm home,' telepathically from Katy, 'and I've brought Robin and Vicky back with me. It was too crowded in town and we've left Robert there to enjoy it on his own. We were absolutely frozen out there.'

They walked into the lounge and Lillian welcomed Robin and Vicky while Katy went into the kitchen to put the kettle on.

'Happy New Year everybody,' said Katy as she came back into the room and she went and kissed her mum, dad and brother.

The TV was on BBC1 and a brilliant firework display from the banks of the Thames was being broadcast. The London Eye was the focus of the display and the new arrivals were just in time to see the grand finale. It was a truly spectacular ending. It showed the crowds gathered on the opposite bank and all seemed to be in a jolly mood and quite enjoying the occasion though they were all well wrapped against the freezing conditions. There were families there too with young children and all appeared smiling and happy as they waved to the TV cameras. Ashley wondered if the Anztarzans were also watching this on their own TV monitors. Were they also enjoying the spectacle and Ashley couldn't help wondering what they made of these earthly celebrations. He immediately received a multitude of good wishes from the Anztarzan people who said what a grand and colourful display they had witnessed not only from London but from all the other Capital cities of the world. Sydney and Shanghai had been two of the most magnificent. New York was yet to reach the New Year. The Anztarzans hoped this year would be a stepping stone for their two cultures. Ashley knew exactly what they meant.

'Come and sit down you people,' said Alex. 'You look chilled to the bone. Would you like a sherry or something? Lets all drink a toast to 2004.'

'Yes please,' said Vicky, 'I'd love a sherry and also a hot cup of tea Katy. It's still just milk and no sugar.'

'Tea for me please,' said Robin, 'and a tiny bit of sherry for the toast. I've still got to drive home and I can drop Vicky on the way.'

'I'll ring Robert and tell him where I am in case he's searching for me in the bar,' said Vicky and she went into the kitchen with Katy to make the call on her mobile.

But there was no response from Robert so Vicky left him a voice message. She also sent him a text to say she had gone home.

When all had settled down comfortably with their drinks both hot and cold, an atmosphere of love and peace filled the room.

'I think that 2004 is going to be a very special year for all of us. So cheers everybody, here's to a happy and prosperous New Year,' said Ashley and he raised his glass as did the others.

'Cheers, Happy New Year all,' from Katy and repeated by everyone in the room.

'I think it's time for a snack,' said Lillian with a big grin, 'I've got it all ready on the trolley. I just need to add a few more plates and napkins.'

She then wheeled in the serving trolley loaded with mince pies, pork pies, sausage rolls and fruit cake slices. And there was a separate box of variety biscuits.

'I'll just have a biscuit,' said Alex, 'or I shall be up half the night with heartburn. But you lot please carry on.'

'Looking forward to our holiday Katy?' asked Ashley.

'Yes,' said Katy, and to Vicky, 'we're all off to sunny Tenerife for two weeks. Even Uncle Ron and Aunt Brenda are coming with us. Granddad Eric was complaining about the cold so mum and dad suggested somewhere warm and Tenerife came up. We're off on the seventeenth of this month. Uncle Robin will be minding the shop on his own. Why don't you and your mum pop in and give him a little company sometime. He'll treat you to doughnuts from the bakery opposite. He and Mrs Hollings are getting quite close and I dare say she'll be looking in on him too.'

Ashley winked at Katy and conveyed that she'd make an excellent story teller.

'That sounds great,' said Vicky. 'You must tell me all about it when you get back.'

At one o'clock Ashley said he was ready for bed and planted a telepathic suggestion in Robin's mind that it was time to drop Vicky home.

'Well thanks for a lovely scoff,' he said to Lillian and Alex, 'I think I'd better be on my way and drop Vicky home.'

He shook hands all around and Katy walked with him and Vicky to the front door and then outside to the car.

It was only later in the day that they heard the news that fighting had erupted in a corner of Centenary Square just after the fireworks had finished and that one person had been stabbed and was seriously ill in hospital. Several people were reported as helping police with their enquiries.

Initially Robert had been annoyed at Vicky for leaving the bar but when she told him about the fighting and the stabbing he was apologetic and grateful to Robin for dropping her home. He reckoned that far too many people had been allowed onto the square and that the police or the council should have limited the entry. Crowd control was one of the topics at the academy that Robert had taken a special interest in.

McGill's Antiques reopened as usual on January 2nd and all the Christmas decorations came down on the 6th as was traditional for the twelfth night. The place suddenly looked quite bare and Robin suggested that something alternative be put in place. Milly said she'd think about it.

And so the days rolled on and the seventeenth of January approached. Robin was given charge of the shop and he was keen to do his best. Milly had taken great pains to show him how the accounts must be kept and suggested he make notes of everything. In fact for the last two weeks Robin had been doing all the accounting under the watchful eyes of both Ashley and Milly.

'Don't you worry my dears,' said Robin as the final week before the holiday commenced, 'I know exactly what to do and after all it's only a shop. It is a quiet time of the year for business anyway. Lorraine said she'd come over as often as she could for a chat and to ease my boredom. I hope they have doughnuts in Tenerife for I shan't be saving you any. Is the shop mine if you don't come back?'

They all laughed at the suggestion. But you never can tell can you?

Telepathic conversations continued all week with Brazjaf and Muznant as the pickup arrangements were finalised. While in Anztarza the anticipation of the visit was at a peak of excitement and speculation. For them this was to be an historic occasion comparable to the return to Nazmos of that first exploratory expedition to Earth all those thousands of years ago.

And so on Friday the sixteenth of January 2004 Ashley and Milly shut up shop at 5 o'clock and handed all the keys to Robin and wished him good luck.

'See you in a fortnight Uncle Robin,' said Milly, 'I hope you enjoy the experience and thank you for taking it on.'

'Now you just go and enjoy yourselves and come back with a nice tan. And don't forget my chocolates, fudge and toffees from there,' said Robin.

They reminded him about the alarm system and that ADT always sent someone around on patrol at weekends to check their clients' premises. If at all the alarm system did not monitor on their system at the prescribed times then Robin could expect a phone call from them. So far they had proved extremely reliable.

Saturday arrived cold and miserable and the drive to Aberporth was uninteresting and dull with a thin mist covering the hills. Once in the Welsh hills the sleet and snow commenced and the driving was slowed right down. Luckily it didn't settle.

They had all driven up in three cars as per the last visit in November. Ashley and Tania rode together while their parents each travelled in their own cars. Lillian and Alex picked up Eric and made an early start. Ashley had driven to the Marsh residence and then with Tania seated beside him had followed behind Milly and Jerry in their own car. The decision to travel in three cars had arisen from the need to accommodate each person's ample luggage. The ladies were out to impress the Anztarzans with their dress sense.

Muznant had indicated that they could bring as much baggage as they pleased since she wished them to feel at home in the allotted accommodation in Anztarza and on the craft when cruising in space.

During the journey all parties were in telepathic contact with each other and so knew exactly where each was. Alex, Lillian and Eric were the first to arrive at the B&B and were welcomed by Ron and Brenda even before they'd got out of their car. Ron and Brenda were pleased to see them and Lillian noticed the two average sized cases already in the hallway. Alex placed their own cases beside the others and all went into the lounge for a hot cup of tea or coffee.

It was 2 o'clock when the others arrived and joined them in the lounge. The clouds had given way to intermittent sunshine but it was still bitterly cold out in the open. The sky didn't get dark till nearly five which was a half hour later than at Christmas.

'Hello my friends,' communicated the recognisable thought structure pattern peculiar to Muznant, 'we are here just as before. We shall be with you in about an hour and there will be no need for that rendezvous on the beach. We will be in an old coach bus and will come to your car park and stop beside the front door of Ron and Brenda's home. It is in fact one of our platform craft that has been suitably modified and disguised. It will not be necessary to walk any further than a few feet from your front door. There is enough room aboard for everyone and ample storage space for all your bags. We will contact you again as we arrive.'

The Anztarzans did not end their communications with a goodbye but rather sent over an emotion of affection and goodwill. This now came across powerfully and all smiled at the pleasantness of it. Ashley also felt something that was akin to love and adoration. But then all this was new to him and perhaps he had misunderstood the farewell from Muznant. Or perhaps it was the Anztarzan style to love everybody.

The specially modified platform craft had been made to look like a 45 seater 1955 British Leyland holiday coach bus. It had the typical 50's styling with small windows and curving back. The front had a long rectangular snout for the engine housing and the body was painted a dark red from the window line downwards. The roof was painted in a pale cream colour as were the wheel arches in a backward sweeping streamlined pattern. A few scratch marks had been contrived on the paintwork to give it an aged look. To all purposes and intents it looked and functioned as an ordinary motor coach.

However, the bus also had the Anztarzan technology built into it. As such it had the ability to rise silently above the ground and function just as the other Deck Transporter craft in Anztarza. It would of course require a trained operator to drive it about although the Zanos onboard bio-computer would perform to the thought commands of its operator.

Currently it sat quietly in the cargo hold of a craft much larger than the 8962-Green craft that had collected Muznant and Brazjaf in November. This was 11701-Red and was 400 feet long, 175 feet wide and 60 feet high. It had an overall oval shape with four deck levels. The rear 100 feet of the craft was split into two decks each with a ceiling height close to thirty feet and spanned the width of the craft. Currently it held a number of Transporters similar to Kazaztan's 536-Orange back in Anztarza but with the tops enclosed for operation as shuttles between craft out in space. These had a single sliding door at the rear with several steps leading up from ground to platform level. There were rectangular view panels all around the sides and these were at the four to five feet height level. There was seating inside on either side of a central aisle. Each seat had a lightweight clamp arrangement for use in space as a supplement to the electrostatic suits worn in non-gravity conditions.

The oddity in the cargo hold was of course the 1955 British Leyland holiday coach bus. It was much smaller at twenty feet long and eight feet wide as compared to the other Transporters in the bay. The Anztarzans had reproduced it to look authentic from recorded data obtained during one of their clandestine visits to a motor museum. The bus craft was designated 326-Red and would hopefully be used again on many future occasions.

The operator was Shufzaz and she was relatively young at 60 years. She had pulled strings to train for this pickup and drop-off task. She was a close friend of Partuzna and Ripozatan and had begged and pleaded to be given the privilege. Her pleas had also gone out to all of Anztarza and her enthusiasm had won her the day.

'Be careful,' was Muznant's advice to her during her training and briefing, 'you will easily fall in love with this Ashley when you meet him. I nearly did I think.'

11701-Red dipped down towards the sea and slowed to a velocity of a few hundred mph. At just a few feet above the water it levelled off and raced eastwards towards the coastal town of Aberporth. When it was about fifty miles out from the shore it slowed to a complete halt. Large bay doors at the rear opened silently and 326-Red floated swiftly out and turned in a half circle to head for the coast and the Aberporth rendezvous. 11701-Red then shut its bay doors and sank down quietly into the sea depths to await their visitors.

Shufzaz knew exactly where the craft must beach and standing beside her were Brazjaf and Muznant. Both were smiling and a sense of keen anticipation permeated the craft. They looked forward to meeting their new friends again.

The night was dark and overcast and from high up during their flight from Anztarza Muznant had noticed the crescent moon low on the western horizon. It was a good night for flying. The bio-computer had its own locator orientation that would guide it to within a few feet of its intended destination. It was now just after ten pm GMT.

Once on land and near Aberporth Shufzaz drove 326-Red on the left side of the road and kept to a speed of just under 30 miles per hour. They did not pass another vehicle and were soon driving into the B&B car park. Shufzaz brought it right up close to the B&B front entrance. Muznant had already conveyed their progress from the moment they had crossed the shoreline. Now she communicated that their transport had arrived and that they bring themselves to the transport with their baggage.

There was great excitement within and the ladies came out first and boarded the bus. Ashley, Alex and Ron made two trips each with all the cases and soon all were aboard and being greeted by Muznant and Brazjaf. Shufzaz was introduced to everyone in turn but the face mask and over clothing hid her features from them.

The door was shut tight and bus craft 326-Red turned around smoothly and made its slow progress back along the roadway. When the road reached the shore Shufzaz turned off all the lights and the craft floated up just above the ground and then headed swiftly out over the sea. There were gasps of astonishment from the women aboard as the craft increased its speed to just over 100 mph and the wind began to whistle over its non-streamlined superstructure.

Muznant and Brazjaf were already in the process of removing their facial masks and the all-over clothing and both were soon greeting their guests with a customary Earth handshake and kiss on both cheeks. They also performed the general two-way communication of 'Sewa' questions and answers. Muznant had on a pale blue tunic and leggings while Brazjaf displayed an orange outfit edged in dark brown. Shufzaz then followed suit and exposed her own bright green tunic edged in red and Muznant gave her a cautionary reminder that Ashley was spoken for. Shufzaz conveyed her pleasure at finally meeting Ashley's family members and all took an instant liking to this very small and vivaciously pretty Oannes woman. She had a childlike appearance with very delicate and exquisitely moulded facial features. She was much shorter than Muznant or Brazjaf and was about four and a half feet in height and also very much slimmer though a bit on the skinny side. Her webbing was more prominent as a result and the wing on her back was of a stronger colour than that of her companions. Muznant read their minds and explained that the heightened colour indicated her excitement at meeting them all; the wing colour tended to change according to their emotional state. Ashley thought that Shufzaz was beautiful and when he conveyed this to her she changed to an even stronger colouring. Muznant smiled at this and thought to herself what a wonderful politician Ashley would make. Anztarzans would simply love this Earth human.

Communication was made with Captain Lyzongpan of the waiting craft 11701-Red and instructions were confirmed for the reception of their transport 326-Red into the cargo bay. Muznant conveyed all this to her guests and also details of the second part of the journey all the way to Anztarza in the larger spacecraft.

The night was dark and Ashley and company could see absolutely nothing through the windows of their speeding coach. A dull phosphorescent glow pervaded the inside of the craft and the only inkling they had of approach to a docking was the reduction in wind noise on the outside skin. Their badges conveyed all progress information and Shufzaz indicated how they would dock inside the larger craft.

Very suddenly they were in the bright daylight luminance inside the cargo bay of 11701-Red and Ashley could see two Oannes people at the far end. They appeared to be standing and watching 326-Red settle onto the deck between the other craft there. Ashley wondered at what their duties might entail and Muznant immediately informed him that they were crew members of the larger craft and were there to witness their safe arrival and to make sure the cargo bay was returned to a secure sealed status.

Shufzaz opened the sliding door and asked her passengers to follow her outside. She would take them to the control centre to meet Captain Lyzongpan. The cases could all be left on 326-Red and would be delivered to their allotted accommodation in Anztarza.

The walk to the control centre was along a broad corridor that ran the length of the craft and there Captain Lyzongpan greeted each of them. Ashley performed the Sewa ritual on all their behalves and could sense the pleasant surprise among the other crew members. In his own mind Ashley gave thanks to Andrew Pando for his extensive notes about the Dogon tribe and their customs. It was amazing how a polite tradition had prevailed all through the millennia.

Captain Lyzongpan was older looking and was 190 years of age and had been put in charge of 11701-Red only two years previously. He was originally from Wentazta just like Brazjaf and had come to Anztarza some fifty years ago. He had been back to Nazmos only twice since then. His wife Dazulteng was here with him on the craft and they were comfortable in their ample quarters. She was 160 years of age and chose to travel with her husband on all his journeys; especially when transporting passengers to and from the FTL starships. They also had a house accommodation in Dome-17 adjacent to the food Domes 21 and 22. They had three offspring two female and one male who were all in their nineties. They had chosen to live on Nazmos and each year the FTL craft brought back recorded holographic communications from each. They were a close family even though they lived light years apart.

The captain conveyed that their route to Anztarza would be a quick one today. They could rise to their eighty miles height almost immediately and then cruise southwards at a velocity of 12,000mph. The craft would remain under normal Earth gravity as they would not be entering anywhere near an orbital path. At eighty miles altitude they would go unnoticed. The captain stated that there would be splendid views from the control room's reinforced polycarbonate type windows during the flight and they were all welcome to stay. The journey to sea re-entry would be an hour and then underwater towards the Anztarza tunnel would take another hour or so. The hundred mile tunnel journey was under water and would take about two hours. This would allow them a rest of three hours at least in the allocated cabins prior to docking in Anztarza Bay. Eric conveyed that he would like to sit down and the captain indicated the padded benches located around the control centre. These were near the outer walls but set slightly away from them and were designed backless for the Oannes to sit on. Eric found a comfortable seat with a forward view and was soon joined by most of the others. Only Ashley, Tania and Katy remained beside the captain as did Muznant and Brazjaf. Shufzaz had gone to see her friends in the crew recreation area and for an invigorating drink of Wazu.

The Zanos-447 bio computer was thought commanded by the captain to proceed home at all speed. Immediately the slight surge of impulse magnetic power was sensed by all and 11701-Red rose smoothly upwards towards the clouds as it also changed to a southerly direction. It remained perfectly level as it increased in altitude and other impulse generators gave it its forward velocity. This ensured the absolute comfort of its passengers. The craft burst through the clouds at 12,000 feet and a sky brilliant with stars and heightened by the Milky Way luminance was suddenly and brilliantly brought into view. The sound of the pleasant wowing gasps from his passengers brought a pleased emotion to Captain Lyzongpan and he turned to them and conveyed that many other spectacular sights were yet to be viewed. The corners of his mouth turned upwards in the hint of a human smile. He had practiced this at length in front of his mirror and his wife confirmed that it produced a pleasing expression.

Within moments the craft had achieved its cruising height and speed and soon the cloudless west coast of Africa came into view. The coastal towns' lighting was visible from the control room left side window panels and the visitors were all keen to get a view. These soon receded from sight behind them. The night below was pitch-black and there was no sensation of speed or of movement. Ashley was surprised how comfortable he felt standing on the control deck of this Anztarzan spaceship. The captain read Ashley's thoughts and conveyed that journeys in space were just as comfortable though rather uneventful. At least here on Earth there were changing views to admire.

The captain explained how tennis-ball sized beacons had been placed strategically at locations on the Earth which functioned as the guidance system that allowed the Zanos controllers to navigate anywhere on the planet. This was currently being used to get them back to Anztarza.

It was just about thirty minutes into the journey when Captain Lyzongpan pointed directly ahead to the beginnings of a faint glow of light on the horizon. He conveyed that they were approaching the white continent of Antarctica which was in the middle of its summer period.

'This is a view of pure beauty,' he conveyed to the group, 'please join me here and see it for yourself. It never ceases to amaze me.'

The light ahead increased rapidly and suddenly the sun flashed its brilliance at them. Immediately a tint developed within the control room windows and the glare was lessened. The whiteness of Antarctica was soon below them and they were racing over its shadow strewn white mass. Ashley realised they were looking over the top of the world to the other side where daylight prevailed. What a way to travel. The vast whiteness of Antarctica spread from horizon to horizon without a break. Alex had his arm around Lillian's shoulders as they stood side by side looking at the view passing below. Katy and Tania stood either side of Ashley and they each had a tight hold on one of his hands and were quite unconscious about it. And not a thought passed between them as they were mesmerised by what they were witnessing. An emotion of awe and wonder pervaded the area surrounding them and the captain looked at Muznant and Brazjaf and expressed a good humoured wide mouthed Oannes smile.

Ron and Brenda stood together a bit separate from the others and seemed quite amused that they were actually in such a situation high above the Earth. Jerry stood behind his wife Milly and was smiling as he watched the views of the Earth below. He had his hands on Milly's shoulders and one of her hands had reached up and covered his as she nestled back against him.

Captain Lyzongpan looked at his visitors and felt the love and goodwill that existed between them and he was pleased to be with them. If only this was representative of Earth's people then there was great hope for their future together. But he knew that such was not the case. There was still a wide base of aggression and greed upon the Earth amongst the vast variety of cultures. Ashley was special and so was his family. Lyzongpan had taken in everything expressed at the conference when Muznant and Brazjaf had returned from their first visit in November and now he confirmed in his own mind all that Muznant had stated. Ashley was exactly as he appeared.

The captain conveyed for the benefit of his guests that the scene passing below was not very different from Nazmos in the wintertime zones and it was times like this that he was reminded of his love for it. Yet he conveyed that he had also come to love this planet Earth just as much and longed for the day when Oannes could roam freely over it. He could live here forever and now that a first close communication contact had been realised the chance of integration with the Earth people had come just one small step closer to reality. The thought was a very pleasing one.

It was not long before 11701-Red passed across this white vastness and began a gradual descent towards its destination for entry into the Davis Sea. The journey had been nearly an hour long and the craft had passed over the South Pole at an altitude of 50 miles and a speed that was gradually lessening. It passed over Queen Mary Land at 8000mph and 30 miles altitude and in bright daylight. The Shackleton Ice Shelf was soon under them and the captain's thought commands prepared Zanos-447 and his crew for sea entry. In places the ice was quite thick and Zanos must ensure that sea entry was well clear of it.

The craft slowed considerably as it approached the open sea beyond the ice shelf and eventually hovered silently a few feet above the ice-free waters. Then without further delay the Zanos bio-computer sent the craft downwards and into the sea. Its speed increased as it sped downwards below the waves while making a gradual turn around as it navigated for the Anztarza Tunnel entrance 2000 feet down. Beacons placed strategically guided the craft towards the tunnel and would also control its journey along the hundred mile long stretch upwards into Anztarza Bay.

Captain Lyzongpan conveyed all this to his guests and indicated that this was now the slowest part of their journey and it would be nearly three hours to their Anztarza Bay destination. It would be an hour to the tunnel entrance and then another two hours within it. As there was nothing more to view he advised that they go to their cabins and get some rest.

All this time a crew member had been standing quietly in the background near the door to the control room. He was an unassuming person and now came forward and stood beside his captain.

'This is Difuntaz my second in command,' conveyed the captain, 'he will guide you to your resting rooms. He will also return for you at the appropriate time just prior to our arrival in Anztarza.'

Difuntaz was 120 years of age and a keen advocate of the integration lobby. He did not approve of Puzlwat's attitude and hoped that Ashley would prove him wrong. Difuntaz knew of the testing program, as did all of Anztarza, and was sure that it would help persuade Puzlwat otherwise. But he also knew that Puzlwat was openly against any form of integration and the one exception might not be good enough. Ashley would have to prove himself repeatedly to win Puzlwat's admiration. Nogozat might make the difference. Puzlwat admired and listened to his wife and she had moderated his attitude considerably. But he was yet to be fully converted to moderation.

Difuntaz had been observing the guests and noticed that Ashley was pleasant and quietly unassuming. Difuntaz searched for and found the confidence and power within the man and this drew him to like and respect Ashley. His chest swelled with pride that he could have had the privilege of being near an icon. An icon born in an ancient myth and now come true right here before his eyes. Difuntaz felt extremely proud. If only there was someone close he could share this with.

Difuntaz was single mainly because he had not as yet met anyone special. Maybe it was because he had been more occupied with his career than with matters of the heart. He was due to return to Nazmos next year and hoped to travel the big cities and towns. Perhaps his luck would change and the partner of his dreams might appear. Yet somehow he found the Earth females very attractive and there was one actress on terrestrial TV that he found particularly beautiful. And now seeing these Earth people close up in the control room especially the younger ones Katy and Tania, his opinion of their general beauty was reinforced. Muznant nudged against him and told him to be careful as they could all read his emotions not to mention his thoughts.

Integration would not happen in their lifetime and perhaps not for a thousand years. But the seed had now been sown. Muznant of course referred to the telepathic skill that would spread gradually and continually through Margaret Dutton and Dutton Consultants. Ashley picked up Muznant's thoughts and realised the importance and significance of his recent London trip. Telepathy was a key factor in the peaceful society and culture of the Oannes people. Perhaps this would eventually pervade all of Earth. Ashley wondered if contact with Margaret might occur through the stone tablet he had returned to her. Would they eventually expand their contacts and bring others too to visit Anztarza? It would all boil down to trust in keeping a secret.

Difuntaz led the way back down the corridor and up a ramp to the top floor level of the craft. He pointed down the corridor and conveyed that their rooms had been prepared and each door would convey who was to enter. A light flashed above the first door and all their badges conveyed that Ron and Brenda should enter. The door slid open and from curiosity all entered behind the chosen two.

Ron and Brenda's room was large though a third of the floor space was taken up with the sleep tank that was full of crystal clear water. The rest of the room had been arranged like a spacious bed-sit. There was a cloth covered twin sofa suite around a coffee table and at the far end of the room were two beds spaced about three feet apart and separated by a chest of drawers.

'This craft's Zanos system has been authorised to recognise your thoughts,' conveyed Difuntaz, 'so any queries you have will be instantly resolved for you. All facilities in each of your rooms are yours to command. You may wish to rest now. I will come for you later.'

Ron and Brenda could see their cases beside the beds and immediately their query was answered that these had been placed there to make them comfortable and should they require any item from within. Ron and Brenda sat down on the large soft sofa and smiling up at the others humorously conveyed for them to get off to their own rooms. Apart from the sleep tank it was just like any ordinary hotel room they had visited.

Muznant indicated that she herself could do with a rest and 'forty winks'. She knew all the Earth slang expressions. She then led the way out of the room and Difuntaz led the remainder to their rooms and the surprise was when Tania and Katy found that they were lodged together.

'Perhaps they think us oldies need our little privacy,' said Milly winking at Lillian. 'Anyway I shall follow Muznant's suggestion and grab a quick forty winks myself. It has been a long exciting night after all. Mind you with all this excitement I'm wide awake as I'll ever be.'

Difuntaz smiled his affection for these Earth people as he turned about and returned to his captain.

Ashley and Eric were placed together and this pleased Eric. He had been afraid that he might be on his own. Ever since Jenny had been taken from him he had been classed as a single supplement whenever he went on holiday. He had revisited all those holiday locations they had once so enjoyed together but that had not worked out at all. There'd been no fun in it anymore and it had only brought back the feeling of aloneness far more. He still thought of her but the pain had gone and he could look back at their moments with pleasantness and affection. Ashley was the prominent factor now and Eric wondered how he would cope with Ashley being taken away by these people to do that big task whatever it was. Yes, Ashley would have to travel far but Eric decided not to worry about that now. As far as he was concerned it was late and he would normally have been in bed by now. His wrist watch showed well past one o'clock so he lay down on the bed with arms folded behind his head and legs crossed lengthways and shut his eyes.

'I think I might do the same granddad,' said Ashley aloud and then asked telepathically of the others how they were all doing. The response was about the same. They were all quite excited but would also take advantage of the next three hours to get some sleep; fully dressed of course.

'Tea and coffee are being delivered to each cabin this very moment. A pot of each will be placed in the food cubicle by the entrance door along with the milk and sweeteners as you prefer,' conveyed Muznant. She had read their emotions for a hot drink when they had first entered their rooms and had conveyed the desire to the Zanos system. She then conveyed through their badge communication devices that Wazu was her favourite drink and when they were all comfortably housed in Anztarza she would introduce them to it. But for now both she and Brazjaf would also rest in their sleep tank.

Captain Lyzongpan stayed at his post in the control room and Difuntaz stood silently by his side. It was now completely dark outside their viewing windows and the craft cruised at close to 90 mph. The water pressure contracted the hull of the craft by only a marginal amount. The 14 inch thickness of the outer skin was well within the designed limit. It could venture down to the deepest parts of Earth's oceans. The hull material was similar to that used in the lining of the walls of Anztarza's domes. The alloy composite had been discovered by accident when Nazmos scientists had been experimenting with neutron star material prior to the construction of their first FTL starships. It had the unique property that resulted in the fusion of two surfaces that were in contact. When two flat surfaces were forced together and left like that for a year or so then complete fusion of those surfaces occurred. The two blocks would become as one. On average a space going craft such as 11701-Red would have taken about fifty years or more to complete. On the other hand an FTL starship took at least two hundred years in the making if not more. And it not only had to be made off planet but far out in inter-stellar space. For Earth, inter-stellar space commenced somewhere beyond the Oort-Cloud; a spherical cloud of up to a trillion icy objects that surrounds the Solar System at a distance of about one light-year. The same would probably apply for the Raznat System.

Ashley closed his eyes as he lay on the bed beside his granddad but sleep eluded him. So he tuned in and listened to the thoughts within the ship. Ashley found his reading and listening skills had increased tremendously and in fact had even surpassed those of the Oannes. But the block in their thoughts still resisted his probing efforts. It stood like an impenetrable wall within which that secret was sheathed. The captain was busy with thoughts of the journey and also of the changes to the décor of his home in Dome-17 that Dazulteng his wife was planning. They would have to get their material orders ready for the next FTL starship which was due anytime now.

Shufzaz was still in the crew recreation lounge drinking Wazu and in thought communication with two others who lived in the same dome as him. They were planning an excursion to one of the remote pine forests of Canada during the start of the spring season when few might be about. The lakes there were ideal for their purposes and quite similar to the conditions in the Sea of Peruga during their own summer season. The oceans of Earth were uncomfortable for the Oannes and were not for prolonged habitation.

In the cargo area at the back end of the ship a group of crew members were checking the join locking of the large bay doors, always a bone of contention with the maintenance staff when deep underwater travel was in progress as it was now.

Gradually all activity on the ship dulled to a quiet thought background and Ashley sensed that many had gone to their quarters for a few moments rest before arriving in Anztarza.

'Hi Tania, can you sleep?' from Ashley.

'So you're awake too. Is granddad asleep?'

'Yes, completely so.' Ashley liked the way Tania referred to Eric as her granddad too.

'How about Katy?'

'Yes, she's out like a light. I'm on the bed with my eyes shut but no sleep I'm afraid.'

Ashley smiled to himself. 'I'm the same.'

'I just yawned. Actually I am a bit sleepy I think.'

'I'll keep communicating and when you don't respond I'll know you've drifted off.'

'Okay, I'll keep listening.'

'I love you Tania' and Ashley conveyed the emotion too.

'Dang, there goes my sleep.' there was the emotion of humour with the message.

'Would a lullaby help?'

'Can you sing telepathically?'

'No.'

'Try.'

'Okay.' A brief pause was followed by, 'did you get that?'

'No, nothing. Your voice doesn't carry.'

'Actually I didn't try, I was just joking. I'll have to ask Muznant about that,' from Ashley generally.

'Muznant is luxuriating in her sleep tank fast asleep,' came from Brazjaf. 'In answer to your query you can convey only what you have observed. Like a concert in which there is music, singing and dancing. But someone else needs to convey what you sing because then it is their experience that is conveyed. Unfortunately only you Ashley from among all your family can do that as we Oannes can. But in time the art will be acquired by all.'

'Thank you Brazjaf,' conveyed Tania smiling, 'but I don't think Ashley can sing at all. Trust me he has a terrible singing voice. It is agony just thinking about it.'

Brazjaf conveyed back a humorous emotion and stated that although he enjoyed musical entertainment programs on his TV he didn't think that any Oannes in Anztarza had singing voice skills.

'Of course I can sing,' conveyed Ashley light-heartedly, 'you should hear me in the shower.'

'I'd rather not,' conveyed Tania. 'And I shall put a 'No Singing' notice in our bathroom to that effect.'

No response came from Ashley though he conveyed that he was tired now and perhaps a bit of quiet time would be beneficial.

'Okay,' from Tania. 'I'll just close my eyes and think for a bit. Perhaps my forty winks will find me.'

'Granddad Eric is snoring,' conveyed Ashley. 'It's been a long day for him.'

'It's been a long day for all of us. Now go to sleep Ashley, over and out.'

'Ten four,'

'Shut up.'

'Goodnight.'

'Goodnight.'

In the control room Lyzongpan stood with his wife Dazulteng beside him. Difuntaz his number two had gone to the crew recreation lounge for some refreshment. He preferred plain water with a hint of fruity flavouring. Wazu was not quite his cup of tea though he used it as a pep-me-up when he was tired or needed to be up for long periods on duty. It was surprising how invigorating Wazu could be but Difuntaz found the taste bland. Whenever he added flavouring to the glass the furry seeds all sank to the bottom as if dead and bitterness spread through the drink especially near the end.

Dazulteng touched her captain husband's hand loosely with hers and they communicated conversational trivialities with each other. The redecorating of their home was one of the topics with colour schemes being top of the agenda. They each had a preferred theme but Lyzongpan knew that his wife had a better understanding and artistic skill where interior design was concerned. Hers would be the right choice but he knew that she desired an input from him.

They had known one another since before they had partnered and their legal document had been drawn up to declare them man and wife over 110 years ago. He had been a young man of eighty when he had plucked up the courage to settle down with this woman who was then just approaching her fiftieth year. Their three children on Nazmos had not yet married and seemed to be enjoying their lives. Their annual communications did not mention their friends but Dazulteng was sure that they were promiscuous and only shy of mentioning it. Communications between their generations had its restrictions.

11701-Red had now entered the Anztarza Tunnel and was proceeding at just 50 mph. The Zanos bio-computer had complete control of speed and course and the hundred mile length would be covered in about two hours.

In the domed city of Anztarza many were making their way to the Bay area and the Deck Transporters were kept busy ferrying people. All were keen to get a first glimpse of their visitors. And once again Kazaztan and 536-Orange had the privileged task of conveying the visitors to Dome-4 and the amphitheatre meeting place. 536-Orange had enhanced ornamentation added to its perimeter railings and carpet richness compared to the other Deck Transporters. It was ideal for the purpose of conveying visitors and top brass dignitaries around Anztarza and Kazaztan was extremely proud and excited at the prospect. He reckoned that his age of 256 years might have been a factor in the equation.

Pzandab at 306 years was the oldest person in Anztarza and her job was supervising the mooring of craft in Anztarza Bay. No one over the age of 310 years was permitted to remain on Earth and Pzandab had opted to leave for Nazmos on the FTL ship due in 2006. She had been in Anztarza for nearly half of her lifetime. The pains of age were beginning to be felt continuously, especially in the restlessness that she experienced when she entered her sleep tank. The Wazu had been a help for quite some time but now even that didn't seem to benefit her and sleep came fitfully. But she loved Anztarza and had many friends here. She loved this planet Earth and had often walked its remote forests when she was younger. She missed the greenery she had been permitted to visit then and now she tired easily and such forays were out of the question. So instead she watched the programs on her TV and lived vicariously through the nature documentaries shown there. She had never partnered and preferred the company of other women although she had many men friends too. The men were just good friends and never companions.

Pzandab had taken a keen interest with regard to their earthly visitors and had made a special study of Ashley and all that he had revealed to the 'thinking stone'. Her instincts were very strong and these confirmed in her mind that Ashley was indeed the person foretold in their myths. He would make Nazmos as green as the Earth providing that his telekinetic gift was strong enough to avert the impending danger of Zarama.

'Yes,' she thought, 'this Ashley person has got to be the one to stop it. He just has to be the one.'

As 11701-Red approached the end of its journey Lyzongpan conveyed the information to his passengers and invited them back to the control room. Brazjaf and Muznant collected their guests and were met in the corridor by Difuntaz who took them all down to the control centre. Lyzongpan introduced his wife to Ashley and the others and Dazulteng conveyed her pleasure after a brief 'Sewa' formality that Ashley responded to easily and with finesse.

The craft was still submerged and moving slowly with a dull lightness now visible through the control room windows. Suddenly they were out of the water and the lights of the Bay Dome burst in upon them all with a dazzling brightness. The marina was about a half mile away and was similar to those on Earth except for the variety of the craft moored there. Ashley and Tania stood side by side holding hands as they watched the approaching shore.

The Anztarza berthing was done to perfection by the onboard Zanos controller in coordination with the Central Zanos Anztarzan system. Captain Lyzongpan conveyed his final instructions to Difuntaz his deputy regarding the maintenance checks to be performed on the craft before he handed over control. The onboard Zanos bio-computer would now take all thought commands from Difuntaz. The wetness in the mating join of the cargo bay doors had been reported during the trip and would be given priority for immediate attention.

Ashley and family had observed the crowds behind the small group assembled on the marina platform and felt slightly apprehensive. They were being treated as celebrities which was a first for them and rather embarrassing. How should they behave and what should be said?

'Please don't worry,' conveyed Muznant reading their anxiety, 'nothing is expected of you apart from your presence. Anztarza just wants to see you and welcome you. They already know all about you and are keen to see and greet you. Just behave as you did with Brazjaf and me when we first met. We are all ordinary people the same as you.'

Lyzongpan and his Dazulteng led the way from the control room and out onto the quay and the waiting crowd. At the front were the three Chief Ministers Rymtakza, Zarzint and Tzatzorf along with some of Anztarza's other leading citizens. Puzlwat and Mytanzto were among these. The visitors would be treated with full respect according to the strong Oannes tradition and any personal views or feelings of dissention would be kept hidden. Puzlwat kept an open mind though he secretly hoped his scepticism and distrust with regard to Ashley would be proved correct. He would in fairness give Ashley every chance and opportunity to prove otherwise. Puzlwat was for the good of Anztarza and nothing more and nothing less. His doubts about Ashley were ingrained from his belief that humans were a primitive race and had nothing to offer the Oannes. Their history had so far proved him right.

Each of the ministers greeted their guests informally. The rubbing of noses and touching of foreheads was omitted as this only took place between the Oannes. But Ashley indicated that he would however like the Sewa ritual to be fulfilled. This took but an instant by Tzatzorf the senior-most minister and when Ashley responded he opened his mind and projected his Sewa enquiries to all of Anztarza. The response was vast and Puzlwat was taken by surprise though pleasantly so. So, the Earth people could be polite he thought. Or was this another trick that Ashley had up his sleeve? His wife Nogozat who was beside him on the pier decided on impulse that she liked this Ashley person. She sensed an abundance of goodness in him and her instincts were never wrong.

When all greetings were completed Tzatzorf led the way to the large Deck Transporter 536-Orange that sat slightly further back but in front of the assembled Oannes. Kazaztan had a wide-mouth expression of utter pride in his privileged role today as he stood beside the steps at the rear of his Transporter. The chief ministers led the way up the steps and onto the luxuriously blue carpeted floor of the platform. This time Kazaztan's wife Zarpralt stood at the top of the steps and welcomed her husband's passengers aboard. Kazaztan's plan had been approved as appropriate when he had requested it. It was standard practice for wives to accompany the husband on the craft under his command. Deck Transporters were as important as any space-going craft at least in this instance. Ashley and his family were considered extremely important.

Standing positions were communicated to all and Ashley and his family were given positions at the railings near the front of the platform. Ashley immediately understood the reason for this. They were special guests and were meant to be seen by the welcoming Oannes people. Chief Minister Rymtakza conveyed that it had been agreed that a circuitous route from Dome-1 through to the Dome-4 amphitheatre be navigated where the official welcoming ceremony was to be held. This would take in Domes-2 and 3 and so allow maximum viewing exposure of the visitors to the crowds below.

The onboard Zanos bio-computer responded to Kazaztan's thought command and 536-Orange rose smoothly and silently upwards till it reached a height of 15 feet. The watching Oannes could see the visitors very clearly and all thought how beautiful these Earth people really are. 536-Orange then began to move forwards at a sedate 10 mph.

'There is no waving or clapping or gesture making,' thought Lillian and conveyed this to the others. Then she felt it; a powerful emotion of gladness and good cheer was being transmitted upwards to envelope them all. One or two thoughts also filtered through but these were hospitality requests inviting Ashley and family to visit them in their homes.

At the back end of the Bay Dome were two tunnels. These were 100 feet wide with an arched construction that peaked at 200 feet at its centre. The base had a 30 feet wide canal filled with water which was not connected to the water in the bay area. It was at a higher level than the bay and the water in these Anztarzan canals was lake water similar to that on Nazmos.

536-Orange headed towards the right side tunnel and floated into it. The tunnel was half a mile long and before long they were in another dome only marginally smaller than the Bay Dome. This was Dome-1 and the first to be constructed over six thousand years ago and differed from the Bay area in that it had a magnificent architectural design about it. It was full of block style housing no more than two storeys tall and with a considerable diversity in appearance. There were geometrically parallel streets with a spacious plaza at the central area. Trees grew along many streets and there was even a small grassy park with shrubs planted in circular beds. It all looked very pleasant with a distinct Earth-like feel about it. When the visitors looked downwards at the gathered people it was noticed that many wore re-fashioned Earth design clothes in place of their usual tunic and leggings.

'I have a dress like that,' said Milly pointing to an Oannes lady in a yellow floral dress. Of course the backs of all garments had to be adapted to accommodate the large back butterfly type webbed wing. There was laughter and jollity as Eric and Alex both pointed out an Oannes man in a large loose fitting red coloured short-sleeved bush shirt which both recognised as a Magnum design from the TV program of the same name. Lillian conveyed that somehow she didn't think that Earth clothes quite suited the Oannes figure. Perhaps they ought to evolve a design of their own more suited to their physical makeup. The webs on their arms, faces and backs somehow did not blend in with the clothes' patterns.

536-Orange floated on over the central plaza and then turned left towards the tunnel at the far end that led to Dome-2. There were even some Oannes people standing inside the tunnel area to get a glimpse of their visitors.

Dome-2 was similar in appearance to Dome-1 except in the design of some of the buildings and in the shape of the central square. Their park was smaller and quite plain though still green. On the far left was the tunnel that led back to the Bay Dome while on the right was the tunnel entrance leading to Dome-9. Straight ahead was the way to Dome-3 their next destination. The Oannes were spread thinner here in Dome-2 but all expressed the emotion of joy at seeing their visitors floating overhead. They were dressed mostly in colourful tunics and leggings and a few among them had on a sort of floral head adornment. Muznant explained that these were the objectors and were simply expressing their views of disapproval. In all of Anztarza there had been 23 Oannes who had voted against allowing this visit. Puzlwat was their leader along with Mytanzto. Ashley smiled as he leaned over the Transporter railing and had a good look at the people passing below.

The next Dome-3 was very similar only there was a bigger crowd waiting. All looked up eagerly and Ashley saw only one head adornment on display. Ashley kept his mind open and conveyed generally that his thoughts were available for scrutiny by anyone. As the Transporter floated on Ashley and the others were pleased to see the one head adornment being removed and held behind the back of the Oannes person who had been wearing it. Could it be a change of heart he thought?

As they emerged from the next tunnel and into Dome-4 there was a surprise waiting for them. The crowd of Oannes people was absolutely phenomenal. There must have been close to 3000 people filling the amphitheatre and surrounding areas.

536-Orange settled gently onto the floor to one side of the amphitheatre and after alighting down the steps of the Transporter the visitors were led through the assembled people and onto the raised dais of a large square platform near its centre. Ashley knew that he was the celebrity they had all come to see and his mind filled with pleasant emotions of welcome. There was an air of expectancy in the people around him and Ashley understood that he must stand up before them all and express his joy at being here among them.

There weren't any seats on the dais as there were no speeches or announcements planned. This was to be just a showing off of the visitors to their welcoming hosts, the people of Anztarza. All had seen what humans were like from the TV programs they all watched and monitored but to be so close to them was a new experience. So standing as a group though slightly apart from the chief ministers' entourage Ashley stepped forward and raised both his arms up in the air in front of him. A mental hush descended in the amphitheatre as Ashley faced first right and then left. Slowly he brought his palms together in a silent series of clapping gestures. Then he turned towards the chief ministers behind him and gave them a shallow bow slow and deliberate. Turning to Muznant and Brazjaf he did the same. They all responded with a similar bow in return and in their minds wondered how Ashley could have known of this lost custom of their ancestors recorded only in the ancient texts. A feeling of awe and respect overcame them all and their chests swelled with wonder. Even Puzlwat was temporarily choked by an emotion of wonder which rather confused him. But then he thought that this Ashley was cleverer than he had expected. He must be more wary in his antagonistic approach.

Lillian's heart filled with pride at this boy becoming a man right before her eyes. Her eyes also welled with tears of joy and a mixture of every emotion under the sun filled her being. Alex felt the same and slowly put his arm around his wife's waist and squeezed her to him.

In response to Ashley's request he was given approval and authority from the chief ministers to address the expectant crowd. And so he faced the people and putting his right hand to his lips he made a gesture sending a kiss out to them. Ashley made a series of these while he slowly turned to left and right a number of times. There was an emotion of delight and humour and joyousness from the assembled Oannes and they also began imitating Ashley's gesture of hand kisses up at their visitors. All on the dais responded in kind. Ashley knew he must now express his joy and thanks at the lovely welcome they had all just received.

'My friends,' he conveyed in a powerful thought signal, 'my family and I are overcome with the joyousness of your welcome. Anztarza is a great and beautiful city from what we have seen so far and we are very pleased to have been invited here to be among you. We all look forward to meeting as many of you personally as will be possible in the next couple of weeks and getting to know you as we have Brazjaf and Muznant. My family join with me in saying that we think you are a beautiful people and that is the truth and that we are sure that we shall become good companions and friends. As for myself I do not know why these gifts of strength have been bestowed on me and I am quite in awe of the power at my command. I believe that it is all towards a good purpose which at the moment is unknown to me but I am willing to do whatever is required. I have been informed that a great task awaits me and I will need guidance from you who have a civilization well in advance of our own. I also ask you to teach us your ways for us to better understand you. At the moment our societies on Earth are not deserving of you but the seeds of mental communication have been sown among a business family in London called the Duttons and I believe the way forward has begun. They possess the very same communication tablet that was used by me and which I referred to as the 'thinking stone'. It led me to you and perhaps it might do the same for them.'

Ashley paused and looking back at his family he smiled at them. He then went and stood between Tania and his mother and put an arm around each.

'My family and I are your first Earth guests and I feel proud that we were chosen to meet you. I sincerely hope that in the future you will choose others to follow in our footsteps. But you must choose carefully and wisely. One day many lifetimes from now I believe that a full integration will be achieved and the Oannes people shall then also become full citizens of a peaceful Earth to roam freely across its varied landscape. And Earth people will also do the same on Nazmos. But for now you must maintain your secrecy and peaceful way of life here in Anztarza and on Nazmos.'

Ashley took hold of Tania's hand and stepped forward off the dais. Slowly they walked together to where the crowd was assembled and stopped in front of the first person there. Ashley looked into the gentle eyes staring up at him and knew it was a woman. Ashley reached forward and touched her shoulder and expressed an emotion of affection as his greeting to her. This was similar to what Muznant had done with Ashley when they had their first meeting at Ron and Brenda's B&B back in November. Tania then also did the same with the Oannes person standing in front of her. Lillian and Alex and the others had all followed Ashley and Tania down to the assembled people and each found someone to greet.

Gradually the gathered hosts began to relax and a feeling of comradeship developed within the assembly. There was now a lot of touching and little by little Ashley was separated from his family members. They too had become separated from each other as the Oannes surrounded them and took them deeper into the excited crowd. Tania received as much attention as did Lillian and Katy.

Before any of the Oannes reached out to touch they would first request permission to do so which was always given. Of great interest was the hair on the heads of the visitors and there was a great desire to feel its texture. Invitations of hospitality poured out from the people who wished the visitors presence in their homes. Each would give their name and then invite the visitor before them to their house to share a glass of Wazu with them.

'I am Mazontaz and would be honoured if you came to my house,' was the general style of invitation conveyed.

However in all of this a very small group remained separated from the activity and simply stood apart and watched with amusement. This was a group of about ten persons who stood alongside Puzlwat and Mytanzto. They found it interesting to listen to Ashley as he made his play with the assembled Oannes. Watching Ashley's performance only increased Puzlwat's doubts in Ashley's suitability for the task ahead. Action spoke louder than words and so far they had seen none of the former. Nogozat was not beside her husband since she did not share his opinions. She had actually sensed Ashley's goodness of mind as some Oannes are wont to do and she had conveyed this to her husband. But he said that he had sensed no such thing and in fact felt quite the opposite. He knew he was right and would bide his time and so be proved right in his distrust of Ashley's intentions.

All this lasted about an hour and would have gone on for longer had not chief minister Zarzint conveyed to the assembled crowd that the visitors needed rest from their journey. They would now be transported to the accommodation set out for them and be given refreshment. It was late in their body clock time and he requested that they be brought back to the dais. Almost immediately paths were opened up within the melee of people from wherever Ashley and the members of his family happened to be. As Ashley walked back to the dais he held out his hands and gently touched palms with the people as he progressed past them.

On the dais Ashley again faced towards the assembled crowd and raised his hands in the clapping gesture of before. He was surprised to see several arms raised similarly in response. Then more were added and suddenly the whole assembly had their arms up and were silently emulating Ashley's movements. A new form of greeting appreciation had been coined and adopted by the Oannes here in Anztarza. Behind Ashley on the dais the chief ministers and others also joined in and all were smiling their characteristic wide mouth expressions. Ashley faced the crowd and his face was aglow with pride. It was a humble pride that came with the knowledge that finally all his gifts were out in the open in this place and known by every single Anztarzan.

Ashley did not have to operate secretly here and apparently the Oannes believed that he was capable of preventing whatever impending disaster threatened. Ashley stood tall and with him his family also stood tall with pride in one of their own.

From this moment a new man came into being. The old Ashley had been part boy but now a maturity descended upon his manner that was apparent to all his family. This is what the Oannes had seen and this is what Lillian and Alex now saw in their son. Tania too noticed this new maturity that had been added to Ashley's demeanour and with this she knew that she not only loved him as before but now also looked up at her man suddenly grown in stature and wisdom.

A new power seemed to emit from Ashley's personality and both Lillian and Tania wondered if he had been granted another gift. Up until now Lillian had always feared that his gifts would somehow endanger Ashley and possibly take him away forever. That fear now dispersed and was replaced by a new confidence in Ashley's ability to look after himself. However, she did wonder whether their mother and son relationship might change. She needn't have been concerned for Ashley sensed her thoughts and turned towards his mother and his girl and gave them that same old charming smile that said 'I'm still me and always will be. Nothing has changed for us.'

This was something new for Ashley to sense another's unease and he concluded that the communication badge must have picked up his mother's concerns and relayed them to him. And immediately Ashley understood the secret behind the Anztarzans peace and why the Oannes were such a calm people. They had a built-in remedy for allaying problems and concerns. Help was always at hand and all worries or fears were openly shared and appeased.

Muznant and Brazjaf then stepped forward and touching Ashley gently indicated that they board the Deck Transporter for conveyance to their arranged accommodation beside their own in Dome-7. Muznant led the way and once again a path was opened for their walk to 536-Orange.

The surprising thing in all this was the verbal silence that prevailed throughout the proceedings. But as the visitors walked through the gathered Oannes a few softly spoken verbal 'goodbyes' were clearly heard. Ashley and his family responded enthusiastically with several 'goodbye friends' while once again touching with outstretched palms those closest to their path.

As 536-Orange rose up slowly Ashley and his family lined the side rails looking down at the people. Several arms were raised in a half clapping half waving gesture. And so the group on the floating deck waved back at the crowds below as they continued across towards the tunnel leading to the next dome.

When they entered Dome-7 it seemed deserted in comparison and Muznant explained that this was their own habitation dome and that the people had agreed the visitors be given their privacy here. Muznant conveyed that the amphitheatre crowds had been the official welcoming party and that from now onwards they would be granted a partial anonymity and the freedom to see as much of Anztarza as they desired. The freedom of access meant that they would be treated as ordinary citizens free to meet and communicate with whomsoever they wished. However a program of special visits had also been organised and hopefully would be adhered to over the next few days. Among these was a trip into space and hopefully also to see the FTL starship if it arrived as expected within its scheduled period.

536-Orange settled to the floor of the central plaza area and Brazjaf led the way towards his street. Muznant referred to her dome as 7-Blue and their house was on Fifth Street by the dome wall. To avoid any contention among the people the chief ministers had decided that Muznant and Brazjaf have the privilege of housing Ashley and his grandfather Eric in their own home. Theirs was the first house on Fifth Street which was on the corner with the broader main street running the length of the dome at right angles to all the habitation streets. Fifth Street also happened to house families who were all close friends of Muznant and Brazjaf. Most were in administrative and monitoring functions similar to Brazjaf's governmental job. Anztarza's citizens all had jobs of one form or another that related to the monitoring and recording of data on the culture of the vast variety of sects of humans on the Earth. Some studied the flora diversity while others chose to study the animal species on the Earth. Each Anztarzan was multitasked and the chief ministers had requested the home government for higher staffing levels to cover further areas of interest.

On the street the first neighbours were Laztraban and his wife Niktukaz and they had been chosen to accommodate Lillian, Alex and Katy in their home. Laztraban was 196 years old and his wife whom he called Niktu for short was just 166. They originally came from a small town alongside a remote lake quite distant from the capital city of Wentazta. They had lived in Anztarza for over seventy years and had visited Nazmos only twice in all that time. They had fallen in love with the views of Earth when they first arrived and often roamed a remote isolated island forest somewhere off the coast of the vast landmass known as Canada. They also had a great affection and admiration for Earth's peoples and one of their tasks in Anztarza had been to pick up the languages and living cultures among the diverse Inuit people. They were currently studying a small nomadic tribe in Outer Mongolia and were fascinated at the diversity of culture and dialect. They loved watching Earth's TV programs and thought that one day Nazmos too might become similar to Earth in its lushness of vegetation. Somehow Ashley entered into this scenario and both husband and wife considered themselves privileged to be given the honour of housing his parents and sister. Their home was large and two rooms had been converted into bedrooms for them; twin beds in one and a single bed in the other.

The next house was that of a young couple Fruztriv and his wife Rontuzaj. He was 70 years of age while she was ten years his junior. At the moment the house was unoccupied due to the couple being on a visit to Nazmos.

The house was very similar to the others and had plenty of room to accommodate five people comfortably. And so Ron and Brenda were housed here with Jerry, Milly and Tania. Laztraban and Niktukaz had agreed to supervise and look after their needs too.

The Oannes had a thorough understanding of the habits and diet preferences of all their guests and everything had been thoroughly looked into for their comfort. The Oannes could read the minds of each person just as Ashley had been able to from the moment he had met the Polish plumbers at the Aberporth B&B, and so all their likes could be catered for and the dislikes avoided.

The family found all their suitcases in their allotted rooms and already most of the clothes had been put onto hangers and placed in the wall storage spaces. There was never any confusion as each badge conveyed complete clarification whenever required. A confused thought or query was immediately responded to and answer given. When Eric thought that a cup of tea would be nice he knew immediately that he must go to the recess in the wall of his room and all the makings were there including the constant hot water. Eric did not know it but another local Oannes drink was to play a very important role in his welfare. And that was the drink of Wazu.

Ashley had his own room and after a drink of cool water he said goodnight to all through his badge and settled onto his bed for a well earned rest. The response was similar from all the others and before long quietness descended within the three houses on Fifth Street of Dome-7. Even Brazjaf and Muznant reposed peacefully in their sleep-tank. A busy activity schedule lay in the days ahead.

The lights of the dome were dimmed for the internal simulation of nighttimes to give the Anztarzans the routine perspective of nights and days. It also helped in establishing continuity between activity and rest periods not to emphasise the balancing of the Oannes body clock. Day and night sequences were each twelve hours in duration and the Oannes adhered to the Earth time and date calendar. Times were synchronised to conform to Greenwich Mean Time.

Muznant and Brazjaf were up first and sent out a mental thought to the rest of the group that a new day had begun. Similarly Laztraban and Niktukaz had begun preparations for the morning refreshments and nourishment items for their guests. Although they knew the preferences of each guest they also included a jug of the Oannes favourite Wazu drink. When Muznant offered a glass of this to Eric and Ashley they both looked hesitantly at the furry seeds lazily floating around in the clear liquid. The seeds seemed to be moving around the glass of their own accord.

'Do not chew the seeds when you drink as they have a bitter taste,' conveyed Brazjaf as the four of them were seated on stools at the food table, 'you must just drink it as you do water. You will find it very refreshing and invigorating. We find the Wazu gives us nourishment and energy.'

Ashley sipped at his glass gingerly and put on a worried expression before breaking into a smile.

'Not bad at all,' he conveyed, 'the flavour reminds me a bit of rose water.'

When he looked up Eric had already emptied his glass and moved it forward for a refill.

'I need to drink plenty of fluid everyday,' he said aloud, 'it helps with all my aches and pains. Also for all the pills I've got to swallow daily.'

Brazjaf and Muznant smiled at each other conspiratorially and then conveyed that it was with Eric in mind that they had requested a stronger version of the Wazu drink. It usually took about an hour for the energy effects to be felt. Muznant explained that Anztarzans tended to drink it at regular intervals during the day especially if their work involved physical activity. It had also proved to be a great remedy for space sickness.

The other items on the breakfast table were cheese and bread. Earth bread was a favourite among the Anztarzans and this was usually accompanied with a wide variety of cheeses from all over the world. Tea and coffee were also on the table and pre-made in pots. The Oannes thought-read all the favourite eating habits of their guests and apart from meat products could provide all the rest. Even Soya type simulated meat was anathema to the Oannes who abhorred eating the flesh of other creatures. Most of the items on the breakfast table had been procured in an English town.

Laztraban and Niktukaz also served up similar tables for their two sets of guests and suggested that afterwards they all make their way to the first house to meet up with Ashley and the others. All the guests had drunk of the Wazu and only Katy and Tania were put off by the floating bug-like seeds. They said it was like having to drink medicine. Niktukaz explained that the Oannes found it gave them added energy and helped the older ones cope with the pains of age.

All the badges were open so thoughts went back and forth between the party members. All said what a wonderfully quiet night's rest they'd had and wondered what this new day had in store. Brazjaf conveyed an emotion of humour and the simple suggestion of wait and see. The chief ministers were expected a little later which allowed them all time to stroll out to the central square and plaza to take in the sights within the dome. It was very bright and reminded Ashley of a bright summer's day in the middle of Dudley.

The Wazu took effect gradually and Eric was the first to remark how well he felt this morning. He said he actually felt as if he'd like to do a bit of a jog around the block. When Muznant explained that the Wazu had that effect on a lot of their people Eric said he was definitely staying with the Wazu diet. Eric's feeling of wellbeing and energy came as a pleasant surprise to Ashley and his query as to the origins of the Wazu drink seeds were immediately answered by Brazjaf and Muznant.

They conveyed that the actual origin was unknown but that it was suspected that some Earth contamination had been carried back to Nazmos from that first expedition that had proved so disastrous on the return journey ten thousand years ago. Somehow the seeds had entered the food plateau in the Great Sea of Peruga on Nazmos and must have found the conditions favourable and subsequently evolved to their present state. Initially the seeds had been ornamental as many found them fascinating when displayed in glass jars since they never settled and had this weird floating type of movement at all levels. Some child or other had accidentally drunk from one such display jar and suffered no ill effects except to complain that the drink was tasteless and the seeds horribly bitter. And the rest was history. The Oannes discovered the very high protein content of the Wazu seeds and the fact that it not only gave them a renewable energy supply but in the long term illness and disease seemed to diminish among the population who drank it.

'You have fluoride in your water supply in Dudley and Birmingham that prevents tooth decay yet you do not know how it works. I suppose Wazu is the same', conveyed Brazjaf.

Attempts had been made to cultivate the plant on Earth but alas without success. The food domes 21, 22 and 23 in Anztarza failed in all their attempts even though they had duplicated all the conditions of the food plateau on Nazmos. However the Wazu seeds could be brought to Earth in their dried form and the subsequent drink made up in Anztarza. It was just as good as any created on Nazmos. Eric said that was good to know else he might have considered emigrating to Nazmos.

It was Jerry again who posed the question of their much longer lifespan as compared to humans.

'Was it always so or have you gradually increased your longevity with progress in the medical field?' asked Jerry aloud.

'Our history shows that we did not always live this long,' said Muznant in her low tone melodic voice that Ashley so loved. 'However our earliest records did show that we lived to over two hundred years. Our evolution like yours is a state of mind desiring a quality such as this very desperately. Perhaps that could be a key factor in its achievement. All Oannes have such a desire inbred in them and of chief concern is the need to explore our galaxy as much as possible. For this we need to live long even with our FTL starships. Our technology is continually advancing and even at much greater FTL speeds time is a critical factor. Future expeditions to other star systems might require hundreds of travel years and so a captain and his crew must be able to enjoy the fruits of their discoveries. So we all crave a longer lifespan and over the last million years it has increased by a considerable amount. We are lucky to have Earth and Nazmos in such close proximity. Perhaps if you on Earth had a similar intense craving your future generations might benefit.'

'I never thought of it like that,' replied Jerry. 'I always imagined that the answer lay purely in medical science discovering the secret of long life.'

'Evolution is sure but very slow,' conveyed Brazjaf telepathically. 'Whatever you desire must be for the future only. A desire to improve your race must exist but there must also be a strong survival reason behind it. Otherwise it may never happen.'

They reached the central plaza just as Deck Transporter 536-Orange operated by Kazaztan arrived with the three chief ministers and a few others. As it settled down gently chief minister Rymtakza conveyed for his guests to climb aboard for a general information tour of all the 23 domes that made up the City of Anztarza. The Dome-24 was still under construction and so was out of bounds to all Anztarzans including chief ministers such as him. Only specialist construction workers and their associates went within.

Muznant had already had Ashley read her mind at that first visit in November and all his family knew of the history of Anztarza which had been conceived just over six thousand years ago. But now Rymtakza told how the first domes that were constructed were the Bay Dome and Domes-1 & 2 with their adjoining link tunnels. This had taken 250 years to complete after the 200 years it had taken to make the hundred mile sea tunnel access to the Bay Dome. Underwater work was not difficult for the Oannes but Earth's sea water had been an unfriendly environment for them. In addition it had taken nearly twenty years of research and test bores and geological mapping to establish the perfect long term site for the future city. Of course all this had depended upon the FTL space cruiser starships that had brought men and materials to Earth from Nazmos several times each year. Rymtakza continued his tale telepathically.

'Initially the FTL starships travelled at six to seven times light speed and took about a year each way. Now at ten times light speed the journey takes between seven and eight months. There had initially been a single such ship but the current fleet now extends to nine. More were in the making but neutron star material involved a painstakingly slow construction of the ships shield and all had to be done well out in interstellar space. So far only one Starship 1110-Green had been lost when it struck a seven mile wide ice block within the Oort-Cloud just a light year from Earth. Since then regular patrols were made to break up any such threats.'

'Another Starship 2110-Blue was unknown when it had set out from the Raznat system some 1400 years ago. With a full family complement of 1500 Oannes it had journeyed towards an interesting star system under the leadership of Captain Chamzalt. He had not only been specially chosen for his leadership qualities but also for being a natural born explorer. He had taken his family with him as was the custom and alas there had been no contact or message from the FTL ship in all that time. One could only hope that they still survive somewhere.'

'As for Anztarza, a new dome had been completed at the more leisurely pace of about four domes per millennium. The last habitable Dome-20 was completed about 1500 years ago and at that time the population of the city was a mere three thousand Oannes. All food was then still ferried from Nazmos although a few products were purchased on Earth. Gold coin was easy to make and was generally accepted everywhere.'

'Nazmos policy changed and it was then decided to gradually increase the Oannes presence on Earth to a maximum of ten thousand. Subsequently three food growing domes were constructed about a thousand years ago and are fully operational and supply nearly all our requirements. The only general import from Nazmos was the Wazu and all construction materials. We hope to increase our staffing levels even further since undertaking worldwide monitoring and currently Dome-24 is in the process of construction. This will become our fourth food dome and completion is anticipated in about fifty years.'

536-Orange floated about thirty feet up in the air and proceeded slowly across towards the entrance to Dome-8. It kept to its height as all connecting tunnels were two hundred feet at the arched apex. As the Transporter proceeded from one dome to another the chief ministers in turn gave a commentary about who lived there and what duties they performed. Each dome had its proportion of mentoring governmental administrators since each Anztarzan had an allocated work function. Most of these were monitoring Earth's varied population and learning the customs, languages and rituals of their daily life. Detailed records had to be kept and regularly sent back to Nazmos. Much of the records had to do with the forays into Earth territory for shopping and other purposes. Some of these were purely recreational such as simply enjoying a stroll through one of the remote island forests. One day all this would come in useful towards the limited integration between the two peoples; a fervent hope of all the Oannes people both here in Anztarza and back on Nazmos.

Lillian was bursting with curiosity and her emotion was immediately sensed and understood by all. But Muznant only responded for her to be patient. After the tour all would be revealed at a moment of the chief ministers choosing. The Oannes people loved making revelations if only to see the looks of wonder on the faces of their listeners. And so it was with the chief ministers after all basically they were just Oannes like everyone else.

Muznant however did not quite share the same feelings especially with regard to her new found friends whom she had taken into her heart. Subsequently she dropped her mental guard briefly and brushed her hand gently against Ashley and conveyed the one word 'look' in her low tone voice. This was to let Ashley know her mind was open. When he was done she looked up at him and smiled. Tania read the look and knew that Ashley had made another conquest. She didn't mind in the least because she knew that people were naturally drawn to his personality and so easily fell in love with what they saw. His gentle manner and winning smile, though a little crooked, just made a girl want to hug and smother him with her love. Tania gradually sidled closer towards little Muznant and when alongside reached down and gave her hand a gentle squeeze just to say 'I understand.' She wondered what Brazjaf made of his wife's attraction towards Ashley. The answer came immediately as a correction for her thoughts. Muznant didn't just love Ashley; she admired and adored him as if he were some deity. Tania realised that Brazjaf also looked on Ashley in a similar manner to his wife with an equal amount of admiration. Both husband and wife reckoned that Ashley had been specially gifted so that he might rescue both their worlds from the approaching menace. Ashley now knew what that was.

Ashley moved slightly apart from the group at the rails of the Transporter as it floated over the tops of houses and on through the connecting tunnels. He stood there looking downwards at the passing scenery but his mind was miles away. In fact hundreds of light years away at a White Dwarf star racing through space. There was serenity on his face that had not been there before. He must keep this and the other things he had picked up from Muznant's mind to himself but only till the end of the tour today. Rymtakza would then have the privilege of explaining all in his own way. Muznant had requested that Ashley not indicate any knowledge of the planned program of events that was scheduled for him before then.

And so the tour continued. One dome was very like any other apart from minor housing variations. However when they traversed from Dome-16 across to Dome-21 the connecting tunnel had no water canal at its base and a completely different scenario unfolded in the dome below. This dome seemed larger than the others. Perhaps this was because apart from a small crescent shaped beach area covered with shrubs and trees the remainder was covered in water a bit like the Bay Dome without the quayside.

The chief minister explained that all food was grown at a depth of about twenty feet and the dome was modelled on the food plateau of the Great Sea Peruga on Nazmos. Apart from the Wazu seeds everything that was grown on Nazmos could also be grown here. The water in the food domes was from Earth's freshwater lakes and treated to resemble that on the home planet.

536-Orange momentarily stopped near the centre of the dome and Rymtakza pointed downwards at the tiny figures swimming around underwater.

'This dome is currently being harvested of its crop which is mainly Raizna, a favourite among us Oannes,' he conveyed along with its pictorial image of long flowing leaves. 'After that the dome bed will lie fallow for a month and then be planted with another crop called Starztal which should partially return to the sediment some of the nutrients used up by the Raizna. Then for about three weeks no one may enter the dome. We have found that any living mammal presence tends to slow the initial development of the seedlings. This also affects the taste of the vegetables when harvested. We can give no reason for this other than that it is what happens.' Rymtakza smiled up at his guests when he communicated this.

The Raizna vegetable looked like a cross between a small potato and a Brussels sprout but with a hollow centre. The taste conveyed by Rymtakza was of something a little bit spicy and minty. On the other hand the Starztal was like a pea but rather flat. The taste was bland but could be mixed with certain condiments or served with a gravy or broth mixture. Herbs and spices from Earth's produce were now also a part of the Oannes diet and had also been exported to Nazmos. It was in great demand there. Bread and rice had also become an Anztarzan favourite that was likewise exported to Nazmos.

An emotion of regret was expressed by Rymtakza about the fact that meat was eaten by the people of Earth. He expressed the hope that in time alternatives would be found and the practice might cease. On Nazmos too there had been creatures on land and in the sea that lived long ago according to a pecking order of kill or be killed. In other words eat or be eaten. That was nature's way and they'd had no alternatives. Sadly all had since become extinct both on land and in the sea.

Ashley had the oddest mental sensation about this that the subject was anathema to the Oannes and discussion on the matter was discouraged.

536-Orange then progressed to Dome-17 and then across to the next Dome-22 where another crop was still a few weeks away from harvesting. There was no direct tunnel connection between food domes and this was for the sole purpose of keeping growing areas completely separated from one another. The food domes were similar except that the underwater crop here was much taller and its yellow colour was clearly visible from above. Rymtakza explained that the crop was Yaztraka which had a longer growth period and produced fruit that was about three feet long and two inches in cross-section. Harvesting was very easy and the sticklike fruit floated to the surface when cut. The flesh of the fruit was high in protein but also had a high fibre content which was good for the Oannes digestion habits. The Yaztraka fruit was an annual harvest and each plant produced an abundance that survived well in cold storage. In fact surplus amounts in storage usually had to be discarded to make room for the arrival of the next harvested batch.

'I hope we get to taste these sometime,' said Jerry aloud. 'I think I just might have been persuaded to go vegetarian.'

'You will certainly taste everything we eat,' said Rymtakza in a high pitched melodic voice,' but I must warn you that to change your diet suddenly is not recommended unless you have the proper alternatives to prevent deficiency. You should convert gradually and let your body adjust to the change.' He then reverted to telepathy and conveyed that the Oannes diet was ideal for them and contained high levels of protein and also included the right ingredients essential to a healthy body.

While all this had been going on Eric had moved across to Kazaztan who was standing at the railings near the back steps of the Transporter. Eric asked him telepathically what it was like living inside a domed city. Kazaztan recognised Eric as being close to the same lifespan bracket as him. Kazaztan was just over 250 years old in the Oannes lifespan while Eric would be eighty later in the year.

'I like it here in Anztarza,' conveyed Kazaztan. 'My wife Zarpralt also likes it here and I enjoy all the privileges of seniority. I have lived here for nearly ninety years and before that I served on many spacecraft and lived quite an adventurous life. I can tell you a few interesting stories about those times. Now I enjoy ferrying people around Anztarza especially important people like you. You are the first human I have met and I relish this experience. Though I do see a lot of the Earth's people on my TV and think I know them well. But it is nice to talk to you personally. And what about you, what do you think of our city under the ground?'

'I do like it,' said Eric aloud though softly as in a whisper, 'it is not as I at first imagined for a place that is far under the surface. Your technology has made it into a beautiful place and so expansive and open. The clouds in England tend to scud lower than the heights of these domes and so it does not feel confining in the least bit. And what do you think of our girls?' added Eric with a smile and a teasing twinkle in his eye.

Kazaztan looked up at Eric and smiled back conspiratorially. He looked across at the group at the railings at the front of the craft and stared at them for a while. Then turning to Eric he conveyed that he found them acceptable. Eric laughed out aloud and all looked back towards him.

'What do you mean acceptable?' said Eric in a laughing whisper.

This time it was Kazaztan's turn to show his own sense of humour.

'Why I simply mean that I would be happy to become a partner to any one of them if I were a single man. Our young men will go crazy over the beauty of Ashley's partner and his sister. The more senior women have the beauty of maturity in them which appeals to me more. I believe and have believed for some time now that an integration of our two peoples has interesting possibilities.' Kazaztan had the distant future in mind when he conveyed this.

'Yes,' said Eric verbally again, 'I do think we have a future together. But I'm ashamed to say that I do not believe we are ready for you just yet. A proportion of our people are corrupt and filled with greed for their own pleasures. This pervades all our races and cultures across the Earth. But we live in hope that one day we shall all reach your level of civilization.'

Kazaztan had looked into Eric's mind and smiled as he asked what Eric thought of their Oannes girls especially the lovely Muznant. Eric blushed and knew that Kazaztan had looked into his thoughts and already knew the answer.

'I love all beauty,' he said. 'I love being in the presence of beauty. In fact I love being in the presence of all women, full stop. And when I first saw Muznant in November last my heart did a flip flop at her quaintness and her charm. Yes, to me she is beautiful. You Oannes people especially your women have an adornment of facial and body features that is pleasant to me and I believe to us all in general. We are similar in structuring and your relative smallness is most endearing. Many of our own women are as tiny and we feel that quite normal. So yes, I do find Muznant most attractive.'

'And I think she in turn is attracted to your Ashley,' conveyed a smiling Kazaztan. 'So in this respect we have already taken a step towards a favourable future integration.'

'Yes, Ashley,' said Eric pensively, 'now there is a one. As my grandson I have known him since the day he was born. I have never heard an unkind word or deed come from him. His gifts, great as they are have not gone to his head and he has always listened to and done as his parents advised. My son Alex advised Ashley to keep his gifts secret from the world and what a good decision that was. But what is this big task that he must perform? I believe that everyone in Anztarza knows the answer but we have not been told.'

'Yes we do know,' replied Kazaztan, 'and Ashley and his gifts give us hope. But we the citizens of Anztarza are all commanded by the chief ministers that it must be for them and them only to reveal this secret to you and hope that Ashley will agree to try to help. With all our advanced technology at our disposal we could never with all our efforts expect to deflect such a massive object.'

Not only had Kazaztan accidentally revealed what he was not supposed to but he now looked appealingly at Eric and begged his forgiveness.

Muznant came over to them and she placed her hand on Kazaztan's shoulder. Whatever she did or conveyed to him seemed to relax him. He looked at her and then at Eric and smiled his affection and relief.

Muznant then conveyed to Eric that she had already revealed everything to Ashley. There were now no secrets between the Oannes and Ashley so Kazaztan's slip-up was no great blunder. In fact later today at the Dome-4 banquet the chief ministers had agreed to reveal everything to their guests.

Eric put his hand on Kazaztan's shoulder and conveyed his affection for the man and that he should like to visit him and his wife at their home. Kazaztan was quite pleased by this gesture and immediately communicated the news to his wife. Apparently every Oannes person possessed a communication badge like the ones given to Ashley and his family which made this possible wherever they were. The badge could be in selective communication mode and therefore on a one to one basis simply by intending it to be so. An open mode allowed all of Anztarza to receive a persons thoughts but through a central command system. This facility was restricted generally to the chief ministers or the hierarchy in government.

Eric said that he should like to get to know Kazaztan and his wife better and learn their ways. Just the three of them would be ideal he conveyed and not a burden for entertaining. Kazaztan conveyed his instant agreement as did his wife Zarpralt. Communication was instant and so wonderful thought Eric to himself.

536-Orange was then piloted on by Kazaztan's thought commands through Anztarza's tunnels and domes till they were back in the Bay Dome area. This was slightly larger than the habitable or the food domes and the visitors now had a chance to view the quay area from above. The larger of the crafts moored there were similar to the one that had brought them from Aberporth. There must have been about thirty craft of various sizes and none were less than about 200 feet in length. On the outside they were not of the same design and Rymtakza explained that this was because of their differing manufactured ages. All craft were constructed on Nazmos by one or another of the spacecraft builders there. Each had their own design signature but internally all craft had to conform to a set layout specification. They were ferried to Earth in FTL starships as and when necessary. For major repairs or modifications they were ferried back to Nazmos as no such facilities existed in Anztarza. The newest spacecraft was nearly 200 years old. The oldest were aged at about a thousand years from date of manufacture though many had been modernised since then. This obviously had necessitated trips back to Nazmos.

From the Bay Dome 536-Orange went through the connecting tunnel on the left and then across the left side of Dome-2 to the connecting tunnel there. It was then straight across Dome-3 and finally back to Dome-4. It was nearly eight hours since their first meeting with the Oannes people and in that time a huge luncheon banquet had been organised and set up in the central square. Rows of tables and stools sat in ordered lines and the tables seemed covered in a variety of steaming dishes.

536-Orange settled down at one corner of the square and Kazaztan stepped down the Transporter steps and as usual stood to one side as his passengers disembarked. The chief ministers led the way to a table at the head of the central row and conveyed for all to be seated. There must have been about a thousand Oannes standing around and these all moved in orderly fashion to their allocated seating.

Eric conveyed that he would like Kazaztan to join them and to be seated near their table. Immediately room was made and Kazaztan invited to sit directly opposite Eric. The Oannes were a polite and respectful people and any request made by their guests was an honour to fulfil.

The tables were laden with cooked foods as the Oannes had acquired many earthly recipes but without the meat ingredient. Jugs of Wazu drink were evenly spaced on every table and all helped themselves to this first. Eric did the same and waited till Kazaztan filled his own glass. He then raised his glass and said 'cheers friend' before he drank. Kazaztan and several others at the table did the same before they too took a sip. Then 'cheers friend' seemed to echo around the tables as everyone followed suit. Even the chief ministers joined in with this new Earth convention with a smile.

Chief Minister Tzatzorf then conveyed that the banquet should begin. He apologised to those who could not be accommodated here today but opportunities would be made for them to dine with the visitors on other occasions. There was a great emotion of general happiness and goodwill in the plaza that seemed to fill the dome.

Ashley began by conveying his thanks to all the people of Anztarza for such a wonderful welcome and in making their visit such a happy one. Then one by one starting with Lillian the visitors also expressed their thanks to the Oannes people and communicated this through their badges. When it was Eric's turn he gave Kazaztan a special mention for driving them around so smoothly. There was not a single bump he added and a ripple of humour passed down the tables. Kazaztan looked across at Eric who also happened to be looking towards him and both smiled at each other. The whole of Anztarza sensed the affection between these two old men from different worlds and the emotion of satisfaction that such a friendship had developed so quickly filled the Oannes with pleasure. Another small step towards the fervent hope of integration had been taken without command or contrivance. This was a friendship pure and simple between equals.

The dishes of Raizna were mixed with peas and carrots that were diced and mixed in rich gravy. The Starztal looked just like a lentil dish and Ron and Brenda thought it tasted very similar. The Yaztraka dish was unrecognisable from the fruit image conveyed earlier and its rich sweetish taste was definitely flavoured with earthly spices. It resembled a sweet potato in masked form. There were also colourful and flavoured dishes of Mirzondip, Lazzonta, Tartonta and Yantza to name but a few. Muznant and Brazjaf helped explain to their guests exactly what these dishes were and how they had been prepared. There was a dish of plain boiled white rice which the Oannes had adopted just like baked bread.

Jerry conveyed that as he had just been converted to the Oannes way for food that he would taste all the dishes on the table even if his stomach burst with the effort. Chief Minister Rymtakza expressed his concern at this but Brazjaf quickly explained to him that Jerry was showing a typical Earth type sense of humour and being polite at the same time. It was a humorous compliment for all the delicious looking foods on display.

'In that case,' conveyed a smiling Rymtakza to Jerry, 'may your stomach burst in any direction other than mine. I have on my best tunic.'

Jerry laughed out aloud and clapped his hands and commended Rymtakza on his joke. Jerry then suggested that during the meal some of the communication be in the form of verbal talk if only to drown out the sounds of vigorous munching and swallowing that could be quite off-putting.

'Besides,' he added verbally, 'a happy meal is one where people can be heard laughing and chattering. Silence during a meal for us Earth people can sometimes be thought of as being secretive and unfriendly – although we know that this is not the case here in Anztarza.'

'Then so it shall be,' said Chief Minister Zarzint. 'We shall all talk and communicate as well if only to drown out the loud champing noises of my fellow ministers.'

There was laughter from both Rymtakza and Tzatzorf who were seated either side of him.

From one of the adjacent tables Ashley sensed the stares of Puzlwat and Mytanzto. These were not aggressive or intrusive but Ashley sensed a curiosity on their part. They were trying to understand him and whether he was truly the possessor of such powerful gifts. It seemed improbable that such an innocent looking young man could actually do all the things indicated in the life story he had conveyed through the communication tablet back in October.

Ashley conveyed this to the others at the table and immediately sensed an emotion of embarrassment coming from the other table and some little wonder that Ashley had read and knew of their current sentiments and thoughts. So Ashley looked across towards Puzlwat and somehow he knew of his innermost thoughts. There was no malice there but only protectionism for the Oannes way of life. There was also a strong distrust towards all of Earth's population but underneath all this was the fervent wish that what Ashley had conveyed and Muznant had portrayed could really all be true. The doubt was that he could not see how this could be. And therefore he suspected Ashley of some gross ulterior motive in claiming all those fantastic gifts. So far he had seen no evidence of it. Nor did Ashley behave like a man who possessed such a quality. Such a man should and would show a great amount of pride and confidence.

Ashley sensed all this and smiled inwardly. He was not a show-off and never would be since it was not in his character. He would wait for the right moment to show his skills. Whether these were enough for the big task ahead he could not be sure but he knew that the Oannes would help him to develop skilfully towards that end.

Ashley realised now that he had just received another quality. His gifts had been extended to a new level of mind reading. Most times the Oannes could sense when their mind was being probed but Puzlwat showed no sign or emotion to this effect. Briefly their eyes met and Ashley nodded an acknowledgement of recognition and then sent across a brief version of a Sewa greeting which seemed to pleasantly surprise Puzlwat. Ashley sensed that a thaw in relations might have been initiated. There was still a long way to go to before Puzlwat could accept that Ashley's visit to Anztarza was justified.

The banquet progressed and was near its end with many of the guests and invitees getting up and moving around to talk to friends. Ashley and Tania had moved together and had mixed with the Oannes by sitting briefly at several other tables. At each a brief Sewa had been conducted and Ashley held out his hands so that others could touch and acquire a deep mind read if they wished. Several did and left smiling and exhilarated.

Ashley's example was emulated first by Eric and then by Ron and Brenda. They were followed in kind by Alex and Lillian. All of their thoughts and experiences were subsequently an open book to the Oannes people just as Ashley's had been.

Jerry and Milly looked towards Katy but she was with another Oannes girl with whom she seemed wholly involved. They subsequently went off to mingle at the tables.

Katy's companion Jantuzno was fifty years old and quite fresh and innocent looking. She was slightly shorter than Katy and had a slight and slim body. She was nearly half of Katy's weight with arms and legs that appeared extremely fragile. The webbing on her face and arms seemed larger and slightly out of proportion to her stature. Her facial webbing was more colourful and vibrant than that on other Oannes but all this paled into insignificance with her gesturing mannerisms. She was an avid terrestrial TV addict and would sit in front of her large wall screen and imitate the verbal conversations she heard. She would love to be one of those actresses on her screen. Some of the programs were rudely intimate and she disliked these and switched channels immediately.

Initially she had been at another table but when people began moving around to socialise she was drawn to the table where Katy was and to this beautiful TV-like personality whose brother was the famed Ashley. So Jantuzno came and sat down opposite Katy and gave a big smile of greeting.

'Hello,' she said aloud in a posh though soft acting type practiced voice, 'I'm Jantuzno and I'd like to talk with you.' and with that she telepathically conveyed her life story and how much she enjoyed the English programs on her TV. She had been to a couple of remote Earth cities on assignments and in disguise of course and would like to visit many more especially near where Ashley lived. Language was not a problem since this could be acquired more or less instantaneously through a local mind read.

'Hello Jantuzno,' said Katy and instinctively extended her right hand for a handshake greeting. This was met by an equally firm grip and lasted just a second or two longer than was usual. Katy smiled at this and conveyed that she welcomed the mind read contact.

'Friends shouldn't hide secrets from one another,' said Katy.

'What is a secret,' asked a puzzled Jantuzno?

Katy realised that the Oannes didn't hide information from one another and that everything they did or thought was a common sharing with almost everyone else. They had no desire or need to keep secrets from one another and as such the word held no meaning. Katy did know that Ashley had been given total access to Muznant's mind but that he had been sworn to silence for the present. She felt that whatever the big task was the Oannes were not telling their visitors perhaps by order of their chief ministers. For some reason the Oannes people did not want Ashley or his family to know anything about the big task that awaited him as yet. That information was being kept from them until such time that one of the chief ministers divulged it in a grand gesture of announcements. Katy conveyed her thoughts to Jantuzno but did not reveal the fact that Muznant had already given Ashley that information.

'And that is what I call a secret,' said Katy verbally but in a gentle low voice. 'We already knew from our friend Philip that Ashley had a great task ahead of him but we do not know the details. Ashley has kept his mind open and accessible to all and hides nothing from you. But your people decided that we should not be told of these tasks that you have waiting for him to fulfil. Why is that?'

'I did not agree with that decision,' said Jantuzno, 'but it was made for a reason. We were not sure if Ashley would be capable of such a huge task so it was decided to wait and see. We Oannes could cope with the knowledge of it but we did not think you could without preparation. We did not wish to induce a mental panic scenario even though it does not affect us in the short term. Please forgive me but this information cannot come from me. You must wait a little longer for the full announcement to be made. You should know that I do not like this hiding of information and never will. I do not like secrets and I am conveying my dislike of it to all my fellow Anztarzans at this very moment.'

There had been a buzz of verbal conversation and jollity at the banqueting tables when suddenly all this ceased and an emotion of discomfort and embarrassment filled the room. Jantuzno's message had been picked up by the Anztarzans and now that they had seen and met Ashley and his family members they agreed with her opinion and expressed their discomfort at the lack of total openness towards their guests. This deception was not the Oannes way of doing things and the rare feeling of guilt was most unwelcome.

Rymtakza the youngest of the chief ministers suddenly stood up and raised his arms above his head.

'The people are right,' he conveyed to all, 'it was wrong and misguided of us to shield our visitors from the truth. To think that our guests must not be burdened with the truth of the impending danger was wrong. It was also wrong to think that they might panic when faced with the facts. I speak for my fellow chief ministers when I say that we apologise for any lack of confidence in you and ask forgiveness for our ignorance in the matter. We did not wish to upset our own people or to insult our visitors. We say sorry to all of you and so will now set it right.'

He then turned towards where Ashley sat some three tables away and walked towards him. He then sat down at the same table in a seat directly opposite him and closing his eyes conveyed for Ashley to read his mind completely and deeply. There would be no blocks or shielding encountered.

It took but a moment for Ashley to scan through Rymtakza's mind and to then convey the same information to all his family members via the communication badges. In that moment the tension in Anztarza was eased and replaced by an emotion of affection and peace again. It would take a while for all that Rymtakza had revealed to sink in. For now all continued as before. The danger was not immediate or even within the bounds of several lifetimes, Oannes or human.

Gradually the buzz of conversation returned and it was noticed by Ashley that the Oannes quite enjoyed the sound of their own voices. Jantuzno was smiling at Katy now that they could be friends with no secrets between them. She had already given Katy her life story and had also read Katy's mind and so knew all there was to know. Katy's years included Ashley as well so Jantuzno got an added perspective of him from an onlooker's point of view. So now they discussed the things they liked to do. Katy said she read a lot of books and Jantuzno talked about the TV programs she liked. Many of these Katy had also seen so they had a lively discussion about them. Jantuzno said she found the actress women very attractive and beautiful and she would like to be made up like some of them. She also said that the male actors were very handsome too and she wondered if they actually fell in love with their leading ladies. Katy explained that it happened quite often but that actors and actresses had a very poor homely life since they tended to be kept busy filming at different locations around the country most of the time. As such they soon drifted apart and were soon lost to each other.

'I don't think I'd like to be an actress,' said Katy. 'I like to be with my family and friends every day. I think actors live beautiful artificial lives on the screen but I think they are all really very lonely people when not on the set. And if they did have a family and children how often are they able to be with them? Not very often I would think,'

'I never realised it was like that,' said Jantuzno. 'I don't think I'd like that at all.'

'Oh don't get me wrong,' said Katy, 'they are not all as bad as that. In fact they all love the work they do and wouldn't change it for the world. Theirs is a world of glamour and fun but I was just indicating that I don't think I'd like it. After all we are all different and have our own preferences.'

They then moved to the topic of books and Jantuzno said that one of her work functions was to review books both old ones and newly published ones for the records. Katy then brought up drama and poetry books and Jantuzno said she loved the old ones especially Shakespeare. And so the discussion continued and both developed a liking for each other when they talked about their personal likes and dislikes. Katy mentioned Robin Nesters and how they planned a life together one day. Jantuzno said she was too young and would not partner for at least another forty years or so. Then she would return to Nazmos to her family there and they would take her around to friends' houses in the hope she might meet someone nice. She said there was a lot she planned to do with her life before settling down to raise a family. Katy called Tania over from the next table and the three girls had a chat on topics that was of concern to girls only. Tania hoped that they would see a lot of Jantuzno during their stay in Anztarza since they got on so well. The topic went back to the TV programs and then to the art of lipstick and mascara and general makeup cosmetics. Jantuzno was fascinated by it all and her eyes sparkled with interest. She had never used any makeup but would like to try some on. Katy and Tania were both delighted to accommodate her and before you could blink an eye they had Jantuzno leaning back and were applying light blusher to her cheeks, mascara to her eyes and a pale pink lipstick to her lips. Jantuzno looked at herself in the compact mirror and her eyes opened wide in surprise. By this time they had an interested audience gathered around them buzzing with conversation. Some remarked that it was too bright while others said it was not enough. But in general they all said they wanted to try on a bit of the makeup; all of the Oannes women that is of course. Ashley was pleased at what he saw going on with Katy and Tania and the Oannes girl Jantuzno and decided to leave them to enjoy the moment.

The Oannes mind thought patterns were intensely more powerful than what the human brain would have been able to cope with or else Rymtakza could simply have conveyed his information directly to all his visitors. But to be cautious was his intention when he asked Ashley to read his mind at his own pace. Ashley could then safely convey everything he read in Rymtakza's mind to his family members. This had also been Muznant's strategy when she had conveyed information about Anztarza to him back in Aberporth.

Of course Ashley had only recently been granted access to Muznant's mind and so none of this information from Rymtakza came as a surprise. But the others were quite startled at the enormity of the task facing Ashley. Philip was right in saying that a big task lay ahead of him. Lillian went to her son and conveyed her doubts as to the level of his powers and whether he would be able to achieve what the Oannes were asking. She remembered how he had become fatigued after the events of the tree vandals. The telekinetic effort of pushing the huge logs through the entrance doors of the buildings had exerted his brain to extreme tiredness and he had slept for hours afterwards. There were other occasions too when he had been in need of sleep and rest after a telekinetic exertion. Lillian conveyed this to Ashley with an open mind and it was picked up by all the Oannes in the dome. In fact her communication badge transmitted her concerns to all of Anztarza. This was the mother of Ashley expressing concern for her son. Ashley was not some miracle worker or deity with infinite power at his fingertips. He was a common human being who had a few extraordinary gifts. All this was conveyed to the Oannes people.

Alex came and stood beside his wife and put an arm around her. Ashley was that little boy who caught butterflies and birds and made holes in tree trunks. Lillian could see him running around with Brenda's dog Barclay and how they would snuggle up together at night. Katy also came into this picture as a child who looked up to and adored her big brother. And now at the youthful age of twenty two he was being asked to move worlds. Would it be too much for him?

'Whoever granted Ashley his gifts did it with a purpose in mind,' said Alex to Lillian reading her thoughts. 'I don't think a limit has been set for what is possible. Surely our son was born for this moment and even Philip conveyed a big challenge. I have confidence in our son and I believe that so do these people. Let us see what Brazjaf and Muznant have to say.'

Muznant came over to them having heard their concerns through the communication badges. She looked up at them with sympathetic understanding and carefully chose her words.

'Ashley will never be asked to do anything that is beyond his capability,' she said in her melodic low tone voice. 'We know of everything that he has achieved so far and we believe that his strengths need to be nurtured and developed. We also think that he has not as yet achieved the full potential of his powers. We have told you what is desired of him ultimately but what was not made clear is when we hope that all of this might be achieved. We expect the period of nurturing to span many years in fact even decades. There will be many trials to test his telekinetic powers over a time span that could be as long as twenty years or more. So Ashley should be able to live a normal family life on Earth. We hope he and Tania have many children and even see them grow to maturity. We Oannes are a patient people and hope that Ashley will succeed. If not then it is our future generations who will suffer the anguish of the approaching disaster. We ourselves would be a distant memory long before then. But I am certain that Ashley is the one foretold of in our myths and I know he will try his utmost in whatever way he can.'

Muznant paused for a moment as she always did when making a lengthy communication. Then she continued.

'Tomorrow we shall all venture out into space to the asteroid belt. This contains mostly dust and small debris particles but there are a few larger asteroids. This is to be Ashley's first testing ground with asteroid rocks that vary in size. Ashley can attempt his first telekinetic push upon these. We know it will fatigue him but as we go through his planned program we hope his powers develop to overcome this side effect.'

Lillian reviewed in her mind all that Rymtakza had revealed to them indirectly through Ashley.

A White Dwarf star slightly larger than the Earth was speeding on a course that would bring it close to Raznat and then on towards Earth's Sun. The White Dwarf star was a stellar remnant composed mostly of electron-proton degenerate matter compressed down to near Earth size from a star that was a third larger than the Sun. Its mass however remained the same and so this White Dwarf star was composed of extremely dense matter with a mass a third greater than that of the Sun.

White Dwarf stars are the final evolutionary state of all stars whose mass is not high enough to become a Neutron Star. In the normal course of events 97% of all stars in the Milky Way would end up as White Dwarfs. After the Hydrogen fusion lifetime of a main sequence star of low or medium mass like the Sun ends, it will expand to a Red Giant which fuses Helium to Carbon and Oxygen in its core. If the Red Giant has insufficient mass to generate the higher core temperatures required for Carbon Fusion then an inert mass of the Carbon and Oxygen will build up at its centre. It will then shed its outer layers to form a Planetary Nebula and leave behind this core which forms the stellar remnant called a White Dwarf Star. White Dwarf stars are composed of one of the densest forms of matter known, surpassed only by Neutron stars and Black Hole objects.

The effect of the close approach of this White Dwarf star to another star system would be to distort its orbital path and then to attract away the planets around them. The worst case scenario was that Earth and Nazmos would both be drawn away from their parent stars to travel through a dank and dark interstellar space on their own. The planets might even be drawn into the White Dwarf star itself and so into oblivion. The Oannes had named this star Zarama which meant 'time of reckoning'. Currently Zarama was 525 light years distant from Raznat and on the side opposite to Earth's position. It was travelling at close to 33,000 miles a second towards Raznat which was a little over a sixth of light speed. For some previously unknown reason its speed was increasing marginally.

The Oannes scientists had first analysed Zarama some 195 Earth years ago though they knew about it thousands of years earlier than this. Most stars had some relative angular motion yet this faint distant star seemed not to deviate at all. The Red Shift of the lines within its spectrum indicated its motion which came out as being directly towards the viewer. Also that motion was indicated as being extremely large. In fact this velocity was calculated as 33,000 miles per second or 17.7% of light speed in a path directly towards Nazmos. At that time Zarama was calculated as being 566 light years distant. As to accuracy of distance the Oannes scientists could footprint any ray of light to determine the total time from when it was originally emitted. A bit like carbon dating is done on Earth. Today Zarama was checked out as being 525 light years distant and still travelling towards Nazmos but at an increased velocity of 33,074 miles per second. In 195 years Zarama had accelerated its velocity by 74 miles per second. Ashley's insight into the make-up and functioning of the universe had explained to the Oannes how this was possible.

Although the light seen today had left Zarama 525 years ago it was calculated that because of Zarama's velocity it was really a bit closer than that. Zanos had worked out that in 525 years Zarama at an average velocity of 17.76% of light speed would have traversed an additional distance of 93.2 light years towards Nazmos. So in reality Zarama was now at an invisible location of 431.8 light years away.

Ashley had conveyed all his knowledge to the Oannes and their most recent calculation had concluded that Zarama would increase its velocity by another 200 miles per second by the time it reached Nazmos. This put the star's arrival approximately 2,421 years in the future. The Oannes had known of Zarama's existence for considerably longer but it was then too distant to be considered a threat. Stars can deviate as they travel past other masses but Zarama had not done so in the many thousands of years since first being observed.

Yet how could a star accelerate of its own accord out in interstellar space? The answer was simple according to Ashley. The universe was a dispersal of mass in both gaseous and solid form. The universe was in its sixth cyclic phase and all mass was now in slow decay. This meant that a flow of energy-medium was continually emanating from every proton and neutron of each mass item according to Einstein's mass to energy conversion formula $E = mc^2$. Now take any particular point within the universe and these energy-medium flows arrive at that position continuously from practically every direction. One of the properties of energy-medium flows is that they can pass or phase through each other without any resistance or change. Thus during phasing their individual concentrations or intensities become added. Also each energy-medium flow diminishes in intensity level the further out it travels. Since the mass positions can be considered relatively constant in the short term then all energy-medium flow intensities arriving at a selected point will also remain constant. The same will be true for an infinite number of selected points across the entire universe. But each will be slightly different in energy-medium intensity level. This then is what constitutes our universe's space grid; a grid which possesses a difference of energy-medium intensity levels between any two points. As such an energy-medium gradient will exist there in some particular direction. This essentially is what causes the property of gravity that exists throughout our universe.

Consider protons inside all mass objects as little round balls that are emitting energy medium flows outwards uniformly from their entire spherical surface. The rate of this decay emission depends upon the position of the proton within the spatial grid. The higher the grid energy-medium intensity level the less will be the proton emission and vice versa. But if a space grid gradient prevails around our round ball proton then one side will be at a marginally higher energy intensity level than the other. The rate of emission will subsequently be lesser on the side of the higher grid density. As such the uneven emission flow across the surface of the proton will result in a jet effect impulse that causes the proton to be pushed in the direction of the increasing grid gradient. Higher space grid intensities exist close to all emitting mass objects and so it appears as if they are drawn towards each other; we call this the pull of gravity. As far as Zarama was concerned there had to be an increasing space grid gradient between its current position and Nazmos causing it to accelerate.

Understanding the complexity of the universe was something that had been revealed to Ashley and he had decided to one day write it all down in simplified form as an educational text. The Oannes interplanetary starships had prompted him to choose the perfect title for this futuristic work. He would title his work as 'Faster than Light'. Ashley's notes were well advanced but he was yet to compose its style and sequence. Alex his father and the rest of the family had encouraged him to do this and were all quite impatient to see the finished article. Ashley had already conveyed all his knowledge to them and the Oannes scientists and its people. The arrival of the FTL starship was keenly awaited and many would embark on the return journey to take this knowledge back to the homeland.

Lillian thought of the other plans that Rymtakza had revealed. A program of testing and telekinetic practice had been drawn up for Ashley within the solar system. After initial testing on several small objects in the Asteroid Belt which lay just beyond the orbit of Mars he would progress to Neptune's smaller moons. There were several that were about thirty miles in diameter. Others got progressively larger. And finally there was Triton which was two-thirds the size of Earth's moon. Strangely Triton had an atmosphere albeit extremely thin. It was only one of three such moons in the entire solar system, the other two being Jupiter's Io and Saturn's Titan. Triton also had a retrograde orbit around Neptune which meant that its orbit was the opposite way to the planet's rotation about its axis. This was a strong indication that Triton must have been captured by the gravity of Neptune at some time in the distant past.

Ashley would practice by moving Triton from its current orbit to one that moved in the same direction as Neptune's rotation. The Oannes hoped that in time Ashley would be able to apply differing levels of telekinetic power at will. The Oannes scientists would make the calculations and then position Ashley precisely relative to the object to be affected. The rest would be up to Ashley. Also to be tested would be the effect of Ashley's telekinesis upon any living beings that were on Triton's surface. This would be affected by positioning one of Anztarza's large spacecraft with full crew at different locations down upon it.

Rymtakza had revealed that far in the distant future Nazmos would be the future of Earth. This was based on the fact that the life cycle of the sun was small compared to that of Raznat.

The Sun was about halfway through its main-sequence evolution during which nuclear fusion reactions in its core fused hydrogen into helium. Each second, four million tons of matter was converted to energy. So far, since its birth four and a half billion years ago, the Sun had converted only around 100 Earth masses of matter into energy. The Sun did not have enough mass to explode as a Supernova and so Earth was relatively safe. Instead in about another five billion years it would enter a red-giant phase when most of its hydrogen fuel would have been consumed and helium fusion would take over at a much hotter core temperature. The Sun would spend a total of approximately ten billion years as a main-sequence star.

Earth's fate was precarious though. As a red giant the Sun would increase to 250 times its present size and expand to beyond Earth's current orbit. Fortunately the Earth's orbit would by then have moved outward because of the Sun having lost roughly 30% of its present mass. But even if Earth escaped incineration in the Sun, still all its water would have boiled away and most of its atmosphere lost into space. During its current life the Sun has gradually become more luminous at a rate of about 10% in every one billion years. And its surface temperature was slowly rising. The Sun used to be fainter in the past which is possibly the reason that life on Earth had only existed since about one billion years on the land. The increase in solar temperatures is such that in about another one billion years the surface of the Earth would become too hot for liquid water to exist so ending all terrestrial life.

Raznat on the other hand was a low mass red-dwarf star at about 20% the size of Earth's Sun. It was considerably older at between ten to twelve billion years of age and could be among the oldest stars of the universe.

It was heated by fusion and convection currents within it and so was likely to last about a trillion years in its present state. This would give Nazmos a lifetime that was a thousand times longer than the one billion years remaining for life on Earth.

Nazmos orbited Raznat at a distance of 25 to 31 million miles and was the only planet of four to sustain life. The surface of Nazmos was 70% covered by sea and the land areas were largely cold and semi-arid. The Oannes lived mostly in or close to water with city habitation similar to Anztarza. Wentazta had an old quarter that was under water and just off its shore. Some of the poorer class of the Oannes lived there and were considered rather weird and hermit like. They kept themselves separated from the general community and opted for a simple way of life. They were called the Rimzi which meant 'the estranged'. They were recognisable by their larger water-breathing webbed fin structuring. They were a kindly people but strict with their young and very few tended to wander out of the community. Some thought that as the Rimzi population had increased many had migrated into the deeper areas of the Peruga Sea.

Unlike Earth, Nazmos was considered a rather cool planet with tundra like conditions at the best of times. In its winter periods a thin layer of ice spread over the sea. All plant life grew in the sea and the lush vegetation that the Oannes saw on Earth became a thing of wonder and hope. While Earth was in the central area of the ideal habitation zone around the sun, Nazmos was nearer its outer limits. The Oannes on Nazmos had speculated about conditions if their planet had been a few million miles closer to Raznat. Their scientists had researched upon ways and means whereby this might be achieved but without success. The Oannes had calculated that if Nazmos was to be repositioned closer to Raznat at about 20 million miles then its weather would warm considerably and lush greenery on land like that on Earth could develop in time. And this is where Ashley came into the picture.

The Oannes had calculated that Ashley would need to slow Nazmos slightly at each perigee of its orbit to achieve this goal. The effort should not be greater than that exerted on Neptune's Triton and if that proved successful then Nazmos would be next on Ashley's agenda. Twenty years or so would not be a lifetime and the Oannes were a patient race. But as yet agreement on this issue had not been reached by the Nazmos governing body.

Lillian felt pride in all of this and knew that Ashley would succeed. She conveyed her thoughts and emotions to all around her and Muznant responded with her own thoughts. All this was incidental to the real big task; that of Zarama. So far there was no set plan but it was hoped that the current FTL starships would gradually become capable of much greater velocities. The Oannes were looking at power sources to supplement the existing ones by a factor of ten at least. Theoretically their scientists believed that 100 times light speed was a possibility in about fifty years or so.

Of course all of this information had to be conveyed to the people on the home planet but there was no reason why the first phase of testing Ashley's telekinetic power should not continue as planned by the chief ministers. The results of the asteroid experiment would be sent back with the returning FTL starship and the chief ministers were sure that there would be considerable excitement back home. There was no doubt in their minds of Ashley's credentials and authenticity. Perhaps they should send Muznant and Brazjaf as their ambassadors to take back a full memory report of the recent events. They would discuss this with the captain of the FTL starship.

The buzz of verbal conversation and jollity at the banqueting tables returned once more and Ashley read great relief in the emotions of the Oannes in the amphitheatre. A new closeness was apparent in the way the guests were viewed and an emotion of well-being was evident within the dome. In fact there were messages and thoughts of congratulations for the Anztarzan visitors for their acceptance of Rymtakza's apology and the plans laid out for Ashley. Lillian especially felt this emotion strongly and conveyed her own messages of thanks and emotional relief that the planned program for Ashley mainly involved his gift of telekinesis. Now that she herself had been a passenger on one of their spacecraft she felt no qualms at her son being flown across interstellar space. In fact it was pleasing to know that they could all accompany him wherever he went if they so wished. So far as the rogue White Dwarf star Zarama was concerned Lillian was certain in her mother's mind that Ashley would triumph and would either stop it dead or else divert it onto another path.

Alex still had his arm around his wife's waist and he too felt the same relief that the task facing Ashley did not seem an exceptionally dangerous one. Neither did it seem to be beyond his capability. There was the briefest of communication between husband and wife before they walked up to where the chief ministers had regrouped at one of the banqueting tables. A hush of expectancy descended in the amphitheatre as everyone anticipated an announcement.

It was Lillian who conveyed her feelings in both words and thoughts.

'Alex and I would like to thank you for revealing all these plans to us,' she began. 'We are also pleased that you are not demanding something excessive or anything that could be construed as dangerous. Whether or not Ashley succeeds in these tasks is immaterial to us since it does not put his person in any form of jeopardy. As his parents we put no restrictions on him. We hope that with your help and guidance he will develop his telekinetic gift to such an extent that it will enable him to successfully complete the program you have planned for him. We know that the long term future of Earth is tied to that of Nazmos and we welcome the idea and the prospect of harmony between our cultures. It will be a good partnership. However, tackling the problem of Zarama is another matter. Zarama's mass is immense and a third more than that of Earth's Sun. As such it has an average density of matter that is over a million times the average density of the Sun. White Dwarfs are composed of one of the densest forms of matter known and surpassed only by Neutron Stars. We hope and pray that Ashley's gifted powers are sufficiently developed to compete with what will be required. The journey towards Zarama will be long and we should like to accompany him all the way. His success will be a success for us all and I pray that our God be with him in all his endeavours and keep the expedition safe.'

Muznant and Brazjaf had come up behind Alex and Lillian and stood silently. An emotion of love and affection filled the dome and Lillian looking around saw Muznant and leaning down drew her into a gentle hug. Alex reached over and touched Brazjaf on the shoulder. The emotion of calmness and well-being prevailed in the area and was felt and understood by all. The chief ministers conveyed their gratitude at Lillian's words and indicated that as of now all minds would be kept open to them as was the normal Oannes custom. It was regretted by them that such had not been the case at the start of their association.

Gradually the assembly began to disperse and many tables were now empty. The food dishes and plates had also been removed by the very people who had sat at the particular table. Ashley presumed that each Oannes person had been allocated a duty which had been performed on cue.

Jantuzno, Katy and Tania still had their little assembly of Oannes women around them and many now sported varying degrees of make-up on their faces. Jantuzno conveyed that she would like Katy and Tania to spend the rest of the day in her care. She would take them to her home in Dome-14 which was adjacent to Muznant and Brazjaf's Dome-7. Several of the partly made up Oannes ladies expressed a desire to also accompany them for the day and Jantuzno gave them her welcoming agreement. The plan was conveyed to all and agreement received. Both Lillian and Milly were quite happy to leave their girls in the company of these peaceful people.

'I want you all home before dark,' conveyed a smiling Lillian to the group. Both Katy and Tania laughed out aloud though Jantuzno and the other Oannes girls seemed puzzled by Lillian's remark. Katy explained that on Earth it was considered unsafe for young unescorted girls to be out very late at night. Her mother had said this as a joke but also that they should return to their abodes at a reasonable time so as not to cause anxiety. Though in Anztarza there was little chance of that since they were all in continuous telepathic communication with each other.

The last that Ashley saw of his sister and fiancé was of them boarding one of the Deck Transporters along with several of the other Oannes women. The Transporter lifted and headed towards the entrance tunnel to Dome-7. Ashley knew somehow that their destination was Dome-14 on the other end of that tunnel. He was pleased that Tania and Katy had made friends and were quite enjoying their Oannes experience.

Eric conveyed that he would stay with Kazaztan on 536-Orange and go home with him when his duty rota finished. Kazaztan wanted Eric to meet his wife Zarpralt and see where they lived in Dome-11. Eric conveyed that his badge would keep everyone informed of his whereabouts at all times. As yet he was not sure of Kazaztan's plans and so would play along with events as the day progressed. He enjoyed Kazaztan's conversation and they discussed their life experiences which both found mutually fascinating. It gave each an insight into the others lifestyle and upbringing. History does not impart this in its scenarios but personal experiences bring those times to vivid life.

Ashley had his own entourage and many expressed the wish for him to visit their homes. Ashley conveyed that he was at their disposal for the rest of the day and so it was agreed that he would be taken by Deck Transporter to each of their homes in turn for a very brief visit. At each place a small glass of Wazu would be drunk to commemorate the visit. Ashley was not only an esteemed guest but also the man of their ancient mythology; at least that was what they all wished to believe.

At first they were very respectful and rather in awe of him. To them this was the person who would change history and do marvellous things. But Ashley's personality and charm won through when he laughed and joked with them. Like Jantuzno they too watched a lot of terrestrial TV and so discussed many of the programs with him. It was the comedy in life that was not quite understood by them and Ashley had to explain how humour was built up and he gave a few examples which brought forth a few smiles. Each country had a different sense of humour which was not always appreciated outside its boundaries. It was also usually a culture thing where one class of people joked about another. Ashley noted that humour was not a strongpoint among the Oannes and so he moved on to other topics.

Sport was not played on Nazmos as it was on Earth. The Oannes found the sports channels rather pointless and Ashley tried to explain the theory of competitiveness in all walks of life. They simply could not see the reason for wanting to arrive before anyone else or hit a small ball into a hole in the ground. Ashley conveyed the range of sporting activities from team sports like football, rugby, cricket, baseball etc. When Ashley came to individual prowess in athletics and swimming they became interested. When they asked if the use of their power capsules was permitted Ashley replied that it must be each person's own ability only that came into play. However, Ashley conveyed that a new water sport might be initiated for a race over a set distance using power capsules. He then conveyed mental images of the latest Olympics swim trials held in Coventry the previous summer.

The first house they stopped at was in Dome-5 and it was very much like the accommodation in Muznant and Brazjaf's house. The owner introduced himself as Frazazato and he lived currently on his own. His wife and daughter were back on Nazmos and had been gone two years. He did not expect them back anytime soon. She had gone to see her parents and brother which he conveyed might have been an excuse to get away from Anztarza which she had never ever liked. He personally liked it immensely and felt very much at home here. He especially loved Earth and often made forays to secluded forests of the northern continents. Frazazato was 110 years old and so relatively young and had been on Earth just nine years. His job was to monitor the strife and war patterns on the continent of Africa and as such he was kept extremely busy maintaining his records.

Ashley was taken around the rooms and noted the large sleep tank in one of the upper floor rooms. The other eight Oannes stayed back in the main living area down below and two busied themselves in preparing the glasses of Wazu. Ashley complimented Frazazato on his house and thanked him for his hospitality as he raised his glass of Wazu ceremoniously. There were smiles all around and a sense of pleasure filled the room as they all expressed happiness in adopting this pleasant Earth custom. When Ashley said 'Cheers' they all followed suit in lifting their glasses. Perhaps later Ashley would complete this with the touching or 'clinking' of glasses. However his mind was read and instantly a few did exactly that. Luckily no breakage occurred in spite of the roughness of their touch.

'I drink to your health and well-being Frazazato and may we be friends forever,' said Ashley with raised glass above his head before lowering for another sip. All did the same with beaming smiles.

And so the process was repeated over the next few hours as the Transporter took them from one house to another across the spread of Anztarza's twenty habitation domes. Eventually the Transporter returned to Dome-7 when Ashley received communication that Brazjaf and Muznant had returned to their Street-5 house. The Transporter settled down in the central plaza and everyone alighted full of exuberant energy from all the Wazu they had consumed. They were keen to make a show of escorting Ashley safely home but also to visit the home of the now famous Brazjaf and Muznant the first present day Oannes to have made direct contact with Earth people. They were the pioneers who would go down in the annals of the Oannes people.

The happy group were welcomed into the house on 5th Street and again a table had been set up with jugs of Wazu and enough thimble-size glasses. It was polite to offer refreshment to visitors and it was impolite not to accept. And so the happy chattering group around Ashley drank to the health and well-being of all just as they had repeated at all the homes. He requested to be excused to use the washroom and on this communication of his need to pee all the others expressed a similar desire. They had been holding back through embarrassment but now their desperation could be eased. As such it was a good hour before Ashley's new friends all left to walk back to the plaza to await the summoned Transporter. Night times were different and a Transporter had to be given a special call when required. Normally night time was rest time.

Ashley settled down on one of the sofa seats in the living room area and communicated his relief at this peace and quiet as he rested his tiredness. Eric had not returned as yet and upon the thought a communication was received from Kazaztan that they would return Eric after their evening meal. A similar thought message came from Jantuzno that Katy and Tania would be eating with her and a few other friends.

Laztraban communicated that the evening meal was being prepared and that Ashley's parents and Aunt and Uncle were currently resting in their rooms. Milly and Jerry had been commandeered by another group but were now on their way back and should arrive shortly. Laztraban politely conveyed that he and his wife would be pleased if Ashley along with the esteemed Brazjaf and Muznant could join them at their table for the evening meal. Muznant immediately conveyed her pleasure and was happy to accept. Although Muznant had made her own plans for Ashley's dinner these could be put on hold and food items returned to storage. It was impolite to take anything of your own when invited out to a friends house. The entire pleasure of providing for guests must be with the hosts. That was the Oannes custom.

To Ashley's surprise Brazjaf communicated that he had a gift for Ashley. He entered Ashley's room carrying a hanger with a tunic and leggings in one hand and light coloured footwear in the other. The tunic had been specially made to fit and was a pale yellow with bright green borders. The leggings were pale green with a pale yellow bottom cuff and made to be loose fitting like trousers. The shoes were like moccasins in a light tan colour.

Brazjaf conveyed that similar outfits had been made for all the guests with measurements taken from their current wardrobe selections. Mind reading earlier had indicated each person's preferences of colour and styling.

Niktukaz smiled her pleasure when she saw Ashley walk in all dressed in his new standard Oannes styled clothes. She came forward and touched her nose with Ashley's and performed a brief Oannes Sewa greeting. And Ashley responded with polite replies and asked his own Sewa questions as he was followed into the room by Brazjaf.

Sewa was basically a hello and welcome greeting with the added 'I hope all is well with you and yours'. Ashley favoured the custom immensely and so had the people of the Dogon Tribe of West Africa to have kept the ritual going over the millennia.

Laztraban was standing beside his other guests and what a colourful assembly they made. All had been provided with clothes similar in basic design to Ashley's except in differing colour combinations. The tunics were slightly different from the ones worn by the Oannes since these had been made with three-quarter length sleeves. The Oannes did not have sleeves because of the webbed fins on their arms. However the styling on the outside of the sleeves from elbow to cuff had a frill to imitate the Oannes' physical quality. There was also a colourful deep stiff frill down the middle of the back where the Oannes had their butterfly style webbed fin.

The men's tunics were all similar and Ron looked dapper in his green and gold colours. Alex's tunic was similar in colour to Ashley's and he realised then that colours were considered a family trait; a sort of coat of arms association. However Alex's leggings were not green but a pale yellow though the footwear was the same. Ron had a more brown orientation in his tunic with a darker border and matching loose leggings. Jerry's outfit was a military khaki or olive colouring but with a bright red edging on both tunic and leggings.

The ladies clothes were in brilliant colours with embroidery patterns across the chest area. Each was different and had a silky shine to its quality. Lillian's tunic was a yellow colour with sleeves that flared out slightly. Again these were of three-quarter lengths just like the men's but with the cuffs embroidered in a gold lace pattern. The trousers were a colour match but with a broad gold pattern down the outside length of the leg. Brenda had a very similar outfit in colour except the embroidery pattern was different and more brown than gold. Milly's outfit was dusky green that sat beautifully on her slimmer figure. Her tunic had a pale yellow belt that allowed a slight flare near the hem which had a pale yellow edging. Her trousers matched the tunic in design and colouring with the sewn-in belt feature being at the knee position. The stiff frill on the ladies tunics was larger than the men's and stood out stiff and proud with more varied and brighter colours. This frill stood out about six inches compared to the men's three and gave the ladies quite an Oannes appearance.

Ashley showed his delight by his beaming grin and by kissing his mother, aunt and future mother-in-law on both their cheeks. The men received a hand clasp and a man hug in turn. Then were all laughing as they commended one another on their dress sense and did twirls to exhibit their new clothes.

'I think I can set a new fashion trend when we get back home,' said Lillian, 'I'm sure this could catch on.'

'Some of your fashion outlets already have something similar in their design ranges,' said Muznant, 'but they remain quite exclusive and expensive. We have simply adapted a couple of the favoured designs to suit our pattern of wear. Do you like it?'

'They're wonderful,' said Milly, 'now I really do feel quite posh, but nice. You men look really smart too.' and Milly winked at Lillian and Brenda and communicated that they certainly were a colourful lot.

The meal that Laztraban and Niktukaz served was lightly spiced but with a strong flavouring of coriander and mint. There was Raizna with a sprinkling of pepper and salt in a large bowl-shaped dish. The Starztal was cooked with Yantza in the traditional Oannes style. The other dishes were a mash of Yaztraka, boiled Lazzonta that had been chopped into inch long lengths and mixed in pale gravy and steamed Tartonta cut into wedges and placed in a clear syrupy liquid. And of course there had to be a large basket of assorted types of bread at the centre of the table with creamy butter to go with it. There were a couple of jugs of Wazu beside the bread and small glasses at each place setting.

The cutlery items were similar in style to Earth knives, forks and spoons except these were made of the Oannes greyish composite material and quite lightweight in comparison.

Ashley noticed that Muznant and Brazjaf ate sparingly though they sampled all the dishes in turn. Muznant sensed Ashley's observation and looking up smiled at him and telepathically indicated that she was watching her figure. The baby that she suspected within her would grow and grow and she did not want to look monstrous in the months ahead. Brazjaf supported her by eating similar amounts which was perfectly in keeping with the Oannes traditions. Most couples returned to Nazmos for the confinement but Muznant wished her baby to be Earthborn. She had at least another seven months to go. Oannes babies had a gestation period of just less than nine Earth months.

Ashley conveyed all this to the others at the table and all looked up towards Muznant and offered their congratulations while smiling their support.

Lillian said that Muznant looked even more beautiful now in her pregnancy and conveyed that Earth women approaching motherhood tended to have a glow of beauty and health about them too. Muznant seemed to blush slightly and Brazjaf leaned towards his wife and wiggled his shoulder against hers in affection.

Messages were simultaneously received from Katy and Tania that they would be back in Dome-7 within the hour. Ashley conveyed back to them the visual of them all sitting at the dinner table dressed up in their new Oannes finery and he received a 'wow' in return and the emotion of impatience to see it all for themselves. Jantuzno conveyed that she would hasten their return and would also accompany her friends into the house. She too wished to see the visitors all dressed up in their new clothes. Eric's communication badge had relayed all this to him as well and he too said that he was on his way. Kazaztan and Zarpralt had been wonderful and had invited him back again as soon as it would be possible. Eric had thought about spending the night period at their house but firstly they did not have a suitable bed for him and secondly he did not wish to miss the space flight to the asteroid belt set for the morrow. And now he too was keen to not only see how the others looked in their Oannes costume finery but also to try on his own set. This Wazu had given him added energy and a new zest for life and he planned to get the very best out of it.

'Dad is like a little boy eager to open his Christmas present,' conveyed Alex smiling and he received an emotion of general gaiety from them all.

After they had all eaten their fill Laztraban and Niktukaz cleared the table but left a refilled jug of Wazu and fresh glasses for their guests. Lillian conveyed that next time she would have liked her hosts to have joined them in the meal at the table. Niktukaz indicated that when there were a lot of guests then it was easier for all if someone did the serving and waiting at table. Besides she and Laztraban had already eaten earlier when they were preparing the items. With a smile on her face she said it took an awful lot of tasting to ensure that everything was cooked just right, and everyone laughed at her excellent sense of humour.

Lillian conveyed the image of their large Christmas dinner gatherings when she and Katy would serve up the various items before sitting down themselves. They would then be the first to rise when clearing away began though everyone usually joined in helping with this. Niktukaz said that she would follow suit at the next meal and a pleased emotion came from both her and her husband that such was to be the case. It was an honour to serve their guests but the effort could be rather wearisome. With the meal over the verbal conversation continued as they all sat around the large table. Lillian and Milly insisted that Laztraban and his wife join them and so two more backless chairs were drawn up to the table and everyone shuffled around to make space.

An emotion of excitement filled the room just before Katy and Tania burst in. Jantuzno followed closely behind and her eyes opened wide as she stared at Ashley and the others in their finery. Ashley looked so handsome in his yellow and green colour combination that Jantuzno involuntarily conveyed that he was the most beautiful man she had ever seen. And she included all the actors in the TV programs she had watched. She blushed profusely when she realised what she had just conveyed but Katy quickly touched her arm and said her brother had that effect on a lot of girls. Muznant blushed at that but then gave a lovely cover-up smile.

'My, my,' exclaimed Tania aloud, 'gosh you all look fabulous. I can't wait to try on my own outfit. I do have one too don't I?' She looked keenly across at Muznant.

Muznant conveyed that costumes had been made for all and that more was in progress for other occasions too. Immediately Tania excused herself and the three girls went off to Tania's room first. Her outfit was hanging up in the wall space and both Jantuzno and Katy helped her get out of her current clothes and into the new ones. The pattern was similar to the ladies ones with flared ends to both tunic and trouser leg. The colour was a dusky green that was similar to her mother's outfit.

Katy was impatient to get to her room which was in the next house so all three girls immediately trooped across to it. Katy's outfit was pale yellow with brilliant gold edging and she looked quite stunning in it. She had a pleased smile on her face as she thought that it also matched what her mum was wearing. Jantuzno conveyed that the stiff upright frill down the middle of the back of the tunic gave them an Oannes appearance which she thought was extremely innovative of the dress designer.

The girls returned to the Laztraban house and Katy and Tania paraded themselves down one side of the room. Katy put one hand on her hip and with the other extended out she did an exaggerated hip swaying fashion parade style walk back towards the seated family causing everyone to laugh. Muznant and Brazjaf looked on with pride at the appreciation shown by these people for such a minor gesture as being given new clothes. Muznant's meaningful glance at her husband and partner was noted by all. Brazjaf conveyed that it had been the chief ministers' idea for the new outfits to be made. They thought that the Earth clothes were rather ordinary and so decided on something more colourful and Oannes like. Brazjaf communicated the dressed up images of the guests in their finery to the chief ministers and an emotion of pleased satisfaction was conveyed back.

There was a relaxed atmosphere in the house when Eric walked in with Kazaztan. Laztraban and Kazaztan exchanged a quick mental Sewa greeting after which the customary small glass of Wazu was offered. This was gratefully accepted and downed in three quick gulps. Eric conveyed that he now felt full of energy and good health which he had not felt prior to this visit to Anztarza. Kazaztan exclaimed his pleasure at seeing the visitors in such smart appearance and expressed a wish to see Eric in his outfit before he left. He of course knew of the chief ministers' idea for the clothes and he said he must convey this image back to his wife Zarpralt. She would be pleased. He and Brazjaf then accompanied Eric back to the first house and it was not long before they all came back with Eric kitted out in his new outfit.

'Good grief dad,' exclaimed Alex, 'you look like Errol Flynn in the film 'Robin Hood'. Mind you a few extra pounds would not go amiss.'

Eric smiled and said, 'Thanks son and the rest of you can stop gawping too. And don't worry about me I reckon with all this Wazu I've been drinking I might even put on those few pounds. It really makes me feel great.'

Eric was indeed dressed in the green tunic and loose leggings of Sherwood's merry men as depicted in the film. The only difference was the stiff gold coloured frills down the back of the arm sleeves and down the middle of his back. Alex conveyed that the missing item was Errol Flynn's cap with the feather sticking up. There was a pensive look on Eric's face.

Muznant recorded his thoughts and looked across at Ashley. Ashley nodded to her and conveyed that he understood and approved.

Lillian and Tania had both seen this exchange and conveyed a strong query across to them.

Ashley then conveyed only to Lillian and then Tania in turn that a seed of a thought was growing strongly in Eric's mind of a desire to stay on in Anztarza. Not permanently but for an extended duration at least. He had begun to believe that he would regain his health and fitness here and was thinking of staying on for about a year or so if the Oannes would have him. But this was just a thought at the moment and he had yet to come to a firm decision. If he did decide then he would like the privilege of making that announcement personally.

Muznant smiled at Tania and gave a long slow blink with both eyes. This was more usual between Oannes courting couples but Tania understood that Muznant was telling her of her love and admiration for Ashley as well. Tania looked at this quaint tiny woman from another planet and was filled with an admiration and affection for her. She conveyed this to Muznant and responded with a similar slow blink in return. This didn't go unnoticed by Ashley and he expressed his pleasure at the mutual love and understanding between these two people who meant so much to him.

Again it was Jerry who brought everyone back to reality.

'Right then,' he said, 'I believe we have a long space trek tomorrow. I think we should be getting some rest. It's been a long and interesting day and I'm ready to hit the sack. How about you lot?'

Everyone agreed and said they were really looking forward to the new experience. Having travelled here in the spacecraft 11701-Red under Captain Lyzongpan they all felt confident and safe in the hands of their Oannes hosts. After all, the Oannes had only begun their space travelling some twenty thousand years ago; plenty of time to have got it right so to speak.

Brazjaf conveyed all the plans for the journey. They would travel on a craft similar to 11701-Red that had brought them to Anztarza; only this one was rather larger in both size and capacity. It could comfortably accommodate just over a hundred persons which of course also included twenty of the crew. On the craft would also be the chief ministers and several of their leading scientists. Puzlwat and Mytanzto had requested attendance as they personally wished to witness the experiment on the asteroids. Secretly they were sure Ashley would fail; at least they hoped he would.

Due to the gravitational forces exerted by the planet Jupiter the asteroid belt was pulled open into three main circular zones. Earth scientists had named the spacing between the zones as the Kirkwood Gaps. As such all asteroids were recognised by the Oannes scientists by their Earth designated names. 2867 Steins was in the central zone and was currently at an orbital position that was just 150 million miles from Earth. Steins had a rough diameter of approximately three miles and its mass would be a good first trial for Ashley's telekinetic gift.

The next asteroid that the Oannes had chosen for experiment was 2685 Masursky which was slightly larger being ten miles wide by twelve miles long. It was also in the main central belt and about 55 million miles from Stein's present position.

The final test asteroid would be 253 Mathilde which was considerably larger at thirty three miles in approximate diameter. It was also in the main central zone of the asteroid belt and orbiting at a position only 30 million miles from Masursky.

'And how many months will all this take?' enquired Jerry concerned by the great distances to be travelled and the limited fortnight time they had planned for their stay away from work.

Brazjaf smiled his humour at this enquiry and conveyed to all that the journey time to the Steins asteroid should take no longer than 13 hours of fast space travel. Travel from Steins to Masursky would take about five hours and then from Masursky to Mathilde just another three.

'My goodness,' exclaimed Jerry, 'what speeds do you propose to travel at on these journeys?'

'Only a fraction of what we are capable of,' conveyed Brazjaf,' after all these are only local journeys to us. I don't expect Zanos will take us beyond about 10,000 miles a second.'

Brazjaf referred to their bio-computer system with a familiarity borne from confidence.

Jerry was not convinced. 'But I thought you said that all space travel was under normal gravity conditions,' he stated. 'Surely to achieve such speeds so quickly the acceleration would have to be phenomenal. No living being would be able to survive such huge gravitational forces.'

Brazjaf smiled again and indicated that Jerry had raised a very relevant point. He then conveyed a science lesson in detail with regard to the propulsion systems on their spacecraft and indicated his regrets for not having done so earlier. Ashley also smiled since he had read Brazjaf's mind and knew exactly what he was to reveal.

Brazjaf conveyed that so far he had only indicated that their craft were powered by magnetic type impulse generators. This was a very general form of propulsion system used on all craft including the Deck Transporters. They were also used to maintain the gravity effect within spacecraft on long space journeys through its constant 1g acceleration as Jerry had rightly stated.

However there was another motive system which could only be used far out in space remote from any planets or mass objects. This was the neutron material generator. The impulse generator was a magnetic system that gave the spacecraft a push in a given direction. But the neutron material generator artificially altered the spatial grid gradient in front of the spacecraft's line of travel. Travel in space was always in a direction vertically upwards from the spacecraft's floor plane. The functioning of gravity had been explained to the Oannes recently by Ashley in full detail although they had already developed their gravity drive through their own principles of cause and effect.

From points all around the perimeter of the spacecraft's upper structure a myriad of energy-medium beams were focussed on a point about three miles ahead of the crafts direct line of travel. The focal point of all these beams of energy resulted in an extremely high energy-medium intensity level such that an infinitesimal amount of neutron type matter was created. Being unstable this matter immediately reverted back to a dissipating energy medium flow similar to that emanating from every mass object of the universe. This then resulted in raising the level of the spatial grid pattern in the zone around that focal point. This zone by calculation extended all the way to the spacecraft and the grid gradient therefore caused the craft to be gravitationally drawn towards that focal point.

Brazjaf conveyed that Earth scientists would consider this to be comparable to the creation of a temporary singularity or 'black hole' phenomenon. The gravitational pull towards the focal point was so intense that a spacecraft could be accelerated to a velocity of thousands of miles per second in a very brief time. And yet neither the structure nor the occupants of the spacecraft tended to experience adverse g-forces. The principle was that of a body free-falling to Earth - or towards the mythical 'black hole'.

'The Oannes scientists have worked this out to an exact science,' conveyed Brazjaf. 'The focal point for the energy beams at three miles distance is just enough to alter the steepness of the spatial grid gradient to result in a gravitational pull on the spacecraft without tearing it apart. Some occupants feel a light-headed sensation at these moments and so we have recommended that all lie down to horizontal positions whenever the neutron material generator is activated.'

Brazjaf explained that this neutron generator action was repeated till the desired velocity was achieved. He conveyed that the magnetic impulse motors would continue to provide the spacecraft with normal acceleration throughout the space bound journey to provide the gravity effect needed for comfortable and normal living. When arriving at their destination the neutron generator would again be brought into action to slow down the spacecraft – facing in the direction it had come from of course. They would also undergo a marginal slowdown in the pace of time and should gain several minutes on the journey. However Zanos would make the necessary clock corrections.

'Wow,' said Jerry, 'I see where you are coming from. This is amazing. I shall look forward to our journey tomorrow.'

'There is one other factor that I haven't covered,' conveyed Brazjaf, 'and that is how Ashley's push experiment is to be performed upon the asteroids.'

Brazjaf looked towards Muznant and she subsequently took over the briefing.

'As you know, Ashley needs to be in a specific position relative to the asteroid in order to give it a push in the desired direction,' she conveyed. 'You also know that the spacecraft must continue under a constant acceleration for normal gravity conditions to be maintained. We would of course be in a closed loop trajectory of travel to remain in the general location of the specified asteroid.'

Muznant paused and smiled.

Jerry looked puzzled and said, 'So then if we can't stop where we want how is Ashley to apply his telekinetic power in an accurate manner? And how will you measure the results of the experiment?'

'By means of a smaller shuttle craft,' said Muznant aloud. 'There are several of these in every spacecraft and each can accommodate up to forty persons. But there will be no gravity effect in these once they exit the spacecraft to arrive on location. However to prevent people from floating around inside it all must wear an electrostatic body suit. These provide the suit with a small electric charge that is attractive to the body of the shuttle craft. The suits themselves are insulators and so 'shocking experiences' are avoided.' The emotion of Muznant's humour filled the room which was the closest that an Oannes person came to laughter.

'With practice one is able to slowly walk its floor area,' continued Muznant. 'However for the most part we shall all remain seated on special seating. The slit gap in the back rests is designed for an Oannes person but should not inconvenience you at all. A clamping arrangement across the thighs will ensure that you are secure and comfortable. The onboard Zanos system will take the shuttle to the designated position a few miles away from the asteroid. There are large viewing panels at the front and sides of the shuttle and all occupants will get a good view through them. Ashley will then be requested to carry out his task,' concluded Muznant.

Then Brazjaf added that a second shuttle carrying their scientists and test equipment would follow closely in order to measure and monitor everything that occurred. Both shuttles would afterwards return to the spacecraft which could then make passage to the next asteroid.

'So if all goes to plan we should be back in Anztarza within two days?' asked Jerry.

'That is very likely,' conveyed Brazjaf.

The conversation covered many other topics till eventually Kazaztan and Jantuzno thought that it was time for them to leave. They conveyed the pleasure of the whole day and hoped to meet again on their return from what was widely acknowledged as the 'Ashley tests'. Eric came forward and clasped Kazaztan's hand and shook it vigorously while conveying that he would definitely see him again. Kazaztan looked at his hand afterwards and nodded a smile. Yes, he quite liked this Earth custom of hand contact as both a greeting and a farewell gesture.

Jantuzno said goodbye to Katy and Tania and they gently rubbed noses. Then Tania went forward again and kissed Jantuzno on the cheek. Katy followed suit and did the same while mumbling a 'goodbye' and 'see you soon'.

Shortly after the friends had left, the lighting in the dome began to dim and all decided that it was time to bed down for the night. They said 'Goodnight' and departed for their respective accommodation bedrooms.

Ashley lay awake for a long time wondering whether his telekinetic gift was strong enough to move the proverbial mountain; because that is literally what these asteroids could be compared with. He finally drifted off into a dreamless sleep with his final thoughts being of Tania, Katy and their friend Jantuzno laughing together. Somehow the face of Margaret Dutton seemed also to be mixed in amongst them. How very odd indeed was his last thought.

CHAPTER 12

Asteroid Tests

It was only our third day in Anztarza and already it seemed like weeks since we'd arrived here. I woke this morning with a feeling of boyish exhilaration and expectation. Exhilaration that we were to travel out into space as no other human had done and an expectation of an adventure that was yet to unfold. I had a fairly clear idea of what was expected of me and I had no doubt that my telekinetic gift would exert a hefty force upon those great lumps of asteroid rock when the time came. But as yet I had no measure or proper control of that power that had been granted to me. The whole idea of this experiment was to test my ability to shift the selected three asteroids from their current orbits to another much further out.

I had conveyed this to Muznant and Brazjaf and indeed to all of Anztarza with my open mind and had received encouragement in response that with the supporting help of their scientists my skills could be perfected. I certainly hoped so. Somehow these Oannes seemed not to worry or even to be concerned about their future. Their faith that things would turn out right was a philosophy bred from millennia of peaceful living. Their lives were without intrigue and this was a direct result of keeping their minds and thoughts open to one another. I wonder what Freud would have made of it.

Although they were remote from their home planet Nazmos there was little or no nostalgia for an immediate return. They had all come to love their underground city and those who hadn't liked its limitations soon returned home. I too felt a fascination for Anztarza as had granddad Eric. Our tour of all its huge domes had impressed upon me how well the needs of the general living here were catered for.

But living was not confined to the domes. The Oannes had access to Earth's beauty. Its greenery fascinated them to enchantment. Nothing like this was to be seen on Nazmos. They could roam Earth's remote forests albeit in secrecy. They cherished the hope that perhaps one day, though not in their lifetime, that Oannes and humans could harmonise openly and live in peace with each other.

I understood that the Oannes had been monitoring life on Earth for about ten thousand years. Their 'thinking stones' were everywhere. At first they had tried living among humans and were able to implant a fair amount of their own knowledge into the minds of some of the big city dwellers. Babylon was one such city. But Earth prejudices were against these 'strange fish people' and wealth ambitions were too great for peaceful living. As such integration was quite impossible. The two mind sets were much too different and gradually the Oannes withdrew from the cities.

The Oannes then colonised an area in a remote northern area and developed there successfully for nearly two millennia. But regular bouts of illnesses and plagues caused great suffering and distress among their population. The great freshwater lakes in the area were so much like the seas at home that it was with much sadness when the decision from Nazmos came for the building of Anztarza. The reason given was that the people of the colonies were developing immunity to the Earth bacteria but at the same time were becoming dormant carriers of diseases which they brought with them back to Nazmos whenever they visited. It was simply the history of an early failure.

The Oannes were an extremely peace loving people and never in all the millennia of years here on Earth had they considered claiming this primitively occupied planet as a conquered prize. According to their code an indigenous people lived on the Earth prior to their arrival and as such the Earth belonged to them. The Oannes were simply visitors and as such must behave politely. The principle of Sewa was strong. The hope and belief that Nazmos would one day become like Earth was also strong and on this they placed great faith in me. The ancient myth legend was clear and firm in all their minds.

We'd had a relaxed morning and breakfast had been light, mainly of toasted bread with butter, jam and cheese. Kazaztan was waiting for us in the central plaza with 536-Orange and we were soon floating through the domes and tunnels towards the dome of Anztarza Bay. Tania was beside me and the others were close by at the rails. I looked at Tania as her hair whisked gently about in the slipstream flow from our Deck Transporter's easy pace.

'What?' she said looking up at me and smiling that knowing confident smile I had got to love so much.

'Just admiring,' I replied and conveyed how I felt.

Tania sidled closer and the emotion enveloping us must have spread to the others for we received knowing expressions of regard with a little sympathy mixed in. I wonder who that could have come from. It didn't matter, I was happy and so was Tania.

Muznant and Brazjaf stood slightly apart from the rest but their minds were open to me. Muznant was supposedly in the early stages of pregnancy and I wondered if it was safe for her to journey with us today. She read my mind and conveyed back thoughts of reassurance and that once I had experienced space travel the Oannes way I would understand. She conveyed that the Oannes travelled in space with such comfort and ease that it just became a normal everyday type of event. I conveyed that I was certainly looking forward to the experience.

Kazaztan settled the Transporter to one side of the Bay and quite near the dome wall. A craft much larger that 11701-Red was moored there. This was 520-Green and we were welcomed aboard by a smartly dressed elderly looking Oannes lady. She was short and stocky but had a gentle and pleasantly smiling face. There was an air of confidence about her that exuded authority. I knew instantly that she was the captain. There were two much younger looking Oannes men standing either side of her. All had pleasant expressions on their faces and they came up to us.

Muznant and Brazjaf were at the front with the chief ministers and our group was right behind them. A brief Sewa was performed by the lady who introduced herself as Captain Bulzezatna and the two beside her were her deputies, First Deputy Tatizblay and Second Deputy Rubandiz. Each was skilled in the mechanics of space flight and had captained smaller spacecraft prior to their transfer request to their current post.

We were all dressed in our smart new outfits and I personally felt quite posh with my side and back frills. As I found myself being introduced to the captain I made a slight bow of acknowledgement and performed a brief mental Sewa greeting on behalf of us all as was the custom. I kept my mind open and realised that Captain Bulzezatna and her deputies also did the same. I could see that they were pleased and complimented by my presence here and I knew they had picked up my essentials as I had theirs.

Bulzezatna was 200 years old and had been captain of 520-Green for eight years. She originally hailed from the City of Wentazta the same as Brazjaf. She was an only child and had been flying in space ever since she could mind read which happened to be at the young age of thirteen. There had never been a time or inclination for romantic ideas and she was happy with her unattached and uncomplicated single status. Bulzezatna had served as a crew member on a variety of ships including an expeditionary FTL starship early in her career. She had put herself forward for transfer about every ten years or so citing that she wanted to gain as wide an experience as was possible.

For a short period she had been a middle ranked technical crew member on 17366-Brown a Nazmos interplanetary ferry ship. She had then visited Anztarza as a crew member aboard a starship on several occasions. Earth for her became the most beautiful place in the universe. After a dozen such trips Bulzezatna requested that Anztarza become her home base. That was eighty years ago and she had loved every minute of it ever since.

She had been captain of another ship similar to 11701-Red for eleven years before being transferred to 520-Green as First Deputy. Six years later she succeeded her captain an elder of 250 years when he retired back to Nazmos with his even older and ailing wife. Bulzezatna had been captain of 520-Green for just over eight years and was well known in Anztarza and very well liked by her crew of just twenty Oannes. She valued her independence and privacy and had a few close friends whom she frequently entertained. Brazjaf and Muznant were among those whom she liked and favoured with her leisure moments. She was pleased they were aboard her spacecraft.

First Deputy Tatizblay was 120 years of age and still single though he did like a young thing of eighty called Niztrabt. She worked as one of the food staff in the section for underwater crop cultivating and harvesting plus other general duties in Dome-22. Both had lived in Anztarza for a little over twenty years and loved it. Many of their best romantic moments were spent roaming a particular remote forested area in the north of present day Canada. The winter climate there was just as it was on much of Nazmos. They had known each other for about three years and had secretly agreed a date a couple of years away. I smiled at this since nothing was ever kept secret among the Oannes.

Second Deputy Rubandiz was 110 years old and already had a wife called Hazarzym of the same age. They had known each other from living in the same street of the small town of Zoztarnt on the shores of Lake Voolzort. Zoztarnt was literally on the opposite shore of the lake to Muznant's home city of Latipuzan and was faintly visible in the distance on a clear day. They had been married for twelve years but as yet had not decided on children. Hazarzym worked as a monitor and enjoyed her tasks. She had Jantuzno under her wing and was quite fond of her.

I conveyed all this information to the rest of our group and mum acknowledged with thanks. It would be some time before any of them would read minds. Somehow Margaret Dutton's face came to mind as a passing thought. I wondered if any contact progress had been made there.

With the introductory formalities over we were shown to our cabins personally by deputy Tatizblay. I could read an excitement in his manner and I only hope I don't get a swollen head from all this attention. Everyone seemed excited to meet me and I must confess I found that I quite liked the celebrity status feeling. But more so because it brought a glow of pride to mum's face. And also to Tania's and Katy's too. Granddad Eric was in his element ever since he'd drunk his first Wazu. And I was pleased that he looked and felt so well. I also knew from reading his thoughts that he had an inclination to settle permanently here in Anztarza. He hoped to put his request to the chief ministers when we had returned from this trip.

Our cabins were very similar to the ones we'd occupied on spacecraft 11701-Red under Captain Lyzongpan for our journey to Anztarza. We were situated on the upper habitation deck which was on the same level as the control room. As before granddad Eric and I shared a cabin. Katy and Tania were together again as were mum and dad, Uncle Ron and Aunt Brenda and Jerry and Milly. Muznant and Brazjaf were also close and conveyed that it would be well over four hours before our journey proper began when the neutron generators could operate.

The craft would take nearly two hours to traverse the hundred mile Anztarza Tunnel to its exit point 2000 feet below sea level and then another hour up to the ice-free surface point in the Davis sea. Brazjaf conveyed that Captain Bulzezatna would call us to the control room to visually experience the exhilaration of the climb upwards into space from the Davis sea exit point. Brazjaf conveyed that both he and Muznant never missed these occasions and would certainly not miss this one.

I was curious about this spacecraft and immediately received a communication through my badge giving me all its main features. 520-Green had accommodation of nearly a hundred cabins on four levels. There were recreation rooms on each level for both crew and guests. Only twenty two crew members were required for normal functions aboard the ship but four extra had been included for this trip. The ship was operated by the Zanos-537 bio-computer which was the very latest system. It was far more advanced than the Zanos-447 aboard 11701-Red in that it anticipated the captains command and all the needs of the ship. It also responded to thought queries from anyone aboard just as it was currently conveying all this information to me.

The craft was 550 feet long and 250 feet wide at its centre and was oval in shape. The rear and front were quite similar except for the large viewing panels delineating the front and upper areas. It had six decks which gave it a height of ninety feet. The upper deck was where all the electric power was generated through direct atom nuclei stimulation. The neutron generators were also on this level close to their power source but were arrayed as nodules around the outer perimeter of the ship and facing upwards. The nodules were large and looked grossly menacing according to the visual images I received. The ship needed to be at least one million miles from any planet or large mass object before the neutron generators could be safely operated. The impulse motors that were the main motive power for the ship were all housed within the lower deck six.

The outer hull and each deck floor were 14 inches thick and similar in material to the Anztarza dome structuring. At the centre of the craft and going in a perpendicular fashion through all the deck levels was a continuous six feet diameter circular pillar. This was the composite material electric field generator for the creation of the fifty mile Van Allen type magnetic protection belt around the spacecraft. This was only made functional when in outer space.

A ten feet wide pedestrian corridor encircled the interior of the ship on each of the four habitation levels and gave access to all the cabins and recreation rooms. All interior walls were also 14 inches thick and the construction layout of each cabin deck was similar. As such each wall and partition was continuous from top to bottom of the ship which gave it tremendous structural strength especially when at extreme depths in the seas of both Earth and Nazmos.

150 feet of the rear portion of the spacecraft was the cargo area on three deep decks. Each deck was twice the height of the inner decks. One deck was for stores, another for a variety of shuttle craft and the third was for maintenance work and to receive visiting craft.

All this detail wasn't explained as bits of information but came as a complete pictorial package of knowledge. I was quite astounded by the advanced technology the Oannes had achieved and I was given reassurance that military defence was obsolete. I had been about to think on those lines but Zanos on board had pre-empted my intended query.

I was informed that should anyone intend an aggressive action to harm the ship or its occupants then intense thought control would be exerted to alter that intent and cause the person to favour a more peaceful course.

Once again Zanos-537 anticipated my thoughts and informed us that 520-Green had not left Anztarza Bay and was still moored to the quay. Zanos had sensed the unease of one of the crew and that they were about to become ill. A replacement was found and was on his way. Technician Voznoliz was 200 years old and something he had eaten last night must have disagreed with him and he was getting odd rumblings in his gut. Zanos-537 diagnosed an infection within the digestive system and that Voznoliz required treatment and isolation for 48 hours in the sick quarter facility of Dome-1.

When 520-Green finally got underway Zanos informed us of the event. Yet inside the ship I got no sensation of movement. We all received a pictorial image of 520-Green heading slowly away from the shoreline and then gradually submerging under the water surface. This was done by the impulse motors which then took the craft down into the Anztarza Tunnel. It would be at least two hours to the tunnel exit and then nearly another hour to the Davis sea surface point beyond the melting ice-shelf. In places the sea ice was quite thick and Zanos must ensure the craft was well clear of it.

Captain Bulzezatna conveyed that we would be invited to the control room shortly before the craft was scheduled to surface so that we could experience the exhilaration of the climb into space. It was always an interesting moment to see the Earth's horizon falling away and the sky change to a deeper blue before eventually giving way to the blackness of space. But that was at least three hours away.

I contacted Tania on open communication and suggested we all go to the recreation lounge just down the corridor. There was an immediate 'yes' from everyone and even Muznant said she would meet us there. Brazjaf was in the control room with Captain Bulzezatna catching up on the latest gossip. They were old friends and often talked about their home city of Wentazta when visiting each other. Brazjaf kept a few bottles of Earth-made sparkling wine which Bulzezatna had become partial to with her Wazu. All this was open knowledge and other Anztarzans also liked to flavour their Wazu drink with a dash of lemon which apparently didn't seem to affect the fuzzy floating seeds at all. Anything stronger was not tolerated by the floating seeds and had to be consumed as a chaser. I smiled at this piece of knowledge and wondered how long it would be before a liking became a craving.

Granddad and I walked the short distance to the lounge and found that Katy and Tania were already there. The rest of the family soon joined us and we sat on sofa style armchair seats with slotted backrests very nicely designed to accommodate the Oannes back butterfly wing webs. We found them extremely comfortable and managed to sit so that our tunic back frill fitted neatly into the backrest openings. Once settled down we helped ourselves from the Wazu dispenser. I thought I would have liked a nice cup of tea with milk and one sugar at that point.

Muznant had been the last to have joined us and now she stood up and conveyed that I follow her. We walked the ten steps to the end of the room and around a small partition into a sort of kitchenette area. There was a worktop there and placed neatly on one side was a kettle, carton of milk and sachets of sugar and artificial sweetener. Tea, coffee and biscuits were in neat round capped containers also placed alongside on the worktop. It was near enough to what you would find in any B&B or hotel room on Earth. There was a shelf above the worktop on which a dozen small mugs sat and I couldn't stop myself from giving a 'Wow' and chuckle of subdued laughter.

'What is it Ashley?' asked mum when she heard me and I replied for her to come and have a look for herself.

Of course everyone was curious and followed her and tried to crowd into the kitchenette for a look. I received a strong emotion of pleasure and joy along with eager anticipation. I think we are all tea or coffee addicts which of course was quite normal for us earthlings. I personally like my tea fix several times a day.

'Alright everybody,' said mum aloud, 'I'll be mother. So who wants tea and who wants coffee? But give me some room in here so go and seat yourselves down.'

'I'll give you a hand,' said Tania and mum smiled at that. She definitely liked Tania and I suspect had done so from that first moment at the Navigation Pub darts match. Tania was only thirteen then and mum had met Milly and Jerry for the first time also. Thoughts of the moment came to my mind and I wondered what Harry the pub landlord was doing at this precise moment. I thought of the two crooks and especially of Quigley Thorn the converted one. Was he still entertaining people with his card tricks? I hoped he was. I then went and sat down but Muznant stayed behind to show mum how the kettle worked.

Tania carried two mugs of tea over to us shortly after and mum followed right behind. Tania, mum and I were the only ones drinking tea the rest all had coffee. Even Katy had recently taken to coffee. She liked hers weak and black but with two sweeteners.

Muznant shook her head when mum asked what she would like. She touched her abdomen to indicate that she was being careful. Anyway I knew she couldn't stand the taste of anything hot. She said she'd stick with the Wazu with the slight flavouring of lemon.

My wrist watch showed nearly midday GMT. Zanos anticipated my query and indicated our asteroid destination arrival time as 5 o'clock in the morning which was a journey lasting seventeen hours in total. That would enable us to have a good night's rest prior to arrival at the Steins asteroid rendezvous.

Brazjaf came and joined us a while later and conveyed that Captain Bulzezatna would be sending one of her deputies around to see us.

We were all in general gossiping conversation when our communication badges conveyed that Second Deputy Rubandiz was offering to give us a tour of the ship. There was an eager 'yes' from all and we were asked to make our way to the control room.

Once again we were welcomed by Captain Bulzezatna. Rubandiz then came forward and guided us towards the rear part of the room. The front viewing panels were completely dark and it was conveyed to us that the ship was still within the Anztarza Tunnel. Only when the ship approached the sea surface would there be a glow of light. But for our benefit powerful lights were switched on and the front panels took on a greenish glow. It was only then that I noticed the view panels across the ceiling area too which also had a greenish glow though I couldn't make out physical features of any kind. Zanos clarified this by indicating that nothing was discernible because of the smooth featureless walls of the Anztarza Tunnel through which we were speeding at 60mph or just under 90 feet per second. I also knew the purpose of the ceiling view panels. They were to become our forward travel views when travelling in space.

Rubandiz saw me looking upwards and immediately conveyed that all seating could be reclined for more comfortable upward viewing. He then informed us that all crew and passengers would be requested to take up reclining positions whenever the neutron generators were to be operated. This was a precaution against the feeling of space disorientation which could and did affect a small proportion of passengers. Rubandiz explained that space disorientation or sickness was basically a feeling of nausea and vertigo caused by the fractional variation in the pull of gravity over the distance between the top and bottom of ones body. Hence the reclining posture recommended at critical moments of neutron generator forces. The impulse motors produced their gravity effect simply by keeping the spacecraft at a constant acceleration of 0.9g throughout the journey in space. Rubandiz conveyed that gravity in the ship should feel no different out in space from what we were currently feeling. Mum smiled at this reassurance of what we had been told earlier. The external flood lights were extinguished and suddenly the control room felt less bright. Rubandiz then led us out of the control room and into the corridor and so our interesting tour of the ship began.

I noticed that the design within the ship was very block-like as we walked along the encircling corridor passing our cabins on the way towards the rear of the ship. There were doors to other cabins and lounges as we progressed.

At the rear we walked down a gentle slope and entered the first of the three Cargo Bay levels. This was like a large warehouse filled with cartons and boxes arranged in rows from floor to ceiling. I saw a small unmanned floating platform moving down one of the aisles at near ceiling level. I was not sure what it was doing but my mental curiosity was read by our guide who conveyed that it was a Zanos probe doing a stock-take of the ships supplies for our coming journey. I also noticed that this bay was at a much lower temperature than the living areas.

We then went down to the second Cargo level and upon entering this bay I was fascinated by the variety of small spacecraft I saw neatly parked together in the 150ft by 200ft floor area. There were craft of various sizes the largest being about 40ft long by 15ft wide and 10ft high. There were only two of these and both were painted a bright yellow colour. All the others were smaller shuttle craft being just above half the size of the bigger craft. All sat on the deck floor and were neatly parked side by side and nose to tail and I counted twenty in all. I noticed that all their bases were a chunky 4ft thick. Rubandiz answered my thought query by explaining that all the motive power systems for the spacecraft and shuttles were contained within this under floor area.

I could see only three crew members in the bay but they didn't seem to be doing anything. Rubandiz explained that they were there to monitor the readiness levels of all craft but this was simply to ensure that their internal bio-computer systems were in constant communication with Zanos-537. Zanos would update the captain if anything was amiss. The principle was essentially one of 'no news is good news' reporting.

Our guide informed us that these craft were all transporters for shuttling people and material from one craft to another while travelling in space. They were also essential for ferry work to and from the FTL starships when necessary. Or in the event of main craft failure, which could be a result of mechanical breakdown or a space meteor strike. Zanos immediately answered my query by informing that the last incident occurred exactly 2867 years ago when spacecraft 820-Sapphire suffered an overload shutdown of its power systems. All personnel had to be evacuated while on a journey from the FTL starship which was parked way out in the Kuiper Belt on the fringes of the solar system. Barely an hour into the journey towards Earth and shortly after the neutron generators had functioned a temperature anomaly on the electricity power generator deck was reported by the Zanos bio-computer. The ship was travelling at thirty thousand miles a second and the captain had the foresight to reverse the ship's attitude and operate the neutron generators at the 200% emergency level. At this point the overload shutdown occurred with the ship still travelling at a thousand miles a second.

Everyone on board had to put on their electrostatic suits and the ingenious Captain Gotsmazn ordered all shuttle craft to use their small impulse motors inside the cargo bay to help slow the ship down to near standstill status. The rescue ship arrived in about six hours and all the people on board still wearing their electrostatic suits were shuttled across. 820-Sapphire was towed to the FTL ship and then returned to Nazmos for investigation and repair. The reason for overheating was established and modifications made to all craft in service. 820-Sapphire was never returned to Earth service but kept usefully occupied around Nazmos. It was considered quite old by Oannes standards and was eventually used as a space cadet training facility.

We moved along and went down towards the third Cargo Bay level. We entered this and I was surprised to see it completely empty. The area looked huge and I looked towards Jerry and he raised his eyebrows.

'Looks like all the parties are held here,' he smiled. 'Gosh, you could hold a mini Fair down here.'

The emotion of humour filled our space and I couldn't help smiling too. Rubandiz explained that this was the bay for receiving the shuttle craft from other ships. I wondered why Zanos had not anticipated my curiosity and offered an explanation. It was only then that I knew by instinct why that was. A protocol of etiquette must exist that did not allow Zanos to over-ride or precede what our guide could and would reveal. Oh, I did like this and I developed an even greater respect for Zanos for this act of politeness. I conveyed my thoughts to all the others and Rubandiz smiled at me with pleasure and intimated his admiration at my inference.

Tania was beside me and smiled up at me and conveyed something intimate that I shall keep private – thank you very much. But I squeezed her hand in return and conveyed my own thoughts. Rubandiz glowed with pride and smiled while looking away at the rear wall of the empty cargo area. He'd obviously read our thoughts as must have all of Anztarza. The Oannes had a soft spot for couples who conveyed their deep affection for one another. Peace, love and openness were central to the Oannes way of life. And both Tania and I loved it.

I was now quite used to the Oannes appearance. Their large round eyes, full lips and fine aquiline nose gave them an appearance of gentleness and calm. The web fins down each cheek at the side of their face reminded me of pictures I had seen of Victorian gentlemen sporting large bushy sideburns. All in all I think they had striking features especially the ladies and Muznant in particular.

I was happy to wear our new Oannes clothes as it brought us nearer to their appearance with our arm and back material frills. It was only when I received the emotion of affection in a general manner did I realise I had kept my mind open and all my inner thoughts and feelings had been picked up by the entire crew and perhaps even all of Anztarza. I wonder what Puzlwat thought of my opinions. He and Mytanzto were on this spacecraft to witness my attempt to move the asteroids and my instincts indicated that he hoped for a failure. I think I did care what he thought and I sincerely wished I could win him over to trusting in me. I hoped I would.

The asteroids were large by my current standards and last year this time I had never even considered that such a task would be put before me. I considered myself a novice but a good one. I had confidence in my gifts and knew that if I did not succeed initially I would develop in time; with the help and guidance of the Oannes of course.

We spent quite a long time in this empty hold and Rubandiz walked us towards the rear section. He touched the wall and indicated that these were large bay doors that could be opened wide to give an opening of 100ft across and the full height of the bay. This would allow access to any size of shuttle craft and even to some of the smaller privately owned spaceships on Nazmos.

Zanos now informed everyone generally that 520-Green had exited the Anztarza Tunnel and was heading up to the surface in the Davis Sea area. The craft would arrive at this surface position in about forty minutes. A large opening in the ice cover had been reported by an earlier craft and that is where we were now heading.

There was one more item essential to the spacecraft that Rubandiz wanted to show us and that was the composite core magnetic system responsible for the fifty mile wide Van Allen type magnetic field that would operate whenever 520-Green was in outer space. This was currently inactive.

We made our way to the interior corridor on this lower habitation level leading in a curved fashion towards the front of the ship but we stopped about halfway. Rubandiz used his authority to thought command an inner-side door to open. All habitation levels were of course identical in cabin layout and design and the room we stepped into would be the same at each level. There was a large hall before us and at its centre was a circular pillared construction from floor to ceiling. It was perfectly smooth and similar in texture to the internal walls of the spacecraft. The circular pillar was about twenty feet in diameter and Rubandiz explained that inside it was a concentric composite material core of about ten feet diameter which extended the full height of the ship. Around this central core was a myriad of complex woven coils and counter coils that generated the massive magnetic field that was essential for the safety of the ship travelling in the hazardous cosmic ray filled environment of outer space.

Jerry asked if it was dangerous for anyone to be in this room when the magnetic system was active. Rubandiz explained that all of the magnetic field's strength was purely at each end of the column and as such this room was perfectly safe at all times.

It was while we were making our way back to the upper habitation level that we received the message from Zanos that 520-Green was approaching the Davis Sea surface opening and we should return to the control room. Time does seem to go by quick.

As soon as we entered the rear of the control room I noticed a decided glow of pale greenish light in all the viewing panels. We were only just in time and a few minutes later the ship gave a slight judder as it popped up onto the surface of the Davis Sea and into brilliant daylight. There was a ring of bluish white cliffs of ice a few hundred feet away to the front and either side of us and I imagined around our rear as well. Zanos then took the ship out of the water and we began a swift rise upwards towards the clear blue sky. The acceleration was smooth and vertically upwards and the flat horizon gradually took on a mystical fuzzy curvature. I noticed how quickly the sky above us turned to a deeper blue before becoming completely black. Zanos conveyed we were passing above 100 miles and continuing to accelerate at the prescribed 90% of gravity. This would remain constant throughout our journey towards Steins. I had no sensation of speed since we could not see the Earth anymore. The horizon had disappeared and Earth was somewhere under our feet. I continued to look upwards and suddenly the blackness of the view altered and I saw a brilliance that I could never have imagined. The stars overhead were everywhere and I wondered at their crowded abundance. There was the section of the Milky Pathway that delineated our galaxy and I could just make it out at the upper edge of the view panels. It was brighter than I imagined and its dark patches were unusually pronounced. I looked at the others and they were just as mesmerised as I was. But what puzzled me was the fact that there had been nothing there to view when we had first reached the blackness of space. My thoughts must have been read by the captain for she smiled and conveyed that the brilliance of space is a wonder that comes upon one suddenly. Eyesight is a funny thing and often has a delayed action response to what is sent to it. It might only be a few seconds but is enough to confuse. Captain Bulzezatna then conveyed that later another view awaited us when the ship was at cruise velocity after the neutron generators had operated and when she could rotate the ship to view the receding Earth and sun. Then the stars would again disappear as if by magic to leave just the Earth and sun visible; and maybe Venus if it was in the right aspect. I conveyed that I keenly looked forward to that as did all the others. Looking upwards grew wearisome and my neck felt an ache which I didn't think normal. Everything about me felt heavy.

Zanos pre-empted my thoughts and conveyed that the neutron generators would operate in three and a half hours time when 520-Green was a million miles from Earth. Under normal gravity acceleration this position would have been reached in about five hours. However Captain Bulzezatna had commanded that acceleration was increased so that the jump to 15,000 miles per second could be accomplished sooner. After that the gravity would return to the normal level which was a relief to me since I did not know how long I would be able to tolerate such a weight increase.

Captain Bulzezatna conveyed that it was quite the norm for personnel to occupy their sleep tank facility during these periods of high acceleration. She suggested we do likewise and return to our cabins and rest on our beds. Suddenly I thought that was an excellent idea.

Zanos informed me that 520-Green was now at the 1.5g level of acceleration and gradually increasing to 1.8g in the next few minutes. I must confess that I did not feel any different until we began the walk back to our cabins. I noticed that I was stamping my feet as I walked even though I did not intend it. However, once I become conscious of the fact I made a concerted effort to measure my steps and so gradually walked in a more normal fashion; at least that is what I thought. I had to smile when the thought about a drunken person attempting a semblance of normality in the pattern of their walk rhythm came into my mind. There was quiet laughter when I conveyed my thoughts to the others walking with me. All said that they were coping well and that arms and legs felt especially weighty. We would be glad when we reached our beds. Mum conveyed that the women had a special problem in that their bra straps were becoming excessively uncomfortable and the sooner they lay down the better.

We finally got to our cabins and felt much easier once we had settled down on our beds. Muznant and Brazjaf conveyed that they too were eager for the sleep tank in their room; though they would require the float tunics to improve their buoyancy under the higher gravity conditions. I received an emotion of satisfaction from the women of our group and all expressed their relief to be lying down on their beds.

I looked at my wrist watch and it showed the time to be nearly 4 pm GMT. I guessed that it would be sometime in the early morning that we should arrive near asteroid Steins. Zanos had indicated this as 5 am. It had been an interesting day and the extra gravity made me feel pleasantly tired. I removed my tunic and hung it in the hanging space provided but kept my leggings on when I lay down. I really liked my new clothes and I'm sure the others did as well. They were comfortable and made me feel good. My eyes seemed heavy and I thought a little shuteye could not go amiss. I conveyed this to the others generally and both Katy and Tania replied that they felt the same. I'm sure I received the emotion of a sleepy yawn from someone. I began to doze off but not before I got the impression that granddad was attempting to saw the legs of his bed.

I dreamt one of my recurring dreams. It seemed that this time I was not going to miss my bus to school like I had done so often before. I knew that this was a dream but nevertheless I had decided that once and for all I would sort this out. I collected all my books and homework and walked to the bus stop across the street. The odd thing was that our house was different and somewhere out in the country. From across the street I saw my bus approaching the stop and I ran to catch it. But there was no one at the stop and the driver didn't see me and continued on. I ran towards the bus hoping to hop onto the open running board at the back but suddenly my legs seemed to operate only in slow motion. So there I was running about ten feet behind the bus but unable to catch it exactly as in all the other dreams. Gradually the bus drew further away but I kept up my futile chase at which time the dream just faded away. I knew that I would think about the dream in the morning when I woke and wonder why I had not gone 'pink' and so caught the bus quite easily. Over the years I must have had this dream several times but this time my slow motion running was accompanied by a feeling of lead in my legs.

Somehow the Oannes came into my thoughts as I dreamt on and I wondered if my dreams were being picked up as thought waves. I must ask Muznant about this aspect I thought as I dreamt on. And suddenly there she was swimming towards me just above a field of ripening barley or was it wheat? It seemed quite normal for her to be swimming in the air and an emotion of joy enveloped me at the sight of her. But this dream then changed and I was looking into a large mirror and I could see the reflection image of a huge brightly glowing ball coming up behind me. I tried to turn around to see it directly but I couldn't move my head and remained transfixed on the mirror view. It was just about up my back and I could feel its heat. Then suddenly I was able to spin around but there was nothing there. I could still feel its heat on my back and so I turned back towards the mirror and there it was inside the mirror view and receding away into the reflection distance. I watched as it grew smaller and smaller till it was just a tiny dot. I must have then fallen into a deeper sleep for I cannot remember dreaming of anything else. Gradually I woke to the sound of a buzzing bee and realised that granddad was still asleep and in gentle snore mode.

My watch showed just after 7pm and my weight felt normal. Zanos immediately answered my intended query and stated that the neutron generators had operated as planned about twenty minutes ago in a succession of bursts to take 520-Green to a velocity of 15,000 miles per sec. The impulse motors had also reverted back to maintain the ship at a normal 0.9 Earth gravity level. We should arrive at the Steins asteroid locality in approximately eleven hours time. I had been asleep for nearly three hours. A good afternoon kip and I felt refreshed.

Granddad Eric was now awake and conveyed that he was starving. Apart from the few biscuits with our tea earlier we'd not eaten anything since our late breakfast. My communication badge conveyed that the others were also awake after a good rest and were feeling the same. I think our minds were read and we were requested to be in the food lounge just down the corridor in half an hour. A pictorial image of its location was conveyed along with the message. The suggestion that we should appear smartly dressed in our Oannes outfits also came across strongly.

We were a perfectly attired group as we entered the food lounge and I was surprised and pleased to see Captain Bulzezatna already there along with Brazjaf and Muznant and First Deputy Tatizblay. The captain welcomed us all with a brief Sewa formality and inquired if we'd had a good rest. This time mum responded with all her charm and smiles. I could see that this pleased the captain no end that the mother of the group had chosen to be the representative. It was a woman to woman thing I imagined but I also felt that mum had taken an instant liking to the captain and the captain to mum. I think I got my easy-going manner from mum and Tania had often said how much alike we were in some of the things we said and did. I suppose this must be obvious to others as well including our Oannes hosts.

We sat at a long table which had seating room to spare. Jugs of Wazu and small glasses had already been spread strategically on it and I sat down between Tania and Katy and opposite the captain as directed. Mum and Milly were either side of Bulzezatna with the others spread closely around them and us. The two ends of the table were left unoccupied and I wondered if there was any significance in that. Muznant was across to one side and she looked at me and seemed puzzled by my observation. In the Oannes tradition the privileged and preferred places were near the centres of the table as then you were in the middle of everything that went on. It was definitely the best seat for being entertained.

After the Wazu drinking ceremonial was over Muznant, Brazjaf and Tatizblay stood up and went towards a cupboard at one end of the room. Captain Bulzezatna conveyed to us that all our cooked food dishes had been placed in readiness for us in the hot food dispenser and would be brought to the table by our three volunteers. But mum was having none of this and immediately stood up and called up Katy and Tania as well and the three of them quickly caught up with Muznant.

'Many hands make light work,' conveyed mum, 'and the men can do the clearing up afterwards.'

I could see that Bulzezatna was pleasantly amused at this and gave her approval with a gentle nodding of her head.

The dishes of food were similar to what Laztraban and Niktukaz had served up the previous evening but with a slightly different flavouring. And to our great surprise and delight there was a large bowl of boiled potatoes with the skins left on.

'We knew you all liked your potatoes so we had plenty placed on board,' said Bulzezatna in a pleasant falsetto voice. 'And you can also have scrambled eggs with your breakfasts to go with your toast.'

I smiled and conveyed that we were being treated like royalty. Muznant replied that we were considered more than special. We were the first Earth guests to have ever been entertained by the Oannes people. That made us extra special she said. We were the first contact between the two races and she hoped that this would lead on to greater things.

We all ate heartily and again I noticed that Muznant and Brazjaf ate sparingly though perhaps a bit more than previously. Mum remarked to Bulzezatna that she could give them a few Earth recipes which she was sure they might like. There was a smile on Bulzezatna's face as she conveyed that not only did they possess a library of Earth recipes but they also knew the favourite dish and pudding for each of them. Of course I thought how silly of me to forget that with their mind read capabilities the Oannes knew the inside and out of each one of us. Bulzezatna reached across and touched mum's arm and said in her softest voice, 'We shall have your omelette prepared for you in the morning just the way you like it with bits of cheese and chopped onions.'

All mum could say was 'Lovely' as she smiled at the captain. I think they were bonded for life.

Now again Zanos anticipated my thoughts and informed us that we were indeed racing towards our objective Steins at just over 15,000miles per sec and gradually increasing this with our 0.9g acceleration. No loop tactics were planned until we were in the steins vicinity and as such spaceship 520-Green's velocity would increase by about 300mps during the journey time.

The conversation around the dinner table was just like it had been at the banquet in the Dome-4 amphitheatre and I noticed that First Deputy Tatizblay said very little. He kept looking keenly at the women folk and I noticed especially at mum, Milly and Aunt Brenda. He had at first been interested in Tania and Katy and looked into their minds in order to compare their thought patterns with those of his companion Niztrabt. But it was only when he shifted his attention towards the older women did he discover their mature and very interesting thought patterns. These women were half of Niztrabt's 80 years and yet they thought with the maturity of an Oannes person of Bulzezatna's age. It was a wonder to him how quickly the Earth people matured intellectually and also how rapidly they aged to finality. Their lifespan was less than a third that of the Oannes' and Tatizblay fully expected his people to extend towards 400 years one day. Perhaps with integration the Earth people might progress along a similar path. Who knew what discoveries lay ahead?

Suddenly my inner voice gave me an insight of Tatizblay's future. He was destined for great things and would lead the Oannes in a completely new lifestyle on Nazmos. This spoke volumes for me also and I felt a surge of confidence in the outcome of all that the Oannes would ask of us. Nazmos would change and I was to be its architect in a manner of speaking. And Tatizblay would rise to the new challenges and become a great leader. I thought of Philip and wondered whether my inner voice was his or was it someone else; or was it the much greater being who had granted me all my gifts. What else lay dormant within me was a thought that seemed to recur often? Zanos must be reading all this but unable to resolve an answer. Perhaps Zanos did not get involved in personal issues.

After dinner Captain Bulzezatna invited us all back to the control room. She said she planned a short loop tactic to show us a view of the now distant Earth and sun. She conveyed that the Earth under normal view would only just be discernible at our current distance. I sensed an emotion of humour coming from her and was not quite certain what little secret she had up her sleeve. But I knew she was anticipating with some relish a new revelation she was about to divulge.

Muznant and Brazjaf did not come with us to the control room as Muznant was not feeling at all well. Brazjaf said that it might be the after-effect of the high gravity push. They returned to their cabin and conveyed that a few hours in the sleep tank should do Muznant a world of good. I expressed my concern and so did the entire group, including Captain Bulzezatna. Since Zanos had not picked up anything medically unusual on the ship, conveyed the captain, then there was nothing serious to be worried about. Women in Muznant's condition often had a few ups and downs comfort wise.

We entered the control room and 2nd Deputy Rubandiz was the only occupant there. He bowed slightly to the captain and retreated slowly to the rear of the room and stood there for a few minutes. He then appeared to receive a communication after which he conveyed a brief Sewa farewell before exiting through the door to the corridor. I gathered that he had been relieved of his duty and would probably go to one of the crew recreation lounges for some well deserved nourishment and the latest gossip; and then perhaps to his cabin and sleep tank.

I looked up at the starry view and was still fascinated by the clarity of the picture in the viewing panels. There were couches at spaced intervals around the room and Captain Bulzezatna suggested we settle down on one and go into the semi-reclining position for better viewing comfort. She was right; it was much easier looking up at the star-filled heavens from this position. It was like looking straight in front of you and was much more comfortable.

The lighting was dimmed considerably and Zanos conveyed that the ship would now commence a slow 180 degrees rotation towards the left. It was a very gradual motion and the starry view in front of me began to shift slowly to my right. Also very gradually brightness began to dawn upon the framework of the view panel edges and the stars seemed to fade from view. A darker tint appeared in the view panel clarity which was meant to shield us from this new solar brightness entering the control room. It was only then that I realised we were experiencing a spacecraft sunrise.

There was a 'Wow' exclamation from some of the group as the full sun appeared in our view, though adequately shielded by the window tint. It was the same size as when viewed on Earth but now it was a clear round ball object that shone dazzlingly bright even through the tinted effect. When the sun became fixed in its position I knew that 520-Green had completed its rotating manoeuvre.

There were no stars visible to us now and Zanos conveyed that we should concentrate our sight upon the large view panel to the right side of the sun. But my mind conveyed such confusion that I could not see anything there. It was only when the sun was completely shielded from us by the end panel turning a much darker tint that a quarter moon shaped object which I concluded was the Earth came into view. Zanos conveyed that we were a little over two million miles from Earth and it would appear in size at about a third the diameter of the visible sun.

Captain Bulzezatna conveyed that 520-Green's course towards the Steins asteroid was such that the two directional lines from the Earth and from the sun to the craft made an angle of 26 degrees. I concentrated my look upon the Earth but could not see where the moon might be. Zanos conveyed that from this vantage point the moon would be a dark object. I'm afraid I was not at all impressed by the view before me and my thoughts must have been read by the captain. Again I sensed the emotion of amusement in the room and it was only when I felt a light touch upon my shoulder did I realise that Bulzezatna had come to stand silently behind my recliner.

Bulzezatna squeezed my shoulder again and her thoughts entered mine and the emotion of humour once again came through. In an instant I understood what she had found so funny. The view panels each had the ability to magnify the object being viewed nearly without limit and the humorous part for Bulzezatna was that she and her crew had simply forgotten to mention the fact to their guests. It was generally assumed that everyone knew about it. The Oannes took their technologies for granted as just an ordinary part of everyday living. It was a bit like a chair that people used to sit on. No one needed to explain what the chair was there for; you just went and sat on it if you wished.

The view panels were a complex arrangement – a bit like the 'thinking stone' tablet – and had the ability to convey a closer view of the object in question simply at the thought command of the viewer. It was a mind thing and consequently two viewers could mentally see the same object quite differently magnified. Bulzezatna conveyed that we did not see with the eyes but with the mind. The eyes simply conveyed a signal to the brain which then interpreted this as vision. Bulzezatna conveyed that the African continent and Europe were currently in her view and I could see the same if I wished it. The magnification was absolutely stupendous she conveyed.

I looked at the distant quarter moon of Earth and wished to see a bigger image. I was surprised when I saw a much larger Earth emerge in front of me inside the view panel. I wished it closer and that happened instantly. I laughed when the Earth's image filled the panel. There was Africa with a sort of cloud band across its central zone but I concentrated on Europe and instantly this became magnified. My thought wishes were to see a part of England but all that came into my view was a mass of white cloud cover. I concentrated my thoughts to the east of this but Europe also seemed covered in cloud though this became patchy as the scene approached the Earth's night shadow area. I went back to the smaller view where I could see the entire quarter-Earth image inside the window panel. Earth had colour and beauty that quite took my breath away and I gazed in wonder at its loveliness in the vast blackness all around it.

This had to be shared and so I immediately conveyed all of this knowledge to Tania first and then to the rest of the group and waited for the expected reaction.

Suddenly the emotions of wonder and awe and pleasure just filled the room. And of course there was Bulzezatna's humour that came across as a sort of mental laughter emerging through it all. Finally after a few moments my own earthly chuckle grew into jolly laughter and I was soon joined by the others whom I'm sure saw the funny side of it all. Bulzezatna certainly did.

Finally after about twenty minutes of magnified Earth viewing Zanos conveyed that the ship would now make a slow rotation to return to the original heading towards Steins. I had seen enough for now and my mind was a little fatigued. Bulzezatna conveyed that the receiving of mental signals from the view panel plates needed getting used to. The fatigue effect was not unusual for a first viewing; it would get easier with frequent use.

As I lay on the recliner thinking about the Oannes and their technologies I wondered what other revelations lay in store for us. Suddenly I was thinking of Robin and how he might be coping in the shop. Would he be expecting a phone call from one of us? Perhaps a call from Anztarza on our return might be in order. Zanos immediately replied that such a communication facility did not exist on Anztarza. An alternative path would have to be explored. Oh well, it was just a thought.

Speeding through space at 15,000 miles a second now seemed quite an ordinary feat especially with normal gravity under our feet. I looked through the view panels and once again the myriad of stars filled the area overhead. I desired a magnified image and instantly I was looking at something similar to the Hubble telescope pictures I had seen displayed on the internet. The screen was full of galaxies of every shape and size with many in full spiral configuration. I chose one and again this just filled the view panel and I tried to look into its central core. The magnification increased till suddenly there was nothing on view. My inner voice confirmed that the centre of this galaxy was its proton giant or 'black hole' which was what held the galaxy together. I knew that a very long time ago when the phasing realms were into their Circle-4 phase, that proton giants had formed in such abundance that they filled the universe. Most of the universe energy-medium was thus locked within them but enough remained for today's ordinary sized protons to evolve in the following Circle-5 phase. These primary atoms congregated to evolve into stars of varying masses and followed their burning cycles to form the more complex atoms. They would then be attracted towards one or another of these proton giants. They'd be pulled into orbit around the 'giant' and we would assume the orbital path to follow Newton's laws for planetary motion. This would in fact be incorrect. As one gets closer towards the proton giant there is an increasing component of repulsion action causing a diminishment in the gravitational attraction component. As such the stable orbital paths would be comparatively slower and are actually seen to synchronise with the orbital velocity of the stars that are farther out. This is termed as the galaxy 'Cartwheel Effect'. In the early age of galaxy formation there would have been many collisions of stars that were being drawn into orbit; some perhaps even orbiting in opposite directions. It was a turbulent period but in time stability was achieved as we see today. The cartwheel effect has actually been observed when Earth scientists looked at distant spiral galaxies that happened to be orientated flat wise to our view. The rest is history with stars forming and exploding and eventually giving light to the universe as it entered its present circle 6 phase. Galaxies live because it is impossible for anything to fall into the proton giant or 'black hole'. There is such an emission of proton decay energy-medium being emitted from the proton in general that any object approaching close to it is pushed away on a simple principle of mechanics. This is also why 'black holes' have always remained as separate entities. I shall need to give a more detailed analysis and explanation when I put all this in written form.

Captain Bulzezatna conveyed that we could stay as long as we wished but I felt fatigued mentally and anyway I could always return when I'd had a good rest. I conveyed that the view was beautiful but I had seen enough for the present. I suggested we all return to the lounge for a nightcap before heading to our cabins and a good night's rest. Zanos had estimated our arrival near Steins sometime around 5 am GMT. It was now just after 10pm on my wrist watch and I looked forward to my cabin bed. Physically I felt fine but my brain said 'more sleep please'.

The lounge was deserted when we got there. This time the men folk made the tea and coffee in mugs and brought them to the seating area. We were thinking of having a second round of hot drinks when Puzlwat and Mytanzto walked in. They did not seem surprised to see us and were heading towards a set of stool seats in the far corner of the room. I conveyed a brief Sewa greeting and requested their company among our group. There were plenty of slit-back seats and I conveyed that these were quite comfortable. After a very brief but noticeable hesitation both came over to us and sat down where I had indicated.

'Greetings friend Puzlwat,' I said aloud, 'I am glad we finally meet; and greetings to you too Mytanzto. We consider all of Anztarza as a friend even though you did not agree to this visit. I hope I can prove to you that it is all worthwhile.'

'I too am glad we meet face to face with you Ashley,' replied Puzlwat in a slightly squeaky high pitch voice, 'and I must welcome you to Anztarza now that you are already with us. I hope you find your stay of interest. But what will you do when you return to your homes? No good can come of you telling the world of our presence here on Earth.'

'But why should we do that?' said mum in a kindly way. 'Earth is not ready for that news and probably won't be for another thousand years or more. Your people want integration but that can only happen when we are at peace among ourselves and when our communication system is fully telepathic like yours. Would you not agree with what I am saying?'

Puzlwat hesitated again and I read a little confusion in his thoughts. But it was Mytanzto who conveyed that he knew Earth mentality from his job as a general monitor and that self interest was paramount in our thinking.

'You take great pride in your status and popularity,' he conveyed. 'So why would you not tell everyone you know about us? You would achieve nothing for yourselves by keeping this secret.' He looked at us in a very sceptical and distrustful manner.

I was silent and then I conveyed that our minds were open to them. They must look in and read for themselves all our innermost thoughts and cravings using the touch method. I reached forward with my right hand and gave each of them a firm earthly handshake and in that brief moment felt a deep probe of my mind. Then dad, mum and all the others in turn reached forward and did the same.

At the end of this ceremony I noticed a puzzled expression appear on Puzlwat's face. He communicated to Mytanzto that we had been clever in clearing our minds of incriminating thoughts. But how we had managed to do this is what puzzled him since even the Oannes did not have that ability. I read all this and immediately conveyed to them that we on earth were not advanced mentally as the Oannes and had only recently acquired the gift of telepathic communication and that too to a limited extent. As such our brains were not as extensively utilised; hence the open spaces.

During the handshakes I had managed a deep probed reading of their minds as well and what I had found pleased me though with an edge of sadness at their mistrust of our motives. Puzlwat was a very genuine person with pure motives and he loved Anztarza and his people. Monitoring all aspects on Earth gave him the worst possible impression of our mindset. The seven deadly sins were only a minor part of Puzlwat's overall understanding of the human trait. And so to him it was impossible that no trace of those characteristics had been found in our minds. He simply concluded that somehow we must be cleverly concealing our true intentions. And nothing I could do or say was going to make him change his opinion.

'And what will you do when we reach the Steins asteroid and you find yourself unable to affect its position or orbit?' Mytanzto asked aloud in quite a base toned voice which I found surprisingly different from all the other Oannes voices I'd heard.

'Well, if I am unable to move Steins with my telekinetic ability,' I said slowly in my softest and gentlest voice, 'then I must ask for your help in further developing my gift so that one day I will be able to achieve exactly that. I have never moved anything larger than a log of wood so I too have my doubts as to whether or not I am able to move this three mile piece of rock.'

I stopped here and gave my most innocent of smiles. I was tempted to demonstrate my telekinetic gift by moving my mug of tea to the far end of the table but I could see it would achieve nothing with these two. Their real fears were for a threat to their lifestyle being corrupted by too early an integration with humans.

'Let us not diverge in our intentions at the moment,' I said in the same low voice, 'so I would ask you to drink a glass of Wazu with us. And let us agree that what has been done has been done and so we must make the best of it. What can't be helped must be endured. Let us also agree that no further contact is to be made with humans and that we are to be the only exceptions. I believe I am the cause of that choice of contact because of the extraordinary gifts that were given to me and which I revealed to you through the 'thinking stone'. You know of our religious beliefs and I have this faith that my gifts were given to me for a specific purpose. My family believe the same. I believe that one of the reasons may be to divert Zarama from its current path. The other reason also affects Earth but in the longer term. And that is to alter the orbital path of Nazmos bringing it closer to Raznat and giving it a more Earth-like climate. In a billion years Earth will become too hot for survival but Nazmos will continue on for a further trillion years at least. As such full integration with the Oannes nation would be in Earth's best interest.'

I could see I had Puzlwat's attention but I don't think that Mytanzto was even listening. I could see his thoughts were in a closed loop of objection at our presence in Anztarza. His mind had been made up for him by arguments that Puzlwat had presented earlier in November and I now realised that his intelligence level was of a somewhat limited calibre and considerably below that of Puzlwat. He was like a faithful bulldog that had been given a command and would not diverge from his original perceived task. I decided to try a different approach.

'Mytanzto,' I said to him directly, 'let me ask you this. If all that has occurred could be undone completely would that be a solution you might wish for? Just say the word and I will request Muznant and Brazjaf to cancel all arrangements and return us to our home on Earth. I am not just saying this but I mean it as well. If that would make you comfortable then so it shall be. But think what happens in 2,421 years time when Zarama approaches both our worlds. We will not be alive then but your descendents will say that there was once a chance to stop Zarama but it was not taken up. Do you think that another will come by then with the gifts I possess? Can you take that chance? I am here now and I have agreed to do everything in my power to prevent this disaster. You have lived with knowledge of Zarama's approach for hundreds of years. We have just learned of it and already I feel sad for both our peoples. Perhaps I may not possess enough telekinetic power to stop Zarama but I do know that I will try my utmost to succeed even unto my very last breath.'

I paused here not for a rest but because a coldness of fear came over me and I felt quite light headed. I put my head in my hands with my elbows on the table. The emotion of concern from my family filled the room and I knew that I had spoken some fateful words. Mum had come up behind me and pushing my hands aside she began to gently massage my temples. Her cool hands felt good and I soon felt better so I continued.

'The people of Anztarza saw me for what I was and made their choice to take up this option now,' I said. 'The chance that such a moment would arrive was the reason for all the monitoring tablets distributed around on the Earth all these thousands of years. Ever since you have known about Zarama you have also had recourse to your ancient mythology. What does it say? Did it refer to someone from Earth coming forth to deliver? And if such a person was picked up on your monitors would you not investigate to see if that was the one? Or should you avoid contact with Earth people altogether simply because many of them are not fit to meet?'

Puzlwat sat mentally quiet while all forms of confusion raced through Mytanzto's mind. I realised that I needed to calm Mytanzto so I sent him an emotion of peace and affection of such intensity that even I was surprised by it. Mytanzto breathed a sigh and I'm not sure if it was of relief or the realisation that he had simply objected to contact with us because at the time he felt we were a threat to Anztarza. Suddenly he saw the wider picture and became convinced that the chief ministers may have been right after all. Was not Anztarza's purpose to monitor the Earth people with the aim of discovering that gifted person from their mythology?

Mum still stood behind me and I sensed her sadness. She too had felt a chill when I spoke those fateful words. Puzlwat read our emotions and I'm sure he felt a twinge of regret. I sensed a change in him but he remained stoic and conveyed nothing. He had closed his mind completely and aimed a communication at Mytanzto who suddenly stood up and left the room. I was surprised at this since it was usual for a farewell Sewa to be politely adhered to.

'Forgive my friend,' said Puzlwat in his squeaky voice, 'but I think he suddenly felt unwell and needs a rest in his sleep tank. As you so rightly say we cannot undo what has been done and so must make the best of it. I do not know if you are the foretold one so I cannot comment upon it. But I shall not object to your presence among us Oannes as the stark choice has already been made. Perhaps the chief ministers were right to bring you to Anztarza to confirm your credentials. I personally will keep an open mind on the matter. You have been most persuasive in your argument and your threat to withdraw from it all at my instigation would not bode well for my political standing. I will not be the cause of dissention in Anztarza and that an available option was not investigated. You may be that option but personally I do not think so. You have done nothing so far to make me think otherwise and in my mind I have a faint hope that I may be mistaken in my opinion of you. However I must continue in my distrust of you and your motives until I see proof to the contrary. Our communication has been polite and constructive and I thank you for it. Perhaps we can meet again after you have finished with Steins. You and your family are not as I imagined you to be. I find you a pleasant and honest group of people. Have a pleasant evening.'

Puzlwat stood up slowly and performed a polite farewell Sewa greeting before turning and walking briskly through the door to the corridor. I then reached up and briefly put my hand over mum's and conveyed my thanks for her care and that I was feeling quite well now. She leaned down and kissed the top of my head before returning to her seat. Inwardly I had a feeling of jubilation with regard to Puzlwat though I had qualms for Mytanzto's attitude. He was not one to be persuaded by intelligent argument. For some reason Jimmy Marshal whom we used to call 'General' at school came into my mind. I smiled when I thought of the red spots I had marked on his face and how he'd gone to the school nurse Angela Stevens. Other names also came to mind; David Jacobs, Rory Matthews and Mike Marr and I wondered how they had fared after leaving school.

As far as Mytanzto was concerned I decided to let time do its work. He must come to his own conclusions about us but I was sure that Puzlwat would be the main factor in influencing Mytanzto's opinion. And behind both I knew was someone who had looked favourably on me at our first contact in Dome-4 amphitheatre and later at the arranged banquet. And that person was Puzlwat's wife Nogozat. I sensed her excitement at my presence in Anztarza and I had noticed her often looking in my direction. I'm not that naïve that I don't know when someone is attracted to me and keen to become a friend. Though I think the anticipation and hype created prior to my arrival in Anztarza had a lot to do with it. I was a celebrity and all were eager to see what I was like. It was very welcome and I knew that Nogozat would be a great influence in our favour. I would certainly hope so.

I conveyed all my thoughts to the group and Tania squeezed my hand to show her support. I looked down at her as she looked up at me and our eyes and hearts met in a brief moment of intense desire. A pain spread across my chest as if it were being pumped up to near bursting. I thought that love must be a solid thing to cause such sweetness in its pain. So this is what is meant by the pangs of love. Tania was the sweetest, loveliest, gentlest most lovable of women and I was proud to call her mine. I loved her with all my heart and soul and being and knew we were meant for each other and to be together for always. I was impatient for Tania to finish college when we could marry and live together. I could not see into the future but knew by instinct that our life together would be a happy one. Roll on 2006.

'I love you,' I whispered as we stared at each other.

'And I love you too, Ashley Bonner,' she said calmly, 'and don't you forget it with all these women throwing looks at you.'

I had to laugh. Tania had such a wonderful way of easing the moment. I wonder if she read my thoughts just now. But she couldn't control the emotion of love that filled the room. There was also quite a bit of pride emotion mixed in and I knew this came from our parents as they watched us.

We stayed on for another cup of tea and some chatty banter when Uncle Ron came out with a few of his long drawn out jokes with a moral to the punch line. I liked the one about the ancient African chief who collected the thrones of all his defeated enemies and stored them in his loft. Eventually at a big feast they all crashed down upon him and his guests. Uncle Ron dragged out the punch line by asking us what we thought was the moral to the story. Even then he wouldn't say till I threatened to read his mind.

'Okay then,' he said. 'Here it is. People who live in grass houses shouldn't stow thrones.'

General laughter ensued with a few moans as well. Eventually we all went to our cabins for a well earned rest; it had been a long and exciting day. It was now near midnight by my watch and I couldn't believe that we were zipping through space at 15,000 miles each second.

I thought of my life together with Tania as I lay on my bed with granddad already beginning to snore. I expected a long and happy one. I thought of green meadows, village lanes, dense forests, warm sunshine and gentle warm breezes blowing through my hair as I drifted into sleep. And the very last thought that pervaded my subconscious was that I was not on Earth but on Nazmos. How strange is that I thought?

When I awoke I knew I had overslept because granddad was already up and washed and dressed. I looked at my watch and it showed just after six o'clock. Zanos answered my query and conveyed that 520-Green had reached destination and we were approaching the Steins asteroid under impulse power and had been for the last hour. We were now a few thousand miles away and would approach to within a few hundred miles before beginning the parking loop manoeuvre.

Granddad said that everyone was up too and a standard breakfast of bread and toast with butter, cheese, jam and marmalade was ready in the dining lounge. I wondered who must prepare all this for us as we hadn't as yet met our chef. I must ask Bulzezatna about this.

The other adults were already there and I conveyed a good morning through my communication badge. I received many pleasantries in return and special ones from the captain, Brazjaf and Muznant who were together in the control room. We were all to be taken there once we had breakfasted.

I had a quick shower and shave before granddad and I walked into the dining lounge. Tania and Katy had only just come in ahead of us and I thought how smart everyone looked fresh faced and smart in their colourful Oannes outfits. I felt just as smart in mine.

I wasn't particularly hungry but mum and dad insisted I have some toast which I did. After all they said I had some work to do today with the asteroid experiments. I think there were two for today and one on the morrow. Tania poured my tea lovingly but I buttered my own toast. I liked it plain without jam or marmalade. Katy found this odd because she knew that when I had fried eggs for breakfast I always put a dollop of jam on my plate. Mum had usually smiled at this idiosyncrasy of mine but never said anything one way or the other. I had support from granddad though who said he had tried it and quite liked it too; a bit like having cranberry sauce with your turkey at Christmas. I don't suppose we'll be doing that anymore.

I was on my second cup of tea when deputy Tatizblay entered the lounge and conveyed that everything was prepared. He sat with us for a while as we finished up and watched us clear the table. He had an amused expression on his face but also one of approval. I could see that he was impressed with our good manners and our family bond. I conveyed that most families on Earth behaved in a similar manner especially the older generation. It was only some of those youngsters who didn't have a particular ambition or aim in life who became bored and caused trouble on the streets. This was a worldwide problem which I often put down to a failure in our societies for not providing good and proper guidance during the formative years. At present this was a contentious issue among most politicians. There was the hope that that in the future we would learn from our mistakes. Tatizblay smiled and then suggested we make our way to the control room which we did.

Captain Bulzezatna welcomed us again with our own greeting of 'Good morning' and we all responded in unison. The captain pointed to a lower view panel and there sat a small marble sized bright whitish-looking rock. Zanos conveyed that 2867 Steins asteroid was fifty miles away and the ship was doing a slow flyby under 0.9g of constant acceleration. 520-Green was performing a standard 100 mile flat loop pattern in order to keep Steins within view for all.

I had to smile when I conveyed that to me Steins looked like the face of a bird with a beaky protuberance and two dips for eyes in just the right places. Tania said she couldn't see this and neither could Katy. Mum said she did notice the eyes and the nose but nothing else. The others just shook their heads as a negative. I guess I was always the imaginative one especially with the billowing clouds at home. I once saw a cat chasing a dog and found it quite funny but it all changed to nothing within moments.

Steins looked small at this distance even though it was over three miles in rough diameter. Zanos indicated that the ship was near stationary at the moment but was accelerating towards its next loop turn in about fifteen minutes. The Oannes were never in a hurry and Captain Bulzezatna conveyed for us to spend as long as we wished here looking at Steins. I think we all took the opportunity to get a closer magnified look at the surface of the asteroid. Surprisingly the surface was really quite granulated as though it was a bit volcanic. However there was not much of interest here and I returned to normal view. I think the others did the same.

Bulzezatna then conveyed to us the procedure we would follow prior to boarding the shuttle craft. There would in fact be two shuttle craft leaving together and each under the command of one of the deputies.

I looked at Steins as it gradually sank in view to the lower part of the view panel and then disappeared from sight. Zanos conveyed that the loop turn would begin in two minutes so we all stayed to witness it. The sky was devoid of stars because of the reflected brightness from Steins so nothing was visible above us. Then gradually Steins once again came rapidly into view till it stopped at the edge of the top view panel. I had no sensation whatsoever of the ships turn manoeuvre and thought what a lovely way to travel in space.

I then indicated that I was ready for the next stage of the plan and Tatizblay asked us to follow him. We left the control room and walked the length of the craft towards the cargo bay area. We went down the ramp to the shuttle bay and then along the balcony overlooking the parked craft. Tatizblay opened a door off this and we entered a large rectangular hall. Along each of the walls were ranged lots of open storage facilities within which hung arrays of gold coloured very shiny overall type garments. Tatizblay conveyed that these were our space electro-static suits which must be worn by all passengers and crew whenever shuttle journeys were undertaken. Although the shuttles could function in a similar manner to a spaceship and provide a small amount of gravity there were moments when there was no gravity effect whatsoever.

The electro-static suits were internally charged with static electricity so that the suit was attracted to the material of the shuttle which was at an opposite electrostatic charge. However the suit was mainly a precaution only since all passengers were held firmly in their seats with gentle thigh clamps. I couldn't wait to see how all this worked.

Because of our size special static suits had been made up for us just as they had made us our tunics and leggings. I loved the way I knew exactly where my suit was hanging as did the rest of our group. Our badges had communicated the information to us but it was as though our suits had a mind of their own asking us to come to them. We also knew exactly how the suits must be put on and had to be first opened from neck down to crotch. I think Zanos was behind the direction of all this information.

The suit itself was very loose fitting and baggy so we didn't have to remove any of our clothes or footwear. But once I had closed up the long front flap the suit seemed to tighten slightly around me though without causing any discomfort. And yet on the outside it still gave the appearance of being loose and baggy. I realised that there was an inner layer to the suit which was somehow internally separated from the outer layer. There were no mirrors so we just looked at each other to see how we must look. We looked like posh mechanics wearing shiny gold coloured overalls.

I noticed that Tatizblay had also got on an electro-static suit and with his back web fin totally enclosed. He immediately responded to my query and conveyed that the fin was folded sideways and was not the least bit uncomfortable. A full length padding allowed normal seating posture inside the shuttle.

We left the hall and went through another doorway and down a ramp to the floor of the shuttle bay. Our suits were practically weightless and we walked with a surprising degree of comfort. They were silky quiet with none of that rustling noise one associates with ordinary fabrics; especially in the region where arms and legs rubbed adjacent material.

Tatizblay led us to our shuttle which was rather large at over thirty feet in length and bright yellow in colour. Like the Anztarza deck transporters we had to climb the six steps at the rear up into the shuttle seating area. There were about forty well spaced seats in two rows of three seats each and some were already occupied by smiling Oannes in suits similar to ours.

The view panels around the shuttle sides and front gave a good all-round view and I felt as if I was on Kazaztan's 536-Orange Transporter. Except in this case we had seating and a full enclosure around us. Our shuttle was 5202-Green and was to be commanded by deputy Tatizblay. The other shuttle that would accompany ours was 5201-Green and Rubandiz was its commander.

I could see across to the gold decked Oannes entering the other shuttle beside us and both shuttles seemed to fill up quite quickly. There were three aisles along the length of our shuttle; narrower ones on the sides and a broad one down the centre. The rear three seats on the left side were a raised affair where the commander of the shuttle sat along with any of his crew.

Tatizblay took us to the very front of the shuttle and got us seated and clamped down. On the left front row were Katy, Tania and then me. On my right were mum, dad and granddad Eric. Behind them were Jerry and Milly and behind me were Uncle Ron and Aunt Brenda. Then there were the three chief ministers on one side in our row with Brazjaf and Muznant behind. And on the other side of the chief ministers were Puzlwat and Mytanzto. The rest of the seats were filled by other keen Oannes such that we were about twenty persons on our shuttle. The other shuttle beside us looked rather fuller.

Zanos then conveyed that all shuttles must be made ready for departure. All hatches and doors were slowly shut including those of all other craft parked in the bay. All crew personnel exited the bay and the bay lights began to dim. Zanos conveyed that 520-Green was approaching zero velocity in its loop pattern and opening of bay doors was about to commence.

Then a very surprising thing happened. I sensed that all our electrostatic suits must have been activated for suddenly the hairs on our heads stood out on end. We men didn't look too odd but the women looked decidedly ridiculous. We saw the funny side and began laughing at the situation. I conveyed generally that head scarves or something similar were required for the women,

Since the Oannes had no hair on their bodies this had never been a problem for them. Zanos intimated that departure would be delayed to the next zero velocity status to facilitate the supply of suitable head scarves for the Earth women.

The lights in the shuttle bay were normalised and eventually a crew member arrived with a roll of eighteen inch wide silky material similar to the gold of the static suits along with a cutting and sealing tool. As he boarded our shuttle mum conveyed to him that one yard lengths would make perfect head scarves. These were then handed out and once again the shuttle made secure. I must say Tania looked quite school girlish in her golden rain hat. She gave me a dig and a frown when I conveyed this across to her.

Once again the departure procedure was initiated and this time both shuttles rose upwards and closer to the bay ceiling. They gradually rotated outwards away from each other till we were facing the rear of the ship. Very slowly the entire back of the shuttle bay seemed to fold open and our shuttle moved towards the open blackness beyond. Zanos-onboard was in complete control and gradually the huge bulk of 520-Green seemed to accelerate away from us.

Although the large soft thigh clamps gripped and held us down to our seats firmly we were now under no gravitational influence whatsoever. I had never been weightless before and a kind of nausea crept up into my head. I peered across at Tania and Katy on my left and then at mum on my right and all looked as I felt. I imagine we were all feeling queasy. I didn't think the asteroid experiment was going to work at least not with me feeling like this.

But then I began to receive a very strong hypnotic type suggestion and suddenly it was as if I couldn't think for myself. It was as if someone else was in control of my thoughts. I began to feel euphoric and I looked at Tania beside me and from a pale wan appearance of a moment ago she was transformed into someone with a radiant glow on her face and seemed to be enjoying herself. It was like when were on a ride at Alton Towers. I had felt sick to my stomach while she screamed with delight at the thrill of it all. Just thinking about it made me want to laugh out aloud and I think I may have done just that for Tania squeezed my hand hard and mum looked smilingly across at me.

Anyway I was myself again and realised that the nausea had vanished out of my system. It was as though I had been given a travel sickness tablet that had worked instantly. I then knew that this was the work of Zanos-onboard and I was thankful. I glanced around and everyone looked comfortable and seemed to be enjoying the ride in the nil-gravity conditions.

The shuttle had worked its way around so that Steins was now ahead of us and clearly visible in the front view panels. Gradually it grew in size until it nearly filled one whole window panel. I looked at its rough surface and now it seemed ugly and menacing. The other shuttle craft was about a mile away to our right.

Zanos-onboard now conveyed that we were stationary relative to the asteroid and needed to move around to the correct position for my telekinetic push. Without any sensation of shuttle motion the asteroid seemed to slowly rotate from left to right for a few minutes. It then became stationary again which really meant that we had completed our manoeuvre.

Deputy Tatizblay conveyed that the shuttle was correctly positioned and that the planned experiment could begin. I conveyed back a quick open message of thanks and that I was ready. I then went into 'pink' mode and applied a concentrated telekinetic push with my greatest degree of effort and for as long as I could hold my breath. I had gone to a very deep rosy pink status when everything was silent and shrouded in a foggy mist. To me this was the largest object I had ever encountered or tried to move. I considered that it would require a maximum effort on my part. I regret to say this was a big mistake and a gross miscalculation.

My first mistake was to return to normal mode in an instant. The second was that I did not know the calibre of my telekinetic gift and so had applied an excessive force. What an error that was.

As I returned to normal mode the asteroid Steins sped away from the shuttle position with such ferocity of acceleration that within a split second it suddenly disintegrated into a pile of expanding debris and dust. Within seconds even the dust cloud had receded into the distance and was not visible anymore.

I put my head in my hands and expressed my sorrow for an experiment gone wrong. But all I got in return was an all-pervading emotion of wonder and awe for what had just occurred. It was as though the Oannes observers had hoped for something powerful and spectacular and their wishes had been dramatically fulfilled. It was conveyed to me by many that if only that could have been the threatening Zarama then a great problem would have been solved.

I looked up and around the shuttle and was relieved that the Oannes people saw this in a different light. But I now realised that my gift of telekinesis was raw and wild and I definitely needed to acquire a more positive control of the awesome power that had just been displayed.

I needed to calibrate the output from this gift so that I could apply it in a systematic and safe manner. I conveyed to all in general that I required a lot more practice in the art of telekinesis and I hoped that the larger asteroid Masursky with an average rough diameter of eleven miles would present a better challenge. I would also like to be positioned at a much greater distance away for the next experiment. My inner voice gave me a solution in how I must apply my telekinetic push in the future. It would be a staged affair but I had much to resolve prior to it.

Suddenly I began to feel fatigued and drowsy. My eyes felt a heaviness descend upon them and I just couldn't keep them open. Sleep definitely beckoned and I closed my eyes to rest them. I became oblivious to everything around me apart from a tight squeeze upon my hand. I was at peace with my Tania by my side. I sensed an emotion of concern and a command that the shuttle return immediately to the mother craft.

I must have dozed off for the next thing I remember was that we were in the bright lights of the shuttle bay and gravity had returned. The thigh clamps had released and I was awake again. I thought that sleep in a weightless condition was most relaxing. Mum said that it had taken nearly half an hour of manoeuvring to get the two craft together at the predetermined loop position before the shuttle could enter the open bay. I expressed the wish for a further rest in my cabin and it was with some considerable leaden effort that I managed to reach the static room and then my cabin bed. It looked so inviting that I flopped facedown upon it and fell instantly into a deep sleep.

When I awoke I was somehow in my under-shorts and vest and lying face up with my head on the pillow and bed covering up to my shoulders. I hadn't a clue as to how long I had been out but I did feel refreshed and full of vibrant energy. My watch was on the table and I sat up, reached across and picked it up. It showed the time as half past two, but which day. How long had I been asleep?

Obviously my thoughts had been picked up and the door opened and in trooped all the gang plus Brazjaf and Muznant. They conveyed that it was the same day and that I had been asleep for nearly five hours. Katy had a jug of Wazu and she poured me out a glass which I drank in double quick time and then held it out for a refill. My throat felt dry and I felt really thirsty but decided to stop at the second glass.

'So what's been happening while I've been passed out?' I asked aloud.

There was a brief silence and then Brazjaf conveyed a full account of the events since I'd returned to my cabin this morning. The ship had got under way quite quickly and the neutron generators had accelerated it to its planned 15,000 mps velocity towards the asteroid Masursky. Arrival time was approximately about an hour away.

Again another short mental silence ensued. This time Muznant conveyed the news. The scientists on board the second shuttle were mystified by the lack of readings on their analytical instruments. Even Zanos-onboard had got nothing. They recorded a nil force being exerted on Steins but then for no apparent reason it had suddenly accelerated away and disintegrated. There was confusion as to when and how I had worked my telekinetic push upon the asteroid.

'But you already know the answer to that,' I conveyed trying to be as patient as I could although I believe a note of exasperation showed in my emotion. I then reiterated about my gift of making time in the universe slow down to a near standstill. Quite obviously while I was in this phase all their bio-analysers and technology also came to a near standstill and so did not and could not recognise what I was doing. And since I had exerted my telekinetic efforts while I was in 'pink' mode they could not sense or record anything. So I asked the obvious question. How much force would have been required to cause the late Steins to undergo such acceleration as to result in its annihilation?

Zanos immediately answered the query and conveyed that the amount of force energy expended upon the asteroid would have been in the region of about thirty to forty times the neutron generator power necessary to accelerate 520-Green close to the speed of light. This surprised me no end as I'm sure it also did for everyone on the ship.

I conveyed my regret for the excessive use of force upon Steins and that in future I would be more circumspect in how I applied my telekinetic push. My inner voice had already given me a solution and I knew the path I must adopt. However, I would as a first course apply my telekinetic push upon Masursky without going into 'pink' mode. Zanos could then indicate how much force had been applied as I gradually increased my efforts. This would give me an initial evaluation of my telekinetic gift. I knew that by going into a lighter shade of 'pink' mode where Time was slowed to about half normal rate then any force I exerted would be magnified to double that force when normal mode was resumed. If I slowed Time to a fifth then the force exerted by me would be magnified to five times that effort. I would need to regulate myself positively while in the pink zone and know exactly the amount of force I was applying at every stage. Unfortunately I could receive no real assistance from the Oannes scientists upon this matter and I must conduct this learning experience on my own.

I must practice controlling the relative variances in Time pace using a normal clock as a measure. I would use the simple measure of counting out the seconds mentally against the slowed ticking of that clock or digital timer. I must practice this often and in my mind I knew exactly how I would go about it.

I conveyed all these thoughts as an open communication and received back a general note of approval. I wondered that I had not thought to follow this course long ago. But then I knew that I was on a learning cycle and there was yet much more that I could learn. It was a matter of horses for courses. A solution only presented itself when I encountered a new problem or specific task. I had plenty of time for practice in the days, weeks and years ahead.

I don't know why but Robert Black came into my mind and I remembered our sessions in the cricket practice nets when I threw the ball to give him that extra needed batting practice. I would throw the hard red ball at a variety of speeds and angles to give him the necessary experience in recognising the different strokes he must use. And he did improve tremendously and we became good friends as a result. The thought soon passed and I returned to thinking about my control of Time.

I thought that once I was in 'pink' mode I could go towards the darker shades for a greater slowing of Time. It would be interesting to see how I could vary my control of it. What would be my first 'pink' setting? My inner voice seemed to indicate that this should be a fifth of normal Time pace. I was ready for Masursky and was feeling quite refreshed from my sleep. But I was rather famished and conveyed as much.

'You get dressed and we shall wait for you in the dining lounge,' said mum as they left the cabin. Tania stayed back and came and sat beside me on the bed and said she'd wait here with me; for which I was glad. I had a quick shower as I felt rather grubby after my sleep. Tania went to the clothes storage space and chose an outfit for me to wear and placed it on the bed. She also placed a clean vest and boxer shorts beside these and conveyed this to me.

When she handed me my bath towel I was half tempted to pull her towards me but she sensed this and told me to behave myself.

'There'll be plenty of time for that after we are married,' she said with a mischievous grin. She busied herself looking through my wardrobe of tunics and leggings as I got dressed and we were soon walking hand in hand towards the dining lounge. We'd only spent about a minute after I got ready in a spell of light kisses.

Muznant sat opposite me and conveyed that I should eat an extra portion of Yaztraka mash as it was rich in protein. I couldn't wait to tuck in and happily did as was suggested. But I'm a small eater and in no time was feeling quite full. But once again I was thirsty so had two glasses of the Wazu drink which was nicely flavoured with its hint of roses. A pinch of salt was added to my glass just before I drank it. Apparently the Wazu seeds are adversely affected by the salt and so you must never add the salt to the jug. The salt made the Wazu more potent and the reason given to me by Brazjaf was that the seeds got agitated by the presence of the salt and so gave out a boost of their goodness. I wasn't so sure about this but thought that the salt definitely improved the Wazu in taste.

A message came through from Zanos that a reverse slow down of the craft would begin in ten minutes. For personal comfort all crew and passengers were recommended to remain in a seated or reclining position. Brazjaf conveyed that we should be alright as we were.

'In that case,' said Milly, 'I have enough time to make us all a nice pot of tea. Come on Jerry you can give me a hand in the kitchen.'

'Elderly husband and wife sloping off on their own for a kiss and a cuddle I suppose,' I conveyed to the group who all smiled back at me. They knew I was joking of course especially about the 'elderly' connotation.

'You watch yourself Ashley Bonner,' said Milly aloud from the kitchen area, 'a bit of respect for your future in-laws please, thank you very much. I see Tania has a lot of training to do.'

We all laughed.

Muznant and Brazjaf were getting used to our sense of humour and I think they quite liked our light-hearted banter. With their telepathic prowess the Oannes could never tell jokes with a surprise punch line ending since the listener instantly knew the whole tale. But an idea came to me that if the joke was in written form then no one would know the ending until it was actually reached. A joke book was definitely the answer. I had one at home and decided to bring it along on my next visit. I wonder if it would make the rounds in Anztarza or would they even find it amusing. But then I thought that surely their monitoring people had already picked up on the theme and I was out of date with my idea.

Zanos now communicated that a very precise chronometer existed in my cabin. This could read at thousands of a second of elapsing time and would be ideal for my time practice when I was in 'pink' mode. I had a mental conception of the duration of a normal time second and I could use this as a measure in my practice sessions.

Zanos now conveyed that the ship had been directionally reversed and that the neutron generators would operate in the next minute. Here at the dining table I relaxed myself against the seat backrest and waited for the sensation of the acceleration that was to come. Nothing seemed to happen at least as far as any gravitational sensation was concerned. I waited another minute and was just about to query Zanos when I received the communication that all had gone to plan and 520-Green was now just several thousand miles from the Masursky asteroid. The space craft would approach to within a few hundred miles before going into its parking loop pattern.

It was about half an hour later that the captain invited us to the control room. The moment I entered I sensed something was different. The captain had dimmed the room lighting but it still remained bright inside. I then saw this large bright rock-like object floating just outside the left lower view panel. As I approached closer I recognised it as the Masursky asteroid. Zanos answered my query and conveyed that the asteroid was 120 miles away and was currently in the full sunny side position relative to us. It shone brilliantly like a full moon did on Earth only it seemed much brighter out here in the darkness of space. It looked cold and foreboding and suddenly I grew afraid of it. It sat out there in front of us just staring at us and I knew it to be just a lifeless experimental object. I still didn't feel kindly towards it and wondered that I should have any emotion for it at all.

Perhaps it represented a challenge that I was not as yet fully prepared for. My subconscious feared what I might do to Masursky as I remembered the disaster that had occurred to Steins. And then an irritation and impatience grew inside me that seemed to want it all over and done with. I conveyed my feelings to the captain and everyone else on board. The Oannes were really open with their minds and I liked that I had got this irritation off my chest and into the open.

I think mum and dad and the others sensed that I was in an odd mood and they came around me for support. Tania put both her arms around me and gave me a tight hug. Then mum and Milly also joined her in a group hug and dad put his hand on my shoulder.

'Don't worry son,' he said, 'we are all here with you. Just take this one easy at first.'

And I knew exactly what he meant and what I was to do. Granddad and Katy stood right close to me and Jerry had his hand on Milly. There was a great atmosphere of affection around me and I could sense support coming from Bulzezatna and her deputies. Captain Bulzezatna conveyed that there was no requirement for haste. The asteroid was not going anywhere at least not just yet and 520-Green was content in its parking loop manoeuvre. The shuttle craft were in full readiness and simply awaited my pleasure.

If anything the Oannes possess a great degree of patience. They never seemed to be in a hurry in anything they did. Perhaps this philosophy of calmness contributed to their longevity. They were so different from us humans with our inbred impatience for getting everything done to a time scale.

I let myself relax and conveyed to the captain that I would like about half an hour before starting the experiment on Masursky. For the moment I'd just like to take it easy and look out at the asteroid through the view panels.

When I magnified the image of Masursky I noticed its similarity to Steins. And suddenly it appeared quite benign and didn't feel menacing at all. The affection and goodwill surrounding me infiltrated my inner thoughts and spread out to Masursky. Steins had been utterly destroyed; annihilated by me and I felt sadness for it. Masursky was growing on me as though it was alive and had the right to exist. I'd like to meet it and knew instantly what I was going to do.

When I conveyed my request to the captain she understood my reason and gave her assent and conveyed her pleasure that I felt obliged to land upon Masursky's surface. It was to be a sort of touch greeting before the experiment. Bulzezatna however stressed that I must on no account leave the safe environment of the shuttle craft, to which I readily agreed.

The Oannes considered all objects in space as having the right of respect and Bulzezatna was pleased that I had adopted such a philosophy. Masursky to me had altered from its initial menacing impression to one of a benign neighbour that reminded me of Earth's moon.

So once again we all got into our electro-static suits and trudged down to the shuttle bay. We repeated our seating positions on the shuttle 5202-Green and waited for the appropriate moment to exit the mother craft at the end of its parking loop manoeuvre. The lights dimmed and the bay doors then opened slowly. Both shuttles rose upwards and passed through the open doors and into the blackness beyond. They kept in line abreast formation as we accelerated towards the asteroid. I did not feel nauseous at my weightlessness and assumed that I had got used to it even though it was only my second such flight. As we approached Masursky the shuttles moved further apart till we must have had a few miles of separation. We approached Masursky to within fifty miles and it just filled the front view panel. I could make out a graininess to its surface texture and the small strike craters were very apparent with their little dip shadows. There was a large flattened area close to the curve of the lee night shadow and I mentally conveyed this as a good landing location. Our accompanying shuttle now drew back to a standstill as we continued on.

Masursky grew ever larger and suddenly it was no longer an asteroid but part of a desert plain on some foreign land. It filled our view and as we approached closer it was all around us. I no longer recognised my selected landing area but I reckoned that Zanos-onboard had made the computation correctly. The reflected light was quite dazzling and the shuttle windows compensated by developing a deepening tint to adjust to the brightness.

I'm not sure when the shuttle actually touched down on the asteroid since I felt no bump or sudden deceleration. Tatizblay conveyed that we were now upon the asteroid surface and would remain here for five minutes.

Everyone peered this way and that but there was nothing to see really; just a white sand textured surface that stretched to right and left of the shuttle. To the front there was the shadow of the shuttle stretching all the way to the edge of the asteroid which disappeared into the darkness of its own night. Tatizblay had settled the shuttle down with its back to the sunlight which I welcomed and considered a most discerning decision.

We were all mesmerized by our shuttle's shadow which seemed to possess a life of its own as we lifted slowly upwards. The shuttle shadow separated itself from us and raced away into the asteroid night where it completely disappeared.

We rose up and away from Masursky and the shuttle manoeuvred around so we could see it recede. We retreated to a position that Zanos-onboard conveyed as being sixty miles distant. The other shuttle then came into view on our right and about two miles away. We were stationary with respect to each other and I imagined also stationary as regards the asteroid. Once again I looked keenly at Masursky and at the point where we had settled. I wondered what the view must have been for the occupants of 5201-Green looking down on us sitting there close to the asteroid's night shadow. Our own shuttle's shadow must have been large and clearly visible and immediately I received a clear pictorial image of the scene in question. This was conveyed by deputy Rubandiz who was in command of the other shuttle. I sent him my thanks and best wishes and stressed that the image of us on the asteroid surface looked more exciting as a view than actually being on the surface. The Eiffel Tower at night is more exciting to view from the top of the Mont Parnesse building than from being on the Tower itself. I should have remembered that.

The two shuttles were now side by side facing the asteroid and it was conveyed to me that we were in the correct calculated directional position for me to exert my telekinetic push. However I waited another ten minutes or so and just thought about Masursky and where it was destined to travel after I had done with it. I kept my mind open so all were receiving my thoughts and I wondered at the Oannes patience. So we just sat there in our static suits with the clamps exerting a gentle pressure upon our thighs. Even Zanos-onboard conveyed nothing.

Gradually I thought about the large object in our front view panel and decided that I should begin moving it away from us. I did not concentrate my mind as intensely as I had done with Steins but just kept up a controlled telekinetic effort. I did not realise that as the asteroid began to slowly move away from us so also did Zanos-onboard decide to keep pace with it. I thought nothing was happening so decided to go 'pink' and apply a similar small push before returning to normal Time mode.

It was only after that that I felt the shuttle's acceleration as it tried to keep up with the receding Masursky. Zanos then conveyed to me that the intention was to maintain a constant sixty mile distance from the asteroid as the experiment continued and to give me the best chance of success. Zanos conveyed that the asteroid had received a good push that had boosted its perihelion orbital velocity by 3 mps and it was still accelerating. I wondered at this since I had ceased my concentration upon the asteroid. But then I remembered the sandbag suspended in our garage when I had first discovered I could move objects through telekinesis at the age of eighteen. I had discovered then that I had only to look at the sand bag and think about moving it and the deed was accomplished. I could move the sandbag just as I wished by simply thinking it even if my back was turned or I was in another room. So I now decided to stop any push action against the asteroid and conveyed that I was done with the experiment.

I felt great since I had hardly strained myself pushing Masursky. There was no tiredness or sleepiness as I had experienced the last time with Steins. I wondered why that was. I suppose I was on a learning curve and I felt keen now to go on to the next asteroid Mathilde which at thirty three miles in diameter was by far the largest of the three by quite a margin. I also felt rather smug in my new found confidence. But I knew also that I had a long way to develop if I was to have any success with Nazmos. And Zarama was another spectre lurking on the distant horizon. How and when would I ever be ready for that challenge; certainly not at the present time?

We had to wait some considerable time before we could approach the rendezvous point with the mother ship. It had been at the opposite end of the loop pattern and would take about fifteen minutes to be within docking acceptance.

I looked for Masursky but it had receded rapidly and was now just a tiny bright speck in the distance. And that too soon disappeared as the stars around us once more became visible. The universe looked even more spectacular now since we seemed to be so alone in the middle of it. I could imagine what it must really look like if our own sun were dimmed to just a distant star. Such would be the case if we were just outside Neptune's orbit. It dumbfounded me how the brilliance of the Milky Way and all the stars in the heavens could be damped out by a local light source.

Zanos-on-board took us to the new waiting point and it was not long before the familiar sight of 520-Green came into view. The view was of its underside and it was obviously decelerating as it got closer. It got slower and slower and I noticed its rear bay doors were wide open. Both shuttles moved towards it then and suddenly we were inside the shuttle bay with each setting down on its designated parking spot. We settled with a very slight bump and immediately I felt the joy of gravity back upon my system. The bay doors closed and the lights inside brightened to indicate that normal atmosphere had been restored. As we exited the shuttle I found I had to control my walk and not slap my feet. Mum and dad smiled at me as we walked to the static suits dressing room and I felt quite euphoric at what I had achieved today. But for me the icing on the cake was the look of admiration I got from both Puzlwat and Mytanzto as I passed them in the shuttle aisle. I think I may have won them over for now.

Muznant conveyed that she was not feeling too good so she and Brazjaf went to their cabin for a rest. Although by the time the two deputies had led us to Captain Bulzezatna in the control room Brazjaf also entered a few minutes later. We all expressed our concern for Muznant. Brazjaf conveyed has appreciation and said that this wife was going through a body adjustment for the child within her. She was partial to her sleep tank and had raised the water temperature slightly for greater comfort. He conveyed that she would probably feel better after a couple of hours rest.

Captain Bulzezatna conveyed that in general such discomforts during the Oannes pregnancies were not uncommon. Oannes mothers considered themselves lucky to undergo mild discomfiture though many relished the more violent reactions. Mum, Milly and Brenda all showed their concern and hoped Muznant would feel better soon.

Zanos-537 anticipated my thoughts and conveyed that the Masursky experiment had revealed that I had increased the force energy I had expended on Steins by a factor of three. I was surprised by this and wondered how it could be. I had simply wanted Masursky to move and had hardly made a concentrated push upon it. But the effort had been over a much longer period and perhaps that had been the difference. I was beginning to see the light and to understand some of the rules behind telekinetic activity. I wondered what the effect would be if I applied a constant push and then went in and out of 'pink' mode several times. But I definitely needed to calibrate, in my mind, the various levels of 'pink' mode that I should be able to adopt whenever necessary. I needed to be able to apply an exact amount of force intelligently and correctly. I wanted proper control of this gift that was correct and precise.

My inner voice had already told me how I could achieve this and Zanos had conveyed earlier that a digital timer capable of thousandths of a second already existed in every cabin. I simply needed to activate it to my purpose. Zanos conveyed that this had been done. Oh I did like Zanos, it made life so uncomplicated.

The captain and the crew and passenger guests had all received Zanos' conclusions on the experiment and general satisfaction had been expressed at the results. This was all relayed back to Anztarza in a special Zanos transmission.

I anticipated the captain's thoughts and conveyed that I was more than ready for Mathilde. But I was rather thirsty and after a glass or two of Wazu I should love a nice mug of tea. Bulzezatna was amused by my preference for tea since she saw no value in it; the Oannes did not like their drinks hot.

It was now five o'clock by my watch which was an afternoon or evening time on Earth. Bulzezatna conveyed that Mathilde was about three hours away if we went to neutron generator speed in ten minutes. She suggested we relax on our recliners here in the control room and visually experience our first 'black hole' acceleration.

The split back seats could be reclined backwards and we all made ourselves comfortable. I looked up through the ceiling view panels and was completely taken with the display of stars. Although I knew the intricacies of our universe I did not have the recognition ability for individual stars. I would need to acquire that skill from an astronomer. But one thing I did know simply by looking at a pinpoint of light was the distance of it from me. Somehow this just came to me like my skill at knowing the history of every antique. For me the Milky Way always took centre stage and I just loved to follow its flowing course from one extreme side of the sky to the other. Here in open space I could see all of its 180 degrees of arc; and yet I could not be sure exactly where it ended and where the outer galactic spiral arms took over.

I was in this thought reverie when the sky went blank. What looked like a shower of sparks seemed to emanate from a point high above the view panel and this was repeated several times. Then all was normal again and the myriad of stars returned to view in their normal un-twinkling brilliance. So that is what the neutron generators produced ahead of the ships travel path for the required gravitational style acceleration. I queried the others to see if they had seen the same as me. Yes, they had but had felt no other sensation. An emotion of humour filled the control room and I guessed that the captain and her deputies were amused at the sense of wonder at our first experience of the neutron generator phenomenon. It was something that they obviously considered as quite an ordinary occurrence as far as space travel was concerned. Perhaps seeing it through our eyes and emotions might bring back a little of its initial thrill; after all for them it had been around for more than nine thousand years and was old hat. It was sometime after the Oannes first visit to Earth 10,000 years ago that Faster than Light travel had been realised. Although electrons had always been extracted from the nuclei of atoms to produce their required abundance of electrical energy, it was a new discovered form of stimulation that had since resulted in a thousand fold increase in those emissions. Today those electron emissions were being further enhanced and the Oannes hoped one day to achieve a hundred times Faster than Light speeds in space.

At the top of my mind was my need to be able to regulate the varying levels for slowing of Time that I needed to achieve every time I went into 'pink' mode. Once the chronometer in my cabin was set up as I required then I should be able to experiment with my rates of time. I conveyed what it was that I wanted to achieve and I would be able to do this if I didn't have any distractions. I wanted to be alone in my cabin to be able to do this.

But first we all went to the dining lounge where I drank a glass of Wazu and then mum and Aunt Brenda made tea and coffee for everyone. I had my tea and said I would return here in about half an hour.

As I walked down the corridor I saw Puzlwat and Mytanzto coming towards me but they were still some distance away. For some unknown reason I did not want to enter into a conversation with them just yet even though I knew that they were now amenable towards me after the two successful experiments with the asteroids. I'm not sure if they saw me or not but I went 'pink' and just walked on past the two near stationary figures. I returned to normal when I came to my cabin door and entered silently. But I sent a message to Puzlwat through my badge apologising for my rudeness for silently passing them in the corridor as I had urgent business of my own to attend to and didn't want to be distracted just then. I added that I would be in the dining lounge in half an hour with my family if he wished to talk. Puzlwat declined the invitation politely and said that he would wait till after the last asteroid experiment had concluded successfully and we were on our way back to Anztarza. He would meet me then as he had much on his mind. Mytanzto also wished to discuss matters. I got a distinct feeling of the emotion of respect coming across. Also a bit of humour for Mytanzto had seen me one moment only for me to suddenly disappear in front of his eyes. Puzlwat and I were beginning to develop a rapport of sorts which I thought of as quite favourable.

Zanos anticipated my need and set up the wall chronometer to run in thousandths of a second. I needed to calibrate my mind at the various possible 'pink' levels. I decided to grade the levels from one to ten for the moment. The chronometer was racing through the milliseconds at a phenomenal rate as I stared at it. The clock display was on a 24 hour basis and currently showed 17 hours and 23 minutes with the seconds clicking upwards continually. The milliseconds raced through the numbers towards 999 before reverting to zero and beginning the count again.

'Here goes,' I thought to myself and set my mind to go 'pink' but at the most minimum level whatever that might be. A thought came into my mind which said 'calibrate'. This was a command and I wondered where or from whom it came. I looked at the chronometer as the milliseconds began to click over more slowly. My mental clock indicated that it was taking about ten of my seconds to go through the thousand milliseconds which made up one second.

My inner voice said that this should be level two in my calibrated 'pink' levels. So now I willed the chronometer to speed up so that it took my five seconds to its one. I calibrated this as 'pink level one' which was one fifth the pace of normal Time. And 'pink level two' was one tenth of normal Time. Level three became one twentieth and so on with a doubling of the denominator number for each successive stage in pink levels.

I remained in pink mode and stepped mentally from one level to the next while carefully monitoring myself on the chronometer. When I reached level ten I noticed that the fogginess I had experienced at times had not yet been reached. So I went on up the levels and it was only when I reached level fifteen that I noticed the visibility in the room becoming hazy and indistinct. When I finally went up to pink level sixteen I recognised the thick fog of invisibility that filled the room. I recognised this as the extreme pink level I had visited as a child and when I had heard mysterious telepathic thoughts coming at me. My inner voice commanded me to go no further as danger lay beyond this. The hairs on my neck stood on end like bristles and I felt a cold sweat run down the middle of my back. I knew I must never ever exceed 'pink' level sixteen under any circumstance.

I had pegged my mind for all these pink levels as I progressed so that I only had to wish the necessary level and it would be so. And so for the next several minutes I practiced hopping from level to level while keeping my eye on the chronometer. I felt much happier now that I could be in proper control of my pink zone levels. This also meant that I had a better ability to control my telekinetic pushes in a far more skilled manner. Yes, I think I was ready for 253-Mathilde.

I returned to normal mode and the practicality of the audible sounds of the ship returned to my senses. I had never felt fearful anxiety like this before but what I had just experienced simply took my breath away. For me there was a forbidden territory and I think it would be wise to heed the warning of my inner voice. For some intuitive reason I knew that I might have to venture beyond level sixteen but only as a very last resort. There was extreme sadness associated with this thought that filled my whole being and I gave a choking cry of despair and sorrow. This mood of melancholy and wretchedness clung to me and I knew that I needed Tania more than ever now in order to shake it off. It might be a very distant prospect but I just knew that the sorrow I had felt here would be passed on to all those that I loved.

I looked at myself in the full length mirror and realised that I was slouching. I stood up straight and then went closer and looked directly into my own eyes. I had felt the run of tears at my sadness and I thought I could see dark rings under my eyes. I decided to freshen up and so got into the shower and had the temperature increased to as much as I could tolerate. I followed this with a lukewarm rinse before getting out. A fresh outfit was hanging up and I wondered again who did all these things on this spaceship. I must ask Bulzezatna. I got dressed and put on a forced smile before communicating that I was on my way to the lounge.

I had been on my own for nearly half an hour and when I walked into the lounge the mugs of tea looked freshly made.

'So where is my tea?' I said with as light hearted a voice as I could muster but I knew I was not fooling anyone. Tania got up and came to me and put her arms around my waist. It was just what I needed.

'What is it Ashley?' said mum, 'you look as if you've seen a ghost.'

'Metaphorically speaking I think I have,' I replied and then proceeded to convey everything that had occurred in the cabin.

'I believe I now have full control of the different levels I can go to in the pink zone all the way up to level sixteen. The ghost I encountered was my inner voice warning me not to venture further,' I said. 'But I just know that circumstances will be such that one day in the distant future my only alternative will be to go beyond it. That is when I got hit by this overwhelming sense of despair and sorrow. This mood of melancholy and wretchedness was accompanied by a terrible feeling of fear and a sense of loss. I don't understand it but somehow I know the sadness will affect you all.'

My voice broke slightly near the end and I just had to put my arms around Tania and give her the fiercest hug ever. The tears were back in my eyes but I managed to look up and produce the semblance of a smile.

The mug of tea that Milly put in my hand was hot and welcome. It was a bit sweeter than usual but I still liked it. Milly knew me well from the shop and I suspected she added that little bit of extra sweetness whenever she thought I was tired from one of my antiques foraging trips. With my family around me I gradually felt better and I realised how much Tania meant to me. O God, I do love this woman so and never want her sad or upset because of me. I must protect her from the sadness that I felt must come one day. My inner voice seemed to laugh out at me and I then knew that the sadness was not a certainty and being in the far distant future might never happen. My son by then would be a middle aged man. My son? Till this moment I didn't know that I was going to have a son. I laughed at the joy of the news and happily conveyed the thought to the family. Tania blushed but had a quizzical expression on her face that I read as a moment of unsure pride.

'I want more than just one,' she said to me in a whisper. 'Actually a boy and two girls would be nice.'

I conveyed my hearty agreement to that.

'What are you two whispering about?' asked Katy anxious not to be left out.

I was about to tell her when a dig in the ribs stopped me. So I just laughed and said, 'Just sweet nothings, sis.' I don't think she was convinced.

I was nearly back to my former good humour and thanked my lucky stars for such a close knit family. I thought of Philip and wished he could have been here with us. And perhaps he was. I had suspected that my inner voice might be Philip but don't expect me to even try to explain it, for I wouldn't know where to begin. Oddly I also thought of Margaret Dutton and her mother Mary and wondered what they might be doing at this precise moment. It was nearly six in the evening in London and already night there.

Mum brought some biscuits out then and I had a second mug of tea to go with them. I liked the plain Digestives because they dunked well. We were then joined by Brazjaf and I sensed an emotion of deep concern in his manner. Muznant was not having a nice time and he had left her in their cabin sleep tank. She was restless and twitched and turned in her sleep quite a bit. We should be back in Anztarza tomorrow and he had decided that a visit to the sick facility in Dome-1 was to be considered.

I was worried for him and wished I could help. I then realised that maybe I could help. I conveyed about my gift of physical diagnosis just in case it was something more than pregnancy pains. I explained that this was another of my gifts and that I simply needed to touch Muznant to receive complete information on her condition. Perhaps my gift of reading histories of objects was linked to this diagnostic skill. I conveyed to Brazjaf about the case in which I had by pure chance diagnosed Oliver Ramirez's brain tumour when he had jostled past me in getting off the train. I wondered how he had got on at the hospital later on.

I could see that Brazjaf was mildly uncomfortable with this but I insisted and he agreed for me to go and see Muznant right away. Brazjaf looked a bit relieved but also embarrassed since Muznant was still asleep in the sleep tank. But then he came to a decision and said to follow him. I knew that the Oannes usually were nude in their sleep tanks and did not like to be seen then by anyone outside their immediate family. But Brazjaf called me in and conveyed that I would have a doctor's privilege.

Muznant was totally nude and fast asleep facing downwards as she floated in the tank of clear water. She was gloriously beautiful and slender with her web fins nicely puffed and rigid. The large butterfly wing on her back seemed to be woven into her back with streams of colourful lines spreading to her sides which gave her a beautiful delicateness. She had a pert round buttock and a completely flat stomach with no sign of a pregnancy swelling as yet. She had quite a flat chest like that of a child and so different from earthy women with their breasts. But I noticed two recessed folds of skin halfway down her front and knew right away that a suckling infant would go there for nourishment. There was a frown on Muznant's face and I reckoned that when she finally went to sleep that she must have been experiencing some degree of pain.

'How beautiful she looks,' I conveyed to Brazjaf and he appeared a bit embarrassed when Muznant expelled a stream of air bubbles from between her legs. As she was quite near the edge of the tank close to us I reached forward and down into the water. I had to reach down quite far but just managed to touch her shoulder. I received all the information I needed and felt quite pleased that there was nothing physically the matter with Muznant. And she was not pregnant at all but undergoing an extreme phantom pregnancy. Brazjaf and Muznant had both intensely desired a family and had been trying for one for sometime now. And when Muznant had a stomach upset both she and her husband believed it might be the first symptoms of her pregnancy. In such cases the mind and body of the person became such that the mother produced the relevant hormones to support that belief. Subsequent superficial tests indicated that her body was with child. The Oannes do not conduct invasive examinations of any kind as these had the potential for harm. Muznant's extensive knowledge of the history of Oannes pregnancies was the chief culprit and from her early symptoms she had decided that hers was the worst case scenario.

I conveyed all this to Brazjaf and he immediately seemed to stand taller with relief, although I did sense a slight disappointment too. I also conveyed that Muznant's mental psyche would not accept anyone's word right away since the disappointment would be too great. A mother always has the instinct to know best. I told Brazjaf that I might be able to help Muznant accept her disappointment at not being pregnant by means of deep hypnosis to the contrary but she would need to be awake for that. I said I would leave now and if necessary see them later. I left the cabin and returned slowly to the recreation lounge.

'How is our Muznant?' was the immediate question from more than one voice. We were all very fond of the little lady.

'She's fine,' I said and left a very pregnant pause. When the eyebrows began to be raised I added, 'She's not pregnant at all. She has what is called a Symptomatic Phantom Pregnancy and her body and mind have adjusted her hormonal levels accordingly. She believes hers is a typical worst case Oannes scenario pregnancy and so suffered all the associated sympathetic discomforts. She may not believe otherwise even from Brazjaf or me. But Muznant is extremely knowledgeable and she just might review her own case and come out of it unscarred. I certainly hope that is the case. However she must also divest her body of the symptomatic hormonal build-up before all normality can return. As a backup I mentioned to Brazjaf that I was prepared to carry out a deep hypnosis to help her accept her loss. Nevertheless I fear that even when the pregnancy symptoms begin to subside she will still undergo a feeling of sadness for what could have been. She might retreat into the trauma of a lost pregnancy but I feel her rationality will override this. But no one knows precisely how a grieving mother may react.'

There must be cases in the Oannes medical history of other similar cases. I conveyed this to Brazjaf via my communication badge and he replied that the clinic in Anztarza would have the information in their databases for Nazmos. If it could happen to Muznant then surely hers couldn't possibly be an isolated incident. There must be records of other cases.

I was not hungry but from habit picked up a digestive biscuit and went to dunk it in my tea but my mug was empty. Seeing this mum said she'd get me another and before she could get up there were multiple requests from nearly all the others as well.

'Not for me,' said Milly, 'but I'll come and give you a hand making this lot of lazy of beggars their cuppas. Not you Ashley dear, you've been busy playing doctor.'

She was smiling mischievously as she said this and both slim ladies did exaggerated fashion catwalk strides as they walked towards the kitchen area. Jerry gave a low wolf whistle and we all clapped in feigned appreciation. I wondered if all this camaraderie was being picked up by the captain and her crew. I hoped it was as it would put us in a favourable light.

Tania and I sat side by side and we just enjoyed our nearness. But a dark shadow had been cast earlier and although I had pushed it to one side I knew it was still hovering around somewhere in the back of our minds. I couldn't help wondering what lay beyond that last pink level that made it a danger. I trusted my inner voice and would never go against it, but that didn't stop me being curious. Perhaps it was a danger to the entire working of the universe and if I brought it to a total stop it might never get going again. I was not one to experiment with the unknown. I shall leave this sleeping dog alone.

But then pleasanter thoughts overrode and I thought of my future life with Tania. And I knew we would have a good long life together with plenty of loving and understanding. The children factor was something I had never considered till now. Of course there would be kids and I was keen to see who they would turn out to be like. I knew one thing for sure and that was that mum and Milly would spoil them rotten. And suddenly there was Margaret Dutton's face in front of me. Why did she keep cropping up in my mind? Did she have a role to play in the link between Nazmos and Earth; and between Oannes and humans? I wondered about that.

Zanos interrupted these thoughts by conveying that 520-Green was to decelerate in ten minutes. This meant that the craft would reverse its directional attitude before applying its neutron generators. These would be done in a series of short bursts so that the ship slowed while it was still many thousands of miles from Mathilde. The ship would continue to decelerate over a period of time till it was close enough to the asteroid to begin its pattern of looped space parking.

I must be getting used to this space travelling lark for it all seemed quite ordinary now. But this was only the result of the efficiency with which the ship operated under Zanos' extraordinary mastery. Being on 520-Green was not too dissimilar from being inside Anztarza. But I would still like to see the sparks that the neutron generators set off when accelerating the ship towards the simulated singularity point. Zanos anticipated my request and informed us that Captain Bulzezatna would be pleased for us to re-enter the control room to witness the decelerating approach to destination. We did not need a seconds thought on the matter for we were on the edge of becoming bored with having waited in the recreation lounge for nearly three hours.

When we entered the control room the view panels had already been dimmed which meant that the ship had already been manoeuvred around and was facing towards where Masursky had been. The sun was now on our left and just visible near the rim of the lowest window. We were greeted by the captain and we gave our own 'Thanks for having us' greeting in return. This was not a Sewa formality but just a 'Hope you are well' affair; but was politeness as usual nevertheless.

We settled down on the reclining seats and I patiently gazed up through the ceiling panels. The first series of sparks caught us by surprise. There was then a pause of a couple of seconds before a second series of sparks was repeated. This was repeated several times before Zanos informed us that the operation had completed successfully. We were now seven thousand miles from Mathilde and the distance was reducing rapidly. We should fly by the asteroid within thirty minutes when our speed would have reduced considerably. This would enable the ship to enter its holding loop pattern about a thousand miles away from Mathilde.

The ship's attitude slowly changed and a very bright marble sized round object came into our view. Had we been a bit further away I would have thought it a luminous star. I was surprised how round and bright it was and how it grew in size as we approached it. Eventually it looked the size of the moon on Earth but about twice as bright. I magnified it in my view panel so that I could see its surface clearly. I had to squint at its luminosity but then again Zanos anticipated my discomfort and increased the window tint. Mathilde's surface was much like Masursky's only it seemed slightly more pitted in several places. Then suddenly the surface began to move sideways at speed which surprised me until I realised the ship was rotating away from the asteroid to begin its hundred mile loop manoeuvre.

Mathilde looked large as life and I thought it was rather beautiful. I did not feel it cold or forbidding in any way as I had first experienced with Masursky. Maybe that was because I was now surer of myself with confidence in my ability to apply my telekinetic power in a scientific and controlled manner. Mathilde was large at thirty three miles in diameter and I estimated that I ought to be about three times that distance away when I applied my push. Once again I decided that I should like the shuttle to touch down upon the asteroid surface before I began the experiment. I felt a degree of over-confidence which made me hesitate and wonder if I had overlooked something. I conveyed this feeling to the others including the captain and she conveyed back that one should always be on the lookout for the unexpected. That is why the shuttle had not been allowed to let its full weight rest upon the asteroid surface. While it sat upon the asteroid only a tenth of its weight bore down upon it. The rest was held up in hover mode by the impulse motors. It was most discerning of the captain to reveal this to me now when its revelation meant more to me. Earlier I would have just digested it as a piece of factual safety information. I knew the course I would follow during the experiment and would make allowances for any adjustment or modification that I felt was relevant. My heartfelt thanks went out to Bulzezatna.

So once again we walked towards the cargo bay at the rear of the ship, along the balcony overlooking the shuttle craft and through the door into the large rectangular room housing the electrostatic suits. And it was not long before we were seated and clamped by our thighs inside shuttle craft 5202-Green.

The area was evacuated, the lights dimmed and the bay doors were slowly opened. We had to wait a few minutes before Zanos-onboard took the shuttle craft out into the vast blackness of space. I looked for the stars but they had vanished. The twin brilliance of our sun and the reflected light of Mathilde outshone everything else in the heavens. We backed away from the large mother craft which seemed to accelerate rapidly from us and it too soon became a small and distant shiny point of light. The other shuttle remained to one side of us as on the previous occasions and together we approached Mathilde. Gradually the asteroid grew in size to fill our view. The reflected light was rather dazzling though Zanos-onboard increased the tint to the windows progressively as we got nearer.

Tania and Katy were on my left and I could sense their excitement at the relative closeness and size of Mathilde. As we drew nearer Tania put her hand in mine and smiled up at me. I think she was trying to reassure me that we were all together. What more could anyone want? Your girl smiling up at you, family close at hand and a huge thirty three mile rock on your doorstep. All this as you sat in a tiny gravity-less fragile looking shuttle craft manoeuvring ever closer towards a mini moon. The mother craft was out of sight now and yet I wouldn't wish to be anywhere else at this moment.

Muznant and Brazjaf were not onboard though Puzlwat and Mytanzto were in their usual seats behind Milly and Jerry. There were some new Oannes faces farther behind and the shuttle craft seemed rather fuller than on either of the previous flights. Tatizblay was in command of our shuttle as Rubandiz was of shuttle 5201-Green. I looked back and conveyed that I should like a touchdown on Mathilde before the experiment. This would become my trademark pattern for each experiment whenever possible.

'It shall be so,' communicated Tatizblay and our shuttle edged ever closer to Mathilde till we were moving in on our own.

I could see the granular surface features of the surface and was surprised at the concentrations of crater pitting that seemed localised in places while others were quite smooth. The larger impact depressions were relatively few and far between but I could now make out shallow undulations in the surface pattern. The shuttle manoeuvred around and I lost sight of the surface but only for a moment. As we settled lower Mathilde's horizon came into view and suddenly the landscape surrounded us. It was a desert view with hardly a shadow to be seen. We settled down a few miles from the night shadow and faced away from the sun. Once again the shuttle shadow stretched ominously into the distance. It looked like a dark path leading away from the shuttle and into the unknown. There was a very faint gravity on Mathilde but I hardly noticed it. I was as light as a feather and grateful for our seat clamps. Zanos-onboard informed us that the asteroid had a very slow rotation about an axis. It took seventeen Earth days to complete one rotation and we would not notice any movement during our brief stay on its surface.

I now noticed that Mathilde had a pale ochre tint in its surface and everywhere was a dispersal of scintillating shiny grains. Our settling had caused a slight stirring of surface dust which had yet to settle completely. We were soon rising up again and our shadow did a magical disappearing act as if it were retreating up into the underbelly of the shuttle.

Zanos-onboard took us rapidly out and away from Mathilde till we got alongside the other shuttle craft. We retreated further towards the planned hundred mile position where the asteroid image just fitted into the front view panel. We stopped, manoeuvred sideways and then stopped again and I knew then that we were in the correct relative position for my push experiment.

Mathilde was now showing as a three quarter moon and I imagined that my telekinetic push might very well take it into the outer asteroid zone. Perhaps it would pass Masursky on the way and say 'hello'. Just a joke which I conveyed as an open thought but got nothing in reply. I think they were all waiting keenly for me to begin.

I took my time and when I felt ready I just willed a push upon the asteroid and for it to move away from us. Nothing seemed to happen so I continued with another willed push. I felt that surely the asteroid must be affected by now so asked Zanos-onboard for an analysis. Mathilde had acquired an additional velocity of five inches per second away from our position. Rather disappointing I thought so I went to pink zone one and applied a prolonged telekinetic push lasting several of my mental seconds. I returned to normal mode and Zanos confirmed a new velocity of six feet per second. That's better I thought and I went to pink zone two. I was determined to conduct this experiment exactly in the stages I had planned. I did not want anything disastrous to happen as had been the case with Steins. Nor did I want to feel the exhaustion I'd felt after that event.

Mathilde had a natural orbital velocity of 10.6 miles per second in its middle zone path and was currently near its Aphelion position. Boosting its velocity by a third should see it comfortably on its way. I calculated that an addition of 18,000 fps was required. Zanos was monitoring each speed increase and this certainly helped me affect full control of the experiment.

I went through pink zone two and three successively and Zanos indicated that a further push was necessary. The asteroid had now acquired an additional velocity of 9,700 fps through my telekinetic efforts. I was beginning to get a little impatient with this slow build up of velocity. If I was really expert with my gift I should be able to do it all in one or two calculated pushes. I let my mind think that what if Mathilde was really Nazmos. Would I want to risk disaster? No definitely not and so I went readily to the next pink zone four. Here I gave another prolonged push that I thought was needed and hoped for the best. Slow and steady does it I philosophised. Returning to normal I could sense that I had achieved the desired result and Zanos confirmed that Mathilde had indeed acquired slightly more than the necessary velocity. If this were Nazmos I would need to slow it down slightly for the sake of accuracy of orbit. But here that did not matter as much. This was simply an experiment and practice for me to use my telekinetic power.

The shuttles had now both increased their forward velocity in order to keep pace with the receding asteroid in case I needed to apply further force. Zanos-onboard conveyed that Mathilde had been given an additional velocity of 18,500 fps. I had increased its orbital velocity from 56,300 fps to 74,800 fps which should see it well on its way towards the outer zone. Not that it would become a permanent member there unless we gave it another push at its new Aphelion position. But for now I judged this experiment a success as far as I was concerned. I hoped that this was the opinion of the Oannes too. I wondered what astronomers on Earth would think when they realised that Mathilde was no longer where they had expected it to be. They'd be speculating about its change of orbit for years to come. Perhaps they might consider that an unforeseen asteroid collision had taken place.

It was when I looked at my watch that I realised how short a time had elapsed since we'd started the experiment. Barely fifteen minutes had elapsed and yet it seemed so much longer. Of course I had spent quite some time in the pink zones which would not have been recorded as time spent in action. I conveyed to Tatizblay that I was done and that I deemed the experiment a complete success. When I added that I was starving for my dinner the emotion of humour filled the shuttle.

Tatizblay caused Zanos to rock the shuttle from side to side a couple of times and when I looked across at the other shuttle it also did the same though rather more gently. I conveyed to Tatizblay that his Earth humour had definitely improved and I appreciated what I called a 'victory roll'. Though I'm glad he didn't do one literally. He read my thoughts and that is exactly what he did but rather smoothly and slowly. There was no sensation of a spin apart from the fact that the other shuttle seemed to make a complete circuit around us. And as I looked it too did a slow rotation about its own length axis. And very good it looked too from where I sat. It was pleasing to know that many of our humorous qualities were filtering through to the Oannes. By reading our minds surely they must be picking up many of our traits. I hope we were creating a good impression of all that was commendable in the human race. It would be wonderful if we could get our natural sense of humour into the Oannes mentality. A sense of playful mischievousness might not go amiss.

I looked across to my right and all were smiling. Jerry gave me a wink and behind him was a smiling Puzlwat. Mytanzto saw my glance and immediately looked away at his view panel and I sensed embarrassment in his manner. I think he needed some encouragement so I sent him a personal message through my badge. I said I was glad he had been close at hand to see everything and I asked what he thought of the experiment. He looked around and I caught his eye and smiled at him. My emotion of affection must have got through to him for he also smiled back in return. He then did a very unusual thing for an Oannes person. He raised his right arm up in the air and gave me a clenched fist greeting. I returned the gesture and immediately nearly everyone in the shuttle did the same. And yet not a sound was uttered though I did receive a shuttle full of affectionate emotions. I felt more satisfaction from Mytanzto's conversion than from everyone else's acclaim. I would meet them when we got back to the ship.

'Well done son,' said dad loud and clear for all to hear, 'very well done indeed. I knew you would do it in style.'

'Yes,' said mum, 'very well done Ashley.' There was great pride in her voice and dad's for that matter and that meant the world to me.

'I could do with a glass of Wazu,' said granddad with a smile. 'I feel a bit tired. Oh yes, and hungry too like Ashley.'

Tania had my hand gripped fiercely in hers and I could see the watery emotion just under the surface. I knew she was proud of her man and that emotion came through clearly. I know Katy was the same, extremely proud of her big brother. She looked across from Tania and winked.

'You were better at catching birds at home than you are with asteroids,' she said. 'You keep on losing these.'

We all laughed and good humour returned to the shuttle.

It was not long before we were back in the shuttle bay of 520-Green and the large bay doors had closed. The bay lights became bright when normal atmosphere was restored and we were unclamped. It was near to nine o'clock and I did feel a bit like granddad. I looked forward to dinner and then a good nights rest.

We divested ourselves of the static suits and then made our way forward and into our general lounge. Captain Bulzezatna was already there to greet us and she seemed particularly enthusiastic in her greeting. I realised that it would look good on her record that this mission that she commanded had been a complete success. The spacecraft had been a few hundred miles away and Zanos had conveyed everything that had occurred in a minute by minute commentary of events. To the Oannes watchers it must have seemed to have happened quite quickly since they would not be aware of the time I spent in pink mode. I thought for a moment that Bulzezatna was going to hug me in her joy but then she held out her hand and we did a good earthly handshake. And why not, since they had been monitoring Earth customs for thousands of years and surely must have adopted quite a few; at least those to their liking. After a while she left.

Brazjaf and a shrunken looking Muznant were also there to greet us and this time I could not stop my tears when I saw her. She looked drawn and feeble but there was no stopping the smile beaming out at me when our eyes met. Tania gave me a push and I walked forward and reaching where Muznant sat I leaned down and gave her a gentle kiss on her upturned lips. I also gave her a light squeeze across her shoulders and conveyed that I had missed her supporting presence on the shuttle. As I moved back I had to make way for the others as they all came forward to crowd around our little Muznant. The emotion of love and sympathy for Muznant filled the room and I wondered what Brazjaf had said to his wife when she woke from her sleep. Muznant had now stood up and was quite enjoying all the hugging even from the men.

When I had kissed her I had automatically done a deep mind probe and this told me that Muznant had accepted my diagnosis that there had been no pregnancy at all; she just had a deep rooted desire for a baby of her own. When Brazjaf had first told her of my skill in diagnosing illnesses and how I had offered to check her condition she accepted that I did have such a skill. It had been revealed to her when she had read my mind way back in November. So when Brazjaf had given her my diagnosis that she was undergoing a phantom pregnancy she had accepted it without question.

331

She remembered her friend Partuzna telling her about her own mother's friend Myrzbaza who'd also had a phantom pregnancy experience. Myrzbaza's condition had gone into many months and when she discovered that no additional weight had been put on began to suspect that something was wrong. Although hers had been a normal easy pregnancy she was nevertheless upset and disappointed not to really be with child. It had taken her several weeks of friendly advice and therapy to accept her loss. Unfortunately she had been rather mature in years and tests had proven that she would never be able to conceive. All this was in Muznant's memories and gave her the inner strength not only to accept her feigned loss but also to look forward to the real thing. After all she was only 100 years of age and in her prime. I thought she looked gorgeous and she smiled when I conveyed this. Brazjaf at 112 years was not very much older. Child bearing with the Oannes could continue up to the good age of 200 years if lucky.

I realised now that Muznant had a much stronger constitution and psychological makeup than I had given her credit for. But I still thought that she ought to be among friends and I hoped that we could fit that bill and give her the necessary support. Back in Anztarza she would also get the consolation and sympathy from her Oannes friends. Brazjaf was very appreciative of our concerns for them both and he knew he had been right in forcing Muznant to come to the lounge and be amongst us. And Muznant conveyed her emotion of pleasure and thanks to us for our presence around her. She had sat down again and now looked across at me and spoke in her low tone sing-song voice.

'Ashley,' she said, 'thank you for all you have done. I am proud of you. You have proved me right when I first tried to convince the Anztarzans about you when I returned from our first meeting. I know you are special for us. But more than that I believe you will change the face of Nazmos and turn Zarama away. My blessings are on you always.'

'And bless you Muznant,' said mum, 'for saying such a lovely thing about my son. I hope one day you do have a child of your own to love and cherish. In fact I hope you have many.'

Muznant looked up at mum and smiled but with a hint of sadness that her pregnancy hadn't been real. It made me think about how this might affect Muznant in the long term. There was nothing I could do to ease her mind. Although her thoughts would accept a healing and the mental anguish would fade yet it could never be completely forgotten. There had been a lot of physical discomfort during the experience. The only positive remedy would be for a child to be born of her and Brazjaf's making for the past to be finally laid to rest. The child would bring her joy and reconciliation.

Granddad Eric brought us all back to reality when he asked if dinner was ready. Suddenly we felt famished and thanked granddad for the reminder. We received a communication from Bulzezatna that she and her deputy Tatizblay were in the food hall and would await our arrival. I suspect our badges had been relaying our thoughts and conversations to all on the ship.

Once again we were a perfectly attired group as we entered the food hall and took our usual places at table. A brief Sewa was communicated and then Wazu was drunk by all. As the ladies got up to make their way to the cupboard at the end of the room mum put her hand on Muznant's shoulder and told her to remain seated. So it was just mum, Milly and Brenda who brought all the dishes to the table. Again I expressed my curiosity about who prepared all our food and did all the other things too. Bulzezatna read my query and gave me an insider's view of the kitchens. There were several and they had a minimum of staff; just one in fact. But there were a number of Zanos style bio robots that did most of the work. Communication was essential but not a problem. The intentions of the Oannes staff person was read and jobs done accordingly. Dishes were placed on floatation trays which then automatically took them through special corridors to the required food lounge kitchenette area. They were similarly collected later when thoughts were picked up that dinner had been satisfactorily completed. The same applied to our cabins where similar robotics was used as general duty valets. The whole scenario of work on board was portrayed by Bulzezatna and I had to laugh at the simplicity of it all. Of course this had also been conveyed to the others and there was astonishment at the advanced domestic technology of the Oannes. Life in Anztarza must be very easy conveyed mum. Brenda said that she could do with similar help at the B&B. I was pleased to have had this little glimpse of the lifestyle of an advanced civilization. I suspected that there was a lot more to know but Bulzezatna kept it simple.

'The men will do the clearing up after dinner, won't you darling?' said mum as she smiled sweetly at dad.

'Yes my good lady,' said dad with a fixed toothy grin that was meant to resemble a grimace. This was followed by general laughter.

Dinner was tasty as usual and flavoured with Earth herbs and soft spices. I hardly recognised the Yaztraka mash on top of the small rounds of Raizna. There was also boiled potatoes in a bowl and thick slices of brown bread with a block of soft butter on an adjacent plate.

The other dishes were well camouflaged and as tasty. It was surprising what a variety of dishes the Oannes could concoct out of their limited larder. The surprise of the evening was the cheese and biscuits as an after treat. There were six types of cheeses and I tried a small amount of them all. I had to be careful with cheese as sometimes it caused me to react with a mild itch.

While we were at table Zanos conveyed to Captain Bulzezatna and all crew and passengers that the neutron generators had been successful in accelerating 520-Green on its homeward journey at a velocity of 20,000 miles per sec.

Captain Bulzezatna then conveyed an explanation that we were in a special spatial position rather further out from Earth than had been the initial distance to Steins and hence the increased ship velocity. The journey time to neutron generator operation a million miles out from Earth should take seven hours. Then the normal gravitational deceleration to Earth's atmosphere would be another six hours which incidentally was the slowest and most time consuming part of the journey. The ship would then be facing away from Earth which would not be visible from the control room. Bulzezatna conveyed that there were side view panels at certain positions along the length of the ship which might afford some good views. The sea journey into Anztarza would be nearly three hours long. So in sixteen hours we should be back in Anztarza.

After a moments thought Jerry gave his opinion.

'Well that would allow us a good nights rest,' he said. 'Its ten o'clock now. If we get to bed by eleven or eleven thirty then we should be nearly there by breakfast time.'

'Oh I don't know,' said Milly very seriously and we all wondered what she was about to reveal. And after a prolonged pause she added, 'I feel so full now I can't even think about a breakfast.'

This time even the Oannes present at the table joined in our laughter. Their sense of humour had definitely improved.

'In that case,' said Bulzezatna in her falsetto voice which I found quite pleasant and unique, 'would you all like to come up to the control room and get a sighting of Earth from this distance? It should be across towards the farther side of the sun in a three quarter moon image. We shall be cutting across the orbital path of Venus which fortunately for us is across on the other side of the sun. The view of Earth will be stunning.'

Five minutes later we were all comfortably settled on our recliners in the control room and I noticed a faint glow ahead of 520-Green. Zanos anticipated my question and informed us that this came from the magnetic field around the ship and the deflection of a recent burst of solar particles. The magnetic field strength had been increased to reflect this increase in activity from the sun. That was very comforting to know and I felt safe here inside the ship as a result. The sun was smaller than when seen from Earth and was maybe a little more than half its usual size. The control room was still brightly lit by its filtered light and as I gazed at our sun it seemed to possess a life of its own. It actually vibrated as it sent its beams across towards us. As I continued to stare at it through the tinted panel it looked like there was a hole in the darkened room through which the outside daylight was bursting in.

I looked for Earth and suddenly there it was like a brightly shining star. It was to the right of the sun and I found it fascinating that we should be racing towards it at 20,000 mps and yet had no sensation of our velocity. We seemed quite stationary relative to everything around us. Earth was 500 million miles from our current position and yet we would reach our deceleration point in just seven hours. I decided to relax and just look at this bright star that was really Earth and pondered at the wonder of the life pulsating upon it. This was all still fascinating for us as it was our first venture out into the depths of space. The Oannes were of course quite used to space travel and for them it was like an everyday event; like having breakfast, lunch or dinner. I however longed to be back on Earth under its blue sky and to feel and breathe its aromas. I knew then that I was not a space ranger and would only travel in space out of necessity. I'd much rather be in a position where I could look up at the night sky and just think of all our Oannes friends racing about up there. I missed our good old England and I thought about Dudley and Erdington and Aberporth and the crashing of waves on the shore. I felt Bulzezatna's hand on my shoulder and I knew she had read my open thoughts and had come to reassure me with her own kind thoughts. It would be another week before I saw Robin again. I wondered what revelations this next week would bring.

For now though I decided to get a closer peek at Earth. My will for magnification brought Earth into sharp focus and I could see a lot of ocean and much of the east coast of South America. I looked at my watch and it was well after 10 pm. This would also be GMT and so it would be night in England and Europe. I went for greater magnification and mentally asked for England. And there it was rather well lit up but unrecognisable. There was quite a bit of cloud covering the Midlands area but London appeared as a bright patch of light. I tried for greater magnification but the picture became progressively blurry. So I retreated to an overall view of Europe and I was surprised at how bright the Belgium and Holland area looked. I then panned around the night areas just to see which places were more brightly lit than others. I drew back further and just looked at our lovely planet with South America clearly defined in daylight. I was surprised how far east it was. It jutted so far towards Africa that it would soon be night on its east coast. I could see that the entire continent of South America was wholly east of Florida. I called up my mental query and I got this answer. The 80 degree west longitude line went southward through Hudson Bay in Canada, a few miles west of Hamilton on Lake Ontario, through the centres of Pittsburgh and Charleston in the USA to skim past West Palm Beach in Florida, through the middle of Cuba, and then through

Colón on the Atlantic side of the Panama Canal, and finally after taking a very thin slice off Ecuador and Peru on the South American west coast it dived down into Antarctica. Only seventeen degrees of longitude separated the west coast of Africa from the tip of the South American east coast. This was quite a revelation and I wish I had paid more attention to geography at school.

I conveyed all this to our group and they began a renewed look at Earth. I lay there on my recliner for several minutes with my eyes closed reading the thoughts of the others. Perhaps it was time I returned to my cabin but then a thought came to my mind and I conveyed this to Bulzezatna. She expressed mild surprise but also pleasure. Zanos had already anticipated my request and after getting the okay from the captain conveyed that the ship would realign in five minutes. This was conveyed to the ships crew and other passengers and a keen sense of anticipation seemed to fill the ship.

I noticed the slow rotation in our view panels as the sun disappeared behind us. The stars once more became visible in all their brilliance as we faced to the outside of the solar system. After a minor adjustment I knew we were facing slightly towards where the centre of the galaxy lay. On Earth Barnard's star is visible just above the horizon in the northern hemisphere and so nearly in line with the plane of our solar system.

Since we didn't know what to look for Zanos conveyed that it would control the view panel magnification to bring the red image of Raznat into general view. And there it was as large as life. An emotion of joy came through as the image was mentally relayed to all on the ship. Raznat was a bright red glowing ball and as I increased the magnification it filled the view panel above us. So finally I had got to see the Oannes sun. I looked for Nazmos the home planet and after scanning left and right and then up and down I finally found it; or so I thought. But this was one of the other three planets so I continued my search nearer to the red sun. And suddenly there it was with a very fuzzy atmosphere but nevertheless quite as beautiful as Earth. Nazmos was on the far side of Raznat and well above it and so was well illuminated for us. Obviously its plane of rotation was in a plane inclined differently to our plane of view. Relative to our solar system it was orbiting in a plane at nearly 40 degrees of angle north and south of Raznat.

I zoomed in closer to the planet but fuzziness prevailed and I could not make out the land or sea areas. I could however make out a large polar icecap. Bulzezatna conveyed that only the central equatorial zone was where the Oannes had the majority of their population. The Rimzi water people tended to spread farther afield but underwater of course. I found it staggering that such magnification could be achieved for something that was the size of Earth and six light years distant. I conveyed as much to the captain.

When Zanos returned the ship to face back towards Earth I spent just five minutes zooming in to the forests of Brazil before I began to blink my eyes through tiredness. I rose from my recliner and conveyed to all that I was returning to my cabin and my bed. There was this weariness in my head that seemed to have a will of its own. Put me to bed it kept on saying to which I simply gave my full agreement. And so did all the others as there was nothing new to see. It was apparent that the luxury of space travel in this Oannes ship was making everything seem quite routine and ordinary.

I thanked the captain for showing us the wonders of space travel and the views of Earth and Nazmos and hoped that we might meet also on dry land in Anztarza during the following week. She in turn conveyed for us all to get a good nights rest and that 520-Green should be in Earth atmosphere in about thirteen hours. We performed a brief but formal Sewa farewell before making our way out to the corridor.

Tania came up to me and we exchanged thoughts as we walked hand in hand down the corridor. And we continued our private conversation through our communication badges as we lay on our beds in our separate cabins. The lights dimmed as granddad began his gentle cello symphony and I hoped I'd be asleep before it went to crescendo. I never remember the exact moment that I fall asleep but this time I knew that Tania had dropped off before me. The total silence in the ship was amazing and most peaceful. We on Earth had a lot to benefit from all this technology and I'm not sure if we were ready to absorb any of it just yet. Perhaps when the explosion of telepathic skill took hold we might advance to an open minded society with all the advantages that came with it.

I woke once sometime later and went to the wall recess for a glass of Wazu. I found myself drinking this instead of plain water because it refreshed me. Back in bed I thought about the view panels in the control room and wondered if the sidewalls of the ship did the same but I drifted off to sleep again before I could think further upon it.

The sound of flowing water woke me and I felt confused for a moment before I realised it was granddad having his morning wash. I leaned up on one elbow and said a good morning greeting telepathically. It was now just past 7 o'clock on my wristwatch so I must have slept for nearly eight hours. I felt refreshed and conveyed a general good morning to the rest of the group.

'Six of us have been up for ages,' was the reply communication from mum. 'We are in the dining lounge on our second mugs of tea and were just about to call up breakfast. But we'll wait a bit longer for you lazy lot to arrive.'

'Give me twenty minutes to get ready and I'll be with you,' I conveyed. 'Granddad is nearly ready and will be with you before me.'

When I got there Tania had only just come in before me but Katy had yet to arrive. I sat in my usual seat and Aunt Brenda placed a steaming mug of tea on the table in front of me. I think a mug of hot lightly sweetened tea is the best drink for starting every morning. It invigorates and gets you into gear for whatever the day might hold.

Muznant and Brazjaf did not join us this morning as they were never really the breakfasting type. In fact most Oannes were not either but I think they probably joined us mainly to listen to our lively conversations. We are so different from the Oannes in both physical and psychological makeup and yet a great affection has developed between us. I find that fascinating and extremely encouraging.

Tania had done her hair in a ponytail and she looked stunning with just a hint of makeup. I told her so and she smiled at me and said, 'Thanks.'

I said, 'You're welcome.'

She said, 'Not so bad yourself.'

I said, 'What, my ponytail?'

She said, 'No, your backside you ass,' and poked her tongue out at me.

I acknowledged with a wink and my head to one side.

'Now, now children,' said Milly smiling at the others, 'do control yourselves after all you are in civilized company.'

Katy came in then all made up and looking beautiful and everyone said so. Katy preened herself by doing a slow fashion turnabout with hands prominently on both hips and wide cheesy grin before sitting down and asking in a feigned thick country accent, 'Where's me coop o' cha then?'

We all clapped and laughed.

Breakfast was of the continental type and I had quite a few slices of toast with marmalade and jam. I left the cheese alone. I was on my fourth piece of toast when Bulzezatna and deputy Rubandiz came into the room.

We got a pleasant greeting in the Sewa tradition and information that we were on the backward approach to Earth. The neutron generators had operated successfully over an hour ago at the million mile distance and the ship was decelerating at the normal gravity rate. Zanos would of course vary this by up to 1.2g if the need arose. We should be in Earth atmosphere in less than six hours time.

Bulzezatna invited us to the control room after we had completed our breakfast so that we could get a five minute close-up glimpse of the Earth and the moon. We all conveyed an emotion of great interest and accepted heartedly.

We had a lot of time to kill so spent a leisurely time over breakfast. The captain and her deputy spent some time with us and I could see they were keen to listen to our voices in conversation. They were quite fascinated by the varied sounds we put in our voiced conversations, especially our laughter patterns.

We spoke about the latest antiques that Milly and Robin had acquired for McGill's and how I intended to add the histories to each when we returned. Ron and Brenda discussed whether or not to add a larger conservatory onto the southwest face of their B&B which could double as both a breakfasting room and an evening lounge in the summer months.

Granddad was silent and I knew exactly where his thoughts were. And so did Bulzezatna for she gave me a curious look as if to ask if he knew what he might be getting himself into. I conveyed my opinion privately to her that my granddad's health and physical constitution had vastly improved since we had come to Anztarza. And he wanted the diet and the Wazu to continue. I certainly saw him looking and behaving like a younger person and I wondered if his roving eye had alighted on someone of Muznant's stature and good looks. Perhaps his flirting days with Milly were over. Bulzezatna smiled and very nearly laughed as she read these thoughts.

I conveyed that we still had another week in Anztarza and would cross that bridge when we came to it. Bulzezatna was puzzled, 'What bridge?' she asked. I explained and then conveyed a whole lot of other sayings we used in our conversations like 'Don't cry over spilt milk', don't count your chickens before they're hatched', 'every cloud has a silver lining', and so on. She was appreciative of my little lesson and said that observation and monitoring of human languages and customs never quite gave the whole picture.

However I knew in my mind that granddad had decided to stay on in Anztarza but the question was for how long. I wondered if he secretly hoped to travel to Nazmos eventually on one of the FTL journeys. I might have to dissuade him from that course because of the colder conditions there. Bulzezatna nodded her agreement and conveyed her understanding.

When I conveyed all this to mum and dad they said they felt quite happy about Eric staying on. He might not have the same quality of life back home as he was having here. This Wazu drink and the Oannes diet seemed to suit him perfectly and had perked him up no end. In fact the Oannes way of life might even be like the proverbial Shangri la for him. I said Amen to that. I decided not to mention my suspicion about a possible visit to Nazmos.

We were just about to leave for the control room when Brazjaf and Muznant walked in. Muznant looked beautiful and radiant just as she had when we first met in Aberporth. Brazjaf too looked happy and contented. I guessed that they had been busy making plans for the future and creating a family anew. My thoughts somehow got a general airing and Muznant turned a bright rainbow colour in all her fins, especially the one on her back. However her smile of pleasure won through and her emotion of affection for us filled the room.

Milly went over to her and stooping down gave her a gentle hug. She was followed by mum and Aunt Brenda. I could see that Muznant expected more so I grabbed Tania's hand and we surrounded her in a sort of huddle cuddle. I instinctively knew what she would like so I leaned downwards. Muznant gave Tania a kiss on the cheek and then turning to me planted a brief though firm kiss straight on my pursed lips. Although brief I felt it lingered that fraction more than just friendly. No one else followed us and I could see granddad pondering about coming forward too. In the end he did and got a tight hug and a kiss on the lips too for his efforts. He came away smiling.

We stayed in the dining lounge just a bit longer before eventually making our way behind Bulzezatna and Rubandiz to the control room. Tatizblay welcomed us all and signalled to the recliners. We took our usual places.

Looking out of the view panels I could again see the brightness of the stars and the spread of the Milky Way. I think I could lie here forever just gazing at that majestic sight. This was an astronomer's paradise and I thought I should meet some and acquire their catalogued knowledge of the stars. I might then appreciate what was spread before me in a more factual manner. Although I had a general knowledge and insight of our universe realm domain I did not know specific names and relative locations of the visible stars.

While I was in this reverie I suddenly noticed the stars begin to move across the view panel and towards the right. I realised that Zanos was rotating the ship for us to get a view of the Earth. Gradually, brightness built up on the left of the windows and then the stars all just faded to nothingness. I found this odd but rather fascinating. The faint glow of our magnetic field also became prominently visible.

When the Earth did come into view it showed up as a half moon and I was surprised at how close it appeared. We were just over half a million miles from it and at this distance it was the same size as the moon when viewed from Earth. I zoomed in and knew I was looking at the eastern side of Asia. Japan was already in night shadow but I could see the glimmer of lights within the darkness. I looked for more lights but realised there would be none in the Pacific Ocean. Australia was not visible being hidden by the curvature of the Earth, but India and its mountains could be clearly seen. I panned for Mount Everest by zooming even closer but was disappointed how flat everything looked. The shadows cast by the mountains were equally unimpressive. I went back to the wider view and panned west. But here again there was a lot of cloud especially in the northern areas and I didn't recognise any particular features. The shape of Africa's east coast was just discernable though much of it was hidden by the Earth's curvature as was most of Europe.

After about five minutes of this the Earth view slowly drifted back to the left of the view panel as 520-Green gradually returned to its former position facing away from the Earth. Zanos conveyed that morning was just beginning in England with the local time being at 8:40 GMT. For some reason the Anztarzans had adopted GMT as their universal time pattern throughout the year. I suppose they had long ago chosen the time at zero meridian longitude to be a logical place to start their day. They kept to GMT even when England put its clocks forward for summertime.

Zanos conveyed to all that it would be another four hours before 520-Green entered the outer fringe of Earth's atmosphere and that we would be entering it somewhere over the continent of Antarctica. I was feeling quite refreshed from my long sleep and wondered what we could do during the next several hours. It would be at least seven hours before we entered Anztarza Bay.

Captain Bulzezatna read my thoughts and after a brief pause suggested that we all venture into the crew recreation lounge on the second deck and meet a few of them. Most would be there at some time or other and she was sure that they would find the experience a welcome treat. It was to prove most interesting in more ways than I expected.

Tatizblay was relieved of his duty and he escorted us to the crew lounge. We had to go down one level and then along a corridor to a position that I thought must be directly underneath our own lounge. But this was rather larger and reminded me of the airport lounges for Business and First Class passengers. I think the captain must have conveyed her intention to the crew for when we arrived there a seating area had been cleared and prepared for us.

There must have been about fifteen Oannes in there of whom two were women and these were quite middle aged like their captain. They were the first to welcome us and conveyed that they had been members of Captain Bulzezatna's crew on her two previous craft appointments. One of them was a distant cousin and about the same age. Her name was Nuztazm and she was born on the island of Ventrazta which was far out in the Peruga Sea. Ventrazta was a large island and had a number of towns one of which was located inland. The town was Krintozat and was a popular holiday centre. Its name implied landlocked which was unusual for an Oannes town most of which were located beside large bodies of water. It was in a hilly area and so no canals or waterways existed there. Incidentally Ventrazta had been the original name chosen for the underground city planned on Earth but had been changed to its present name after construction began.

Several of the crew came and communicated with us but I was especially taken by a very small young looking man named Sudzarnt. He tried saying how pleased he was to meet us but I could barely hear his whispering voice. I read his mind and ascertained that he was only 60 years of age and the youngest member of Bulzezatna's crew. And also the smallest for he was barely four feet in height. He was stocky in build and I just discerned a slight belly bulge under his tunic. But an emotion of humour exuded from him and he seemed as though he was on the point of laughter. The slightly bulbous nose and chin gave the impression that with a little makeup he could be dressed to look like a circus clown. The laughing twinkling eyes were what instantly attracted me to him. This was his most outstanding feature and I guessed that he must be very well liked and popular with the rest of the crew.

He originally came from a small town on the extreme north of the Great Sea of Peruga and had developed a natural dislike for the cold climate up there. Panztarna was within the northern freeze zone and remained frozen for half of the Nazmos year. If anything Sudzarnt hated being cold. Most Oannes didn't mind cold temperatures but Sudzarnt detested it and so when he was just thirty years old he migrated to a small town on Lake Voolzort not far from Latipuzan the city that Muznant came from. After a year there he heard about the life in Wentazta and decided to move there. It was to prove a good move for he met and became friends with Wasagga the 170 year old owner of a café that he frequented. It was from Wasagga that Sudzarnt heard exciting stories about Anztarza and Earth. And when he saw images of Earth's lush vegetation and heard of its milder climate he knew that it was where he would like to live. He found out all he could about Earth and Anztarza and there was no doubt in his mind that he'd like to go and live there.

Subsequently with Wasagga's help he applied for a monitoring task in the Anztarza organisation and was eventually successful and given passage to Earth on the FTL starship 6110-Red two years later. For the next twenty years he was placed in a variety of monitoring team positions and gained a good knowledge of the makeup of Earth's cultures. Somehow he seemed to connect with Earth philosophy and came to understand much of their aspirations, frustrations and anguish. He was at first confused by their aspects of anger but began to understand some of the reasons behind it. Sudzarnt stated openly that he would love to live among the Earth's population and experience at first hand all their trials and tribulations. He also found much loving among them and this gave him the encouragement to be among them. In other words he found the perfectionist lifestyle of the Oannes to border on the boring though he did not express it in quite that way.

On the upside however were his excursions into the lush Canadian forests during the hot summer months. And when Muznant returned from her first visit to Aberporth in November he avidly listened to her speech about me and my family.

About a year previously he had been accepted as a trainee crew member on 520-Green and so was not at the grand welcoming banquet held in Dome-4. But here I was with my family sitting right before him and him quite unable to utter the words he had intended.

So I read his mind and understood his unease through his excitement at meeting us face to face; quite an unforeseen event for him. I was rather flattered and telepathically conveyed to him that I was an ordinary person just like him and if he wished he could see into my mind and so know all about me. It took but a moment and suddenly he seemed to relax and even smiled. I asked him to sit with us and if he wished to just listen to our conversation.

Of one thing I was sure and that was that he had never felt conscious of his size. Although he was unusually short he had never been teased about it. Perhaps there were others as small. He was also different from the other Oannes I had seen in that his fins were practically half the normal size. But more so were the webs on the side cheeks of his face. These were only slight ridges and when he smiled his face looked quite human. So I queried this aspect about him and he just shrugged his shoulders with a gentle smile. I liked this little fellow and conveyed as much. And then he spoke again and his voice was still a whisper but now much more measured and audible.

'Please may I visit you in Anztarza,' he said and immediately there was silence from our group as they strained to hear what he had to say. 'I heard about you well before this visit just like everybody else and I did not believe everything that was said. But now I know it is all true. I saw you move the asteroids and that to me was a wonder. I have something to confess and I believe I might get what I desire,' and here his voice gave out as his throat went dry. He had simply run out of the ability to make a sound. I read his thoughts and conveyed this to the others.

Firstly he did not like the cold of Nazmos. And surprise, surprise he did not like the feel of water either which was extremely odd for an Oannes. And thirdly he didn't like the enclosed living inside Anztarza. This probably resulted from the fact that he was not a natural spaceman as most Oannes were. He suffered from something called 'space anxiety' in which he felt extreme insecurity of status during prolonged space flights.

He had discovered this on the seven month FTL journey to Earth. After the first week he had begun to feel depressed and then anxious that they were lost in the blackness of space. He had to be sedated when Zanos had reported his condition and he swore never to make such a long space journey ever again. He was on 520-Green because he had the desire to learn about space flight in a local environment and also that he might discover a way of coping with the space anxiety problem. Sudzarnt had been a year with Captain Bulzezatna and had grown to like and admire her immensely. And she too had noticed this diminutive Oannes person under her command and had taken a liking to him. His job on board was in the food supply cargo bay and was basically the fetch, carry and store away tasks. Perhaps it was Sudzarnt that we had seen on that first ships tour we had made.

And it was also Sudzarnt who had arranged the cabins for us. He had tested the beds and found that lying on his belly was quite comfortable and had one placed in his own shared cabin. He alternated between the bed and the sleep tank but felt that with a softer mattress cushioning on the bed he could gravitate there permanently. Sudzarnt had an inventive mind and already he was mentally considering the possibility of living among humans albeit secretly. Being with us was a dream come true and at the back of his mind was the hope that I might help find a solution to his dream. And perhaps I could help but he'd have to get the approval of his ministers. I knew what he was thinking and he knew that I was amenable to the idea, with a few reservations of course. I reached forward with my hand and took his tiny one in mine and conveyed that I would indeed help with his aspirations for integration with humans in any way I could.

I also found out from my mind probe that here was someone who appreciated Earth's variety of humour. During his years of monitoring it was the jokes and ribald crude humour that had caught his fancy and he had found it an amazing new emotion. When he had approached his superiors and tried to get this categorised as a facet of Earth culture he had been turned away. Sudzarnt's recorded opinion on the matter had been given a sub-file status which meant it was not relevant for onward transmission to Nazmos.

Sudzarnt had a light hearted attitude to life and this setback did not worry him in the least. He was widely liked and I considered him to be quite human in his demeanour and probably the first of the Oannes to fit right in with Earth ways. I conveyed that we should certainly like to see him again in Anztarza if that were possible and that I would speak up for him. I must ask Muznant and Brazjaf about him and of the options that were available to him. I had this vague thought in my mind for just an instant. Perhaps I thought but only perhaps.

Sudzarnt left us then and went back to the group of crew members at another seating area. Others then came and also greeted us and communicated their politeness and some even stopped for a brief verbal conversation that centred on the asteroid experiments.

It was then that I received the greeting from Puzlwat. He invited me to his table in the far corner of the room and conveyed an image of its location. I looked around and could just make him out in a far corner. I waited for a break in crew attendance and then excused myself. I walked across to where Puzlwat and Mytanzto sat along with another Oannes person. I was welcomed in a brief Sewa to which I responded before sitting down beside Mytanzto. An emotion of admiration now exuded from Mytanzto and I welcomed it as a pleasant change from his previous antagonistic attitude. His mind was open so I smiled at him and touched his bare arm for a deep mind probe. Immediately I understood everything about him.

Mytanzto was not the smartest of people and relied on others to tell him what he should think and do. Puzlwat had been such an influence and when I came along he had been confused. It was easy to push me to one side as an impostor but all of that crashed around him after witnessing the asteroid tests. Initially he could not understand why I had not gone for glory from the very start by showing off my skills as he would have done. However the realisation dawned upon him that I was a very different kind of person to what he expected. That I was a private family man who just wanted to help and be done with Zarama and all the rest and to lead a quiet life with his family. This would be quite impossible if I were to become an icon in the public domain. I'm glad of dad's wisdom in making me keep my gifts a general secret.

'Greetings to you Puzlwat and Mytanzto and to your companion here,' I said softly as I smiled at them. 'I was pleased to receive your invitation to join you. How may I be of service?'

'Thank you Ashley for coming so promptly,' Puzlwat said in his falsetto tone, 'this is Brajam and he is keen to talk with you. He specifically asked me to arrange this meeting. He is chief scientist on this mission and wishes to discuss certain issues with you. However before I leave you with him I should like to apologise to you personally for the injustices of my attitude towards you and your family before this trip. You have proved you are everything that Muznant communicated about you and I'm sorry I did not trust her judgement. I have already communicated my feelings to her and Brazjaf and they have been most generous and understanding. From now on you will only experience our acclaim.'

'Oh I think a good opposing viewpoint is extremely healthy for keeping one focussed,' I said aloud with a smile, 'it gave me something to aim for since even I was not sure I could do what I did with the asteroids. This experiment has taught me a lot; the chief of which was how to regulate my telekinetic gift. I was horrified by my destruction of Steins and I feel sorry for it. That will never be allowed to happen again.'

'Thank you,' said Puzlwat, 'you are most understanding and I hope we shall meet again in Anztarza. We will leave you now as I believe Brajam has much to discuss.'

Puzlwat and Mytanzto then slowly stood up and it was only then that I noticed that Mytanzto was quite a bit taller and heavier built than most; the proverbial Oannes bouncer.

I turned my attention towards Brajam and was struck by the deep piercing look of his eyes. I could see that he was keen to come to the point of this meeting and so without hesitation I conveyed that I was at his disposal. He seemed confused at my meaning so I reached my hand forward and he did the same. He had a firm handshake and in that brief moment we both completed a mutual deep mind probe. He was 150 years old and had been in Anztarza for ten years. Before that he was a research scientist on every available FTL starship. It was his ambition to discover ways of increasing their FTL velocities even further. Although the first FTL starships that had achieved several times light velocity was a tremendous breakthrough it was still considered too slow for effective space travel further afield. Even now the Oannes scientists were dreaming about an FTL ship achieving one hundred times light speed. The energy requirements would be phenomenal especially in the acceleration stages. However with the development of improved nucleus stimulation the emission of electrons had increased nearly a thousand-fold over what had been available before. This was a very positive and encouraging step forward.

Brajam's inner mind was a mass of scientific facts and data all pointing in that one direction. Brajam was ambitious to achieve recognition and had been so inclined from the youthful age of twenty. He had remained single and had no interest in girls apart from being with his mother and five sisters. He was born in Wentazta and had lived there with his parents all his life before coming to Earth. He returned there often and was due back on the next FTL starship home mainly to report back on a project he had been working on. Of course he would also like to give his own first hand account of the asteroid experiment and this meeting with me.

More recently thoughts of Zarama and the extinction of life on Nazmos had had been deeply persistent in his thoughts. He loved his home planet but a similar affiliation towards Earth had gradually developed within him. After all the city of Anztarza was also on Earth and it was wholly Oannes in culture. Earth's beauty was different from Nazmos and some might say more beautiful but to him he remained faithful to the land of his birth. A planet was its people and as yet Earth was a primitive place but with hopes for great improvement. The Oannes were a benevolent people and I felt that a great harmonious future lay before us. Brajam thought the same except he had doubts as to whether I could accomplish the big task of removing Zarama from the equation. Personally I also had my own doubts on the matter.

I had read his thoughts and had an idea of his fears and doubts but I now waited patiently for him to speak and indicated as much. His communication was however in the telepathic form as it was something he was more at home with.

'I was impressed by your power of telekinesis,' he conveyed, 'and I commend you on your restraint in its use.'

'Thank you,' I said aloud and simply inclined my head to one side to await his next statement. He was of course referring to the fact that I was not an exhibitionist and had not showed off my telekinetic prowess prior to the asteroids event. Dad had instilled in me the need for secrecy and I had abided by that advice always. I had never ever felt the least desire to show off. Having read my mind Brajam must have understood this.

'I have no doubt that you will be able to affect an orbit adjustment for Nazmos. It will take time for the climate to adjust and for new vegetation to take hold. But I fear that Zarama may not allow us that time,' conveyed Brajam.

I had never seen a sad expression on an Oannes person but such an expression was on Brajam's face. This was accompanied by an emotion of sadness that now surrounded us.

He continued. 'Zarama's arrival is a little over two thousand four hundred years away and I fear that may not be enough for Nazmos. Earth will suffer the same fate. Zarama is 431 light years distant and travelling towards us at just over a sixth of light speed. With our current technology we can only hope to reach near Zarama in about fifty years. We have begun work on an idea for a FTL ship to achieve 100 times light velocity but this will not be available for at least another hundred years – possibly longer.'

I could see where he was going with this and I felt saddened at the thought. But I waited for him to continue.

'The people think you are the saviour that was foretold in our mythology and I believe in it just as much as the next Oannes. But if you are the person foretold then I fear you may have come upon us too soon. Your lifespan is short at barely a hundred years and Zarama is too far away.' He paused and looked at me with his keen piercing gaze.

'But what do I know of the extent of your power,' he conveyed. 'Perhaps it has far greater potential than even you can know. And there lies my hope and purpose for communicating with you.'

I knew the question and conveyed to Brajam that without a trial of sorts I could not know the extent of my gifts. I did not know if I could move the asteroids but when the test came I actually exceeded my wildest expectations.

'But I do know this,' I said aloud, 'that these gifts have been granted me for a purpose. I also know that a very big task lies ahead of me and I do have an inbuilt sense and intuition that says I will achieve success. Someone is watching over us all and so will not allow failure especially if this is part of an overall plan.'

Brajam looked puzzled but only briefly. He recalled Earth's history and knew that I was referring to our religious beliefs and nodded his understanding.

'I certainly hope that such is the case,' he conveyed.

'So what is the issue you wish to raise?' I said knowing full well what he was about to ask.

'It is this,' he finally spoke in a low tone alto voice which rather surprised me. 'Do you think that with your telekinetic power you can affect an object a very long distance away?'

'I don't know the answer to that until I try,' I replied, 'what distance do you have in mind?'

I knew the answer before he said it.

'The distance to Zarama,' he said and stared piercingly at my face.

I looked calmly back at him and smiled before saying, 'Maybe, all things are possible.' But at that moment I did not know for sure.

I thought about the size of our galaxy at 100,000 light years in approximate diametric distance and in my imagination I reduced it in size to the scale of an aspirin. Then our nearest galaxy Andromeda would be another aspirin about five inches away. This plus a few other galaxies form our local group. The next similar group of galaxies called the Sculptor Group would be two feet away. The Virgo Cluster of about 200 galaxies spread over the size of a football is only three yards away. The Virgo Cluster is the hub of a loose swarm of galaxies called the Local Super-Cluster of which we are a part. On this scale just 40 yards away is another Super-Cluster called the Coma Cluster containing thousands of galaxies. Everything we can see through our telescopes on Earth - which is the entire visible universe - can be contained in a sphere roughly a mile in diameter (on the scale where an aspirin represents our Milky Way galaxy).

I conveyed my thoughts to Brajam and let him know that all distances were relative and so Zarama did not seem unreachable. I felt I could stretch out my arm and touch it. My inner voice however prompted that I was not quite ready and I conveyed as much to Brajam.

'This is good,' he said, 'very good. I am exceedingly encouraged by your attitude Ashley. It could all come true.'

I knew he was referring to their ancient myths and all I could say was, 'We shall see.'

Tania had quietly come and sat down beside me and there was a gentle slowness in her manner that she reserved for me when I was with someone she thought could be distressing me. In an instant I conveyed to her everything that had just transpired with Brajam and she seemed relieved.

'You two seemed to be glaring at one another so intensely that I was sure something was wrong,' she said. 'But I see now you were discussing an impossible situation regarding Zarama. Sorry if I barged in.'

Tania was my saviour in more ways than I could count. Without her love and caring I think I'd be at a total loss. I just cannot imagine my life without her around me.

Once again I could see that Brajam was lost in his thoughts. As a scientist he would be analysing a problem from every angle to make certain that the solution was realistic. He was staring at the far wall and seemed quite oblivious of us in front of him. Tania and I looked at each other and I shook my head slightly to indicate that we should not interrupt his current thoughts. I was seeing another side of the Oannes personality in which their mental process went into high gear which I found rather intriguing.

'It will not work,' Brajam suddenly announced looking at me directly and conveyed all his analysis data over to me. Fortunately I was able to absorb this concentrated telepathic information though with a slight degree of confusion at first. Brajam had not thought that the human brain had only just begun to operate in telepathic mode and had not as yet any degree of refinement. Any other Oannes person would have no problem receiving such a burst of compressed data and information. If the blast had been directed at Tania then I fear she could have suffered adversely either as a pang of pain or a dull throbbing in the head. Either way the information would not have been received. I conveyed as much to Brajam and he was quite shocked by his oversight.

'I'm so sorry,' he said aloud, 'I fear my excitement got the better of me. Yet you Ashley seem to have been able to accept my message. Are you alright?'

'Only just,' I said, 'only just. Perhaps this is because I am the only human who is also able to probe and read the Oannes mind. Perhaps I have acquired your mental agility by doing so. But on the subject of Zarama I do see the problem.'

'Yes, it is unfortunate and we shall have to find other solutions,' he said.

Tania looked confused and was looking quizzically from me to Brajam and back at me. So I conveyed Brajam's analysis across to her.

My intended effort to work upon Zarama from this perceivable distance of 525 light years would not work for the simple reason that it would not be there. What I would be seeing in a spaceship's view panel would be simply the image of Zarama as it had been location-wise 525 years ago. Any telekinetic pulse that I sent out against it would therefore not be directed at the White Dwarf star itself but at its virtual past image. I knew in my mind that I must be able to view the object in question in real time physically in front of me for me to apply any telekinetic force upon it.

Then the question came up that even if I did manage to guess where Zarama was actually located and direct my force to that point how long would it take for my impulse to actually span the distance? I did not know.

And of course we would not know whether I had succeeded for another 500 years or so. Brajam had analysed all this at depth and had come up against barrier after barrier. His next thoughts had been for me to get closer to Zarama in an FTL ship but here again my shorter life-span would mean that for me it would be a one way trip. This was not acceptable to the Oannes morally or otherwise. Another solution had to be found. It was my inner voice that brought a possible solution to mind.

I conveyed this to both Brajam and Tania and he immediately went into his analytical trance-like fixed staring stance. He then looked at me and smiled and conveyed his thoughts slowly to Tania and me. Basically I had suggested that I might be able to increase the speed of a current FTL ship with my telekinetic push force if it were suitably modified for that purpose. Of course I would have to be on the FTL ship and my push would simply be a supplement to the ship's own impulse power. I did not know by how much I could increase the velocity of the FTL ship so trials would need to be conducted. Nor did I know for how long I must sustain such an effort. Also the acceleration forces caused by my telekinetic push might be too great for its passengers including myself. Brajam smiled at this and conveyed the principle of gravity that was applied as a result of the ships massive neutron star material shield.

So that was how the passengers on current FTL starships were kept at a constant 0.9g gravity level throughout the seven month journey to and from Earth. Once the FTL ship was cruising at ten times light speed its velocity remained constant unlike 520-Green which had to be under constant acceleration for the comfort of its passengers.

The visual I received from Brajam was that of a mushroom shaped head behind which was a slightly tapered circular body that was nearly half a mile in diameter and two miles long. The mushroom head was made from neutron star material and was three quarters of a mile in diameter and nearly a quarter of an inch thick. The thickness increased marginally with each prolonged FTL journey. Within the rear mile and a half length of the ship was housed the power plant complex of electron generators and impulse motors. The mushroom head was the main factor that shielded the structure of the ship and its occupants from the energy-medium of the realm grid that would have destroyed any atoms that fell in its path at the ten times FTL velocity. As such there was no time dilation factor inside the ship.

There was only one passenger habitation level and this was on a movable platform parallel to and behind the mushroomed head and normally located about 500 to 600 feet from it. The habitation floor faced away from the neutron shield which was placed some distance underfoot. The layout of the passenger accommodation was similar to that of the domes of Anztarza except there were no streets only pathways between the blocks of houses. And there was no central plaza either though the centre point was marked by a circular column of twenty feet diameter that went up into the high ceiling above the habitation level. There was a protective safety barrier wall around the column at floor level. The column was part of the platform's movable mechanism complementing those that existed at six peripheral locations.

Under stationary or constant velocity cruise conditions the habitation platform needed to be at a distance slightly less than 600 feet from the neutron material shield for normal Nazmos gravity levels. When the floor moved downwards and closer to the neutron shield the gravity level increased exponentially. At 400 feet position the gravity increased a hundredfold. At 300 feet the increase was a thousand fold. And if closer this could be made to reach unimaginable levels.

As such the ship could be accelerated at a phenomenal rate towards its FTL cruise speed without causing gravitational stress upon its passengers.

Each FTL ship had a committee of twenty three Zanos type bio-computers with each capable of operating all of the ships functions in complete harmony. One of the key tasks performed was the raising and lowering of the habitation platform to ensure correct Nazmos gravity levels in all the phases of the FTL journey.

Under the habitation level and closer to the front neutron material shield were the food growing tanks which had the capacity to produce a continuous supply of Raizna, Starztal, Yaztraka, Lazzonta and Yantza enough for two thousand Oannes the maximum accommodation level. The passenger and crew levels however seldom exceeded a thousand per trip.

Brajam conveyed that as yet he did not know how my telekinetic power could be applied to accelerating the spaceship but that his teams would soon be working upon it. Of course the essential factor was that I would have to remain at habitation level on the ship the same as all other passengers.

Suddenly it did not look that daunting a problem after all and I conveyed all this to Tania cuddled up beside me. She looked up at me and smiled her full support for anything I should decide. A sudden thought came to me and I conveyed this to Brajam. What if my efforts took the ship to a hundred times FTL velocity or even higher? Could the structure of the ship withstand the stresses of such a velocity?

Again Brajam gave an Oannes style telepathic chuckle followed by an outward smile. He conveyed that the only limitation on the FTL starship was its power source not being sufficient to push it to the required multiple FTL velocity. He indicated that the greatest power expenditure was in actually accelerating the spacecraft to the specified multiple FTL velocity. Keeping it there required less power. Other design considerations could also be taken into account but this would require the construction of a whole new type of craft taking several hundred years and not an option for us. The neutron shield was the all important factor that sheltered the ship and its passengers from the spatial grid energy medium that it was crashing through. The greater the FTL velocity the greater was the mass absorption rate by the neutron shield. No normal atomic structure could withstand such a direct onslaught of energy medium. It would only take a matter of moments for the atoms to be stripped of their protective shell and oblivion. Hence the importance of the neutron shields. Brajam conveyed that we should stick to the current ship modification plan which could be available for trial in a decade or so.

I sensed another doubt of sorts arising in Brajam's mind and then picked up the factor that was causing it. He had no doubt that Nazmos could be moved by me as required. The doubt he registered was the effect my telekinetic effort might have upon the population of the planet. There were people and animals who could not all be evacuated to the safety of space. And what effect would there be upon the oceanic mass? Would there be cataclysmic tidal waves or atmospheric storms?

This came as a shock and I could make no response to any of these questions because frankly I did not know. But what I did know was that I now had a complete and accurate control of my telekinetic power and could apply the gentlest of force over a longer period of time and so cause the least amount of disturbance on Nazmos. I conveyed this to Brajam and suggested that an asteroid type experiment be conducted but with shuttles of Oannes personnel positioned upon and around its surface.

Brajam had a fantastic computing brain and instantly his mind was whirling with computations, calculations and the practicalities for such a complex experiment the conclusions of which he then conveyed to me.

Of the three other planets orbiting further out in the Raznat system there was one named Platwuz that was larger than Nazmos but which also had a thin atmosphere of methane. There were several research and mining camps upon it and this might be the ideal testing ground for my telekinetic trials. Brajam conveyed that he would of course need to put the idea to the Nazmos Governing Council for not only agreement but also for further detailed planning to be formulated. It might also be an advantage to bring Platwuz to an orbit nearer to Raznat and one in which the planet would not remain such a frozen wasteland. The concept seemed to grow on Brajam and his eyes sparkled with inner excitement.

If anything I had learned that the Oannes were an extremely patient people. They took their time in all things and believed in thoroughness. So when I queried the timescale that Brajam had in mind for any of these things to occur he conveyed that it might all happen rather quickly; perhaps as soon as ten or twenty years from now.

When I conveyed all this to Tania she burst out laughing.

'Call that quickly,' she said aloud with laughter still in her voice but I could sense relief there too. 'Why I think that's wonderful. I wonder what they would call something that we do urgently on the spot on Earth.'

Brajam seemed confused by this but then he probed Tania's mind and immediately understood her thinking. He smiled at the humour and conveyed that Oannes legislation and plan approval was extremely thorough with mental simulations being conducted a multitude of times prior to sanction. The asteroid experiment had been formulated over a period of a month and a half and many of the Oannes scientists had not been happy with the rapid approval by the chief ministers. They had hoped for a much longer process of thought and analysis.

Mum, dad and the others had walked across to our corner of the room and now stood around us. I noticed that Muznant and Brazjaf had remained back at the table. With their Oannes minds they would know all that went on here. I introduced Brajam to our group and conveyed to them all that had just transpired between him and me. He of course knew who everyone was and conveyed a Sewa greeting to them all.

'So are further experiments with Ashley's telekinetic gift about ten to twenty years in the future?' asked Jerry.

'Not necessarily,' conveyed Brajam. 'Perhaps others back on Nazmos may feel it necessary for a much larger mini-planet size experiment for Ashley. There is a large strange moon around your planet Neptune that might be considered for an orbital adjustment.'

'Oh,' said Jerry our spokesman, 'and what is this strange moon you talk of?'

Brajam conveyed his thoughts in a single concentrated blast of telepathy that was lost to all but me.

Quickly I relayed his information to the others while at the same time communicating to Brajam that he must remember to slow his telepathy style to suit our slower human brain.

'Sorry,' he said aloud in his whispering voice and continued for the benefit of all. 'This body or moon orbiting around planet Neptune is known to your astronomers as Triton. It is about two thirds the size of your own moon and strangely enough has a thin atmosphere of nitrogen gas. What is even stranger is that it has a retro-grade orbit which means that it orbits Neptune in the opposite direction to the planet's rotation. It is therefore highly probable that Triton was a capture event and may have collided with one of the original moons or even bounced off Neptune's atmosphere. It is very cold on Triton at just a few degrees above absolute zero and yet there are active geysers upon it. These spew out a gaseous form of Nitrogen which is what creates Triton's atmosphere.'

Brajam paused here and reading Jerry's mind answered his query before it was voiced.

'Yes, it would be a most interesting test of Ashley's telekinetic skills if he could alter Triton's path from its current retro-grade orbit to a normal one in the opposite direction,' said Brajam looking at Jerry directly.

He then slowly conveyed his thoughts on how this could be done without actually stopping Triton's orbital motion. His idea was to gradually alter Triton's orbit direction from its present to a more polar one in successive stages. By continuing this process Triton could be made to eventually orbit in the same direction as Neptune's rotation. At no stage would Triton be in danger of crashing downwards upon its planet.

'And when is this experiment likely to be conducted?' asked Jerry.

Brajam again conveyed his slow telepathic answer that it was just a thought on his part and on the spur of the moment. To be realised it would have to get the approval of the Nazmos Governing Council and be given a thorough mental simulation and evaluation of all possible probabilities. The repercussions among Earth's astronomers would also need to be taken into consideration. If this meant that they might conclude that an alien influence had been involved then the experiment might not receive permission at all. Again a timescale of ten to twenty years was envisaged by Brajam.

'What about the recent asteroids experiments,' asked Jerry? 'Won't the orbital changes of Masursky and Mathilde cause speculation?'

'Yes they will,' Brajam replied, 'but asteroids in the central zone are being jostled about continually by collisions among themselves. That is the reason we chose the central zone for our experiment. Some are even struck by large external non-asteroid objects and such an event may be attributed for the disintegration of Steins. I mean no unkindness Ashley but I believe that Steins was an important part of the overall experiment for it brought to your notice the necessity for you to accurately control your telekinetic power. And I know that you have accomplished this to your own complete satisfaction.'

Tania squeezed my hand at this and reading her thoughts I knew exactly what she was thinking about. She was relieved that we would have our life together back in Dudley without any immediate complicated experimentation requirements from our Anztarzan friends. My inner voice was silent and that reassured me somewhat. But I knew that the task ahead of me that Philip had referred to in his final communication lay just over the distant horizon. And would my gifts diminish with my advancing years? And what part would this fantastic energy drink Wazu have to play in all of this? Many questions came to my mind but no answers. And yet a confidence was building up inside me that made me look to the future with growing joy and exuberance. Was this some newfound cockiness on my part or just an exhilarating insight of the goodness of my life ahead?

On impulse I turned my face towards Tania and planted a firm kiss upon her soft surprised lips and held it there for an eternity. Not that she or anyone knew it for I had gone to pink mode the moment my lips touched hers. Remaining in pink mode level one I gazed at Tania's face close up. Her eyes were half closed and her mouth had a hint of a smile at its corners. I stood up then and walked back a few paces and viewed the scene before me. There was a beautiful slow-motion effect to everyone's movement which quite fascinated me. Without exception all had their eyes in Tania's direction and all had gentle smiles on their faces including Brajam. And even though time was near motionless I could sense the emotion of love all around me. I soaked this in and felt quite overwhelmed by it all. I was a lucky man and was thankful for it. My communication of thanks went up like a prayer into the unknown reaches of the eternity we call heaven. There was a great deal I had to say and I said it all before once again sitting down beside Tania and returning to normal time mode. The buzz of sound returned and it was only then that I noticed how beautifully silent everything had been during the pink mode session.

A smiling Brajam now stood up slowly and conveyed his thanks to me for meeting with him. Many issues had been clarified and he had much to report. He conveyed that he must return to Nazmos on the next FTL starship so that he could give all his information to the Governing Council. He said he was pleased to have also met my family and wished us happiness and success in our endeavours.

A brief Sewa was conducted by him and I followed suit and I wondered if we should ever meet like this again. The probability was high that we would and I hoped for it too as he had come across as a gentle and very likeable personality. He must have read my thoughts and felt my emotion for he smiled with pleasure as he slowly turned and walked to the door. I watched him leave and he did not look back until he was nearly out of the doorway. Then he paused briefly and looked back at us for a moment before stepping out into the corridor. The sliding door closed silently behind him.

'What a nice gentleman,' said Brenda, 'but then they are all like that.'

'Yes,' agreed Milly, 'I'm afraid they put us to shame.'

We went back to our table and sat down with Muznant and Brazjaf. Muznant conveyed that Brajam was a well known and liked figure and brilliant in his work and exceptionally thorough in everything he did. I guessed as much. They had known Brajam for many years and admired him. Brazjaf had dealings with him in his governmental administration work. He was married to his work and as such had no time for socialising or romantic notions. He was definitely a confirmed bachelor.

My wrist watch was now showing 10:30am and I thought we must be nearing Earth. Captain Bulzezatna had promised us a control room view of our entry into Earth atmosphere above Antarctica and I wondered how much longer that could be. I knew that we were continually slowing down to preserve normal gravity on board and were currently in the slowest phase of our journey.

Zanos communicated an instant reply that 520-Green should be in Earth's gravity grip within the hour which prompted a desire for a nice cup of tea. Tania must have read my thought through her badge and relayed this to the others.

Granddad Eric suggested we return to the quiet of our own dining lounge as he'd like to flake out and rest his eyes while sitting on the comfy sofa there. Besides he said we had our own tea making things all to hand in the kitchenette there.

I thought it a good idea as did Tania and the others so we performed a general Sewa to the occupants here and slowly filed out of the room. We had to go up one level and it was Katy who led the way back to our lounge. Granddad poured himself a glass of Wazu and I did the same as I was rather thirsty. Milly and Brenda went to make the tea and I wondered if there was any hot chocolate to be had. There was, so I opted for that instead of tea. Granddad Eric went across to another sofa and taking his shoes off got up into a sideways semi-reclining position. He put his head on the soft armrest and shut his eyes.

I conveyed that it wouldn't be long before the wood sawing sounds began. But I was wrong and though he seemed sound asleep from his deep breathing there was not the hint of a snore. Perhaps the angle of his head must have been just right for him.

The hot chocolate was okay but I think I should have stayed with the tea. Mum sensed this and said I should leave it if I didn't like it.

'Perhaps another half spoon of sugar might make it just right,' I said grinning sheepishly.

'Oops,' said Aunt Brenda, 'I'm afraid I didn't put any in at all. I'll get some right away.'

She came back with the sugar container and a long handled teaspoon and I helped myself to a heaped spoonful. I gave it a good stir and then took a sip.

'Aah,' I said, 'that's more like it.'

'My son has a sweet tooth,' said mum to everyone with a big smile. 'He's always had one sugar in his tea and probably always will.'

'That's because I'm a sweet guy,' I said and everyone smiled.

We had finished our drinks and were talking generally about Anztarza and that we should be back home soon when a communication came from the captain for us to return to the control room if we wished to see the view.

We were about to settle into our usual places when Captain Bulzezatna suggested we remain standing and close to the view panels. She said we should soon be in Earth's gravity hold and travelling in a forward direction. There was an eerie brightness about the ship and I realised that this was the sunlight shining on the craft and also that reflected up off the Earth's atmosphere.

Zanos conveyed that the ship was now held by Earth's gravity and that a forward impulse was being applied. We were still dropping downwards but soon the impulse motors would keep us at a planned height. There was no need for aerodynamics since the impulse motors performed all functions to balance with the Earth's gravity. The current cruising height was 100,000 feet. But this would not be for long as 520-Green had entered the Earth's upper atmosphere over the southern tip of Argentina and was heading south towards the whiteness of Antarctica.

It was exhilarating to see the glow around the ship suddenly burst open and the Earth's curvature of brightness came into our view. My heart jumped and I felt an emotion that I cannot find eloquent enough words to describe. Perhaps the chest pain emotion of love at first sight might be an adequate description of how I felt. I could feel other minds entering mine and I knew that Captain Bulzezatna along with several of her crew had sampled my exhilarating moment just as if it were their own. Once you share such an emotion then affections are born that last between you forever. This joy of meeting with one's homeland must be what FTL passengers experienced upon returning to Nazmos after a prolonged stay away in space or on another planet.

The horizon flattened and brightened as we dropped to a lower altitude and when we cruised over Antarctica the bare whiteness was amazingly beautiful. Although I had seen this before when we first journeyed to Anztarza somehow you forget how beautiful it can look. The sun was behind us so it was just the glare of reflected light from below that made us squint initially. Then Zanos must have recognised our discomfort for the view panels slowly acquired a darker colour tint.

The ship was cruising at several thousand miles per hour and I thought what a far cry it was from the 20,000 miles per second velocity from Mathilde towards Earth. There was little sensation of our speed since my view was mainly forwards and slightly downwards and so I was not able to see Antarctica speeding beneath the ship. Captain Bulzezatna received my thoughts and suggested I go right up to the view panel and look downwards from there. I did as told and what a sight met my eyes. The others had also come forward and their expressions of awe were clearly heard by all. Tania squeezed my hand as she exclaimed her appreciation in an 'ooh aah' fashion.

Zanos conveyed that 520-Green was still at 100,000 feet and 6000 mph forward speed which accounted for the fast moving panorama beneath us. The sun was at a shallow angle and the mountains cast deep dark shadows that gave the flatness below a semblance of depth. And as we raced above our velocity became quite apparent. The view was mesmerising and I thought how fortunate we were to be witnessing all this at firsthand.

Captain Bulzezatna was pleased at our emotional response to the beauty passing below and conveyed that it also reminded her of the polar zones of her own Nazmos. She was pleased also by the response to our home coming simply because it showed how alike our two peoples really were. There was love of country in both our hearts which was one of the essential ingredients for compatibility and a harmonious relationship.

As I watched the frozen landscape passing below we suddenly seemed to drop right down to near ground level and I felt dizzy at the tremendous sensation of speed. Someone's thoughts infiltrated mine and immediately we were back at the previous altitude.

'It is not wise to magnify the view image when travelling at this relative rate,' was the telepathic message from Bulzezatna and I could sense a humour in her tone. 'I suggest you look forward at the approaching coastline as we shall soon be descending towards our sea entry point.'

I realised that I must have subconsciously willed to see the detail of the passing landscape beneath us and the view panel had interpreted this as a request for telescopic magnification of the ground below. I looked across to the captain and bowed my head in thanks for her intervention and she smiled her acknowledgement of my appreciation. This also made me realise that our minds were being constantly monitored along with all our emotional responses so that best efforts could be made for our comfort. I wondered how long it would take for our societies on Earth to reach this level of pleasant harmonious living.

I conveyed all this to the others of our group and Jerry responded with the thought that he had already tried it though in a partial manner only. Since he had wilfully intended it he knew what to expect and had been exhilarated by the sensation of speed that it gave. But now he had again gone to magnification of the distant coast ahead and enjoyed seeing its approach though at a much less sensational rate. We all followed suit and the broken ice near the coastline seemed to have large blocks of ice bunched close together so that it appeared quite ominous. But this was simply the effect of the view panel's magnification of the scene before us. The magnification seemed to compress distant objects close together such that relative depth of field was falsified.

Suddenly the horizon rose higher in the panels and I saw that the ships attitude had altered and that it had gone into a shallow descent. We were descending quite rapidly. I returned to normal view and keenly watched as the coast approached and then passed beneath us. We were now over the broken ice packs and still descending. Zanos answered my query and indicated our height was now 5500 feet and speed 1500 mph and decreasing fast.

Time goes by quickly when events are rapidly unfolding and it seemed like only minutes had passed before we were practically at sea level and hovering above the waves of the Davis Sea.

Sea entry was a slow gentle process of first settling on the water and gradually submerging downwards. The ship then proceeded forwards in a shallow underwater descent till it reached its target depth of 2000 feet.

But we didn't wait for this as there was nothing more to see. The view panels had gone dark quite quickly and Captain Bulzezatna suggested that we return to the lounge and relax. A light lunch was available if we wished since it would still be a few hours before 520-Green reached our Anztarza Bay destination.

Granddad Eric conveyed that he would certainly like a bite to eat but that he would also like a couple of hours rest in his cabin afterwards.

I wasn't hungry at all but had a glass of Wazu to keep the others company.

'It seems like ages since we set out on this trip,' said dad wistfully, 'and it's a little sad that it's coming to an end.'

'I never imagined that travelling in space could be so simple and comfortable,' said mum. 'They really have solved a lot of things. At times I thought I was back in Anztarza. I shan't worry about Ashley if he does have to make other journeys with them and I'm sure that many will be made.'

Then turning to Muznant she added, 'Excuse me Muznant and Brazjaf what I mean is that you are a wonderful and skilled people and I hope we see a lot of each other in the future.'

'And so we shall,' Brazjaf conveyed, 'and we are grateful to you for thinking so. We are really more indebted to you because Ashley is yours and we wish him to help us. So you see we are quite mercenary really. However there is much we can teach you so in that way we are really partners in all of this. Nazmos and Earth will both benefit from Ashley's actions.'

He smiled after he had conveyed this and I knew exactly what he meant.

If we are to harmonise with the Oannes people we must literally come to their way of thinking. Telepathic communication was the key factor in all of this and I hoped that Margaret Dutton was successful in her teaching endeavours. Once a nucleus of people acquired the skill it could grow throughout the population quite rapidly. That was my hope anyway. I wondered if there was any way the Oannes could help. Perhaps not as I knew that the Oannes way was never to interfere. It was a very strict code that they had always adhered to.

And yet my guess for us to attain the Oannes level of telepathy and communication was that it would take possibly a thousand years of constant development. Hopefully by then Nazmos will have begun to develop a flora comparable to Earth. Our future was there and perhaps even somewhere far beyond. When Earth is a hot dried up shell in a billion years time Nazmos will be a haven for the next trillion years. What a wonderful hope that was; somewhere for us to seek refuge.

I suppose we were all in our own deep thoughts wondering what adventures lay around the corner. The asteroid experiment was certainly high adventure for us. And yet there was no concept of danger throughout it all. Space travel could certainly be made safe through technological development. I'm certain Tania was beginning to enhance her telepathic skills through association with me and acquire the ability of actually picking up my thoughts. She squeezed my hand as if to reassure me that I was not alone. And I was not because I had my family around me for support and I was grateful that it was so. I am not a loner and in a couple of years when Tania and I tie the knot our two families will really become one and be always there for us as we shall be for them.

With lunch over we agreed to return to our cabins for a rest or even forty winks as granddad put it, after all we had about three hours to kill.

I lay on my bed and thought about granddad Eric who was already well into sleep mode. I knew he had definitely decided to prolong his stay in Anztarza at least until our next visit. But I sensed that he was quite likely to make this his second home. I only hope he does not overstay his welcome. When the news gets back to Nazmos I wonder what their reaction will be to this visit. There has got to be a prejudice against such a visit by humans just as Puzlwat initially reacted. But the Oannes were a goodly people and if they could believe that I had the power to divert Zarama then that could only be good for us. Brajam would have much to show in our defence along with testaments from Muznant and all who had met us. I do feel that we have much in common.

I also wondered whether granddad Eric was actually thinking of visiting Nazmos as his ultimate adventure. I could see no harm in it other than the fact that we should not be in contact with him for a long time. Also it might be a good thing for the Nazmos Oannes to see granddad and wonder at the aged appearance of an eighty year old human. I'm sure he would be the perfect ambassador to represent us all. Also he would be my granddad and recognised as such. I had no doubt that we should be visiting there also. But that was not just yet. As Brajam had indicated the Oannes took their time about things and I reckon we have a grace period of about twenty years. Our communication badges would keep us in touch with granddad while he was here on Earth but never when we were six light years apart.

'What are you thinking Ashley?' It was Tania enquiring as usual through my badge so I conveyed all my thoughts about granddad back to her.

'Hmmm, you certainly are a deep thinker my love. I thought I might at least have been a bit more in your thoughts,' conveyed Tania. She was a saucy one but I didn't send that to her.

'I don't need to think of you because you are permanently inside my head,' I replied.

'Do you think about my body Ashley?' She certainly was in a saucy mood.

'Yes and no.'

'Do you love me?'

'Yes I do, very much so.'

'How much?'

'From one side of my finger to the other.'

'That's not very much.'

'It is if you go from one side of my finger and all around the universe to get to the other side.'

'That's very clever. But I want to hear the words of how you love me.'

'How do I love thee? Ah, let me count the ways. I love thee to the depth and breadth and height my soul can reach, when feeling out of sight for the ends of being and …..'

'Shut up and go to sleep you fool.' I sensed laughter in her tone and I knew I had said it right.

'See you later Tania,' and I conveyed my emotion of love through my badge which I knew it was fully capable of doing.

Silence ensued and I knew why and I loved her even more for it. Tania had the knack of concluding conversations not by having the final say but by shutting it down with a silent withdrawal. I do not know of any one else who can do that with such finesse.

I must have drifted off for when I awoke I thought for a moment that I was on a sailing ship gently rocking at its moorings. We were in fact in Anztarza Bay and the motion I sensed was the ship being gently buffeted by lapping waves caused by its arrival at the surface.

I queried Zanos and was informed that 520-Green was at the quayside and I was the only one still in my cabin. The others had all gone to the control room when Bulzezatna had communicated that the ship was about to surface in Anztarza Bay. My badge must have sensed my deep sleep and not disturbed me. I was thankful for that as I now felt quite refreshed and on top of the world. I was ready to meet the world on any level so to speak.

'Where is everybody,' I queried in general and received an immediate reply.

'Wake up sleepy head,' communicated Tania. 'We had to request Zanos to wake you nearly five minutes ago.'

Only Zanos could do that by triggering a thought pulse of the right frequency and modulation. And yet I had felt no sense of being awakened intentionally by anyone. It seemed a perfectly natural moment. I shall know next time to request Zanos for a similar alarm call as necessary.

I entered the control room and saw that the chief ministers were also present though not together as on previous occasions but dispersed among the others there. Rymtakza stood near Muznant and Brazjaf and was listening to granddad Eric saying something. I gathered this to be his formal request to stay on in Anztarza after the rest of us had returned home. And Rymtakza seemed to be smiling back agreeably. Zarzint was with our little group to one side and in verbal conversation with mum and dad. He seemed to be making a point for I could see Jerry nodding agreement. The senior chief Minister Tzatzorf stood beside Captain Bulzezatna and quite separate from the rest of the roomful.

Puzlwat and Mizpalto were at the view panels looking out at the Bay view. Upon my entry they walked towards me in a very welcoming manner. Mizpalto was all smiles and fawning so I made a point of shaking palms with him first. We both conveyed our Sewa greetings to each other and I added the word 'friend' somewhere in mine. I then did the same with Puzlwat and he also added the phrase 'pleased to meet you' during our handshake.

'I have been in communication with Nogozat and she is keen to see you again; this time as the returning hero,' he said aloud.

'Thank you,' I said, 'it will be a pleasure to visit your home.'

The Oannes never issued a direct invitation but offered to show hospitality without the pressure of an obligatory response. It was then up to the recipient to take up the offer and suggest a visit to their home – a supreme honour for the host.

'The honour will be mine and it would be an even greater pleasure if you brought your family with you,' said Puzlwat in a most agreeable tone.

Somehow I just could not imagine that this was the same Puzlwat who had been antagonistic to our visit here. But then he had genuinely believed me to be false and had been quite open about it.

Neither of Bulzezatna's deputies was in the control room and I suspected that they were about their duties securing the ship alongside the quay. The slight rocking motion of the ship had now ceased and Zanos answered my unasked question. Underwater supports had been raised to lift the ship just sufficiently to allow the passengers and crew to disembark along a level walkway. The Oannes saw to their every comfort and convenience even to the little inconsequential factors such as a level connecting ramp. Such was the height of their civilization.

As we walked onto the quayside I found it hard to believe where all I had just travelled. The Oannes had made it seem as though I had taken a simple trip to the seaside for a short holiday. The normality of space travel by this Oannes civilization was truly a wonder in itself. Space was not that hostile environment that we on Earth envisaged but just another place to roam freely. All the essentials were there on board the Oannes' ships the chief of which was the comfort of the ever present normal Earth type gravity; a veritable home from home atmosphere.

I shall look forward to any future trips into space with them especially the trip to see the FTL starship when it arrives. Also this trip had proved to mum and dad that it was quite the safest thing to travel with the Oannes. I know that they are completely reassured that I shall be safe in their care. Besides, the Oannes people are a most civilized society, their chief aspect being their open-mindedness. They kept no secrets from one another. If there was dissension then it was open and apparent as had been the case with Puzlwat. But there had never been any malice attached to his opinions. My chest swelled with hope because I knew that one day far in the future we humans would also reach such a stage in our civilization. And with the help of the Oannes people that might be realised perhaps a little bit sooner.

There was quite a crowd gathered on the quayside and I recognised a few. Katy's friend Jantuzno was there and came forward to meet us. She got into step beside Tania and Katy and it was a typical girl's reunion of sorts. Kazaztan welcomed us telepathically through our badges and although I could not see him I imagined him standing beside his Deck Transporter 536-Orange somewhere behind the crowds.

I felt like the returning conquering hero, after all I had just proven myself in the 'battle of the asteroids' so to speak. The Oannes now had a greater confidence in me as I myself had also become more assured of my ability. I decided to do a walkabout among the crowds and conveyed this to our group members. On my initiative we all split up and headed into the crowd in different directions. Handshakes seem to have been adopted as a norm by the Oannes as it also doubled as a good body contact for mind reading.

As I made my way forward shaking hands and being touched on my shoulders and arms I wondered how this popularity would affect me mentally. I had never wanted glory or acclaim of any kind and here I felt I was giving something of myself to please these people rather than the boosting of any personal ego trip. My gifts had been given to me freely and I would ensure that they would be available to all whenever I was able to accommodate a need. These gifts could just as easily be taken from me and then I'd be just another ordinary human being. I wanted the Oannes to see me for what I was as a human being and to realise that I wanted nothing more than that. I could not and would not change my views just because I was able to perform something out of the ordinary.

Sometimes I feel the weight of the responsibility that has been thrust upon me but then I count my blessings in that I am able to lead an ordinary life with my family and my girl. I get a great satisfaction from my McGill's Antiques and Museum business and I shall ensure that it continues for as long as I am able.

Nazmos and then Zarama were on my future agenda but that was many years away as indicated by Brajam. Before that I could foresee many years of happy married life with Tania and our two cohesive families. And joy of joys granddad seemed on the mend and doing extremely well. This Wazu had given him a whole new lease of life.

I was shaken from these thoughts by a hand clasping mine. It was Sudzarnt and he was looking up at me with a pleading expression. I knew what it was that he wanted but I was quite helpless to oblige. On Earth he would be looked on as a dwarf and not a pretty one at that. I would speak to Muznant about him and perhaps she would have some idea of what could be done. Yes, Muznant and Brazjaf would be the ones to make approaches on Sudzarnt's behalf. I conveyed this to my little friend and I felt his emotion of joy come back at me. A quick squeeze of my hand and he was gone. I shall pass on the subject of Sudzarnt's immigration request at the dinner table tonight for further discussion.

We made our slow way towards the bright colours of 536-Orange and as we got closer Kazaztan came out to us though his flood of affectionate emotions preceded him by several yards. Granddad rushed ahead of us and the two men clasped hands and smiled into each others faces. I noticed that when Kazaztan got emotional his head bobbed up and down quite rapidly. I was beginning to recognise certain characteristics pertaining to individuals as I got used to seeing them more often. I wondered how they saw me. Perhaps I walked in a certain manner that was uniquely recognisable as pertaining only to me. Or did I move my head in a certain way each time I spoke? I suppose all these particular mannerisms are what make us different from one another; our own unique blend of personality.

We were just about to board the Deck Transporter when a command came to stop. I turned and there coming towards us was our Captain Bulzezatna and her two deputies Tatizblay and Rubandiz. They had come to say farewell. I put my hand out towards Bulzezatna but she brushed it aside and reaching up with both hands drew my face downwards and planted a brief soft kiss on my lips. I responded by giving her a hug and happily returning her kiss. I was kissing a two hundred year old woman and loving it. Her emotion of affection came through strongly and she communicated that initially she'd had qualms about transporting me on the asteroid experiment trip but that was before we'd met. Since then after meeting me she had come to admire my character and openness. She was also impressed by our family affiliations and how we blended together in affection. She said that there were few uncomplicated personalities around but that I was one of them. I'm not sure what that meant but it had drawn me to her. I think with all her years of experience Bulzezatna must be a shrewd judge of character. Whatever it was she had judged me as being okay in her book. She had to be akin to my great, great, great grandmother if her age was anything to go by. Did she look upon me in a similar vein? Perhaps, though I rather think not.

She performed a brief mental Sewa and then turned about and walked briskly away. I sensed an emotion of love welling up inside her and I expect she did not want it seen publicly. She was a very private person. I then got a firm handshake from both her deputies and a brief communication about how it had been a privilege having me on their ship. I replied in kind and we then performed another brief mental Sewa after which they too turned about and followed their captain.

Jantuzno also said a farewell to us all and promised to see us in the morning when she would take Tania and Katy to meet a few of her girl friends. Katy said she looked forward to it.

The deck Transporter took us directly to Dome-2 then through -9 and -8 and into Dome-7 where it settled down in the central plaza area. The chief ministers bade us a farewell Sewa and conveyed that they had Anztarza business to attend to and would be in contact with us later during our stay.

At our accommodation houses we were enthusiastically greeted and welcomed by Laztraban and his wife Nicky. Everyone in Anztarza knew of the success of the asteroid experiments and also of my own accomplishment in acquiring proper control of my telekinetic power with a degree of accuracy that I'd not had previously. Steins had taught me a lesson I was never to forget.

We had a welcoming glass of Wazu and then a nice hot drink. We sat around the table chatting and both Laztraban and his wife sat with us and listened to our conversation. We told them that it was unbelievable how simple the Oannes had made travelling through space and that it had been a thrilling experience for us. After about an hour of this some decided to retire to their rooms and return at about 7 o'clock for dinner. I wasn't tired since I'd only just woken after a two hour kip on 520-Green. Tania felt the same and we thought we might take a stroll around the dome.

Muznant was seated at the table and I thought she looked a bit wistful. She read my thoughts and looked up at me and smiled. Tania noticed Muznant's mood too and we both went and sat near her. I reached out and held her hand by the fingertips and did a brief Sewa. It was instead of asking if she was feeling okay. The memory of her recent experience must still be quite traumatic with the realisation that her baby had never been real. It would have been a disappointment in the extreme and rather like a miscarriage of sorts. I probed her mind and the scars were quite evident in her memory. I conveyed the love and affection from both Tania and me and her response was an instant aura of companionship and goodwill emotion that surrounded us. Brazjaf watched us from the end of the table.

'I will recover from this,' Muznant said in her low tonal melodic voice, 'with friends and a loving husband around me I definitely will put this behind me. I feel saddened that you will soon be leaving Anztarza to return home again. But we shall keep in constant communication contact through our badges so I will not really miss your thoughts. You two are my very good friends and I appreciate your love for me. I also have a great love for you.'

I think the last bit was aimed at me personally and I knew what she was alluding to. It was the fact that she had developed a love and admiration for me and Tania didn't mind this in the least. Even Brazjaf understood and didn't let it spoil or sour our relationship. In fact Tania was quite chuffed that I had a serious admirer among the Oannes. But Muznant was special since she was the first Oannes woman we had met and a pretty one at that. I too had been enamoured by her looks. I had told Tania that I suspected I must also be a little in love with Muznant as well. I feel it enhances a friendship if the feelings of affection and love go just that little bit deeper. All in all it was a very pleasant sensation within one's chest.

At dinner Nicky had prepared her usual wonderfully diverse spread of tasty dishes and it was after we had finished and were chatting generally that I raised the topic of Sudzarnt's request. I conveyed all of my conversation with him in the ship's crew lounge. I stressed that he disliked his sleep tank because of his aversion to water and also hated the cold temperatures of Panztarna his home town on Nazmos. He considered Nazmos itself a rather cold place in general.

There was a brief silence before Brazjaf responded. He looked towards Muznant and after she gave him a nod he conveyed that Sudzarnt would not be the first such case. Then followed a history of the many cases over the centuries when an Oannes person had elected to live among humans as a matter of preference. On most occasions it was a request to live near the shores of a deep freshwater lake. Each had their individual reasons but none like that of Sudzarnt. Brazjaf conveyed that the establishment had known for some time the mood of Sudzarnt's mind and his wish to even appear human. There was no problem with this since his physical appearance could be altered quite easily; it was a case of where he would settle. Now it appeared he had support and possible help from within the Earth community. Brazjaf was I imagine referring to us here. Would one of us be prepared to take him on, at least for a settling in period? Since I had agreed to help Sudzarnt I suppose it was up to me to volunteer my assistance.

Aunt Brenda looked at Uncle Ron and a brief telepathic tête-à-tête ensued after which Brenda said she had a suggestion. Sudzarnt could come to work at their B&B in Aberporth. Muznant conveyed that it was a good choice of location. She also stated in her communication that since Sudzarnt's case was like no other that his physique might take on a permanent change. All web appendages would disappear and he would appear remarkably human though a rather hairless one. Tinted spectacles and a woolly hat or hair piece could complete the disguise.

Muznant paused and Jerry questioned the time scale at which all this might happen. I think Jerry suspected a long drawn out issue especially from Brajam's description of the Oannes thoroughness in analysing every situation.

It was Brazjaf who gave the answer. Sudzarnt would first need to return to Nazmos where his request would go before the Governing Council of Ministers. Conditions would be set and approval given. No similar logical request had ever been refused provided the conditions were accepted. Then Sudzarnt would have to undergo the physical alterations set in the conditions followed by the appropriate healing time. Then he must undergo a further period of psychological adjustment to get him to function and think as a human before returning to Earth. Brazjaf estimated a time scale of between three and four years for this to be achieved.

'Well then,' said Jerry, 'I suppose the sooner the process is started the better for him. So he had best return to Nazmos on the next FTL starship. That won't be a problem will it?'

'The maximum capacity of an FTL starship on the Earth run is upto two thousand persons but there are seldom more that six to eight hundred on board,' said Muznant. 'Two FTL starships out of a total fleet of nine have been allocated to the Earth run and all are of similar size and design. The last FTL ship to leave Earth was in May last year and was under the command of Captain Zakatanz of the starship 8110-Gold. This and 9110-Red are the most recent FTL fleet acquisitions. They were completed just over a thousand years ago. Others are under manufacture but will not be operational for several hundred years. The 100-FTL ships are still in the thought stage and the first may be available in perhaps a thousand years time.'

I could sense a slight relief in Aunt Brenda that she wouldn't have to provide accommodation for Sudzarnt right away. But both she and Uncle Ron were keen that he came to them eventually. So they asked Brazjaf if they could meet Sudzarnt and get to know him personally over the remainder of our stay in Anztarza and personally tell him how keen they were to have him.

As it happened there were visits to various homes planned for us and Brazjaf conveyed that it would be more convenient if we split ourselves into smaller groups or even as couples. But Katy said that she and Tania were already booked to go out with Jantuzno tomorrow and probably other days as well to meet with her friends. So it was agreed for the senior couples of mum and dad, Ron and Brenda, Milly and Jerry and finally me with granddad to group together. But then granddad said that he had already agreed to spend time with Kazaztan and his wife Zarpralt. He looked at me and mouthed a silent 'sorry'. I noticed a twinkle of mischief in Muznant's eyes when she volunteered herself to accompany me and be my guide on the visiting rounds. Brazjaf would of course be busy with his governmental affairs and so would not accompany us.

While we had been away on the asteroid a second body of ministers had drawn up a complete schedule of tours and house visits. Each host would get release from whatever duties they performed for that day to entertain their guests. This was good because I believed that we would be meeting with the ordinary Oannes citizens and so get a good feel of everyday life in Anztarza.

Tania and Muznant held a very private telepathic conversation from the way they were looking at each other. It was in an extremely conspiratorial manner and I saw the hint of a smile break out on their faces. I knew that it must have something to do with me and of Muznant's known open affections but what was communicated remained hidden from me. I did not probe their minds as that would not have been the honourable thing to do. I was beginning to think like the Oannes.

Next morning after a leisurely breakfast several Oannes arrived to take us on the designated tours. Jerry and Milly were to go to a science and maintenance area and then to a house visit with an Oannes family till the evening. Mum and dad were to visit where the main administration of Anztarza was conducted and from there to another family home. Uncle Ron and Aunt Brenda were similarly to be shown another facet of Anztarzan life and then to a family home. I was to be given a full tour of a food dome and I would be meeting all the people who worked there. And afterwards I'd spend time with a family in their home.

Muznant said that I must expect a degree of deferential treatment bordering on adoration; after all my achievements with the asteroids was considered quite awesome by the Oannes in general. I sincerely hoped that this would not be the case as I did not approve of any kind of obsequiousness or fawning for whatever reason. There was no need for such behaviour and I hoped to express my disapproval in clear terms. I shall overcome any such reticence by keeping my mind open and encouraging access to all I met. They must see me as an ordinary person who thinks just like them. If they could see the history of my gifts then maybe they would know me as quite ordinary.

My tour guide was a very slim and tiny looking Oannes lady who appeared a bit on the shy side but who also knew all the right things to convey. Her name was Muzzalt and she was nearly the same height and build as Muznant but not quite. She looked more delicate. Muzzalt was one of the inspectors of food Dome-21 and had been on Anztarza for 75 years. She was 183 years of age but looked very much younger. I found her shy aspect very attractive and I think she sensed it too. I suppose it was the quaint manner in which she glanced sideways at you when she communicated that was so enchanting.

I read her mind and discovered a modicum of sadness to her past. She like Muznant came originally from Wentazta where her parents and two brothers still lived. But she had been a romantic and a flirt and at the extremely young age of 35 had fallen in love. Zatfortz was also young being just a couple of years older than her and had proposed a partnership marriage. Muzzalt's parents had objected but her brothers liked Zatfortz and the marriage went ahead. But after a honeymoon period of two years Muzzalt realised that her wise parents had been right and that Zatfortz was too immature. Another year passed and the marriage was dissolved and Muzzalt went back to live in her parents house.

But she became restless after a few years and soon formed another friendship with a much older gentleman named Nozatap. He was 210 years old and a very understanding and loving person. They saw a lot of each other and enjoyed one another's company. Nozatap got on well with Muzzalt's parents and brothers and it was the parents who finally suggested the two get married. They did so three years later and lived happily together for fifteen years. Then after a short painful illness Nozatap died and Muzzalt was quite distraught as were all her family. She swore never to marry again and she didn't for 45 years.

One day while out shopping she bumped into a young man. He had a commanding aspect about him but seemed lost in the big city. He was here to deliver a personal message from a friend but had been unable to find the address. Muzzalt gave him directions but also volunteered to take him there personally. They got on the right Transporter and while on it they talked. He told her he lived on another planet called Earth and was back on Nazmos on leave for a year and had only just arrived. He worked in an underground city called Anztarza and made frequent visits to the lush green forests that were abundant on the surface. His name was Ramtazan and he was 110 years of age. By then Muzzalt was 115 years old and once again in love.

Muzzalt found him romantic and exciting with all his tales of space travel and living on another planet. They saw each other every day and even Muzzalt's parents approved of him. They finally professed their love for one another and Muzzalt suggested marriage. But he said no, not just yet He said he wanted her to spend time alone after he returned to Anztarza. If she still felt she wanted him then she must follow him to Anztarza where he would wait for her arrival. He said he loved her and would wait for her forever.

At first the shock of his proposal made her angry. She said she hated him and never wanted to see him again. But then as time went on she began to miss him and all the things he used to say. Her parents watched her behaviour change and could see clearly what she refused to accept. Then one day about a year later they decided they could take no more of their daughter's misery.

'For our sake child,' they said to her, 'go to him and end this misery for us. Ever since he left you've been a lost person. He said he would wait for you, so go. We will make the arrangements.'

And so they did. Muzzalt came to Anztarza 75 years ago and has been married to her Ramtazan ever since. They were currently living in Dome-17 and had two lovely girls aged 65 and 57. Both had left Anztarza a few years ago for a prolonged visit to Wentazta and were currently living in the family home of her parents and brothers.

I presumed that Muzzalt had read my mind also and so also knew my history. I realised that she and everyone on Anztarza knew all about me from before my visit; from me divulging my life story to the 'thinking stone' way back after my first visit to the Duttons.

We all went as a group on the deck Transporter 536-Orange under the command of our smiling Kazaztan. Mum, dad, Milly and Jerry were dropped off in Dome-4 near to the amphitheatre while Uncle Ron and Aunt Brenda were left in Dome-2 to visit the air purification plant complex. Muzzalt then asked Kazaztan to proceed to Food Dome-21. It was a long journey that took us through six residential domes before arriving to settle down near the wall inside the dome. Granddad said this looked interesting enough for him to stay with me after consulting with Kazaztan.

We were met by a young looking dome supervisor named Shumpazon accompanied by his assistant and were taken to the store rooms after having first performed our respective Sewa greetings. The store rooms were up against the dome wall and were much cooler inside. There were rows and rows of storage racks that went from floor to ceiling. The ceilings were high and the higher levels could only be accessed by using small floating platforms. One in particular was being unloaded manually of crate-like boxes of Raizna. These were pushed off the platform and directly onto the shelf. Shumpazon informed us that the platform collected the harvest at an underwater location and brought it here to store temporarily prior to its ultimate distribution as required.

Also growing underwater was Starztal and Yaztraka and these were being constantly harvested. Later other crops would be planted under a rotation cycle dictated by the central administrators. All supply had to be matched by what the other food domes were also supplying. There was a lot to see but unfortunately I was not able to see the actual underwater parts of the operation. But Shumpazon conveyed an excellent visual imaging of the processes there so I felt I didn't miss anything.

After an hour of this Shumpazon invited us to a small luncheon in the large dining hall but Muzzalt conveyed that one was already prepared for us in her house in Dome-17 where her husband Ramtazan awaited with another couple. However I expressed a wish to see the dining area and would be pleased to drink a glass of Wazu with our host. This pleased him no end and here was another Oannes that I had impressed with my politeness and good manners. The Oannes were not only a very gentile people but they placed etiquette and politeness high on their agenda. And I found it very easy to please them. A simple polite act was the road to a firm friendship. And so Shumpazon made me promise to pay him and his family a visit at sometime during the remainder of our stay in Anztarza. I could see Muznant smiling with a semblance of pride at my friendliness with Shumpazon. She had taken it upon her shoulders to vouch for me from the very start when she and Brazjaf had returned from their first visit to Aberporth last November. So anything I did to impress the Oannes reflected on her and reinforced everything she had said about me. I also think that her opinion of me was being continually upgraded perhaps because she wanted me to do well. Love can be a bit blind I think especially where Muznant was concerned with regard to me. I conveyed this to Tania via my badge and received a well done accolade in return. I sent her a thought kiss if there was such a thing.

The Oannes were ever so easy to please at least that was my current impression and one that I was to correct in the distant future. Later Kazaztan transported us to Muzzalt's house in the neighbouring Dome-17 and I met her husband Ramtazan and another couple. Muznant was most polite since she was meeting them for the first time and they in turn were most deferential towards her. After all who hadn't heard of the great Muznant who had brought the first Earth people to Anztarza?

I was impressed by Ramtazan for he was the first Oannes person to initiate a verbal conversation with me immediately after we had completed our Sewa greetings. And I noticed that he was quite relaxed about it too. He had a pleasant alto tone to his voice and he spoke with an excitement when he described an event or journey. One of his tasks was the procurement of food items such as bread making ingredients along with dairy products for their warehouses on Earth. These were large structures for temporary storage and as collection points for eventual transportation to Anztarza. A great deal of deception was involved but with their telepathic abilities there was never a problem. And so the system had gone on for a thousand years and more. It was easier of late when the container system of bulk transportation had become common practice. Money was no problem either as vast amounts lay in numbered accounts transferred from the ill-gotten hoardings of any deceased despot.

Muzzalt was entertaining too and presented a lovely meal of Raizna, Starztal and Tartonta dishes. Somehow the thick blocks of bread went well when dipped in the spicy gravy that she put in small bowls along the centre of the table. Granddad had not stayed with us and had gone on with Kazaztan to his house where a private meal had been prepared just for him. I presumed he'd stay there for the night.

I conveyed to our hosts that I was having a most enjoyable visit and really getting to know Anztarza. I wondered what I would see tomorrow. I received a complex reply of a visual of a number of places of interest. There was the immaculate purification plant that kept Anztarza clean of all the waste products of both personnel and domestic effluent. The image was of something that resembled a miniature oil refinery shiny and new looking. A lot of the functional stuff was underneath the city and did not encroach upon the habitation areas.

Then there was the power plant very much like what was on their spacecraft but a lot larger. Again it was mostly under Anztarza's floor level. There was the air purification plant which Muznant said was the most important functionary over all the others. A failure here could be the end for living conditions in Anztarza. As such there was a backup system of three separate such plants.

In Dome-4 under the amphitheatre were the monitoring rooms and memory files. And keeping charge of everything was the main Zanos bio-computer system. This was a series of control banks through which all monitoring functioned. My initial contact with the Oannes through Chief Ogemtali's 'thinking stone' had come through here. The 'thinking stone' plates placed on Earth all those thousands of years ago were still being monitored after a fashion.

I couldn't begin to think of the complex organisation taking place here in Anztarza and I knew that over the next few days I would get to see or know a large proportion of the city's functioning. The Oannes were keen for me to know everything about their way of life and any query I expressed in my mind was immediately answered and clarified. The Zanos bio-computer was a thinking computer and as on 520-Green could anticipate my thought trends and so give answers to a question I had not even posed. I suspect that Zanos knew me better than I knew myself.

Muznant and I spent a lovely day with Ramtazan and Muzzalt and I hoped to see them again sometime in the future. We thanked them and made our Sewa farewells just before our transport was requested. This time another deck Transporter operated by a very youthful looking Oannes lady returned us to Dome-7.

As expected granddad Eric conveyed through his badge that he would be staying for the night with his friend Kazaztan and wife Zarpralt. He then mentioned that it might be another night as well. Katy and Tania came in much later with Jantuzno and two other girls and all were full of smiles. I imagine they'd had a fun time together. They planned to do the same again tomorrow and hoped to meet several others of Jantuzno's friends, an all girl affair.

When I asked Tania what they had done all day she just laughed and said, 'Just had fun of course. O Ashley, it's so nice to go out with the girls. They have such lovely manners and are so friendly; Katy and I just love being with them.'

I had to smile as I watched both Tania and Katy in such high spirits. They looked like young carefree school girls out on a picnic. It was a side of Tania that I could sit back and watch for hours. I was happy that both she and Katy were enjoying themselves so much. I realised that the Oannes of Anztarza were not just of the older generation. Jantuzno and her friends were part of a much younger population as could be clearly seen.

Mum, dad, Milly, Jerry, Ron and Brenda came back together and they also seemed quite flushed with excitement from their visits around Anztarza.

'O, I don't think I can do this everyday for the remainder of our stay here,' said Milly, 'I'm absolutely pooped. But it was nice seeing those plants and meeting those people. They are all so pleasant and polite not to mention affectionate towards us. I've never felt so important in all my life.'

'Look ladies,' said Jerry, 'why don't you do what Katy and Tania are doing. I'm sure Muznant wouldn't mind showing you around to meet some of her friends; while we men can visit the business end of things.'

I looked across at Muznant and she had a great big smile on her face. She conveyed that she thought it a very good idea and would be happy to spend a day out with the ladies.

The next few days were easy happy ones for all and plenty of Wazu was drunk at every location. We visited Puzlwat and his wife Nogozat and even went to Mytanzto's house. We made many new interesting acquaintances and friends and all tried to get us to visit them at home as well. Sadly we had to decline quite a few. There just wasn't the time.

On the last but one day I said I'd just like to wander around our own dome and meet our immediate neighbours. I didn't realise that my thoughts were being received by all of Anztarza. Subsequently on the day as I walked around people kept arriving in crammed Deck Transporters. They came up to me and said a Sewa farewell and also shook my hand which they knew as an Earth custom. Some walked with me for a short while and then left as others arrived. Some even brought container jugs of Wazu with small matching glasses. There was many a house I knocked on just so I could use their washroom facility.

Towards the end of the day Brazjaf came around with the chief ministers in tow and we all strolled back to the house on Fifth Street.

The chief ministers were most pleasant and we talked of life on Nazmos and compared it with my description of our life in Dudley as we sat around the table in Muznant and Brazjaf's house.

I felt I had come to know these people and believed that I loved them for what they were. And from them I received a continual flow of the emotion of affection and goodwill. I fear that we humans are so far behind the Oannes in social development that Earth was definitely not ready to meet with them. No, and possibly not for another thousand years to come. By then I suppose I and whatever I might have achieved in my lifetime would only be a distant memory. Perhaps I might be lucky and become something of a myth in their records.

I believe I knew the purpose for which I was here and I felt confident that I would fulfil all the tasks set before me, especially Zarama.

Our final day in Anztarza was partly spent floating around on 536-Orange waving to the Oannes people below as we traversed through each dome in turn. I knew we would return often and I mustn't lose touch with our new friends. Our communication badges would keep us in constant contact.

Granddad had made up his mind to stay on and we all supported him in this. The Wazu had certainly made a great improvement in his health and perhaps it was wise for him to remain here for a longer period. I should of course prefer him back in his own home eventually. My inner voice was silent on the matter so I was not sure how to think.

Before we left Anztarza I must stress for granddad to keep his badge near or on him at all times.

I wondered with a bit of trepidation what we would say to Robin when we got back about our holiday in Tenerife. But I was looking forward to Lorraine Hollings' fresh hot doughnuts.

And I wondered too how Margaret was getting on with her telepathy course. Tania and I must make another visit there.

Sadly the starship from Nazmos had not arrived at rendezvous so no trip to see it could be organised. Perhaps another time said Brazjaf.

Things however looked promising.

PART TWO

2016

Chapter 13

Summer 2016

Ashley awoke to the sounds of the morning birds announcing the new day. But on top of this chattering and twittering came also the sounds from the zoo. Traditionally on farms the cockerel should be the one to announce the new day but here it seemed that one particular elephant liked to trumpet the world awake. Or was he just calling the keeper to say someone was hungry.

Ashley's bedroom clock was aglow with a dull red 5:20am but the sun had already brightened the day though from behind a thick umbrella of cloud. A pale light tried to sneak around the edges of the pale orange curtains. There was the slight tapping of raindrops against the double glazing and the sound told Ashley that it was just a light rain. There must be a light east wind to push the drops against the glass and the sills which meant it should be a milder day. The North Wind fairy must have gone to bed. Thank goodness for that, thought Ashley.

The house was quiet except for the creaks of the floorboards expanding and contracting as the central heating water flowed through the hidden copper piping. The summer had been a wet and chilly one so far and was characteristic of the persistent low pressure zone that had settled over France. Some blamed the weather on El Nino but others said that the Jet Stream having drifted too far south was the culprit.

So far this century there had been no rise in the average global temperatures and in fact the reverse was true. Weathermen had finally come to the conclusion that Earth was prone to a series of cyclic temperature fluctuations that lasted approximately thirty to forty years. So according to them Earth was currently in a dipped temperature cycle and had about another fifteen or twenty years to run. Yet the previous summer had been a fairly decent one so far as Ashley could remember.

Ashley listened out but no sounds came from the kids' bedrooms. Simon would be eight in another month while Rachel had turned five in June. She might as well be ten for all the run-around she gave Simon. But then girls tended to be far in advance of boys especially where organising things was concerned. All in preparation for motherhood perhaps thought Ashley.

He could sense that Tania was still fast asleep beside him on the right side of their king size from her muffled breathing. Tania slept with her head completely under the covers. Even at night when she sometimes poked a bare leg out from under the duvet she kept her head well hidden.

Ashley found this fascinating and knew that it was a longstanding habit within her sleep pattern. Mind you with the light summer mornings with sunrise at five o'clock it was an advantage to shut out the light and sleep on. Perhaps that is why Ashley woke early. But then he had always done so and could remember that as a child he'd wake early, get dressed, sit in the enclosed front porch and watch the torn strips of cloud turn pink in succession and the sky become brilliant with streaks of sunlight over the roofs of the houses across the Close. In the winter the sun rose much too far to the south and that too at near eight o'clock. Besides it was too cold in the porch to sit and admire anything other than the falling snow.

It was July now and in another two months Tania would be thirty-one. Ashley would himself turn thirty-five a couple of weeks before that. Tania had kept her slim size ten figure even after Simon in 2008 and Rachel in 2011.

Tania had finished her teacher training in 2006 and she and Ashley had been married that same year. Soon it would be their tenth anniversary and Ashley was hard pressed to think of something appropriate. Tania did not like surprises and preferred to discuss their celebration plans openly. After all it was meant to be a joint celebration. With birthdays she liked to include the whole family but considered their wedding anniversary as a private thing. So perhaps they could go away somewhere by the sea with just the children.

Ashley looked back on the year they got married and remembered how Muznant and Brazjaf had delighted the whole family with a trip far out into space in the November of that year. It was like a late wedding present after their fortnight honeymoon trip to the Algarve. Muznant had conveyed that the FTL ship 8110-Gold had arrived in late September and nearly a month earlier than expected. It was then parked in the outer solar system eight billion miles from Earth in the Sagittarius sector of our sky; this being in the direct line between Nazmos and Earth.

Ron and Brenda did not want to miss out on this trip of a lifetime but regretfully it was a busy time at the B&B with full bookings. They just could not spare another week away. Julie Griffiths overheard them discussing the issue and said that she and Barbara should manage quite well. If need be they could always get additional supply staff from the agency. They could ask for Shirley Rudd who had helped before. They did need a break and should go said Julie.

Muznant picked up on all of this and conveyed that the trip to the FTL ship would take just three days and that too from Monday night to the early hours of Friday morning. Ron and Brenda were quite pleased with that and agreed to go.

Ashley remembered how excited they had all been when Brazjaf communicated the details of the journey to the outer solar system. They would be picked up in mid-November as usual from Aberporth by Shufzaz operating the bus craft 326-Red and ferried to 520-Green captained by Bulzezatna. After the initial million miles distance from Earth position the ship would accelerate to its cruise velocity of a hundred thousand miles per second or just over half the speed of light for the next eight billion miles in the direction of the Sagittarius constellation. The journey would take a little over twenty-two hours of Earth time to reach the vicinity of FTL starship 8110-Gold.

At this velocity the time-dilation factor was 1.185 and passengers would experience a slowdown of their time by about three and a half hours relative to Earth actual time. So it would feel more like a journey close to nineteen hours instead of twenty-two. However Brazjaf conveyed that Zanos-on-board had a micro functionary timing system in a specially constructed tiny neutron shield material case that allowed universal time to be maintained under all velocity time dilation conditions. At eight billion miles from Earth there would of course be a twelve hours time delay in Anztarza communications.

Ashley looked across at Tania still fast asleep and thought how Brazjaf had assured them that at the planned half light speed velocity there would be no adverse effects whatsoever. At this velocity the Oannes had never experienced any noticeable increase in weight or a physical alteration in any form to the ship or to them personally. However no Oannes spaceship was permitted to exceed this maximum velocity when carrying passengers and crew. Some ships Brazjaf had said had a form of space shielding that permitted a slighter greater velocity but these were mainly research vessels.

520-Green would operate its deceleration at a distance of a few thousand miles from 8110-Gold and then manoeuvre closer towards the backend of the FTL ship and well away from the front end shield. The FTL starships all had three deck levels but only one access. This was the shuttle or cargo bay and was large enough to accommodate a vessel the size of 520-Green. This had to be so that these ships could be transported to and from Nazmos. This was one level above the habitation area. The lower level below the habitation area contained the food growing tanks. Natural gravity was created by the neutron star material shield at the front of the ship and as had been described by Brajam when they were returning from the asteroids experiments.

520-Green however would be parked in a loop about a hundred miles astern of 8110-Gold and shuttles would then ferry them across and into the cargo bay. The entire tour should take about one hour as the food growing areas would not be accessible for the practical reason that humans were not amphibious.

The purpose of the journey was mainly to ferry Oannes people to the FTL starship for them to settle in prior to their journey to Nazmos. There were also material goods including monitoring records to be transported back to the home planet.

Ashley remembered how like clockwork the trip had gone. But one of his main memories was the astonishing first visual he got of the FTL starship. As 520-Green had manoeuvred closer the size of 8110-Gold became apparent. There was a broad stripe in gold colouring longitudinally along its tapering two mile length that made the image even more impressive. Ashley had magnified his view through the control room view panels and had visually inspected the entire length of the FTL starship. It had a totally smooth exterior and not a single viewing panel in sight. But when he'd tried to focus on the front of the ship to view the neutron shield he could not. All he had got was a blurred fuzzy image across the front of the ship where the three quarters of a mile diameter mushroom shaped shield was supposed to be. At least according to the description that Brajam had given them. And Ashley had known immediately then why this was so. There was an Event Horizon very close to the shield material that prevented light waves from maintaining their wave pattern of synchronicity.

The next spatial memory that Ashley valued was of the shuttle approaching the rear area of 8110-Gold. As they got closer the immense size of the FTL starship overwhelmed them completely. At two miles long and half a mile in diameter it took several minutes to actually reach the cargo bay area and the open airlock chamber.

The internal tour went as planned and as expected and for a brief moment Ashley thought he was back in Anztarza. Brazjaf was happy that his guests were enjoying the trip and Ashley could see a personal pride for 8110-Gold. It was a great Oannes achievement for all concerned.

Brazjaf then took them to meet Captain Zakatanz in the central area control room. This was also part of the captain's living quarters and from where he issued orders and held meetings with his officers. It was very different from 520-Green but impressive nonetheless. After a brief Sewa greeting the captain formally invited them to share the customary glass of Wazu. There was a polite formality about the captain's manner and Ashley got the impression that he was not enamoured with humans. He did not refer to his deputies or introduce any of the other personnel in the control room; and after an appropriate interval of polite conversation offered them the freedom of the ship before excusing himself back to his duties.

Brazjaf and Muznant then led the group out onto the open habitation platform area and only then gave a characterisation of the captain. Ashley remembered all this like it was yesterday. The captain was 215 years of age, a confirmed bachelor and a very private person Muznant had explained. He was a thinker and a writer who had compiled many memory texts on a variety of subjects. One of these was on the subject of one-way expeditions to faraway star systems. Perhaps Captain Zakatanz was gifted in some special way but for some reason he had made an indelible imprint in Ashley's memory. Just like Margaret had after that first meeting in London and before all this began. Even now Ashley often thought of the taciturn Captain Zakatanz of the FTL starship 8110-Gold. Perhaps he had some role to play in Ashley's future. Recently Ashley had often wondered about that.

There was one factor that Ashley had queried Brazjaf about. And that was that on their return journey the neutron generators had been initiated when 520-Green was barely a thousand miles from the FTL starship. Brazjaf had explained that any gravity effects on the FTL starship could be corrected by its impulse motors. For Earth however a minimum distance of a million miles had to be maintained to ensure a negligible gravity effect upon it. It was purely a safety consideration.

The return journey had been as uneventful as the outward journey and earth-fall to Aberporth was accomplished on time in the early hours of Friday morning. Surprisingly, apart from resetting their watches the journeys had caused no discomfort whatsoever. It could have been just a simple trip to the seaside.

Ashley kept all his memory thoughts blocked so that they did not accidentally intrude into the sleep thoughts of Tania or the children. Ashley's telepathic skills had improved considerably and could now be rated on a par with the average Oannes person. However the human brain was still behind the Oannes mind in development and capacity for memory; but this would change with future generations evolving to accommodate the need for a more advanced form of telepathic communication. It may have to follow a natural process of evolution that could take a long time; though it might also depend somewhat on the urgency felt by the individual.

So far Ashley had sheltered his children from any telepathic process but had decided to begin their initiation next year when Rachel turned six and Simon approached nine. Rachel was a precocious little child and so the difference in years would not matter. Tania had wanted the process sooner but when consulted Muznant had advised a delay. The Oannes children were not initiated into the mind process till they were fifteen. It was essential to both Tania and Ashley that the children learn and practice their telepathy together.

Simon who was soon to be eight on the 26th of August looked very much like Tania. He had her slim build and colouring right down to the hair and eyes. Rachel who had just turned five on the 15th of June was quite unlike either of them. Milly said Rachel reminded her of her mother Mona with her very deep brown wavy hair and greyish eyes. Simon was the quiet one compared to Rachel's bubbly talkative manner. Simon would sometimes tease Rachel by imitating her hand mannerisms when talking. Even Ashley once commented that if you tied Rachel's hands behind her back she would be unable to speak. She rolled her eyes upward when describing the other girls at school. Simon would do the arm waving, eyes rolling and head shaking to extremes and cause Rachel to pout and moan to her mum. Ashley simply laughed and told Simon to behave better towards his sister.

Tania had never taken up teaching after completing her three year training course as she preferred to work in the shop with her mum. She had only done the Teacher Training at Newman College to please her mum and dad. But her heart had not been in it and she wanted to be free to look after her own children when they came. It was not as though the money side was tight since McGill's was doing extremely well.

The shop had been extended finally in 2010 just as had been discussed with Robin so long ago and Robin had been thrilled with the result. The adjoining shop selling home furnishings had never been available since it too was doing a roaring trade. The recession of 2008 had not affected either of the two shops but a premises two doors away had become available in 2011 and Ashley had snapped up the lease. It was a local council controlled property and Ashley acquired a new 99 year lease upon it.

Jerry had been due to retire soon and Ashley had offered him a partnership if he was prepared to manage affairs at the new premises. Jerry accepted, took an early retirement and enthusiastically set about designing a layout for the interior. In six months it looked quite the twin of the original McGill's shop. Jerry argued that customers should find a familiarity in both shops and Ashley said he was absolutely right about that.

Ashley remembered how Uncle Robin Morris had got stuck into the extension idea to the original shop and set about his own layout plans. He was like a dog with two tails when the builders finally came in and work began. It was all completed inside a three month period though they'd had to get special approval for some modifications at the ground level. So finally McGill's had an extra large store room on ground level at the rear and the upstairs was twice its former size with its own kitchen and washroom facilities. Ashley had let Robin do as he pleased though Milly didn't quite trust him and wanted to know his plans throughout the revamp process.

It was in late 2014 that Robin had shakily come downstairs with the complaint that there were flies everywhere. They were even down here he said. But Milly could see nothing and realising that something was wrong summoned Ashley over right away. She sat Robin down and gave him a drink as they waited for Ashley who was with Jerry at the time. Ashley rushed in and taking hold of Robin's hand did his diagnostic thing. He saw clearly what the matter was. Uncle Robin had had a mini stroke but it could get worse and he needed immediate hospital treatment. An ambulance was called and he was taken to the Russell Hall Hospital. Lucky for Robin he recovered quickly and was put on the appropriate medication. He would be 80 next February and the whole family suggested he take it easy from now on. But Robin loved the antiques business and especially the old toys and models and begged to stay on. Milly and Ashley had agreed provided he worked part-time. As such there were days when Robin just came in to chat and make the tea. It was good that he still felt a part of the business.

Perhaps a factor had been when Lorraine Hollings retired from the bakery and had moved South to look after her ailing younger sister Marjorie in New Quay. At first Robin had kept in touch regularly by phone but gradually this diminished to every now and then. Robin complained that she never actually rang him back. Perhaps she's found someone else he said one day. Milly explained that it must be very difficult looking after an ailing relative.

It was about this time that the idea of hiring an assistant for each of the shops was raised by Ashley. Robin was no longer a viable alternative employee and so a notice was sent to the local Job Centre for suitable candidates. Over a period of six months Ashley and Milly interviewed several candidates but none seemed to be really interested in the antiques business. But eventually in late 2015 they struck lucky in a forty-two year old named Mark Tinman. He had been a manager in a home for the elderly for fifteen years until it was closed down by the council under a reorganisation plan. He was an avid fan of the Antiques Road Show program on TV and keen to work for McGill's Antiques. Jerry was impressed by the man and offered him a trial period of three months. Mark had done well and was now a permanent employee covering in both shops. He was single and Milly conveyed her feelings to Ashley that Mark would always be single. She said the signs were obvious. His outward manner was always polite and considerate and even Robin thought he was great. He soon became quite good at the job and it was obvious that he had a love for antiques.

Les Gibson was only thirty and had been a teaching assistant at a village school in Alrewas that had shut and its pupils transferred to another school nearby. That was in 2013 and Les had been unemployed ever since. One of the interests listed on his CV had been the collecting of antiques. One thing led to another by chance and eventually he was interviewed by McGill's Antiques in March of 2015. He passed with flying colours and was now a valued employee. He was not married but had a steady girlfriend called Agnes Thomas who was six years his junior and worked as a secretary with the police at their Headquarters in Lloyd's House in the Birmingham city centre. Their plans to get married had been dashed when Les lost his school job and so far no further plans had been made other than the fact that one day they would definitely wed.

The two assistants had settled in well and life for Milly and Jerry became a lot easier. It was good to have someone reliable in the shop and Ashley thought that maybe one day they might be offered enhanced privileges or even a partnership.

Ashley thought about the year of the London Olympics. That was the year that both his maternal grandparents had died. Beryl had gone suddenly one evening in May while watching TV. She was 93 years of age and had never been ill a day in her life or so she'd said. Grandpa David was lost without her and within months had suffered a stroke. He spent hardly a week in hospital when a second more severe stroke finished him off. Lillian managed to see her dad in the hospital after the first stroke but he had hardly recognised her. His mind was wandering and he kept asking for Beryl. But Ron and Brenda just missed seeing him in hospital by a few hours. Of course both sisters had visited him in Aberdare on a number of occasions and offered him a home with them. But he declined and said he wanted to be in familiar surroundings, which was understandable.

'Beryl is still here,' he had said more than once.

The house remained quiet and all still slept on though the outside chorus seemed a bit more frantic with the rain having stopped. At least it wasn't tap tapping against the bedroom window. Ashley wondered whether he should go downstairs and make himself a mug of tea but thought better of it. Tania would probably wake with the motion of the mattress readjusting to one person. No, thought Ashley, it's still only 5:30 so I'll stick with my thoughts.

Ron and Brenda looked on Sudzarnt like an adopted son. He came over to them in 2008 with a very human appearance. The alteration was quite amazing and even his feet had been reconfigured close to the human foot. He said he hadn't minded the journey to Nazmos and back to Earth because of what he had to look forward to. Under his tutelage Ron and Brenda's telepathic skills had improved in leaps and bounds. Aberporth seemed to have become the contact base for all trips to Anztarza and Shufzaz was a frequent visitor in his imitation Leyland coach 326-Red.

After the visit to the FTL starship 8110-Gold in 2006 Eric had requested a visit to Nazmos. But so far his request had not produced a positive response one way or the other. Muznant conveyed that the Oannes hierarchy were wary of humans visiting their planet for the reason that integration was not deemed possible at present. And so time had rolled along and now Eric was 92 years of age and it was beginning to show. The Wazu was a good tonic but it did not slow the aging process. He slept well into mid morning and then complained that he hadn't slept a wink all night. He watched TV a lot too. His trips to see his friend Kazaztan had become less frequent and the news that he and his wife Zarpralt were to return to Nazmos soon was a sad moment for Eric. They had talked about visiting Nazmos together but now that didn't seem likely.

Alex had retired finally and now he and Lillian lived the relaxed quiet life making frequent trips to Aberporth. Occasionally they visited the shop but didn't feel there was a need to help out. They were concerned for Eric as he took longer to recover from his coughs and colds. But of greater concern was that he often forgot things. Simple things like writing out a card and then forgetting to post it. The communication badge was a god-send as it allowed all the family members to talk to him everyday. Milly especially kept her communication open so that Eric could know what they were up to in the shop. But there were also good days when Eric got perky and said he'd like to go out and about. Someone usually volunteered to pick him up and take him to where he wanted to go.

Weekends were often spent with Ashley, Tania and the kids. Ashley had bought the adjoining Semi-detached house when it became available and had doors put through both upstairs and down to connect up the two houses. They were now registered as one property and the council tax band had jumped from a B for each to an E for the combination. It was a very comfortable arrangement with two kitchens, four reception rooms and six bedrooms. Tania had the reception rooms converted into two large through rooms so that a twelve-seater dining table could be accommodated in one and extra settees in the other. The six bedrooms were most useful with Lillian, Alex, Milly and Jerry going straight to their usually allotted rooms whenever they visited. Though Milly said she preferred her own bed and pillows and so would drive the short distance back to their own place even if it was in the early hours. The greatest asset of all was that they were in constant thought communication through their badges.

Uncle Robin was not in the communication loop though Ashley had wanted to include him. However Milly had overruled this by advising against it on account of Robin having a compulsive desire to tell someone what he knew. He could get friendly with a total stranger at his Saturday night pub outing and tell all. But so that he was not completely out of it Ashley had sent him on a couple of courses to Margaret Dutton in London. Robin liked his London trips and even though he was extremely slow with his telepathic skills nevertheless it allowed the others in the shop to effectively communicate with him. Apparently he'd made a friend at the hotel where he had lodged and Ashley on Milly's prompting had ascertained that this was a lady member of the staff there. Ashley refused to pry further and Milly just showed her amusement at her Uncle's flirting ways.

But such had not been the case with Robin Nestors. Katy had completed her teacher training in 2005 and had then gone on to do a degree course lasting three years. She got a teaching job in a primary school in Handsworth and quite enjoyed her work. She and Robin had been engaged for a while and finally tied the knot in 2009. They had two girls after a couple of years; Fiona was born on 19th November 2011 and Sarah on 1st June 2013. Fiona the elder one had Robin's looks and sedate ways but Sarah was pure Katy including her mischievous ways.

Ashley had taken Robin aside a couple of months before the wedding and divulged all. He also implanted Dr Mario's Spanish memories into Robin's mind just as he had done for Katy so long ago. Robin found all this fascinating and subsequently an immediate bond that went beyond friendship developed between the two men. Telepathy was something that had to be acquired through practice and Katy took it upon herself to instruct Robin.

More recently Robin had been given a promotion at the bank and was now on the annual bonus listing. Katy had thought about giving up teaching but realised she enjoyed it too much and would miss the working environment with its camaraderie and contact with kids.

Vicky Chambers and Robert Black had missed Ashley and Tania's wedding in the summer of 2006 due to Mavis Chambers being involved in a serious car accident a month earlier. It had happened at a busy crossroads near Bordesley Green when for some reason the traffic lights in both directions remained at green. A fault in the electronic controller was blamed and a dried snail track was later seen across an integrated circuit board and analysed as the probable cause.

Mavis Chambers had to be cut from the crumpled car and remained in a coma in The Heartlands hospital for two days afterwards. Robert was now a member of the local constabulary and ensured that all the investigation information was relayed immediately to Vicky. He was a great support to Vicky in her moment of need.

Mavis was six weeks in hospital recovering from her multiple fractures and was eventually allowed home in a wheel chair. The prognosis was good for a near full recovery and that Mavis should be able to walk again but with the aid of a walking cane.

During Mavis' stay in the hospital Robert visited every day after his shifts. Vicky of course was an ever present comfort to her mum and at first an adjoining room had been set up for her. Robert went frequently to the cafeteria for a quick cuppa during his visits and it was there that he met staff nurse Roberta. With similar names they had something in common and a spark was kindled. In the following weeks Robert and Roberta met often and both looked forward to their moments together. Robert looked out for her chatter and her smile and realised how elated he became when in her presence. Vicky met Roberta too and straightway noticed the sparkle in Robert's eyes. Roberta too had eyes only for Robert and Vicky felt an inner relief. She knew now that she had never really loved Robert though he had been quite possessive towards her. She also knew that her heart was elsewhere but there had been nothing she could do about that. These things just could not be helped.

So Vicky told Robert that her mum would be an invalid for a long time and it was her duty to look after her fulltime and it would be unfair to Robert for their engagement to continue. So under mutual agreement they decided to end their relationship. Robert was quite relieved with this outcome and also realised that Vicky had been more a fascination of possession than true love. Roberta did things to his insides that he had never felt before and he realised that this was it. A feeling of calmness came upon Robert and he could sense that the aggressive part of his nature was just not there any more. Someone at work had mentioned that he looked like he'd had a very good night's sleep.

A year later Robert and Roberta had a quiet registry wedding and over the years had three beautiful girls. Vicky was pleased for Robert and they had remained good friends. She was surprised by the completely different personality he presented and at how happy he looked. But she lost contact with him when the family moved up north to Aberdeen the year of the London Olympics.

Vicky cared for her mother full time and the compensation came in very handy. Mavis got around with the aid of two sticks with some degree of difficulty at first but eventually she managed with just the one. Eric had been a frequent visitor until his own problems came into play and he could just manage the occasional visit; though he kept in touch over the phone. Sadly, the accident had aged Mavis prematurely and she now looked twice her age though she kept up her happy appearance. She became deeply involved in the affairs of her local church and sang in their choir.

Vicky too was a much happier person and kept her mum company in all that she did. The reverend Stephens was single and quite young and Vicky like many others had her eye on him. She still had a yen for Ashley but now in a mellowed more friendship sort of way. Vicky, Muznant and Margaret all had a similar leaning towards Ashley. Tania recognised this in each and didn't mind in the least. Let the whole world love Ashley her husband and her lover. Tania was happy in her own love for Ashley which came with her long-term confidence of his love for her. Telepathy added to their love-making in a way that increased it a hundredfold in both excitement and passion.

Lillian and Mavis were good friends and saw each other frequently and with this Vicky and Tania also became good friends. And both Simon and Rachel were fond of their auntie Vicky whom they referred to as the sweet lady. Vicky tended to carry a small bag of sweets in her handbag and offered them a couple each whenever she visited. And each time they were of a different variety and the kids tried to guess what they might be. It was a vicarious sort of fulfilment for her.

Margaret Dutton had made great strides in her telepathic skills and had split from her father's business. She had set up her own Dutton Telepathic Institute in London and had just recently expanded to a branch in Edinburgh. All she did was to run four-day workshops and had developed a band of very skilled staff around her. Ashley drew her into his confidence and invited her to Aberporth to meet Brazjaf and Muznant. From there she was taken to Anztarza on one of Ashley's many visits. She like Vicky and Muznant had an open admiration for Ashley but kept her emotions in check; though not hidden from Tania's discerning eye.

Muznant liked Margaret and saw in her someone of dedication but with little self interest. Her mind set was to get telepathy as a universal tool in the improvement of the human race. Muznant wanted the same thing and said she would help with the telepathy workshops. The communication tablet would help but Muznant received approval for a personal communication badge for Margaret. Of course it was stressed that all this be kept secret from all including her own family members. Margaret was not one to parade her assets and so was happy to agree. This made her feel closer to Ashley and to his family.

Subsequently Margaret's telepathy workshops became renowned for the efficiency and ease with which telepathic skills were acquired. Students came from all over the world and the Dutton Telepathic Institute stressed that each student must be obliged to try to pass on the skill in the manner they themselves had been taught. The philosophy of the Institute was that the whole world should become telepathically literate. It had more to do with the awakening of the human mind to this form of communication than being taught something new. There were the usual objectors of course who claimed that this was an intrusion into the mind of a person which took away their privacy of thought. However the majority welcomed the skill.

Muznant was still without child but it was a well known fact that that the Oannes had a very low fertility rate; probably a natural factor that attached to their longer life span. It was perhaps nature's way of keeping the overall population in check. Or was it the Wazu that somehow acted as a form of contraceptive? The Oannes did not think so. But Muznant was young at 112 years of age and her peak years lay ahead of her and she was hopeful. In Margaret she had met someone who professed no interest in marriage or of children of her own. Somehow this eased Muznant's mind.

After that first meeting with Ashley on 520-Green back in 2004 Brajam had returned to Nazmos where he had presented his opinions and suggestions to the governing council of Ministers. The communications that Ashley received back from Brajam with the arrival of each FTL starship was that progress was being made on the modifications to the starship 4110-Silver. This was not one of the regular Earth starship ferries but was of a similar design to all the others and had been pulled out of space duty at Brajam's request. The latest report last year was that 4110-Silver was being made a half mile longer than previously; with the installation of additional power generators and impulse motors in the extended zone. The current power plants were also being updated. Brajam anticipated a complete operational readiness in fifteen to twenty years. Still to be determined was Ashley's physical location within the FTL habitation platform from where he could best apply his telekinetic push. A central zone area was the probable best location. Tania was pleased that Ashley's trip to quell Zarama was still far into the future. She did not expect anything to precipitate events till well beyond the year 2035. Ashley felt the same but his inner voice was saying something different.

Brajam also conveyed that scientific opinions were very much divided with regard to the relocation of Nazmos. There was resistance to change and many felt that Nazmos was good as it was. However science logic had prevailed and the Nazmos governing council allowed the debate and arguments to be ongoing. No decision either way would be made till further detailed scenarios were presented by both lobbies. The Rimzi had been consulted but they wanted nothing to do with the decision. Temperatures would not affect them one way or the other as they were exclusively an underwater living people.

However the governing council members had been impressed by the visuals of the asteroid experiment and were considering the next stage as proposed by Brajam. And that was the Triton moon experiment.

After a thorough and very lengthy consideration this had been rejected on the grounds that it would bring attention to an intelligent outside influence. But a modification was proposed by Brajam and this was eventually agreed. And that was to put Triton into a polar orbit and allow it to make only one full circuit of Neptune. A full orbit took approximately six Earth days and this could be done within the period when Neptune was hidden from Earth by the sun. Ashley would then re-exert his influence and return Triton back to its original contra-orbit. Brajam and his team would be on hand to make sure that Triton was in the exact time and place location as if nothing had changed.

Neptune was a little less than three billion miles from the sun and took roughly 165 years to make one orbit. The Oannes had introduced to the Babylonians a system of dividing the sky into what we now know as the zodiac signs. Each sign had its divisions and along with the north-south inclination could pinpoint a particular straight line direction from the Sun. As such Neptune being on the Sun's equatorial line entered Pisces in early April 2011 and would leave it in early June 2024 a period of just over thirteen years. The Oannes were a very thorough and patient people and it was more than nine years after that first contact and the asteroids experiment that the Triton moon trial was finally to be performed.

It was the year 2013 then and the experiment had to be performed with Earth in early Virgo. So a date near the end of August was chosen when Neptune was just two years into Pisces. This would allow about three weeks when the Sun would effectively hide Neptune from Earth's astronomers; ample time for the experiment to be fine tuned on completion.

Ashley was accompanied by his mum and dad only. Eric had wanted to join them but had only just returned from a month long stay with his friend Kazaztan in Anztarza and was not feeling too energetic. Travelling with the Oannes in space had become rather a routine experience for them all.

Ashley could remember that it was a Tuesday 20th August and the school holidays were in full swing. However this didn't apply to either Tania or Katy since they both had toddlers in their care. Rachel was two and Sarah just one then and as such both mothers had decided to stay at home.

Brajam had returned from Nazmos with his team of Oannes scientists and they would decide on precise locations for Ashley's telekinetic pushes. They would also monitor everything and ensure that Triton was returned exactly to where it would have been as if no experiment had been conducted. It was important to the governing council on Nazmos that their precise requirements be strictly met. There must be no error in the execution of the completed experiment. The Oannes had the expertise and Ashley knew then that the experiment would be a total success and so had been the case.

Brajam had then indicated that he hoped for the next experiment to be the Platwuz one though this was still in the consideration phase. So far no human was permitted to travel to Nazmos as a matter of Oannes' regulations. But this might be changed Brajam had hoped. The politics of the rule were complex. And the Nazmos relocation envisaged by Brajam was still resisted strongly by quite a large faction of their population. Brajam toyed with the idea of blackmail since Ashley was the key to stopping Zarama. If the Platwuz relocation did happen then when they saw the beneficial result the doubters might even begin to consider something similar for their home planet.

All was still quiet in the Ashley household as all slept soundly on. Ashley felt the need to go downstairs and make up a cup of tea but knew that his absence from the bed would immediately be sensed by Tania and she would sleepily ask where he was going. It never ceased to amaze Ashley how Tania had a desire to know everything he planned to do. If he felt the need to go to the other kitchen to get himself a banana then the moment he stood up he received the telepathic query 'Where are you going?'

Ashley had jokingly once replied that he was off to look for hidden treasure, but that had gone down like a lead balloon; and a slightly hurt expression. Ashley had begun to understand his wife's ways and accept them as part of the feminine psyche. So he had begun to convey his intentions prior to movement. I think I'll get myself a cup of tea, or I think I'll just take a little stroll in the garden to get some fresh air and check out how the new plants are doing.

Ashley loved Tania and loved her as she was. She was his lovely Rembrandt and he wasn't about to retouch any part of it just because a corner of the oils had changed colour. No, he was lucky to have her love even though he knew he himself was no Goya. He was much more likely a Picasso with his hand coming out of the top of his head. Let them sleep on while he continued his reverie of the events of the past years.

Ashley and his parents had motored up to Aberporth on the Sunday prior and had been welcomed by Ron and Brenda and Sudzarnt. Of course all were in constant communication through their badges and Ashley had promised to keep up the contact even from nearly three billion miles away near Neptune with its four hours time delay. Conversations had been estimated as a no-no so just news would be relayed.

Shufzaz had ferried them on time in craft 326-Red under its guise of a 1955 British Leyland coach. When they had entered the shuttle bay of the spacecraft Ashley recognised it as the same as the one on the asteroid trip. They had been welcomed by deputy Tatizblay and greeted quite enthusiastically though the usual Sewa had still to be ritually performed. In the control room Captain Bulzezatna had repeated the warm welcome. Funny how Ashley remembered that Zanos had also got into the act and conveyed a fairly decent welcome to each of them in turn and by personal name; all telepathically of course.

After the preliminary exchange between Oannes and humans of the niceties of how well everyone looked Zanos took over and briefed everyone on the statistics of the journey. Neptune was 2.8 billion miles from Earth and would be reached in a total of seventeen hours. That was an initial four hours of 1.1g acceleration before the neutron generators operated. 520-Green would then travel at 80,000 miles per second for ten hours to reach the vicinity of Neptune. Another three hours would bring the spaceship to the required position near Triton. Neptune was 30,000 miles in diameter and Triton which had a diameter of 1690 miles orbited around it once every six days at the safe distance of 220,000 miles. With time dilation the ten hours high speed section would appear shortened by one hour.

Tania shuffled around under the duvet and one leg went across Ashley's as she mumbled something. Ashley ignored what was mumbled since he'd heard it all before. It was simply Tania's waking pattern. She was now in light sleep mode and it would be another half hour before she'd peep out from under the covers with squinting eyes to ask what time it was. Ashley decided to continue his reverie.

Brajam had been on board having returned from Nazmos on the most recent FTL ship. He was not the most socially gifted person and his PR skills had a lot to be desired but he was a brilliant scientist. Ashley and company met him in the old ship lounge and he immediately got down to 'brass tacks'.

The Oannes were extreme scientists and also very thorough leaving nothing to chance. Under their guidance Ashley would apply telekinetic power to Triton to put it into a polar orbit. They must then wait six days for one full orbit to be achieved. Triton must then be returned back exactly to the same position in its previous orbit as if nothing had altered. Earth's astronomers must see no change in Triton's position to raise the least amount of suspicion.

Ashley was desperate for a cup of tea and now conveyed a desire for the bathroom and slipped out from under Tania's leg and the bed. He stood beside the bed for an instant before moving barefooted quietly into the en-suite. Ashley had got into the habit of sitting down as this enabled a good scratch around his middle not to mention being more hygienic for the surroundings. It had also received favourable approval from Tania. It had the advantage that he could wake up in the dead of night, find his way there and then get back into bed without once really having opened his eyes. Ashley now smiled at the thought.

Still barefooted Ashley made his way downstairs and into the kitchen. Closing the door he switched on the light and put the kettle on. He was down to half a sugar now and had gotten used to his tea like that. He wondered if he'd ever get to no sugar at all. He went into the lounge with his mug, drew back the curtains to let in the morning light and stood peering out at the sky. It seemed to be lightening a bit though still with a dense cloud cover. The forecast was for a dry day with a bit of sunshine later in the afternoon.

The trip out to Neptune had gone as planned. Triton had been moved into polar orbit and the wait of six days had been taxing on the human patience. The Oannes took it in their stride as they were a patient people. When Ashley had applied his first push on Triton there had been two fully loaded shuttle craft parked upon its surface. These had been positioned strategically to evaluate any side effects of Ashley's power push on Triton. There had been none. In fact the shuttle occupants couldn't believe that the first phase of the experiment had been completed and they were asked to return to the mother ship 520-Green.

During the initial part of the experiment Ashley's shuttle craft had been positioned just over 2000 miles from Triton. Ashley remembered how massive the moon had appeared at first and of the little doubts that had flickered in his mind.

His initial telekinetic effort had been in pink mode at the level five for a full minute. Ashley had looked across at Brajam and received a shrug from him. There seemed to have been no change so Ashley had gone back into pink mode and jumped to an effort level eight and maintained this for nearly five minutes. At the end of this effort a slight dizziness had come over Ashley but this had soon passed.

Ashley queried Brajam again and received a positive 'yes' from him but also that much more needed to be done.

The shuttle had kept pace with Triton's changing location so that Ashley's telekinetic pushes could be applied exactly right. Subsequently Ashley had begun to push the moon at level eight efforts for one minute at a time. Each time Brajam had indicated further action. The polar orbit had finally been achieved after Ashley's sixth push.

It was only then that Brajam had noticed Ashley's exhausted aspect and pale facial colouring. Ashley could remember putting his head back against the seat headrest and closing his eyes. He had also picked up on Lillian conveying to Brajam that excessive telekinetic efforts tended to tire him out. She'd conveyed that a couple of glasses of Wazu to assuage his thirst followed by a good sleep would restore her son back to his former self. Being in pink mode always seemed to cause a thirst in Ashley she conveyed. Ashley had sensed Brajam's relief at this information.

When he'd got back to his cabin Ashley had gone out like a light for fourteen hours straight. He'd learned later that Zanos had kept a zone monitor on his condition at his mother's request.

The Oannes and especially Brajam had subsequently developed a greater respect and understanding of Ashley's gifts. They realised that Ashley's gifts were not without limit and that Zarama would present a greater challenge.

For the six day wait period Bulzezatna had taken 520-Green into a larger and more distant loop pattern. Ashley remembered meeting most of the crew in their lounge over the following days and had even told them a few jokes and explained the humour to them. They especially liked it when Ashley had got on to the pun side of earthly humour. They finally got the one about the sailor who fell off the rigging of a tall ship to land upon the deck. The other sailors had laughed and remarked that Jack was not used to hardships. Ashley had to explain that the ship's deck was made of a very hard wood, hence the hard-ship factor.

Brajam and his team had gone over their calculations over and over again and each time making fine-tuning corrections. Brajam had even included Ashley's part and the effort he must apply and for how long. He had also concluded that he must not over-exert Ashley and that two minutes of rest must follow each minute of telekinetic push. The Oannes now understood how Ashley applied his gift of telekinesis and his need to recover from each such exertion. Ashley had felt the awe of the Oannes towards him and it made him feel good that he could connect with these people.

On the sixth day 520-Green had returned to its previous short loop pattern and Ashley's shuttle repositioned according to Brajam's instructions given to Zanos-on-board. Triton had been returned to its former contra-orbit and the very last effort on Ashley's part had been to increase its velocity a fraction and then ten minutes later to slow it down again. Brajam had explained that this had been the fine tuning to relocate Triton exactly where it should be had the experiment never been undertaken.

Ashley remembered that he had not felt the same exhaustion as on the previous occasion of six days ago. This time he had not experienced any dizzy spell nor had he been excessively fatigued afterwards. But he had felt his usual thirst and two glasses of Wazu had soon remedied that.

With Triton's orbit confirmed after a few hours Brajam conveyed to Captain Bulzezatna that the return journey to Earth could commence at her convenience. The Oannes were an extremely polite race and went out of their way never to give offence by word or deed. By his manner Brajam had conveyed that Bulzezatna was in charge and not him.

The return journey was a reverse of the outward journey with the neutron generators being activated when 520-green was a million miles from Neptune. Ashley remembered that he had slept rather a lot of the time on the return trip and had put this down to a delayed reaction to his telekinetic efforts.

Ashley then thought about Katy and Robin and their two girls. Fiona and Rachel had become good friends and played well together whenever they all met up at the family home in Erdington. Simon used to join in their games but gradually opted out of what he called girls' games; except when they got Ashley to do his magic tricks for them. There was the card trick in which he could make them pick a card from the pack and then produce it out of one of their pockets. But they loved his disappearing tricks most of all. He'd put a button in one hand, close and then open it and the button would have disappeared. Or he'd put a small item under a mug and make it disappear only to reappear somewhere else. Tania used to smile and tell the children that he was cheating.

'Yes I am,' Ashley always said, 'but you don't know how. So it really is magic isn't it Simon?'

Since Simon was the oldest, Rachel and Fiona accepted that he knew more than them. One day they would get to know his secret of going into pink mode to do his tricks for them. And that day would not be very far away.

Ashley sensed Tania just before the kitchen door opened and she walked in sleepily. She came up behind him and placed her hands on his shoulders before sliding them down the front of his night shirt. She then kissed the top of his head before snuggling down to place her cheek against his.

With her hand on his belly she said, 'And where is my cup mister? By the way I think you could do with a bit more exercise as I believe I can pinch more than an inch of flab on your tum.'

Ashley turned his head towards her and fleetingly kissed the corner of her lips.

'If you release me madam I'll make thee a cup. And its not flab, it's just my posture,' he said.

But Ashley knew that what she said was true. He had put on a bit of weight and perhaps a bit of concerted exercise would be good for him. He had grown stockier as he had matured. From being a thin tall lad he had gradually broadened in both face and chest and now looked quite a bit like his dad Alex.

'It's Tania's love and cooking that's made him look so good,' Lillian had commented to Milly one day when they had been talking about Ashley in general.

Tania and Ashley continued to sit at the kitchen table and were now into their second mugs of tea.

Although they were both adept at communicating telepathically Tania still preferred to talk verbally when they were alone together. But she also loved the way they had contact with all the family even when they were as far away as Aberporth. She couldn't wait for her own children to join this select group but Ashley had thought that they ought to wait another year till Rachel was six. Simon would by then be approaching nine and Ashley was already planning in his mind how he should go about their induction. He had discussed his ideas with Tania and both had agreed that they could begin by implanting small doses of information at first. On this they had sought Muznant and Brazjaf's advice and had queried how their own young were initiated. But the Oannes brain was physically more developed than the human one and so loading up had to be done in a more gradual manner.

'I think I hear stirring sounds upstairs,' said Tania with her head inclined to one side.

'Ah yes, it's our little five year old lady,' said Ashley after having listened in telepathically. 'She's gone to our room and is wondering where we are,' he said as he continued to listen to his daughter's thoughts.

'I wish I could do that,' said Tania wistfully, 'when will I be able to read minds? The Oannes too can read thoughts; I'm quite envious.'

'I don't think it's something you can learn. It's a gift I suppose. Maybe when we get the kids their communication badges you'll be able to listen to their thoughts. Sorry my darling it's not something I can just transfer to you. I suppose it's like my telekinetic gift, you either have it or you don't. Even the Oannes don't have that.' Ashley reached across to Tania and squeezed her arm.

Rachel came into the kitchen and silently climbed into Ashley's lap. Ashley put his arms around her middle and squeezed her in a gentle hug.

'Morning mummy,' she smiled across at her mum, 'can I have a cup of tea please.'

Tania came across and leaning down kissed her daughter lightly on her upturned lips. As she turned to walk away Rachel grabbed hold of her hand and said, 'And one for daddy too,'

So Tania turned and laughingly kissed Ashley lightly on the forehead.

'Your daddy gets too many kisses from all of us and I think it's making him fat,' laughed Tania.

'Oh, daddy eats well,' said Rachel seriously, 'he's not living on just love and fresh air.'

Both Tania and Ashley laughed at that. Rachel picked up on things other people said and would wait for the right opportunity to repeat them. She loved important sounding words too and would fit them into her conversation whenever she thought fit. Her latest words were 'coronary' and 'paramedic' from last week when one of their neighbours had been taken ill.

Simon referred to her as 'The Newspaper' since she couldn't keep anything to herself. Everyone just had to hear her news.

Tania made Rachel's tea with plenty of milk and half a teaspoon of honey, just the way she'd had it since a year ago.

'Yummy,' purred Rachel when she took her first sip and wiggled her bottom on Ashley's lap. She always did her wiggling when she found something to be delicious. Simon teased her about it and even imitated the motion to show her how tasty something was that Rachel didn't like. Like her dislike of prawns. Rachel just didn't like the look of them and so nothing would induce her to even try one.

Simon was still fast asleep and Tania had to wake him up on school mornings at least twice before he finally got up and washed. But once he'd had his breakfast of jam on toast he became a livewire of energy and chat. Milly said that he not only looked like Tania but also behaved just like Tania had as a child. Both Milly and Lillian were proud of their grandchildren and were keen to see them whenever they could, though it was mostly at weekends.

Eric had proudly claimed himself a great granddad when Simon was born way back in 2008 and jokingly announced that he'd expect a bit more deferential respect from everyone as a result.

'But dad,' Alex had said, 'we have always given you the respect an old man deserves.'

'Less of the old please,' Eric had retorted and everyone had laughed. He was a much fitter man then and had been sometimes referred to as the 'Wazu man'.

Being a Saturday and also the school summer holidays it was another hour before Simon finally woke. And then another half hour as he just lay in bed with his eyes closed trying to sleep some more. But sleep didn't return and finally the thought of breakfast brought him downstairs to the empty kitchen where he made himself a mug of hot chocolate. He had no liking for tea or coffee.

And he was rather hungry this morning.

Tania and Ashley had washed and dressed and now came down again for their breakfast. Rachel had already had her cereal and a slice of toast with plain margarine on it and was now playing in her room. She'd dress herself and she'd come down again when she was good and ready.

Ashley always had a bowl of porridge with milk and sugar while Tania preferred a toast with just margarine on it followed by a small pot of fruity yogurt. This morning it was raspberry flavoured.

They were greeted by their seated son who had sleepiness still written all over him. Perhaps the odour of Rachel's toast browning nicely had permeated up to his room to awaken his hunger.

Simon said a quiet 'Good morning' to his mum and dad as he sat drinking his chocolate. He looked up and smiled at his mother and Tania immediately understood his look.

'Toast and jam Simon?' she asked matter-of-factly and Simon responded with a nod and a broad smile.

The time was right now and Tania went over to him and gave her son a kiss on the cheek and then nuzzled her cheek against his. He had such soft skin that she'd love to do this more often. But Simon was a boy and he feigned that boys did not kiss or nuzzle up. And first thing in the morning was not a good time for kissing or cuddling Simon. However Tania knew that her son became amenable when he wanted something, like his toast and jam now. And when she took him to school she understood that she must not fuss or caress him and even not walk too close beside him.

'All the other boys are looking mum,' he would say, 'and I need to maintain my image.'

Tania understood and couldn't wait for when she could talk to him telepathically. That would be some awakening for him.

Simon usually slept well through the night but occasionally Tania sensed him awake and restless. She'd go over to his room and sit on his bed and stroke his forehead. Tania remembered well the first time several years ago when he reached out and put his arms around her and pulled her towards him. She lay down beside him and they cuddled together and Simon mumbled 'Mummy I love you' bringing tears to Tania's eyes. She had stayed with him till he'd finally fallen asleep.

Simon also liked to read in bed and often Tania had to go up and say it was time for lights out if he had school next day. He'd look up and say, 'Okay mum' and reach out for a hug. But Tania knew she must wait for the initiative to come from him. Once when she had tried to kiss him he had turned his face to the side. And never in public, as that would have been the ultimate sacrilege.

Simon and Eric had a special bond in their relationship for Simon always gave his great granddad a hug and a kiss whenever they met. Simon said that he could hear great-dad Eric thinking. This was due to Eric going into telepathic mode accidentally at times when Simon was about which the lad picked up easily but not knowing how.

Eric felt that Simon should have been told all about telepathy years ago when he was six. But Ashley said that with a much younger sister this may have led to awkwardness for the younger child. But now that Rachel was five and going on ten, Eric tried to persuade Ashley and Tania that surely the time was right for it now. Girls had a mental age far beyond their years and to wait another year would be such a shame. Eric said that Rachel was ready now.

Although Margaret Dutton's workshops and classes were well known locally and very well advertised it was still viewed by the general public as an innovative new idea that was not really practical. It was talked about in the more intellectual circles but the ordinary general public didn't really know much about it. But knowledge of it was growing slowly and Margaret was confident it would spread faster as time went on. As yet Simon had not heard of anything among his classmates that could be considered telepathic. Ashley had confirmation of this when he visited the school for parent's evenings.

But Simon did have an unusual gift too but over which he had no control. And this was the very occasional premonitions that came to him. When queried about it he shrugged his shoulders and said the thought just came into his head. It wasn't a voice or dream or anything like that but just an unconscious thought that popped up into his head out of the blue. However there was forcefulness in the thought that was convincing in its truthfulness and clarity.

He had been proved right about the car breaking down two days after he said it would. Then there was the time last year when he announced that Aunt Brenda was ill. When Ashley conveyed this to her she laughed and said she never felt better. And yet the following day she came down with the vomiting bug and was violently ill. She took a week to recover. Yet these were occasional only and so far there had been just four that Simon had mentioned. A fifth was about to unfold.

'When are you going away dad?' Simon now asked in a nonchalant way as he munched on his toast.

'How do you mean son?' asked Ashley as he quickly read Simon's mind.

According to Simon his father would be going away on a very long journey. No other details were given.

Tania exchanged thoughts with Ashley and there was concern in her look. She and Ashley both knew that he would one day travel to Nazmos and then on to try to stop the rogue White Dwarf star Zarama but Brajam had indicated that all that was years in the future. They had both expected another ten years at least before the Nazmos Council of Ministers came to an agreement for a visit to the Oannes homeland.

'Just one of my thoughts that came to me on the spur of the moment just this minute,' said Simon quite unaware of the consternation he had caused.

'Are you going away somewhere dad?' he then asked.

'There is a matter I have to attend to,' replied Ashley, 'but I had not expected it to come up just yet. I had thought it was at least ten years or so in the future. Conditions may have changed but as far as I know at this moment I have no plans to go anywhere.'

Simon didn't say any more and continued into his second toast quite unconcerned.

'This is yummy. I do like this new bread mum, its nice and crispy,' said Simon.

'It's the new bread from Asda. Its called Oatilicious so I thought I'd give it a try,' said Tania smiling down at her son. 'Your dad thinks the slices are smaller though.'

Simon smiled up at his mum and continued munching.

Rachel had come into the room all dressed and caught the tail end of the conversation. She now walked around to Simon.

'Can I have a bite please Simon?' she said looking at the half piece of toast in his hand.

'Okay,' said Simon, 'but only a small one little minx.'

He held a corner of the toast and lowered it towards Rachel's mouth. She took a small bite which crunched quite loudly and then rolled her eyes with pleasure.

'It is crunchy and nice. Can I have one please mummy and just like Simon's,' she said.

Ashley conveyed Simon's premonition to Muznant and Brazjaf but they were none the wiser. Ashley had mentioned Simon's premonitions once before to them when they had enquired whether any of Ashley's gifts had shown up in his children. However they said the FTL ship from Nazmos was due soon and they would communicate any news when it arrived.

It was two days later that Muznant contacted Ashley with the news that the FTL ship had arrived. Tania also picked up the conversation through her own communication badge.

'The FTL ship 9110-Red under Captain Natazlat has just arrived and we have received communication that all is well,' conveyed Muznant. 'Captain Natazlat is known to me personally and she is also my confidant. She is the only female FTL captain and quite young at 190 years of age. I would like you to meet her when you come to Anztarza sometime soon. But the reason I am also calling is that Brajam has also returned and brings good news. The information pulse we received indicates that the Platwuz experiment has been approved by the Council of Ministers on Nazmos. You alone will be permitted on Nazmos as the first human allowed there; though there will be conditions and restrictions to be applied. These will be detailed to you by Brajam when you meet with him in Anztarza.'

'This is a great honour for all of us and Brajam and I hope that you are available for this visit to Nazmos. Starship 9110-Red will remain at the parked location for three months before commencing the return journey to Nazmos. Brajam would like you to accompany him on the journey back. You are of course at liberty to postpone this visit for the next FTL ship if this is too soon for you. Brazjaf and I will also accompany you whenever you make the journey as we could never miss such an historic moment. Besides we could never envisage you going to a strange land without your oldest Oannes friends being there beside you to assist.'

'I will consider it,' communicated Ashley, but he and Tania both knew that he had already made up his mind to accept right away. He would have to go alone and leave his family behind. He sensed from Muznant's message that this was one of the conditions imposed by the Council of Ministers. They were being cautious and circumspect and wished to take no risks in an unknown field. Ashley also felt that they wished to see him at firsthand to make their own assessment of him. So far they only had the reports and visual records of the things he had done. Brajam must have claimed some things about Ashley's prowess that he may have to literally demonstrate before the council.

Ashley was prepared to go along with any suspicions if this could all be towards the Nazmos orbital adjustment and eventually stopping of Zarama. He thought about his son Simon and knew that he had been right in his prediction about the long journey. Ashley also knew that consecutive FTL starship journeys took about a year and a half in time and so he could expect to be away from his family for at least that long. Unless of course he could speed things up!

But he knew that Simon was not a clairvoyant as someone who could see future events at will. All of Simon's predictions had been in the short term, a matter of a couple of days notice at best. And each time it had to do with one of the family members. A long journey as predicted by Simon could refer to distance mainly and not include time as well.

It was while Ashley was thinking about all this that his inner voice spoke to him as never before. It told him of the things he might do to hasten his journey to Nazmos. The instructions were precise and full of technicalities and exact science computations. Ashley absorbed all of this and wondered who or what had given him this guidance. To Ashley it was quite clear what he must do and he was quite excited by the prospect. It would certainly surprise the Oannes and especially Captain Natazlat. It would be a development beyond all expectations. The citizens of Nazmos would also be dumbfounded.

Long ago Ashley had named his inner voice as the Lych Gate informer and he wondered if it was the same instructor prompting Simon's premonitions also. Someone was definitely looking after their interests. Ashley thought it might be Philip since it must all have a link to the great task that Philip had mentioned so long ago. Ashley felt a confidence in being successful in the big task as he had not been before. He knew also that a much greater power was behind all of this and was there to help and guide him; the inner voice might just be the intermediary.

Ashley was brought back to reality by Tania touching his arm.

'Before you go off around the universe darling I think we should educate our two, don't you think?' she communicated telepathically.

'Absolutely,' replied Ashley in like fashion. Then he added, 'Something fantastic just occurred,' and went on to communicate the instructions he had just been given.

Tania smiled at what her husband had revealed and her concern for his wellbeing was considerably lessened. She was now convinced that Ashley had a special protector looking out for him.

'I will be going to the Raznat system to put the mining planet Platwuz into an orbit that is much closer to its sun if only to prove to the Oannes population that it can be done without imperilling the existing mining population,' conveyed Ashley. 'The task may require two efforts to place Platwuz in a stable orbit which means a slightly longer stay there. I shall then return to Earth and await the next action which I presume will be Nazmos' orbital change. Zarama can wait for another ten years or so as I want us to tackle the Big Task together as a family. I shall be dictating the timetable and I shall make that perfectly clear to the Oannes population on Nazmos. Earth's future is tied to Nazmos and it must have a temperate climate to benefit all. You can see how favourable they find Earth especially it's green forests. Well I shall stress that Nazmos can be the same. I will not tackle Zarama until Nazmos agrees to an orbital change and I shall make that my final offer.'

'Oh Ashley,' said Tania aloud with a quiver in her voice, 'I do love you and I hope it all works.'

'Be sure of it,' he said seriously and put his arms around Tania and hugged her tightly. They communicated their emotions quietly and intensely.

'Let's tell all the family,' whispered Tania and Ashley agreed.

'But first I want the children to know what's going to happen,' communicated Tania.

'Yes,' conveyed Ashley, 'and I think that the time has come upon us to start initiating them with telepathic lessons and practice. Rachel has quite a mature little mind for her five years and will cope well. Simon is quite a thinker in his own right and I'm not at all concerned for him. But I think they need to be told about their dad and some of the things he can do. I trust you to cover that area better than I would darling.'

'Flattery will get you everywhere,' laughed Tania.

Ashley willed his communication badge to stay in open mode and then conveyed all of this to the family members. He was in no doubt that it was received in all of Anztarza as well. The response was immediate with a flood of congratulatory happiness wrapped within an abundant emotion of affection and goodwill.

Muznant conveyed that individual thought badges in the form of tiny communication devices had already been prepared for Ashley's children. For Rachel this would be in the form of an ear stud for which she would need to have her ears pierced while Simon would have it inside a small signet ring for his middle finger. As it tightened he could change it to the next finger and finally the little finger. Both devices would be in gold coloured Oannes composite material the same as was used in the construction of their spacecraft. As a matter of course when the children matured they would be supplied with communication badges similar to the rest of the family.

'Before we leave for Nazmos,' conveyed Ashley to all, 'I should very much like my children to meet the people of Anztarza. I would like for them to see first hand the things I shall be telling them about. I want them to know everything about me and what I am involved with. In addition as a special favour to me I should like for them to experience space travel in one of your craft, perhaps in 520-Green with Captain Bulzezatna.'

Muznant immediately responded with, 'It would be a pleasure and great honour for us to meet Simon and Rachel. We shall plan for your visit whenever you wish.'

Obviously everyone in Anztarza had received all of this and once again an emotion of joyous expectation came through to them over their badges.

Over the years the Oannes in Anztarza had diligently followed the life events of Ashley and his family. But they had never met or seen Simon and Rachel though they held visual images of them.

'I look forward to meeting you again Ashley,' came through from Puzlwat, 'and it would be a great honour to meet Simon and Rachel. My wife joins me in giving you good wishes.'

Ashley smiled at this for he had found Puzlwat to be an Oannes of great conviction. His initial doubts about Ashley had been allayed on witnessing the Asteroid experiments way back in January 2004 and he was now an ardent Ashley fan. He had even gone back to Nazmos to argue the case for Ashley to relocate the home planet closer to Raznat. He sincerely believed that Nazmos could become like Earth in climate and flora.

'Thank you my good friend,' conveyed Ashley, 'we too look forward to seeing you again.'

'We the Chief Ministers also welcome you and your proposed visit to us,' came from Rymtakza. 'You and all your family will always be welcome in Anztarza. We shall arrange something special.'

'It has already been scheduled that I be the one to meet you and your family at the usual pick-up point in Aberporth,' came through from Bulzezatna. 'And I shall have a special space-trip treat for Rachel and Simon prior to proceeding to our destination of Anztarza. I look forward to meeting you all again.'

'That would be wonderful,' said Ashley. 'Thank you very much Captain Bulzezatna. We look forward to it and to seeing you and your lovely crew once again.'

'At your visit we shall fit the communication devices for Simon and Rachel,' came from Muznant.

Ashley thought how excellent all this was. It was easy to know who was communicating as all messaging was accompanied by a visual of the communicator. Which is the reason why in the Oannes culture only first names were sufficient? And actually even names were immaterial as a means of identification. The Oannes had found it fascinating that on Earth names were an essential part of the people's identification. And some even listed their father's name alongside theirs to further the distinction of identity. For the Oannes thought communication was their norm and a visual image was a complete identification in itself. In communication if a third party or a group was being referred to then a complete visual would accompany the thought message.

Ashley thought that this was an ideal situation for a people as advanced in the art of telepathic thought communication as the Oannes were. It proves what a great civilization they are.

'Would you like me to tutor Simon and Rachel in thought communication while you are away?' came through from Sudzarnt in Aberporth. 'I could teach it to them in the Oannes fashion.'

'That would be very nice Sudzarnt,' replied Tania, 'but you would have to come and stay with us here as I don't want the children to miss school. Rachel starts Primary in September.'

'Of course it would be a pleasure to come to Dudley,' conveyed Sudzarnt, 'but that will be quite unnecessary since all my tutoring can be imparted through their communication devices when they get them. I received everything that has been discussed so far. Maybe I could give you a few lessons as well then.'

'That would be super,' replied Tania.

'That would be very good of you,' added Ashley. 'In the meantime we shall give them a good grounding and practice in telepathy over these months before I leave.'

'Sorry we can't come with you to Anztarza much as we would like to,' conveyed Brenda from her B&B, 'it's a very busy time of year. Business is good and we are running around in small circles. Sudzarnt is a great help to us and he's a good manager too.'

'I'm afraid we can't leave either,' came from Milly and Jerry, 'the world has gone mad and everybody wants to look at antiques'

'Then that leaves just us,' said Lillian. 'I'm sure we'd love to join you and our grandchildren on their first space flight.'

'Oh, I'd love to come too,' from Katy, 'but I can't leave the babies just yet. Sarah will be only four in August.'

'I'll give it a miss too,' came from Eric, 'I get tired very easily these days. My friend Kazaztan is no longer there and I do miss his thoughts and that of Zarpralt. We did cover some good years as close friends. And besides I'm too old to make these journeys into space. I'll send him a thought package and I'd appreciate one from him in return.'

'It'll be my pleasure granddad,' said Ashley. 'I'll make a point of visiting him on Nazmos and I'll tell him all about you.'

Ashley realised that his granddad had confused the trip to Anztarza with that of Ashley's pending journey to Nazmos. He thought it best to leave the matter alone as it might only confuse his granddad even more.

'Thanks Ashley you're a good 'un,' from Eric.

'You know Katy,' conveyed Robin who was at his desk in the bank, 'I sometimes feel that my mobile phone is so very obsolete. But I need it for my customers. I still wonder at how lucky I am to be involved with your family. A whole new horizon of adventure now lies at our feet. It's a shame we can't make this trip with Ashley and the kids. I wonder how long the visit to Anztarza is planned for.'

'Ah, Robin,' said Ashley to his badge, 'we don't often pick you up. We only plan to spend two nights in Anztarza. We need a full day in Anztarza to show the kids around. With the journeys there and back that's maybe three days of which two could be in the weekend.'

'I'm tempted but perhaps another time. Maybe when the kids are older,' conveyed Robin who knew Katy was listening.

Katy confined her badge for Robin only and sent him her thoughts.

But everyone heard Robin's reply which was a simple, 'I love you too Katy.'

Perhaps he just forgot to think 'private'.

'About my trip to Nazmos I'll be back before you know it,' conveyed Ashley to all.

So far he kept those thoughts blocked and would not reveal his plans till after they had been accomplished. Only Tania knew in advance what his inner voice had revealed to him. There was one question Ashley intended to raise with Zanos the bio-computer system the Oannes used on their ships. The question was to learn of the method by which the FTL ships were decelerated down to sub-light velocity.

Zanos picked up the query from Ashley's thoughts and no sooner had it been posed than the solution was revealed.

By turning off the impulse power that was keeping the FTL starship at its cruise velocity there would be a rapid deceleration to sub-light speed. But this would cause very high gravitational forces which would crush every living creature on the ship. The forward neutron shield could not assist with deceleration forces.

During the start of each journey it was only the impulse generator power that accelerated the starship to its FTL velocity. Constant 0.9g gravity was maintained by the movement of the habitation platform closer to the dense shield material which had its own fierce gravitational pull. But in the deceleration process the neutron shield was unhelpful. At FTL velocities the inhabitants and the very structure of the ship must never be subjected to even the least amount of the energy-medium of the spatial grid that was racing by. Only the massive forward neutron shield was able to absorb this 'invisible matter' and prevent its destructive power from stripping ordinary atoms of their cohesive structural shell.

For slowing the starship the backward facing neutron generators were operated towards around the tail end of the ship. They would operate in harmony with each decrease in the ship's impulsive power to rapidly bring the FTL starship to sub-light velocity. After that the ship could be rotated 180 degrees and slowed to a standstill in a matter of minutes as if it were being accelerated in a new direction. Here the massive forward neutron shield would assist and the habitation platform would adjust itself accordingly as at the start of the journey.

The question was asked by Ashley what the conditions of deceleration would be if the ship had to be slowed from a velocity of 100 times FTL speed? And what about 200 times FTL speed? Here his inner voice remained silent and Ashley didn't know what to make of it. Was Zanos confused or was it doing a calculation or even a simulation.

It was later that night that Brajam's thoughts conveyed to Ashley that deceleration from 100 times FTL speeds would simply involve a longer period of neutron generator activity toward the rear of the ship. The same would apply all the way up to 500 times FTL velocity. The research had used an Oannes simulator on Nazmos while Brajam had been working with the team modifying the FTL starship 4110-Silver.

Ashley queried Brajam how he had known that this was a question that had arisen in his mind. Brajam simply replied that he had meant to inform Ashley of the progress on 4110-Silver's upgrading to 100-FTL capacity but it had simply slipped his mind. He seemed worried by his omission.

Oannes scientists had established that no upgrading to the neutron generators was necessary. They had ample capacity to function up to 500-FTL velocities at least. They were of course the same type neutron generators that also accelerated ordinary spaceships.

Their main purpose in the decelerating process was not to slow the craft through the decreasing FTL velocities but to apply a backward pull on the inhabitants of the ship during that process. Ashley decided to keep his thoughts private and placed a block against them being read by the Oannes when he visited Anztarza. He would divulge his plan with full technicalities and exact science computations to Captain Natazlat once 9110-Red was underway. Bio-computer Zanos could be called upon to confirm Ashley's plans.

And so over the next few days Tania primed her children little by little that their dad was a very special man. And then gradually she told them of each of his special gifts. She also made stories of some of the things that Ashley had done to bring some criminals to justice. They loved the court stories that Ashley had passed on to her and also the ones she had personally attended with him after she and her parents had been brought into the Bonner family fold.

Tania showed great patience with her children and every night she told them that there was more to tell but they would have to wait till the next day if they went to sleep nicely. Simon wanted to ask questions but Tania said that the time for all their questions would come a bit later after she had told them all about their father.

Finally Tania felt she had completed her task having conveyed everything to Ashley on a daily basis. So now it was question time. Apparently the one gift of Ashley's that seemed to fascinate Rachel the most was where her daddy could not be hurt. Even by a bullet from a high powered rifle.

'And when did he find out about this?' asked Rachel.

'Well,' said Tania, 'I think it was during a cricket match when he was at school. Your dad was fielding quite close to the batsman who happened to hit the ball really hard and straight at daddy. But the ball suddenly stopped when it touched his chest and he wasn't hurt at all. In fact he then held the ball in his hand and the batsman was given out. Everyone thought your dad had made a brilliant catch. When he got home he told Grandpa Alex what had happened so they tested him with an airgun and the same thing happened. So that was how they discovered another one of daddy's gifts, purely by accident. We still think that there might be other gifts that he has not as yet discovered. So there you have it.'

I like the one where dad can push things with his mind,' said Simon. 'Which one do you like best mum?'

'Pushing things like that is called telekinesis. And which do I like best? Well let me see,' said Tania pretending to look puzzled. 'Oh yes, I think it has to be where your dad can read my thoughts and talk to me telepathically. And this is one gift we can all learn. So daddy taught me how to talk to him telepathically with my mind and he hopes that one day everyone on Earth will have that ability.

'Will he teach us also?' said Rachel.

'Yes my darling,' said Tania with a smile, 'and I think he will start on you very soon.'

'Why can't he start now?' asked Rachel.

'He wanted me to talk to you first to get you to understand what this is all about,' said Tania, 'so that you are not surprised when you see the things he intends to show you.'

'Wow,' exclaimed Simon, 'my dad is a superman.'

'Not quite Simon,' said Tania in a more serious tone, 'and I don't think your dad will quite like you saying that either. He likes to think of himself as being given a big job to do. And he thinks that when it is done that whoever gave him these powers might just take them away again.'

'What does he have to do?' asked Rachel.

'Well,' said Tania with her eyes shut tight and head turned upwards, 'there's this great big bad star that is racing towards Earth and other close planets. At the moment it is a very long way away but one day about two thousand years from now it will reach here and swallow up the Earth and all the planets. Your dad thinks that his job is to stop it before it gets to us.'

'How will he do that?' asked Simon.

'Now that is another part of our story,' said Tania. 'There is another world like ours in another solar system not too far away. Well, many thousands of years ago the people from that world managed to travel to Earth and set up a secret camp here. They are very much cleverer than us and are a gentle and peaceful people. They have been listening to all our thoughts with special devices and so managed to find out about your dad's special gifts. They contacted him and told him about this rogue star and asked if he could help stop it. Your dad said yes he would try. These people are called Oannes and they have big fast spaceships that can take daddy close to the star for him to use his powers on it to stop it coming towards us. And that is it I guess.'

'Do you think daddy will stop it?' asked Rachel.

'Of course he'll stop it,' said an impatient Simon, 'why else has he been given all his powers.'

'Yes I think he will darling,' added Tania smiling at her two children despite the very small doubt niggling at the back of her mind. 'I certainly hope so.'

The children were silent for quite a while as they thought about what their mum had told them. Simon's thoughts were about the spaceships and the travel in space which had always interested him.

Tania knew that boys tended to look at the adventurous side of things and was quite prepared for Simon's next question.

'Will I be able to travel in one of their spaceships mum?' he asked. 'I'll be the only boy in class who would have done so.'

'The answer to that is yes. A trip has been arranged for us to be taken up into space as a special treat for you Simon and you Rachel on our way to their underground city Anztarza,' said Tania and then changed to a more serious voice.

'And that brings me to another point. You cannot tell anyone about the things I have told you. Not even to your best friend, is that understood.' She paused for effect and waited till they had promised.

'And you cannot even mention any of the things your dad can do. If you did then our lives would be made a hell by news people and photographers with everyone wanting to know more. We would not be a family anymore and we would have no privacy. They would want your father to keep showing off his powers like in a circus. And he even might get his powers taken away from him. Your father was a little boy when he discovered his powers and granddad Alex and grandma Lillian kept all of this as a secret to protect him. So please don't tell any one about your dad or about the people from outer space living on Earth. Besides people do not understand as we do and they might panic and want to hurt these people. These are gifts of power that have been given to your dad for a special reason and so must be kept as a secret.'

Tania finished and looked intensely at each child in turn. They both nodded to their mother and Tania knew that she could trust her children to say and do nothing to bring attention to the things they now knew. Rachel was quiet for a while before giving her opinion.

'I think God must have given daddy his powers,' she said which Tania found most perceptive for a five year old.

'Quite possibly,' replied Tania and said nothing further as she did not want to expand on that theme.

'Do you think that when I'm older I might be able to do some of the things dad can do?' asked Simon.

'My darling son, you already have a precious gift and that is your premonition of things happening in the future. Like you knew that dad was to go away on a long journey two days before we actually got the news. So who knows that one day you might be chosen for some great task and given a power to help you in that task? You must be patient with what you have and let things roll along of their own accord.'

'And we mustn't tell anybody anything at all or daddy will be in trouble,' said Rachel in her most serious voice. 'Isn't that so mummy?'

'Yes darling,' said Tania, 'that is perfectly right. So let's practice from now and say no more about it, okay?'

Both children nodded their heads with a big smile on each of their faces.

'Can we have some ice-cream,' asked Simon.

He knew that whenever they were asked to do something and they agreed on it then a treat could be expected. And Simon's favourite was ice-cream.

'And what would you like on it,' asked Tania.

'Can I have lots of squirty on mine please,' asked Rachel.

'And I'll have chocolate sauce on mine please,' said Simon.

Tania knew in her mind that once Ashley began his telepathy lessons with these two that their childhood attitudes would suddenly vanish. They would become mini-adults. Hopefully Ashley would put enough in their minds to make them proud to be his children – and hers.

Their journey to Anztarza would be a thrilling one for them especially for Simon with what Bulzezatna planned in space as a treat. Hopefully it would keep a part of their childhood excitement alive. Simon would be in awe of the spaceship 520-Green and a tour of its interior would show how advanced the Oannes were. This would generate a respect for its peoples from both her children and was something Tania could look forward to. Of course Ashley would be on hand to explain things but Tania was sure that Bulzezatna would have arranged everything to a fine tuned level. In the end all Tania could hope for was an understanding from her children that their father needed to make the journey Simon had foreseen.

And she knew that it might only be for a short while – at least this first journey to Nazmos. Zarama still caused nightmares in Tania's thoughts. She feared that there was considerably more to Zarama than they suspected.

Ashley received all of this through his communication badge while he was with Milly in McGill's Antiques original shop premises. Tania had kept her badge in open mode so all could receive her thoughts and everything she had said to the children.

Katy responded with a message of support and conveyed that she could expect the same from her two girls when they were of a suitable age. But by then hopefully telepathy would have expanded to a much wider fraternity and perhaps even been brought onto the schools' curriculum as a second language.

The Dutton Telepathic Institute was due to expand and Margaret had encouraged her skilled staff to spread their wings and set up independently if they wished. Margaret and Ashley were of similar minds in that the sooner telepathy became a world wide phenomenon so much the better for mankind. Already telepathy was being talked about in the news but not as frequently as Ashley could have wished. The seed had been planted and it was just a matter of time now for the harvest to ripen. Nevertheless steady progress was being made. Opening branches of the Dutton Telepathic Institute in Scotland and Wales was a step that would push things along.

Ashley conveyed to Tania that he would spend time with the kids tomorrow. He would not only brief them about himself but also demonstrate his telekinetic prowess. He would also implant a visual knowledge in their minds of the Oannes people and their city of Anztarza. He would include a visual of the many trips he'd made into space with the Oannes and especially Captain Bulzezatna and her ship 520-Green. The asteroids and Triton experiments would be another block of information to impart as would his tour to and within the FTL starship 8110-Gold. There were lots of other little things that Ashley wanted his children to know about but he would impart all of this slowly and carefully over the months he had remaining before setting off to Nazmos.

Ashley and Tania both worried that Rachel might be a bit young to absorb everything Ashley imparted but Muznant sent a message to allay this concern. They had seen that Rachel had a very strong mind and in fact her brain's absorptive capacity was slightly greater than Simon's despite the age difference. The Oannes had monitored Simon and Rachel through the badges of their parents just as they were doing with Katy's Fiona and Sarah.

Nevertheless Ashley's policy was to give his children this knowledge in a slow and steady manner. And while he was away on Nazmos he was happy for Sudzarnt to continue the tutoring process not only in telepathic skills but also to impart knowledge of the history and culture of the Oannes people. This would naturally include their space odysseys and subsequent Earth contact.

In fact it was two days later that Ashley managed a whole free day with his children. There had been some urgent matters that Milly and Jerry wanted Ashley to decide on and also an important Stately Home house auction which had been on the cards for sometime. Milly had looked through the catalogue of items again and noticed a few odd items that were puzzling. Ashley had gone along to the auction and clarified the listing by using his gift of recognising the history of each piece and their probable value. Because the glazing on the vases had appeared cracked someone had tried a coat of high gloss blue enamel paint over the entire piece. Not only did McGill's Antiques acquire these 18th century pieces at a bargain price but also a couple of rare mantel clocks. Robin had gone along for he loved auctions but complained about the number of long case clocks in 'every bloody corner'. But Ashley and Milly could see him quite enjoying the outing despite his 79 years.

So finally after they'd had their breakfasts and usual morning chatter Ashley drew his wife and kids into the living room. And the first thing he did there was to put his finger on his lips and telepathically tell them that from now on there was to be no verbal talking. The kids must think in their minds what they meant to say.

'I will read your thoughts,' conveyed Ashley to them, 'and I will answer. I am going to teach you the art of telepathy; which is talking with ones mind.'

Ashley paused and looked at Rachel and then at Simon and both nodded back at him to confirm that they understood. So he decided to make a start while Tania seated herself in a corner of the room.

'Hello my children,' conveyed Ashley telepathically, 'I trust that you can hear my thoughts as if I was talking to you. I shall communicate like this and you can talk back the same way. Just say in your mind exactly what you want to say as if you were talking to me, okay?'

Rachel screamed aloud with glee.

'I can hear you in my head daddy,' she shouted aloud, 'I heard everything you said.'

Simon was about to say something too as his expression was full of excitement. But Ashley raised one hand up in the air and used his other hand to put one finger on his lips.

'Now, now Rachel,' he conveyed telepathically, 'you must calm yourself. We must remain quiet and work at this telepathic thing. You must practice it to learn it. So just think what you want to say and I will hear you.'

Of course neither child had any telepathic skill as yet so Ashley would read their minds to pick up their messages.

'Can mummy talk to us as well?' were the thoughts from Rachel while Simon asked how long it would take for them to communicate telepathically.

Ashley conveyed this to Tania who immediately replied to Rachel's question.

'Of course I can Rachel,' she conveyed, 'I've been with your daddy a long time and he's a very good teacher. So it won't be very long before we are all talking telepathically.'

Tania had sent her message to Simon as well in answer to his question.

'Oh mummy, we can talk girl talk and Simon won't be able to listen like he always does,' were Rachel's thoughts that Ashley conveyed on to Tania.

'Yes my darling we can certainly do that,' conveyed Tania to Rachel. 'But don't forget Simon will also be able to say things that you won't hear either. We are a family and we shouldn't keep secrets from one another should we?'

'No, I guess you're right. I'm sorry,' were the thoughts from Rachel.

'That's okay darling. But this is exciting isn't it?' conveyed Tania. 'I've waited a long time for this moment.'

They practiced talking telepathically all morning and finally Ashley called a break as his mind was getting tired out with the constant mind reading and transmissions back and forth. So far nothing telepathic had emanated from either Rachel's or Simon's minds according to Tania. She had not picked up a single syllable or word. So Tania suggested that they go and play quietly in their rooms till lunch time. They could resume practice again after lunch.

Tania conveyed her concern to Ashley that the children's minds might be too immature to cope with the telepathy at the present time. After all they were only five and eight years of age.

Ashley only smiled back at Tania and she read confidence in his expression which partially reassured her.

'Give it time,' was all that Ashley conveyed still smiling.

There was so much more to Ashley that Tania knew she would never fathom his entire makeup. His confidence with respect to his children was unshakable and must come from another reservoir of gifted power that Tania knew nothing about. Perhaps he too had premonitions of future events and had passed a bit of it on to his son. She knew and loved her husband and had done so from when she was a thirteen year old, but she knew that a facet of him would forever remain a mystery to her; which made life with him so exciting.

Lunch was at the kitchen table and was usually sandwiches, fruit and pots of fruity yogurt. Ashley conveyed that lunch must be a silent affair for today only. There must be no talking in order to give their little minds time to adjust further. As far as telepathy learning was concerned verbal discourse was a distraction. Telepathy lessons would recommence immediately after lunch in the living room.

After lunch was over they all settled into their favourite seats in the living room and Ashley conveyed his plan. The human brain could be stimulated towards telepathic awakening by the continual reception of incoming telepathic messages. And it took a few seconds only for Ashley to convey to his children a brief pictorial history of his life. How he had discovered each of his gifts one by one as if by chance.

He flashed through the events of his early life in school including the lesson he taught the bully Brian Charles. Then the cricket match between the first and second eleven teams and his immunity from hurt. The darts match in the pub which led to the discovery of his telekinetic gift. And how he had caught the pub thieves red handed. He could regress to past events in his mind exactly as they had happened and so was able to see what the thieves had done. His inner voice had shown him how to do this. He would slow time and then concentrate his mind on a particular spot and past events would come to life all over again in his minds eye.

He told them how he had started work at McGill's Antiques shop and eventually become a partner to Philip Stevens. Of the tragic mugging that led to Philip's death. How Ashley had found the guilty pair and taught them a lesson.

Then he told them how he had also discovered another gift by accident. By simply touching someone he could diagnose if they had a serious illness. This had happened as he got off the train at Dudley Port station and had lightly bumped against someone. This was the case of big Oliver Ramirez. Out of the blue Ashley had suddenly received a medical diagnosis on the man. There was apparently a pea sized fast growing tumour inside the man's brain. Ashley took action and caused the man to pass out on the ground. Paramedics attended him and concussion was suspected. A CT-scan was suggested by Ashley that would hopefully highlight the tumour.

Ashley had done a similar diagnosis on Uncle Robin Morris when he'd had a minor stroke in the shop.

And how at McGill's Antiques he had shown he knew the history of every antique by simply touching the item. And as a result of attaching history cards to each antique how the business had thrived. And how having attended many house clearance sales one in particular had brought him in contact with Andrew Pando's travel diaries and notes and more importantly of the 'thinking stone' given to Andrew by Chief Ogemtali of the Dogon tribe on the Niger River in Africa. One thing had led to another and contact was made with representatives of the Oannes people who lived in an underground city called Anztarza somewhere beneath Antarctica. He then conveyed all his experiences with the Oannes and his trips into space.

Throughout Ashley's telepathic communication with his children he had also imparted detailed visuals of each event, person and place. So that by the time he had finished both Simon and Rachel had a very clear picture of all the events their father had been through as if they had been with him throughout.

Simon thought that the first trip on spacecraft 11701-Red under Captain Lyzongpan to Anztarza was good. But the trips on 520-Green to the asteroids and then to the FTL starship 9110-Red outside the solar planets was something much more stupendous.

With a pure involuntary and unintentional response Simon's brain sent out a single telepathic exclamation which both Ashley and Tania picked up. Simon's 'Wow' was accompanied by his sense of wonder mixed with pride and affection.

'Well done Simon,' conveyed Ashley, 'you have just sent out your first telepathic message.'

'I sent you a message too daddy,' said Rachel aloud, 'didn't you get it?'

'Try again darling,' said Ashley, 'I must have missed it while I was listening to Simon's message.'

Rachel's thoughts were on the Oannes people especially Muznant. Muznant seemed a very nice person and Rachel thought it would be nice to have her for a friend or even an aunty personality whom she could meet.

'Well done Rachel,' conveyed Ashley having read Rachel's thoughts, 'I did get your message but it needs more practice as it was a bit broken up. Yes, Muznant is very nice and I'm sure she would be thrilled to be your friend or aunty especially as she doesn't have any children of her own as yet. Should we ask her?'

Ashley had kept his badge open and immediately Muznant responded through the badge communication system directly to all which Rachel also received into her thoughts.

'Hello Rachel,' conveyed Muznant also sending a visual of herself and Brazjaf with her message. 'Yes I would love to be your friend and even more I would love for you to call me your aunty. I will look on it as a special privilege and we shall be good friends forever just as your mummy and daddy are our special friends.'

Then she added for Simon's benefit. 'And I look forward to meeting you as well Simon. Captain Bulzezatna has arranged a special space flight adventure for you and I shall be happy to show you all over the inside of spacecraft 520-Green.'

A feeling of love and affection then filled the room and Ashley knew that Muznant had been overwhelmed by what Rachel had just conveyed. If the deep love of Rachel's father was out of her reach then the love of his child was nearly as satisfying. Also her desire for a child would be somewhat assuaged by this connection with Rachel.

Ashley was puzzled by the visual that Muznant had sent over to them just prior to receiving the emotion of love and affection from her. He knew that it had been primarily meant for Rachel and Simon but obviously had been picked up by him and Tania. It was a visual of a vast tangled arrangement like a huge scintillating colourful ball of entangled spaghetti-like strings floating in mid-air. It only lasted for a micro second before it was gone. Ashley was much too polite to query Muznant about its meaning.

'I think I like Muznant very much,' was a telepathic message that came from Rachel.

Both Ashley and Tania received it as a strong clear telepathic message and they were quite astounded by such rapid progress from her. But of course they were very pleased about it.

Ashley's inner voice gave him the answer. The Oannes coached their children in normal telepathic communication from a very early age. And that is all it remained as a simple form of communication that worked for them both above and under water. Yet when they reached a certain age which was between fifteen and twenty their brain had to be triggered by a complex message implant in order for them to progress to the next stage of telepathic ability. This gave them the ability to read others thoughts. With training and practice this progressed to the art of deep mind reading through physical contact. Further skills evolved naturally such as blocking ones mind to probing from other mind readers. Ashley remembered that this is what Muznant and Brazjaf had done when they all had met for the first time way back in November 2003 in the B&B in Aberporth.

Ashley had all these skills as gifts given to him naturally and the Oannes had been quite astounded that a human being could be so skilled in their own art. Having monitored Earth for the thousands of years since their first arrival they knew the capabilities and limitations of the human mind. So Ashley was a real surprise to them. And yet Ashley had been unable to impart his mind reading ability to Tania as he wished he could.

Ashley conveyed all this to Tania and she confirmed that she too had received the fleeting visual mental configuration during Muznant's message. Tania instinctively knew that she too now possessed the skill to read minds just as Ashley could. She was thrilled that her children would also have that ability but she would make sure that they never had reason to misuse it or access other people's minds indiscriminately. They must become responsible adults.

'Thank you Muznant,' conveyed Tania, 'I shall value this gift of yours to us.'

She added 'Aunty to my children' as a quick after-thought. The emotion of pleasure and humour filled the room. The Oannes were learning the art of human laughter but in a telepathic manner which they found most pleasurable.

Ashley knew that he must let the natural development of his children's minds grow slowly and without interference from him. The seed had been planted and he was certain that in time they would progress to deep mind reading as well.

Ashley had been concerned that the quantity of information he had to impart to Rachel and Simon might be rather fatiguing for their young minds. But now he could be as brief as possible and in time when their skill matured they could read his mind and glean all the information they desired at their own pace.

They would see how Ashley had learnt new languages by simply reading another's mind and also acquiring their life history and memories. They would see his connection with the Dutton family and how he had read the history of Mary Dutton's Star Brooch and her ancestry connections from it. They would understand about Margaret Dutton and her Telepathic Institute workshops and her aspirations to teach the entire world the skills of telepathy. They would learn that progress was being made though rather slowly.

They would pick up Ashley's knowledge of the universe and also the history of the Oannes people. How they had arrived here on Earth so long ago and the building of their underground city of Anztarza.

Simon had been curious about the Oannes spaceships and he would now be able to satisfy that curiosity through his father's memories and travel vicariously through space. Simon could then also see the interior of 520-Green including the cargo and shuttle decks. He would also learn about the Big Task that lay before his father though this might cause him some concern. But before attempting that task he would know that Ashley had aspirations of creating Earth-like conditions on the Oannes home planet Nazmos; because ultimately Earth's future was Nazmos. Simon would also pick up his father's concern that he did not overload his young mind too quickly.

Ashley was happy to let his children awaken their minds slowly for as yet they had not realised their full potential. Their brains were young and uncluttered and could absorb a great deal. But they also had their limitations. However if they began to rush things and acquire too much then they would get drowsy and lose interest temporarily. This was a natural protective barrier that the brain put up against excessive input. Ashley would make sure that they knew about this.

Tania could now also acquire much of this information but as yet her brain cells did not have the same capacity as the Oannes. The human brain had some way to go in its evolution to reach such a stage. Even Ashley had great difficulty in picking up a concentrated blast of compacted Oannes telepathic data.

'I feel tired mummy,' said Rachel aloud and gave a big yawn. All this new telepathic reception had been too much for her young brain. She was not yet acclimatised to any of it.

'I think you should lie down for a bit darling,' said Tania. 'Come on we'll go to your room and we can chat.'

'Yes I'd like that,' said Rachel and turning around headed for the door and the stairs.

'I'm not tired,' said Simon sitting up straight.

But Ashley looked into his mind and saw that he too showed signs of brain fatigue.

'I must be getting old,' said Ashley for Simon's benefit. 'All this telepathic storytelling has mentally tired me out so I think I'll rest up for a bit too. Perhaps later this evening we can practice it a bit more.

Simon still pretended that he was fine but conveyed telepathically that he would go to his room and read his story book. Ashley conveyed back that that was a good idea. Simon didn't as yet know that he could read minds and Ashley thought it best that he discover it sometime later of his own accord.

Ashley sat on his bed and conveyed to the rest of the family everything that had occurred. He left the good bit to the end when he mentioned how Muznant had given Rachel, Simon and Tania the skill of looking into another persons mind just as he himself was able to do.

Tania came in and sat on the bed beside Ashley and conveyed that poor little Rachel must have been mentally exhausted. She was asleep within moments of placing her head on her pillow. Ashley remembered his own experiences of exhaustion after his own mental exertions. It was like after teaching the tree vandals a lesson.

'I peeped in on Simon,' whispered Tania, 'and I'm sure he was just pretending to read. He looked ever so sleepy and I think he too will soon be in the land of nod.'

Ashley concentrated his thoughts and then smiled.

'Yes,' he whispered back to Tania, 'Simon's fast asleep now.'

'How do you do that?' said Tania. 'Now that Muznant has given me the ability to read minds I still don't know what I must do. Will you show me how it's done? How do you know Simon's asleep?'

'Well I listened for his mental activity and felt none. I can recognise a sleep mode. You forget that I've been doing this for years and years,' said Ashley. 'It'll come to you gradually. It's nothing I can teach. It's like recognising a taste or smell. It all comes with experience. And don't forget I didn't have to learn my skill. It was given to me as a gift. But I shall try and coach you by showing you what to look out for.'

'Thank you darling,' said Tania and snuggled up close beside Ashley. 'Both kids are fast asleep you know,' she added with a twinkle in her eye.

Ashley kissed Tania tenderly on the lips and conveyed that he had only come up to persuade Simon to rest up. But now he was thirsty from all his telepathic conversing and was dying for a mug of tea.

'Coward,' said Tania laughing and giving Ashley a sideways push, 'come on then let's go back down to the kitchen.'

They held hands strolling down the stairs and Ashley conveyed a suggestion of his own. He got a giggle and a good firm hand squeeze in return.

'We shall have to be careful what we think from now on,' said Ashley, 'especially when the kids are in the house. Soon they too will be able to probe our minds and the younger you are the quicker you are to learn new tricks.'

'Oh my goodness,' exclaimed Tania, 'do you think they picked up my thoughts while we were upstairs?'

'I don't think so,' laughed Ashley. 'Not only were they asleep but they've not had an awakening to that skill as yet. That usually gets triggered when the need arises to understand something being said near them, like a foreign language. That was how I learnt my Polish from Jan Bogdan and Sarul Kwaitkowski at Aunt Brenda's B&B way back when I was still at school.'

'Well then,' said Tania, 'I should have no problem listening to a foreign language since we are such a multi-ethnic community. I shall go shopping and listen out for someone talking in their home language. If I don't succeed at first I shall keep trying till I get the hang of it.' She had a knowing smile on her face as she finished.

They sat facing each other and Tania tried looking into Ashley's mind but she couldn't. Ashley knew when a mind probe was being attempted and he had felt Tania's weak effort. He conveyed this to her and she was encouraged that at least her probe had reached that far. She'd try again later but not today as that one effort had left her mentally exhausted. She now understood exactly how Ashley must feel after his big telekinetic pushes on asteroids and such.

The kids slept for a good few hours and when they awoke they still looked drowsy. Ashley decided that he would not try any further telepathic practice with them today. The needed a longer rest. But tomorrow he'd do something different and show off his telekinetic skills. When he conveyed this to them verbally they seemed to liven up a bit and became quite excited at the prospect.

The next morning at breakfast both Rachel and Simon kept looking up at their father expectantly.

'When are you going to show us how you push things around dad?' asked Rachel telepathically.

'When we finish our breakfasts and mummy says we can go and play,' conveyed Ashley with humour in his tone.

'Who wants another piece of toast?' asked Tania aloud and also with a smile.

'Yes please I do,' said Ashley smiling and moving his head from child to child in a tease.

Then laughingly he added, 'I do need extra energy if I'm to start pushing and shoving things around don't you think so?'

Both Simon and Rachel had finished their breakfasts and were impatiently waiting for their father who was taking tiny bites off his toast. When that was finished he poured himself a top up of tea, added a spoonful of sugar and then some milk before stirring slowly. He still varied between half and full spoons of sugar. Tania passed him the bottle of A-Z vitamins which Ashley slowly opened. He placed one large oval pill beside his mug.

The children were looking up at him and didn't see the pill slowly roll across the table to Simon's place-mat.

'Simon,' said Ashley nonchalantly, 'would you be so kind as to pass me back my vitamin pill that seems to have rolled over to you.'

Both children knew instantly that their father had pushed the pill towards Simon with his mind power. Tania smiled up at Ashley with pride at his gesture and placed the pill back in front of Ashley.

Rachel shrieked for her father to do it again.

'I don't know what you mean young lady,' said Ashley with a mischievous grin on his face, 'it must have rolled across of its own accord.'

'No it didn't daddy,' said Rachel, 'you made it go, and I know you did.'

'And just how do you know that missy?' said Ashley.

'Because I just know that's how. Please do it again daddy and this time towards me,' pleaded Rachel as Simon looked on smiling.

So Ashley picked up the pill and placed it the other side of his mug so that it was in a direct line between him and Rachel.

Very slowly the pill began to roll towards Rachel but it had got to about halfway when Tania reached forward, picked it up and placed it back beside Ashley.

'Do stop playing with your food you three children,' she said laughing, 'just swallow the darn pill and go out into the garden and play your little games.'

Ashley popped the pill into his mouth and took two big gulps of tea while throwing his head backwards. He found it ever so difficult to swallow pills especially large oval ones.

In the garden both Rachel and Simon walked slightly behind and to one side of their father as he rolled their football in front of them. After two circuits Ashley decided a different demonstration was called for. He conveyed to the children that he would throw a stone up into the air, go into pink mode and then propel it upwards with such force that the friction with the air would hopefully cause it to disintegrate into fine powder. He explained that he couldn't do what he had done at Aberporth by propelling the stone far out to sea. There were too many houses around here which made it not safe to do.

Simon searched in a flower bed and found a nice large pebble about the size of a pigeon's egg.

'That'll do nicely,' said Ashley as he took the pebble from his son.

He then tossed it up in the air above his head and going into a high level of pink mode gave the pebble a full exerted telekinetic push. He then returned to normal mode and they all watched as the pebble accelerated upwards with a hiss and a streaming smoky trail. When it reached about a mile in height above them it suddenly exploded into a shower of bright sparks and a second later they heard a muffled bang. Then all that remained was a small cloud of white dust which quickly dispersed with the wind.

Both children just stood open mouthed looking upwards. Even Ashley was taken by what he had just witnessed as it never ceased to amaze him at what he could do.

Tania came out and said she too had seen the show and it was amazing to see.

'Well children,' she said as she put her arms loosely around them, 'what do you think of your father's gifts?'

Simon looked up at his mum and tried to say something but only choked with a great big lump in his throat. All he could do was to nod his head repeatedly. There were tears in his eyes that he tried to rapidly blink away.

Rachel was more verbal. 'Daddy, you were great,' she said.

To cover up his embarrassment Simon had found another pebble but Ashley shook his head and conveyed that he didn't want the neighbours getting curious about what was going on. But it was time for another demonstration and this one would be indoors.

Ashley led them into the garage from where Tania returned to her chores in the house.

Ashley went to an old wooden box in which he kept an assortment of the larger nuts and bolts. He picked up a six inch long steel bolt which was about half an inch in diameter and held it for his children to see.

'What are the chances of me bending this backwards on itself with my bare hands? I shall wear gloves of course,' he said passing the bolt to Simon.

Simon looked at the bolt and tried its stiffness before passing it to Rachel.

'I don't think an ordinary man could but I know you can or you wouldn't be showing it to us,' he said.

'You're quite right, Simon,' said Ashley, 'in normal mode I couldn't. However, in slow time or pink mode I can bend it and quite easily too. Now you won't actually see me do it but you will see the result. But be careful and don't touch the bent bolt straight away as it will be rather hot.'

Ashley began his exertion as they watched before going into pink level six mode. He bent the bolt easily then and returning to normal showed it to the kids before placing it on the workbench.

'Wow,' said Simon and Rachel together as they saw the bolt in its new U-shape.

Ashley removed his gloves and touched the bolt lightly but drew his finger rapidly away.

'It's still rather warm,' he said, 'but leave it for a minute and it should have cooled down by then.'

When Ashley finally picked it up again it was just warm. He passed it to Simon who held it and examined it with interest before passing it to an impatient Rachel.

'Can you straighten it again daddy?' she asked, 'just like it was before.'

'I can try,' said Ashley, 'but I don't think I can get it exactly straight. There'll be a slight kink in it from where it was dent.'

So Ashley picked up the U-bolt and soon a reasonably straight bolt lay on the workbench. This time it had not heated up quite as much and so he passed it to Rachel.

She looked at it and said, 'Well done daddy. Will I ever be able to do that?'

'I'm afraid not darling,' said Ashley, 'and that's because it's a special gift to me which I can't pass on to anyone. But I'll do something special for you two. Just watch this.'

So taking the straightened bolt in his hands he said the feigned magic word 'Abracadabra' and the next thing he had the bolt in two pieces.

'There you are,' he said, 'one piece of bolt for each of my children to keep as a souvenir.'

Ashley had gone pink to a level ten and applied a finger pinch at the centre of the bolt and then pulled it apart. A cup and cone fracture was visible at the area of the break. Simon had the bolt head while Rachel had the screw threaded bit.

Ashley conveyed to them exactly what he had done along with a visual of the event actually taking place. Only Ashley would have seen this in pink mode.

For a brief instant Ashley felt a mind intrusion taking place but it was a very weak one. Instantly he knew it was Rachel trying to find out what her father planned next. Ashley was rather pleased and impressed that his daughter of five years of age should be the first one to attempt a mind read.

'Well done Rachel,' he conveyed to her alone, 'that was a good effort. Did you learn anything?'

'I don't know what you mean daddy,' she conveyed back, 'I was only wondering what you planned to show us next but I didn't get an answer.'

'So,' thought Ashley, 'it was an automatic mind probe. It must be in the Oannes style since it was Muznant's gift.'

Ashley realised that what Muznant had passed on to his family must be the skill that the Oannes themselves possessed; which was an involuntary mind reading ability. He conveyed his thoughts to all the family through their badge communicators and suggested they be on their guard when the children were near.

Lillian and Alex responded with an immediate 'Thanks for the warning' but also a joyous congratulation on the children's step up to this new skill.

Ashley would watch out for further probes but for now decided to say no more.

Simon looked puzzled as he was picking up a mixture of message bits. Ashley felt another mind probe attempt and knew it was Simon trying to find out what was to happen next.

Ashley decided not to keep any secrets from his children and so conveyed what he thought had just happened. He conveyed that he was pleased that both had attempted a mind probe with their father as a matter of simple curiosity. He told them that in time they would enhance this mind reading skill and not only be able to communicate telepathically through the badges that they would receive in Anztarza but that they would be able to look into people's minds to see what they were thinking. But most of all they'd be able to learn that person's complete life history including their language if different from their own.

Ashley then stressed that when they became proficient they must never abuse the privilege. People's minds were a private zone and that must be respected. Ashley then conveyed the visual of his first contact with the Polish plumbers and how he had acquired their memories and language.

'How many languages can you speak dad?' asked Simon after a moments thought.

'Oh, I don't quite know,' replied Ashley, 'maybe ten or eleven. I stopped probing too deeply when I realised that my brain capacity must have a limit. I wouldn't want to overload my mind would I? After all our brains are still developing. We are quite behind the Oannes in development since they can do so much more than we can; and much faster too. At their highest mode of telepathic communication we would not be able to pick up or understand a single thought. But enough of that for now, it'll all come to you in time.'

He then conveyed that the next demonstration would be a little game of hide and seek; something he had just invented on the spur of the moment. So they all went back into the garden and this time Tania went as well.

'Mummy, are you going to play as well?' asked Rachel.

'No darling,' replied Tania, 'I'll just watch you enjoy yourselves with daddy.'

Ashley explained the rule of the game which was very simple. He would go behind a bush or a tree in the garden, go into pink mode and move to another hiding spot and they must guess where. He would then come out to prove them right or wrong.

There were just three trees and four decent sized bushes around the garden and they didn't have to actually go in search of him; just shout out where he was. But Ashley also had a special trick up his sleeve as a treat.

And so the game began much to Tania's amusement. The first place that Ashley went to was behind the large Viburnum bush. He then went pink and walked up behind the flowering cherry tree in the opposite corner of the garden.

Rachel had seen her father go behind the Viburnum and so pointed that he was there. Simon called out and pointed to the next bush along. So when Ashley stepped out from behind the cherry tree Rachel was quite astounded. Tania laughed and explained to Rachel what her father had just done. It was as if he'd made himself invisible and then moved to the other hiding place.

'Oh, now I understand,' said Rachel, 'it's just a matter of guessing right. Thanks mummy.'

Then to Simon she said, 'Simon, you go for the bushes and I'll go for the trees. That way we can guess better.'

But they still got it wrong more often that right. Until after about fifteen minutes into the game. Then Simon began to get it right more and more often. Then he got it right every time.

Ashley then decided to play his little trick.

'Okay,' he said, 'you'll never guess this one.'

He went behind a bush and called out, 'Where am I?'

He then went pink and walked up to and behind where his family stood before returning to normal mode.

Rachel pointed to the Viburnum bush but Simon slowly turned around and smiled at his dad. Ashley was astounded. How could he have known? There had to be an explanation. Could Simon see into the future whenever he liked? How else could all his correct answers be accounted for?

Tania got Ashley's message and she too was amazed at Simon's ability yet pleasantly pleased and proud of him at the same time.

'How did you know I'd be here?' asked Ashley of Simon.

'I don't know dad,' replied Simon, 'I just felt you were here so I looked around. The other times the thought just came to me where you might be and I was right nearly every time.'

Ashley remembered his own inner voice giving him the answers to his questions and he wondered if Simon had something similar. Ashley decided not to confuse the child and so decided to say no more about it. However Ashley was pleased and proud just as Tania had been. But he wondered where it might lead to especially for his son. Was he to fulfil some role in the future of Earth and Nazmos? Could this even be linked to Zarama in some way?

Ashley kept his thoughts to himself and put a block on his mind from any probing that might come from Tania or his children. He'd keep his concerns to himself for now. Tania as a mother could worry herself sick with her habit of making a mountain out of a molehill.

'Okay kids and dutiful wives,' he said cheerfully, 'let's go in and have a cup of tea and a biscuit. You've all done very well.'

The kids ran into the house while Tania linked arms with her husband and walked with him but in perfect telepathic silence.

Ashley recognised the mood and knew that something was niggling within her subconscious. He didn't probe as he knew that she was still in the process of identifying and trying to work out why her woman's intuition was ringing alarm bells of inner concern. It had to be something about her son Simon's newly discovered talent and she needed to be alone with her thoughts and let them mature to a discerning conclusion. She could then share her thoughts, concerns or worries with her husband. Ashley knew this from experience and so knew that he must not push the issue. Tania in her turn was thankful that Ashley remained silent though she too sensed that his thoughts were similar to her own. He always knew when not to say anything and it was one of his traits that made him so dear to her. Silence is golden and Ashley knew the art of it.

Tania looked up at his quite serious aspect and wondered at his true thoughts. This time she got a hint of the same concern about Simon that she herself was in puzzlement over. Then suddenly her thoughts became quite clear and she knew she was not alone in those thoughts. Ashley felt them just as much.

'What do you think Simon might be needed for?' Tania asked Ashley telepathically.

'He will help you with Zarama,' was the statement made by Ashley's inner voice. This was a matter of fact announcement without an explanation of any kind. Ashley knew not to question these statements as no clarification had ever been given. Ashley would have to work this one out for himself.

When Ashley relayed this to Tania she gave the telepathic equivalent of a cry of anguish.

'O Ashley,' she said aloud in a soft quivering voice, 'I worry so about you tackling this 'Big Task' and now must I worry for my son as well? I think I know how your mum had felt about you when she learned of your gifts.'

Tears filled her eyes and trickled down both her cheeks. Ashley stopped and enfolded her in his strong arms. He then flooded her mind with all his love when suddenly both of them were surrounded with an immense emotion of care and understanding from thousands of minds. Joyousness pervaded their thoughts and it was as though a mental miracle had melted their concerns and replaced them by a glorious anticipation of a blissful and happy future.

From within this feeling of euphoria Ashley knew that Muznant and Brazjaf had received their emotional distress and had got their Oannes people to lend a hand. What a wonderful way to treat a melancholy mood. No wonder their civilization had remained so prosperous and peaceful. Any thoughts of anger or aggressiveness were simply melted away to be replaced by other much more pleasant emotions. This was a most powerful defence against any feigned aggressor.

Ashley conveyed all of this to Tania and then to the other family members through their communication badges. Simon was to help Ashley in the big task of quelling Zarama. Yet what his role would be was unclear. However Ashley had no intention of pursuing that course for at least another fifteen years. By then Simon would be a young man in his mid twenties and Rachel a very pretty lady. She might even be married with children of her own. After all Tania had been just twenty when they married and Simon had arrived on the scene a couple of years later.

Zarama could definitely wait as Ashley had his own agenda for Nazmos. Earth's future wellbeing lay tied to Nazmos as the alternative Earth in the far distant future.

As a star in the main sequence of its current life cycle the Sun was gradually becoming more luminous at a rate of about 10% every one billion years. As a consequence its surface temperature was slowly rising. In the past the Sun used to be fainter which is possibly the reason life on Earth has only existed for about one billion years. The increase in solar temperature would be such that in a billion years from now the surface of the Earth would become too hot for liquid water to exist, so ending all terrestrial life.

On the other hand Nazmos' star Raznat would remain as a stable Red Dwarf star for another trillion years from the present time. That was a life for the planet Nazmos well beyond what Earth could hope for. Currently the Raznat system had a lateral velocity in space relative to Earth of about 85 miles per second. But it was also getting closer to Earth. In about 10,000 years it would approach to within a mere 3.8 light years distance. After this however it would steadily recede at the same rate. In a million years Raznat would be 200 light years away. So in a billion years in the future it would be a thousand times this distance and Earth perhaps a forgotten memory. Travellers would find it a dried up hot planet similar to what the planet mercury appears today.

Ashley came out of this reverie when Rachel came running out with the biscuit tin to show that it was empty.

'Oh dear,' smirked Tania leaving go of Ashley, 'whatever shall we do? Perhaps I'd better bake some more quickly.'

'No mummy,' giggled Rachel, 'just get some more down from the top.'

Of course Rachel meant the top shelf of the kitchen cupboard where all the unopened biscuits were stored.

'Okay then,' said Tania seriously, 'I wonder which the next one is according to sell-by date?'

'I'll have a Shortcake biscuit and a Custard Cream,' said Rachel, and then quickly added her 'please.'

'What two whole biscuits for madam,' asked Ashley feigning surprise? 'Why missy, before you know it you'll be big and round and fit for the circus. Lunch is not too far away.'

'Oh daddy you are being silly,' said Rachel, 'I can never get fat because I have the same metabolism as you and mummy. Anyway I'm growing and my bones need the extra 'thingies'.

'The word is 'nourishment' little madam,' said Ashley because he knew how Rachel loved the use of large words and phrases.

'Yes,' she immediately repeated, 'I need my nur-ish-ment thingies,' in a slow measured way.

She kept repeating it as she walked into the kitchen behind her parents.

'I can have two biscuits,' she said to Simon proudly, 'because my bones need lots of nur-ish-ment.'

Ashley could see how cunningly Rachel had manipulated his words to suit her own interests, but he smiled at Tania and said nothing. Rachel was a little live wire and the joy of his heart.

Children are the sunshine in our lives Ashley thought but how quickly they grow up. He would savour its freshness while it lasted. He would definitely not tackle Zarama for about twenty years. Fifteen might be too soon. By then he'd be in his mid fifties and happy to have savoured his family to the full. He could sit back and relax except for this rogue star Zarama. He looked forward to seeing Simon as a grown man and wondered what sort of assistance he would give.

Muznant conveyed that Ashley's next visit to Anztarza was set for the end of August when most of the ferrying to and from the FTL starship 9110-Red should have been completed. Captain Bulzezatna would then be free to carry out her surprise space trip treat for Simon. The visit would be simply over a weekend though much could be accomplished in that time.

Ashley gave his thanks and conveyed the news about Simon's ability to predict certain events and that he had received an inner voice message stating that his son would assist with Zarama. Muznant replied with the humorous remark that Simon was simply his father's son. She also conveyed that Anztarza monitors had received everything that Ashley had been attempting with his children and that the general consensus was one of complete approval. Anztarza listened with great interest.

The succeeding days went by quickly and Ashley had to spend several days every week at the two McGill's shops with Milly and Jerry. The history cards for the newest items had to be dictated and made up. And only Ashley had the gift for delivering that. Word had spread around and people were bringing in their own antique items and personal heirlooms for history cards to be written up. Of course it was all business and McGills made a reasonable charge in every case which added to the shops' profits. A few items had to be retained and reported to the police as having been stolen ages ago from this or that stately home and bought in all innocence by the current owner. Criminal charges were not usually instituted but where possible the item was returned to its original home. In several cases the heirs did not know that such an item even existed. Of course old police records in their archives showed up the reported thefts having occurred twenty, thirty or even forty years previous. It was an interesting time for McGill's and the antiques business in Dudley.

In the mean time Tania had taken Rachel into town and had her ears pierced and 9.ct gold studs fitted. Rachel was ever so proud afterwards and said she now felt like a proper lady. She kept rotating the studs as instructed and Tania gave them a regular dab of white spirit to make sure no infection occurred. It took about a week for the healing process to complete.

Rachel and Simon had become proficient in their telepathic communication and had begun to pick up the art of mind reading quite well.

Tania had not progressed greatly with the mind reading but Ashley gave her plenty of encouragement. She had ventured into town with the explicit intention of listening out for people speaking a foreign language and had attempted to look into their minds but without much success. Ashley told her to keep trying and it was a good few weeks later that she thought she had reached a memory. She saw a rather drab grey coloured block of flats in a street and lots of trams and buses speeding passed. Then she saw St. Basil's Cathedral in Red Square with its brilliantly coloured multiple onion domes. A street name Utilsa Kul'neva came through but not much else.

Tania guessed that that the scene was in the memory of the person who obviously was from Russia since the scene was definitely Moscow's Red Square and the street must be somewhere in the city where the person had lived.

It was a big step forward for Tania and she felt encouraged. But it was not like the Spanish memories that Ashley had given her from Dr Mario's mind. Madrid would always be a familiar haunt as if she had actually lived there. She communicated her experience to Ashley and he gave her encouragement and said that it would all get easier with time. She should keep at it and her mind would eventually know what to do and it would become quite involuntary. Probing another's mind required a greater brain effort than ordinary run of the mill telepathy.

As the August Bank Holiday approached Muznant conveyed the details of their pickup in Aberporth. Ashley conveyed that the children and Tania were looking forward to it. Simon was especially excited about his first space trip and was curious about what Captain Bulzezatna had planned as a treat for him.

Only Lillian and Alex were to accompany Ashley, Tania and the kids on this Anztarza visit which had been set for Friday August 26th with pickup in the late evening from the Aberporth B&B. The return was planned for late Monday night so the visit was for a long weekend only.

For Ashley the news was that the FTL starship 9110-Red planned to head back towards Nazmos about the middle of October and Ashley would be the only human among the Oannes on board.

For now though Simon got more and more excited as the Anztarza visit approached. Rachel on the other hand was dubious about aeroplanes and ships. She thought that sometimes they crashed or sank.

'Will it be scary mummy?' she asked more than once.

'No darling,' Tania always replied, 'you won't feel anything. And daddy and I and also grandma and grandpa will be there beside you. And Muznant too will take care of you after all she is your new aunty.'

'I hope so,' said Rachel showing her baby side for a change.

'I want to see everything on the spaceship,' conveyed Simon, 'I just can't wait. Will I be allowed on the flight deck?'

Ashley once again conveyed a complete visual of his first journey to Anztarza on the spacecraft 11701-Red under Captain Lyzongpan. The view from its Control Room was what intrigued Simon and he was now even keener to experience space flight at first hand; a personal experience that was fated to change his life forever.

Ashley smiled inwardly at his son's enthusiasm and conveyed that the Oannes were so advanced in space travel that for them it was as simple and comfortable as being on an ocean liner on Earth. Even their FTL starships catered wholly to the comfort of the passengers by maintaining constant normal gravity conditions throughout the months of their interplanetary journeys.

Simon had always had a schoolboy fascination for aeroplanes and especially for military type jet fighter aircraft. He had visited the RAF Cosford Museum many times and loved to just take in the sleek aerodynamic shapes of the aircraft exhibited.

Little did Ashley then realise where all this enthusiasm would lead and later it did not surprise or displease him in the least. After all it was the right course if Simon was to assist his father with Zarama. But more of that in its proper place.

Lillian and Alex motored up to Aberporth on Tuesday 23rd August. This was at Ron and Brenda's request for the sisters had not seen each other since Rachel's birthday. Much of their talk was about the kids and how they had progressed with their telepathy. And now that Muznant had implanted the skill of mind reading they'd all have to be careful of their thought trends when the kids were around. However they said that Tania had stressed that it was rude and impolite to look into another person's thoughts as that was an invasion of that person's privacy. However their skill was not yet as advanced as Ashley's. Tania they said had not made much headway with the mind reading skill and her few attempts with foreign speaking strangers had met with only partial success. But Ashley was her guiding light and encouraged her to persevere. He said that her skills would develop as her mind adapted to its demands. From then her progress would be rapid and they could play mind reading games between each other and then with the children. Lillian said that perhaps this visit to Anztarza would boost that development.

They took regular evening walks along the coastal path and once even stopped off at the hillside railway carriage bungalow of Peter and Fiona Ellis, who were quite pleased to see them.

Ashley, Tania and the kids travelled up on the Friday and arrived in time for lunch. Rachel gave her great aunt Brenda a big hug as the two of them had always got on well. But then Rachel was the bubbly sort and her cheerful outlook was quite infectious. There seemed to be a special bond of love between them which filled Lillian with pride. The sisters were close and Lillian felt it that Brenda had never had children of her own and so this rapport with Rachel pleased her no end.

As the day wore on into evening the sky became heavily overcast and a light rain commenced which put paid to any notions of a coastal path walk.

Dinner was at 7 o'clock in the dining room and Ashley thought of the time so long ago when he'd heard and understood the conversation of the two Polish plumbers at breakfast in this very room. He still wasn't sure how it had all come about but it must have been an automatic and involuntary mind read for it to have happened.

Rachel ate well but Simon only picked at his food. He was far to excited to be hungry and kept looking out of the window to see if it was dark outside. It was well after 9 o'clock when it did get dark.

Muznant had been keeping in constant badge communication and gave her own progress report. 520-Green would descend into the sea when it was dark enough for secrecy and remained there till it was time for the bus craft 326-Red to be sent out for them. The rendezvous point was at a location fifty miles out and west of Aberporth. Ashley relayed Muznant's information continually to Simon who appeared to be in a constant 'are we there yet' mode. But very soon Ashley felt Simon's mind probing into his searching for this information. Simon's mind reading skills had suddenly improved by several levels because of this keen desire to know when the Oannes visitors were arriving.

By now the rain was coming down quite heavily and Rachel had fallen asleep on the sofa with her head in Lillian's lap. Tania looked at her little cherub and her heart filled with love and pride. She was a true beauty and more so as she slept. Ashley put his arm around his wife's shoulders and hugged her to him. He too was admiring his little princess. Muznant would be quite taken with her.

The rain was still sheeting down when the bus craft drew into the B&B car park but this time it came right up to the front entrance. It was now well past 10 o'clock.

Muznant and Brazjaf conveyed a telepathic greeting to all along with the usual Sewa ritual of welfare and conveyed how lovely the rain felt to them. It felt nearly as good as their sleep tanks. They were dripping wet when they entered the hallway from having paused outside to especially enjoy the rain. They removed their large loose fitting overcoats and hats. They still wore their humanised face masks but which they removed once Ashley met them and brought them into the living room where the others were. No other guests were present as all had gone to their bedrooms.

Muznant said 'Hello' to Simon and remarked how much like Tania he looked and yet had his father's bearing and manner. She came up to him and carefully looked him over to see where the changes would occur as he matured. She concluded that he would be tall and broad with strong features in his chin and cheek bones. He would definitely be of great comfort to his father especially as foretold for Zarama. And yet there would be another who would outshine him. Muznant kept her conclusions to herself as things had a way of deviating onto other paths.

Turning away from Simon she caught sight of the sleeping Rachel and something within her tightened and generated a fleeting twinge of pain in the very centre of her chest. And yet there was sweetness to the pain that produced a feeling of exhilaration. Ashley recognised that Muznant was emotionally moved at the sight of Rachel and her emotion was transmitted to them all. It was an emotion of love, wonder, gratefulness and desire all rolled into one. Muznant's hand stretched outwards towards Rachel but had to stop short since she was across the room. Slowly she approached the sofa and Lillian reached up and touched hands with Muznant. She then bent down to look more closely at Rachel's face.

At this point Rachel awoke, opened her big eyes and smiled up at the peering face of Muznant. Private telepathic thoughts raced between them of greetings and questions and answers. Each gave general explanations of their likes and dislikes and preferences as to give the other a better understanding of their nature and inner being. All this took place within the blink of an eye as they looked at each other in that first moment of meeting.

Muznant felt her heart skip a beat and in that instant a bond was established between them that would echo into eternity. The Oannes had an openness of culture and Muznant's mind would be read by all her people now; and in the future would be seen as the first major step forward in Nazmos' Earth relations.

Lillian smiled as she looked at Muznant's profile and saw a hint of Earth style cosmetic make-up. Katy's friend Jantuzno and her circle of friends had been experimenting with lipsticks and blushers for some years now since their first meeting in 2004 and the fad had gradually spread across Anztarza. And perhaps it had carried all the way to Nazmos as well with the FTL starships.

Muznant had on a very pale shade of pink lip-gloss and just a hint of matching blusher blended cleverly over her cheek bones. It enhanced her looks and Rachel's mind conveyed that she thought

Muznant had a pretty face.

'Hello Rachel,' said Muznant aloud in her low tone singsong voice, 'I'm happy to meet you. And I'm happy to meet you too Simon. I hope we can all become good friends. This is my husband Brazjaf. It is nice that you have decided to visit our city and I hope you get to like it. Our people are also looking forward to meeting you.'

Ashley suspected that the Oannes had more in their telepathic repertoire than he had at first thought. If they could quell moods of temper or violence aimed at them then perhaps they might also be able to induce in others a desire for affection in their direction. Ashley thought of what they could have achieved over the millennia with regard to suppressing all those struggles in which nations fought wars against each other. But perhaps it was never the Oannes policy to interfere and to let nature take its course. Ashley realised that they themselves must have learnt from their own history that peace only came from the ultimate realisation that strife was completely wasteful and achieved nothing. Earth had as yet to learn such lessons; lessons that must be learnt through painful experiences. The spread of telepathy and ultimately of mind reading would go a long way towards bringing the desired tranquillity of thoughts within the human mind. Ashley had that firm belief.

'Hello auntie Muznant,' said Rachel a little hesitantly, 'you have a pretty face.'

'And you are very beautiful Rachel,' replied Muznant.

Brazjaf now came forward and stood beside his wife and smiled at the children.

'We have also brought each of you a little gift,' he said. 'A signet ring for Simon and an ear stud for Rachel. These are telepathic communication devices similar in function to the badges that were given to the other members of your family. It will help us to have telepathic communication with each other at all times.'

Muznant then produced a gold coloured medium sized ear stud which she handed to Lillian. Rachel sat up eagerly and removed her left ear stud and replaced it with the larger one Muznant had given. Brazjaf also handed a signet ring to Simon which he immediately put onto the middle finger of his right hand. Muznant then conveyed complete instructions on how they were to be used. Both children expressed their thanks and immediately said a hello to the other members of the family. They were initially surprised when great granddad said hello in return and by Aunt Katy's congratulations. Rachel wanted to begin a conversation but was interrupted by Brazjaf's voice.

'I think Captain Bulzezatna is waiting for us to return to the ship,' he said in his own particular voice similar to Muznant's but with a slightly heavier resonance to it. 'She is keen to meet you Simon as she has a special space treat for you. So shall we board the deck Transporter Bus as Shufzaz awaits us outside?'

Simon and Rachel had their small backpacks which contained their night clothes, changes of underwear and tooth brushes. It had been conveyed by Muznant that tunics and leggings would be provided for all just as always. Ashley and Tania shared a small carry-bag as did Lillian and Alex. Travelling light was the theme and Muznant smiled when she read their thoughts.

It was still raining outside but had lessened a little. The Oannes loved the cool rain on their bared heads and were humoured when they saw how humans used umbrellas and rain capes to shield themselves from the rain. Muznant and Brazjaf replaced their face masks and overcoats before going outside. Craft 326-Red in its disguised form as a 1955 British Leyland tourist coach was parked just outside the B&B entrance facing the car park so they all only had a short distance to walk. A smiling Shufzaz sat in the driver's seat and greeted them telepathically as they came aboard.

Ron and Brenda with Sudzarnt standing behind waved goodbye as the bus seemed to spin around and head towards the car park exit. From there it turned right and then straight towards the sea shore. It was in a completely darkened mode and its sensors indicated an absence of human presence in the vicinity. Subsequently Shufzaz allowed 326-Red to lift upwards about fifty feet and accelerate rapidly out over the sea.

'Wow,' exclaimed Simon, 'this is really great,' at the sensation of speed when Shufzaz gunned the bus forward. They headed out into the rain lashed sea mist at 95mph. The rain had increased again and was drumming viciously against the front of the bus craft.

Simon sat in the front seat beside Shufzaz even though he could hardly see anything ahead. Shufzaz immediately received his thoughts and explained that it wasn't him driving the craft but that Zanos the on-board bio-computer was in full control. All he had to do was to command a manoeuvre or operation. Zanos had already communicated with 520-Green which was now also above the sea and heading towards them. It would take about twenty minutes to rendezvous with it.

It wasn't long before the bus craft began to slow noticeably and then suddenly they were all dazzled by the brightness of the interior of 520-Green's shuttle bay.

Another 'Wow' of surprise passed Simon's lips and even Rachel looked up in astonishment at Muznant seated on her left. Rachel had chosen the security of sitting between her mother and Muznant both of whom made her feel secure. Throughout the bus journey Muznant had telepathically explained what was happening with full visual imagery.

326-Red settled down silently and smoothly onto the shuttle deck without even the slightest of bumps. The spaceship was already rising upwards fluidly as the bay doors closed tight and suddenly they were above the clouds where Bulzezatna held it stationary. She wanted her passengers to experience the climb into space.

The moon was above the eastern horizon and just past its last quarter. Yet it shone its faint light on the turbulent clouds below showing up their changing raggedness of design. It would be quite a sight for an enthusiastic young Simon.

First Deputy Tatizblay met the visitors as they stepped down off the bus craft and welcomed them in the usual Sewa fashion performed telepathically with Ashley. Ashley was deemed the leader of the group because of his status with the Oannes people. Tatizblay conveyed that the captain awaited them in the control room if they would kindly follow him there. He paid special attention to the children and offered his hand. Simon accepted by eagerly stepping forward but Rachel shook her head and conveyed that she would stay between mother and aunty.

Tatizblay smiled and so led the way all the while conducting a vigorous telepathic visual communication with Simon. Bulzezatna had instructed her crew and staff to keep free and open minds with regard to their guests and especially the boy. Bulzezatna considered him special.

All of Anztarza had picked up everything that had gone on over the past month with regard to Simon and subsequently Bulzezatna had generated plans of her own; plans that she kept lock away in a secret compartment of her mind and which she would only reveal once her intuition was confirmed. If it proved true then it could be a first historical step towards that harmony that was desired by so many.

As they entered the control room Simon let go of Tatizblay's cool hand and stepped resolutely to where Bulzezatna stood. There was good lighting here and Simon was at once impressed by the captain's imposing and dignified stature. The face that Simon saw was quite lined but had a noticeable kindly aspect though with a hint of mischievous humour behind the gentle looking eyes. And yet there was authority in her manner which bordered on an imperiousness of dignified majesty. Here was someone who was not to be trifled with and yet someone who commanded involuntary respect.

Simon liked her at once and instead of a Sewa greeting he gave her a slight bow from his hips. He then conveyed that he was pleased to meet the captain of 520-Green and was looking forward to his first space trip. He also asked to be forgiven for his young age but time would soon remedy that.

Bulzezatna smiled broadly at this humorous remark and immediately took a liking to the boy. He was proving to be everything she had hoped for. She came forward still smiling and put both her hands on Simon's shoulders.

What happened next took even Ashley by surprise. Bulzezatna poured the entire details of the ship's makeup and operation and command structure into Simon's memory. There was much more that also filtered across for suddenly Simon seemed to stand straighter and taller. Ashley already knew much of what Simon had been given from his own earlier trips in the ship with Bulzezatna and her crew and now he was pleased when his inner voice revealed the captain's hidden motives.

Bulzezatna was surprised when Ashley conveyed that he was complimented by her faith in Simon and of her long term plans for him. Not even another Oannes could have probed the locked compartment of her mind and yet Ashley had done so or so she believed. How else could he have discovered her plans for Simon? A new found admiration and respect grew inside her for Ashley and she thought that the son might become as great as his father but in an entirely different way. What chance could Zarama have against a team such as this? Legend or myth, Bulzezatna could see the reality developing right here in her time and she felt its awesomeness.

520-Green now accelerated upwards and forwards and turned to face the West. Simon looked upwards and the sight of the abundance of stars above them filled him with awe. The Earth might be an interesting object to view he knew but the stars were what filled his heart with wonder and an unreserved longing. It was as though the brilliance above beckoned him. The Milky Way stars splashed right across the view panels from one side to the other in pure dazzling showmanship.

One hundred miles up, then two and three and still rising as the ship silently raced west at 4000mph.

The visitors on board saw the sun rise up in the west as the control room flooded with sunlight and the stars disappeared. The view panels changed automatically to a darker tint for their comfort. The ship climbed higher still and from 2000 miles up the day and night zones on Earth were clearly discernable. There were twinkling lights from the cities within the darkened zone and the bluish hazy brightness of the cloud filled daylight area. From even higher up the Earth looked like a bald headed monk with the dazzling arctic brilliancy as his pate. Although the ship's acceleration was upwards, at 10,000 miles distance Bulzezatna commanded Zanos to execute a looped turn so that her guests got a good view of the retreating Earth. The lower part of the southern hemisphere was in darkness so Bulzezatna had decided on the longer route to Anztarza as a treat for Simon. The Earth was now a truly magnificent sight as 520-Green turned towards it.

Simon stood glued close up to the view panels and looked downwards at the land in astonishment and wonder. And queries that came into his thoughts were immediately answered by Zanos as had been commanded by the captain. The Pacific area was clearly visible and as the ship retreated further the Earth lost its identity and took on a purely planetary conception. The ship rotated once again in order to accelerate upwards. At 80,000 miles distance after just another hour's travel and another looped turn the Earth resembled a three quarter hazy moon as the night side blended into the blackness of space behind it. Bulzezatna had linked her mind to Simon's in order to experience his reactions and she was amazed at the sensations that came across to her. The longing to be among the previous viewed array of stars spoke wonders and confirmed in her mind what course she must pursue. She communicated this to Ashley and received an affirmation of confidence in her judgement. Simon's apprenticeship seemed to have already begun. 520-Green rotated once again and brilliant sunlight re-entered the control room from above. They were heading sunwards and this time also in the direction of the moon and a surprise special for the guests.

The Earth was somewhere underneath the spaceship and out of sight for the time being. The brightness of the Sun prevented the stars from being seen and Simon expressed his disappointment at this. Bulzezatna conveyed that between the brightness of the fully illuminated Earth and the Sun the stars themselves had little chance of being in the visible zone.

For now however Bulzezatna conveyed to her guests what had been planned as a treat for Simon. 520-Green would begin a slow circuit around the Earth at the same distance as the moon's orbital path. The moon was currently in a position roughly between the Earth and the Sun and therefore its blind side would be in sunlight. The plan was to use the shuttle craft on board to make a lunar landing at a location from which a brilliantly lit Earth was visible.

Simon took all this in and wondered that it was all being done for him. He felt quite chuffed about it till it dawned on him that it was his dad who had the main telekinetic power and it was to compliment him that the son was being entertained. Simon hadn't a clue as to the true reason for Bulzezatna's interest in him. And yet his father had indicated that Simon would be of assistance in the battle against Zarama.

Simon had always imagined that spaceflight would have lots of dramatic moments and he now wondered at how normal it felt here in the control room. He could in fact be back at home playing a computer game under normal Earth conditions. Here gravity was just as normal and there was no sensation of speed. 520-Green was continuing upwards from the Earth and it then began its circuit towards the moon's position in the same direction as the Earth's rotation along the lunar orbital path. The thin crescent of the Earth appeared in the forward view panel but then suddenly it disappeared from view completely. A sort of halo of light was faintly discernable though the brightness of the Sun above it spoiled the image. Then after about five minutes of travel the Earth reappeared as a right-side crescent of light which rapidly grew ever larger. Soon there was half the Earth visible and Bulzezatna conveyed that another smaller half globe was visible further above in the view panel.

Ashley watched his son's fascination and excitement with everything that was unfolding before his eyes as he appeared glued to the view panels looking this way and that. Bulzezatna was living vicariously and enjoying the emotions she picked up from Simon's mind.

Rachel however had lost all interest in the events of the moment as she had got quite sleepy and tired. It was late for her and way past her normal bedtime. Lillian suggested that she take Rachel back to their cabin and put her to bed. Lillian had enjoyed seeing Simon's exuberance but she too was now rather tired and said she would stay with Rachel. Tiredly Rachel reached out and asked that Muznant come too. Tania thanked Lillian and said she'd like to stay a while longer up here to see Simon experience the moment. She'd like to remember the expressions of delight shown by him at this his first space flight. Little did she know that this moment would decide Simon's future career.

'Where did all the stars go?' queried Simon again and Bulzezatna explained that the Sun's light was far too bright to allow star shine to be seen. Just like on Earth no stars were visible during daytime. But soon the ship would go into a parking loop pattern of flight when nearing the moon and the stars would again become visible when it faced in a direction away from the Sun.

The spaceship was now in a position between the Sun and moon. The Earth was behind and slightly above the moon and both were in full sunshine. Because the Moon was nearer it loomed extremely large and bright. The Earth was a distant small colourful ball but still shiny bright in the darkness of space. 520-Green rotated around in order to decelerate and soon slowed to near zero at about a thousand miles from the moon and on its sunny side. Zanos now put the ship into a parking loop spanning about one hundred miles. The loop direction was at right angles to the imaginary line joining Earth, Moon and Sun such that they were always visible in its view panels. No stars were visible at all.

Preparations were now made for the boarding of the shuttle craft that would ferry the guests to a lunar landing. Ashley, Tania and Alex had all experienced the shuttle mode of travel on the asteroid experiment occasions and also when they visited the FTL starship 8110-Gold and so knew what to expect. Simon however now also knew what to expect from the visual imagery of those experiences that were conveyed to him. He felt as though he had actually been there with his dad. He even looked forward to the zero gravity conditions on the shuttle.

Captain Bulzezatna was pleased at Simon's sense of adventure and fearless reaction to the coming shuttle experience and drew her own favourable conclusions. Yes, she thought, Simon would make a good space traveller not to mention an asset as a crew member after suitable training.

Detailed instructions were conveyed and both deputies then led the way out of the control room and on towards the rear of the ship where the shuttle bay was located. As per the normal procedure two shuttle craft would be deployed out on the journey but only the one with the guests would land. They went down the ramp to the shuttle bay and then along a balcony overlooking the parked craft.

Tatizblay then led them through a doorway off this and they entered a large rectangular hall. This was the shuttle suiting up room where the electrostatic spacesuits were stored. There were the storage recesses along each wall and Ashley remembered the gold coloured overall type garments hanging in each.

For Simon's benefit Tatizblay conveyed that the electrostatic suit was a must for all passengers and crew on the shuttle journeys. The shuttle craft did not operate like the larger spaceships and so its journeys tended to be at zero gravity conditions. The electrostatic suits were therefore essential to prevent passengers or crew from floating around. The suit was internally charged with static electricity which caused it to be attracted to the shuttle structure. Simon smiled at his mum and dad and conveyed that he'd already known all this.

Tatizblay led Simon to a special storage section and held up a smaller item specially made to size. The suits were loose fitting baggy garments that were meant to be worn over everyday clothes. Ashley remembered that once the long front flap was closed the suit tended to tighten up slightly without causing any discomfort. He conveyed this to Simon who smiled back at his dad.

Once they had all put on their zero gravity suits they looked just like mechanics in shiny gold coloured overalls. The crew were also similarly dressed and Tatizblay then led the way out of the hall, through another doorway and then down the ramp to the shuttle bay floor. Rubandiz and his small crew were already down there and ready to board. Rubandiz would be in command of the shuttle craft 5201-Green that would fly as backup alongside 5202-Green commanded by Tatizblay.

Tatizblay led his charges onto his shuttle which was actually a bright yellow colour for good visibility in space. He took them down the central aisle and to the front seats where he got them seated and thigh clamps engaged. Simon sat between his mum and dad on the left side of the aisle while Alex sat just the other side of the aisle. There were about a dozen of the crew dispersed about the shuttle seating which could have accommodated a maximum of forty persons.

Tania had on a head scarf to keep her hair in place for when the electrostatic suits were activated. Tania remembered that first occasion on the shuttle prior to the Steins asteroid experiment when the electrostatic suits were energised. The men didn't look too odd but the women had looked decidedly ridiculous with their long hair standing on end. All had seen the funny side but it was remedied when headscarves had been provided.

The shuttle bay was made ready for their departure. All hatches and doors were slowly shut including those of all other craft in the bay. All maintenance crews exited the bay and the general lighting was dimmed.

Zanos was given the command and both shuttles rose upwards and gradually rotated about to face the rear of the ship. Slowly and fluidly the huge bay doors opened and both shuttles floated easily out into the open blackness of space. Zanos was in full control and turning around they saw the massive bulk of their spaceship 520-Green rapidly accelerating away from them. Soon it was a tiny speck in the distance and could have been mistaken for a distant star.

The shuttles were in brilliant sunlight but the viewing panels all around the shuttle had darkened for the comfort of the passengers. The two shuttles separated to positions about a mile apart and sped towards the looming ball of the moon which was barely a thousand miles distant.

Ashley looked at Simon and expected to find him feeling a bit of the nausea that was common with being weightless for the first time. But Simon looked perfectly at ease by which Ashley guessed that Zanos on board must have anticipated the situation and applied telepathic hypnosis therapy to help ease the condition. After the first few shuttle occasions Ashley realised that he had begun to look forward to the feeling of hypnotic euphoria that followed shortly afterwards.

The lunar landscape now filled the view ahead as their shuttle drew ever closer. The second shuttle under Deputy Rubandiz now held back and seemed to withdraw backwards. It would hold position about three hundred miles from the lunar surface and keep a careful monitor of everything that occurred.

Simon was all eyes looking this way and that and Ashley could sense that he was receiving a constant commentary from Zanos. Ashley could see the Earth as a bright ball on the far left while the glowing orb of the Sun was to the far right. The lunar landscape was right there in front of the shuttle and less than a hundred miles away. It seemed to speed up as they got closer and when the shuttle changed attitude for a landfall the faint effects of the lunar gravity became apparent. Zanos conveyed the intended landing zone which brought excitement among the human passengers.

Tania looked at her son's glowing facial expression and smiled across at her husband. Ashley smiled back and conveyed that he too was looking forward to the expected view.

The shuttle slowed as it approached the shadow line that separated the light and darker sides of the moon and then smoothly settled on a relatively flat plateau near it. Gravity was a welcome feature now and Simon looked around at the grey looking lunar landscape below the shuttle. He knew that he would have to make do with the visual experience since Bulzezatna had forbidden them to leave the shuttle. Simon then looked at his father and grandfather with the pride of a child receiving a most longed for Christmas present.

'Thanks dad,' he said in a soft emotion filled voice but filled with a new tone of confidence. Simon had now found what he had been unknowingly longing for without being able to pinpoint exactly what it was that he wanted. It was like his destiny had suddenly been revealed to him and he was pleased about it.

Ashley read his son's intent and said nothing though he reached down and squeezed Simon's hand. Tania had also suddenly understood what her son really meant and placed her hand on top of Ashley's to also give her blessing. Both smiled at their son. Simon was destined to become a true spaceman.

But all this was lost in the view that greeted them. For there to their left was the full Earth, a brightly shining ball of hazy blue, brown and white suspended in the magic of space. As their eyes got used to this full moon like apparition a faint background of stars became visible. But these were faint as the Earth's luminosity was too great to allow any but the brightest to be seen. Because of the shuttle's position Simon was seeing the Earth sideways. The bright North Pole was on the right and darkened hidden South Pole was to the left. Africa was at the top, India near the centre with Asia's eastern coastline near the bottom of the Earth image. India which was central to the image had quite a bit of cloud over its central area which Ashley reckoned to be the remnants of the monsoon season. At the top of the image was Africa which was only just visible within the curvature of the globe though China and Thailand showed up clearer. Australia was out of sight round the edge of the bright circle and inside the haze surrounding the Earth. There was an abundance of clouds generally over Asia and when Ashley tried to zoom in on a particular area it didn't happen. Zanos conveyed to Ashley that only the control room of 520-Green had that facility which would be available as soon as they returned to the main craft.

After several minutes on the lunar surface had elapsed Zanos informed them that the shuttle craft would now lift off and proceed into the darkened zone of the moon. The view of Earth should then become even more spectacular. Smoothly the shuttle craft rose up off the lunar surface to a height of a few miles and gradually made headway into the darkened area of the moon that faced earthwards. The Sun disappeared from view below the lunar horizon and suddenly there was Earth above them and now more brightly displayed than before. There was no Sun's brightness to dazzle the eyes and the Earth's identity became much more gloriously apparent. Simon tried to make out its rotational movement but could discern none. The cloud patterns showed up their own activity and from this Earth was definitely seen as a vibrant living entity.

The inside of the shuttle was now completely darkened by Zanos so that the occupants might see outwards clearly. As such Ashley could make out the lunar features below them. It was lit by Earthlight similar to that of a full moon only three times as bright. Earthshine created a magnificent sight with the lunar landscape clearly illuminated for them to make out the smooth and the rough areas. The shuttle ascended higher and the earthlight shadows in the myriad of craters were clear to see. On Earth all this was invisible since this dark phase of the moon was always in Earth's daytime. Yet here it showed up in all its earthshine glory. This was a sight to remember.

Ashley conveyed his thoughts to the others as the shuttle was commanded to increase speed and height across the darkened surface of the moon. The Earth was directly overhead and the lunar surface now seemed to get a bit remote as they sped over it. The Earth was like a mirror for the sun to reflect its brightness onto the shadowed side of the moon to bring relief to future generations of settlers on it.

Simon felt his senses awakened by this awareness and his enthusiasm for the vastness of the structure of open space increased considerably. It was a great feeling to view the valleys and patchwork of meadows from a hilltop back in England but to view something like this from the isolation of space far exceeded anything he could have remotely imagined.

Although it was supposedly in its night time phase yet the moon's surface was crowded by the detail that a lunar map would have highlighted. Looking up at the Earth was another glorious sight and Zanos indicated that further out in space on the African direction was a bright looking star. This was Venus a planet shrouded in cloud which was even brighter than Earth for its reflected brilliance. Perhaps one day it would cool and become inhabitable.

Ashley watched Simon wildly awake in his excitement of the moment and conveyed to Tania that their son seemed to be enjoying this treat from Bulzezatna. Ashley felt that he also enjoyed this experience as a first and knew that there was something more for them to see when they returned to the ship.

The shuttle finally drew away from the moon and back into sunlight and headed at speed to the rendezvous with the sister shuttle craft 5201-Green. Zanos then conveyed that 520-Green was on the return phase of its parking loop and both shuttles sped forwards to the meeting point. It was not long before the approaching under body profile of the spacecraft could be seen and both shuttles manoeuvred towards the inviting open bay doors.

389

The entrance into the shuttle bay occurred as the spaceship neared the end of its parking loop when its velocity status was near zero. The sudden brightness of the ships interior was always a surprise event but as the two craft settled onto the bay floor it felt nice to be back under normal gravity conditions again.

The bay doors closed and air pressure was restored to this area of the spaceship. Crew re-entered the bay and went about their normal business as Tatizblay opened the shuttle door and all disembarked. And it was not long before he got his passengers to divest themselves of the bulky electrostatic suits and led the way back to the control room.

Although Ashley's wristwatch showed that it was a few minutes after 5:00am BST he could see that Simon was wide awake and full of pep despite the late hour. For him his first experience of space had kept any semblance of tiredness or sleepiness at bay. Ashley could not say the same for himself or for Tania and Alex.

When they entered the control room Simon went up to the captain and conveyed his thanks for an experience he would never forget. Captain Bulzezatna smiled back at the boy and conveyed that there was one more treat in store for him before they set course back to Earth and Anztarza.

520-Green now raced away directly towards the Sun which appeared directly overhead through the heavily tinted view panels. The acceleration was slightly greater than normal gravity but Simon found the experience rather exhilarating. At about 2000 miles from the moon the ship did a complete about face so that now the fully sunlit moon was above them. It was a massive circle of brightly shining lunar landscape but one that was never visible from Earth. This was the far side of the moon and rather different in its greater pockmarked appearance and hardly any flat sea areas. Beyond and slightly above this huge brightly lit orb was the diminutive though colourful ball of the Earth.

Simon was glued to the view panels and moved from one to the other. For some reason the lunar landscape seemed not to interest him very much. He was more taken by the view of Earth and zoomed into its detail as best he could. India was still visible at the Earth's centre and Simon zoomed in for a look at some of their major cities. Simon could make out some main streets in the conglomeration of buildings but it became rather fuzzy and indistinct when he tried for greater magnification.

Zanos responded with the instruction that images might get sharper as 520-Green got closer to Earth if the atmospheric conditions allowed. Zanos' own scanning system was much more sophisticated and so it had to be for Zanos to exercise proper directional control of the spaceship. This was crucial in space when the cruise path ahead was being constantly scanned for matter of any kind that might be a danger to the craft.

520-Green was now accelerating at 1.0g in a direction that seemed to be aimed directly at the moon. It was then that the captain decided to test her new apprentice and ask what the right course should be to take the ship past the approaching Lunar mass. Simon was jerked out of his thoughts on the views of Earth and appeared taken aback by Bulzezatna's question. But he recovered well and his mind went into gear. He replied that he was not captain of the ship and it was not his place or responsibility. But if in the event that he was put in a position that required him to make such a command then he would not do so directly for the simple reason that he did not possess the necessary knowledge. Instead he would pass the course judgement on to Zanos to fulfil with the proviso that the course to follow must be such that there was no danger to the ship.

Ashley and Tania picked up this open telepathic response and were pleasantly surprised by their son's maturity. Bulzezatna was also pleased at Simon's response and conveyed her pleasure to him.

'Then we must set our course direction from now if we are to skim past the Lunar surface without getting closer than 200 miles,' conveyed Bulzezatna. 'That should make it quite spectacular at the velocity that we shall achieve. Our flypast should commence shortly.'

520-Green rotated slightly so that the huge orb of the brightly lit moon was just overhead in the forward facing view panel. The ship was now travelling at approximately 4000mph and accelerating. It seemed to be heading straight towards one edge of the moon as it loomed ever closer. Then suddenly there it was right in front of the control room view panel. The curvature of the moon seemed to rise towards them ever so quickly and when they were at the closest point the sensation of speed was tremendous. Suddenly they zoomed over the shadow line and over the darkened face of the moon. This could be seen quite clearly but fleetingly as the ship raced over it as its curvature began to roll away from them. Within a few minutes the dark face of the moon changed to a crescent and more and the prospect of the approaching Earth lay ahead. The ship was travelling at close to 8000 mph.

The Earth was still a very distant brightly shining fuzzy ball of colour and it would be some time before they got close. This was because of the need to maintain normal gravity conditions on the ship. As such the deceleration for low velocity entry into Earth's atmosphere must begin at about 100,000 miles.

Again a 'Wow' exclamation at the sight before them escaped not only from Simon but from Tania as well. Captain Bulzezatna just stood looking unconcerned and yet there was a hint of a smile on her old face. She was pleased her guests appreciated this spatial treat that she had arranged for Simon. Their thoughts of pleasure and excitement came through to her mind and she quite enjoyed the vicarious thrill of it. No doubt others on the ship had also received the same.

For some minutes Simon stood looking at the Earth view when a big yawn of tiredness made itself obvious. Bulzezatna conveyed that it would be about seven hours before Earth fall and arrival in Anztarza and suggested that they all retire to their cabins for a well earned rest. After all it had been a very long day for them all.

Ashley, Tania and Alex all accepted this with relief since it was showing 6:00am on Ashley's wrist watch. Sleep was definitely an essential item now though Simon at first denied that he was tired. He was reluctant to miss out on anything especially the re-entry into Earth's atmosphere. However he gave in when Captain Bulzezatna suggested otherwise. There would be other times such as the return journey back to Aberporth at the end of the Anztarza visit.

Bulzezatna handed over control room command to First Deputy Tatizblay and then led her four guests to their cabin area.

Lillian got up from a light sleep on one of the beds when Tania and Ashley entered with Simon. Alex had gone straight into his adjoining cabin and Lillian conveyed that she would join him right away. Rachel stayed asleep as Simon undressed down to his shorts and got into the bed his grandma Lillian had lain on. Tania and Ashley waved a silent goodnight and plodded into their adjoining cabin bedroom.

As they finally got into their own bed Ashley paused momentarily as if listening out for something and then conveyed that Simon had already dropped off to sleep. It had been a day to remember for him as it had for them all.

'Oh Ashley,' exclaimed Tania feigning her distress, 'I wish I could do that.'

'It will come to you one day darling,' whispered Ashley, 'don't fret about it my love, it'll come one day when you least expect it.'

'I love you Ashley Bonner,' said Tania also whispering. She still found that words sounded so much nicer.

'And I love all of you my darling Tania,' replied Ashley, 'and Rachel and Simon. I feel proud that Bulzezatna in all her years of wisdom has seen fit to take Simon under her wing. We have a budding spaceman in our family. Did you see the way he gloried in all that he experienced today?'

'Yes,' said Tania, 'he may have just discovered what he'd like to do when he grows up. I think he'll love anything to do with space travel. But I first want him to see and appreciate a lot more of Earth's beautiful places. I'd like for him to be able to take all those images and memories with him wherever he goes. Space travel with the Oannes is so well established that it holds no risks and as a mother I shan't worry too much about him being inside one of their spaceships. But I shall miss him when he's away.'

Ashley remained silent and was already halfway down the sleep ladder. Tania smiled to herself and this time succeeded in recognising his nil-thought brain pattern confirming that for him sleep was imminent.

Tiredness crept under her own eyelids and she never could remember the exact moment when she fell into a tired sleep.

It was nearly seven hours later that they were awakened by Zanos conveying that 520-Green would be entering Anztarza Bay shortly.

At the breakfast table in the dining lounge Simon started to tell Rachel all he had seen. He told her how his small shuttle craft had actually landed on the moon which by the way was not made of cheese.

'Of course I know that silly,' said Rachel, 'that was only in the story books for little children. And I'm not little anymore.'

Ashley and Tania smiled at this remark. Oh how quickly their children had become mini-adults.

Now Simon conveyed to Rachel's mind the images of much of his recent adventure. After all he had been glued to the control room view panels for most of the journey around the moon. But Rachel was more interested in the image of the Earth that Simon projected and wondered at how small and round it looked from the moon.

When they all went back to the control room Rachel walked between her mum and Muznant. Captain Bulzezatna was already there and conveyed a Sewa and a welcome back to them all. She had slowed the ship's progress through the Anztarza tunnel so that her guests could witness the ship actually surfacing in the Bay. She conveyed this to them and within minutes of their arrival the view panels went from a complete blackness to a shade like early dawn. This continued to lighten rapidly to a brighter hue before the ship suddenly broke into the open air of Anztarza Bay. The surfacing of the large spaceship was done slowly and smoothly so as not to cause any excessive waves to the water surface. As such only a gentle wave ripple spread out from the ship.

520-Green now slowly progressed the half mile to the quayside and before long was secured to its berth position where a small committee of Anztarza citizens stood waiting.

There was Puzlwat with his wife Nogozat and a few friends and interested Anztarza residents. This was the usual reception on most of Ashley's recent visits which was not considered unusual anymore.

Deputy Tatizblay had the honour of escorting the visitors onto the quayside and handing them over to the reception committee. Ashley and Puzlwat exchanged a friendly Sewa and Nogozat came forward specially to give a greeting to Rachel and Simon. She was surprised and pleased at how small Rachel was but her eyes rested for a long moment on Simon as being Ashley's son.

Nogozat had a very perceptive mind and something about Rachel puzzled her. She read a quality in the child's mind that would blossom with maturity and have an impact upon the people of both worlds. But the sense of it was lost as soon as it was perceived and Nogozat wondered whether the feeling had just been her imagination. Muznant who was beside Rachel picked up Nogozat's thought and she too wondered at the truth of the interpretation.

Puzlwat then conveyed that they needed to board the Deck Transporter which would take them to Dome 4 where an assembly was gathered to greet and welcome them; this being Simon and Rachel's first visit. Only two of the chief ministers would be there as Tzatzorf the eldest was indisposed and confined to his sleep tank.

They boarded the usual 536-Orange Transporter but there was no elderly Kazaztan to welcome them. Instead a very young Oannes male named Fritvazi aged 90 was the new operator and he greeted them accordingly. He was very small at barely 4½ feet tall and of extremely light build. But this went unnoticed as he exhibited the widest smile that Ashley had seen in all of Anztarza; a pleasant and most welcoming manner.

Simon took a liking to him straight away and made a point of saying 'Hello' in a low voice. He received a high pitched 'Hello' in return and the smile of course. They were to become friends and would serve together on Simon's first Starship duty emplacement but that was some considerable time in the future.

At Ashley's request Fritvazi commanded the 536-Orange to make a circuitous route through several of the Domes before arriving at Dome-4. Rachel was fascinated by the views of the city type scenes passing so closely below them and felt sad that there was so little visible vegetation. She thought about it but said nothing. One day she'd do something about it. Her thoughts however did not go unread.

Simon on the other hand found the journey and its aerial views disappointing but only in comparison to the experiences of his trip out in space. He'd much rather be up there than confined inside a habitation dome even ones as large as these.

Fritvazi finally settled the Transporter in the central plaza of Dome-4 where a large group of the Oannes community was waiting to greet them. This time a fair proportion of them were the Oannes' wives who were keen to see and get to know Ashley's children. And for some reason the women were more interested in Rachel and grouped around her when the formal welcoming by the chief ministers was over.

Formalities had always to be strictly adhered to on every occasion without exception. The Sewa tradition was strong in the Oannes civilization and Ashley considered this a most endearing asset. Politeness and genteel etiquette could never be ignored or taken lightly.

Jantuzno introduced herself to Rachel saying that she had much to thank Katy for. Consequently Rachel took an immediate liking to Jantuzno who appeared both youthful and pretty. There was more than just a hint of cosmetic makeup on Jantuzno as was also the case for many of the other Oannes ladies gathered around her. Lipstick, blusher and eye shadow makeup did a lot for the Oannes appearance. Apparently the fad had also travelled to Nazmos over the years.

Chief Minister Rymtakza had finished his welcoming address by adding that a welcome banquet was planned for later in the evening period when more of Anztarza's citizens would attend. This would be after the new young visitors had been given a general aerial tour of Anztarza's many features and had rested in the accommodation Muznant and Brazjaf had arranged.

Muznant had read the lack of interest in Simon's demeanour for a further floating tour and so suggested that the party be split up. She would take Rachel and anyone else who wished to join them on a special tour of the dome habitation areas while Brazjaf would take Simon and the men back to the Bay Dome and a walk-on tour of the spacecraft moored there.

'Oh yes please,' came the exclamation from a smiling Simon who immediately agreed to the plan.

'I want mummy to come with me,' said Rachel and Tania said she'd love to go with her darling daughter. Of course Lillian and Muznant would join her too.

And so it was that the women went one way and the men another.

However Ashley and Alex both expressed a wish to return to their usual habitation Dome and just meet some of their old friends in the plaza there. Ashley thought that Simon could then get the full attention from Brazjaf and whoever accompanied them into the various craft there. Simon needed to develop on his own towards the future he had set his heart on.

536-Orange commanded by Fritvazi took the ladies while another Transporter was called and took the men to Dome-7 where Ashley and Alex disembarked. It then went on to Anztarza Bay.

Rachel simply loved the aspect of looking down upon the residential areas and the upward looking Oannes residents as she floated overhead. She received greetings through her ear stud communication badge and responded likewise. She was only five years of age but a mothering instinct seemed to well up within her for these people.

She had never experienced such a sensation before and an instinct within her being grew in intensity to reveal just a tiny part of the destiny that lay before her. Yes, they would become her charge and she would belong to them. Then all this fragmented into a haziness of confusion and the moment was lost as if awakening from a dream that is soon forgotten.

Simon on the other hand had very satisfying informative tours of the various spacecraft parked along the crescent curve of the Bay shoreline.

There was 520-Green and two others very similar in size and shape though with a variation of several features such as the access ports and side view panels. Brazjaf explained that there was a difference of about 500 years in each ones manufacture with 520-Green being one of the more recent at only 100 years of age. Each was 550 feet long and 250 feet wide with six decks, though the upper and lower decks were mainly for housing the power units.

Also further along was 11701-Red commanded by Captain Lyzongpan which had brought Ashley on his first visit to Anztarza years ago. This was 400 feet long and 175 feet wide with four decks. It was usual for the rear of all spacecraft to have large bays to house shuttle craft and cargo.

Others like 8962-Green and 6310-Yellow were of a smaller class of vessel meant mainly for limited local planetary travel and were 300feet in length with three decks only.

And others were even smaller craft being just 100 feet in length and 40 feet wide and one passenger deck. Yet all were of varying design and capability.

All could venture into space though the smallest ones at 100 feet in length were used mainly within Earth's atmosphere for journeys to the northern forests and for picking up items purchased by their agents on Earth. These were by far the greatest in number within the Anztarza fleet.

Simon's enthusiasm was picked up by Brazjaf and an inside tour of 8962-Green and one of the smaller ships was agreed. Captain Nazaztal was not on board his ship but conveyed his permission for Simon's tour within. He expressed his regret that he was not there personally but his deputy Bynztal was already looking forward to showing them around the ship and considered it a privilege to have Ashley's son on board. Senior crew member Byuzlit was away on Nazmos visiting his parents at Arznat.

Simon also noticed the dozen or so deck transporters parked close to the dome wall well away from the shoreline. These were unattended and Brazjaf explained that this was their usual parking location. At one time they used to be left in singles to one side of the central plaza of each dome but this practice had been changed several hundred years ago. They were also programmed to accept private usage by certain delegated persons or by agreed advisement. Communication in Anztarza was never a problem.

Simon expressed a wish to look more closely at the deck transporters so Brazjaf led the way across to them; a ten minute stroll as Simon stopped briefly to gaze at the moored spacecraft as they passed by them. Simon showed his keenness by examining and determining the small differences in the design of each Transporter. Brazjaf always replied to Simon's queries with visually illustrated telepathic explanations and reading Simon's mind he conveyed that on Nazmos they were the usual form of transportation. Of course some Transporter craft were larger than others.

'Maybe one day we shall have similar transport in general use on Earth,' conveyed Simon wistfully.

'One day perhaps when contact is widely accepted.' conveyed Brazjaf. He knew it would be millennia rather than centuries and indicated as much to his young protégé.

Simon thought about the future when none of them would be around. Would they even be remembered? Brazjaf read these thoughts and added his own.

'I think that Ashley and his family will always be remembered as the historic first civilized contact between our peoples' said Brazjaf, 'after all our myths had foretold about someone like Ashley from ancient times. So why should we not remember him and his family over the millennia to come?'

'Gosh,' said Simon verbally, 'that does make me feel important.'

Brazjaf smiled. He liked this son of Ashley. He in turn might make his own mark on history.

They then returned to spacecraft 8962-Green and were welcomed by Bynztal and another of the crew. A brief Sewa was exchanged and Simon responded for himself which pleased Bynztal and surprised the crew member a relative Oannes youngster.

Deputy Bynztal was 120 years of age and had been in Anztarza for only four years. His home on Nazmos was another small town on the shores of the Great Sea Peruga but quite distant from the big city of Wentazta that was Brazjaf's home. He too like the absent senior crew member Byuzlit was single with parents, a brother and a sister back on Nazmos.

The young crew member with Bynztal was a recent arrival from the home planet and had a cadet trainee status on 8962-Green. He was 60 years old and very keen to progress to a position on a FTL Starship. His name was Mipzanti and he was small even for an Oannes person being just 4 feet tall the same as Sudzarnt. He had pleasant youthful features highlighted by a rather upward pointing perky nose. This gave him a childlike appearance and

Simon liked him immediately. They would in fact become firm friends and serve together on several space cruisers. With his relatively large mouth his wide smile was extremely infectious. But for now he remained a silent attendant.

Bynztal led the way into his ship and went straight to the control room. It was similar to most of the Oannes spacecraft but 8962-Green had just the one habitation deck. The other two decks were for power generation and impulse units and for general cargo storage.

He then conveyed an image of the ship to Simon and also its general dimensions. It was 300 feet long and 150 feet in width and 50 feet in height. This not only gave the ship strength underwater but more importantly enabled the central electro-magnetic core to generate a strong polar magnetic field that extended approximately for 50 miles around the ship when out in space. This was similar to the Van Allen magnetic field around the Earth but on a much smaller scale.

There was a corridor that circled the interior of the ship and the habitation level layout was similar in design to what it had been on 520-Green. Each cabin had a sleep tank and all the usual facilities.

Moving on they approached the crew quarters and Mipzanti conveyed a thought to Bynztal. Brazjaf picked up the thought as did Simon and he became quite excited at the prospect.

Apparently when Mipzanti left home his parents had provided him with several new tunic outfits in increasing sizes. As parents they hoped that their son would gradually grow to at least 4½ feet. So some outfits were currently much too large. Mipzanti noticed that Simon was near that height and perhaps might like to try on one of these oversize outfits.

'I would love to,' conveyed Simon with thanks and a generous smile. 'Can we do so right away please?' He conveyed that here in Anztarza his Earth clothes made him feel out of place. He liked the Oannes dress style of tunic and leggings and knew outfits awaited him back at their host's house. He looked up at Brazjaf and smiled. But he would like to surprise Rachel by arriving back all dressed in his new outfit.

Mipzanti had his own cabin which was of a reasonable size and appeared comfortable. The sleep tank was slightly smaller and Brazjaf and Bynztal stood to one side as Mipzanti brought out two outfits. One was beige with yellow flashing and with an emblem design on the tunic chest. The other was a pale green with blue and orange flashing side by side. Simon immediately pointed to this and was quite unembarrassed when he stripped to his underwear in front of the others. He put on the leggings first and the fit was perfect. The tunic was slightly on the loose side but he preferred this to be so. The slit opening in its back was kept closed by a couple of fine clips. There was corresponding footwear but this was definitely much too large. The Oannes must have big feet thought Simon, or did he just have smaller feet. So for the time being Simon put his own shoes back on.

Brazjaf smiled at the oddity but said, 'Do not worry Simon other outfits await you at my house so that for the banquet you shall be suitably attired.'

Simon looked at himself in the wall mirror and was impressed by his appearance. He wondered what his spaceship uniforms would look like. But that was years and years in the future.

Mipzanti was all smiles as he looked at Simon. He liked what he saw of the boy.

They then progressed to a hall which had at its centre a circular pillared construction from floor to ceiling. It was smooth and similar to the internal walls of the craft. It was twenty feet in diameter and Bynztal explained its purpose. Inside the circular wall was a concentric core ten feet in diameter which extended through the entire height of the craft. A myriad of coils and counter-coils within were meant to generate a powerful magnetic field around the ship when it was out in space. The field protected the inhabitants of the craft from the harsh cosmic rays that pervaded the entire space environment.

Simon queried several aspects which Bynztal promptly clarified. Zanos on-board would never permit operation of the magnetic field inside the Earth's atmosphere or for that matter here in Anztarza. When approaching another spaceship in open space one of the fields would be neutralised by agreement.

Simon felt quite perky in his new colourful tunic and the banquet event was something that he was now keenly looking forward to. Wait till Rachel saw him in these pale green colours. Funny, he thought, he would never in a million years have dared to wear such colours back at home or in school. Yet now he would be proud to do so because his future lay with these people.

Brazjaf conveyed that much time had passed and it was time to leave. Mipzanti regretted not having been able to show Simon some of the smaller craft but then they could do that tomorrow when they had a full day for it.

Brazjaf and Simon said their Sewa farewells to Bynztal and Mipzanti and made their way to the waiting Transporter. Simon's own clothes were to be sent on to Brazjaf's house in Dome-7 as would the new outfits for him and Rachel. But first they all needed to rest up before the evening gathering and the banquet prepared for them.

It was a matter of etiquette that no one was permitted to be transported directly over the banqueting preparations and so they went to Dome-7 via a roundabout route. By coincidence 536-Orange arrived from the direction of the Dome-14 connecting tunnel just as Brazjaf and Simon alighted from theirs in the central plaza.

Simon waved enthusiastically to Rachel whom he could see leaning over her Transporter rail and looking downwards at him. She waved back and conveyed that he looked very smart in his Oannes outfit. She especially liked the blue and orange coloured flashing.

536-Orange settled down quietly on the other side of the plaza as telepathic thoughts were conveyed back and forth between them all. Tania and Lillian repeated how smart Simon looked. Muznant had mixed thoughts about this child and thought how Ashley must have been when at a similar age. Her love and admiration grew just that little bit more. She then gave Simon a complete image view of all that they had done and seen. Surprisingly Rachel had shown a greater interest in the Food Domes than she had with the habitation ones.

But one place they could not view was what lay underneath the city floor levels. That was where the power plants were housed which supplied Anztarza with all of its energy needs. Also below was the purification plant that kept the city clean of all personal and domestic waste products. An image of something resembling an oil refinery was conveyed to the visitors. The air purification system was housed as three separate plants each capable on its own of coping with all of Anztarza's needs.

The administration and Earth monitoring memory banks were located underneath Dome-4. And keeping control of everything was the main bio-computer Zanos system; a series of control systems that backed up one another. This was from where all the 'thinking stones' and communication badges functioned and were monitored.

Brazjaf then conveyed to Rachel all about Simon's visit to the spaceships moored in the Bay dome and his tour inside the ship 8962-Green. He also conveyed images of the crew members Bynztal and Mipzanti who had conducted the tour for Simon. Rachel was glad that Simon had enjoyed his visit just as she had hers and suggested that he might have found the food domes rather interesting. Perhaps he would like to make his own visit there.

They all walked the short distance towards the Dome wall and to Muznant and Brazjaf's housing accommodation. Laztraban and his wife Niktukaz were there to greet them and showed great interest in the children, especially since some of the family were also staying in their accommodation. Lillian and Alex would sleep in Muznant's house and all would dine and breakfast there together.

Of course Wazu was the welcoming drink after the polite Sewas were exchanged. In the Oannes fashion telepathic Sewas were extremely quick. It was now early afternoon since Anztarza kept to GMT all year round, and Muznant suggested that they all have a rest period of a few hours in their rooms prior to the banquet event which was scheduled for seven o'clock.

Ashley and Tania took the children to the house next door accompanied by Niktukaz who conveyed that two rooms with Earth beds had been prepared. The dining and recreation rooms had been converted to bedrooms since all dining was arranged to be in Muznant's house. She and her husband Laztraban would of course occupy the room with the sleep tank. It was assumed that all catering would be performed by Niktukaz with Laztraban assisting.

Ashley and Tania's tunics etc were already in their room from previous visits while the new outfits for the children had only just been placed alongside. There were two outfits each and both kids rushed to view them. Simon's was the slightly larger and he quite liked the colour designs in each. One was similar in colour to the one Mipzanti had given him but the other was a pale yellow with bright red flashing. Rachel had a bright green outfit with yellow flashing while the other one was a pale pink with a shiny dark magenta flashing. The flashing was down the outside of the leggings and on the lower border of the tunics.

Of course pink was Rachel's favourite colour and she decided that was the one she would wear to the banquet. The footwear was a good match to each outfit and fitted them perfectly.

There was one difference with the Oannes' tunic and that was the short sleeves that had been added to the top of their design. Also the material was of a softer texture. Muznant conveyed that the Oannes tunics and leggings were made from a water impervious material to ensure it did not absorb moisture during their underwater activities. Like when Muznant and Brazjaf had first met Ashley in Aberporth and had left via the sea to aqua-dive out towards the craft that had brought them. Once out of the sea in the ship's hold the water had simply drained away leaving their outfits feeling quite dry.

Ashley, Tania and the kids were left to settle down into their accommodation and Niktukaz once again welcomed them to her hospitality. She did not enter their bedrooms but simply conveyed that she hoped they rested well. Being out in space had brought its own kind of fatigue and so a suitable period of rest was always recommended at some time prior to a major engagement such as the banquet gathering. She and her husband would spend a quiet time in their sleep tank as would also Muznant and Brazjaf.

A quietness descended in this little quarter of Dome-7 as its residents slept for a few hours. Sleep was never a problem in Anztarza. The desire for sleep was read by the Zanos bio-computer and a corresponding sleep thought induced in the person. The 'thinking stones' of Chief Ogemtali often performed such a function when placed close to the person at night. There was no need for an alarm call since a wake up stimulation would be initiated at the desired time.

At the banquet Rachel was seated between Tania and Muznant. Also at the same table were Jantuzno and some of her friends. Tania noticed that many of them had on light cosmetic make-up in the forms of blusher and lipstick.

Wazu was on every table and the guests helped themselves as they sat down. Rachel was extremely wary of drinking it as its appearance put her off. She didn't like anything that had seemingly live fuzzy things floating in it. So she asked for plain water and was given it.

'My mummy says I'm too young to wear make-up in public; but I put some on when I'm at home,' conveyed Rachel. 'And when I'm older I shall have my hair streaked and put extensions in it.'

'We do like this enhancing of our best features,' conveyed a young girl of 60 called Zizarnta, 'but we don't have hair like you.'

Tania couldn't help interrupting with, 'But there is such a thing as a wig for women who have lost their hair for some reason. These are artificial and come in such a variety that there is bound to be one to your liking. Many of the actresses on TV put a wig on top of their natural hair if they wish to change their look from blonde to brunette without going through the elaborate colouring processes.'

Here Tania conveyed an image of a shop displaying wigs of all shapes and sizes.

Muznant had a smile on her face and conveyed to Tania and the others at the table that she'd just had a visual of a lady's wig floating upwards in a sleep tank as it separated itself from the head of its owner. This brought general humour all around and even to some of the other tables who had been listening to the thoughts coming from this guests' table.

Simon was at an adjacent table seated between Ashley and Brazjaf. Also at the table was the diminutive smiling face of Mipzanti and some of his space cadet friends.

Simon finally had the chance to query Mipzanti regarding how he got to be a cadet on a spaceship.

Apparently like Simon he'd been taken with space when he'd travelled on the FTL starship to come to Anztarza about a year ago. His interest had been noted and if anything the Oannes recognised an aptitude and encouraged the corresponding enthusiasm in its citizens. How good the person was at the job would be seen in practice. So far Mipzanti had shown he was quick to learn and displayed a continued keenness and intelligence with his questions.

Simon conveyed that he had always had an interest in aeroplanes and had wished one day to fly in them. He enjoyed films with an Air Force theme. But flying through space was what he really wanted as a career. He did not convey the fact that Bulzezatna had already vetted him for when he was old enough. Simon said that he hoped to become a space cadet just like Mipzanti.

'I shall look out for you then,' conveyed Mipzanti, 'and perhaps one day we shall be fortunate enough to serve on the same ship.'

'I certainly hope so,' said Simon aloud, and in his mind the possibility was forecast as a certainty. Had he just had another one of his premonitions? Yes, it did seem like it and he felt quite elated.

This was to be an informal banquet and dishes made from Raizna, Starztal, Yaztraka, Mirzondip and other things grown in Anztarza's domes were placed on the tables.

Ashley recognised many of them but some were new combinations or recipes. He pointed to the ones he recognised and explained them to his son.

'Get used to this fare spaceman,' he said, 'for when you are in space for great lengths of time only this will be available having been grown in-house.'

'It looks quite nice dad,' said Simon tentatively, 'so I shall try them all in turn. I might even have a favourite.'

'I think that the Oannes have adopted some of our spices for their foods but in general they prefer their food simple as always,' explained Ashley.

There was silence while everyone served themselves from a number of dishes. Ashley looked to see how Simon was getting on.

'I find the Raizna very similar in taste to our own potato mash,' commented Simon, 'and you know that potato mash is one of my favourites.'

'Well then,' said Ashley pointing to one of the dishes piled up in the shape of a mound, 'that dish is made from Yaztraka. It is from a tree with long hanging fruit and is always cooked in a mash. Try it and tell me what you think'

So the dish was passed to Simon. He looked at it before slowly putting a spoonful on his plate. He thought it had a firm body though with a slightly sticky consistency. He put a little on the tip of his spoon and gingerly tasted it. He found it nice and sweet.

'That is really very nice dad,' he said with a smile, 'I might have a bit more of that.'

There were smiles all around and from the other tables also as Simon's pleasant thoughts were generally read. His emotion of liking the dish of Yaztraka was an emotion that could not be feigned.

Brazjaf conveyed that Simon obviously liked his food sweet since Yaztraka was also a favourite with most of the Oannes youngsters on Nazmos. The older generation however gravitated towards the potato type diet of Raizna.

The conversation among the Oannes on the visitors' tables was light hearted and generally solicitous about their general daily lifestyle. Although they knew much from their monitoring they still wanted to know how they enjoyed day to day living. There was so much recreational space on the lush green Earth that this was an opportunity to get first hand opinions.

They were interested to know how Simon and Rachel coped with the mundane tasks of verbal education and were surprised at how slowly Earth children learned their facts in history and geography. Simon showed his own interest in the Oannes style of acquiring knowledge and hoped one day that Earth would follow suit.

'One day we also will learn things the easier telepathic way,' he said to the young Mipzanti sitting opposite.

'But first the human brain needs to develop further,' said Brazjaf. 'At present your brain would find it hard to cope with large amounts of data in a rapid flow. You must still acquire knowledge gradually even via telepathy. I'm sure that one day you will become proficient like us. But I fear that is a long way away; perhaps even as far as a few millennia away.'

After the meal had been cleared off the tables there was a general moving around by the guests though the visitors remained at their places. Chief Minister Rymtakza and his wife Mizpalto came and sat at Rachel's table and communicated telepathically. They were pleased that Ashley had brought his children to meet them. After etiquette was observed they moved on to other tables before visiting Ashley and Simon. Rymtakza was quite impressed by Simon and what he had heard from Bulzezatna and conveyed that he would be happy to sponsor Simon's entry into the spaceship program.

'Thank you Minister,' was the thought message that came from none other than Captain Bulzezatna who was not present at the banquet. 'That is greatly appreciated since I have seen the latent talent in Ashley's son. He has a love for the vastness of space and a predisposition for space travel. He is young and I look forward to his development into maturity.'

Simon had a moment of contemplative reverie as he digested this conversation.

'Come,' said Mipzanti, 'let us walk around and meet some of my other friends and cadets. You will find that not all are as young as I. Some who are on Nazmos only developed a keenness for space travel in their senior years.'

And so Simon and Mipzanti went around to the other tables, sipped their Wazu offers and exchanged their space travel experiences. Simon remarked on how wonderful it had been for him his first time ever. He said how grateful he was to captain Bulzezatna for arranging the trip onto and around the moon.

The others mentioned how envious they all were of Rizaltz who had been on 520-Green during the time of Ashley's asteroid experiments. She had actually been on one of the shuttles that took Ashley out for the 253 Mathilde asteroid push and seen it disappear into the distance. She was currently on Nazmos with her family and possibly to get married; she was nearing 100 years of age.

She'd suffered a bout of space nausea and had received advice against extended space travelling. She had worked for two years in the food domes of Anztarza before deciding to return to the home planet on a permanent basis.

One cadet in particular said he missed her company and would have liked to have started a relationship with her. His name was Grizamitan but at 60 years of age the others all said he was far too young for her. He hoped to meet her again some day.

Simon enjoyed their space experiences vicariously as they conveyed vivid images of all their trips. Part of their learning curve was to know the intricacies of spaceship functionality especially with regard to the technical detail. This included operating procedures according to the rules laid down over thousands of years. There was also a behaviour code with regard to Earth and its inhabitants. The strict rule in general was against any form of contact. Ashley had been the exception because it was believed that his coming had been mentioned in their ancient myths.

Simon sensed that they hesitated when the myths topic was broached and realised that there was much more there that was not talked about. In fact he received the notion that it was an area of conversation that was discouraged generally even for the Oannes people. Misinterpretation was dangerous and so it was left to the expert committees to discuss and deduce. This was not the moment for Simon to query but he would raise the issue with Muznant and Brazjaf later.

Rachel too had plenty of pleasant conversational chatter and was happy to leave Muznant and go around with Jantuzno and her girl friends. Rachel felt grownup with them and realised that she looked upon them as a mother did towards her brood. A very odd thought indeed since Rachel was just five. Jantuzno and the others read these thoughts and looked at each other with knowing looks. Perhaps the myths did extend further. But it was unclear how Rachel fitted in with their future. The link between their two worlds was as mysterious to them as were the myths themselves.

Rachel quite enjoyed this all-girl company and chatter and this sentiment was picked up by the others and appreciated. They had taken a liking to the presence of this child among them. Girls aged five can be extremely precocious. Rachel was a fast learner and one of those who just couldn't wait to grow up into motherhood. It was subsequently agreed as a matter of choice that Jantuzno and some of her friends would pick Rachel up the next morning and show her their little world of activity; an Anztarza from a woman's perspective. Rachel was thrilled at the idea and both Tania and Muznant conveyed that it was a good plan.

Simon too had been invited out the next day. Mipzanti conveyed that there was still a lot for Simon to see. Among them was a surprise item that was essential to FTL space travel. Simon could only guess at what this might be and to actually see it at close quarters was something he found hard to imagine.

Ashley conveyed a visual diary of their trip so far to the badges of the family back home and received pleasant emotions in return.

'Its lovely to know that Rachel and Simon have made friends and are enjoying themselves,' was the response from Katy. 'Jantuzno and I often communicate and I'm glad that Rachel has met her.'

'We feel like we are there with you,' conveyed Brenda, 'and hope to see you again on Monday night. Don't leave it too late or I shall be asleep in bed. Sleep tank to our friends who I know are listening in.'

There was general amusement at this added remark.

'We shall be there before midnight,' conveyed a humorous Bulzezatna, 'after all we are still on the same planet.'

Lillian and Brenda then had a closed private conversation although it was just general chatter but it made Brenda feel as though she was not really missing any of this visit's excitement.

Eventually the time drew on and both Rachel and Simon showed signs of tiredness. Yawning was something that quite fascinated the Oannes as they had never experienced the phenomenon at such close hand. Ashley thought that they had yet to witness a sneeze at close range. They may have seen it on TV but never in real life and at close quarters. The Oannes monitored Earth TV and of course coughs, sneezes and yawns were portrayed. But now with Rachel and Simon they could connect the physical state of tiredness with the proverbial yawn.

After the usual farewell Sewas Muznant accompanied Rachel and the lively group of Jantuzno's friends on the deck Transporter to Dome-7 and their accommodation quarters. Simon was similarly accompanied by Brazjaf and Mipzanti's fellow cadets. Ashley and Tania came marginally later with Lillian and Alex.

Within the hour all had retired to their rooms. Rachel and Simon were the first to drop off into an exhausted sleep. It had been a long and event filled day. Even Brazjaf and Muznant floated peacefully in their sleep tank.

Ashley however lay awake for a while beside a sleeping Tania and thought lightly and generally of what the future held. Not just tomorrow or the day after that but in the millennia to come. The future should be bright he thought just before sleep claimed him. The dome lights had already dimmed considerably to imitate night in the GMT zone and all was quiet as Anztarza slept.

Next morning Laztraban and his wife Niktukaz helped Muznant lay out the breakfast meal so that when the guests awoke all would appear in readiness. And so it was. Simon and Rachel both awoke early and were already at table when Lillian and Alex joined them. Tania was next but Ashley was considerably later. Breakfast was simple and Lillian was pleased to see bread, butter and cheese laid out along with a bowl of strawberry jam.

Muznant looked at Lillian with a smile and conveyed that everything had been made on Earth and brought here for them. Bread had become quite a favourite in the Oannes diet not only here in Anztarza but also as far away as Nazmos.

Jantuzno and a couple of her friends were the first to arrive and ready to whisk Rachel off for the day. Rachel was as keen to be off but Tania had a moment of hesitation. A mother's protective instinct came into play which Muznant immediately read.

'If it is to be an all girl outing then perhaps an older person could be made to feel young again in your lively company,' conveyed Muznant to Jantuzno with all the imagery and meaning attached.

'Oh Aunty Muznant,' exclaimed Rachel excitedly, 'you must come with us. You can hold my hand and show mummy I'm safe.'

Muznant looked at Ashley and Tania and smiled at Rachel's perception of the situation.

'Oh yes,' conveyed Jantuzno immediately, 'we can then go to places we as juniors are not permitted.'

'The more the merrier,' commented Ashley quietly to himself.

At first he got a puzzled look from Muznant but then understanding dawned. She was getting used to the variations of earthly humour with its humorous witticisms.

It was sometime after Rachel had left with her new friends that the diminutive Mipzanti arrived alone to collect Simon. He seemed overly excited and when queried stated that permission had been granted for them to tour any one of the smaller ships moored in the Bay. But apart from this they would also see a tiny aspect of an FTL starship. What that was Mipzanti would not reveal but it did excite Simon no end. The other cadets awaited them in the Bay dome beside one of the moored ships.

Rachel didn't seem very interested in the habitation areas passing below the Transporter or even in the Bay dome with all its moored spaceships. It was only when they floated above the still waters of Food Dome-21 did she become interested and asked to see it all in detail.

'To do that you will need to enter the water and swim down to where the plants are growing,' conveyed Jantuzno, 'which is not possible for you.'

'No it isn't, 'conveyed Muznant smiling, 'but I can take Rachel down to see it all.'

'But I don't swim very well,' said a dejected looking Rachel, 'and I couldn't hold my breath for so long either. But I don't mind getting wet.'

Jantuzno now understood what Muznant was intending as did the other friends who immediately volunteered for the job in hand.

'Don't worry Rachel,' said Muznant, 'your Aunty Muznant won't let you get wet at all. I shall go down myself and you will see everything through my eyes.' And Muznant conveyed her plan and full intentions.

'Oh that would be absolutely lovely,' exclaimed Rachel and gave Muznant a hug. Muznant also put her arms around Rachel and pressed her lightly towards herself. Her heart skipped a beat as the emotions flooded within her chest. It was a rare sensation but an extremely pleasant one. A bit like the kiss she had given Ashley at their first meeting when she had probed deep into his mind.

The Transporter settled down near the dome wall and Muznant communicated with the dome supervisor Myzantra who appeared up out of the water quite near them. She was 150 years old and quite pretty and had been in Anztarza for nearly twelve years now. Her husband worked in the monitoring section under Dome-4. She had replaced Shumpazon the senior food supervisor aged 220 years about ten years ago. He had returned to Nazmos with his wife and son and would remain there until his son's education and career was formulated. The current food inspector Muzzalt was elsewhere in Anztarza at the present time.

The shoreline was a thin crescent of land across a quarter of the dome floor area and was covered in shrubs and dwarf trees. It then dropped quite steeply to the growing depth of twenty feet where it flattened out. This then extended across the entire dome area. The actual dome floor was another twenty feet below this indicating the true depth of the growing soil.

Myzantra had two small cylinders with her. They were cigar shaped and slender and just over a foot long and similar to the ones that Muznant and Brazjaf had used when they left Aberporth after their first meeting with Ashley and family.

Since most Oannes wore tunics with the circular metallic bulge at each side Muznant was quite prepared when she was handed the pair by Myzantra. She clipped these into place and communicated that she was ready to follow where Myzantra led.

They walked to the shoreline and stepped into the water and soon disappeared under the surface. Muznant sent her visual views as a constant stream of mental images to Rachel's badge that she found quite fascinating seeing the underwater scenes unfold before her.

Myzantra led the way and Muznant followed. They went all the way down to where the Yaztraka trees grew with their long hanging fruit. Some were as long as the Oannes themselves. As they proceeded further they came to shorter shrubs with small pink pods. This was Starztal and they extended along the soil in a broad straight line. Further along was another little forest of tree-like growth but devoid of any fruit. Myzantra conveyed that this was Lazzonta and similar to Earth's runner beans but all had recently been harvested. It would produce another full crop in a few months time. It was usual to get about three harvestings per year from most of the crops grown here.

They then came to a blank floor area which was quite extensive. Myzantra explained that this was where Raizna was grown but had just been harvested. Since the Raizna fruit was an underground product the harvesting involved pulling out the entire shrub to get its crop. She explained that Raizna was similar to Earth's potato.

Rachel found this interesting and stimulating and somewhere in the back of her mind she knew that something in what she had seen would be of great importance one day. But how this was to impact on them was unclear to her. Her instincts were strong though and when Muznant received her thoughts she too puzzled on its meaning. She decided to look again into the records of the old myths and ancient legends to see if there was some connection.

And Rachel insisted that a similar tour be made of the other food domes as her instincts pushed her. However apart from different crops and layout the domes proved to be fairly similar in function.

Muznant conveyed the history of the domes to Rachel. Anztarza's last habitable dome had been completed just over 1500 years ago and the third food Dome-23 completed 500 years later. Construction on food Dome-24 had been started 300 years ago and would need about another fifty years to complete. The need for additional food domes had arisen as the population of Anztarza had gradually increased from an initial few thousand to the current ten thousand.

Dome-24 was currently quite empty and was out of bounds to all except those involved in its construction. No exception could be allowed though Rachel pleaded with Muznant for just a tiny peek at the overall dome shell. Sadly she showed her disappointment when their Transporter was turned away. But because Rachel was the daughter of Ashley the construction supervisor on duty agreed to meet with Rachel.

He was a 187 years old Oannes named Wizgotal and had been on the Dome's construction since the age of 102. He climbed aboard one of the many small construction craft and floated out to where Rachel's larger Transporter waited. A brief Sewa was conducted and he conveyed what a pleasure and honour it was to meet Ashley's daughter.

'You may see through my mind all there is about this domes construction from when I started years ago to its present near completed state,' conveyed Wizgotal.

But Rachel was not as yet proficient in reading minds and so Muznant did it for her. She read Wizgotal's mind in an instant and then slowly conveyed the visual images to Rachel.

It was wonderful how Rachel saw the work progress over the years. Wizgotal had been on the project for 85 years apart from his occasional trips to Nazmos. The view at present was of a completed dome roof structure but blocks of composite material were still being laid in the floor central area. A gap of about a hundred square yards remained. There was a massive construction machine straddled like a giant spider over the deep floor covering the central area. The floor was about sixty feet lower than the water level of the other food domes and Wizgotal explained that soil from Nazmos would fill much of it. The blocks being laid were nearly ten feet square by five feet thick. Those in the roof area were twice as thick being as ten feet cubes. All blocks were perfectly smooth and accurate by dimension. Perfect face to face contact was necessary for effective fusion of the blocks to occur. Fusion took place in a slow manner like the setting of concrete. Only in this case it took nearly a year to achieve 90% bonding. 100% bonding took a further five years. Then all blocks became as one continuous wall. Spaceship construction was very similar. During FTL transportation from the factories on Nazmos the composite blocks were encased in an isolating protective coating to prevent accidental contact fusion. Viewing the construction through Wizgotal's memory the dome roof had been nearly 75% complete when he arrived in Anztarza. The roof blocks were laid from the floor level and gradually progressed upwards to make the dome walls and arched form. Rachel thought it resembled the building of an Eskimo's igloo from blocks of ice.

Wizgotal explained that prior to block placement the dome roof and walls had to be machined precisely so that the composite blocks from Nazmos fitted against the rock face perfectly. It was essential that the rock face and blocks be flush against each other for construction integrity. The blocks when fused together would reinforce the natural rock of the Earth above it in an absolute manner.

Rachel closed her eyes and visualised all of this through Wizgotal's memories and wondered at the preciseness of it all.

'I'd like to see it again when it is complete and when the first crops have been planted,' said Rachel. 'I'll be much older then,' she added wistfully.

Wizgotal conveyed that he also hoped to be around then and would welcome her back. But for now he must return to his supervising work and hoped that Rachel enjoyed the rest of her visit.

Brief Sewas were exchanged before Wizgotal's small construction platform retreated along the wide tunnel and back into the dome and out of sight.

Something was niggling at the back of Rachel's mind and it was only when they were back over the habitation of Dome-19 that she queried Muznant about it.

'Why do you grow all your crops underwater?' she asked.

'Because that is how they are grown on Nazmos,' replied Muznant. 'That way they can be grown all year round even when it is the winter season.'

'But what about growing them on land here on Earth?' Surely there must be somewhere suitable,' continued Rachel.

Muznant paused to think about Rachel's suggestion before answering.

'It might work and it might not,' she said. 'The weather on Earth can be quite variable while here in the domes we can control the conditions for best growth. But I suppose it could be tried one day in the future. Though introducing a new plant species to Earth environment might lead to problems. We Oannes must keep our presence here on Earth a complete secret for now.'

'I understand,' said Rachel. 'But maybe one day it could be tried.'

Muznant probed Rachel's mind for the purpose behind her question but found nothing relevant. She assumed that it was just an innocent though intelligent query. She would definitely look through the ancient records. Perhaps Zanos might have to be brought in to help trace a possible link.

Next Muznant took the group back to the central assembly area of Dome-4. The Transporter settled down and they all disembarked and followed Muznant down a long flight of shallow stairs into a huge underground hall. The place was packed with rows upon rows of consoles and monitor screens. There must have been at least several hundred Oannes personnel seated on split back arm chairs and most seemed to be in a semi-hypnotic state as though listening to instructions.

The little group stood still near the bottom of the stairs and Muznant conveyed that they all keep silent and not communicate unnecessarily. Rachel knew that this was the Earth monitoring centre and detailed images would be preserved and sent back to Nazmos on the next FTL starship; the one that her father would be travelling on.

After several minutes of viewing the hall Muznant led the way back up the stairs and gave Rachel a full explanation of the work and importance of the monitoring section. But she stressed that it was never Oannes policy to interfere or even warn of any unpleasantness being planned by any section of Earth's communities. There had been an occasion when a sympathetic Oannes monitor had conveyed a doubt into the mind of a war leader in May 1940 and a crucial advance had been delayed altering the course of events. This had been discovered only when the Zanos records had been reviewed on Nazmos. The Oannes involved was traced and returned back to Nazmos. The punishment was that neither she nor any member of her family would be permitted to set foot on Earth ever again. There had been other incidents prior to this one but they were few and went back to historical times.

Now Jantuzno took over the tour agenda and they went to meet some of her friends in Dome-14. Rachel was treated as one of them and she just loved the attention and female camaraderie.

Muznant felt she was out of place with all the youthful chatter and so communicated this to Ashley and Tania and it was agreed that she could leave Rachel in the care of Jantuzno; provided of course that Rachel kept her communication badge in open mode.

So Muznant conveyed this to the girls and took her leave of them. She got a big hug from Rachel which nearly persuaded her to change her mind. But that might restrict their fun.

Meanwhile Simon had gone with Mipzanti to the Bay Dome where five of the other cadets were waiting. Simon had already had a tour inside 8962-Green and now expressed a wish to see a smaller craft.

One of the subjects all space cadets had to master and store in their memory was not only the complete history of the Oannes space age but general historical events before that. Their records were detailed and extensive and Mipzanti conveyed that acquiring such detail was dull and laborious. But Simon said that he was keen to learn as much as possible about the Oannes people and everything they had achieved. In fact he would like to become like them in all but physical makeup.

Mipzanti then conveyed to Simon that it might be in his interest for him to know a little about the Oannes space development. And since Simon's was an Earth brain he would not be able to receive a concentrated data burst. As such Mipzanti said he would convey the essential facts relating to their Earth connection in normal telepathic mode.

He conveyed that the Oannes first went into space some 20,000 years ago. There were many shortcomings and disasters in the early programs but lessons were soon learnt. Considerable historical detail existed for this early period which mainly involved space travel to the three other planets, Rubabriz, Zraplat and Platwuz around Raznat. All of these were in orbits further out from Raznat than Nazmos.

Mipzanti then conveyed the geographical positions of Raznat's four planets. Nazmos was the closest with an orbit varying between 26 and 31 million miles from Raznat. Next was Rubabriz which was about the size of Mars. It had a barren landscape with a very thin atmosphere. It was quite uninhabitable and orbited at a distance of 250 to 265 million miles out from Raznat. Next was the huge gas planet of Zraplat that was about eleven times the size of Nazmos. It orbited Raznat at a distance of 630 million miles. The fourth was the useful planet of Platwuz 1,230 million miles out. It was nearly one and a half times the size of Nazmos and its gravity level was 2½ times that of Nazmos. A colony was established on Platwuz for research and mining.

Longer ranging travel outside the Raznat system commenced about 12,000 years ago and finally the first such trip to reach Earth occurred 10,000 years ago at half light speed; the journey time being fifteen years each way. Contact was made with the human species then and attempts to educate them in Oannes ways proved fruitless. Yet some of the knowledge was absorbed and led to great advances in their sciences.

At that time there was no faster than light travel but work was progressing well. The first ships could barely approach light speed but gradually this was raised and five times light velocities were achieved. These early ships took over a year to reach Earth and the same time back to Nazmos. Progress was made over the centuries with manufacturing techniques such that now FTL speeds of ten were achieved easily. Journey times to Earth were reduced to seven months. The total fleet of FTL starships was nine until recently. However one of these namely 4110-Silver was taken out of service for experimental modification work; to increase its FTL capability by a factor of ten. But this was estimated to take close to 100 years before trials could commence.

'FTL starship 2110-Blue went out towards another star system 1,400 years ago and nothing has been heard of it since. Perhaps it will return one day in the distant future,' said Mipzanti. 'A replacement ship was built and brought into service about 500 years ago.'

At present only two FTL ships operated on the Earth to Nazmos run and these were 8110-Gold and 9110-Red. The latter was currently on station in Sagittarius awaiting its return journey to Nazmos.

Simon knew that this was the ship that would take his dad to Nazmos come mid-October. He would be gone for more than a year- maybe even longer. But one of his premonitions indicated something quite different which made him think it was wrong; though he sincerely wished it were not. But that would be impossible with the Nazmos to Earth distance being so great.

Mipzanti continued his slow data flow to Simon. On Earth duty were nine medium sized craft.

8962-Green moored over there alongside 6310-Yellow and both were in the 300 feet length category. There was the slightly larger 11701-Red at 400 feet. But by far the largest ship was 520-Green at 550 feet length. There were a range of ships similar to both 11701-Red and 520-Green but these were out in the distant Ort Cloud zone patrolling for space debris. This was in the Sagittarius sector and nearly one light year from Earth. A complete mapping of large objects was carried out regularly and an avoidance course set for the FTL starships leaving for Nazmos. Detection of any danger had to be detected and the space lane between Earth and Nazmos kept safe.

Then there were the much smaller craft of which there were fourteen. These were eighty feet long and used for the shorter earthbound trips to the northern forests etc. They functioned mainly as shuttles for terrestrial transportation. One of them could quite easily fit inside the shuttle bay of the bigger ships such as 520-Green. These did not have a set crew but could be operated by deputies and other designated qualified Oannes with special permission. They were numbered similar to Anztarza's Deck Transporters, e.g. 321-Orange, 625-Blue, 951-White and so on. The cabins were small and did not contain any sleep-tank facility. All were a dull grey in colour with an anti-radar coating. All of Anztarza's space craft were equally suited to space, atmosphere or ocean travel; and if need be were capable of settling down on the deepest ocean floor.

None of the ships were capable of travelling between Nazmos and Earth and as such all had to be ferried inside an FTL starship if necessary. The FTL starships were two miles long and half a mile in circular diameter with the forward proton shield umbrella being three quarters of a mile across. As such there was plenty of space in the cargo hold for a ship the size of 520-Green and more if desired.

Simon took in the wonder of it all and then expressed a wish to see inside one of the smaller craft. One of the cadets suggested 625-Blue because it was the most accessible and close to the shoreline.

Mipzanti had received authorisation earlier and so he had contact with the onboard Zanos bio-computer. When they were alongside the ship it didn't look small at all to Simon being eighty feet in length. Mipzanti gave a thought command and a side panel door opened for them to enter. They were welcomed aboard by Zanos individually by name. This was simply another form of a Sewa greeting.

Simon was first taken to the control room which was quite small with split-back seating for three persons only. The craft was half as wide as it was long and only twenty feet from top to base. There was a single deck corridor down the middle with three cabins on one side and lounge rooms on the other. Apart from the control room there were no view panels anywhere else. Above the ceiling was the power plant and under the flooring were the impulse motors. The ship had the same manoeuvrability as the larger ships and the only construction difference was that there was no central magnetic core. So really these were not meant for prolonged periods in space unless attached to a bigger craft.

Simon took a liking to 625-Blue and said he would like to go for a trip in it. But this was not permitted on the ground that there was insufficient time for it. Captain Bulzezatna had other plans for Simon's entertainment.

After wandering around this craft for some time Mipzanti suggested that they visit something quite different. He said the air purification plant would prove interesting and Anztarza's main power plant was not far from it either. All this was under the floor levels of several habitation domes.

And then there was the space beyond that. Mipzanti looked at his fellow cadets in a conspiratorial manner and Simon sensed that they were planning a surprise for him. He began to anticipate what it might be but all had blocked their minds and Simon's probing proved fruitless.

The power plant was out of bounds for most Oannes but the air purification plant was not. It smelled good in there but there was not a lot to see. Mipzanti conveyed the functionality of the plant and its main purpose before suggesting the tour moved on.

They had a fair walk through a long curving corridor coming to a door that led into a huge empty chamber. It was well lit but Simon could not make out what was supposed to be in there. It seemed as if they had forgotten about the room altogether.

Mipzanti smiled as did the other cadets.

'I always feel exhilarated when I come in here,' he conveyed to Simon. 'Maybe it's because what is here is at the very heart of space travel. Come let me show you.'

They walked towards the central point in the room and came to a clear circular panel about two feet in diameter set level with the floor.

Simon looked down and noticed that the recess below the clear panel was only inches deep. Set at its centre was a greyish but foggy coin sized object that seemed to scintillate and vibrate from side to side. He was fascinated by it and when Mipzanti suggested that Simon move around to another position he did so and noticed that the side to side motion followed with him.

Simon puzzled over this and only knew what it was when the cadets let their mental guard ease in order that he read their minds. Wonder filled Simon and he looked down again at the shimmering fuzzy coin with renewed interest. He was looking at a very thin layer of Neutron Star material which had been compounded by Nazmos' scientists right here on earth. He just stared at it and it seemed to mesmerise him. It fascinated and thrilled him and yet sent a faint chill through him. It was what made FTL starships possible. It was a shield and a life saver. It was a case of love at first sight and Simon was completely overwhelmed.

The emotion was not lost on the cadets around him. Even they had never experienced such euphoria at their first encounter with this material. But more importantly Simon's emotion of thrill was joyously picked up by all of Anztarza.

Bulzezatna choked back her own emotions of joy and relief. Simon had passed his first fitness test for space as no one had before him. He would make a true spaceman and she wondered at what he would ultimately achieve with him being Ashley's son. Simon's fascination and exhilaration with the various spacecraft he had toured was minute in comparison.

Ashley picked up Simon's euphoria as did the others of his family. Tania was proud of her son just as Lillian was of hers.

The telepathic queries came rushing in at the wonder and intensity of this thing that had happened.

It was Muznant who conveyed the full visual that she had received from Mipzanti and explained that a spaceman had been born. A boy had become enamoured of a tiny piece of a Neutron Star.

Gradually Simon's mind settled back to normal and he looked carefully again at the material patch before him. He knelt low and put his palm flat onto the view panel right above the grey patch and thought he felt a slight tingling sensation. But it passed as his hand got used to the coldness of the floor and the sensation was gone.

Mipzanti conveyed to Simon how this material had been placed there. Actually it hadn't. It had to be manufactured right there by the special process perfected by the Oannes scientists for their FTL starship shields. The compounding machines had been assembled right here in this hall and had taken up every square foot of space. Then the energy beams had been focussed on the one spot and masses of I-protons beamed at it. At first some had adhered though many had not. Gradually as a grouping developed more of the I-protons adhered to the ones already there. It had taken nearly fifty years of constant compounding to create the present thin coat of this dense material. If it were possible to weigh the patch then it would be the equivalent of ninety tons here in Earth's gravity conditions.

'So that little skin of proton shield material weighs ninety tons?' exclaimed Simon in wonder.

'Yes,' conveyed Mipzanti, 'and it is only a hundred or so protons thick. Imagine how much the full shield of an FTL starship must contain. And it increases in mass each time the starship makes an FTL journey.'

Listening to this conversation Captain Bulzezatna was impressed by Simon's correct use of the terminology for FTL shielding. It was a natural aptitude that few had.

Simon remained silent in thought. He had a lot to learn in the years ahead.

Mipzanti continued. 'It shields the ship's structure and its occupants from the electron stripping effects of the space grid energy-medium when the relative velocity is ten times FTL. At this velocity all atoms absorb enormous amounts of this dark space matter and would soon cease to exist. The entire FTL starship would dissipate into its composite nuclei including its occupants.'

Simon understood completely how essential the three quarter mile diameter proton shield was for the survival of the ship.

'Another thing,' continued Mipzanti, 'it provides essential normal gravity conditions for the occupants on the habitation platform during the long FTL space journey. It has been noted that the mass of the proton shield increases with each FTL journey. This not only increases its effectiveness but also enhances the gravity effect inside the starship. Subsequently the habitation platform can be positioned further away. However the acceleration power needs also increase and so must be continually upgraded with improvements to achieve the intended FTL velocity.'

Simon took all this in and it simply increased his appetite for space travel. He thought that the Oannes were so far in advance of the Earth's human technology that even if they imparted some of this knowledge to Earth scientists they would not know how to effectively apply it. They were 20,000 years ahead in space travel technology and Simon realised with joy in his heart that he could jump those years by simply becoming a part of their space program.

That night as he lay on his bed in Dome-7 he had much to think about. Impatience grew in him to actually view an FTL starship. A thought came to him but it was dismissed immediately. His dad wouldn't want him there when he left for Nazmos. But he so wished to go partway and see 9110-Red. He would have to wait till he was much older.

The whole of the next day was taken up with prearranged visits to several of the Oannes homes being part of the compulsory etiquette commitment for Ashley. And of course his children were included as an essential part of these visits. So he made the unhurried ten visits along with Tania and the kids. Lillian and Alex made their own visits as the parents of Ashley and they were given near equal importance.

Simon was rather bored by all the Sewas and formal pleasantries but Rachel revelled in it. When Ashley conveyed to Simon that all this was important etiquette education for his future command as a Starship captain a new interest was kindled in him.

Rachel basked in the adulation of these people whom she had taken to her heart. There was something in her being that wanted to be protective towards them. In her mind they were her people and she was like a mother to them or one day hoped to be. This surprised even her for she did not know where the mood came from. She only knew it was there.

Muznant received these thoughts from Rachel's stud badge and they continued to puzzle her. Nothing in the ancient recordings gave any clues. As Ashley's offspring Rachel must have something of her father in her and so may have a part to play in the combined Earth-Nazmos future. What surprises would that bring?

Finally Anztarza entered its evening and the time had come for Ashley and his party to begin their journey back to Aberporth.

536-Orange under the command of a youthful Fritvazi transported them to the Bay Dome where they were met by Captain Bulzezatna. She had on a very different tunic outfit that lent her a certain regal appearance. The base colour was of pale gold with the neck, arm holes and tunic hem banded by a broad strip of bright green. The stripe down the outside of each leg was also in the same bright green. The base of the tunic was cut in a complex wave pattern that gave it its aristocratic appearance. Also each of the ten chest holes was ringed in the same green colouring.

Brief thought Sewas were exchanged and Ashley commented on the regal appearance of the captain.

She was pleased by this and smilingly said, 'Wait till you see my deputies, they are even smarter than I.'

'How dare they look better than you,' commented Ashley with humour in his tone and all laughed including a big smile from Bulzezatna.

'If this is how we interact,' she thought to herself, 'then a bright future lies before us.'

Ashley read the thought and was pleased. He conveyed his agreement to the captain. She in turn praised Ashley for his skill and concluded that she must be careful with her thoughts in Ashley's presence. Telepathically he was practically at the Oannes skill level.

After the visitors had entered 520-Green's control room and been greeted with Sewas from the deputies the spacecraft got underway. The deputies were both very smart in their colours but Simon thought not as striking as the captain. Perhaps it was her face that gave her the advantage.

Simon watched the quayside twist around to their right as 520-Green headed out into the centre of the bay. He hoped to return one day as he had formed a great affection for this underground city. He felt like he was in a place of peace; a place where everyone was at peace which was a particularly nice feeling. He just liked being here.

Gradually the view panels dipped into the water and the visibility became occluded and rapidly changed from a pale green to a much darker shade before finally going into total blackness.

Captain Bulzezatna conveyed that refreshments were available in the crew's lounge where they could sit and communicate. She would accompany them there. It would be nearly three hours before 520-Green could begin the climb into space. So the time could be spent in relaxed comfort.

It had been a busy weekend filled with activity and now Rachel appeared quite tired. Tania indicated that she'd like to take Rachel to their cabin to rest. After all she was only five. It would be nice if Rachel had a sleep prior to her arrival in Aberporth.

Bulzezatna conveyed that the return journey would take about five hours in all and that a rest in their cabins for part of the journey was advisable. She suggested that after a refreshing drink they all retire for the next few hours; at least during the ships underwater part of the journey. Zanos would alert them just prior to arrival at the Davis Sea and when the flight into the upper atmosphere commenced. Looking at Simon she conveyed that he would enjoy the exhilaration of the dash upwards from the sea to space.

Tania put Rachel in Ashley's bed and lay down in her own to keep Rachel in sight. She conveyed the desire not to be woken till they were about to arrive in Aberporth. Ashley and Simon went to the other cabin while Lillian and Alex went to theirs.

As soon as they had lain down Zanos conveyed a sense of peace and calm and blocked any wandering thoughts. Even Simon who would not normally have been able to relax in his energetic excitement managed to drift off to an untroubled sleep. They were all lying on top of their beds and fully clothed; less the footwear of course.

It only seemed a short while later when Zanos roused them, except Tania and Rachel, and indicated that 520-Green was about to surface in the Davis Sea. Telepathy indicated that Lillian and Alex were ready and would meet with them in the corridor.

In the control room Captain Bulzezatna and her deputies were already present. The room had the dull tones of background illumination. The view panels were in total darkness but as Simon stared he thought he noticed a faint greenish glow. He was not wrong for the glow lightened considerably and he had to squint from the glare and whiteness of the Antarctic ice floes. The ship did not rest there but continued smoothly out of the sea to rise rapidly upwards into the sky.

The sun was low on the horizon announcing the start to the long polar day. The view looking down at the long shadows of the icecap was beauty personified. It was now 10pm BST and Ron and Brenda conveyed that the nights were closing in a little earlier each evening. She said to Lillian that both she and Ron had felt a part of the trip through the constant information being relayed to them from keeping their communication badges in open mode. Muznant replied that they hoped to be with them around midnight and Brenda said that a nice hot drink would be ready for them when they arrived.

Simon, in his youthful exhilaration exclaimed that he wished he could live permanently on a spaceship; any spaceship belonging to the Oannes. Bulzezatna feigned indignation at this and a flustered Simon jumbled an apology saying that so far 520-Green was the best spaceship ever.

'Wait till you see some of the truly large ones on Nazmos,' she said and conveyed several images of their mammoth space cruisers. 'Some are three times the size of the largest in Anztarza. But of course nothing can compare with the size and complexity of the FTL starships.'

520-Green was now fifty miles up and the vastness of Antarctica was spread like a bright white desert below them and stretching to beyond the hazy horizon. Simon stood beside his father at the view panel and gazed in wonder at the passing Earth below. The ship was now travelling across a segment of the continent and approaching 2000mph. Bulzezatna conveyed that their route would traverse Africa and up into southern Europe as they curved westwards towards England.

'We hope to make the 12,000 mile journey in about two hours,' she told Simon, 'and I hope you enjoy the night time views that you shall see.'

The ship continued to rise higher and also accelerate in the forward direction. At 100 miles above the Earth the ship steadied and attained its cruising speed of 8000mph.

There were ridges and mountains that moved by under them and the landscape below was made prominent by the long shadows. 520-Green raced around the Earth's curvature and the white sheet of Antarctica seemed to reflect its brightness straight up at them.

But soon they left Antarctica behind and headed towards the southern tip of Africa. To Simon the ship seemed poised in mid-air with the vast curvature of the Earth slowly rotating underneath. They were over a darkening sea now and the bright glow to the left of the ship was rapidly diminishing as the darkness of night slowly spread like a vast blanket below them. Simon's query was answered by Zanos that their course would take them intentionally directly over Cape Town at their midnight hour. It was a course laid on for Simon's benefit for him to see the beauty of a large city at night.

The Earth continued to roll by and then there far below and ahead appeared the lights of a city shining up at them through the clear darkness. Cape Town was easy to see at night as its lights were brightly spread over a large area. There was no shape to the city, only a conglomeration of concentrated lighting. Pinpricks of light were dotted around at random. In some places the lights were orange and stood out prominently. The street patterns were apparent as they were outlined by the streetlights. The coastline was also clearly demarcated by the outline of the city lights. All this went by under the ship as it headed up over the western coast of this vast night shrouded continent.

It was completely dark and as 520-Green approached central Africa it passed over a widespread thunderstorm. Simon could see lightning everywhere. Bright flashes went from cloud to cloud illuminating them as it arced from one to another. It was better than a firework spectacular. Except there was no sound and both father and son gazed in wonder at the sight. There were several flashes of light occurring simultaneously with each one extremely brief. The colours were enchanting and ranged from orange to blue to white. Some were like balls of light while others had the characteristic lightning streak shape.

The storm though large was beginning to thin as the ship continued on its journey. The Earth unfurled below and a city passed by underneath the clouds. It was only seen because of its lights that shone through against the backdrop of the diminishing pulses of lightning.

Soon the thunderstorm was left behind and a small city could be seen as a cluster of lights like a miniature galaxy. The night sky was inky black as the ship glided noiselessly over the Sahara desert. From 100 miles up, even though the Earth's horizon was dark, light provided by the distant clouds and the city lights reflecting off them provided enough illumination for Ashley and Simon to discern the difference between Earth and space. And the night sky sparkled with countless points of light. Some were white, some red, and some orange and all of different sizes. They were everywhere. The beauty of the heavens was what drew Simon to want to be a space traveller and Ashley seeing all this could understand.

The stars surrounded the Earth and wrapped around it like a blanket. 520-Green was swimming in a sea of beautiful lights which of course could only be seen in the darkness of night. The Milky Way was clearly evident as it arose from behind the Earth like a glowing white path that led off into the distance. Ashley found it humbling just to see his galaxy spread there before him. It was one thing to see the vastness of space in your minds eye but it was immensely more satisfying to see a part of it spread out before you. It was mesmerising, awe inspiring and overwhelming all at once; and oh so beautiful.

The Earth continued to roll by and Ashley saw that by his watch it was nearly half past eleven. The time had flown by and he hadn't noticed because of the events with the passing landscape below.

520-Green had turned slightly westward as it passed over the southern shore of the Mediterranean Sea. The lights of the small island of Malta were to the far right of the ship and were like a bright jewel in its surrounding blackness. They then traversed directly over Tunis which showed up as a coastal town with its shoreline clearly highlighted.

There appeared a brighter glow ahead and Bulzezatna conveyed that they were approaching the lights of night-time Europe in the region of Southern France. They passed over the towns of Toulouse and Bordeaux with a sprinkling of lights showing across the entire area. Many big city lights could be clearly discerned in the far distance to either side of their course. Europe had cities that were considerably more brightly lit up than those in Africa. Their density spread was apparent and Ashley thought that was because of the area being more developed and ancient.

As 520-Green crossed over the Bay of Biscay it made a wide sweep over the Atlantic as it approached its destination. It slowed and descended towards the sea to the west of Aberporth. There was much more cloud over the Atlantic area and over England as well. Subsequently it was in total darkness that 520-Green settled down above the sea far out from the west coast of Cornwall. It had just gone past midnight when the guests conveyed their thanks to all and especially to Captain Bulzezatna. Simon even went forward to the captain and said 'Thank you for everything captain,' and put out his little hand. Bulzezatna took it and a firm handshake ensued; the first of many between these two. Bulzezatna found herself drawn to this child of Ashley and she pondered over the emotion. Again the customary Sewas were exchanged before the guests left the control room.

Rachel was carried down to the shuttle bay and onto the bus-craft 326-Red while still fast asleep. Simon was wide awake though and saddened that his adventure had ended. He conveyed to the captain and the deputies that one day he would be back; and quite a bit older.

Earlier Captain Bulzezatna had had a private communication with Ashley about his forthcoming FTL rendezvous in mid-October only a month away. Ashley was pleased at what was conveyed and said as much.

326-Red sped through the night and it was close to one o'clock when Ron and Brenda welcomed them back in through the doors of their B&B.

Muznant and Brazjaf had come along but did not leave the bus. Sewa farewells were repeated telepathically, the bus door closed and 326-Red turned about where it was and then rapidly disappeared into the night.

Simon suddenly felt very tired and Ron said he'd show him to his room. Simon said a sleepy goodnight to all and followed Ron up the stairs. And it wasn't long before the others followed suit. Tania had taken Rachel to her bed straight after they had arrived and stayed with her till Simon entered. Rachel and Simon usually shared a room when visiting Aberporth.

'Sleep as long as you like,' conveyed Brenda, 'we can brunch when you come down.'

Ashley had worrying thoughts with regard to the approaching FTL trip to Nazmos. He still didn't know much about the planet Platwuz. And he looked forward to meeting with Brajam again. He reckoned that he had much to learn.

CHAPTER 14

A Starship Journey

October 2016

September 2016 went into the record books as one of the warmest for 100 years. And October seemed to be carrying on in the same vein. So far there had been little rain and predictions abounded for drought conditions and a hose pipe ban in the coming year. Yet despite the mild weather the shops were already promoting Christmas. Cotton wool snow was a common theme in the decorated window displays.

I'd heard of Christmas coming early in the shops but I usually considered this to be sometime in November. Though the kids loved it and were making big hints at what they would like Santa to bring them. Anyway the shop decorations and festive lights looked very colourful and nice. Robin had suggested that McGill's should also follow suit but both Milly and Jerry said that it was far too early; and I agreed with them. Robin persisted and Milly finally agreed that when freshly cut Christmas Trees went on sale on the High Street he could then put up his decorations.

My trip to Nazmos was still a week away and I had mixed feelings about it. I knew what had to be done but the journey itself was into unfamiliar territory and I kept my eye on Simon to see if he came up with one of his premonition predictions. But none came and Simon just smiled back at me when I rather blatantly enquired after his welfare.

Tania had her own qualms about the coming trip but kept her emotions hidden under a calm façade. She had finally mastered the art of reading minds and was currently fluent in two Eastern European languages. She had a yen to visit some of the places she felt familiar with through the memories of the people she had read. She had visited these places vicariously of course and now felt a need to actually go there. September had been a thrilling month for her and I was pleased.

Both Rachel and Simon had advanced dramatically in their telepathic skill and Muznant's gift to them had borne fruit in more ways than I had thought possible. They were both proficient in reading minds and also in conveying their thoughts with imagery just as I could. Tania however had not yet reached that level.

What was a puzzle was that both children said that at times they received telepathic thoughts from a range of individuals who were quite unfamiliar. The thoughts were ordinary mundane ones such as a decision to watch a particular program on TV; or of thoughts about what to cook for the evening meal.

It didn't bother them one way or another but it did make them curious. Anyway they found they could block them out completely if they wished. Rachel however commented that she found it interesting to know what other people thought.

I queried Muznant and Brazjaf about this and they said that they would investigate the matter. I was surprised at what they found out.

Having read Simon and Rachel's minds the monitoring section in Anztarza could only conclude that the thoughts being picked up were similar to what they themselves received from the 'thinking stone' tablets dispersed around the Earth. It was highly likely that one of these had a telepathic rhythm that was compatible with the minds of the children. Perhaps this mind pattern development arose from Muznant's initiation which had been bestowed as her gift to them. It may have allowed these background thoughts to be recognised and interpreted. No Oannes person had developed such ability and the matter was put before the Anztarza governing council.

Muznant stated the fact of her implanting the seed of mind reading to the children and wondered if this might be responsible. The analysts discounted this on the basis that a similar initial induction was also imparted to all their youth without such a resulting effect.

Their conclusion was that Simon and Rachel must have something of their father's gifts lying dormant inside their minds. I was pleased that no blame was attached to Muznant.

I began to think about my own inner voice and wondered if they could be linked to the same source. I didn't think so since they spoke directly to me. But the matter regarding my information queries still puzzled me. Could I have been inadvertently accessing the Zanos bio-computer system in Anztarza through the stone tablets? I really couldn't say.

As it didn't seem to bother either Simon or Rachel we let the matter rest. Tania and I had also picked up Muznant's mind reading prescription but had not detected anything similar. Secretly Tania hoped she would and I told her she might find it tedious and bothersome; like noisy neighbours. Our children seemed to be acquiring gifted tendencies very different from my own.

I had only a week with my family before the scheduled FTL starship trip to Nazmos and I intended to soak up every precious moment. Rachel gave me lots of cuddles and sat on my lap at every opportunity. Simon too tried to stay close as much as possible. He had received a premonition about my FTL journey during the recent trip to Anztarza and had thought it not possible yet wished it could be true.

My inner voice had instructed me clearly but I was not sure of the outcome. I had my doubts though I hoped it would work out. I would find out soon enough.

Tania on the other hand was confident that what my inner voice had revealed had to be right.

I had not been confident enough to divulge any of this to anyone else other than my wife; not even to the children.

'I'll miss you daddy,' Rachel had said, 'so please hurry back. I don't want to be old when you return.'

'I shall be home sooner than you think,' I said to her nearly divulging my secret. She immediately probed my mind deeply to see what I meant but could not get past the block I had placed around my secret.

I spent a full day at the shop and tried to keep it as normal as possible. Milly showed her concern for me but Jerry said I should be alright with the Oannes on Nazmos. After all they'd had years of information about me and would be used to my appearance. Yet I would be the first human on their precious home planet. I was glad that I should have the familiar company of my old friends beside me; Muznant and Brazjaf, Puzlwat and Nogozat and of course Brajam the scientist and engineer.

Granddad had asked me to contact his old friends Kazaztan and Zarpralt on Nazmos. I was to tell them all about him from a personal level even though regular communications were exchanged via the FTL starships.

Muznant and Margaret had developed a fondness for one another and regular communication took place between them via Margaret's badge. Margaret was like one of the family now and I was surprised when she drove up to Dudley for the day. She'd not conveyed anything beforehand but turned up around mid-morning. She said she just had to wish me 'Bon voyage' personally. It could be a couple of years before I returned she said.

The kids were at school so Tania and I took her out to the Kashmir Diner for lunch. It was a pleasant and friendly meal and she left for London about 4 o'clock having planted a farewell kiss on my lips. I read her mind as did Tania and knew she had planned it for sometime.

Tania smiled and conveyed that only Vicky Chambers had yet to do that. But I knew that Vicky could never be as bold. Muznant's kiss had been a curiosity thing way back in November 2003 and partly because I had initiated it. Gosh, how time had flown and what a lot had happened since then. For me the world had changed from one to two.

'Ashley Bonner.' Tania said aloud, 'I want to know of all the women you conquer on Nazmos. I shall ask Muznant to keep her eye on you.'

A pleasant emotion came through her badge and a message from Muznant that all the women on Nazmos would be at Ashley's feet. I had to laugh and conveyed a 'Thank you very much' to Muznant for stirring her great big wooden spoon. I also conveyed what this meant and she conveyed her humour.

And so the days passed and Simon and Rachel grew restless and clingy. I did have some guilt attached to my remaining days with them before my interplanetary trip. I looked upon it as the first step towards that big task mentioned by Philip. I remember that I had initially thought it to involve an asteroid or comet that was on a collision path with Earth. That was before I met Muznant and Brazjaf and the Oannes people. I wondered about what other revelations or discoveries were yet to unravel.

Zarama was the mystery for me. I must ask Brajam for more information about it. How fast was it spinning and what was its size and overall mass? But most of all how was I to tackle it and from what distance? Just thinking about these issues brought me out in a cold sweat.

I felt Tania's arm about me.

'What is it?' she asked telepathically.

'Zarama,' I replied. 'It scares me.'

Tania was silent. She knew that nothing she said could allay my fears. She just squeezed tighter.

Then she whispered, 'Let's put Zarama aside for the next twenty years or so. Maybe for even longer while you get Nazmos sorted first.'

I put my cheek against her hair and felt eased. I was not alone. I also felt a bit stupid. I moved my head to look down into her eyes and I just nodded. There was a shiny wetness in her eyes and suddenly her face went all blurred as I blinked away my own emotion.

I felt two little arms around my waist and Rachel conveyed that there were only two days left.

I knew what she meant and I reached around and drew her in between us. I looked up and Simon was standing awkwardly in the open doorway. I raised my hand in a mini-wave to him and he waved back from hip level. Simon was not a hugger but I could feel his love just the same.

'Okay then,' I said as I broke away from our huddle, 'who wants a doughnut?'

'A jam one,' said Simon coming forward.

'Me too,' said Rachel.

Milly was pleased to see us and understood why the kids were not at school. Today was Wednesday the twelfth of October and I was due to be picked up in Aberporth on Friday night. Tania and the children would come up to see me off. I still had mixed feelings about the trip. I had never been away from my family for that long before.

After our double dose of doughnuts we went to see Jerry in the other branch and he was pleased to see us.

'Its one thing being in thought communication,' he said, 'but I prefer to see people in the flesh.'

Rachel giggled at this and Tania picked up on the theme.

'Oh dad you mustn't talk like that in front of innocent children,' she said with a mischievous expression on her face, 'fancy wanting to see people in the buff?'

We all laughed at the witty word-play and I conveyed to Rachel the real meaning of Jerry's remark.

Jerry closed up early and we all went back to Milly. Robin had returned from his nap and was upstairs fussing over his little domain. We just sat around chatting and drinking mugs of tea.

'Let's all go out for a meal,' I suggested. 'It'll be like a farewell supper before my trip.'

'Actually I was about to ask you over to ours instead,' said Milly. 'I've got some steak and Yorkshires and baking potatoes. And you can relax and stay as long as you like.'

Tania looked at me with eyebrows raised but Rachel got in first.

'Yes let's,' she shrieked and so it was decided. Actually I was quite pleased and conveyed that I could take off my shoes and sit in comfort.

'Yes,' I said to Rachel, 'and tomorrow we can go to your other grandma's for dinner.'

I conveyed this to mum and got a delighted 'Come a bit earlier so we can sit out on the patio in the evening sun.'

Everyone knew of our plans to leave for Aberporth on Friday morning. Muznant and Brazjaf would be on the bus to meet me. I was glad that they and some others were to accompany me to Nazmos.

I also knew that Simon desperately wanted to view the FTL ship and I considered whether to let my family travel out with me on 520-Green. I conveyed this privately to Tania but she responded that Simon needed to show patience and concentrate his efforts more on his school work. Since we'd returned from Anztarza both Simon and Rachel had been walking on air and neglecting lots of little things. Tania had told them that this was irresponsible and that they could only get their ambitions fulfilled through hard work and keeping their feet firmly on the ground. It was one thing to dream but it was another thing to work towards that dream. There was so much about Earth and their home life that was important towards building their character and social skills. They must remain realistic and enjoy the present. One day they would look back on all of this with joy and longing. Looking at the past can be a pleasurable pastime especially if you happen to be on a spaceship in another part of the galaxy.

I had a thought and after a private communication with Captain Bulzezatna I received agreement for what I had in mind. And that was for my family to welcome me back when I returned. Since 520-Green was to be one of the spaceships sent out to meet the FTL ship then it should be no extra effort for my family to be aboard. And that way Simon would get to see and possibly board the Starship.

When I conveyed this privately to Tania she thought it a very good idea and could act as a spur for the kids to knuckle down to their school work. I could see she was thrilled at the idea and she conveyed that she would talk to the kids about it. I imagined that there would be a considerable amount of blackmail involved. Be good and sensible or else! But things worked out differently.

Thursday was a day I shall remember. Mum had cooked a lovely meal and had also invited Katy, Robin and their two lovely girls Fiona and Sarah. Fiona would be five this November and she was the same height as Rachel. Sarah was only three but quite a little charmer. She was so much like Katy used to be that I was taken back to our childhood days of birds in little cages. She had the same mischievous expression that Katy so often exhibited and I know that mum was very taken with her. And she was a little chatterbox and was currently sitting on her grandma's lap and enjoying every second.

The cousins got on well and Rachel had to be extra careful how she communicated.

And of course granddad Eric was there in the special reclining armchair with extending footrest. Dad had bought it some time ago for his own comfort but granddad commandeered it whenever he visited. He was looking much better today than when I visited him last week.

'I'm ninety two now,' he said, 'and I feel really good today. Tomorrow will be another matter but I shall hope for the best. Mavis and Vicky usually visit me on a Friday afternoon and I do look forward to Mavis' chat. She still has to use both sticks for walking though. I think Vicky should get a medal for the way she looks after her mum.'

I think that granddad believes that one visit on a Friday becomes the rule. I know that Mavis tries to keep in touch with all her friends and so granddad would be lucky to see her once a month if that. Perhaps the previous visit was a Friday. He does forget things quite a lot now.

We sat on the patio in the bright evening sunlight as it was a really mild and windless day. But as the sun dipped into the tree line on the rise it got a bit chilly so we went in again.

Granddad hadn't come out with us and was now fast asleep in the recliner. But our chatter soon woke him. Dad went and turned the central heating up a bit as the house felt a little chilly.

Mum served up dinner just after six and I think I might have overdone it with that second helping of Tiramisu.

There was a program on TV that granddad wanted to watch so we all chilled out where we sat. I must confess to having forty winks in my corner of the room. A ten or fifteen minute kip was a most satisfying experience and I felt quite refreshed after it.

I really enjoyed being home again especially with Katy there to remind me of long ago times. It was a happy childhood.

We all left for our homes just before ten and Rachel was fast asleep in the car within minutes. Simon stayed awake though but only just as I could see the sandman attacking his eyes. I imagine that his thoughts were on my forthcoming trip. I know he wished he too could be on that trip.

Friday morning was wet and slightly foggy with a decided chill in the air. Was this the first sign of approaching winter? I suppose Christmas wouldn't be the same without a bit of cold weather and ice and snow.

I received my goodbyes via our communication badges and it was as if I had everyone still around me giving me their good wishes. Even when we were well into our journey I received little conversation pieces from mum, Milly and Jerry. Katy and Robin also had their little say and conveyed that Fiona and Sarah had loved being at mum's house yesterday. Ron and Brenda said that they were looking forward to seeing us and hoped Tania and the kids could stay on a bit beyond the weekend. Tania replied that the kids had school on Monday which they mustn't miss. Brenda said she understood.

We arrived at the B&B about mid-afternoon and Ron expressed surprise at how little travel luggage I had. Everything I needed was loosely pressed into my medium sized backpack which I deposited in the hallway. Tania had a pull-along case with the kids and her stuff crammed inside. We then all went into the lounge where Brenda had a small tea laid out for us. The kids' eyes lit up when they saw the scones and jam. Suddenly I felt rather hungry and Brenda stood back smiling as she watched us tuck in.

'Don't fill yourselves up too much as I have a lovely Shepherds Pie and dessert for dinner,' she said

'O yummy,' said Rachel and we all looked at each other knowingly. Rachel loved her food and Tania had often remarked that their little girl was putting on a few extra pounds and we would soon have to watch her diet. Simon on the other hand ate like a caterpillar and never put on an ounce. His metabolism must be very good.

After my second mug of tea I had a little doze where I sat as everyone chatted away. I found that these little naps of an afternoon were becoming quite a habit and I wondered if this had to do with my increasing age. What would I be like as I got even older? Probably a bit like granddad by the time I reach sixty. Gosh, that was only twenty-five years way. Tania would be fifty-six then and the kids into the thirty age bracket. And Simon was to assist me in some way when I was to tackle Zarama. It would be great if we humans could have a lifespan like that of the Oannes.

Brenda put off serving dinner till about 8:30pm when the kids started looking around for things to nibble. We were still in British Summer Time and it had only just got dark outside. It was while we were relaxing in front of the TV afterwards that Muznant conveyed that the pick-up bus would be with us in about an hour. Both she and Brazjaf would ride along as she didn't want to miss an opportunity to see Rachel in person. Rachel smiled at this and perked up. She liked to go to bed quite early and I could see that she had been flagging a bit.

'We are here,' conveyed Muznant. It had barely been an hour since her earlier message.

As there were other guests residing at the B&B Muznant suggested we all meet on the bus. It had dried up nicely and even the chill had eased. Rachel was the first to climb aboard the bus and she gave Muznant a goodly hug. Also on the bus were Puzlwat and his wife Nogozat and brief Sewas were exchanged all around. Puzlwat said he looked forward to travelling with me once again and to the events that were to unfold when we were on Nazmos.

I had said my goodbyes to Tania and the kids just before I had picked up my backpack to board the bus. However I now got more dainty kisses from them again as they retreated back to the warmth of the B&B.

As the bus turned full circle I waved to Tania where she stood out on the open porch. We had a continued private conversation as the bus raced across the sea towards the waiting spaceship. I conveyed that I would stick to the plan I had been given and hoped it all worked just as per the instructions.

I think Muznant and the others read my emotions and so there was a complete lack of telepathic conversation as we journeyed to our rendezvous. I was in a world of my own thinking about the future as I stared into the pitch black of the night view ahead. The wind made a hissing-rustling sound as we sped through the night at what I estimated must be close to 100mph.

The first inkling I had that we were approaching our destination was when the wind sounds began to diminish and went to a lower pitch. Then suddenly the brightness of the shuttle bay appeared before us as its doors opened and I had to squint to reduce the glare effect.

The bus settled to the floor of the shuttle deck and I was welcomed on board by Captain Bulzezatna and invited up to the control room. The large bay doors had closed and First Deputy Tatizblay led the way after a brief Sewa greeting. As we entered the control room I could see from the view panel that the ship was already in the sky above the clouds. The clouds were illuminated by a three quarter moon shining brilliantly. The moon looked so close and I was reminded of my view of the asteroid Mathilde.

Once again a telepathic Sewa was exchanged with the captain who then conveyed full details of our intended journey to the FTL Starship 9110-Red. I would like Captain Natazlat she conveyed. Captain Natazlat was the only female FTL Starship captain and a personal friend of hers. She was ten years younger and an excellent commander. The image that Bulzezatna conveyed to me was of a Muznant look-alike and I felt I was already developing a partiality towards her. Beauty seems to play an important part in how favourably I felt towards a person at a first meeting. Sadly the looks did not always portray the character.

I then went forward and the captain and I exchanged a firm hand clasp. I looked into her eyes and she into mine and the understanding of respect and admiration was mutual. My emotions toward Bulzezatna went beyond simple affection. It was something greater and more lasting which I could only compare to that of family ties. Something a child would feel for a mother or father. Or even a favourite Aunt.

I had kept my mind open along with my badge so that Tania and the others could know how I was faring. I suspect that my immediate thoughts and emotions must have filtered through to the captain for she smiled at me with pride. I discerned a modicum of embarrassment too. I think all of Anztarza must know of how I regarded Bulzezatna. How can I help myself from admiring these people who to me are the most gentle and straightforward of beings? The Oannes are to be greatly admired and emulated.

I knew that the journey to the Starship would take 520-Green about 25 hours in all. That was the initial three hours to the million mile distance when the neutron generators would operate and then another 22 hours at the high velocity of 100,000 mps to cover the eight billion miles to 9110-Red. To us on the spaceship the journey would seem shorter because of the time dilation factor of 1.185 at the higher velocity. The 22 hour journey would register only 19 hours on my wristwatch.

Earth was currently in the zodiac sign towards the latter part of Libra. Raznat or Bernard's Star was in Sagittarius which meant that it lay on the diagonal line passing through Earth and Sun in early December. 9110-Red was parked on this imaginary line on the outer fringe of the solar system and 520-Green was accelerating towards it.

Captain Bulzezatna and I had a private conversation in which I expressed my aspirations for Simon. Zarama entered as a non-urgent topic though I did indicate my agenda for tackling it in about twenty year's time. I hoped that Simon would be at my side then since I valued his gifted judgement. Captain Bulzezatna knew exactly what I meant by this. Five hundred light years was a vast uncharted distance and the journey line to Zarama might contain hazardous objects. Simon's premonition gift on such a journey at the intended FTL velocity might prove extremely useful. It would be a great comfort to me to have him at my side.

After about half an hour in the control room I decided to retire to my cabin. The ship was now under a nearly twice gravitation level and I had to measure my steps carefully as I tramped to my cabin. Zanos-on-board led me directly to it and I realised I was quite fatigued both mentally and physically. Mentally I think from the subconscious anxiety of the day's events. It had not been a nice feeling having to leave my family behind. Tania must be as tired out as I was. When I contacted her she just sent me a huge emotion of love. The kids were fast asleep and she was just about to drift off herself when my message got to her.

'Goodnight darling,' she conveyed, 'go to sleep and come back soon.'

'I will,' I replied and sent my very best emotion of deep love as I too settled down onto my bed.

Zanos conveyed the time as 11:35pm BST when I queried it.

Just before I fell asleep I wondered if I should refer to Zanos as male or female. I think I might prefer Zanos as a 'she' rather than an 'it'.

When I awoke nearly eight hours later 520-Green was travelling towards 9110-Red at 100,000 miles per second and was a quarter of the way there. Zanos indicated that two billion miles had been travelled and we were now beyond the orbit of Uranus. Pluto's orbit was nearly half the distance to where the Starship was parked.

411

I stayed in my cabin for the next hour relaxing with my thoughts. We were now well out of telepathic communication range as far as Earth was concerned so I reminisced on the varied events of my life so far. I thought of Philip and when I had first met him. I wondered if he had been expecting me then apart from the fact that Jerry had said I was coming. That was indeed a turning point in my life. The other was when I had met the Duttons and got possession of Andrew Pando's diaries and the 'thinking stone' tablet. I looked around at the comfort of my spacious cabin and thought that with the Oannes I had leapt forward into their technological era; a jump of at least twenty thousand years for that was when they had first ventured into space. Earth technology was that far behind. And here I was in an Oannes spaceship travelling through space at more than half the speed of light. And soon on the FTL Starship I should be exceeding that a hundredfold or more if I followed my inner voice instructions. Perhaps it was time for me to reveal my plans to the captain and to Brajam the chief scientist onboard.

I was somewhat famished and decided to get something to eat in the main lounge and dining area. But first a mug of tea would be most welcome. It took a few minutes before I received intimation that my tea awaited me in the food recess. That first sip was absolutely divine as I sat on my bed and cupped the hot mug in both hands. The thoughts continued but this time with regard to how future events would turn out on Nazmos. I was not confident of any outcome but then Tania had said that my diffidence was an asset because it made me more likeable.

I remember Puzlwat and Mytanzto being dubious about me and doubted whether I possessed any telekinetic powers at all. Their reasoning had been that if I did have such a power then as an earthling why hadn't I used it to further my image and fortune. I think that their friendship towards me grew strong because they realised I was no showman. Dad had been wise in his demand that I keep all my gifts a secret from the outside world. And I had never felt alone in this since I always had my family for support. I was glad that Margaret Dutton had joined that select circle.

I placed my empty mug back in the food recess and walked out to the dining area. It was now nearly ten o'clock. There were just two crew members seated in a far corner of the room. I was about to make my way to the control room when I received a communication from Muznant to remain where I was and they would join me shortly. And so they did. Brajam was the first to enter followed seconds later by Puzlwat and Nogozat. Then all the others came in which included Captain Bulzezatna and deputy Rubandiz. A brief Sewa was conducted and mainly as to my well being and my night's rest. I replied that everything was good.

It was Brajam who looked at me in a peculiar manner that made me feel as is he was expecting me to make some announcement. I realised what it was. I may have let my mind block lapse for an instant during my reverie last night just before I had dozed off and so my thoughts on the instructions with regard to the FTL journey must have been pick up.

'We believe you have some plan with regard to the journey to Nazmos,' conveyed Brajam. 'Please let us know what it is that you propose.'

I blanked my mind and could not meet his gaze. Leaning back in my seat I looked down into my lap. I stayed like this for nearly a minute with my mind racing. I was tempted to go into pink mode and retreat to my cabin but discarded that course immediately. These were my friends and I must treat them as such with the respect and trust they deserved.

'Yes,' I said in my softest tone as I looked back up at them. 'Yes, a detailed plan was revealed to me by my inner voice. I had hoped to convey everything to you when we were on the Starship and with Captain Natazlat present. I also need to communicate with Zanos on starship 9110-Red so that proper control of the journey was in hand at all times. There is no doubt in my mind that the plan is sound and will shorten our journey time considerably,' I conveyed.

Muznant then came and sat on the seat beside me after she had pulled it up against mine. She reached down and took my hand in hers and lifted it up and placed it on the table with her hand on top. I looked at the others and placing my other hand also on the table conveyed that all should follow Muznant's example. I splayed my fingers wide apart so that all may make contact. I then nodded at them and closed my eyes. My mind was open to them and I sensed rather than felt their deep mind probing.

This time I heard the indrawn breaths and one gasp of astonishment from Nogozat.

'Is this possible?' came from her as she looked around the table.

'If Ashley has been given this plan then I believe it to be factual,' conveyed Muznant keeping her hand on mine. 'He has been granted many gifts and one more does not surprise me. Our myths do not mislead.'

The others had all withdrawn their hands and now all looked at Brajam. There was a look of wonder on his face and gradually his head began a gentle nodding action.

'Yes of course,' he said. '4110-Silver is under modification with additional power plant being added for it to achieve 100FTL velocities. Our FTL starships are designed for the shields to cope easily with 500FTL speeds if only there was that power capability. This is a logical plan for such a power to be applied in a controlled and effective manner linked to the Zanos system on board. Navigation is the key factor here if we are not to be lost somewhere beyond our intended destination. We must relay this information to 9110-Red immediately.'

'No,' I said as firmly as I could without sounding rude or aggressive. 'It would be better if I communicated this to the captain and her crew on a personal and direct level as I did with you. There would be too many questions needing clarification and the five hours in communication delay would not be convenient. I would also need to be in direct contact with the Zanos-on-board system. We must not create doubts in anyone's mind just as you now have none in yours.'

'I fully agree with Ashley,' communicated Bulzezatna, 'and when I meet my friend Captain Natazlat I shall convey to her my full support for this plan.'

'I too agree with that,' said Muznant. 'Direct contact is the best way for the intricacies of the plan to be understood.'

'Yes,' said Brajam, 'in my excitement I did not think clearly. So Ashley, tell us how long you expect the journey last.'

I smiled before I replied and very conscious that Muznant still held my hand. Gently I freed it from under hers and then conveyed my affection as I reached up and touched her cheek lightly with the back of my hand. I thought of Tania and for a moment felt a little less lonely.

'I understand that the normal journey is somewhere between six and seven Earth months,' I said. 'I do not know the ultimate velocity that we will achieve but I imagine it to be around the 200FTL mark. Brajam my friend, you led me to understand that this is well within the design limits of the FTL Starships. So there is nothing for us to be concerned about on that score. Zanos-on-board must deal with the navigation side of the journey which I expect it is fully capable of doing.'

I paused as I looked across at Puzlwat and smiled.

'When I first visited Anztarza you were right to doubt me,' I said. 'But the asteroid experiment persuaded you otherwise. However what you did not know then was that I was quite unsure of myself. At the time I did not know if my telekinetic power was enough to move Steins not to mention the much larger Mathilde. It was only then that I learned how to properly control the forces that I exert. With respect to 9110-Red I know what I must attempt but I am as yet unsure of the result. Just as I learned from the disaster of Steins I shall rely on Zanos to keep me informed of the FTL velocity that is progressively achieved. I shall learn from the experience because then when I do head towards Zarama I shall be considerably more confident in what I can do.'

'Have you had anything to eat this morning?' asked Muznant changing the subject.

'Just a mug of tea,' I replied. 'Actually I do feel rather hungry now that you have mentioned it and a breakfast would be most welcome. Though I should like to conform and have an Oannes meal as is the custom. I would not want the council of ministers on Nazmos to think me strange.'

A message was conveyed and before I knew it there were dishes of Raizna, Starztal and Yaztraka brought to the table with jugs of Wazu by a member of the crew. This Raizna was very much like porridge in its consistency which was different from when it was served in the evenings. It was also much sweeter and definitely to my liking as such.

'You eat like an Oannes,' said Nogozat, 'and I should be happy to cook for you anytime.'

'Thank you,' I replied and conveyed my affection to her.

'Be aware Ashley,' said Muznant aloud, 'Nogozat is very pretty and quite forward even in front of her husband. I am to report back to Tania don't forget.'

The emotion of humour filled the area and I smiled at Muznant. A smile I know she understood.

We spent a while drinking Wazu and conversing generally. The one topic no one mentioned was about the various religious beliefs among us earthlings. I think the fact that Philip had once communicated with me was something that quite intrigued them and was outside their parameter of logic. Had I created Philip in my mind or did he really exist in another form. The big question was what would happen to them, the Oannes person, when death finally came. I know that some of the older generation in Anztarza had considered adopting some of this religious philosophy on the basis that there just might be something in it.

After spending over an hour like this we decided to retire to the control room with the captain. My watch registered midday but I knew that with time dilation and the length of the journey so far that it would be an hour behind the actual. I also knew that our time of arrival at 9110-Red's location would be 11pm BST but our watches and body clocks would be showing 8pm. Zanos however would have the correct Earth time.

Tatizblay greeted us in Sewa fashion and when Captain Bulzezatna passed on my information a pleasant surprised look came to his face. I sensed the emotion of admiration from him. I walked over and put my hand out to him. We exchanged a firm handclasp and I opened my mind and let him see that our futures were linked. One day in his changed world he would become a leading voice for a new lifestyle; a lifestyle to suit the changed climate on Nazmos. My inner voice had revealed this to me long ago when we were journeying towards the asteroid experiments. And it had revealed a lot more to me in that I knew then that my efforts to get Nazmos into a closer orbit around Raznat would achieve the success I wished. Of course Tatizblay would be quite old by then and possibly approaching his 300th year and the conditions on Nazmos would have begun to change towards a milder climate.

Perhaps over the next millennia there might be forests on Nazmos accompanied by abundant rainfall. The polar region would however still remain cold and frozen. I wondered how the Rimzi people would adapt if the seas got warmer.

My thoughts were interrupted by Muznant warning me to close my mind when I had these futuristic thoughts for the good of all. It was something I must learn to do automatically. I thanked Muznant for the reminder.

Tatizblay stood to one side and I feared that I had embarrassed him in front of his peers. But when I saw his glowing face I knew that I had not. He seemed to have a new set to his posture. He looked taller or was that just my imagination. I read his mind and saw a new resolve for him to achieve something with his life. All I had done was to let him see through an open window to what lay before him. I was pleased that I had done so.

I spent nearly an hour in the control room before deciding to return to my cabin. The views of space appeared static even though they were still brilliant. I think I had just got used to it though I dare say that Simon would have thought otherwise.

I lay on my bed and thought of Tania and the kids and imagined them on their way back home to Dudley. Or had they been persuaded to stay on another day. Aunt Brenda could be quite persuasive.

I must have drifted off to sleep for when I awoke and looked at my wristwatch again it was well past six o'clock. I wished for another mug of tea and waited a few moments before collecting it from the food recess.

By seven o'clock I had freshened up with a shower and a shave and had on my favourite pale yellow and green tunic and leggings. Tania had liked me in them.

I conveyed a request to Captain Bulzezatna and was given immediate permission to enter the control room. I wished to experience the journey transition when the neutron generators operated to slow the ship to an approachable velocity for rendezvous with the Starship. On the last occasion when we had visited 8110-Gold on a tour 520-Green had slowed to a position a few thousand miles to one side of the Starship and then manoeuvred closer to its rear end. From there the shuttle craft had transported us into the Starship's airlock alongside the upper deck cargo platform. I expected the same to be repeated with 9110-Red.

In the control room I was welcomed and Bulzezatna suggested I occupy a recliner to view the brilliance of the stars through the upper view panels. I did so and at once noticed that the brilliancy of the stars and the Milky Way had a decided bluish tint in their colouring. Of course at half light speed all visible wavelengths shifted proportionally towards the blue end of the spectrum.

Zanos then conveyed that the velocity reversing manoeuvre would be activated in twenty minutes. This simply meant that 520-Green would rotate through a 180° angle to face in the opposite direction to its travel. I looked forward to this as I wished to witness the wavelength shift in the colour of the receding stars. How much would the red shift be I wondered?

I didn't have long to wait. The image of the stars above me began to move slowly to my right. It was a very gradual manoeuvre and if I didn't have the stars as reference I should never have known we were turning about. When the manoeuvre was completed and I was looking at a very bright star in the distance I knew that it was our sun. It didn't look as sparkling and bright as I had expected because it now had a slight rosy tint to its colour. The abundance of the visible stars also had a rose tint in their colour. This was a familiar setting for me since I often experienced this whenever I went into pink mode.

Captain Bulzezatna conveyed that the procedure for slowing down the ship would be operated in several stages so that 520-Green did not overshoot the rendezvous point excessively. The first neutron generator blasts would commence in five minutes. I looked at my watch and it showed the time to be 7:55pm.

Zanos conveyed that the rendezvous point at a thousand miles from 9110-Red should be attained at 8:30pm ship time. But Zanos time or Earth time would actually be 11:30pm BST and it was approximately 24 hours since we set out from Earth.

Suddenly the stars all disappeared and the view panels went blank. Then what was like a shower of sparks seemed to emanate from a point far out in space and central to the overhead view panel. This repeated itself several times before all was normal again and the stars were once more visible in all their abundance. Zanos conveyed that the ship's velocity had been reduced by 20% and was now 80,000mps.

Thereafter every few minutes the neutron generators operated till finally the ship had slowed considerably more and Zanos conveyed that 9110-Red should be in sight as a star-like object about 10,000 miles away. But as we were not facing in that direction we could not see it. 520-Green finally rotated around again and I was still unable to discern which star object it was. Captain Bulzezatna came over to me and touched my shoulder and suddenly there it was. I had forgotten to demand magnification and I could now see the rear view of 9110-Red filling the view panel. It looked so elegant and sleek and I felt good that I would be travelling in it.

As we approached closer and to one side the Starship gained in size and its massiveness became apparent. It was simply huge. 520-Green was now close enough to the Starship to commence its parking loop well to its rear end. The loop never came closer than 100 miles from 9110-Red and Zanos also conveyed that spacecraft in general never ventured anywhere near the forward neutron shield of a Starship.

From what I could see there was a pattern of red colouring longitudinally painted along the two mile length of the shiny circular body of the Starship. I magnified my view through the control room view panels and so inspected the Starship's entire length. It had a completely smooth exterior with no windows or view ports of any description. When I attempted a magnification of the forward neutron shield zone I could not get a proper focus. All I got was a blurred fuzzy image across the visible front section of the ship where the mushroom shaped neutron shield was supposed to be. I remember my view of 8110-Gold way back in the November 2006. The visit had been a gift from Muznant and Brazjaf on the occasion of our marriage earlier that year.

9110-Red was absolutely awesome to look at and represented to me something of both beauty and immense power. At two miles long and with its circular profile tapering slightly and red stripe it gave the impression of a ship that was sleek and fast. I think I may just have fallen in love with the sight of it. I couldn't help thinking that I should soon be inside it and causing it to speed through space as it had never done before. I wondered how fast that would be; I would find out soon enough.

There were to be several shuttle journeys to the Starship and passengers would be taken over first. I went with Muznant, Brazjaf and the others to suit up with the electrostatic gear and then down to the shuttle bay. I was surprised to see Captain Bulzezatna join us.

'I wish to meet my friend Captain Natazlat personally and I should like to see her expression when the new journey plan is revealed to her,' she said generally. 'And I should also like her to get at first-hand my mindset with regard to Ashley and know of my regard for him.'

I was complimented and thanked Bulzezatna for her faith in me. As our shuttle approached the Starship I needed no magnification to see its immensity and detail. We approached at an angle from its rear and before long it filled the view panels from side to side and top to bottom. Its outer surface was quite smooth with no view panels or apertures anywhere along its length. I could see no joins either.

As the shuttle got closer I began to feel a slight gravitational effect which gradually increased. Our shuttle then rotated so that the front of the Starship was below us and its gravity effect was in that downward direction. I looked up at the length of the rear section and was surprised at how far into the distance it reached.

Then suddenly before us an airlock opening was exposed and we drifted in. There was a slight judder as the shuttle adjusted to the full gravity of the ship. As we settled onto the airlock deck I could feel the gravity effect which was nearly as normal as that which we felt on 520-Green. The dimmed lighting brightened when the airlock doors were closed.

I could see that two other shuttles had accompanied us and these were both positioned on our right hand side. Then a smaller sliding door opened and I could see the extent of this cargo platform. My thought query was answered immediately and I was given a complete view of this entire platform level. It was for cargo storage and at nearly half a mile in diameter could also accommodate spaceships the size of 520-Green. Of course the much larger bay doors on the other side of the platform would have had to be used and a different procedure initiated. This platform was fifty feet above the habitation platform level and had a marginally lesser gravity being slightly further from the neutron shield.

Muznant was beside me and conveyed that much cargo was to be brought aboard from 520-Green requiring several more shuttle trips. But for now we were to proceed down to the next level where accommodation had been prepared. 9110-Red would be 60% occupied for the return journey to Nazmos and so there was plenty of spare living space available.

Captain Bulzezatna led the way to a large room that reminded me of the floor of one of Anztarza's deck transporters. When the sliding door closed I got a light headed sensation. I realised we were moving downwards like in an elevator. When the side panel opened again I saw a mini-city spread out in front of me and I thought of one of the domes in Anztarza. We were then led to a large room and took off our gold electrostatic suits. The design was similar to the room on 520-Green but much more extensive. Muznant conveyed that there were several of these rooms around this level.

It was then a fair walk to the centre of the platform to the control room and the central platform pillar. We were welcomed aboard by Captain Natazlat and I performed my own professional Sewa which quite pleased her. She seemed much younger looking than I had imagined and she smiled as she read my thoughts. I think we took an instant liking to each other.

Then a puzzled expression came to her face and she turned to Bulzezatna who immediately explained that a plan had been given to me, Ashley, by my inner voice.

'What plan is this?' she turned to me with a modicum of anxiety and displeasure.

Before Bulzezatna could say anything further I put my hand out and Natazlat grasped it. I could feel her deep mind probe and a sudden lightening of her grip.

'Why wasn't I informed of this plan prior to your arrival?' she said looking keenly at me. She had such piercing large green eyes that I felt her looking right down into my thoughts. I couldn't help thinking how fascinating those eyes were.

Again she read this thought but her expression remained unchanged.

'I'm sorry but I prevented it,' I said aloud. 'The detail of the plan could not be conveyed to you via telepathy in case some aspect of it got left out. It had to be done in the most direct manner so that I could be sure you received the complete scenario. Also the distance was too great for effective discussion. What is your opinion of the journey plan?'

'We must first consult Zanos and see if adjustments can be accommodated,' Natazlat replied.

'All aspects have been analysed apart from the supplementary power aspect,' came from Zanos almost immediately. 'A variable power input will be applied and navigation adjusted accordingly. The path is clear.'

I then communicated directly with Zanos and indicated that my mind would remain open at all times for access to all aspects of the plan. I also conveyed that a journey velocity approaching 200FTL was probable.

Zanos again replied that all factors would be recognised and destination arrival times adjusted.

Zanos-onboard was a complex of 23 interconnected bio-computers with each capable of operating the Starship's functions independently.

I thought it worthwhile to inform Zanos on how my telekinetic power worked and that there might be a directional variation of applied force depending upon my location on the habitation platform. I would of course remain within the central area at all times.

One of the conditions in my instructions had been that I must on no account go into pink mode when applying my push on the ship. At no time must I do anything outside of normal time zone and hidden from Zanos' sensors. As such there would be no limit to the push level that I would be able to apply. That only applied in pink mode when my inner voice had stopped me from going above pink level 16 because of some danger beyond.

I knew that when I tackled Zarama I would go up to that level and if that wasn't sufficient I would have to go further and suffer the consequences. What that might do to me I did not know but I was prepared to stop Zarama at all cost. I hoped that it would not come to that.

Captain Natazlat seemed very pleasant but I think I had put her off her stride when my plan of action had been sprung on her. However Captain Bulzezatna and the others including Puzlwat had all expressed their utmost confidence in me which reassured her to some extent. No captain of a Starship likes their routine being upset at the very last minute before a journey began. But I think that Natazlat had rationalised the condition and now viewed me simply as a supplementary power source – and quite a prodigious one at that. She knew of my achievements with the asteroids and with massive Triton and so had confidence in my ability to deliver the necessary power as planned.

The Oannes do not keep secrets and so the plan in all its detail was conveyed through Zanos to everyone on board. There were a few questions but nothing of major importance. The fact that the journey time would be considerably shortened brought general acceptance. My reputation had preceded me and I for once was pleased that it had. I hoped I could live up to the expectation.

For some reason I felt slightly uncomfortable in my mind but realised that this was because Zanos-onboard was continually drawing me into its calculations. Whatever force I applied to accelerate the Starship must inevitably and instantly be compensated for by Zanos repositioning the habitation platforms closer to the forward shield as a gravity adjustment.

The ferrying of the shuttles between the Starship and 520-Green was finally completed and we passengers were shown our relative allotted accommodation. I suppose all were generally similar in basic design. Mine consisted of two large rooms one of which contained a fair sized sleep tank. Otherwise all the usual facilities were in place and a bed had been specially set up for me similar to the one I had on 520-Green. My apartment if you can call it that was as close as possible to the centre of the circular habitation platform. And yet I was about fifty feet from the central column.

I knew what I had to do from what I had been instructed. I had been shown the general plan of the Starship. I was to stand with my feet apart as close to the central column safety barrier and concentrate my mental push effort downwards at the floor between my feet and on to a wide area near the centre of the neutron shield which would be between 400 and 600 feet below me.

I queried Zanos on the detail of the journey acceleration in order to make my own plan for my successive telekinetic efforts. The information I received was that a gradual build-up to maximum acceleration would be initiated at the commencement of the journey and then maximum impulse power maintained for the remainder of the travel period. When the ship attained 10 FTL speed the impulse power would exactly balance the impact of the grid energy-medium being absorbed by the neutron shield. My own efforts should raise this threshold of power by a considerable amount. But by how much I could not be sure. It had been indicated that a 200 FTL speed should be aimed for. I would need Zanos to advise me as the speed built up.

Muznant, Brazjaf and the others had been placed in accommodation adjacent to mine. Captain Natazlat invited us to join her for the farewell meal as was the usual custom. Captain Bulzezatna would attend along with several of her crew. Departure was flexible and scheduled for 4 am GMT which was a couple of hours away.

The control room was in the area close to the central column and directly opposite to where my own accommodation was. This not only functioned as the heart of the Starship but was also the living quarters for its captain and his or her family. Captain Natazlat was single like Bulzezatna and so lived alone. I wondered about Simon. Would he one day be captain of such a ship and would he have his family with him? I felt a pleasant sensation when I thought of the prospect.

The meal was a decent spread of the usual Oannes dishes. There must have been about twenty persons seated at this ample table and the telepathic conversation was polite and formal. I sat between Muznant and Bulzezatna with the Starship captain sitting opposite me.

As the only Earthman sitting at the table I thought I might as well assert my human side to the proceedings. So I tapped my Wazu container with my spoon and then slowly stood up. I looked around the table and then very slowly picked up my glass of Wazu and raised it up to head level.

'I propose a toast,' I said aloud and paused briefly. Then added, 'May this journey to your home on Nazmos be swift, sure and safe my friends,' and I took a sip of my Wazu.

I sensed general approval from all as they too stood up with Wazu glasses raised and repeated the words, 'Swift, sure and safe,' and took a drink of their Wazu.

The formality seemed to dissipate and a feeling of ease and camaraderie prevailed instead.

Captain Natazlat looked at me and conveyed her thanks for my words of distinction.

'I shall remember you Ashley,' she added, 'since I will from now on repeat your toast before the start of every journey. Perhaps it will become a custom on other Starship's as well. Yes I do like it; swift, sure and safe. Thank you.'

I'd had a good rest on 520-Green on the journey here and it was now time to say farewell to Captain Bulzezatna and her crew. Sewas were exchanged and I thought there was a longer one between the two captains. I read a great friendship and respect between them and a pride in their achievement as women. For some reason I was glad that Natazlat was our captain and not Zakatanz. I wondered how he would have received the news about the change to the flight plan. I don't suppose he would have been too pleased but would probably have gone along with it but in a grudging sort of way.

I watched as Captain Bulzezatna and her crew walked into the distance towards the deck transfer room. I did not see them leave as Captain Natazlat put a hand on my shoulder and conveyed that we should make ready for departure. I think she had accepted the change of plan and was looking forward to seeing me in action. Obviously my reputation with regard to the asteroids was well known in general but to see me in action on her Starship had built up an excitement of anticipation. Brajam was also near and conveyed that he hoped a velocity close to 200 FTL could be reached. I said that I would do my best and that Zanos would be guiding me progressively in all aspects.

When we received Captain Bulzezatna's message that 520-Green had commenced its journey back to Anztarza, Captain Natazlat gave her command to Zanos to initiate departure for Nazmos in five minutes. She smiled at me and said in a very conspiratorial and Muznant like voice, 'shift, sure and safe.' My affection went out to her and Muznant looked at me sideways with an expression bordering between pride and love. I think I understood her better just now knowing it was not any jealousy but an admiration of a quality that saw my affection grow also for another Oannes person; one whom I would come to respect a great deal. Our species were not that far apart after all.

I heard a whispering sound behind me and looking back noticed that the central column was moving upwards. Natazlat conveyed that 9110-Red had begun its acceleration and the whole of the complex platform structure was moving closer to the neutron shield in compensation. The acceleration would gradually peak at several thousand gravity levels and the Starship should be at the first light speed quite quickly. Thereafter the acceleration would progressively diminish as velocity through the space grid increased and an increasing quantity of energy-medium impact against the forward neutron shield was absorbed. The captain suggested that I begin applying my telekinetic force in about ten minutes.

'Zanos will link with you and give you feedback as you apply your increasing telekinetic force levels,' she conveyed.

I couldn't help a slight nervous tension in my head and yet I was keen to begin. This Starship was really fantastic. There had been absolutely no sensation of the ship beginning its journey apart from the central column indicator that the platform had repositioned. Even now we could be approaching the velocity of light-waves and it felt as if the ship was still at rest. There was no feeling of speed or of movement. As there were no viewing ports we could see nothing of the outside. Zanos did it all; the navigating and the platform adjustments for maintaining normal gravity conditions and also monitoring the desires and welfare of all six hundred persons aboard. Since the interior of the Starship was shielded from the effects of the energy-medium grid then all clocks would keep to normal Nazmos or Earth time.

I was interrupted in these thoughts by Zanos that I should now commence my telekinetic effort. 9110-Red was approaching twice light velocity.

Captain Natazlat looked at me and smiled. She was keen to see me in action.

I was resting with my back against the central column safety rail and I now gripped it firmly with a hand each side of me. I spread my legs just a bit more and looked downwards. I imagined the neutron shield below me which Zanos indicated was just 400 feet distant and I began a push at level ten. I heard the familiar whispering sound of the central column behind me and knew that Zanos was compensating for an increase in acceleration.

I did not have to continue my concentration since I knew that the telekinetic force would continue at the set level until I either increased it or willed it to stop. I had progressed considerably since the day of the darts match in the navigation pub all those years ago. Tania was just thirteen years old then and had just visually come into my life. It seemed such a long time ago that I had first applied my telekinetic effort on the sand filled canvas bag hanging from the beam in our garage.

Again Zanos came through to me clearly and very matter of fact. The ship had been accelerating for nearly an hour and had attained the velocity of 10 FTL which was still increasing. It was time to increase my telekinetic effort again. So I went to level 20.

The whispering sound from the central column returned and I'm not sure if I also felt a very faint judder in the floor beneath me. Zanos conveyed that I should not increase the power level in such a big jump. I was surprised at this but accepted that perhaps I didn't properly know my own strength. I waited for Zanos for feedback on a new FTL reading.

It was twenty minutes later that Zanos intimated the ship's new velocity. It was 35 FTL and increasing. The captain and Brajam looked at each other and nodded a mutual approval. I do believe that the captain was proud that hers was the first Starship to attain such a velocity.

Now that I realised what I was capable of I began to increase my telekinetic force by two levels every fifteen minutes. At the end of another hour Zanos confirmed that 9110-Red had accelerated to a velocity of 60 FTL and was still accelerating. And as yet I did not feel any stress or fatigue.

From my past experiences I had expected a certain amount of tiredness to creep up on me but now I realised that perhaps that only applied when I operated in pink mode.

I continued increasing my push effort and now did so by 3 levels at ten minute intervals. There was still no sensation of speed or even of movement but then Zanos conveyed that the ship had exceeded 100 FTL speed.

Natazlat and Brajam appeared ecstatic. My push effort was now at level 50 and I felt as normal as when I had begun. It felt like I was applying a simple effort pushing the bowling balls around my dad's garden. I decided to stop applying any further telekinetic effort to see what velocity level would be attained. I conveyed this to the captain and the others.

After twenty minutes Zanos conveyed that the ship had stabilised at a velocity of 126 FTL. As this needed to increase further I once again commenced increasing my push effort by two levels every few minutes.

I had not realised I was thirsty until Muznant brought me a glass of cool Wazu. I drained it in seconds and asked for another which I held in my hand and sipped at intervals. I learned that Zanos had instructed her to do so.

I decided to query Zanos about the performance of the Starship and should I continue increasing the push levels. All I got in return was that everything was normal and 9110-Red was travelling at 151 FTL and accelerating.

I smiled at Natazlat and Brajam and felt Muznant beside me with her hand subconsciously resting lightly on my forearm; the same arm in which I held a half drunk glass of Wazu. It was additionally nice when Captain Natazlat also touched my other arm and looking directly into my eyes conveyed that it would be nice for her Starship to achieve the 200 FTL speed. Her green eyes were so mesmerising that I don't know what my thoughts were telling me. I felt a brief squeeze of warning from Muznant and I was brought back to the present. Whatever would Tania think of me?

I nodded to Natazlat and requested a computation from Zanos as to what push level would be so required. Zanos had been monitoring each of my telekinetic efforts and suggested that I pause at push level 70.

I continued with the gradual stepped increases until I reached this level. I looked around and over to the accommodation houses as far as the curved wall of this fantastic Starship. I could not see any difference in size or colour and that was due to the effectiveness of the neutron shield. As far as we inside the ship were concerned we were not moving relative to any energy-medium grid. Our spatial environment within the confines of this Starship was being maintained in total isolation from the outside universe. The neutron star material of which the forward three quarter mile diameter mushroom shield was composed kept all matter behind it safe from the destructive forces racing against it. I wondered by what amount the neutron shield mass would increase during this journey.

I noticed that the platform was moving very gradually up the central column. Finally it slowed to a stop and Zanos conveyed that 9110-Red was now cruising at a steady 215 FTL velocity and had been achieved in a little over three hours. What happened next came as a complete surprise.

Captain Natazlat turned towards me, reached up and pulled my head down to her level and kissed me first on one cheek, then on the other cheek and finally a slightly prolonged one on my lips albeit a bit off centre. I couldn't help but put my arms around her tunic, avoiding the back 'butterfly wing', and gently pressing her against me.

When I let her go Muznant swung around and did the same. But she had learnt to kiss and so softened her lips when they met mine.

'Oh dear me,' I said aloud looking at Brajam and Brazjaf after Muznant had released me, 'I hope you two aren't going to follow suit.'

There was a half second of confusion on their faces before they got the humour and began to laugh in the Oannes way. Natazlat, Muznant and I just had to join in.

'Congratulations Captain,' I said again still smiling, 'I trust that your journey will be swift, sure and safe. Incidentally, I think Muznant has a slight edge in the kissing stakes. Perhaps she could give you a few tips.' There was a mischievous tone in my voice and expression.

'I shall report back to Tania about your behaviour here today,' said Muznant, 'and that you kissed a Starship captain and quite enjoyed it.'

I looked across at Natazlat and instantly read her mind – and she knew it. It was a most enigmatic smile and sideways glance that I got from her and I knew that I had made another conquest. I was flattered by what Tania had referred to as my 'harem' of women admirers. And I admired them in turn but in a most friendly though loveable way. I suppose I always have and always shall look twice at an attractive woman.

I thought of my Tania and I remember her asking me when it was that I had first begun to love her. I remember replying that I didn't quite know the moment nor the hour, day or place, or the look or the words that had laid the foundation. It was too long ago, I had said, and that I realised I was in the middle of it before I knew I had begun to love her. I remember her saying nothing except to come over onto my lap and begin to kiss me. It was the summer of 2006 and we were on our honeymoon in the Algarve. I do remember it so well and I had to smile at the thought.

I was in mind reading company and my mind had been open to all before I realised everyone on board the Starship had taken part in my nostalgic reverie. It was only when the emotion of immense goodwill and affection reached me that I knew they liked me more for it.

'Ashley,' Muznant conveyed only to me, 'whatever you do, say and think makes people love and admire you more and more; as I do.'

'Thank you Muznant,' I said aloud. I had to keep my mind open for Zanos.

Zanos then conveyed that at the current Starship's velocity the Raznat system would be reached in 11.4 Earth days. Navigation and computations would be based upon the current velocity conditions and the gradual reductions in velocity towards the latter part of the journey.

There was an emotion of euphoria and excitement that filled the habitation platform and quite a few of the Oannes passengers came out of their accommodation and wandered over to the central area to see the captain and express their joy and wonder. I knew that they had also come to get a look at me close-up since I was well known by reputation. I hope I got a similar reception in Wentazta when I went before the governing council of ministers.

Muznant looked at me again and I read that she found my diffident nature a delight to her senses. To her I had all these fantastic gifts and yet I did not seem to assert myself in front of others. She found that quality rare and loveable. I was flattered that she should think so.

There was one thing I understood and that was never to presume. I had not been sure of many things just like before the asteroids experiment. But I had learned. And on this Starship I had not been certain of the extent to which I might accelerate it. But with the assistance of Zanos I do believe that we could have taken the speed a lot further. And yet I still did not know the ultimate level to which my telekinetic capabilities extended.

However I feel certain that with a Starship modified and enhanced as 4110-Silver was undergoing that the 500 FTL target was within reach. After all we had exceeded 9110-Red's capability twenty times over. Zarama might even be just a six month journey away if I could have my way.

Brajam looked at me and smiled. I guessed he had read my thoughts and I knew that he agreed with the direction in which I was thinking.

Captain Natazlat asked me how I was feeling in my physical self. I replied honestly that I was surprised that I did not feel more fatigued. I was however still rather thirsty and felt that a snack would be most welcome. The thing about telepathy is that an emotion or mood gets conveyed instantly and words are immaterial. Meanings are clear as imagery is usually attached. Nazaztal nodded and agreed that they could all do with a light meal too.

Puzlwat and Nogozat had been silent spectators during the past few hours and now came up to me and shook my hand. There was admiration in Puzlwat's eyes before he added that he was not a good Starship traveller and needed to retire to his cabin. It was an attitude of mind he said and the fact that they were flying blind behind a neutron shield seemed to unsettle him.

Nogozat on the other hand was quite at home. She came up to me as Puzlwat began to walk away and expressed a wish to give me a kiss. I smiled and leaned down and presented my right cheek. But her firm hands grabbed my face in both of her cool hands, turned it straight on and then planted a kiss just like Muznant's firm but soft. I think I blushed at her forwardness but couldn't help a big smile. These Oannes ladies were getting rather skilled at it. Nogozat smiled at that, let go my face and turning about walked slowly to where a smiling Puzlwat had stopped to wait for her.

The thought crossed my mind about the women on Nazmos. Would they also follow this trend? Not that I'm complaining since I find it a pleasant experience but whatever will Tania think? And little Rachel for I shall have to tell her. Oh, I did miss them. In future I shall insist that they accompany me on these long journeys. I had eleven days to while away.

After the repast in the captain's quarters and a decent interval of polite conversation I gave my thanks and indicated that tiredness seemed to be creeping up on me and I could do with retiring to my accommodation for a rest. Muznant and Brazjaf came back with me and stayed awhile. I felt very close to these two; practically as close as family. They were the first Oannes I had met and Muznant's feelings towards me brought our relationship ever closer. She was over the trauma of her phantom pregnancy but as yet had not conceived. Both she and Brazjaf were matter of fact about it and sincerely believed that it would all happen when the time was right. Perhaps once the spectre of Zarama had been removed things might prove more propitious. Although the Oannes did not have religion they did believe in a sort of destiny. They were extremely placid in their outlook.

For them as a nation they had accepted that Zarama had been destined to follow a path to Raznat. They had the technology to build Starship's and so search out other worlds for a new beginning. And yet they also held onto a solution foretold in ancient mythology that a being from another world would intervene to save them from disaster. They put two and two together and listed Zarama as the disaster and me from Earth as the other half of the equation. So far I think they were right for why else would I have been given such gifts and such power. It had certainly taken no great effort on my part to accelerate this Starship to its present velocity. Also I was fairly confident that Zarama would be stopped for I had seen that Tatizblay would play an important role in a new Nazmos. In the distant future many millennia away I saw a Nazmos that was very Earth-like.

When Muznant and Brazjaf left me I drank another glass of Wazu and then lay on top of my bed and thought pleasant thoughts of home. For some odd reason my thoughts went back to my childhood days of playing in the park on the slides and swings and running across the green. Mum and dad were ever so young but somehow little Katy wasn't in the picture anywhere. Funny I thought as I dosed off only to dream of a tiny Katy dragging me off to the kitchen for something off an upper shelf. The dream then switched to a Starship long, sleek and silvery; only I was on the outside watching it speed through space in front of me.

I awoke hours later and just lay there. I had eleven days to kill and still had to keep my telekinetic push active to keep the ship at its above 200 FTL speed. I just willed it so and yet felt no mental strain from the effort. I queried Zanos on the ship's status and on the true time. Everything was normal and it was now 1:37pm BST or more precisely 12:37 GMT and I had been asleep for nearly six hours. The Oannes in Anztarza stayed with Earth's zero-meridian Greenwich Mean Time zone throughout the year. Zanos conveyed also that the Starship's velocity had reduced to 210 FTL by slightly easing up on the output of the ship's own impulse power.

And so the days passed and Captain Natazlat insisted that I be her guest at meal times. We got on well and when we happened to be alone on occasions she behaved in a very proper manner. I liked her and I know she liked me because I could sense her interest and curiosity; just like from Vicky and Muznant. But I think there was a certain amount of awe mixed in with her admiration of me and of my reputation which preceded me wherever I went. And so I got to know more about her from each successive discussion. I could never have dared to probe her mind as it just was not done for politeness sake.

She liked to talk about herself, of her history and her aspirations. And I was a good listener. She was 190 years of age and originally came from Wentazta on the shores of the Great Sea of Peruga. But later in her youth she had moved to a smaller town not far from Latipuzan where Muznant came from. But that was many years before Muznant was even born. They had met only by chance about forty years ago when both happened to be travelling to

Earth on the same Starship. Yes, Natazlat had been to Anztarza but she had preferred the openness of outer space as space travel was in her blood. She had been an only child to an ageing couple who both passed away some hundred years ago when Natazlat was ninety.

Like Bulzezatna she had been career minded from an early age. She had met Bulzezatna when they had served together on an expeditionary FTL starship to another star system. She had been hooked on space ever since and had dreamed of commanding her own Starship one day. And so had volunteered for every possible Starship venture even to the extent of foregoing the captaincy of a vessel twice the size of 520-Green to serve under a variety of Starship captains.

Her tenure of some nine years under Captain Zakatanz had been most fruitful in that she had learned a lot from him. She liked his style and it was ultimately from his recommendation that she was finally considered for captaincy of 9110-Red just fifteen years ago. I was pleasantly surprised at her liking for Captain Zakatanz but then I did not know him apart from our brief meeting on that visit to 8110-Gold all those years ago in 2006. At the time he may have been otherwise involved with matters on the ship and we were a distraction. Yet he had been polite though formal in his manner to us visitors. I hoped to renew his acquaintanceship one day. Perhaps on my next Starship trip to Nazmos.

Natazlat had read all of Zakatanz's theories and treatises about one-way journeys and she had been quite fascinated by his ideas. She had no family ties and as such would be willing to make such a trip. So I asked the question whether she would give up the captaincy of 9110-Red if such an opportunity presented itself. She thought about my question and then replied that she didn't know for sure. It would have to be a decision made at that time with fuller information on the trip and the prospect of where it was targeted. I understood exactly what she meant.

And so the days passed and I got to know Brajam, and Muznant and Brazjaf a lot better. Daily living had such an effect. Even Puzlwat and Nogozat became quite friendly, especially Nogozat. She had a very gentle manner about her and had the habit of looking directly into your eyes whenever speaking to you. At 180 years of age she was past middle age but had the mischievous mannerisms one would associate with a much younger person, someone of Jantuzno's age. Puzlwat was twenty years her senior and had a more serious outlook but with a very pleasant manner about him if he was partial towards you. And he was very partial towards me I knew. Where Muznant and Brazjaf looked upon me as a kind of 'saviour-of-the-world' figure, Puzlwat treated me with the respect he'd give to another human or Oannes person. There was no favouritism in his nature. I had proved myself to him and that was that. He made me feel ordinary and I liked that and realised that subconsciously he could be a sort of father figure to me on Nazmos when my own was absent. I do believe that I could look up to him in that respect.

I was glad when the tenth day of the journey arrived. It was partway through and we had just finished our afternoon meal when Zanos informed the captain and me that the ships velocity needed to begin to reduce. Zanos instructed that I should reduce my telekinetic effort gradually and in the same stages as had been initially applied. And so over the next three hours I dropped my push upon the neutron shield about two levels every five minutes or so; sometimes a bit more and sometimes a bit less; a total reduction of 70 push levels. The deceleration had to be counteracted by the operation of the neutron generators operating towards the back end of the ship and with the moveable platform at its highest point. When I had totally ceased all my telekinetic efforts Zanos conveyed that the Starship was now solely under its own impulse power and cruising at 12 FTL speed. This was a relief to me personally in that I felt decidedly lighter in my head. Also I was now free to wander around the habitation platform of which I was quite curious. Zanos informed us that 9110-Red should reach its parked location in approximately six hours time.

The Starship had now reduced to 5 FTL velocity and was progressively slowing. The neutron generators were in constant operation during these deceleration periods. Zanos was in complete control and coordinated exactly the operation of the reverse neutron generator with the ship's power reductions. Conditions on the habitation platform seemed quite normal with regard to the level of gravity felt.

I had nothing more to do and so I conveyed to the captain that I should like to wander around for a bit and meet some of the other passengers. I decided to walk directly towards the far wall and on the way I met quite a few fellow passengers. We communicated in general terms though I sensed their excitement at so early an arrival. I suppose when you expect a six month journey only to have it reduced to eleven days then joy and relief could be expected.

When I reached the wall of the ship I noticed a column there similar to the central one. I looked around and saw others in similar locations around the habitation platform periphery. Nearly half a mile away and opposite to my position was another. All in all there were six columns equally spaced. So the habitation platform structure was supported by seven columns which allowed it to move up and down smoothly. I found this ship rather fascinating.

Unlike for Earth the Starship could be brought to a much closer location in the Raznat system since there was no need of secrecy from Nazmos. It would still have to be parked about 100 million miles outside the orbit of Platwuz which was the furthest planet from Raznat. This was a safety rule that was instituted when the first FTL starship was under construction. Platwuz was a mineral source for Nazmos and it was nearly 800 million miles from Nazmos depending upon the time of year and relative orbital positions; a journey of about four hours by spaceship.

I did not want to look tired when I appeared in public on Nazmos and so I decided to get a little rest time after a light meal with the captain. The captain was sympathetic and wondered at my resilience after pushing her ship continuously for so long. I myself had to wonder where all that push energy came from. My inner voice remained silent on the matter.

When I got into my bedroom and lay on the bed I thought to just shut my eyes for a moment. But I was mistaken for when I reopened them it was nearly six hours later. I felt considerably refreshed though and full of energy and keen to see what surprises Nazmos had in store.

Zanos informed us that 9110-Red had attained its parked position with 94% accuracy of intended location. The last reduction in speed from 150,000 mps to near stationary had been accomplished by turning the Starship completely about and then applying normal acceleration.

Communication with Nazmos from here took just over an hour each way and Captain Natazlat was keen to hear the surprise from the general public and the governing council of ministers with regard to the early arrival of 9110-Red. Natazlat informed me that a full report of the journey had been despatched in which a large section was about my part in the ship's acceleration to over 200 FTL velocity. Natazlat said that she had laid claim to being the first Starship captain to have operated her ship at the phenomenal velocity of 215 FTL for the entire journey from Earth to Raznat. She said she wanted all of this to go into the records for posterity. I agreed and suggested that on my return journey to Earth we could go for a velocity in excess of 300 FTL. She looked at me sideways and gave me a rather enigmatic smile. I think she was flirting but only a bit. And I liked that. I could see Muznant smiling too and the emotion of fun humour came across to me from her and this time there was no admonition to be careful. I think Muznant understood me very well.

'Tania where are you darling,' I conveyed with an open mind, 'I miss you.'

Natazlat conveyed that spaceships would head out to us in a couple of hours after receiving her arrival message. Journey time was about four hours and so we had close to six hours of waiting. I didn't mind this since there was now plenty of time for a nice meal with the captain and friends and possibly a stroll around the platform. I was still amazed at the size and complexity of the ship and especially the fact that the Starship was stationary in the middle of nowhere and yet I felt I was somewhere on Earth or in Anztarza. I imagine that so long as the food growing section that was on the level below produced enough food then this ship functioned like a mini-planet of sorts. With the prospect of Zarama's approaching destructive power I could see how the Oannes held out hope for some form of survival in a fleet of Starship's. With me on the scene I had brought hope that it may never come to that. But I had an agenda of my own that I wished to implement and which I would push for with the council of ministers when I met them.

Muznant, Brazjaf, Brajam, Puzlwat and Nogozat plus a few others were seated with me at Captain Natazlat's table when the first message from Nazmos was relayed to all on the ship by Zanos. The message expressed wonder at the news that the journey from Earth to Nazmos had been reduced to just eleven days. Scientists and engineers were being assembled in order that a complete inspection of the ship's structure could be carried out. However there was a sense of elation in the latter part of the message that was quite apparent and I couldn't help but smile. In a way this was a demonstration of my telekinetic gift and I hoped that it would help in persuading the council to agree to Nazmos' relocation closer to Raznat.

With hindsight I felt that had Zanos not restricted me a greater FTL velocity could have been achieved. At the time there were many unknowns and mainly on my part. But swift, sure and safe was to be the guideline and future space fleet motto and I was very happy to go along with that.

Captain Natazlat read my thoughts and smiled at me. Yes, she conveyed we may have been able to achieve greater velocities but again swift, sure and safe was a good motto to follow. Was a new chapter in my life beginning? I would soon see.

CHAPTER 15

Nazmos

2016

The shuttle that took Ashley and the others to the waiting spaceship was much larger than any he had been on previously. And the spaceship itself which came around in its loop cycle to meet them looked massive as it drew closer into their view. Its large bay doors were open wide and all three shuttles entered together and settled smoothly on its bay deck. It took a while for the bay to be secured and pressurised before the shuttle doors were opened. When Ashley alighted he could see that this bay was at least three times larger than that on Bulzezatna's spaceship 520-Green.

This was more like the design of the Starship upper level in that it could hold a varied design of ships and in some considerable quantity. Ashley estimated this shuttle bay to be about a thousand feet square with a ceiling that was at least fifty feet in height. The shuttles were parked to a pattern which reminded Ashley of an airport hub on Earth.

Because of the vast distances on this ship the Oannes made use of smaller Anztarza type deck transporters to move about the ships interior. One such internal Transporter took them to the electrostatic suits hall along a corridor within the ship. The hall was similar to all the others and everyone took off their gold electrostatic suits in the normal manner and hung them in the wall recesses.

Muznant and Brazjaf and the others were on home territory and their expressions showed it. They were proud of this ship and of their Raznat system. Brazjaf conveyed that it had been requested that they go to the control room where Captain Rojazonto wished to welcome them personally. Muznant secretly conveyed to Ashley that the captain was especially keen to meet him face to face.

'You have become a legend on Nazmos,' she conveyed, 'so expect a lot of welcoming formalities when you meet him; especially since you brought a Starship all the way from Earth in just eleven days.'

Ashley felt embarrassed at this accolade from Muznant but he could see the pride in her emotion with regard to him. Muznant had taken Ashley under her protection and she felt obliged to look after his interests. After all she had been the first Oannes woman to have met him and had supported his case for visiting Anztarza. And Ashley could be the one to stop Zarama. It was a great expectation and he would have to continually live up to it. Oh how he wished for Tania and the kids to be here at his side; perhaps on the next visit.

Brazjaf conveyed that he knew Captain Rojazonto very well. He was comparatively young at 152 years of age and he came from Wentazta. He had a wife and a son who was aged 23 years and whose chief interest was in architecture. Rojazonto had been 1st deputy on this ship 8962-Orange for eight years before being given temporary command as acting captain when the previous captain aged 280 years had retired on grounds of ill health. Rojazonto had fulfilled his command with distinction and after three years was promoted as permanent captain. That was nearly fifteen years ago and he had then been the youngest captain for this class of Spaceship.

When the select group entered the control room extensive Sewas were performed and Ashley conducted his own detailed Sewa with the captain. Although Rojazonto had expected Ashley to be familiar with the Oannes custom of greeting he was nevertheless surprised and pleased at the ease, politeness and fluency with which Ashley conducted his Sewa greeting.

With a wide smile on his face Rojazonto came forward and reached out his hand to Ashley. On Nazmos it was known that the Earth custom was to shake hands as a form of greeting with a very simple Sewa question of 'How do you do?'

Ashley took the offered hand and responded with, 'I'm very pleased to meet you Captain.'

The two looked briefly into each others minds and read the emotions of goodwill towards the other.

'You have a magnificent ship here Captain,' said Ashley aloud and conveyed that it was the largest he had seen apart from the Starship. 'May I be granted a mental tour of it through your esteemed Zanos on-board?'

'Of course,' replied Rojazonto in a rather gravel like low tone voice, 'I shall instruct Zanos to do so at once.'

'Thank you Captain,' said Ashley smiling his best. He liked this captain.

The captain then made a sweeping gesture to Ashley and the others and conveyed that they had the freedom to wander around the control room and see the sights through the view panels which were on all sides. It was only when Ashley queried Zanos was he shown the control room as a bubble structure perched centrally at the very top of the ship.

The ship was in an extended parking loop and Zanos had kept its orientation so that the FTL Starship was visible from one of the surrounding view panels. The captain conveyed that they had another few hours of shuttle loading and unloading before he could begin the journey home. Natazlat's Starship 9110-Red was nearly two hundred miles away but still looked large and impressive.

Ashley looked out at the stars that shone brilliantly all around them and he realised that he felt quite at home. For there was the Milky Way stretching right across their view from upper left to lower right. And the stars also seemed to be vaguely familiar, the brighter ones being the same as seen from Earth. Orion's belt was clearly visible although Betelgeuse and Bellatrix seemed closer together. And of course Sirius was as bright as ever and to the left of Orion's lower star Saiph. He also recognised the bluish white cluster of stars known as The Seven Sisters. Orion's belt, the Hyades cluster around Aldebaran and the sisters were all in the same general extended line.

Ashley thought about Earth and home. He tried to analyse where it could be in amongst this display of stars. His inner voice answered his query along with Zanos on-board. They told him to look at Orion's Saiph and then to move his gaze towards Sirius. Not quite halfway was a small yellowish star rather on its own. This was Earth's sun. Ashley felt his heart leap in excitement when he managed to pinpoint Sol. He went to magnification mode and gradually increased this till the sun was enlarged sufficiently to look familiar. So now where was Earth in its orbital position he thought. Here again the answer was provided. The ecliptic of the solar system planets was inclined at quite an angle to the Raznat system and Earth would be seen as just a thin crescent of light at a position to the lower right side of the sun. Ashley searched in the area but in vain until Captain Rojazonto came alongside him and placing his hand on Ashley's shoulder directed his mental gaze to the thin Earth crescent. It was very faint and as Ashley tried a further magnification it went rather blurred and fuzzy. But it still gave him a joy that he had never expected. He stared at his home planet and wetness came to his eyes as he thought of his family just six light years away.

'No, not six light years,' he thought, 'but more like just six days away now.'

He felt a squeeze on his arm and he looked down to see Muznant there. She conveyed her thoughts of companionship to him and the emotion filled the control room and eased the feeling of homesickness in his heart. It was nice to have such understanding friends around him and he thought of them as his 'other family' now. This was picked up telepathically and the emotion of love and affection pervaded the area.

For the next half hour Zanos gave Ashley a tour of the stars visible around them. Chief among these were the eighteen star systems that were well within range of the Oannes Starships. These were categorised as those that were at less than fifty light years distance. But among them there were only five that were really close. Although Alpha Centauri was closest to Earth at 4.3 light years distance it was eight light years from Raznat. Sirius was just 8.6 light years from Earth but on the opposite side to Raznat. As such Raznat and Sirius were nearly fifteen light years apart.

On the other hand the very bright star Altair was 16.6 light years from Earth but only eleven light years from Raznat. Zanos conveyed that Starships had already been to this star but had kept a good distance from its mass which was twice that of Earth's Sol. There was nothing of interest there other than it being a good navigation exercise for Oannes space cadets. Ashley wondered if Simon would need to make such trips during his space training.

Then Ashley thought about Zarama. It was visibly some 525 light years from Raznat but in which direction? He was curious to get a look at it after all it was the reason behind all of his gifts. He had no idea of its position since none had been even mentioned. Ashley guessed that the Oannes actually avoided the subject simply because it was full of bad intent. Zarama was the fiery dragon of their myths and was intent upon destroying Nazmos.

Ashley queried Zanos but received nothing from there. His mind was open and all must have read his thoughts that he wished to see the thing he must conquer. Still silence so he rephrased his thoughts in a more positive form and conveyed that he must see his enemy before he could vanquish it. This time Captain Rojazonto came up to him and put his hand on Ashley's arm.

'You must look in the direction opposite to Earth,' he conveyed.

Slowly the ship began to rotate towards a new direction which brought a section of the Milky Way directly ahead of them.

'Now imagine yourself back on Earth and look in the direction of where you would expect our Raznat to be,' conveyed Rojazonto.

Ashley looked for the Sagittarius section in the Milky Way structure and found it. Then he was directed towards the bright star Altair and then across to the right to another bright star that was Rasalhague. Then Rojazonto mentally directed Ashley's view slightly above and to the left from there to a spot that seemed empty of bright stars. Ashley knew that far back in that space was where Zarama lurked. The view panel zoomed in on this space and had to really extend its magnification power such that eventually a tiny dot of dim light became visible. The object slowly enlarged to a round fuzzy ball of light and Ashley knew he was looking at Zarama. A chill went through him at the sight and he was immediately reminded of his glowing ball dream of so long ago.

Although Zarama was very far away Ashley could feel the menace emanating from it. And yet it was just another dwarf star object in space that happened to be travelling a dangerous path. It seemed so tiny and inconsequent now but in time it would be the opposite causing disaster and mayhem.

Ashley closed his eyes and looked away and conveyed that he had seen enough. But he was glad that he had satisfied his curiosity and gone through the experience of searching out and looking at Zarama. He knew now the direction in which Zarama lay; and the path his starship must travel for a rendezvous.

'Thank you Captain,' said Ashley, 'that was most enlightening. May I now be shown around your ship; by Zanos of course?'

'Certainly,' conveyed the captain, 'Zanos has been so instructed'

Zanos on-board then began to slowly convey blocks of information about Captain Rojazonto's ship 9632-Orange to Ashley. It was only when Ashley communicated back with speed that Zanos transmitted all the information about the ship's detail in one massive block of data. Ashley was proficient enough to absorb it all and so see clearly the location of the control room with regard to the rest of the ship.

The control room was a large shallow domed structure at the top centre of the ship's upper outer surface. It was the only feature that upset the smooth flowing contour of the ship's profile.

9632-Orange was nearly half a mile in length, a quarter of a mile in width and six hundred feet in height at its central region. There were ample viewing panels throughout its length near the central region perimeter. There were thirty decks within it and the view panels were on its fifteenth. Four of the decks housed the power plant and impulse devices. These were paired in the two upper and two lower decks and functioned as a backup for one another.

Three other deck levels had been converted to house the food growing tanks. The visual that Ashley got was something similar to the food domes of Anztarza with a roof structure that was forty feet above the water level.

The remaining decks were the accommodation cabins for nearly two thousand passengers. This was about the same as could be accommodated on a Starship. A spaceship of this class could travel in space indefinitely and many had been constructed and more were still being constructed since the Zarama threat had been confirmed some 1600 years ago. It was far easier to manufacture a spaceship of this type than a Starship with its complex shielding structure. Also spaceships could actually make landfall on some remote planet while Starships could not. But all of this had become somewhat irrelevant with the news that an earthman had been discovered who could possibly fulfil what their myths had foretold.

Ashley had been invited to visit Nazmos in order that the Oannes governing council of ministers could evaluate the man and his motives in person. They also wished to further test his gifted power of telekinesis in the repositioning of one of their outer planets. Platwuz was their outermost planet and it was desired to have it in a much closer orbit around their sun.

Brajam had conveyed to Ashley the geographical positions of Raznat's four planets. Nazmos was the closest with an orbit varying between 26 and 31 million miles from Raznat. Next was Rubabriz which was about the size of Mars. It had a barren landscape and a very thin atmosphere. The dust storms on it were fierce and could last for months. It was quite uninhabitable and orbited at a distance of 250 to 265 million miles from Raznat.

Next was the huge gas planet of Zraplat that was eleven times the size of Nazmos. It orbited Raznat at a distance of 630 million miles and was the brightest of the stars in the Nazmos night sky.

Then last but not least was the useful planet of Platwuz. It was nearly one and a half times the size of Nazmos, had a dense atmosphere of methane and a terrain covered in mountains and ravines. It was a solid planet and its gravity level was 2½ times that of Nazmos. It was very cold on the surface which registered at minus 100°C. However there were essential deposits of minerals underground and so mining there had been developed.

The Oannes were tolerant of cold temperatures but not that cold so special gear had to be worn outside the habitation domes. However there was a detectable heat source at the planet's core which kept it above the expected minus 200°C temperature; probably from its inception ten or so billion years ago. As such the Oannes had built their habitation domes in the ravine areas and had managed to tap down towards this heat source.

The Oannes had mined Platwuz for nearly 15,000 years. An essential ingredient in the manufacture of neutron star material existed deep down below the surface. It would be beneficial if Platwuz could be relocated closer to Raznat; somewhere between the orbits of Nazmos and Rubabriz. An orbit at 100 million miles from Raznat had been computed as the ideal location and had been agreed by the governing council of ministers.

Platwuz had a slow rotation about its own axis that took nearly three Nazmos days. Its orbital period around Raznat was 62 years. The Oannes had calculated that slowing it down sufficiently would cause it to drop to an elliptical orbit with perigee at the required 100 million mile distance from Raznat. A further slowing down at this point would stabilise Platwuz into a circular orbit around Raznat just as desired. The half period of the elliptic was estimated to take thirty years. However an initial acceleration of Platwuz at the start of its elliptic journey could reduce this time to twenty-two years.

Ashley considered all of this and knew that his main aim was the relocation of Nazmos to an orbit closer to its heat source of Raznat. He hoped to raise the issue with the governing council of ministers at the forthcoming meeting. However he would not push the issue at the present time but he would lay a foundation for his argument. He would ask for a decision once Platwuz was properly relocated. That meant a decision did not have to be made for some twenty-two years.

Ashley now felt a greater confidence in his telekinetic ability and realised that his gifted power seemed to get enhanced the more he exercised it. The mass of Platwuz would of course require him to operate in pink mode and it would be useful practice for when he had to tackle Zarama. That was a complete unknown and Ashley's confidence evaporated just at the very thought of it.

Muznant conveyed to Ashley that the Starship 8110-Gold under Captain Zakatanz had not as yet left for Earth and was scheduled to do so in another fifteen days time. Hopefully they could all be on it for the return journey to Earth. She conveyed that Captain Zakatanz had been informed about this and had expressed his pleasure and anticipation of having Ashley aboard. He conveyed his thoughts to Captain Natazlat that her FTL speed record would be exceeded if he had his wish.

Captain Natazlat had replied with affection and humour that she would still go down in history as the first captain to exceed 200 FTL velocity. Perhaps Captain Zakatanz could set another benchmark at above 300 FTL. The reply came that he would do his best to oblige. There was humour in the Oannes after all thought Ashley when he read this. A full team of 140 Oannes scientists were to be aboard the Starship to check it out at the Solar system end of the journey.

Ashley had hoped to be home for Christmas and this now seemed most likely.

Ashley's demeanour lifted at the thought and suddenly Tania, Simon and Rachel didn't seem that far away. He thought of the song 'I'll be home for Christmas' but couldn't quite remember more than the first line.

Muznant noticed this cheeriness in his thoughts and puzzled over it. An emotion of light heartedness and anticipated pleasure seemed to emanate out of Ashley and she went across to him and touched his arm. She did not expect what happened next. Nor did any of the others present in the control room expect him to do what he did.

Ashley being full of exhilaration and joy at the expectation of his early trip home just had to express his feelings in the only way he knew how. And Muznant who happened to be the nearest was pulled into the fever of the moment.

Ashley reached down and wrapping both arms around this diminutive Oannes woman squeezed her to him in a ferocious bear hug and planted several kisses on her face, lips included. He was laughing as he did this quite forgetting that Muznant was wincing with pain as her butterfly wing was crushed against her back. Yet she thought it was worth seeing the person she adored expressing his joy through her.

It was only when he eventually released her and stood up straight again did he realise what he had done and what it must have looked like to those watching. He turned a bright red when the thought hit him. But the Oannes could all read his thoughts and knew that thoughts of love for his wife and children were paramount in his heart and this expression of joyousness was simply a release of that emotion.

Brazjaf came and stood behind his wife and gently smoothed her reddened back vane by repeatedly running it between his two palms. Muznant looked back at him and gave him an affectionate smile as she turned about to face him. A private communication ensued and Brazjaf smiled lovingly at his wife.

Ashley came over to Brazjaf and also communicated his own thoughts. Brazjaf smiled and then in open communication to all conveyed, 'I am very relieved that it was Muznant who came up to you just then and not me.'

Ashley had to laugh at Brazjaf's sense of humour as did all the others too.

'Yes, I suppose the thought that I should be back home with my family soon just overwhelmed me,' he said aloud. 'I'm sorry if I hurt you Muznant but it was just instinctive reaction to my emotions that made me want to hug someone. And you were the closest to me; and the prettiest if I may add.'

'I heard that and I am jealous,' came from Captain Natazlat in the shuttle bay.

It was the custom for spaceship captains to meet aboard one of the ships and greet each other personally especially if they happened to be good friends.

The Starship 9110-Red was under extensive examination by the Oannes scientists and engineers after its extraordinary trip and Captain Natazlat had left them to their task. She would return to Nazmos as commanded and appear before the governing council of ministers to personally deliver a full report of all events on the journey from Earth. She would also receive a commendation in the Starship's log and be feted for the ship's accomplishments under her command. Ashley would be included in this report and so receive recognition of sorts. There were some among the ministers who considered Ashley a lucky chance happening and not the usual unacceptable Earth person.

They were in for a surprise. And the instrument would be that thorn in their proverbial side named Puzlwat. Ashley was grateful that Puzlwat was a good friend and would prove to be an ally in Ashley's case for Nazmos' relocation.

An emotion of alarm and stress suddenly filled the control room. Captain Rojazonto conveyed his anxiety that a shuttle was approaching the front shield of the distant Starship 9110-Red. It appeared to be getting much too close to the shield and could be in danger of being disastrously drawn into it.

'It's that engineer Niztukan again,' he said, 'he's out there checking the mass gain in the shield after its most recent FTL journey. It usually has a fraction of a percent increase but may be a bit more this time.'

Niztukan was 144 years of age and had spent quite a few years on Platwuz as a mining engineer. He had got used to the gravity there and claimed that a stint at the higher gravity level did wonders for one's physiology. He recommended it as treatment for certain ills. But then he had failed his annual medical blood analysis and been diagnosed with high bone density and unusual calcium levels. As such he had been returned to Nazmos and given corrective treatment over a two year period. As an engineer he was exceptional and had joined the teams that generally monitored Starships. It was important that the shield's mass gain be measured accurately soon after each FTL journey in order that its true total mass may be computed and fed to Zanos on-board. It also indicated the intensity of the energy-medium in the space grid zone between Earth and Nazmos.

All eyes in the control room were on the shuttle craft approaching the Starship's neutron shield. Captain Natazlat had by now entered the control room and after a brief Sewa with her friend Captain Rojazonto also looked out at the drama unfolding 200 miles in front of them.

Apparently Niztukan had done this many times before and it had always caused the alarm bells to ring in the minds of those observing his manoeuvre so close to the ship's neutron shield.

Captain Natazlat communicated with Zanos on board 9110-Red to monitor and control the shuttle carrying Niztukan on his task. Captain Rojazonto asked his own Zanos on-board for a status report. Both bio-computer systems reported that currently neither Niztukan nor his shuttle were in any danger. There was of course enough shuttle power available to retreat from a 9g environment if necessary. It was however not permitted to approach to closer than a 4g level. The shuttle was loaded with delicate instrumentation and when Ashley went to a greater magnification view he could see into the shuttle and Niztukan was calmly going about his business. The blurred image of the neutron shield seemed awfully close but then these Oannes must know what they were doing thought Ashley. So far the bio-computers did not indicate any danger.

'Niztukan takes too many unnecessary risks in his measurement task,' conveyed Captain Natazlat to her colleague Captain Rojazonto, 'one day he will go too close to the forward shield. I get nervous just watching him as he does this.'

Ashley like everyone was also watching the scene unfold and wondered whether he should intervene should Niztukan express alarm at any stage. But all that came back was a mild emotion of humour from this Oannes man in the shuttle. It seemed as though Niztukan was teasing his watchers into thinking he was putting himself in danger.

Suddenly the shuttle began a swift acceleration towards the outer edge of the neutron shield and all seemed to hold their breath. But the appearance was deceptive at this distance. The shuttle was actually beginning a high velocity orbital flyby that would take it to within a couple of hundred feet from the centre of the shield. This was a safe procedure yet still fraught with unforeseen dangers. Any error in orbit velocity calculation could end in disaster. But Niztukan knew his business and the shuttle appeared to skim the forward shield and disappear into the blurry haze of its event horizon.

Once again there was an intake of breath from everyone and even Ashley felt a constriction in his chest from the anxiety of the event unfolding right there in front of them. However it was a relief when Zanos informed them that the shuttle 9604-Orange had successfully completed its measurements of 9110-Red's neutron shield mass increase and was currently enroute to Starship docking through airlock-4. Apparently the mass increase was similar to that of all the other previous FTL journeys.

Ashley accepted this as the norm since the sweep up of energy-medium by the neutron shield through the space grid was the same in all cases for similar distance travelled no matter what the FTL velocity. If one considered a ¾ mile diameter tube extending all the way between Earth and Nazmos then the energy-medium quantity inside this cylinder is what would have been absorbed by 9110-Red's neutron shield.

There was relief all around at Niztukan's safe completion of the task and Ashley queried whether Zanos on-board the shuttle could not have handled the operation instead. Brajam replied to this in the affirmative but added that Niztukan was an exceptional engineer and simply preferred the excitement of doing it his way. Niztukan had argued that there were aspects of the skim over the neutron shield which he could judge better than any bio-computer. The height sensors became erratic on close approach to the shield's event horizon. The Nazmos governing council of ministers could not refute this and so gave him the authority to do as he felt necessary.

Ashley received a visual of Niztukan and was surprised at how young he looked. He had got used to the age appearances of the Oannes and would have judged Niztukan to be under a hundred years in age. Perhaps one day they would meet.

'You most certainly will,' conveyed Brajam having picked up Ashley's thought, 'for he is to travel on 8110-Gold on our return journey to Earth with Captain Zakatanz.

It was now nearly eight hours since 9110-Red had arrived at its present location and it would be at least another hour for all shuttle activity to complete. Only then could Captain Rojazonto give the command to begin their journey to Nazmos.

Muznant and Brazjaf conveyed that a meal was to be served up in the dining hall close to their allotted cabins on deck-21 and central to the ship. Puzlwat informed them that he was not hungry and would stay on in the control room. He had aspects he wished to discuss with Captain Rojazonto with regard to their return journey and also of the relocation of Platwuz. Nogozat however said she would join the others as it was not good for her to go for long periods without a meal of sorts.

They did not have to wait long before a small internal Transporter craft arrived outside the control room and they all got aboard including both captains. Puzlwat changed his mind and joined them. There were shaft connections between all the decks and Ashley's stomach did a flip as they ventured down one of these. They were soon brought to the dining hall destination and they all alighted there. It was a large hall but practically empty. There were a few crew members present but mainly to supervise the buffet style layout of the food dishes. The group settled at one of the tables near the entrance before going up to view the dishes on offer.

Ashley served himself portions from three dishes which he recognised and knew he liked and returned to the table. It was the usual fare of Raizna, Starztal, Yaztraka and a few others. Those that Ashley did not recognise were explained to him by Brazjaf or Muznant. Obviously there was a greater variety of home grown food here as compared with that in Anztarza.

When Ashley had cleared his plate he decided to try some of the new dishes. Their taste was not too dissimilar from the known ones except for one that had a very spicy flavour. A sip of Wazu helped to ease the hot spicy taste. Muznant explained that this was a seaweed product called Milsony which left a strong after taste. It was very high in protein but did not take to cultivation. It was a natural product and did not survive outside the Peruga Sea.

It was now nearly nine hours since their arrival and Ashley expressed a wish to relax in his cabin before setting foot on Nazmos; he was feeling rather tired it being near the end of a busy day. It had been a long journey from Earth and Ashley felt mentally and physically drained. Had the eleven days of continuous telekinetic activity finally caught up with him? Perhaps.

Captain Rojazonto conveyed that the journey to Nazmos would take about six hours. It would be three and a half hours to within a million miles of Nazmos and then two and a half hours of decelerating travel down to the surface. As per the norm the neutron generators could not be operated closer than a million miles from any planet.

Muznant and Brazjaf also decided that a rest before arriving on Nazmos would be beneficial and the others agreed. The captain returned to the domain of his control room. Nogozat went to her cabin alone as Puzlwat said he'd first go to the control dome with Captain Rojazonto.

A bed had been specially provided in Ashley's cabin which was similar to all the others he had used. It was not long before he relaxed on it and eventually dozed off into a deep sleep. Zanos was a great facilitator in that respect.

In the control room Captain Rojazonto gave the command to Zanos that departure for Nazmos be initiated as soon as all facilities with regard to the Starship 9110-Red had been concluded; and that the neutron generators were to be operated shortly after to take the ship to its cruising velocity of 100,000 miles per second.

There had been a slight delay as one of the shuttles from 9110-Red had to wait for one of the engineers to complete an inspection task on the Starship. He wished to return to Nazmos with the completed results. Niztukan however would remain on the Starship for another few days as there were many things that he wished to check. Chief among these was the fluid operational functioning of the Starship's central platform. It was suspected that Niztukan might imitate the gravity of Platwuz just to remind himself of his time on that planet.

The Starship's food growing tanks did not need replenishment since the growing cycle had not had the opportunity to mature in the eleven days of travel from Earth. The arrival and departure locations for Starships on the Earth run were kept 200 million miles apart. When Captain Zakatanz's Starship 8110-Gold departed for Earth with Ashley in about two weeks time then 9110-Red would be moved across to that location.

9632-Orange began its journey to Nazmos just as Ashley had dozed off. And when he awoke again several hours later the ship was within the million mile distance from the home planet Nazmos. He queried Zanos on-board and was informed that arrival on the surface would be in a little less than two hours. Zanos then replied to Ashley's thoughts that Captain Rojazonto would be pleased to welcome him in the control room.

A mini Transporter was ready for Ashley when he came out of his cabin a while later. On entering the control room Ashley saw that his friends from Earth were already there. It had been several years since they had seen the home planet and they did not want to miss the first sight of it from space.

9632-Orange was in deceleration mode and so was travelling backwards towards its destination. The planet was thus not visible but overhead the Milky Way was brilliant among the clusters of stars on display. The whole sky was one mass of glorious shining pinpoints of light and Ashley thought how familiar it all looked. He could just as easily have been somewhere in the Solar System. He looked to see where it was in amongst all this lot but Orion was nowhere in sight. He was not discouraged since he knew exactly where to look in the overall background of stars.

The deceleration was going according to plan and so Captain Rojazonto conveyed that a glimpse of Nazmos was in order – especially for the new guest from Earth. The stars and Milky Way then began a slow traverse across the view panels till they faded from view as the brilliance of Raznat appeared. This was followed by Nazmos appearing with its night view foremost.

Raznat had a warm bright pinkish glow about it and did not dazzle the eyes like Earth's sun. Yet it brightened the surrounding sky such that no stars were visible. And it appeared slightly smaller than Sol but gave a brightness that was the equivalent of about 100 full moons. This came as a reply to Ashley's unspoken thought query as to Raznat's luminosity.

'Gosh,' thought Ashley, 'if there were a hundred full moons shining in Earth's night it would be practically as bright as day.'

For some odd reason Ashley felt a lump in his throat when he saw Nazmos for the first time. It was very unlike the colourful Earth in appearance. There was a light blue haze around it and hints of brown in the visible quarter crescent but in general it gave the appearance of a barren landscape. On magnification through the view panel the visible sea and land areas seemed to blend together as if they were one feature. But then on further magnification the towns and cities became apparent especially those lit up in the night areas. It was only then that Ashley noticed that there were no widespread clouds shrouding any part of the planet but rather a kind of hazy mistiness in areas; some more dense than others.

Ashley felt sadness at the lack of visible flora around the cities but knew that all this would change one day. At least if he had his way. The lump in his throat returned when he thought that in the very long term – like a billion years from now – Nazmos would be the future for mankind. A mankind who would by then have abandoned the hot, dry and waterless Earth.

If only Tania could see this she'd feel just as he did. Earth and Nazmos were both alive with vibrant life and deserved to continue as such forever. Zarama must be stopped at all cost. A pang went through Ashley's chest at the thought. Yes, he would stop it at all cost. The words were a poignant reminder of what he was prepared to sacrifice if necessary.

Ashley felt a love for Nazmos just as he could see it now and Muznant reading his thoughts felt proud that she had chosen the path taken way back in 2003 when first contact had been made with Ashley; the person she now believed was the future for her planet and her people. Ashley had learned to keep his mind open to hold nothing back from these people. His thoughts were his personality and he wanted to be known and understood for what he was; a genuine person with malice towards none.

Rojazonto then had the ship turn about to resume its proper deceleration status and Nazmos and Raznat disappeared from view. Once again the stars became brilliantly displayed overhead and all around in the view panels. The time went by quickly and Ashley came out of his reverie when Zanos conveyed that 9632-Orange had entered the outer limits of the Nazmos atmosphere.

Gradually the sky colour went from black to a deep blue and the ship slowly changed its course to follow a sideways velocity as the gravity of Nazmos took a hold. As the ship descended to an altitude of fifty miles the curvature of the planet became visible. Ashley thought of his first trip to Anztarza in November 2003 with Captain Lyzongpan in 11701-Red and how the Earth's horizon had looked as they sped across Antarctica at eighty miles up and 12,000mph velocity.

Zanos conveyed that Wentazta was a thousand miles away and that landfall would occur in twenty minutes. The spaceship parking area or spaceport was a few miles outside the city and fleets of Transporter craft awaited their arrival. As the ship got lower and slower the visible scenery became more enchanting. The land was predominantly light brown in colour but also had large patches of pale green and yellow. Ashley assumed that this was the type of vegetation that survived on Nazmos. In general he knew that Nazmos was a planet that was much cooler than Earth overall.

He thought about returning to his cabin to retrieve his overnight pack but Rojazonto said that all his items would be delivered to his allotted accommodation on Nazmos. Ashley smiled at this and thought 'was nothing private?' Apparently not in this telepathic mind reading society but that had been his choice to have kept his mind and thoughts in open mode.

Then suddenly as if by magic the city of Wentazta was there below them. Ashley could make out buildings, domes and cones of structures that continued into the distance as far as he could see. 9632-Orange was now barely moving and then stopped as they approached the spaceport. He did not feel anything as the ship settled to the ground. Apparently the ship remained in a partial hover mode as multiple antennae like legs extended to the ground.

'Welcome to Nazmos,' said Captain Rojazonto to Ashley and the others. 'You are all to accompany me to meet the governing council of ministers. They await you in the Great Domed Hall.'

Muznant and Brazjaf came up on either side of Ashley and Muznant mischievously whispered, 'There is no escape now.'

Puzlwat and Nogozat followed behind with Brajam bringing up the rear. They boarded the small internal Transporter and floated along for a distance then entered a vertical shaft that went down through all the decks till it exited into the open air underneath the ship.

It looked impossible but the massive bulk of 9632-Orange seemed to be balanced on about ten very long slim antennae type legs. Surely they could never support the entire weight of such a huge ship thought Ashley. The captain smiled at this thought and conveyed that only a very small percentage of the ship's mass was on these legs. The main mass of the ship was still supported upwards against Nazmos' gravity by the ship's impulse motors. The legs were there only to keep the ship at a set position upon the ground. Ashley nodded his understanding.

The small Transporter moved along under the spaceship and manoeuvred onto a much larger Transporter some distance away. Captain Rojazonto transferred to the deck of this Transporter and the others followed suit. The small Transporter lifted off and returned to the spaceship. There was a constant stream of these to and from the underbelly of 9632-Orange and all seemed to follow a similar pattern.

Ashley looked at the Transporter and noticed that it was about twice the size of the ones in Anztarza. However these had no handrail but instead had a three feet high parapet wall surrounding the outer perimeter of the deck. And it was about a foot in width at its top with holes at regular large intervals. Muznant conveyed that these were for use when erecting a canopy over the decking in adverse weather conditions. Today was fine as would be the case for the next few weeks according to the forecast. The weather on Nazmos was very stable and so quite predictable. Ashley replied that such conditions might alter when Nazmos was warmer. He noticed a slight chill in the air though it did not seem to bother the Oannes who thrived on the cool conditions. And yet those who lived in Anztarza loved the green forests of Earth and its warmer climate.

Captain Rojazonto conveyed that they must first and foremost meet up with the governing council of ministers as a matter of priority and etiquette. This was in response to Ashley's thought request for a brief aerial tour of Wentazta.

The operator of the Transporter was given the okay by the captain and the lift off was quiet and smooth. They rose to a height of 150 feet and then proceeded at a slow even pace towards a visible large domed structure some three miles distant. It stood out among the surrounding structures which in the main were a block type of construction and not as tall. Otherwise the buildings which Muznant pointed out as residential homes were not laid out in any symmetrical or rigid line pattern. The streets were only pathways between accommodation areas since all transportation was of the aerial type. Many of the houses had smaller Transporter like vehicles in varying designs perched on their roof terraces.

Ashley looked into the distance and the houses seemed to continue on forever and he queried this. Puzlwat supplied the answer and said that Wentazta itself could be considered larger than all of London including the greater London area as well. It took up an area the equivalent of two thousand square miles in a quadrangle approximating 50 miles by 40 miles. The larger section bordered the shore of the Peruga Sea.

In fact a large portion of the old city went beyond the shoreline and down into the sea bed area which was where the Rimzi people preferred to live. They kept to themselves and seldom ventured onto the land areas. They were deemed strange and had little to do with the Oannes on land. Once a year a member of the governing council of ministers who was known to the Rimzi ventured into their domain and briefed them about the main decisions made by the council. But there was never any objection to whatever had been planned. They had no system of organised officials but had a handpicked few who met and politely listened to the communication by the Oannes council member. Although they were polite and formal they never offered a Sewa as a welcome or a farewell. The annual meetings seldom lasted more than a few minutes. Ashley could recall similar communities on Earth; each to his own he thought. Then a thought entered Ashley's mind that the Rimzi had other colonies and cities spread about in the Peruga Sea and at considerable depths. They had their own undersea culture and divulged nothing to the land based Oannes. A vision of a densely populated sea flashed before him. Ashley puzzled over this but made sure his mind blocked off all this information permanently and hid it deep down in his subconscious. He sensed a dislike between the two cultures that went back eons. It was a danger area never to be raised. A thought flashed through Ashley's mind but was gone before he could make anything of it. One day he would recall the moment.

The Transporter then entered a large portal to one side of the large domed structure and it took a while for Ashley and the others to get used to the relative dimness of the building's interior. As the Transporter settled down in the central plaza he thought it was very much like the Dome-4 of Anztarza.

Waiting to one side was a group of very distinguished and brightly dressed Oannes men and women. These were the governing council of ministers' representatives who had been delegated to welcome Ashley to Nazmos.

When Ashley alighted off the transporter he did not hesitate in proceeding forward on his own. He stopped a few paces in front of this group of distinguished Oannes and stood ramrod straight with arms stiffly at his side and feet firmly together. He then gave a slight bow at the waist before returning to stand stiffly upright and waited for his hosts to make the next move.

The leader of the representatives Nerbtazwi knew all about Ashley from the reports over the years and was pleased that he had observed their custom of coming forward and presenting himself and then waiting acknowledgment by his hosts.

By now Muznant and the others had also come up to stand beside Ashley with Muznant being right beside him. This was to indicate that she alone was to be his sponsor before the council.

Nerbtazwi was 320 years of age and she smiled with pleasure at this polite and handsome earthling standing so tall and trim before her. By comparison she was just four feet in height having shrunk considerably with age. She had to look upwards to see Ashley's stiff lipped seriously composed face. But when Ashley saw her smiling at him he too turned on the full force of his charming smile and relaxed his stance. He liked what he saw in this diminutive lady and suddenly his chest filled with instinctive affection for her. The emotion was mutual and it filled the room with an aura of charm. And Muznant thought 'not again' when she realised that Nerbtazwi had fallen under the spell of Ashley's charm and taken an instant liking to him.

The formality of Sewa was then performed telepathically which covered a detailed enquiry that took but an instant. Ashley responded to each and every solicitous enquiry with an eloquence that surprised his hosts. And that too was over in an instant.

Now Nerbtazwi stepped up to Ashley and raised an arm up towards him. Ashley went down on one knee and took the hand offered and allowed his mind to be deeply probed. But he did not respond in kind. It was not the etiquette for him to have done so as it would indicate mistrust on his part.

'I see what it is that you wish,' conveyed a more serious Nerbtazwi, 'but that has yet to be decided.'

'Yes,' replied Ashley, 'and that is for me to convince you that what I desire is the right path to follow.'

'Come then and meet with our governing council of ministers up on the dais,' she conveyed.

'It will be my duty and my pleasure,' said Ashley aloud but in a soft and respectful voice.

Nerbtazwi smiled broadly at this and said aloud in a surprising clear soprano type singsong voice, 'Come follow me and have a care what you say.'

She turned then and Ashley stood up and followed as she walked rather speedily towards the far end of the hall. They passed groups of Oannes some of whom were seated while others stayed standing. Ashley looked from side to side as he followed Nerbtazwi and made eye contact with as many of the Oannes people there as he could.

Finally when they stopped before a large dais on which sat about twenty or so very elderly and distinguished looking Oannes personages. Nerbtazwi did the formality of presenting Ashley to the Nazmos governing council of ministers and conveyed that she had read his mind and he was in fact the person Ashley Bonner that had been invited to Nazmos. This was a custom of verification whenever a guest was presented for the very first time.

Again Ashley stood stiffly to attention and made that slight bow to his esteemed hosts. But this time he smiled as he looked up towards those seated on the dais. In the process Ashley was not aware that Nerbtazwi had taken a place beside him and also faced upwards to the council of ministers. This was a surprise to all present especially to Muznant. It indicated that Nerbtazwi had accepted Ashley and was prepared to personally sponsor him too. Muznant stepped forward and stood on Ashley's other side. And then Puzlwat also came up and stood beside Muznant. This came as a surprise to the council of ministers for Puzlwat was well known to them.

Korizazit was a senior member within the council of ministers and he now came forward to the edge of the dais and beckoned for Ashley to approach. Ashley did so and again the handshake was repeated. Of course this was a personal verification by Korizazit of Ashley's inner intentions and Ashley let it happen. But this time he felt a deep probing of his thoughts and allowed his affection for his Oannes friends to become a prominent emotion.

Just then Ashley's inner voice revealed everything there was to know about all the members of the council of ministers there on the dais as well as those that were absent. Korizazit jerked backwards and pulled his hand away from Ashley but there was wonder on his facial expression.

431

'How did you do that?' he queried telepathically. 'You have not only learnt everything about me but also about all the other ministers including those not present here today.'

'Forgive me,' said Ashley aloud, 'but that was not a voluntary intention. I have been granted many gifts and one of them is that information is given to me by an inner voice should I but query a subject. It happens automatically so please believe me when I say I meant no disrespect.'

'I thought I had been briefed about you Ashley,' conveyed Korizazit, 'but this feature was never indicated.'

Korizazit was 290 years of age and single in status and had been on the governing council for nearly ninety years. He was most discerning in his intuitiveness and could instinctively sense when things were not right. As such the council of ministers trusted his opinion and so he had been nominated to probe Ashley's inner being. And in the process of that deep probing he had triggered Ashley's inner voice which had seemed to speak to him also. And now that same inner voice seemed to have taken root in his own head too. The gift that Ashley possessed was now also his to be employed whenever convenient. Korizazit was elated and felt like a child with a new found toy. He felt youthful again and his emotion of joyousness welled up and filled the hall. He conveyed all this to the council of ministers and they too wondered at what had taken place.

Then another member of the council stood up and invited Korizazit to return to his place. This was Ritozanan who was a prominent decision maker within the council. She was 310 years of age and well respected by the people of Nazmos. She too was of single status and renowned for her astuteness and dedication to the council.

'I should like to address Ashley in a manner that can leave no doubt about his ultimate intentions in regard to Nazmos and our Oannes people,' she conveyed to her fellow council members.

She then turned and looked directly at Ashley. She was not smiling.

'Ashley,' she said telepathically, 'please inform the council of the thing that you most desire. We know that you can relocate Platwuz for us as we desire it to be closer to Nazmos. Our scientists will guide you in this just as they did with the Triton experiment. That was most successful. We also know from Brajam who supports you in this that you desire Nazmos to become more like Earth. We in the council cannot agree with this view as the change in Nazmos' climate may not be to the advantage of our people. We also have the Rimzi to consider and what effect a new climate would have upon them and their lifestyle. We understand that your intentions are altruistic and you are well known and respected by all in Anztarza. But here on Nazmos it is different. Our people like Nazmos just as it is so why should they desire a change? So Ashley, we respect you and will listen to what you have to say. Please speak openly and freely.'

Ashley had never seen Muznant look so dejected. To her it seemed as if the council had already made up its mind against Ashley's plan for Nazmos. Even Puzlwat appeared downcast and his thoughts went out to the council to present his own argument in support of Ashley. But he could not do so unless given explicit permission. The council was strict in its code and had already read the minds of all those standing before the dais. As far as Puzlwat was concerned he felt their case was lost.

He looked at Ashley's back and noticed a change in stance there. Suddenly Ashley looked taller and a new resolve seemed to emanate from him. This was a new and very different Ashley. He saw Ashley turn to the left and slowly and purposefully walk in even measured loud-heeled steps to one side of the room. And he stood there for a minute which seemed like an eternity to his friends. And then he spun around to face the room. His face had reddened and the fierceness in his eyes was clearly visible. His jaw line had a hard set to it.

Muznant's heart did a flip when she saw this new aspect of the man she adored. And suddenly she felt sorry for the twenty council members on the dais. They had no idea of the true measure of the person they were dealing with.

Ritozanan watched Ashley with a sardonic smile on her face and thought he was being dramatic before he presented his argument. She had seen Puzlwat do the same when he had presented his objection to a particular project he didn't like. She then tried a quick mental probe of Ashley's mind but was shocked at the protective shield around him that prevented this. It was not a mind block as was normal but this was something much more potent. A chill went through her as she realised she had made an error in judgement. She had not only grossly underestimated this person but she had foolishly antagonised his inner being. Her premonition was a dread of what he was about to say to them. All she could now do was to wait.

'I speak to you aloud so that my words will be remembered,' said Ashley in a surprisingly calm and mellow voice but with a serious expression on his face.

He looked around and then smiled at his friends grouped in front of the dais before he continued.

'I also speak with a telepathy that is powerful and will reach to all of Nazmos' citizens including the Rimzi. I thank the council for giving me this opportunity to speak to you all as I have much to say.'

'But first I must tell you about Gozmanot. She was the wisest Oannes on Nazmos and she lived 36,520 years ago on the island of Vaz far out in the Peruga Sea. She had been confined to her sleep tank for nearly fifty years with a sickness others believed was in her head. But as she approached her 500th year of life, older than any Oannes person before or since, she began to see visions of the future. It was only after nearly a year that the local council members began to take her seriously and kept a record of everything she conveyed. Much of it was repetitive and confusing but because of her age and previous wisdom many took her visions seriously; though others did not. Shortly afterwards she died and was soon forgotten apart from the fact of her having reached such a great age. But even that gradually faded from memory. At that time Nazmos and Earth were twice their current distance apart.'

Ashley paused for a moment to allow what he had said to sink in. Then he continued.

'Some 500 years passed and a new generation lived on Nazmos. It was a young Oannes male in his seventies named Duntazaf who accidentally rediscovered the records of Gozmanot's visions. Of course he did not know of her or even about her but the abstract predictions seemed to strike a chord in his psyche and he finally brought it all to the attention of the central governing council. He also managed to interpret some of the records and to connect them to reality. Throughout his life of nearly 400 years he continued to unravel the records of Gozmanot's visions but had only partial success. As the millennia passed the old records got altered and misinterpreted though only slightly and so became legend. That is how your myths originated.'

There was another moment of pause for Ashley to gather the thoughts he was receiving before he continued.

'You know much of what is recorded there and it was only upon your discovery of Zarama's approach that you began to consider the myths more seriously. Disaster loomed but the myths said that a being from another world would be the instrument of salvation. Zarama was described as the 'fiery monster in the sky' and Earth was simply 'a faraway sky-place'. 'And it will bloom anew' is also referred to. Let me tell you of Gozmanot's visions before any recording began. That first year all she saw was beauty. People around her thought she was dreaming when she conveyed images of vegetation climbing out of the sea and covering Nazmos. In her mind Gozmanot saw Nazmos as a lush green planet – or was she seeing Earth? 'It will bloom anew' are the words written and can you doubt what she saw in her mind? Earth was already lush with vegetation and so was not being referred to. No, she was seeing a vision of Nazmos of the future; a future that approaches and which you can do something about. What I have told you is true and you know it is because of my gift for seeing the history of the past.'

Ashley paused again to rest the dryness in his mouth.

'I have told you of their origins and ask why you would wish to go contra to your myths. What Gozmanot saw was the truth that will come to pass and I request the council not to fight against it. The next question I must ask you to consider is that why it was that someone from Earth was given the power to stop Zarama. I will tell you. It is because Earth and Nazmos are to become one civilization.'

'Yes, Earth will in time progress to your level and integrate in a manner to your liking. Earth has only about one billion years of life left to it before its Sun scorches it into a waterless arid planet. Nazmos on the other hand will continue comfortably around Raznat for at least another trillion years without change. So Gozmanot's vision 'others will come' saw that Earth people in the very long term must find a home on Nazmos if not elsewhere.'

Ashley then walked to the food recess behind him and picked up the glass of Wazu that he had requested. Returning to his previous position he took a few sips of the Wazu and then looked up at the council members.

'Here is what I propose on the basis that none of you has the reality experience of what Earth is like. So I ask you to come and see Earth, its forests, its permanently frozen tundra areas and its lakes and seas. All those in Anztarza love to wander the northern forests, albeit in secrecy, and they go there whenever the opportunity permits.'

'I will take you there in six days travel time even faster than our journey here. Spend a few days in Anztarza and communicate with its people and hear what they think. And most important of all I would like you to go and walk in the northern forests and experience the chill of the northern Tundra in their summer time. I want this so that you have a first hand experience of at least a part of the vision that Gozmanot saw. Earth still has vast regions that remain frozen all year round just as Nazmos has. Those areas will not change even when Nazmos is nearer to Raznat. And when you are satisfied that you have seen enough I shall bring you back to Nazmos in another six days of travel.'

Once again Ashley paused as he sipped his Wazu.

'I would then ask you to consider more logically about relocating Nazmos as Gozmanot foresaw its future. What she saw was the truth and I believe she could not have seen it if it did not actually exist in the future. That future exists and nothing you decide can change it. I have yet to move Platwuz closer to Raznat and will do so before we journey together to Earth. Nazmos would be an even simpler operation.'

'Your citizens have all heard what I have just said to you and I shall relay to them all the images and experiences of your visit to Earth. They will see for themselves what Nazmos could be like. If you still reject the idea then I shall say that Gozmanot weeps for her vision and I shall be sorry for her memory.'

'But your decision does not need to be made then or even after I have returned to Earth for the second time after your visit. No you have a period of about twenty two years in which to make up your minds. The movement of Platwuz will be initiated in a few days. I shall start its elliptic journey to a position around Raznat as you desire but I must finalise its orbit when it reaches location in twenty two years time. That is when I must return and that is when I will desire your decision. In that period I hope that more of your citizens will travel to Earth and see for themselves what the future of Nazmos could be.'

Ashley now turned about and replaced the empty glass in the food recess and then walked back to where Muznant and the others were waiting. But this was not an idle walk for while he was doing so he was also sending out a very strong hypnotic auto-suggestion to the whole planet and implanting a curiosity for the conditions on Earth. It was like an emotion of affection that went out to the council of ministers, those in the hall and out to everyone on Nazmos. Even the Rimzi living deep in the Sea of Peruga received Ashley's message.

There was a long wait before the elderly Ritozanan stepped down from the dais and approached Ashley and the group. She reached out and upwards to touch Ashley's face and he let her with a smile on his lips. She stepped hastily back and stared at him.

'How have you done this,' she said, 'it is unheard of?'

'I have a protector and a shield has been put around me,' conveyed Ashley. 'I know what you are trying to do and it will not work. I am a private person and from now on my thoughts will also remain private if I wish it. Those who know me trust me in all things. Perhaps you will come to know me on our journey to Earth.'

'How do you know that we will agree to that,' said Ritozanan in a whispered voice, 'for we have not said we would visit Earth?'

'It has already been agreed in the minds of the council,' said Ashley, 'I was informed of it. Korizazit will confirm this.'

'Yes,' conveyed Korizazit, 'the inner voice that tells Ashley everything has foretold that our decision will be to agree to the visit even though we have not as yet discussed it.'

Now Ritozanan appeared downcast. Her frame seemed to slump as she realised that Ashley was the stronger of them. But it was in her nature to accept what she could not control. Ashley saw what was going through her mind and couldn't help but like the little old lady. She had been like Puzlwat with the initial antagonism but had accepted that Ashley might get his way.

So he came up to her and took hold of her tiny wrinkled hand and leaned down as he held it to his cheek while opening his mind to her. Like a thirsty sponge she probed deep and intensely and all she came up with was a mind that was pure and full of love; a love that longed to be back with his wife and children and a secret wish that these powers had never been bestowed upon him. She also saw that he offered his life in exchange for the destruction of Zarama. And he actually believed that such might be the case and yet still persisted in fulfilling the big task. Ritozanan puzzled at this expression but then read that Ashley had known that a big task lay ahead of him before ever meeting the Oannes of Anztarza. Perhaps there was something to this Earth religion thing after all.

She lowered her hand slowly and thoughtfully returned to her seat on the dais. Ashley knew that a telepathic conference was in session but which lasted barely a minute. He also knew that every aspect of his speech was discussed and all the pros and cons highlighted.

Then another member of the council named Dultarzent who was extremely thin stood up. He was the senior most council member with an age of 320 years and he conveyed that the decision of the council was to visit Earth as suggested by Ashley and that the journey would commence aboard 8110-Gold commanded by Captain Zakatanz in six days from now. The meeting was over and the council members prepared to leave.

Ashley conveyed his thanks and a brief farewell Sewa in which he wished them well. After the council members had all left there was a shuffling in the hall and the general public also prepared to leave. But when Ashley looked around at them they just remained standing and seemed to be waiting for something to happen.

Muznant nudged Ashley and conveyed that they were all waiting for him to leave first. It was the respectful thing to do for someone whom they considered worthy. Ashley felt embarrassed by the attention and began the walk to where the Transporters were parked. He looked to right and left as he walked and made respectful gestures with his head to all in general. As he nodded his head in acknowledgement he received similar gestures in return.

When the Transporter rose upwards and headed out of the building into the brightness of the day Ashley noticed that Raznat was low in the sky. He felt at home here though the air had a much chillier feel to it. And this was mid-summer here in the equatorial zone of Nazmos.

The nights will get quite cold,' conveyed Puzlwat, 'even though it is summer as you call it on Earth. In our winter time the days seldom get above freezing for a third of the Raznat cycle.'

'Then that is like many places in Earth's northern regions,' conveyed Ashley, 'so you see things will not alter that much when Nazmos is relocated.'

'That was a good suggestion you made about the council members visiting Earth,' conveyed Brajam, 'they will see how similar our two worlds are or will be afterwards.'

Ashley said nothing about his hypnotic auto-suggestion. The council must believe that the decision was entirely theirs. Muznant however looked at him in a most peculiar manner as if accusing him of an underhanded manoeuvre. But then she smiled and Ashley could feel her emotion of pride in him. He wondered what it was that she suspected.

'You must tell me more about Gozmanot,' she conveyed, 'I feel a connection with her but I don't know why.'

'That is because she is your very distant ancestor,' said Ashley. 'Perhaps you too may see visions one day.'

The look she gave Ashley could not be mistaken.

'I'm already seeing one,' she said in her soft low tone voice.

Ashley smiled back at her and then screwed up his face, looked upwards and said, 'Help Tania, I'm being waylaid by a designing woman.'

Muznant made a face at him and then turned and snuggled up against a smiling Brazjaf. He knew that his wife adored Ashley and he didn't mind it in the least. In fact he felt very much the same as also did most that met and came to know him.

The Transporter was up at 150 feet and moving gently towards the setting Raznat. Eventually after about twenty minutes it began a descent and settled in a plaza area that had only low type buildings around it. All disembarked and Muznant led the way through a gap between two of them. After a short walk Brazjaf pushed at a large arched door which opened fully of its own accord. They entered and Ashley found himself in a covered courtyard. There were plants in large glass tanks which Ashley recognised as Yaztraka trees that he had been conveyed images of when visiting the food domes in Anztarza. With subtle backlighting the effect was quite picturesque and surprisingly soothing to the eye. All the greenery in Nazmos grew in the seas.

An elderly couple were waiting by one of the tanks and Muznant guided Ashley towards them.

'This is Zazfrapiz and his wife Jazzatnit,' said a smirking Muznant to Ashley, 'this is their home and they have been given the pleasure of looking after us.'

Then she added, 'Jazzatnit is also my mother's oldest sister and so I too share the honour as do all my family.' Muznant was smiling broadly as she said this.

Ashley reckoned that she knew all along about this and had kept it a secret. Now he smiled as he stepped forward and looked at Jazzatnit. She had Muznant's eyes and general facial outline and Ashley thought she must have been very beautiful in her youthful years. A real beauty and he thought that Zazfrapiz must have been a looker too to have done so well.

The Oannes were past masters in reading expressions and thoughts and both elders were pleased at Ashley's admiration of Jazzatnit.

Ashley stood before them and waited as was the custom. The Sewa that followed was a formal one and quite extensive in its coverage. Ashley replied appropriately. Yes, his wife and children were all well as of eleven days ago. In fact everything was fine. However telepathy takes but an instant and then it was Ashley's turn to enquire after the wellbeing of his hosts. All in all his hosts were impressed by Ashley's politeness and custom awareness and his skill at telepathy.

'We have heard much about you over the years especially from Muznant's communications. You have many admirers here on Nazmos,' said Jazzatnit aloud and with a smile.

Her voice was a contralto with a slight quivering lilt in it which Ashley thought most enchanting. Ashley also thought it very polite of her to use his normal form of voice communication to make him feel at ease. Muznant would be jealous if she knew his thoughts.

'I am jealous,' conveyed Muznant privately. 'I shall tell Tania that you have a favourable tendency or should that be inclination towards presentable women regardless of age.'

'Tut, tut,' conveyed Ashley back to her,' I am only responding to the beauty I see before me. And may I add that it is not polite on Earth to make reference to a woman's age.'

It was then that Ashley learnt from Muznant that her Aunt was 329 years of age and her husband one year older. Ashley conveyed his amazement at this and how well they looked.

'Everything you do or say makes you more likeable to those around you,' said Muznant, 'and now Jazzatnit has become another ardent admirer. She finds you extremely handsome Ashley.'

Ashley didn't know how to reply to that and felt rather embarrassed. If only Tania were here at his side he'd feel more at home.

'Come,' said Zazfrapiz, 'I will show you to your quarters where you can rest and refresh yourself before our meal together.'

Both husband and wife led the way and Ashley followed with Muznant, Brazjaf and the others coming along behind out of curiosity. They stopped before a large single door which Zazfrapiz pushed open. Husband and wife entered and stood to one side as Ashley and the others all trooped in. They looked around in wonder at the large room which was divided into open plan sections. The sections were only obvious by different types of furniture in each. An Earth type bedroom was the one with the sleep tank alongside it. Beside it was a glazed door that went into the bathroom and shower facilities which was normally used by the Oannes prior to entering the sleep tank. The dining table and seating around it was clearly another section. There were no windows anywhere but a soft glow of lighting displayed beautiful holographic pictures of not only Nazmos scenes but some of Earth's greenery as well.

'We did not expect you so soon,' said Zazfrapiz. 'We expected your arrival after the normal journey time from Earth.

'It is just perfect,' said Ashley, 'I shall feel quite at home here thank you. I do like the paintings of Nazmos and of Earth. Perhaps it foretells of our future together.'

'When you are rested,' conveyed Zazfrapiz, 'please feel free to enter the courtyard and view all our displays. Jazzatnit and I are usually there during the day. We find it pleasant and relaxing.'

'Thank you I will,' replied Ashley telepathically.

It was nearly two hours before Ashley re-emerged and walked around the courtyard. He hadn't noticed how large an area it covered and the number of glass tanks on display. Each housed a variety of water plants that gave a brilliant effect. As he wandered from one to the other the names of the plants came automatically to him. There were many that were new to him and one seemed to intrigue him more than the others. It reminded him of a rose bush and had several red and yellow coloured blooms upon it. No name came into his head but he noticed that the glass of the tank had an uneven surface which slightly distorted the image of the plant. It seemed to ripple as Ashley moved. He then sensed a presence behind him and turned to see a smiling Jazzatnit.

'This one intrigues you does it not?' she asked.

'Yes,' replied Ashley, 'it is so much like a bush rose that I have in my garden on Earth.'

'That's because it is a rose plant,' she said aloud, 'but this one is artificial. It is the only such representation here and I had it made especially when we knew you were to be invited to visit Nazmos. Perhaps you could give it a name.'

Ashley thought for a moment and then said, 'I shall call it Rachel.'

He didn't know why he had chosen that when he had actually been thinking of Tania. But Rachel it was and his inner voice confirmed it to be the right choice.

'Rachel it shall be. You must bring her here on your return visit,' said Jazzatnit. 'You must bring your whole family to meet me and the pleasure will be entirely mine.'

'They will be with me on all my visits from now on,' said Ashley with a firmness coming to his lips. 'They will be with me when I return with the council of ministers after their trip to Earth.'

'It will be an honour to meet them,' said Jazzatnit, 'and any others of your family whom you wish to bring with you. And that is an offer of an invitation from me. You may tell the council as much.'

'Thank you, you are most kind. But you can meet them all if you wish,' conveyed Ashley, 'by travelling to Earth with us on this approaching trip.'

'Zazfrapiz and I are not good space travellers I'm afraid,' conveyed Jazzatnit. 'You see we both suffer from space sickness. Even short journeys leave us confused. But our age also restricts us from Starship travel except in exceptional circumstances. Thank you just the same but we would prefer to wait here for you to bring them to us. I shall instruct the council that you are to be permitted to bring all whom you wish. Zazfrapiz served on the council for a number of years before deciding that he did not like the decision-making processes. So we do have a little influence there. I would very much like to meet your parents.'

'Then I shall bring them with me,' said Ashley smiling. 'I know my grandfather would love to come too but I'm afraid that he has become much too frail to travel. He would love to meet up with his old friend Kazaztan and wife Zarpralt again.'

'Of course,' conveyed Jazzatnit, 'they knew of your visit and I have arranged for them to come here to meet you sometime tomorrow. They were taken by surprise at the early arrival of the Starship bringing you from Earth and insisted that they come to meet you. And they will be even more pleased to learn that you plan to bring other members of your family on your next visit. It is a shame that they themselves cannot travel back with you; their health and age prevent it. Ah, here come the others.'

Puzlwat and Brajam walked up together followed by Muznant and Nogozat. They were in the same clothing as when they had arrived except that both the ladies had fresh blusher and a faint lip colouring. In contrast Jazzatnit wore no makeup at all and Ashley thought she was the most regal looking of them all. It was her bearing and easy confidence of manner that made you like her instantly. And her smile although slight was very suggestive and quite meaningful. A hint of a promise was there for the discerning.

Muznant came up beside Ashley and linked her arm around his. Nogozat did the same on the other side as if to tell Jazzatnit that Ashley was theirs as they had seen him first.

'Ladies please,' exclaimed Ashley aloud but smiling, 'you mustn't embarrass our hostess with any lurid displays. After all whatever she wishes must be acceded to.'

'Come,' said Jazzatnit, 'Zazfrapiz awaits us at the dining table. He informs me that all is ready.'

The dining room was through a doorway more or less opposite to where Ashley had his rooms. It was rather bigger but had only a single long table with split backed chairs on each side. It had seating for twenty persons. There were several doors in the walls that Ashley knew must lead to rooms where the food was prepared before being served up. Zazfrapiz was there waiting for them.

The table was covered with about seven or eight different dishes and none of them gave off any steamy vapours. Most Oannes liked their food only slightly above room temperature as Ashley had discovered in Anztarza. And yet Ashley had also found it to his liking as the tastes were always fresh. Anyway most hot food on Earth tended to cool rapidly as the meal progressed. Tania had remarked that the second half of the food on her dinner plate tended to be about the same temperature as that served on the Oannes tables anyway.

The conversation at the table was pleasant and interesting. Jazzatnit liked the visuals that Ashley conveyed to her when he described his childhood days. She was fascinated that Ashley had loved the little dog Barclay so much. To her it said a lot about humans and their pet animals. No such comparisons existed for the Oannes.

Somehow the topic of conversation turned to Earth sunsets and their varied beauty especially after a storm had passed.

'Ours is due in about an hour,' said Zazfrapiz. 'You might find it interesting. We shall go up on the terrace to see it after the dinner Wazu.'

There was a zigzag path up to the roof terrace which they all went to soon afterwards. Raznat was low over the horizon and already its bright glow seemed to have lessened. Then Ashley noticed a faint pink halo around it which gradually deepened in colour to red and then to magenta. The sky too was beginning to darken when Raznat had sunk halfway into the distant horizon. A decided chill came over them as it sank even lower till finally with a sparkling wink it shut its eye and sank into the ground completely. The darkness held back for a minute before descending rapidly over them.

Zazfrapiz looked at Ashley and smiled as though to say 'Wait, there's more'. It was only then that Ashley noticed his reflection in the ten feet high glass panelling that surrounded the terrace on all sides.

At first a darkened hush settled over the entire area and then gradually a distant whispering sound came from behind them that grew in volume. Suddenly the glass panels vibrated with the shock of a strong gust of wind that seemed to race towards where Raznat had set. It only lasted a minute before diminishing as rapidly as it had begun. For some reason a total Lunar eclipse on Earth came into Ashley's mind. There were similarities of effects when its darkness occurred.

'We call it the 'Dark Wind' as it only occurs at Raznat set,' said Zazfrapiz.

Ashley understood immediately. As Raznat had set and its heat was lost the remaining warm air rose upwards and the cold ground air raced in to replace it. This cold air then settled over them and the wind ceased. He shivered visibly and seeing this Jazzatnit suggested they go back down into the warmth of the courtyard.

'The cold air does not affect us,' she said aloud to Ashley, 'as we are quite used to severe winters. But you will feel it because Earth has a much warmer climate.'

'Not everywhere on Earth is warm,' said Ashley, 'we have our colder latitudes too which are very much like Nazmos is in winter. Few people live there but those who do have become quite used to it.'

When they were in the courtyard again Jazzatnit conveyed her opinion of Ashley's desire to bring a more temperate climate to Nazmos. She said she was both for and against it. She was for it because it would bring land vegetation; but was against it because a way of life would be lost forever.

Ashley said he understood this and conveyed images of Earth's far northerly regions and of the Eskimo people and their way of life.

'On Nazmos conditions in its polar regions would still be frozen wastes just like it is on Earth today,' he explained.

'Then I am all for it,' said Jazzatnit. 'I only wish I could visit Earth and see it all for myself.'

'So do I,' said Ashley, 'so do I.'

In the courtyard it was quite mild but Ashley asked for an over-garment to put over his tunic. After some confusion one was provided but it was a sort of loose open sided soft tunic that fitted Ashley like a poncho. But it was nice and warm and he said so with his thanks.

'I would like to go up on the terrace again,' he said, 'I'd like to view the city of Wentazta and also the night sky if you please. The stars are not too different here and it would make me feel as if I was back on Earth.'

So they all trooped up onto the terrace again and Ashley looked all around. The city was mainly on three sides with the expanse of the Peruga Sea on the sunset side. It was really cold now but the city's glow lent imaginary warmth that was reassuring. There was no breeze but already a slight frost had settled on the terrace floor and on the composite furniture there.

Ashley looked upwards and the glow from the city reduced the number of stars that could be seen. But the main ones were there. He recognised Orion and it's slightly squeezed together pattern. He looked for the Plough but could not find it. But the Pleiades or Seven Sisters was clearly visible as was the cluster of stars highlighted by Aldebaran partway to Orion. Earth would be about there he thought on the opposite side of Orion and partway towards Sirius. The Milky Way was extremely faint and Ashley could just make it out. But all in all he felt that Earth was not so very distant after all. The star pattern was similar albeit viewed from a slightly offset angle. And of course there was no moon around Nazmos.

Ashley began to feel the cold through his extra clothing and looking at his Oannes comrades they seemed quite unaffected.

'I think I'll go down before I freeze to death,' said Ashley with a shiver.

He looked at Jazzatnit's horrified expression and quickly explained that it was just a humorous Earth expression signifying discomfort of some sort. He gave other examples such as melting in the heat, scared to death, frozen to the bone, loving someone to bits and many others.

The next day after breakfast when Raznat was well up in the sky, Kazaztan and his wife Zarpralt came to see Ashley. Kazaztan looked old with a tired expression in his manner. It was apparent that he was not in the best of health considering he was only 274 years of age. Ashley knew that although the Oannes lifespan was usually over 300 – nevertheless some aged more rapidly and fell far short of that mark. However Zarpralt his wife looked fit and well.

Both were overjoyed to see Ashley again and asked why none of his family had come with him. Ashley conveyed all he could about his family with full visual images of them. He also told them about Eric his granddad and they were sorry to hear that he was not as strong or his health as good as before and that his age was telling on him.

'He has never mentioned this in his yearly communications,' said Zarpralt, 'and we had hoped that one day he would travel to see us. But Kazaztan's health has also diminished and he begins to feel the cold of the nights. He longs for Anztarza's domes with its controlled climate conditions. The hundred years we spent there were most memorable.'

There was a nostalgic sadness in her thoughts but also concern for the current health of her husband. They had got used to Anztarza and the cold of Nazmos was not to their liking. They would welcome the warmer conditions from a Nazmos change of orbit.

They stayed just over an hour and left a communication package for their friend Eric. Ashley said he would see his grandfather soon and convey in detail the images of this visit. There was a hint of sadness in their parting Sewa.

After they had left Brajam conveyed that a plan was needed from Ashley with regard to the Platwuz operation. But today was to be Ashley's day and he was to be given a grand tour of part of Nazmos. Tomorrow they would travel to Platwuz.

When a Transporter was summoned to take them to the spaceport both Zazfrapiz and Jazzatnit said that they would not be accompanying the group but would await their return that evening. Spaceship travel – no matter how local – was not to their liking. However all the others said they would come along for they had not done such a trip for a very long time.

The spaceport was twenty minutes on the Transporter and the blue striped craft they boarded was quite small at 90 feet long and 40 feet wide. It was 30 feet high and had large view panels all around its oval shape. It had two levels and was divided into several compartments.

They were welcomed aboard by Captain Lyozonpa who appeared very young. Muznant conveyed that he was 95 years of age and this was at a primary stage in his spaceship career. The craft was designated as a tour craft numbered 566-Blue and was restricted to local Nazmos duty. He had a deputy and two trainee cadets on board but they were in another part of the craft.

Captain Lyozonpa seemed in awe of Ashley and the others as he had heard much of their adventures – especially the Asteroids and Triton events. And now Starship 9110-Red had exceeded 200 FTL velocity and travelled from Earth to Nazmos in just eleven days. He was a keen spaceman and aspired to commanding a Starship one day. And now Ashley was to take the council of ministers to Earth and back to Nazmos at even greater FTL velocities.

The Sewa that Lyozonpa performed was extremely respectful and Ashley responded in kind. Then Ashley reached out and shook hands with the young captain and allowed his mind to be read. This was a gesture that was both polite and friendly and Lyozonpa was to remember it in the years to come. Perhaps Simon and he would meet one day, thought Ashley.

566-Blue rose silently up into the sky and Ashley looked downwards through a large rectangular view panel to see Wentazta spread out widely underneath. Gradually it seemed to diminish as they rose higher and at 100 miles up the ragged outline of the city could be made out. The outlying areas were very much like cities on Earth – except there was no greenery. There were no trees at all and Ashley hoped that one day it would be different.

The Sea of Peruga was vast and it had several large islands dotted around. One was particularly larger than the others and Muznant conveyed that this was Ventrazta and was where Nuztazm, a cousin of Captain Bulzezatna came from. As they proceeded there was an island on its own and about half the size of Ventrazta. Muznant said that this was the island of Vaz that Ashley had told the council of ministers where Gozmanot had lived all those millennia ago. Ashley looked at it and requested a pause above it. Looking down upon its barren landscape Ashley suddenly got a vision of it covered in lush forest but only for an instant. But that was enough for the view to be transmitted to all those on board 566-Blue. Little did Ashley know that it had also been seen by the council of ministers and most of Wentazta?

The tour then continued back to the shore and towards a large lake north of Wentazta. There were several towns on the lake shoreline but relatively small when compared to the big city of Wentazta. Muznant pointed and conveyed that one of these was Latipuzan her home town and that the lake was Voolzort. Ashley magnified his view panel image and Muznant mentally pointed out the street on which she had lived. There was much to see today otherwise Muznant would have taken Ashley there where her parents still lived. She would visit them soon even though she had been in communication with them last night and again this morning.

The craft 566-Blue then went on at great speed across the Peruga Sea and apart from islands dotted at intervals there was no large land mass to be seen. Muznant conveyed information on the extent of Peruga which surprised Ashley. It was larger than Earth's Pacific Ocean and yet the Oannes still referred to it as a sea. The surface area of Nazmos was 70% water and the landmass was just one large continent that spread north and south like an octopus with multiple arms. One of these arms spread north and made up the north shore of the Peruga Sea. A town there was called Partuzna and it was where Sudzarnt had originated from. He hadn't liked the cold there and had moved to a town on Lake Voolzort. After a year there he had gone to Wentazta and eventually to Earth. Now of course he was humanised and was Ron and Brenda's adopted son.

The flight continued and cruised over the upper polar region. Ashley wasn't surprised at the wilderness aspect of it. The Polar Regions on Earth were the same and little of it would alter when Nazmos moved to the intended closer orbit around Raznat.

The Raznat system was very much older than the solar system by up to three times. As such the core of Nazmos must have cooled rather more over the longer period. Ashley wondered if his inner voice had taken this into account when computing the amount of the change to Nazmos' orbital position. Brajam and the Oannes scientists had made their own calculations anyway and so far they had not disagreed with Ashley's inner voice instruction for the new circular orbital distance of approximately 19 million miles from Raznat.

566-Blue now turned into the night zone and really there was nothing to see below. But Ashley looked upwards at the sky and was stunned by the dazzling brilliance of the stars stacked in all their abundance. The Milky Way stood out grandly as a brilliantly bright pathway across the sky. It was stunning and Ashley tried to imagine where Earth and Sol could be. He looked for and found Orion but it was very low down near the horizon and looked different from this angle. In actual fact it was inverted to Ashley's view which confused him. Anyway his consolation was that Earth was in that general direction which was a pleasing thought.

He had been thinking of Tania and the kids and of their surprise when he contacted them on his early return. He must convince them to come back with him for the short return visit. Simon would get on well with Lyozonpa and would probably have a lot of questions to ask too.

Muznant was beside Ashley and gently squeezed his arm in sympathetic support; there was understanding in the looks he received from the others as well. Ashley was an open book as far as his thoughts were concerned and the Oannes read him well. And it drew them to him.

The craft once more entered into Raznat's light and Ashley could see the arid landscape below dotted with quite large lakes at fairly wide intervals. The Oannes towns and cities were concentrated within the equatorial zone though a few like Partuzna were further north and south. All of this could be dense forest one day thought Ashley. He couldn't help wondering how the sea plants would fare in the warmer climate. The answer was in Anztarza. The food domes there were at considerably warmer temperatures and the sea flora did perfectly well. At least that wasn't a concern. Hopefully the Wazu would also thrive where it grew.

During all of this 966-Blue had been cruising at an altitude of close to 100 miles and a telepathic running commentary was being delivered by its captain. Ashley thought of Lyozonpa like the captain of a tourist boat on the Thames at Westminster in London. He gave a very enlightening description of all the features passing below. When Muznant and her friends Wigzolta and Partuzna had first visited Wentazta Ashley wondered if they had gone on such a trip; after all they had also been tourists then. Muznant immediately picked up on this and said they'd had other interests then. Ashley smiled at this as he knew exactly what she meant. Girls at that age were no different on Earth.

Eventually Lyozonpa brought 966-Blue to a lower altitude as they approached Wentazta from the landward side and Ashley got a wonderful aerial view of the city. The tour around Nazmos had taken nearly four hours and now Ashley had a pretty good idea of the planets limitations on land. His case for orbital change was quite confirmed in his mind and now made more sense than ever.

They were welcomed back by Jazzatnit who informed them that her husband would join them shortly after his daily afternoon rest. She herself had decided to wait up for their return as she was much too wound up about this visit. She also mentioned that some friends would be joining them for the evening meal as all were keen to see Ashley in the flesh. They were of the older generation on Nazmos and were supporters of the plan to relocate their planet closer to Raznat. They all felt the cold which came with age to most. A couple of them had been to Earth and Anztarza a long time ago in their youthful years and the impression of a warm green planet had remained vividly in their memory.

Jazzatnit had arranged for a pot of tea with milk and sugar to be ready and placed in Ashley's room so that when he retired there his favourite hot drink would be at hand. And most welcome it was too when Ashley decided a rest would be good.

After a restful two hours he freshened up with a shower and fresh tunic and leggings before returning to the courtyard. The place was quite busy with about ten or so elderly looking Oannes couples dressed up in their finest tunics. But there were some single persons there too.

Ashley smiled his best smile as he came forward to meet them. But first he conducted his own form of Sewa which had a slight Earth flavour to it with a 'Hello and how do you do' followed by a hand shake. All replied easily and wished him and his family well. Being among them was a pleasant moment for Ashley and he communicated telepathically in an easy manner as if he were the host.

Jazzatnit and Zazfrapiz were not present and Ashley took the lead as substitute host. He said he was very pleased to make their acquaintance and hoped he would get to know them well in time. He also said that they all looked exceeding handsome. The colourful back vane gave each Oannes person a unique appearance but together in a milling group such as this it created a spectacle of synchronous beauty.

'But Jazzatnit is my favourite lady as I find her the most exquisite woman in style and beauty that I have met on Nazmos on this my first visit,' he said aloud, 'and of course Muznant is a close second, don't you think?'

It was obvious that they liked what they saw and were enthralled by his voice. So out of politeness they too began to converse with him aloud. Ashley was fascinated by the musicality of their delivery and thought how much Tania would have loved them for it.

Eventually Muznant and the others appeared at a far end but stopped to watch Ashley entertaining these senior citizens. They could see that he was perfectly at home in his role as host and Nogozat turning to her husband Puzlwat said aloud in a respectful voice, 'Now that is what you would call a perfect Oannes gentleman.'

'Yes,' he replied, 'and to think that I had mistrusted him and opposed his coming among us. I was so very mistaken and wrong in my opinion.'

Muznant touched his arm in reassurance and said, 'It grows stronger every time I see him do these things.'

'Yes,' came the voice of Jazzatnit right behind her, 'if only I was 200 years younger,' she said wistfully. 'But come, let us do our duty to our guests and that includes Ashley as well.'

The meal was in the large dining hall and all fitted along the long table with several seats to spare. Ashley was seated near the centre with hosts Jazzatnit and Zazfrapiz on either side. Because of the distance to those nearer the ends most conversation was telepathic. Ashley was quite at home with this and noticed that Muznant and the others of their group had taken seats farther out. This was to allow the new people to be entertained closer to the guest of honour.

There was a lot of food on the table and some dishes that Ashley had not seen before. But all were described in detail by Jazzatnit or one of the guests and Ashley tasted them all. He had to stop when he felt rather full up and as a joke he remarked that the strings from his stomach were causing his eyelids to close. A curiosity developed among the guests until Muznant explained that it was just an Earth expression to indicate when one was sated. The Oannes said they also got sleepy after a big meal especially now they were in their senior years. But they liked Ashley's remark and would try it out on their friends. It was so true they said but had never considered it like that. Of course no strings existed but it did give a connection of sorts and it was humorous to think so.

Ashley remained the centre of attention and proved his worth as a celebrity guest. Finally the party ended and the senior guests all made their Sewas and drifted away.

Jazzatnit and Zazfrapiz were immensely pleased with Ashley's performance today and wished he could stay on for longer. Perhaps he would when he returned with his family.

'When you return with your family,' said Jazzatnit, 'this is where you will be very welcome if you choose to stay.'

'Of course,' said Ashley, 'I would like nothing better than to be in the house of Muznant's very beautiful Aunt and her handsome husband. I have felt quite at home here and I'm sure I always will.'

But a sad thought crossed Ashley's mind when he thought of the distant future when he would return to conclude the Platwuz orbit change.

The next morning pleasant farewell Sewas were performed before Ashley and the others boarded the Transporter taking them to the spaceport. As they approached one of the large ships Ashley recognised it as 9632-Orange. The Transporter settled to one side of it and once again Ashley noticed the anomaly of its spindly support legs.

They disembarked and Ashley stood still for a moment looking up at the massive structure before him. It was as tall as a forty storey building and extended sideways to a length of nearly half a mile. The ring of viewing panels formed a curve along its length about its middle area. Its size was on a massive scale and Ashley knew that these ships were planned as the future for the Oannes population against the pending disaster that was Zarama.

The little group then boarded a much smaller Transporter belonging to the ship itself for internal use. It proceeded under the belly of the ship and then smoothly rose upwards to enter a portal. They kept going upwards for some time before venturing sideways into a corridor or passageway. It then settled to the floor and Ashley realised that they must be just outside the control room dome.

They were welcomed by a smiling Captain Rojazonto who was dressed in bright orange and red tunic colours. With the formalities of the Sewa greeting completed the captain asked Ashley what he thought of Nazmos.

'Wentazta is a beautiful city and I have met some beautiful people too. The tour of your world was most enlightening but I missed seeing the colours that exist on Earth. Perhaps one day,' said Ashley. He intentionally left his ending hanging in the air.

Ashley could be a politician when he needed to be for then he added that the Polar Regions were in fact very similar to Earth so in that respect he had felt quite at home.

Rojazonto understood what Ashley was trying to say. He had been there at the governing council of ministers with Ashley and knew of the orbital change plan put forward. He in fact agreed with Ashley whole heartedly and hoped the council would agree to it eventually. Then he conveyed the details of the task ahead with regard to Platwuz. It would be at least a couple of hours before the ship was ready to begin the journey. A large group of scientists and engineers had requested to be aboard the ship for its journey in order to monitor the event. Some were aboard already but some had yet to arrive from farther afield. Most were there to monitor and direct the telekinetic effort but others simply wished to witness the event.

Ashley requested permission to remain in the control dome until departure time. In the meantime there was plenty to see of Wentazta from this high vantage point. There in the distance was the high Domed Hall of the governing council of ministers. That had been a life changing moment for Ashley. He had discovered then that events were being controlled for him and not by him. Words and phrases had been formulated for him that he had not planned beforehand. He only knew instinctively that he had something to say and he'd said it. The history thing about Gozmanot was true and had come to him only when he had begun to speak. And all of Nazmos now knew that the island of Vaz had been a special place and would be from now on. Ashley wondered what new evidence might be discovered there. Little did he suspect the surprise that awaited him there?

Ashley then looked over the space port area and it seemed to continue on for a great distance. And further away he could make out a spaceship that appeared even larger than 9632-Orange. It stood apart from the others and was of a very different design. It seemed as if several conventional 9632-Orange type ships had been brought together to form this huge bulbous looking spaceship. Captain Rojazonto had been observing Ashley keenly and picked up his thoughts and puzzlement about the ship in his view.

'That is 98103-Pink that you are looking at Ashley,' he conveyed. 'It is our latest experimental vessel and was completed about forty years ago. It was conceived in answer to Zarama and would allow the evacuation of 90,000 of Nazmos' citizens for an indefinite period. The plan was to keep on constructing these ships until Zarama's arrival was imminent. This one has just returned from a ten year space trial with only 20,000 people on board. I believe the trial met all our objectives and has been declared successful.

'Where would you go and which star system would you select?' asked Ashley.

'That is for our scientists to reveal,' replied Rojazonto. 'But so far they have not found a suitable planet. Perhaps all this may prove to be unnecessary now that you are with us.'

Ashley knew what he meant and smiled back at him.

'Let's hope I am the one to stop the 'sky monster' as foretold by Gozmanot. But it is good to plan ahead as you are doing,' he said.

It was not very much later that all passengers had boarded and Zanos on-board informed the captain that all was ready for departure to Platwuz. Although Ashley felt no movement he realised that the ship was slowly gaining height from the wider view of the city that became apparent. The acceleration was not noticeable but as the land fell away and the sky began to change shade to a darker hue Ashley noticed the horizon curving in the distance. The sky became black though Raznat was still brightly visible on Ashley's upper right. Nazmos had disappeared below them. At an altitude of about 500 miles the ship shifted its angle to begin an orbit towards the northern polar region. Now Nazmos was visible again through the view panels in front of Ashley but he could also feel the increased acceleration pushing the ship to greater velocity. Suddenly the polar region was below them and then the night side of Nazmos became visible.

Nazmos rapidly fell away as 9632-Orange raced towards the outer limits of the Raznat system and where Platwuz was currently located. Soon Nazmos and Raznat were behind them and all Ashley could see was the glory of the star studded universe.

Platwuz had an orbit at one and a quarter billion miles from Raznat and was the farthermost of the four planets. The path to Platwuz was clear as both Rubabriz and Zraplat were far from the travel line. Zanos responded to Ashley's query and conveyed that it would take 8½ hours of comfortable travel to reach Platwuz. There was of course the million mile distance from Nazmos within which the neutron generators must not be activated. The central journey time would be 3½ hours when the ship would cruise at 100,000mps.

The stars were at their most brilliant and Ashley just could not get tired of gazing at the sight. The Milky Way was for him the most fascinating aspect of the heavens spread out all around him. The control room dome gave an exceptional all round view of the sky which he found most pleasant. The acceleration increased further and Ashley felt his extra weight especially when he tried to walk; he had to be careful not to stamp his feet as he stepped. The Oannes who worked on Platwuz had to endure a gravity that was 2½ times that on Nazmos. Ashley thought that he would like to experience that gravity by having his shuttle craft settle on Platwuz prior to the orbital change operation. Zanos informed Ashley that the ship's gravity level was currently 1.8 times normal in order to attain the million mile distance as quickly as possible.

'I think I'll go to my cabin and rest there,' conveyed Ashley to the others. 'I'd like to be fresh when we reach Platwuz.'

'That is a good idea,' said Brajam, 'I will do the same.'

The others decided to follow suit and when they got permission from the captain an internal Transporter took them to their allotted cabins on deck 21.

Ashley stamped into his cabin and flopped down on the bed provided. It was soft and he was glad to lie down in this higher gravity. Eight hours was a long time to kill and he began it with thoughts of home.

The days and nights on Nazmos did not coincide in time with Earth and Ashley had lost the relativity of each. But he thought of Tania and the kids and wondered what they might be doing at this very moment. Simon would still be star gazing and would be thrilled when told about the trip on the Starship. What might Tania say about that? And Rachel what would she have to say?

He hoped that his mom and dad could be persuaded to come to Nazmos too. Then there was Jerry and Milly and of course Margaret. Why did she keep coming into the picture?

And then Ashley switched his thoughts to his life during the intervening years between now and after 22 years when he must return to Nazmos to finalise Platwuz's orbit. He hoped then to also move Nazmos to its new orbit. He decided that for those intervening years he would just enjoy life with his family and watch his children grow to maturity. An emotion of joy enveloped him when he thought of the prospect.

And then Gozmanot's visionary 'sky monster' came into his thoughts and he knew that he must decide upon a timeframe for tackling it. He got a prickly sensation at the back of his neck when he thought about it. Gradually his eyes grew tired and he dozed. But then he dreamt of the old glowing ball all over again. All the flowers in his dad's garden were being sucked up by it and disappearing. The garden became barren and brown but then suddenly the glowing ball burst open and became a lovely big bunch of colourful flowers. And distant laughter could be heard just as Ashley drifted off into a deeper and dreamless sleep.

When he awoke hours later he felt rested and refreshed and the burden of Zarama had lessened. Was his dream a good omen telling of the future? A successful outcome, with Zarama vanquished?

Zanos responded to Ashley's time query and stated that the neutron generators were operating intermittently to slow the ship as it approached its destination. The operation would be complete in twenty minutes and then Platwuz should be visible at its distance of one million miles.

Ashley was surprised that he had slept for so long. But at least he would be fresh and alert for the Platwuz operation. He thought of a hot mug of tea with milk and sugar and after a brief moment went to the food recess across the cabin to collect it. His thoughts were of home as he sat on his bed with the mug cupped in both hands.

Brazjaf and Muznant communicated that they were making their way to the dining hall close to their cabins where a meal was to be served up shortly. For Ashley the thought of food brought on immediate pangs of hunger and he was keen to see what was served up. He found the Oannes food varied and full of surprises and had become quite fond of many of them especially the sweetened ones.

When he entered the hall there were a few others there and he greeted them generally. And then he saw Brajam with Puzlwat and Nogozat at a table on his right and walked across to them. It was a large hall and could probably accommodate at least a hundred if not a few more. Currently it was nearly empty and Brajam said it seldom got full since people came and went at random. Muznant and Brazjaf soon joined them at the table and said that they'd had to wait for a Transporter.

The food was laid out buffet style with some crew members present to supervise things and replace the empty dishes. The usual fare of Raizna, Starztal and Yaztraka were recognisable with a few others that Ashley had seen on Zazfrapiz and Jazzatnit's table. After he had a first course Ashley decided to try the seaweed product that he knew to have a spicy flavour and a strong aftertaste. But this time he had it alongside the sweetened Yaztraka mash. The Milsony was definitely better with the very sweet Yaztraka to remove the aftertaste. There was always plenty of Wazu in jugs and Ashley felt rather thirsty after the spicy dish.

The friends sat communicating for quite a while afterwards and then Brajam suggested they return to the control room dome to experience the landfall on Platwuz. This confused Ashley and he asked Brajam to explain. Brajam had a huge smile on his face as he answered.

'The ship does not need to enter a parking loop like it did for the asteroids or for the Starship,' he conveyed. 'We will use the gravity of Platwuz to good effect by occupying a position above it where the gravity conditions are the same as if we were on the surface of Nazmos. We began to refer to this position as 'Nazmos landfall' because that is what it feels like.'

'Does this mean that we do not need to use the shuttle craft for the operation?' asked Ashley.

'That depends upon you,' said Brajam, 'and whether you wish to be at a further distance from Platwuz to apply your telekinetic effort upon it.'

'And what is the 'landfall' position?' asked Ashley.

'That would be about 1,200 miles above the planet surface,' said Brajam.

Ashley considered this and computed that if Platwuz was nearly eleven thousand miles in diameter then at the landfall position its size in his field of vision would be much too large. He needed to narrow that down by moving further away. His inner voice came up with the answer as the number one. This meant that Ashley needed to be at a distance of one planet diameter away.

'I need to be positioned at a distance of eleven thousand miles from the surface of the planet,' said Ashley in a very matter of fact way.

'Then we shall need to make use of the shuttle craft,' said Brajam and conveyed this to Zanos and to Captain Rojazonto.

Zanos conveyed that the neutron generators had completed their operation and 9632-Orange had slowed sufficiently to approach Platwuz in normal deceleration mode. Landfall would be another two hours.

Ashley was curious about what Platwuz looked like from this distance and realised that there were view panels all around the central zone of the ship at the 15th deck level. Zanos had given him full plans of the ship's layout when they had first come aboard from the Starship. So now he conveyed a desire to go to that deck to view the planet for the first time. Muznant said that she would accompany Ashley. Neither she nor Brazjaf had ever been there or even near it. Puzlwat however said he had no desire to set foot upon Platwuz again as once was enough. The gravity and the cold were both excessive. Although the domes had been warm enough it was the gravity effect that was too oppressive for him. He didn't know how the mining crews tolerated the conditions. Apparently they became used to it like Niztukan but body calcium levels and bone density needed to be monitored closely. Yet the mining function was important for their Starships and for the essential ingredients used in electron stimulation. Their very existence depended upon it.

Muznant led the way out of the hall and onto the waiting Transporter. Brajam was hesitant since he had wanted to go directly to the control dome. But then he too agreed to accompany Ashley. He didn't want to miss out on what else Ashley might plan. Besides it would be nice to get his first view of Platwuz.

It was a smooth ride across the ship and then down to deck 15. They arrived in a thirty feet wide passageway that circled the perimeter of the deck. The out-facing wall contained the view panels which were six feet square and spaced at intervals of about fifty feet. They were positioned low to the deck floor so there was good viewing up, down, left and right.

As Ashley stood looking out at the star-studded sky he pondered over the coincidence that a Transporter always seemed to be at hand whenever they needed one.

Reading his thoughts Muznant conveyed, 'That's because you are a special guest and Captain Rojazonto has instructed Zanos to look after your needs. We ordinary Oannes are not so fortunate and might have to wait several minutes for the same facility. I'm glad that we are with you.'

Ashley hid his embarrassment by staring out through the view panel and searching downwards for a glimpse of Platwuz. Brajam was beside him and conveyed that Platwuz would be small and probably hidden under them by the ships floor. But a communication to the captain caused Zanos to alter the angle of descent and then Brajam pointed out the faint small ball of Platwuz among the starry background. Raznat was too far away to offer a great deal of light but once Ashley saw the planet he magnified his image and noticed its hazy outline.

There was an atmosphere around it which gave it its fuzzy appearance. Further magnification showed the rugged terrain on the surface. The mountains looked quite threatening but the whole planet looked exceedingly desolate. With even higher magnification some smooth circular features became apparent which were dotted at wide-ranging intervals. Ashley guessed these to be the habitation domes for the mining crews. On the whole the planet did not appear inviting and Ashley had second thoughts about having his shuttle touch down on its surface. Yet he would like to experience the gravity effect. Then the ship altered its position back to the original angle of descent and the planet disappeared under the belly of the ship.

Ashley stood back from the window panel and looked up and down the wide passageway and saw quite a few Oannes at the other viewing panels. The passageway disappeared as it rounded the curvature of the ship. He thought about the Oannes ships on Earth and realised that they were limited in size so that they could negotiate the undersea Anztarza access tunnel. Also they must fit into the hold of the transporting Starship. But on Nazmos no such limit existed. This was proven by 98103-Pink that Ashley had observed in the Nazmos spaceport. It was a true behemoth capable of carrying 90,000 Oannes for an indefinite period as Captain Rojazonto had described.

There was nothing more to see so Ashley and his friends decided to return to the dining hall and drink a few glasses of Wazu while conversing generally.

Brajam conveyed that it might be a good idea for his science team to meet up again and go over the Platwuz operation plan. Ashley and Brajam had already discussed the plan many times and a final sequence of action had been agreed.

A message was sent out through Zanos and over the next half hour about thirty Oannes scientists arrived in the dining hall. They arrived in small groups of twos and threes. Some had not met Ashley before and so came up and shook his hand in a friendly gesture. And of course Brajam and Puzlwat were well known to them. In fact all knew Puzlwat if not personally then by reputation.

These were the cream of the Oannes space scientists and although they could compute precisely what needed to be done their technology as yet did not extend to being able to affect the movement of a planet. They were here simply to assist Ashley in accurately performing that task. They would direct the shuttles into exact spatial positions for Ashley to apply his telekinetic gift. The other shuttles would be there to measure and confirm any changes in orbital velocity of the planet; and confirm when the required status had been achieved.

Platwuz was currently orbiting at a radial distance of 1.23 billion miles from Raznat and at an orbital velocity of 750 mph. This needed to be reduced down to 600 mph for Platwuz to begin its slow journey towards a perigee that was 100 million miles from Raznat. It would take 35 years for this to occur. Ashley had stated to Brajam and the Oannes scientists that he did not wish to wait that long. The human lifespan was short in comparison to the Oannes and so he suggested that Platwuz be given an additional push towards Raznat and so reduce that journey time to 22 years instead.

There had been general agreement to this proposal but Ashley suggested one further alteration.

'All of your planets follow a near circular path around Raznat that is close to a flat reference plane which you call the ecliptic,' he conveyed. 'I would like to alter Platwuz's orbit to one that is inclined to that ecliptic by about 15°. You and your instruments must be my guide in this. I do it for two reasons. The first is that I wish to avoid any effect that Platwuz may have upon either of its neighbours Zraplat or Rubabriz. The second is purely a safety consideration for the longer term in case of unforeseen circumstances.'

The Oannes scientists had nodded an agreement to this after some discussion and Ashley allowed his mind to be read for them to know exactly what he was referring to. If Ashley couldn't slow Platwuz when needed at its perigee position then he would not be able to stop Zarama either.

It was agreed that this second phase telekinetic push be initiated 24 hours after completion of the initial slowdown of Platwuz.

Brajam conveyed that Platwuz would enter its perigee position in 22 years at an orbital velocity of 27,200 mph. Ashley must then slow it down to 9,000 mph to stabilise it in its new orbit; a rather big task indeed.

The next part of the operation plan was delicate and for the benefit of the population inhabiting Platwuz in the habitation domes. It was to take account of the adverse weather conditions that were bound to arise as a result of the deceleration and acceleration of the planet.

Fortunately Platwuz had no large expanses of open water and so it was only the atmosphere that would be affected.

The Oannes scientists had calculated that Ashley's telekinetic push upon the planet must not cause an acceleration factor that was greater than 1% of Nazmos gravity. For this to be achieved they would monitor the planet accurately to direct Ashley in his push effort.

Ashley had conveyed that he would apply his telekinetic push in a graded manner commencing at his graded push level one. He would remain in normal mode just as he had done when accelerating the starships. Depending on the results Ashley could then increase the push level in steps of one push level whenever instructed. He said he hoped that all would go according to plan.

The Oannes scientists had calculated that to reduce Platwuz's velocity from 750mph down to 600mph at the required 1% of Nazmos gravity would take 113 minutes.

Ashley had specified that in order to effectively apply his telekinetic push uniformly upon Platwuz he needed to be able to view it as a whole. This meant his angular field of vision from the distance of 11,000 miles.

'I hope I shall be successful in all these things,' said Ashley, 'but it will be our success as a team.'

There were smiles all around and a telepathic hush as all aboard had listened in to the plan being reviewed.

Muznant then came forward and touching Ashley communicated that they should go up to the control dome. It was the proper etiquette to personally convey his entire thoughts to the captain who was in charge of this operation. It was the Oannes custom.

Captain Rojazonto was pleased to welcome Ashley and his friends back into the control dome. Mind contact was made when Ashley reached out and shook hands with the captain. Landfall would be achieved in the next half hour and already a faint glow could be seen at the lower edges of the view panels here.

Zanos then conveyed that 9632-Orange was stationary 1,150 miles above the planet's surface and that gravity was at the Nazmos level. Ashley thought this quite marvellous as the ship did not need to execute a parking loop in space. Also when his shuttle was moved out to the 11,000 mile location he should still feel some of the gravity of Platwuz. It would make the shuttle trip that little bit more comfortable.

In the meantime Ashley was at a loose end. So he made a suggestion to the captain for an adventure of sorts. He would like to experience the massive gravity of Platwuz and wondered if the captain could land 9632-Orange on its surface.

Ashley also had an information request of Zanos which was for a computation of the exact positions of the gas giant Zraplat and the small planet Rubabriz when Platwuz passed across their orbital paths. Zanos replied instantly that Zraplat would be at a position in its orbit that was 46° behind where Platwuz would pass above its ecliptic. And in the case of Rubabriz it would be 76° ahead in its ecliptic path around Raznat when Platwuz passed by.

Captain Rojazonto replied to Ashley's request to land his ship on Platwuz in the affirmative and for an altogether different reason. He had been in communication with the mining authorities and non-urgent issues had been diagnosed on several of the longer term residents. These were mainly staff members who provided support in the recreation and catering departments. They were showing abnormal levels of salts and irregularities in their blood analysis and had been listed for posting back into normal gravity conditions. In other words they were to be evacuated back to Nazmos. Just like Niztukan and others before him long stays on Platwuz often led to such a condition. The maximum period of duty was regulated at five years but many were rotated for two years on and one year off planet.

Since 9632-Orange was available on site the men in question could be picked up and eventually returned to Nazmos for treatment. All aboard were informed of the pickup request and that the ship would begin its descent towards Dome 32-Blue near the polar zone in exactly one hour. The stay on Platwuz would last a maximum of two hours and all personnel on 9632-Orange were given the option of using the reclining couches in their cabins to ease the high gravity conditions. They could also avail of their sleep tanks for the duration if they felt the need.

Ashley was pleased that he would get the opportunity to experience the high gravity of Platwuz. The maximum he had undergone was during the trips out to the asteroids on 520-Green under Captain Bulzezatna and that had been close to 1.9 times normal gravity. He remembered having difficulty in controlling his walk to avoid stamping around. He wondered how he would fare at the greater 2½ times gravity level. He would of course remain on the ship throughout the stopover.

Eventually Zanos informed all aboard that the descent to Platwuz ground level had commenced and that the ship was also moving in a transverse direction towards Dome 32-Blue. Estimated time of arrival was a little over two hours.

As 9632-Orange descended Ashley began to feel the increased gravity. After an hour he decided that he'd like to go to the viewing corridor on deck-15. He'd get a good view of the Platwuz surface from there. Muznant and Brazjaf agreed to join him as did Brajam. But Puzlwat and Nogozat said that they would ride out the increased gravity on the recliners in their cabin until normal gravity was achieved.

The ship was now about a hundred miles above the surface and the gravity pull was quite intense. Ashley thought it must be well above twice normal gravity. When Ashley got to the deck-15 corridor he decided to stay up against the view panel since walking about had become difficult.

The Platwuz landscape looked cold and arid and quite dark. However there were spots of illuminated features dotted around. The ship was traversing the landscape rather slower and at an altitude of twenty miles until suddenly a regular structure appeared right below them.

'That is the Dome-32 Blue,' conveyed Brajam to Ashley. 'We must settle on the flat area beside it and send a shuttle into the dome to collect the staff to be relieved.'

The ship was now quite close to the dome and moving towards it slowly. The gravity pull was now at its maximum of 2½ times normal. After several minutes Ashley felt that it eased as his body got used to it. It was interesting to watch the dome getting ever closer and it reminded him of the sea ferries docking at Dover and Calais. The scene was rather mesmerising for them all.

Ashley sensed that Brajam had a question to ask and so turned to him and asked what he wished to know. Brajam showed his surprise and then pleasure at this.

'I have been puzzling over why you decided on changing Platwuz's plane of orbit when it was known that neither of the other planets was under threat,' he said.

Ashley put his hand on Brajam's shoulder and conveyed his thoughts.

'It was done not as a whim my friend,' he said, 'but as a precaution. Nothing is certain in this life and it was just something that was stated by my inner voice. Twenty two years is a long time and I cannot be sure that an unforeseen event may not occur in that time. Let us hope that is not the case. And if I am unable to return for whatever reason then at least all of your planets will remain safe.'

'But what of Zarama' conveyed Brajam?

'Don't worry,' he conveyed with humour in his message, 'I intend to be here for a long time. At least as long as a normal human lifetime and long enough to fulfil Gozmanot's vision. And that includes the defeat of her sky monster Zarama. But I still believe that it was wise to be cautious and that was my reason for altering Platwuz's orbital plane.'

Muznant was dismayed that Ashley should even have contemplated his future being cut short. Brazjaf sensed his wife's emotional state and stepped sideways to bring his body up against hers. This was the first time that the awareness of the human lifespan being short as compared to the Oannes had been brought into the forefront of her thoughts. She would have at least another hundred years of life after Ashley and all his family were gone. It was not a pleasant thought for her. She would miss seeing him but would look back on these days with fond memories. Contemplating that future was a sad thought for her.

Their attention was diverted when Zanos announced that 9632-Orange had secured a footing beside Dome 32-Blue. Ashley had not felt the slightest judder or bump when this had occurred. All he could see was that the ship's lateral travel relative to the surrounding landscape had ceased. The Platwuz gravity did not seem all that much now that he had been under its effects for some time. Ashley reckoned that he could get used to it and begin to function quite normally. He now understood how the miners and dome crews could work in such an environment. As long as they worked indoors of course under the protection of their dome structure.

Ashley thought about the layout under the dome and instantly received a visual from Brajam that it was similar to the domes of Anztarza. The exception was that mining shafts existed therein that went down deep under the floor level. The mined ores were stored in large shuttle sized containers that were then placed in special areas outside the domes. Transport ships came from Nazmos and collected these at regular intervals.

It was just over an hour later when Ashley noticed movement of the landscape below. The ship was moving and began to rise upwards making the Platwuz ground fall rapidly away. The acceleration was only a fraction of Nazmos gravity but the build up of speed was continuous. When they reached the 500 mile altitude the ship was allowed to coast upwards as the pull of the planet continually decreased. Minor adjustments of power brought the ship back to the Nazmos landfall position and it was maintained there in hover mode by the ship's impulse motors. Once the gravity was at normal level all could once again relax in comfort.

The Oannes were in no hurry to begin the operation and last minute computations and calibrations were the order of the day. Typical Oannes thoroughness thought Ashley.

Zanos on board 9632-Orange would keep in constant communication with Zanos on all the three shuttles to be used for the orbital change operation.

Ashley knew exactly what he had to do as the operation had been worked out in such detail. He was just one factor in the overall plan. Without the Oannes expertise and technology he would have no idea how his push effort was progressing.

Captain Rojazonto smiled at Ashley and conveyed that they should all toast the success of the operation by drinking a glass of Wazu.

A food recess near the control dome entrance contained a number of jugs of Wazu along with an ample supply of drinking vessels. These were different from the ones in the dining hall being opaque in appearance with a bluish tint on the outer surface. Ashley thought they looked very elegant. A telepathic toast was said for the success of the operation and Ashley added an aside to it. Rojazonto raised his head at this but then nodded his agreement. Ashley had simply added that he hoped this to be a practice run for the Nazmos operation. In his heart Ashley felt that his speech before the council of ministers had found favour with a fair proportion of the Oannes population. The essential factor had been his revelation of the source behind their acclaimed myths; namely Gozmanot.

Perhaps his history gift had been given to him for this very purpose; so that Gozmanot's memory could be resurrected in the annals of Nazmos' forgotten history. Many of the Oannes could claim to be descended from members of Gozmanot's family though she had no direct offspring of her own. Ashley had conveyed to Muznant that she was descended from Gozmanot's family line through an older brother.

Ashley reckoned that this would be a major factor in the council's decision. And now he had an ally among them in the person of Korizazit who was a senior member of that august governing body. Perhaps Korizazit would also be guided by his newly acquired inner voice just as it did for Ashley. Perhaps the event back in the Domed Hall had not been accidental at all but followed a predestined purpose. The thought lifted a burden of doubt from Ashley's mind and suddenly he knew what the final decision about Nazmos would be. The Oannes liked to be certain of their decisions and did so slowly and carefully. Twenty two years should give them ample time for that.

But today Muznant and Brazjaf along with Puzlwat would be on the shuttle with Ashley. Brajam planned to be on one of the other shuttles with his scientific colleagues and their measuring equipment. The three shuttles would triangulate the velocity of Platwuz with a high degree of accuracy. It was important for Ashley to receive information on the result of his telekinetic push and thereby judge the correct push level to be applied by him. All communication would be through Zanos on-board and linked to the main bio-computer on 9632-Orange.

Captain Rojazonto conveyed that preparations be initiated for the commencement of the Platwuz operation. All persons for shuttle embarkation must first proceed to the suiting-up rooms. The mini-Transporter took Ashley and several others towards the rear of the ship and to the large room where the electro-static suits were stored. Once inside Ashley was thought directed to the correct size suits made especially for him. When they were all suited up in gold they made their way back to the Transporter which then ferried them down to the shuttle parking bay.

Ashley boarded shuttle 96324-Orange and took a seat at the front. The other two shuttles were 96326-Orange and 96329-Orange. On board the Oannes referred to the shuttles simply as numbers 4, 6 and 9. Brajam would be on shuttle 6. These were part of the shuttle fleet that had ferried them across from Natazlat's Starship 9110-Red. Beside Ashley were the others of his group but how he wished that his family were here with him as they had been during the Asteroids experiments.

The thigh clamps tightened and this made Ashley feel secure. He looked around and noticed that the shuttle was only half occupied. At the rear was a rather stocky looking Oannes who was obviously the crew member in command of the shuttle. Ashley discovered that this was Labztrazi and he was third deputy to Rojazonto with general responsibility in the upper decks habitation areas. This was the reason Ashley had not seen him in the control dome. He was 130 years of age and still single. He sensed Ashley's mind probe and nodded slowly to acknowledge that he accepted the query. A brief polite Sewa passed between them and the hint of a smile came across Labztrazi's face which made Ashley feel at home.

The other shuttles alongside filled up slowly and then the bay lighting dimmed. Shuttle doors were secured shut and then the large bay doors began to open. Silently all three shuttles lifted upwards and began a synchronised slow rotation to face the blackness of space outside. Brajam's shuttle was the first to exit the bay doors followed closely by Ashley's. The third Shuttle 9 followed behind and Ashley did not see it again until the end of the operation.

Things happened rapidly as the shuttle ahead raced away from both ship and planet. Ashley could not see the ship as it was somewhere below the shuttle floor. However the planet began to recede noticeably.

Then the shuttle began a traverse across from the planet that would bring it onto the line forward of Platwuz's orbit. It took half an hour for this to be achieved and Ashley felt the gravity effect from the shuttles acceleration towards its designated location. Then the deceleration began just as fiercely but with the planet in full view overhead. Shuttle 6 was a tiny speck several miles away but the third shuttle was nowhere to be seen though Ashley knew that it must be strategically positioned.

Ashley waited patiently in his seat for Zanos to confirm when the shuttle was correctly placed for the operation to begin. The thigh clamps kept Ashley and the others firmly in their seats as the shuttle rotated slowly for Ashley's benefit. As planned he now sat facing directly at the centre of Platwuz when Zanos confirmed that the shuttle was exactly on station 11,000 miles above the surface of Platwuz. The planet's gravity upon the shuttle was now only a small fraction of its earlier strength which was fortunate for the seated passengers. Shoulder clamps were activated to keep them in their seats.

Ashley closed his eyes and in his mind went over the plan they had agreed. He decided that a Level-one push would be too little a telekinetic effort. Somehow he just knew. So looking directly at the planet as a whole he concentrated his mind and applied a Level-two telekinetic push upon its entire visible surface. He kept this constant like he had for the starship and waited for Zanos to confirm the effect. After about a minute Zanos conveyed that Platwuz was slowing at the deceleration rate that was equivalent to 0.3% of Nazmos gravity. Consequently Ashley increased his push action to Level-3. Again it took Zanos a minute to report back and confirm that the planet was now under a deceleration equivalent to 0.7% of Nazmos gravity. So now Ashley increased his telekinetic push to Level-4 and decided that whatever the outcome he would not increase it any further. He closed his eyes and locked his mind at this push level. Zanos subsequently confirmed that Platwuz was decelerating at just under 1% of Nazmos gravity.

Zanos then commenced a minute by minute countdown of the gradually decreasing orbital velocity of Platwuz. It was to be a long slow process which took nearly two hours of continuous telekinetic push by Ashley and one that he had done before on the starship. It was at the 114th minute that Zanos confirmed that the target 600mph orbital velocity had been achieved. Ashley immediately ceased his telekinetic push and breathed a sigh of relief. Although his immediate task had been completed he was concerned about the effect all this had had upon the planet's atmosphere.

Zanos conveyed that high winds were raging all across the planet's surface with dust clouds rising a couple of miles up into the atmosphere. It was predicted that this could last for several weeks or even months but was not considered disastrous. In fact this had been predicted and the mining population had earlier been instructed to cease all mining operations and to remain inside their habitation domes. It was reported that they considered it all one great big adventure not to mention a well deserved rest. The sound of the wind could be heard by them inside the domes.

The next stage of increasing the velocity of the planet's elliptic path towards Raznat and also of changing the ecliptic angle of orbit would be done after 24 hours as suggested in the agreed plan. And so the shuttles returned to 9632-Orange and messages of congratulations came through to them. As his shuttle finally entered the shuttle bay and settled down on the deck floor Ashley felt the tiredness creep up on him. When the thigh clamps were released and he stood up he realised how tired and thirsty he felt. Muznant sensed this and both she and Brazjaf walked either side of Ashley as he disembarked and got onto the Transporter.

In the robe room where they all divested themselves of the gold static suits Ashley found that jugs of Wazu had been provided. Muznant was a most caring person he thought gratefully. He looked up at her as he sat drinking his second glass and smiled tiredly at her and the others watching him. Many had a look of wonder at what this human had achieved and all with the power of his mind. And yet he had not felt the least bit tired when he'd pushed the Starship to its record velocity for eleven days non stop. Also it might help if he spaced out the telekinetic pushes with longer intervals in between. He'd do that tomorrow he thought drowsily.

He conveyed a desire to return to his cabin for a rest and immediately the Transporter took him there. Ashley entered the cabin and flopped backwards onto the bed. The others had entered to see that he was alright but Ashley looked up at them in a half daze, closed his eyes and fell instantly into a deep blank sleep.

The others turned to leave but Muznant stopped them.

'Just look at how peacefully he lies there,' she conveyed. 'I want us to remember this moment forever so we can tell our children. This is Ashley as he was meant to be seen; a man without guile and with a pure heart. How can you not feel the utmost affection towards him? Let this image be conveyed to all.'

They stayed a moment longer and then quietly left to return to the dining hall for refreshment. Muznant knew that Ashley too would be hungry when he awoke from his rest whenever that was.

Ashley slept unmoving for nearly seven hours. When he did awake he just lay there on the bed thinking. He wondered about Simon and the wonderful expression he would exude when given the news of his forthcoming Starship journey. And what would Tania think? They could all stay a week with Jazzatnit and Zazfrapiz and meet lots of the Oannes people. Ashley thought he would like to visit the island of Vaz personally. His history skill might give him more information about Gozmanot. The thought came to him that he'd like to see Rachel and Jazzatnit together. Something in Jazzatnit reminded him of Rachel but he couldn't quite put his finger on any particular aspect.

Then he thought about Anztarza and their surprise at the arrival of the most august council of ministers from Nazmos. What would be the effect in attitudes? Their stay might only be a week but much could be accomplished in that time of that Ashley was certain. It was important for the ministers to experience Earth's tundra areas for a comparison with similar areas on Nazmos.

Then there was the question of permission from the council to bring his family back with him. What if they refused him? He thought of a plan but discarded it immediately. He had already promised to return them to Nazmos in six days. He could appeal to Korizazit's good sense and indebtedness. And then there was Jazzatnit's invitation for the family to visit. But although this was all tentative Ashley was confident he would get his way.

Finally Ashley got up and went into the washroom to freshen up with a shower and a shave. He put on a different set of clothes before contacting the others about a meal.

'We will meet you in the dining hall,' conveyed Muznant who had been waiting for him for hours.

'Thank you,' conveyed Ashley, 'and yes I feel refreshed and ready for the next task. But first I must fill my demanding stomach.'

In the dining hall they were eventually joined by Captain Rojazonto and several of his crew. They had come to see the man who had moved a planet. For Ashley to have affected Platwuz's orbital change so easily was looked upon by all as a great feat. They'd known of his reputation with regard to the Asteroids experiment and even Neptune's Triton. But now it had been done without any dramatics and Captain Rojazonto showed a respectful attitude towards his guest. Ashley was the man of the moment and it showed in the deferential attitude of those around him. For them it was history in the making and they felt privileged to have been present when it happened. It was absolutely stupendous to have witnessed such a feat.

And yet the man before them did not exhibit any exhilaration or emotions of grandeur. He just behaved in the most unassuming normal manner. This on its own was a wonder to them; that someone with such immense power did not desire fame or fortune. From looking into Ashley's mind they knew that all he desired was to be with his family on Earth and to live out a normal peaceful life with them. And so it would be for the next 22 years.

After the meal Ashley spent time in the control dome with Captain Rojazonto. He found the captain a pleasant conversationalist but most of all Ashley was asked about Earth as Rojazonto had never been there. Perhaps now that he had met Ashley he would think about such a visit.

There was another meal six hours later followed by a short rest in his cabin prior to returning for another bout in space in the shuttle craft. It all went smoothly according to plan and this time Ashley restricted his telekinetic push to just a Level-3 for the duration. The aim was to increase the velocity of Platwuz in its new orbital path towards Raznat to 700mph. and also to alter the plane of the orbit so that it was inclined at an angle of 15° to the ecliptic of the other planets.

Because of the storms still raging over Platwuz's surface Ashley had decided to keep the acceleration factor less than before. Zanos subsequently conveyed that the current acceleration was at 0.68% of Nazmos gravity and would require an operation lasting 109 minutes for the required orbital velocity to be attained. This would put the planet into an eccentric orbit that would bring it to a perigee of 100 million miles from Raznat in 22 years.

Ashley would have to return in January of the year 2038 to slow it into its new circular orbit. Zanos computed that the perigee orbital velocity would have reached 27,000 mph by then. He would need to slow it to 9,000 mph for a stable circular orbit around Raznat to be achieved.

Zanos gave a minute by minute readout of its velocity with Ashley's continued push effort upon Platwuz. Again this was a lengthy process but at the end of 109 minutes exactly Zanos conveyed that the required velocity had been achieved. Ashley ceased his telekinetic push effort and again enquired after the welfare of the population in the habitation domes. The report came back from one of the domes that the storms were still raging but did not appear to have increased in their intensity. Ashley felt relieved and Zanos confirmed its previous prediction for the expected duration of the storms. The higher gravity level of Platwuz would assist the dust clouds to settle sooner and for normality to return as predicted.

Ashley wondered how all this would appear to the governing council and whether it would affect their decision for Nazmos. He had faith that Gozmanot's vision would be taken into account for any decision that they might make.

Ashley repeated his request for the exact positions of the gas giant Zraplat and the smaller planet Rubabriz when Platwuz crossed above their orbital paths. Zraplat would be 46° behind and Rubabriz 76° ahead in their ecliptic paths as previously indicated.

There were still two days to go before they could join the Starship 8110-Gold for the return journey to Earth. Ashley was informed that Captain Natazlat was still on Nazmos with her family and her Starship had been relocated to another location by her deputies and the scientists on board. Captain Zakatanz had however rejoined his Starship and this would be moved to the normal rendezvous location within the next 24 hours; a location 100 million miles further out from the original Platwuz orbit.

Captain Rojazonto informed everyone on board that the 8632-Orange would remain at its current location for another 24 hours. It would then make its way to the rendezvous with the Starship 8110-Gold commanded by Captain Zakatanz.

Ashley thought of Simon and how enthusiastic he was about all things spatial. It had surprised Ashley then but he had been pleased about it. Simon would definitely be with him when he travelled at speed to meet Zarama.

In 22 years he would probably be a well travelled spaceman approaching his thirtieth year. And Rachel, what were her prospects? Ashley's inner voice had already told him that she would achieve much but not how. Ashley's joy was mainly in the fact that for the next 22 years he could forget about Nazmos and Zarama and just enjoy normal family living. He could watch his kids grow to maturity and looked forward to seeing Rachel blossom into womanhood. Would she still talk with her hands waving about? He thought of Tania and how he just wanted to hold her tight to his chest. And with these thoughts his chest filled with that lovely ache of love for her. He was sure that they would all have a pleasant future together.

Then he thought of the immediate future with the council of ministers on the Starship 8110-Gold on the trip to Earth. He would work his most gracious charm on them for permission to bring his family back to Nazmos with him. Korizazit and Ritozanan must be especially pandered to and they hopefully would sway the others. All he wanted was a week on Nazmos and for his family to meet the elderly and charming Jazzatnit and her husband Zazfrapiz. And then there were their charming friends who had all expressed a desire to meet Tania and the kids. He could then also make a visit to the island of Vaz and to Gozmanot's home location. Only he would know where to find it.

The next twenty four hours passed pleasantly for Ashley in the company of his friends. The captain had taken kindly to this person from Earth and had developed an admiration of sorts after having witnessed the operation on Platwuz. They were not so different after all since one's being was in the mind and not in the outward physical appearance. Rojazonto like Muznant and the others was impressed by Ashley's ease of behaviour and diffident approach to what lay ahead for him. At the final count for these Oannes Ashley was just one likeable human. Some said that it was no wonder that he had been chosen for the task of subduing Zarama by being given such powerful gifts.

Ashley was quite rested when the ship began its journey to the rendezvous location with the starship 8110-Gold. He was keen to return to Earth and his darling Tania, Simon and Rachel. He even looked forward to seeing the familiar faces of the shoppers who simply walked passed McGill's Antiques and Museum shop every morning on their way to work or wherever. They were all strangers by name but familiar by appearance. Dudley was his home in more ways than he'd thought possible. Familiarity of places and its people had become a binding force.

The council of ministers was a formidable group but Ashley knew that he had an edge in his ally Korizazit. He too now possessed the gift of inner voice to guide him and Ashley was sure that his requests would be granted eventually.

It was eight hours later when the Starship 8110-Gold came into view and 8632-Orange entered into a parking loop just over 200 miles away. Ashley was again impressed by the starship's size and beautiful streamlined appearance. A gold coloured stripe ran along its length and already it seemed as if it was travelling at speed.

The council of ministers had not arrived but would do so within the next few hours. They usually travelled accompanied by a husband or wife aboard a ship very much like Bulzezatna's 520-Green. But it had a unique design and was numbered 103-Silverstar. There was a fleet of eight such prestigious ships and this one was commanded by Captain Duntazent and his crew of fifty.

The ship was a special one with a central meeting chamber for council activities. The council's entourage consisted of some 220 Oannes and all would be travelling on the starship to Earth. No other passengers were permitted aboard 103-Silverstar. The captain and his crew kept to their own space once the ministers were aboard and all communication was through Zanos on-board.

The transfer from 8632-Orange to the Starship was a slow and easy process. When Ashley and the others had changed out of the electrostatic over-clothes they descended from the Cargo to the Habitation platform and were guided towards the centrally located control room.

Captain Zakatanz appeared very different from the last time Ashley had met him in the November of 2006. Tania had been with him then and the trip to the Starship had been a belated wedding gift from Muznant and Brazjaf. Ashley had thought the captain as a polite though taciturn individual. Yet now there was a hint of welcoming pleasantness in his manner towards Ashley.

After the formalities of Sewa had been completed and a glass of Wazu had been drunk the captain invited Ashley and his friends to have a wander around the spacious habitation platform. Zanos would then guide them to their allotted accommodation. Ashley's was more or less similar to the one he had on 9110-Red in both location and comfort. Location meant that it was as central to the platform as it could be. The captain had been primed as to Ashley's needs by Captain Natazlat. After all it would be his home for the week long journey to Earth.

There was an exception however and that was the area for housing the council of ministers and their retinue. This was to be located in zone 31 of the habitation deck and would be a restricted area for all other passengers. Anyone wandering too close would be informed by Zanos accordingly.

Just after the Sewa greeting Ashley had come forward and offered a handshake in the Earth custom. Ashley had then opened his mind and let Zakatanz probe deeply. What the captain read was a pleasantness of character that was simple and uncomplicated. There was no personal grandiose plan for him but rather an earnest desire to just spend all his time with his family. But there was also a sense of dedication to fulfil the big task that had been bestowed upon him even if it cost him dearly. Zakatanz's awe turned to admiration and he could now understand how Ashley was so widely respected and in many cases loved.

Captain Zakatanz was much too polite to enquire after the journey velocity that Ashley intended but hoped that it would be around the 300 FTL mark or greater. Zakatanz and Natazlat had a friendly rivalry in that area and Zakatanz was keen to meet her on his return. He had also decided that he would like to know more of this earthling with such powers. Word about Gozmanot had spread and how both Ashley and Zarama had been foretold by her. If anything Zakatanz was extremely impressionable and he had come to look upon Ashley with a certain awe that generated a natural respect from him. Any antagonism that he had initially harboured towards the Earth people had been dispelled. There must be a good reason that an Earthling had received such gifts as opposed to an Oannes person instead.

He then thought about his expeditionary views for one way journeys to the further away stars and considered how much easier it would be when four figure FTL velocities were attainable. But that would be in a very distant future. Unless of course someone like Ashley were there to assist.

Ashley, Muznant and Brazjaf then walked towards the general living areas and were greeted by many of the Oannes there who had come aboard the previous day. The Starship was very similar to Captain Natazlat's 9110-Red Starship and Ashley felt a familiarity with the place in general. For some reason he also felt that Zakatanz was a rather likeable fellow.

It was much later that Zanos informed the captain that shuttles carrying the governing council of ministers and their party were due to board the Starship. Ashley showed his surprise that the ministers should be granted such preferential treatment. But the others informed him that such had always been the case from time immemorial and if anything the Oannes did not like to deviate from what had become a tradition. For some reason Ashley felt bemused by this and knew in his heart that tradition was about to get thrown out of the proverbial window. After all hadn't the ministers agreed to the Anztarza visit to see for themselves the climatic conditions on Earth and the forests there? And wouldn't they also be meeting and mixing with the common Oannes folk?

And another thing came to Ashley's mind. The accommodation on the Starship was for small family groups only. There were no large meeting rooms or halls for them to conduct their business; if business they had to conduct. They would travel to Earth as ordinary passengers and Ashley found this to their credit that knowing this they had nevertheless agreed to the journey.

Therefore it came as no surprise to him when later that day a message came from Korizazit requesting Ashley's presence to a meal in his accommodation in about three hours time.

Ashley responded immediately but requested permission to be accompanied by some of his friends. The request was granted though with a perceived hesitation. Ashley conveyed this to Muznant and Brazjaf and was surprised that there was hesitation in their reply.

'It would be better if you went on your own,' conveyed Brazjaf, 'for Korizazit may have a special reason behind his invitation and our presence would restrict that communication. But if you insist then we will accompany you. There may be others of the council there who may not take kindly to our presence.'

Ashley replied that he understood and would therefore go alone. He conveyed this to Korizazit who replied that he was glad of it. There would in fact be two others at the meal. They were to be Nerbtazwi and Ritozanan. This invitation had been expressly requested by them as they wished to know more of him. The occasion was to be an informal one in which friendly relations could be established and Ashley replied that he looked forward to it.

When he conveyed this to his friends they were surprised but very pleased. Only Ashley could have made such an impression on these august Oannes persons and they saw a bright future blossoming from it. Muznant was choked with the emotion that this news caused within her such that she was unable to communicate further. But her pride and joy for Ashley exploded to all around her. Ashley smiled at this and thoughts of another admirer came into his mind. Margaret Dutton had a funny way of cropping up at the most unexpected of moments.

It was a bit later that Zanos on-board conveyed that the Starship 8110-Gold would leave for Earth in seven hours time. Ashley had to keep his own emotion in check as thoughts of seeing Tania, Simon and Rachel filled his being. Journeys on Starship's were becoming routine and Ashley looked forward to seeing Zakatanz's emotion when a record FTL velocity was attained. Ashley hoped to surprise them all.

After the meal and once the Starship had begun its journey Ashley would need to remain near the central zone of the habitation platform. A smile came to his face at a thought that came into his head. Another step forward to a new future with the Oannes was just beginning.

Chapter 16

An Earth Visit

November 2016

It had been a long day for me. I'd had qualms about my invitation to visit Korizazit in his quarters. But these had proved groundless as the welcome was genuine by my host and his two female governing council colleagues. Nerbtazwi and Ritozanan welcomed me in the Earth style of a firm handshake. Both Oannes ladies performed a brief Sewa followed by a verbal enquiry.

'And how is our friend Ashley today?' they conveyed.

This put me quite at ease and on the spur of the moment I decided to go one step further. Stooping low I kissed the ladies in turn on both cheeks and then for good measure placed a light kiss on their lips. When I stood upright again both ladies looked rather flushed with pleasure.

I conveyed that this was a custom mainly between opposite sexes though the kiss on the lips was not a part of that custom. That had been my own spur of the moment decision because of my affection for them.

I had taken a liking to both these ladies at our first meeting in the Great Domed Hall of the council of ministers in Wentazta. At that meeting Nerbtazwi had taken an instant liking to me as had I to her. But Ritozanan had been suspicious and antagonistic at first contact. Later after my speech and our sparring of minds she had changed her opinion of me. I had felt sorry for her but also got to like what I saw in her mind. She had character and a conviction for what was just and right.

'Come and sit here with us Ashley,' said Korizazit, 'and let us communicate as friends. We would know more of your thoughts on matters that interest you.'

'And how do you find yourself adapting to this new gift of inner voice,' I queried when we were seated? I could see that the table before us was laden with a variety of the usual Oannes dishes.

'It has not spoken to me since,' conveyed Korizazit, 'but I know that it is there. I expect that when an important decision is to be made I will be guided by it.'

'You may not hear from it again,' I said, 'but you must believe that it is there and it shapes your thoughts. Your decision making will become easier.'

Then Ritozanan queried my other gifts and asked how I coped with such an arsenal of dormant power. I replied that each had come upon me gradually in accidental discovery or revelation; and I had just accepted that each must have a purpose. I said that my history gift must have been given so that I could reveal to the council of ministers the origin of their myths.

The fact of Gozmanot was extremely important to the future of Nazmos and I hoped to find out a bit more about her life when I visited the Island of Vaz. But I kept these thoughts to myself.

'And yet you did not use the latent authority of those gifts to force the council to accept your will,' said Korizazit.

'That is only partly true,' I replied. 'Persuasive argument is always the better route to winning over a person's opinion. My history gift was my most powerful tool this time.'

'It did not seem so at the time,' conveyed my friend, 'and that is what impressed us so greatly.'

Both Ritozanan and Nerbtazwi were silent for quite some while. They then conveyed that I had caused a great stir of controversy among the council members. Suddenly none of them were as sure of their opinions as they once had been. To them Gozmanot was the key to Nazmos' long term future and her visions could not be taken lightly. I knew exactly what was being referred to and I felt elated by it. There was another moment of silence when it was suggested we begin our meal.

I felt rather hungry then and each of us started with a favourite dish. I liked the sweetness of the Yaztraka mash but both Korizazit and Ritozanan preferred to start with Milsony together with the Starztal alongside it. Nerbtazwi took a little of nearly everything.

Nerbtazwi surprised me not only by the amount she put on her plate but also how quickly she made it disappear. My thoughts of surprise were obviously read by my hosts and there was humour in their thoughts.

'What does hollow legs mean,' queried Korizazit?

I had to smile at this and conveyed that it was just an expression of wonder at where all the food must be going. Surely one's stomach was not large enough to accommodate all that went in through the mouth; hence the alternative hollow legs theory as a joke. I think they liked the analogy.

I felt affection for these three Oannes persons and it grew as I spent more time with them; and I felt their affection in return. Nerbtazwi as leader of the representatives had taken an instant liking for me back then in the Domed Hall on Nazmos. Both Korizazit and Ritozanan were esteemed council ministers but here with me around the meal table they were quite informal and had let their guard down. They were relaxed in my presence and I knew that they liked how they felt. Was this to be the forerunner of how the council of ministers functioned? I certainly hoped so. For on Earth and in Anztarza the entire squad of ministers would be in common communication with the ordinary Oannes people. Hopefully the influence of my three friends here would act like a catalyst for changed ways.

As our meal neared an end I sensed that there was a question at the back of their minds which they seemed hesitant to put to me. Oannes custom seldom allowed undue favours to be requested so I took the lead in order to overcome their reticence.

'You have a request you wish to make and if my guess is correct it is something to do with Gozmanot,' I said aloud.

I expected surprise from them but not wonder.

'How could you have known this,' conveyed Ritozanan, 'it is impossible to retrieve such information from our minds when we wish to keep it locked from all forms of probing.'

Again I smiled and conveyed that it was a common human trait called intuition. The body gives out a language of its own when people try to deceive or keep something secret within.

'When I mentioned Gozmanot in relation to my history gift you responded with a degree of silence,' I added. 'I suspected then that you did not wish to discus anything in relation to her life for fear that you might reveal what you have been commissioned to request. Your continued silence confirms this and I think I know exactly what it is you want me to do.'

The silence both verbal and telepathic was deafening, so I continued.

'You are my friends and we should hide nothing from one another. So my answer is in the affirmative and I will make the attempt on my return to Nazmos. I have never searched that far back before but then my history gift had never needed to.'

I paused to see if one of them might respond but none did, so I continued again. This time I had the advantage of a revelation by my inner voice.

'I believe that the council wish me to acquire a visual imaging of a part of Gozmanot's life with my gift of bringing the past to life in my own mind. I have done this many times and brought criminals to a sense of justice. My gift of seeing the past also revealed to me the truth of what took place as in the case of Lucy Hambling and her dog Bluey in order to exonerate young Peter Hindle. You know of this from my own life history.'

'Thank you Ashley,' conveyed Korizazit, 'thank you very much for that. Yes, we are commissioned by the council to learn more from you about Gozmanot. 36,500 Nazmos years is a very long time ago in the past but for some reason my confidence in your ability to do this has suddenly increased greatly. This gift of inner voice is extremely powerful and I feel that we shall get to know this visionary ancestor of ours very well.'

'I must be upon the Island of Vaz to pick up on her life and I shall want representatives of the council members present there when I make the attempt,' I conveyed. 'They must see what I see.'

'Well if we can travel all the way to Earth,' said Ritozanan, 'surely a little trip to Vaz would not be difficult. But the council must make the decision.'

'The council has already decided to be there,' I said with a smile.

'How is this so?' queried Ritozanan.

I smiled again and looking directly into her pale grey eyes said, 'Because you are the council.'

'That cannot be,' she replied rather forcefully though with a hint of confusion.

'It is so,' I said again. 'Look back to your hundred and twenty years with the council and tell me from all the things that you ever supported was one ever turned down?'

There was a shocked look of discernment on Ritozanan's face and then a hint of a smile.

Korizazit then stepped in with a wide smile and said in his gentlest manner, 'It is true. If Ritozanan supported a case it went through. And if she was against it then it failed. But that is because her arguments and reasoning are logical and persuasive in the extreme and I have always admired her for her skill.'

I then gently whispered a questioning, 'So?'

And as quietly Ritozanan replied, 'Yes, the council or its representatives will attend on Vaz as I will support it.'

'I too have a request to make of the council,' I said looking earnestly at Ritozanan.

She read my mind and nodded.

'It is only right that your family should accompany you on your journeys,' she conveyed. 'I shall speak for you at the council.'

'Thank you,' I conveyed.

'Good,' said Korizazit, 'so now let us enjoy the rest of our meal together.'

And a most pleasant hour followed of happy conversation both verbal and telepathic. When I finally took my leave to return to my allotted accommodation Nerbtazwi accompanied me part of the way.

Just before we parted she whispered, 'The council members are in awe of you Ashley. But tread carefully as there are some who would cling to authority inside the council. Vindictiveness is not an unknown feature among our people especially where personal authority is concerned. So do not pre-empt them. Let them feel that the decisions they make are entirely their own.'

This was sound advice from a good friend and I would heed it. I suddenly felt an even greater admiration and affection for this elderly Oannes lady. I would not forget her advice. I shall keep my revelations to myself in future and play the servant and not the king as I had done today. Was I becoming arrogant? Probably, and I felt ashamed at how I had demonstrated this; but not any more. If only Tania were here to keep me in check. Or was I just showing off?

Back in my bed I slept for several hours and awoke quite refreshed. Zanos conveyed that the Starship had begun its journey towards Earth and was currently accelerating towards the 4 FTL velocity mark. I decided that it was time for me to attend Captain Zakatanz in the control room. The next several hours proved fruitful for the captain because at the end of it I had accelerated his Starship to a final velocity of 523 FTL.

I had progressively increased my telekinetic effort by one level every twenty seconds or so. The effect was a smooth and continuous acceleration which the starship's platform could accommodate quite easily. I was however surprised that when I paused at the 70 telekinetic push level the Starship was at a velocity close to 300 FTL. This was far greater than when I had applied the same level of effort on Captain Natazlat's Starship 9110-Red. I could only conclude that my telekinetic power was still in the development stage and getting stronger with time for when I was to tackle Zarama. Perhaps after another two decades I might be considered ready.

At the 100 telekinetic push level the Starship achieved 500 FTL and was still accelerating. I increased this to a push level of 110 and locked my mind at this position. I dared go no further than this. I felt no strain or tiredness and informed Zanos and the captain that I was done. When the Starship 8110-Gold finally settled at a cruise velocity of 523 FTL the captain came to me all smiles, clamped his hand upon my shoulder and conveyed his thanks and admiration. The whole process had taken just over four hours. We read each others' minds and I believe that a deep friendship was conceived at that instant. A friendship that was full of respect between two professionals.

'When your son Simon qualifies for space duty I would be happy to have him aboard my Starship and give him the benefit of all my experience,' conveyed the captain.

'Thank you,' I replied. 'You shall meet him on the return journey as I intend to have my family with me always from now on.'

'I look forward to meeting them,' he conveyed.

'Perhaps we could achieve 600 FTL on the return journey,' I said, 'if your scientists deem it safe of course.'

'I will communicate with them,' he beamed.

I read his thoughts and knew that he was dreaming of a four figure FTL velocity. I also learned that once their scientists concluded that the Starship's shields could withstand these high velocities then efforts to build larger and more powerful propulsive units would be accelerated. The crucial factor in this was the ship's neutron material shield. How would it bear up to the tremendous absorption of space-grid energy medium at the higher velocities? So far the indications had been encouraging.

Zanos on-board conveyed that with the Starship's current velocity they should arrive at destination station in six days and five hours approximately. Deceleration at the destination end would take slightly longer than for previous trips. I would be required to reduce my telekinetic push in small steps in conjunction with the reverse acting neutron generators.

But for now however we were to have six days of peaceful cruising. Muznant and Brazjaf along with Brajam were with me just outside the control room. We stood beside the handrail that circled the central pillar and looked around at the habitation platform profile.

The Oannes engineers tended to build in the same general patterns and I understood why the Anztarza domes were as they are. Although Wentazta was huge as a city I had found familiarity in its house designs generally. And I realised I had felt quite at home there. If only the climate was more congenial. Hopefully if I got my way it would be just as Gozmanot had envisioned.

Captain Zakatanz then came out and joined our little group and before long Puzlwat and Nogozat joined us too. There were also some others whom I knew to be passengers for Anztarza. They were curious to get a look at me to see how I was keeping the Starship at its current velocity. I answered their query by conveying to them that I had willed my mind to continue to exert a 110 level telekinetic push upon the neutron shield and left it at that. The push action would continue without further conscious effort on my part even when I slept as I would need to. The essential factor was for me to be on the Starship and at a fairly central location on the habitation platform. There were a few more questions which I answered with directness and honesty. I had no need for any sort of pretence or cover-up.

Captain Zakatanz smiled at my responses to the questions and then made a show of inviting me to have all my meals with him in the rooms alongside the control room. He also invited Muznant, Brazjaf, Puzlwat and Nogozat to keep me company. He would join us as often as he could. I accepted and said that he was most considerate. The others too did the same.

Brajam was not asked since he was to be kept busy with his scientific colleagues monitoring various aspects of the ship as it cruised at this phenomenal velocity; a first in their history records. I believe that Brajam had tried to get me interested in the dynamics of the Realm Grid impacting upon the starship's protective neutron material shield. I understood the mechanics of it but knowing that the ship's structure was isolated from the fierceness of the impacting energy-medium I tended not to think any more about it. But all this was new physics territory for the Oannes scientists such that there was quite an atmosphere of exhilaration emanating from them. I was pleased for them but the matter did not seem to be anything out of the ordinary for me. I was here to push the Starship and that is exactly what I was doing.

During mealtimes Captain Zakatanz and I made small talk conversations and gradually we got to know more about each other. Although I knew a lot about him from having read his mind nevertheless it was nice to learn of his likes and dislikes and of his ambitions in general.

There was sadness in his past which he tended to keep locked away from prying minds. But gradually he came out with little bits of his early life. And then he mentioned Hazazamunt purely by accident. I was pleased that he had chosen to trust me with something he had not spoken to anyone about. It was a part of his life that he treasured most. His most joyous years had been spent in the company of someone he loved more than life itself. And it was also the saddest moment of his life when it ended.

Zakatanz had left his parents house in Wentazta when he was just eighty years of age in order to forge a career for himself. He had approached the Rimzi but they had wanted nothing to do with him. He then joined a Peruga farm and did well for himself and achieved the level of a supervisor. At the age of ninety five he met and fell in love with Hazazamunt a beautiful Wentazta girl twelve years his senior. When his parents met her they strongly disapproved of the match. Despite this Zakatanz and Hazazamunt continued their courtship and a deep love and understanding grew up between them. It was obvious to all who knew them that this was a unique love affair. After a period of ten gloriously happy years a legal partnership was agreed and this time Zakatanz's parents accepted their son's love for Hazazamunt. And finally her parents too gave their wholehearted agreement to the partnership. When both sets of parents met an immediate friendship developed between them and this was a most happy moment for the soon to be joined couple. The romance was widely known and messages of joy for their future were conveyed.

It was a week before the official certification for the sealing of their partnership that Hazazamunt disappeared. After a day of searching and enquiries across the planet panic began to set in for Zakatanz. No one knew what could have happened. The Zanos system of monitoring reported Hazazamunt's small spacecraft heading out low over the Peruga Sea and at great speed when all contact was lost. At about that time there had occurred an intense stellar flare on the surface of Raznat but not directly towards Nazmos. Only slight communication interference had resulted.

Hazazamunt was a proficient pilot of her craft and even ventured out into space with Zakatanz by her side. She loved to bypass Zanos on-board so she could perform daring manoeuvres manually. At one time she aimed the craft at Raznat and yelled to Zakatanz that the controls were not responding. She went halfway to the glowing orb of Raznat before pulling away with peels of laughter at her stoic boyfriend. There were many such happy memories of his time with her. She was so full of life and fun that he loved her to the utmost core of his being.

Although she was missing he felt sure she would return within a day at the most. But when a week went by he began to fear the worst and his heart filled with sorrow. He thought he would go mad; and then doubt entered his mind. Did she not want him?

Her spacecraft was capable of achieving great velocity in space as she had often demonstrated with Zakatanz beside her. Both had felt the exhilaration of the speed and it made him love her even more when he viewed the mischievous expression on her face as she performed high gravity manoeuvres to tease him. And she loved him too because he shared her sense of adventure just as much as she did.

Deep space communication was attempted but no response was ever received. As more time elapsed Zakatanz became inconsolable and withdrew into a mind shell. He left the farm and after a year could not bear to be anywhere near Wentazta City and so decided on a career in outer space. He enlisted in the space cadet facility and put all his thoughts and energy into his cadetship. He excelled in all of its aspects such that Hazazamunt became a distant memory. There were bad days though that followed when she appeared in his occasional dreams. His heart would nearly burst with the awakened love for her but then he would become taciturn and morose for weeks afterwards.

He said he could never forget her even though it was now over a hundred years later. They had shared ten years of love which for him had been a lifetime. He carried visual images of her in his memory and I was complimented when he conveyed this to me. She was a very pretty Oannes lady and reminded me a bit of Muznant. No, not Muznant but her Aunt Jazzatnit. But what I suddenly saw also shocked me for I had just received a diagnostic on her condition.

Although I had quickly blocked my thoughts from outside probing, Zakatanz saw something in my expression that made him ask what I had seen. I said nothing at first and he just waited patiently for me to speak. I was trying to sort out what had been diagnosed which was not quite as definitive as I would have wished. But when I did get the gist of it I conveyed this to Zakatanz.

Hazazamunt had a bulbous growth inside her brain. As it grew larger it began to impress on neighbouring blood vessels and caused them to balloon into aneurisms. There was more than just the one ballooning. Sooner or later one or more of these would rupture with tragic consequences. That is all I could convey with regard to the diagnosis. As to what really happened on the day Hazazamunt went missing I did not know.

Zakatanz remained silent for quite some time. He then thanked me for the revelation and getting slowly up from his seat left the room. After a brief moment I too stood up and followed him out onto the open habitation platform. He stood just outside and was staring at the far wall of the Starship before slowly walking away. I felt he was gathering his thoughts and picturing Hazazamunt's last reported flight. Her craft had last been recorded as heading out over the sea of Peruga on a bright sunny morning. There had been no trace of her craft anywhere afterwards and I think that Zakatanz had to conclude that somewhere in her flight she had lost consciousness. Could her pilot-less craft then have continued out into space and then directly into Raznat? That was one scenario only but a major one to consider. The captain was probably thinking of the many times they had flown together and of the daring manoeuvres she made purely for the thrills it gave her.

I did not see Zakatanz again that day and decided not to reveal any of this to my other friends. I then went to my accommodation to think and I eventually fell into a deep sleep. I dreamed of Tania, Simon and Rachel and then also saw Hazazamunt walking and talking to Margaret. That Margaret again, she just seemed to crop up everywhere.

When I saw Zakatanz again the next simulated day at our normal mealtime he seemed his usual self. I couldn't help reading his mind and found that a great burden had been lifted from his conscience. There had always been a niggling doubt in his mind that he had done or said something that had upset his love; and that in a fit of disappointment she had run away. Although it was an illogical thought it nevertheless did pry on his conscience. It was like a bereavement giving rise to feelings of guilt.

Knowing I had seen into his thoughts Zakatanz looked at me and smiled.

'Thank you my friend,' he conveyed only to me, 'finally I think I am at peace with myself. I shall convey this to Hazazamunt's family on my return. It will mean much to them too.'

After that for the rest of the journey towards Earth Zakatanz made no further mention of his past and behaved exactly as a Starship captain should. I think Muznant suspected that something had transpired between the captain and me for she looked at me quizzically. I told her that a matter had been discussed and was now resolved to our complete mutual satisfaction. It was something very personal and important to the captain. One day I would divulge it all to her but not just yet. Muznant was very understanding and made no further enquiry.

Towards the end of our sixth simulated day on the Starship Zanos communicated that deceleration action was to commence shortly. This was to let me know that I was to coordinate with Zanos in reducing my telekinetic push as the reversing neutron generators were operated. We must synchronise our efforts. Zanos left it to me to begin when I was ready. I responded with the information that commencing in five minutes from now I would begin to reduce my telekinetic push by one level at approximately one minute intervals.

I had short pauses at the ninety, seventy, fifty and thirty push levels to rest my mind from its concentration on the various factors involved. It was just over two hours later that I released my mind from all telekinetic activity on the starship's neutron shield. It was now entirely under its own motive power and Zanos would control and complete the remainder of the Starship journey as it usually did.

The Starship was now at 12 FTL velocity and Zanos conveyed that arrival at the Solar parking rendezvous was to be in approximately six hours. I had been restricted to the central area of the habitation platform and now felt the need to stretch my legs and stroll around. I had the desire to first walk diametrically across from one wall to the other and expressed this wish. My friends said they would accompany me and were surprised that I wanted to do it right away. So I loosely linked arms with Muznant and Nogozat and the five of us strolled easily along the pathways between the blocks of apartment houses. It was nice to stretch my legs even though I kept my steps small for the benefit of my Oannes friends. When we reached the opposite wall I put my ear to it to listen for any sounds from the outside. There were none and I was quite taken by the pleasantness of our journey through space. Tania and Simon would love this though I was not quite certain about Rachel.

Muznant looked at me and smiled for she had read my thoughts about my family and how surprised they would be at my early return. I had a tingling sensation inside my chest at the thought of being with my darlings again and I think my emotion of joy spread to the area around us.

We began our stroll back in the opposite direction and were met by Brajam and another scientist as we passed the central column on our way to the other wall. The scientist's name was Vazlodip and her speciality was the structural bond between the forward section of the Starship and the neutron shield. She had monitored the compression in the bonding beams when the Starship had been at its maximum velocity of 523 FTL and her readings indicated that these were close to an allowable limit. With suitable strengthening modifications there was no reason the ship could not be taken to double the speed just achieved.

'And how long would such a modification require to be completed?' I asked.

Vazlodip read my mind and knew exactly what I was thinking.

'Oh I expect somewhere in the region of ten to fifteen years,' she said aloud. 'It is a hazardous operation being so near to the neutron shield. And it is rather a large area of work that needs to be done. We could have one ready for the trip to Zarama.'

I smiled back at her and we opened our minds to each other. She was 180 years of age and reminded me a bit of Bulzezatna in her mannerisms. She was from Wentazta and had been involved in the design philosophy behind the huge spaceship 98103-Pink that I had seen on Nazmos. But Starships and FTL considerations had always been her main interest. She had gone diligently through the recent Zanos records of Captain Natazlat's 9110-Red Starship after its epic eleven day journey from Earth and found nothing untoward. The integrity of the ship was absolute. And then she had been delegated to travel to Earth on this trip and was quite astonished at the 523 FTL velocity achieved. However she said that there were signs of strain but only in the one area. And that was the linkage between neutron shield and Starship structure.

We communicated as we strolled to the other wall of the habitation platform and I was surprised at how rapidly the time had passed when Zanos conveyed that the Starship was just four hours from its parking destination though still travelling at a 4 FTL velocity.

It was time for another meal and the captain requested for me and my friends to eat it with him. It was a happy meal in more ways than I expected. I was happy that I was nearly home. Zakatanz was happy for many reasons. Not only was he the proud captain of a record achieving Starship but also because a great burden had been lifted from his mind. A burden he had subconsciously carried around for approximately one hundred years. Vazlodip was elated by her discussions with Brajam not only about the starship's performance but also about the structure of the space grid impacting and being absorbed by the neutron shield.

Muznant and Brazjaf were exchanging frequent looks at one another and I noticed something special going on between them. I didn't wish to intrude by reading their thoughts but by outward signs I guessed that Muznant was actually flirting with her husband. She was in fact expressing her fertility and I sincerely hoped that they would be successful. Mischievously I conveyed my best wishes and got a playful poke in the ribs from a deliriously happy Muznant. It was interesting for me to observe how an Oannes couple behaved in courtship. It was the same chemical interaction as I had seen on Earth. No different from how young lovers carried on in Dudley. In fact it reminded me of those heady days when I first realised that I loved Tania. How we had laughed and rubbed noses when we were together. Zakatanz and Hazazamunt must have enjoyed a similar relationship. I had a great optimism for our two civilizations harmonising and integrating one day in the very distant future.

Because of the happy atmosphere around this table I ate rather more than I had intended. As a result my stomach strings began to pull upon my eyelids and giving a stifled yawn I thanked the captain for a lovely meal and to everybody for being so entertaining. But now could I be forgiven and be allowed to retire to my accommodation bed for an overdue siesta. By now all knew of my many earthly expressions and immediately offered to escort me to my bed. Although I said that I could manage on my own it was Vazlodip who begged to be allowed to see where I slept.

So off we trudged and when we entered my apartment and then the bedroom Vazlodip sat on the edge of the bed and tested the springiness of the mattress. I like a firm bed which is what I had but Vazlodip thought it would be most uncomfortable in comparison to her sleep-tank.

'How do you sleep on such a hard and rough surface?' she commented.

'Well it is what I am used to,' I said. 'I tried a water bed once but it was too wishy washy for my liking.'

'What is wishy washy?' they all seemed to ask in unison.

'Oh that simply means that I found it unstable like a sea with waves,' I said with a laugh, 'and I thought I might get sea sick.'

I conveyed a visual of a ship in a stormy sea with people getting sick over the ship's rails. There was general humour at this visualisation. Communication with telepathy is so much simpler and exact compared to a lengthy description with words.

I then showed Vazlodip how I slept by lying down on the bed on my back fully clothed. I closed my eyes and gave a pretended snore.

'What was that you did?' she queried.

'That was a snore caused by restricted air passages in the nose and throat,' I said, 'and most humans snore at sometime in their lives especially as they get older. And it can be quite noisy and most disturbing for the partner.'

'Then give me my sleep tank anytime,' said Vazlodip.

I laughed and said, 'Wait till you are older and fall asleep sitting up in a chair.'

They all laughed for they had heard stories of elderly Oannes nodding off during meetings and of them making deep breathing noises not too dissimilar to the description of snoring that I had given. So now they knew what snoring was all about.

'My Aunt Brenda had a pet dog called Barclay when I was a child,' I said, 'and he used to snore loudly when he slept. I think it must have been a trait in that breed of dog.'

I conveyed some of my visual memories of Barclay and they seemed quite taken with him.

I now really began to feel drowsy and getting up I walked to the door and opened it wider. There I bowed low and gave a sweeping gesture with my right arm and said that we must all get some rest. Muznant and Brazjaf exchanged fluid glances and said they would return to their sleep-tank as well.

I shut the door behind the last one out who just happened to be Vazlodip and then taking off my shoes, tunic and leggings got into the bed and snuggled down. My thoughts were of Tania, Simon and Rachel and how I should feel when I saw them again. Love nearly burst out through my chest. I thought also of mum, dad, granddad and Tania's parents Milly and Jerry. Then of Katy and her kids and then all our friends just before I drifted off into a deep sleep. I think my last thought was of myself and whether I snored while asleep.

When I awoke some hours later Zanos informed me that 8110-Gold was now at its planned nine billion mile distance from Earth parking station rendezvous and that communication had been sent to Anztarza. A reply was not expected for twenty-six hours at least. And then it might be another day for the first spaceship to arrive.

I smiled to myself when I tried to visualise the consternation among Anztarza's chief ministers of the news that a majority of the Nazmos governing council was about to descend upon them. This would be a first in the history of Anztarza and I could guess at the furious activity at making the necessary preparations. But that was not my concern as I intended to be taken directly to Aunt Brenda's B&B.

When I queried Zanos about the ferrying arrangements I was informed that at least two ships had been requested. Again I surmised that one of these would be for the for the benefit of the governing council members and their accompanying retinue.

I felt quite elated at this news and wondered if Bulzezatna's 520-Green would be one of the ships sent to meet us. I certainly hoped so. My emotion of elation must have been picked up by the others for I received a message from Muznant that Captain Zakatanz wished to see me in his quarters. I expressed a desire for a mug of hot sweetened tea and Muznant conveyed that one would be waiting for me when I got there.

I splashed some water over my face, brushed my hair straight back as usual and then got dressed. I was out of my cabin door and on my way across to the central control room in ten minutes flat. When I entered the control room I was greeted by the captain with a big smile and firm handshake. No Sewa was conducted as we were all fellow travellers on the same journey.

'A detailed communication was sent to Anztarza just over an hour ago,' he said, 'and I have requested that three ships are sent out to us initially. A reply will not be received for another day at least and the first ships will take another day after that. Then it will be another day to travel to Earth and I have instructed for you to be taken directly to your Aberporth destination. I also included in my communication that all your family be informed of your safe return and of your expected arrival in Aberporth in approximately three days time.'

The emotion of the moment overwhelmed me and tears of joy rolled down my cheeks. I didn't know whether to laugh or cry. I think I did both. I went up to the captain and grasped his hand in both of mine and pumped it up and down and just kept nodding my head. I had clamped my lips tight as a control against any blabbing noise I might make. My thoughts conveyed my thanks but I knew I must also voice my gratitude.

'Thank you Captain,' I whispered hoarsely, 'thank you a thousand times for that. You are truly a most understanding person. I shall always remember this moment.'

The captain stood quietly after I let go of his hand and although he had a smile on his face I could see emotion written all over him. I instinctively knew that he must be thinking of his Hazazamunt and the love they had shared before she was taken from him. And I know that he was happy to share in my own moment of joy with the love I had for Tania and all my family. Muznant and Brazjaf came on either side of me and made me aware of their presence by placing a hand on each of my arms.

I wiped my eyes and cheeks with the back of my hands as a child would do and then rubbed my hands together to dry them. The moment had passed and I was just happy that Tania and the others would receive news of my return and make preparations to get to the Aberporth B&B.

The next couple of simulated days were busy ones. This time I took Muznant and Brazjaf with me when Nerbtazwi invited me for a meal at her lodgings. Korizazit and Ritozanan were there as before along with another council member called Wetzarnti. He looked very old and at the age of 331 years was rather wizened and frail in appearance. But he spoke with a briskness that contradicted his age. He had requested to be invited as he said he wanted to talk to me personally. He was friends with Zazfrapiz who had mentioned me in their communications. Muznant apparently knew Wetzarnti from having met him at her Aunt's house; but a very long time ago on a previous visit.

Zazfrapiz had served as a council member in his younger days about a hundred years ago. He had resigned his position after a few years only because he did not like the decision making process that was being used. He believed that not all factors were always taken into account and at times the deciding outcome had not been reached democratically. He had made many friends there and continued to meet them socially. Occasionally his opinion or advice was requested on a particular matter. Wetzarnti was one of those who kept a close friendly relationship with Zazfrapiz and Jazzatnit.

'You have given the council much to think about Ashley,' he said, 'and chief among this is the matter of our relationship with Earth people. You and your family are acceptable to us because we have got to know and understand you. I believe that there must be others like you and I hold that the long term future is encouraging for thoughts on our integration.'

I smiled back at him and said, 'Please be circumspect on how you proceed. I do not believe that Earth is anywhere near ready for any form of integration. Our evolution towards the Oannes mentality and culture will be slow and we just might be ready in about a thousand year's time. Telepathic communication is an important factor for that integration and it has only just been introduced into a part of Earth's awareness. It will progress slowly. Only when it becomes universal may we then be deemed as an open society like yours. I believe Gozmanot saw more than we know from the existing records of her visions. I hope to go to Vaz on our return to see what more I may learn.'

A private communication then came to me from Korizazit and I replied that I was pleased for him. His inner voice had finally spoken and clarified something he had been puzzling over. He had then also received a very positive image for the future of Nazmos; the very long term future when no Zarama threatened and Nazmos was on a path to Gozmanot's vision of it.

'Ashley,' he communicated, 'I believe that success will be yours in all that you undertake. There must have been a purpose that such a gift, which I call the gift of voice, has been passed on to me a council member. If only I could pass it on to the others. Perhaps an opportunity may present itself one day.'

Muznant and Wetzarnti were in earnest open communication and they were discussing the decorative features in Jazzatnit and Zazfrapiz's house courtyard. Wetzarnti conveyed that Jazzatnit had a great gift for artistic innovation and arrangement and that he so looked forward to his next visit just to view her new creations.

Brazjaf was rather quiet but I sensed a joyous exhilaration inside him. My instinct told me that it had something to do with having a child and all the emotional signs from Muznant corresponded exactly with those of her husband; a perfect recipe for success. In my heart I wished for them to achieve their desire.

It was a pleasant meal in which the elders ate frugally. It was Muznant, Brazjaf and I who ate a lot of what had been spread on Nerbtazwi's table. I was beginning to like the flavour of the Milsony dish and its spicy after-taste. I knew that when the stocks on board the Starship ran out I'd have to wait for our return to Nazmos before more was available. I wondered if Milsony had an ingredient that could cause an addiction like craving. But of course my favourite was the sweetened Yaztraka mash. I always had a portion at the end of each meal as a substitute for dessert.

Afterwards I thought of the meal and the conversation topics. I wondered whether Wetzarnti had been sent by the council in general to get to know me and my views better. I didn't mind in the least as I had nothing to hide. It was unlikely that I would meet any of the council members on Earth. They would be in Anztarza and I would be in Dudley. Of course communication could be initiated but I doubted very much that it would happen. I only hoped that they got to see the places I had referred to in my big speech back in the Domed Hall on Nazmos.

Nerbtazwi had communicated that the governing council ministers were to spend the prescribed six days on Earth before returning to the Starship. That meant that I too would have those days at home with my family. And since the return stay on Nazmos was to be short, no more than a few days, I would convince all to travel with me. I must have Tania at my side at all times as I certainly missed her very much on this last trip. Ritozanan had agreed to my request earlier and I knew the governing council members as a whole could not refuse her. And I also wanted the governing council to meet my family as much as I wanted my family to meet Jazzatnit and Zazfrapiz. Mum and dad would love their house and especially the artistic courtyard features.

When I gave my thanks to Nerbtazwi for a lovely meal she again agreed to walk me to my accommodation. We talked of many things as we walked and felt I had a good friend here. No more advice followed and I think she knew that I had heeded her warning.

Time went by slowly and communication was received back from Earth. And it was not long before Zanos was able to inform us that five craft were approaching and each was identified by its captain. Two of these were Captain Bulzezatna in 520-Green and Captain Lyzongpan in 11701-Red. The others were also very similar craft but I hoped to travel with either one of the captains known to me.

I had hoped to meet and make friends with the engineer Niztukan during this trip from Nazmos. But Brajam informed me of the private nature of the man and that he was not one for socialising since he did not like inconsequent chatter. However I hoped that our paths would cross on the return journey. I would go out of my way to intercept him with Brajam's help of course.

As it turned out the entire governing council and retinue were to be taken on board 520-Green under Captain Bulzezatna. Thankfully I was to go with Captain Lyzongpan on his ship. The captain was to take me to Aberporth directly before continuing on to Anztarza. Shufzaz and her 326-Red bus craft had transferred from 520-Green to the shuttle bay on 11701-Red for my benefit when the allocations had been confirmed after arrival here. This was easy since shuttles from all five spaceships worked tirelessly and continuously making multiple trips to and from the Starship.

Before I lift the Starship I got a firm handshake and a friendly farewell Sewa from Captain Zakatanz. I could not be certain but I believed I read emotion in his thoughts. I know that he and Simon will get on well in a respected master and favourite pupil sort of relationship. I did not realise how well till I actually saw them together on the return trip.

I was greeted affectionately by Captain Lyzongpan when I entered his control room and Sewas were exchanged. He told me of the surprise in Anztarza when Captain Zakatanz's detailed communication was received. Urgent preparations were begun immediately to empty a dome and make it available for the esteemed guests. The Anztarza chief ministers however took the news favourably and were pleased that such an opportunity had presented itself. The full details of meeting with the Nazmos governing council had been relayed to the Anztarzans and so they knew what was expected of them; a subsequent program of events and visits was drawn up. The Anztarzans were in favour of my proposal for a warmer Nazmos and so would do their utmost to present Earth in a most favourable light. I only hoped that they didn't overdo it.

Also in the general communication to Anztarza was my adventure with regard to Platwuz and the intended orbit fixing in twenty two years time. Captain Bulzezatna had received this news with I imagined a quiet pride since I knew her feelings for me and my family. I had communication with her and she conveyed much of how she felt. I think I might get a swollen ego but I thanked her for her praise.

The trip to Earth in 11701-Red was at the slightly slower pace of 80,000mps and as usual the last million miles took nearly five hours to complete. It had been an unusually long trip for me as I had difficulty sleeping in my cabin. I was far too excited thinking of Tania and the kids and what I would say to them. I'm sure they must be just as excited as I. I had never been away from them for this long before; or this far away. I would ensure that it would not happen again. They were definitely coming with me on the return journey.

Muznant and Brazjaf had come with me on 11701-Red but Puzlwat and Nogozat were on another ship. I was still intrigued by the ecstatic mood emanating from my friends and could only hope for every success for them.

It was twenty four hours from the start of our earthward journey that we finally entered Earth atmosphere and cruised to location just out from Aberporth. It was a month ago on October 15th that I had left this same spot and my time sense was quite out of sink. Zanos on-board conveyed that it was six o'clock on the evening of Tuesday November 15th and it was very dark outside.

Earlier as we were approaching Earth Zanos had conveyed that the ship was now in badge communication distance from Anztarza. But of course my primary interest was to communicate with Tania and all the family as soon as possible. I did this immediately in open transmission format so all would receive it simultaneously.

Tania and the kids were at Aunt Brenda's but the others had all stayed home and would see me back in Dudley and Birmingham. Granddad said he was quite impatient to hear about my trip so without further ado I conveyed to all a visual detail of the entire three weeks that I was away. I did this slowly and in stages and it took an unusually long five minutes in time. Of course I was interrupted on occasion for little clarifications mainly from Simon.

But I got a 'wow' from him and an even bigger exclamation when I conveyed my intention to have them all with me for future journeys. Simon began to ask me for more information but I said I'd talk to him further when I was home.

'I'm on my way to you now,' I conveyed to Tania as I boarded the bus craft in the shuttle bay along with the image of the old style 1950s coach which she knew so well.

I'd received a great welcome from the young Shufzaz as I boarded and I performed a brief Sewa with her. She was now 73 years of age and seemed to get prettier with age. And I said so too. I don't think that Muznant took much notice of this as she and Brazjaf were in a world of their own. It was lovely to see them so affectionate and I thought they were not unlike us even though our origins were so different.

11701-Red was in hover mode just above the darkened sea when it opened its bay doors to let us out. Shufzaz left the ship smoothly but with some considerable acceleration. We reached landfall in half an hour and then descended onto a road and slowly wound our way to the B&B car park. I had conveyed a running commentary of our approach and the door had barely opened when I saw Tania and the kids rush out to meet me. I dropped my backpack on the ground as I stepped down and instantly Tania was in my arms kissing me fiercely on my lips and then all over my face. I squeezed her tightly to me and oh how I savoured the warmth of her body against mine. I breathed in the scent of her hair with my pulse racing. Then the kids were there too and I reached out and wrapped them both into my arm circle. Simon had had a slight hesitation but I pulled him close and got him into our big threesome hug. He seemed to like fitting in this way.

Muznant and Brazjaf looked on from inside the bus and smiled their approval at the spectacle. I read their emotions and knew how much they hoped for a family of their own. And suddenly I knew they would not have long to wait.

I waved to them and Shufzaz and conveyed a brief farewell Sewa before the bus performed a spin turn and moved quite rapidly into the darkness and out of sight. I knew that they would soon be speeding to their rendezvous with 11701-Red.

I picked Rachel up and Tania put an arm around my waist as we walked into the B&B with my free arm on Simon's shoulder. What a glorious feeling I had in my chest.

Putting Rachel down I went forward and gave Aunt Brenda a big tight hug and a kiss and at the same time reached out and shook Uncle Ron's outstretched hand. It was so grand to be on home ground that I could feel the watery stuff just behind my eyes desperately trying to burst out.

Sudzarnt came forward then and we conducted a brief Sewa. He was smiling and looked happy in his adopted home and family. He conveyed his good wishes and pleasure that I had returned safely.

Tania and I now stood side by side with an arm around each other. We were both smiling and happy. I made no further mention of the return trip but would bring it up again later. I had a whole week for it.

'Welcome home Ashley,' came through from mum and dad and this was followed by a similar message from Tania's parents Milly and Jerry.

It was one thing being able to converse through our badges but being with someone physically was infinitely more satisfying.

Tania had driven up in our car so I planned on leaving Aberporth sometime late in the morning tomorrow. I fancied a nice drive behind the wheel and looked forward to the scenery unfolding as we headed through the Welsh hills and into the English countryside. But first for a nice mug of tea which Aunt Brenda said was ready for us in the lounge. Somehow the tea tasted so much nicer here than on the Starship. I guess it must be the hard water that gives it an added flavour.

Aunt Brenda had also prepared a lovely roast and I tucked in when we sat down for dinner. I thanked her for it and was glad that none of the Oannes were around to see me enjoying myself on a meat dish. Aunt Brenda said I deserved a treat for being away so long.

We sat and chatted till quite late when Rachel dropped off to sleep beside Tania and me. I carried her up to her bed and Simon then also went into his room. That left Tania and me to say our goodnights as well and to go to our room. Tania had a mischievous glint in her eye as she shut the door behind us and I read the signs clearly. And what a homecoming that was.

We came down to breakfast at near 10 o'clock and Rachel scolded us for being so lazy. I just smiled and gave her a loving hug and nibbled her cheek. She giggled and clung tightly to me. Simon was sitting quietly so I told him about the Starship and the speeds we had achieved.

'How long are you staying dad?' he asked.

'Well let me see,' I said. 'The Nazmos governing council are here on a week long visit to see the conditions on Earth especially the Northern forests and the Tundra regions. I asked that they experience all these for themselves and get a proper feel for what Earth is and what a possible future Nazmos will be like. I then promised to take them back after that which means another week's journey to Nazmos. Then I propose to spend a week on Nazmos where I can show off my family to Muznant's Aunt and Uncle.'

Tania already knew of my plans since we had discussed much of it last night before dropping off to sleep. And she had approved wholeheartedly of her and the children accompanying me back to Nazmos.

There was a quiet few seconds before Simon whooped with joy.

'You mean we're coming back with you dad?' he exclaimed. 'And is Rachel coming too?'

'Yes and anyone else of our family who would like to come,' I said. 'Except granddad Eric as I'm afraid he's not well enough to travel. The Oannes have rules about that sort of thing unfortunately.'

'And how long would you be away for this time Ashley?' asked Uncle Ron.

I looked at him and smiled.

'Not more than three weeks,' I said. 'One to travel there and one to travel back and I propose to stay a week on Nazmos. I'd like you all to meet Jazzatnit and Zazfrapiz. They have a lovely house and a massive enclosed courtyard most tastefully decorated.'

I conveyed visual images as I spoke.

I changed the subject by telling Simon that some of their latest ships could carry 90,000 persons for an indefinite period. 'They began constructing these when the threat of Zarama first became known to them,' I added. Again I conveyed a visual of the ship 98103-Pink.

Brenda looked at Ron and I could pick up their telepathic discussion. This was a chance of a lifetime to visit another world and three weeks away from the B&B would be like taking a holiday abroad.

'There is one thing more I need to tell you,' I conveyed in open badge communication and this went to Margaret as well. 'After this trip I intend staying home on Earth for the next twenty two years and watch my children grow up. This does not mean that we shall not be visiting our friends in Anztarza. I hope we can all keep up our ties there.'

'Then at the ripe age of fifty six in early 2038 I shall return to Nazmos to fix the mining planet Platwuz in its new 100 million mile orbit around Raznat. I also hope to have a go at the repositioning of Nazmos, if the governing council have agreed it. I expect that they will have made a decision by then.' I added this especially as I knew that all my badge communications were being monitored in Anztarza. And I remembered Nerbtazwi's advice to tread carefully with regard to any decisions pending with the governing council. I would indeed heed that advice.

'I would like to meet aunty Muznant's aunty,' said Rachel wistfully.

'And so you shall Rachel,' came the reply from Muznant through the badge communicator.

'Hello aunty Muznant,' conveyed Rachel, 'when will I see you again?'

'You will see me next week on the Starship,' said Muznant. 'We can walk around all the houses on the living platform. And on Nazmos you shall meet my own aunty Jazzatnit who looks a bit like me. I think you will like her even though she is a bit older than me.'

Uncle Ron was still undecided in his own way but I knew that Aunt Brenda had made up her mind to come on the trip. Uncle Ron was thinking of the B&B and of leaving it in the care of Sudzarnt, Julie and Barbara for all of three weeks.

'We are definitely coming with you Ashley,' said Milly and Jerry. 'And we're not standing on ceremony to be asked either.'

Then mum and dad came through the badge to say that they were happy to also go on the trip.

Uncle Ron still seemed undecided though I knew that the idea was growing favourably.

Katy and Robin came through separately and both felt that Sarah was much too young at the moment being only three. And Fiona would be all of five this Saturday. I said I understood and would be there to give Fiona her present.

Tania had bought a large Rag-doll and had wrapped it in shiny gold paper she conveyed to me.

'Goodness,' I thought, 'don't these children grow up fast'

It seemed like only yesterday that Fiona was in nappies and struggling with her first steps.

I could see that Aunt Brenda was keen to go but Ron said that he would consider it only when he was happy with the cover arrangements. Sudzarnt had been listening to all of this and didn't wish to intrude so remained telepathically silent. It was only when he came in to clear away the breakfast things that he made the comment that they would all simply love Wentazta. It was a huge and beautiful city, the best on Nazmos.

'And the sunsets are spectacular,' he added. 'You can trust Julie, Barbara and me with the running of the B&B for three weeks Ron. I won't forgive you if you don't see the world I came from.' He was smiling as he said this as was Aunt Brenda.

She came forward and put an arm around Uncle Ron and gave him a peck on the cheek and conveyed something privately.

Uncle Ron was a worrier in many ways and when it came to the B&B he worried doubly about it. When they'd go away even for a short holiday he would be constantly ringing up to see how things were going. It was his nature to think about things that might go wrong. And by going away to Nazmos he'd have no way of finding out how things were. Six light years is too great a distance for that.

But now looking at Sudzarnt he realised that not only was it the low November period but he could depend upon him as one of his own. He had come to love this diminutive Oannes humanised person as if he were his own son.

So now he let out a laugh and said, 'Okay Bren you win. Sudzarnt will be in charge of the B&B while we go away on the holiday of a lifetime with our nephew. And Barbara and Julie can do what they do best in helping to assist wherever they need to. We'll tie up the details as soon as we can.'

Sudzarnt smiled at this and said, 'Thank you Ron, I will do my best to keep the B&B running at its very best. Have a good trip.'

Sudzarnt had always been on first name terms with his employers from the day he returned from Nazmos in 2008 fully transformed and looking quite human. That was eight years ago and since then he had developed a great affection not only for Earth but for this little town of Aberporth and all the people in it. Because he was small and had a soft singsong lilt to his voice all the shop owners had taken an instant liking to him. Of course Sudzarnt cheated by using his telepathic skills to create pleasurable emotions in those around him; which was why so many of them remarked that they felt good when Sudzarnt was around.

Tania had packed her cases earlier and we loaded up the car by midday. Aunt Brenda put out some tea and biscuits and suggested we all have a drink before setting off. There's nothing like a good cup of tea and a biscuit before a long drive. It would be over three hours to Dudley though we'd probably make a stop at Aberystwyth. Then Tania could take over the driving to get us home. I felt comfortable when Tania was behind the wheel and often shut my eyes for a relaxing bit of shuteye; but I don't expect I'll get that with both Rachel and Simon in the back seat.

We said our goodbyes and conveyed our intentions to be back en-mass at the end of a week. Aunt Brenda and now Uncle Ron both said they were quite excited at the prospect of going to Nazmos with me. I know our friends in Wentazta would love them. I smiled when I recalled some of the events of the trip I'd just returned from.

We made a stop in Aberystwyth and found a little café where we all had cream teas with huge scones. Rachel said she was full up and would probably have a sleep in the back if Simon would stop talking. I said I might do the same if the need arose. Tania smiled and rolled her eyes. She knew me well and that I could drop off anytime and anywhere.

There were no hold-ups on the way and after Welshpool the going was even faster. We finally pulled onto our driveway just after five in the evening though it was quite dark already. Tania hadn't minded because the last stretch was all on the M54 Motorway. We'd left at Junction 2 and down the A449 around Wolverhampton to Tipton and our home near Dudley Zoo.

In preparation for my home-coming Tania had made a nice lasagne and frozen it in the freezer. She took this out and put it in the micro on the defrost cycle. We had soup from packets while we waited. There was always a variety of these in the kitchen cupboard and my favourite was cream of tomato. In fact today we all chose the same and sat in comfort watching the news on TV. Nothing had changed in the three weeks I'd been away.

Milly and Jerry conveyed that they had closed up shop and were on their way home and wondered if we would like to come over a bit later. But Tania said that we were all tired from the long drive and just wanted to chill out at home. Probably watch a bit of TV and then have an early night. Tania looked at me with those mischievous eyes and I just rolled mine upwards and smiled back. However she told them that we'd see them at the shop about mid-morning tomorrow. Being a Thursday it would be a normal working day for all the shops.

Milly conveyed that they hadn't as yet mentioned about going away to Uncle Robin, Mark or Les. But both she and Jerry had the utmost confidence that they'd keep both shops ticking over nicely. On previous occasions when Milly and Jerry had gone on week long holidays they'd found everything quite normal on their return. A three week holiday would appear no different.

Mum then came through and invited everyone over for lunch on Saturday. It would also be Fiona's birthday and we could all have a little celebration. Katy came on and said that would be just lovely. It would be like old times and I said I quite looked forward to the day. In fact I was especially looking forward to seeing my two little nieces again.

'Can I come too,' came through from Margaret in London and immediately mum said she'd be most welcome to join the family.

'No,' conveyed Margaret, 'I meant can I come on the trip to Nazmos with you all?'

'I don't see why not,' I replied, 'after all you have been to Anztarza and are no stranger to the Oannes. I'll let you know the pickup time in Aberporth. I expect it to be on Monday sometime late in the evening.'

'Then I'll be there by midday on Monday,' she replied. 'I hope that's okay with Ron and Brenda.'

'That'll be fine Margaret,' conveyed Brenda, 'we look forward to seeing you again.'

'Thanks,' was the reply.

I sensed she wanted to convey more but couldn't. I thought about the Dutton Institute which now operated in both London and Edinburgh. The 4-day workshops had worked well and occasionally Muznant had assisted with the more difficult cases. There were techniques in the Oannes' tutoring arsenal that Muznant could and did use.

The next day Tania and I took the kids to school and I had a word with Mrs Gillespie the Head Teacher. I requested permission for our Simon and Rachel to be given leave of absence up to the Christmas holidays as we planned a three week trip abroad. When she enquired where I conveyed a telepathic image of somewhere remote in the wilds of South Africa and that it was to be a once in a lifetime trip. I said it would be educational and would have a big impact on their future careers. I wished to keep it a secret so could say no more.

Mrs Gillespie smiled and said she understood and that my telepathic skills were remarkable. I conveyed an image of Margaret and the Dutton Telepathic Institute in London and that she should try one of the workshops. I said that the founder Margaret was a family friend.

Later, Tania and I walked through the doors of McGill's Antiques and Museum and Milly came forward and gave me a big hug and kiss. She stood back and looked up at me with a most loving aspect on her face.

'Oh Ashley my wonderful son-in-law it's so wonderful to have you back,' she whispered.

'And I love you too,' I said, 'and I have missed you all terribly. I thought of you all often and vowed that never again would I travel without my family by my side.'

I then conveyed my plans to be home for the next twenty two years and Milly said she was glad for me and Tania.

Robin wasn't in today but Mark Tinman came down from the upstairs room when he heard our voices and gave a smiling hello. I shook his hand warmly and asked how he was. If this had been on Nazmos we would have had an elaborate Sewa of questions and answers. Was I beginning to think like the Oannes? Perhaps, but that was not such a bad thing. After all, one day in the very distant future, we on Earth would need to communicate just like them and at their level.

I spent an hour chatting to Milly and Mark and I mentioned about being away again soon and hoped to take the family with me this time. Milly would brief Mark with all the necessary details. I then decided to visit our other shop two doors down. After all I was the most senior partner of both and so ought to make my presence felt. And yet I was also happy to let it continue as a family business with Tania's mum and dad really managing things. Tania said she'd stay and help her mum for a while. I really needed to also help out with the History Cards as only I could dictate what must go on them. Being away three weeks had created a backlog for many of the latest acquisitions. I'd do as much as possible over the next few days before the next trip.

Jerry was outside the door of the shop and smiled as he saw me leave the one shop and walk towards the other. I looked into the house-furnishings shop as I passed it and it looked empty of customers. But then afternoons were often quiet periods, even in our antiques trade.

Jerry and I shook hands and I could see he was pleased to see me. Reading his thoughts I knew that he had been concerned for me when I went off on my first Starship journey. My safe return had been a great relief to his mindset. Now that the entire trip details had been conveyed his mind was quite allayed by the non-hazardous nature of the journey. Also being on hand during the next trip would make it an easier situation to deal with.

'Welcome back son,' he said. He called me son ever since Simon had been born. Milly though preferred to call me her darling son-in-law and I liked that. And I think I reciprocated with either 'my dear mum-in-law' or 'hello Tania's mum'. We were a close family and not only because we shared a unique secret.

'Thanks Jerry,' I said. Somehow it seemed natural for me to continue this way and ever since that fateful darts match when we'd first met.

Les Gibson came and said hello and asked how my trip had gone. Again I conveyed telepathically that it had been a success and I had acquired several great items. I could be economical with the truth as any of the others. I then conveyed that I should be travelling abroad again soon maybe within a week and this time I hoped to take the family with me. Again this trip might last up to three weeks but it would probably be the last trip abroad for a long time to come. It was rather lonely being on my own but then the kids could not miss their schooling. I said I expected the shops to flourish in the capable hands of our two able assistants. Les assured me that both he and Mark would continue to do their very best. There was a glow of pride on his face and I knew he was complimented by the trust I had in him. We were lucky to have two such dedicated assistants. I thought about it and knew that one day I should promote them to junior partner in the business. I must first consult with Milly and Jerry on the matter. But for now they would each get a generous Christmas bonus. After all, the shops were doing very good business. The history cards accounted for a lot of that.

That evening we had another early night and I wondered if there was such a thing as Starship-lag. My body clock must definitely be slightly out of kilter. Tania didn't complain and explained to the kids that daddy was still not used to Earth time. She put Rachel to bed as usual knowing that Simon often read in his room before he too got into bed. She then followed me up to our room. She had a knowing smile as she got into bed and snuggled up beside me. Who was I to complain after all I was home with my wife and kids?

We got to mum and dad's place about noon on Saturday just before Katy, Robin and the girls arrived. It had been a busy two days in the shops dictating the histories of the various items into the recording system. We had found this to be the most efficient method for doing this. One day with the latest Oannes technology it might become even simpler; and then again perhaps not – at least not in my lifetime.

I got hugs from both my parents and dad said he was glad they were all coming with me on the return to Nazmos. Here too I read the anxiety that had been in their minds when I'd left in October. They had all kept their emotions well under control then.

But today was to be a celebration. It was Fiona's fifth birthday and Tania had bought a Barbie doll for her which came with a complete little wardrobe of clothes. Fiona looked a lot like Robin and even had his hesitant sedate mannerisms. She said 'Thank you' very politely and came and gave each of us a kiss. Simon backed away so she gave him a smile instead.

She looked at me and said, 'Uncle Ashley please will you show me some more magic tricks?'

'Most certainly I will young lady,' I said, 'and which ones would you like to see?'

'The disappearing ones,' she said immediately.

'Okay,' I said, 'but can we do it a bit later when we've had lunch and everyone can see it too?'

Sarah who was three and the little minx came up to me and took my hand and pulled downwards. I knelt down and put my arm around her and gave her a big hug and kiss. She put both her arms around my neck and gave me a big wet kiss on the lips. She then did the same to Tania and worked her way around to mum and dad. She then pulled herself up onto mum's lap and looked around the room with a big satisfied smile on her face. I could see that Sarah was mum's favourite since she was a young Katy all over again. And once she actually did start talking there was no stopping her. She just bubbled over with enthusiasm.

Mum and dad had bought Fiona a compact dolls house that was folded in its case and could be opened up. There was a box of matching furniture and lots of little bits and soon all three girls were seriously discussing where to put the pieces. I looked on and thought how quickly they went into organisation mode; a mode that would eventually be useful in their adult lives, like motherhood.

I'd often watched Rachel set up all her dolls and cuddly toys in a circle around her and talk to them quite seriously like a reception class teacher would. Many of the expressions and words she used were recognisable as coming from a grownup. Rachel often used phrases she'd heard Tania repeat. Like 'If you insist on doing that then the consequences will be on your own head'. Or 'I'll not be responsible for the consequences' and phrases like that; the bigger the word the better. At one time about a year ago the word 'consequences' had been Rachel's absolute favourite.

Simon on the other hand led an uncomplicated lifestyle. There were mealtimes, playtimes, reading times and bedtimes. But underlying this was a fierce ambition to achieve something. And now that he'd had a taste of spaceflight he was set upon a career in that field. Space the final frontier was deep within his subconscious thoughts and nothing else would be good enough. I had given him an idea of how vast our miniscule region of space was within the universe realm and how no one could ever travel across an even small part of it.

'Ah dad,' he had said, 'but at least I'd see it all around me knowing I was a part of it.'

I wonder what Captain Zakatanz would have thought of that remark.

Dad went out in his car to fetch granddad and while he was gone Milly and Jerry arrived. They too had cards and a present for Fiona. It was a pop-up story book of Hansel & Gretel and she was quite taken with it.

When granddad arrived he'd bought a present called 'Headbands' which we all played later that evening. I tried not to cheat but it was difficult blocking my mind from everyone's thoughts. So I purposely guessed something different.

Ron and Brenda had said they couldn't make it but would see us all on Monday prior to the pickup. They had posted their card to Katy earlier in the week and included a £20 gift voucher.

It was a nice sunny day but with an icy chill in the north-westerly breeze so we all kept indoors. Mum had prepared a very nice cold meat platter with a beautiful egg and potato salad. There was also a lot of finger food in the form of chicken nuggets, fish sticks, pizza, cocktail sausages and scotch eggs. And of course a pile of oven baked potato wedges. The roast potatoes were plentiful but served cold and just the way I liked. They are very good for nibbling at later in the evening.

There was jelly and ice cream as afters for the kids and a Costco Tiramisu for us grownups. Although it seemed an odd assortment of eats mum had done it as a party for Fiona from knowing all the child's likes and dislikes. I thought of the many dishes that the Oannes served up and rather missed seeing them here. I conveyed the thought and granddad said he'd like a glass of Wazu anytime. It had been so invigorating when he'd first had it all those years ago.

I had a bit of this and a bit of that and by the end of it all I felt quite full up. We had served ourselves like a buffet and had found somewhere to sit. Of course a place was made for granddad at the dining table along with the kids. Katy and Tania sat there also but mainly to supervise the girls. Simon brought his plate quite loaded with mainly finger food and came and sat beside me on the sofa.

Afterwards when I had drunk my mug of tea I do believe I had a bit of a doze in the sitting up position on mum's very comfy settee. Granddad settled into dad's big recliner padded chair and had shut his eyes within minutes. He'd eaten his fill or maybe a bit beyond and looked content. This was one of his better days I think. He had conveyed his regret that he could not make the trip to Nazmos as he would have liked to have met up with Kazaztan again. Visual messages are all very well he said but not quite the same as meeting someone face to face and feeling their presence. I said nothing as there wasn't anything to say. A trait that Tania said she loved in me. She said I just knew when silence was golden.

When I opened my eyes after my kip there was little Fiona standing right in front of my knees. Beside her was my little Rachel also with a wide mouthed smile.

'The disappearing tricks please Uncle Ashley,' said Fiona, 'you promised.'

'So I did,' I said, 'so I did and I do keep my promises, don't I my darling. And what have you got for me this time?'

It was always up to Fiona to produce some small article that she wanted me to do the disappearing trick with. She held out her tiny hand and produced a large red button. I knew she had carefully chosen it from her mum's sewing box when she knew I was to be here. The last time when I visited her house just before the Nazmos trip it had been a glass marble.

I took the button and placed it on my thigh and then put my hand over it. When I lifted my hand the button had disappeared. I then pointed at Rachel's shoulder and there it sat. Of course I had gone into pink mode to move the button from one place to the next – a simple operation for me but a real bit of magic for Fiona. I repeated the trick several times in a varied fashion much to Fiona's delight. Rachel of course knew my secret but remained silent but with a knowing smile. Little Sarah had been watching and clapped with delight and asked for more. And of course I obliged till Katy said that they'd been entertained by their clever Uncle long enough. Katy came and sat beside me and we chatted telepathically on many subjects. Katy knew me well and asked about Margaret.

'You do know that she has a crush on you Ash,' she said, 'just like Vicky and Muznant.'

'I know it and so does Tania,' I conveyed. 'But who am I to turn my admirers away. In a way it boosts my ego and I quite like it; a bit like basking in the sunshine.'

'Just don't get carried away,' she advised.

'You know I could never do that,' I said and I meant it.

Tania then came and joined us and we talked about the old court cases that I had helped with. It was nice chatting like this and I realised how much one missed the simple things in life like family companionship when alone and far away. I wished that Katy was coming on this trip but she said perhaps when the girls were older. I agreed with her reasoning.

Later mum stuck five candles on a home baked cake with 'Happy Birthday Fiona' in chocolate uneven writing on it and brought it to the dining table. I helped light the candles and we all sang 'happy birthday' as Fiona stood in front of it. She had a big smile as she stood between Katy and little Sarah. Robin stood behind and sang rather flat. I smiled at Tania who had the camera clicking away at the scene before her. Milly also took pictures and when Fiona blew out the candles she told her to make a secret wish. In fact I think we all made a wish.

After we'd all had a slice of the cake Jerry raised his mug of coffee and proposed a toast.

'Here's to a safe trip out on Monday and a safe return,' he conveyed telepathically so as not to alert Sarah or Fiona.

'Here, here,' we all added and sipped from whatever drinks we had. Mine was a mug of tea.

'We are not going this Monday,' was the telepathic message from my son Simon.

This was out of the blue and when we all looked in his direction he just shrugged his shoulders and shook his head as if to disclaim what he had just conveyed. But I had learned to trust Simon's premonitions and knew that his was a gift just like my inner voice.

I conveyed this to Muznant and Brazjaf through my communication badge and waited for their response.

Muznant was surprised to receive my query and conveyed that the Nazmos governing council members wished to see more of Earth and so extend their visit by a few more days. They had seen much but believed there was a lot more to experience especially in the northern tundra regions. The duration of the extension had not as yet been decided upon but Muznant expected it to be no longer than a week.

Simon's reputation was growing and within moments all of Anztarza came to know of his premonition. Muznant conveyed that even the council members were astounded and expressed a wish to meet with him when on board the Starship. By this I knew that Ritozanan had spoken for me and had received council approval for my family to accompany me to Nazmos. I conveyed this to all via our badge communicators. I was quite relieved that I would not have to resort to plan B and of which I had not quite made up my mind about.

But I was pleased that my stay on Earth was also to be extended. Though this was cause for worry to Uncle Ron. He wished to be back at the B&B over the busy Christmas period. The same applied to McGill's Antiques and I conveyed all this to Muznant. She said she understood and the council would have already picked up on my communication and would act accordingly.

'Did you get that Uncle Ron?' I conveyed through my badge.

'Yes I did,' he replied, 'but I wonder how long they plan the delay.'

'I got that too,' was the communication from Margaret, 'so I shall hold my arrival plans till I hear again from you.'

'I'm sure that we shall be given ample notice for the trip,' I conveyed to all. This telepathic badge communicator was certainly the ultimate in the contact field.

'I didn't know we weren't to go on Monday,' said Simon apologetically, 'it just came out without me thinking.'

'I understand son,' I said, 'but that is the nature of the gift. It's the same with me and my inner voice; its quite awe inspiring don't you think so?'

'I suppose so dad,' he said, 'but it's as if it is not me but someone else saying it.'

'It'll get better and probably also develop in technique as time goes by. It will be a great asset in space especially at the FTL speeds we shall need to travel at,' I said as I put my arm across his shoulders.

Zakatanz would hear of this in time since he was still on his Starship at its parked location. He would be pleased that he had made his offer to take Simon under his wing when the time came. Simon's gift would be of immense value on expeditions ventured into virgin space territory. But that would be many years in the future.

A great feeling of satisfaction came over me as I sat looking at my family. I had thought about this when I was on Nazmos looking up at the night sky and searching out the Orion Constellation and then picking out the yellow star that was our Sun. Now that I was here I did not look forward to another long trip away. Unlike my son Simon I was not very enamoured by space travel and would much rather keep my feet on terra firma. But my consolation this time was that I would at least have most of my family with me. I could sense Simon's elation at the prospect of the Starship journey and at meeting its enthusiastic captain. I expect the feeling was reciprocated by the captain; a captain who I think is finally at ease with himself.

As it got later in the evening granddad Eric grew tired and asked to be taken home. Dad did the honours and I went with him. On arrival the house was chilly so I turned the thermostat from its economy 15ºC up to 18ºC and flicked the timer switch to the 'Constant' setting. I'd repeatedly told granddad not to try to save on the heating bill but old habits die hard. Dad boiled some water for tea and also filled a hot water bottle after adding a spot of cold water first. The water bottle was encased in a fleece cover and dad placed it in the central part of granddad's bed.

We didn't stay long and said goodnight as granddad said he'd be in bed before we got back to the house. We are lucky that granddad could still look after himself though mum went over every day just to make sure he was okay.

When we got back Sarah had dropped off to sleep on mum's lap. So Katy and Robin decided that it was time to take the children home. After all it was past ten o'clock and late for little kids especially a three year old. Fiona and Rachel seemed wide awake but I did notice the occasional yawn. We left for home about half an hour after Katy and Robin and the same time as Milly and Jerry. Rachel fell asleep in the car and I had to carry her up to her room. My goodness she did feel a dead weight and my legs felt the strain as I climbed the stairs. Tania took over then and did the undressing and tucking into bed part. Simon mumbled a goodnight and went to his room under his own steam.

Although it was lovely being at the old family home with everyone I still find that there is no place like ones own home with your own wife and kids. Tania and I sat silent in the kitchen sipping our hot cups of tea listening to the settling sounds of the house in the night time. The occasional click here and there or the creak of the central heating pipes expanding or contracting.

Tania then reached out for my hand and said it was time for us to go to bed.

'But I've not finished my tea,' I smiled teasingly.

'Finish it later,' said Tania with an impish grin and I took the hint. I was still being treated to the grand home-coming and I loved it. It was like being on honeymoon all over again.

The days then just flew by and the kids were loath to attend school for this extra week. But Tania insisted that they did. Muznant and Brazjaf were in constant communication with us and were none the wiser as to when the council planned to return to Nazmos. I hoped it would be soon since I wished to be back here well before Christmas.

In the meantime I worked full time at the shops and was pleased at how the business was flourishing. McGill's had quite a reputation all over England and I suspected that many of our customers made a small profit by putting the items purchased from us up for auction in some of the well known auction houses in London. Subsequently Jerry suggested that we revise our marked prices by ten percent. Milly and I didn't like the idea since we were quite profitable as it was and a price hike would be noticed by our regular customers. Milly said she didn't want someone reconsidering the purchase of a particular item only to find it had gone up in price. We compromised by agreeing that all future items be initially assessed with Jerry's 10% suggestion in mind and marked up accordingly. Since both shops were crammed full of antique items I reckoned that this would not be noticed as a blatant price hike. There was the matter of inflation and the increase in the cost of living to be taken into consideration. And I'm sure the public understood this.

Jerry also suggested that the history cards be redesigned with a more colourful boarder edging. Again Milly was against the idea because she said that the previous purchases might lose value if their history cards appeared too plain by contrast. Jerry said he hadn't considered that side of it and so withdrew his suggestion. I however put in my own compromise by suggesting that all cards should be laminated prior to display. This would include the current ones as well.

Lamination machines were plentiful and cheap on the market and soon a couple of tabletop versions were purchased from Staples and immediately put into use. Mark and Les were quite enthusiastic when the first trial laminations were carried out on blank cards and after a few hiccups things went smoothly.

It was on the afternoon of Friday 25th just prior to closing time that Muznant communicated the council's decision for departure for Nazmos. The return journey would now commence on Tuesday 29th November. This implied that the actual Starship journey would commence on that date. So we needed to be picked up on the evening of Sunday to begin the 22 hour trip to the Starship rendezvous point.

There was a change of plan however. Of the council's entourage of 220 Oannes only 150 would be returning with the council to Nazmos. This meant that although all the council ministers would be returning to Nazmos only two-thirds of the associated council staff would do so.

Originally quite a few of the council ministers had decided to stay on to see more of the Earth's flora but none fancied the later six month return trip that would be without my assistance. So the council had selected 70 of their best Oannes personnel to stay on instead and report accurately what they observed. They would return to Nazmos on the next available Starship hopefully when I returned from this trip.

'I've got that,' came through from Margaret in London, 'I shall try to be at the B&B by mid-afternoon on Sunday if that is alright with you Brenda?'

Brenda conveyed that it would be just fine. The rest of us would probably arrive about the same time and we also conveyed this to Ron and Brenda.

Simon was quite excited by all of this now that a journey date had been set. Rachel was slightly nervous and asked if aunty Muznant would be travelling too.

'Yes I will Rachel,' conveyed Muznant, 'and I shall show you all around the Starship living platform. It looks just like one of the domes in Anztarza.'

'I wish I could go too,' conveyed granddad Eric, 'but I shall be with you in spirit nevertheless. Have a safe journey there and back,' he added.

Ron conveyed his doubts again about whether they'd get back before Christmas. I told him that if we left within a week of arriving at the Raznat parking location then we should certainly be back by mid-December; or the 17th at the latest. I did want my family to see Nazmos just as I had. A tour of the planet with Captain Lyozonpa was a must for Simon's benefit. I also wanted them to meet Jazzatnit and to see her house just as I wanted her to meet my family. And of course I had to visit Vaz and sense the history of the place where Gozmanot lived. I must attempt to recall the picture of a part of her life which had been requested by the governing council and which I had agreed to do. I had my doubts of receiving any visions from that long gone past. 36,520 years ago on the island of Vaz is a very unlikely recallable situation. Nevertheless I would make the effort. I believe the past is factual and is always worth looking at. Or why should I have been given this gift?

In my mind I had thought to increase the Starship's velocity to about 550 FTL a slight increase on what we had achieved on the journey here. Captain Zakatanz would be pleased though it would not be the 600 FTL he might have hoped for. However I must consult with Brajam about this of course.

My communication badge must have picked up these thoughts and relayed them for I immediately received a reply from Brajam. Vazlodip had revised her figures on the structural bonding between Starship and its neutron shield. Since our arrival in the solar system she had taken further extensive measurements on the bonding beams and established that the beams were of a redundant nature meaning that there was six times the numbers that were actually required. The original purpose had been to design against any unusual impact upon the shield from large space objects and such. Velocity had not been the only consideration. It meant that under the compression forces of high FTL velocity it was perfectly within its strength limits for the Starship to travel at near twice the speed it had travelled at on its journey to Earth. But the problem would be in the deceleration action when approaching destination. The neutron generators were not powerful enough to cope with slowing the Starship from above 600 FTL speed while keeping the comfort of its passengers to within 1g limits. I guess a restriction existed in one form or another. I wondered when 4110-Silver would be ready. I'd been told about fifty years but perhaps this was a rough estimate and it could be sooner – or later. I hoped not too much later since I didn't have the lifespan of an Oannes person. I'm sure my thoughts were picked up in Anztarza as Zarama was an ever present issue in their thoughts.

A thought came into my mind based on this new data and I conveyed it to Uncle Ron.

'Why Ashley that would be perfect,' he replied. 'It means that we could be back here on Earth by mid December.'

Of course Muznant, Brajam and the others had also picked up my communication and I received mixed emotions in return. But all bordered on elation.

Tania looked at me and just smiled. And I liked that in a woman, especially her. I don't think that anything I did could surprise Tania. Yet all I had conveyed to Uncle Ron was that at a projected 600 FTL velocity the Starship could make the journey to the Raznat system in a little less than four days travelling time. And that four or five days on Nazmos should be ample for all that I planned to do including a visit to Vaz.

By the afternoon of Sunday 27th November which was cold and wet, everyone for the trip had arrived at the B&B in Aberporth. Margaret had been the first to arrive just before noon. She said that she had wanted to avoid possible delays on the motorways. But she'd had a clear run and hence her earlier arrival.

Uncle Ron and Aunt Brenda had set out a buffet luncheon in the dining room with plenty of finger food items which would go down well with all including the children.

The rest of us all arrived within an hour or so and the gathering was complete just after one o'clock. We were all travelling light since we knew that tunics, leggings and footwear would be provided as always. Margaret had visited Anztarza several times and so knew the dress code. She was the best prepared from among us and in the evening changed to an Oannes outfit given to her on a previous visit.

All went according to plan and the bus craft 326-Red arrived to pick us up at 9:30pm a bit earlier than I expected. But perhaps this was because it was a dark, wet and miserably cold night. The craft operator was not Shufzaz and when I queried him I was informed that Shufzaz was on leave to visit her family and so would be a passenger with us on the Starship. The current operator was a male Oannes named Myzpazba and very much older at 160 years. He had been on Earth for nearly twenty years and simply loved it. He added that he looked forward to the change on Nazmos whenever it came about. He said that he'd like to see Nazmos develop on land as Earth had but was not sure whether he'd live to see it unfold. But he certainly could imagine it. I conveyed that none of us alive today would see that since I estimated a period of about a thousand years for the climate change to bear fruit. But benefits in warmer temperatures should be apparent as soon as the orbital change was completed; that is if the governing council approved the plan. Myzpazba expressed his views with an expression I had not seen on an Oannes face before. I hesitated to draw any conclusion from this but wondered if that was the general viewpoint in Anztarza. Or for that matter on Nazmos.

I also conveyed that with more energy arriving from Raznat there were bound to be anomalies and a big shift in atmospheric conditions. Thunder and lightning and clouds were not common on Nazmos but could become frequent occurrences under the new conditions. Also with the increased evaporation from the seas it was possible that their levels might drop under the new weather conditions. These were factors that I'm sure the Nazmos governing council would have their scientists and professional people study closely.

'I would still like it to happen,' conveyed Myzpazba. 'I have witnessed storms and hurricanes on the Earth and find them quite exciting.'

'Yes, but how would the citizens of Nazmos feel when they experienced their first storm or hurricane?' I asked.

'They will get used to it,' said Myzpazba in a very matter of fact manner. Again that dismissive expression appeared on his face but this time with the hint of a smile.

In many respects the Oannes were quite stoic in their philosophy towards life and I expect that they might even welcome these side effects in a warmer Nazmos. So I just smiled back at Myzpazba and nodded my agreement.

The spacecraft taking us out to the Starship rendezvous was 520-Green and Captain Bulzezatna had already conveyed her anticipation of welcoming us all aboard once again. We were all becoming seasoned space travellers and Simon was especially overjoyed by her communication.

The trip out over the sea in the bus craft was quite a bumpy one and I was pleased when Myzpazba chose to slow down a bit. When we did see the dull glow coming from the open bay doors of 520-Green I felt somewhat relieved. I knew that spaceship journeys were always ultra smooth. We were soon out of the bus and making our way to the control room behind a smiling first deputy Tatizblay.

Muznant and Brazjaf were already in the control room and Rachel raced up to give her aunty Muznant a big hug. In a few years they might be the same height. I could see that Muznant was pleased at Rachel's display of affection for she looked at her husband and smiled. That smile said a lot and I could guess what that was. I'm not absolutely certain but I read the body language between them and it seemed to say, 'Soon we shall have one of our own.' Could I be mistaken? I think not.

Simon had gone up to the captain and waited as I had instructed him on Oannes custom. I came up beside my son and also waited till Captain Bulzeatna performed a welcoming Sewa to which I responded in kind. Our Sewas were rather less formal than those that would have been performed between strangers meeting for the first time. Children were not required to become involved in any Sewa until they attained a certain developmental age.

We spent about half an hour with the captain during which time 520-Green had accelerated up out of the Earth's atmosphere. The night was dark as we climbed through the clouds since there was no moon visible. We headed away from both Earth and Sun and in a direct line towards the far away Starship 8110-Gold rendezvous location. Initially we saw plenty of stars but as we climbed away further the brightness from the sun came at us from one edge of the Earth and blanked them out.

We were then shown to our cabins and I'm sure they were the same ones that we'd had on all the previous occasions. Tania and I were both quite tired and so was Rachel. But Simon seemed to go into overdrive in a most ebullient mood of anticipation. However Zanos advised us all to take to our beds as gravity acceleration was about to increase to twice the normal level. It would be about three hours before the neutron generators could be operated to take the ship to its cruise velocity of 100,000 miles per second. Rendezvous with the Starship would then be in 18 hours time for us though the actual duration would be 22 hours in actual time. The Time Dilation factor at this velocity was 1.185. Zanos would however advise us of the actual Earth clock time.

I was happy that the family were to be with me on this trip. I had missed Tania and the kids on the last trip and now that they were with me that empty feeling was gone and it was like old times when we had first visited Anztarza. Only granddad was missing but we had Margaret instead. She and Muznant had become good friends and I could tell when they were in private communication as I had an instinct for that sort of thing. But I dared not guess the subject matter being discussed. I was indeed attracted to both of them but simply as a response to their own attraction for me. Margaret had been the enigma from the very start of our acquaintance and seemed to keep cropping up in my thoughts. I was glad when Vicky and Robert had split up because I knew her heart had never been in the relationship. It had been a false romance and entirely one-sided. I knew where her affections really had been and Tania had noticed it too. But now Vicky had a new purpose to her life which was to take care of her mum. Subsequently her attraction for me had mellowed to a sincere affection which I much preferred and actually liked. We were better friends now and Tania said I should show her a bit more affection than I was wont to do. But when I know of a woman's general affection towards me I tend to act a bit reserved in my chatter. It was the same with Margaret and Muznant. I look back with embarrassment at that distracted momentary lapse of joyous elation when I hugged and kissed Muznant. Tania had laughed when I mentioned it to her with full visuals of course. She had looked at me and I sensed the deep love and pride that she flung at me – all because I had confessed an emotional moment of joy at seeing Earth's location from Nazmos.

And yet it gave me a sense of fulfilment and a boost to my ego that Muznant and Margaret felt that way towards me. Recently however Muznant was on another wavelength and I think it was another case like Vicky finding a new purpose in her life. Having a child of her own was paramount in both her and Brazjaf's thoughts.

But it is Tania whose love I crave and whom I could never do without. I never want the slightest shadow to creep between us. I want no woman to be in a position to say they have one up on her. That very thought keeps me focussed and I know that I shall never stray. I hope it remains so for as long as we both shall live.

Tania must have sensed my thoughts as she lay in the twin bed beside me. I read her thoughts just before I drifted off to sleep and the phrase, 'You men have such silly insecure ideas,' came through loud and clear. 'Odd but very true' was my last thought as I fell asleep. Tania read minds very well.

When I opened my eyes I was alone in the cabin. Zanos conveyed that it was 9:20am Earth time.

'Good morning sleepy,' came through to me from Tania and Rachel followed by sundry remarks from the others. I took it all in good humour as I felt good and fresh and full of energy. They said they had woken just after eight o'clock and were now in the dining room having breakfast. I passed some inane remark and then conveyed privately to Tania that I would love a nice big mug of tea.

'Ashley Bonner,' she replied privately to me, 'curb your passions and get yourself washed and dressed and over here pronto. A mug of tea will be waiting for you. I don't want my hair messed up again.'

Tania knew me well but I hadn't that sort of tea in mind at all and I said so. There was laughter and a promise in her thoughts so I said I'd be there in twenty minutes.

And so I was. And as I was in an affectionate mood I gave all the ladies a good morning kiss. I got a big hug from Rachel and she conveyed that I looked like Simon when I was asleep.

Margaret blushed slightly when I kissed her lightly on the lips but Muznant took it in her stride as she smiled at her husband. Something lovely was going on between them and Muznant was glowing with whatever she was getting. I watched with interest at this foreplay that they exhibited and I guess the Oannes were no different in biological make up than us earthlings. We are all animals really. I did hope that success would be theirs this time.

After my first mug of tea I had four slices of toast successively with cheese, marmalade and jam before I felt comfortable again. I followed this with another two mugs of tea as we sat and talked both verbally and telepathically.

Brajam came over and joined us along with a couple of his engineer friends. I could see him avoiding a topic so I just mentioned that I might try 600 FTL on the return trip. He smiled at me and nodded.

'You always seem to know how to answer my question before I have even asked it,' he said aloud with admiration in his voice.

'I just knew that there was something you were avoiding in your conversation and it was just a guess that you might be interested to know my intentions for the return trip,' I conveyed.

He then looked at mum and dad and said, 'You must be very proud to have Ashley as your son.'

They just smiled back at him. Then mum came round to the back of my seat, leaned down and put her arms around me.

'Ever since he was a little boy I knew he was destined for something,' she said in a soft low voice. 'At first it worried me and made me sad and to think I might lose him to others for some great purpose. I would often have tears in my eyes thinking about this and wondering what was to be. But as time went on and our Ashley grew older we saw new gifts bestowed upon him and my anxious moments lessened. I realised then that there was a greater power looking after him and I stopped worrying. Then you all came along and a more benevolent people I have never known. But a danger threatened both our planets and our future lives are threatened by this Zarama. I know that Ashley will meet and defeat this intruder and we shall be safe again. Yes, he is the perfect son to us and we his family are proud of him and I thank you Brajam for your compliment and your thoughts.'

I reached up and squeezed mum's hand and simply conveyed my love. I did not look up as I knew what I would see and that would only set me off too.

Brajam nodded and smiled his understanding.

Later we all went to the control room and spent nearly an hour looking at the brilliant stars and the Milky-Way spread across the sky view. The slight distortion in their colours did not detract in the least from their stunning display.

Simon was totally mesmerised by what he could see and I'm sure with his youthful and keener eyesight he saw it all in a better perspective than I did. At one stage I could see the captain standing slightly behind him but with her hand resting lightly on his shoulder. I knew she was explaining things to him in a private telepathic communication for he kept looking to right and left to view the different aspects visible. She must have shown him where Raznat was since our path towards the Starship just happened to also be in the direction of the Sagittarius Constellation. I reckoned that Simon might be getting his first lesson in astro-navigation and spatial recognition.

I looked at my wristwatch and saw that it was midday. But I knew all my systems were running slow and I queried Zanos for Earth time. Zanos conveyed that our times were slowed by 3¼ hours due to the time dilation from travelling at just over half of light velocity. And we should lose another half hour before our arrival at the Starship rendezvous point in about four hours time.

I wasn't hungry as I'd had my breakfast not so long ago. But the captain suggested we return to the dining room for a drink and a snack and meet some of the other passengers. And that is what we did.

Captain Bulzezatna must have known that there was someone special eager to meet us for as we entered the dining area we were met by our old friend Shufzaz. She didn't look a day older than her 72 years and she was as cheerful as ever. She performed a brief Sewa with me and I replied on behalf of our group. I queried her about this trip and she conveyed images of her family that she was to visit in Wentazta. She was the eldest of two other siblings both male whom she had not seen in 18 years. She knew that some arrangements were in hand regarding a partnership but she had yet to meet the one that her parents had suggested in their last communication. Apparently he too was from Wentazta and somewhat older than her by about 35 years. But in the lifespan of the Oannes this was of minor consequence. She had seen visuals of him and thought he was rather handsome.

Although we had exchanged greetings and light banter with Shufzaz on the bus craft 326-Red there had never been time for any lengthy social exchanges. I now wish that I had taken the time and effort to have socialised more since she had been a part of the crew on all those trips for which she had ferried us. But now I found that I had plenty to talk about with her. She was not overly attractive from the beauty aspect but her cheerful demeanour was what drew me to her. I wondered how Muznant and Margaret viewed my interest in Shufzaz's conversation.

The issue she found most exciting was the prospect of Nazmos being relocated closer to Raznat. She said she looked forward to the governing council accepting the idea and giving the go-ahead for it to be so. We also discussed Gozmanot and she hoped that more could be discovered about that person's life.

'It is wonderful to know that our myths actually have an origin,' she conveyed, 'and we must try to find out more about her.'

'I hope to attempt that when I visit Vaz,' I said and then changed the subject by asking why she wished Nazmos to be closer to Raznat.

'Well,' she replied, 'anyone who has lived in Anztarza and wandered the northern forests could not but want Nazmos to be the same. Is that not a good reason?'

'Yes it is,' I said. 'That is a perfectly good reason and it is why I requested that the governing council members all visited Earth and experienced for themselves what you have just said. All the visual reports they have received in the past cannot possibly carry the same weight of persuasion. Nor does it breed a love for that which surrounds you. They now have 22 years to decide on what they have seen on this visit. I feel it in my inner being that an agreement is nearly reached. But it will be Gozmanot who will be the ultimate persuader.'

'I hope so,' said Shufzaz, 'I certainly hope that our myths will govern the final outcome.'

'But you do realise that many conditions will change and not all for the better,' chimed in Jerry. 'How will you cope with the hotter weather which may come to a big city like Wentazta?'

Shufzaz was silent for a moment before answering.

'We have coped with the weather on the cold side,' she said, 'so coping with the opposite will not be that different.'

A good answer I thought, in fact a very good answer. I was impressed at how Shufzaz put her opinions with logical and thoughtful reasoning. She could go far with that sort of a mindset.

And so time went by with other passengers coming forward to talk to us. But I knew that it was Simon and me that they were keen to meet. Word certainly spreads in this Oannes open society. I hope that one day we on Earth shall be like them. It also gives me hope for our own future.

We drank glasses of Wazu and ate a few spoonfuls of very sweet Yaztraka until Zanos informed us that we were close to rendezvous point. The ship was to turn about and the neutron generators would operate in successive bursts for accurate deceleration. Captain Bulzezatna invited us to the control room to witness this operation. I knew that it was Simon whom she had in mind for this and I was pleased by her thought and regard for him.

We subsequently made our way to the control room and settled on the recliners. The ship had turned about and a diminutive sun was directly overhead. Then came that sparkling action like distant fireworks exploding high overhead. The effect was spectacular and I could see a 'wow' shaping on Simon's lips. The effect was repeated several times and when there was a long pause I knew it was over and we had reached our destination.

The ship 520-Green rotated around again and suddenly there in the distance was 8110-Gold in all its sleekness and defined glory. It was distant and though Zanos confirmed it as being nearly a thousand miles away the view panels brought us an image that belied this. And suddenly I was impatient to start this next phase of our adventure. I did so want Tania and the kids to meet Jazzatnit and to see her lovely home. I wondered if she had made any changes. Perhaps not as it would be too short an interval between successive visits. Captain Bulzezatna brought the ship to within a hundred miles of the Starship before 520-Green entered its parking loop.

After a communication with the Starship Captain Bulzezatna was able to inform me that several other spaceships were in transit but not due to arrive here for several hours. Our transfer to the Starship was not a priority at this moment and therefore no need for a hasty departure. As usual the Oannes did everything at a calm and steady pace.

My watch indicated that it was after 4 pm Earth time and I realised that we had not had anything substantial to eat since breakfast. Captain Bulzezatna picked up my thoughts and suggested we return to the dining hall shortly for a meal that was being laid out for us.

'It would have been nice to have had a glass of Wazu as a farewell gesture but I think a meal as well would be more fitting,' she conveyed.

'That would be delightful and much appreciated,' said Milly. 'I am rather in need of something.'

'I think we all are,' I added. 'I'm sure Rachel and Simon are too.'

Rachel looked up at me with large rounded eyes and nodded vigorously. I thing Simon agreed but wouldn't own up to it. He wanted to appear grown up.

'Then let us return to the dining hall and while we wait for the meal to be served up perhaps we could all share some lively conversation and a glass of refreshing Wazu,' said the captain.

When we entered, the hall food was in the process of being laid out by several of the ships crew though jugs of Wazu and glasses had already been set up. And so sitting around the table we all raised our filled glasses and wished each other well. Each of us toasted our captain for looking after us so well and transporting us to all our destinations in such good comfort. Of course our toast was done telepathically with the added emotion of affection mixed in. I could see that Margaret who was seated near the captain was deep into her own thoughts and I wondered what she was thinking. I'm sure she was impressed by how advanced the Oannes were in the ease and speed with which they travelled through deep space. I was a seasoned traveller and took it all for granted. Margaret on the other hand had only made the short journeys between Aberporth and Anztarza.

Rachel who was sitting between Tania and Muznant refused politely to drink any of the Wazu. Her glass remained untouched and I knew why. The Wazu seeds seemed alive and Rachel was quite put off by their jerky movement. Perhaps one day when she was older things might change for her. Tania passed her glass to me and I conveyed that I was drinking it on Rachel's behalf.

Quite quickly Muznant placed a glass of plain looking water in front of Rachel and implied that she give it a try. I was sure that it had been sweetened with Earth sugar especially for her. Muznant knew that Rachel did not like the Wazu seeds and so had this alternative drink ready.

'Try this darling,' said Tania, 'and tell me what you think of it.'

Rachel was hesitant at first but then remembered that her auntie Muznant would not give her something distasteful to drink. Nevertheless she had a good look at the clear liquid before slowly lifting the glass to her lips and taking a tiny sip.

'Hmm,' she hummed, 'this is nice. It tastes just like lemonade without the fizz.'

She drank half the glass before putting it down and then smiling at all around her. She looked at Muznant and conveyed her thanks. I think they then had a private little conversation after which both smiled at each other.

I could see that Captain Bulzezatna was impressed and moved with affection for our little daughter. I don't think she had taken extra special notice of her before but Rachel's refusal of the Wazu drink had shown up the strength of character of the child. Rachel had taken a lone stand among a room full of grownups and this said much to a fellow female with much authority.

It was a pleasant meal with the usual dishes and we all ate well. I liked the way Simon tried many of the dishes but I think he felt that if this was space fare then he must like it. Rachel was a bit more circumspect in her approach but the sweetened Yaztraka mash was definitely to her liking. Margaret too tucked in with a smile that said a lot. Was she doing it for my benefit? We all ate a lot of what was on the table. I was even beginning to like the flavour of the Milsony dish and its spicy after-taste. As an added bonus there was bread, butter, cheese, biscuits and jam served towards the end of the meal not to mention tea and coffee. Rachel and Simon went for the jam with their biscuits while we grownups favoured the cheese.

It was a pleasant fulfilling hour in more ways than one before it was agreed that we begin preparations for our transfer to the Starship. We said our farewell Sewas to the captain and crew generally before 1st deputy Tatizblay led us out and to the rear of the ship to where the electrostatic suits were housed. And it was not long after that we were in the shuttles and exiting the bay doors into the blackness of space. Again all the women wore headscarves to keep their hair in place. Rachel as usual had to investigate and took hers off in mid-journey. She did look funny and Simon laughed. But she managed to get the scarf back on - after a fashion!

As usual we approached the Starship 8110-Gold at an angle from its tail end which still gave us a good view of its immense size. At two miles long with a slight taper to its circular profile it gave the impression of a ship that was sleek and fast. Looking at Simon I could read his expression and knew that for him this was simply a case of love at first sight.

We slowed as we crept up the side of the Starship and as we advanced I detected a slight gravity effect upon ourselves. This increased gradually until Tatizblay decided to rotate the shuttle so that we became more comfortable in our clamped seating. The gravity effect was now in the downward direction and the rear of the Starship was visible overhead. I was surprised how elongated it appeared and Simon looked sideways at me with wonder on his face. I think he must have tired of repeating his 'wow' expression at everything new to him.

Then quite suddenly an airlock opening appeared in the side of the Starship and the shuttle slowly glided into it. There was a minor judder as the shuttle settled on the decking and I could feel that I was at normal gravity again.

Two other shuttles had accompanied us into the airlock and were now sitting towards our right side. The dimmed lighting brightened as the airlock door was closed. Then another sliding door opened ahead of the shuttle and we could all see into the massive extent of the cargo platform.

I conveyed to the others that this platform was fifty feet above the habitation platform level and both were half a mile in diametric size; and that this was for cargo storage mainly but could accommodate spaceships the size of 520-Green. It was how all the ships in Anztarza had been transported from Nazmos to Earth.

We left the shuttle and Tatizblay led our party to a large room which I knew to be the elevator that would take us down to the habitation level. When the sliding door closed I immediately recognised the slight sensation associated with dropping downwards. I heard an 'oops' exclamation from Rachel as she was not prepared for the hollow feeling in her tum. When the sliding door opened again there was a gasp of amazement from Simon and Rachel plus a few others. Margaret was totally speechless for a moment before commenting that it was huge and just like Anztarza.

Before us was a mini-city that still caused me amazement. I could see pride in the faces of our Oannes companions after all it was a great achievement especially for a Starship.

'Wow,' said Simon for the umpteenth time, 'it's just huge and its all inside a spaceship.'

'Actually son this is a Starship,' I corrected. I was just doing what my kids often did to me. I often said 'thing' to describe some object and I would get corrected immediately by one of them giving the proper name of what I'd had in mind and should have said.

Simon ignored my riposte and said, 'I never ever imagined that it could be this big.'

We were then led to a large room and took off our gold electrostatic suits. It was similar to the room on 520-Green but much more extensive. I conveyed to the others that there were several of these at this level.

Tatizblay then led us out to the central column area where the control room and captain's quarters was situated. As we approached it Captain Zakatanz came out into the open and stood near the railing that surrounded the central column. There was a pleasant expression on his face as he greeted us with the briefest and most congenial of Sewas. I responded in kind and we made a firm handshake.

Captain Zakatanz had met some of my family way back in 2006 but it had then been just a formality for him. It was his first human encounter and he had not looked favourably upon it. And after an appropriate interval of polite remarks he had offered us the freedom to tour the ship and had excused himself to attend other matters. But that was then.

'Captain,' I said aloud, 'I am very pleased to be back aboard your ship. Please let me introduce you to my family.'

And with that I conveyed a detailed relationship of all those present including Margaret as a family friend. I conveyed details of her telepathic workshops and how important that was for the eventual integration with Oannes society. I saved Simon and Rachel for the last.

'And these Captain, are my children. This is Simon my son and this is my daughter Rachel,' I said with pride. 'Simon as you know would dearly love to follow in your footsteps. I fear he has visions of grandeur and hopes one day to be a Starship captain like you.'

'I am very pleased to meet you all,' said Captain Zakatanz, 'and of course especially a future Starship captain. I would be happy to have him aboard with me when the time comes and I look forward to the prospect. I am now 225 years of age and Simon is only eight but I already sense a connection between us. Over the years I have compiled many memory texts on a variety of space travel subjects which I shall make available to him when the time comes.'

He then did something that surprised even me not to mention the other Oannes present. He communicated directly with Simon and allowed his own mind to be read. Simon responded in kind and I noticed a look of wonder appear on the captain's face. What had he seen that I had not? In our conversations over the next few days I might query this. I had a great faith in Simon's gift of premonition and perhaps Zakatanz had seen something more.

After a few seconds of direct private conversation Zakatanz turned his attention back to us with an invitation that we have all our meals with him in the captain's quarters. Muznant and Brazjaf were also included in the invitation and I was pleased that they were. Rachel would not have liked her auntie Muznant not to be there.

I then conveyed to the captain that I had been invited to Korizazit's apartment for a meal on the journey to Earth and suspected that the same might be repeated. But since I did not want to exclude members of my family I asked his advice on how a refusal or a decline would be seen. I did not wish to upset any member of the council of ministers in what could be looked upon as an insult or rudeness. I conveyed this in open minded mode hoping that it would be picked up by my friend Korizazit.

When Simon had had his premonition about the delay to our journey it had caused surprise among the ministers and they had expressed a desire to meet Simon. I think they considered Simon's gift akin to that of Gozmanot's visions. After a moments thought Zakatanz conveyed in open mind mode that I should willingly accept any invitation but request that it be postponed for when we are on Nazmos. Now why hadn't I thought of that? I conveyed my thanks to Zakatanz and he just smiled back.

Tatizblay now made his presence felt and wished us a safe journey to Nazmos and would we please excuse him and allow him to return to his duties under Captain Bulzezatna.

'May your journey be swift, safe and sure,' he smiled.

So, Captain Natazlat had passed on the catch phrase motto we had initiated on my earlier journey to Nazmos. I was pleased about that.

We performed our brief Sewas and as I watched him walk towards the electrostatic suits dressing rooms I again sensed that he was destined for a great future. A future I think that was linked to a changed Nazmos. He would become a leading voice for a new lifestyle to suit the changed climatic conditions on Nazmos. He would of course be very much older then even by Oannes standards. He and Niztrabt were still in a relationship but as yet no contract had been made between them. She was still young at 90 years of age to Tatizblay's 130 years in this year of 2016. I wished them well and hoped to see much of them in the future.

Jerry broke into my thoughts by asking a question.

'Tell me Captain,' he said, 'how does one person manage a Starship of this size and complexity?'

Captain Zakatanz smiled and conveyed a complete visual image of the Starship and its crew. There were engineers and administrators all over the ship. The cargo level above was managed separately as were the food growing tanks below them. There were deputies to look after the welfare of the passengers and crew for looking to the catering needs. But most important of all were the 23 Zanos bio-computers that controlled and monitored every aspect of the ship's functions including the health of all persons aboard. This was essential when journeys of six or seven months were undertaken; the normal travel time between Nazmos and Earth. Of course when all this detail was conveyed telepathically with full visual imagery it became much easier to understand. And it had all taken just seconds.

'Thank you Captain,' said Jerry, 'that is very clear and I now understand what a complex organisation is working under you. However, does that not make you feel somewhat redundant as its leader?'

Captain Zakatanz smiled his understanding and coming forward reached out and touched Jerry's arm.

'Yes my friend it does,' he said smiling, 'and I hope it stays that way. But every ship needs a focal point in someone to give the necessary commands and it just so happens that I was elected to it. Our system of communication allows me to know everything that is going on in the Starship which then makes me the person responsible. As captain I must allow things to run smoothly without undue interference on my part by trusting that my crew are performing their duties well. But if something untoward occurs then I am responsible and will give the necessary commands for its solution. There is much power under my control in both quality of personnel and machinery. In Earth language you would say that you had men and material in abundance under the authority of a commander. So it is with me and my Starship. I say 'my Starship' because it is my sole responsibility that every journey be uneventful and routine as I hope this journey to Nazmos will be.'

He again smiled at Jerry and then around at all of us.

'It is customary that special guests drink a glass of Wazu with the captain before a journey such as ours,' he said, 'and I would be honoured if you could all join me at the captain's table.'

I accepted for all of us and we followed him into his quarters and he gestured us to our table places. For Simon he pointed to a place beside his but Simon politely declined and conveyed that he would sit with his parents. Zakatanz smiled at this and changed his own position to be central with his guests. Simon would make a good leader he conveyed to me and Tania and with Gozmanot's gift to guide him he would be extraordinary. Tania squeezed my hand and her face glowed with pride. And I felt the same.

I conveyed to Zakatanz that I thought Simon's premonition gift was for one purpose only and that was to guide me safely through unknown space towards Zarama. After that my inner voice communicated nothing at all. We conversed for another twenty minutes before Zakatanz conveyed that we must be in need of settling into our allotted accommodation which was prepared and ready for us. Mine was to be the same as before and Zanos would communicate guidance where each of the others was located.

As it happened mine was the first and second apartment connected by a through doorway. And then were mum and dad, Ron and Brenda, Milly and Jerry and finally Margaret with an apartment to her self. Muznant and Brazjaf were across the pathway from us and I could guess that they preferred to keep separate at this moment in time. Among the Oannes people they were my dearest friends and I wished the very best for them. Muznant loved Rachel and I could see her loving her own even more. I could not help thinking that if I had read the signs right then success would soon be theirs. I dearly wished it for them. Muznant didn't even think about her phantom pregnancy such was the breeding euphoria that had come over her. And Brazjaf was just as euphoric about it all.

In our apartments we each went to see what the other's was like just out of curiosity and I think that a slight disappointment showed when all were found to be similar. What little luggage we had brought with us was in each of the rooms plus brand new Oannes style outfits complete in all aspects. We sat chatting together in our double apartment for some time when Zanos conveyed that two more ships had arrived on location and one of these was carrying the Nazmos governing council of ministers. Zanos pre-empted my query by informing us that hopefully in about ten hours from now all transfers would be complete and the journey to Nazmos could commence.

I wondered again if I would get another invite to visit my council member friends Korizazit, Ritozanan and Nerbtazwi. The council had expressed a wish to meet Simon and I would suggest that it would be better done in the Great Hall on Nazmos. I would follow Zakatanz's advice.

Also I must make an effort to meet and get to know the engineer Niztukan. Perhaps he might like to be a direct witness when I accelerated the Starship to the planned 600 FTL velocity. Or I could request Brajam to arrange the meeting at some workplace location. I would very much like to know him better as I think he is a brave Oannes person from when I saw him racing over the neutron shield of 9110-Red.

Our accommodation was generous and comfortable though Simon was not overly happy about sharing a room with Rachel. In Dudley he had got used to the privacy in his own room. He worried that Rachel would mind him keeping the light on so that he could read the books he had brought along. I said that it was only for four days and a bit and besides there would be so much else to think about.

Tania also did not think that twin beds were ideal but I thought it best not to have any distraction while I was maintaining the Starship at its planned FTL velocity; if you can guess what I mean!

None of our group was tired but I felt that I needed to rest within this ten hour interlude before the Starship began its journey. Tania said she'd ensure I got that and took the kids with her to their grandma's rooms. I lay down on my twin bed and thought of my plan for accelerating the Starship. I'd do it much the same as on the journey here and see what telekinetic force level needed to be applied. Zanos and I would work together and I would try not to exceed my target velocity. My telekinetic gift seemed to increase in strength each time I used it so I was curious to see at what force level the target velocity would be attained. And those were my last thoughts before my eyes closed and I drifted off into sleep. It's funny that we are unable to know the exact moment that sleep takes over from conscious thought.

When I awoke I thought I must have slept for ages; six or seven hours at least since I felt wide awake and refreshed. However Zanos conveyed that I had slept for just four hours which I found as rather disappointing.

I sat up and went to the washroom and splashed water on my face and dried vigorously before venturing out onto the habitation platform. None of our group was around so I walked across to the control room. There was no sign of Captain Zakatanz there but one of his deputies welcomed me in. This was Pzabandiz and he was of middle age at 160 years but most alert in his posture. He was from Wentazta and quite pleased to meet me on his own. He had followed all that I had achieved and I was rather embarrassed when he mentioned some of the things I had done that had really impressed him. He said it was wonderful how I had managed to shift a large planet like Platwuz. He hoped that I could do the same with Zarama but I read a hint of doubt in his mind. I too had a similar uncertainty but then I was relying upon the fact that I had been called for this task and must surely get the required assistance from that greater power behind all of this. I had to keep faith in that belief and in myself.

All our communication was telepathic and he conveyed that I was the first Earth person he had ever talked to. He had never been to Earth or Anztarza for that matter and so knew nothing about us humans other than what the reports showed. To Pzabandiz Earth civilization was very far behind that of the Oannes. I think he was trying hard not to show rudeness in his thoughts about humans. I simply replied that change was on the way and I hoped that one day we too would approach the civilization level that the Oannes had achieved. I hoped that integration between our peoples might take place then. But that possibility was at least a couple of millennia away.

I then turned the topic to news of the captain's whereabouts and was informed that he was personally giving my family members a tour of the ship. They had been gone well over an hour and were probably on their way back. Zanos automatically took this as a query and immediately informed me that the party were currently on the cargo deck above us but were about to make their way back down to the control room. I decided that I liked the company of Pzabandiz and his diverse conversational variety. Eventually I opened my mind to him and he did the same for me.

He was an engineer by training but had opted for spaceship and then Starship duties when a friendship had turned sour. She was a fellow engineer much like Vazlodip but extremely career minded and according to Pzabandiz rather selfish. Her name was Zazrantiz and she was the same age as him. He thought her pretty but noticed that she had a very sharp and impolite manner whenever she did not get her way. They had been friendly for well over a year when she decided that Pzabandiz was not for her. He had been saddened and upset at losing her and decided to forge a career far away from her.

My thoughts went to the relationship of Zakatanz and Hazazamunt and of how their own relationship had been broken. There was no comparison but the sadness was there just the same. In that respect the Oannes were no different emotionally from us humans and I felt a connection there.

I queried Pzabandiz about the arrival of the other ships and he informed me that all transfers had been completed during the last few hours and the council of ministers and their entourage were comfortably aboard the Starship. They had been located in their own privileged sector of the habitation platform as previously and Zanos was instructed to maintain their privacy. I thought about Korizazit and whether he'd had any further inner voice experiences.

I noticed that there was one topic that Pzabandiz did not mention and that was with regard to the relocation of Nazmos closer to Raznat. By this I understood that he was not keen about it or that he was uncertain as to its merits. I considered that had he been totally opposed to the idea then his attitude towards me would have been very different and I should have sensed the underlying strain in his conversation. I had detected none. However I decided not to bring up the subject either.

Subsequently our conversation drifted to the passengers aboard and their accommodation facilities. Normal journeys took over six months to complete and I asked how they coped overall. Food was the main issue he said and so our conversation turned to our likes and dislikes in this field. I said the sweetened Yaztraka was among my favourite dishes. He said he too liked it but his favourite was only available on Nazmos and was a concocted dish called Ribzonta. This was a new dish with known ingredients but mixed according to a recipe. Pzabandiz said that it was quite spicy from the added Milsony but also had Mirzondip and Raizna in it and cooked as elongated shapes with a thin coating of Starztal granules. I thought that this would be ideal finger food for the kids and I must remember to request a sample from Jazzatnit when I see her. There must be other recipes in the Oannes cookery repertoire which I must ask about. Rachel had conveyed a secret thought that the Oannes food in Anztarza had been boring. Well perhaps with the appropriate recipe book it could be made not so 'boring'.

Just then Captain Zakatanz and my tourist family arrived back with a buzz.

'We wondered where you might have got to,' said a flushed Tania. 'We've had the grandest tour of this magnificent Starship. It is truly impressive. Do you know it took over five hundred years to build and even now they are adding bits and pieces to it? We went to wake you but you were gone.'

Rachel came up to me and privately conveyed that she was thirsty and hungry. I conveyed this to the captain and he immediately had tea, bread, biscuits, cheese, butter and jam set out for us. I think we were of the same mind and politely sat down and tucked in. I just love plain bread and butter.

I noticed that Simon stayed close to the captain and seemed to await the next bit of information from him. And the captain did not seem to mind this in the least.

'Thank you captain for showing my family around your Starship,' I conveyed. 'I'm sure they all appreciated it especially Simon.'

'Yes Captain,' said Jerry aloud, 'we all thank you for showing and explaining everything to us. It was wonderful of you to take such an interest. It was most generous of you.'

'It has been a pleasure to return something that Ashley has given me. Only he can know what I mean,' said the captain looking directly at me and nodding an acknowledgment.

I knew exactly what he was referring to. He loved Hazazamunt from the bottom of his very being and I had eased a guilt he had carried around for a hundred years.

'Perhaps one day I shall do more,' he added looking towards Simon.

There was an aura of admiration and respectfulness emanating from Simon that was quite obvious to all. I wonder what he would make of his dad when I accelerated the Starship to its cruise velocity and saw the reaction of his idolised captain. Was there a hint of envy lurking somewhere? I hoped not since I looked forward to Simon making his own way in a career he would love. And Captain Zakatanz was someone even I could look up to. Simon would be in good hands.

I remember Simon returning from school one day and all he could talk about was his new teacher Mr Waites. I think the whole of the class of twenty seven kids, boys and girls had been taken by his youthful looks and manner. In fact so was I when I did meet him. He seemed to connect with the kids and used street expressions that they all thought quite 'cool'. Simon came home with stories about his teacher saying this and saying that. Tania and I always made an effort to listen as best we could.

Perhaps a similar sort of relationship had developed in Simon's mind with regard to the Starship captain; which I don't think was a bad thing for his future career. I mentioned this to Tania and she didn't seem to mind it at all. I conveyed that once we were on Nazmos he'd have plenty of other things to consider. Like the huge ship 98103-Pink and then the tour of the planet on the Nazmos based craft 556-Blue under the young Captain Lyozonpa.

There was plenty to think about and with our conversation time seemed to fly. And so it was no surprise when Zanos informed us that the Starship was 'secured' and ready to begin its journey to Nazmos as planned. It was then up to the captain to give the command.

The Oannes technology was so advanced and so stable that no preamble was really necessary for the ship to start its full operations. Starships are always in readiness with all the functions continually operating to keep the internal systems going. It was like a miniature Anztarza including the gravity effect from the neutron shield. So all it required was for the impulse generators and motors to begin their task of accelerating the ship. What a culture.

As such I believe that Captain Zakatanz must have commanded Zanos to proceed with the journey immediately. I only knew that acceleration of the Starship had been initiated when I heard the whisper of relative movement between the platform and central column. The platform complex was moving closer to the front of the Starship to negate the tremendous backward g-force of acceleration that was being imposed. I would not be applying my own telekinetic push for another hour at least or until the Starship had attained a velocity close to its normal cruise speed.

I conveyed all this to the family group and they expressed surprise that the ship was moving at all. No one had felt the slightest effect of it. Zanos then conveyed to all that the Starship 8110-Gold had just exceeded light velocity and was still accelerating.

I noticed that the platform was very gradually adjusting back upwards relative to the central column. I knew that as the velocity of the ship increased into the multiple FTL area the space grid energy-medium impacting upon the neutron shield would cause greater resistance to its progress. As such the ship's acceleration level would reduce. I was impatient to commence my own contribution so I conveyed my thoughts to the captain. He suggested that I wait till Zanos confirmed the ship's velocity as approaching 7 or 8 FTL. When I queried Zanos on this I was informed that this velocity should be approached in just over two hours from commencement of the journey. I felt that was a long wait for me and I would have liked to begin applying my telekinetic push considerably sooner. Captain Zakatanz conveyed that he would be happy for me to start my push whenever I considered it appropriate. I then liaised with Zanos and intimated that I would like to begin sooner rather than later.

It was nearly half an hour later that Zanos conveyed that the ship was approaching 4 FTL. That was good enough for me so I informed both Zanos and the captain that I would commence my own push upon the ship in five minutes time.

I then progressively increased my telekinetic effort upon the neutron shield at the rate of one push level every few seconds. I felt I was climbing up a stairway. Zanos continually informed me of the ship's velocity. I paused for twenty minutes at the fifty push level in order to compare the velocity with that on the previous occasion. Zanos conveyed that the ship was approaching 295 FTL. That told me that my telekinetic power had indeed developed further. Zarama here I come I said to myself though with not quite the confidence I should have felt.

At the ninety push level the Starship achieved 560 FTL though it was still accelerating. I waited before I applied any further force. I now went one push step at a time with adequate pauses in between as the velocity approached 600 FTL. It was at the 97 push level that the Starship finally attained a steady velocity that was just under 600 FTL so I left it at that. I remembered what Brajam and Vazlodip had said so I was loath to exceed this velocity. I locked my mind at this push level and then informed the captain that I was done. He conveyed his heartfelt thanks and hoped we could share many more Starship journeys together. Starship captains tended to hide their emotions but I knew he was elated at the ship's new record velocity.

'One more journey back to Earth,' I conveyed, 'and then I can put my feet up and relax for the next twenty two years.'

I sensed his amusement at this.

Muznant came over to me and conveyed a private message to Tania who was beside me. I hadn't realised it but I had been involved with the acceleration of the ship for several hours now. Simon had been beside his mum and dad all through the above acceleration process and I had felt his admiring eyes upon me. I sensed his pride that I was his dad. Yes, it was a very good feeling which I conveyed privately to Tania.

Muznant thought I needed refreshment and Captain Zakatanz conveyed that we should all retreat to the captain's quarters for a well earned meal. And a lavish meal it was too. I suspect it had been specially laid on for my benefit and to celebrate a velocity never achieved before by an Oannes Starship. I wondered what Captain Natazlat would make of it when it became known on Nazmos. I received a thought out of the blue that she would expect a similar treatment for her Starship. But that could only occur if her ship conveyed me back to Earth. Surely Zakatanz had already laid claim to that privilege.

Before the meal I drank two glasses of Wazu and only then realised how hungry I was. Tania sat across from me but Simon was right beside me. The fact that I was continuing to maintain the Starship at its cruise velocity without any visible effort on my part seemed to surprise and impress him.

'How do you do it dad,' he asked?

'I really don't know son,' I replied. 'The initial acceleration did require considerable effort and concentration on my part. But once cruise velocity was achieved I just locked my mind at that push level and left it at that. My mind seems to be able to take over the burden of maintaining the necessary force and I don't need to even think about it. When the time comes for deceleration of the Starship in four and a half days time I shall have to voluntarily reduce my push levels in a gradual step down process. This would be the reverse of what I did to accelerate it. I'm getting better at it with practice and find that my telekinetic power seems to be increasing with each application. But I don't think I'm quite ready for Zarama just yet.'

I could see admiration and pride in Simon's eyes but my heart skipped a beat when I thought that I would be relying on his premonition gift when the modified Starship 4110-Silver carried me the 525 light-years distance to Zarama. And this reminded me of Philip. I wondered where he could be. I'd not felt his presence since that first time when he informed me about the 'big task'.

Rachel sat between Muznant and Margaret and I could see her trying several of the dishes that Muznant suggested. Margaret and Muznant often spoke directly to one another and I sensed a conspiracy of sorts being hatched. Margaret had fitted in well with the Oannes society and I admired her for it. There was still a vague mystery about her that I felt in the back of my mind.

Tania and I then had a private conversation across the table and she suggested we return to our rooms after the meal for a rest. It was well past midnight according to my wristwatch and I realised that our body clocks must be in overdrive. Simon said that he wasn't feeling tired at all but Tania said he must also think how Rachel felt and make her get her rest.

It was another hour before we thanked the captain for his hospitality and retreated to our individual rooms. Muznant and Brazjaf were rather keen to get to their sleep tank I thought. I believe Zanos had been instructed to induce a mood for sleep among the passengers in general which I thought was an excellent system.

The Oannes had simulated periods of day and night which was the norm on their entire spaceship fleet just as it was in Anztarza. Without it there would not be the sense of elapsing days and weeks.

And so here on the Starship 8110-Gold the first journey night descended upon us at least in our quarter and we all slept in our comfortable beds. Tania reached across and we held hands before sleep came. I sensed her love strong and powerful and I went to sleep looking forward to our return to Earth and twenty two years of wonderful companionship. She makes my life so worthwhile that nothing else really matters. Other thoughts came too but sleep took over before I could dwell upon them.

And so the next few days passed and I had visits from Korizazit and Nerbtazwi. Ritozanan didn't come though she communicated telepathically. We agreed that Simon be presented to the council in the Domed Hall on Nazmos just as I had been. They missed Simon because he stuck like glue to the captain's side.

I conveyed my request to Brajam about meeting up with Niztukan but received a vague reply about the man being busy with his duties monitoring the shield etc. Niztukan however conveyed his own message of regards to me and said he would try to meet with me before the end of the journey. I expressed my admiration for his work and his bravery and would like to get to know him personally. This seemed to amuse him somewhat that I who was quite famous should want to get to know an obscure engineer from Platwuz. I conveyed my own feeling on that and we came to a mutual understanding and regard for one another and left it at that. But I feel that I have made the first contact and will see more of him. I felt good about it.

Apart from a reasonable breakfast we were given two main meals each simulated day. One was at about 2.pm and the other quite late about 9.pm. But Rachel and Simon had snacks in between these times. Tea and Wazu was always available; and biscuits of course.

Simon came up to me frequently and I could see that he was looking for any signs of strain on my part with regard to the fact that I was still applying a continuous telekinetic effort to maintain the Starship at its cruise FTL velocity. I always smiled down at him and conveyed that the push effort took care of itself as an involuntary action without my even being aware of it. I think Simon was quite in awe of my powers; more so now that I was demonstrating it in a practical fashion.

About the third day in the evening period about 5.pm a very slight judder was felt throughout the ship. I looked around at Tania and she too had felt it. I queried Zanos about it but was informed that all systems aboard 8110-Gold were normal. At the time Tania and I were in our apartment sitting at the small table. Rachel was out somewhere with Muznant and Margaret while Simon was in the control room as he had been for most of the day.

I then queried Zanos more specifically as to the reason for that single vibration effect but again was simply informed that all systems were functioning normally. I picked up a lot of emotional stress from among the passengers in general and I guessed this had to do with their concern for the safety of the ship. I queried my inner voice but got no response. Simon then came in and I looked questioningly at him but he shrugged his shoulders and shook his head. He too knew nothing about it.

Tania, Simon and I then went outside and were met by others of our group. Muznant and Margaret were there too with Rachel who was wondering what all the agitation was about. Apparently she hadn't felt anything. Margaret seemed the most agitated and I said that Zanos had reported all as normal. The ship's velocity hadn't altered and I decided to wait for the captain to make an announcement – telepathic of course. I wondered what Brajam, Niztukan and all the other crew members would make of what had just occurred.

I then saw Brajam along with quite a few new Oannes faces walk hastily into the control room. I presumed that they had been summoned there by Captain Zakatanz for a full report. Everything seemed to continue as smoothly as before and I wondered if it might happen again. I sincerely hoped not.

It was nearly an hour before the captain made his telepathic broadcast. Apparently Zanos had computed that a minor object had been in collision with the outer surface of the neutron shield. From the impact effect Zanos analysed that the space object had an inertial mass equivalent to sixty-two and a half tons. The neutron shield had absorbed the impact without endangering the integrity of the Starship. Velocity loss had been negligible and the previous velocity resumed. Anticipated arrival at Raznat destination was one and a half days from now.

Since I was essential to the Starship's velocity I decided to enter the control room on my own and ask my questions directly. I needed to know as much as possible about FTL travel and of the dangers that existed in space. I was thinking about my trip towards Zarama one day.

I entered the old dining area and immediately saw several very serious looking Oannes sitting around it. The captain gestured me to a seat beside him which I took quietly. All communication was telepathic and I tried to link my mind into it to see what was being discussed. As soon as I did this I realised that the focal point was Zanos. Rapid fire questions were being put to the bio-computer system and equally rapid answers given in return. One of those in the room was Niztukan and I could see why. Anything to do with the neutron shield was his concern.

Captain Zakatanz had a most serious demeanour about him and I could see that he was extremely annoyed that the presence of a rogue object in space had gone undetected prior to setting out from Earth. He did not like excuses or vague explanations and plainly conveyed this. Niztukan conveyed that he could offer nothing towards the identification of the mass until the Starship was at destination. He could then carry out a scan of the outer surface of the neutron shield. The presence of aggregations of heavy atom nuclei might help him towards an analysis of a probable object. However one aspect came to his mind and that was of an Oannes private spacecraft. Although this was close to the correct inertial mass it was too far out from Raznat to be plausible. At nearly two light years distance what private craft could venture so far unless it had no pilot aboard?

A sudden thought came into my mind but I immediately blocked it from any mental probing. But Zakatanz had been about to query me about my opinion on the matter in hand at that precise moment and caught part of this thought. His eyes widened as he stared at me and in the room there was an expectant telepathic silence.

I shook my head vigorously at the captain, shut my eyes and closed my mind. I remained silent like this for a full minute trying to make sense of what that thought entailed and then slowly stood up and walked out of the room and onto the open platform. Tania was close to our apartments with our little group of travellers and she immediately saw my expression and walked over to me. I conveyed only to her in a selectively private communication the thought that had come into my mind but which I could not quite understand. Not as yet anyway. I needed to speak to the captain privately and also with Zanos to sort this out. Tania put her hand in mine and gave it a supportive squeeze. I'm so glad she is by my side on this trip.

Slowly we made our way back to our rooms though all were curious about what had gone on in the captain's quarters. I told them as much as I could of the situation with regard to an object impacting against the neutron shield but that at the moment no one really had any idea of an explanation.

'What are you thinking,' asked mum for she had read my body language? She had always known when I was concerned about something. I suppose all mums are like that.

'It's the Captain,' I replied. 'I feel I need to discuss something with him concerning what has just occurred but I think it might upset him. It really is a very delicate matter. He has a great responsibility for the safety of this ship and the last thing I want is to confuse his mindset or his concentration towards his duties. But he knows that I have a notion about the impact so I shall have to wait till he calls me to him. For now though I'd love a nice hot mug of tea?'

'And a biscuit,' chimed in Rachel.

'Was it another spacecraft dad,' asked Simon?

'Why do you say that son,' I replied?

'Oh, just a thought,' he said. 'Don't worry dad I've not had a premonition of any kind. I didn't know that a collision or anything like that would happen.'

Simon smiled at me for he knew exactly what I had been thinking. I sometimes think that these kids are better at reading minds than some Oannes.

So far this was the first serious thing that had happened on this interstellar journey. I thought of that other journey I would have to make to reach Zarama; a journey distance of some 525 apparent light-years. What objects would we encounter as 4110-Silver sped towards it. I should like to have Simon's premonition gift at hand then to warn of any dangers lurking in our FTL pathway.

It was wonderful to have my family and friends around me and I thought back to the previous three weeks when I had been without them. I had certainly missed them then and remember promising myself that I would never go anywhere again without at least Tania by my side.

I often reminisced and saw her as that thirteen year old girl, tall for her age with wide staring hazel eyes looking across the pub at me. Her hair had been a reddish brown colour then and looking at her I could still see quite a bit of the young girl in her now more mature features. I had never known when she'd made up her mind about me but I wouldn't be surprised if it was right then. On my part I had simply considered her to be someone who was rather mysterious and struck a chord in my thoughts. I should be content with my life which really is quite complete; except for this persistent worry about Zarama.

I got no call from the captain which rather surprised me. But he knew what he was about and it was much later after our evening meal that he requested that I stay behind for a private moment with him. I conveyed this to Tania and the others so that they would not be concerned when I remained behind afterwards.

I poured myself another glass of Wazu and stared at the captain awaiting his query. A visible sadness seemed to descend upon him and I knew that he had caught more of my earlier thought than I suspected.

'Can it be true,' he asked of me?

'What has been established,' I replied?

'The spacecraft that I flew in with Hazazamunt was catalogued as 17426-Black. I have queried Zanos about the Nazmos records and am informed that her ship's gross inertial mass was recorded as sixty two and a half tons. This is the same as the mass that impacted against the shield of this Starship. Most ships of this class were slightly less than this because they were standard built. Hazazamunt had improvements made to the size and power of her impulse motors and generators which resulted in the additional mass.'

We were both silent and thoughtful for a while during which time my mind raced and bubbled uncontrollably with an effervescence of thoughts. I believed in fate or divine intervention or call it what you will. How else could I have met the Marsh family and through them Philip Stevens? And then there came the diaries of Andrew Pando and the 'thinking stone' leading to a meeting with the Oannes people. And here I was married to my Tania and with two beautiful children and racing through interstellar space at a faster-than-light velocity.

Captain Zakatanz picked up all my thoughts and could not help but smile.

'I wish I had this grounding of faith that you humans possess,' he said aloud, 'but sadly I do not. For me every event follows a pattern of logical sense many of which I cannot explain. I accept each for the very fact that it is there. Something tragic took place a hundred years ago and another event has just occurred. Both are of concern to me. Because of your thoughts Ashley I now begin to suspect that the two might be linked by some strange coincidence. But I cannot know for sure although I trust in your intuition on the connection.'

There was a pleading aspect to his statement.

'There are many things we can never be sure about,' I said. 'But of one thing I am certain and that is the caring love that existed between you and Hazazamunt was a solid fact and that it will continue on forever in your very being. It is alive inside you and there is nothing you can do about it. The past is an indelible fact and no one can expunge it. History is history my friend.'

I paused to let what I had said sink in.

'If it was 17426-Black that crossed our path then it is now an integral part of this Starship,' I added. 'Think of it like this that Hazazamunt has returned to you in a way you never expected. And she has done it without endangering your Starship. As its captain you are a part of this ship and now she is too. I can say no more that that.'

There was a long moment of silence between us before Zakatanz stood up slowly. Again there was a brief pause and after nodding to me he turned and walked pensively out into the open space of the habitation platform. I expect he'll be walking for quite a while in a sort of meditation of the probable events of the past one hundred years. He had done the same when I first revealed Hazazamunt's condition to him.

I knew that I must keep all this from my family for even a stray thought from any one of them might be picked up and Captain Zakatanz's privacy would be no more. Only Tania knew about a little part of it that I'd been forced to reveal to her. But once we are back on Earth I shall reveal it to everyone. Oh, how I was looking forward to the peace and quiet of family life in Dudley for the next couple of decades.

I then stood up and left the room to stand outside near the pillar railing. I could see no sign of the captain but the habitation platform is a large area densely packed with many structures so he could be anywhere. I stood still for several minutes thinking about the possible event that we had just discussed. I could see that the past had returned for Zakatanz and that this could bring an end to the saga. At least I hoped it would.

'Where are you?' I conveyed to Tania and the others generally.

'We thought to stroll around the platform area,' came from mum. 'We won't be long now.'

481

I walked to our apartment and lay on my back on the bed. I couldn't help thinking about Hazazamunt and what must have occurred all those years ago before even granddad was born. But as I tried to concentrate on her pretty looks the vision of Jazzatnit kept popping up. I thought about the courtyard in Wentazta and how I should love to see Tania's expression as she walked around all the glass tanks with their Nazmos flora displayed. I wondered if there were any additions on the artificial rose that I had named after Rachel. And they must definitely experience the fabulous sunset 'Dark Wind' phenomenon up there on the glass sided terrace.

I must have dozed off and only came wide awake again when I heard the shuffling feet and the voices. I sat up, blinked my sleep away and then stretched my arms wide in a sort of animal stretching action. I mustn't forget the accompanying big yawn as they all walked in.

'Oh look he's been asleep again,' said Tania teasing but coming up to me and putting her arms around my neck. My face was in her tummy area as she kissed the top of my head before setting down beside me. She was all smiles as were the others. Margaret's face had an odd expression but knowing her I understood what it meant; another Vicky-like expression.

'Did you say that this was a four and a half day journey to Nazmos,' asked Jerry, 'because if it is then we have just over a day to go?'

I queried Zanos on this and we were all informed that estimated time to destination was thirty two and a half hours from now. And so tomorrow roughly about this time I would need to coordinate with Zanos and commence reducing my telekinetic push effort. That should take between three and four hours and after that it would be about six hours to destination. It was easier for Zanos to plot a more exact course when below 3 FTL velocity. Journey time at two-thirds of light velocity took approximately two hours and the destination location could then be reached with pinpoint accuracy. The Starship would complete its journey facing backwards. I conveyed this to all but mainly for Simon's benefit, our future space cadet.

That night when we had our evening meal with the captain he appeared to be his normal charming self. But I knew that he had not fully recovered from the thought that it somehow might have been Hazazamunt's spacecraft that struck the Starship. He had assumed that her spacecraft probably disappeared by flying into Raznat all those years ago. And now the possibility arose that the scenario might have been slightly different. Had she headed towards her sun but somehow missed it fractionally and instead received tremendous acceleration from a slingshot effect? Had her craft then continued burnt and blind to its fated rendezvous with Zakatanz's Starship one hundred years later? Was this the scenario that was haunting the captain? Possibly but I couldn't be sure. The big question was why hadn't the craft been spotted by the survey teams roaming space to keep the Sol to Raznat space lane free of craft or space debris?

After the meal I again stayed behind and this time I asked the captain if there had been any further analysis by Niztukan and the engineering team.

'I was not expecting any,' he conveyed, 'and possibly we shall never know for sure. But I thank you Ashley for both your revelations. You have many gifts and I have benefited from them in more ways than I expected. However I came to a decision yesterday as I walked the platform and that was that I shall not be making the return journey to Earth with you. 8110-Gold has made both the trips to Earth and back and needs to be checked out thoroughly. I shall let Captain Natazlat or another have that honour. I need to visit family on Nazmos.'

My heart skipped a beat as I had a great affection and respect for Natazlat the youngish looking female captain of 9110-Red. I also realised that Captain Zakatanz needed a break and to come to terms with the news of Hazazamunt. He would probably first visit his family and give them his thoughts on the matter of Hazazamunt's disappearance. Then he might go to the old haunts that he and his love spent time at and relive some of their past. I hope he didn't come to any rash conclusion regarding his career as Starship captain. I was counting on him to look after Simon's cadetship.

I hoped it would be Natazlat who took us back to Earth and not another. I'm sure I shall be happy with whoever it was but Natazlat would be my first choice. I could promise her a record velocity that would stand for at least twenty two years; a sort of bribe for her reputation. I wonder if 4110-Silver would be ready by then and what maximum FTL velocity it would be permitted. Would a four figure FTL velocity be allowed in its design makeup? After all Zarama was an apparent 525 light years distant. Or was it less?

Although the light seen today had left Zarama 525 years ago it was calculated that because of Zarama's approach velocity it was closer than that. Zanos had worked out that in those 525 years Zarama would have covered a distance of 93.2 light years towards Nazmos. So in reality Zarama was now at an invisible location of 431.8 light years from Nazmos.

As to Captain Zakatanz's visit to his family on Nazmos I wondered what he would say about Hazazamunt. If I knew the captain he would not keep anything back. He would divulge everything that had been discussed between us and let them draw their own conclusions. It would be the end of a chapter for them but only the beginning of a new life for him; at least in his thoughts and his memories of Hazazamunt. We drank another glass of Wazu as a gesture of goodwill and I couldn't help but raise my glass in a final toast to this sad but very likeable captain.

'To tomorrow and to all the tomorrows after that,' I said and made a point of touching my glass towards his. Zakatanz raised his glass too and repeated my toast. There was a great respect between us and I thought how my opinion of him had changed from that brief contact with the taciturn Oannes captain of ten years ago. It was after another hour of inconsequential pleasant conversation that I finally left to return to my apartment.

The next morning at breakfast I enquired of the captain as to the journey remaining. He understood what I meant and queried Zanos about it. Deceleration was to begin at noon which was just two hours away. Because of our extreme velocity the deceleration was to be a slower process than usual at least down to 500 FTL. Thereafter I would proceed as on the previous occasion. When I had ceased my telekinetic effort and the ship was entirely under its own impulse power then Zanos estimated the time to rendezvous would be about six hours. Zanos also conveyed that all was ready with the reverse directed neutron generators and I confirmed my own readiness for the noon deadline. This was also relayed to all passengers on board. The engineering crew were ready with whatever they were tasked to do. It looked as if Niztukan would be too busy to meet up with me after all.

And so at precisely one minute past noon I contacted Zanos and then commenced to reduce my telekinetic push effort by one level every two minutes. After two hours of this my push effort was down to level 67 and the Starship's velocity had reduced to 365 FTL. Zanos confirmed that I could now reduce my push levels at the slightly faster rate of one a minute. However I decided to rest my mind with short pauses after each drop of ten push levels. And so it was just over two hours later that I was able to release my mind of all telekinetic activity. The Starship was now entirely under its own impulse power and Zanos confirmed that its velocity was at 12.5 FTL. Time to Raznat parking location would be six hours from now.

After being restricted to the central zone of the habitation platform I felt the desire for a good walk-about to stretch my legs. I conveyed this to Tania and she replied that she would accompany me. We did a brisk walk from our apartment to the far wall and then back and across to the opposite side then returned to our rooms. I reckon we must have walked a mile and I felt quite good after the exercise. Of course there were interruptions when we met and talked to other passengers.

Although the walk had been invigorating having lasted nearly an hour I realised I felt quite fatigued in my head. I put it down to all the telekinetic effort of the past four days. It was not long to go before the evening meal and I told Tania to wake me in time for it. I would just shut my eyes for half an hour. Tania suggested that I sleep as necessary and she would have something brought for me later. She leaned over and kissed me lightly on my lips and whispered something that sounded like 'my hero'. I think I went to sleep smiling.

When I did wake I queried Zanos and was surprised that I had been asleep for nearly six hours. The Starship was at its Raznat parking location and spaceships were already on their way to meet us.

I was ravenous and thirsty and raring to go. Tania said I was to go to the captain as soon as I awoke. But I decided I'd freshen up with a shower and shave and then put on my best colourful tunic outfit before venturing out. I felt invigorated from my sleep.

My watch indicated that it was 5.am and most of our group were still asleep. They'd had their evening meal while I slept and returned to the rooms just after 10.pm.

As I showered I could see Tania watching and I read her mind. At my suggestion we both got into the sleep tank in the next room completely naked and frolicked quietly so as not to wake the kids. It was a lovely feeling of freedom and I understood how naturists must feel. We swam around and hugged and kissed above and below water and in the end resorted to our twin beds. I felt sated afterwards and thought Tania the most wonderful and gifted of wives. It was a joyful experience and it made me wonder if I should have a sleep tank installed at home in Dudley. Maybe one day when the kids had grown up was a last thought before I fell into another deep sleep.

It was close to 9.am when I awoke again and definitely feeling very hungry. Tania was still fast asleep so I dressed quietly and made my way to the captain's quarters.

Captain Zakatanz was sitting at the table and I understood he had been there the whole night. After my greeting I conveyed a desire for a mug of tea and something to eat. I had a glass of Wazu while I waited for my tea which came soon enough. This was followed by the breakfast items which were brought by a couple of crew members. I tucked into the toasted bread with the butter, cheese and jam. It was not long before Tania appeared with Simon and Rachel in tow. Then a bit later the others of our group also joined us. I got a rather curious knowing look from Margaret as though she knew what Tania and I had been up to earlier. The last to appear were a cheerful Muznant and Brazjaf.

After my fifth toast my tum began to feel happy again. Then as I was having my third mug of tea I sensed Zakatanz's gaze and knew he wished to communicate something. Now why did I suspect that it also involved the engineer Niztukan? Perhaps my inner voice was becoming secretive.

So again I remained seated as the others all left after the meal. Zakatanz then conveyed that he had a special request of me. For him it was a complicated issue and he hesitated in his communication. It was not that I feared for my safety but the prospect of skimming over the neutron shield was not something that I had envisaged.

Niztukan then came in smiling a very smug sort of a smile. Quite obviously the captain had already conveyed his intentions to him. The task was normal for Niztukan since he did it after every Starship journey. The captain conveyed that he had thought long and hard about his proposal and was convinced that it was what he wanted.

I knew that the captain had told Niztukan everything regarding Hazazamunt's disappearance and of my theory that the impact on the Starship's neutron shield was possibly her spacecraft 17426-Black.

In view of this Niztukan said he'd not only do his normal checks but also needed to add equipment for a complete scan of the shield surface. This would show up the structural peaks on its surface left by any striking object. Although minor the scan would reveal its extent and possibly type of object. Niztukan said that all this was necessary for the starship's records and to show up in future scans the rate of neutron particle flow across the surface of the shield with time. The Oannes were always very thorough in their analysis of any such event.

At first Niztukan had initially not liked the idea of the captain being aboard but relented when the purpose of his and my presence was explained. The captain required positive proof and hopefully I could give that to him.

This was a recent event and the captain wanted me to mentally regress to the moment just prior to the impact in order to view the striking object. I had done this in the case of Quigley Thorn and Johnny Price and then repeated it often to bring other criminals to justice. It had been a sad moment for me to see Philip Stevens being attacked and burgled. And the Nazmos council wanted me to try to do the same on the island of Vaz in order to find out more about Gozmanot. Of course I would do my best there but she did live a very long time ago. Yet I know that the past is indelibly fixed so I was hoping for success.

I then laid down my own conditions. And that was that Niztukan must take no risks and so not get too close to the neutron shield surface. He could do that on his own on another occasion. With me and Zakatanz on board it must be a case of swift, safe and sure as for all space flights.

Niztukan smiled at me and conveyed that we would be safe with him, especially on this trip. It would not be necessary for a separate lower level scan as it could all be done from a higher altitude orbit. The results produced would be slightly less accurate but good enough for the Starship's records.

I knew that I had to do this but also knew that mum and dad and the others would not want me to take the risk. I'd have to convince them that for Zakatanz's sake I needed to do it. So when I did tell Tania and the others it was as I expected. They were absolutely against it. There was only one way I could persuade them. So I told them all about Hazazamunt. I left nothing out.

'Oh Ashley,' said mum nearly in tears when I finished, 'why didn't you tell us all this before? The poor, poor man I do so feel for him. It's the saddest story ever; what a huge loss for him. Of course you must do what you can to put any doubts to rest.'

'I did tell Tania about my thoughts just after the impact occurred,' I said. 'I had to tell her why I was expecting a call from the captain then. I had intended to tell you all about it when we got back to Earth and not before. The captain is a very private individual and any loose thoughts about his secret could have been picked up by others on the ship. But now he has had to inform the Nazmos governing council aboard this ship and request their permission for Niztukan's cooperation and for my assistance as well. So his secret is out and everyone aboard knows. And now so do you.'

'He is a very courageous Oannes captain to wish to do this and I would do exactly the same,' said Jerry looking across at Milly. 'Besides I'm curious to know the truth and only Ashley can provide the answer.'

I looked at Muznant and Brazjaf but they said nothing. I suppose they knew what I would do. I also suspected that they had known about Hazazamunt's disappearance but in general terms only from the extensive Nazmos records.

Margaret however looked quite upset initially but now gave a recovering smile. I could imagine her in front of her TV with a box full of tissues watching some sad late night movie. The old film 'An Affair to Remember' came to mind. The ending even got me all choked up.

Simon looked up at me questioningly but I conveyed a very private negative. Captain Zakatanz did not wish for any unnecessary company on this trip. It would be quite nostalgic and sad for him. Simon was quite adult about it and conveyed his understanding.

I was relieved that I could now do what I had wanted to do when Zakatanz had first made his request. Of course if Tania had said no I would have abided by her decision but then I might have found an alternative. However

I knew that being close to the site of the event gave the greatest chance of success. I hoped for a positive result too when I visited Vaz and the site of Gozmanot's home. As I said before the past is there as if set in concrete and one merely needed the skill to search it out.

I sent the captain a brief message and received an immediate response. The earlier the better he conveyed.

And so it was about an hour later that I was dressed in a gold electrostatic suit and clamped to my seat at the front of the starship's shuttle with Captain Zakatanz in the seat beside me. Our feet were in contact so he could read my mind immediately after the experiment. Niztukan was at the rear of the shuttle in the command position. We exited the cargo airlock and headed at speed away from the Starship in a slightly southward direction; south being the tail end. We continued like this for nearly ten minutes so I managed to get a good look at the abundance of stars all around us. It was nice to be in open space again. I think I was getting used to space travel especially the Oannes way. I looked for Orion but it must be somewhere behind us. The Milky Way however was clearly visible as it stretched across the sky from left to right in my view.

Now the shuttle slowed and turned in a wide curve to head back towards the Starship. I felt the extra force of acceleration as we shot forward and I could see the top of the Starship approaching rapidly. I thought we would shoot up and away from the neutron shield area but the enormous gravity effect pulled us over towards it. I guessed that we were in a sort of orbital trajectory over the top of it.

I looked back and could see that Niztukan was enjoying the exhilaration of the moment. I'm certain that this must act like a drug for him and something that he looked forward to after each Starship journey.

We must have been a mile out when the pull on the shuttle began in earnest and we seemed to rapidly close this distance. Niztukan had gauged our velocity exactly and we must have gone over the edge of the neutron shield at a distance of around six hundred feet above it. The shield was shrouded in a foggy mist below our shuttle as our race over it commenced.

Zakatanz looked sideways at me and I could see that he was curious about what I was going to do. This reminded me that perhaps the time was right for me to begin my act. I went into pink mode and as before it all happened as if in a dream. The universe turned rosy pink and I shut my eyes tight and concentrated on the neutron shield of the Starship 8110-Gold moments before the impact event of the previous day.

At first nothing seemed to show apart from the vast concentration of stars all around me. There was no Starship anywhere in my view. So I then concentrated on the narrow time frame close to 5.pm yesterday. I looked towards where Nazmos would be and suddenly there it was. It was like seeing things in a dream with me in the role of a detached observer. And yet it was all very real and the imagery as sharp as if I was viewing it all on a bright clear day.

A small spacecraft was approaching my position and as it got nearer I looked closely at it. I then found myself inside the craft viewing its contents. The interior was colourless and seemed to have suffered from smoke damage but I couldn't make out how this might have occurred. There was room to seat about ten persons at various locations and not in any particular arrangement. The craft was completely without power and I sensed extreme coldness inside it. From my observer position near the rear of the cabin I could see that there was a form sitting on the front pilot's seat. There were the usual view panels and a sloping console in front of this seat but it too had smoke damage to it. I noticed that the view panels were quite opaque and I guessed this was from some heat source. The scene changed and now I was at the front looking down towards the object in the pilot's seat. Whatever it was I found it as unrecognisable because of the frozen state it was in. It then came to me that this was an Oannes person long since deceased. The figure was completely covered by a frosting of large ice crystals which gave it the appearance of a frosty snowman of sorts. There were no recognisable features; not on the face, arms, legs or body. But it was small in my estimation.

Suddenly I was an outside spectator again watching the collision scenario unfold in slow motion.

To my left side I could see a huge long fuzzy cone shaped object advancing rapidly towards me. On my right side was the small spacecraft approaching slowly but at a slight angle. The huge cone shaped ship went past me and straight into the path of the smaller craft which then disappeared.

The vision was suddenly completed and I was returned to normal mode. I was back again on the shuttle craft with Zakatanz by my side and racing above the neutron shield. It was over within moments and the Starship was once again rapidly receding behind us. I was saddened by what I had seen and was fairly certain that my initial thoughts had been correct. The sadness was like a heavy blanket covering me. My eyes remained dry but there was a constriction in my throat that threatened to choke me. Should I convey my vision to Zakatanz or delete the frozen body bit? No, it must be all or nothing. I owed it to Zakatanz to be wholly honest about what I had seen.

Niztukan conveyed that he had got all his data and was pleased at another successful neutron shield scan.

Zakatanz kept looking at me and I gave him a brief nod before conveying to him and to Niztukan everything that I had seen when I had gone into pink mode and concentrated my mind around the timeframe of the collision. I conveyed the full detail of my vision and left nothing out.

As the shuttle turned about and headed back towards the Starship airlock Captain Zakatanz conveyed his thanks and requested that I see him alone back in the control room. There was a sombre expression on his face which was turned down towards his feet. Niztukan conveyed a private message to the captain which I believe may have been a sort of condolence offering.

There was a companionable silence between us as the shuttle entered the airlock and settled on its floor. I let the captain precede me out of the craft. I said I would see him shortly after I had been to my rooms.

'Well what did you see?' asked Tania on behalf of our waiting group.

Again I conveyed telepathically a complete visual of everything I had seen; the small spacecraft and the detail of its interior and the ensuing collision. I conveyed that only Zakatanz would know if this was the same 17426-Black spacecraft that he and Hazazamunt had flown in. Only he could identify the uniqueness of the ship's interior and its control console. There could be no doubt now that the impact on the neutron shield of the Starship was caused be a small spacecraft.

Muznant brought me a glass of Wazu just before I left for the control room on my own. As I approached I met Niztukan on his way out. He paused when he saw me and waited for me to get near him. He then placed a hand on my arm and conveyed his respect and affection for me.

'We will meet again one day my friend,' he conveyed before walking away towards the buildings opposite to my mine. I thought what a fine Oannes person he was and glad that I'd finally spent a little time with him.

I entered the control room then and poured myself another glass of Wazu before sitting down at the table opposite the captain. I waited for him to begin the conversation.

'I'm not sure if I should have asked you to do this,' he said. 'Perhaps I was better off not seeing these things. After all these years the interior of the spacecraft looked different but recognisable in many ways. It is definitely the same kind of craft and where the body sat was Hazazamunt's seat. It could be any Oannes person but I feel it was her that we saw.'

He paused before he continued, but slowly and wistfully.

'She would look sideways at me and smile wickedly before throwing the spacecraft into a high gravity manoeuvre. It seems like only yesterday that she was by my side.'

Again he paused and the emotion of grief came across to me strongly. That feeling of the loss that he had felt when she first went missing was rekindled afresh in his thoughts. I too felt sadness in my heart simply from seeing how my regressed vision had affected him.

'I will convey all these images to those who modified Hazazamunt's ship and get further confirmation. We Oannes are like that,' he said, 'we must know for certain.'

I then saw a side of Zakatanz that I had not seen before. He talked from the heart about Hazazamunt and how she had permeated his inner being. He talked of how her touch had thrilled him beyond what he had ever expected and of the many times that they had lain together in and out of their sleep tanks. Somehow this did not shock or surprise me. It simply painted a glowing picture of the love that they had for one another. He said that at the time he did not realise it but they were putting a lifetime of joy into the few years that they had spent together. They were the most wonderfully memorable ten years of his life for which he was extremely thankful.

Zakatanz talked like this for nearly an hour and I just listened. As he talked my own thoughts were about my darling Tania in comparison. Finally he paused and I could see that the major burden of his grief had been eased. I think a lot of emotion had been kept bottled up inside him but not any more. And I'm glad he chose me as his confidante.

'But come my friend let us share a meal together again before your departure for Nazmos,' he said with a smile that was a bit more natural, 'it may be our last together for some time.'

Perhaps he saw me as different and special. After all I did have these special gifts that no Oannes had been bestowed with. To him was I a sort of Father confessor figurehead? I didn't feel like it but then I am a good listener. Even Tania says that I know when not to say anything. To me Captain Zakatanz appeared very different now from that taciturn captain I had met briefly all those years ago. But then I hadn't known the Oannes personality within him.

Our family group was informed of the pending meal by Zanos and subsequently a very pleasant hour was spent sampling all the special dishes that the captain had organised for us. It was a big surprise when partway into our meal two new members joined us. These were my friends from the council of ministers namely Korizazit and Nerbtazwi.

'Thank you captain for inviting us,' said Nerbtazwi in a most formal manner, 'and may we on behalf of the council members offer you our own sadness empathy for your betrothed Hazazamunt. It was most worthy of you to consider sharing this tragic experience with us.'

What I hadn't known earlier was that when the captain and Niztukan had been discussing the pros and cons of my regressed dreamlike vision that Zakatanz had conveyed a full report not only to the council of ministers but to all the Starship's passengers and crew as well. He had done this through the medium of Zanos. He had kept nothing back. He had even included the disappearance of Hazazamunt's spacecraft all those years ago. Because I had used my special gift to see into a past event my regressed vision was accepted as factual. It was also what the Nazmos governing council of ministers hoped from me in regard to looking into the life of Gozmanot's past life on the Island of Vaz.

Because of this Zakatanz informed me that the burden of secrecy that he had maintained for so long was now eased and he felt better for it. I knew exactly how he must feel. I had always preferred openness to secrecy and had made it a code within my lifestyle.

We were ultimately nearly two hours at the meal table engaged in pleasant and light hearted conversation. We had long since finished eating when Zanos informed us that a fleet of spaceships had arrived including the spacecraft 103-Silverstar. This was the special spacecraft allocated for the transportation of the Nazmos governing council of ministers. They would be shuttled across to this craft as a priority.

Nerbtazwi had informed me that the council of ministers expected me to formally present my family members to them at the Domed Hall on Nazmos as soon as we landed on the home planet later today. After that we would be free to do as we pleased. For me that would be a repeat of most of what I had done on my previous trip there. Nevertheless I felt excited at the prospect; especially the meeting with Jazzatnit and Zazfrapiz in their beautiful home. I was glad to learn that Captain Rojazonto would be ferrying our group to Nazmos as I was keen for him to meet my family.

It was a sad moment for me when I performed my farewell Sewa with Captain Zakatanz. I knew I should not see him again for a very long time. I could see that he too was moved by the emotion of the moment and by the affection that had developed between us. It was an automatic reflex when we both went forward for a firm handshake with both our hands. We remained so for several seconds before separating. He then shook hands enthusiastically with all the others in the group but not Muznant or Brazjaf. A special Sewa was reserved for them.

'Take good care of Ashley,' he said to Muznant and to Brazjaf, 'for he is a very special being.'

I liked that phrase because it classed me on a par with the Oannes people. When Simon started his cadetship I would make it a point to look for this man. I in turn had classed Zakatanz as one of us. I think he read my thoughts and showed an emotion of pleasure.

'Goodbye my friend,' I conveyed.

We were in one of a fleet of shuttles sent out from the spaceship 8962-Orange commanded by Captain Rojazonto. These shuttles were larger than the usual ones we had been on and I could see Simon looking around at its spaciousness and size. We were not the only passengers aboard as it was rather full with Oannes who had travelled with us from Earth.

I looked around but all I could see was an expanse of starry space until the spaceship 8962-Orange came into view. It was approaching the end of its parking loop cycle and was moving quite slowly. Its massive bulk became apparent as we drew nearer and I could see that its large bay doors were wide open. Simon seemed enthralled by the spectacle as we approached and then entered through it to settle gently upon the bay deck. I think at least three other shuttles entered with ours. Gravity returned instantly as we settled and then after several minutes the bay doors closed and atmosphere was restored to the bay. Only then did our shuttle doors open and we were allowed to disembark.

I had seen all of this before and although I had communicated all my previous trip experiences in detail to the family I could see that they still looked around in awe. This shuttle bay was about a thousand feet square with a ceiling height of over fifty feet. I still found it impressive nevertheless. And the myriad of shuttles filling the bay all seemed parked to a pattern which I could see won Simon's admiration.

Tania was beside me so I reached out and held her hand. Simon was alongside Jerry and was pointing things out but mainly as an exclamation of discovery. Rachel was holding onto Muznant with Margaret on her other side. Ron and Brenda stayed with mum and dad and I could see that they were quite enjoying this new experience.

I explained to them about the distances within the ship that necessitated the use of internal deck transporters to get from one point to another. One such Transporter appeared near us and we were all invited to get on it which we did. There was ample room on it for us plus maybe a few more.

It lifted off the bay deck very smoothly and took us directly to the electrostatics suit hall which was similar to that on 520-Green. I imagine that there must be several of these to cater to a ship of this size. We took off our gold suits and were directed by Zanos on-board where to hang them. I could see that Simon was really enjoying the sophistication of the Oannes technology and I knew that he had already formed a great respect for this on-board predictive Zanos bio-computer species. I too could not help but think of it in a similar manner.

Brazjaf then conveyed that Captain Rojazonto wished to welcome us personally and requested that we meet him in the ship's control room. So once more we embarked onto the mini Transporter and were smoothly whizzed through wide corridors and up vertical shafts to finally arrive at the door of the control room. We entered and Captain Rojazonto and I exchanged polite Sewas before getting closer for a firm handshake.

'I'm very pleased to be on your ship again captain,' I said aloud, 'please let me introduce you to my family.'

He acknowledged this and then took each introduction seriously memorising the connection with me and placing it firmly in his mind. He said he hoped to get to know them as individuals. He was looking at Simon as he said this and I could see that news of Simon's future cadetship had reached Nazmos. Goodness, news did travel fast. But then in an open society like the Oannes I could hardly feign surprise or expect anything less. I could see that Simon was pleased by the attention and Tania beamed with pride. I suppose I did too.

Then Jerry conveyed to the captain that this was a magnificent ship and requested a tour of it sometime.

'Of course,' replied the captain in his husky throaty voice, 'I shall instruct Zanos on-board to do so at once.'

Jerry had not expected such a reply nor did he expect it to be a mental tour. Rather he thought it might be a physical one on one of the transporters. But he was pleasantly surprised when detailed images and views appeared in his mind along with a complete description of each facet of the ship.

The same was also received by each of the others including myself. It was done with a fluent speed of delivery but slowed enough for the human mind to cope with. It was over in a matter of minutes and suddenly the actual size and capability of this spaceship could be really appreciated. Simon looked at me with a glowing smile on his face. I read his thoughts and knew then that all his ambitions were definitely to do with space travel and spaceships.

We were in the control room of 8962-Orange that was actually a large structural bubble at its very top centre. The ship was nearly half a mile in length, a quarter of a mile in width and just over six hundred feet at its centre. There were thirty decks within the ship and the main passenger viewing panels were along a perimeter corridor internally circling the fifteenth deck. The power plants were on the two upper and the two lower decks. Three other decks were essentially for food growing with the remainder being used for the accommodation of two thousand passengers and crew. The spaceship had the capability to travel in space indefinitely and many had been constructed when a probable threat from a white dwarf star had first been discovered some 1,600 years ago. It was then too distant for accurate analysis and any certainty of its course.

I suddenly thought about Simon and understood that when he did become a space cadet with the Oannes that his training and competence would exceed my wildest expectations. The Oannes had education facilities like nothing on Earth. The future for Simon looked good.

The captain then made a sweeping gesture and conveyed that we were all free to move around the control room and see the sights of the universe through the large view panels that completely surrounded us.

The ship was in an extended parking loop and Zanos on-board kept its orientation in a set direction so that the Starship 8110-Gold was always in view. Although it was some 300 miles from us it still looked massively impressive.

We began to look at the stars all around us and Simon pointed to the obvious Milky Way stretching across our view. The stars were not very different from those viewed from Earth especially the brighter ones. They were all there even if some appeared slightly closer together.

'Dad,' asked Simon, 'where among all this lot can I find our Sun?'

If I remembered correctly I'd had the same query on my last trip here. So I told Simon to look for the Orion constellation. It was nowhere to be seen until the ship rotated around at the midpoint of its parking loop.

'There it is,' exclaimed Simon pointing out Orion's belt of three stars.

'Well then,' I said, 'now where is Sirius?'

'There,' pointed Simon, 'it's the brightest star in all this lot.'

I then conveyed in detail the configuration of the constellation of Orion with respect to Sirius. I told Simon to look at the two lower stars of Rigel and Saiph that were below Orion's belt. I paused while he did this. Then I told him to draw an imaginary line between Saiph and Sirius. He did this in his mind.

'Not quite halfway to Sirius is a rather small yellowish star rather on its own,' I said, 'that is our Sun and where Earth is.'

'Got it,' exclaimed Simon joyously. 'This is fabulous.'

What I hadn't realised was that not only were our entire group listening in to my communication with my son but so was Captain Rojazonto. I could see that he was impressed by Simon's enthusiasm and knowing Simon's desires he concluded him to be excellent space cadet material.

Simon was now looking at Earth's Sun through the view panels but in magnification mode. I looked into his mind and saw what he could see. He was searching for Earth's illuminated crescent shape but was unable to do so. I conveyed to him that at best it would be a very thin crescent but currently was at the midnight position as far as Nazmos was concerned and conveyed what this meant. The positioning of Earth, Sun and Raznat were in a direct straight view line.

We spent just over half an hour in the control room before Brazjaf suggested that we retire to our allotted cabins. Muznant asked if anyone was hungry but we all said no except for Rachel. So it was decided that we all go anyway to the dining hall. It was now 4.pm on my watch and the captain said that it would be another few hours before all transfers were complete. The journey to Nazmos would take six hours of which over two hours would be the decelerating action to landfall.

We were taken to the food hall via mini Transporter where I had a glass of Wazu and then a nice mug of hot sweet tea. Rachel tucked into the biscuits as did Simon who opted for a hot chocolate drink. I confess that I had a couple of biscuits too which I disgracefully dunked into my tea. Tania pretended to look away but I could see a smile around the corners of her mouth. We were being well looked after, a thought that Muznant picked up which made her smile. We were asked if we wished for anything more substantial but Brazjaf said that a proper meal was planned in a couple of hours after which we should get a proper rest. I think he meant sleep.

We spent just over an hour in our cabins during which I managed to freshen up a bit before dinner was announced by Zanos. Although I had managed to relax on my comfortable bed Simon had kept me awake with a host of questions, all telepathic of course. I responded as best as I could and in the end said that he'd just have to wait and see what turned up.

The meal in the food hall was excellent as usual and the place was quite packed with Oannes passengers and crew. There must be several of these halls on every deck level because there was room for just about a hundred in this hall. As a general rule it was served buffet style so we were quite happy to help ourselves as necessary.

Muznant and Brazjaf again surprised me at the quantity they served themselves which was happily put away. There was most definitely something in the air or should I say in waiting. I'm very suspicious about signs like that even though my inner voice was silent.

Finally we just sat around at the table drinking Wazu and mugs of tea when Zanos on-board informed us that all transfers were complete and the journey to Nazmos was about to commence. My watch showed just after 6pm and when I queried Zanos I was informed that it was currently night time in Wentazta with Raznat rise in about three hours time. I decided to leave my watch set as it was at least for now. When I conveyed this to Tania she said that she'd like the kids to get some sleep before arriving on Nazmos. I agreed because I also felt I needed a good nights rest before meeting with the governing council in the Domed Hall.

We had two cabins with a connecting doorway. Rachel was asleep in no time at all and Simon lay on his bed in intense thought though before long he too dropped off to sleep. Quietly we closed the connecting door and snuggled up in bed. It was some while before we went into an exhausted sleep! My last thought was wondering how Muznant and Brazjaf were enjoying the privacy of their own sleep tank.

I awoke many hours later and Zanos answered my query and said that I had slept for nearly seven hours. 8962-Orange had landed in the Wentazta space park but disembarkation had yet to commence. Captain Rojazonto had decreed that the spaceship be used as a first base for us to get freshened up and breakfasted in preparation for our audience before the Nazmos governing council of ministers later on today. As such we took our time getting ready and so it was over an hour later that we finally all met up in the food hall. Captain Rojazonto was waiting for us there with rather an unusual breakfast. It was more of a full blown meal and yet looking at all the food on display made me quite hungry. Was this another Zanos anticipation of our needs? Perhaps it was. Anyway I decided to make this a sort of a 'brunch' meal and I think the others decided the same. As such we sampled most of the dishes presented. I'm sure I was putting on weight but Tania said I looked the same as ever. I'm not exactly sure what she was trying to say but I enjoyed my food just the same.

Captain Rojazonto finally announced that the Nazmos governing council of ministers were now all assembled in the Domed Hall and conveyed that they were ready to see us. I gathered that we were the only item on the day's agenda and this would be their way of formally welcoming me and my party to their homeland. I also understood that they wished to agree a time for a visit to the island of Vaz. I had no reservations about that.

'Come my friends,' said the captain, 'I am commissioned to escort you to the Domed Hall to meet the governing council. I have also opted to be your sponsor if you will allow it and which will be my privilege and honour.'

There was a certain formality in Rojazonto's manner which I quite understood. The governing council of ministers was a most august and distinct body of Oannes persons.

An internal Transporter took us along corridors and down vertical shafts till we finally exited down through the underside of the spaceship. As before the ship appeared to be delicately balanced on ten or so very spindly antennae-like legs. So I explained to Simon that the main mass of the ship was still supported upwards by its own impulse motors. The legs were simply there to maintain the ship at a set position relative to the ground and to keep it there.

The Transporter moved along underneath 8962-Orange till it cleared the ship's mass and out into the bright Raznat light. Ahead and some distance away we could see a much larger Transporter to which we were headed. We settled beside it and transferred onto it quite easily. The small Transporter then lifted off and returned to Rojazonto's ship.

I think this could be the same Transporter that took me to my first meeting with the council on my previous trip. The colours were familiar but the operator was not. Captain Rojazonto had also escorted me to that meeting then.

The operator received a command from Rojazonto and the Transporter lifted upwards smoothly and quietly. We rose to a height of about a hundred feet and then proceeded at a leisurely pace into the heart of Wentazta. The captain communicated a running commentary of all the structural features passing beneath us which I still found interesting. Rachel and Margaret were very fascinated by the passing scenery of houses and I wondered if it had something to do with their future on Nazmos. I noticed that Rachel had got close to Margaret and the two seemed to enjoy frequent small conversations. At first I thought that perhaps Margaret was attempting to curry favour with me through friendship with my daughter but then I could see that they were genuine towards one another. Am I getting paranoiac in my old age?

Simon was looking back at the retreating space park which seemed to extend across the horizon. The large spaceship 98103-Pink was nowhere in sight which was rather disappointing for Simon. Anyway he'd had a visual of it from the images I had conveyed when describing it to him earlier.

Wentazta seemed to extend on forever into the distance and Jerry queried its actual size. Captain Rojazonto conveyed that it took up an area of two thousand square miles in a rough rectangular shape whose sides approximated fifty miles by forty miles with the largest section bordering the Peruga Sea. Of course he said that this did not include a part of the city that descended down into the sea bed area which was where some of the Rimzi people lived. He then gave a brief explanation of these reserved Oannes underwater people.

I could see the large dome some miles ahead of us and I pointed this out to the others as our destination. The Transporter continued its leisurely pace until we finally approached the Domed Hall building. We entered through the large portal at one side and our eyes had to adjust to the change from direct light to shadow. The Transporter settled down in a centralised plaza which again reminded me of the Dome-4 in Anztarza. In fact both Jerry and Margaret remarked about it and the others nodded agreement.

When we stepped off the Transporter we were met by a group of very distinguished Oannes standing as tall as they could dare. I knew the formalities from my previous visit so I stepped slightly ahead of our group and made a slight bow of recognition. I then waited for our hosts to make the next move.

I spied my friend Nerbtazwi coming towards us and I relaxed mentally. Suddenly it all became less formal and even the distinguished Oannes seemed to relax physically.

'Come,' said Nerbtazwi in her clear sing-song soprano voice, 'the council eagerly await you and have bid me escort you to them.'

She had not quite reached us but her welcoming smile was Sewa enough. She then turned about and beckoned us to follow. We did so and marched through an auditorium quite full of seated Oannes before arriving at the large dais upon which the governing council of ministers sat. There were about twenty seated there and I instantly recognised Korizazit, Ritozanan and a few others.

There was a pleasant atmosphere all around us and I could see that we were being looked upon favourably. At our first meeting weeks ago there had been just me here. But now my whole family was here including our friend Margaret. The Oannes who had kept their presence and their culture a secret were now beginning to make contact with the human race. It was a selective process of which I think the council had approved. I hoped this to be the forerunner of things to come with more contacts in time. Yet I knew that in general Earth was not ready for the Oannes.

My mind had been in open mode and I could see that my thoughts had been read. There were knowing smiles on the faces of the council members.

Formal Sewas were then exchanged in which I represented our group. Muznant, Brazjaf and Rojazonto were also recognised and Sewas exchanged. This was so different in emotional atmosphere from that first meeting of several weeks ago.

At the council's request or should I say command I was asked to present each member of my family group in turn. I did this and also made a special mention of Margaret as a close friend and of the work she did in training groups of humans in telepathy; a very difficult task and not always successful.

'She shall have assistance,' conveyed Ritozanan and I believe she communicated privately with Muznant causing a smile to appear on that pretty face. I was partial to Muznant my very first Oannes lady.

However I could see that it was Simon whom they were really interested in getting to know.

'My son wishes to captain a Starship one day,' I said with pride. 'And already he has impressed Captain Zakatanz such that the captain has offered his tutelage. It is important to me that he accompany me when I journey towards Zarama when 4110-Silver has been fully modified.'

I was surprised by the next question

'Does Gozmanot's gift of prophesy continue in your son?' asked Ritozanan.

Simon was about to answer for himself but I put out my open palm in front of him and stopped him.

'I do not think so,' I said. 'But Korizazit knows about this that it is not something that one can command at will as I'm sure neither could Gozmanot. Like the inner voice that appears at random so it is with Simon. His premonitions have not been many but they have been accurate. I have enough understanding to believe in them explicitly when they do occur.'

I then conveyed all the instances of Simon's premonitions that had occurred so far; the last being with regard to the delay in the return travel to Nazmos.

After a momentary pause Ritozanan asked me point blank when it was that I wished to return to Earth. I believe the question had been proposed by another council member and one who knew my thoughts on the matter. I wished to be home well in time before Christmas as promised to Ron and Brenda for their B&B events.

'In three days not including today,' I replied instinctively.

'Then so it shall be,' said Ritozanan. 'Captain Natazlat will be so informed and 9110-Red will convey you to Earth.'

There was then a pause although rather brief but lengthy enough for me to understand that I was expected to volunteer something. The Oannes do not like to impose themselves or their wishes unnecessarily. Instinctively I knew that a visit to Gozmanot's home had been mentioned earlier for me to attempt an observation into the past with regard to her life there. I remember agreeing to attempt a visual imaging of a part of Gozmanot's life at that meal with Nerbtazwi, Korizazit and Ritozanan onboard Captain Zakatanz's Starship 8110-Gold just prior to its departure for Earth.

'When does the council wish to come with me to Gozmanot's home place on the island of Vaz?' I conveyed to all.

Ritozanan smiled at me and I could see pride in her expression. I had passed a little test.

'Arrangements have been made for your family to be given an aerial tour over Nazmos just as you did,' she conveyed. 'If it is agreeable this will take place tomorrow and occupy most of the day period. Captain Lyozonpa will do the honours just as he did for you. You Ashley will not be on this trip as we wish you to go to the island of Vaz with six council members accompanying you.'

This had been conveyed as an open communication and Tania though surprised by its commanding content looked at me and smiled. She squeezed my hand in support. Mum. Dad and the others all conveyed their acceptance too. But Rachel conveyed a very private message to me which rather surprised me. Why did she have a keen desire to know everything about Gozmanot and to see the place where she had lived? When I looked around at her she was holding Margaret's hand and was quite apart from Muznant. I queried my inner voice but nothing came back to me. I sent a short sharp message that basically said no.

'Thank you,' I then replied to the council in general, 'I shall be at your disposal as desired.'

Ritozanan smiled at me and I got this feeling that I was under her protective wing. Somehow she made this august assembly of ministers appear less formidable. I'd had a great respect for this governing body of administrators all along but which had been laced with a measure of caution. Now however Ritozanan made me feel politically safe. Yet I would do everything by the rules to maintain that status.

'Then go now for Jazzatnit and Zazfrapiz eagerly await you in their home for they requested the council not to keep you unduly long,' she said pleasantly as the entire council rose to leave.

I waited for about a minute to allow for politeness before also turning about to return to the central plaza where our Transporter was parked and soon we were moving easily back over the panorama of Wentazta. I remembered that on the previous occasion I had travelled in the direction of the setting Raznat. But this was midday and Raznat was directly overhead and everything was bright beneath us. Still I recognised many of the features passing below us and eventually after about twenty minutes or so we began a descent towards a large plaza area. There were only low single storey buildings around us and after we disembarked Muznant and Brazjaf led the way along a path between them. It took several minutes of walking and we came to the large arched doorway that I remembered as the house of Jazzatnit and Zazfrapiz.

The door was easily pushed open and we entered their lovely courtyard.

'My, what a beautiful place,' exclaimed Tania even though I had prepared her for this with my visual imaged descriptions. The others were equally impressed.

Our hosts were waiting beside one of the large glass tank displays and now came forward to meet us while conveying their welcome. A brief Sewa was conducted as they walked towards us and I replied for all of us.

I then introduced each member of my family in turn and included Margaret as a very close friend. I could see Muznant smile at this.

Jazzatnit then went straight to Tania and reached out both her hands towards her. It was lovely to see such easy affection delivered in the Oannes way with nothing verbal said. All was telepathic – instant and extensive. Then she did the same for Simon and Rachel before moving on to mum and dad. And then all the others as well which included Muznant and Brazjaf.

It was like a royal line-up with Jazzatnit leading and Zazfrapiz following close behind. There was a look of understanding when our hosts held Margaret's hands giving her a nod and a smile. I think she was simply welcoming another admirer into my little fan club. At 329 years of age I thought Jazzatnit possessed a great deal of charm along with the handsomeness of the mature Oannes lady. I noticed admiring looks from both dad and Jerry. I think mum whispered a soft 'close your mouth dear,' in a humorous way and I'm sure that Milly did the same to Jerry. I remember thinking that she must have been a very pretty version of Muznant in her youth. Jazzatnit still had her perfect posture and I could see her revelling in the silent admiration beamed at her.

'I welcome you all,' she then said. 'I have looked forward to this moment ever since Ashley promised to bring you back with him. It is nice to see so many of you and I hope you enjoy your stay here. We have ample accommodation for you all and I have made arrangements for some of our friends to meet you during your visit. Perhaps tomorrow would be a good time before our evening meal. It is not often that I get the privilege of entertaining what you would term as royalty but that is exactly what I consider Ashley's family to be to me.'

It was dad who surprised me with his next words.

'You do us a great honour but it is I who feel privileged to meet you. Lillian and I are most grateful to be your guests and I am sure that the rest of our family and friends feel the same. Thank you for having us visit and stay in your lovely home. It is entirely our pleasure. Thank you.'

Jazzatnit smiled widely and slowly came forward and kissed dad on both cheeks and then lightly on his lips.

'Like father like son,' was all she said and I knew exactly what she meant. The accent was on the word 'like' which could easily have been substituted by the word 'love'.

I'd never seen dad blush so quickly but he tuned to smile at mum with a sheepish grin. She smiled back at him and we all saw the pride and love in her look. I'd swear that dad seemed to grow an inch or two taller.

'Come,' said Zazfrapiz smiling mischievously, 'let us walk about the courtyard together and look at Jazzatnit's hobby handiwork. Of course you must say it all looks nice or she shall be extremely upset.'

'Will you walk with me Rachel,' asked Jazzatnit and before I knew it there was Rachel trotting alongside her and even holding her hand.

Muznant looked at me and smilingly shrugged her shoulders as if to say, 'I don't mind.' But then she left Brazjaf's side and walked about with Margaret. I was curious to know what was being discussed between them – but then I'm sure I could guess.

We walked in our little groups and swapped around as questions were asked. But Simon stayed with me throughout our stroll around the displays. The plants were in large glass tanks and Simon recognised quite a few of them. The Yaztraka tree was easily recognisable since we had seen it grown in the food domes of Anztarza.

I received a communication from Rachel and realised she and Jazzatnit were beside the artificial rose bush named after her. She said it looked real and was glad it was given her name.

Mum and dad walked together most of the time and dad remarked with amazement at how large an area the courtyard covered. I conveyed that all the Nazmos plants shown grew underwater in the sea and so could not normally have been seen by us humans. With the backlighting and artificial sea bed arrangement the presentation inside the tanks was extremely artistic.

I could see that Simon was bored after the first few minutes but he blocked his emotions so as not to offend our hosts. This was very mature of him and it pleased me since I got a glimpse of the man in him. Rachel on the other hand was a bubbling delight and thrilled by everything she saw. Jazzatnit had taken to her in a big way and kept looking down at her with affection. I thought that they must make the most of this visit for they might never meet again. I couldn't help thinking about how long the Oannes lived on average and wondered if Jazzatnit would still be around aged 351 years in the year 2038 when we next returned. I would hope so but one can never be certain.

'Do not worry Ashley,' came through to me from Jazzatnit, 'I shall be here then, at least I hope so. My parents lived to nearly 400 years before they passed away so there is hope for me too.'

'I'm sorry but I couldn't help my thoughts,' I replied very apologetically.

'Please don't be concerned' she conveyed back, 'Zazfrapiz and I talk about it all the time. We even discuss things like which one of us could be the first to go.'

There was nothing I could say or add to this topic so I remained telepathically silent.

After a very pleasant hour spent in the courtyard chatting and wandering around looking at the fine exhibits Zazfrapiz suggested we all freshen up before our evening meal.

'Come,' he said, 'I will show you to your rooms where you can rest and refresh yourselves before our little banquet together.'

Husband and wife led the way and we followed. The house was large overall and comprised seven suites of rooms like the one I had occupied the last time. Each had its incumbent sleep-tank but this did not detract from its spaciousness. I believe there was also accommodation below ground level in the area which extended underneath the courtyard. But this may have been for other purposes. It somehow reminded me of a castle with its many rooms. And of course there was the terrace above from which I had experienced the setting of Raznat and its accompanying 'dark wind' phenomenon. I had conveyed images of it to the family but I was keen for them to experience it for themselves.

And so they did. After a rest during which I had lain down for an hour Tania and I decided to wander around the courtyard again. Mum and dad were already out there but the others must have stayed in their rooms either resting or waiting to be called. Our hosts were also nowhere to be seen. I knew that Zazfrapiz rested during the day so I had not expected to see him till the meal.

I stopped again to look at the rose plant named after Rachel and I had to admire the craftsmanship. The detail was excellent and it was so true to the colours as well. Whoever did this most certainly did it from actually observing a live plant on Earth. He or she must have been in Anztarza at some time. Tania and I were holding hands quite loosely as we stood before this exhibit when Jazzatnit came to stand silently behind us. When I sensed her presence she said that an Oannes male had crafted it over a hundred years ago when he was already in his old age. Sadly he was no more she said in a matter of fact way. This statement which was said without any emotion gave me an insight into the Oannes philosophy about death. To die was simply a matter of ceasing to exist. Instinctively I knew that much would change when Oannes and humans integrated in the millennia of the future.

'Come,' said Jazzatnit, 'all is ready and the banquet waits. Today it will be just us but tomorrow you shall meet some of our friends.

The dining hall was through a doorway opposite to where our rooms were and it was big and the table able to seat about twenty people. Zazfrapiz was already there and waiting for us and directed each to an allotted place. The table was laden with lovely looking dishes though none gave off steamy vapours or aromas. I knew that the Oannes did not like their food to be hot but rather just above room temperature and I had got used to it and now liked it so.

There was no one at either table end which was much cosier. Zazfrapiz and Jazzatnit sat at the centre of one side with mum and dad beside them. Tania and I sat opposite them with Rachel beside Tania and Simon beside me. The others were all suitably located on both sides of the table. Some thought had gone into the arrangement.

The conversation at dinner was quite animated with Jerry making comparisons with Earth living. Nazmos and Earth were really very similar apart from the climatic conditions he said and I could see Zazfrapiz warming to the topic. The discussion progressed and finally came to the subject of the beautiful and varied nature of the sunrise and sunsets on Earth.

'Our Raznat is still well above the horizon,' said Zazfrapiz, 'but it will set in about three hour's time. We shall give you the pleasure of observing it from our upper terrace location if you wish.'

'That would be excellent,' replied Jerry who had viewed the event vicariously from my conveyed images of it back on Earth but would like to see it for real.

And so eventually with all our appetites assuaged we found ourselves up on the glassed in terrace in bright daylight with about an hour to go for Raznat to dip below the distant sea horizon.

Rachel grew impatient as she watched the bright orange globe slowly making its way lower and lower. She was shifting from one side of the glassed-in terrace to the other watching the effects of the fading light upon the panorama that was Wentazta around us.

Raznat was now very low and close to the horizon and its bright glow had lessened considerably. A faint pink halo appeared to surround it and it gradually deepened in colour from bright to dark red and then to magenta. There were no clouds near it since these were rare at the equatorial zone of Nazmos. The sky began to dim as Raznat's ball touched the Peruga Sea and begin to dip down into it. Finally it was completely swallowed up and disappeared from view. The darkness seemed to hold back for a good minute before rather suddenly descending upon the city. I looked at Simon and conveyed a silent 'Wait for it' message. I was quite excited by the forthcoming prospect.

A hush settled over the area before a distant whispering sound became audible. In seconds this sound began to grow in volume till suddenly it became a roar. It was as I expected and the ten feet high glass panelling surrounding the terrace juddered and shook violently. It seemed fiercer than I remembered but diminished as rapidly as it had begun. There were looks of wonder all around.

I could see that the suddenness of the violence had scared Rachel so I picked her up in my arms and held her snugly to my chest. I conveyed to her the physics of the phenomenon and she visibly relaxed.

'I thought it was a bad angel flying past and it scared me,' she whispered in my ear, 'it felt evil.'

Tania came up and stroked Rachel's back gently and conveyed a private message. Rachel turned in my arms and I passed her over to her mum.

The air then got rapidly colder up here so we made our way back down to the warmth of the covered courtyard.

'Oh, this is lovely and cosy, 'said Margaret to no one in particular. But we all did agree.

In our conversation over the next hour I enquired after Kazaztan and his wife Zarpralt whom I had seen only weeks ago.

'He is not a well Oannes,' said Zazfrapiz. 'I do not think he will come to visit you this time though I feel that Zarpralt will. She is in excellent health.'

As the Nazmos night wore on I began to feel tired and conveyed this to our hosts. They also tended to retire early considering their age and so we said our goodnights in Sewa fashion and retired to our rooms. Except for Milly and Jerry who decided to stay up a bit longer and make another round viewing Jazzatnit's artwork displays.

Tania looked at me and raised an eyebrow in a gesture I quite understood. A little romantic interlude entering late in ones life was encouraging to say the least.

'I'm an only child,' said Tania in a private message, 'and I want it to stay that way.'

I had to smile at the thought and it didn't bother me in the least.

'I wish you were coming with us dad,' said Simon when were back in our rooms. He was referring to tomorrow's trip with Captain Lyozonpa.

'Don't worry son,' I said, 'Captain Lyozonpa is young and you will get on well with him. Ask him if you wish to see anything special and he will be more than willing to oblige. 566-Blue is a relatively small craft and gives you a tremendous sensation of flight even at altitude. And I think that with me being absent will be to your advantage. Trust him and just be yourself Simon.'

I was proud of my boy who I hoped would one day be a space captain with the Oannes fleet.

'Thanks dad,' he said sounding more confident.

That night I slept like the proverbial log and felt absolutely refreshed when I washed and dressed in the morning. I wore my favourite tunic outfit. Breakfast was an informal affair as we individually made our way across the courtyard and into the dining hall.

Jazzatnit was already there and her manner was quite cheerful. I really do admire this lady and made my feelings known through an open mind. She made apologies for her husband not being there but he was a late riser and loved to just wallow in their sleep tank first thing each morning. However we would see him later in the day and definitely this evening along with some friends who had been invited to meet us. I had met some on my last visit and I had quite enjoyed the experience. I looked forward to meeting them again. Jazzatnit smiled when she picked up my thoughts and nodded to me.

I felt it odd that our group was to separate from me today. But the governing council had been adamant that I go on my own to Gozmanot's home on the Island of Vaz. I expect they wanted me to be free of all distractions at least from those of my family. Perhaps they were right.

And so after we had finished breakfast I was left alone with Jazzatnit when Muznant and Brazjaf shepherded Tania, the kids and the others to the plaza area where the Deck Transporter awaited that Captain Lyozonpa had sent for them. I'm sure Simon would enjoy this aerial tour of Nazmos tremendously. It was just his cup of tea.

They all knew what to expect on this tour from the graphic images I had given of it when I'd arrived back on Earth. But seeing it for real was bound to be far more interesting. I looked forward to their comments when they got back. Rachel had become slightly nervous about the trip when she learned that I was not to accompany them but I said I had other important work and that Margaret and Muznant would both hold her hands throughout. I said for her to watch Simon's expressions on the trip and to tell me if he enjoyed it. I leant down and she gave me a big hug and a kiss and said she would look after Simon. She said it in a most motherly fashion which made me smile with pride. Rachel was a gem and little did I know that both she and Margaret would have important roles to play in the future of Nazmos.

Jazzatnit and I were up on the terrace looking across at the city when Zazfrapiz came up and joined us. We looked at the city view and he pointed out many salient features.

'I prefer to be up here in the late mornings,' he said. 'It is the freshest and best time of the day for me.'

It was nice and warm now and I knew exactly what he meant. His bones felt the cold much more now than when he was a younger man. There was a huge contrast in the temperatures between day and night and I hoped that this would mellow after the Nazmos orbital adjustment.

I now received a communication from Simon that the small craft 566-Blue was up in the sky and heading out over the Peruga Sea. Captain Lyozonpa had given him a detailed itinerary of their intended tour of Nazmos and I could sense the excitement in the tone of the message. The image I received of the Nazmos landscape was of the Peruga Sea far below with the coastline retreating behind them. The sea had several large islands dotted around and one was particularly large. This would be Ventrazta and I remembered Captain Bulzezatna mentioning it because it was where her cousin Nuztazm grew up.

I was glad that the trip was going well and I hoped that Rachel too was enjoying it. I know that Captain Lyozonpa would do his best to make it all very interesting. I queried Tania about Rachel and she replied instantly that my daughter was quite into the trip now and enjoying the views from the panel window that she and Margaret had to themselves. Tania understood my concerns for our little girl and made sure I knew that all was well.

We now received a communication from Nerbtazwi that six of them were on their way to the space park and that a deck Transporter was on its way to collect me. And so Zazfrapiz and Jazzatnit walked with me to the plaza area. As we approached it we saw the deck Transporter coming in. It settled down quietly and as we went to it the operator alighted and came towards me. He conveyed his Sewa greetings and that his errand was to transport me to the spaceship 561-Silverlake. Zazfrapiz said that this was one of the governing council's special ships for their exclusive use around Nazmos. It could ferry its passengers anywhere on Nazmos and I imagined it to be similar to the craft currently taking my family on their tour.

'It is truly a magnificent craft for short journeys,' said Zazfrapiz with a reminiscent smile. 'I have travelled in it many times when I was a council member. You will enjoy the experience. I only wish I was fit enough to accompany you and relive old memories.'

I received a visual image of a fairly large ship; about twice the size of Lyzonpa's 566-Blue. It was a shiny silver colour with a gold stripe band around its centre. It had three decks of ship-encircling view panels two of which were either side of the gold stripe. The inside was sumptuously decorated with large rooms covered in lush carpets and heavy curtains festooned over the inner walls. The furniture looked soft and comfortable and this surprised me as I did not think the Oannes went in for this sort of adornment.

Zazfrapiz then conveyed that the long travel spaceships like 103-Silverstar were just as luxurious. In fact some were even more opulent and geared for extreme comfort. Nothing was too good for the members of the governing council of Nazmos.

'Well,' I thought, 'if the homes like that of Jazzatnit and Zazfrapiz could be grand then why not their spaceships also. After all a spaceship was like a home in space.'

The operator kept to a telepathic formality when communicating his duty to me and I acknowledged him in a similar manner. I thought I must keep to the rules at least as far as the governing council was concerned.

I gave my thanks to my hosts Jazzatnit and Zazfrapiz and conducted a brief and informal farewell Sewa as I boarded the Deck Transporter. This then lifted upwards and I smiled down as I rose above them. I stood alone at one side of the Transporter deck while the operator remained embarrassingly silent near the rear. I guessed he was under strict protocol rules and so I did not venture familiarity. Yet I felt uncomfortable with this and decided that I would speak to Muznant or Brazjaf about it.

My badge must have automatically communicated my quandary to her and she immediately conveyed back the strict discipline that applied to all who were connected in service duties with any governing council business. This included all staff and assistants. Muznant conveyed that I should find that all council associated Oannes kept a formal communicative distance from the ordinary Oannes people. If I ever travelled on 103-Silverstar I should find that its Captain Duntazent also behaved with a similar formality. And yet my thoughts went to Nerbtazwi who had become a friend just as Korizazit and Ritozanan.

'That is different,' conveyed Muznant, 'they are part of the upper hierarchy within the council and may do as they please.'

I expressed my confusion at this and found it hard to understand the system.

Muznant then explained that an Oannes person must achieve a certain grade level of confidence within the council for the disciplinary code to be relaxed. She said it was just the way of things within the governing council.

I think I understood part of it but it simply reinforced my determination to play and act according to those rules.

The Transporter took some twenty minutes to traverse the distance to the space park but then it continued right across to the far end of it. As it settled down I noticed the magnificent form of a spaceship sitting on the ground some fifty paces away which the operator confirmed was indeed 561-Silverlake.

It resembled the spacecraft of Anztarza with side doors that allowed direct entry via a ramp approach. I remember the manner I had entered the spacecraft 11701-Red and 520-Green from the moorings in the Bay Dome of Anztarza.

As I disembarked I saw Nerbtazwi coming to meet me. I received a telepathic welcome and Sewa as we were still walking towards one another.

'Welcome Ashley,' she said, 'the others are already inside the craft and await you. I trust that your family are having a pleasant tour of our Nazmos.'

'Yes thank you,' I said. 'They have been in contact with me and my son is especially thrilled.'

Somehow Margaret was considered as part of my family and I didn't mind it in the least.

I noticed again that the Oannes never referred to Nazmos as a planet. That was reserved for Platwuz and Rubabriz. Zraplat was neither and was just referred to as Zraplat. I am happy to say that Earth was Earth and never planet Earth. Though travel between Earth and Nazmos was referred to as inter-planetary.

On board the spacecraft Silverlake I was led by Nerbtazwi to a large ornately decorated hall-sized room in which were seated Korizazit, Ritozanan, Dultarzent and two other elderly male Oannes whom I understood to be council members. They were introduced to me as Maztatont and Zutadintz and were brothers. Maztatont was 290 years of age and Zutadintz was five years older. They had both been on the Nazmos governing council for twenty years and were both highly qualified as experts in the science field. They were pleasant in appearance but had seriousness written all over them. They were not the bubbly social type but their scientific acumen was prodigious. They came originally from the Island of Ventrazta in the Sea of Peruga and had often visited the not too distant smaller Island of Vaz.

I got all this information from a polite mind scan that had been permitted by them which also told me that they were on this trip to help in the search for the probable location of Gozmanot's home on the Island; wherever that might have been. I had my doubts that scientific means could locate something that had existed 36,520 years ago. Perhaps my inner voice could do something to help in that respect. I certainly hoped so for at the present time I just did not have a clue as to where or how I should begin my search. But I expected something to turn up.

Ritozanan came forward and touched my arm in a most comforting and reassuring manner. I suppose the gesture was meant to say she understood my doubts and that I should simply do my best. I had the utmost respect for this elderly lady and the more I saw of her the more my affection for her grew. And I knew that she felt the same about me for her open thoughts conveyed much.

Tania said that my easy laidback attitude towards things made people in general which included the Oannes, to trust and like me. Tania made me aware of a lot of things about myself that I would not normally have even considered. I just liked to behave in a casual manner and achieve or do what I wanted to do in the most stress-free way possible. The other thing that Tania made me aware of was that I was a good listener and that I knew when to keep my mouth shut.

The Oannes ways suited me just fine. I loved their openness of mind and ease of communication and the calm in their lives. And yet there was also plenty of tragedy and sadness woven into their lives as I thought of Zakatanz. Hazazamunt had been a great loss to him and as yet he had not got over her. She was forever in his thoughts. And then there was Muznant's phantom pregnancy which had been so upsetting for her. And Muzzalt the Anztarza Dome-21's Food-Inspector who'd had a disastrous first marriage to the immature Zatfortz whom she'd had to divorce. Her older second husband Nozatap had died after only fifteen years and she'd sworn never to marry again. And yet after forty five years alone she had met Ramtazan with whom she had found happiness and was still happily partnered.

My thoughts were interrupted when Zanos on-board informed us that the craft had lifted off and was heading across the Peruga Sea towards the Island of Vaz. I had felt nothing of the lift-off and again wondered at the smoothness of the ride. The Oannes technology certainly had travelling to a fine art whether it was to be in space or simply over the Nazmos landscape.

It was not long before the captain communicated that the craft was now stationary over the Island of Vaz at an altitude of just over sixty miles. He requested that we state the location where we wished to land on the island.

Korizazit conveyed back that the destination was as yet unknown since the exact location of Gozmanot's home was a mystery. Some intuition must have caused him to request the captain to descend to a lower altitude so that an aerial survey could be carried out. Perhaps a feature might reveal itself which could then be investigated. The brothers Maztatont and Zutadintz agreed with this and said we should go to the room where the view panels were located. Korizazit sent me a private message and I replied in the negative. My inner voice was silent.

It was the usual clear day and when we got to the room with view panels and I looked downwards at the Island of Vaz growing larger as we descended. The island was oval in shape but with a large bite taken out at one side. To me it had the form of a child's mitten with the fat thumb jutting outwards. For some reason this fat finger of land drew my attention and a curiosity formed in my mind to see it more closely. Was my inner voice guiding me or was it just an intuitive instinct? I had always trusted these notions and for want of something more positive I decided to follow it through. So I conveyed my desire to the captain and the ship noticeably altered course and headed towards this part of Vaz. At about ten miles up my instinctive feelings grew in strength and a level of confidence began to build in me. Something was drawing me there and who was I to contradict this urge. I still knew nothing about Gozmanot's home location but the nature of what was pulling me towards this peninsular of land was a curiosity I could not resist.

The brothers Maztatont and Zutadintz looked at me with considerable doubt and I could tell that they thought I was just going through the motions of trying to locate Gozmanot's home. They had not tried to read my thoughts as Ritozanan had. She saw that I was onto something and gave me a nod of approval. The brothers' thoughts were that scientifically how could I remotely know where Gozmanot had lived when there was absolutely no trace or records of the site? There wasn't the least hint of where on the entire island we should begin to look. And I must confess that I had no faith about the matter either but a greater power had given me a gift and I trusted implicitly any instinct that was fed to me. Something was leading me towards this part of the island.

As we got lower I directed the captain towards the broad peninsular strip of land. The island of Vaz was about eighty miles at its widest stretch and maybe forty miles across at the central part. The peninsular was like a fat thumb that was ten miles at its base and extended out to about twenty miles. It narrowed to a nicely rounded curve near its end. There were no steep cliffs anywhere on this peninsular section and it had pleasant shallow beaches all along it. The island itself was a mixture of soil and rock and the central part rose to several hundred feet above the sea.

I directed the craft towards the centre of the rounded end of the peninsular and just about half a mile from the shore and asked the captain to land there. When he did this I got a very strong feeling about the place. But the place was totally barren and not a ruin of sorts anywhere in sight. It was like virgin land where no one had ever lived.

Nerbtazwi led the way as we disembarked and walked away from the craft. There was the crunch of grittiness under our feet as we walked along. We had gone hardly ten yards when Korizazit stopped and stared at the ground. I thought that perhaps he had received some sort of inner voice message.

'I have a piece of grit in my shoe,' he conveyed and looked around for somewhere to sit.

There was a clump of rocks to our left and he made his way there. We watched as he chose a suitable seat and settled down lightly upon it. He took off his left footwear, shook it upside down and checked inside it with his hand before putting it back on. We waited but he did not stand up again. I then saw him close his eyes and shake his head from side to side. Something was the matter with him so I quickly went to him with the others following closely behind.

'What is the matter Korizazit,' I asked, 'are you unwell?'

'I think I am,' he replied, 'I feel dizzy. Perhaps I sat down too quick.'

Suddenly I too felt lightness in my head and conveyed this to the others. Then they all said that they too felt rather odd.

'We must get away from this place,' I said instinctively and helping Korizazit to his feet we walked slowly back in the direction of the craft. After just a few yards the heady feeling disappeared completely and we all stopped and looked back at the pile of rocks that Korizazit had sat upon. There was a shape to the pile and I immediately thought that it resembled a cairn. I looked around and noticed the barrenness of the surrounding area. Further inland there was shrub growing but nothing between us and the sea.

'We have instruments on board the craft which we brought along for just such an event,' said Zutadintz looking keenly at me. 'Perhaps it might be wise to analyse this area before we proceed with our search.'

Suddenly it became obvious to me. The pile of rocks was Oannes made. It was like a cairn used to mark some location. But what was it marking? I conveyed my thoughts to the others but they knew nothing of its origin.

The brothers re-entered the craft and I waited for their return. But instead they conveyed a message that we should move further from the rock pile. The craft lifted off the ground and very slowly went up to a height of about a hundred feet. Then gradually it positioned itself right above the cairn. It remained stationary there for several minutes before returning to the ground at its previous position.

The brothers had done a complete scientific analysis of the rocks and its surround and in addition had called upon Zanos on-board to also do an independent analysis of the area. What had been a piece of grit in a shoe had developed into a confusing puzzle.

The brothers conveyed that their instruments had found nothing other than the usual normal ground analysis. There was no radioactivity or gas emission of any sort. And Zanos on-board reported that there was nothing unusual there and that the cairn was just a pile of inert rocks.

But why had my instinct drawn me here to this spot when the craft was as high as sixty miles above it. Again on instinct I decided to make a slow walking circuit of the cairn. I conveyed my intentions and requested that the others remain where they were but to keep in tune with my open mind.

When I got to the opposite side of the cairn I noticed a shallow dip in the ground. The dip was about twenty feet around and just a foot or so down at its centre. My inner voice cried out to me that this was the place I was searching for. I walked down into the dip and felt a warm emotional feeling when I got there. It was a most pleasant sensation and I looked down at the ground for any clues. I then sensed that the others had come up beside me and I knew that they too were feeling as I was. When I looked up I found myself standing in dense jungle. A forest of tall trees and lush green grass and bushes was all around me. This vision was there for only an instant before it was gone. I looked at the cairn of rocks and realised that whoever had built it must have had the same sensations that we'd had. And that would remain a mystery for generations to come. I could not help my thoughts that the cairn was a haunted place; purely a human impression. The Oannes had no religion and they did not believe in an after-life. Well not as yet.

Ritozanan who had been reading all my thoughts came and put her hand on my arm as did Korizazit and Nerbtazwi. The two brothers stood to one side but were looking keenly at me. I knew that all had seen my brief jungle vision and were curious to learn more.

'Do it now,' conveyed Ritozanan to me in a keen though anxious tone.

'Yes,' joined in both Korizazit and Nerbtazwi, 'we wish to know.'

I still wasn't sure that this was Gozmanot's house location but the signs had been positive so far and my instincts had brought me here; and my inner voice had said 'this was the place'.

'I'll give it a try,' I conveyed.

I hadn't a clue as to what Gozmanot might look like even if I could regress to her time. So I concentrated my mind on her name and her time of 36,520 years ago. At least I was sure of that because it had been clearly revealed to me through my history gift.

I went into pink mode with my eyes shut tight hoping that something might be revealed to me. But nothing appeared and I opened my eyes again. The landscape before me was unchanged except that it all appeared with a rosy pink colouring. There was also a mist hovering over the island which began to descend lower down to my level. Gradually this became more dense and I could just make out the statue-like still forms of Nerbtazwi and the others standing beside me. The brothers being a bit further away had disappeared in this mist.

Then dizziness came upon me forcing me to sit down upon the ground. It all happened as if in a dream and I instantly recognised the event. I was that spectator again viewing the events of the past. I was suspended above the island and suddenly my consciousness became aware that I was thousands of years in the past but still on Vaz.

I looked down and there below me was a small village of some forty or fifty block type houses. The houses were spaced apart though not by very much. There were no defined streets but paths between the houses were clearly visible. There were also several defined and well used paths leading away from the village and down towards the sea shore. The name of the village or should I say township was thrown at me and sounded like Razfarrant.

I then felt my spectator self being pulled downwards towards a house near the seaward edge of the village. This house was rather more apart from the others and closer to the shoreline. I felt an odd emotion as I approached it and soon found myself viewing it from the inside. The interior was quite gloomy and sparsely furnished but I didn't take much notice of this. My attention was drawn towards a doorway at the back of the room and towards which I was being pulled. I seemed not to be in control of where I went or what I viewed. Some other force was guiding me and I floated through the doorway and into another larger more open room. Here there was a sleep tank the like of which I had not seen before. It was constructed of wide wall-like pillars that formed a complete circle at the centre of the room. Between the pillars clear panels were fitted such that the whole formed a container feature. This was nearly full of water which to my spectator view seemed rather hazy. I was then drawn into the tank interior and the haziness seemed to clear. And then I saw her. My consciousness told me that this was Gozmanot so I ventured closer in order to see her face. Her back was towards me and I could see that she was awake and apparently searching for something or someone. Then she turned towards me as if by instinct and a big smile lit up her face. But how could this be? How could she know that I was looking at her?

'Welcome,' she conveyed and her hands reached out towards me.

My dream vision took my spectator-self forward and into her arms. Her arms seemed to close around my form and yet I could not feel them. But her emotion of joy and affection was so real that I in turn could not help but respond in kind. An emotion filled my being and it was a beautiful feeling; a love-at-first-sight feeling. In that instant I felt there was a communion of emotions between the two of us.

I looked into Gozmanot's eyes and could feel hers focussed on mine. Her face was old even by Oannes' standards. Although very old looking she was not wrinkled or ugly in any way. Her head was unusually large and she had a wide face and the biggest smile I had ever seen. I saw no resemblance to anyone I knew and yet there was a familiarity about her looks. She then backed away from me with a serious expression as her mouth took on a pronounced droop at its edges. She was certainly not pretty but that was because of her age. She was nearly five hundred years old for my dreamlike vision had brought me into the latter part of her life. Instinctively I knew that she had not long to live. She had seen all her visions and I think my appearance to her at this moment was simply a continuation of that theme. I somehow felt that I had been expected.

'At last I am satisfied and can go in peace,' she conveyed generally. And then forced into me a concentrated data blast of every vision she had ever experienced in her lifetime. She then retreated away from me and the water once again became hazy and her form faded from my vision and consciousness.

Suddenly it was all over and I was back on the ground of the barren Island of Vaz. The dizziness I had initially experienced was no more and I made to stand. But my legs seemed frozen and would not respond. Or was it my mind? Eventually I stood up with Nerbtazwi's assistance though she had a puzzled and concerned look on her face. I realised that for them only an instant of time had elapsed and they had no notion that I had fulfilled their wish to know more of Gozmanot. I also knew in my heart that my regression into Gozmanot's time was not so much my doing as hers. She had drawn me towards her time just so that she could look into my eyes and know for certain that what she had seen as a vision would one day become reality through the person who was in fact me. Only such a person as she had envisioned would be able to venture back in time to fulfil her wish. Suddenly I began to see the wonder of it and my whole being was swamped by an emotion of sadness; a sadness that arose through the loss of another being. The sadness struck into the core of my soul and overwhelmed my thoughts such that I had no control over my emotion. I covered my face with the palms of my hands and I wept like a child. The tears poured out and soaked my palms and my whole body shook with sorrow. I remained stricken for quite a while till the emotion passed. My eyes dried up and I realised that tears were a proper release for that emotion of sadness that came when you knew that you would never see your friend again.

I had been drawn into the heart of this woman now long gone and yet that fleeting moment of our meeting would live in my heart forever. She had conveyed all her thoughts and visions in that brief moment and it was as though she had kept this spot sacred solely for when I arrived.

I looked around me now and up towards the cairn of rocks and instantly knew that a release had occurred and that it was safe to approach them. And this I did with first Nerbtazwi and then the others following close behind. I stood proud beside the cairn and felt a new calm and sereneness about the place. My friends looked at me and expressed their surprise. Whatever had been here had gone and in my subconscious I just knew who that was but kept the thought to myself.

'What has happened here,' asked a very worried Ritozanan?

I made my decision then that I would convey my dream-like vision experience in all its fine detail once only. The moment and the emotions were still poignant and fresh in my mind and I wanted it conveyed exactly as I was feeling it now. I would convey the images in exact detail through my communication badge to every living being on Nazmos. It would then become a permanent record in Nazmos' history and all would see the face of Gozmanot just as I had seen her. They too would see her looking directly at them just as she had done with me. They would get a first hand view of all her visions just as they had been passed on to me by Gozmanot herself.

It took a few seconds for me to convey to all the images and thoughts of my regression experience. I knew that those on board 566-Blue would also receive it since I had phased my thought transmission to suit their slower mental capability. I wanted Tania, the kids and all the family including Margaret to know that I had succeeded in my mission regarding Gozmanot and for them to be proud of my achievement.

There followed a momentary telepathic silence for what seemed like ages. Then suddenly a clamour arose in my mind that was a mixture of exclamations, good wishes and congratulations. This was an historic moment for Nazmos and I and my six companions were in an historic place. Then I saw the captain and his ten crew members come out of the craft 561-Silverlake and make their way towards us. I believe their request to do so was granted by Ritozanan.

When Gozmanot had first begun to see her visions it had confused her. But then she began to see a beauty in them. And as she watched, her view of Nazmos began to alter. The formless barren heights had begun to resolve into high grassy hills and wide valleys. In the valley bottoms rivers twisted among trees that seemed to be springing up everywhere as if in slow motion. And solid building structures appeared as if by magic among the islands of cultivated land in which the bright green early shoots of crops were showing themselves in abundance. This tide of green exploded across the land in an ever-widening circle that spread in every direction towards the distant horizon. It was a glorious sight that Gozmanot conveyed to me and I found it pleasing and exhilarating to watch. And over all of this was the sensation of a brightly glowing Raznat spilling renewed warmth over the land. She saw what looked like a lush green Earth in all its glorious detail with its beautifully clouded blue skies. She saw a variety of landscapes and in it a variety of people, some Oannes and some not. Other visions showed the progressive transformation of Nazmos towards that of the other completed visions. These visions repeated themselves but each time with a slightly different aspect. Initially she had not understood what these dream-like visions were telling her. Then the realisation came that a path was being shown to her of a new and better Nazmos. A Nazmos that would be much more beautiful than it was now. It was a Nazmos that would be much warmer and greener for them to live on; a Nazmos where food could be grown on the land areas just as well as it was in the sea. All this was gradual but when she thought of all that could and would be done to Nazmos a joy of conviction exploded into her awareness. She began to ask questions but only some of these were clarified. Others she worked out for herself.

And then the bad visions began alongside the previous ones. A huge monster of fire was lurking far beyond Raznat and creeping forward slowly but surely with the aim of swallowing Nazmos into its fiery belly. This brought confusion, worry and doubt into Gozmanot's mind. She began to doubt her visions until suddenly a new development entered the picture. At first she thought it was an Oannes person she could see but then realised it was not. It was a form that was totally alien to any Oannes she had seen before. The creature was much taller than an Oannes person and it had bushy hair on its head and face. The clothes too were alien and her awareness told her that this being would go out to the fiery monster and push it aside to keep Nazmos safe. It came from another world and Gozmanot tried desperately to see its face more clearly but she could not. She knew it was there but the face would not appear close to her and this caused her to despair.

As the years passed Gozmanot conveyed her visions to others who visited her and gradually she became ill and frail spending long periods in her sleep tank. Her visions became less frequent but she held out hoping to get that longed for close-up glimpse of her alien. A deep affection grew in her heart for this creature from another world and she would look into her visions intensely with the hope of manipulating a better and closer view of its face.

I saw the look of wonder and joy that had come upon Gozmanot's broad face when my dream-like vision brought me right close up to her. Her wish had been fulfilled when she looked closely into my eyes and saw my face. She must have liked what she saw for she reached out her webbed arms to enfold me. I now wish that I could have felt those arms about me.

In that brief moment my heart had skipped a beat and I had felt a very great affection for this visionary. And I hoped that all of Nazmos would feel the same.

I wiped my eyes and looked upon my companions and smiled a slow tired smile. I felt like I had been on a great journey into the past and now I was back. I felt emotionally drained and exhausted by the experience and with a sense of loss that I could not explain.

'It is truly wonderful what you have done today Ashley,' said Ritozanan looking up at me. 'I think you know that all will be just as you wish it.'

I think I knew what she was referring to but I was not in a mood for hasty decisions and certainly not for any kind of victory celebration. I wanted my own time on Earth and nothing was going to alter that.

'What has happened here today is truly amazing,' conveyed Zutadintz. 'No science can explain it but it is your gift that permits it. Thank you for showing us the mystery that was Gozmanot.'

He then came forward and offered me his hand now widely known as an Earth custom. I clasped it firmly and felt a good grip in return. We smiled at each other. Then his brother also came forward and offered me his hand with a smile and a nodded acknowledgement.

'This place will become known to all and many will wish to visit it,' said Korizazit, 'and I acknowledge that this is an historic moment. A very important event occurred here today and its significance will be wide ranging.'

'Yes,' I thought to myself, 'far more than you or I can ever imagine.'

My own belief is that Gozmanot's soul was locked to this place seeking reassurance which I had brought to her by showing her my face in her vision. We had felt the force of her presence at the cairn when we first approached it but not anymore. The realisation of this fact would eventually dawn upon the Oannes culture and theism might be born. I wonder what slant that might take and whether any influence from Earth's religious philosophies would endure.

I hesitate to admit the impact that my visual meeting with Gozmanot has had upon me. If I were a superstitious person I might say that she had cast a spell over me. I feel as if something transpired between us when her eyes looked into mine even though it was in my dream-like condition. An emotion of raw passionate desire came alive inside me and I had an impatient urge to be with my Tania. I wanted to hold her against me, feel her lips on mine and do everything we had done on our honeymoon; again and again. I could barely contain myself. And in amongst all this emotion was a desire to be home in Dudley. Home there for the next twenty two years at least.

I spun around as a gentle hand touched my arm and the love in me exploded. It was Nerbtazwi showing concern for the topsy-turvy state of my mind. Without a semblance of voluntary control I then did to her what I had done to Muznant when the joy of going home to Earth had overwhelmed me. I stooped, put my arms around this 320 year old Oannes lady and lifting her up I squeezed her to my chest. I was laughing as I nuzzled my cheek against hers and I felt her arms squeezing me in return. Then realising what I was doing I put her down and made an attempt to smooth her large back fin. My embarrassment was obvious and nothing came into my mind for me to communicate. For an instant I thought about going pink and disappearing into the confines of the ship but that would not have solved anything.

'Thank you Ashley,' she said smiling, 'that was rather enjoyable. Tania is a lucky wife.'

'Please excuse me Nerbtazwi,' I said, 'I don't know what came over me. I think that Gozmanot has had a peculiar influence over me.'

'You may not be excused,' said a smiling Ritozanan, 'unless I am granted an example of the same.'

I liked and respected this lady so who was I to disobey a governing council member's request.

With a flourish I gestured with a deep bow and said, 'Your wish is my command most august lady,' and I repeated the embrace but in a much gentler manner.

Ritozanan's arms that went about me were lightly caressing but the chill in the cheek that touched mine set alarm bells ringing. She was not a well Oannes. Age had caught up with her and would soon overwhelm her being. My diagnosis revealed nothing wrong apart from exceptional aging. She must have sensed or read my thoughts.

'What have you seen Ashley,' she asked after I had put her down.

Wetness came into my eyes as I looked down at this lady. Thoughts and words failed me again so I just blinked back my tears and shook my head.

'You have a unique gift and it is a sad gift in many ways,' she said with understanding in her eyes and for a moment I was reminded of Gozmanot. 'But age gets to all of us and some sooner than others.'

She had read my mind and my emotion perfectly.

'Come,' she then conveyed to all in general, 'let us return to the comfort of our ship and then to Wentazta. Ashley is tired from his experience and must rest.'

What else had she seen in my mind? I blushed at the thought.

'O Tania where are you when I need you most,' I thought privately to myself.

I must exert more control over my thoughts and emotions. But the feelings of passion would not be stemmed.

The journey to the space park was uneventful. Throughout the trip back I sat on a comfy lounge sofa with my head back and eyes shut as I feigned tiredness. To take my mind away from the present I let my thoughts wander to the streets of Dudley and home. I stood outside Philip's house on Griffin Street and then I strolled over to the Black Dog pub. Next I was on King Street looking at McGills Antiques and Museum shop and then turning around to see the Bakery shop where Lorraine Hollings once worked. A myriad of people and places passed through my mind and then I knew I was definitely homesick. I must have dozed off for a bit.

At the space park just before we disembarked Ritozanan conveyed a request for me and my family to be available for a celebration in the Domed Hall on the day before our planned departure back to Earth. I was not sure what was intended but agreed to her request. That meant the day after tomorrow and it would complete the three days that I had said was to be our planned visit.

But tomorrow was to be Muznant and Brazjaf's treat. They wished to show us the sights of Wentazta and especially where she and Brazjaf had first met. I looked forward to the day.

I conveyed my Sewa farewells to my companions as they boarded a separate Deck Transporter. Mine was to be the same one that had brought me here.

When I arrived at the plaza area Jazzatnit and Zazfrapiz were there to greet me. The sight of Jazzatnit reignited my passions and I was glad this had not happened on my previous visit. She looked beautiful and I did not resist the urge to go up to her and plant a light kiss on her lips which she permitted with a smile. Muznant must have spoken at length about me. She had warm lips and I immediately thought of the contrast with Ritozanan's ice cold face. A sad thought indeed.

'Come,' conveyed an amused Zazfrapiz, 'you have done well with revealing Gozmanot to us. It has been a great success for us all and you must be drained of energy. After light refreshment you must rest before the evening's celebration. Our friends look forward to meeting you again. Your family are still on their tour and will be gone for some time yet.'

I realised I was quite hungry when we sat down at the table and a few dishes appeared before me. I drank two glasses of Wazu before I served myself to some sweetened Yaztraka. This was my favourite Oannes dish but I took some Raizna as well to please my hosts. Neither of them touched anything and conveyed that they had eaten earlier. They would save their appetites for this evening's banquet when all their friends would be visiting.

Having finished my snack meal I began to feel rather tired and a bit drowsy. I thought that perhaps my regression to Gozmanot's time had taken its toll on my energy. Jazzatnit saw me like this and suggested I get a few hours of rest before the others arrived back. I welcomed her suggestion and immediately acquiesced and allowed them to lead me to my room. I sat upon the bed to remove my footwear and looking up was just in time to see my hosts exit the door which gently closed behind them.

The next thing I remember was Tania's lips pressed hard against mine. I woke to that raging passion being reignited in the core of my being.

'I knew something was up when I got your message hours ago and sensed your emotion,' she said.

I stared at her and raised my eyebrows and suddenly we both burst our laughing at the words she had just used.

She then smacked me quite hard on the side of my head.

'Ashley Bonner must you always be so crude,' she chuckled and we started laughing even harder.

When I reached out for her she shook her head and conveyed that I'd have to wait till tonight when we were really alone. I agreed reluctantly but still grabbed her and squashed her against me. Her body was so warm against mine that I accepted it as a consolation prize. Her eyes looked into mine and understood all too well.

'How was the tour?' I asked to take my mind away from other things.

'Quite an experience,' she replied understanding what I was doing, 'but for me it was wonderful watching Simon and Rachel so taken by everything the captain showed them. Simon and Captain Lyozonpa got on like a house on fire. There was a mutual interest between them. Though Rachel surprised me with the interest she showed. She actually went and stood beside Simon and listened to everything that Lyozonpa conveyed. O Ashley, the whole view below us looked so drab that I can't wait for Nazmos' orbital change to bring some greenery into the scenery.'

I thought of Ritozanan and told Tania about her aging body. I knew that Ritozanan had made up her mind in favour of the orbital change but I said I would not affect it before I had completed the Platwuz orbit stabilisation. The intervening twenty two years were to be mine and free from any onerous thoughts. Of course I would keep in touch with Anztarza and all our friends there but I wished to remain on Earth and be a part of my children's growing to maturity.

Simon would be the first to leave home for the adventures of space but I puzzled over Rachel and the role she would play. My inner instincts had paired Rachel and Margaret together but their future was as yet unclear. I suspected however that it would be something to do with Nazmos.

The next thing I knew was that all the others of our group had trooped into our room full of the excitement from their tour of Nazmos. But there was the added excitement that I had regressed successfully to Gozmanot's time and gained the information that the governing council had desired.

'That was beautifully done,' said mum to me and I could see how impressed and proud she was of the fact. I could see her visualising me as that little boy she once worried about for having such gifts.

'Thanks mum,' I said, 'but I'm really glad that it is over. I've never felt so unsure about anything before. I'd no idea where or what to do beforehand. Something just drew me to that place and I felt as if it was Gozmanot who was doing the guiding.'

I had a brief insight into Margaret and Rachel's future but it was gone before I could comprehend its meaning. I puzzled over the moment for many years afterwards and thought that these gifts could be quite confusing.

We chatted for nearly an hour about their trip and mine before someone mentioned about getting ready for the evening do. Jazzatnit's local guests were due in just over an hour. It was wonderful how we could know this without being told specifically. That is the wonder of the openness of the thoughts that flowed around in this Oannes society.

When we were alone again I went for my shower hoping but Tania insisted I go in alone. 'Spoilsport' I conveyed but she ignored the insinuation. Afterwards I felt refreshed and smart in a yellow and red combination; yellow tunic with red leggings and footwear.

We walked out into the courtyard as a family and found that some of Jazzatnit's guests had already arrived. Polite Sewas were exchanged and introductions conducted. No details were necessary since visual images were transmitted with each person's name.

Mum, dad and the others soon also came out and I went around performing my duty. Tania said she was impressed by the friendliness and politeness of the general conversation. And no one mentioned Gozmanot specifically though I saw many admiring glances. Since I had universally conveyed my regression experience in explicit detail there was nothing to query or discuss and for which I was most grateful. I felt that the decision had been a good one.

Once again we spent quite a while wandering around the courtyard and I found myself often alone with an Oannes couple talking about conditions on Earth and my own home in Dudley. And in return they gave me information of their own town origins. I was getting to know and like these people more and more. I often saw Muznant looking in my direction with pride as if I was her discovery. She and Brazjaf were my first Oannes experience not to mention that first Oannes kiss.

At the dining table Jazzatnit surpassed herself with a myriad of old and new recipes. I thought I must try the new ones and I found that most were rather good. However there were two that were definitely not to my liking. One was very grey in colour and a texture that was rather slimy. The other was the opposite that tasted of nothing and with the consistency of sand. I decided I would avoid these in future. I think they were called Bizzony and Trozbit respectively. I noticed that some of Jazzatnit's guests quite enjoyed them so I guess it was just a question of taste. Simon had his own derogatory terms for them which I'd rather not mention.

After the meal we all wandered up onto the terrace to experience the setting of Raznat. As before the effects were again exciting and this time Rachel was rather keen to feel it all. But she made sure that she held a hand on each side of her. One of these just happened to be Jazzatnit who felt rather privileged and complimented. Rachel had taken to her because she looked and sounded a lot like Muznant. And of course Rachel conducted most of the conversation. I saw Margaret say a few words as well since hers was the other hand that Rachel had latched onto. Again that brief insight flitted across my mind but I was none the wiser. My inner voice seemed to hint that the two of them Rachel and Margaret had a connection with a future aspect on Nazmos.

It was as we were walking back down into the courtyard that the truth of Gozmanot's desire to look closely into my eyes hit me. Somehow she knew that her view of me in her vision represented a real person; her alien so to speak. The fact of the cairn and me being guided to that spot was not chance but a planned event. How she could know that I would arrive on time was beyond me. And it was not to just me that she was conveying all her visions. No, she was using me as her transmitter to all of Nazmos both now and in the forever future. In her time of 36,520 years ago she had expected a visitor to enter her visions and for her it had not been a long wait. I had regressed into her domain and been given her message. Her eyes had bored into mine and now those same eyes bored into everyone to whom I had conveyed her vision imagery. Each person on Nazmos would feel the eyes of their myth originator focussing on them as an individual. The impact of this direct contact with each person was immense and I had no doubt that she had understood the difficulty of getting a decision from a governing council. She knew that many had to be convinced that her vision of a greener and warmer Nazmos must be approved to attain reality. She knew that persuasive means were necessary and she had fulfilled that task most ingeniously. I thought, 'What a woman,'

I wish I could have found out more about her earlier years before her visions had begun. But I'd not had the desire to read her mind since I had not thought of her as a physical being. And now I knew I could never go back for another try. I realised that it was a one time thing only and was now done. I simply carried back what she had given me; nothing more and nothing less. Gozmanot had executed a brilliant strategy and had come out on top.

I must have hesitated in my stride for Muznant came to me sensing something was the matter.

'What have you seen now Ashley?' she conveyed privately.

I conveyed back my recent thoughts and I could see the expression of wonder appear on her face. She looked at me for a long moment before it dawned on her that Gozmanot was no ordinary visionary. She had managed to manipulate a being to cross a time span of some thirty-six thousand years and had relayed a message of hope to all of the Oannes people.

'You must convey these thoughts to the governing council members,' Muznant conveyed. 'It is important that they too realise what Gozmanot has achieved.'

'I think it would be wiser to let them come to this conclusion for themselves,' I replied. 'After all they know everything that I know and saw and felt. The communion of feelings between me and Gozmanot is also known to them.'

'Yes,' said Muznant, 'perhaps that is best.'

She looked directly up into my face and I felt her love and admiration. I smiled at her before I turned away to continue my way down towards the courtyard. I think my smile said more than I intended. I must be careful.

The evening wore on and Jazzatnit's local friends gradually left us. Each performed an elaborately polite Sewa with me and then their hosts and conveyed that they hoped to see us all again soon. I wished them the same.

When Zazfrapiz announced that it was his sleep tank time we took the hint and said that we also must retire to our beds. Actually Rachel was already half asleep though Simon seemed as alert as ever. However I had my own agenda and persuaded him to get his rest because tomorrow was to be a long and for him rather boring tour of the city of Wentazta. He'd certainly need all his reserves of energy for that. I conveyed what Muznant and Brazjaf had planned and Simon rolled his eyes and settled into his room with Rachel. I wished them both a pleasant night and shut their door.

My own emotions were peaking again and I could barely wait for Tania and our bed. We stripped and got in together and cuddled up.

'I have ulterior designs on you my husband,' she conveyed in a mischievous tone as her hands roamed over me.

My impatience and passion grew to such an extent that I erupted quite involuntarily. Tania looked at me and frowned but I reassured her that I had plenty in reserve and was quite undiminished in that aspect.

'What kind of a spell has Gozmanot cast on me,' I thought privately as Tania wiped herself clean. My passion was as fierce and keen as ever and I couldn't think beyond my desire for my beautiful wife. I think she felt the same if not even more so.

It was well over an hour later that we both slept from exhaustion though quite sated. I loved the feel of Tania against me especially as it was skin to silky skin.

I did not dream at all for which I was pleased and relieved. With the quenching of my passionate emotions the look from Gozmanot that I thought would haunt me forever now began to fade and become an abstract visual memory. I was glad that this was so and grateful that she had let go of me. Or was it simply that the power of the mutual love between Tania and me had overridden this interference. For a while I had feared that my thoughts and emotions would be swamped by that vision of Gozmanot's look. I am happy that it is not so. I am also immensely glad that I had the foresight to convey the event and her visions to all of Nazmos when it was fresh in my mind. I could not have done so now with the event fading so rapidly. This was because I had been willing it out of my mind. It is now all a matter of history and I shall let it rest there. Gozmanot had fulfilled her mission and I'm proud that I helped her to accomplish it.

Tania and I slept late and when we did wake we lazed in bed just chatting for another half hour. I was not hungry and yesterday seemed like a distant memory – albeit an important one for the Oannes. I had fulfilled the duty requested of me and I believe the Nazmos governing council members were well pleased. Well at least satisfied. I could happily have set course for home then and there but I had promised a stay of three days on Nazmos and shall abide by it. It would be impolite not to do so. Today was the second day and Muznant had arranged to show us the sights of this great city of Wentazta. It was where she had first met Brazjaf and I think that in her brooding state she wished to show us the exact street of that event. She also indicated a surprise for us and I wondered what form that could take.

Breakfast was a continental affair with bread and toast, jam and marmalade with cheese and a type of butter; and tea of course. I was not particularly hungry in spite of last night but Tania made sure I had a couple of slices of bread with butter and jam. I did however have three mugs of tea each with a little extra sugar in. I believe all this had been brought over from Earth on the Starship 8110-Gold. I briefly wondered how Captain Zakatanz was faring.

After breakfast was over and Raznat was higher up in the sky Muznant informed us that a Transporter had been summoned and should be in the plaza area in about twenty minutes.

Jazzatnit had stayed with us during breakfast and listened to our chatter with an amused expression on her face. She didn't eat anything but just sipped on a glass of Wazu. She said that Zazfrapiz was a late riser and she would eat with him when he got ready later. She then conveyed her thanks and appreciation of our friendly attitude towards her local guests. They had all said how much they enjoyed our company and how likeable we were. This was a good indicator for the long term relations between humans and Oannes in general. Well at least it was a good start in that direction.

Jazzatnit told Muznant something as we left the courtyard for the walk to the plaza. I expect it was for Muznant to look after us properly and perhaps a tip on what to show us. The pace of life was slow here on Nazmos and it suited me just fine. Mum always said I was too easy going in everything I did. Well that is exactly what I planned to do for the next twenty two years I hoped. But I'm sure I shall get plenty of excitement not only from my own immediate family but also from Katy's two minxes Fiona and Sarah.

Tania's tug on my arm brought me back to reality and I wondered where we were to go and see as I boarded the colourful deck type Transporter craft. The operator was a pleasant looking Oannes and smiled as we walked up the steps past him.

It was a bright day and a bit warmer than usual for which I was grateful. The Transporter craft lifted upwards smoothly and rose to a height of about a hundred feet. As it did so glass panels rose up all around its perimeter. This would shield us from the wind effect of its forward travelling velocity.

Muznant conveyed a running commentary with regard to the scenery passing below and I thought there was a definite purpose to the direction we were travelling. At first we progressed along at a rather leisurely pace but gradually this increased to about fifty miles per hour. After about fifteen minutes we slowed and then settled down in a plaza area not too many miles from the Domed Hall which was visible on the skyline. Muznant led the way off the Transporter and towards some buildings on one side.

We entered a street and Rachel gave a squeal of delight when she recognised where we were. We were in an Oannes shopping mall. The street was most ornately decorated with colourful signs depicting each shop. This was the first time I had encountered the Oannes written script and I thought it most unusual. Each word was like a snowflake and after looking into Muznant's mind I was able to read what each sign meant. It was like putting thoughts into pictures and I found it rather fascinating. The street was about a mile in length with many other streets branching off it on either side.

There were shops displaying all sorts of wares and I recognised an arts and crafts shop amongst them. There were restaurants too and I wondered if Muznant would treat us in one of them. She must have read my thoughts and looking at me gave a nod – and a smile I must add.

Mum, Milly and Margaret were all attracted to a clothes shop window which displayed quite a variety of tunics in designs a bit different from those that we had been given. I caught a brief facet of a partially shielded thought and I knew that we should soon see our ladies in similar outfits. Earth must have had some influence on Oannes fashion after all visual images from us humans must abound in the Oannes conscious. Facial makeup had become quite the thing among the young Oannes females. I wondered if wigs for the ladies would ever become fashionable. Sudzarnt wore a hair piece but that was from necessity for him to fit in as a human.

We passed many Oannes people wandering around and received pleasant smiles from most as they walked by us. We walked on for a bit and then turned left into one of the side streets. This was as decorated as the first and just as wide. It too was full of shops which were just as interesting and exciting. I did not recognise some of the goods and suspected they might be appliances suitable only to an Oannes household or kitchen. We went a fair way down this street before stopping. Muznant smiled and conveyed something to Brazjaf. He then walked on a few yards by himself before stopping and turning to face us. There were smiles on both their faces.

'That is where Brazjaf and his two friends were when I first saw him. I and my friends Wigzolta and Partuzna happened to be visiting Wentazta from our small home town of Latipuzan. I sensed an emotion and discovered that I was being admired by this person. I think we fell for each other right here and I'm glad of it. That was nearly forty years ago and we still come to this street whenever we are on Nazmos,' said Muznant.

Brazjaf then walked back to us and stood beside Muznant and I could see that this place meant a great deal to them. So there it was that the Oannes are also like us and quite romantic at heart. I felt I knew these people a little better for this. And I thought of the Navigation Pub when I had first laid eyes on a very young thirteen year old hazel eyed Tania. Of course I'd no idea then of how we would eventually get together and it wasn't love at first sight for me. I'm still not sure if Tania had made up her mind about me right then and there. She never lets on but I suspect that the die had been cast in that pub.

Some time during our romance Tania had asked me about the exact moment that I had fallen in love with her. I remember giving a vague reply about how I seemed to be in the middle of it before I even knew it had begun. I suppose it must be like that for a lot of people; but not Muznant and Brazjaf. They had been attracted to one another from the very first instant of their meeting. It had definitely been a case of love at first meeting.

We spent some time in this street before Rachel said she was thirsty. Muznant took us into one of the many restaurants and we sat down at a long table. The room was fairly cool and the table was alongside a large window giving us a street view. I had some Wazu as did the others but Rachel was given a special glass by Muznant. It had a pink coloured liquid in it that Rachel eyed suspiciously. Muznant prompted her to try it so she gingerly took a small sip. Her face then broke into a smile and a 'yummy' ensued from her lips as she drank more of it. Muznant looked at me and smiled as she conveyed that the drink was cool and sweet just as Rachel's liked.

'We have another surprise for you all,' she said but I caught a brief glimpse of her thought image and instantly knew what that surprise was to be.

But I said nothing to the others and feigned ignorance myself. Far be it for me to spoil Muznant's surprise moment.

So we returned to the plaza and boarded the Transporter once again. This time it progressed at some speed in a direction away from the now quite distant Domed Hall structure. The glass wind protection panels were up but we still felt a faint breeze around our heads. I quite enjoy the feel of the gentle wind rippling through my hair and so does Tania.

Eventually we settled in another plaza and this time it was very recognisable. It was a cross between London's Trafalgar Square but without the column or the lions and Rome's Piazza Novona. I was pleasantly surprised by the accuracy of the fountains adornment and the general feeling of Earth. We alighted and wandered around for a bit admiring the various features before Muznant led the way to a nearby street. As we entered it I instantly recognised it as being a very good copy of the famous Oxford Street in London. The shops looked authentic apart from the fact that they were manned by Oannes personnel. Muznant conveyed that there were also copies of other famous streets from many of Earth's famous cities.

We walked into several shops and everything in them must have been brought over from Earth. There were original brands of most things and the ladies glowed with pleasure at the sight of all these goodies. Mum said it was close to Christmas and it would be nice to take something back with them. Muznant suggested we all choose one item and it would be put on our account. She smiled at me and I could have sworn I saw her wink. I think mum had a perfume as did Aunt Brenda, Milly and Margaret. They said they would never use them but keep them as a souvenir from Nazmos. I think the men stuck with aftershaves but I just couldn't decide. There was nothing I really wanted so Tania bought me some thermal socks. She chose a couple of nice silk scarves for herself from another shop. Rachel chose a toy doll while Simon just couldn't make up his mind. He said he'd prefer a model of a Nazmos spaceship for his room and Muznant smiled and said she'd do her best for him. Of course Simon quickly asked for it to be a Starship like the one he'd just travelled on. Again Muznant just smiled at the enthusiasm of this youngster.

We then walked further along into a side street which had an India theme to it. There were jewellery stalls everywhere just like in the bazaars of an Indian town like Delhi and Calcutta that I had seen on travel programs on TV. Another street was like a market place which I didn't think was exciting for the men of our group; though the ladies were quite enthralled. They wanted to browse at each and every stall. I followed behind and noticed some interesting handcrafted figurines.

Brazjaf then conveyed that it was time for the afternoon meal and indicated that we return along the street and to the plaza where the Transporter awaited. I saw Rachel and Simon's eyes light up as they always seemed ready for something to eat.

The Transporter whizzed us to the Oannes shopping mall we had first visited. The restaurant we entered there must have been expecting us and a long table had been set up for us. Muznant and Brazjaf had most certainly been busy organising this day. The table had the usual Oannes fare and I found myself quite enjoying all the dishes especially as my hunger had suddenly picked up. Rachel and Simon had gotten into a choice of a few dishes that they preferred. Of course the sweetened Yaztraka was among their favourites. I in turn seemed to have a craving for the spicy Milsony though none of the others would even try it today. Tania said that one taste had been enough for her as the after-taste lingered on forever.

We'd done a fair bit of walking today and I quite relished the sitting down in the restaurant. I think the others felt the same especially mum who always said that she had never found a really comfortable pair of shoes that also had a bit of style. Dad said that flats were the best which is why men did not complain about their feet. Of course here on Nazmos the footwear was really comfortable but not conducive for long treks. The Oannes were not adventurous like that at all. Their transportation facilities were far too convenient. Perhaps long ago they might have been but I doubted it. They were more used to the sea than land.

I think Muznant read the mood and so conveyed to us that the rest of the tour would be conducted aboard one of the many Transporters. There was much to see but an appreciation of Wentazta's many features could just as easily be gained from the comfort of the transporter system.

She looked at Simon as she conveyed this and I think a secret message passed between them as he seemed keen to continue the tour.

When we had finished our meal we thanked the restaurant staff and returned to the plaza and the Transporter. With wind shields raised we were soon speeding at some height towards a distant rendezvous. I thought we must be approaching the edge of Wentazta's city limits and I was right.

We continued for at least another fifteen minutes over what appeared to be bare scrubland before approaching a vast complex of buildings. And alongside this was what seemed to be a space park.

The Transporter slowed and descended towards this and Brazjaf informed us that we were approaching the one and only Nazmos Space Academy. I knew now why Simon had got so excited earlier on. Muznant had told him of our destination.

The Transporter settled down in the space park and we seemed surrounded by a vast variety of spacecraft. Some were small like the one that Zakatanz and Hazazamunt had travelled in. Others were much larger but not as large as 520-Green commanded by Captain Bulzezatna. But many were in a variety of designs which I had not seen before and which I found quite strange. However I accepted that they must all be very functional.

As we disembarked I heard mum and Milly complain that there was more walking on the agenda. Muznant heard this and just smiled. She then conveyed that a mini-Transporter called a ground Transporter had been summoned and was to arrive shortly. And arrive it did after barely another minute had passed. It was small being just ten feet long and seven feet wide. It had a waist high railing all around its perimeter except for a gap of two feet at one end.

It settled down where we stood as a group and the operator instructed us to step aboard which we did. It was just a single step up onto the platform and even Rachel had no difficulty climbing aboard. It then rose up about a foot only before beginning a slow traverse forward between the parked spacecraft. It headed in the general direction of the large buildings a few hundred feet away. The ride was smooth but we still held onto the perimeter handrail because the ground seemed to move by rather rapidly. I suspect we were travelling at a speed of no more than about fifteen miles per hour. However as we got near the building entrance the mini-Transporter slowed to an easy walking pace. We entered through a large arched doorway and progressed forward slowly.

I now noticed that the operator was more than she had seemed at first. I discovered her name was Venzaztan and she was to be our tour guide through the space academy buildings. She was a staff member here and had been granted the honour of conducting this tour for us. I'm not sure if her interest was in me or my son. But I expect the interest was general and directed at all of us humans; quite a new prospect for her.

I noticed her looking at me and I received her open mind invitation. I read her mind and in return let her read mine. It was a fair exchange and a gesture of politeness on both our parts.

She was 130 years of age and originally came from a small town called Arznat nearly a thousand miles south of Wentazta but also on the shores of the Sea of Peruga. She had come to Wentazta as a child some hundred years before and had shown astronomy perceptive skills that were quite extraordinary. She had joined the space academy at the age of sixty and was a teacher here in the subject of extrapolation astronomy. This meant that space cadets should acquire the skill to recognise exactly where they are within the space zone of one hundred light years radius around Raznat. This was a subject that I found rather intriguing. It would be most useful to a seasoned space traveller. I conveyed all this to the others and received a 'wow' from Simon. I think that Venzaztan was looked at by him with a greater respect. I expect he would see more of her during his intended academy terms.

As we now progressed or should I say floated into the building our guide Venzaztan gave us a running commentary of everything happening before us. We saw small groups of Oannes youths being lectured in a demonstrative manner by a more senior looking person. Venzaztan explained that the academy accepted youth as young as thirty years of age. But most didn't come till several years beyond this age. There was of course a pre-academy establishment that all must first progress through. From there only about half proved suitable. The space academy training proper then lasted some ten to fifteen years depending upon the student and much of that was practical training and experience in outer space.

Our tour lasted nearly an hour after which time my brain felt like it had been bombarded with far too many facts and figures. There was so much to learn and master that I worried a bit for Simon. Would he cope among these Oannes with their superior brain power? But Simon had so much enthusiasm for this career that I was confident he would succeed. My inner voice added the word 'magnificently' at which I felt pleasantly reassured.

Finally we exited the complex of the academy buildings and floated towards our original Transporter. Venzaztan had been an excellent guide and I was impressed by her style of delivery. I felt I liked her especially as she might have much to do with Simon in the future. So when we disembarked I exchanged a farewell Sewa on behalf of our entire group. I also felt affection coming from her and I think our quiet unassuming manner had impressed her. Our eyes had met briefly at one point in the tour and I wondered if another conquest was in the offing. I think both Muznant and Tania noticed the moment. I'm sure I shall hear about this later.

Simon then went up to Venzaztan and conveyed a private comment at which the lady smiled. She put a hand on Simon's shoulder and conveyed something that brought a pleasurable smile to Simon's face.

'Thank you,' he said aloud and waved as he boarded the larger Transporter.

I did not wish to query what had passed between them but I did realise that Venzaztan among others at the academy would play an important role in forming Simon's future. This was a visit that was well worth our while. I could visualise Simon being here in about ten or fifteen years time from now. I also think that the fact of his being my son would be a positive advantage to him. In the back of my mind was the thought that there was much here that would come to assist me in my dealings with Zarama. Simon's gift was to be a great asset.

As our Transporter rose upwards I was pleased that Venzaztan had made no mention of my vision of Gozmanot. That was a chapter though very recent that I considered best put behind me. I only hope that her image does not resurrect to haunt me. I did not like the overpowering nature of her influence on my emotions especially with regard to the passionate desires I had felt. Thank goodness for Tania being here with me to help assuage those desires. Had it occurred on my previous trip I don't know what I might have done. I was practically out of control with desire and that was not a nice position to be in. I remember when Tania and I were together with the 'thinking stone' and wondering what it was. Our passions had nearly got the better of us then and Tania had gained control of herself before I did. I realise now the power over ones thought and emotions that telepathy can exert.

With the wind shielding raised we sped to several other Wentazta locations. We passed slowly over the food growing colleges and the general research establishments that were located adjacent to one another. On the edges of the city were the huge factory units that manufactured a variety of basic supply materials. These made not only technical products of a mechanical and electrical nature but also the simpler household items such as sleep-tanks, furniture and tableware to mention a few. Spacecraft required a myriad of components and most were made in the factory units that were here and spread around the other towns and cities as well.

The Transporter operator was an accomplished guide and I'm sure he must make similar tours for Oannes visitors to Wentazta quite often. I was impressed by both his knowledge and the delivery of the information he provided.

When we hovered over the Infant Education Centre I could see that both Margaret and Rachel appeared interested. They queried our operator and tour guide and received information in return which seemed to satisfy them. After visiting several other tour spots the Transporter finally flew over the coastal area. The Rimzi lived here and apparently their underwater city extended for many miles beyond the shoreline. They were a secretive people and there was no estimate of their population. Some Oannes thought that it might even rival Wentazta itself in both size and content.

There was however one place that we did not visit and could not. This was the bio-factory involved in the manufacture of the Zanos computer's systems. Muznant explained that not even the Oannes were allowed within the shielded zone in case of corruption of the processes being used. Apparently Oannes stem cells were used in a cloning fashion to develop the complex fusion between microchips and Oannes brain cells. The process took years of normal growth for them to harmonise into the coherent form that they had aboard their spaceships and in general domestic use.

We were a tired group of humans who finally trudged from the plaza where the Transporter dropped us to the courtyard of our hosts Jazzatnit and Zazfrapiz. I think that both Brazjaf and Muznant had also found it a long and fatiguing day. Only Simon appeared as fresh as when we had left this morning. There was a remarkable keenness to the sparkle in his demeanour that could only have come from his meeting with Venzaztan at the space academy. Perhaps this was a first mental step towards his spaceman career.

We all went directly to our rooms to rest and then freshen up for the evening meal which was not for a couple of hours yet. We had not been met by our hosts when we arrived but a message was conveyed by them welcoming us back and leaving us to recover from our travels. I thought this was very considerate of them and most perfect behaviour. They would see us at dinner.

Tania and I rested on our beds for about half an hour chatting with Rachel sitting between us. The infant education centre had struck a chord with both her and Margaret and I wondered what this interest could mean for them in the long term. Was Rachel wishing to become a teacher like her mum? Or was it something that was more Oannes orientated? I finally gave up on any further speculation and decided that a hot shower was in order. Tania said she'd follow suit after I was done. I was glad that Rachel was with us to quell any ideas I might have had.

When I came out of the shower I saw that Rachel was fast asleep on my bed. A brief thought came into my head and I looked at Tania quizzically. But she shook her head which I took to be a postponement for later tonight. The remnants of Gozmanot's induced urge had not completely dissipated for which I was rather glad. And I'm sure Tania was too.

The evening meal was excellent as were our lovely hosts. They asked what we thought of their city and we each gave a different viewpoint though all were generally in praise of its many aspects. The conversation at the meal was therefore mostly about our tour. The ladies talked about the shop streets while Simon had to mention the space academy. Jazzatnit and Zazfrapiz both sat listening to all this chatter and I noticed that each sported satisfied expressions as they looked around at their guests.

We gave the sunset phenomenon a miss as I don't think any of us fancied any further activity. We all felt rather full of the day's adventure; except Simon and Rachel who went with Muznant up onto the terrace. It was not long before they came down again having experienced the setting of Raznat and the accompanying wind. Rachel said that it got very cold very quickly and she had to rush down to the warmth here.

That night Tania and I snuggled up again but not like the night before. It had been a long day and tiredness took its toll. Tomorrow was to be our last day on Nazmos and we were to be guests of the governing council at a banquet in the Domed Hall. I wondered who else we might meet there.

When I awoke in the morning I had a strange feeling that something was odd. I then received a message from Muznant that I was to come up onto the terrace as soon as possible. Tania was still asleep so I had a quick wash, got dressed and made my way up towards the terrace. As I climbed the stairs I noticed the strangest glow coming from above. There were six people already on the terrace when I got there and looking upwards I saw the sky was a deep rosy pink colour. It was eerie and yet quite beautiful. Mum and dad were there along with our hosts Zazfrapiz and Jazzatnit. Muznant and Brazjaf smiled at my puzzled expression. There was no wind but I sensed that the mist-like glow above us was in motion. It was quite high up and seemed to be moving in a direction away from where Raznat usually set.

Jazzatnit then explained that the phenomenon was a sea mist that came up off the coastal area and gradually rose upwards as it moved inland. Since the house was several miles from the shore the mist had risen to a height of several hundred feet and was getting higher as it progressed further inland. She said that as Raznat got higher up in the sky the mist would disappear altogether and all would be normal again.

It was fascinating to see as the rosy glow seemed to pulsate with a life of its own. I felt a hand enter mine and there was Tania beside me along with Rachel and Simon. We all stood silently looking up at the sight above us. There was nothing to see except the beauty of a pink coloured sky that flowed above us. I looked across at the city and saw it bathed in the same reflected glow that gave it a beauty all of its own.

'Does this occur very often,' I asked?

'Only about once or twice a year,' replied Jazzatnit, 'and it usually gets very cold afterwards. You will feel the cold later today.'

'And what causes it,' I asked?

'We think that when a cold deep sea current shifts close to the shore it rises and cools the surface layer and the mist occurs but only at night or early morning before Raznat has risen,' conveyed Brazjaf.

'Do you think that the Rimzi could have something to do with the current shift,' was my next question?

There was a moment of shocked telepathic silence before Muznant replied.

'It is not something we have considered. It is just a natural phenomenon. What makes you think that the Rimzi have anything to do with it?' there was concern in her tone.

'It is just a thought since they live in the coastal regions,' I said.

'It causes no harm,' said Jazzatnit, 'so it is quite unimportant who might be responsible.'

I felt ashamed that I had made the suggestion.

'I'm sorry I did not mean to accuse anyone,' I said, 'please ignore my remark about the Rimzi.'

'I think it is beautiful,' chimed in Rachel. 'I think I like Nazmos'.

We all smiled at this since it was her first real compliment for this world.

The Oannes are a very gentle people and would never place blame on anyone without good reason. I felt I had overstepped a mark and I conveyed my emotion of contriteness over the matter. I had spoilt a beautiful moment and nothing I could say or do would make amends.

Jazzatnit and Zazfrapiz however came over to me and both touched me on the shoulder in a most affectionate and forgiving gesture and conveyed that it was forgotten. However it was a thought worth investigating they said. I still wish that I had not voiced my thoughts. I shall endeavour to be more circumspect in future.

We stayed up on the terrace for another half hour before coming down again. It was certainly quite cold up there and breakfast drew us to the dining hall. We went up again about an hour later for a quick look and noticed that the mist had nearly all gone and you could see the glowing round ball of Raznat through the light pink haze. It reminded me of our own sun viewed through an early morning mist on Earth.

The banquet in the Domed Hall was set for later in the day and Jazzatnit suggested we pass the time in the courtyard. Today would not be a good day to spend time out in the open outside as the air temperature was likely to be colder than usual.

Dad and I attached ourselves to Zazfrapiz and listened to stories of his earlier life. When I asked him about his time with the governing council he was hesitant to talk about it. But what he did say was that it had not been to his manner of thinking or in its approach to making decisions for the general good. Although he didn't say it I guessed that he disagreed with the style and that a bias of opinion existed in their thinking. He had been a council member for just five years before tendering his resignation. He had not specified a reason for his leaving and remained good friends with most of the current members. As a past member his opinion was often sought on certain matters. And he did give the matter serious consideration before offering a balanced opinion. He never ever recommended a course of action since he said it was not his place to do so.

We then briefly discussed the relocation of Nazmos to a closer orbital position around Raznat and the reply he gave was that it could do no harm. Changes would obviously occur in the climatic conditions he said after all wasn't that the purpose behind the orbital change. And people would adapt as they always did. I sensed regret in his tone and I suspected that he felt he might not be around to see all the benefits resulting from such a change. I mentioned the fact that most wouldn't since it might be many lifetimes before Nazmos produced any real benefits.

I noticed that Zazfrapiz did not say if he disapproved of the orbital change idea. And yet neither did he say anything in its favour. I guess he was an Oannes man who went with the flow and the decisions of the Nazmos governing council. Here was someone whom I had begun to understand and respect. He was easy going in his manner and I could see how Jazzatnit had come to love him. He was her perfect partner in life.

They had made a decision early on in their partnership that children were not in their plans. Both had agreed this and had been happy with the commitment. I briefly let my thoughts wander to the topic of Muznant and Brazjaf and their keenness for a child and Zazfrapiz gave a big smile on picking up this thought.

'They will have at least two I think,' he said privately to me, 'Muznant is of the typical mothering sort. Jazzatnit will be pleased.'

'What are you men discussing,' came from Jazzatnit when her group approached ours?

Mum, Brenda and Milly were with her at the time. I just smiled and waited for Zazfrapiz to answer his wife. But he too just smiled and remained telepathically silent. As he wished to make no response to the question he simply ignored it. The least said the better and a man after my own heart. Tania would most certainly think so.

Our larger group now walked around the exhibits and we were soon joined by the others. Margaret and Muznant had Ron and the kids with them and Rachel came to me and took hold of my hand. Brazjaf had returned to his room briefly before this but now came back and joined us.

'Let us take some refreshment and drink a glass of Wazu to our friendship,' he said, 'and then we can all get ready for our departure to the Domed Hall. You will be coming too will you not,' he asked our hosts?

'Of course we are,' said Zazfrapiz, 'it is after all a great honour that is being conferred upon our Earth visitors. But we may not stay the duration as it will depend on how tired I feel.'

He looked at Jazzatnit as he said this and she nodded agreement.

Zazfrapiz had a peculiar mannerism whenever he spoke or conveyed something. He would begin his discourse looking upwards at some imaginary point over your head. It was as though he was avoiding direct eye contact. But as he neared the conclusion of his argument or opinion he would lower his gaze and look directly into your eyes. It was as if he was asking for your response whether agreement or otherwise to what he had just said. He would keep his gaze fixed for a moment and then close his eyes in a slow blinking action as he listened to the reply. And if no reply was necessary then he would simply give that slow blink and follow it with his wide friendly smile.

Oh, I did like this man. He was so unique and so different in his gentility of manner from other Oannes I had met that I just had to admire him.

We had been standing around for a good part of the morning and it was now near midday. The refreshment in the dining hall was most welcome especially the sitting down part.

Rachel and Simon helped themselves to the biscuits on the table and I couldn't help thinking if this was an influence from Earth or was it the other way around. The Oannes had brought much of their knowledge to Earth all those millennia ago. Surely some of their food culture had been transferred to us. Why else would our ancestors have left a plentiful supply of meat on the hoof to pursue the more laborious industry of farming the land?

After a glass of Wazu I requested my more favourite drink; a mug of hot sweet milky tea. Simon and Rachel immediately went for their hot chocolate favourite. The others too chose their own preferences. After a while here we went to our rooms to freshen up and get ready for the special banquet gathering. I thought to put on my most colourful tunic outfit.

However when we got to our rooms we found new outfits had been laid out for us on each of our beds. Mine was a pale yellow one with gold and red edging. Tania's was similar to mine but in a pale lime green colour. Simon had his in the space cadet colours of purple and white but without the gold flashing on the shoulders. Rachel had the same as her mother.

When we assembled in the courtyard again we all looked extremely regal. Jazzatnit and Zazfrapiz came in simple white outfits that had a more flowing pattern which I thought was most elegant. There is something about dressing simply that says far more than an elaborate colouring. It carries the weight of a senator or dignitary and needs no introduction in its assertion of authority.

I thought we must now make our way to the plaza for our transport. But Zazfrapiz conveyed that we only needed to climb up to the terrace area where a special transport shuttle awaited us.

The terrace had a separate area that was over the courtyard which had no glass panelling around it. Two small shuttle craft rested lightly there and we divided ourselves between them. Each could seat about ten people and was completely enclosed like the spacecraft shuttles. An operator greeted us with a brief Sewa which needed no reply and we were soon speeding towards our rendezvous. I was with our hosts and Zazfrapiz had a broad smile on his face for the entire journey.

We disembarked in the large reception area and were led slowly towards the main hall. We were met at its entrance by Nerbtazwi and a few of her younger associates. The hall was laid out with tables and seating in rows upon rows and reminded me of the similar layout in the Dome-4 of Anztarza except on a much bigger scale. I think there would be a lot more people accommodated in here.

We were led to a position near the top end of the hall close the ever present dais of the governing council though currently unoccupied. None of the tables in the hall had so far been taken up but behind us I could see that our arrival had been anticipated and guests were now proceeding to their allocated positions. By the time we settled down on our seats the hall began to fill rapidly.

And behind us near the fixed dais a door opened and I recognised our other friends of the council. Ritozanan and Korizazit entered along with all the governing council members. They too like Zazfrapiz and Jazzatnit dressed in pure white flowing outfits but with a hit of gold speckling all over them. They settled at the tables either side of ours and all seemed in a pleasant mood.

Each and every table had jugs of Wazu and fine glasses and we were informed telepathically of the protocol for the evening celebration. And this was that the governing council members would initiate the pouring of Wazu into their glasses and all would then follow suit. Ritozanan would then telepathically make a toast for the health and well being of Nazmos' distinguished visitors from Earth. Glasses would be raised and Wazu drunk as all repeated the thoughts of the toast while still seated. Oannes custom did not require them to stand on such occasions. The empty glasses would then be put down again but with a positive tap on the table. The idea was not to do it all at the same time but in a random delayed sequence so that a rattling effect was heard.

But it did not go quite as planned. The glasses of Wazu were poured at the governing council tables and followed through by all the others. But a toast was not made; at least not then. Instead Ritozanan, all 320 years and four feet of her stood up and made a telepathic speech.

'I cannot propose a simple toast to our visitors from Earth,' she conveyed and briefly paused before continuing, 'because that would just not be good enough. Instead I must tell you my fellow Oannes people what is really in my heart.'

Tania looked at me with shock written all over her face but I just smiled back at her and winked to indicate I knew exactly what was coming.

Ritozanan continued but without that earlier smile or was I mistaken.

'We have known of the Earth and of its barbaric and primitive peoples for a very long time and had given up on them. They were considered beneath our culture and we avoided any contact with them. Yet we continued to monitor their ways by maintaining an outpost on their world. For what reason we did not know other than as a curiosity.'

She paused for a moment before continuing.

'For sometime now we have known that a threat existed in Zarama. We made preparations for the eventual evacuation of Nazmos and hoped that one day a place of refuge would be found somewhere out in space. Zarama was to arrive many generations in the future and so we of today had no fear or sense of urgency. There was one remote hope however and that was given to us within the vagueness of our ancient myths. Many did not believe in them and the truth is that neither did I. Few of us on the Nazmos governing council did and who can blame us for we deal in facts and not in dreams.'

The little woman paused to take a sip of her Wazu before continuing. I could see that she was visibly overcome with emotion for her legs seemed to quiver beneath her.

'But these ancient tales are myths no more. They are real. Gozmanot is real and we have all seen her in our own minds and everything that she foresaw that must come to pass for Nazmos. We may fear Zarama no more for she also saw what will happen there.'

She took another sip and placed one hand on the table for support.

'There is a family in this hall that we have come here to honour,' she said and the image she conveyed included Margaret. 'They are humans from Earth whom we rejected as a people that were unworthy of us. How wrong we have been. But Gozmanot was not wrong and we saw her joy when she at last came face to face with Ashley. She was expecting him and she knew him instantly as we do too. It is as if Ashley has travelled to us by chance or is it called fate. Earth people follow many religions and all have a central theme. Unfortunately we Oannes do not but I begin to wonder. There is more to our being than just life and death. Gozmanot lived and died over 36,000 years ago but yet she has come into our minds afresh. And for that we have Ashley to thank.'

Ritozanan now stood straight and lifted her glass of Wazu above her head and said, 'I wish to propose two toasts. The first is for the health and wellbeing of Ashley and all his family and friends here with us. And the second is for a continued fellowship in the longer term between the peoples of Nazmos and the peoples of Earth. So please all raise your glasses and drink to our friends here and on Earth.'

I watched as a great rustling of raised arms filled the hall and then the rattle of empty glasses being popped back on the tables. When the last one went down a silence descended and I knew that I must respond to the words of honour that Ritozanan had just bestowed upon me and mine. She had included Margaret in that listing.

Tania squeezed my hand as I now stood and faced the hall full of tables and Oannes. I decided I would speak aloud and let my voice be heard and recognised. My thoughts would also be picked up as I spoke. The Oannes are very skilled in that way.

'On behalf of all my family I wish to thank my dear friend the honourable Ritozanan for her most generous wishes,' I said knowing that the Oannes loved the formality of such occasions. 'And ever since I came among you both here and back in Anztarza I have come to know and love all whom I have met. I now have more close friendships among the Oannes people than I do with my own people back on Earth. And that is because you all have an openness of thought that is both caring and considerate. But that is only natural since your civilization is so greatly advanced beyond ours. One day we hope that with your assistance we too on Earth will become like you. It is my fervent hope that we do. But that is a very long way away in the distant future.'

I paused to let what I had said sink in and also to take a sip of my Wazu.

'For a large part of my life I did not understand the reason behind my gifts. I simply made use of them when necessary especially the history gift and that of regression to view past events. But I was only employing them and I did not feel any urgency of purpose. Then along came Muznant and Brazjaf who became my very good friends and whom I now love dearly. I visited Anztarza and saw what a wonderful city it is. And now here I am in Wentazta the biggest and best city of Nazmos. And yet there is one small place that has an importance all of its own. And that is the Island of Vaz where Gozmanot lived. You have all seen the images of my visit to her in her time. I have a confession to make about that. I did not go there by using my gift of seeing past events. No, there was something far more forceful that not only drew me to that part of Vaz but pulled me to the very spot where Gozmanot lived. My mind was suddenly taken over and I was drawn powerfully in towards Gozmanot where she awaited me in her sleep tank. I did nothing, she did it all. How she did this I do not know but it is a thought I must leave for you to ponder over.'

I paused for another sip of my Wazu. Words and images flashed through my brain.

'From all those years ago a vision has been passed on to you. It is a vision of a different Nazmos that is much like Earth. Zarama too appeared in the vision but that is as it must be. Now I know the reason I was granted these gifts and I can feel the urgency of purpose behind this power given to me. I shall use it to the best of my ability against Zarama and hope that Gozmanot's vision is true. So today I celebrate with you but must also take my leave of Nazmos and return to Earth. Hopefully we shall meet again twenty two years from now.'

I paused briefly.

'And now I too have two toasts I wish to propose. The first is for the health and wellbeing of Nazmos and all its peoples everywhere. And the second is just as sincere. May the memory of Gozmanot be forever in your hearts and minds and may she convey to us the true love she felt for the future of her people. So please refill your glasses and drink to the future of Nazmos and to the memory of Gozmanot.'

Again a great rustle filled the hall followed by the random tapping of empty glasses being replaced back on the tables. My own glass had been raised with all the others but I did not put it down. I raised it as high as I could and stretched it out towards the entire assembly turning a semicircle as I did so. It was only then that I realised that Tania had been holding my other hand throughout. I looked down at Simon and Rachel and I sensed their approval, love and pride. Then mum and dad began to clap and this was quickly followed by others and soon the clapping was a din from all around the Domed Hall. I was relieved when it gradually died down and to show my appreciation I made bows from the waist in several directions. It was an embarrassing moment for me but at the same time I felt tremendously uplifted. Who would not be? I conveyed my thanks to the council and to the hall in general and hoped that they understood how I felt.

When silence once again descended Ritozanan stood up.

'The formalities are completed,' she conveyed to all, 'let us now enjoy the occasion. The meal will be served and then afterwards all may mingle as they please. I'm sure our guests would be happy to meet with any of you who wish to do so.'

She sat down and smiled at me and I sensed the emotion of affection that came out to me. Her private message also came through loud and clear and I got great satisfaction from it.

Out of a bank of doors either side of the hall a hoard of servers suddenly appeared with food dishes on small floating pallets the size of large tea trays. These settled beside each table and the dishes were transferred by hand. Many of the seated guests gave the servers a helping hand in this. It was quite fascinating to watch and I thought it had not been like this at any of my previous banquets either here or in Anztarza. Within minutes the process of transfer was completed and the servers all withdrew. Then a general clatter commenced as cutlery made contact with plates as everyone began their meal.

It was the usual variety of dishes and I think we all had a personal favourite. I tried a bit of each dish in turn except for the Trozbit. I definitely did not like this dish at all. It reminded me of the mussels I had once tried from a seaside street vendor when we were holidaying in Dawlish Warren. Fine sand must have got into the container and the grittiness between my teeth put me off this type of seafood forever. And again in Rome I had tried the Risotto but again the crunchy bits got to me which I found unpleasant.

However I'd developed a taste for the spicy Milsony though none of the others had. Of course I was sure to put a dollop of Yaztraka on my plate to help with the spiciness. I think we were all quite hungry so for a while there was not much conversation. But nowadays I find I get full up rather quickly and I found that mum, dad, Ron and Brenda had stopped eating before I did. Ones appetite must diminish with age I think. Muznant and Margaret were still tucking in and I noticed that they were again in a private conversation. I was glad that they had become good friends.

Jazzatnit and Zazfrapiz were at the next table to ours and had Ritozanan, Korizazit and Nerbtazwi for company. I could see that they were all most friendly. Jazzatnit sat at her table but we faced each other and I began to notice her constant looks in my direction. There was no way I could have a private conversation with her so decided I'd enquire later. Or perhaps she just liked looking at the cut of my jib. A little vanity never did any harm!

When we had finished with our meal as had everyone else, I decided that a walkabout to the other tables would be the right thing to do. So out of curiosity I went across to the next table and seated myself right opposite Jazzatnit. In private communication I brought up my observation and asked what it was that she found about me that made her glance repeatedly at me.

She laughed silently and said, 'Oh Ashley do you not know? I am not the only one who stares at you. You have a pleasant manner about you and I have been trying to read what it is that makes you so amenable to all around you. I think it must be something that comes with all the gifts you have. But there is another reason also. When you leave tomorrow I shall not see you again until you return after twenty two years. You will have aged some more and I was wondering how you would look then.'

'I'll have a lot more white hairs on my head and wrinkles on my face not to mention a thicker waistline,' I said with a smile and conveyed an image of my dad to her. I meant this as a joke but I think Jazzatnit took me literally. I conveyed all this to Tania and from the other table she conveyed her response in one word. I'm not sure if she called me an ass or the longer version of the same. Either way I got the message.

I spent a few minutes talking to my council member friends before moving on to the other tables. I stayed a few minutes at each making small talk and allowing my mind to be read. That way each of the Oannes that I spoke to received a direct personal image of me. I always spoke aloud as I wished people to know my voice. Telepathy has it advantages but a voice has a unique and recognisable quality all of its own.

By now a lot of people had risen from their tables and were socialising with friends. So as I moved around I received a very pleasant surprise. Or should I say two surprises in two Starship captains. For there standing before me were the Captains Zakatanz and Natazlat. And both were smiling broadly and seemed pleased to see me as I was in seeing them. Zakatanz looked a very different person. Gone was the taciturn captain to be replaced by a pleasant looking and happy Oannes person. He was relaxed in his manner and smiling. I had never seen him like this before and I said as much.

'I shall tell you all about that in a moment after you have greeted my fellow captain,' he said.

I then greeted Captain Natazlat and knowing how she favoured me I went a step further and planted a kiss lightly on her lips.

I am pleased to meet you again Captain,' I said, 'and I look forward to our record journey back to Earth.'

I winked at her to let her know what I intended. She laughed silently and patted Zakatanz on the shoulder and jokingly said, 'I shall exceed your record by a decimal point my friend and that will stand for the next 22 years.'

I had missed the person who had stood behind Zakatanz. She now came forward and I received the shock of my life. She looked the spitting image of Hazazamunt of a hundred years ago. That was the image that Zakatanz had conveyed to me on board his Starship when he had first confided in me. This person also laughed silently at Natazlat's joke and looking up at Zakatanz she gave him a most affectionate look.

'Please let me introduce Azatamunt to you,' said Zakatanz as he faced towards this lady. 'She is Hazazamunt's younger sister and looks a lot like her. She was keen to meet you Ashley so I brought her along. I knew you wouldn't mind.'

I went forward and offered my hand to Azatamunt. When she took it I bowed low at the waist and gently touched my lips to the back of her hand. I noticed how smooth and cool it felt.

'I am very pleased to make your acquaintance Azatamunt,' I said, 'I feel as if I've known about you from before as you look so much like your sister.'

She smiled at me and then looked up at Zakatanz. He nodded ever so slightly as if giving her permission to speak. It was polite of her to do so and I felt an instant affection for her.

'And I am proud to meet you Ashley as there has been so much that we have received about you,' she said in a low husky voice. 'You are very different from what I imagined.'

I laughed out loud with my head thrown backwards. Heads were turned to look at us.

'Oh dear,' I finally said, 'I'm sorry to have disappointed you.'

'No, no,' she said, 'you are much nicer than what I thought. You behave quite ordinary and I like that very much.'

I sensed an emotion of great affection and admiration coming from her and thought was this another to join my growing fan club? I felt complimented and I said so.

'Thank you very much,' I said to her smiling widely, 'that is the best compliment I have had in a long time.'

She looked at me and then again at Zakatanz. I could see something there and wondered if Zakatanz had even noticed. The chemistry was mainly flowing in one direction at the present but I could see a future for my bereft captain. Azatamunt would win in the long run of that I was certain. There was a certain beauty about her that seemed a little boyish. I expect that she had some of the bravado for adventure that Hazazamunt had possessed which Zakatanz had found so fascinating. I also knew that Zakatanz had turned a corner in his thoughts for his Hazazamunt. It was as if there was closure to that long gone tragedy. She had left him and then returned in a most dramatic way.

Zakatanz then told me his story. I listened while he related all that had occurred over the last few days. He had gone to Hazazamunt's family and told them everything. Of the unknown tumour in her brain area and the aneurisms that would have resulted. Her disappearance into space was connected to it of that there could be no doubt and his speculation that she and her craft may have sped into Raznat. And then after a hundred years of guilt and grieving something had crashed into the forward shield of his Starship.

He told them of my gift of regressing to witness events in an earlier time frame. How I had seen the image of the craft and its interior which left little doubt in his mind about whose craft it was. But he had to have confirmation and so had visited the ships manufacturer. From the images he had conveyed to them they had confirmed that the collision craft was indeed 17426-Black. This was Hazazamunt's craft and Zakatanz felt that a chapter in his life had finally come to an end. He knew with certainty what had happened to Hazazamunt and now so did her family. He had closure and would forever treasure her memory. Although he had lost his dearest love he could now accept the loss and move on with his life.

He had spent the last few days with Hazazamunt's family and the initial grieving had relaxed to the point that there was no real sorrow left in their hearts. No feelings of guilt or remorse either. There was a relief at knowing that her going must have been instant.

Zakatanz had really looked around him for the first time since Hazazamunt's loss and he had not been oblivious to the admiring glances from Azatamunt. She was twenty years younger than Hazazamunt and bore a striking resemblance to her sister. Zakatanz was a Starship captain and had the bearing to match. He was handsome in an older sort of way and now that he had begun to smile more often it gave him a very pleasant appearance. An Oannes such as he could not remain aloof to the emotional signals sent out by one such as Azatamunt; especially someone who looked like his beloved Hazazamunt.

I think a new life would open up for Zakatanz when he finally decided that his period of mourning was over. It would be hard for him to think about partnering anyone other than Hazazamunt but his thoughts must be about life and living. And sooner or later a new affection and joy would awaken in his being and he would let go of Hazazamunt. Azatamunt would be patient and I knew she would win him over in the end. I secretly wished them well.

In three days a great transformation had occurred in Zakatanz's demeanour and I wondered what I should find when I returned twenty two years from now. I shall ask for regular news of him in the interval.

I communicated for a further few moments with the two captains as Azatamunt looked on before moving along to other tables and groups. No one referred to the recent events on Vaz for which I was grateful. Instead we talked about the morning's rising mist phenomenon. It was interesting to see the images from across the city and listen to the differing viewpoints.

I came across Brajam and Niztukan and both said they would be on the return trip to Earth tomorrow. I was pleased about this and had a long discussion about the forward shield with Niztukan. He told me also that he had received news about the progress being made by Platwuz in its new orbital path towards Raznat. All was going according to plan and they reckoned that it should be in position when I returned to fix it into its new orbit in twenty two years time.

'Perhaps Gozmanot's visions will become reality,' he said with a twinkle in his eyes.

'That will depend upon the decision of the governing council,' I said in a more serious tone.

'Yes,' he said, 'that is so. But after what we saw of Gozmanot and her visions will they dare go against all that?'

I had to smile at this. Gozmanot had had her final say through me and I had to agree with Niztukan's view. I could see where his thoughts lay and he conveyed to me that the majority on Nazmos felt as he did. This was a politically dangerous topic to be on and I wished to avoid it completely. There would be plenty to say in the year 2038 when I returned.

I was then approached by Captain Rojazonto and I took my leave of Niztukan. Rojazonto and I exchanged pleasantries and he informed me that he would be transporting me tomorrow to the Starship 9110-Red. A shuttle would pick us up about midmorning to convey us to his ship in the space park. Rojazonto was not the conversational type and we talked mainly about the facilities on his spaceship.

After a while we parted and I strolled on to another group and met up with the governing council brothers Maztatont and Zutadintz who had travelled with me to Vaz. Dultarzent, Ritozanan and Korizazit were with them and all seemed in pleasant mood. I sensed that a decision had been reached individually which made me feel quite optimistic for the future of Nazmos.

As I looked around and across the Hall I could make out where each member of our group was. The Oannes are shorter than humans by about a head. But what struck me was that each of us was on our own and mixing well with the Oannes invitees. We were dispersed randomly and all seemed to be in earnest conversation with those around them. I could not see Rachel or Simon but I knew that they were being perfectly looked after by these gentle people. And I'm sure Rachel my little chatterbox was holding her own. I learned later that she had got into a discussion with a group of Oannes ladies about their way of life. Jazzatnit told me that she had kept her eye on Rachel and was always near her as she wandered around.

One of the couples that I met and spent some time with was Kazaztan and his wife Zarpralt. I had met them at Jazzatnit's house the last time I was here and it was lovely to be able to talk to them again. Tagging along with them was Shufzaz who had been on the Starship trip out with us and when we had met aboard it in the dining hall. I told Kazaztan that I had no fresh news of my granddad Eric except that he had sent his very best wishes to both him and his wife. Kazaztan looked tired from the day's proceedings and we conducted our farewell Sewa. I wondered if I should see him again in twenty two year's time. I hoped so but doubted if I would. Shufzaz too said she would go along with her friends. It had been great for her to meet up with them again after Anztarza.

I would remember this moment as the time in which we few humans were representing Earth and it seemed as if we were ambassadors on Nazmos. Perhaps this would go down as an historic moment when viewed by future generations many millennia from now. I certainly hoped so.

My gifts have set me apart from my fellow humans and I am grateful for the privilege. My future is not secure however because of the burden that Zarama imposes upon me. I feel I must value the next twenty two years of my life and get maximum joy from the time. A moment of melancholy passed through me at the thought but my inner voice remained silent. I must fulfil the Big Task that Philip had referred to all those years ago. Where are you Philip I thought? I kept all these thoughts locked away so none may probe, not even Tania. What was that premonition that had brought on this sad mood? I would know one day.

Gradually the numbers in the Domed Hall began to diminish as people left. I guessed this must be by governing council arrangement. A time had been set for the departure of each guest. I then saw Simon in communication with Zakatanz and Natazlat with Azatamunt close by. Poor Azatamunt could only look on quietly but she seemed quite content to be beside her captain. Eventually they too took their leave as did most of the governing council members. Ritozanan and Korizazit however remained and we talked about the future. In my heart I felt a pang of sorrow for some inner instinct told me that I might not see her again after today. At least not like this. She was a frail looking 310 year old lady in poor health. Age was no respecter of persons and had not been kind to Ritozanan. My diagnostics indicated that she was just worn out and sooner or later something must give. And I think she knew this.

When we parted and said our farewell Sewas I kissed her on both cheeks and then cupping her cool face in both my palms and stooping low I kissed her lightly on the lips. She smiled up at me and must have known exactly how I felt. Slowly she turned and walked away. Would I ever see that ancient face again I thought?

Night had fallen and we'd felt nothing of the Raznat-setting phenomenon here inside the Domed Hall. The enclosed shuttles carried us over an illuminated city and back onto the terrace landing of Jazzatnit and Zazfrapiz's home. We sat around the dining table and talked about whom we had met at the banquet and what had been discussed or communicated.

There were snacks on the table along with drinks. I had my usual mug of hot tea while each of the others had their preferred choice. Both Rachel and Simon had their hot chocolate with a few biscuits which they infamously dunked.

It had been a memorable day for all of us and I was pleased how well everything had gone. We had met a lot of lovely Oannes people and I think we had mingled well to give a good impression of human socialising. On Nazmos we were the aliens and yet had been treated with the utmost respect and affection. I feel no different among the Oannes than if I was on a Dudley street; such has been their behaviour towards us. If the roles were reversed I very much doubt that they in turn might have received such fine treatment. Well not for some millennia at least.

I went to bed thinking these thoughts and conveyed them to Tania. She agreed with me wholeheartedly. My thoughts went on to tomorrow as the day when we began our journey back to Earth and home. Oh how I looked forward to the prospect; which was my last remembered pleasant thought before I drifted off into a deep sleep.

I awoke early before Tania or anyone else. After a few minutes of just lying there with my usual thoughts I decided to get up and wander into the courtyard area. It was peaceful here though complex thoughts were still whirling around in my head. I welcomed the tranquillity. I wandered around and found a seat near the Rachel Rose exhibit. I was deep in thought when I heard a rustle of sound behind me. It was Jazzatnit. She smiled at me and then quietly settled herself on a seat nearby. Nothing was said but the companionship of her presence was most comforting. We stayed like this for ages just looking at the exhibit and deep in our private thoughts.

Finally she stood and walking up behind me placed her hands upon my shoulders. I felt her press her cheek lightly to the top of my head and after a gentle squeeze from her hands she walked away. I stayed seated for another half hour or so at perfect peace with myself and the world. The earlier moment of mental turmoil had vanished and I now felt full of an emotion of goodness and love. If Jazzatnit were still near I would probably have put my arms around her in a hug of affection; perhaps given her a kiss as well. It was amazing how her presence had calmed me so completely.

When I walked back into our room Tania was awake and smiled at me.

'Jazzatnit was here,' she said, 'and she told me that you were in the courtyard finding peace.'

'Yes I was,' I replied and I then conveyed to my beautiful wife all that had transpired there.

'And not a word was spoken or conveyed?' she asked.

'That's the lovely thing,' I said. 'We just sat there immersed in our own thoughts while looking at the Rachel Rose. It was so peaceful there. I'm ready to go home now.'

'Good, so am I,' she said.

Tania then got up and came to me. She put her arms around me and hugged me tight. I did the same to her. Then I felt another little pair of hands creep around me. So lowering one arm I encircled it around my little Rachel and drew her into our hug. Simon stood in the doorway looking on and smiling. He was not the demonstrative type but he gave me a half wave with his hand down near his waist. Both Tania and I waved back.

Later at the breakfast meal there was a buzz of verbal conversation. The fact of our imminent departure today was cause for much excitement. Our hosts had not joined us this morning unlike yesterday when the pink fog had brought us all together on the terrace. Consequently breakfast was a slow casual affair this morning for I was not particularly hungry. Tania however insisted that I at least have a slice of toast with butter and jam so I politely obliged; though I did down three mugs of lovely hot tea. I was on my third mug when Jazzatnit came in and sat down at her usual place. She looked lovely in a pale cream outfit and mum said so. Jazzatnit smiled and nodded and then she told us that Zazfrapiz was making a special effort to get ready. He wished to see us before we left and to greet us with a special farewell Sewa.

Jazzatnit smiled generally at us all around the table but I sensed a prolonged glance in my direction. I conveyed a thank you to her for my moment of peace in the courtyard. And I received the barest of acknowledgement signals I'd ever seen. She just changed the angle of her head slightly while continuing her smile. I knew that she had understood exactly what I was trying to say. There was much I could learn from this lady. We were then joined by a smartly clad and smiling Zazfrapiz.

Muznant informed us that a Transporter was assigned to meet us in the plaza in about one hour so we returned to our rooms to freshen up. The time of our departure was drawing near and soon it would be time to say goodbye to our wonderful hosts. It was a sad moment for me as I feared I might not see Zazfrapiz again after today. I could only hope otherwise.

I will forever remember this morning's quiet moment with Jazzatnit and I shall think of her like an Aunt or even adoptive mum. That last gesture in the courtyard when she placed her cheek against the top of my head was so maternal that it is beyond words. It was an emotional gesture in the extreme.

And now it was time to say our farewells. I thanked Jazzatnit and Zazfrapiz for their hospitality to all of us. And as I conducted my farewell Sewa her eyes bored into mine and I received her affectionate message of goodwill and love. Except it was more than that. It was like a mother telling her son to be careful and to look after himself. Without children of her own any yearning she may have had now released itself as she looked upon me. I conveyed a private message and she smiled with pleasure.

The walk to the plaza was a dreary one for me with our hosts not accompanying us. But we were soon aboard the Transporter and floating above Wentazta and speeding our way towards the space park. It was a lovely bright and fairly warm morning but the operator kept the clear shielding raised up around the Transporter perimeter.

Tania was beside me and I conveyed to her how I felt. She squeezed my hand in support for she understood the sadness that comes when you must part from someone whom you love and admire. It must have been like that for her when I left her on that first trip back in mid October. Twenty two years is a long time and much can happen but I hoped I would find Jazzatnit and Zazfrapiz still here when I returned.

At the space park we transferred to one of Captain Rojazonto's internal mini transporters that then took us up into the bowels of his ship 9632-Orange. We were taken directly to the control room bubble at the very top of the ship. As we entered we were greeted by the captain with a rather formal Sewa though he did have a smile for us. The Oannes do love to do things in a formal and correct manner. I replied in a similar serious tone for all of our group but also with a smile. After all we had been together as recent as yesterday at the Domed Hall banquet.

We were given to understand that all passengers had now arrived and the ship would be ready to begin its journey in the next half hour or so. That is another trait of the Oannes people they are never in a hurry.

Simon was in his element once again and went from one side of the control room to the other looking at all the ships parked around us. Sadly the huge 98103-Pink behemoth had not returned so Simon did not get to see it.

Simon then gave a sudden whoop as he noticed that the other ships in the space park slowly began to sink down and out of sight. If it hadn't been for Simon's exclamation I would never have realised that our journey home had begun. It was not long before the sky changed colour from a light to a deeper blue and then to black. Raznat was still above us but all this changed as the ship veered to the left and away towards the utter blackness of space. It took a moment for our eyes to adjust and then there before us was the brilliance of the universe stars in all their glory. The Milky Way was the most brilliant like a pathway across the sky and I immediately thought that it was much the same as when viewed from Earth. Nazmos and Earth were really quite close together.

The ship continued its directional turn towards our rendezvous destination which was about six hours away. That was 2½ hours before the neutron generators could operate. And then 3½ hours at the high speed of 100,000mps to reach Captain Natazlat's 9110-Red Starship. Of course the 3½ hours would seem less to us because of the time dilation factor at this velocity of more than half the speed of light. Our wrist watches would show the journey duration as just three hours.

When the ship had completed its course change I noticed that the stars overhead now remained stationary. The acceleration had been smooth and the gravity feel had remained normal. What a way to travel in space. I'm continually amazed by it even though by now I should be quite a seasoned traveller.

I hadn't been hungry at breakfast in Jazzatnit's house but I now suddenly felt rather famished. It was near midday by Wentazta time so I expected a wait of at least another hour or so for the next meal. Captain Rojazonto must have read my thoughts and so suggested a welcoming meal in the dining hall near to our cabins in about thirty minutes.

Simon was happy to stay here for longer. He was enchanted by the view from this control room bubble and I could see that he had begun to recognise the positions of the different star groupings. I admired his keen desire to know as much as possible but there was only so much he could take in. He'd have to become more patient and let time come onto his side as currently his youth and inexperience were against him. There was much to absorb and he had plenty of time ahead of him in which to do so. I was very proud of my son and one day I'd probably travel in a spaceship commanded by him.

For now however hunger called and we gladly hopped onto the mini-Transporter that took us to our dining hall. There were no other Oannes there and service was fluid. It was not long after I had eaten my fill that a certain amount of drowsiness began to creep up on me. I'd had a disturbed sleep last night and had got up early to sit alone with my thoughts in the courtyard. A complexity of thoughts had been churning around in my head until Jazzatnit's silent companionship had banished them from my mind. An inner peace had descended upon me and I was sure that Jazzatnit must have woven some magical mental potion of her own. I think the Oannes must have the skill to exert an influence over other people's emotional state in order to induce a relaxing calmness within their minds. I thought back to the 'thinking stone' and its relaxing potential. Chief Ogemtali had said this to Andrew Pando when they had exchanged gifts. He'd suggested to Andrew that he place the tablet under his pillow at night and it would bring him inner peace.

Towards the end of our meal I had a nice hot mug of tea which I only half drank for the increase in the drowsiness that overcame me. I wished to arrive fresh at the Starship rendezvous point and conveyed this to the others and suggested a rest in our cabins. Muznant and Brazjaf agreed but the others all wanted to return to the control room to witness the spectacle of the neutron generators. Tania changed her mind and said she'd come to the cabin with me. It would be nearly an hour before the neutron generators operated and I didn't think I could stay awake for that long.

I'm not sure if I disappointed my wife but within minutes of us reaching our cabin I slumped onto my bed and fell into a deep sleep.

When I awoke I was inside the covers of my bed and in my shorts only. I felt quite refreshed and raring to go. I queried Zanos and was informed that four hours had elapsed since I'd returned to the cabin. A quick calculation indicated that we must be approaching our rendezvous position. And Zanos confirmed that our rendezvous with the Starship was just thirty five minutes away.

I decided to freshen up with a hot shower and then go up to meet the captain in the control room. Just then Tania came into the cabin along with Rachel and Margaret. They were followed by Milly and mum. They had requested Zanos on-board to inform them when I woke up which is how they knew when to enter. They said they'd been concerned for me and wished to know if I was alright. Mum said she'd seen my drowsy condition after the meal and knew something was not quite right with me. I explained about my early morning adventure with Jazzatnit and of the fact that I'd had a restless night. I didn't say anything about the turmoil of whirling thoughts within my mind. No need to create unnecessary worry. I assured them all that I felt refreshed and invigorated now. Tania raised an eyebrow at this and I nearly laughed out loud. I knew exactly what she was alluding to and hoped no one else had picked it up. Tania can be very wicked at times. I conveyed a private message to her and she smiled back at me. I definitely looked forward to being home again.

It would be soon be Christmas after we got back and I thought about the presents we usually bought. I knew that Tania had been shopping when I was away on Nazmos the first time. She normally picked up things when she saw them throughout the year. But she usually put in a concerted effort in November and early December. Merry Hill was a favourite of hers because it had everything in one area. It is surprising how early the shops begin to ply their Christmas trade. I've seen some start their window displays as early as October.

I learned that after witnessing the spectacle of the neutron generators all had returned to their cabins for a rest. Three and a half hours was a long time to be standing around just staring at an unmoving starry sky. After I had fallen asleep Tania had also returned to the control room but with the sole aim of bringing the kids back with her. She had come back with only Rachel as Simon had begged to be allowed to remain. Captain Rojazonto was quite taken by Simon's enthusiasm and gave permission for his continued stay.

Tania said that she and Rachel had lain on the bed together and just chatted about things in general. Later by agreement all had gone on to the dining hall for liquid refreshments. It was from there that they had received the information that I was awake. The ladies all came to check that I was alright but the men stayed put.

Having seen that I was fine I told them all to buzz off back to the dining hall where I would join them after I'd freshened up with a hot shower. So twenty minutes later I was in the dining hall with them sipping a delicious mug of tea. I was surprised to see Simon there also. Perhaps the lure of the chocolate drink and biscuits had enticed him away from the stars.

'What day is today?' asked Ron. 'According to my calculations I think its December 9th but I'm not sure.'

'I think you're right,' said Jerry, 'but days on Nazmos are different from days on Earth so we could be a day out either way.'

'The reason I'm asking is that I'm trying to calculate when we shall arrive back in Aberporth,' said Ron.

'If all goes to plan,' I said looking around the room, 'we should be home by December 15th. Christmas at home is a lovely thought is it not?'

'I'd like everyone at ours for Christmas dinner,' said mum and then quickly added, 'that is if no one has other plans, except Ron and Brenda of course. The B&B comes first for them.'

It was nice to hear talk like this and I do believe I might be a little homesick. The chat continued about Christmas and presents and the best way to make Christmas cakes and puddings.

It was then that we received a message from Zanos that the spaceship was turning about prior to operation of the neutron generators for the slowing down phase of our journey. The slowing down would commence in ten minutes.

We were all keen to witness the sparkly spectacle again especially Simon so we requested permission for this. Captain Rojazonto gave his permission and we all exited the dining hall to find a mini Transporter ready and waiting in the large corridor. We had barely settled ourselves in the recliners when the overhead view exploded in multiple lightning flashes of spectacular sparks exploding above the spaceship. This continued for several minutes and then just as suddenly ceased. I knew then that we must have arrived at our destination.

Our gravity conditions remained normal as the ship entered a parking loop some three hundred miles from the Starship 9110-Red. Contact with Captain Natazlat was made by the onboard Zanos systems communicating all information as was the norm.

Simon was glued to the control room view panels and I knew that he had spied the Starship in the distance. I too followed his gaze and at once saw 9110-Red far out there among the stars and I was amazed at how impressive it always appeared even at this distance. I think the red stripe down its length stands out brilliantly and more so than the gold stripe of Captain Zakatanz's Starship.

Captain Natazlat conveyed to us that her Starship was in full readiness for its trip to Earth. This would commence sometime after we had all come aboard. Other passengers and cargoes had already arrived in the days previous and we were the last passengers.

The Oannes never rush so it came as no surprise when Captain Rojazonto suggested a return to the dining hall where a final glass of Wazu could be drunk to the success of our journey home. I knew exactly the toast that he would propose. And so in the dining hall we raised our glasses and waited for the captain to speak.

'It has been a great pleasure and a privilege to have you all aboard my ship,' he said. 'And I am happy to hand you over to Captain Natazlat for your journey to Earth. I wish that your voyage be swift, safe and sure'

We all repeated that last sentence and gulped at our glass of Wazu. Simon was getting into the theme and repeated it twice. He imagined that he might be doing this one day as captain of his own craft. Rachel still wouldn't touch the Wazu so had a glass of her pink drink instead. Muznant knew exactly what she liked.

Our transfer to the Starship was uneventful after we had suited up in the gold electrostatic gear. Head scarves were now supplied to all our women as a norm. I smiled when I remembered the first shuttle trip during the asteroids experiment and how comical they looked with their long hair standing on end. For myself I quite liked the tickling sensation I felt on my scalp when my short hair stiffened outwards.

Captain Natazlat welcomed us as we came out of the lift that had transferred us down from the cargo platform. We divested ourselves of the gold overalls in the electrostatic robing room before she led the way back towards the central pillar and the Starship's control room; being also the captain's quarters. She was dressed in a very smart outfit that I thought had been specially laid on for our arrival. There was also a hint of colour in her face that I had not noticed before. Was it possible that a bit of cosmetic use had found its way into her quarters? She was after all a good looking Oannes female and a Starship captain to boot. At 190 years of age she was still in her prime. She looked back at me and smiled. I suspect she had picked up my thoughts and considered them a compliment. She was a very likeable person.

'We shall be on our way shortly,' she said when we were seated at her table, 'but before we do let us partake of a glass of Wazu and hope that our journey be swift, safe and sure.'

'And uneventful,' Jerry added remembering the collision with Hazazamunt's derelict spaceship.

Captain Natazlat looked keenly towards where Jerry sat and nodded her head with a slight sideways angle to it. A smile appeared on her face before she repeated her toast.

'May our journey to Earth be swift, safe and sure and also uneventful?'

After the toast she looked at me and I read a query in her expression. I am not a tease so I decided to ease her suspense.

'Captain Zakatanz's ship achieved the record speed of just a fraction below a 600 FTL velocity on the journey here. I'm given to understand by the eminent Brajam that the ship's reversing neutron generators cannot cope with velocities much above 600 FTL. So perhaps on this trip we might venture a velocity of a fraction over this figure.' I smiled my most charming and innocent smile.

'That would be wonderful,' she said with a pleased smile. 'It will remain as a record until you return. Captain Zakatanz will be informed in time.'

I knew that she was indirectly referring to the duration of her return trip to Nazmos; a journey at the relatively slower 10 FTL velocity that would take just over six months to complete.

We were informed that our quarters would be similar to the ones we had occupied on 8110-Gold. For now however a welcoming meal and been arranged here in the captain's quarters. It had been over five hours since my last wholesome meal and so I welcomed the impending one. Captain Rojazonto must have conveyed details of our trip on 9632-Orange or had the Zanos on-board bio-computer systems simply communicated with each other. It was wonderful how all our needs were anticipated and catered for.

The meal was laid out progressively by a couple of the Starship's crew and before long the table was quite laden. Captain Natazlat conveyed that the journey to Earth would commence in about an hour so we could relax during our meal. My appetite had returned and I felt rather hungry as the fragrance off the various dishes reached my senses. I helped myself to the Raizna and some of the sweet Yaztraka. I decided to give the Milsony a miss this time round. I noticed that there was no Bizzony or Trozbit on the menu which was a pleasant surprise. I reckon our preferences had become known and neither of those dishes was on that list. Thank goodness for that.

Later I tried the Starztal which is like a lentils dish and very tasty. I had this with the Mirzondip as I thought they complimented one another for taste and odour. And that was my lot apart from my usual mug of hot tea. I still take one sugar but Tania wants me to cut this to half.

I communicated with the captain throughout the meal and it was while I was sipping my tea that Zanos on-board informed us that the journey towards Earth had just commenced. I had not felt the slightest tremor or sense of movement. The sophistication and ease with which the Oannes have developed their space travel is absolutely marvellous. It is beyond words.

In my mind I decided to wait till the Starship had attained a velocity of about 5 FTL before I began to apply my own telekinetic effort. Zanos informed me that it should take about forty minutes for that to be achieved. I remembered that on the last trip with Captain Zakatanz I had commenced my action slightly before this. I had been impatient to begin. I conveyed my plan to Captain Natazlat and she replied pleasantly that she was happy with anything I planned. I opened my mind so that Zanos and I could coordinate our respective efforts.

My plan was a repeat of my previous effort. I would increase the telekinetic push by one level every few seconds. Zanos would of course keep me informed on the velocity of the Starship throughout my exertions. This was my fourth Starship journey and my second with Captain Natazlat. I was getting used to applying my telekinetic gift to push these magnificent Starship's to the higher FTL velocities. I'm sure I could do better and faster if allowed. Brajam had warned me of the ship's limitations in the deceleration aspect. So for now I must try not to exceed a velocity of 600 FTL.

I wondered how my telekinetic gift had developed since the last time. I noticed that each time it had become slightly more powerful. With 8110-Gold just a week ago the Starship had attained a steady velocity of just under 600 FTL. My push effort had been at level 97 then. What would it be this time? I'm sure it would be a bit less; I was impatient to find out.

Since I would be restricted to a position near the central column when I did commence my push I decided that a walkabout beforehand to stretch my legs would do me good. Tania said she'd accompany me as did some of the others. Muznant and Brazjaf said they were returning to their cabin and would see us later on. They kept their minds blocked to outsiders which drew a smile within my mind. I had noticed earlier that Muznant had developed a glow of joyousness about her manner. Or was it just my imagination?

Simon wished to stay close to the captain hoping to learn more about Starship procedures. I don't think he did since every aspect was managed by the onboard Zanos bio-computers. But it was good for him to see how a Starship captain behaved.

By the time we had walked to the far wall of the habitation platform and then back to the central area the Starship had attained a velocity of slightly above 2 FTL. The acceleration of the ship under its own propulsion would gradually lessen as it attained a higher FTL velocity. This was purely due to the increase in the volume of the space grid energy-medium impacting upon and being absorbed into the ship's neutron shield. Since the maximum impulsive power of the motors was limited the resultant force to accelerate gradually became less. A balance was achieved when the ship reached a velocity of approximately 10 FTL.

We continued our walk to the opposite far wall and while there became involved in conversation with some of the other travellers. They all knew of me and my recent regression to Gozmanot's time and were keen to meet me personally. Many of them were returning to Anztarza after a year long stay on Nazmos meeting their family and friends. All said that they were looking forward to the return to Earth. Most interesting I thought. I took my time walking back and stopped frequently to talk with other interested Oannes. They were keen to practice their verbal skills and what a varied tone of voice each had. It was during one of these verbal discussions that Zanos informed me that the Starship had just exceeded 4 FTL speed.

When we finally reached the control room again Captain Natazlat and Simon were waiting for me at the central column rails. The Starship was now approaching a velocity of 5 FTL so I conveyed that I would commence my part in accelerating the ship as of this moment.

I stood beside Simon and leaned back against the waist high railing and with a smile at my son I commenced my push effort. I applied the telekinetic force downwards and between my slightly parted legs. I imagined the location of the distant neutron shield and concentrated my mind upon it. Again I looked and smiled at my son and giving a nod I shut my eyes and began my first level push at that neutron shield monster.

I progressively increased my effort at a rate of one additional push level every few seconds and let Zanos inform me of the change in velocity. I paused for twenty minutes at the 40 push level. I wished to compare the ship's current velocity with that attained previously with 8110-Gold at this push level. At the end of the twenty minutes Zanos conveyed that the Starship had just exceeded a velocity of 310 FTL. This was well up on the previous velocity. I remember stopping at the 50 push level on 8110-Gold which then had achieved a velocity of 295 FTL. Goodness, my telekinetic power had certainly developed further.

At the 60 telekinetic push level I paused again and this time the Starship settled at a speed of 526 FTL. I was then careful how I applied the next few push efforts and stopped again for sometime to let the Starship velocity settle. This occurred at a velocity of just over 592 FTL. From now on I would increase by one push level at a time and wait to receive velocity confirmation from Zanos. It was at the 72 telekinetic push level that the Starship finally attained a steady 600¼ FTL so I left it at that. I locked my mind at this level and informed Zanos and the captain that my initial task was completed.

Captain Natazlat touched my arm for she had been beside me for the whole period of nearly four hours and conveyed her thanks. I detected a note of triumph in her posture. She and Zakatanz had a friendly rivalry as did most other Starship captains and this time she was slightly ahead of them all. This competitiveness had come down over the years when they had been on assorted spaceships. Professionalism counted massively for them in their respective careers as spaceship officers and now that they were Starship captains it was more so than ever.

Having been involved in accelerating this Starship for such a long period had resulted in an innate feeling of general tiredness in me. I also felt rather thirsty which seemed to be the norm on these occasions. Simon had been close to me all along and I sensed his pride in his dad. With all of these bestowed gifts it is impossible that people are not impressed by the things that I achieve.

Sensing my needs Captain Natazlat immediately persuaded me along with the others to retreat into her quarters for some liquid refreshment. Once inside I drank two glasses of Wazu though not too quickly as I was supervised by all the women of our group. I did feel a bit revived but it was while I was having my mug of tea that the tiredness seemed to resurrect itself. My arms and legs felt as if they were made of lead. Then a drowsy lethargy overcame me and I craved my bed. Tania saw me flagging and Rachel thought I was ill.

Tania tugged at my arm and I jerked into a wide awake reaction. It was like when I had got drowsy while driving on the motorway and hit the rumble strip. Dad and Jerry came either side of me and helped me to my feet and though I said I was okay they kept a hold on me. They walked me fairly briskly to our apartment room with the others following close behind. I think that the captain came as far as the entrance door before turning back. I must have been half asleep when I was placed on my bed. I felt someone lift my feet up onto the bed and a vague sensation of clothes being pulled off me.

The lethargy in my system made it seem as if I was asleep but I was not. I desperately wanted to get rid of this paralytic feeling. I wanted to yawn and stretch my arms and tense all my muscles in an animal-like stance but I could not. I briefly opened my eyes with difficulty and smiled at the concerned faces peering down at me. Then gradually my body eased and a peace descended in place of the tiredness and I knew that sleep was not far away.

'Let him rest,' I heard a whispered voice say followed by the sound of a closing door.

I was left to my thoughts which also slowed from an earlier whirling momentum and came down to a single thought. I was going home; home to live with my Tania, my Simon and my Rachel. I felt a hand in mine and knew that it belonged to Tania. She was sitting on the bed with me. She had not left with the others. And I could forget about Nazmos and Platwuz and Zarama for a long long time.

Sleep came and soon a new chapter in my life would commence. An anticipated chapter of twenty two lovely years of peace and calm in which Tania and I could watch our children grow slowly into adulthood.

PART THREE

2038/2039

Chapter 17

December 2038

Ashley and Tania were driving towards Birmingham on the motorway. They'd got onto the M5 going north and then joined the M6 going south indicating London. But the aim was to get off at Spaghetti Junction and then make their way to his mum's house in Erdington. It was the 12th of December 2038 and the anniversary of Eric Bonner's death eighteen years ago in 2020. Being so near to Christmas it had been a sad occasion then and one that the family commemorated each year with flowers for his grave on the day. It had become a part of their Christmas tradition.

Today the weather was clear but with a decided chill in the air. The sunshine felt warm inside the car but Ashley knew that there'd been a moderate frost during the night. Clear night skies in winter tended to be cold and frosty. His dad Alex would need to wrap up warm when they visited the grave in Witton Cemetery.

When Ashley had returned from his last trip to Nazmos he had visited his granddad every week. His contact via their Oannes communication badges was frequent and they spoke at length daily as did Lillian and Alex. Eric Bonner never really felt alone since he got to talk to all the other members of the family too.

Ashley noticed a drop in his granddad's enthusiasm for chat as the years rolled by. And for the last year of his life he'd lost interest generally and preferred to stay home even when invited to one of Lillian's dinners. He was however pleased to receive visitors though tended to drop off to sleep sometime during the chatting. Lillian went everyday to see to his needs and he always called her his angel.

On this particular morning when Ashley attempted a badge communication he got no response and immediately suspected the worst. Alex and Lillian were over in a flash when Ashley communicated his fears and they found Eric lying peacefully in his bed as though still asleep. It was a quiet and peaceful passing for Eric Bonner aged 96 years.

Ashley had bought his granddad a lovely big colourful woolly scarf for Christmas that year and decided to keep it for himself as a memento in his memory. He thought of his granddad with a fondness that had grown from when he was a boy playing catch the ball in their back garden. It had been his granddad who had first noticed his special gifts and had told his parents.

The funeral had been a week later at the St Barnabas Church and had been well attended. The weather was unusually mild that year and the sun had shone warmly on them all as they assembled around the grave plot in Witton Cemetery. Afterwards a reception was held in the upstairs party room of the revamped Roebuck pub a short walk from the church. The landlord was an old friend and knew Eric well. The buffet was excellent and the first two drinks were on the house with money Alex had put up behind the bar.

Ever since then Lillian and Alex had made it with flowers for his grave on each anniversary. Today was to be no different except that Ashley and Tania would do the chauffeuring to the graveside as they had done for the past so many years since Alex's illness.

Ashley was now fifty seven years of age and had kept his youthful looks remarkably well. Tania thought it might be another one of the gifts given to him. But Ashley's inner voice simply mentioned 'Gozmanot' whenever the thought about his age came into his mind. Ashley felt that perhaps she had passed something on to him at their regressed meeting which had somehow altered his genetic coding. Would he now live like the Oannes did? He very much doubted it.

Ashley had fully enjoyed these past years at home with his family and friends. He had led a normal life away from the worry of Zarama or Nazmos' climate change. McGill's Antiques and Museum shops had prospered and he had even managed to put his knowledge of the universe down in print. He had of course titled his work 'Faster than Light' in recognition of the Oannes Starships. Tania had sent copies on disc to several publishers but none had accepted it as suitable material. Too controversial they said and by an unknown in the field. A friend suggested Amazon Books and they were happy to let Ashley publish it on the internet. It received a considerable number of 'hits' on a regular basis and Ashley earned reasonable amounts of money from it. But no fame or notoriety came to him which was just as he wanted it. One day in the distant future its relevance and truth would be realised of that he was sure; perhaps well after he had departed this earthly life.

In 2018 two years after that return from Nazmos the other half of their semi-detached property came up for sale. Tom and Judy were moving to Weston for their retirement years and being friendly neighbours offered Ashley and Tania first refusal. Tania became quite excited at the prospect of enlarging their home and after discussing it or rather begging for it Ashley gave in and agreed to the purchase. Tom and Judy were pleased and the conveyance formalities were all completed within a couple of months.

Tania loved the larger garden area and a builder friend did all the modification and conversion work inside the house within a fortnight. It was simply a matter of putting an internal doorway access to the adjoining property both upstairs and downstairs. The documents for the two houses were then amalgamated and registered with the city council as one detached property which caused the council tax valuation to jump from Band B to the much higher Band E.

Simon and Tania moved into the master bedroom that used to be Tom and Judy's and Rachel took their old room. She didn't fancy moving to the other end of the house and further away from her mum and dad. Tania had had a field day in redecorating the entire new house and included new furniture in her plans. She looked back often upon her decision to acquire the other semi and to amalgamate the two halves into one house and had no regrets. She was now fifty three years of age and was only a few pounds heavier though still between a ten and twelve dress size. A few grey hairs had appeared in her auburn hair but were regularly attacked with the appropriate dye.

Tania was enjoying her life with Ashley and she frequently helped her mum and dad in the shops. She loved the bigger house even though now both Simon and Rachel had grown up and left home. There was a bit more housework but not more than she could cope with. It never occurred to her to want to downsize to a smaller property. Where would she put all her stuff if they got a smaller place? She could not bear to think about it; at least not yet anyway. Besides she called it her 'mansion' and how many could boast one of those. There were other considerations as well with both sets of parents getting on in years.

As they drove along the M6 Tania thought about her son Simon who was now thirty years old. My goodness she thought, how time flies. Simon had completed his A-Levels at the young age of seventeen and then gone to live in Anztarza at the suggestion of Captain Bulzezatna. She had taken him under her tutelage for a year before sending him off to Nazmos to join the Space Academy there as a junior cadet in training; the most junior posting possible. His first communication arrived a year later. He said that he thought the six month Starship journey to Nazmos a most informative one and he had learned the patience that was required for any long distance space travel.

Within ten years he had leapfrogged into his qualifying years and received an outstanding passing-out commendation. By 2036 he was a third officer on a spaceship for ferrying passengers and cargo to and from Platwuz. The ship had a capacity for up to a thousand passengers.

His visual communications to Earth and home came regularly as clockwork through Anztarza. Both Tania and Ashley not to mention the rest of the family were amazed at how mature he had grown and how adult he looked. There was much of his father's confident bearing in Simon's manner and Rachel had to laugh when she saw her brother sporting a thin moustache above his upper lip. Tania thought it quite suited him and enhanced his handsomeness.

But Simon continually conveyed that his heart was set on a Starship posting and mentioned that he had applied for a position on the modified experimental 100 FTL Starship 4110-Silver. This was the Starship that was meant to take Ashley towards Zarama one day.

Updated reports were continually received through Anztarza's council of ministers and apparently the modifications were progressing well. Trials were expected to begin in about ten year's time and would last for another two years at least. Commissioning would then take place after that provided that all went well. Further modifications might or might not be necessary.

Simon conveyed that crew allocation was being considered and among these would be five junior officers. Simon hoped to be one of them.

When Tania and Ashley arrived at the Bonner house Katy and Robin's car was already on the drive. They went in quickly as the outside air was cold compared to the warmth of the car. Lillian kept her house warm especially these last few winters for Alex's benefit. He was now eighty four years old and suffered from rheumatoid arthritis but never complained.

He'd had a hip replacement ten years ago and then the other one as well a few years later. He was on a complex array of coloured pills that Lillian carefully monitored and dispensed. A low level of steroids was among these which helped considerably. It gave him rather a healthy appearance. He got about fairly well and used a walking stick quite often. Ashley felt rather helpless knowing that there was nothing he could do to help his dad.

Alex could still drive their car though more often than not Lillian told him to get in the passenger seat and do the navigating. Lillian herself was now eighty but was healthy and very fit not to mention her youngish appearance. This was because she had few wrinkles or lines on her face. Perhaps it was her genes that Ashley had inherited. Or was it the special cream she had always applied to her face each night.

Alex's repeat prescriptions were taken care of by the local Lloyds pharmacy attached to the Stockland Primary Care Trust where their GP practiced.

'Hello Tania, hello Ash,' said Katy and gave each a hug and a kiss, 'fancy a nice hot mug of tea?'

'Yes please,' said Tania as she went to say hello to Lillian and Alex. 'And how is everyone?'

'Dad didn't have a very good night but is feeling better now,' said Lillian and then to Alex, 'aren't you darling?'

Ashley looked at his dad and went over to where he was seated and they shook hands.

'Hi dad,' he said, 'how's tricks?'

'Oh I can't complain son. Your mum just exaggerates a bit. I was fine but just couldn't get to sleep. I felt restless especially in my legs but I guess that's because I'm not getting the exercise I need. I should walk more and I will once the weather gets better.'

Katy came and stood beside her dad and asked if he would like another mug of tea.

'No thanks my girl,' he said smiling, 'I'll have one when we get back from the cemetery.'

'Okay dad,' said Katy 'I'll just go and make one for these two.'

'You stay and chat,' Lillian said, 'I'll do the needful.'

Katy was fifty three now and her features had turned heavyset and matronly. She was the Assistant Head Teacher at a large comprehensive school in Yardley. She had decided against going for a Headship even though she had done the head-teacher's course. This was on the advice of close friends in the teaching profession who stated that she would have to cope with a high level of stress and responsibility which played hell with ones home life. Katy had discussed this with Robin and he agreed with the advice. This was when Fiona and Sarah were still at home under their care.

Robin Nestors was fifty seven years old the same as Ashley and he had moved jobs to the Nat West Bank in West Bromwich when he was offered the post of assistant Bank Manager. He enjoyed his work and hoped to become Bank manager one day. Katy said he looked the part. Robin had put on a bit of weight and looked quite prosperous in his ample suit.

He and Katy had bought a large detached house in Sutton Coldfield off Maney Hill nearly twenty years ago and had just finished paying off the mortgage. They loved Spain and went there every summer for their holidays; usually during the month of August for about three or four weeks.

Both girls were well settled in their jobs but were still living at home to Katy's satisfaction.

Fiona was twenty seven the same age as Rachel and it was odd how both had gone towards the medical profession.

Rachel had completed her A-Levels and then gone to medical college in London. She qualified as an MD with honours and attained the very highest of marks possible. Her telepathic skills had helped especially with her ability to read other's minds. Her practical exams astounded her tutors as she understood and interpreted the patient's symptoms exactly. She cheated a bit by consulting her dad through her communication badge occasionally to confirm her diagnoses when in doubt. When she got a job as junior registrar at the City hospital she never erred in diagnostic decisions. She had a rented flat not far from the hospital because of the long and odd hours she worked. She liked the quiet privacy when she had to catch up on lost sleep. But she still had her room at home and often returned there when her shifts were more amenable. And Tania loved it when she did stay.

She'd had a few suitors both at college and afterwards but had never taken any seriously. There was no one on the cards at the moment though one of the doctors seemed to look often in her direction.

However Nazmos was often in her thoughts and she felt that her future lay there. She hoped to return there one day. Maybe she could go back on this coming trip with her dad. In the back of her mind was a pull towards Nazmos that she didn't quite understand. Perhaps she'd like to monitor the changing environment there after the orbital change. There seemed to be no doubt in her mind that it would occur.

In the summer of 2017 Troy arrived in the Bonner household. Troy was a small black Cocker Spaniel dog pup just four months old and quite a playful little chap. Ashley remembered Barclay from Aberporth and had then hoped to have one of his own some day. And now that yen had been fulfilled. Troy originally belonged to another couple who lived on Gervais Drive not far from them and had been a Christmas gift from the husband's parents. Without children of their own the young couple found it hard looking after the little pup. Tania and Heather knew each other from the church and the long and short of it was that Heather offered Troy to Tania for nothing. When Tania mentioned the offer to Ashley and the kids they were over the moon with delight. Needless to say Troy became the focal of attention in the Bonner house for the next fifteen years. Rachel and Simon just loved Troy and they did so openly. They were often seen hugging and kissing him on top of his head. Rachel sometimes even let Troy lick her all over her face.

At first Troy chewed at everything available but that soon stopped. He was house trained from the start and never once did anything inside the house. But he was a lap dog. He would jump up onto your lap and snuggle down and seem to be asleep in minutes. He was also a hawker and stared with drooling mouth whenever you were eating something. Troy loved his daily walks around Priory Park and Wren's Nest nature reserve which was a little further away but still a treat. Tania and Ashley discussed Troy often and both agreed that he brought out and calmed hidden emotional and adolescent issues in the kid's growing-up development.

'I know that Troy is good for us because he has increased the loving feeling within our family,' said Ashley one day when Troy was about five or six.

'Definitely,' agreed Tania, 'and I believe it's taken the glory aspect slightly off of you as far as the kids are concerned. You're just daddy now.'

'Yes,' said Ashley with a twinkle in his eyes while jiggling his eyebrows up and down, 'and we have plenty of time for ourselves.'

'Ashley Bonner', she said pouting at him though with a hint of a smile too,' you men have one track minds.' If others had been present Tania would have simply blushed profusely.

When Simon was seventeen he had left for Anztarza to prepare for the space academy under Captain Bulzezatna. And it was a sad day for him when he came on that last visit before his departure for Nazmos and had to say goodbye to his middle aged dog. There were lots of kisses, tears and hugs; Simon knew that this was a last farewell.

Rachel however had Troy for company to the very end; after the age of twelve Troy had repeated bouts of ill health. And then at age fourteen the vet diagnosed a series of mini strokes. When Troy was fifteen his back legs began to give way quite frequently and he became frail and incontinent. He could not climb onto your lap anymore and had to be lifted up. Tania wanted to continue nursing him but Rachel the medical student thought that they were being unkind to a proud dog. She said Troy was lingering towards a slow death. There was no quality to his life anymore and it showed in his expression.

Troy went to sleep for the last time at 3:16pm on 22nd July 2032. Ashley and Tania both wept when Troy closed his eyes and his head flopped back in the cradle of Ashley's arms as the vet administered the overdose of intravenous anaesthetic. The vet offered a cremation service but Ashley said no. Troy would be taken home and buried deep near his favourite spot in the back garden. It would remain unmarked but troy would never be forgotten.

Fiona unlike Rachel had qualified as an SRN nurse with a BSc Honours from Bristol University. She spent three years in the NHS but left when the opportunity came for exciting research work with a private medical company called Revolux. This company did contract work for the government Ministry of Health and Fiona travelled around the country in her company car giving talks and demonstrations on the usage of various new drugs, diets and medical appliances. She also visited GP surgeries around the country getting information about the drugs that had been administered. Fiona and her line manager Gail got on well and Fiona hoped to head her own team one day.

She'd had a succession of boyfriends though none recently since being with Revolux. She still had a room at home with her mum and dad but was looking at a first floor maisonette in the local area.

Sarah her younger sister was twenty five now and had qualified as a teacher at Newman College and had gone on to do a B.Ed Honours before starting her teaching career. She'd got a teaching post at Copeley Primary in Sutton but had moved to St Bartholomew's in Handsworth after eighteen months. She became friendly with a teacher there called Brian Walters who was seven years older than her. They got on well and saw a lot of each other out of school hours and at weekends. Sarah brought him home to meet her parents and they thought him a likeable chap.

Brian had a sister Tamsin who was two and a half years older than him and to whom he was very close. Their mum and dad had separated amicably when Brian was twenty four. They'd just drifted apart when the kids left home. At Tamsin's wedding a few years ago both had attended and seemed to get on well. But the dad had been restless for adventure and soon disappeared from view. No news had come back since then.

Brian had finally proposed to Sarah when he'd taken her out for dinner on his birthday this last September. He presented her with a wishbone patterned ring and asked her to be his wife. The ring had six diamonds embedded flush in the surface in white gold. The size was correct and it was the one that Sarah had actually tried on way back in June on her own 25th birthday. Brian confessed that it had set him thinking and so had decided to pop the question on his own 32nd birthday date.

The engagement was welcomed by Robin and Katy and also by the entire family when they were informed. As Brian was a football enthusiast and a staunch Villa supporter he suggested a date in the coming spring. He had attended every FA Cup Final since he was a teenager and so suggested a week later on May 21st would be a good date. But Sarah revised that to another week later to May 28th which would also be the end of the school term. Brian agreed that it was a good decision.

Sarah had then moved in with Brian at his home in Harborne after announcing their plans to everyone. They planned a simple church wedding which they would arrange themselves.

When Fiona and Sarah were growing up in their early teens Katy had noted how headstrong both her girls were. She and Robin debated whether they ought to reveal everything about Ashley's gifts to them. There had been an incident of shoplifting by a group of girls from their school and both Fiona and Sarah were somehow implicated. Two girls were named as the main culprits but they named Fiona as part of their shoplifting gang. Fiona denied that she was involved and Katy got Ashley to get to the truth of the matter. Although Fiona was innocent of the claim brought by the other two on this occasion Ashley discovered that she had shoplifted an item two months previous as a dare by this same gang of girls. Katy and Robin were furious and the thirteen year old Fiona burst into tears when confronted with the evidence. She swore never to do it again and she didn't.

As a result Fiona and Sarah were told about Ashley's telepathic mind reading gifts along with his gift of seeing past events. They were also told of his gift of knowing the history of any item he touched and of the famous History Cards in McGill's Antiques shop. But they said nothing of his other gifts or anything about Anztarza or Nazmos. One day they would be told all but not until Ashley and the family saw fit. Sadly that moment had been deferred continually and Katy had only a month ago discussed the matter again with her brother. Ashley had agreed to do the needful soon; perhaps by the first week of January. A visit to Anztarza could be arranged later when Ashley got back from Nazmos. But this might change as he thought more on it.

Very little mention was made to them of their cousin Simon and they thought of him as a prodigal son who had run off to foreign parts with a girlfriend or two. As such neither girl had been given a communication badge though Ashley had trained them well in the art of general telepathy. They were not able to read minds as yet.

'I managed to get some nice artificial flowers for the two vases,' said Lillian. 'I know they fade with time but at least they'll last longer than the fresh ones will, especially with the night frosts we are having. It was dad's idea really.'

'Excellent mum,' said Ashley, 'they look so realistic. I'm sure granddad will like them. We can change them again at Easter if we need to.'

'Yes we can indeed,' said Lillian. 'The other bunch is on behalf of Ron and Brenda. They asked for me to get one from them as usual.'

'Thanks sis I'm sure they look lovely,' came through on the communication badge from Brenda in Wales.

'See for yourselves,' said Ashley as he conveyed images of the flowers to his Aunt and Uncle.

'They're nice,' said Brenda, 'you chose well sis. I'm sure Eric will love them.'

Alex smiled at this but said nothing.

'Just sorry we can't be with you this Christmas,' said Ron, 'but you know how it is.'

Ron was eighty two years of age now and feeling it too. He'd been diagnosed with glaucoma about ten years ago and at first the eye drops had brought the eye pressures close to normal. Gradually however the pressures had begun to climb again and when they approached close to a fifty level the eye specialists decided that drainage grommets needed to be fitted to each eye. These had proved successful but not before Ron's right eye optic nerve suffered some permanent damage causing diminished vision in that eye. The left eye was perfectly normal.

Brenda who was four years younger than her husband was perfectly well like her sister Lillian. She and Ron had legally adopted Sudzarnt as their son and heir and were happy to hand the running of the B&B over to him. They had moved into the recently built annex that was attached to the back of the main building and were very comfortable in it. Brenda helped her adopted son whenever they were short staffed or if she was at a loose end and needed an excuse to do something. Julie Griffiths had left to get married nearly twenty years ago and now lived in Cardigan with her husband Barry and two teenage sons Giles and Andrew. The B&B had other staff but usually on a short term basis.

Sudzarnt made some significant changes in the running of the B&B the most notable of which was an alteration in the basic food menu. He decided to trial converting the cuisine to one that was totally vegetarian based. He had been after Brenda and Ron with his ideas and they finally agreed when Sudzarnt presented them with his new food menu. Both Ron and Brenda were surprised by it since to them it looked exactly like the previous one. Sudzarnt explained that there was such a disparate assortment of meat-like products made from Soya that few would actually notice any difference. And so it proved and once word got around the business boomed. Ron said that he never knew that so many people favoured vegetarianism. The B&B had a new sign with the word Vegetarian printed underneath in large bold lettering. Of course visits by the food inspectorate increased in frequency. Sudzarnt always treated them to a meal of their choice as a means of proving a point.

Ron and Brenda went for long walks everyday and apart from his right eye partial vision Ron was a very fit and energetic walker for his age. Since returning from Nazmos just in time for that Christmas of 2016 they had all made annual visits to Anztarza but only for short durations. Sudzarnt had never accompanied them on these trips as he said his life and happiness was on Earth. Nazmos and Anztarza were in his past and should remain there.

Robin looked at the mantel clock and suggested that they make tracks for the cemetery while the sun was still bright.

'We'll need to go in two cars,' he suggested.

'Hi mum and dad,' communicated Tania, 'we are on our way to the cemetery to pay our respects at granddad Eric's grave with some flowers. Do you want us to pop around to Uncle Robin's as well and put something on it?'

'No darling,' replied Milly, 'but you could go around to it and tidy things up a bit. We put some silk flowers in his vase last month so they should be alright for now. But have a look anyway. Your dad has a touch of the flu or so he says but I think it's really a bad cold so we are staying in for now. You know how men are; can't tolerate a little sniffle.'

'Aw mum, have a little compassion,' said Tania smiling, 'and give dad my love.'

Ashley smiled at this exchange and said nothing but had to agree. Alex smiled too and winked at his son.

The trip to the cemetery was a short one because of the cold. The ladies did all the tidying up and Ashley held the empty carrier bag for all the old flowers and rubbish. Lillian gave the black headstone a brief wipe with the damp J-cloth that she had brought along and which she dumped in the carrier bag that Ashley was holding.

Alex stood in front of his dad's grave with a thoughtful look on his face. The sun shone low in the blue sky and there was a decided chilliness in the air. Alex didn't have to lean on his cane but he kept it with him at all times just in case and because his wife told him to.

Ashley thought about his granddad and how sprightly he had become after drinking those glasses of Wazu on that first trip to Anztarza. It was sad that its effect had not continued to benefit him in the longer term. It was as if its benefits had simply ceased to exist.

'Shall we go over to Robin's plot,' said Alex after a few minutes as he turned and began walking towards his left. He knew where the grave was situated.

Ever since that first mild stroke in the shop in 2014 aged seventy seven 'Uncle' Robin Morris had gradually gone downhill. After a series of mini strokes five years later he was diagnosed with bowel cancer. He had extensive surgery in early 2022 but sadly passed away a year later in September 2023 aged eighty seven. The Macmillan nurses had been excellent throughout the last year of his illness and his final days were in the John Taylor Hospice.

Alex Bonner was using his walking cane now as he had been standing for quite a while. He had kept on walking between the rows of headstones when Lillian called to him.

'He's here Alex, in this next row,' she said.

'So he is,' said Alex turning back, 'I'm always losing my bearings among this crowd of headstones.'

They all stopped in front of the grave and stood silently for a moment.

'The flowers still look quite fresh mum,' said Tania as she communicated with Milly and conveyed a visual of the view before her.

'And so they do,' replied Milly. 'Perhaps you could bunch them closer together. The wind seems to have rustled them about a bit.'

'Sure mum,' replied Tania and bending down used both her hands to cup the flowers closer together in the metal drop-in vase.

'How's that,' she said when she had finished and conveyed the new image.

'That is lovely darling, and dad sends his love,' came back from Milly.

'I can speak for myself,' came from Jerry. 'I'm hoping to shift this bug well before Christmas.'

'Right then,' said Katy, 'lets get back home and into the warmth before we catch our death of cold. Oops sorry, I shouldn't say that here should I?'

Everyone couldn't help a smile but all moved back to the cars.

Back at the house Ashley settled into his favourite chair as did Alex. Lillian brought them all mugs of tea or coffee and Katy put out two plates of biscuits. The room was warm and the tea was hot and the biscuits could be dunked just as Ashley liked.

It had been agreed earlier that all would stay for the evening meal and it was something to look forward to as Lillian was an excellent cook.

'I've kept the meal simple,' said Lillian, 'and I hope you like it as I've made it slightly spicy.'

She paused and looked around at her family. Ashley knew what it was but pretended ignorance.

'Come on Lil,' said Alex, 'I'm sure they already know. They can read minds you know.'

She made a face at her husband before announcing that it was her special beef lasagne.

'I've added in some herbs and spices with a bit of pepper,' she added. 'We'll have it with a baked potato and some salad. I'll place some pickles and salad cream on the table so you can please yourselves. It's nearly four now so it should all be ready to serve up by about five if that's okay.'

'That will be perfect mum,' said Ashley, 'I might just grab my forty winks before then.'

But Katy came and sat beside her brother and asked about his forthcoming trip to Nazmos. They all knew that Ashley had been contacted by the Anztarza council of ministers in October when the Starship from Nazmos had arrived on station. The plan was for it to return to Nazmos in the middle of January with Ashley aboard. Platwuz needed to be stabilised in its new orbit and Brajam was in Anztarza ready to accompany Ashley.

'I think Robin and I would like to come along with you this time,' said Katy.

'That would be lovely sis,' said Ashley. 'I don't think any of our seniors will be coming along this time. I know Rachel wants to go and I feel that Margaret might also. What about Fiona and Sarah? I shall have to reveal all to them sometime soon. They need to know and perhaps they may want to come along. I feel a bit guilty for not having told them before this. Talk to them and perhaps we can make a trip to Anztarza to introduce them to our Oannes friends.'

'Robin and I will speak to them tonight. Sarah may want to tell Brian but perhaps we can ask her to keep it secret till after their wedding,' said Katy. Then she leaned over, gave him a kiss and added, 'You know bro I do love you very much and I'm so proud of you.'

'Thanks sis,' was all Ashley could say.

Lillian heard this and smiled over at Alex. There was a lot of emotion in the room.

Tania agreed with Ashley about the seniors. Her mum and dad may or may not wish to make the journey to Nazmos. They had seen it all the last time and might just be content to receive all the visuals when they got back.

Jerry Marsh was now seventy-seven years old and apart from being on medication for high blood pressure was otherwise quite fit and healthy. And Milly who was a year younger than her husband and was well and fit just like Lillian; both she and Jerry worked full time in the shop.

Mark Tinman who had reached the ripe age of sixty-seven was now a junior partner in the McGill's Antique business. Ashley along with Milly and Jerry had voted him in nearly ten years ago. Sadly his mother with whom he'd lived had passed away in late 2030 and Mark had put extra energy into his work in the shop to help overcome his grief. He proved himself to be a very resilient human being.

Les Gibson was also made a junior partner the same time as Mark and was recognised as being the more enterprising of the two. Les had married his girlfriend Agnes in the summer of 2018 and they now had a lovely daughter Rebecca who had just turned eighteen. Les was fifty-five and Agnes six years younger at forty-nine and Ashley could see that they would be the backbone of the business in future years.

Ashley had weekly meetings with all present and Les kept pushing his ideas for expansion of the business for more shops on other premises. He said he envisioned a chain of shops across the country. Ashley instinctively did not like the idea and both Milly and Jerry were against it. Milly thought that they risked the shops becoming impersonal supermarket style venues. Besides, their business had thrived mainly because of the history cards that were attached to each item. Since Ashley was the only person who could dictate this information how would they cope with the increased requirement at the various new sites?

Ashley's instinct told him that it was not what Grace and David McGill would have wanted the business to become. It was a family run business and so it should remain. Although the original family members were no longer alive the principle was the same. Ashley felt that Philip was watching and perhaps guiding. For that matter so might Grace and David.

But Les and Agnes were both enthusiastic about the business and felt profits could be even greater with more shops. They understood the matter about the history cards and hoped to at least get another shop in the Dudley area. Ashley smiled and liked their ambitions for promotion of the business and relied on Milly to keep a rein on their ideas.

Katy put the TV on for the latest news but there was nothing surprising. She switched it off when Lillian called out that dinner was ready to be served.

'Alright everyone,' called Lillian from the kitchen, 'wash your hands or whatever else you need to do and get yourselves to the dining table. I'm serving up in five minutes.'

Ashley looked at his hands and smiled. It was exactly what his mum used to say from way back when he was little. So nothing had changed. But like an obedient boy he went and rinsed his hands at the kitchen sink and then dried them on the kitchen towel while smiling down at his shrinking mum. Tania went to the downstairs loo and left the door wide open as she washed. Katy stood right behind talking to her sister-in-law. Robin went upstairs while Alex went straight to his place at the table.

At the centre of the table on heat mats were two large lasagne dishes with rich brown burnt looking top layers. Beside them was a basket of baked potatoes still in their silver foil wrapping. Lillian said they stayed hot for longer that way. Then there was the large glass bowl with the salad full to the brim on the other side with pale green plastic salad tongs placed on top.

Also on the table were an assortment of bottles and jars one of which was the salad cream and the other Ashley's tomato ketchup. There were two bottles of Shloer on the table. It was a sparkling grape juice drink which was a favourite with the girls.

'This is lovely mum,' said Katy helping herself to a spade of the lasagne, 'and you've made such a lot.'

'What you can't finish today your dad and I will have tomorrow,' said Lillian with a smile. 'And then again we can always freeze some for another day.'

Ashley and Robin had a second helping of the lasagne but not a second baked potato. Tania was a small eater and just had lasagne with some salad. The salad cream went well with it. You could see both Tania and Katy wince when Ashley squeezed the ketchup over his potato and lasagne. Lillian just looked up from her own plate and smiled knowingly. Alex was hungry and tucked in. Of course he had his bottle of pills beside his plate and a glass of water for them for when he finished his meal. His rule was never to have his pills on an empty stomach.

After the main meal Lillian brought out a medium size Asda's own Chocolate Gateaux. There was a large canister of squirty cream that she placed on the table. After serving reasonable slices she suggested they do their own topping as they wished. Lillian knew her family well for all had a good squirt of the cream on their cake. Tania and Katy decorated theirs rather artistically to the smiles of the others.

Tea and coffee followed later as they watched the next episode of 'Strictly' on the telly. The finals were to be aired on Boxing Day which was a Sunday.

'It's much more fun watching this together,' said Katy. 'I wonder if anyone in Anztarza is also watching.'

During the program both Ashley and his dad had a little shut eye. Robin looked a bit tired but Katy kept him alert. She always was a bit of a 'bossy boots' Ashley thought.

After the program ended at 8 o'clock they sat around chatting for another hour when Tania looked at Ashley and suggested they make tracks for home; in private telepathy mode of course.

'Thanks for a lovely day and my favourite meal mum,' said Ashley aloud. 'We shall see you again soon. Tania says it's my beddy-byes time.'

Alex laughed out aloud as he looked at Tania's expression.

'Ashley Bonner you just behave yourself,' she said blushing.

Katy quickly came in with 'Yes it's been lovely meeting like this again. Granddad has left us a legacy of meeting up just before Christmas. I'm not sure what's happening yet about Christmas day but we'll let you know. You're all at Ashley's this year aren't you?'

'Yes,' said Ashley, 'bring the girls over and I'll bring them up to speed with everything.'

This had been a sudden spur of the moment decision that came into his mind. Perhaps his inner voice could do that to him as well.

'Oh Ash,' said Katy 'that would be lovely, wouldn't it Robin?'

'Yes,' said Robin and smiled at Ashley. 'Thanks mate,' he added.

'Then it's a date,' said Katy. 'What about Brian? What if Sarah wants to bring him along too?'

There was silence for a moment before Ashley announced that they might as well include him now sooner than later on. They could then also take him on the proposed visit to Anztarza. Ashley had met Brian and liked what he had seen of his inner thoughts.

Tania looked at Ashley and felt a warm glow. Even after all these years, she thought, he's still as handsome and charming as when I first saw him at that darts game.

Katy came over to her brother and putting her arms around his waist gave him a tight hug. There was a glistening wetness in her eyes as she drew away.

There was then the usual round of goodbyes and kisses and firm handshakes between the men. It was odd to say goodbye when they would be in constant communication through their badges. But old ways and customs remained and possibly would forever.

There was a thin coating of frost on the roofs of the cars but the windscreens looked clear so everyone just drove off. It was freezing in the car but the heating would soon kick in Ashley knew. And it did.

As he drove along he reflected that it had been a good day for his parents especially as it had been such a fine sunny day. The cold hadn't bothered them too much.

He looked back over the years and thought it had been a most contented period for him. In these twenty-two years he had achieved the satisfaction of watching his children grow into adulthood. He had enjoyed each and every remembered moment. He missed his son Simon but was happy for him to be in the career he loved. There was now a spaceman in the family.

And Rachel was well into a career she had planned but there was something more she wished to achieve; and Ashley knew what that might be. She wished to be on Nazmos but it was not clear what she wished to do there. She and Margaret communicated constantly.

Fiona and Sarah had done exceptionally well in their preferred careers. Fiona loved travelling about the country doing the work she did. She felt she was doing something of use for the country and the National Health Service. Sarah loved her teaching and was looking forward to her spring wedding to Brian and to becoming Mrs Sarah Walters.

Ashley drove slowly past the entrance to the zoo and noted how dark the front looked. There was not a single floodlight to illuminate it except for the usual street lighting across the road. This light reflected off the zoo's massive iron gates and the high railings on either side. An equally high brick wall then took over which Ashley knew was the perimeter structure that kept Dudley Zoo and the Castle ruins safe from the outside.

Ashley drove around the castle grounds keeping the wall on his right hand side until he came to Paganel Drive just off The Broadway. He turned in and eventually drove onto his now double fronted driveway. He and Tania sat in the car for a few moments before he switched off the engine.

'Aren't you putting the car away,' queried Tania?

'O yes, of course,' said Ashley, 'sorry, I was miles away.'

He handed over the house keys from his door pocket and Tania stepped out and opened the right hand side up and over garage door. She entered and turned on the inside garage light and then went to open up the front door of the house. Ashley drove into the garage, stepped out and then lowered the door before entering the house. They had always used the right side of the semi as their main entrance.

Tania turned the central heating thermostat up a few degrees and went around drawing all the curtains downstairs and then those upstairs. She then made mugs of tea and they sat and flicked through the TV channels for something interesting. But nothing caught their fancy so they decided to go to bed.

Next morning Ashley woke early and looked towards Tania's outline under the bed covers. As usual she was asleep with her head completely covered. The curtain edges remained dark in the window even though the luminous infrared digital radio clock showed that it was a few minutes after seven. It was still dark outside so Ashley just lay on his back with his thoughts.

Why did Margaret always pop up into his thoughts like this? She was fifty nine now and looked exceptionally good for her age. She had plenty of grey interlaced within her dark blond hair but it seemed not to worry her at all. It was now cut quite short and Ashley thought it suited her round face. In fact it gave her a slightly pixie appearance. She'd never gone out with anyone and so had remained single. Like Katy she had put on several pounds all over but always dressed well and chose the right type of outfits. She and Rachel had become close friends. Ashley thought about this and realised that both had a common love for Nazmos. He didn't know what they planned between them but it definitely had something to do with Nazmos.

The Telepathic Institute had done well and spread to other countries around the world. Former students who'd mastered the art had set up their own businesses by agreement and so the skill had spread. Originally Muznant had helped with the difficult cases but then she and Brazjaf had left Earth to have their child on Nazmos. Telepathic learning continued apace however and Ashley and Sudzarnt helped whenever they could.

Dutton Consultants was now run by the eldest brother Andrew who was sixty four with David as partner. Geraldine had married in 2020 and had moved to Canada with her businessman husband Terry. Margaret had visited Geraldine only once several years ago and it had not been a pleasant sisterly experience.

Lester Dutton had died at the age of eighty eight in 2021 after a bout of pneumonia in the very cold winter of that year. Mary his wife was still alive at the ripe old age of ninety five but only just. She now resided in a care home in Staines and Ashley and Tania had visited her there on several occasions. Margaret and Rachel had also visited her but she hadn't recognized them. The care staff said that Mary had very few good days now as her dementia symptoms were very advanced. They did say that the only thing she did talk about on her better days was a star brooch that she said she possessed. Ashley had to smile at the memory of all those years ago when he had told her its history from Halley's Comet of 1835. Margaret had said that Andrew had put their mother's entire jewellery collection in a safety deposit box at the bank. She thought that the brooch would eventually go to Andrew's wife Marcia or to the eldest of their three daughters. The history card that Lester had printed would obviously go along with it.

Ashley again looked across at the sleeping form of his wife and a satisfied glow crept into his chest. They were good together and Ashley thought of her as his companion in life.

'I still wake up in the morning and the first thing I want to see is your face,' he whispered quietly to the mound of the duvet beside him. Tania was well covered and didn't hear this. A brief sadness came over him then with the fleeting thought that one day in the future one of them would be left alone. He hoped it would not be her as she would be lost without him; and lonely. His eyes moistened at the thought. He quickly pushed it out of his mind as best he could but knew that it would return as the time to tackle Zarama drew near.

Thinking about Mary in her care home brought Mavis Chambers to mind. She was eighty one now and getting increasingly frail in her body. She used a wheelchair to get about and Vicky who was the same age as Ashley did all her caring. Vicky looked older than her fifty seven years and was now rather stocky in appearance. Her hair was very white but she kept it short and neat. Ashley and Tania visited often and Mavis was very chatty on all the occasions. Ashley and Tania both noted what an alert mind Mavis had.

About two years ago Mavis and Vicky were visited by the Chief Superintendent of the West Midlands police in full uniform. Vicky had recognised him instantly and threw her arms around him in a big hug. It was Robert Black and he had been promoted recently and posted to his home town. He and Vicky were the same age and they sat and chatted alongside Mavis in her wheelchair. Mavis joined in the conversation and listened to all of Robert's news.

Robert had asked after his old friends and said he was sorry for not keeping in closer contact. As such Robert and Roberta visited Ashley and Tania in Dudley and they got on famously. It was as if Robert had never been away. Roberta and Tania became friends and this pleased Robert immensely. Their three daughters were grown up and all had married Scotsmen and had stayed in the Aberdeen area with their families. Robert proudly said that he was a grandfather many times over. The eldest grandchild was five now and he showed Ashley and Tania pictures of them all.

Robert and Roberta visited Mavis and Vicky often and like Tania, Roberta developed a liking for Vicky. A close friendship grew between them and the two went on shopping trips together and often took Mavis along with them in her wheelchair.

Ashley looked back on these events and thought how wonderful it was for old friends to rekindle former friendships. People drift away in their jobs but it was nice when they returned and took up where they had left off.

Ashley and Tania had celebrated their 32nd wedding anniversary this past summer. He remembered that Vicky and Robert had still been together on their wedding day in 2006 but they had missed it due to Mavis Chamber's horrific car accident a few days before. And that was when Robert also met Nurse Roberta for the first time in the hospital cafeteria. They'd married a year later and in five years had three lovely baby girls. They'd moved to Aberdeen in 2012.

Tania then stirred and pushed the covers back and opened her eyes. Ashley looked at her and winked. She smiled back and turning on her side reached out towards him and got a hug in return.

'Good morning darling,' she said with a smile, 'I've been reading your thoughts you know ever since you whispered about wanting to see me first thing every morning and I liked seeing things from your perspective. It is nice that Roberta and Vicky are friends. I like Roberta and I think she's good for Robert.'

Ashley smiled back and began to get out of bed and Tania asked where he was going. It was one of her little habits and done quite involuntarily. And Ashley had learned never to give a sarcastic answer. He had got to know her ways and this was one of them.

'I thought I'd bring us up mugs of tea,' he replied dutifully.

'That'll be lovely darling,' giving him her most charming smile.

Ashley went down the stairs thinking about the time he'd replied to a similar question with a drawn out tale of going to Anztarza for a glass of Wazu. It had been a frosty day after that and he remembered thinking that it had not been worth the humour on his part. He'd said he was sorry later and had been forgiven with a hug and a session of combined laughter. She had called him a silly ass or words to that effect as they laughed.

He put water in the kettle and switched it on and thought about Anztarza and his friends there. Muznant and Brazjaf had returned to Nazmos when they discovered that Muznant was really pregnant. Their daughter Farzant was born in 2017 and they were thrilled at her cuteness. They'd sent images of the infant to Ashley in their regular communications from Nazmos. They had stayed on Nazmos for the sake of their child and had no plans to return to Earth. They said they were looking forward to his coming visit next month when he was due to stabilise the path of Platwuz in its new orbit around Raznat.

Although Brazjaf was not a member of the Nazmos governing council he nevertheless had an important position with them as Advisor on Earth Affairs. This kept him busy on Nazmos to the exclusion of all else – except his beautiful daughter of course. Muznant communicated that her greatest wish had been fulfilled with the birth of Farzant.

Zakatanz also kept in regular communication with Ashley from which it became obvious that he quite enjoyed the company of Azatamunt. But it took him five long years to realise that Azatamunt had entered his heart as had her sister Hazazamunt so very long ago. Then it had been the excitement of a passionate romance; while now with Azatamunt it was a loving and peaceful companionship. Zakatanz thought about it and felt that if Hazazamunt had lived they would probably have mellowed in their relationship; a state similar to what he now found himself in with Azatamunt. It was as though there was a continuum in the events of his life. But he was not displeased with the outcome and so it was that a legal contract of partnership was finally sealed between him and Azatamunt in 2022. And three years later a daughter was born to them whom they named Hazazamunt. Azatamunt agreed with the name choice because she too had loved and admired her elder sister whose memory would now live on in their daughter. The images of the child that they conveyed to Ashley showed a pretty girl who looked a lot like her mother.

Ashley thought back and smiled his pleasure for the happiness that had finally come to this great starship Captain. Zakatanz had his family as also did Muznant.

Captain Natazlat who had arrived at the Earth rendezvous location in October this year was unchanged and still unattached. She had no desire to partner anyone as she was totally dedicated to her starship. She had indicated a willingness to take on the newly modified starship 4110-Silver when it was eventually commissioned. No starship had ever ventured as far out as Zarama's position an apparent distance of some 525 light years. The furthest expedition had been to the star system of Aldebaran in Taurus which was just 68 light years distant. More commonly visited were the star systems that were within 30 light years from Nazmos. No conditions similar to Earth or Nazmos were ever found on the planets orbiting these stars. Perhaps Captain Chamzalt in 2110-Blue had succeeded where everyone else had failed. Sadly no communication had been received back from him since he'd left Nazmos over 1400 years ago.

Simon's regular communications to his mum and dad were full of interesting facts about the Oannes' space fleet. The current fleet of starships was down to seven from the original nine. Starship 1110-Green under Captain Latinuzart had been lost when it collided at near light velocity with a seven mile ice block in the Oort-Cloud half a light year out from Earth. The fate of starship 2110-Blue under Captain Chamzalt was unknown since it left in the direction of the Ursa Major star Mizar sixty light years distant.

Simon gave details of five new series 20-starships far out in space. Construction on the first of these had begun some thousand years previously. However as a result of the modifications being made to starship 4110-Silver all the newer starships would also follow similar enhancements to upgrade their performance to 100 FTL achievement. The first would not be available for service for at least 500 years. Others would then follow at approximate 100 to 200 year intervals.

Eventually with the expected success of 4110-Silver all of the remaining fleet starships would progressively undergo a similar transformation. Ashley wondered where this would all lead in time. Who knows what these starships could be capable of in a million years from now?

Ashley thought about Captain Bulzezatna and how wonderful she had been with regard to coaching Simon in preparation for his entrance to the space academy. She would make a good starship captain but it was not in her ambition at all. At 234 years of age she was still younger than Captain Zakatanz who was 249 and yet there was only one Oannes female among all the starship captains; and that was the 212 year old Captain Natazlat.

Bulzezatna had remained captain of 520-Green but her crew had changed. Tatizblay had left the ship to become a tutor at the space academy on Nazmos. Simon had met him there and was full of praise for him. Tatizblay's wife Niztrabt had borne him a son some eight years ago and they were both overjoyed. The issue of climate change was high on Tatizblay's agenda and he had begun a private research into all the probabilities. Ashley knew that the future was bright for this young Oannes now aged just 154 years.

Rubandiz who had just passed his 144th birth date had succeeded to the position of First deputy. In time he might move on but not for many years yet. He seemed not to aspire towards starship duties at all claiming that he did not like to fly blind. He was still young and impressionable.

News of Kazaztan and his wife Zarpralt filtered through from Simon who visited them whenever he could. Both were fine though Kazaztan often complained of his 285 years and a general tiredness.

Ashley and Tania had said farewell to Puzlwat and Nogozat on their last visit to Anztarza last year. Both had decided to return home to Nazmos on a permanent basis. Puzlwat said he wished to experience first hand all the changes that might take place when the orbital change came about. Ashley had to smile at this since the Nazmos governing council had not as yet conveyed their final decision. At least not that he was aware of. Perhaps Puzlwat had other sources. There may be the doubters but Gozmanot was a ruling influence.

Ashley did not wish to go against what he felt must be a minority opinion. And so he kept a backup plan which he hoped to put to the council. It had been at the back of his mind ever since returning from Nazmos all those years ago. It would be like a trial period impinging upon both phases of the current and the future. He could let that continue for the years between the coming visit and when he'd return again to tackle Zarama. And that would be when the starship 4110-Silver was commissioned for duty. Ashley reckoned that this could be a period of maybe ten years give or take a year or two. The orbit of Nazmos had to be done in two phases -just like Platwuz –and so its second orbit fixing phase could wait for when Ashley returned again. Subsequently Ashley planned for the coming trip to Nazmos to be a short one; a stay of not more than a week or two. Unless of course he received news that he might meet up with Simon.

Although Ashley and Tania received regular communications from Muznant's Aunt Jazzatnit that all was well there was never any particular mention of their council member friends Ritozanan, Korizazit and Nerbtazwi. It was about Ritozanan that Ashley particularly wished to hear news of since at their last parting he had got the notion that he might not be seeing her again. After all she had appeared rather frail at that farewell banquet in the Domed Hall on Nazmos the day before his return trip to Earth. In all his communications to Jazzatnit and Zazfrapiz, Ashley had requested them to convey his best regards to those three but no return response was ever mentioned. Perhaps council members were not allowed to be discussed or mentioned in the Earth communication packages.

Ritozanan had great influence with the council's decisions and after the Gozmanot episode she had indicated that Ashley's wish would be granted. Had she already got the council to confirm this decision?

The kettle boiled and clicked off but Ashley waited till it had stopped bubbling. He poured the hot water into their mugs, gave a good stir and then added the milk. Tania had one Splenda sweetener in hers while Ashley put sugar in his. The vitamin pills were already on the tray and he carefully walked up the stairs.

They sat up in bed with the pillows raised against the headboard and chatted generally. The subject of Katy's Fiona and Sarah came up and also of Brian. Now that Sarah and Brian had set a wedding date Tania reckoned that they should treat Brian as one of the family; just as they had done with Katy's Robin.

'Why don't we have them over this Saturday for dinner and you can do it then,' suggested Tania.

'Sounds good to me,' replied Ashley.

'I think we'll just have them over and no one else,' said Tania, 'that way it would be simpler for you.'

'Would there need to be some form of demonstrations or do you think the information would be enough,' asked Ashley.

'Oh, a few demonstrations definitely,' said Tania.

'In that case an afternoon lunch might be the better option,' said Ashley. 'That way we could go outside in the garden as I demonstrate my telekinetic gift. And also the hide and seek affair I played with Simon and Rachel.'

'Speaking of Rachel, I wonder if she is on duty on Saturday,' said Tania and conveyed the query through her badge.

'Unfortunately I am mum,' came the reply, 'but let me know how you get on. Its about time those two ladies were in the know. By the way I'm planning a leave of absence so I can come on this trip to Nazmos next month. And Margaret is coming too if that's okay.'

'Sure it is darling,' conveyed Ashley, 'and I'm hoping we get a chance to meet Simon while we are there. We could extend our stay a bit if we know he is due from wherever he gets to. We'll only know when we get there.'

'I'm not worried about how long we stay as I've booked myself a sabbatical. Sorry I didn't mention this before but it's something Margaret and I have been discussing for some time now. Would you be awfully upset if I chucked in my job here and stayed indefinitely on Nazmos?'

'Where would you stay darling,' asked Tania.

'Oh, I'm sure one of dad's friends would be happy to accommodate us,' she replied. Rachel was very positive in her outlook when she had her mind set on a particular course.

A humorous emotion came through before Rachel added, 'I think the daughter of Ashley would be welcome anywhere.' She was playing the Ashley card.

Ashley had to smile. Rachel could certainly look after herself. And Simon was the same if not even more so if the reports coming back were anything to go by. But what were Rachel and Margaret planning to start on Nazmos? He was curious to find out.

'Fancy another mug?' asked Ashley.

'Why not,' replied Tania, 'it's still early. We could get to the shop for 9:30 or so. We'll let our partners start the day without interference from us. We must contact Katy about Fiona and Sarah for Saturday.'

'Sorry mum but I don't think this Saturday is a good date for those two,' came through from Katy. 'Fiona is away on her travels and Sarah and Brian are booked to see a show at the Alex. Since we're all at yours for Christmas day you'll have to leave it till then. I hope that doesn't ruin things for you?'

'It might be better that way,' conveyed Tania to her daughter. 'I'm sure your dad can work things just as easily then.'

'That'll be better because I can get the badges for them by then,' said Ashley.

'Thanks dad,' from Katy.

Ashley went downstairs to the kitchen and made two fresh mugs of tea and brought them up.

It was after they had washed and dressed and at the breakfast table that Ashley thought about Jill Prior's picnics. Sadly Jill had got food poisoning at a friend's wedding though no one else had been affected and the hotel had disclaimed all liability. Health inspectors had found nothing either. But Gary was certain that something she ate at the wedding had caused her illness. Jill never did recover fully despite all the hospital tests each time the same symptoms recurred. Then Jill got two bouts of pneumonia six months apart and the second one proved fatal. That was nearly ten years ago. Ashley and Tania had attended the funeral in Mansfield and met the grown up children. Malcolm and Mary had left home but returned for their mum's funeral and stayed for a week afterwards. Maura was still living at home then but had since got married and moved to Edinburgh where her husband Richard worked.

Surprisingly Gary had been very composed during the funeral service and at the reception afterwards he had moved around and spoken to all the guests. Since then Gary had lived alone and became a leading light in his church. He joined the choir and helped in their fund raising events throughout the year. He had visited Ashley at the shop on several occasions, the last being about four years ago. Since then the only contact was through their Christmas and Easter cards.

It was near ten o'clock when Ashley and Tania got to the shop and said hello to Milly, Les and Agnes. Agnes' daughter Rebecca was also there and she came out of the kitchen to ask if they'd like a cuppa.

'O yes please,' said Tania.

She got on well with Rebecca who at eighteen was a lot like Rachel had been at that age. Rebecca had finished her A-Levels and joined Teacher Training College at Bordesley this past September.

'There's been a problem with the heating system so they've closed the college to students but not to the teaching staff,' she explained with a big smile. 'They hope to have it fixed for tomorrow.'

Ashley looked out across the road from habit when the bakery had been open and when Lorraine Hollings would visit with a bag of doughnuts. But that was long ago and Lorraine had moved south to New Quay. Uncle Robin had missed her then especially after his first stroke in 2014. The bakery had done well and McGill's Antiques was a regular client. But three years ago the bombshell had dropped and the bakery had closed. The management said that it was simply an economy slimming down operation and that was that. There were other confectioners around but they were a bit further away on the next street. As always Milly kept a tin of well stocked assorted biscuits in the kitchen cupboard. She made sure that there were plenty of Ashley's favourite Custard Creams in it. It would be a sad day indeed for Ashley if the Custard Cream Factory ever closed Milly always remarked.

'Thanks Rebecca that's very nice of you,' said Ashley, 'and how are you today?'

'Great,' replied Rebecca, 'good as gold. I've got some new history card designs for you to look at later. I did some at college with help from my tutor.'

'What does Milly think?'

'She says they're fine generally,'

'Then they're okay by me too but I will have a peep at them later just the same,' said Ashley giving Rebecca his most charming smile.

Agnes was looking on and smiling too. She was proud of her Rebecca.

Agnes liked her boss and had taken a liking to him from the moment she'd first met him. There was a dynamic magnetism that emanated from Ashley to all those around him. And he exuded an air of confidence that she had never seen with anyone else. She and Les were happy working here now that Les was a junior partner in McGill's Antiques. She sometimes worked with Jerry and Mark at the other branch. She thought that if only the business would expand to other additional premises then perhaps she and Les could be put in charge of one as a husband and wife team. But so far all her suggestions had not been favoured by the senior partners. Agnes thought this to be short-sighted of them but she would be patient in her ambitions.

Ashley came into the shop most days and enjoyed the mundane calm of his life among his fellow beings. He knew that soon he'd be back on his travels to change the course of worlds. These past twenty two years had been heavenly and seemed to have zipped by. And yet such a lot had happened in that time. What would the next decade bring he thought? More of the same he hoped.

There were house auctions to attend and antiques to purchase. They would go to these on a turn by turn basis but often he would accompany Milly or Jerry just for the thrill of the auction. The Andrew Pando auction had been a milestone in his life. How things had changed when Graham had mentioned that Andrew also turned his interest to ancient history and archaeology and yet there was nothing to show for it in the house contents. It was then that Graham had learned from the auctioneers that Andrew had a cousin Lester who had inherited everything and who had a consultancy business in London.

'I wouldn't be surprised if this Lester cousin didn't have some of Andrew's archaeological artefacts stashed away somewhere,' Graham had said to Ashley as an aside remark.

And so a friendship had begun that lasted for years.

Sadly, Graham had developed a cancer of the stomach and it had taken just six months for it to prove fatal. That was a sad day for Ashley in 2020 when he and Tania had attended their friend's funeral. All of Graham's 1940s Revival Club members had attended with most dressed up in the military uniforms of the 1940s. And there were vintage cars there too. An Austin seven and a couple of khaki coloured army jeeps. Later at the reception in the church hall Ashley was surprised by the display of photos of Graham that were stuck on the walls all around the room; a most memorable event and a fitting farewell to a lovely man.

The days leading up to Christmas Day 2038 seemed to get milder though there was always a frost at night. Christmas Day was bright and sunny and Tania was kept busy with all her cooking. The large turkey had gone into the oven at six that morning and with two kitchens and two electric ovens the cooking progressed smoothly.

Katy had confirmed it with her daughters for Christmas to be spent at their Uncle Ashley's. They said they were looking forward to it as was Brian. Somehow they'd got the notion that an important announcement was to be made but they had no idea what it was to be about. In order to convince them to attend Katy may have hinted vaguely at some important revelation that affected them all.

Ashley had communicated with Anztarza chief minister Rymtakza about his plans and three communication badges had been delivered to the B&B in Aberporth. Each would automatically lock onto the telepathic thought mode of the initial user and become their individual communicator badge. From then on it would become uniquely theirs.

Sudzarnt had driven down to Dudley in his fairly new Honda car to deliver them personally to Ashley and had stayed to help in the shops for a couple of days. He usually visited Dudley about twice or thrice each year just to keep in contact with Mark Tinman.

Mark had been on a short holiday to Aberporth way back in 2017 and stayed at Ron and Brenda's B&B. He and Sudzarnt became friends then and the friendship had grown stronger each time they met. Mark never suspected that Sudzarnt was anything other than what he appeared to be, not that it would have made any difference. Sudzarnt coached Mark in basic telepathy and was pleased when Mark picked it up with enthusiasm. What Sudzarnt saw inside Mark's mind drew him to the man and he told Ron that Mark was a truly genuine human being.

He returned to Aberporth several days before Christmas as it was a very busy time for the B&B.

Lillian and Alex were the first to arrive after having attended the morning service at their local St Barnabas church. Ashley and Tania had been to the midnight service though it had been changed to begin at 10:30pm. The first half hour had been taken up just singing carols with the small choir leading the singing. It was just after midnight when they'd got back home for a port and a mince pie prior to bed.

'We're on our way,' said Katy through her communication badge, 'and I think so are Brian and Sarah. Fiona is with us and believes you have a special treat for her. She's been pestering us with all sorts of questions.'

'We've arrived,' came through from Milly as Jerry drove onto the double drive.

Of course both Lillian and Milly were keen to help in the kitchen. But Tania had everything under control so the three of them chatted in the main kitchen as mugs were put out for tea and coffee.

The dining table had been laid for twelve and Jerry and Alex placed their bottles of red and white wine along the centre. Everyone seemed to bring bottles of wine with them and because no one really drank a lot Ashley found that he ended up with more bottles than he started with.

The noise began when Sarah and Fiona walked in. Brian stayed close to Sarah though he was not a complete stranger to any of the others. He had a great discernment in his psyche and had always felt there was some greatness in Ashley. Sarah had passed on to Brian the fact that something important was to be announced but she had no idea what it was.

Both Sarah and Fiona remembered the apparent magic tricks that Ashley used to entertain them with when they were children and it was all still a mystery to them. Of course they were now fully adult and deported themselves as such. But the niggling mystery of Ashley's tricks remained in the hidden recesses of their minds.

Rachel had wanted to be home on Christmas Eve but duty had called for the extra cover needed in the hospital. She had gone back to her flat just before midnight and conveyed to her mum that she would be in time for the Christmas lunch; hopefully a little before 2:00pm. And so she did.

The cousins got on well and always had. They talked about women's fashions and how much they liked each other's dresses and earrings. Brian got a chance to talk to Ashley as they sipped their pints of beer. Only, Ashley's was a weak shandy which he'd made just the way he liked it with plenty of lemonade.

Rachel had been primed about Ashley's revelations for her cousins and she was pleased that Brian was to be included. She nearly slipped up when she was talking to her dad about the coming trip to Nazmos. Ashley quickly turned the subject around to where he intended to go on holiday this summer. Majorca seemed nice he said and Rachel raised her eyebrows and smiled her agreement.

'I'm definitely coming along with you and mum this time dad,' she said aloud and Ashley smiled back with an 'Of course that would be lovely darling.'

Tania then announced that dinner would be up in five minutes and helpers were needed in both kitchens to carry the dishes to the table.

'Dad,' she said to her father Jerry, 'could you see to the wine please?'

'With pleasure,' he replied with a smile.

When all were finally seated Ashley stood up from his position at the head of the table with carving knife and fork in his hands.

'Brian,' he said, 'since you are the youngest male among us would you like to have a go at carving this bird for us?'

And with that Ashley moved to where Brian was seated and offered him the carving implements.

'Oh please sir,' he said still seated, 'I'm rubbish at carving anything. Besides I'd rather you did it as head of this house. Sarah would never forgive me for making a hash of it. So I beg of you to do the honours yourself.'

Ashley smiled at this. Brian had passed the test with flying colours. He had shown his respect for his seniors and Sarah squeezed his hand under the table while smiling at him with love and pride. Brian just kept his gaze fixed on his empty plate but there was a hint of a smile there.

When Jerry had gone around pouring wine into all the glasses he sat down and nodded that all was ready. Ashley remained seated but raised his glass in front of him.

'Here's to our beautiful chef for all that looks so delicious here in front of us,' he said.

Everyone repeated 'cheers' and took a sip from their raised glasses.

Ashley then stood and added, 'And here's to absent friends.'

He conveyed images of his granddad Eric and of Philip Stevens done mainly for the benefit of Brian. Again all stood and repeated 'To absent friends.'

'And finally,' said Ashley, 'lets us drink to all those who are away from us and cannot be here today,' and conveyed images of Simon, Ron and Brenda.

Rachel added, 'To my brother Simon wherever he may be. May God bless him and keep him safe.'

Tania smiled as both her daughter and her husband blinked furiously.

Fiona and Sarah looked puzzled because not much had been mentioned about their cousin Simon before. They thought he'd left home as the proverbial prodigal son. Obviously there must be much more to it than that.

Ashley planned his revelations for after dinner when all would be seated back in the lounge. It would certainly be a surprise for his nieces; especially the badges. Brian would probably take it all in his stride but be pleased that he was a part of this family.

The Christmas dinner was a beautiful chatty event and all complained that they had eaten too much. They stayed at the dining table for some time afterwards just talking and it was near 5 o'clock before someone suggested the move to the lounge and the more comfortable seating. A couple of cushioned garden chairs were brought to accommodate everyone.

'Is it time to open our presents,' hinted Lillian looking towards the pile of assorted packages under Tania's artificial six foot tree.

'Yes it is,' said Ashley, 'but first I must give something special to Fiona, Sarah and Brian.'

Ashley then went forward and took the hand of each of his nieces and gave them a squeeze.

'Sarah and Fiona, I must apologise to you for not including you into our family secret before now. But now seems to be the right time and I shall reveal all. And Brian, you have chosen Sarah as your partner in life and are now part of this family. So you too have the right to know all our secrets.'

Ashley paused and moved back a step and took in their serious expressions, part puzzled and part excitedly expectant.

'You must never reveal to anyone outside of this family what I am about to tell and show you,' he said with a most intense look at each of them. 'You will understand the need for this secrecy in a moment.'

Fiona and Sarah knew of Ashley's telepathic and history gifts but little else. And Brian knew as much from all that Sarah had told him. So he simply thought there must be another aspect to Ashley's gifts. Could he do real magic thought the girls remembering those times with their uncle when they were children? The three of them waited expectantly.

Katy and Robin stood behind their children. Katy put a hand on Fiona's shoulder while Robin put one on Sarah's and the other on Brian's.

Ashley then conveyed his entire life story slowly and relentlessly into their minds. He began with the ball games he played with Eric his granddad and then the feats the family arranged to determine the extent of his abilities. His telepathic and mind reading ability. His inner voice. The cricket match and the discovery that nothing could hurt him. The darts match, telekinesis and mental regression. Philip Stevens and McGill's Antiques Shop. The Thinking Stone and the discovery of the Oannes people living on Earth in Anztarza. Barnard's Star and Nazmos. The asteroid tests. Platwuz's orbital change and the intended one for Nazmos. Gozmanot's visions and finally Zarama that threatened all of their existence. All this and more was given to them with full imagery in the space of a few minutes.

'Wow,' exclaimed Sarah as she blinked back the tears that had welled up in her eyes. Sarah had always been the intensely emotional one. She gazed up at her Uncle Ashley with a look bordering on adoration.

'It's like suddenly discovering we have a superman right here in our own family,' she said squeezing Brian's hand and looking to see his expression. He looked to be in shock.

'Is this all really true?' he couldn't help asking the question despite knowing that it was.

'Yes,' said Ashley, 'it is all true. I don't know why I was chosen but I do believe that all these gifts were given to me for a reason. I wish they hadn't but then the choice was not mine to make. Someone thought I was suitable.'

Tania came and stood beside her husband and put her arm around his waist.

'Apart from everything that you have just been told,' she said, 'we are all just an ordinary loving family. We discussed this between us and felt it was the right time for you to be told everything. There will be no secrets between us anymore. And for this we have these Oannes communication badges made especially for each of you. Keep them on or near you at all times.'

And with that Tania handed out a coin shaped object to each of them and telepathically explained how they worked. She got a thought 'wow' from Sarah who was looking at the badge in her hand.

Katy said, 'This does not replace your mobile phones so you will still need those. These are for your thought communications with us and the Oannes when you meet them. They are effective anywhere on Earth. Try it out by saying hello to your great Aunt Brenda in Aberporth if you wish. Just think of her and in your mind say how you feel.'

'Hello Aunt,' thought Sarah, 'is it true what Uncle Ashley has told us?'

'Hello Sarah welcome to our exclusive club. Yes it is all true and isn't it wonderful? I'm glad Ashley has finally given up his secrets to you; and hello Fiona and Brian, greetings to you all from Aberporth. You will like the Oannes people when you meet them one day. They are a very gentle people and you will love Anztarza too. But when you see Wentazta on Nazmos you will be even more impressed.'

'Thank you Aunt Brenda,' conveyed Ashley, 'I was just about to come to that part.'

Then he conveyed to Fiona, Sarah and Brian that he was due to visit Anztarza soon and then from there the family group would journey onward to Nazmos on a starship. It would be their first trip in an Oannes spaceship and a good first experience if they wished to come along.

'That would be wonderful,' said Brian aloud not quite used to the badge thought communicators.

'O yes please,' was Fiona's and Sarah's joint thought response. 'Who all will be going,' they asked?

'Why just us,' said Ashley, 'less our mums and dads.'

'Yes, I think we're too old for this trip now. Besides we've seen it all last time around,' said Jerry.

'Robin and I are definitely coming,' said Katy, 'we missed it last time.'

'So are Margaret and I,' said Rachel. 'So that makes us a party of seven.'

Fiona stood up and came up to Ashley. She put her arms around him in a hug and kissed his cheek.

Then looking him in the eye she asked if he could demonstrate some of his gifts for them.

'I've already given you all the information about what my gifts entail,' conveyed Ashley, 'so which one would you like to see first?'

'This bit about going into pink mode,' asked Brian, 'does it really cause Time itself to slow down or even stop everywhere around you?'

'I really don't know how it works or what really happens,' replied Ashley. 'I only know that everything slows down relative to me; even clocks seem to tick slower.'

'I see,' said Brian as he concentrated his thoughts for several long seconds.

Then he added, 'Perhaps it is only you who have changed in time mode and the rest of us and the world continue on as normal.'

Ashley smiled broadly as if something new had just been revealed to him.

'Thank you Brian, I never thought of it like that,' said Ashley. 'That seems much more plausible than the other way around. Perhaps that is why I feel tired out after prolonged bouts in Pink mode. I'm probably moving around much too fast.'

The more Ashley thought about it the more logical it became in his mind. He thought back to just before he had tackled the asteroid 253 Mathilde when he was calibrating his telekinetic push effort in the various Pink mode levels. He understood now why his inner voice had set him an upper limit then at the Pink mode level sixteen.

Ashley had left his communication badge in open mode and all in the room picked up these thoughts. In fact so did all of Anztarza and it was a revelation for Ashley and he had Brian to thank for it.

'Brian, you are a good man to have around,' conveyed Ashley privately to Brian, 'I hope there's more where that came from. Sarah is a lucky lady.'

Brian smiled back but puzzled over a part of Ashley's message indicating something for something. But then suddenly understood when he began to receive an intense communication from his host. Ashley had just conveyed into Brian's mind all the memories he had retrieved long ago from a certain Spanish doctor Mario Gonzalez of Madrid. Ashley conversed aloud with Brian in Spanish and Brian replied fluently. Sarah was not only surprised but flabbergasted. Katy smiled and joined in the conversation. She then conveyed to both her daughters what Ashley had just done. He'd done the same for her at her own introduction to his gifts so very long ago. The Spanish was to help in her college work on that subject and how pleased her Spanish teacher had been.

'Please can I also be made able to speak Spanish,' begged Sarah, 'then I can converse with my future husband in secret when his mates are around.'

'Of course,' said Ashley and immediately conveyed the same to both his nieces easily and fluently.

'Good gracious,' exclaimed Fiona and before you knew it both sisters were chattering away in Spanish to each other as well as to their mum and Brian.

Ashley had done the same with all the family long ago so they all understood what was being said.

'So what's next?' asked Sarah.

'Well,' conveyed Ashley, 'I could go into Pink mode and move around the room without being seen by you.'

'We could play the same game you did with Simon and me,' said Rachel.

'I think that might be better for outdoors,' said Ashley to his daughter, 'but I suppose I could move to different places in this room.'

And so Ashley demonstrated how he could be in one corner of the room one instant and then suddenly be in the next as if by magic.

To do this he moved behind one of the drawn back curtains beside the patio glass doors. Then he went into Pink mode and moved across behind the set of curtains on the opposite side of the same doors. When he returned to normal mode and stepped out he got an ovation from his new fans.

'It's just like the magic you used to do with buttons in your hands when we were kids,' said Fiona laughing.

'But now the magic has gone out of it because we know your secret,' said Sarah.

'I think it's still wonderful to have a gift that allows you to do that,' said Brian seriously.

'Okay then,' said Katy, 'I think the next item on the magic agenda is a demonstration of my brother's telekinetic gift; if that's okay with you bro?'

'Sure it is,' said Ashley. 'But it will have to be something small within this room. Perhaps I could demonstrate with a small book on the dining table. Shall we go back in there?'

Katy directed Fiona, Sarah and Brian along one end of the long dining table and Ashley stood on the opposite end. Then Katy picked a novel sized hardback book from the shelf, placed it flat on the table in front of Ashley and moved to one side.

'Just look at the book,' said Ashley, 'and I will move it towards you as gently as I can'

Fiona, Sarah and Brian kept their eyes on the book and slowly it slid on the table towards them. Gradually it increased speed till Katy put out a hand and stopped it before it fell off the table.

Ashley was surprised at how the book had begun to move in the first instance. He had not been conscious of any effort on his part as on other occasions. This time he had simply desired the book to move in a certain manner and it was done exactly as he required. For Ashley this was a new development. In the past twenty two years he had never once exercised the use of his telekinetic gift. He began to wonder by how much that power had increased. He was determined to find out but would have to wait for when it became necessary to accelerate the starship during the coming journey.

However Ashley did not reveal this aspect but gave them a more mundane explanation. He conveyed that he had remained in normal mode and applied the gentlest of telekinetic pushes upon the book to get the desired result. He then conveyed to them graphic images of his disastrous effort upon the asteroid Steins-1867 which was 3½ miles in diameter. He showed the effect of having applied too much force upon it causing it to disintegrate. He conveyed that since then he'd learned to calibrate and precisely control the amount of telekinetic force he applied. He also explained that he could only push things directly away from him and it was with this telekinetic push that he could accelerate the starships in which he travelled.

'Would you like to feel a gentle push effort applied upon your person?' asked Ashley.

Sarah looked at Brian before stepping forward and nodding her head. She conveyed through her badge that she was willing to experience something new. So Ashley told her to go to the opposite end of the room and then to begin a slow walk towards him.

Sarah did as instructed and turning around began to step towards Ashley. It was at the third step forward that she found she could not progress forward anymore. Something spongy was pushing against her body and stopping all movement forward. She could move backwards but not forwards. She called for Brian to help her and he immediately came to her side. Together they tried again but with the same result. Brian too could feel this soft force pushing against his body. It did not hurt but felt extremely alien.

Katy watched their struggles and began to giggle. She remembered how Ashley had dealt with the Brown Hills New Town Estate hooligans who had made a nuisance of themselves in Parkview Drive. She remembered how the three boys had got so spooked and scared when Ashley prevented them leaving the cul-de-sac that they had literally wet their pants. But then they were only aged twelve or so at the time. Parkview Drive was never troubled again after that. Katy conveyed all these images to the others to explain why she found it all so funny.

Ashley eased off now and let Sarah and Brian walk forward as normal.

'Do you know I quite enjoyed the experience,' said Brian. 'It was like an invisible sponge pushing against your body and not uncomfortable at all since I knew what was causing it. But if I was alone on a dark night and I experienced that again I'd be in a blue funk. I'd think it was something supernatural. What do you think Sarah?'

Sarah nodded but didn't say anything. Katy could see how she had been affected so came and put an arm around her daughter. Suddenly Sarah burst into tears and Katy hugged her even tighter. Ashley came forward and put his arms around both of them and conveyed an emotion of peace, love and tranquillity just as the Oannes had done for him all those years ago.

Sarah looked up at her Uncle Ashley and with her now relaxed face conveyed a big 'Thank you' to him. She understood the emotion of calm he had just wrapped around her.

'Forgive me Sarah,' said Ashley, 'that was not meant to upset you. We'll have no more demonstrations of my gifts for now, okay? Let's all snuggle down and have a nice hot drink or something stronger and just chat. I'll answer any questions you may have.'

And so the evening wore on. There were a few questions that Brian put to Ashley but these were mainly about how Ashley felt towards the Oannes and how they felt about him. From Ashley's answers Brian got the impression that the Oannes were a very likeable and gentle people. Ashley conveyed that he considered the Oannes to be a smart and good looking people; in their own way of course. Brian thought that the image of Muznant that Ashley conveyed showed a very good looking Oannes person.

Tania butted in and said that Ashley had made many conquests and had gained the admiration and affection of several Oannes women. She cited Muznant as the first among these.

Brian's final question was about Zarama and whether Ashley thought that it could be stopped or turned away. Ashley remained silent for a whole minute before answering.

'I'm not sure about that since I don't know too much of this White Dwarf star,' said Ashley. 'But I do know that I shall do my utmost in that respect. My only consolation is that the seer Gozmanot predicted that 'the fiery dragon will be vanquished' which I take to be a view of my success. In her visions Gozmanot also saw Nazmos become like Earth in its climate and flora. So there you have it Brian what do you think?'

'You will succeed,' said Brian in a matter of fact manner.

It was the way that he said it as a statement rather than an opinion that struck a chord in Ashley's inner being. Brian had simply stated a result and nothing more. A sadness emotion welled up inside Ashley just as it had when he had been given the upper limit of sixteen for his Pink mode force calibrations. On no account must he attempt to exceed this value; or what? And that was the sadness; not for himself but for Tania. Ashley did not want her to be alone. She needed him to be with her. And her aloneness would cause him grief – extreme grief - sadness and regret if it came to pass. He must do everything in his power to avoid that. If only – and he could think no further. But Zarama had to be stopped at all cost.

Poor Tania, she would be lost without him beside her; as would Simon and Rachel and all the others. The vision he received was of them, of Earth, the galaxy all diminishing in size and becoming ever more distant till he lost sight of them all. And he found himself alone in the infinite darkness of the cosmos heading towards some distant region.

Ashley cleared his head and looked at Brian and nodded.

'Yes, I believe I shall,' he said in the same matter of fact manner, 'I most certainly shall.'

He didn't add 'at any cost'.

The evening concluded with both Sarah and Fiona sitting on either side of their Uncle Ashley in a snuggled up sort of way. They had always been extremely fond of him when they were young and had respected his wisdom sense as they matured. But now a new feeling had exploded to life inside their consciousness that bordered on pagan idolatry. Or was it just hero worship; perhaps a mixture of both. And for them the wonderful thing was that he was of their own flesh and blood family. This brought them into a closer bond with him and of which they felt extremely proud.

Eventually Sarah went and sat beside Brian but Fiona remained with Ashley. Tania came and sat where Sarah had been and Rachel sat between her two grandmothers Lillian and Milly. They were all adults and the conversation had a mature content.

'Uncle Ashley,' said Fiona in a whisper, 'I'd like to know more about Philip Stevens. What kind of a man was he? Did he laugh and joke or was he very serious?'

'Both,' replied Ashley and then conveyed images of their last Christmas together. He conveyed the story Philip had told them about the rifle cleaning incident when he was doing National Service in Cyprus and how they had all found it extremely amusing. And how granddad Eric and Philip had then got on famously relating stories of that time making it sound full of camaraderie with all their mates. They had all listened with interest and laughed at all the funny episodes. Fiona listened to all this with a smile on her face and said she'd have loved to have met him.

Later that night Ashley pondered over Fiona's desire to know more about Philip. All had departed for their own homes well after midnight. The cars had been frost free and the night air relatively mild. There had been no plans made for New Year's Eve but that was not unusual. Over the last few years Ashley and Tania had brought in the New Year quietly together. They'd get a Takeaway pack from ASDA with a bottle of sparkling wine and settle down for the evening watching a DVD before switching over to BBC1 at about 11:30pm. After the twelve gongs of Big Ben they'd watch the firework spectacular at the London Eye before going to bed.

Several years ago they had actually stood on the Embankment on the Thames right across from the big wheel. They'd had a fantastic experience of the fireworks display in both sound and colour even though it had been a freezing night. It had been six hours of standing in one location against the front barriers but it had been worth every second of the fifteen minute firework fantasia. The crowds around them had been so full of jollity and humorous banter that Ashley thought they might do it again one day. But they never did; perhaps another year soon.

Of course there was continuous communication between the badge holders and the newest members found it quite a novelty. Thoughts went to and fro with such ease that Ashley remembered his own fascination with them when he and Tania had first received theirs. But it was all commonplace now and quite taken for granted. However had they managed before then? Ashley smiled at the thought and yet it was what had pulled the family even closer together. It had been a terrific boon for granddad Eric and made it possible for him to live independently and yet not feel alone. Yes, thought Ashley the Oannes were a great civilization and a wonderfully advanced people. Would that Earth could one day achieve a similar harmony and inter-relationship between its peoples.

Fiona had asked about Philip and this had set Ashley's thoughts also in that direction. After that early communication there had been total silence. Was Philip still out there or had he other business to attend elsewhere? Ashley could never know. But what he did know was that Philip was ever present in his thoughts. It was also when Ashley had been told about the 'Big task' that must be undertaken. Philip could only have known about it if it had been shown to him by another. Was Gozmanot also at work here?

The year 2039 arrived quietly without fuss or bother even on the international stage. The daytime temperatures had dropped considerably and night frosts returned with a vengeance often getting down to a cold 10°C below freezing. The starship trip to Nazmos was due for January 15th but Ashley requested an Anztarza visit for a few days before that for the benefit of Fiona, Sarah and Brian so that they could meet the council of chief ministers. Ashley told them that he planned for a return to Earth by mid-February and so they must arrange for a leave of absence from their work till then. Rachel put in for a prolonged and indefinite sabbatical from the City Hospital. She cited family issues. As such the Aberporth pickup would occur on the night of Monday 10th Jan. The flight to starship rendezvous would commence late on Thursday and had usually been of twenty two hours duration from Aberporth. From Anztarza however another three hours would have to be added due to the slower underwater part of the journey.

Ashley was keen to meet up again with Captain Natazlat whom he'd seen only once since arriving back on Earth twenty two years ago. That was on a visit to Anztarza several years ago by arrangement between them. He was also keen to determine the extent by which his telekinetic powers had increased. Would a simple desire be sufficient or must he still go through the ritual of push levels stage by stage? He would soon find out.

Margaret came over from London on Friday 7th and stayed at Rachel's flat. Apparently the two of them had a lot to discuss and Margaret didn't trust the weather. A sudden freeze-up could spell long delays on the roads.

There was to be a full moon on the night of the Aberporth pickup but snow had been forecast for Scotland that would gradually work its way south and possibly spread to the Midlands and Wales by nightfall. Brenda had communicated that the B&B was exceptionally busy and they had no spare accommodation to offer; which was why the Ashley party of nine planned to arrive there on the afternoon of the pickup. But lunch and dinner would be laid on. Sudzarnt conveyed that it would be a pleasure to look after them all until the pickup arrived.

The group would drive up in three cars. Katy, Robin and Fiona would travel together; then Ashley and Tania with Rachel and Margaret; and finally Sarah and Brian would come in Brian's Toyota.

All went according to plan with each car arriving within half an hour of the other. Sarah and Brian were the last to arrive at just after 2:30pm. They'd all been in continual communication through their badges so that Sudzarnt could have the lunch ready to serve on arrival.

Although the B&B had the 'No Vacancies' sign the spacious lounge area was quite empty of people when they arrived. Ron and Brenda sat with them and talked about the future. Ashley guessed that they meant the future of Nazmos. Brenda said that there was so much to consider that she just hoped that everything went according to plan.

'Zarama is not on the agenda on this trip is it Ashley?' she asked.

'No Aunt,' he replied, 'the starship modifications have not been completed and won't be for many years at the very least. I'm guessing at about ten years or so.'

'Good,' she said slowly, 'because I have a funny feeling about that thing.'

Ashley knew she meant the White Dwarf star and not the starship.

Ashley conveyed that Simon was to be a member of the crew on 4110-Silver and so would be with him and Tania when they ventured out towards Zarama. Simon's presence was essential for the success of the journey over that vast distance. No Oannes starship had ever ventured the 525 light years distance that was the light travelling time from Zarama to Raznat. But in reality this had been recalculated as 431.8 light years due to the velocity of the rogue star directly towards Nazmos.

They all knew of Simon's gift and Ashley had extreme faith in his son's ability to avoid hidden hazards enroute.

'Where is Simon now?' asked Ron.

'I'm not sure,' replied Ashley, 'but he does know of our arrival schedule. In fact I think all of Nazmos knows. Tania and I are hoping that he can come and meet us then. Although we get regular communication packs from him we haven't spoken face to face for nearly twelve years since he went to the space academy on Nazmos; he was eighteen then.

'That is just one of the reasons I'd like to live on Nazmos,' said Rachel. 'I'd get to see my spaceman brother more often among other things as well.'

Ashley knew what Rachel was implying. But he had a plan of his own for the Nazmos orbital change. Rachel thought that her dad would slow Nazmos in its orbit now and then wait the five months till it attained the new perigee position at twenty million miles from Raznat to fix its orbit there. But that was not Ashley's plan at all. He intended to stay only about a week on this trip before returning to Earth. He would return when the starship 4110-Silver was commissioned and ready for service and then at the appropriate time arrive to fix the orbit of Nazmos or not as the governing council finally decided. But Ashley said nothing and conveyed nothing; he just smiled pleasantly at his doctor daughter.

The day had started sunny and cold in Dudley but by late afternoon when they arrived in Aberporth grey clouds had crept over the sky from the north and the predicted snow seemed imminent. The sun lay hidden somewhere to the west and the air seemed to feel just that little bit milder. Tania said that was a sure sign that it would snow. Ashley smiled at his wife and at her childlike expectancy for a white landscape. He remembered her watching the snowflakes floating down in their back garden only last winter. She had been quite thrilled by their slow motion descent towards the ground. After all it did have that same mesmerising effect as watching flames dancing in a log fire or white ribbons of froth cascading down a waterfall.

His thoughts were interrupted by a communication from Bulzezatna that 520-Green was on its way and would be at station fifty miles out from Aberporth in about two hours. The pickup would be an hour after that. Of course the communication had included the initial niceties of an enquiring Sewa which reminded Ashley to explain this Oannes etiquette to Fiona, Sarah and Brian; which he did right away. He also told them about the customary welcoming glass of Wazu and he conveyed images of what it looked like. He conveyed to their minds the pleasant taste that came with drinking it.

'I never liked it as a child,' said Rachel, 'because I thought it looked alive. But I can tolerate it now for politeness sake. And the floating seeds do have a medicinal value in that it raises your energy level; especially in your mental concentration ability.'

Brenda laughed and said that the Wazu seeds did behave like little furry bugs darting around inside the glass.

'It gave Ashley's granddad Eric a tremendous boost of health and energy and it seemed to rejuvenate him for quite some time,' she said. 'I wonder how he would have fared if he had gone to live on Nazmos.'

'Is that why the Oannes have such a long lifespan?' asked Fiona.

'I don't think so,' said Ashley. 'The Wazu was a relatively recent discovery and just after their first visit to Earth some ten thousand years ago. They already had a long lifespan before that. The seer Gozmanot lived to five hundred years and she lived over thirty-six thousand years ago'

'Can't the Wazu be grown here for us on earth?' asked Fiona.

'Unfortunately it can't. I don't know why but they have tried. It only grows under the Sea of Peruga on Nazmos and that too at certain depths only,' said Ashley.

He could see Fiona pondering over this and wondered where her medical thoughts were taking her. Though she said nothing more Ashley knew she would pursue the subject further.

It was now 6:30pm and the pickup was expected at 9:30pm according to Bulzezatna's communication. Sudzarnt had been prepared for this and conveyed that a full dinner would be ready in the dining hall for them in half an hour. It was important that they ate well now for their next meal would be in Anztarza tomorrow morning at breakfast.

The meal was vegetarian though you would not have thought so. The B&B was classified as a vegetarian establishment ever since Sudzarnt had decided the conversion all those years ago. The escallops were made from Soya bean but tasted and looked like proper chicken or turkey burgers. The rest was potatoes, peas, carrots and cauliflower with nice thick gravy. There were sauces in bottles but these went untouched. For dessert Sudzarnt had prepared a nice apple crumble which one could have either with hot custard or ice cream. Ashley had his with custard as did all except Margaret who preferred ice cream. Afterwards all relaxed in the lounge where coffee and tea was served.

Ashley had finished his second mug of tea and was just dozing off in his armchair when Bulzezatna's communication came through that she had arrived on station and that the pickup bus was just about to get under way. It should arrive at the B&B within the hour. And so it did.

Myzpazba was the bus operator and gave them all a welcoming Sewa as they boarded. Sudzarnt came aboard briefly and had a pleasant private communication with his friend and fellow countryman. They actually shook hands as per the Earth custom just before Sudzarnt disembarked.

Sudzarnt had acted as the perfect host to them and Ashley felt sure that the B&B was doing so well not simply because of its vegetarianism but also because Sudzarnt used his Oannes skill to induce an atmosphere of emotional well-being and calm in all his customers.

All this was new for Fiona, Sarah and Brian but they took it all in as if it was quite normal. The initial surprise had been when Sudzarnt had been introduced to them as being an Oannes originally from Nazmos; he looked so human to them but that was because of the hair-piece he wore. Myzpazba had his mask on so they had yet to see an Oannes in real life. However Ashley had prepared them well so that there'd be no surprises in store for them when they entered the spaceship 520-Green.

With their small bags of clothes etc stowed aboard the bus the passengers settled into the empty seats. Myzpazba then turned the imitation coach-bus around and slowly moved it down the road towards the sea. The night was dark and sky overcast so that when they reached the end of the road the bus lifted a foot off the ground and made straight for the waterline. It gathered speed as it headed out over the sea into the darkness beyond. The whistling noise outside the bus increased and Ashley estimated a speed of close to 100mph. Apart from a dull glow inside the transport nothing could be seen of the outside.

After about half an hour the wind sound lessened indicating a slowing down and then a bright light became visible not too far ahead. Myzpazba glided the slowed transport in through the large bay doors of 520-Green and brought it down onto the deck beside one of the ship's shuttlecraft. By the time Ashley and the others had walked to the control room the spaceship was already well above the cloud layer and in the bright light of a full moon.

The visitors were welcomed by Captain Bulzezatna in a grand ritual of Sewa to which Ashley replied on behalf of them all. Ashley and the captain greeted each other with smiles and a firm handshake before the captain made a sweeping gesture and conveyed to her visitors especially the new ones that they were free to wander around the spacious control room at will. She pointed to the view panels and conveyed how they could be used as a magnifying screen whenever necessary. Captain Bulzezatna gave them the route the ship would take and hoped they enjoyed the sights passing below. The ship would rise to a height of sixty miles and head south towards Antarctica at a velocity of 8,000mph. The time was now 10:20pm GMT and the sun had long since set in the northern hemisphere. However as they rose to cruise height and moved further south they would see the sun rise again on their right hand side.

Ashley acted as guide for his nieces and Brian and tried to point out features passing below mostly from the pinpoints of light in a darkened world. As the west coast of Africa approached so did the sunrise though the land was still in semi-darkness. As the journey progressed and there was just the dull ocean below them Captain Bulzezatna caused the ship to alter course slightly towards the east. She explained that this was for their benefit so that Cape Town could be viewed as it appeared on their left. And so it did and nearly an hour had passed without them even noticing. The odd thing was that although the city itself was in shadow the top of Table Mountain glowed in the last remnants of its day.

'It all looks so flat from up here,' said Fiona and Ashley could see how fascinated she was by this new experience. Sarah and Brian stood together at another view panel and both seemed quite in awe of all that was happening to them.

The sun was bright and high on their right but there seemed nothing but ocean below them. And then a dazzling whiteness appeared in the distance in front of the ship. The Earth glowed with a whiteness that hid any visible features and Ashley conveyed that this was the vast continent of Antarctica. A tint developed inside the view panels and the glare diminished. The vast whiteness of Antarctica was soon spread from horizon to horizon without a break and it appeared shadow-less and flat as a pancake.

'What a way to travel,' was a thought that Ashley picked up from Brian.

It was now an hour an a half since they'd entered the control room and none of them noticed standing for so long. It was all so interesting even for Ashley. Every journey in a spacecraft was a fascination for him with something of new interest to be seen each time.

Gradually over the next half hour the ship descended and slowed marginally till the captain announced that they were passing over Queen Mary Land at 4,000mph and twenty miles up and must soon be over the Shackleton Ice Shelf. After that they must continue at the same heading to beyond where any ice sheet existed and prepare for sea entry.

The craft had slowed progressively as it approached open sea and eventually came to a hover silently above a section of the Davis Sea. Sea entry was done at a measured slow pace though a slight judder was felt through the ship for just an instant. The view panels soon went quite dark and nothing could be seen through them.

Ashley conveyed that the ship's course underwater was to be a lengthy one. First it must drop down to a depth of two thousand feet and then traverse a fair distance towards the entrance to the Anztarza tunnel. Thereafter the journey up this hundred mile tunnel would consume another two hours before they arrived in Anztarza Bay. All in all they could expect to be in Anztarza in just less than four hours. And since there was nothing further to see he suggested they retire to their allotted cabins and rest. After all it was now midnight and way past normal bedtime. The captain suggested that they all sleep as normal and the arrival in Anztarza Bay would be delayed accordingly. At half speed their arrival would be in eight hours time.

First Deputy Rubandiz showed them to their cabins on the floor below and suggested that refreshment could be availed in the dining hall at any time that they wished. But the general wish was for bed as the day had been exciting in the extreme especially for the new travellers.

'I think us oldies could do with a good nights sleep,' said Ashley, 'so I'll see you in the morning.'

They were given five cabins. Rachel shared with Margaret and Sarah with Brian. Robin and Katy had one for themselves as did Tania and Ashley. Only Fiona had a cabin to herself which made her feel quite privileged.

Captain Bulzezatna suggested that 520-Green be used as a base for this night and a breakfast would be available at about 9:00am in the morning. They would then be transported to the usual accommodation in Dome-7 where their friends Laztraban and his wife Niktukaz awaited them. The meeting with the Anztarza council of ministers was scheduled for the early afternoon between one and two pm GMT.

It really had been a long day for them and Ashley undressed and got into his bed within minutes of closing their cabin door. Tania too yawned went into the washroom before also getting into her own twin bed. Ashley monitored the others and communicated briefly with them. But soon a telepathic silence took hold and he knew that they were all asleep. He conveyed where they were to the others in Birmingham, Dudley and Aberporth and explained the journey and the excitement of the newest travellers Fiona, Sarah and Brian. Only the women were still awake communicated Milly and that the men had all gone to bed a good hour ago. Ashley said goodnight and signed off and before long he too had dropped off into a tired sleep.

When he awoke his query was anticipated by Zanos and he learned that it was nearly eight o'clock in the morning and the ship was safely moored against the shoreline of Anztarza Bay. Tania was not in the room and on enquiry she replied that she was with Fiona in her cabin chatting. Fiona was in a state of excitement and asking all sorts of questions; mainly about Anztarza.

Ashley washed, shaved and dressed and as he made his way to Fiona's cabin he was met outside the door by Brian and Sarah. Badge communication is a wonderful tool that allows everyone to keep in touch with updates on personal events and thoughts.

'Come on everybody,' conveyed Katy, 'Robin and I are off to the dining hall for a cuppa and breakfast. We're starving. Shall we meet up there now? It's just across the passageway from us.'

'See you when you come in,' conveyed Rachel. 'Margaret and I have been in here for ages and have already had a nice cuppa. We thought you were all sleepy heads.'

It wasn't long before they were all together seated at one of the long tables. A crew member placed jugs of Wazu on the table but no one had any apart from Ashley who always seemed to have a thirst.

The buffet table was well stocked with the usual earthly breakfast things but all first went for the tea and coffee dispensers placed to one side. Then a bit later it was toast with marmalade, jam and cheese that was attacked and Ashley felt sated after his fourth toast. The bread was seeded and cut thick and was delicious when toasted. The Oannes certainly served a good continental style of breakfast.

It was about nine o'clock that they received communication from Captain Bulzezatna that transport awaited them on the Bay Dome shore which was ready to take them to the usual lodging apartments in Dome-7. Their Anztarza hosts were to be the husband and wife team of Laztraban and Niktukaz as had been on all previous occasions. First Deputy Rubandiz arrived in the dining hall and took a seat with the others and helped himself to a glass of Wazu. He said there was no need for haste as they had the whole day before them. The Oannes were a patient lot thought Ashley but then he knew them well.

After a pleasant interval of general conversation Ashley suggested they all follow their guide Rubandiz and head for the exit port. They followed Rubandiz down the passageway and turned to the left along another short corridor before arriving at a large open door. The quayside was clearly visible as the ship was right alongside it. A short step-down was required for them to get onto the quay and from there it was a distance of about forty feet to the awaiting deck Transporter.

Ashley immediately recognised Fritvazi as its operator and thought that it might be 536-Orange that Kazaztan used to operate. But it was a different colouring and when they got aboard Fritvazi conveyed that 536-Orange was undergoing maintenance and refurbishment. The present Transporter was a very similar one and being used as a temporary replacement.

Fiona, Sarah and Brian were at the rails near the front as the Transporter headed through the first tunnel leading to Dome-1. It cruised at a height of about thirty feet but at the fast walking pace of five miles per hour. Fritvazi had of course performed an initial polite welcoming Sewa to which Ashley had responded prior to boarding earlier. They had shaken hands and said what a pleasure it was to meet again. Ashley had last visited Anztarza about eighteen months ago.

Ashley introduced Fiona, Sarah and Brian to Fritvazi and he conducted a more formal Sewa to which Brian made a polite reply. Ashley was pleasantly surprised and complimented Brian on his Oannes social skills. Brian shrugged and conveyed it was simple politeness to reply. Sarah looked proudly at Brian and her emotion of pride and love was clearly sensed by all.

Ashley requested Fritvazi to do a mini guided tour on their way to the apartments which is what he did. The slow speed of the Transporter enabled the passengers to leisurely view the scenery of buildings and streets passing below them as Fritvazi gave a brief commentary.

Fiona looked around her with a degree of astonishment. She said that she had expected the domes to be large but these exceeded her wildest expectations. At roughly a mile across and over 2000 feet high at their centre the domes to her were a wonder and a work of art. She could happily live in one of these she said.

There were Oannes people on the ground looking up and waving as they floated by. Everyone on the Transporter waved back and accepted the Sewa wishes conveyed. Some Oannes even gave their names and dome address along with an invitation for a visit if desired. Ashley knew that all of Anztarza had been informed of this visit and it was most heartening to receive such a welcome.

'Perhaps when we return next time,' had been Ashley's communication back to them.

The Transporter then entered the 100 feet wide and 200 feet high connecting tunnel that led to Dome-10. The tunnel was well lit and half a mile in length.

Fritvazi then conveyed images of the extent of Anztarza along with a brief description. The domes were arranged in a square geometric layout pattern with interconnecting tunnels. In all there were twenty habitation domes arranged in a grid pattern of four rows with five domes in each row. Then there were four food growing domes which made up the fifth row in this grid layout. All domes were interconnected by tunnels to their neighbouring ones. The Food-Dome-24 was not as yet completed. All that was left was for soil to be transported from Nazmos to make up its food growing base. Conditions had to be exactly as they are on the sea bed of Peruga.

As they entered Dome-10 Fritvazi explained that this too was a habitation dome and just like all the others. Fiona, Sarah and Brian did notice a similarity of construction and layout to the earlier one. The Transporter floated through Domes-9 and 8 and arrived inside Dome-7 their intended destination. It went towards the central square and settled down gently. All disembarked and Rubandiz led the way down the broad central street. There were five other lesser streets branching out on each side and Rubandiz led them to the last one quite close to the dome wall. They turned to their left and immediately Ashley recognised their usual lodgings. Muznant and Brazjaf had lived in the first apartment but which was now vacant. Muznant had referred to this dome as 7-Blue and as her home on Earth.

The next house was for the couple Fruztriv and wife Rontuzaj but they were still away on Nazmos. Ashley had never met them as they had been away since before his first visit to Anztarza. Zanos answered Ashley's query and conveyed that the couple were due back sometime soon. Their option had always been to return to work in Anztarza.

Just then a smiling couple came out onto the street to meet them. They were Laztraban and his wife Niktukaz. Sewas were exchanged, a welcome conveyed and all were ushered into the large dining room of the first house where Muznant and Brazjaf had lived. Refreshments in the form of jugs of Wazu and a nice looking orange coloured drink were already on the long table. Rachel's dislike for Wazu was well known and so now a sweetened orange drink was always made available as an alternative. The Oannes always did their best to please their guests. Rachel's reputation had preceded her from all those years ago. The journey from Anztarza Bay had taken over an hour in a pleasant but warm atmosphere and the cool drinks were very welcome.

There was much telepathic communication between Ashley and his hosts but they were mostly of past pleasant memories. Niktukaz was quite taken with Fiona and before long a dialogue began between them; telepathic of course. Ashley found this most interesting and polite protocol prevented him from any attempt to listen in to their thoughts. He would ask Fiona later what she thought about her Oannes friend and the Oannes in general.

Rubandiz then took his leave rather formally specifying that he must return to his ship duties. He said he would see them again soon when they made the trip out to the starship rendezvous. Apparently the passenger listing was quite an unusual one. Many who would not normally have ventured out had decided to make the journey because of Ashley's presence aboard. They knew of the shortened journey time. Ashley wondered if somehow he had let his mental guard down and his thoughts had been monitored with his plan details that he'd intended to put before the Nazmos governing council. It was quite possible that his intentions for the Nazmos orbital change were now common knowledge in Anztarza. Perhaps he ought to consider this aspect more carefully. But then decided he would not change his views and the plan must stand.

Communication was then received that the presentation before the chief ministers in the assembly dome would be later than originally planned. The time conveyed was for just after 4:30pm GMT. From this Ashley knew that not only was a grand reception arranged but that there was also a request to be made. That request was probably in the form of an assurance that a certain schedule would be adhered to. The Oannes' ways were well known to Ashley.

No one was tired so it was suggested that a walking tour of this dome be undertaken. Niktukaz thought it a good idea and told her husband to be their guide. He would be able to introduce them to any of the neighbours they happened to meet.

'Oh goody,' exclaimed Fiona smiling, 'I'm ready as of now.'

But Niktukaz conveyed a negative on this which quite puzzled Fiona as well as Sarah and Brian. Ashley laughed because he had seen the tunic outfits hanging up in his and Tania's room when he had gone in to look around and to freshen up.

'You'd stand out like a sore thumb if you went dressed as you are,' smiled Ashley. 'We are expected to follow a certain dress code while we are here by wearing the Oannes outfits provided. They should be hanging up in your room if you didn't notice before.'

'I wondered who those clothes were for,' said Fiona, 'I thought they'd been left by the previous occupant.'

'You'll find that they've been specially made for you and to your tastes,' said Tania. 'All your measurement and colour preferences would have been thought read when it first became known that you were to come on this trip.'

'I like it,' sighed Fiona, 'yes I do like it very much. Right then, I'm off to change. Can you come with me Aunt Tania and tell me how I look when I put it all on.'

'Of course dear,' said Tania, 'and Zanos will instruct you on what goes where. You really can't go wrong here in Anztarza.'

'I think we'll go in and change too,' said Sarah grabbing Brian by the hand and leading him away.

'We might as well all follow suit,' said Katy.

She burst out laughing when Robin raised his eyebrows and said, 'Boom, boom,' conveying the aptness in her use of words.

Katy bowed and said it was pure coincidence but maybe she was just naturally clever.

'And none of that smiling please thank you very much,' she added.

It was twenty five minutes later that they returned to the dining room all dressed in their new Oannes outfits. Niktukaz conveyed an emotion of admiration at their general appearance.

'This feels very comfortable,' said Brian, 'and also I feel quite dressy and posh. I do like the ruff on the back of the tunic. I expect its there to harmonise with the Oannes back vane.'

There was much complimentary discussion among the women and both Fiona and Sarah sought repeated assurances that their outfits matched well with their hair and makeup.

'Does it suit me?' asked Sarah and immediately blushed when everyone laughed again at the suit word. 'I shall never use that word again,' she added smiling.

Each outfit was a good combination of colour with brilliant contrasts in edging and legging stripes. And when they all walked out onto the street they looked very much like the dome inhabitants that they encountered. They walked up the broad central avenue and soon arrived at the central square. Laztraban explained that this was the Transporter pick up and drop off area for the dome. And each dome had a similar area.

Sarah asked about everyday living needs and Laztraban explained the system. Requirements were thought-read by the Zanos system on an individual or family basis and delivered by Transporter to the storage facility and pickup points around the square. These were usually below ground level. Individuals did their own collections and transferred the items to their homes using the porter-pallets which worked like a mini-Transporter. A record was maintained of all transactions and adjustments made at their workplace. Any anomalies were brought before the administrators and then reported to the chief ministers. The Oannes were very thorough in applying rules and regulations but these were generally of a sensible nature. Detailed reports were included in the information sent back to Nazmos.

As the group strolled down a particular street many of its residents came out to say hello; some even inviting them into their homes for the proverbial glass of Wazu. However Laztraban politely declined these offers with the excuse that there was a lot to show the visitors and time was short. Perhaps another time he said.

It was interesting how many houses had ornamentation features added to their frontages. It was a personalisation of their homes and Ashley guessed the Oannes to be very house proud. In that respect they were similar to humans who considered their homes to be their castle.

The walking tour took a circuitous route and many polite refusals had to be made before they arrived back at their apartments. It had been an interesting tour that had lasted over an hour.

Niktukaz had tea and coffee ready for her guests and she suggested a rest in their rooms afterwards and prior to them setting off to meet the chief ministers. It could be a long evening she conveyed.

And so it was that later they found the deck Transporter waiting for them in the central square was none other than that operated by Fritvazi as before.

The moment that they entered the Dome-4, Ashley recognised the layout of the tables as being for a banquet occasion; but perhaps to a somewhat lesser degree. This was to be a lower level celebration to welcome the three latest new visitors. From being extremely secretive the Oannes were now getting to meet an increased number of humans. It was still only Ashley's family and close friends who were allowed that privilege. 'One day,' thought Ashley and let the thought just hang there.

There was a general milling of Oannes people between the tables with small groups standing around in silent communication. The chief ministers had not as yet made an appearance at the top tables and Ashley was glad they had arrived early. It was considered poor etiquette to arrive late.

Fritvazi lowered the Transporter gently to the central plaza floor and all disembarked. Ashley led the way and knew exactly where to go. He was guided to their allotted table places by Zanos conveying the information.

They saw many acquaintances among the Oannes guests and Ashley stopped for a handshake every so often. Sewas were not conducted since this was not necessary among guests at a social though there were many enquiries into Ashley's well being. On each occasion Ashley took the opportunity to introduce Fiona and then Sarah and Brian as a couple. When they all remarked how pretty Fiona looked Katy beamed and said, 'Well after all she is my daughter.' Sarah didn't mind the attention being towards her sister since she was totally in love with her own man.

When she was a child Fiona had her dad's general features. But as she matured and grew to womanhood her features lengthened and a beauty erupted that was a surprise to all. She kept her hair long and it framed her face as though by an artist. The slight waviness in her hair was most becoming and it was only when she smiled and exposed her perfect teeth that you could see a part of Robin represented.

Sarah had Katy's looks and still did and they were easily recognised as mother and daughter. She had a great sense of fun but her mischievous ways had mellowed once she became a teacher. She was now so in love with her Brian that she believed she'd achieved the ultimate happiness. At twenty five years of age she considered herself to be at an advanced age; though her students didn't think so.

As they arrived at their prescribed table a sudden lowering of the conversation buzz descended in the assembly area and looking up Ashley saw the chief ministers walk in from a large house nearby. They were accompanied not only by their wives but by close friends and their wives. Immediately Ashley relaxed and knew that this was to be an informal occasion albeit an important one. He conveyed this to the others and both Tania and Katy whispered a relieved 'Thank goodness'.

Chief Minister Rymtakza led the way with his wife Mizpalto by his side. They were followed by chief ministers Zarzint and Tzatzorf accompanied by both of their wives. Behind came a group of friends accompanied by their wives or partners. All seemed relaxed and smiled generally at their guests. Ashley felt pleased by the thought that the chief ministers had probably been on the lookout for Ashley's arrival before venturing out; a compliment indeed.

'They must have a keen request to make,' smiled Ashley at the thought.

Mizpalto spied Ashley and pulling her husband with her made a bee-line towards their table. The others naturally followed and all of course knew Ashley by sight. Sewa greetings and handshakes were followed by Ashley introducing his nieces and then Brian as Sarah's partner. A lively communication ensued during which both Sarah and Fiona were complimented on their youth and beauty.

The remark that they looked 'Just like the people we see on TV programs' was considered by the Oannes the ultimate in makeup and good looks.

Katy was tapped on the shoulder and showed her delight when she recognised her friend Jantuzno. They had not seen each other for years as Jantuzno had returned to Nazmos over ten years ago. Her parents had chosen a partner for her but she needed to approve the choice. She had indeed got on well with the fellow and grew to like him and his ways and they had legalised their partnership some four years ago. Jantuzno was now 85 years of age and looked just as young as Katy remembered her.

'This is Chaztalit my husband,' she said turning to the Oannes man standing slightly behind and to one side of her. He was her height and rather stocky but with a youthful and smiling face. Jantuzno conveyed his details as being twelve years her senior and both worked in the monitoring section here in Anztarza. They had arrived back a year ago. And they looked forward to the Nazmos orbital change. Chaztalit had told Jantuzno how twenty two years ago he had received Ashley's memory transmission of that feted meeting with the seer Gozmanot. It was something he could never forget. Looking at Ashley across there with the chief ministers was like a dream come true for him. Many on Nazmos felt exactly as he did.

Ashley received these thoughts and turning gave Chaztalit a brief nod and smile.

Katy then introduced her daughters whom Jantuzno had never met but had heard about. There was much to tell and catch up between these two friends and they had the whole of the evening to do just that.

This was also the first time that Ashley had a closer look at Zantonomaz the wife of chief minister Zarzint. And then he also got a look at Rajoltaz who was the wife of chief minister Tzatzorf. Both Oannes ladies were behind the scene personalities and very rarely communicated in public.

However Mizpalto was very different and quite liked the limelight with her husband. She came forward to Tania and putting her hand on Tania's arm conveyed her own silent Sewa to which Tania happily responded. Tania then introduced Fiona, Sarah and Brian to this elite group of chief ministers and their friends.

Rymtakza came forward and expressed his pleasure at meeting more members of Ashley's family. He shook the hands of each in turn and this was followed through by others in his group. When these formalities were completed Rymtakza again asked Ashley how he was. Ashley replied that he was well and this time the chief minister smiled back and conveyed privately to Ashley that there was a matter to discuss.

'I knew it,' thought Ashley keeping his mind blocked, 'it has got to be a request.'

'Yes of course,' conveyed Ashley in reply, 'whatever the chief minister desires I am at your service.'

It was one of those situations in which he knew that they knew that he knew. But the proper words had to be conveyed formally nevertheless.

As this event was a general welcoming one it would also maintain a degree of informality in its nature. And so there were to be no speeches as such. There were about two hundred guests only and mainly those who were known to Ashley personally from his previous visits. Those left out would not mind due to the informal nature of the occasion. Etiquette was high on the Oannes agenda and always would be.

A telepathic request was sent out through the Zanos bio-computer system for all guests to take their places at table. The chief ministers' group retreated to the top table allocated to them as did everyone else to theirs.

Jugs of Wazu and the new orange coloured drink were already on the tables and now volunteers brought out a variety of food dishes on small floating pallets. From these the dishes were transferred onto the tables. Soon all the tables were well laden with exotic looking foods in a variety of shaped dishes.

There were the usual dishes of Raizna and Starztal along with Yaztraka and Mirzondip that Ashley easily recognised. The others of Lazzonta, Tartonta, Yantza and Milsony were not recognised by him straight away but he eventually was informed by Zanos as he mentally queried each one. Ashley noted gratefully that Bizzony and Trozbit were not among these although he noticed them on the other tables.

Ashley had explained the various Oannes cooked dishes to his nieces and now pointed out each one individually along with a taste emotion; telepathically of course. He also made some recommendations one of which was the sweet tasting Yaztraka. He thought Brian might like to try the Milsony since he was known to be partial to spicy Indian curry dishes. But he did recommend that they at least taste a bit of each and decide their own likes or dislikes.

Although no formal speeches were made a general communication of welcome to the Earth visitors came through from Zanos on behalf of the people of Anztarza. Ashley knew that this must have come through the express wishes of the administration body of Anztarza, namely the chief ministers.

And so towards the end of the evening when all appeared to have ceased eating Ashley in his turn – through Zanos – conveyed a grateful thanks to all the people of Anztarza for their generous and gracious hospitality in making their human guests feel so welcome.

Someone began to clap and soon the whole dome echoed this drumming of hands coming together. This was something Ashley had introduced sometime ago during his first visit to show his appreciation of a polite act shown him. It had subsequently been liked by the Oannes and was adapted into their culture as an approving gesture. The TV programs they monitored also showed this as a likeable human trait similar to the greetings handshake. Ashley thought that they must see a lot of kissing on their monitors but as yet there was no evidence of it in public. In the privacy of their homes or sleep tanks it was probably another matter.

Gradually the Oannes guests started to rise off their seats and began to mix with friends from other tables. Some came up to Ashley and conveyed a personal greeting before moving on. A few began to retreat to where the parked deck transporters were floating overhead.

Ashley and his group stayed seated until Brian said that it was time he stretched his stiffened legs. He took Sarah with him and they moved towards another table where some Oannes were standing and began a tentative conversation. Brian seemed very interested in these people which impressed Ashley. Brian continued to impress and surprise him in many ways. Sarah had certainly found herself a good man there and he conveyed this to Robin and Katy.

Fiona stayed next to her mum as though for protection and listened to her conversation with Jantuzno and Chaztalit. She was fascinated by the superior intelligence display of these people at every turn. They seemed to know everything about the human psyche and yet never once had they mentioned anything derogatory in that respect; even though Fiona was sure they must see a lot of Earth's savagery on their monitors. They had ten thousand years of watching the Earth's peoples and yet they conveyed a hope for integration in the longer term.

Then Ashley received a communication to approach the top table where the chief ministers and their friends sat. He acknowledged and conveyed the request to Tania and asked her to accompany him.

Ashley sensed an emotion of mild annoyance that he did not come alone. However he allayed this feeling by saying that Tania could communicate with the wives while he listened to them.

'This is an awkward request but one that our wives wish us to make,' said chief minister Rymtakza. 'We would be obliged immensely if you could consider it.'

Ashley decided to impress them with his instinctive reply. He suspected that they knew of his Nazmos plan but out of respect pretended ignorance.

'I believe I will be able to fulfil the wishes of your esteemed wives,' said Ashley and paused before continuing. 'Is it your wish to journey with me on this trip to Nazmos?'

'It is,' conveyed a surprised Rymtakza. 'It has been our wives wish for some time now and we wish to oblige. But there is a problem in that as chief ministers we cannot stay away too long from our duty here. Not more than a few weeks at most.'

He paused to let this sink in.

'We know that you have the task of stabilising Platwuz in its new orbit. But then there is also the possibility of the Nazmos orbital change which we believe is very likely since it adheres to the wishes of the seer Gozmanot. However that is up to the decision of the Nazmos governing council,' he added quickly.

Ashley waited for his plan to be voiced and to his very great relief it was not. Rymtakza continued.

'We know that the Nazmos orbital change – should it go ahead – must be done in two stages. The first stage to be concluded right away and the second stage approximately five months later when Nazmos approaches its orbital perigee position. Our request is that you return to Earth with us after the first stage and then return later to Nazmos to complete the orbital stabilisation.'

Ashley looked at them and knew with relief that they had no idea of his plans for the orbital adjustment. So he gave them his broadest smile and said he would do exactly as they wished. They should be back in Anztarza within three weeks from departure. Journey times would be roughly a week to Nazmos and a similar week to return to Earth. Personally he would like to stay at least a week on Nazmos to meet old friends and possibly his son Simon whom he'd not seen since he joined the space academy in 2026, over twelve years ago. Ashley did not add anything further and let them assume that he would return to Nazmos within that period.

'That is excellent,' said Rymtakza. 'Since the visit to Anztarza by the Nazmos governing council twenty two years ago we too have longed to make a similar round trip journey. There are many who wish to go also and we will accommodate their wishes if convenient. A week on Nazmos will be sufficient. Who knows but the next time we return it may be an entirely different scenario.'

Ashley smiled and said that this gave him an idea that he would put before the Nazmos governing council. He did not elaborate and made sure he kept his mind blocked to any probing enquiries.

'May I make a request of the chief ministers,' conveyed Ashley, 'and that is your permission for a tour of Anztarza to be given for the benefit of my nieces who have never been here before.'

Although this did not require such high approval it nevertheless did relieve the minds of the high command that they were not getting something for nothing. It was Ashley's way of balancing the books so to speak. It was in his general style to put others at their ease.

'That has already been arranged for tomorrow,' smiled Rymtakza for he knew exactly why the request was made. 'It is always a pleasure to show off our city to welcome visitors. Fritvazi has been instructed to be at your disposal for the entire day. He will also be your tour guide.'

'My grateful thanks chief minister,' said Ashley making a slight bow which drew a smile from the ladies. They considered Ashley the most chivalrous of humans. He was instantly likeable and this proved it yet again.

Ashley had already mentioned the possibility of a general tour of the city domes so he now conveyed to them that it was to go ahead for tomorrow.

'Oh that would be grand,' exclaimed Fiona, 'I am quite looking forward to it.'

'So are we,' conveyed Sarah and Brian together.

'Well as a matter of fact so am I,' conveyed Ashley. 'I'd like to see the progress made on the food Dome-24. It was nearly completed the last time I was here.'

The general patter of conversation continued and Ashley was surprised when Zantonomaz the wife of chief minister Zarzint actually made a comment about the winter on Nazmos and whether the orbital change would improve conditions by any great amount. It was obvious that she did not like the cold.

Eventually as the assembly area depleted of guests the chief ministers made their brief farewell Sewas and departed just as they had come in. This was the cue for Ashley to prompt their own departure which they did as soon as the chief ministers were lost to view. Zanos informed Ashley that it was just after ten o'clock.

Fritvazi brought the Transporter down when he saw Ashley approach and before long the tired looking group were floating towards Dome-7 which was adjacent to Dome-4.

The walk to their street was a slow one but once in the apartment they all begged forgiveness of their hosts Laztraban and Niktukaz and said they wished to go straight to their rooms and to bed. Ashley conveyed the news about the city tour in the morning and he was informed that breakfast would be ready about nine o'clock.

Once in their room Ashley kissed Tania goodnight and stripped to his shorts and hopped into his twin letting out a great big sigh. Within minutes he was asleep. Tania came out of the bathroom and looked at him and thought, 'We're getting old.' Then she too got into her twin but sleep came slowly. Many thoughts passed through her mind the last of which was a disturbing one about Zarama. Poor Ashley had such a lot to do.

The next morning all were aboard the deck Transporter just before 10 am. Fritvazi had arrived with the Transporter at 9.am and walked to the fifth street apartments to meet his guests. They'd all been up and ready earlier but were now having breakfast. Fritvazi was invited to sit with them and was offered something to drink. A mug of tea was suggested but he politely declined. He said he could not understand how anyone could pour scalding hot water down their throat.

'We could make it cold for you like iced tea,' offered Rachel but Fritvazi said that the taste was not to his liking.

'It's not quite my cup of tea,' he smiled and everyone laughed.

'Your humour is excellent,' conveyed Ashley, 'you're almost human.'

'Thank you,' he replied and then went onto explain that as guide he considered that an overhead tour was the initial feature to be considered. However many of Anztarza's other essentials were in under-floor places and might not be accessible. These were the sewage and water purification facilities and also the power plant and Zanos rooms. The air ventilation room was however quite safe to view. Those not seen would be conveyed as mental images for a full appreciation of their features.

They all walked to the central plaza and boarded the Transporter which soon rose to its normal height of thirty feet and cruised slowly towards the tunnel leading to Dome-4. Gradually the Transporter increased to a faster pace and Ashley and the others faced the direction of travel to relish the massage effect of the gentle warm wind ruffling through their hair. A very pleasant sensation indeed thought Ashley. The dome temperature was kept at an ambient 18°C throughout the Anztarza year. Ashley thought that most of the Oannes who had lived in Anztarza for many years found that the conditions back on Nazmos as rather harsh whenever they returned for a visit. Secretly they wished for a warmer Nazmos and Ashley offered such a possibility.

The Transporter now entered Dome-4 and all immediately recognised the venue of the previous evening. But it had other secrets and Fritvazi explained that under its floor was a large hall with banks upon banks of monitoring equipment set up in rows at which hundreds of Oannes personnel were busily employed at all hours. Fritvazi conveyed detailed images of the large hall and its layout. He then explained how the information was categorised and stored in vast banks of interconnected bio-computer systems with a virtually near infinite memory capacity. However each year most of the information was sifted through and transferred to Nazmos via the ferrying starships. Direct communication with Nazmos was not conveniently possible. Fritvazi asked if this information was sufficient as access to the monitoring room was possible but only from a viewing platform vantage point. The tasks performed there could not be intruded upon.

Ashley looked around and conveyed to Fritvazi their general thoughts that entry into the area was not necessary. They all had a good insight into the functioning of the monitoring system from the excellent imagery conveyed by him.

Fritvazi let the Transporter float on and mentioned that the huge Power Plant for the general functioning of Anztarza was also contained in halls under several habitation domes. It was obviously out of bounds to any other than the engineers who supervised its functioning.

However he could show them one of the air purification plants all of which were well away from any sensitive or dangerous areas. And close by would be another intriguing feature that they might find most interesting. He looked at Ashley and smiled for Ashley knew exactly the item Fritvazi was referring to. He thought of Simon for whom it had been quite an experience all those years ago. Fritvazi conveyed that they would enter this underground feature well away from any power plant interface which meant travelling into the next Dome-3.

He settled down in the central plaza there and led the group down a shallow flight of stairs. It smelled fresh down there and Fritvazi explained about the huge vat-like features before them. He showed them how the air was purified and how sea water was essential to the function. The hall was expansive and bare of any Oannes personnel. Actually there was little to see here apart from the impression that everything seemed to be functioning perfectly.

'Yes,' thought Ashley, 'the air does feel very fresh down here.'

Fritvazi smiled and explained that the air down here was that which had been newly processed and so would be the freshest in Anztarza. If it were not so then something was not functioning correctly. Ashley smiled as it was obvious to him that his thoughts had been picked up and read by their guide.

Fritvazi then led them through a side door and into a fairly wide though long and curving passageway. Ashley noticed that they passed several closed doors before their guide stopped before one of them. He looked at his guests as if to say 'are you ready for this?' He opened this door and they all entered what was a huge though empty looking hall. Fritvazi once again gave his guests a look of pride and conveyed that he always felt exhilarated when he came in here.

'Maybe it's because of the very important item that is housed in here which is at the very crux of FTL travel,' he said aloud while smiling broadly.

'But there's nothing here,' said Brian as he continued looking around the hall.

'Ah let me show you,' said Fritvazi leading the way to the very centre of the hall. He stopped near a circular glass panel set flush in the floor and looked down at it. He drew them in a circle around this panel and asked them to look down more closely.

The glass panel was about two feet in diameter and clearly a couple of inches thick. Set under it and at its very central point was a fuzzy greyish coin sized flat object. It seemed to scintillate in the light and also vibrate very slightly from side to side from whichever angle you looked at it.

Ashley knew what it was for he had been here before with Muznant and Brazjaf as also had some of the others. So what interested him now was to see the expressions on the faces of Brian and his nieces when Fritvazi explained that they were observing a piece of neutron star material. Brian's eyes lit up with a new discerning interest as he looked more closely at this fuzzy object. Fiona and Sarah were still not impressed and appeared rather puzzled. Until Fritvazi explained that it was what made FTL starships possible. The material was the shield that prevented the realm grid energy-medium or dark matter of space from stripping the atoms inside the starship of its entire molecular structure when it was speeding through space at multiple FTL velocities. He conveyed an image of a starship and it massive forward umbrella-like shield made entirely of this material. Current starships were two miles long and half a mile in diameter with the shield in front shaped like a mushroom head three quarters of a mile across.

Fritvazi then explained how this coin sized piece of neutron star material got to be here. It had to be manufactured right where it sat by the compounding machines that were assembled within this very hall. The energy-medium particles generated by the machines had to be focussed at the one spot and masses of I-Protons beamed onto it. It was a complicated process that took fifty years of constant compounding to create the present coin-sized amount of material.

'So how much does it weigh?' asked Brian still full of interest and knowing that it must be many tons at least.

'Here on Earth we estimate it to possess an inertial mass of about ninety tons,' said Fritvazi.

'Amazing,' chimed in Sarah.

'Yes, and this is thin compared to the actual proton shield of a starship,' added Fritvazi.

Ashley remembered when Simon had returned from a similar tour that all he could talk about was the fact that he had actually seen neutron star material and had felt it pulsate when he placed his hand over its glass cover. Ashley knew that it had been a turning point for Simon's career when Bulzezatna and others had felt Simon's initial euphoric reaction at his witnessing that fuzzy coin in the floor. They all knew instantly of Simon's potential and love for space.

Fritvazi interrupted Ashley's thoughts to guide the party back to the upper floor level and thence onto the deck Transporter. There was much more to see he conveyed.

They cruised through Dome-2 and turned right towards the tunnel leading into the Bay Dome. This was slightly larger than the habitation ones and Fritvazi communicated its general layout. There were a large number of craft of varying sizes moored along the crescent shaped shoreline. Fritvazi pointed out the more common larger craft like 520-Green which was the largest of them all at 550 feet in length. Next in size were the craft like 11701-Red at about 400 feet. Fritvazi said that there were a range of ships similar in size to these two but most were currently out on space patrol somewhere in the Ort Cloud area checking for space debris and the like in the space-lane zone between Earth and Nazmos.

He then pointed out two craft further along the crescent shore that he said were about 300 feet long. And then there were the twenty or so smaller craft which were between eighty and a hundred feet in length. These he said were mainly for Earth duties one of which was for the purchase of Earth products like wheat flour; bread was an adopted Oannes favourite and had been so for millennia. Many other vegetarian products were also on this purchase list. Like Sudzarnt they had many Oannes in key areas. Fritvazi did not elaborate further.

All Anztarza craft had a unique identity in their numbering and were usually a dull grey in colour. All were covered with a thick anti-radar coating.

'Could you travel to Nazmos in one of the larger craft?' asked Brian.

'That would not be advisable,' replied Fritvazi, 'but it is a possibility if circumstances were extreme. All Anztarza craft are equally suited to space, atmosphere or underneath the ocean. The first journey to Earth from Nazmos was in a ship like these and took fifteen years to accomplish. Since then we have our starships which normally do the journey in six months. With Ashley on board it becomes a matter of a few days.'

Ashley smiled at this and gave Fritvazi an acknowledgement bow.

Sarah and Fiona looked at their uncle with pride.

Fritvazi then brought the Transporter to a lower level so that his guests could get a closer look at the moored craft. Even Sarah and Fiona took an interest in the view below.

There were quite a few Oannes on the shoreline and they looked up with interest at the tunic clad faces peering down at them. Of course greeting messages were exchanged telepathically but the invitation to descend and drink a glass of Wazu had to be declined on the grounds that there was a lot as yet to be seen by the group.

And so Fritvazi lifted the Transporter back to its travelling height and moved towards the other tunnel on the right which led to Dome-1. Again this looked similar to all the other habitation domes so Fritvazi said he would continue on toward the food domes which they should find interesting.

But just then a message was received from Niktukaz that refreshments were ready for them if they wished to take a short break. This certainly came as a relief for Sarah and Margaret. Brian too said he could use a break back at the apartments on account of the three mugs of tea he'd had at breakfast. Fritvazi looked at Ashley who gave a brief nod. The message had been understood.

The Transporter then speeded up and went straight through to Dome-10. It then turned left for the tunnel to Dome-9 and continued straight on to Dome-8 and so on into their Dome-7 where it settled down in the central plaza. An easy walk brought them to their Anztarza accommodation and a welcome from their host couple Niktukaz and Laztraban.

There were snacks on the main dining table that included sliced bread with cheese, butter and jams laid out. Jugs of Wazu and orange drink were also on the table along with three of the common main meal dishes. These were Yaztraka, Raizna and Yantza. Niktukaz invited her guests to help themselves to anything they liked and that a proper main meal would be served that evening when they returned at the end of their tour.

'I think I'll go easy on the drinks,' said Brian after he had returned from his room, 'just in case it is another long session.'

All knew exactly what he meant and Fritvazi quickly apologised for his oversight. Washroom facilities existed in every dome as part of the general facilities for Oannes personnel in the area. He should have mentioned this when he commenced the tour. Ashley smiled as even he had not known about this. However when he queried Fritvazi about it he learned that Fritvazi was elaborating on a theme. Every house would welcome visitors into their home even if it was just to use their convenience; it would bring honour to the house. The Oannes were a hospitable people and kept an open house to anyone who wished to visit be it Oannes or human. Fritvazi wished his guests to feel comfortable about using someone's home without them thinking it as an imposition.

It was roughly an hour after arriving that they were once again on the Transporter. This time it went through into Dome-6 which was at the end position of a row of domes. As usual there was very little activity going on here though several Oannes in the central plaza sent their greetings and invitations. Ashley conveyed a reply that they were on a tour and were heading for the food growing Dome-21 and perhaps would visit another time. Back came the reply that they understood and wished them a pleasant voyage for the next day. All of Anztarza knew of their plans.

The Transporter turned to the right and headed for the next tunnel leading to Dome-15. Then they proceeded straight on to Dome-16 before forking right to the tunnel leading to the food Dome-21. When they entered the dome Brian thought it resembled the Bay Dome but without the mooring features. Fiona and Sarah found it much more interesting than the built up habitation domes and asked to see more. So Fritvazi floated the Transporter just above the water near the centre of the dome and conveyed a detailed imagery of the underwater features with the plants grown below in their disciplined rows.

'I should very much like to go down there and see it all for myself if only that were possible,' said Fiona in a whisper to Sarah.

'Yes,' replied Sarah, 'wouldn't that be wonderful.'

'To do that you would need to enter the water and swim down twenty feet to where the plants are being cultivated,' said Fritvazi having overheard their comments.

But neither of us is capable of that,' said Fiona sounding disappointed. 'We can barely swim as it is.'

Both ladies had shown a keen interest in seeing more of this important feature that fed Anztarza and openly showed their disappointment. Fritvazi smiled and conveyed that it still might be possible for them to gain the experience by viewing it all live and through the eyes of another.

He then took the Transporter to the thin crescent of land and settled it down there beside the towering dome wall. His communication with the dome supervisor brought her up out of the water after a couple of minutes and Rachel instantly recognised her as Myzantra. She was now 172 years of age and remembered Rachel as a child.

The shoreline was a thin crescent of land covered in shrubs of various colours which looked quite decorative. Ashley noticed that the nursery of dwarf trees had disappeared from here though he had seen evidence of a few such trees dotted around within the habitation domes. Perhaps an attempt was being made to make Anztarza a bit greener. Ashley wondered whether the vision of Gozmanot had anything to do with it; it was more than likely he thought.

Brief Sewas were performed and also introductions. Rachel and Myzantra touched hands and a mutual reading of minds took place. She did the same with Katy and looking at Fiona and Sarah said they were very pretty just like on TV. After meeting all the guests Fritvazi conveyed the wishes of Sarah and Fiona to view the underwater features of the dome. Myzantra said that she would be happy to oblige Katy's children. She came forward and briefly touched each of their hands and conveyed that she would swim down to the food beds and convey all her mental images back to them just as they occurred. Turning about she stepped to the shore edge and waded into the water. She gave a backward hand gesture before disappearing down into the depths.

Fiona and Sarah and the others too saw the view appearing before Myzantra as she descended and the Yaztraka trees gradually come into view. The water was surprisingly clear with a dull lucidity from the dome lights filtering down. Twenty feet was not all that deep and conditions had been made similar to the Peruga Sea. The trees had long hanging fruit on them and Myzantra conveyed that they were now ready for harvesting. She cruised between the trees and their fruit breaking one off in the process to demonstrate to the visitors how easy it was to harvest. Fiona and Sarah conveyed their joy and fascination at this experience.

'This is wonderful,' said Fiona, 'I know what Yaztraka tastes like and now I can see it growing in its natural habitat. I feel as if I'm right down there among it all and I'm not even wet.'

Everyone laughed and Myzantra conveyed that she would go to the next growing plot.

As she cruised along she came to shorter shrubs with small pink pods. The shrubs were grown in long straight rows. This she informed them was Starztal and not yet ready. Further along were the Lazzonta trees but these had just been harvested she conveyed so none of the runner-bean-like fruits was visible. However another crop of its fruit would be ready in a few months. It was usual for there to be three harvestings in each year. That was the benefit of underwater cultivation.

Myzantra then came to an area which was covered in another shrub-like ground cover. This was the Raizna crop which also was ready for harvesting she said. Raizna she explained was similar to earth's potato and harvesting involved pulling out the entire shrub and then replanting from scratch. Because of its growing characteristics only two crops were grown each year.

Ashley and the others who knew all this from previous visits still found it all interesting. The underwater views transmitted by Myzantra were phenomenal. Rachel remembered her first time when she was a child. Then Muznant had gone down with Myzantra and had conveyed back similar images. The image of Gozmanot floating lazily in her sleep tank passed through Ashley's mind.

With the food dome underwater experience completed Fritvazi conveyed that apart from the different crops being grown the general layout and functioning of the other two remaining food domes was fairly similar. The need for additional food growing domes had arisen as the population of Anztarza had increased over the years. It currently stood at ten thousand. Construction of the fourth food Dome-24 had commenced over three hundred years ago and was now close to completion; perhaps in another thirty years or so. The Oannes had a very different concept of time in that nothing was ever done in haste. That was because there never was any need to. They planned well.

'Could we see how it is progressing?' asked Rachel remembering her first visit there as a child.

'I'm afraid that would not be possible,' said Fritvazi, 'as even I am not permitted onto a construction site.'

'Perhaps we could get a communication from Wizgotal,' suggested Rachel. 'He could convey images of the construction progress as he did the last time.'

'Yes, I have just communicated with Wizgotal and he replies he will meet us in the central plaza of Dome-19 not too far from the tunnel entrance to his Dome-24,' said Fritvazi.

With thanks and brief farewell Sewas to Myzantra the Transporter lifted away and floated towards the tunnel leading to Dome-17. Fritvazi was a good guide and because Dome-19 was five domes away he decided to zigzag there by visiting each of the other two food domes as well. Each time he intentionally floated the Transporter into the centre of the food dome in question so that his visitors could see for themselves the similarity of appearance between the domes. They finally exited Dome-23 and entered Dome-19 and settled down in its central plaza. And it was not long before a tiny floating Transporter emerged from another tunnel to settle down beside them.

A brief Sewa was conducted and Wizgotal's greeting conveyed that it was always a pleasure to meet Ashley and his family again. It was only when he was reintroduced to Rachel that he showed his surprise at her appearance from that of the little girl he had seen all those years ago. He was very pleased to meet Sarah, Fiona and Brian as first time visitors to Anztarza.

Ashley explained that the purpose of the tour was really for the benefit of these newcomers and it would be kind if Wizgotal could give them a general understanding of the construction progress of his food dome.

'It will be my pleasure,' he said and then added, 'you may look into my mind if you wish and see for yourself all there is to know about this dome's progressive construction.'

Since neither Fiona, Sarah or Brian had the skill to do that Ashley did it for them. He read Wizgotal's mind and slowly in stages conveyed the visual images to all members of the group.

Wizgotal had now been on the project for 107 years and in that time had made several recreational journeys back to Nazmos. Ashley conveyed the progress of the dome's construction since Wizgotal had arrived there and the technical specifications involved. This included the physical sizes of the dome roof blocks as well as the lesser floor ones. All the construction blocks had now been laid and full fusion between them had taken place. The dome was now one complete integral piece and finalising work was in progress. This meant that sediment from the bed of the Peruga Sea was being transported to Earth and laid out evenly over the floor of the currently dry dome. The soil had to be built up to a level that had a depth of forty feet. When this had been completed a rest period of a few years had to be allowed for settling and compaction. Then finally water from the Sea of Peruga would be added and this would bring the water level up to that of the other domes. Several years would then be allowed during which time nutrients would be added to boost future food growth. Only then would attempts at cultivation commence.

The large construction machine that had straddled the dome floor like a giant spider for much of the construction period was gone and in its place was a cabling and bucket system for depositing the Peruga soil.

Ashley could see that Fiona was inwardly marvelling at the early construction work in her minds eye and the sheer immensity of the task undertaken considering the size and weight of the building blocks used. With all of this so vividly presented Brian could see how very much more advanced the Oannes were in comparison with Earth technology. Ashley could see him nodding his head as the images appeared before him.

Sarah and Fiona asked the same question that Rachel had asked of Muznant all those years ago and they received the same answers. The crops were grown underwater because that was the normal growing technique used on Nazmos. Land on the Earth's surface had too varied a climate and it was essential that the Oannes keep their presence on Earth a secret.

Fritvazi finally conveyed that it was time to conclude the tour as it was getting into the evening period. All agreed as it had been a long day full of events and places worth seeing. Much had been learned by Fiona, Sarah and Brian and so they all said a farewell Sewa to Wizgotal and thanked him for his time and images. He in turn replied with his own Sewa and that meeting Ashley's family was always a privilege and a pleasure. The Transporter lifted upwards and cruised at a leisurely pace through tunnels and domes to arrive and settle down in the plaza of Dome-7. It was now 6 pm and Ashley thanked Fritvazi for the excellent tour. A Sewa was conducted and they said farewell to their guide and began the short walk to the apartments.

Ashley thought a shower would invigorate him and Tania agreed that it was an excellent idea. Ashley read her mind and smiled inwardly. The others said they might do the same.

Niktukaz and Laztraban were nowhere to be seen and Ashley reckoned they must be resting in their own private apartment. The dining table had jugs of Wazu and orange drink laid out with plenty of glasses so all sat there for a while sipping their preferred drink before retiring to their rooms. They agreed to meet back there when they were refreshed in maybe an hour or two. They would communicate with each other through their badges just before.

Ashley decided that a shower would freshen him up and Tania agreed to follow. But she didn't wait for him to finish as she undressed and got into the large cubicle right behind him.

'I can do your back for you better than you can,' she said with a wicked smile on her face.

And it began from there. A shower area is all very well but not very comfortable for two with ardour in their minds. So they dried off and made their way onto the bed together.

'This is much nicer,' said Tania giggling.

'Definitely,' agreed a smiling Ashley entwining his arms around his wife.

Afterwards they still had their arms wrapped firmly around each other and just before Ashley dropped off to sleep he requested a wake up call from Zanos in exactly one hour.

Tania too had thoughts of her own just before falling asleep. They were sad instinctive thoughts that her darling Ashley must surely be taken from her one day; hopefully not as yet but perhaps in the not so distant future. She offered up a little prayer begging for it not to happen.

The evening meal was served up by Laztraban and Niktukaz about 8:30pm and was a lively affair with Fiona extolling the virtues of living in a place like Anztarza. For her the domes felt quite natural and not the least bit confining. It was their size that did it for her she said. Brian made a discerning comment that all things considered they could be living on a large spaceship. Ashley conveyed an image of the huge ship 98103-Pink that he had seen on Nazmos and which was capable of supporting 90,000 Oannes in space for an indefinite period; nine times the population of Anztarza. He conveyed that it was the first of an experimental vessel that was completed just over sixty years ago in answer to the Zarama threat. Basically it was an evacuation plan vessel to transport as many of the Oannes population to safety as was possible. A ten year space trial had been completed successfully with 20,000 Oannes aboard when Ashley was last on Nazmos and the plan was to continue constructing similar spaceships for the next two thousand years. That was when Zarama was expected.

'Wow,' said Brian having seen the image that Ashley conveyed, 'that ship is huge.'

'Will they stop making these ships now that you have arrived on the scene to stop Zarama?' asked Fiona.

'Lets hope that I can stop Zarama,' replied Ashley, 'but it is good to plan for every eventuality. There is no guarantee that I will be successful.'

Fiona smiled back but in her mind there could be only one outcome. She had a supreme faith in the gifts of her Uncle Ashley.

Since all had had a brief rest or sleep earlier no one was really tired even though the time was close to 10.pm. So they just sat around the table chatting about all they had seen that day. Their hosts stayed up with them and listened keenly to all that was said. It made them feel proud of their city. It must have been around midnight time when all finally said goodnight and retired to their rooms.

'See you all at breakfast,' conveyed Ashley as he and Tania shut the door of their room.

Next morning after breakfast information was received that all must begin preparations to board the fleet of ships waiting to take them to the starship rendezvous location. Nearly two thousand Oannes planned to make this journey; a full starship passenger loading.

Fritvazi conveyed his message that he was on location in the central plaza in readiness to transport them to the Bay Dome and their allocated spaceship. It was to be 520-Green.

Captain Bulzezatna conveyed that she had a special treat for Ashley's nieces but wished it to be a pleasurable surprise. This time Ashley had no idea what was being planned by his favourite captain. Affection between them had grown that was akin to a teacher and favourite pupil relationship. Ashley had his gifts and Bulzezatna had her extensive experience.

Farewell Sewas were conducted between the visitors and their Dome-7 hosts Laztraban and Niktukaz. Ashley was wished a pleasant and successful journey to Nazmos as were each of the others. Ashley knew that the success part referred to the Nazmos orbital change. All was conveyed in a most seriously formal manner.

Fritvazi too was quite formal in his farewell Sewas when he deposited them on the quayside close to where 520-Green was moored. All of Anztarza knew the purpose of Ashley's trip to Nazmos and somehow knew that Gozmanot's visions would come true. The Nazmos governing council must consent to the orbit change just as they had for Platwuz. Integration between human and Oannes would be that much easier with both worlds having similar climatic conditions; or so they thought.

After boarding 520-Green Ashley and his group were met by First Deputy Rubandiz and formal Sewas were exchanged. Rubandiz suggested that they all go straight to the dining hall for a welcoming glass of Wazu or orange drink and he led the way. The ship was to get underway in about an hour when all passengers had boarded. The Oannes never rushed things as Ashley knew.

It was while they were sipping a second glass of drink that Captain Bulzezatna conveyed that they could come into the control room if they wished to visually witness the departure process brief though it might be. This was probably for the benefit of Fiona, Sarah and Brian.

In the control room Sewas were brief since communication had already been effected earlier. Ashley responded for them all. Bulzezatna intimated that 520-Green would break its mooring connection in five minutes and move out to the centre of the Bay Dome. There it would submerge to begin its journey through the 100 mile connecting tunnel towards the Davis Sea exit. This part of the journey would take two hours and then another hour and a half to reach clear water at the sea surface.

Captain Bulzezatna paused in her message and smiled at her guests.

'We are to make a slight detour before we begin the actual journey towards rendezvous point,' she conveyed still smiling and looking at Fiona and Sarah.

She now let her mental guard down and indicated that her mind was open for any who wished to see what was planned.

Ashley did so and quickly conveyed the captain's thoughts to the others.

Apparently there was a massive unusual physical storm over the central Pacific Ocean in the equatorial region south of the Hawaiian Islands. Anztarza monitoring had picked up unusually high magnetic effects there with storm clouds reaching to unusual high altitudes. 520-Green was to make a pass over the area so that more accurate data may be collected for transmission back to Anztarza. Captain Bulzezatna's information indicated that the nature of the storm should provide a spectacle worth seeing from above; even for someone with her experience. But that would not be for another four hours at best so there was plenty of time for other things first.

So now 520-Green broke from its mooring ties and commenced a slow movement away from the quayside. They all got a very good view of the entire shoreline as the ship rotated about.

Ashley noted that the captain stood quite close to Fiona pointing out various features on the shoreline. Fiona in turn was quite enjoying the briefing and asked many pertinent questions. The captain picked up Ashley's thoughts and looking in his direction gave him a brief nod. She had given Simon the same attention and coaching. There must be something about Fiona's thought trend that had gained the interest of Bulzezatna, thought Ashley; something that only the advanced mind of an experienced Oannes was able to discern.

The spaceship 520-Green then began to slowly submerge and when the view panels went under only a greenish tint could be seen through them. Soon this darkened into a complete blackness and Ashley noticed the slightest of angle change in the deck floor as the ship speeded up to enter the sea tunnel. But this soon corrected itself to near normal.

The tunnel had a drop of two thousand feet over a distance of a hundred miles which gave it a slope of just one fifth of a degree downward angle. The ship adjusted its attitude such that the deck remained horizontal throughout.

Since there were now nearly four hours of underwater travel the captain suggested that his guests either pass the time in recreation in their cabins or in the dining hall where they might meet some of the other passengers.

Ashley thanked the captain and conveyed that he had a request to make for the benefit of the new travellers in his party namely Fiona, Sarah and Brian.

Bulzezatna read Ashley's mind and conveyed back her decision which Ashley immediately accepted. The requested tour of the ship would be conducted later when 520-Green was cruising towards rendezvous point after the neutron generators had operated.

And so for now all opted for the dining hall except Fiona who requested that she be allowed to stay in the control room a bit longer. She had much she wished to learn from the captain she said. Her request was granted with a smile from Bulzezatna who assured Ashley that she would personally escort Fiona to the dining hall in half an hour. 'A captain must also eat,' she conveyed to everyone's amusement.

It was now approaching midday GMT on Ashley's wristwatch and Zanos informed them that a light meal was ready to be served up in all the dining halls. The mention of food was a most welcome topic and Ashley suddenly felt quite hungry. He'd only had a few toasts for breakfast which seemed like it was ages ago.

Ashley was on his second mug of hot tea when the captain and Fiona entered and took a place at their table. Fiona was quite flushed and Ashley guessed that it was the excitement of the moment and of what was expected. The captain conveyed to Simon privately that Fiona was a bit like Simon in mentality. Where Simon had developed a keen desire for all things to do with space Fiona was ultra-keen to explore what to her was the unknown. Her sense of adventure was tremendous and therefore a source of potential danger if someone did not look out for her. Bulzezatna said that she had decided to do her best for the girl. So over the past half hour she had been imaging for her what she could expect in the days and weeks ahead. Bulzezatna said it was refreshing to read the thoughts of such a mind and that it brought back distant memories of her own youth and development.

'Ah, I see the buffet is being laid out,' said Bulzezatna aloud looking towards the far end of the hall. 'Perhaps a good meal inside us and then a rest in our cabins will prepare us for the spectacle ahead.'

She of course meant the storm in the Pacific Ocean. She explained that monitoring of weather conditions there had been ongoing for the last month and it now seemed to be reaching a peak of activity.

'I don't understand the situation,' said Fiona looking keenly at Bulzezatna, 'what is so different about this storm? Perhaps you could tell us more.'

So Bulzezatna conveyed what the analysts in Anztarza had passed on to her.

Apparently the warm west flowing North Equatorial Ocean Current had dipped southwards causing it to run into a section of the east flowing warm Equatorial Counter Current. This then dipped southwards causing it in turn to interfere with the west flowing South Equatorial Ocean Current. All this occurred months ago with the result that had possibly caused these currents and counter currents to dip down into deeper ocean depths. A distorted El Nino effect had resulted and the energy of the storm had gradually built up over several months culminating in the present anomaly of electrostatic and magnetic effects within the hurricane-like conditions.

'I see,' said Fiona with a measure of excitement in her voice, 'and will this ship have to fly into the storm?'

'Most definitely not,' said Bulzezatna. 'The electrostatic and magnetic effects within it are unknown precisely and may cause interference with the ship's functions. Even we are wary of such effects. No, we shall cruise over the storm at an altitude of sixty miles and our sensors will do the rest. However it will be night time there and the storm's effects may prove to be quite a colourful spectacle even for me.'

Fiona's face went from an initial disappointment to one of excitement as Bulzezatna spoke.

'I shall look forward to it,' she said.

'How long will we be over the storm,' asked Brian?

'At a height of sixty miles and travelling at 8,000mph I imagine no more than a few minutes. Perhaps five minutes at the most,' said the captain.

'Wow,' exclaimed Fiona.

Ashley had to smile as he thought that it would also have been Simon's reaction all those years ago.

'I believe the buffet table is now ready for us to serve ourselves,' said Bulzezatna as she began to stand up.

Ashley and the captain walked side by side down the hall and began to help themselves to the food. Ashley was surprised at the amount that Bulzezatna piled upon her plate before returning to their table. She had chosen from the section of dishes that were not sweetened like the Yaztraka which was Ashley's favourite. Captain Bulzezatna seemed to prefer the savoury and slightly bland dishes. Ashley remembered that Jazzatnit also had a similar taste. Perhaps the mature Oannes palate had a more conservative preference.

By now all the others were familiar with the Oannes dishes and knew which choices to avoid. Fortunately Bizzony and Trozbit were not among the dishes displayed. But Milsony was there and Ashley took a bit. Fiona was adventurous and put some on her plate but made a face when she tasted it and pushed it to one side. The captain saw this but kept her head down as if concentrating on her food. Ashley however noticed the smile at the corners of her lips. She was being polite because that is what all Oannes are.

The meal concluded but they all stayed at the table. Bulzezatna also remained with them and Ashley noted that she paid special attention to everything Fiona said. Fiona was in the first quarter of her life while Bulzezatna at 234 years of age was near her last. And yet Ashley saw a compatibility of interests between them. Could Fiona's spirit of adventure see her follow a new career in space? Bulzezatna picked up Ashley's thoughts and conveyed her own back to him. All Ashley could do was smile in return. He would see where Bulzezatna's grooming might lead. It would be Fiona's choice in the end as to the course she followed.

They all finally left and went to their cabins for a rest with the knowledge that Zanos would rouse them prior to exit from the Davis Sea. That would be in about three hour's time. With their full bellies an afternoon nap seemed a very welcome option.

Ashley and Tania lay together on the single twin snuggled cosily together. Tania had her head on the upper part of Ashley's outstretched arm while hers was folded neatly underneath with her elbow digging lightly into Ashley's chest. Their free arms were loosely around each other.

'Comfortable?' asked Ashley.

'Not quite, but good enough,' she replied and shuffled to a slightly better position.

They exchanged thoughts; pleasant thoughts about their future; and his plan for Nazmos.

'I like that,' whispered Tania, 'then at least we shall have those ten years at home together.'

'They may not like it,' responded Ashley, 'but that is how I want it to be.'

'Are you afraid then?'

'You know I am but not for me,' he said.

'I know, you don't want me to be on my own.'

'No I don't because you will have the sadness and not me.'

'Will you be able to see me?' she asked.

'I think so. I hope so. And that will be my only consolation.'

'Oh Ash,' conveyed Tania, 'maybe it will be alright. What did Gozmanot see?'

'Perhaps it will. I would like to feel that you are prepared,' he said. 'I don't think Gozmanot saw the minute detail beyond the fact of the vanquishing of Zarama the fiery dragon in the sky. I shall do everything in my power to survive the ordeal.'

'Yes darling I know you will,' whispered Tania as she pressed her lips to his. He felt her moist cheek against his and thought how wonderful it was to love.

They were silent then and just clung to each other as they drifted into their own troubled sleep.

Tania awoke first but didn't shift position. She looked at her sleeping husband and wondered at the innocent looking youthful face. He was still her handsome husband and always would be. She tried to fix this moment in her memory for the day he might not be near. There was a unique calm about him that pervaded through to her. Oh how she loved him and how much she would miss him should he be taken from her.

She thought back to the emotion she felt when she'd first laid eyes on him in the Navigation Pub. The pain had welled up in her chest right where her heart was. It was an emotional pain that had a sweetness of its own. It was the pain that came with love at first sight. He seemed not to notice her at all then and even paid little attention when she helped her mum in the shop. And then one day she knew. That was the best day of her life. They rubbed the tips of their noses together as a normal thing between them but it was when they laughed at it and he hugged her fiercely that she knew. His emotion of love came through to her and had done so ever since. And their love had grown and grown till it evolved into this wonderful companionship they now shared. It was their most prized possession because they belonged to each other.

Recently that pang of emotional pain had recurred inside her chest but this time there was sadness attached. A sadness of possible loss; a sadness filled with anxiety. A sadness that said she must roam the earth alone with only her memories for comfort. Perhaps if she then went to live on Nazmos she might feel closer to him.

Her thoughts were cut short as Ashley stirred and opened his eyes. Seeing Tania still snug against him he pulled her closer and their lips met and lingered together for what seemed like ages.

'I love you,' he conveyed telepathically.

'I know,' was her similar reply as she nibbled at his lower lip.

They cuddled for another long while communicating constantly until Zanos interrupted with the information that the sea exit would occur in twenty minutes.

They met the others in the corridor and made their way to the control room. In moments the view panels lightened from black to pale green and then suddenly the brightness of the sunshine was upon them. 520-Green was on the surface of the Davis Sea; but not for long. As it broke free of the clinging water tension Ashley felt a slight tremor under his feet. But then the smoothness of the ascent through the air took over and the sea horizon seemed to retract away from them. Within moments the curvature of the Earth became apparent as did the blue darkness of the sky. From below and to their right came the glowing brightness of the Antarctic icy landscape. The ship now turned away from the land and began its course towards the central Pacific Ocean.

'The storm will be in its night period,' conveyed Bulzezatna, 'so the spectacle of electric activity should be quite brilliant. At least I expect it to be so. The wait will not be long – perhaps half an hour at best.'

The ship continued to rise higher and to accelerate away from Antarctica towards what seemed like darkness on the distant horizon ahead. At sixty miles altitude the ship steadied having also acquired its forward cruising speed of 8,000mph. There was nothing but ocean beneath them now and this too soon disappeared into the dark flush of Earth's night. For now though not a cloud was to be seen below them.

Zanos conveyed to the captain that the ship needed to increase altitude by another ten miles to be safe from the storm's magnetic effects. Obviously information on the severity of the storm had been relayed to Zanos from Anztarza's monitoring system. The captain handed full control to Zanos to take whatever action was deemed necessary. Zanos could respond to any emergency instantly and without any communication delay.

Soon the effects of the storm which was visible on the distant horizon became evident. Bright flashes illuminated the massive columns of clouds that seemed to tower upwards. They are massively magnificent thought Fiona as she looked on mesmerised by the scene unfolding below the speeding ship. There was a sort of malevolence in the scene and fear flitted briefly through Ashley's mind. He looked at the captain and Zanos was instructed to take the ship up to an eighty mile altitude.

They were over the storm now and it sparkled in multicoloured flashes like some great firework display. The colours ranged from shades of yellow, orange, red and blue. There was lightning everywhere with bright flashes going from cloud to cloud and column to column illuminating them briefly before another took over.

Ashley looked at the structure of the storm and the fear returned. This was much more ominous than the one they had witnessed over Africa when Simon was with him. That was spectacular too but was nothing compared to this. For an instant Ashley thought he glimpsed a pair of eyes peering up at them and he felt threatened. Bulzezatna looked across at him and read these thoughts and conveyed an understanding. She was amazed that Ashley could feel so. But she liked him that much more for his down to earth attitudes. Not an ounce of pride or self aggrandisement presided within this human despite all the gifts he possessed and what he had achieved. He behaved just like any ordinary Oannes person.

Fiona however just enjoyed the spectacle and gaped in wonder at the colourful sight. The flashes of light occurred simultaneously from everywhere across the panorama of the storm. The colours were phasing from orange to blue and white and then repeating constantly. Some were like balls of light while others had the characteristic jagged lightning streak shape. What was amazing was the way these arched across the billowing columns of cloud as if trying to reach upwards.

They were near the centre of the storm when suddenly the ship juddered and jumped upwards. The acceleration approached close to twice gravity level for a brief moment. Zanos had responded to something and had taken 520-Green up to an altitude of two hundred miles. From here the extent of the storm was evident and only now did Ashley feel they were safe. Had some premonition caused him to fear earlier?

Zanos conveyed that a very powerful magnetic field was emanating from the eye of the storm and the ship had very nearly intersected this field. Had they done so then the effect on the ship's systems might have had serious consequences. The monitoring experiment was considered concluded and all data collected was sent on to Anztarza. As such 520-Green could now head towards its starship rendezvous point.

Although Sarah and Brian had been thrilled by the Pacific storm spectacle Fiona was the one glowing with wonder.

'That is a sight I did not ever expect to see and it is one that will stay in my memory forever,' said Fiona to the captain.

'Yes it was certainly quite a sight even for me,' conveyed Bulzezatna. 'And sometimes beautiful can be dangerous,' she added.

She was referring to the ship's evasive action. But also advising Fiona to be wary of things unknown to her no matter how adventurous the aspect may seem.

She then conveyed to her new visitors all the details of the journey time to rendezvous point. The million mile distance from Earth that must be attained before the neutron generators could operate.

520-Green was now headed away from the Earth and Sun such that the darkened sky ahead was highlighted by the brilliance of the universe stars in the view panels around and above them.

'Like the beautiful lights of a big city at night,' thought Fiona.

The Milky Way was clearly visible like a brightly lit pathway that crossed from one side of the sky to the other. All gazed in wonder at the sight displayed in such glorious fashion. Even though Ashley, Tania and the others had seen it all before they could not help but admire the view as if for the first time. Space was always an amazing and exciting sight.

'This is so beautiful,' said Sarah as she held Brian's hand.

'Yes,' said Ashley, 'it is one thing to imagine the vastness of space in your minds eye but it goes beyond your wildest expectation when you actually see it like this spread out in front of you.'

'Oh yes,' said Fiona, 'and if this is so beautiful then can you imagine what heaven must be like.'

Captain Bulzezatna listened and said nothing. Having seen into Fiona's mind she knew her to be very religious with a firm faith conviction. This was something Bulzezatna and all Oannes understood as a human trait that had been fostered for millennia. But it remained as a simple observation for them and nothing more.

Yet Ashley's contact with Gozmanot had brought a new aspect into focus and a curiosity had arisen to find out more. And there was the mystery of that first communication from the one called Philip Stevens after he had deceased. Then there was what Ashley called his 'inner voice' giving him advice. Korizazit a Nazmos council member had also accidentally received the gift of inner voice from Ashley. The Oannes were never one to reject ideas but at the same time tried to seek logical explanations for all such phenomena.

Ashley pondered all this and wondered if Fiona had some role to play in the future mindset of the Oannes people in general. He thought about it but could not sense anything. His inner voice was silent and had been for quite some time.

They all spent nearly an hour in the control room. The captain had shown her new visitors how to magnify the images they saw through the view panels and Brian was over the moon picking out distant stars for a closer look. He had always been interested in astronomy as a teacher but this now opened up a whole new field for him. He was ecstatic and Sarah was pleased for him.

Ashley looked at his wristwatch and was surprised to see it was quite a bit after six pm. The captain conveyed that the ship's acceleration would increase marginally by a quarter and should not prove inconvenient to normal activity. It would however reduce the travel time to about three hours for when the neutron generators could operate.

The evening meal was due to be served up in the dining hall at seven pm so the captain suggested they all make their way there. She would not be joining them but would expect them back in the control room for the neutron generators' spectacle. Zanos would inform them prior to the event.

The dining hall was quite full but a table had been kept free for the Earth visitors. The fare was as usual and Ashley realised that he was quite hungry as were the others. But so much had been going on that no one had felt it till now. They were also thirsty and the jugs of Wazu and orange drink soon emptied and were refilled.

After the meal they sat around talking about the events of the day and surprisingly the storm did not feature as much as the starry sky did. It just went to show what a magnificent display existed which people on Earth hardly got to see. Finally they all trooped to their cabins for a rest. After a couple of hours Zanos prompted a return to the control room for the neutron generators' firing. It was now 9:35pm by Ashley's watch.

In the control room recliners were set out for them for an easier overhead view. They did not have long to wait. What looked like a starburst of sparks seemed to emanate from a point high above the overhead view panel and this was repeated at regular short intervals again and again. The spectacle was quite brilliant for first time viewers though Ashley still found it an exhilarating experience. He thought of Simon and the 'wow' expression he always mouthed on such occasions. This time it was Fiona's turn to do the same. And yet there was no sensation of the tremendous acceleration that the ship underwent. Then all was normal again and the myriad of stars returned to view in their normal un-twinkling brilliance. Ashley knew then that the ship had attained its cruising velocity which Zanos confirmed as 100,000mps; more than half the speed of light and all in a matter of a few minutes.

Zanos conveyed the ship's cruising velocity for the benefit of Fiona, Sarah and Brian which meant a journey time of 25 hours to cover the nine billion miles to rendezvous point. But the spaceship occupants would in fact experience it as a journey of only twenty one hours due to the Time Dilation or slowing of time by a factor of 1.185. Zanos would monitor the true elapsed time with a specially shielded clock monitor.

It was now a simple matter of time for the journey to be completed. But in that time Fiona, Sarah and Brian had been promised a tour of the ship and the captain had not forgotten and commissioned Rubandiz her First Deputy to do the honours. Ashley and the others decided to go along just as a matter of interest. They might see something different. It was now close to 10:00pm and the tour was not expected to take longer than an hour at most. The control room views were still fascinating but they could come back to that anytime they wished.

Zanos conveyed a layout plan of the entire ship including its overall dimensions and number of decks. With this in mind Rubandiz took them first to the cargo and shuttle bays. They walked up to the large bay doors and Rubandiz explained their size and width allowing entry for all shuttle sizes. Even the smaller private spaceships could be accommodated he conveyed.

Ashley could see that Fiona communicated her questions directly to Rubandiz and he responded in turn. Telepathy was quick, simple and efficient.

Rubandiz was thorough and he took the group to all the facilities on board apart from the two power plant decks one and six. They even entered the electrostatic outfitting room and he got Fiona. Sarah and Brian to each try one on. Sarah asked what her head scarf was for and he explained with visual imaging. Both she and Fiona laughed at the view they got.

They were then taken along the wide corridor to a room where a section of the ship's magnetic protective system could be viewed. Rubandiz explained the necessity for the powerful fifty mile wide Van Allen type magnetic field around the ship when travelling in free space. He used his authority as the ship's First Deputy to thought command an inner door to open. Inside he went to great lengths explaining the workings of the large twenty feet diameter central pillar that went from floor to ceiling. He explained that inside this was another core of composite material ten feet in diameter that also extended the full height of the ship. Around this central core were a myriad of complex woven coils and counter-coils that generated the massive magnetic field so essential for the safety of the ship's inhabitants in the fierce environment of outer space.

Fiona, Sarah and Brian asked many questions and Rubandiz answered them all in an easy and encouraging manner; via telepathically of course. The Oannes are a polite and patient people and no question no matter how abstract was ever considered out of context. Sarah and Brian both thought that Rubandiz would have made an excellent teacher. It takes one to know one.

The tour took over an hour and when they returned to the control room Bulzezatna asked her new visitors if they had seen enough. Brian replied for them and thanked her and said it had been interesting and most informative. Rubandiz had been an excellent tour guide.

There was still plenty to see and Ashley asked the captain to point out the position of Raznat in the sky above them. Bulzezatna conveyed to all their minds where to look and it was easy for them to acquire the necessary magnification to see Raznat's glowing reddish ball. Fiona was amazed at how easy it had been but then she began to search for Nazmos without success. Bulzezatna came up behind her and put a hand on her shoulder and led her mind to where Nazmos should be. When she finally did see it, it appeared as a very small dull crescent shaped object. Further magnification did not help as it only increased the fuzzy appearance. Still it was exciting for her to look across six light years to see their destination.

Ashley noted that since the neutron generators had operated the colour of the stars above them had changed towards a slightly bluish tint. He pointed this out to Fiona, Sarah and Brian; and Brian said he understood and had expected it. But Ashley explained it all for Fiona and Sarah's benefit. It was simply the Doppler Effect of their velocity towards those stars. This caused the light waves reaching them to appear at a shorter wavelength than normal. Brian added that travelling at more than half the speed of light felt no different than before.

It was now past 11:00pm and Ashley communicated that it was well past his bedtime. The others all agreed and Bulzezatna conveyed that the ship would commence a simulated night period so that all could get a good rest. It was agreed that it had been a long and exciting day and the beds in their cabins seemed to beckon invitingly. Breakfast would be after 9:00am.

Ashley and Tania conveyed a goodnight to the others as they entered their cabin. Sleep was not top of their agenda and they frolicked in their sleep tank before eventually retiring to their own beds quite exhausted.

It was close to 10:00am when Ashley and Tania went to the dining hall for their breakfast. Rachel and Margaret were already there with Katy and Robin. Tania got mugs of tea for Ashley and herself before sitting down and beginning their morning chatter.

It was while Ashley was on his second toast with marmalade that Fiona came in accompanied by the captain.

'I was up at eight and went to the control room to see the universe sights,' she said. 'I didn't want to disturb you sleepy heads so I kept nice and quiet.' She meant telepathically of course.

Captain Bulzezatna smiled at this as Ashley concentrated on his toast. The captain conveyed that she herself had not entered the control room till quite late which was normal for her. Her deputies were usually there before her anyway. Besides Zanos really ran the ship on its own. Ashley noted that no gender was ascribed to Zanos. It was just a part of the ship's function albeit a very important one.

Breakfast was a pleasant sequence of events with Sarah and Brian coming in at about 10:30am.

'We must have been really tired out from yesterday,' said Sarah, 'I just wasn't able to wake up properly this morning.'

Both were quite hungry and helped themselves to the continental type breakfast items presented. Brian preferred plain bread with butter to which he added cheese, jam or marmalade. Sarah preferred her bread as toast before she buttered it and added her preference which was usually just marmalade; and with plenty of tea to go with it.

With breakfast completed they all followed the captain back to the control room and spent an hour there just looking at the stars and trying to determine which constellations were where. Zanos of course was always available for help. Eventually all went back to their cabins for TV recreation. Zanos could call up all sorts of programs including games and the latest Earth News bulletins available.

A lunch meal was served at 3:00pm which all attacked heartily after which they returned to their cabins for an afternoon siesta. It was becoming a welcome habit especially after a big lunch. Their next meal was likely to be aboard the starship 9110-Red.

It was just before 6:00pm that Zanos conveyed that the neutron generators would operate in fifteen minutes and the captain would welcome them in the control room to witness the spectacle again.

Ashley, Tania and all the others trooped back to the control room but only Fiona, Sarah and Brian settled horizontally on the recliners. Ashley stood close as he wanted to see the expressions on the faces of his nieces, especially Fiona when they first caught sight of the starship.

At 6:10pm the spaceship 520-Green rotated about and the stars disappeared as the distant Sun came into view overhead but only as a very bright large star. At 6:15pm precisely the neutron generators operated by firing repeatedly over a period of several minutes with the usual brilliant display of sparkling fury. Even though the distant Sun was overhead the display was still quite spectacular and drew the proverbial 'wow' exclamation from Fiona. Sarah and Brian smiled delightedly at each other as the grip of their hands tightened. All was over when no further sparks appeared and slowly 520-Green rotated again to its former position.

Zanos then conveyed that the starship 9110-Red was ten thousand miles distant and should be visible in the left side view panel with magnification. And so it was. It appeared at first as a distant silvery inconsequent star, but with magnification it grew to impressive proportions. This time Fiona, Sarah and Brian stood open mouthed as they stared at its sleek beauty. Ashley smiled for starships never failed to impress. The red stripe down 9110-Red's visible side imparted a certain air of majesty in a class of its own. Zanos conveyed the starship's overall dimensions but Ashley had already briefed his nieces about it including the interior general layout.

This view soon disappeared from sight as 520-Green rotated once again. The spaceship needed to decelerate so that it could enter into a parking loop not too far from the starship. It acquired this within half and hour and at a distance of 150 miles that ran parallel to the length of the starship.

There were three other spaceships at various parking loops around the starship and at varying distances. Ashley could see at least one shuttle approaching the starship from the opposite side and as he and the others watched it disappeared from view. Bulzezatna read their thoughts and conveyed that the shuttle had probably entered one of the starship's many airlock entrances around the cargo platform level. It would be their turn soon to begin ferrying their own passengers across as soon as arrangements were completed; probably sometime in the next two hours.

In fact it was just two hours later that Ashley and co. were aboard the starship and being greeted by Captain Natazlat in the central control room area. From the moment they had got into the gold electrostatic suits on 520-Green to boarding the shuttles and then making the gravity-free trek across to the starship, Sarah and Brian said it was an experience they would always remember. There had been anxiety at first but Zanos had allayed this along with any feelings of gravity-free space nausea. There had been a moment of humour aboard the shuttle during the transfer when Sarah's headscarf had slipped slightly causing a few strands of her hair to break free. It looked quite comical before she quickly grabbed it all and pushed it back in place.

Captain Natazlat was pleased to see Ashley and Tania and the others after Fiona, Sarah and Brian were introduced. Brief Sewas were exchanged and again Ashley and the others were invited to have all their meals with the captain in her quarters. Ashley gratefully accepted and expressed his thanks to the captain.

The captain smiled at this formality and her affection for Ashley grew even further. How could he act with such humility when what he was about to achieve was so immense and with such a monumental impact. A whole world would change for the better but to this human it was just another common event in his life. He had been given these tremendous gifts from infancy but it had not made him proud or conceited. He just treated all of it as commonplace and took his gifts for granted. He had been chosen just as easily as another could have been. He considered himself fortunate but the burden of the final task against Zarama was to be a great one. Could he survive it?

Natazlat knew of his thoughts of doubt which made her affection border on love. If she as an Oannes could feel so for a human then there was great hope for the two peoples to integrate one day in the distant future. Certainly a great hope.

It was while she was mulling over these thoughts that Brajam and Niztukan entered the control room. They beamed with pleasure when they saw that Ashley had arrived aboard. They had come to personally give their news to the captain but seeing Ashley and his family threw them off course for a bit. However after the brief Sewa and greetings were completed they quickly conveyed their piece of information before turning their full attention back towards Ashley, Tania and the others.

Ashley introduced Fiona, Sarah and Brian to Brajam and Niztukan as a matter of course but the two made a special point of communicating with them. Ashley thought this a most polite gesture. But knowing what Oannes were like this was not unusual.

'And how is the adventurous Niztukan faring with his daring neutron shield surveys?' asked Ashley.

'Very well thank you,' responded a smiling Niztukan, 'and it is nice of you to enquire. However I no longer perform that task; it is the responsibility of another. I do miss the excitement of the low pass but I have a much more interesting duty now.'

Ashley waited but Niztukan added nothing further. The Oannes were never ones to brag or boast about the importance of their task in hand and it was Brajam who clarified about Niztukan's duties.

'Niztukan is now on my team and has been so for the last ten years,' said Brajam looking towards his colleague. 'He had some interesting ideas which our team have been working on for some time now. Basically Niztukan's idea was to do with the possibility of increasing the power output of the starship's current reversing neutron generators. With further minor changes we believe a ten percent increase in their performance is available. Niztukan spent five years attached to the 4110-Silver project before coming to me with his ideas.'

Apparently Niztukan had volunteered for service on 4110-Silver's redevelopment and was attached there. He enjoyed the thrill of the new development and seeing what was being implemented put forward some ideas of his own. But these had not been considered appropriate at least not for the planned 100 FTL velocity planned for that ship. He had been with Zakatanz on 8110-Gold when it had been limited to 600 FTL. He felt that this limit could be increased and subsequently communicated his idea to Brajam who immediately saw its potential; with Ashley in mind of course. The end result had been to apply the necessary modifications to 9110-Red and 8110-Gold. Both captains had agreed for their ships to get this enhancement but time had been the issue. Both captains had desired that the modification work be completed before Ashley made the journey to stabilise Platwuz in its new orbit.

The work had begun on both starships ten years ago and the information that Brajam now conveyed to Captain Natazlat was that 8110-Red now had the capacity to slow successfully from a velocity of 680 FTL and certainly no more than 700 FTL maximum. Less would be the preferred option.

Captain Natazlat had digested this and beamed a look towards Ashley. The look held all the ingredients of begging a favour.

Ashley laughed out aloud and walked towards the captain. He put out his hand to her and she gripped it firmly though still appearing uncertain.

'I will do my best,' said Ashley in his most serious tone, 'but only if you grant me a favour in return.'

'And what may I do for you Ashley,' she said quickly though with a degree of confusion and also mild puzzlement.

'What could this human want that he does not already have' was her secreted thought.

'Could you please arrange for the Yaztraka to be just a little bit sweeter,' said Ashley with his face breaking out it his widest possible smile.

Captain Natazlat's smile was so broad that she nearly laughed out loud. Oannes did not have that trait and instead emitted a couple of cough-like sounds. However her whole body developed a vibratory shake as if the unexpressed laughter was somewhere deep inside her desperate to get out.

The expression 'laugh and the world will laugh with you' was certainly true. Within seconds Ashley had broken out in peels of laughter as did Tania and the others. Even Brajam and Niztukan saw the humorous side and grinned broadly with just a few coughs.

'Your humour surpasses all understanding,' said Natazlat, 'and I admire you for it.'

An emotion of deep affection came across to Ashley and he recognised it as someone bestowing her love upon him. He had done nothing but act normal and yet they seemed to love him because of it. He felt exhilarated by the feeling and conveyed this to Tania. She beamed with pride that her Ashley could be loved so.

When all had calmed down again Ashley conveyed that he would certainly meet the captain's wishes for a near 700 FTL velocity.

Captain Natazlat beamed by seeming to stand taller and added her own bit of humour.

'I shall boast to Captain Zakatanz that a new power drove my starship to its record velocity. And when he asks me what that was I shall proudly announce that it was Yaztraka power.'

This time it was Ashley's turn to laugh aloud and the others soon joined in.

Captain Natazlat then turned to Fiona and conveyed a private message to her.

'Thank you Captain,' said Fiona aloud, 'that is very kind of you.'

Ashley's instinct told him what had just occurred. Obviously Captain Bulzezatna had communicated with her friend Captain Natazlat about Fiona's interest in space and all things pertaining thereto. Natazlat had simply conveyed an offer to help in any way she could.

She picked up Ashley thoughts and briefly nodded in his direction. 'Nothing gets past this human' she thought.

It was now close to 9:00pm GMT and the captain suggested they all go and settle into their allocated accommodation as she and her admin crew had much work to do. The chief ministers' spacecraft had just arrived on station and they would be aboard the starship within the hour. Other matters had also to be attended to and it was estimated that the starship should get underway in approximately six hours from now. Zanos would confirm this closer to departure.

'All your meals during the journey are to be taken here with me as you will all be my special guests,' said Natazlat to Ashley and the group, 'so if you return here in about two hours a meal will be ready for us.'

Ashley liked the way she said 'us'.

'Can we have a walk around the habitation platform?' asked Fiona of the captain but this time in telepathic mode.

'Perhaps if you could delay that till everyone arriving is properly housed,' conveyed the captain back to Fiona, 'then I shall personally accompany you around. Once we are underway and cruising at our best velocity may be a good time.'

'Yes of course,' replied Fiona. 'And thank you that would be excellent.'

'In the meantime perhaps Ashley who knows the ship well could give you any information about the starship that you wish to ask about,' conveyed Captain Natazlat in open mind mode.

Ashley nodded his agreement and also indicated that Zanos would provide additional information that he could not provide. And so began a communication of information to Fiona which the others also picked up. The information always contained images to illustrate a description. The bits that Ashley was not sure about were referred to Zanos. Zanos always came back with a detailed reply along with visual images of the location being discussed. Fiona was surprised when Zanos anticipated some thing she wished to know and gave her the answer before she had actually worded the intended question. Ashley clarified that Zanos had the ability to anticipate the needs of those in its monitoring care.

Back in their apartment Brian and Sarah discussed the teaching aspect and said wouldn't it be wonderful if the education system on Earth could have just one aspect of Zanos. Visual information tended to be imprinted on the human memory better than normal verbal dialogue teaching.

And so the time passed and they all returned to the captain's central area for the promised meal. This was laid out soon after they arrived and Ashley knew that the Yaztraka would have been sweetened a bit extra for him. He had meant it as a joke then just as a tease but the Oannes captain would have read more into it. A desire had been expressed by none other than Ashley and so must be met of course.

In fact there were two dishes of Yaztraka and Natazlat smilingly pointed out the one that was specially sweetened. Ashley nodded his thanks but took the normal one first. He conveyed that the extra sweet one would serve as his dessert. Natazlat smiled and nodded and Ashley gave her a polite bow in acknowledgement. Here were two people who liked, respected and understood one another. Tania picked up on the theme with pride for the relationship between these two. She admired the captain immensely and it was great to know of her feelings for Ashley. She felt slightly guilty in her possessiveness of her husband; yet she wanted to share his love with everyone. She wanted them to love him because she knew they could not take him from her. A chill entered her heart when she thought about Zarama and her mood changed.

Ashley's watch was showing 9:30pm but Zanos gave the correct Earth time as close to midnight. Ashley had not reset it after the trip from Earth but did so now. He conveyed this to the others and they showed surprise since they were not tired at all.

'Gosh,' said Brian 'does this mean we are younger by two and a half hours because of our speedy trip?'

'I suppose so,' said Ashley, 'but on the starship it will not be like that. The forward neutron shield protects us and all our atoms from any velocity effects so our clocks will remain correct.'

'How long will our journey to Nazmos take?' asked Fiona.

'Well if Ashley gives us his generous assistance,' cut in the captain with a broad smile, 'then we should make it to the Raznat system rendezvous in just four Earth days. That is a considerable improvement over the seven months it took us to reach here.'

'And when does our journey commence?' asked Brian.

'I believe there has been a delay as all passengers are not as yet aboard' said Natazlat. 'They then also have to be settled into their allotted accommodation which all takes time. Zanos will monitor the situation and confirm when all is ready. One does not hurry important people. I expect another six hours at the very least. So have a good rest tonight and by breakfast in the morning we shall probably have begun our journey. Breakfast will be served here from 9:30am. Come when it is convenient.'

Ashley knew that the captain was referring to the chief ministers and their assistants as the important people; and they most certainly were.

With the meal successfully completed Ashley's watch showed the time as 1:00am. He decided that it was time for bed though he did not feel particularly tired. Tomorrow he must apply his telekinetic push on the starship and thought a good rest before would be beneficial. Besides Tania seemed to have certain ideas and who was he to object.

'Well in that case,' said Ashley picking up on the captain's theme, 'I shall bid you all a very good night and hope to see you in the morning at breakfast.'

'Yes,' said Brian and Sarah together, 'goodnight and see you at breakfast.'

'Thank you captain for all your consideration,' said Fiona, 'I look forward to this trip. Just knowing about the journey is like an adventure for me. Goodnight to all.'

Captain Natazlat smiled at this and nodded her appreciation. She must get to know more about this human person she thought.

Ashley and Tania led the way out onto the open platform and all filed slowly across to their nearby apartments. Once inside Tania suggested they relax in the sleep tank before going to bed. Ashley smiled at the suggestion for he knew exactly what his wife really had in mind.

They spent a leisurely hour lazing naked in the sleep tank. Excitement grew and they decided to get out and dry themselves before snuggling together into one of the single beds. It was some considerable time later when they fell into an exhausted though contented sleep.

Captain Natazlat welcomed Ashley and the others as each trooped in for breakfast. She conveyed that the starship had finally begun its journey towards Raznat and that Ashley's telekinetic effort need not commence for quite a while yet. She indicated a possible time frame of two hours though left it entirely at Ashley's convenience. She smiled at Ashley as she conveyed this.

Ashley now remembered the book incident in Aberporth when he was demonstrating his telekinetic gift to his nieces and Brian and decided to share this with the captain. But he did so as a private communication along with the visual of what occurred.

'It was in my mind that the book should move,' conveyed Ashley, 'but before I could apply any voluntary push effort upon it the book began to move. It was as if someone or something was fulfilling my wish. In twenty two years I expected that my telekinetic power would have increased somewhat but this is a completely new development for me; albeit a pleasant one.'

Captain Natazlat smiled and nodded. Then she went into open mode so that all could receive her especially Zanos, and asked Ashley what he wished to do with regard to the starship's acceleration.

Ashley took the hint and repeated his earlier thoughts regarding the book demonstration for the benefit of all before adding, 'I should like to will this starship to accelerate gradually and uniformly to a velocity of 200 FTL and be held at that velocity. If this happens then I would like to check what effect the effort has had upon me physically. Of course Zanos must be in full control at all times.'

'On past occasions your telekinetic push effort was not begun until the starship had attained 4 FTL velocity. At the present moment in our journey we have not yet exceeded light velocity,' conveyed the captain. 'Do you wish to wait till later or is it your desire to commence your telekinetic acceleration as of now?'

'I think now would be good for me if you approve,' conveyed Ashley.

'I do not like experimentation Ashley,' said Natazlat now in full captain mode. 'I will never endanger my starship. However you have pushed this ship before and I am willing to trust your judgement and skill on this. Please proceed cautiously as you have said but up to 50 FTL as a first stage.'

'Thank you Captain,' said Ashley with full respect in his voice.

He then put down his toast and finished chewing what was in his mouth. This he followed by a sip of tea and an audible swallow.

Ashley closed his eyes and visualised the inner face of the starship's neutron shield. Then keeping his mind open he willed it to move at a steady safe acceleration until the ship had attained 50 FTL. Opening his eyes he smiled at the captain and said,' It is done. Perhaps Zanos could confirm to us on the ship's acceleration status.'

The starship seemed to continue on as smoothly as before and no apparent change was felt by its passengers or crew.

Captain Natazlat was staring at the far wall and it was obvious she was in deep telepathic mode with someone. Suddenly she broke out in a smile and looked at Ashley first and then the others there.

'It seems that acceleration has increased marginally over and above what the impulse motors are supplying,' she said. 'Zanos will keep me informed of progress. Now let us proceed with our meal.'

Five minutes later Captain Natazlat paused in her eating and conveyed to all that the starship had exceeded light velocity well ahead of its normal schedule and was rapidly approaching the 2 FTL mark. All this was according to the information that Zanos was continually supplying as per her instructions. She then said aloud that she would not interrupt again until the meal was finished.

Half an hour later Ashley had finished his third mug of tea since the start of breakfast and now placed the empty mug on the table and raised an eyebrow at the smiling captain.

'I am anxious to know of our progress,' said an impatient sounding Ashley.

'And so are we,' said Tania and Fiona together.

The captain bided her time before she said in her most serious voice,' All is going well.' But there was a hint of a smile lurking just in front of her facial webs.

Then she looked directly at Ashley and added, 'All is going well according to your plan Ashley.'

'Yes, yes,' interrupted Tania and Fiona again together, 'but please how well is well?'

Ashley remained silent but smiling for he had read the captain's mind and the captain knew it. After all she had allowed it with a prompt.

'Well,' said the captain in a slow paced manner, 'as of a minute ago this starship just exceeded 22 FTL velocity. Zanos predicts that with current acceleration we shall be at 50 FTL in another thirty five minutes.'

Again Ashley looked at the captain and conveyed a suggestion.

After a brief pause the captain looked keenly at Ashley and said, 'Yes, I agree. Please proceed.'

Ashley nodded and again closed his eyes to better visualise the inner face of the ship's neutron shield. He willed for the starship to achieve 695FTL velocity as rapidly as it was safely possible for the structural integrity of the ship and the normal gravity comfort of its passengers and crew. By keeping an open mind this was also conveyed to Zanos, the captain and all aboard.

Within a minute Zanos conveyed to the captain that the ship's acceleration had increased exponentially to a level that had brought the habitation platforms the closest that they had ever been to the neutron shield. This indicated an acceleration of close to a thousand times the gravity on Nazmos. Zanos also conveyed that normal gravity levels in all parts of the platforms were being maintained.

Captain Natazlat looked at Ashley with a degree of alarm but Ashley simply smiled back.

'Don't be concerned Captain,' he said, 'it will all be done in a safe manner. This is new also for me but I am confident that the giver of my gifts has a purpose in all of this.'

Ashley had received encouragement from his inner voice that all would go as planned.

Captain Natazlat looked away and Ashley could see that she was plainly concerned for her ship and at the pace of events. It was like going too fast towards the unknown.

It was now Ashley's turn to convey an emotion of peacefulness and calm to everyone in the room. The captain then looked at her chief guest and conveyed a request.

'Yes Captain,' said Ashley. 'I will remain here with you until maximum velocity is attained. What does Zanos estimate?'

'Three hours,' conveyed the captain.

'Then perhaps we have time enough for another hot mug of tea,' said Ashley smiling.

'That will be your fourth mug this morning,' said Tania. 'Where is it all going?'

'Don't ask,' said Ashley with a chuckle.

'Perhaps a little portion of extra sweetened Yaztraka?' asked Natazlat with a smile.

It was nice to see the captain back in her usual demeanour. She had been genuinely concerned for the wellbeing of her ship and its passengers.

Tania brought Ashley his mug of tea and sat down beside him.

After a while Ashley conveyed to the captain that he had a query for Zanos. The captain read Ashley's mind and conveyed back that she too would like to know.

Zanos had anticipated the query and responded with a force figure that was quite beyond Ashley's wildest reckoning.

Zanos conveyed that on the occasion of twenty two years ago the telekinetic force corresponding to a final push level factor of seventy two had been applied by Ashley. This had accelerated the starship progressively in stages to 600¼ FTL over a period of four hours.

'A power level comparison please,' conveyed the captain back to Zanos.

'The current acceleration indicates that the power impulse level being applied is 876 times that of the previous occasion,' conveyed Zanos. 'This is enough power to take the starship to 2566 FTL and maintain it at that level.'

Captain Natazlat looked at Ashley in alarm.

And Ashley too looked rather surprised but his inner voice for the second time today said that all would be well and the starship would not exceed 695 FTL.

He conveyed this to the captain and she seemed to regain her composure but instructed Zanos that acceleration levels be communicated to her every five minutes.

It was only after 500 FTL had been attained that Zanos conveyed that a gradual lessening of the ship's acceleration had commenced. The power level had reduced by 5%.

Then at 600 FTL velocity this had reduced by a further 10%.

At 650 FTL the power level was down to 50% and finally after the estimated three hours plus twenty minutes Zanos conveyed that the starship had stabilised at a constant cruising velocity of 695 FTL.

Zanos estimated time to Raznat parking location as four days.

Ashley looked at the captain and smiled broadly and received as broad a smile in return.

Tania and the others looked at Ashley and a common query of concern showed on their faces.

'How are you feeling darling?' Tania finally asked.

'Very detached,' replied Ashley to all. 'It is as though I've had nothing to do with the ship's acceleration. I don't feel the least bit tired or sleepy. And I'm not thirsty either.'

'Let us celebrate the occasion with a glass of Wazu,' said the captain. 'This is a great achievement.'

This time Rachel had a go at the Wazu and took two gentle sips before politely placing her glass back on the table. Ashley appreciated her gesture and gave her a telepathic pat on the back. Rachel acknowledged this and conveyed that it was an acquired taste and she would make more of an effort in future. Tania who was sitting beside her gave her a sideways hug. Ashley read something in this new resolve and guessed that Rachel and Margaret had some plan for themselves on Nazmos. He'd let time do the telling.

The next four days would be a matter of living a routine aboard the starship and Ashley wondered if Captain Rojazonto would come in 9632-Orange as one of the pickup spaceships. There would obviously be a fleet of ships sent out to ferry all two thousand passengers back to Nazmos. Somehow Ashley guessed that his group would be included on Rojazonto's passenger manifest.

A thought entered Ashley's mind. Could he simply will Zarama away like he had accelerated this starship? Or must he do more? His inner voice remained silent.

During the days that followed the captain was true to her word and gave her guests a tour of not only the habitation platform but also of the cargo and food growing levels. With the exception of Ashley of course who remained within the zone close to the central area. Ashley was not certain whether or not to move away from a fairly central location in case this disturbed the force being exerted on the neutron shield. Better to be safe than sorry he thought. Also staying behind with him were Tania and Rachel.

On the tour Fiona was never far from the captain's side and the two seemed to get on well. Later when they all returned Ashley had an instinctive thought about Fiona but pushed it to the back of his mind. He'd received a similar feeling about Rachel and Margaret years ago and so far nothing had matured.

The future was always vague which is what made its prospect so interesting.

'Whatever was going to be would be,' he thought.

CHAPTER 18

New Orbits

January 2039

Once again I found myself standing in the courtyard of Jazzatnit and Zazfrapiz's spacious house and I felt very much at my ease and quite content. For here amongst my own family were Brazjaf, Muznant and their pretty daughter Farzant a coy twenty one year old.

It felt like old times with Muznant and Brazjaf here beside me and I realised only now how much I had missed their presence and companionship these last twenty two years. They had been my very first Oannes contact and had become very dear to me. I still sensed an emotional leaning from Muznant but now received something similar but stronger from their daughter Farzant. Her gaze had been constantly upon me from the moment of our meeting just a few hours ago.

In human terms Farzant was an impressionable teenager and I knew that she had been well and truly briefed by her parents about whom and what I was. I expect that after my mental regression contact with Gozmanot and subsequent telepathic transmission to all on Nazmos, I had attained a certain iconic status among the Oannes in general.

I knew that Oannes children become initiated into the Oannes psyche when they reach their fifteenth year followed by a period of extremely rapid mental development. Farzant was well past that stage and I felt I must make an effort to get to know her better. If she was anything like her mother then I looked forward to the prospect with joyous enthusiasm. There would be plenty of time for that as Brazjaf had conveyed that they intended to accompany me and my family group throughout the current visit.

'Ashley, Tania and all your family members, you are very welcome here,' came the telepathic message from Jazzatnit, 'how nice that we meet again after so long.'

And there walking easily towards us was Jazzatnit in a beautifully long flowing tunic making her a picture of perfection. Somewhat behind her and coming along more slowly was Zazfrapiz. Both had pleasant expressions on their faces and I turned and walked towards them with Tania smiling beside me. We stopped in front of each other and I put my hand out. Jazzatnit gripped it firmly and pulled me towards her and put her face up towards mine. I leaned down and she planted a warm kiss on my lips. Then she did the same to Tania and looked towards the others but they were further back though all smiling broadly. Oannes etiquette now took over and brief Sewas were exchanged between us. I replied in the plural on behalf of all my family members present.

Jazzatnit again looked towards the others some paces behind me and I realised it had been rather remiss of me not to first introduce them to her. So I walked over to Katy and put my arm around her. I then performed a complete telepathic introduction of Katy, Robin, Fiona, Sarah and Brian. Rachel and Margaret were already known to her and performed their own greeting cum Sewa.

Jazzatnit smiled and both she and Zazfrapiz came forward. Jazzatnit then went up to Katy and held out both her delicate hands. Katy took them in hers and a communication ensued which made both of them smile with pleasure. I really have no idea what was said between them but knowing Jazzatnit as I do I'm sure it was very appropriate. She did the same with Robin and then Sarah and Brian together. But with Fiona she took a more serious attitude and her communication was accompanied by a slight nod of her head as if paying a special compliment or praise. Oannes have a special insight of the character of people that still puzzles me.

'Thank you,' said Fiona aloud, 'I will do my best.'

Oannes etiquette prevented me from intruding into those thoughts so I let the moment pass. One day I'm sure Fiona would satisfy my curiosity if she so wished.

Jazzatnit introduced her husband Zazfrapiz to them then before moving to greet Rachel and Margaret. This time I could guess what passed between them. It was about living on Nazmos during the transition period. Rachel did not commit herself or Margaret to anything though her pleased smile told me otherwise.

Jazzatnit then turned back to me.

'And what does our Ashley think of our lovely Farzant? She has been most impatient to meet with you ever since she knew that you were to be here for Platwuz,' she conveyed.

I could see that both Muznant and Brazjaf were keen to hear what I thought.

I looked towards where Farzant stood slightly behind and to one side of her parents and conveyed that I thought she was nearly as pretty as her mother and that I hoped to get to know her better over the next few days.

Muznant smiled at this and conveyed that I had not changed one bit over this past twenty two year period. Brazjaf laughed and said that it was a good thing that their child was a daughter. If it had been a son then Muznant would more than likely have named him Ashley.

'I most certainly would not have,' said Muznant with a feigned pout which quickly turned into a smile, 'but perhaps an Oannes name that sounded a bit like that.'

I too then laughed aloud while conveying an emotion of affection for my old friends. Farzant sensed the easy camaraderie between her parents and I knew she was proud to be their child.

'Come,' said Jazzatnit to me and putting her arm in mine she drew me away. She then took me around her courtyard showing me her new exhibits and discussing other ideas that she also had. She asked my opinion on them and I said it was very clever of her to produce such artistic pieces.

'Oh it's not me who makes them,' she said. 'I just have the design ideas and the craft people do the difficult part of converting my ideas. It is easy to convey a visual image of what it is that I want but it is still a surprise for me when I see the finished product. Do you really like them?'

'Oh yes,' I said. 'I find a peculiar freshness in the carvings and their assembly. And putting them under water seems to add that surreal effect that makes them stand out on their own.'

'Yes I thought so when I first displayed them,' said Jazzatnit. 'But it was Zazfrapiz my husband who first suggested immersing them to see the effect. And he was right of course as I do prefer them this way.'

I noticed that Katy and Muznant were in deep conversation with Margaret listening in and adding an occasional comment or opinion of her own. It was definitely a threesome tête-à-tête.

Brazjaf nodded to me and I excused myself from Jazzatnit and walked up to where he stood with Farzant. Farzant looked embarrassed and I knew she wanted to say something and conveyed as much.

'Is it true that you are just like us,' she asked aloud in a low tone voice like her mother's.

'Yes,' I replied, 'I certainly hope so. It is a product of the gifts given to me before I ever knew about the existence of Anztarza or Nazmos.'

I reached out my hand to her and conveyed that she was free to read my thoughts. But she did not respond.

'I cannot as I am not as yet proficient in that art,' she said, 'but I hope to be within the next few years. Mother has conveyed to me all she knows of you and everything is good. I wish I was there to witness your first meeting with the governing council. For me that conveyed image is a crowning moment.'

I was embarrassed and I think I showed it by becoming very red in the face. It also left me rather speechless so I just inclined my head and then gave a brief nod.

'Oh mother,' exclaimed Farzant, 'he is exactly as you said.'

This time it was Muznant's turn to appear nonplussed. She looked at me with that old admiring look and nodded her head. There was a hint of a smile somewhere too.

Tania was beside me now and put her arm through mine. She then reached out and pulling Farzant close linked her other arm through hers.

'Come Farzant,' she said, 'walk with us around this lovely courtyard and tell us what you see in your aunty Jazzatnit's art displays.'

Tania had a way of diffusing embarrassing situations which I considered an art in itself. I glanced back and saw Brazjaf in near laughter mode as he put his arm around his wife. It was nice to see them happy together.

I thought back to the last few days and of the concern I'd felt about the deceleration aspect for the starship. How was I to affect it I'd thought? Must I simply will the ship to reduce velocity? I had kept hoping for an answer from my inner voice but to no avail. I had conveyed these concerns to the captain. She said she had confidence in me and I must do exactly as I had done in accelerating the starship except in a reversed order. She seemed confident that I was capable of doing it right. Well that gave me a plan though I still had qualms about it all going awry. But it worked out alright in the end.

When the time had come for me to begin reducing my telekinetic effort I simply opened my mind to Zanos and at the same time I willed for the ship's velocity to slowly and continually undergo a reduction over an initial period of an hour. This was then to be repeated hour by hour until the starship was travelling entirely under its own impulse power at the 10 FTL velocity. Zanos made sure that the neutron generators operated in conjunction with the pace of the starship's deceleration for total passenger gravitational comfort.

I think I would have preferred to have been in a situation of voluntary telekinetic push level control as I had two decades ago. However I was grateful and relieved that all had gone according to plan. Also I had not felt the fatigue of those previous occasions. I must get used to these new techniques that are imposed upon me.

During those musings I had received a brief insight into the goings-on from my guiding inner voice. It had been just a flash of information but it was enough for me to begin to understand what had occurred. Whether it had been something implanted in my mind by Gozmanot or whether it was an enhancement of my brain function over the past twenty two year interval I do not know for certain. But my brain had certainly taken over from my voluntary will and acted to fulfil my wishes with regard to any telekinetic push effort.

I realised that I did not need to concentrate my mind on a particular level of telekinetic push anymore but simply to desire an overall result and it would be made so. There was no mysterious element taking control but rather it had been my own mind functioning in a new way. My brain seemed to be evolving of its own accord. And so I had been right to stay within the central area of the starship's habitation platform.

The starship velocity had reduced to 10.8 FTL after four hours and a bit and it was entirely under its own propulsive power. As such I was released from any telekinetic effort responsibility and Zanos had brought the starship to its prescribed Raznat rendezvous location.

Our arrival had been communicated to Nazmos and a pleasant final meal was partaken in the captain's quarters. A fleet of spaceships was sent out to meet us and it was Captain Rojazonto who eventually transported us among others to the Nazmos space park in his spaceship 9632-Orange. I had noticed then that the massive spaceship 98103-Pink was nowhere to be seen and I assumed that it must still be out on its space trials. I wondered about its passenger population this time.

A deck Transporter ferried our little group towards the Peruga Sea but deposited us well short of it in the plaza close to Jazzatnit's lovely home.

Muznant and Brazjaf had come out to meet us and a most pleasant greeting it was too. After a brief Sewa Muznant kissed us all while Brazjaf gave everyone a vigorous handshake. And so here I was walking around a beautiful courtyard arm in arm with two beautiful women Tania and Farzant.

'One day I shall visit Earth and see its beauty for myself,' said Farzant to Tania.

'And one day I hope to see all of Earth's garden glory unfolding right here on Nazmos,' replied Tania with a big smile.

'Yes, I hope it happens,' conveyed Farzant.

'As do I,' said Tania with a nod.

Coming up to the Rachel Rose exhibit Farzant conveyed that it was her favourite.

'Mother says that these grow freely everywhere on Earth on their own through most of the climate seasons,' said Farzant. 'I expect we shall have them here too.'

I knew that Farzant was referring to the arrival of positive summer and winter seasons coming to Nazmos and not just the roses.

'Where we live in England we have a great variety of different coloured flowers and most bloom mainly in our summers,' I said and conveyed images of not only our back garden in bloom but also of those prize ones in stately homes.

'Oh I cannot wait for the same to arrive here,' said Farzant. 'Mother and father said they liked their occasional excursions into the Northern Forests. How long before we have the same on Nazmos?'

'I should think a few hundred years at least,' said Tania and looked at me for confirmation. I simply nodded agreement.

'Oh dear, I shall be an elderly Oannes person by then I suppose.'

Farzant must have picked up our simultaneous thought pattern for she suddenly jerked to a stop.

'Oh, I am so sorry,' she said, 'I did not mean to be crass or unfeeling. Humans have a much shorter lifespan than us Oannes and I didn't think before I spoke. But it is a human who would have made it all possible. Your name Ashley will be remembered here forever even long after I and my family are forgotten in time.'

I leaned around Tania and looked at Farzant and conveyed my emotion of affection for her.

'One day,' I said with a smile, 'one day my dear Farzant you will surely sit on the governing council of Nazmos.'

Tania laughed aloud and everyone looked around at us. What fun were we having that they didn't know about came across loud and clear. I quickly conveyed what had just taken place and there were chuckles and knowing smiles from them.

Tania conveyed privately to me that I had just acquired another fan. I smiled and conveyed back that it was my impish ways people liked. I was joking of course but I got a dig in the ribs for it.

As we rejoined the others Farzant quietly went to her previous position beside her parents. Muznant was glowing with pride and I'm not sure of the exact cause. Perhaps something Farzant conveyed.

It was late evening on Nazmos and Raznat-set was about an hour away. Jazzatnit conveyed that we should all go up onto the terrace and see Raznat slowly sink down into the Sea of Peruga or at least below the distant horizon.

She did not expand on the theme thinking that it would be a new experience for Katy, Robin and the others who had not been here before.

'I should like that very much,' said Katy,' especially the bit afterwards when the wind blows wildly.'

I quickly explained to Jazzatnit that I had long ago conveyed complete visual imagery of the phenomenon when I had returned from my very first trip to Nazmos.

'Sometimes it is fiercer than usual,' said our hostess, 'but you shall see it for yourselves. And afterwards we can come down for our evening meal.'

I sensed she was hiding something from me for she had blocked her mind to any probing. But by the smile in her expression I reckoned that it had to be of a pleasant nature.

Tania looked at me and I guessed that her woman's intuition had an advantage over me.

'What?' I conveyed to her privately.

'Simon,' came back to me with a visual of his face.

I looked towards Jazzatnit and smiled my very best and widest smile.

'Oh Ashley, can nothing be kept secret from you?' she said frowning at me but also smiling. What a pretty comical face she made I thought. She read my mind and the frown quickly disappeared.

'Don't look at me dear lady,' I said, 'it was Tania who guessed. So when is my son coming here?'

'That I cannot say precisely,' replied Jazzatnit, 'but he has planned his duty roster to be on Nazmos for the orbital fixing of Platwuz. He knew you would have to be here. He has visited me whenever he was able over the last few years and promised to be here when you returned. He looks and talks a lot like you but you will see that for yourself. He is really looking forward to seeing you again. Tomorrow you go to meet the governing council for their formal decision on the Nazmos orbital change and later there will be a banquet in your honour. Perhaps Simon will arrive then.'

I knew that the day after tomorrow was scheduled for me to settle Platwuz into its new circular orbit around Raznat. Moving Platwuz from its previous orbit of 1.2 billion miles from Raznat to the new orbit of just 100 million miles out would be a tremendous gain for the processing factories on Nazmos. It had taken twenty two years for Platwuz to drop to this closer position and now it was up to me to slow it sufficiently for it to enter the new orbit permanently. It shouldn't be difficult. But I would like Simon to be beside me as I facilitate it.

And if the governing council gave its approval for the Nazmos orbital change then I could affect that during the same space flight. My private plan was still uppermost in my mind which might come as a surprise to many. I hope the general disappointment among the Oannes population for full implementation is not too great. I know that they will understand the reasons behind my action.

Mention of the governing council brought to my mind the visual image of Ritozanan. I had feared for her health then and now twenty two years later I'd not heard any news of her. No sooner had the thought entered my mind than Jazzatnit communicated about her.

'No one has seen her these last five years or so,' said Jazzatnit, 'for she keeps to herself. I expect she spends most of her hours in her sleep tank. But you may communicate with her as do all of the governing council members whenever the need arises. She may be frail of body but her mind is as keen as it ever was.'

I thought no time like the present.

'Greetings dear Ritozanan,' I conveyed, 'I am very pleased to be able to communicate with you. I am here at Jazzatnit's home and shall be meeting with the governing council in the Great Domed Hall sometime tomorrow. I shall miss your presence there.'

'Thank you Ashley,' was the reply telepathically as powerful as ever. 'It is nice to hear from you and that you are here back on Nazmos. You are the only one who has ever called me dear and I am pleased and complimented by it. Perhaps you will not miss me tomorrow as I have just this instant decided that I shall attempt the journey to the domed Hall. If I cannot then you must come and visit me in my home. You will be most welcome my friend. I would like to touch you once again if you will allow it.'

'That I shall with all my heart,' I replied, 'and I shall keep my mind wholly open to you.'

'Thank you Ashley, you also are most dear to me even though you are human; until tomorrow then or soon thereafter,' she conveyed with a bit of humour emotion finding its way through.

I closed my mind to the communication and stood silently for a full minute deep in my own thoughts. My vision had blurred so I quickly blinked it dry but a tinge of sadness remained locked inside.

My communication with Ritozanan had been an open one just as I had when I conveyed the details of my regressed meeting with Gozmanot to all of Nazmos. So now all of Nazmos would have received my little telepathic chat with Ritozanan. Perhaps it would be some consolation to all those who knew her that she could still get about.

Tania touched my arm to bring me to the present and indicated that we had been requested to move up the stairs to the terrace for the view of the approaching Raznat-set. I had told my family about the 'Dark Wind' phenomenon but they had yet to experience it for real.

I stood arm in arm with my wife and daughter Rachel looking towards the big round dully glowing reddish ball that was Raznat as it gently lowered itself towards the distant flat horizon. It was the Peruga Sea that lay just out of sight beyond the houses but I knew that's where Raznat would set. Those living close to the shoreline would get the best views.

Slowly in stages Raznat sank lower and lower. Its image began to flicker and distort as it got closer to the ground. It seemed like it did not really want to go down further as it feigned a lingering hold upon the bright sky above it. Now only half of Raznat's oval shaped dull orb remained visible which progressively became less and less until finally just a large red drop of Raznat was visible in the distance; and then suddenly that too was gone. The sky remained brilliant over the spot and a wispy haze hung above it as if calling it to return. I expect that Raznat rose up in the morning in a similar fashion. I had yet to witness that.

There was a hush on the terrace as we waited in silence as the dusk crept over the sky and the world of Nazmos rapidly darkened. I had my arm around Rachel and she looked up into my face as soon as she heard it. The sound began as a distant rustling noise somewhere behind us and in the distance. Before we had time to think the whoosh of the wind roared around the house and rattled the glass panels. It felt like an express train was racing past and heading out towards the sea. The glass panels juddered and the whistling rose to a crescendo before gradually diminishing back to a quietness that sounded suddenly quite eerie. It took barely a minute in time but was so very dramatic.

'Wow,' said Fiona to no one in particular, 'that was quite some show. Does it happen with every sunset – I mean Raznat-set?'

'Yes,' said Jazzatnit, 'it does and it is slightly different each time. Perhaps when the climate is milder after the orbital change it might mellow or even cease altogether.'

The air temperature began to plummet so we all went down the stairs to the warmth of the courtyard.

I noticed that Brian had his arm around Sarah and was comforting her. She seemed to have been taken by surprise at the ferocity of the 'Dark Wind' and it had upset her. I noticed her shudder and I decided to lend a hand. I conveyed an emotion of peace and calm to her and saw her visibly relax and smile up at Brian. For once I was glad of all the gifts I had been granted. And especially all that I had learned from my Oannes friends.

'Come all of you,' called Jazzatnit telepathically, 'it is time for our evening meal. I'm sure you are now all quite ready for it just as I am.'

I was about to make my usual joke remark referring to my stomach thinking that my throat had been cut but decided against it. It just might be construed wrongly that I was implying that the meal was overdue. A joke has its place and this was not the time for it. So instead I said that the meal was very welcome. I think I was learning diplomacy. I did however remark after the excellent meal that the strings attached to my stomach were pulling on my eyelids.

Jazzatnit smiled at this and took my hint that I was tired and wished to retire. So after a decent interval of conversation we thanked our hosts for their most gracious hospitality and bade everyone a pleasant nights rest. Tania and I held hands as we walked to our room. Katy and Robin were not far behind.

Breakfast was the biggest surprise of my life. Tania and I were first to arrive at the breakfast table and whom should we see sitting there alone but none other than my son Simon smiling broadly.

'Hi mom, Hi dad,' he said cheerily as he stood up and walked around to us.

Tania got the first hug and kiss while I stood beside them watching full of an inner joy. Then I got a firm handshake and a man hug. My goodness I thought he is a bit taller than me as I felt him patting my back. Our cheeks rubbed and I noticed he had recently shaved for his chin was smooth.

'Let's have a good look at you son,' I said as I held his shoulders at arms length. 'So where's the Errol Flynn moustache?'

'Oh that went months ago, it got a bit itchy and I never could get the two sides exactly right,' he said with his twisted smile. Then, 'Gosh you both look just great.'

'I kind of liked the moustache,' I said. 'It had a character of its own.'

'It'll be easy to grow back,' said Simon pensively, 'so you never know, maybe one day?'

We talked generally and Simon told us that he was still third officer on the Transporter spaceship 7332-Blue under Captain Vikazat who was quite young at 130 years of age. He'd been captain for nearly sixteen years and was strict but likeable. Simon said he was close friends with his fellow First and Second officers who were also both quite young at 75 years each. They had been on the ship when Simon joined. They were Rooztnaz and Brijtook respectively and were keen to meet me.

'They'd like to meet you dad,' said Simon, 'and I said I was sure you wouldn't mind.'

'Not at all son,' I said, 'anytime at all would be fine.'

'Well actually we shall all be with you aboard Captain Rojazonto's 9632-Orange tomorrow when you go to stabilise the Platwuz orbit,' said Simon smiling. 'And we've also wangled a seat on the shuttle that goes out with you when you perform the deed. We got permission ages ago since it was a planned event.'

I had to laugh and Tania smiled as well. Twenty two years ago I had Simon with me when I caused Platwuz to dip towards Raznat. And now I shall have him with me again when I complete that operation. Except Simon was now a spaceship officer and would be accompanied by two other fellow officers. I felt proud of him in the extreme and so did Tania. I was happy for Simon for he was certainly happy in his choice of career and that made me glad.

'So where are your friends now,' I asked?

'Oh, they're still on board ship in the space park,' he said. 'I shall be returning there for the night. It is regulation that ship's officers be aboard at night. So I shall be with you all day today and return to my ship after the evening banquet. And tomorrow I and my fellow officers will be aboard Captain Rojazonto's ship as planned.'

Katy and Robin then walked in and again there were hugs and kisses galore. Katy had been very fond of Simon and linked arms with him and chatted.

'I liked your upper lip fuzz,' said Katy, 'you must grow it back.'

Simon just smiled. He was never one to argue a point yet always followed his own way.

'I thought I'd have a change for a bit,' was all he said.

Rachel and Margaret then came in followed by Fiona, Sarah and Brian. There were exclamations of surprise from the first two and they rushed forward to hug Simon.

Rachel stared at her brother and said how handsome he was. 'How nice to finally see the grown man in the flesh,' she said linking her arm through his.

'You look a lot like your dad when I first met him,' said Margaret, 'perhaps a bit more handsome.'

I had to laugh before turning to my nieces and Brian to perform the necessary introductions.

'Fiona, Sarah, Brian, this is my spaceman son Simon,' I said, 'come and say hello.'

It was Simon who darted forward and kissed his two cousins and shook hands with Brian.

'Very pleased to meet my two beautiful cousins,' he said. 'And you also Brian. Congratulations on your engagement to Sarah. I believe the wedding is in May but regretfully I shall be here on duty. I shall see visuals of it all I'm sure. Mum and dad send me regular communications with full imagery so I have seen you all and know all about you. I'm glad everything is in the open now; better late than never. So here I am and it's the best of me that you see I'm afraid.'

I picked up mixed emotions and thoughts from Fiona. She was staring at Simon as he towered above Rachel beside him. Her eyes were wide open and her admiration was obvious to everyone. Then she turned red with embarrassment when she noticed that all eyes were upon her. Simon laughed his Errol Flynn laugh and I too was mesmerised by his handsomeness. Tania had wet eyes as she went and put her arm around her son. She was a very proud mother indeed.

Simon then did something that surprised even me. With one arm still around his mum he released himself from his sister and moved up to Fiona. He took her chin between finger and thumb and planted a light kiss on her upturned lips.

'That is to thank you for that wonderful admiring look cousin,' he said with accent on the relationship, 'I think we are going to be good friends.'

Now Fiona seemed to relax for she smiled and nodded. She was getting over the surprise and I could see that she was desperate to ask Simon a whole heap of questions. She wanted to know all about him and as told by him. I conveyed my thought readings to Simon.

'So Cousin Fiona, until a week ago you had no idea about my life, so dad informs me,' he said.

'Well actually until a week ago Sarah and I had no notion about Uncle Ashley's fantastic gifts,' said Fiona. 'He did mention that he wished he'd told us sooner and was sorry he hadn't. But no harm done and perhaps it were for the best.'

Although Sarah and Brian showed a keen interest in Simon it was Fiona who wanted to know all about his space travels and adventures as she called them. She also wanted to know about his time in space and if there were any female cadets.

'Oh yes there were many,' explained Simon, 'but only one stayed the course and passed out with me. I believe Mazpazam, for that was her name, is serving on a long range surveying spaceship. I haven't seen her since we left the academy. Perhaps we might meet again one day.'

I thought I read a decided wistfulness in the way that Simon spoke her name. I do believe he had been rather fond of her, but Simon was a career professional and had put her to the back of his mind. He was first and foremost a spaceman. And I needed him to be beside me on the starship journey towards Zarama.

'What must one do to qualify for a place in the space academy?' asked Fiona.

Simon showed surprise at the question.

'Cousin, are you interested in becoming a spacewoman?'

'I don't know,' said Fiona, 'but I do find it absolutely fascinating and thrilling to be out there in the vastness of space. I think I could live in it forever or at least on a spaceship out there.'

'Doesn't it scare you at all?' asked Simon.

'Oh it does, it scares me to bits. But that is what also excites me from what little I have seen. I envy you Simon, I really do.'

'It can get very lonely out there you know. Does that thought not bother you?' said Simon.

Fiona thought for a moment before replying.

'How can one be lonely with all those beautiful stars for company? It would be like a forest of flowers all around you,' she said.

Simon had no reply to this so I stepped in for him. I conveyed to Fiona how Simon had been similarly taken with space travel from when he first encountered it when he was eight years old. Then how Captain Bulzezatna had noticed this keenness and offered to assist when the time came. How starship Captain Zakatanz had also taken Simon to his heart after seeing his potential and offered his help. Then when Simon was eighteen he had moved to live in Anztarza under the tutelage of Bulzezatna. And finally recommendations were made and Simon was accepted into the Nazmos space academy on a trial basis. He had excelled and passed out in the short space of ten years. Normally this training was of a much longer duration as space navigation trips often took years to complete. Simon's gift of premonition always guided his craft to its destination point with an accuracy that surprised his mentors. So now here he was acting as third officer on a class-6 Transporter spaceship.

'Gosh,' said Fiona, 'I didn't realise how much you had to go through Simon. Perhaps I am too old to start such a career now.'

'Ah,' said Simon, 'that was because I had the ambition to one day become a starship captain. But there are many serving aboard spaceships who have never been to the space academy. If you are really interested in being out in space then why not ask to serve as crew on one of the many spaceships out there. You could start within the solar system and serve on Captain Bulzezatna's 520-Green or one of the other ships based in Anztarza. If you show yourself enthusiastic and keen then the Oannes people will be willing to advise and help you. You can pick up a lot as you go along but you can never be a deputy or a captain.'

'Thanks Simon,' said an unsmiling Fiona, 'that is good to know and I shall consider it.'

Katy and Robin looked at one another and smiled. They knew their daughter very well. At least they thought they did. I for myself was not sure what Fiona really intended.

After breakfast and a lot of pleasant chatter there was still no sign of Jazzatnit. Muznant and Farzant had joined us by now and Muznant conveyed that both Jazzatnit and Zazfrapiz slept till quite late. I noticed that neither Muznant nor her daughter ate any breakfast. A glass of Wazu was all they had.

After a while we drifted to the airy courtyard and broke up into three groups. Tania and I stayed with Muznant and Farzant and were soon joined by Brazjaf. Robin, Katy and Margaret formed another group but the energetic ones were Simon, Rachel and their cousins Fiona and Sarah. Brian tagged along with them but was a silent observer. It was nice to see the cousins getting on so well and I think Rachel had missed her brother. She had her arm through his for most of the time. Once I saw Fiona grab Simon's arm to say something but she let go in embarrassment when she realised what she had done. Simon laughed and briefly put an affectionate arm around her waist. It was good to hear Simon's laughter interspersed within the verbal conversational banter and I thought of him commanding a starship one day. Would he laugh as much then? I think he would.

Muznant and Farzant were quite taken by that group's lively chattering sounds and I think they thought it nice to see how a group of youthful humans behaved when having fun together.

I sensed Farzant's gaze upon me but when I looked towards her she quickly averted her face.

I had to smile at the teenage type behaviour of this young Oannes lady. Muznant conveyed a private message and I replied that I understood. I would not embarrass the child with any undue attention on my part. Rather I engaged in verbal conversation with Brazjaf and Muznant and let Farzant listen to it. I know she found it entertaining watching me gesture and explain as part of that communication. For her it must have been like watching something on TV that was interesting mainly because the lead character was known to her. Farzant had yet to develop her social skills and I'm sure she would find all that with her own age group of friends. Maturity came slowly within the Oannes culture. Muznant conveyed that it usually developed near the age of forty or forty five.

I couldn't help it but I kept looking to see what Simon was doing. I just couldn't get enough of the myriad of expressions that crossed his face. He seemed to be enjoying the company of his sister and cousins and made sure that Brian was included in his conversation pieces.

Katy, Robin and Margaret now came and joined us to also look on at Simon's following.

'He's a smart fellow Ashley,' remarked Katy, 'and I fear that Fiona is quite taken with him.'

'But I don't think Simon is quite aware of her admiration,' added Robin. 'There is only one topic on his mind and that is his next venture into space. I don't think he notices women in that way; not yet anyway.'

I could see Tania breathe a sigh of relief and I knew exactly why; affairs between first cousins was taboo as far as she was concerned. I said nothing of my thoughts of Mazpazam. My intuition said she would be an important factor in his life. I wondered how?

It was nice when Simon came over to us and linked arms with his mum.

'Hi again you two,' he said cheerily, 'how's things? Don't answer that as I'm just making conversation. I want to soak up as much of you as I can on this trip. It's nice cruising around in space but I do think of you a lot. Most of all I miss seeing you and having you near. I also miss the others; the old folks as I call them in my mind. Tell me how they were just before you left last week. Grandmas Lillian and Milly and Grandpas Alex and Jerry; I think of them often. And Uncle Ron and Aunt Brenda in Aberporth; I hope business is good.'

So I filled in as much as I could with visual images of our Christmas just gone. Our visit to put flowers on granddad Eric's grave and how cold it was especially for granddad Alex who was now eighty four and needed a stick to get about. We took a stroll around Jazzatnit's exhibits but not really seeing them as Tania and I took turns in talking about things we did as part of our recent life back home. The garden was into its winter mode and looking rather drab though it would not be long before the spring bulbs burst forth their blooms of snowdrops, crocuses and daffs. Simon listened quietly and put in the odd remark about this or that. There was an underlying wistfulness of longing to his questions and I knew what he was thinking. Time was running out for our elderly folk and he might never get to see them again.

'Mom, dad, I make you a promise,' he said with emotion. 'When 4110-Silver is ready and I am part of its crew I shall request that its first run be to Earth to pick you up. I shall visit home then. Please tell them to hang on till then. It could be as little as five or as much as ten years from now but that is my promise.'

There was a glistening of wetness in Simon's eyes as he said this and I knew he was hoping that the time frame would not be too late. He loved his grandparents – all of them, and hoped to meet up with them at least once more.

The morning passed pleasantly in the company of our son till eventually our hosts came out to join us. Jazzatnit was pleased to see Simon there and gave him a grand welcoming hug even though she only came up to his chest. She could not help her partiality towards handsome young men – whether human or Oannes. And Simon was a particularly handsome young man. At least Tania and I thought so.

After a bout of light snacks and liquid refreshment we all returned to our rooms for a bit of smartening up in the Oannes outfits provided for us and made our way to the nearby plaza. We were to meet the Nazmos governing council as arranged. This time both our hosts accompanied us to the Domed Hall for this meeting. Later in the evening we would return again for the official greeting banquet.

'I do not wish to miss the announcement that Ritozanan has engineered,' Jazzatnit had said earlier. 'It will be a momentous occasion for Nazmos and I want to be a part of it.'

'Then you already know what the announcement will contain?' I said with a smile.

'No, not really,' she'd said, 'but how can it be otherwise since Ritozanan more or less gave you her word that it would be so. Also Gozmanot has become a part of our living history and who would wish to offend her.'

There was certainly much to think about there.

It was an easy stroll to the deck Transporter and it made a circuitous ride to the Domed Hall. On the way Muznant gave Fiona, Sarah and Brian details of the areas of Wentazta that were passing below us. Some of the information was new even to me. Eventually we approached the Domed Hall structure and the Transporter took us through the large entrance and proceeded well inside before settling down at the usual place. I noticed that the Hall was empty apart from the odd Oannes going about their business and I realised that the first order of the day was my meeting with the Governing Council which would be a private affair. No one had mentioned this but I realised that our hosts must have been instructed accordingly. I didn't mind it in the least.

Muznant and Brazjaf led the way forward and we all followed. We went to one side of the hall beside the empty dais. Seating had been arranged for us facing the dais and we sat as directed by Brazjaf. Tania and I were at the centre of the row with the others on either side of us. I sensed a pleasant emotion of calm pervading the area around us and I knew this was the Oannes custom of putting their guests at ease. It also pre-empted the thought in my mind that we would have a favourable decision for Nazmos.

I heard a rustling sound and looking to my right saw the retinue of governing council members slowly walking towards us and the dais. They were all dressed in the most exquisite of gown-like outfits that shimmered in the Domed Hall lighting and lent a very august atmosphere to what would be remembered as a most auspicious and eventful occasion.

I then noticed the three chief ministers of Anztarza following just behind which pleased me no end. Tzatzorf, Rymtakza and Zarzint were together and dressed as regally. And their wives were with them. The governing council assistants followed in their own procession which began a few paces behind and they moved to separate seating places at right angles to ours but also facing the dais.

The governing council members slowly mounted the dais and settled into their respective seating positions. Anztarza's chief ministers were near a central position and I immediately surmised that they must have been members of this august council before ever being sent out to Earth and Anztarza as chief ministers. So it was only right that they resumed their former positions on the dais. They obviously were well known to the other council members for they all seemed friendly towards each other. When I queried Zazfrapiz later about this he confirmed that it was so. I wondered if they would have any part to play in today's proceedings or were they here simply as observers.

However I noticed a vacant space on the dais where no seats existed near the front centre and more or less opposite to where I was sitting. I puzzled over this but not for long because on a small floating pallet seated on a throne-like chair was council member Ritozanan.

I thought the pallet would settle into the empty space on the dais but it didn't. It came and settled down right in front of where I was sitting. There was a completeness of silence in the hall before Ritozanan spoke.

'Welcome back Ashley,' she said in a voice that was barely above a whisper, 'it is nice to see you among us again. And welcome to your family.'

I stood up and took two short paces towards her chair. I could say nothing as I was overcome with emotion. An emotion of sadness at the visible shell of the lovely old lady I knew twenty two years ago. Ritozanan had become very thin and all her web fins just flopped flat against her face and arms. I'm sure she was smaller too. Where a perky nose had been was just a flat area with two pinholes for nostrils. Her dress outfit was beautiful but just hung down off her tiny shoulders. I could not see her legs – only her footwear that seemed tiny in the extreme.

I reached out and took her outstretched hands in mine. But all I could do was to close my hands over the fists that could not be straightened. Without thinking I bent forward and kissed first one fist and then the other. I got her message and did as she requested. I leaned close to her and kissed her gently on the lips which drew the old smile from her that I well remembered. Faintly I heard her whispered 'Thank you' and felt the reverence of the moment. My vision was blurred for that short moment and just before I stepped back to my seat. I felt extremely honoured.

Ritozanan's pallet lifted and bore her to the empty place allocated for her on the dais. She seemed to have perked up a bit for she was sitting up straighter but I guessed that this was because she was about to make her announcement and impart the decision made by the governing council of Nazmos. This she did telepathically and in open mind mode for all of Nazmos to hear.

'Ashley you came to us many years ago with a very odd request,' she conveyed. 'At the time we did not welcome this interference in our affairs and I personally did not like you for it. That was a misjudgement on my part for which I am ashamed. I soon discovered that there was far more to you and your gifts than I had thought possible. Then through your history gift you told us of Gozmanot the originator of our ancient myths. And you even regressed to her time to show us her face and give us her thoughts.'

There was a pause during which a powerful emotion of love, affection and gratitude seemed to surround the area around us.

'Ashley I have come to look upon you with great affection and admiration,' she continued. 'And that is not because of all the things you have done and can do, but because none of those things have affected you or your behaviour. How could anyone with such power at their command not become proud and feel that they are the greatest among people. But being close to you I saw none of that. You made us look upon you as an ordinary likeable human. Nothing in what you did or said made us think that you were anything other than ordinary and just like all of us. And for that Ashley I came to admire you and hold you in deep affection along with all your family. They too behave as ordinary human beings without a vestige of any pride accruing from their link with you. I feel there is hope for Oannes and humans to integrate one day. Thank you Ashley for showing us the way.'

Again Ritozanan paused briefly in her communication before continuing.

'And now Ashley the moment has come to respond to the request you made when you first stood before the governing council of Nazmos. The council have deliberated long and consulted with many and have unanimously agreed the decision that Gozmanot will have her dream. The orbit of Nazmos will be changed from its present one to one that revolves closer to Raznat to give it a climate that is warmer than at present and which will be favourable for flora upon the land areas. Our scientists have calculated exact details and will guide you in performing this task.'

After a brief hesitation she added. 'But you must be gentle in your push upon our world so as not to cause undue upset upon it. Our scientists have determined how that should be. We are not as concerned about Platwuz as it has been secured and all its population evacuated.'

I smiled at the pleasure that the overall decision gave me. I had expected it but now that the decision had been conveyed not only to me but to all of Nazmos it brought with it a great mental relief. And I knew that it was Ritozanan to whom I must be grateful. I had to respond so I stood up and gave my most respectful bow to Ritozanan and the council members.

'Thank you council members,' I conveyed in open telepathic mode, 'thank you for a most wise and considerate decision. I'm sure Gozmanot would be pleased that her dream is to be fulfilled. If it is considered appropriate then I would like to begin the Nazmos orbital change as soon as possible. Tomorrow I go to finalise the orbit of Platwuz. Once that has been completed successfully do I have your permission to then also slow Nazmos in its orbit as part of the first phase in its orbital adjustment?'

Again it was Ritozanan who responded for the council.

'Yes, that is to be permitted,' she conveyed. Then added, 'And the second phase in finalising the orbit will be when Nazmos is at perigee after five and a half months. Is that so?'

'So it should be,' was my evasive response and I blocked my mind.

'Good,' conveyed Ritozanan, 'I think our business has been favourably completed here today.'

She was about to turn away and I imagine return to her sleep tank when suddenly her perceptive mind made her turn back to me. She stared in my direction and tried to probe my mind and could not.

'This is like the first meeting between us,' she conveyed with the emotion of annoyance coming through to me. 'You just said that it should be and not that it will be. Are you playing with ideals or are you intending something else? You must explain.'

I felt that I was being commanded now and the council was exerting its authority through this frail looking Oannes lady. But I had prepared myself for this.

'Yes I will,' I replied and conveyed the whole scenario of my planned intentions by opening my mind fully for the council to probe deeply. I saw the mood mellow before me and knew that I was understood.

'I do not wish to be disrespectful but Nazmos and Earth are of minor consequence if the danger from Zarama cannot be averted. It was my inner voice that advised me just as council member Korizazit understands. Much of what I do comes from that source and I always respect its guidance. Without it I am just an ordinary not so very clever human.'

I paused to let this sink in before I continued.

'Tomorrow after I have secured Platwuz into its new orbit I shall slow Nazmos in its forward velocity around Raznat. This will be done in the gentlest possible manner and such that the current position becomes the apogee of its orbit. The amount of slowing down will be as your scientists have calculated such that the orbital perigee is as they have decided; which I understand to be a position nineteen million miles from Raznat. This will be the new intermediate elliptic orbit of Nazmos around Raznat. I hope to return to my home on Earth until the modified starship 4110-Silver is ready to take me to Zarama. I am informed that work on its modifications could be completed in five to ten years time. I will then return here and finalise the orbit of Nazmos. My purpose for this planned delay is so that it will give you on Nazmos the time to adjust gradually to the new climatic changes that will occur.'

'And what of Zarama,' queried Ritozanan, 'have you considered any plan for it?'

I was silent as the question had taken me by surprise. Zarama had been put to the back of my mind pending the announcement of the governing council's decision regarding the new Nazmos orbit.

'I'm sorry,' I conveyed to all, 'I had not given that aspect much thought. I always considered that I must push Zarama to a path that was away from here; a change of direction in its present course through space. But now that you ask I would think that your eminent scientists have drawn up a plan in which my telekinetic gift plays a major role.'

Ritozanan smiled pleasantly at me and nodded her frail head.

'Yes they have,' she conveyed, 'and the details will be conveyed to you.'

I remained thoughtful, silent and unsmiling as a dire thought entered my mind. Tania sensed my unease and lightly touched my arm.

'Your emotion of doubt comes across to me very strongly Ashley,' conveyed Ritozanan, 'what is it that causes this?'

'Zarama is a White Dwarf star and although it is only the size of Earth it has a mass a third greater than to that of our Sun,' I conveyed. 'It is more massive than anything I have yet had to deal with. Gozmanot's vision was that the fiery dragon would be vanquished and not just pushed to one side. How am I to achieve this?'

Ritozanan very nearly laughed out aloud. The amusement was clearly written on her wrinkled face and in the manner that her body shook. She then conveyed to me the full detail of the Zarama plan and I had to smile. Yes, I thought, that should do the trick. Another fiery dragon that was a billion times more massive would swallow up Zarama. And this huge fiery dragon was a benign one and posed no threat to Nazmos or Earth. And its name was Rasalgethi. What a beautiful name I thought. I looked around at the others seated beside me and they all looked quite blank. I then realised that Ritozanan's message had been a private one to me alone. Even Muznant and Brazjaf were unaware of what had been revealed to me although I'm sure they knew generally about the Rasalgethi plan.

'With respect most esteemed council members I keep no secrets from my family,' I said aloud for all to hear. I then began to convey in open mind mode all the information that Ritozanan had just given to me.

'Earth, Nazmos and Zarama are roughly in a straight line distribution and in that order,' I conveyed slowly with my nieces and Brian in mind.

'Although the visible light image left Zarama 525 years ago it was calculated that because of Zarama's velocity it has since travelled a bit closer to us in that time. In 525 years at an average velocity of 17.76% of light speed Zarama would have traversed an additional distance of 93.2 light years towards Nazmos. So in reality it should be at an invisible location of 431.8 light years away in the lower portion of the Constellation Hercules. It can be located in the position slightly above the bright star Rasalhague which is only some 60 Light-years from Raznat. Another bright star visually just a bit further on the right side of it is Rasalgethi and the focus of the Zarama plan.'

I paused briefly for the benefit of the human minds seated around me.

'Rasalgethi is a magnificent red class bright super giant star with a surface temperature 3300 degrees Kelvin. It is 380 Light-years from Raznat and it has a diameter that is close to 400 million miles. If placed at the centre of the Solar System the star Rasalgethi would extend well past the orbit of Mars and into the centre of the Asteroid Belt. It has a mass nine times that of Earth's Sun and forty five times that of Raznat.'

Again I paused but this time for effect as I was quite enjoying my teacher status.

'The Nazmos scientists have computed that Zarama's path towards the Raznat system needs to be directionally deflected towards Rasalgethi by an angular 5.4degrees. The distance between Zarama and Rasalgethi is currently 144 Light-years. This means that at its present velocity Zarama will take approximately 810 years to reach Rasalgethi. So the calculations must be precise and afterwards Zarama's new path must be accurately monitored and verified. This means that the Nazmos scientists on the starship on site will need to track Zarama for a month or more in case any adjustment to its course is necessary. It is extremely fortunate that Rasalgethi is where it is and that the deflection required is so little.'

However a further thought was pushed into my mind which caused me to have some reservations about the plan. The plan lacked two key interrelated factors that had not been considered and the council instantly read my open mind and they reacted immediately.

'Explain what you have been shown,' was the command that came from a Ritozanan of old. There was a degree of fierceness in the conveyed remark that contained within it a deep emotion of slighted indignation.

'My sincere apology if I have caused offence, as none was intended,' I said aloud though in an appeasing tone of voice, 'I only wish for the success of our mission. Two factors have been brought to my attention.'

Ritozanan read my mind and smiled then nodded for me to continue.

'Firstly, although the dwarf star Zarama is fairly small being about Earth size it is a million times greater in its mass. It has a mass slightly greater than Earth's Sun. It is also a rather hot and bright White Dwarf star. My inner voice warns me that a spaceship cannot get too close. Not closer than about a couple of million miles from it. I do not know if my telekinetic ability has the strength to be effective at such a distance. I could venture closer but not by very much I imagine. The shuttles accompanying the effort would need to be specially protected to resist Zarama's inferno. I think there is much to consider.'

There was shocked telepathic silence in the Domed Hall.

It was Korizazit who then conveyed a plan.

'Tomorrow Ashley goes to stabilise Platwuz in its new orbit around Raznat,' he conveyed. 'Let his first effort be done from a distance approaching two million miles. This will show us what needs to be done for Zarama when the time comes.'

'It is a good suggestion and should be tried,' conveyed Ritozanan, 'but what of the other? How close may our shuttles approach this White Dwarf star Zarama in safety?'

Simon then conveyed a private message to me.

I couldn't help a smile as I replied likewise back to him. Why not I thought it would be the perfect try out.

Ritozanan must have seen that an idea had passed between father and son and guessed that we were up to something new. She was too polite to ask though the questioning look she directed at me was enough for me to volunteer our information. However it was Simon's moment and I must let him speak for himself.

'My son Simon has made me a suggestion. If you would permit it he will present it to you,' I said aloud.

I could see that this went against the grain of the governing council code. No one may address or communicate with them except on specific invitation. The pause was brief but it seemed considerable. Obviously the governing council had consulted together before Ritozanan looked up and smiled at Simon.

'Simon, son of Ashley,' she conveyed in open telepathic communication, 'you may give your thoughts to us.'

Simon stood and took a small step forward. He then gave a slight respectful bow before straightening up and standing tall.

'A gracious thank you to the Nazmos governing council for the invitation to speak my thoughts,' he said aloud but at a slow measured pace.

He reminded me of my first meeting with the governing council and I daresay that Ritozanan was reminded of that moment as well for she looked from Simon to me and back again at Simon. I wondered what she was thinking until I saw the faint smile of pride come to her face. Like father like son was the conveyed message I received. And Tania was glowing too.

After a brief pause Simon continued to speak.

'Although I have not personally been to the Sirius star locality I have been trained in the logistics of the system while at the space academy. We know that a White Dwarf star Sirius B orbits the main star Sirius A once every fifty years. As such it is at a conveniently safe distance from its very bright and massive parent star. Sirius A is twice the mass of Earth's s Sun and 25 times as bright. Sirius B orbits it in an ecliptic orbit that compares with Jupiter's orbit at its closest point and out to the Uranus position at it's farthest. Sirius B is similar in size and intensity to the rogue star Zarama.'

Simon paused and looked down at his feet to show his respect for the council. He was well versed in Oannes etiquette. He then raised his eyes again and stared directly at Ritozanan. There was intenseness in his manner that was apparent to us all.

'Starships have visited the Sirius system but have never ventured very close to either star for gravitational reasons. However smaller zero-gravity spaceships carried by the starships have gone in closer to Sirius B but I do not remember the exact distance. Their research was of an unrelated nature so I cannot comment upon the distance factors.'

Again Simon paused briefly.

'What I am proposing is that an expedition be sent out to Sirius B with the sole object of discovering how close a zero-gravity spaceship may approach it safely. White Dwarf stars are degenerate and therefore no fusion of atoms occurs within them thus making them free of the more dangerous cosmic radiation emissions. Sirius A is 14.2 Light-years from Raznat; with my father's telekinetic assistance a starship could travel there in just under eleven days. Proximity to Sirius B tests could then be conducted using zero-gravity spaceships over a period of a day or two before commencing the return journey. I would suggest that a team of scientists accompany the expedition led by our eminent Brajam and afterwards a full report be made to the Nazmos governing council.'

Simon showed he had concluded by stepping back to his previous position and again he kept his head in a respectful bowed manner.

I was proud of Simon for he had adopted the Oannes style of making a brief and to the point proposal and not assuming an agreement or acceptance. Living among the Oannes people for so long had practically made him behave as one of them in thought and deed.

Then Ritozanan broke the seemingly lengthy silence.

'I like you Simon and I like this plan of yours as it has merit,' she conveyed to us all. She then conveyed a private message to me and I immediately replied in the affirmative, privately too of course.

'The council agrees with the suggestion and will see it implemented,' conveyed Ritozanan as a general telepathic statement to all. 'And tomorrow the Platwuz orbit will be finalised in the manner that council member Korizazit suggested earlier in order to test Ashley's telekinetic power from a distance. Also to be implemented after this on the same spaceship flight will be the first stage of the Nazmos orbital change. It will be an historic moment and I hope that I live long enough to witness the benefit to Nazmos.'

This was the first time I had heard an Oannes person talk about their life reaching an end and I was saddened to hear it.

Ritozanan continued.

'The starship 8110-Gold under the command of Captain Zakatanz will undertake the Sirius expedition as suggested by Simon. A squad of zero-gravity spaceships will be placed aboard the starship and used as required. Captain Zakatanz informs me that he will require three days for preparation and will then leave when you have fulfilled your task with Nazmos. I wish you all a safe and successful journey.'

Then without looking at me Ritozanan's pallet raised upwards a fraction, turned around and slowly floated towards the rear exit door. However just before she entered the portal she repeated her private message to me. I replied again in the affirmative. I would visit her on my return from the Nazmos orbital mission. I then wondered whom she would ask to help fulfil her wish.

Standing to one side of the dais with the assistants was little Nerbtazwi and I instantly got a big smile from her. She was ten years older than Ritozanan and still in exceedingly good physical condition. I knew instantly then that she had been chosen by Ritozanan to be my guide and that pleased me.

The dais was soon vacated as the council members took their leave and sedately processed towards the exit that Ritozanan had just gone through. I once again got the chance to admire the grandeur and shimmering colours of the vestments worn by them for this occasion. As they passed by, the three Anztarza chief ministers looked in my direction and gave a brief nod. I smiled back. They were soon followed by Nerbtazwi and the other assistants and we were alone again.

It was still early afternoon in Wentazta and Muznant suggested we board the Transporter for a further tour of the city before returning for the banquet later in the evening. But both Jazzatnit and Zazfrapiz conveyed that they would return home for their afternoon rest.

For some strange reason I felt light-headed and suggested to Tania that I too would like a bit of an afternoon siesta back at Jazzatnit's place. I couldn't understand it but there it was. Perhaps my age was beginning to tell on me. What a thought! But I said to the others that they should continue on. Muznant then suggested that perhaps Simon could take them all to the Shopping Malls for a walk around there.

Tania looked at me with a slight concern on her face but I convinced her that I was fine apart from this feeling of lethargy. Perhaps it was the anticlimax to the stress I must have been under when waiting for the council's decision. I told her to accompany Simon on their little tour. I wanted to be on my own for a bit but made her promise to come and wake me immediately on their return.

It was agreed then that Muznant and Brazjaf would also come back to base with our hosts and me while Simon would have all the others with him including Farzant. She had been of two minds about going with Simon or returning with us but Muznant conveyed for her to assist Simon as tour guide. I think it was what she had really wanted and she readily agreed. Because the Shopping Malls were in a different direction we boarded different transporters and she waved happily as her Transporter moved off. Earlier I had the intuitive notion that both Farzant and Fiona were quite taken by Simon. Tania had read my thoughts then and conveyed that Simon was no different from his father in captivating the hearts of the opposite sex. But then Tania was biased.

'Such compliments never went amiss,' I conveyed to Tania. She just smiled.

Our Transporter dropped us off in the plaza outside Jazzatnit's house and the five of us walked the short distance to the entrance. We went into the dining hall and sat talking over a glass of Wazu.

On impulse I said I wished to ask the advice of my two favourite women. A little bit of butter never hurt anyone. Jazzatnit showed her concern and asked, 'What is it?' rather hurriedly.

There were just us five here at the table and it was where I also felt very much at ease. I had already informed Tania right after Ritozanan had requested it. So I told them that Ritozanan had invited me to visit her in her home and I was to go alone when I got back from my Nazmos space operations. I said I thought that Nerbtazwi would take me to the house. The reason for my concern was why I had been invited to go on my own and not be accompanied by my wife Tania. I was uncertain how I should appear and behave in such a situation. Of course I'd had to accept the invitation but now what should I say or do?

'You have been granted a great privilege and honour,' said Brazjaf. 'For a male to be invited into the private chambers of a senior female Nazmos governing council member is unprecedented. There must be a purpose behind this but only Ritozanan can know that.'

Then Jazzatnit said something that may have hit the nail on the head.

'Your thoughts were read at your last parting twenty two years ago. Even I knew what you were thinking then and they clearly conveyed sadness that perhaps it was the last time you might see Ritozanan. The conveyed sadness emotion said a lot about how you felt for her and she would have liked that. I am thinking that perhaps she now wishes to put into your memory a bit more than just her outward physical appearance. She may want you to see how and where she has lived. Perhaps you will see her in her sleep tank just as you did Gozmanot. You visited Gozmanot as only you could have done. And you were alone when she reached out to embrace you even though it was all ethereal. Perhaps Ritozanan wishes for a comparison and for you to remember her in the same manner. After all it was her and her alone that persuaded the governing council to give a favourable decision for Nazmos so that Gozmanot's dream and vision could be fulfilled.'

'So what should I do or say?' I asked again.

'Nothing,' said Jazzatnit, 'just be your normal self. Behave as you would wish her to remember you too. You have special gifts Ashley that puts great power and insight at your command. But they are as nothing compared to the gentleness of demeanour that spreads out around you. People are drawn to you because they like what they see and feel about you. Perhaps Ritozanan wants to remember you for how you normally are. So Ashley you must behave as you are doing now. Your visit won't be long but it will be enough for Ritozanan.'

I thought about this for a moment and then thanked Jazzatnit for her advice. But now I said I would take that siesta I had promised myself and follow my host Zazfrapiz's example.

'I will walk you to your room,' said Zazfrapiz with a smile, 'and then continue on to mine. We can leave these three to discus their own affairs while we rest.'

I was learning the Oannes ways so I gave a slight head bow after I stood up and turned to walk beside Zazfrapiz and to my room. I could feel the emotion of affection coming to me as I walked away.

'Thank you Ashley for sharing your concerns with us,' came across to me as I shut my door. I wasn't sure whom it came from but it made me feel good. Perhaps it came from all of them. The Oannes are the most polite people that I know.

I went to the washroom first before removing my tunic and leggings. I then lay down upon a bed which I think was on Tania's usual side but it was the closest one for me. I lay awake for a while but with eyes relaxed and shut and my last thought was of Gozmanot reaching out in an attempt to embrace me.

'You've come at last,' were the words she conveyed the moment she saw me.

She was not a thing of beauty at her age but her presence was overpowering in the extreme. And very pleasant at the same time I thought. I think that was the last thought I had before I fell asleep.

The next thing I knew was when I felt soft lips on mine. I had a smile as I awoke.

'Wake up sleepy head,' said Tania leaning over me as she sat on the bed beside me, 'your banquet awaits.'

I put my arm around her and pulled her down onto me. Quickly she conveyed a negative that we were not alone. I relaxed my hold and Tania stood up and her soft laugh filled the room. Oh how I loved that laugh and I heard it often enough. I wondered what she thought of mine. I've never seen it but I do know that there are various degrees of it. The one time I laughed so hard that I had trouble getting a breath in. So I assume that I laugh by breathing outwards as does Tania and most of the people I know. Oannes on the other hand tend not to laugh as we humans do though humour is not far from their conscious thoughts. I think their laughter occurs inside their body for I have seen them shake with humorous emotion. I shall have to observe more closely.

'Hello darling,' I said looking up at this gorgeous wife of mine, 'did you have a nice tour?'

'Oh Ashley,' she said, 'our son was absolutely charming. I think he was enjoying playing up to his fans. He knows so much about Wentazta that he really needed no help from Farzant though occasionally he did ask her opinion. Our son reigns supreme where these ladies are concerned. I feel sorry for them though.'

'And why is that,' I asked.

Tania laughed her soft laugh again.

'I think he's just playing to the gallery,' she said. 'His mind is definitely focussed elsewhere. Space seems to be his only true love.' She said this last rather wistfully.

I blocked my mind – even from my wife - as I went through my own thoughts. I felt Simon had not forgotten a certain lady space cadet named Mazpazam. I'd had a view of a pert little Oannes face when Simon had mentioned her. Survey ships tended to spend extended periods in space and it could be years before they met again.

'And what did our brood think of the Shopping Mall?' I asked.

'Oh they loved it but Simon didn't let them buy anything. He said this was just a window shopping trip and that there was a lot more to see. But Sarah was sorely tempted by a large floral display similar to the ones Jazzatnit has here in her courtyard.'

'Nothing wrong with a little retail therapy,' I said smiling.

'Come on you,' she said to me, 'get yourself sorted and ready for this special banquet. It's in your honour you know.'

'You said we weren't alone.' I conveyed this privately.

'We never are,' she replied in kind, 'someone is always reading our thoughts.'

'Not if you can block them.'

'I forget to,' conveyed Tania with a smile.

'Will you scrub my back?'

'If you wish it.'

'I wish.'

'Okay then,' with a broad smile, 'but you'll have to do mine as well.'

Twenty minutes later we had dried ourselves and put on our best matching tunics, leggings and footwear. Tania looked great with her full make-up and diamond earrings. I'm partial to bright red lipstick especially on Tania. She would be the bell of the banquet today and the envy of the Oannes ladies there.

Sadly Jazzatnit and Zazfrapiz were not attending. One outing a day was as much as Zazfrapiz could endure.

The banquet was well attended and the Domed Hall was packed. There was euphoria in the mood of the Oannes people and I expect that most were thrilled that their hopes for Gozmanot's vision for Nazmos would soon be realised. No one spoke of myths anymore but rather of the foretelling of a wise Oannes sage. This banquet was a celebration of things to come for Nazmos and its people and all knew it. The entire Nazmos governing council of ministers were here and I sensed a change in their mood as well. They seemed pleased with their decision for Nazmos and I expect that Ritozanan had not had too difficult a task of persuasion. But I do think that they were pleased by the euphoric reaction from the majority of their people. It had been a popular decision and therefore an easy one'

Simon was seated between his mum and Rachel. I was beside Tania with Katy on my left. Robin was the other side of Katy.

Facing us and directly opposite Simon were Fiona and Farzant with her parent's Muznant and Brazjaf. Brian and Sarah were the other side of Fiona.

It was conveyed to me that I should enjoy the evening as a celebration without any formalities. There were to be no speeches or toasts of any kind, just friendly communion. Later in the course of the evening after the meal was done then a general mixing among the people could occur.

I looked around and saw many familiar faces at other tables. I think I recognised the back profile of Zakatanz but I was not certain. He must have sensed my thought and looked around and nodded. I smiled back and conveyed that we would meet after the meal. There were two Oannes women with him and I was keen to meet them. I thought one must be Azatamunt and the other his daughter.

Just then the meal was announced telepathically and this was followed by pallets of dishes floating to the tables and supervised by an attendant Oannes person. Everyone was in their finest clothes and I noticed that the Nazmos governing council ministers had on the same finery from the morning meeting. I looked around them but Ritozanan was not among them. I noticed however that this time the ministers had their wives and partners seated beside them and in even greater finery. I had to smile at their beauty as I noticed that some faint tinting of lipstick and blusher had been applied for that little bit of added colour.

The meal was excellent as usual and Rachel had her own special orange drink in place of the Wazu that was distributed around the table.

Oannes normally communicate silently via telepathy – but today I noticed a low pitched hum of verbal conversation throughout the banqueting area. I do not know if the Oannes ever had a language of their own. I had tried to find out but all Muznant could tell me was that telepathic communication had its own intent. No words were necessary since none were spoken. However communication with humans had begun with their first contact ten thousand years ago and since then most of Earth's languages were picked up.

I thought of the time at the Aberporth B&B when I had first come into contact with Jan Bogdan and Sarul Kwiatkowski. It was 1989 and I was eight years old. It was the evening meal and the dining hall was quite full. We were at the next table to the two Polish plumbers when suddenly I realised that I understood every part of their Polish conversation.

The Oannes explorers must have had a similar experience when they first met the human race. And of course since Anztarza all of Earth's languages would have been monitored and understood. I'm sure many were being spoken today here at the banquet.

I was pleased to note that the dishes I disliked had not been put on our table though I recognised them on neighbouring tables. Bizzony and Trozbit are an acquired taste but I preferred to avoid them. I was quite happy with my favourite Yaztraka especially as it came in two separate dishes one with extra sweetening in it.

I noticed that Simon was happy taking a bit from each of the dishes and quite enjoying his meal. He even took a generous portion of the Milsony with its spicy taste. I offered some to Fiona but she politely declined saying she'd eaten enough. Another politician I thought.

I noticed that Fiona and Farzant had become friends and were in intense communication with each other – private of course. But they also were intensely aware of Simon's presence across from them. They asked him about his life in space and Simon regaled them with stories of his academy days and then of the tests they had to endure for their training. Not once did he mention Mazpazam in his adventures and that told me a lot. Good luck Simon I thought but be careful in how you reveal yourself. A spaceman's life is a lonely one but if Zakatanz the formerly taciturn starship captain could find happiness again then who's to know what is and is not possible.

The Oannes servers come out again with empty pallets and cleared the dishes off the tables in a matter of minutes. It was time for the inter-mingling to commence.

The Oannes never do anything in a rush so it was some time before a few stood up and strolled to meet their friends. Tania and I then also stood up and after giving a polite bow to the governing council member's tables I led the way around towards Zakatanz.

He must have sensed our approach for he stood up and turning met me part way. Our mutual affection was evident in the informal greeting and Sewa remarks.

'I'm so very pleased to see you captain and looking so well,' I said with enthusiasm.

'Ah, that is because I am a happy man,' he said, 'and all due to Azatamunt whom you met on your last visit. But you know all about that from my communications.'

He then turned to Tania and gave her a firm handshake and a slight bow. He conveyed a private message that brought a smile to her face along with the hint of a faint blush. Obviously a compliment on her looks had been conveyed.

'Come and meet my daughter Hazazamunt. Azatamunt chose the name and I was pleased to agree. We received special dispensation to bring her to the banquet as she is not yet fifteen years in age.'

Zakatanz smiled with pride as I looked at his daughter.

'She is keen to meet you Ashley,' he added.

'She is beautiful,' I conveyed privately to Zakatanz. I had seen images of her in his communications and thought that she took after her mother – and aunt as well. But she was far prettier in real life as she stood before me.

I shook hands with mother and daughter and conveyed that I was pleased to meet the youngest member of their family.

Hazazamunt had large eyes that were fixed upon my face for some considerable time. I could see that she was trying to reconcile the imagined Ashley person with the legend that had grown up around that name. I stood before her as an ordinary human.

'Do I pass,' I said with my widest possible smile.

I was sorry the moment I had said it for Hazazamunt immediately looked away and then down at the floor.

Tania went around to her and put an arm across the youngster's shoulders. She was still small and much shorter than most Oannes adults.

'Don't mind him my dear,' said Tania winking at me, 'he's just an ordinary unfeeling member of the male species. Aren't you Mr Ashley Bonner?

'Yes I am indeed,' I said, 'and I am sorry if I caused you embarrassment my dear Hazazamunt. Please forgive me. I would like us to be friends.'

I went forward and held out my hand to her. Slowly her small hand lifted and came into mine. I bowed low as I raised her hand to my lips. I let my lips press on the back of her hand before straightening up again. It was a relief to see the smile that appeared on her face. I gave her a big smile in return.

'Have you met my family?' I then asked her, 'I should be pleased for you to meet them all.'

Hazazamunt was shy and only gave a slight nod. So Tania and I took her to our table and I performed the introductions beginning with Simon. She seemed to relax at the sight of Simon and I knew straight away that they had met before and knew each other quite well. A brief communication passed between them which seemed to have a pleasant effect on both. Hazazamunt nodded to each of the others as I introduced them and she seemed to relax noticeably. I then let Simon take over the conversation as I could see her gravitate towards him. Soon a little conversational group had formed around her of Rachel, Fiona and Margaret and Simon gradually withdrew to Sarah and Brian. That left Robin, Katy, Tania and me with Zakatanz and Azatamunt. Muznant and Brazjaf had excused themselves earlier and had gone to meet some friends a few tables away.

I found myself alone with Captain Zakatanz and we discussed our intended trip to the Sirius Star system. Sirius was 8.6 light-years on the other side of where Earth was and the trip from Nazmos would pass within 1.3 light-years of Earth. As such the total journey distance to Sirius was 14.4 light-years and with my assistance should take just under eleven days; Earth days of course. A day was to be spent on the Sirius B tests before journeying to Earth.

Zakatanz had been approached by the Anztarza chief ministers for an alternative program by going to Earth first but had been refused for reasons only a starship captain's command could understand. The trip was to commence in four days after I had completed my tasks here.

I asked the captain if he was to be aboard 9632-Orange tomorrow but after a brief hesitation he conveyed that regrettably he had much to attend to on his starship 8110-Gold. There was a smile on his face as he said this and I then learnt that his ferry spaceship journey was planned to coincide with events and he would be witnessing most of it from another vantage point. I expect there to be a flotilla of spaceships out there for such an historic occasion. Obviously they would be at the proper polite locations so as to cause no hindrance to our shuttles.

Azatamunt then came and touched my arm. She conveyed nothing except I felt an emotion of gratitude and affection coming from her. She had done this once before but this time it was exceedingly strong. I think she was trying to say, 'Thank you for being a friend to my husband.'

I conveyed my own feelings that I admired him immensely and was pleased that my gifts had brought him comfort.

'And love,' she conveyed and I nodded my agreement.

When I had first met him in 2006 he had been a taciturn Oannes captain of very few words. But my revelation regarding his betrothed Hazazamunt's medical condition had shed light on the reason for her disappearance and that had been the start of our friendship. And now here he was a pleasant family man with a loving wife and daughter. What a transformation and I was pleased that I'd had a small part in it.

And so the evening progressed and I got to meet many of the governing council members especially Korizazit and Nerbtazwi. Our main topic was of course about the Nazmos orbital change and the care I would take to ensure that atmospheric and sea conditions were affected to a minimum. My plan was for a 1% of normal gravity deceleration which would have to be over the duration of seventeen hours in six hour period phases. The Oannes scientists had done all the calculations.

Leaving them I passed among the tables with Tania by my side and spoke with all who shook my hand. I was beginning to feel embarrassed by all the admiration, looks and emotions that came through to me. I continually sent back messages that I was just an ordinary human who had been granted certain gifts. I added the thought that as soon as Gozmanot's dream visions had been initiated that those gifts would probably be taken from me – which I was sincerely looking forward to. I imagined that the telepathy part would remain as it was an acquired art currently being pursued generally on Earth. But everything else might go which thought pleased me no end. It was all really quite a burden of responsibility. Anyway we would see what was to be. 'Que-sera-sera' as the song lyrics go.

Although my thoughts must surely have been read by the Oannes people it seemed not to make the slightest difference to their opinion of me. To them I had achieved great things but to me I had simply taken one step at a time. The Asteroids, Neptune's moon Titan, Platwuz and next Nazmos. And then the big task of Zarama to complete the mission and Gozmanot's vision. These would all become a part of Oannes history and I was to be at the centre of it. I suppose I must accept the attention gracefully. And thankfully I'm glad that it was I who was chosen for all of this. The adventure aspect is phenomenal.

And soon I shall return to Earth for a second period of peace until Simon comes for me in the starship 4110-Silver. Oddly, my imagination did not extend to a time beyond my contact with Zarama and yet I felt no sadness at the thought. And so I say again, 'Que-sera-sera'.

The evening continued and I felt that I had been around the Domed Hall venue fairly extensively. I then found myself back to where the governing council members were seated. Many had left but my friends Nerbtazwi and Korizazit were still there. I sensed that they had been waiting for me but had patiently held their thoughts in check when they saw me mixing with the general Oannes public.

'Ashley,' said the diminutive Nerbtazwi, 'you are looking exceptionally buoyant. There is a glow about you that you are enjoying the company here.'

'I am indeed,' I replied. 'It is a wonderful banquet and the people are wonderful. It is nice to think that one day humans will behave like this; though not for some millennia I think. But today I feel I belong here and the thought is a pleasant one.'

Then Korizazit came close to me and touched my arm and conveyed a private message. It had to do with my visit to Ritozanan's house planned for when I returned after I had initiated the Nazmos orbital change. Both Korizazit and Nerbtazwi would accompany me and it would be left to Ritozanan's wishes as to the protocol that was to be followed. But neither of them thought that the visit would be a prolonged one. I conveyed that I would accept whatever Ritozanan wished and that I was looking forward to the visit. Jazzatnit had primed me well.

The governing council members keep their reserve when attending public functions such as this one though in private they mix with a chosen circle of friends and colleagues. I feel privileged to be included in that number.

It was not long after my two friends had left me that I noticed the remaining council members get up and leave through their private exit at the side. The same one that Ritozanan had floated through after our midday meeting. I conveyed to the others of our party that perhaps it was time that we too left. We should take our leave and return to our base at Jazzatnit's house. And so I conveyed a general thanks for the evening and a farewell to all the Oannes people still present in the hall. I became conscious of my embarrassment when they began to clap slowly at first and then with a faster rhythm as our group made its way towards where the Transporters were waiting.

I looked at Simon and he was positively glowing as he looked around and raised his own hands in a clapping gesture. This he did to acknowledge the honour the Oannes were bestowing upon us. So I followed suit as did all our group and we received smiles from every quarter. I must say it all made me feel good inside.

Simon remained on the Transporter when it dropped us off in the plaza near Jazzatnit's house. He said he was required to return to his post on his ship for the night but would meet us aboard the spaceship 9632-Orange tomorrow. He would be accompanied by his fellow officers Rooztnaz and Brijtook.

Muznant, Brazjaf and Farzant also stayed aboard the Transporter and would be dropped off at their own place. They would not be with me on the journey tomorrow as they wished to experience the Nazmos orbital slowdown from down here on its surface. I smiled as I walked away. Muznant was giving me my own space – a wonderful comfort zone.

'How did it go?' queried Jazzatnit when we got back into her courtyard. I conveyed my images of the evening and she was pleased that Korizazit and Nerbtazwi were to accompany me on my visit to Ritozanan. We sat around the dining table chatting informally and drinking a last mug of hot tea before retiring to our rooms for the Nazmos night. Tania and I were mentally tired but that didn't stop us from having our usual bedtime cuddle. We talked about Simon mainly and we both said that we loved what we saw. He was a man now and so full of confidence and the zest of life. We were proud of him and the career he had chosen. I kept my mind closed and feigned sleep when thoughts of his cadet colleague Mazpazam came into my mind. I was not sure how Tania would feel about it.

Next morning after a not too early breakfast the Transporter collected us and took us to the space park and to Captain Rojazonto's ship 9632-Orange. The internal mini-transporter then took us beneath it and then up into the bowel of the ship and before long we were at the control room entrance. I had looked out for Simon and his fellow officers but did not see them anywhere. I immediately received a message through my communication Badge that they were currently enroute to the ship. I conveyed this to Tania and the others.

When we entered the control room Captain Rojazonto greeted us with a smile and a congenial Sewa. I replied in similar vein as we exchanged a firm handshake. It was more like a hand clasp since we used both hands. His deputies came forward then and conveyed their own welcoming greeting with a slight bow of the head. The captain informed us that the ship had been specially prepared for the trip but that all the science personnel were not yet aboard. They were expected and should arrive shortly. Brajam and Niztukan would be among them. Niztukan of course was the dare-devil of the starship neutron shield episodes. I had a great respect for these Oannes scientists and I hoped to meet the others in the team. I imagine that many would be on this trip.

I looked around the space park but could not see the huge bulk of the spaceship 98103-Pink anywhere. I believe it was still out on its long trials somewhere in space.

We spent about twenty minutes paying our respects to captain and control room crew when I received the suggestion that we retire to the dining hall for relaxation and refreshment. We were also informed that our usual cabins had been allocated to our group and we could rest there when the ship was cruising towards its various rendezvous destinations.

I had received a full briefing of the planned agenda and what was expected of me. Platwuz was now approaching the hundred million mile distance from Raznat and beginning its orbital loop around it. It had now attained the very high orbital perigee velocity of 27,200 mph and if allowed to continue it would simply speed out to an apogee even beyond its initial orbital distance. Twenty two years ago I had helped to change the orbit of this planet for it to drop closer to its heat source Raznat. I had done this in two phases in order to reduce the time frame from thirty years down to twenty two. I had not wished to wait the full thirty years since we humans did not have the Oannes lifespan. So here we were twenty two years later and about to consolidate Platwuz into its new orbit.

Brajam had informed me how this was to be achieved. Platwuz must be slowed from its current 27,200 mph velocity down to 9,000 mph. And I was to restrict my telekinetic effort to achieve not more than one percent of normal gravity deceleration on the planet. This was still rather high but with only atmosphere on the planet and all of the mining population evacuated the storms if any should subside within a few months. These science people had done their calculations and the deceleration would involve a period of just over eleven hours. As such I would get a period of rest after five hours when we would return to 9632-Orange for a meal and refreshment. The second stint would recommence after two hours and continue to finality.

A change to the original plan had been instituted by the Nazmos governing council at our Domed Hall meeting to see if my telekinetic gift was effective at a distance of two million miles. This was because Simon had indicated that Oannes spaceships had explored the Sirius star system and that the limit of their approach distance to the dwarf star Sirius B had been this distance. Sirius B was about the mass of our Sun and a third lighter than Zarama but I wished to see it for myself. Hence our intended journey to Sirius after Nazmos had also been slowed.

At two million miles Platwuz would look very small indeed. Brajam estimated a visual image of a pea when viewed at a distance of ten feet. And that too as only a half image since the orbital velocity would be transverse to the position of Raznat and half the planet would be in darkness. I was actually looking forward to the event though a minor doubt did remain.

Would my telekinetic gift be effective at this distance? If not then I'd just have to move in closer. But with Zarama that might not be possible because of the intense heat emanating from it. I would soon find out.

I was into my second mug of tea in the dining hall when Simon appeared through the doorway. Accompanying him were two smartly dressed Oannes officers exuding a very confident manner. I stood up to greet my son and also to receive the introduction to his fellow officers. Both greeted me with great respect and a slight diffidence but I moved forward with outstretched hand which each eagerly shook in turn. I could see that I might be a figure of awe to them but I was confident that I could soon put them at their ease. So I put my arm across Simon's shoulders as I addressed them in my calmest voice and widest smile.

'I do hope that this son of mine obeys all orders given to him,' I said, 'because if he doesn't you have my permission to withdraw all privileges.'

Rooztnaz who was the senior among them immediately conveyed that Simon was an excellent officer and a good friend. He was still not at his ease as I would have preferred.

'I am pleased to hear it,' I said, 'but come and meet the other members of Simon's family.'

And one by one I performed the introductions and tried to convey a little about each.

Simon was nearly in fits of laughter and his eyes sparkled as he watched the awkwardness of his fellow shipmates. I wished Simon had forewarned me that both Rooztnaz and Brijtook were not used to social discourse and had mainly come on this trip to meet me. However I knew how to put them at their ease and that was to discuss this mission with them.

'So will you be on the shuttle with Simon and me when I attempt to slow down Platwuz?' I asked.

They looked at each other with great uncertainty of expression, so I continued.

'Then let me now invite you both to accompany Simon on the same shuttle with me,' I said, 'and you must let me know if there is any other way that I can assist you. Let us hope that we are successful in our mission.'

The confident air returned to them and this time I received a reply.

'Thank you sir,' said Rooztnaz, 'it is a great kindness you show us and which we shall always remember.' I liked his low tone gravelly voice.

Brijtook then also spoke and said something similar. He had a rather husky voice. I said I hoped to get to know them better over time and was glad that Simon had such good companions.

Zanos then came through with the information that 9632-Orange was to begin its journey in the next half hour. I queried Zanos as to the journey time to the destination coordinates and was immediately given a time of five and a half hours. I conveyed this to the others and Fiona said she would like to witness the rise into space from the control room.

'It is always exciting when the blue sky darkens into black and the stars all appear,' she said.

Captain Rojazonto agreed to my request to witness the lift off but suggested that after that all should retire to their cabins until the destination coordinates were attained. The time factor was due to the fact that Platwuz was on the opposite side of Raznat from Nazmos's current orbital position.

Simon and his fellow shipmates conveyed that they would remain in the dining hall. I immediately knew the reason for this. They must show Oannes spaceship etiquette for the captain of the ship on which they were guests. It would have been presumptuous to enter any ship's control room when they were not on duty there. I said that I understood, accepted and respected their decision and would see them on the shuttle with me when the time came.

'Sure dad,' said Simon with a smile, 'see you then.'

Tania looked at me and we exchanged knowing glances. Simon had to behave in a decorous manner when in the company of his fellow officers. Our boy was a grown man and we had to get used to the idea. We made our way to the large control room well in time before the departure.

The lift-off was so smooth that we only knew it was happening when the other craft in the space park seemed to recede downwards. The tint of the overhead sky changed quite rapidly from pale blue to deep blue and then to black as we sped upwards. Some of the brighter stars became visible but Raznat glowed brightly on our right side and would remain so for most of our journey. Our spaceship would have to traverse to the other side of Raznat for our rendezvous with Platwuz.

A decided tint had appeared in the view panels of the control room dome and after half an hour even Fiona felt there was nothing new to see. So we took our leave of the captain and his officers.

Captain Rojazonto conveyed that the plan was for 9632-Orange to accelerate at one and a half times Nazmos gravity for the next 3½ hours until the million mile distance from Nazmos had been achieved. Then the neutron generators would operate to accelerate the ship to 40,000 miles per second to complete the journey to Platwuz in the next 1½ hours. The captain also informed us that a meal was to be served in the dining hall in about 2½ to 3 hours. We should return there then.

'What do you want to do?' was the thought that came through to me from Tania.

I knew what she wanted so I agreed and we got the internal mini-transporter to take us to the dining hall where we expected to find Simon and his colleagues. The others all accompanied us too and that is where we found him alone with Brijtook. We had only the next few days to get to see our son again and catch up with all the visual expressions of our meeting.

'Where is Rooztnaz?' I enquired and was told that as first officer on spaceship 7332-Blue he was duty bound to convey the respects of his Captain Vikazat to the captain of the ship on which he was travelling as a guest.

I looked at Brijtook and saw a sharp eyed Oannes adult keen to make conversation with me. I liked what I saw and as a gesture of goodwill I reached out with my right hand and invited him to an in-depth mind read.

Before he took my hand he looked at Simon who gave him a smile and brief nod signifying okay. The mind read took but an instant and it worked both ways. And I liked what I saw. I had kept my mind open and so had he. We now knew each other well.

Brijtook had been born in Wentazta and had lived there for most of his life before joining the space academy. He loved the city life and was the only child of an elderly couple. Both were still alive, well over 300 years of age and quite frail – a bit like Ritozanan I thought. Age seemed to catch up very suddenly on some Oannes once they crossed the three century mark. I suppose my own parents could now be classed in a similar aged status. I sincerely hope that they are around for Simon's visit to Earth with 4110-Silver whenever that comes to pass. I'm hoping for that to take place sometime within the next five year period. Although Dad will not have quite reached ninety by then I worried that the rheumatoid arthritis was taking its toll on his health.

I sipped my glass of Wazu as we chatted about this and that and eventually the topic of conversation came round to Nazmos and its transition prospects. I said I had no idea how and when the various changes would bear fruit but going by Gozmanot's vision it would be extremely gradual. Some improvement especially climatic might be noticeable in an Oannes lifetime but surely the slowness of change would allow plenty of time for adjustment to the new conditions. Different viewpoints were expressed but in general there was an excitement about it.

Tania squeezed my hand and a sad thought came through to me from her. We personally would not live long enough to see any of it. I then conveyed that we didn't need to since we would be on Earth; or at least she would be. Now why had that separatist thought come into my head? And Tania looked at me wide eyed and questioning.

'Has your inner voice told you something?' she asked silently.

'No,' I replied genuinely puzzled, 'and I don't know why the thought came into my head.'

Simon obviously saw his mum's mood change and he too queried if we were alright.

'Yes,' conveyed Tania, 'it's just that your dad used an odd phrase and he did not include himself in it.'

She then privately conveyed our telepathic discussion. Simon said nothing and I looked at him to see if he had received a premonition, but reading my intent he shook his head.

'Don't worry dad,' he said, 'I'm sure everything will work out just right.'

But he said no more on the matter and I knew that he would not forget the moment.

He soon got back into the conversation around the table with him and Fiona having a lively discussion about the space race back on earth. Fiona said she could understand why humans should not benefit from the energy scientific know-how of the Oannes, at least not as yet. Simon was giving his own point of view when Rooztnaz entered the hall. He had been away for slightly over half an hour and seemed pleased in himself. His Captain Vikazat although much younger had met and got on well with Captain Rojazonto some years ago. And so Rooztnaz was to be given a package of data before the end of the day for onward transmission to Vikazat.

Also as a result Rooztnaz had been granted a tour of 9632-Orange. And it included his fellow officers. It was an opportunity not to be missed so Rooztnaz had come to collect Simon and Brijtook as it would all go towards their career formulation.

I could see that Fiona wished to be asked to join them but she was not. Simon explained that as spaceship crew they would be shown areas of the ship where ordinary passengers were not allowed. So as Simon and his fellow officers took their leave I suggested that we retire to our cabins and return for the meal in two hours time. I said I might just grab forty winks and some quiet time. There was as yet another five hours to rendezvous location.

Tania and I settled down on our beds fully clothed as we were. I think she knew I was keyed up with the uncertainty of whether or not my telekinetic gift would be effective at the two million mile distance of the trial. And so she just reached across and we held hands. I knew that my previous separatist thought was still on her mind.

It was a comfort having her beside me and I hoped that this situation would prevail throughout our lives together. I wanted to be with her always and it was the same with her. I must endeavour for it to be so.

I think I must have drifted off into a doze in which I dreamed I was pushing against this block of stone but it would not budge. And then the stone seemed to melt and turn into a lake. I was standing ankle deep in it but unable to move my feet. This then faded and I was back home in Dudley sipping a mug of tea on our patio – but I was alone. Where was everybody I thought?

When I finally awoke I could hear heavy deep breathing beside me and looked sideways at my sleeping beauty of a wife. We still held hands loosely and looking at her wrinkle-free face with upturned nose my heart filled with love, pride and sadness. How would I fare against Zarama was a thought I did not like to contemplate? Would I win or would I lose?

Just then Tania opened her eyes and a big smile broke her severe expression of a moment before.

I felt sweaty from having slept fully dressed so decided I'd pop into the shower. I thought I needed to feel refreshed before the Platwuz event. Two million miles was a fair distance from which to apply my telekinetic push but we should all find out soon enough. I could always move in closer if need be but then the doubts would remain with regard to Zarama.

Tania did not stir from the bed while I was showering and followed suit as soon as I had finished. It was nice to see her naked body walk past me as I was drying myself and for a moment I thought of following her but decided against it. The mood was not really there for either of us.

We entered the dining hall again and were the last of our group to be seated. Simon was there talking to Fiona and Sarah and he smiled when he saw us. I looked around and could not see the fellow spacemen and Simon quickly conveyed that they were elsewhere communicating with this ship's crew. I perceived a contrivance by them to allow Simon time alone with his family. This was typical Oannes understanding and consideration for others.

The buffet meal was set out and we helped ourselves as usual. Although we sat for some considerable time at the table I noticed crew members coming and going over short periods of time. Ours was a social occasion while theirs was not.

Zanos then conveyed that the spaceship was in a parking loop close to station and that I and my group should prepare to proceed to the shuttle bay area at our convenience. Captain Rojazonto was sending one of his officers to conduct us there.

At about this time Brajam came in with Niztukan and a few others whom I believed to be fellow scientists. They acknowledged us before proceeding to tables nearby. Brajam conveyed a private message to me and I replied in the affirmative that it would be a pleasure. We would be sharing the same shuttle craft for the entire event.

I was surprised when Rojazonto entered the hall and came over to us. I looked around him but he was alone. 'I decided to be with you during this trip,' he conveyed. 'It is an historic moment after all and it is a captain's duty to make sure all goes to plan.' He was smiling broadly as he conveyed this. It would be a pleasure having him on the shuttle with me.

Together we left the dining hall and the internal transporter took us towards the shuttle bay decks where the preparation rooms were. Here we entered one of the rooms and selected and put on the required gold electrostatic overall type suits. We got the transporter again and were taken right up to a fairly large shuttle craft on the deck. There were four shuttles to be used on this trip and each was loading up as we were boarding ours. Each shuttle could carry about fifty persons.

I looked at our ladies and all had their head scarves firmly in place. The Oannes understood what our girls liked to wear on their heads and had fashioned this headwear with that in mind. I smiled as I was again reminded of an old ladies convention heading for an outing on a rainy day. Tania read my thought and elbowed me lightly in the side as a reproof but I noticed a smile on her face. We were in the front row of the shuttle on both sides of the central aisle. Simon was seated beside me and I was grateful for his presence; it was most reassuring. He conveyed that Rooztnaz and Brijtook were also on the shuttle and seated a few rows behind.

Zanos conveyed that departure was imminent and then the bay lights dimmed followed by the slow opening of the large bay doors. The shuttles were all facing outwards and the darkness of space gaped in front of us as the doors opened fully. The other shuttles all left before us and it was a good ten minutes before we too lifted off the deck and floated through the open doors. As before Zanos had primed our minds to cope with the nausea of weightlessness so we felt normal. The thigh clamps held us firmly to our seats. I felt the acceleration in the middle of my back and knew the shuttle was heading out to a set location. Looking back the spaceship 9632-Orange rapidly diminished in size before disappearing altogether.

Brajam and Niztukan were right behind me and I received a private message that the shuttle was nearly at its required location. The other shuttles had spread out to positions of an imaginary triangle that would accurately monitor Platwuz by velocity and spatial position.

It was about twenty minutes before I felt the acceleration diminish and then cease. The shuttle then did an about face to put Raznat on our right hand side. The mass of the universe stars were to be seen on my left. The glow of the Milky Way was truly brilliant but as its pathway rose over the shuttle it gradually faded and then melted into the bright glow of Raznat.

I searched ahead of the shuttle but at first could not see Platwuz anywhere. I blinked to adjust my eyesight from the brightness of Raznat and then felt Brajam's hand on my shoulder. His thoughts directed me towards a point on the front shuttle panel and then to look beyond it for Platwuz. I missed it at first but then saw this very distant half moon shape. It was rather dull and about the size of a pea or should I say half a pea. Brajam conveyed that this was Platwuz and it was currently within the window of its future orbit around Raznat and currently travelling through space at 27,200 mph. It was two million miles from the shuttle's position and I should now begin my telekinetic attempt at slowing it down.

I felt Tania's hand enter mine and rest there. She did not squeeze it or anything like that but I understood that she was just letting me know she was there beside me. For some reason I felt a surge of confidence enter my being and I knew then that my telekinetic efforts would be successful even at this distance. So I looked at the distant tiny half pea of a planet and concentrated my mind upon it and desired that it begin to slow down with a deceleration rate that was 1% of normal gravity. I also desired that the telekinetic push be applied to both land and atmospheric particles alike. I did not want raging hurricanes to sweep across the face of Platwuz hence the low chosen deceleration rate. I knew that having initiated the required telekinetic effort that it would then be controlled as an involuntary action by my mind and would continue uniformly until I willed it to cease.

I knew that some atmospheric disturbance was inevitable on Platwuz but I wished for it to be of minimal intensity. I must slow Platwuz to an orbital velocity of 9,000 mph for its required stable orbit to be achieved. The Oannes scientists had calculated that the time frame for this would take approximately eleven hours in duration.

However this was considered as too long to be in a shuttle under zero gravity and so it had been agreed that I cease my telekinetic effort after five and a half hours. The shuttles would then all return us to the mother spaceship 9632-Orange for a meal and a rest lasting a total of two hours. Then the whole procedure would be repeated to complete the mission.

I looked around at Brajam and then conveyed to all in the shuttle that I had initiated my telekinetic push upon Platwuz. We must now wait for confirmation from the other shuttle crews about the status of Platwuz.

We did not have long to wait when reports came in that a definite slowing down in the velocity of Platwuz had occurred and was continuing at the set rate of just over 1% of Nazmos gravity. A big smile spread across my face as I felt Brajam's hand on my shoulder again and a conveyed 'Well done my friend' message.

Tania's hand gave mine a squeeze and I squeezed hers in return. I looked sideways at my wife and felt excitement build in my groin. I think she recognised the emotion and quickly withdrew her hand from mine and followed this by a rather hard elbow in my ribs. The excitement subsided and I grinned rather sheepishly at her. She avoided my gaze but conveyed a very private one word message instead. And that word was to 'wait' and so I would.

Continuous reports of Platwuz's orbital velocity change kept coming in through Zanos-on-board and for me it simply became a waiting game. After an hour all was still going to plan and the monitoring equipment within Platwuz's domes reported a rising atmospheric wind. All mining operations had been shut down and personnel evacuated to Nazmos. This was because twenty two years ago when I had reduced Platwuz's orbital velocity by a mere 150 mph, great storms had lashed across its surface. This time the planet's velocity must be reduced by 18,200 mph and atmospheric disturbances had to be considered. However at the very low rate of deceleration over eleven hours and my new found telekinetic control it was hoped this would be minimal.

I looked at the distant pea sized half moon and nothing seemed to have changed. Our shuttle was keeping pace and distance from Platwuz as planned as the hours passed.

I sat in my shuttle seat and dozed occasionally as I expect others did as well for nothing seemed to be happening. Every once in a while I looked up into the darkness of space and at the distant planet. Finally the five and a half hours were up and I ceased my telekinetic effort.

It took another half hour for us to enter the shuttle bay of 9632-Orange which had altered its parking loop to suit our arrival. It was an immense relief when I saw the bay doors close behind us and all four shuttles safely on the deck. The return of normal gravity had occurred as soon as our shuttles had entered the ship and settled down. I felt restless and clammy in my electrostatic suit and was pleased when we got out of them.

The internal transporter took us to the dining hall at my request where I not only downed two large glasses of Wazu but also two mugs of sweet tea. I was not hungry then but still felt clammy and I realised that I must have gone through a period of anxiety bringing out the sweat in me. So I expressed a wish to return to my cabin for a shower and fresh change of clothes. Tania said she'd accompany me but I shook my head in a positive 'no.'

'But come for me in a little over an hour,' I said. 'I'm rather drowsy and tired so I shall have a kip after my shower.'

I could see concern on Tania's face as well as the others but conveyed that this was following the usual pattern after such a telekinetic effort. After all Platwuz was a massive planet. It certainly took its toll of my energy.

Brajam conveyed that a meal was about to be served up but they would keep some aside for when I returned to the dining hall. The internal transporter took me to my cabin and within minutes I had showered and lain down on the bed clothed just in my boxer shorts. I must have gone instantly to sleep.

'Wake up sleepy head,' said Tania in a whisper as she also kissed me lightly.

I opened my eyes and smiled up at her and asked if I had been asleep long.

'Yes you have,' she said, 'a little over two hours. I came once before but Zanos forbid me from waking you up then. You were in too deep a sleep and it would have undone any good from your rest. Brajam and the other scientists have reprogrammed the break to three hours. So my dear husband your dinner awaits.'

We entered the dining hall once again and only Brajam and a few of his scientist colleagues were there. All the others had retired to their cabins after their meal for a rest. Some began to return as I was partway through my second helping of Yaztraka. I only drank one glass of Wazu as I did not wish to get a full bladder in the next six hour period. There was such a thing as an absorbent pad that could be worn between your legs and these were stored under each seat on the shuttle. But I would only resort to it if the need was dire.

Brajam conveyed that Platwuz had been slowed to 18,100 mph orbital speed and the second phase to slow it down to 9,000mph was well on target. So once again I was to return to the fray. But this time I had a surprise waiting for me. This time the shuttle went to a position from Platwuz very similar to my first effort of twenty two years ago. Then, the shuttle had been positioned at a distance of one planet diameter or 11,000 miles above the planet's surface. This time however Brajam had thought it prudent to double that distance. I had proved a point at the two million mile position and so didn't need to repeat it.

When our shuttle was in position and stationary relative to Platwuz there was a slight gravity effect felt inside the shuttle that was very welcome. Also the view of the planet below us would be a change from the bland blackness of space with the tiny half pea in the distance.

'There is no further need to distance ourselves from Platwuz as before since we now know that your telekinetic power is effective at the distance you will need to be when you tackle Zarama,' said Brajam. 'So now let us proceed.'

And so I did and just as before. I looked at the planet and concentrated my mind upon it and desired that it begin to slow down with a deceleration rate that was 1% of normal gravity and that the telekinetic push is applied to both land and atmospheric particles alike.

Zanos soon confirmed that Platwuz was slowing down according to our plan. The shuttle angled upwards slightly so that its floor was at a 45° angle to Platwuz. The slight gravity from that massive planet now kept us gently in our seats and eased our long wait. Looking down at the planet I could not make out any features since a dust storm was now planet-wide and had been from my earlier stint. I knew it would get worse over the next five and a half hours but should abate in a few months time. With Nazmos I would reduce its deceleration down to just 0.5% of normal gravity, or half of what I was applying to Platwuz. This was because the water on Nazmos was the greater danger.

As I sat in the shuttle I thought about the past. When Platwuz was at its original orbital distance its velocity had been a mere 750 mph. I had then simply slowed it down to 600 mph and then accelerated it towards Raznat at an inclined orbit. But today I was slowing Platwuz by a considerably greater amount. From 27,200 mph down to 9,000 mph and we were halfway there. I realised that a huge amount of energy was required to do so and the exhaustion I felt afterwards was a consequence of that. I did not feel the same tiredness after my efforts on the starships but that was because the starship is tiny in comparison to a planet the size of Platwuz and thank goodness for that.

What worried me was that Zarama had a mass a third greater than that of Earth's Sun and subsequently 200,000 times greater than Platwuz. Did I have the power capacity to deal with such a mass? I had faith in Gozmanot's vision and so knew that I would succeed but what would it cost me?

I think I must have dozed on my seat in the shuttle occasionally as I looked at the dust shrouded planet below. The hours passed by slowly till eventually Zanos conveyed that Platwuz was approaching the desired velocity of 9,000 mph. I had willed that my telekinetic effort cease when this speed was reached and so it did right on cue. I felt an immediate relief but also a tension ache across my shoulders. Subconsciously I must be tensing my body while my telekinetic push was being applied. I must force myself to relax in future.

We were soon on the shuttle bay deck of 9632-Orange and once again I felt the need to get out of all this gear and back to my cabin for a shower and a kip. After the electrostatic suiting room we went to the dining hall where I downed two large glasses of Wazu. Then the internal transporter took me to my cabin alone and after a quick shower I lay down on the bed naked but for a light sheet as a cover. I think I fell asleep instantly and without any thoughts whatsoever entering my head.

When I awoke I felt refreshed and raring to go and also quite hungry. Tania was sitting on the bed beside me and said I had been asleep for over four hours. She had been sitting here for the last half hour and had let me sleep on.

'Good grief,' I exclaimed, 'that long? Where are we?'

Nearing Nazmos,' she said, 'but don't worry there's plenty of time.'

I smiled for I knew what she meant. That word 'wait' had played on my mind and now the waiting was over.

I drew Tania's face down to mine and then what followed felt perfectly natural and most satisfying for both of us. The cuddle afterwards was what I also liked because of the peaceful and calming emotion that came with it. But it didn't last long this time as my stomach made the most horrendously loud hunger noises.

We entered the dining hall and it was a lovely sight that met me. The place was quite full of Oannes and a meal was being served up. Tania must have telepathically radioed ahead for all of our group were there at our usual table. Simon and his fellow officers were also there as were Brajam and Niztukan.

As I walked to the table there was a rustling sound of people standing up and then they began to clap. Simon was also clapping and I just had to go to my son and give him a big hug. I then raised both my arms in the air and conveyed a grateful thanks to all and gave them a clap of my own. I sat down only briefly so that everyone could return to their former positions.

I realised I had not eaten in over nine hours so now I made my way to the buffet table and served myself to big portions of my favourite dishes. When I go out to meet Zarama I shall indulge myself to a big meal like this. Within half an hour I had eaten my fill and Tania laughed as she patted my bulging belly.

'You'll be getting fat if you keep eating like that,' she said aloud for all to hear.

I just smiled at everyone as I was now a sated happy man. There was nothing I could say.

'Dad will never get fat,' said Rachel, 'he's not the kind.'

Simon laughed his Errol Flynn laugh with head thrown back.

'Perhaps when he is ninety we'll let him get nice and round,' he said.

Suddenly his smile vanished and he looked down at the table. I sensed he'd had a premonition of something and it was not pleasant. I think I knew what that was so I kept my mind blocked. Although my inner voice was not talkative at the moment I nevertheless knew that I would need to use a greater amount of effort on Zarama than I had first expected. 'At any cost' was a phrase that kept coming into my head.

Zanos conveyed that the neutron generators had operated and slowed the ship right down at the million mile distance from Nazmos. It was now cruising at several thousand miles per hour as it approached Nazmos. The plan was to reach a position 100,000 miles from Nazmos but that would not be for several hours.

It would be another day before we could return to the space park on Nazmos and I shall keep my promise to visit Ritozanan then. Zanos would keep her informed of our situation and progress.

It was Simon who suggested that we all proceed to Deck 15 where the passenger view panels circled the ship. From there the ladies would get a good view of Nazmos as the ship decelerated.

'Yes,' I thought, 'what a good idea.' It would take my mind off serious things and help me to relax.

Simon led the way onto the internal transporter that always seemed ready for us. I think Zanos anticipated our every need and had been instructed to fulfil those wishes.

It was a smooth ride across the ship along its corridors and down the shafts to the level of Deck 15. We arrived in the very wide curving passageway that circled the outer perimeter of this deck. The outer wall contained the six feet square viewing panels that were spaced at intervals of about sixty feet. They were positioned low down near the floor and were perfectly aligned for viewing downwards. Simon and the ladies and Brian went to one panel while Tania and I along with Robin and Katy went to another further along.

I could see Nazmos as a half moon but very small in the distance. Beyond it the brilliance of the stars stood clear and still. It always surprised me how static the stars appeared. There was none of the apparent movement or twinkling effect that one saw during the night on Earth or on Nazmos. It felt as if the stars were sitting there staring unblinking to see what you were up to. My thoughts reverted to the white dwarf star Zarama which to me was the dragon of Gozmanot's vision hell bent on destruction. Could it be a living thing or was that just Gozmanot's way of describing a menace?

Tania squeezed my hand and brought me back to reality. She must have read my thoughts.

I stood back from the view panel and looked across at Simon and his entourage. He was busy explaining and pointing to features outside with an exuberance that only his love for space could have endowed. I just loved looking at him as he was and so did Tania. We were proud of our son.

Beyond us there were quite a few Oannes at the other view panels and when I turned around in the other direction down the wide passageway, those too had Oannes peering through them. Of course the corridor disappeared with the curvature of the ship but I'm sure there must be Oannes at every view point.

As we watched I thought that Nazmos gradually increased in size as we drew nearer. Time seemed to pass slowly but eventually Zanos conveyed that 9632-Orange was approaching its parking loop location some 50,000 miles from Nazmos and that the four shuttles would once again be used for this Nazmos operation.

Simon turned to look at me and I nodded that I was ready. The internal transporter took us directly to the electrostatic suiting room where we once again put on the loose fitting shiny overall type suits. And of course the ladies of our group wore their bonnets - as I called them. Again I had to smile at past memories.

Brajam and I had discussed the Nazmos operation at length over the past couple of days and made many compromises. I had realised earlier that it was not a simple matter of applying my telekinetic push upon Nazmos. Nazmos was a complex arrangement of atmosphere, land and water that must be very carefully balanced during the planet's deceleration. We could not allow one to outpace another. Physically I could never have affected such a balance by simply applying a push on the entire planet as I had done with Platwuz.

There was no water on Platwuz and all habitation was either inside the protection of the domes or had been evacuated off planet. The atmosphere upheaval had been severe on that first occasion twenty two years ago and Brajam had said that it had taken several months for normality to return.

But now I had acquired an additional skill to my telekinetic gift. It was now applied more as a willed wish than a physical effort by me.

I realised this when I had tried to demonstrate my telekinetic ability to Fiona, Sarah and Brian back on Earth. I had simply expressed a desire for the book to move and it had done so before I made any voluntary effort in the old way; the old way being levels of push that I applied through a direct mental effort.

So now I could set the parameters for that push and it would be carried out with a precision that would have been beyond anything I could have achieved through a conscious effort.

The plan was for me to reduce Nazmos's current orbital velocity of 28,500 mph down to a velocity of 25,792 mph which was a reduction of 9.5%. This would then allow Nazmos to gradually drop to a lower orbit perigee of 19 million miles from Raznat over a period of five months.

But by then its orbital velocity would have increased to 46,200 mph. The overall orbit would be an elliptical one that varied between a distance of 19 million miles and the current 31 million miles from Raznat. The Nazmos orbital year would then also reduce to 278 days compared to the current 283 days.

I had made clear to the Nazmos governing council that this situation would remain until I returned in five years or so whenever the starship 4110-Silver was commissioned. I would then fix Nazmos in a circular orbit 19 million miles from Raznat by reducing its perigee orbital velocity down to the calculated 44,000 mph.

For now though as a precaution all Oannes were required to remain indoors during the operation and there were to be no craft operating in its atmosphere. As with Platwuz an atmospheric disturbance was to be anticipated but my personal hope was for this to be very minor. The deceleration of Nazmos was to be at 0.5% of normal gravity over the extended period of 17 hours. Of course I hoped to break this into three periods of 5½ hours each. I expected to complete the task in an overall period of 24 hours.

The Nazmos scientists had made exact computations and I would feed these into my thoughts when I applied my telekinetic wish. I would endeavour for this to be applied to every one of Nazmos' land, sea and air particles in an exact manner to cause the least upset. I had already ingested all this information and would only give it the go-ahead when the time came. I believe that the distance for the position of the shuttle above Nazmos was to be just less than 50,000 miles.

My thoughts were interrupted when Zanos conveyed that the shuttles were ready for boarding. Simon was at my side as the internal transporter took us to our shuttle and it did not seem so long ago when I had been directing my efforts at Platwuz. And here I was again clamped by my thighs in the front seat of the same shuttle with Simon and Tania on either side.

The governing council of Nazmos had conveyed guide-lines of conduct to the whole population. All must remain indoors for the next 24 hours and there was to be no aerial activity. Of course this did not prevent craft from venturing out into open space which many did. Although this event was to be an historic moment in the life of Nazmos I hoped that it would be quite undramatic in its execution and visible effects.

The shuttles were now fully loaded and sealed shut. The lights of the bay dimmed and after a short interval the shuttles rose upwards and turned about. I could see the darkness of space through the open bay doors. There was a shuttle ahead of us and it quickly accelerated out into the blackness. We seemed to follow at a more sedate pace but soon we too were alone in the vastness of space and looking back I saw 9632-Orange as a tiny object diminishing in size even faster.

It took about 30 minutes for our shuttle to get to the required position relative to Nazmos. Zanos then conveyed that all shuttles were in position and that Operation Nazmos could commence. This was the go-ahead signal for me to begin my task.

So now I brought all the parameters of information I had put into my brain for the Nazmos telekinetic push and I wished for it to be carried out with a precision that would cause a minimum of disruption to the equilibrium of the planet's constituent parts. I desired the deceleration to be at a rate of 0.5% of Nazmos gravity until I commanded it to cease.

I required a dual feed back from Zanos. One was that the desired slowing in the planet's velocity was being achieved and the other was the status of conditions upon the planets surface. If the second gave me any indication of worsening conditions then I planned to reduce the deceleration rate down to half of the 0.5% of normal gravity that I was applying. This might prolong the operation but I'd rather Nazmos and its people remained safe and secure. I was particularly concerned about any surge in its vast seas.

After a few minutes Zanos reported that Nazmos was slowing perceptibly and that all was near normal on its surface apart from a minor tidal type surge out across the Peruga Sea.

After half an hour the slow moving swell was unchanged but air movement had increased. At the end of an hour a minor gale was reported as blowing across the land and sea areas. I became concerned that such activity might cause the governing council to rescind their decision but after two hours the conditions had not got worse. Information was coming in from the weather people on Nazmos that the storm seemed to have remained at a consistent level.

As I sat staring at Nazmos so close and yet also distant a slight amount of boredom set in and I began to feel drowsy. It was not long before Zanos announced that the first period of 5½ hours had been reached and that we return to the spaceship for a meal and a rest. As such I commanded that my telekinetic push cease forthwith and so it did. This time I did not feel as tired as with Platwuz but I would wait till I was in normal gravity before confirming that opinion.

It was half an hour before all shuttles were back on the shuttle bay deck and not long before I was in the dining hall downing my second glass of Wazu. A meal was also being served and I felt good enough to indulge myself from my favourite dishes. My hunger was not extreme so I ate less than after the Platwuz operation. I still felt the need for a kip and this time I suggested Tania keep me company and definitely wake me at the prescribed time. I received a private message from Tania but replied in the negative. I just did not wish to be alone in the cabin. I think she understood.

This time I lay on the bed fully clothed and Tania lay on the bed beside me. We held hands and before I knew it I had drifted into a deep sleep. Nothing had changed and my mind still required the recharging that came with sleep.

The second phase commenced two and a half hours after the first had ended and I was pleased that we were on schedule. All went exactly as on the previous occasion only this time after two hours I dozed of and slumped sideways against Simon who held me firmly and kept me upright. Of course my mind continued to apply the required push on Nazmos and after an hour I felt somewhat refreshed and sat upright on my own.

Again Zanos conveyed that conditions on Nazmos were no worse than previously although the storm had increased in its severity. But it was not alarming though the seas were being whipped up into a frenzy. The tidal type surge seemed to have abated but perhaps this had been lost to view because of the choppiness of the seas. The time went by slowly till it was time to cease my operation when Zanos conveyed that the second 5½ hours had elapsed.

This break would be our last before the end of the operation when I could relax indefinitely. I thought of Ritozanan and I wondered what she might be thinking. Hers had been the main influence over the governing council's decision and I hope that the conditions that were being experienced on her world did not cause her to regret that decision. But then Gozmanot must have seen all of this in her visions and known that all would go well.

This time after the meal I slept for a shorter duration in our cabin but had a shower and a fresh change of clothes before returning to shuttle duty.

The third phase commenced on time and again all went as before. This would be a slightly longer stint at six hours and hopefully would be the finish of Operation Nazmos. It was a long time ago when I had first requested a change in orbit and there had been fierce opposition to it then. How opinions had changed and I owed it all to Gozmanot and her visions. Without her memory it could never have been envisaged by the Oannes. But Earth had also played its part. Climatic conditions there were the envy of the Oannes and making their planet the same was a great incentive.

Again I dozed off in my seat and this time I think I dreamed but could not remember anything of it. It was barely an hour that I slept but Tania said she had to nudge me awake as I had started to snore.

Zanos conveyed regular reports that all was going according to plan and that conditions on the surface had not changed much. The storm had increased marginally and some damage was being reported. We were into the last hour of the operation and I think this seemed the longest. The six hours were not fully up when Zanos conveyed that the required velocity had been attained and that the mission was completed. I then ceased all telekinetic effort and suddenly exhaustion seemed to hit me. This time I slumped sideways against Tania and within minutes had fallen into a deep sleep; that is what I was told. Simon bolstered me up firmly and Brajam showed his concern by requesting that this shuttle be the first to return to the ship.

Apparently I drank three glasses of Wazu brought to me after the shuttle landed on the bay deck but promptly fell asleep again. When I finally awoke I was told that I had slept for another four hours after being brought into our cabin. Tania said that she had been concerned for a while until Zanos confirmed that all my vital signs were normal though I was in an extremely deep sleep.

'So where are we now?' I asked.

'Still out in space but now stationary above Nazmos at a height of thirty miles,' said Simon who had stayed with his mum to watch over my sleeping form.

'Why,' I asked

Simon smiled as he said, 'There's still a storm blowing across the surface of Nazmos that was caused by you not to mention the rough seas. But it's not as bad as they first thought. They reckon that in another twelve hours the worst will be over and the storm will abate. All craft may then land where they please. So we shall be holding position here till then. We have more or less normal gravity and I believe another meal is about to be served in the dining hall. You missed the first one. Mum and I had ours in turn when you first came in.'

'Would you like me to bring you something here,' asked Tania, 'or can you manage the dining hall?'

I think Simon was laughing when he heard his mum suggest this.

I was fully recovered now and said the dining hall would be fine.

'But I need to shower and change first.'

Tania stayed in the cabin as I showered but Simon said he would see me in the dining area.

I felt refreshed after but extremely hungry. I think I surprised everyone watching on the amount I ate. I had two glasses of Wazu during my meal and then another after I finished my third helping of the sweet Yaztraka. And when I had finally finished I looked around and smiled at everyone and conveyed that I felt normal again. And to prove it I stood up and stretched my arms above my head and lightly beat on my chest in a Tarzan demonstration. I saw a few puzzled Oannes expressions until they read my mind.

It was lovely sitting down with my family and just making small talk. I had finished all my tasks here in the Raznat system and only my visit to Ritozanan remained. And because I had successfully completed the Nazmos operation I looked forward to the meeting and her comments about it if any. I wondered if I would see her again when I returned in 4110-Silver whenever that was. The five years or so would fly by like the last twenty two I suppose. I intend to enjoy those five years with Tania as best I could. Sadness pervaded my thoughts just then but I immediately blocked my mind to it. But I think Tania caught a brief hint of it. I looked away across the dining hall and suggested a nice mug of tea. I don't think I fooled Tania with the diversion.

We remained in the dining hall for well over an hour after this. For some odd reason I suddenly began to appreciate what I had around me as if it were the most precious item in my life. The thought came to me that I would miss all of this one day and so I looked at this family of mine with eyes that took it all in more keenly than I had done previously.

I remember a passing thought I'd had as a teenager wondering how I would feel when my parents eventually died. It had not been a sad thought then but just my curious youthful mind considering an eventuality. Something that would occur in the natural progression of our lives; an inevitable event that came with time. For now however I closed my mind to such morbid thoughts.

Someone suggested we return to the viewing Deck 15 and that is what we did. I held Tania's hand as I stood at one of the view panels looking down at the lights of Wentazta. It was night in the city and the glow flickered hazily up to us and I knew that the storm I had created was still blowing across land and sea. I did not think that twelve hours would be enough time for it to abate but then the Oannes knew better so I would just have to wait and see. Daylight would reveal more. I've decided that the next time when I return to fix Nazmos' in its permanent orbit I would apply my telekinetic push at a lesser rate; perhaps at half of 0.5% of normal gravity.

In 144 days from now Nazmos would have dropped to a perigee position of 19 million miles from Raznat. Its orbital velocity would then be 46,200 mph. It would then race out again to its current apogee position of 31 million miles. So for the next five years or until I return Nazmos will have this elliptic orbit. For a circular orbit the perigee orbital velocity will need to be reduced to 44,000 mph a reduction of 2,200 mph. This would take me 25 hours of telekinetic effort at 0.5% of normal gravity deceleration. Of course I would do this in five hour stints as I had done this time and hope for similar or less disruption to Nazmos' sea and air conditions.

Tania could see I was deep in my thoughts and so suggested we retire to our cabins for the night. She said we would wake refreshed for our return to Wentazta and Jazzatnit and Zazfrapiz's house tomorrow. I should also be rested before my visit to Ritozanan she added. I agreed even though at the moment I wasn't particularly tired or sleepy. But then that could be easily remedied and it was.

At breakfast we received the news that spaceships had begun to return to the Wentazta space park and were continuing to do so. The seas had calmed and the wind had eased sufficiently to allow this. Today was the fourth day since we had set out from Nazmos for Platwuz and the entire Platwuz-Nazmos operations had been completed in the planned time frame. Now all I had to do was to pay my respects to Ritozanan and then bid farewell to Nazmos. I expect that Zakatanz had readied his starship and awaited me and my family and the Oannes scientists to join him aboard 8110-Gold for our trip to the Sirius Star system. I was keen to see the white dwarf star Sirius B up close. It would be like a practice run against Zarama except I would not be taking any action against it. This was to be an observation operation only; or was it?

I enjoyed breakfast as I had woken up rather hungry. Tania was quite the vixen and I loved her for it. The next five years or so back in Dudley would be pure heaven for me and I shall make the most of it. We were still thirty miles above Nazmos and Zanos immediately answered my query by stating that our descent was scheduled to begin in fifty minutes. Apparently the small armada of smaller private spacecraft had been given priority over the much larger vessels. The time passed quickly and eventually Zanos conveyed to all that 9632-Orange had begun its slow descent.

I decided that etiquette demanded I proceed to the control room and take my leave of Captain Rojazonto and thank him for all the care I and my family had received on this extended trip. It would not be long though before we were back on this ship for our rendezvous out to the starship 8110-Gold for the journey to the Sirius star system.

My request was granted and the internal transporter ferried us to the control room. I had especially asked for Simon to accompany me and this too had been accepted. My son Simon stood stiffly tall beside me and I felt pride in his bearing and manner as I began to convey my gracious thanks and farewell Sewa. But I didn't get to finish as the captain came up to me and grasped my hand firmly in both of his.

'It is I who have received the honour of having you and your family aboard my ship,' he conveyed. 'My ship and I will go down in the records of Nazmos beside your name for what has been achieved here. I am forever beholden to you Ashley as are all Oannes everywhere. Thank you.'

Captain Rojazonto then went to each of our group including Simon and shook hands with them. With Simon however I noticed a stay that was prolonged marginally and I suspect a private message passed between them. There was a slight bow of the head from both before they parted. It was generally understood that Simon was to play his part in taking me to meet Zarama when the time came.

When 8632-Orange had settled down in the Wentazta space-park I wondered what the conditions would be like outside. I needn't have worried for all seemed quite normal apart from a steady heavy breeze. The internal transporter had taken us out to the larger Deck Transporter which then ferried us towards Jazzatnit's house. I was surprised at how much the winds had abated and I mentioned this to the transporter operator.

I think he was a bit in awe of me but his face lit up when I conveyed my thought. He was more than willing to give his own opinion. He conveyed that if the dusk Raznat-set could trigger a rush of wind that built up to such frenzy before quickly dying down again then there must be something in the Nazmos atmospheric make-up that prevented the perpetuation of high wind conditions.

I thought about this and queried my inner voice. The answer I received was that the Nazmos atmosphere basically consisted of three main layers with the lowest being just over a mile high but with considerably heavier elements than the rest. Any movement like the strong winds at Raznat-set was not followed by the other two upper atmospheric layers. As such the lower layer motions rapidly ran out of energy and quickly slowed back towards the normal condition with the others. I must remember to query Brajam about this as it could just be part of common gossip; or not.

Both Jazzatnit and Zazfrapiz greeted us enthusiastically in their lovely courtyard and congratulated me on my success. Zazfrapiz conveyed that the governing council were most pleased that I had delivered all as promised and they wished to thank me personally. My heart sank at the thought of another banquet meeting in the Domed Hall with all that it entailed. I quickly blocked my mind as I did not wish to cause offence to my hosts.

I then received the surprise of my life when suddenly from behind many of Jazzatnit's exhibits there suddenly appeared a large number of Nazmos' governing council members and their wives all decked in bright apparel.

'We thought an informal environment would be more suited to you Ashley and to the occasion,' said Dultarzent the most senior member of the council. 'On behalf of all of Nazmos we thank you for initiating Gozmanot's dream. Ritozanan was right to have put her trust in you and I thank her for it. We are happy that we have been able to witness an important part of our history in the making. Thank you Ashley.'

He then came up to me and we did a two handed handshake. His hands felt soft and small in mine and I realised how delicate his stature was. There were a lot of smiling faces around me now and kindly emotions filled the area. I conveyed my thanks to them all and made a special mention of Ritozanan and of her friendship that I so valued and respected.

I was alone among this group of council members and being head and shoulders taller I could see across to where Jazzatnit and my family stood separated from us. This was a great honour for Jazzatnit and Zazfrapiz and their beaming faces showed how proud they were. Then beside Jazzatnit I saw the face of Muznant and my heart did a flip. I had never seen her looking so radiant and beautiful. There was a glow of pride and exuberance in her demeanour that said it all. I had been her discovery and she had argued my case in Anztarza that November day when Puzlwat and some others had been so suspicious about me.

And there beside Muznant appeared her daughter Farzant and she too exuded beauty that seemed to have suddenly blossomed anew. But Tania was there too and the sight of the glow on her face caused that chest pain of love to flood through my being. My cup was full and I could want no more. Simon and Rachel were either side of Tania and it seemed as if all the people I loved most were gathered here together.

I was brought back to reality by Korizazit and Nerbtazwi coming up to me to convey a private message. The meeting with Ritozanan was to be at my convenience though preferably within the next few hours. I conveyed that I was ready to go as soon as honour and etiquette permitted.

Korizazit smiled a knowing smile and conveyed again that it would probably be at least another hour before the council members began to take their leave of their hosts Jazzatnit and Zazfrapiz. Two hours at the very most. The latter proved to be the case. The Oannes are extremely sensitive about doing things in a most proper manner and are never in a hurry about anything. Too early a departure would be impolite and signify displeasure.

Eventually each of the council members took a polite leave of not only our hosts but of me and my family as well. It was a great honour that they bestowed upon us humans. Over the years a great change had taken place in the perception that the Oannes in general had about us humans. And I believe that it was a most favourable one. I sincerely hope that in the years to come disillusion does not set in again.

Korizazit and Nerbtazwi did not leave with the others and stayed to partake of the light meal that Jazzatnit had served up for us. Korizazit was a member of the governing council of ministers and kept a reserved manner at all times – except when he was alone with me. He had received the gift of inner voice purely accidentally from me and was now considered a most valued and important member of the Nazmos governing council; more so than before he received this gift.

'It does not speak to me,' he had said and I had replied that it did not need to. It simply supplied information subconsciously as the occasion demanded.

Finally the time came for my visit to Ritozanan and the three of us left the courtyard and proceeded out to the transporter waiting for us in the plaza. Simon said he'd wait here for my return before leaving to join his colleagues on his transport spaceship 7332-Blue. Captain Vikazat had commanded that all of the ships crew return by evening. I would then be saying goodbye to my son again until he came for me with the starship 4110-Silver. It would be his first visit back to Earth since he'd left to join the space academy all those years ago.

Although the Nazmos air had calmed considerably the heavy breeze remained. Consequently the side panels on the transporter were kept in the raised position and for the added reason that we had a fair distance to cover and so would be travelling at a relatively higher speed. And this proved to be the case as we travelled inland away from the Peruga Sea. The journey lasted some forty minutes at a height of a thousand feet. On the way Nerbtazwi gave me a running commentary of the features passing below us. Gradually the houses and buildings seemed more spread out until we came to a single structure of a quite unique design. From our position high above it looked like three structural bubbles blended together. The sides were straight but were formed into a triangular shape. As we descended I noticed a perimeter wall at some distance from the central structure and it was within this area that the transporter touched down.

'This is Ritozanan's residence,' said Korizazit, 'and she is very proud of it. Her parents lived here until they became deceased quite long ago.'

'There are three sections to the house as you viewed from the air,' added Nerbtazwi, 'and Ritozanan resides in just one.'

I was surprised that neither of them conveyed images of the inside of the house but then I knew that it had not been permitted. Such thoughts could be picked up by others and Ritozanan did not wish this. I understood that all of the governing council members cherished their privacy and jealously guarded it against outside intrusion. By doing so they kept themselves at a reserved distance from the people that they governed. Although their decisions were made with great consultation and deliberation nevertheless once made they could not be questioned. I could accept that as an essential governing precept.

The transporter had landed near one of the entrances and Korizazit led the way into the building. We walked along a wide passageway which had doors at regular intervals but on one side only. We stopped beside the third of these doors and again Korizazit led the way through. We entered a large hall very like the main room in Jazzatnit's house. This one was a truly beautiful room with large view panels located all around it. Each panel was like a picture in a frame and showed sea views, underwater views and even one which I thought was of the northern forests on Earth. It was like being in a room full of windows. It felt light and airy inside and it made me feel very much at home. I could live here I thought.

'Welcome to my home Ashley,' came the conveyed thought from Ritozanan, 'and welcome also to you Korizazit and Nerbtazwi. You may direct Ashley to come to me alone as agreed.'

A humorous emotion came through to me and I knew that Ritozanan had read my earlier thoughts and been pleased by them. Yes, I did feel at home and at peace and I only wish that I had Tania here beside me.

Nerbtazwi then led me to an arched doorway at the far end of the room and turning to me she gestured for me to proceed through it.

'I can go no further,' she said, 'Ritozanan wishes for you to be alone with her. We shall await for you back here.'

I hesitated for an instant before stepping towards the indicated arched doorway. It opened silently at my touch and I entered closing the door behind me. My first impression was that I was outside in an open courtyard area. But I knew I was not. This was a large circular room with view panels from ceiling to floor that went all around the room. The views were similar to those in the previous room but these were cleverly blended to look like a continuous scene.

In the centre of all this was a large square shaped glass sided tank full of water. Inside near its centre I could just make out a motionless Oannes figure floating halfway from the top. So this was Ritozanan's sleep tank and her final domain.

'Yes my dear Ashley, it is my final domain,' conveyed Ritozanan, 'and even I must admit that.'

I felt embarrassment for that thought but knew it would be impolite for me to block my mind here. I simply could not and would not.

'Thank you,' came back from Ritozanan.

Then she added, 'And what do you think of it all?'

'I think it is beautiful and unlike anything I could have imagined,' I said aloud. 'I find it truly magnificent and yet so homely. I love it and Tania would love it.'

'Come close and peer at me through the wall of my sleep tank,' she conveyed, 'and tell me what you see.'

I walked right up to the glass of the tank and looked through it. There was a slight haziness in the water and it was conveyed to me that this had been specially contrived for my visit. Ritozanan conveyed that she did not want me to feel embarrassed and also she wished to preserve an aspect of modesty for she was totally unclothed within.

Suddenly her face appeared right close up to mine and her arms were outstretched as though she would enfold them around me. Her eyes bored into mine and although old she still saw shrewdly. Immediately I thought of my regressed visit to Gozmanot and her first view of me. Then too the water of her sleep tank had the same hazy tint in it.

'So you've come at last,' were Gozmanot's conveyed thoughts to me then and she had reached out to embrace me. Oh, how I wish she had succeeded and suddenly that same feeling arose in my breast towards this Oannes woman today. Ritozanan smiled at my thoughts and after placing her lips against the glass of the tank I saw her in all of her nakedness. I had expected to see a thin frail looking body but the image I saw was quite different within this sleep tank environment. The butterfly type vane on her back seemed huge and so full of colour in comparison to her body. The smaller webbed vanes on her face, arms and legs also stood proudly colourful and all of this gave Ritozanan a very different and majestic appearance. She looked so different to that frail looking Oannes lady of our last Domed Hall meeting. She was like a great bird in full flight and definitely showed herself as in her element. I understood now why she had wished me to visit and see her here. I saw her smile as she read my thoughts. She then retreated back towards the centre of the sleep tank and became just a hazy outline of an Oannes body.

'Go now Ashley and remember me as you have just seen me. I too will remember you though not as of today but of our first meeting in the Domed Hall. That was a clash of our personalities and you won that with your revelation of Gozmanot. I admired you from then on and we became friends.'

There was a hint of sadness in the tone of her thoughts and this time I knew that our parting would be our final one. I expected to receive word of her when I was at my home in Dudley. I conveyed a brief farewell Sewa as politeness required but then added my own sad goodbye to a woman I had come to admire and love. I sensed the abundance of a great love, mine and hers, filling the room and tears came to my eyes.

I retreated slowly backwards towards the arched doorway hoping for a last glimpse of this wonderful lady. I waved my arm just before entering the doorway and was gratified to see a half wave in return. I nearly choked when I saw that fragile arm movement and then suddenly I was back with Korizazit and Nerbtazwi and the door had closed in front of me.

I said nothing as I gestured for Korizazit to lead the way out and back to the transporter. How I held myself in emotional check I do not know. We travelled in silence and soon I was back in the courtyard of Jazzatnit and Zazfrapiz. Korizazit and Nerbtazwi did not come in with me but returned to their own homes aboard the transporter. I think they understood how I felt and did not wish to intrude.

Tania and all my family were there in the courtyard waiting for me and as soon as Tania came close I put my arms tightly around her and hugged her close. I beckoned for Simon and Rachel to come to me too and we had a group hug. I could not hold my emotions in check any longer. I conveyed the visual images of my visit to Ritozanan's house and sleep tank and my tears again flowed freely. Tania and Rachel joined with my tears and Simon too seemed choked into silence. Then the others came around and I felt hands touching me and thoughts of consoling love came through from my Oannes friends. It was a moment of emotion letting and I was pleased I had shared all this and my feelings with them. I don't know what they thought of me for my emotional breakdown but later at the dining table I got the strangest looks from Jazzatnit, Muznant and Farzant. It was as though I had become part of their family and that they were pleased about it.

I know I have always felt ordinary in my life even with all these fantastic gifts. But for them to see me so emotionally upset must have been a revelation. In the end they saw me as no god-like creature but just an ordinary emotionally vulnerable person. They realised that now and I was glad that they had witnessed that part of me.

During our conversation I asked Jazzatnit what it had been like here in Wentazta when I had begun to apply my telekinetic push on Nazmos. I was curious to feel their direct experience of the orbital slowdown.

At first they seemed puzzled at what I wished to know so I clarified by asking if they had felt anything dramatic.

'We had been instructed to stay indoors,' said Jazzatnit, 'and for the initial period when we knew you had begun the operation we felt nothing. Then the wind outside began to blow; slowly at first but gradually with increased intensity. I don't think it reached the peak intensity that we witness at each Raznat-set but we began to be a little concerned at its duration. It seemed to continue on unabated. It was only last night that I noticed a lessening in its intensity and then this morning it had nearly returned to normal and as it is now.'

I smiled when I heard this as Jazzatnit had conveyed full mental images of the experience. When I return to fix the orbit permanently I shall definitely apply my telekinetic effort at the lower level of about half of 0.5% gravity level. I suspect the average Nazmos temperature would have increased somewhat and this would mean more energy in the atmosphere. As such my telekinetic effort could produce a greater storm effect but hopefully all should go well.

Today was my last day on Nazmos and in the company of my son for quite some time. I had seen that he was more than happy and enjoying his chosen career. I could also see that he was very much at ease with his Oannes colleagues and that their attitude towards him was one of camaraderie and acceptance. It might have something to do with the fact that he was my son but at the same time he made friends easily and as such those that got to know him came to like him. He was out to forge a reputation for himself and did not need to play upon his family background. Something tells me that we shall hear more of that space-lady Mazpazam in the years to come.

This had also been a great time for Rachel to catch up with her brother, not to mention his doting cousins Fiona and Sarah. I'm glad that it all came into the open and they got to meet Simon; he was no longer considered as the missing mysterious one.

And so the remainder of the day was spent wandering around Jazzatnit's creative courtyard and sitting around in the lounge and at the dining table just talking about things that came to mind. Light hearted frivolous chatter mixed in with odd bits of humour.

Tania took everything in and I know that she would mull over the things her son said and did on this visit. Simon was understanding and affectionate in his manner especially towards his mum. As we walked around the courtyard he would put his arm around her waist and nuzzle his cheek against hers in affectionate little hugs. He did this with his sister Rachel too and she would respond with a peck on his cheek in return. We were a family together again for this brief time. I wondered at the great change in Simon's makeup and I could only guess that this space colleague Mazpazam might have had something to do with it. When you are in love with someone even if that love is a suppressed one then you share your affection openly with all your other loved ones. I don't think I'm too old to have forgotten what it was like when Tania and I were courting.

The evening seemed to fly by and we all gathered on the terrace for one last Raznat-set. Nothing had altered by much except that I thought the rush of wind seemed just that little bit fiercer. Jazzatnit thought so too but then she said that she had witnessed the odd fierce one on other occasions before. And this time Sarah said that she had been prepared for it and had found it to be quite exhilarating not to mention exciting. She looked at Brian as she said this. I think I detected a sly twinkle in her eye.

Brian said that he now felt like a seasoned space traveller and was looking forward to the next trip out into space. Fiona concurred as she looked wide eyed and enviously towards Simon seated between his mother and sister. I felt inwardly proud at the vision before me and that my son was exactly the sort of person he had turned out to be. I couldn't have wished for better. However I considered myself biased and would have been happy with him in whatever role he'd chosen. I would also happily accept Mazpazam as a partner for him if that is the path he wished. I must raise the prospect with Tania and see what she thought.

Having seen her son as he was now I'm sure she'd be happy for him in whatever he chose to do. It was his life and he had made the career choice which was to live the majority of his life out in space. The human lifespan would limit this to a quarter of that of his Oannes colleagues but I'm sure his candle flame would burn brighter than most.

When the air on the terrace cooled considerably we all returned to the warmth of the courtyard. I suddenly realised that it was time for Simon to rejoin his ship and leave. There was a hint of emotional sadness in the air as Simon went around saying his goodbyes. He gave each of his new-found cousins a hug and a kiss before moving on to the others. Then he went to Muznant and Farzant and gently hugged them too before shaking hands with Brazjaf. Next were Jazzatnit and Zazfrapiz who got the same treatment. He saved us for the last and fiercely hugged Rachel and whispered something in her ear. Then it was his mum and a little sob escaped from between her lips as he hugged her tight. He didn't say anything but held onto her for quite a long while. I sensed he was keeping his own emotions in check. Then he turned to me and we had a smiling man hug and I told him to be good and to look after himself as I hadn't anything else to say. We continued smiling at each other as we went through a two-handed handshake. He touched me on the shoulder before he stepped back.

'I'll see you all back on Earth folks,' he said and gave an imitation of that famous Errol Flynn arm sweeping bow before turning about and walking briskly towards the courtyard gate and the waiting transporter. He walked with his back stiffly upright and head held high and I was certain that he too had a lump in his throat and wetness of eye, for he did not dare to turn for a final wave goodbye.

I stood with Tania and Rachel either side of me and I put an arm around each as we watched Simon turn the corner. Fiona was with her mum and dad while Sarah stood arm in arm with Brian. We'd had a wonderful few days with our son no doubt about that and I looked forward to his eventual arrival back on Earth.

Chapter 19

Sirius B

The next morning Ashley awoke to see Tania staring up at the ceiling. She turned her head towards him and smiled.

'I didn't sleep very well,' she said, 'I kept waking every hour or so and thinking of Simon.'

'So was I,' said Ashley, 'but I kept seeing images of that Oannes girl who was with him at the space academy. I wonder what that could mean.'

'Mazpazam,' said Tania with a teasing twinkle in her eye, 'you think we mothers don't have an instinct for that sort of thing anymore?'

'I wasn't sure if you had guessed,' said Ashley and left it had that. Quietly he smiled to himself. The topic he'd meant to raise didn't need to be raised anymore.

'Ashley darling,' said Tania smiling, 'Simon is your son and cut from the same cloth; what did you expect?'

'Then you don't mind.'

'Not at all, but I feel sorry for her,' said Tania. 'She'll still be a young Oannes lady when Simon is old and retired. In fact none of us will be around then but I'm sure they will be happy together in the years they share.'

'It may not get that far,' said Ashley, 'for Simon will put his career ahead of all else.'

Tania smiled and turned her head to look back at the ceiling. A mother's instinct was practically infallible in such cases and she had guessed at her son's mindset the moment he'd spoken at their breakfast table meeting.

She then turned back to her husband and stretched out her arms and he entered their encirclement. She kissed him lightly on the lips and then placed her cheek against his.

'Let's just snuggle up like this for a while and savour the moment,' she conveyed silently.

Ashley's right arm was tucked tight in front of him and it felt quite awkward but he didn't complain. He put his left arm over Tania's waist and let it lie there. He closed his eyes and images of Simon and Mazpazam together floated in front of him. And then he dozed off into a peaceful sleep.

When he opened his eyes again Tania was not in the bed but he could hear the shower running.

He thought about Sirius B as a White Dwarf star as small in size as Earth but with a mass slightly greater than the Sun. This coming trip to Sirius B was to be a reconnaissance mission without any action of any kind. At least when he did eventually approach Zarama, a similar White Dwarf star, it would not come as a surprise. He would have seen one like it before. The more time he spent in the proximity of Sirius B on this trip the more he could familiarise himself with the conditions around Zarama. It would be just another dwarf star.

Ashley thought of the saying that familiarity breeds contempt – well that is exactly what he wished to do in regard to Zarama. He wished to become familiar with White Dwarf stars and then hold them in contempt. And that contempt would help him to overrule his current fears. But there would always be a certain respect for these massive objects.

However Ashley still feared that Zarama might be too massive an object for him to move. But Sirius B would get him accustomed to its presence and perhaps give him the confidence he needed. And with that his doubts and fears might disappear in time as they usually did. This trip would be his practice run against Zarama and he had Simon to thank for suggesting the visit.

Ashley's thoughts shifted back to Simon and the image of him appearing at Jazzatnit's breakfast table. What a grand figure he had presented and weren't his cousins quite taken with him? And apparently neither were Oannes maidens immune to those charms. Ashley could imagine how Mazpazam must have responded to this exceptional human space cadet. Was it an initial curious fascination? And then could it have grown from that familiarity to something more personal? Only time would tell.

Tania came out of the shower quite naked and smiled at her husband as she walked by him to the shelf where her clothes were stored. Ashley read her emotion and understood that she still felt hollow by the absence of her son. He too missed Simon's company and the dazzling brilliance he exuded when he was among them. Ashley smiled at the memory and his being filled with pride.

'You can't lay there all day, sleepy head,' said Tania now fully dressed, 'get showered and dressed as breakfast awaits. I'm quite famished you know.'

'So am I,' said Ashley with a sly smile.

'You men have just one thing on your minds,' laughed Tania.

'Yes,' replied Ashley laughing.

'Maybe later tonight. Now get up and into the shower with you.'

Ashley did as he was told and soon they were at the breakfast table and the last to arrive.

Everyone was talking about Simon and what a surprising chap he was.

'I suppose the next time we see him will be when he comes to Earth for Uncle Ashley,' said Fiona to Sarah.

'I wonder what he's doing now,' said Brian.

Zanos immediately responded to the query by conveying that the transporter spaceship 7332-Blue had left Nazmos early this morning and was on a mission to supply men and materials to the starship 4110-Silver undergoing upgrading modifications at its orbital location two billion miles from Raznat.

Simon had mentioned that in the next three of four years he hoped to be assigned to that starship on a permanent basis; hopefully as a junior officer on technical operations. Ashley and Tania knew that he was keen for the posting and that other newly qualified spacemen were also likely to be assigned. That was a matter for the Space-Administration Oannes and choices would be purely on a merit and suitability basis.

Ashley wondered if Mazpazam might then appear on the scene. For some reason Ashley thought it highly likely. Would Simon pull a few strings for it to be realised?

Ashley had made it clear that Simon's premonition gift was essential for his trip to Zarama. The corrected 431.8 light-years to Zarama was a great distance and could contain unknown hazards. Simon had proved his navigation instincts time and time again during his cadet years and if he were to make a personal request it would receive fair consideration. To be posted for duties aboard a starship was the ultimate stamp of approval for a young spaceman.

Ashley knew that once he was back on Earth he would receive regular news updates about the progress being made on 4110-Silver. He would also receive Simon's communications through the regular starship visits to Earth giving news about him. Somehow Ashley did not think that Mazpazam would get a mention.

He thought back to his visit to Ritozanan in her home. He would keep that image of her forever in his memory beside that of Gozmanot. He was not looking forward to the news of her passing but knew that eventually such news would come; and that possibly in the next year or so.

Captain Rojazonto had conveyed to Ashley that he expected him with his family group to arrive aboard his ship 9632-Orange sometime later in the afternoon. As such there was no haste to depart Jazzatnit's lovely home. Besides Zazfrapiz did not rise early and Ashley wished to see him and conduct his own farewell Sewa prior to leaving. Jazzatnit joined the group just before midday and all took a pleasant stroll amongst her courtyard exhibits. Ashley and Tania enjoyed these relaxed walks and especially the small talk with their hostess. When Zazfrapiz eventually joined them he seemed glad that they had not left.

To the Oannes mind Earth was considered to be just around the corner and easily accessible. As such Ashley and his family would never be too far away conveyed Zazfrapiz and so they were always welcome in his home whenever they felt the need for a visit. He looked particularly at Rachel and Margaret and conveyed something privately to them. Ashley could only guess what that might be but kept it to himself.

Sadly Ashley could not return the invitation but Anztarza was always a close option. Both Jazzatnit and Zazfrapiz not only abhorred space travel but they were also excluded from it because of their age. The very young and old were discouraged from starship travel except in exceptional circumstances.

Muznant, Brazjaf and Farzant stayed close together and Ashley wondered if they might ever return to Anztarza. Perhaps not thought Ashley since Brazjaf had an important role with the Nazmos governing council.

Jazzatnit was a most conscientious host and she put on a lovely lunchtime meal a couple of hours before her guests were due to leave. Zazfrapiz sat at the head of the table and Jazzatnit sat beside him. There was room for two there and Muznant and Brazjaf sat facing them at the other end. Ashley and Tania sat either side of their hosts and it was all meant to be very formal. This would be their last meal together and Jazzatnit wished it to be remembered with the correct etiquette and dignity.

'We wish you a successful journey to your destination in the Sirius star system,' said Zazfrapiz standing up, 'and we hope you successfully return to your home on Earth. We shall see you again when you return to fix Nazmos in its permanent orbit. And in the interim we shall keep you in our hearts and also inform you of the changes in the weather conditions here as we observe it.'

No mention was made of Zarama and that was typically the Oannes way of maintaining the mood of the moment.

Ashley had to respond so when Zazfrapiz sat down he stood up to say a few words.

'Thank you my dear hosts for being so generous towards us,' he said aloud. 'I feel so very much at home here in this house that I feel sorry to leave. And I speak for all of us who have enjoyed your hospitality; I more than others. I first came here alone twenty two Earth years ago and I was glad that Muznant and Brazjaf brought me to you. I missed my family not being with me but in some ways you made up for it and I thank you for that. As I said we feel sorry to leave but leave we must just so that we can be welcomed back even more when we return. However a greater duty calls which is why we must travel for a look at this Dwarf Star Sirius B.'

Ashley also avoided any mention of Zarama. He then continued.

'This has been a good time for Tania and me as parents and for the rest of the family too because we were able to meet and spend precious time with our son Simon. I think he impressed us all with his gallantry and we shall look forward to seeing him again on Earth in perhaps five years or so. He will hopefully then be an officer on a starship and probably smarter than ever. So my dear Jazzatnit and Zazfrapiz thank you once again for your kind hospitality; we wish you happiness and good living till we meet again.'

Ashley sat down and Tania squeezed his hand in approval.

Brian then stood up to everyone's surprise.

'I would like to add my thanks if I may,' he said and continued after a brief pause.

'I am not as yet a legal partner in this family but I soon will be,' he said, 'and it will be the proudest moment of my life. I have seen some amazing things and met the most wonderful of people here on Nazmos. And it is all thanks to my association with Sarah whom I love very much. I wish to thank our hosts seated here at the head of this table for their kindness and generosity in making us all feel so welcome. I don't know if we will meet again but I know that Sarah and I will treasure these memories all our lives. I also thank Ashley for being instrumental in bringing us here and for introducing us to such beautiful and wonderful Nazmos people. I am overwhelmed and most grateful.'

Brian had got quite emotional as he spoke these words and when he sat down he was very red in the face. But Ashley knew that Brian had spoken from the heart and on impulse; and Ashley was proud of him just as Sarah was. She looked sideways at him and her face said it all; pride in the man she loved.

For Ashley Brian continued to impress in his own quiet way.

Katy and Robin were pleased too and showed it by the smiles on their faces. Sarah had chosen well and that just left Fiona, they thought. Whom would she choose and when? Or had Simon spoilt it for her for the time being?

Muznant and Brazjaf read these thoughts and theirs turned to Farzant. They too thought about her future and where she might lay her fancies – now that she had met Ashley and his family. Muznant knew that the majority of humans on Earth were kind and decent people but often lying dormant beneath their calm exterior was a latent volcano of anger ready to erupt at the slightest provocation. It would be millennia before any form of integration could even be considered.

On board 8110-Gold all was in readiness for the expedition to Sirius B. Two zero-gravity spaceships were settled inside the starship beside all the usual shuttle craft on the upper level cargo platform. Zero-gravity spaceships were used in place of ordinary shuttle craft when environmental conditions were extreme; like trying to approach a Dwarf Star. The zero-gravity factor meant that the spaceship and its occupants could exist in a gravity free state the same as in a shuttle craft. On a zero-g spaceship there were no loose objects or liquids on board. Apart from this they were really normal spaceships but much smaller. The two on board the starship were similar to but half the size of 11701-Red that operated from Anztarza on Earth. As such it was 200 feet long, 90 feet wide and about 35 feet in height. It had just the one deck for crew called the central habitation deck. The upper deck contained the power plant and linear impulse devices for propulsion and the under deck housed water in enclosed tanks along with essential food supplies in secured containers. For extended duties meals could be arranged by putting the ship into a temporary parking type loop to create normal gravity conditions. A zero-gravity spaceship was purpose built and purely as a substitute for the lesser shuttle craft. On this mission to Sirius B the zero-gravity ship would be able to approach closer to the heat of the Dwarf Star than would have been possible with a normal shuttle craft. The heat shielding built into such a ship allowed it to do so; within certain limits of course.

Captain Zakatanz was looking forward to the direct journey to Sirius B. The straight line course from Raznat to the Sirius system would pass within 1.3 LYs (light years) of Earth's Sun. Raznat was 6.3 LYs from Earth and Sirius was 8.6 LYs from it but on the opposite side. As such the total distance to the Sirius system from Raznat had been computed as 14.4 LYs. Captain Zakatanz hoped that with Ashley's telekinetic assistance the journey could be made at a velocity of 695 FTL all the way in a little less than eleven Earth days.

The Anztarza chief ministers had approached the captain about the journey and it had been confirmed that the stay at Sirius B would be no longer than 24 hours. Then the return to Earth with Ashley's assistance would be a little over six days. The Nazmos governing council had initially been surprised by the Anztarza chief ministers' arrival on Nazmos but had accepted their presence for the limited stay period. The chief ministers however had wished to be back on Anztarza as early as possible but Captain Zakatanz had ruled out Earth as their first stop on this outward trip.

The return trip from Earth to Nazmos would be without Ashley aboard and so would be at the normal 10 FTL capability of the starship 8110-Gold. That would entail a journey time of just over six months and as such Captain

Zakatanz had opted to have his family aboard as was the prerogative for starship captains. It had been his daughter Hazazamunt who had requested the privilege. Her reason was that her formal education would begin when she turned fifteen in age and so this would be her last opportunity to get to know Ashley and his family. But Zakatanz guessed that she also wished to see Anztarza for herself having heard so much about it.

Zakatanz was pleased for her but also for himself. The return journey to Nazmos would have been a lonely six months of routine ship affairs without Azatamunt and Hazazamunt beside him. Starship captains did have certain privileges and having ones family aboard for company was one. But Zakatanz would have to forgo this for the duration of Hazazamunt's educational years. The Oannes were rigid on the education of their youth. Azatamunt would maintain their home for her child throughout this period of education which usually lasted beyond the age of twenty five. But what was ten years in a lifetime of three hundred. Zakatanz had been alone before and would see his family between the trips to Earth. He thought back to when his love Hazazamunt had disappeared well over a hundred years ago. He had much to thank Ashley for and he was grateful.

Progress into the modification work on 4110-Silver was now into its third decade. Originally this starship had been two miles long and half a mile in diameter with a mushroom shaped shield at the front three quarters of a mile in diameter. The modifications would only affect the length of the starship when the additional propulsion plant was added.

When the starship had been taken out of regular service for the enhancement modification program its captain had been a 230 year old Oannes male called Wastanomi. He was retained as its resident captain for the duration of the reconstruction program and so would oversee the efficient running of the starship's functions for the benefit of the thousand or so project crew who would be residing on its habitation platform. 4110-Silver was currently in orbit around Raznat at the radial position of two billion miles. The orbital velocity at this distance was a mere 350 mph.

Wastanomi had decided to maintain the habitation platform at a slightly further out position from the forward neutron shield so that the gravity level was held at 80% of normal Nazmos gravity. This would reduce the work effort of his retention crew providing service to the project staff and workers on the habitation platform. It was also less effort for his people on the next lower level which contained the food growing tanks. The starship was self sufficient in this respect though specially requested items could be ferried to them from Nazmos.

Zanos continued to maintain full control of the life support functions within the three levels of cargo, habitation and food growing. The controls for the platform movement had been completely isolated as had all propulsion units under safety procedure regulations. These had all been put offline when the starship had been placed in its current orbit and project work initiated. Most of the original crew had been transferred to other spaceships on other duties but many had also remained especially in the food growing area.

One of the original crew members was 1st deputy Wantrozit aged 180 years. He had served with Captain Wastanomi for over thirty years and had no ambitions for a spaceship of his own if it was not to be a starship. He was a starship Oannes through and through. There were of course the service and catering crew personnel since over a thousand construction engineers and staff had to be cared for on board.

Although Captain Wastanomi oversaw the life support functionality of 4110-Silver's internal operations it was the Chief Engineer Misazatan and his Deputy Chief Engineer Zarndonita who were really in charge overall. Captain Wastanomi was there to ensure all their needs were met. Misazatan was 195 years of age and a brilliant construction manager. His deputy Zarndonita was slightly younger at 180 years and equally brilliant. They were the perfect team. Also in the team was the propulsion drive specialist Sapatizto aged 210 years and the structural engineer Arnztantaz aged 220 years.

But well before any of these had come aboard there was the modification design team headed by Bonuzto who had been called out of retirement by the governing council for this specific task. Bonuzto was 285 years of age and he had put together his team of thirty or so Oannes personnel all close to his own age. It had taken three years for the starship enhancement plans to be finalised and for full material orders to be placed.

Under normal conditions the Oannes way would have been to pace their work for a thorough job to be completed with due care to detail. Each design feature would have been double checked and samples taken and working models made. All this would have extended the workload such that a project of this sort would have spanned about a hundred years of continuous diligent effort. But time was not on their side in this case and depended upon the lifespan of the human Ashley. Ashley alone had the telekinetic gift to stop Zarama from its destructive course and this dictated an early completion date.

Ashley was known to all and Bonuzto's complaining thoughts had been picked up asking why such powers had not been granted to an Oannes person. It would have made his job so much easier and without the need for such haste. To achieve a starship modification in thirty years was according to him pushing things too much. He had originally quoted a hundred year time span for the work but the governing council of Nazmos – especially that council member Ritozanan – had stressed that it be done in a third of the time or sooner. Bonuzto felt that a burden of responsibility was being placed upon him that was beyond reason. Council member Ritozanan had made it plain that if the starship 4110-Silver was not operational while Ashley was still alive and healthy then the entire project would be pointless and the destruction of Nazmos by Zarama would be on his head.

Bonuzto had conveyed this threat to his team and to Misazatan the chief engineer who in turn had passed it on to his own staff. Gradually the message had filtered down to every one involved on the project and the sense of urgency was understood. And it worked. Progress had been rapid and minor errors foreseen and corrected well in time to avoid long delays.

Bonuzto had included the very latest development in linear impulse devices and electron generators into the overall design modifications for the starship. This had meant not only replacement of all existing old equipment but also a complete renewal of the ceramic electric conduction system within the propulsion zones. In addition the rearward facing old neutron generators were to be replaced with newly constructed ones and this was currently in progress. The total number of these had been increased by fifty percent. The new design feature here had been for the slowing down of the starship from a velocity that was double the previous 600 FTL maximum. So at 1200 FTL velocity the starship 4110-Silver should travel the estimated 431.8 LYs distance to Zarama in just under six months.

While all this modification work on the existing starship was in progress, separate construction work on the half mile body for the propulsion extension was well in hand at another location a few hundred miles away. This was being managed as a separate project by deputy chief engineer Katozimob aged 200 years. He had been a close associate of Misazatan the overall chief engineer for over seventy years. Misazatan had put together a team he knew he could rely on not only to get the job done correctly but also within the allotted time-span.

The work pattern was round the clock working in six hour shifts which overlapped each other by an hour for effective continuity.

Then there were the three safety supervisors Divazto, Franzdont, and Gizopanti. They were aged 170, 165 and 180 respectively and would ensure that all safety procedures were followed to the letter. A starship's forward neutron shield could be extremely disastrous for both Oannes and equipment if they got too close. The code of safe practice was in place for all to follow.

And more recently Korizazit along with two other members of the governing council had formed a little team to regularly visit the construction site and report on progress made. It was during one of these visits that Korizazit heard from his inner voice that a facet of the linear impulse devices would cause distress.

He remembered that Ashley had told him to always listen to this voice as it provided information and guidance. Korizazit was not a technical Oannes and could not state categorically where any problem lay and so was hesitant to contact the chief engineer directly. Instead Korizazit simply mentioned this to his team members and reported it back to the council. The council then conveyed a query to the chief engineer Misazatan and propulsion specialist Sapatizto. It was also conveyed to them that Korizazit had received his gift of inner voice directly from Ashley and so the information should be taken seriously.

The teams checked and double checked all impulse devises on 4110-Silver but every connection was firm and locked correctly. It was months later that a chance remark by deputy chief engineer Katozimob about the new linear impulse devices on the half mile starship extension section having a slight difficulty with the mount alignment that had set alarm bells ringing.

Every single one of the thousand or so linear impulse devices had to be aligned in an exact parallel configuration to the ship axis or else the starship could swing laterally when at FTL velocity with disastrous consequences.

Korizazit was proved right and it took a separate team six months to recheck the alignment of all the impulse devices. Out of all only two were found to be outside the alignment tolerances and these were traced to the laser equipment used in their original setting up. The fault was in the calibration interval which was subsequently increased in frequency. This was also applied to other essential checking equipment. The Oannes learned very quickly from their mistakes.

When giving his usual progress reports chief engineer Misazatan estimated that mating of the half mile extension section with the main body of 4110-Silver would commence within three years from now, Earth time. Then after another two years the modified starship could commence the first of its space trials. Another year must elapse before the newly commissioned starship 4110-Silver could be handed over to its resident captain for normal 100 FTL service. Chief engineer Misazatan was being conservative in his time estimates and secretly hoped for the starship to be in service about a year earlier than stated.

The new starship would be two and a half miles long and keep the same 4110-Silver ship identity.

The process would not end there as another starship probably 3110-Orange would be taken out of service for similar upgrading work. This starship was currently under Captain Varloozta aged 198 years who had been its captain for fifteen years. But this time the work time-span would be more near the hundred years or so that the

Oannes engineers were used to. Chief engineer Bonuzto would return to his retirement platform unless some other special task required his skills.

Construction of the Series 20-starships of which there were five had been commenced some two hundred years ago. These starships were designed for travel at 20 FTL velocities and the first of these would have been ready in another three hundred years. However those plans had now been revised and the Series 20 had become Series 100 for 100 FTL travel. And this was all because Ashley must speed towards Zarama 431.8 LYs away. Necessity is the mother of invention.

Back on Nazmos the governing council were to enter into deliberations about the new climate conditions that could be expected from Ashley's success in the planet's orbital change. A committee of climate scientists and experts was set up a year ago when the council had first agreed the orbital change. The plan had then been and still was for all climatic conditions to be monitored over the whole planet and every aspect recorded no matter how minor.

Many long term forecasts had been made and one of these was that there would be considerable rainfall in the equatorial areas and large snowfalls at the poles. It was also expected that this in turn would result in a gradual lowering of the average sea levels by about a hundred feet over the next thousand year period. Another forecast was that atmospheric conditions would become more varied with wind and storm phenomena developing to fiercer levels on account of the greater atmosphere energy content resulting from being closer to Raznat.

There were other committees set up to look at the possibilities of farming on land areas and to advise when this could commence. Gozmanot's visions had shown flora had gradually become widespread over the land. The committee must look carefully at the possibility of introducing some of the Earth crops here on Nazmos. Wheat was one consideration since the Oannes in Anztarza were immensely fond of Earth's bread products.

Then there were the health considerations. With the warmer climate could new viruses and bacteria pose health issues for the Oannes? And the topics went on and on. The Oannes were thorough in everything they did and Gozmanot had visualised many factors with the chief among them being that Nazmos would become like Earth in many ways.

Margaret and Rachel had sought permission from the governing council to extend their stay on Nazmos. They wanted to witness for themselves the climate changes that would occur but permission had been refused. The governing council gave no reason for their decision. But Ashley learned that the next years were considered a transition period alternating between the old and the new orbits and the governing council had been advised that the Oannes should go through this period without any humans on Nazmos. They could however return with Ashley in five years time or thereabouts and then they could stay on indefinitely.

Of course all deliberations and decisions were regularly conveyed to the underwater Rimzi people. They had accepted the information but made no comment. The possibility of sea levels dropping had not seemed of concern to them since their underwater cities were at considerably lower depths and were spread around the central areas of the vast Nazmos seas.

Ashley and his family group had said their gentle goodbyes to Jazzatnit and Zazfrapiz as it was a pleasant friendship that existed between them. They'd also bid farewell to Muznant and Brazjaf though with a bit more emotion. Farzant had held herself back until Tania went to her and taking hold of both her hands gave her light kisses on each side of her face. She was careful to avoid the facial sideburn-like webs that came down on each side. Farzant was a youth prone to easy embarrassment so when Ashley came to say goodbye he simply held her hands in his and conveyed a brief Sewa. Apparently Fiona and Farzant had really hit it off as friends and much was conveyed when they bid each other farewell. There was a promise made that they would communicate often.

The platform Transporter took them directly to the space-park and before long they were being greeted by Captain Rojazonto up in the bubble housing of the control room. There were still a few more passengers on their way and 8632-Orange was not scheduled to depart for the starship rendezvous for another two hours at least. So after fifteen minutes Ashley accepted the captain's suggestion that they retire to the dining hall for refreshments. The internal transporter took them to the dining hall that was close to their allotted cabins and surprisingly there were quite a number of Oannes already there. However their usual table was unoccupied. Ashley suspected that this table had been reserved for their use and the Oannes passengers and crew respected this privilege granted their guests.

None of them were particularly hungry but drinks hot and cold were very welcome. Rojazonto had conveyed that a proper evening meal was to be laid on once all the passengers had boarded and the spaceship began its journey towards the starship rendezvous. The starship 8110-Gold was currently awaiting its passengers at its orbit location that was one billion miles from Raznat.

The journey time would be seven and a half hours in total. It would be four hours to the one million miles from Nazmos distance when the neutron generators could be operated. And then it would be three and a half hours to the starship rendezvous location travelling at 80,000 miles per second. Actually for the passengers on 8632-Orange the journey time with time dilation would appear twenty minutes shorter.

When Captain Rojazonto conveyed to the passengers that there would be a further delay of an hour or so because certain members of the science team had been held up waiting for an essential item of equipment, Ashley suggested that they retreat to their cabins for a rest. Fiona however made a request and was given permission to spend time in the control room prior to commencement of the journey. She liked the view of the receding land and then the deepening of the sky tone when the ship rose up into space. It was an aspect she was determined not to miss.

Raznat was low in the Nazmos sky when the spaceship finally commenced its journey. Fiona had been summoned to the control room at the same time as when the meal was announced. Ashley and the others had had an hours rest in their cabins and now made their way to the dining hall. Fiona said she would join them all as soon as she'd witnessed the spaceship's ascent from the control room bubble. But she and Captain Rojazonto seemed to find something in common and it was half and hour before Fiona joined her family at the dining table.

There were the usual dishes and Ashley and the others had got quite accustomed to the new diet. Ashley as usual tried most of the dishes presented and finished with his favourite in the sweetened Yaztraka. Brian said he quite favoured the Raizna and the Lazzonta. He said he also quite fancied the Milsony but had yet to get used to its spicy taste. The Bizzony and Trozbit were given a wide berth by all.

After several glasses of Wazu – orange drink for Rachel – everyone felt quite sated and ready for their cabins. But they sat chatting for a while longer before glances were exchanged and they finally rose and went to their individual rooms.

The spaceship's acceleration had increased to a quarter above normal Nazmos gravity and Zanos recommended that passengers make use of the sleep tanks in their cabins or recliners in the case of the humans. A good night of rest should find them at the starship rendezvous location when they awoke. Captain Rojazonto had planned the journey to coincide with the night period of Wentazta.

It had been a long and full day for Ashley and Tania and subsequently sleep came readily after their brief moment of passion. Tania lay awake for slightly longer and looked at her sleeping husband's serene expression.

'He's still a little boy at heart,' she thought just before she too fell into a deep sleep.

They awoke after what seemed like only moments but in fact they had slept soundly for the entire seven hours journey to the starship rendezvous.

Ashley felt rested and invigorated and drew Tania into the circle of his arms. The moment seemed to become electrified as they cuddled and kissed and the excitement overrode all. Then once again they lay together sated, quiet and at peace with one another. It was some time before Tania slowly extricated herself from Ashley's arms and went towards the shower cubicle. She looked over her naked shoulder and smiled at her bemused husband. Their mutual emotion of love filled the space between them.

'Five years,' thought Tania, 'at least I have him for the next five years.'

She was being practical about it for she feared that Zarama might be the ultimate challenge for Ashley. His whole life and all his gifts were to fulfil that one Big Task as Philip had so profoundly put it. She thought about Philip and how they had not heard from him at all. Perhaps a greater power had moved him on or had he been filtered in with Ashley's inner voice? Was he still close but in an indirect manner?

Ashley read Tania's thoughts and he too thought the same. A great unknown lay ahead of him but an inner instinct made him feel confident that he would succeed with Zarama.

The family group met again at breakfast and afterwards they were invited to the control room bubble for a sight of the starship 8110-Gold.

Fiona caught her breath when she saw the distant form of the two mile long sleek starship about a hundred miles away. It was mainly an angled tail-end view as 8632-Orange operated along its parking loop. All ferrying shuttles were to approach the starship from this tail position as a matter of course. There were two other spaceships in the vicinity but they were out of sight and operating in prescribed parking loops of their own. There were two shuttles heading for the starship and one could be seen close to it under magnification and making slow progress up along its rear end and towards its central area. Most had seen this sight before but it was especially exciting for Fiona, Sarah and Brian. Ashley and the others including the Oannes present found the sense of their excitement quite fascinating.

There was no immediate urgency to transfer to the starship as others had arrived before them and had priority. So while they talked Fiona queried the position that Sirius occupied amongst all the stars spread before them. Captain Rojazonto heard the query and came over to elucidate. He said that Sirius was not visible from their current orientation but would be the moment that the ship reached the mid-loop position in another ten minutes. The ship then rotated-about to begin the deceleration process towards the parking-loop end. Rojazonto then directed Fiona towards the constellation of Orion with its well defined 'H' configuration of brighter stars. The middle three stars formed the well known Orion's Belt. Rojazonto then pointed out to Fiona that these three stars roughly pointed towards a bright star on both sides and some distance from Orion. The two stars were approximately equidistant from the belt stars. The one which was on the right side was Aldebaran while the other and far brighter one was Sirius. Sirius was also very close to the cloudy brightness that was the Milky Way.

'Thank you,' said Fiona, 'I see it clearly now.'

After a moment of taking all this in she asked where Earth was. Rojazonto conveyed the full configuration of Orion's stars before adding.

'Draw a line from Orion's foot-star Saiph all the way to Sirius. Earth's Sun is not quite halfway along this line. Earth is closer to Nazmos than Sirius and so the starship 8110-Gold will have to speed past Earth on its journey to Sirius.'

'Can you see Earth from here?' asked Fiona.

'You have a better chance of seeing Earth's Sun,' said Rojazonto. 'It is that faint yellow star on the right side of Sirius.'

Fiona looked as did all the others and they were quite taken with the revelation. It was nice for them to know that Earth was not such a great distance away. It gave them a feeling of warmth to realise its closeness. Ashley remembered when he had been shown the position of Earth on his first trip to Nazmos. He had been on his own then and without the comforting presence of Tania and the others. The view had brought a feeling of extreme nostalgia and the emotional state had brought tears to his eyes.

Tania looked at Ashley with a smile of understanding for Ashley had elaborated about this event when he had returned home. That was twenty two years ago and though it seemed like a lifetime ago all the emotion was still vivid in his memory.

Back on Nazmos Ritozanan floated silently in her sleep tank as she too pondered on all that had happened in her lifetime. It had all been quite mundane until the day that Ashley entered into her life. Ashley had come to Nazmos alone and had appeared before the governing council in the Great Domed Hall. His request had been conveyed to the council earlier and she personally had found it ridiculous and had decided to dismiss it as unfeasible. Ritozanan could never forget that event when Ashley a lowly human had humiliated her and made her feel humble. She had never met such a person not even among her own people. None had interested her in the least. None had stood up to her as Ashley had done. It was a clash of wills. The way he had turned his back on her and strutted towards the far wall had angered her. She had thought it was all a show and had instantly despised him for it. She smiled now as she thought of that moment. And then he had turned back towards her and his facial expression was fiercely serious. Again she had thought it was an act on his part and decided to probe his thoughts. But his mind was blocked from her probing and consternation arose within her. How could he do such a thing and who was he to automatically resist her mind probing power. And then he had spoken and his revelation had stunned them all. Ashley had gifts that were beyond her understanding which was when she began in her admiration for him. It was also when she started to love this human. But then he had touched her with his show of compassion and caring and her admiration and love for him had increased a hundredfold. But she could not show it then or later. One day she would let him know and she did. On his visit here she had revealed all and saw the sadness that he had felt in his heart.

About twenty years ago physical pain had entered into Ritozanan's life. At first it had been occasional and slight but gradually over the years there were prolonged, sharper and more intense periods. There were also many good periods lasting several days. She knew what it was and preferred to keep it within her household and to let it take her quietly. She wanted no shadow of its meaning to encroach on her reputation as a governing council member. Ashley had given her Gozmanot's visionary dream for Nazmos and Ritozanan had taken it upon herself to be a champion to the cause.

Her illness was age related and common to the elderly among the Oannes people. The aging tissues within her body had begun to atrophy to hardness in selected areas and so cause stiffness and pain. It was a price one paid for extra long life. Death was creeping up on her just as it did for most Oannes who exceeded 300 years in their age. Very few approached the 400 age mark and Ritozanan, now 332 years of age, knew that she would not be among those. It was a great wonder that Gozmanot had actually achieved 500 years. Her body must have been wracked with pain towards her last days.

Ritozanan pondered over all this and her consolation was that she had met Ashley and through his regression skills she had got to see Gozmanot; as had all of Nazmos. Subsequently she had used her influence to persuade the governing council to accept the idea of the Nazmos orbital change.

'This is our world. What would we be if we did not try to make it better,' were the words she had used to persuade her fellow council members. Gozmanot's vision would be realised.

Also using her authority and influence Ritozanan managed to acquire those drugs which eased the stiffness and the pain that went with her age. And latterly she had begun to consume ever stronger doses such that her mind floated in a misty world of surreal wonder. Was there something beyond death as the religious sects of the humans advocated or was it all wishful thinking. Suddenly she could not be certain of anything.

However the end was not yet and she was glad of Ashley's visit. She knew it was to be their last sighting of each other and so she had conveyed all her inner feelings of love and admiration to him. She had shown herself to him as only a betrothed would do and she had meant it as her ultimate compliment to him. And Ashley had gone away gratified, contemplative and saddened all at the same time. He would not forget her and that had been her sole intention. It brought her comfort to know all this. She wondered what he might be doing at this precise moment. Love had come into her life through him and she savoured its sweetness within her being. It felt good even at this late stage in her life. To actually love someone was an emotion she had found most fulfilling.

Ashley and his family were a billion miles away seated in a spaceship's shuttle that was speeding up the side of starship 8110-Gold and heading for the cargo boarding airlock hatch. The massiveness of the starship was not lost on the humans approaching it and they all felt the greatness of this feat of scientific accomplishment by the Oannes civilization.

As the shuttle approached closer to the front of the starship a faint gravity effect began to make its presence felt. The shuttle then turned about so that its under-surface faced the direction of travel. By the time it entered the cargo hatch the gravity was at normal Nazmos level. And it was not long before they were down on the habitation platform and walking the quarter mile distance to the central column where the control room was situated. And standing there was Captain Zakatanz with his family patiently waiting to greet them. Both Azatamunt and her daughter Hazazamunt looked radiant as they stood either side of the captain.

Ashley noted Zakatanz's happy demeanour and he smiled. He had developed a great fondness for this captain and Ashley felt that he had a shared history with him that began with the tragedy of the first Hazazamunt. It also gave Ashley an insight into the Oannes way of life and he had come to admire and respect them. They really weren't very different from humans.

A smiling Zakatanz stepped forward as Ashley got close and a firm hand clasp was exchanged between them. Of course Zakatanz also conveyed a welcoming Sewa to all his arriving guests. With the formalities completed a more congenial atmosphere prevailed as he took Ashley's party into his private apartments. Light refreshments were served along with the customary glass of Wazu. This time Rachel managed a few delicate sips just to be polite. She was gradually getting used to the taste of this drink but still could not reconcile herself to the furry little creatures she was convinced jerked about inside it.

As before, Ashley and his family were invited to take all their meals here with the captain, his wife and daughter. Ashley was pleased to accept with gracious thanks. He had eleven days ahead of him as empty as blank pages. Somehow he'd have to fill them with the meaningful routine of the starship's journey. He thought about that other journey that he must also take in about five years time to Zarama. That journey would be six months in duration and again he'd have to fill the time usefully. And of course he'd have Tania and Simon to accompany him then. Simon would help fill the empty days, weeks and months. The Oannes were a very patient people and their current starship journeys to Earth from Nazmos also took about six months. And yet none had remarked exceptionally about the duration.

Zanos conveyed that the last of the scheduled passengers had arrived on board and were being shown to their habitation level apartments. The last shuttle had also left the starship but was still enroute to its parent spaceship. Captain Zakatanz explained that only when all the ferrying spaceships had departed the vicinity and were on their way back to Nazmos could 8110-Gold begin its journey towards the Binary Sirius star system.

Sirius A was the large parent star of that system. It was twice as massive as Earth's Sun and twenty five times as bright. This was not a concern since their destination was its companion star Sirius B which was in orbit around Sirius A at a distance of nearly two billion miles; a distance that was equal to the orbit of Uranus around Earth's Sun.

Sirius B had originally been more than twice as massive as Sirius A but then it rapidly consumed its resources to become a Red Giant before shedding its outer layers and collapsing down to its current size as a White Dwarf Star some 120 million years ago. Sirius B was now the mass of Earth's Sun compacted down to the size of Earth. Its current surface temperature was 25,000° C but because there was no internal heat source it would steadily cool as its remaining heat was radiated out into space. This would continue for a period of roughly two billion years. Apart from this radiated heat there was no surface flare activity so a zero-gravity spaceship should theoretically be able to approach to within a reasonable distance. Two million miles might be rather daring hence the need for a trial approach.

Zarama was also a White Dwarf Star but it was a third more massive than Sirius B. The heat conditions should however be very similar.

Zakatanz had worked out a plan of approach for the starship from lengthy consultations with Brajam and his scientific team. The starship would park itself at an initial distance of ten million miles from Sirius B. A zero-gravity spaceship would then be sent out to investigate but not venture far from the starship before returning. Instruments aboard would indicated the conditions prevailing there. By a planned process of forward steps the starship would move ever closer to the star with one of the zero-gravity ships venturing out on each occasion.

The starship had much better heat shielding than the smaller zero-gravity ships and so it could finally park using its impulse drive to counter the gravity effects of the Dwarf Star. From this position if it proved feasible Ashley could venture out in the zero-gravity ship to view Sirius B from the closest safe distance. The zero-gravity ship would also have to resist the gravity pull from the mass of Sirius B which the Oannes scientists had computed as being one and a quarter times the Nazmos gravity at the two million mile distance from the star.

Fiona queried what the gravity conditions might be at ever closer distances and Zanos was happy to oblige. The others including Ashley also found it of interest.

At 1.5 million miles from the star the gravity level increased to 2.3 times Nazmos gravity. At one million miles out this would increase to 8 times Nazmos gravity. At half a million miles out it would be 28 times Nazmos gravity. At the quarter million mile distance which was the distance between the Earth and the Moon the gravity level would be 120 times Nazmos gravity. And finally at the surface of Sirius B the gravity level would increase to a massive 150,000 times Nazmos gravity.

For Zarama these would all be a third greater and Ashley thought that subsequently a greater distance might be advisable. Perhaps two and a half million miles might be the better option.

As to the heat factor Sirius B would be the size of a pea just as Platwuz had appeared to Ashley from the two million mile distance. Except Sirius B would be exceptionally bright and therefore appear much larger and more clearly visible. What would the heat factor be at this distance Ashley wondered?

And approximately 432 light years away was the rogue White Dwarf Star Zarama hurtling on its destructive course towards Earth and Nazmos.

Originally Zarama was part of a binary star system that had evolved along the main sequence of normal star progression about a billion years ago. It had then passed through a Red Giant phase before shedding its outer layers to collapse into its present White Dwarf Star state. It had continued to orbit happily around its giant star companion at the distance of just under one billion miles; an orbital distance that compared favourably with the orbit of Saturn around the Sun.

The companion star was huge being ten times the mass of Earth's Sun. Then about twenty million years ago it went through to the Red Giant phase and when it consumed all its resources it could not sustain its size and collapsed in upon itself. The implosion was massive and caused the star to restart its core fusion process and subsequently it exploded as a Supernova. This resulted in all its material content being blasted outwards with such force that the star remnants attained a velocity of 80,000 miles per second. It took nearly three hours for the long trail of exploded material to impact on the white dwarf star Zarama and force it outwards into the central expanse of the galaxy. Unfortunately the direction it was given happened to lie generally towards Earth and Nazmos.

The Supernova explosion had imbedded debris into the White Dwarf Star Zarama such that certain physical features became a part of its surface geography. Infrared scans highlighted a vague facial image as the star rotated. It was not too unlike the facial image that could be picked out on Earth's moon except this had a leering twisted aspect to it; an aspect that portrayed an evil intent. And that is exactly what came into Ashley's mind when he was shown the infrared pictures.

Zanos now conveyed that all formalities had been met and the starship was ready to commence its journey towards Sirius. Ashley looked up at the captain to see his response and all he gave was a slight nod of his head.

Captain Natazlat of the starship 9110-Red had made a detailed record of the journey from Earth and how Ashley had simply willed his mind to accelerate the starship to 695 FTL in stages. Captain Zakatanz had reviewed all the details of that trip and had conveyed to Ashley that he would be happy if Ashley repeated the process. However he could go for the maximum cruise velocity from the very start of his intentions.

'I would like you to delay your telekinetic push until the starship is well on its way and approaching initial light velocity,' conveyed the captain. 'Zanos will inform you when the time approaches.'

It was barely twenty minutes later that Ashley was informed that light velocity had been achieved. He received a nod from Captain Zakatanz and noticed the gaze of all there upon him. So putting his mug of tea down on the table he looked around at his friends and family and gave them a warm smile. Then closing his eyes and putting his head at a downward angle he visualised the inner face of the starship's neutron shield. He kept his mind open and then willed for the starship to be moved at a steady safe acceleration over a period of just over four hours to a final maximum cruising velocity of 695 FTL. The acceleration was lesser than for 9110-Red which had been a bit over the top. For some reason he also willed that the destination was the Sirius star system with Sirius B as the focus of the rendezvous.

Then opening his eyes and looking up he smiled at the captain and said, 'It is done. Perhaps Zanos could confirm on the starship's acceleration status.'

The starship seemed to continue on as smoothly as before and no apparent change was felt by its passengers and crew.

But then Zanos conveyed that the starship's acceleration had increased exponentially to a level that brought the habitation platform very close to the forward neutron shield. This was once again as on the trip from Earth and indicated an acceleration of close to a thousand times the gravity level on Nazmos. Zanos also conveyed that normal gravity level was being maintained on the habitation platform for all its passengers and crew.

Captain Zakatanz looked at Ashley with a questioning look.

'Please don't be concerned captain it will all be done in a safe manner,' said Ashley. 'I shall remain here with you until maximum velocity is attained. What does Zanos estimate?'

'Four hours and ten minutes,' conveyed the captain.

'Good,' said Ashley smiling, 'then perhaps another glass of Wazu could be arranged.'

There was a curious expression on Hazazamunt's face which Ashley caught at the edge of his vision. He turned to face her and raised an eyebrow and conveyed his query.

'Is that all it took?' she asked, 'just a thought from you.'

'Not a thought but rather a wish,' said Ashley. 'Instead of applying a voluntary telekinetic push at different levels as I used to do, I now let my mind take over and do the needful for the entire process. It makes it easier for me and causes me less fatigue. I suppose the progression to this is all part of my preparation for the big task that is Zarama. I hope I shall succeed there.'

Hazazamunt smiled with embarrassment and looked at her father as if to apologise for her ignorance. He smiled and nodded back at her. All could see that he was proud of his daughter and had liked her asking Ashley the question. Hazazamunt had also liked her communication with Ashley.

He knew that his telekinetic effort always brought on a thirst in his system even though the effort was involuntary. And his mind would need to keep the starship at maximum velocity for the entire journey of approximately eleven days; simulated days of course.

Zanos kept them informed continually of the starship's velocity and it was only after the attainment of 500 FTL that a gradual lessening in the acceleration rate was initiated; a drop of 10%. And at 600 FTL this reduced by a further 20%. At 650 FTL the acceleration was down another 50%. Finally after another hour and thirty one minutes Zanos conveyed that all acceleration had ceased and the starship was now cruising at the prescribed 695 FTL velocity; that is 695 times faster than the speed of light or nearly 130 million miles per second. Zanos estimated Sirius rendezvous in 10 days and 20 hours. The acceleration period had lasted four hours and ten minutes just as estimated.

Ashley looked around and smiled and received exuberant smiles in return especially from the captain.

'Let us celebrate the occasion with a glass of Wazu,' said the captain. 'This is once again a tremendous achievement.'

'Excellent,' agreed Ashley, 'and perhaps a nice hot mug of sweet tea to follow.'

Zakatanz nodded and raised his arm towards Ashley with a glass of Wazu held firmly in his hand. Ashley picked up his glass too and raised it high. This was soon followed by the others doing the same. Even Rachel got into the spirit of it and took a gulp from her glass; with eyes closed of course. Zakatanz passed his own half full glass to his daughter Hazazamunt sitting beside him. Azatamunt smiled and nodded to her daughter who took a sip from the glass before handing it back to her father.

'How are you feeling Uncle Ashley?' queried Fiona.

'I feel quite normal and rather detached if you must know,' said Ashley. 'I feel as if I've had nothing to do with the starship achieving this velocity. I know I'm still applying my telekinetic gift to keep the ship at this speed but I don't at the moment feel tired or sleepy. I expect that will come later.'

Hazazamunt was wide-eyed with admiration for this human called Ashley. She felt awed by his presence and knew that she would remember this moment all her life. Yet he seemed so unaffected and oblivious by what he had just achieved and she admired him all the more because of that. She had seen it achieved in her presence and with her own eyes and it had all been so effortless. And all he wanted was to drink that hot sweet tea which she found tasteless and revolting. She wondered what more she would learn about this human over the next ten days of this journey. All she knew was that she felt good when he was around. She would examine her thoughts as to the reason for that.

Ashley smiled inwardly at this and decided that he would encourage Hazazamunt out of her shyness by letting her get used to the things he did and said over the days they spent together on this trip. He would make sure that Tania and the other members of his family were always with him and they would make general verbal conversation in her presence. Ashley would also keep his mind open even though he knew she was not permitted to probe. He hoped that some of his thoughts might filter through to her. He would also encourage her to ask questions. If possible he would try to elicit her opinion during their light-hearted mealtime conversations.

Ashley had also decided that he would encourage others from among the starship's passengers to come and meet him in the central area. It would be a welcome diversion in what he reckoned to be a rather uneventful journey period. He knew that he must remain within the confines of the central area of the habitation platform for his telekinetic push to remain focussed accurately upon the ship's neutron shield. The apartment allocated to him and Tania was the same as previous being that which was closest to the central column. In distance it was just forty feet away.

Ashley expressed a wish to stretch his legs by going for a small walk-about and asked Tania and the others to accompany him. He would of course remain within the central area between the control room and the circle of the closest apartments. Perhaps five or six circuits would do for a start; with the captain's permission of course.

'That is an excellent suggestion,' said Zakatanz, 'and perhaps I might accompany you on another occasion. A meal will be served here shortly so until then do enjoy your walk.'

Fiona looked at Hazazamunt and said, 'Why don't you come along with us Hazazamunt and you can tell me all about your life on Nazmos and I will tell you about mine on Earth.'

Hazazamunt looked nervously towards her parents as if begging for permission. A quick decision was made between husband and wife such that Hazazamunt got a nodded agreement accompanied by a smile. Zakatanz approved wholeheartedly of Ashley and his family and considered that Hazazamunt would receive a good insight of what was best among the humans. It was important that her first understanding of the human people be a favourable one. In the long run she would compare all others to this group.

'Thank you,' said Hazazamunt in reply to Fiona's invitation, 'I think I would like that very much.'

Fiona noticed that Hazazamunt had a low husky voice when she spoke.

Ashley smiled again to himself and thought that it was clever of Fiona to especially befriend Hazazamunt. He realised her intent which was to gain the favour of the captain her father and perhaps be granted a privileged tour of his starship as had Captain Natazlat on the previous trip out from Earth. She could then compare if the starships were similar within. She would like to see the upper cargo platform and also the food growing areas below. And any other areas the captain might permit her to see.

Fiona was interested in things scientific which came from her nurses background but in this case she was awed by a feat of engineering that exceeded her wildest expectations; the greatest achievement of a civilized society. It would satisfy her ego to actually see the functional part of this starship; her previous tour of 9110-Red with Captain Natazlat had been a brief one that covered general aspects only.

Ashley thought he'd let Fiona get on with her scheming even though he could have conveyed to her all the relevant information. But Fiona had a sense of adventure and she wished to physically visit areas of the starship normally forbidden to passengers. Ashley conveyed his thoughts to Tania and both smiled at what their conniving niece was trying to achieve.

Ashley wished her all the luck in the world hoping she would win through to Zakatanz's favour.

The walkabout was pleasant and Ashley felt he would make it a routine part of the coming days.

The starship was currently keeping to the Wentazta day time-wise and accordingly it was late afternoon when the meal was served in the captain's quarters. It was the usual fare and all partook of it heartily.

Fiona now sat next to the young Hazazamunt who in turn was seated next to her mother and the captain. Fiona had done wonders in so short a time for Hazazamunt was now quite relaxed in her attitude generally. She even smiled occasionally when she spoke to Fiona.

One topic that was generally discussed was about the changes that might occur on Nazmos from the orbital change. Of course there would be a climate change towards the warmer temperatures but of special interest were the types of food crops that could later be selected for land cultivation.

'A lot would depend upon the climate conditions that develop,' said Zakatanz. 'And that will not be known until it actually happens. It would be premature to speculate and I personally will be happy to leave things as they are - for the time being of course.'

'I do agree,' said Ashley. 'But if I did have a choice then I would plumb for a wheat crop. Currently all bread on Nazmos is made from wheat that is imported from Earth. And I do like my toast at breakfast.'

There were smiles at Ashley's remark and a few serious nods.

'I would like to grow potatoes,' said Sarah.

'Ah yes,' said Zakatanz smiling, 'but there we already have something similar in our Raizna crops.'

'Oh yes I forgot,' said Sarah smiling sheepishly.

'What about our fruit trees,' asked Rachel? 'They would add greatly to the forests that we hope will grow up on Nazmos.'

'We shall see,' said Zakatanz. 'It will be up to the governing council to decide what is best.'

'Of course,' said Fiona, 'but it is nice to speculate. In a thousand years I'm sure Nazmos will be very different to what it is now. I hope everything works out for the general good.'

Zakatanz smiled at this. Ashley could see that he approved of Fiona.

After the meal Ashley and Tania decided to do another walkabout in the central platform zone and make themselves available to their fellow passengers. Ashley's thoughts must have been picked up generally and soon small groups of Oannes passengers gathered at the inner fringe of the habitation platform area where the apartments began.

They walked up to one group that was closest and conveyed a brief Sewa. Basically it was a polite form of saying 'Hello, I hope you are well as are we.'

As a general lead-in to the conversation Ashley enquired about their plans when they reached Anztarza and was given a variation of answers. Some were simply returning to their jobs there while others were visiting friends or relatives and making the round trip back to Nazmos on this starship's return journey.

Ashley kept his mind open so that any who wished to probe could do so. Very few did for most thought that it was impolite and considered it an intrusion of privacy. A few asked Ashley how he felt physically after his telekinetic efforts. Ashley conveyed that tiredness and sleep were usually an after-effect but at the moment he was feeling fine; he was after all still applying his telekinetic forces on the starship's forward shield to maintain the ship at its current FTL velocity. He received the odd surprised glance at this bit of information for not all Oannes were scientifically minded. Many were art connoisseurs like Jazzatnit.

This pattern of meeting the passengers continued over the period of the journey and Ashley met many pleasant Oannes couples. No children had been allowed on this trip apart from Hazazamunt. Many extended invitations for Ashley to visit them in their apartment accommodation to share a glass of Wazu but Ashley had politely declined explaining that he must remain in this central area for telekinetic reasons. Tania and the others however would be happy to oblige, conveyed Ashley and the offer was heartily taken up. Tania always came back and gave Ashley a full account of the visits. It was usually after about an hour into the meetings with other passengers that Ashley conveyed a wish for a brief rest in his apartment or until the next meal was served.

Hazazamunt and Fiona were now often together and joined in the Ashley walkabouts. What was discussed between them was kept private. On occasion they were accompanied by Zakatanz and Azatamunt. On these occasions the passengers got a rare opportunity to communicate directly with the starship's captain.

Fiona showed a keen interest in the starship especially as to what was contained within its two mile length. Although Fiona had seen a bit of the starship 9110-Red under Captain Natazlat, nevertheless she also wanted to tour the present one. She thought about Simon and how lucky he was to have joined the Oannes space fleet through its academy. He had looked so debonair with his fellow officers back on Nazmos that Fiona was proud to call him her cousin. She hoped she would see him again one day. She felt a great sisterly love towards him.

When the captain did take her on a tour of the ship Fiona pretended that it was all new to her. She feigned her ignorance very well so that the captain did his best to enlighten her on various aspects of the ship. Fiona was especially interested in the food growing tanks as she wished for a comparison with those on 9110-Red. She asked if these were similar to the Anztarza Food Domes for producing their crops.

'Not quite,' conveyed Zakatanz in reply, 'as these on the starship are far more intensive. A starship is required to feed nearly two thousand persons for an indefinite period. Starship journeys could last for years at a time and food must never run short.'

He explained that the Earth journeys were usually a little over six months in duration and dry stocks were brought on board for the purpose of varying the menu. But out in deep space the crew and passengers would have to rely solely on what was grown in the starship's food growing tanks.

Zakatanz was pleased by the interest Fiona showed in his pride and joy of a starship and heartily approved of the friendship he could see building between her and his daughter. It was good for Hazazamunt to get to know and understand what she could about human behaviour. It would all add to the variety that was to be her future education.

Zakatanz did enjoy his conversations with Ashley not only during their meal times with all present but especially when they walked about on their own and met ship's passengers. It was an insight into Ashley's character to see him conversing so easily with those who were strangers to him. He had such an easy manner of commonality with those he spoke to that they were instantly put at their ease and pleasure was brought to their faces. Both Azatamunt and Hazazamunt were similarly brought under his spell so that they became less formal in his presence. Yet it would be some time before they could be totally at ease with him.

Admiration and a modicum of veneration were aspects generated in the minds of many of the Oannes because of all the things that Ashley had achieved. And only a closeness of association would show them that all he wished for was to be treated as an ordinary person. In time Ashley hoped he could convey this image of himself to all; perhaps after Zarama.

And so the journey to Sirius continued and drew towards the eleventh simulated day. It had been a relaxing time for Tania as she spent the long nights alone with her husband doing the things that husbands and wives are wont to do. It was like being on a celebrity honeymoon all over again. By day they associated with family and friends but at night they were completely alone and private in their beds. Tania's excuse was that Ashley needed his rest since he was still exerting his telekinetic effort to maintain the starship at its cruise velocity.

It was after their breakfast on day eleven that Zanos conveyed to the captain and to Ashley that a gradual reduction in the starship's velocity should commence as of now. It was suggested that this be done over a period of five hours as had been done on the starship 9110-Red under Captain Natazlat on the previous journey from Earth to Nazmos.

Ashley understood that it was far more difficult to decelerate the starship than it was to accelerate it. This was because the forward proton shield played no part in the deceleration. It was the neutron generators that had to operate continuously in order to resist the forward push that passengers received through the deceleration action. Space travel was about maintaining as normal a gravity level for the passengers as was technically possible. The neutron generators produced a reverse acceleration effect and so could do this within limits. So although Ashley had accelerated the starship to its 695 FTL cruise velocity in four hours and a bit it would require a much longer period for its deceleration. Zanos would monitor Ashley's mind and the reverse firing neutron generators would operate in harmony with the reduction in the telekinetic push.

Ashley once again closed his eyes and concentrated his mind on the starship's neutron shield and willed for his telekinetic effort to be gradually reduced until it ceased altogether and this was to be done over a period of five hours from now. His mind was also to be linked in parallel with Zanos-on-board so that normal gravity could be maintained by the synchronous operation of the neutron generators.

Ashley then opened his eyes and looked around at the others. 'It is done,' he said.

Zakatanz nodded and smiled at Ashley as if to say 'Thank you'. Then after several minutes he added. 'Zanos estimates our arrival at rendezvous in fifteen hours and twenty minutes if all goes to plan. Zanos also confirms that the neutron generators have begun to operate in synchronism with Ashley's telekinetic effort reductions and that the starship's velocity has already begun to reduce. The starship will be down to 10 FTL velocity in exactly five hours time.'

Ashley thought about Simon then and wondered if Simon's gift of premonition had also acquired an enhanced performance or was it still a random occurrence. If there was danger on the path towards Zarama would Simon receive warning sufficiently in advance? He certainly hoped so.

Zanos interrupted these thoughts to convey that the starship was now down to 500 FTL and still decreasing in velocity.

A meal was served at the usual time and at the end of it Zanos informed them that the ship's velocity had decreased to 355 FTL. Zanos also confirmed that all neutron generators were operating normally. A starship has no viewing panels but Ashley could visualise the starbursts flaring like a ring of explosions around the circular body of the starship. These functioned like a circle of mini-black holes causing a reverse gravity effect to counteract the deceleration forces caused by the slowing down of the starship.

At the end of the fifth hour the starship 8110-Gold velocity was down to 10.6 FTL and operating entirely under the ships own impulse power. Ashley felt immense relief that all had gone well and suddenly he felt the need for a shower and a lie down on his apartment bed. It was a load off his mind to know that he was no longer exerting any telekinetic effort upon the ship's neutron shield. Perhaps the tiredness was psychological in part but the desire to lie down was still there.

Ashley excused himself from the captain and the others and left for his apartment. Tania went with him to make sure he was alright. By the time they reached the apartment an intense drowsiness came over him and any thought of a shower disappeared. Tania recognised the symptoms and let Ashley lie down on his bed straight away. He was asleep in seconds and Tania carefully removed his footwear and lay down beside him. She ran her fingers through his ample hair and lightly massaged his temples. She felt his forehead and was glad of its coolness. It was mildly warm in the room and after a few minutes Tania decided to leave him alone. He would sleep better without the sense of a presence near him. Quietly she left the room and apartment and returned to the captain's quarters. She conveyed the news that Ashley was soundly asleep on his bed and that she would return for him when the next meal was served. Perhaps he'd freshen up with a shower. The Sirius rendezvous would still be hours away even then.

But it was not to be for when Tania looked in on her hubby he hadn't shifted position at all and continued to sleep soundly. Rather than disturb his well earned rest Tania decided to let him sleep for as long as needed. She returned to the captain's table for the meal that had been served there. Hazazamunt looked keenly at her and Tania conveyed an image of her sleeping husband. She knew this impressed the young Oannes youth for Ashley usually presented a face that appeared serene and all innocence when he was asleep. For one who slept on his back most of the time it was surprising that he did not snore. Apart from a deep breathing hum and occasional lip flutter Ashley slept quietly.

Tania requested Zanos to inform her when Ashley began to stir. And stir he did but not before the starship had parked at its rendezvous position ten million miles from Sirius B.

Tania went into the apartment knowing that Ashley had woken at last. He had been asleep for nearly six hours and the simulated time on the starship was approaching seven in the evening. She found him sitting up on the bed with his head in his hands. Zanos had answered Ashley's query so he knew that the starship was at its initial rendezvous location.

'How are you darling?' she asked and Ashley replied that he felt groggy after his long sleep.

'I think I'll just pop into the shower after I shave,' he said. 'Then a hot mug of tea would be nice.'

He looked up at Tania as he said this and she understood the priority.

'Wait right there, don't move,' she said.

Every apartment had its facilities and it took Tania a moment to pour the hot water and make her husband his most desired drink. In fact she made herself one as well and sat beside him on the bed. She had made Ashley's sweeter than usual and he smiled as he sipped it.

They sat quietly there, thigh touching thigh and Tania felt it normal and intimate as it should be. It was not long before Ashley held out his empty mug. Tania made him another and they finished together.

Ashley liked to wet shave and before long he was in the shower which he kept rather hotter than usual. Tania was of two minds whether or not to join him in the shower but decided he needed to eat first. It would be a busy day with the planned trips outside the starship in the zero-gravity ships.

Ashley had obviously read her thoughts and gave a low laugh. There was no one like Tania for him and he was still so very much taken with her. She was his perfect companion and he hoped his longing for her company would never leave him.

With the openness of their thoughts Tania knew this which was why no jealousy ever entered her mind when she saw the admiring looks that other females sent in his direction. Ashley had told her fully about Ritozanan and Tania felt proud that her husband should be looked upon so.

Ashley had on his brightest coloured tunic and leggings as he and Tania walked to the captain's quarters. The bright green with orange trim suited Ashley perfectly and made him look quite handsome Tania thought. There were looks of approval from all those who saw him both human and Oannes.

'The colours suit you well Ashley,' said Captain Zakatanz, 'and I hope you are well rested.'

'Yes thank you Captain, it is kind of you to enquire,' said Ashley smiling and making a slight bow as he looked around at his family and friends and then at the clear table surface.

The captain smiled and conveyed that a good breakfast type meal had been ordered and would be laid on especially for him. He had missed two meals and a breakfast snack now would not spoil his main evening meal in just over an hour's time.

The captain had barely conveyed this message than toast, butter, cheese and marmalade began to arrive on the table. Ashley excused himself and immediately began to butter a toast while another mug of hot sweet tea was placed in front of him. It was while he was on his third toast that another dish was brought to the table. Tania smiled as she announced that Ashley's dessert had arrived. Of course Ashley recognised this instantly and knew that it would have been sweetened that little bit extra for him. It was the Yaztraka that had been nicely mashed and there was plenty of it.

Ashley was the only one eating and Hazazamunt's eyes could not resist from staring. She noticed that although Ashley must have been very hungry having missed two prior meals nevertheless he ate at a slow and measured pace. He stopped often to talk and smile at his audience. She found him absolutely fascinating and her emotion could not be hidden. It was the idolatry of a child and both Zakatanz and Azatamunt recognised it as such. She saw Ashley serving himself to a fairly large helping of the sweetened Yaztraka and then pausing in between mouthfuls for a sip of his disgusting tea. How could anyone enjoy such a drink she thought?

'I think I'll stop now or I shan't have room for the main meal later,' said Ashley to the room in general and smiled especially for the captain's wife and daughter.

Hazazamunt quickly looked downwards but Azatamunt smiled back and then looked up at her captain husband still smiling.

'Another one on the books,' thought Tania smiling inwardly to her self. 'Ashley just could not help drawing people to him.'

Ashley finished his mug of tea and stood up.

'I think I'll stretch my legs for a bit. I could do with some company though,' he said looking at the captain.

'I will accompany you Ashley,' said Zakatanz, 'and we can discuss what you would like to do about viewing Sirius B from the zero-gravity ship.'

Ashley was silent for a moment while a particular thought raged through his mind. Was it his inner voice telling him what he must do? He looked towards the captain and nodded and a thought passed between them. Ashley then conveyed generally that there was a private matter he'd like to discuss with the captain.

'Come, my friend,' said Zakatanz as he stood up, 'let us discuss our affairs privately as we walk about on the platform.'

He said this pointedly to ensure that they would be alone.

Ashley smiled at his family and conveyed a brief message before going out onto the platform with the captain. They walked silently for several minutes avoiding the other passengers and headed towards the far wall of the habitation platform. They stopped partway and Zakatanz had the patience to wait for Ashley to speak.

'Captain it is a very big task that lies before me,' said Ashley in a slow manner, 'and I feel grave uncertainty about whether I am up to fulfilling what is required of me. I knew that a burden was to be imposed upon me when I was given these gifts so very long ago. Gozmanot seemed to recognise me as being the one she had been waiting for but that does not give me the confidence I need. I have moved planets but a star such as Zarama is another matter. What I need is to test myself on a star like Sirius B.'

Ashley paused for a brief moment to let what he was intending to filter through to Zakatanz's mind.

'So Captain,' he continued, 'I need your permission to test my telekinetic gift on this star that has a mass close to that of Earth's Sun. If I can cause it to change course by the very smallest fraction then it will give me hope that I can also alter the course of Zarama. If I do not succeed against Sirius B then I will have to consider another strategy for Zarama. What do you think Captain?'

Zakatanz was quiet for nearly a minute before he turned and faced Ashley.

'I cannot directly support your wish in this without first consulting with the Nazmos governing council,' he said in a slow thoughtful manner. 'It is against our code to interfere with what is occurring naturally in space and which does not belong to us.'

'Well then Zarama does not belong to you either and yet you desire me to push it aside,' said Ashley.

'Zarama is a threat and the governing council have agreed that it be rerouted towards Rasalgethi,' argued Zakatanz. 'Sirius B however poses no threat at the present time.'

The captain walked on a few paces and then stopped to face Ashley again. Ashley could see a change in his reasoning when he added.

'And again it is essential that you test your telekinetic capability for when you are to meet Zarama. Sirius B on the other hand is a good trial ground and I personally feel that it would be good to know your potential in this. The governing council will understand that a decision had to be made on the spot and I will inform them that it was my judgement of the situation to accede to your request. How do you wish to proceed?'

Ashley had already worked out the details of a plan in his mind and conveyed this to the captain. The captain nodded and added a few points of his own and mainly to do with his starship.

'It is good,' he said, 'and if any change is detected then we must reverse that as you did for Neptune's moon Triton.

'I understand,' said Ashley, 'but first let us see how close we can approach to this dwarf star, the brother or sister of Zarama.'

Zakatanz smiled at the relationship that Ashley had ascribed to Sirius B. He knew from the Oannes logs that no starship had ventured closer than two and a half million miles of Sirius B and that too had been for a very short duration only. Once the data had been obtained from the star the starship had moved out to a safer distance. But a zero-gravity spaceship was another matter. It did not have the bulk of a starship and might not be able to tolerate such a close encounter especially with the marginal shielding of the viewing panels.

As such the plan was to commence at the current position of ten million miles from Sirius B and proceed to a closer position in agreed stages. The starship would cover the distance to the next stage in a matter of minutes and the zero-gravity spaceships need never venture more than a few miles from their starship base.

'Zanos registers a gravity level of just under a twentieth of Nazmos gravity at our current position and so all will need to wear the electrostatic suits when in the zero-gravity spaceships,' said Zakatanz. 'Personally I cannot go with you as my command is here but Brajam and others will accompany you. One of my deputies will be in command of each zero-gravity spaceship.'

'May my family members accompany me on this first trip out,' asked Ashley?

Zakatanz did not agree immediately but after a short pause said, 'We will let the other zero-gravity spaceship venture out first with our scientists aboard and see what conditions they report back. If it is considered safe then you may also proceed outside in the other zero-gravity spaceship and your family may accompany you but only for the experience. It will have to be only this once. On the other trips out at the closer locations only you and our scientists will be permitted. You will of course be in constant mental communication with them as I will not permit the zero-gravity spaceships to proceed more than a few miles from the starship. The airlock will remain open to receive both ships together should the unforeseen occur.'

'Thank you Captain,' said Ashley politely, 'I will inform them personally.'

'Come let us continue our walk,' said Zakatanz. 'It will be a while before the first zero-gravity ship 0G-8110-2 proceeds outside the starship.'

And so the two of them continued their walk and even stopped to meet a few of the starships other passengers over the next half hour. They then returned to the captain's quarters.

Zanos conveyed that 0G-8110-2 was ready to proceed to the large airlock and the captain gave his authorisation for them to proceed.

In the meantime another meal was being laid out slightly later than the normal time. Ashley had of course eaten a breakfast type meal just over an hour ago and so wasn't particularly hungry. But the captain suggested he make an effort as the next real meal would be their breakfast next morning. So Ashley kept everyone company by taking small portions till he felt quite full up; especially with the Yaztraka dish in front of him. The mug of tea that came afterwards was especially welcome.

The first zero-gravity ship had exited from the side of the starship and had speeded out to a distance of ten miles before coming to a complete stop. It gradually rotated so that the control room view panels faced towards Sirius B. At the distance of ten million miles it was no more than a very bright explosion of light from a point source. On their left was a much brighter and larger globe of light which was of course Sirius A the main star in this binary system. Sirius A being twice the mass and size of Earth's Sun was still a body to be reckoned with at its current two billion mile distance. As such all the view panels were kept at a medium tint for general comfort inside the ship.

The pull of Sirius B's gravity was sufficient to prevent any loose objects from freely floating around. It made the trip just that little bit more comfortable though the electrostatic suits were still required to be worn aboard.

Zanos on board 0G-8110-2 reported that a weak magnetic field was present and a medium level of heat effect from the dwarf star was also apparent. It gave the green light for the other zero-gravity ship 0G-8110-1 to proceed out of the starship and it was not long before Ashley and his family group were taken to the electrostatic suiting rooms and thence to the upper cargo platform.

The zero-gravity ship 0G-8110-1 sat here with its ramp open and down to the deck floor. Ashley and his family followed a group of Oannes scientists across to the ship and walked up the ramp slope and into the encircling corridor. In all there must have been about twenty passengers and crew boarding this ship. Although the ship appeared small as it sat on the vast area of the cargo deck nevertheless its 200 feet of length and 90 feet width gave ample accommodation inside.

The commander of 0G-8110-1 was one of Zakatanz's deputy officers named Kalitoza aged 120 years. He was of small build and had a constant smiling expression on his face. Ashley took an instant liking to him as did the others of his family group. When they all reached the enlarged control room area he personally directed each of the passengers to a particular pre-designated bucket type seat. These were quite comfortable and had both shoulder and thigh clamping that was well padded for comfort. Kalitoza explained that gravity forces could come from unexpected sources and it was good to be prepared.

This was very different from the other clear panelled shuttle craft and Ashley felt much more secure here. The bucket seats were inclined slightly backwards which made them most comfortable and Ashley reckoned that he could possibly doze off in one of these if given the chance.

The interior of the control room was quite sparse and completely free of any loose objects. The view panels were similar to those on Bulzezatna's ship 520-Green. Ashley's seat was at the front of the large arrangement and allowed him a good view all around. His emotion was a pleased one and this was picked up by Kalitoza and he instantly conveyed a gracious thank you to Ashley.

When all had boarded and the ramp was secured the ship 0G-8110-1 rose quietly and floated towards the airlock position which was situated in the floor of the cargo deck near the starship's outer wall. On each side of the airlock opening were two huge sliding doors which were meant to seal the airlock from within.

Slowly the zero-gravity ship 0G-8110-1 sank downwards into the airlock space and Ashley saw the large overhead doors slide together above him. There was a brief interval before Ashley looked to one side and saw a large gap open up in the side of the starship. Slowly and smoothly the zero-gravity ship moved through this opening and into the openness of space outside the starship.

The starship 8110-Gold was orientated towards Sirius B which meant that it was positioned so that its front end faced towards the dwarf star.

Ashley could still feel himself at normal gravity which brought a certain degree of puzzlement. Kalitoza conveyed that they were still under the influence of the gravity effect from the starship's forward neutron shield. But as they moved further away from the starship this would decrease and then only the gravity of Sirius B would be felt; a pull of just one twentieth of Nazmos' gravity. And that is exactly what occurred as they drew further from the mass of Zakatanz's starship.

Currently Sirius B was hidden under the belly of Ashley's zero-gravity ship 0G-8110-1 but directly ahead and clearly visible in the front view panel was the bright star Sirius A.

Sirius A was twice the mass and size of Earth's Sun and although 8.6 light years from Earth it had always been the brightest star in Earth's night sky. And here just two billion miles from it that was very apparent as the front view panels automatically went to a darker tint to reduce its glaring brightness. And Ashley could clearly make out its round form in the view panel which appeared as the size of a pea at this distance. All the others aboard seemed to be taken with the view as well for it was not often that a starship visited an alien star system.

Now that 0G-8110-1 and reached a position about six miles from the starship Kalitoza re-orientated his ship to dip its nose downwards and so point directly towards the dwarf star Sirius B. He also rotated the ship so that Sirius A was moved to a position under the belly of the zero-gravity ship. This reduced the glare from that quarter but another beautiful sight caught everyone's attention. And this was the starship 8110-Gold lit up by both stars of the Sirius system. The starship sat there like a dazzling pencil reflecting the starlight and showing off its golden colour stripes making it appear as if it were speeding towards the dwarf star. The effect was enhanced by the blurred haze at its front end where the neutron shield was located. Ashley stared as did Tania and the others and it was Brian who remarked that here was a sight that he would never forget.

Ashley thought how the Oannes had come to this state of progress and knew that it had not been easy. It had taken them twenty thousand years of scientific achievement in space to develop their current technology. Earth science was that far behind and Ashley felt that they must make their own progress in a difficult learning curve to qualify for the status at which the Oannes were now. Little bits of help in key inventions on the way would be no bad thing and Ashley suspected that such had been the case with the early Babylonians. Even the Dogon tribe had been given an understanding of the stars in the heavens above them.

Ashley now turned his attention away from the starship and back to the dwarf star in front of him. His first impression of it was of a continuous explosion of dazzling white light emanating from a point in space. The brightness dazzled his eyes but after a while he got used to it and tried to make out its form. But he could not as it was far too small an object. Being the size of Earth it could only appear as a point at this distance. Perhaps when they got to the next closer position it might appear larger.

The view panel remained at normal tint but Ashley wished for a magnification. He wanted to see into the heart of this dwarf star. And gradually Zanos granted his wish for there before him was this brightly glowing ball of light. Immediately Ashley thought of his dream of so long ago and knew that it had foretold of a vision of Zarama. Had Gozmanot also had such a dream? Perhaps she had in one of her visions.

Ashley got the magnification to increase further as his curiosity got the better of him. He wanted to see inside this star but of course that was impossible. So he just stared at its enlarged image and an ache leapt into his chest like the pangs of love but only different. It caused him to take a sharp intake of breath and that caused Tania to reach her hand out to his and grip it firmly. His thoughts always came through to her at times of emotional upheaval.

Quickly Ashley reverted to normal view and the pinpoint of starlight was resumed. He then conveyed to Kalitoza that he had seen enough for now and was ready to return to the starship whenever it was convenient.

'Uncle Ashley,' queried Fiona in a quiet voice, 'can we see Earth from here?'

She was seated a little to one side and behind Ashley and Tania.

'I know the approximate direction of it,' replied Ashley, 'but ask Kalitoza and I'm sure he will be more than happy to oblige.'

Kalitoza heard Fiona's request and conveyed that he was happy to show them where both Earth and Nazmos were currently located. He conveyed this to all of his human guests and then rotated the zero-gravity ship to point in the direction of the starship's recent journey path. Kalitoza positioned the ship so that both stars of this Sirius system were hidden from view. Sirius B was below the belly of the ship while Sirius A was behind them and in a low-down position.

The universe stars now appeared massively bright and spread out expansively in a full speckled glory that filled their view panels. The Milky Way was a band of brightness that curved across their vision and Kalitoza conveyed that they must look for a particular section of it that was close to the Sagittarius area.

Fiona looked but saw only the bright pathway and wasn't sure exactly where to look and she conveyed as much with her confused thoughts.

'See that section of the Milky Way in front of us in the middle view panel,' said Kalitoza, 'that is the same section we aim for when we travel from Earth to Nazmos.'

Fiona said she saw it but did not know what to look for especially.

Kalitoza was very patient Ashley thought as he continued.

'Can you see those three very bright stars that form a near equal sided triangle but with the apex in the low position,' he asked?

'There are so many bright stars,' said Fiona, 'which three do you mean?'

'I think I can solve that for you,' said Kalitoza, 'I will cause a slight haziness in the view panel which will leave only the very brighter stars visible.'

The view panels developed a very slight smoky tint and Ashley thought it very clever of Kalitoza to use such an aid. He wondered if Simon had received similar tutoring at the space academy. Kalitoza would make a good lecturer he thought.

'I think I can see those three stars now positioned as an upside down triangle,' said Fiona. 'They are spread quite far apart.'

'Yes, that is right,' said Kalitoza. 'Now the star to the upper right is Vega. It is approximately thirty four Light-years from here. It is twice as massive as your Sun and the second brightest star in Earth's northern night sky. The star on the upper left side is Deneb. It is very far away at a distance of nearly 2,600 Light-years but still shows up as very bright. It is 200 times the size of your Sun and if located in the Solar system it would extend as far as the orbit of Earth. The next star is the lower one and it is Altair and the particular one I want you to look at. Altair is 24 Light-years distant and it has twice the mass of your Sun. These three stars make up the Summer Triangle in the northern skies of Earth for there are few other brighter stars in the vicinity. Altair is the brightest of them.'

'Yes I see it,' said Fiona getting excited now. 'It is the brightest.'

'Well concentrate your view on Altair,' conveyed Kalitoza to all. By now even the Oannes on this zero-gravity ship appeared interested and were viewing forward with concentration.

'As you can see,' continued Kalitoza, 'Altair is within the Milky Way cloud configuration. Now draw an imaginary line from the star Altair towards its right hand side that is roughly parallel to another imaginary line that joins the two stars Deneb and Vega.'

Kalitoza paused to let everyone apply this formula before continuing.

'Now move along this imaginary line towards Altair's right side by a distance that is one-third the distance between Deneb and Vega.'

Kalitoza caused the view panels to return to normal clarity as he said this.

'Okay,' said Fiona, 'I've done that. But the area seems empty apart from a few very faint yellow stars.'

'Excellent,' said Kalitoza smiling broadly. 'One of those faint yellow stars is Earth's Sun. So if you now magnify that area in your view panel then the closest star to us - that is your Sun - will appear the more prominent.'

'Yes, I've done it,' said Fiona with excitement in her voice, 'and one has got much bigger than the others.'

'Good, that is your Sun and it is only 8.6 Light-years away from here,' said Kalitoza. 'And if you magnify further you might see some planets. But you won't see Earth as it is in total darkness being this side of the Sun.'

Fiona followed these instructions and could make out the fuzzy outline of two smaller grey coloured circular objects. On query Kalitoza informed her that she was viewing the solar planets Jupiter and Uranus.

'Thank you,' said Fiona, 'that was very nice of you. I feel so close to Earth that I'm not missing it so much anymore.'

As an after thought Fiona asked Kalitoza if the three stars making up the Summer Triangle would appear in a different configuration when seen from Earth.

'Not really,' said Kalitoza, 'because Sirius, Earth and these stars are more or less in a direct line with each other. So from here it is like looking over Earth's shoulder to view these three stars.'

Fiona nodded her understanding and conveyed a thank you to Kalitoza.

Ashley sensed the emotion that filled the room mainly from his family members. Ashley had felt quite choked with nostalgia when he had first seen Earth from space near Nazmos on his trip there alone.

'I've not finished yet,' said Kalitoza, 'there's more to see.'

'Oh,' came from Fiona.

'There are others here who would like to know the position of Nazmos and Raznat,' conveyed Kalitoza, 'and I shall show you how to pinpoint that too.'

He paused before continuing.

'I've shown you where Earth is,' he conveyed, 'and if you continue along the same imaginary line as you did for Earth but onward another one third distance further along then you will come to where Raznat is.'

'There's a cluster of stars there,' said Fiona, 'but which one is Raznat?'

'None of those,' conveyed Kalitoza, 'but just above the centre of that little group of stars is where Raznat should be. However it is too faint to see without magnification. And when you see it, it will be light red in colour.'

Fiona and the others looked in the position indicated by Kalitoza and got the view panel to magnify the area till Raznat came into focus as a fuzzy reddish ball. Fiona knew that Raznat was further away than Earth by another six Light-years and she tried looking for Nazmos but could not find it. She went back to focus on the Sun for another nostalgic look at what was home. It was nice to know where Earth was in this vast array of stars spread out before her. Of course Ashley, Tania and the others had also followed Kalitoza's directions and had been as enchanted by it too. And soon it would be time to go to where they had been looking. Ashley loved the home coming sensations each time he returned to Earth from his starship journeys.

Twenty five minutes later Ashley and his family group were once again back on the starship and seated in the captain's quarters discussing their most recent experience. Ashley conveyed his thoughts to the captain and to Brajam who had joined them that perhaps the next step ought to be at half the current distance from Sirius B. Zakatanz and Brajam conferred telepathically until within seconds Brajam gave a nod of his head. The procedure would remain the same with the scientists going out first in 0G-8110-2. And then Ashley was to be the only human passenger on the follow up trip. Brajam did a quick consultation with Zanos and informed them that the gravity level at five million miles from Sirius B would be a quarter of Nazmos' gravity. He also informed them of the gravity levels at the four, three and two million mile distances. At four million miles it was a third of Nazmos gravity and at three million miles it was 70% of Nazmos gravity. While at the two million mile distance it was 1.2 times the gravity on Nazmos but the heat would be excessive and might prove impractical as well as dangerous.

Fiona then queried how long it would take for the starship to relocate to the new closer-in position as a matter of interest.

'The starship will cover the distance at a leisurely one thousand miles per second velocity,' said Zakatanz smiling, 'so the journey time will be just under an hour and a half.'

He then suggested that the hour was late so they should all return to their apartments for a good nights rest. He would see them at the usual time for breakfast.

'Thank you Captain,' said Fiona, 'and goodnight to you too.'

The captain smiled again but said nothing as his human guests walked out and to their apartments. He personally would not go to his sleep tank until the starship had completed its journey to the new five million mile rendezvous location. Then all on the starship would sleep except for a few deputies with their crew; and of course Zanos the bio-computer system that really ran the starship.

Back in their bedroom Tania looked at Ashley and asked him if he was tired.

'Not really,' he replied, 'are you?'

'No, not me neither,' she replied with a twinkle in her eye.

'So what do you suggest,' asked Ashley knowing full well what the answer would be?

'Let's have a shower together and see where we go from there,' said Tania coming up to Ashley and kissing him lightly on the lips. She then looked him in the eyes and smiled her wickedest possible smile.

'Hmmm,' came from Ashley also smiling as he reached out for her.

Half an hour later they were both asleep cuddled up together in one bed. After an hour Tania awoke and found that one of her arms had gone to a numbed sleep. She extricated herself slowly and shifted across to her own bed and was asleep again in minutes.

Breakfast was as usual in the captain's quarters and all communicated that they'd had a very good night's sleep. Zanos conveyed that the zero-gravity ship OG-8110-2 had gone out earlier with a complement of scientists aboard. They had reported that the environmental conditions were rather more severe than had been expected. At five million miles distance the heat effect from the dwarf star was high but the ship systems were adequate. The cooling system was coping quite well and life support within the ship was secure. However there was a low level of x-ray emissions from Sirius B and the scientists made sure that the zero-gravity ship was orientated with its base section facing the star. The ship contained heavy shielding material that prevented any high intensity emissions such as gamma and x-rays from entering its structure. The view panels however were not so protected so that actual viewing of an emitting object was not recommended for any extended period of time. Even with the view panel filters fully active the danger still existed.

The natural gravity from Sirius B at the current distance was at a level that was a quarter of Nazmos gravity which made it slightly more comfortable for the occupants when the ship was at the correct orientation i.e. with the base of the ship facing the star. Zanos on board the zero-gravity ship was in a protective cocoon of shielding within the base area of the ship and so was safe from the effects of any such emissions.

The scientists also gave the recommendation that it would be unwise for the zero-gravity ships to approach Sirius B much closer than four million miles; though this may have an as yet undetermined risk from the emissions.

They knew that it was important for Ashley to be as close to the Dwarf Star as was safely possible for his telekinetic effort to be effective. Perhaps he would consider remaining at the current distance position to conduct his telekinetic experiments.

Ashley digested all this information and then looked at Captain Zakatanz who was seated across from him. Ashley queried the captain about the safety of the starship being this close to Sirius B as he was concerned about the x-ray emissions impinging upon the starship.

But the captain smiled and conveyed that the starship was well protected against all such emissions but as a precaution he had made sure that the starship was pointed in the direction of the White Dwarf Star. As such the forward neutron shield acted as an impervious umbrella of protection. Nothing could penetrate through it as was proven when the starship was travelling at FTL speeds through the energy-medium space grid.

'This starship could approach safely to within the earlier recorded distance of two million miles so long as we kept the ship to this same orientation,' said Zakatanz. 'But sadly no zero-gravity ship would survive outside for very long. Perhaps it would be wise to take note of the scientists' recommendations and not venture closer.'

Ashley was quiet for a few seconds and realised that no alarm bells sounded within his subconscious and that an emotion of relief made its presence felt within his breast. Was this his inner-voice conveying something?

'I'm quite happy with that Captain,' said Ashley and looking around he saw the relief on Tania's face. If there were dangerous conditions out there then she would rather that her husband did not face them unnecessarily.

'However I would still like to go out there and make my attempt at moving this star,' said Ashley.

'Yes of course,' said Zakatanz, 'but I suggest that you take precautions against the x-ray emissions. Do not view the star overlong.'

'As soon as I have viewed the star and willed for it to be moved I shall get the zero-gravity ship to orientate away for our protection,' said Ashley.

'And how long do you wish to continue with your testing,' asked Zakatanz?

Ashley thought for a moment before answering.

'I would imagine that a half hour should be sufficient to show if a change has occurred,' he said.

Then he added with a smile, 'That is of course if any change is detected at all.'

'Very well,' said Zakatanz, 'but it is a very great task that you set yourself and I wish you success.'

Ashley knew that Sirius B was about the same mass as Earth's Sun and so it was 330,000 times the mass of Earth. And even Platwuz which had a mass more than twice that of Nazmos was minute in comparison. And Zarama was a third more massive than Sirius B and so an even greater challenge.

But Ashley knew that he had to test his telekinetic power against this White Dwarf Star if only to let his mind know what was ultimately required of it. He would not have been given this gift if he was to fail outright and at the first hurdle. His telekinetic strength had increased progressively over the years and he had another five years or so before he went up against Gozmanot's 'fiery dragon'. Would he be ready by then or was another strategy required? He considered this and instantly knew what that might be – but kept the thought blocked from all.

'I think I'll have just one more mug of tea before I venture outside,' said Ashley with a general smile. He reached aside and squeezed Tania's hand. She looked at him and also smiled though with a hint of worry behind it.

And so some thirty minutes later the second zero-gravity ship OG-8110-1 ventured out of the starship's airlock compartment with Ashley, Brajam and several other scientists aboard and all wearing the loose fitting electrostatic shuttle suits over their normal clothing. As soon as they were clear of the starship Ashley sensed the intensity of the White Dwarf Star's heat impacting upon the underside of their ship. Sirius B had a surface temperature of 25,000 degrees Centigrade which was five times greater than that on the surface of Earth's Sun. The Sun however had a core temperature of 15 million degrees Centigrade due to the active nuclear fusion taking place there. White Dwarf Stars were basically inactive having used up all their fusion material and so had no internal heat source. They would steadily cool as their remaining heat was radiated into space over a period of a couple of billion years or so.

Kalitoza was in command of the zero-grav ship and once they had traversed a few miles from the starship he dipped its front so that the view panels faced towards Sirius B. Ashley felt his shoulder and thigh clamps tighten their grip as he was drawn forwards by the low gravity that the star exerted upon them. Although only a quarter of Nazmos gravity nevertheless Ashley was grateful for the restraining clamps that kept him in his seat.

And very apparent was the visual heat of the light rays emanating from the distant spot of light. The view panels had automatically gone into a dark tint mode which allowed Ashley to view the star without discomfort. But he was very aware that x-rays were also reaching out form Sirius B and currently entering the area around him. He then got the view panels to magnify Sirius B so that it increased in size to about that of Earth's moon as seen on Earth.

Ashley then sent a quick message to Zakatanz asking permission to commence his telekinetic attempt upon Sirius B and also to request that would Zanos on the starship as well as both zero-gravity ships be positioned to the appropriate space locations for the correct triangulation monitoring of any change in the orbital status of the star.

It took only twenty minutes for this to be achieved as the scientists on the other zero-gravity ship had anticipated the requirement. Zakatanz conveyed to Ashley that the moment that any change was detected that he should cease any further action. Ashley smiled at this and conveyed back that he would abide by all of the captain's instructions.

'I am commencing my push upon Sirius B as of now,' conveyed Ashley to all as he looked at the enlarged White Dwarf Star in his view panel and willed for it to be moved in its orbital positioning by a fractional amount. Kalitoza then orientated the ship to protect its occupants from the star's ever-present x-ray emissions. Ashley hoped that some change would be recorded but when he queried Zanos after ten minutes he was informed that no change in the motion of Sirius B had been perceived. Ashley felt mildly annoyed and requested Kalitoza to return the orientation of the ship to the previous position so that he could view the star again.

When this was achieved Ashley willed that a maximum telekinetic effort be applied to Sirius B as of now and until he willed for it to cease. But Ashley knew that this was a redundant command as his telekinetic effort was already at its fullest capability. After another ten minutes when no change in the status of Sirius B had occurred Ashley willed for his telekinetic effort to cease completely.

He then conveyed to Zakatanz and the others that apparently his efforts so far had not achieved any result.

'I would like to try a voluntary push in pink mode like I did on the asteroids experiment,' conveyed Ashley to all, 'and here I shall attempt to step towards my personal maximum force level of sixteen. I cannot go beyond this as I was commanded against it.'

For some reason Ashley's inner voice had cautioned him about exceeding a force level of sixteen while in extreme pink mode. It was at the time after the second asteroid Masursky experiment when Ashley had decided to calibrate his 'Pink' levels using the 520-Green spaceship's chronometer. He had worked up from pink level one in slow careful stages. When he reached pink level ten he had found that visibility conditions were still good. It was only when he was at pink level fifteen that the visibility in the cabin became hazy and indistinct. And when he went to pink level sixteen he recognised the thick fog of invisibility that filled the room. He recognised this as the extreme pink level he had visited as a child and when he had heard mysterious telepathic thoughts coming through to him. And it was at this later time of calibrating that his familiar inner voice had cautioned him not to venture further as danger lay beyond. Ashley remembered that command and knew that he must never exceed pink level sixteen under normal circumstances. And he would abide by that ruling with Sirius B.

He then conveyed his plan of action to Captain Zakatanz and all the others and asked for their patience. He would make three levels of push in pink mode starting with pink level five. Then after ten minutes if there was no status change he would go up a notch to pink level ten. If no change again then he would venture to pink level sixteen and apply a maximum effort repeatedly until exhaustion overcame him. This would be his full telekinetic capability and he hoped to achieve some degree of success even if by a very minor amount.

Step by step Ashley went through this plan of action and each step yielded a nil result. When he came to pink level sixteen Ashley shut his eyes and concentrated upon the White Dwarf Star with all his inner mental might. He put all his mental effort towards a full capacity push upon Sirius B. He did this repeatedly for a minute at a time while holding his breath and straining his mental concentration and willing success. He did this ten times and more over a fifteen minute period in pink mode and knew that it would seem like only an instant for all the observers in the starship and zero-gravity ships. Finally Ashley returned to normal mode and queried Zanos. Sirius B was completely unmoved and Ashley felt the disappointment of failure. He now felt drained physically and mentally and requested Kalitoza to return him to the starship and thence home to Earth.

There was confusion for a brief moment until Kalitoza reading Ashley's mind realised that he was confused and needed assistance. Immediately he orientated the ship for the minor gravity effect from the Dwarf Star and Brajam and one of the scientists unclamped and then re-clamped themselves in the seats either side of Ashley.

Ashley's subconscious thoughts were in a dizzying spin and although extremely disappointed he took heart when his inner voice offered encouragement with the knowledge that he had not as yet reached his full telekinetic potential. And in the back of his mind a strategy was evolving for when he did meet Zarama. But that would be as the very last resort and at considerable danger to him.

He now also realised why Sirius B had not been moved. Its inertia was far too great and he compared himself to a man physically pushing against a massive brick wall; a brick wall that could not be moved. A man might as well have attempted pushing against a sky scraper building for all the success which that might achieve.

But Gozmanot had seen a vision of him doing just that; succeeding against the fiery dragon. Ashley knew in his heart of hearts that he would vanquish Zarama – but at what cost? He had been given these gifts and now that his mind knew what he was up against perhaps the giver of those gifts would enhance his power. So although Sirius B had proved to be too massive it had nevertheless given him an indication of what was needed against Zarama.

Ashley's thoughts then became fuzzy and his head drooped forwards onto his chest and it seemed as if he had lost consciousness. But in actual fact the exertion against Sirius B had resulted in an excessive mental fatigue causing sleep to overcome him. Sleep was the great healer for Ashley and always had been.

Brajam and the other Oannes scientist now put their arms across Ashley in a cushioning lock either side of his neck and so kept Ashley's head supported upright. They stayed thus until the zero-gravity ships had both entered into the starship's airlock compartment and then up to the cargo platform.

By now they recognised that Ashley had indeed fallen into a deep sleep through mental fatigue and it was with the help of a floating pallet that he was transported to the habitation platform and to his apartment bed. Tania was not unduly concerned and recognised the symptoms as the norm whenever Ashley had excessively exerted his telekinetic effort. She knew that with a few hours of sleep he would be back to his normal self.

But Fiona and the others who had also come into the apartment bedroom were not used to seeing Ashley like this, apart from Katy, and so they expressed their concern.

'Will Uncle Ashley be alright,' asked Fiona and Sarah together? Brian stood back but showed his concern also. Anything that worried Sarah was his worry as well.

Katy remembered the tree logs incident of long ago and how then too Ashley had needed to sleep to recover. She conveyed her memories to the others for them to understand. She suggested they leave Ashley to his sleep and return to the captain's quarters. Tania said she would stay with Ashley for a while and rejoin them later.

Tania watched her husband lying there on the bed and thought he'd sleep better without his tunic and leggings and so she slowly and carefully removed them off him. She also managed to pull the covers down from under him and then to cover him to just below his shoulders. She looked at him for a moment longer and leaned down and gave him a lingering kiss on his lips. She knew from this that he was in the deepest sleep that she had ever seen him in. She reckoned he would sleep for a quite some time. And so backing out of the room with her eyes always on his cherubic face she returned to the others in the captain's quarters. A meal was to be served soon and suddenly Tania realised she felt quite hungry.

The Oannes are very polite people and never like to intrude into other people's affairs. They wait politely to be informed about matters that might not be normal. Tania realised this and so conveyed to the captain that Ashley was in a deep sleep and might probably remain so for the next several hours at the very least. She conveyed that she had never before seen him so exhausted and drained of energy and wondered if he might sleep for about six hours or more.

'Well then,' said Captain Zakatanz, 'I shall assume that Ashley has completed all he needed to do here and that our expedition to the Sirius system can be considered as concluded. Am I correct in this assumption?'

He looked at Tania as he said this to seek her confirmation as Ashley's partner.

Tania was grateful for Zakatanz's approach and immediately confirmed that she certainly thought that to be the case. She did not want her husband venturing out there again.

'In that case I propose that we make immediate preparations for our journey to the Earth system,' said Zakatanz. 'I shall instruct Zanos to inform all aboard and to commence the journey in one hour from now. The Anztarza chief ministers will be pleased.'

The afternoon meal was then served and all tucked in enthusiastically. At the end of it Tania and Katy went to look in on Ashley. He was still fast asleep and in exactly the same position that Tania had left him over an hour ago. She informed the captain of the situation and confessed that she expected Ashley to stay asleep for several hours longer.

'By then we will be cruising at our maximum 10 FTL velocity towards Earth,' said Zakatanz. 'And when Ashley does awake I trust that he will be refreshed and able to accelerate the starship as he did on our journey here. It is a distance of 8.6 Light-years to the Solar System and with Ashley's assistance I hope to complete the journey in a little over six simulated Earth days.'

'Thank you Captain,' said Tania and she said no more.

The next six days would be her ride home with Ashley. And the next five years at least would be all theirs to do with as they pleased. Her woman's intuition hinted that it could be all that they might have together.

When the journey to Earth commenced there was no sensation of motion apart from the hiss of the relative movement between the habitation platform and central column. As the acceleration of the starship increased the platform complex moved closer towards the front of the ship. The increased gravity pull of the neutron shield counterbalanced the G-forces of acceleration and kept the conditions at normal gravity level for the comfort of the passengers.

It was a couple of hours before Zanos conveyed that the starship 8110-Gold was at its maximum impulse powered cruise velocity of 10.2 FTL. Zakatanz was impatient for Ashley to awake but knew that it must only be when he was fully rested and recovered from his tremendous exertions against Sirius B.

Tania sensed the captain's unease and conveyed that she would go back to the apartment and monitor Ashley's sleep condition. Once there she decided to stay till Ashley awoke. It was an hour later near seven o'clock in the evening simulated time that Tania saw the first hint of Ashley stirring. And that was a big deep breath from Ashley and then a relaxing sigh. There was then another period of sleep for about fifteen minutes before his eyes opened fully. He saw Tania sitting in her chair and smiled.

Tania went to him and sat beside him on the bed and leaning forward kissed him gently on his lips.

'Tea?' she asked.

'Please,' came his instant reply.

Tania had anticipated his awakening after that first big breath and had got a hot mug of sweet tea ready for him. This he downed in quick sips as it had cooled a little and quickly asked for another. He downed two glasses of Wazu from the jug kept beside the bed while Tania prepared his second mug of tea. This he sipped slowly and savoured its sweetness as he and Tania talked.

Ashley had already queried Zanos and been informed of the ship's status and how long he had been asleep. Zanos informed him that the starship was on course for Earth and cruising at its maximum independent velocity.

'I think Captain Zakatanz was getting impatient for you to come awake and to accelerate the starship as before,' said Tania.

'I see,' said Ashley and immediately communicated with the captain and received an affirmative.

'Excuse me darling,' said Ashley as he brushed back the bed covers.

Tania stood up as Ashley swung his legs off the edge of the bed and placed his feet on the floor as he assumed an upright sitting position. He knew that he was close enough to the centre of the habitation platform to affect his telekinetic push upon the central zone of the ship's forward neutron shield. So first he communicated with the captain and then with Zanos what he was about to commence. Then looking down at the floor between his spread feet he visualised the neutron shield far below him and willed for the starship to be accelerated to a final velocity of 695 FTL in a gradual manner over a period of four hours. This would be about the same as it had taken on the journey to Sirius and as such would conform to a standard for the captain. Ashley would keep his mind in open mode for the whole of the journey period mainly for the benefit of Zanos on-board.

'It is done Captain,' Ashley conveyed to his captain and friend Zakatanz, 'and I have willed for the maximum cruise velocity of 695 FTL to be achieved over the same acceleration period of four hours.'

'Thank you Ashley, that is excellent,' conveyed the captain. 'I hope you are well recovered from your Sirius B ordeal. You are probably hungry and I can inform you that a meal will be served up shortly. I hope to see you then.'

'Thank you Captain I feel fine and will be ready in half an hour.'

Ashley then stood up and giving Tania a cuddle conveyed that he would pop into the shower and be out again in a jiffy to get dressed for the captain's table. Tania smiled as she got his meaning and knew that his chief priority at the moment was his stomach. Tania had formed an opinion of her husband long ago and he had remained true to that form throughout the years. But she was still not quite sure which was the more important. She thought it might be his stomach by a whisker as he had grown older. She smiled as she thought about the little belly bulge that was beginning to grow on him. On her own account she reckoned that she too had better take more care of her own figure before it got beyond remedy.

Tania selected Ashley's favourite tunic and leggings with matching footwear and spread them out on the bed which she had quickly made presentable by pulling up the covers.

Ashley came out of the shower rubbing his head with the absorbent towel and Tania had to admire his posture and alert stance even though he was fifty seven years old now. And she herself was not far behind in years at fifty three though she still could admire her figure in the bathroom mirror.

When Ashley had got dressed he smiled his boyish smile and conveyed that he was ready for his dinner. He put his arm around her and pulled her close as they left the apartment. The walk to the captain's quarters was a short one at less than forty feet and they got a grand welcome. Captain Zakatanz stood up and came around to them and greeted Ashley with enthusiasm and a warm double handed handshake and conveyed a private message.

'Welcome Uncle Ashley,' said Fiona aloud, 'I hope you had a good rest,'

'Yes, thank you Fiona,' said Ashley, 'I feel well rested and raring to go.'

'And hungry,' he added as an afterthought.

Tania conveyed that she had given Ashley two mugs of sweetened tea the moment he had woken.

It was not long before the meal was served up but Ashley waited till the others had begun to help themselves before picking up his plate. He served himself to a large helping of the sweetened Yaztraka and conveyed that he considered it to be like his breakfast. After all he had only just awoken from a long six hours sleep.

Ashley could sense young Hazazamunt's gaze and looking back at her he winked and raised his glass of Wazu and made a toast.

'To all my friends here,' he said aloud, 'may we always be in each others hearts and minds with affection.'

He took a big sip as the others did the same and then added the motto he had given Captain Natazlat. 'And may the journey to our respective homes be safe, swift and sure.'

It had become the motto of all Oannes space travellers and was repeated prior to the commencement of each space journey.

Zakatanz repeated this as he also said aloud, 'a safe, swift and sure journey to us all.'

This journey certainly would be swift as no other starship was likely to achieve such a velocity under its own impulse power, thought Zakatanz. And he was right. It would be nearly ten thousand years before an Oannes starship was able to cruise under its own power at such a velocity.

Ashley continued his meal with some Raizna and Starztal which he spiced up with a spoonful of Milsony. And when he was nearly full he returned to a small portion of the extra sweetened Yaztraka that had been placed especially close to him. He was the last one left eating.

'Thank you Captain for an excellent banquet,' he said with a satisfied rub of his tum when he had finally finished, 'I feel somewhat normal again.'

Ashley smiled broadly at everybody around the table as he stretched his arms and stood up.

'I fancy a stroll around the platform,' he said aloud, 'and I would love some company.'

He looked around at the group and received multiple affirmative replies from all except Zakatanz and Azatamunt.

'Come Hazazamunt,' said Fiona to her friend, 'let us follow closely behind Ashley and the others and see what they talk about. And then you can tell me what you think about us humans.'

Hazazamunt was hesitant as she looked at her mother and father. Zakatanz smiled and nodded his approval and Hazazamunt immediately relaxed and smiled her willingness to Fiona.

Zanos then reported that the starship had just exceeded a velocity of 350 FTL and was still under acceleration.

Zakatanz acknowledged the information but was thinking about his daughter. It was good for her education to get familiar with this elite group of humans as they were the best example of those on Earth. She would learn in time of the primitive nature of many of them but it was good to see the ideal side first. First impressions were the lasting ones and upon which she could base her other judgements when she achieved adulthood.

Ashley walked at the front with Tania and Margaret on either side. Katy and Robin had Sarah and Brian with them and were followed closely by Fiona and Hazazamunt.

Hazazamunt was enchanted by Fiona's zest for life and her keen interest in everything around her and said so.

'You mustn't forget that all of this is new to me and so different and so very advanced,' said Fiona. 'On Earth I have a job that involves helping people with advice on their health issues. I travel a lot by car which to you will seem quite outmoded compared to your airborne transporters. I do enjoy my job though but I don't find it very exciting.'

'But I've heard that Earth is very beautiful in all its colours,' said Hazazamunt.

'Oh yes it is,' said Fiona, 'and I hope that you will see it all one day. Your people in Anztarza also think the same and when Gozmanot's visions come to pass then so shall Nazmos. Ashley has already completed the first phase for that. But sadly we may not be around to see the full results as that will happen gradually over a thousand years or so. When you return to Nazmos you must communicate with me and tell me of any changes you think are happening no matter how little.'

'I will try if I am permitted,' said Hazazamunt in her submissive manner.

'I'm sure Uncle Ashley will receive that information from others,' said Fiona, 'but let us keep in touch with each other as friends. And when Uncle Ashley returns to complete the Nazmos orbital change in five years or so I shall accompany him there. I hope I am permitted to stay on after that so I can personally monitor any changes that I notice. All of that is what makes me so excited and glad to be alive at this point in Nazmos' history.'

'I think I understand now how you feel,' said Hazazamunt with a bit of enthusiasm building in her voice, 'and perhaps I too can look forward to the changes that might occur on Nazmos.'

The group walked on in a harmonious mood and chattered on for about half an hour when Zanos conveyed that the starship had achieved a velocity of 520 FTL and was still accelerating.

It was shortly after this communication that Ashley hesitated in his tracks and looked around at the others behind him. They too then paused and asked Ashley if anything was the matter.

Ashley conveyed that he'd just had an odd sensation but perhaps it was his mind playing tricks. He thought he'd felt a light puff of air fleetingly brush through his hair whilst also receiving an emotion of joy and laughter that seemed to surround him; but only for an instant. Perhaps he had imagined it with his mind being still tired from the Sirius ordeal. He conveyed no more as he had thoughts of his own.

'Very odd,' he thought, 'perhaps I imagined it all or did it have something to do with my inner voice trying to tell me something?'

Ashley pushed it from his mind and continued the walk as before but with puzzlement nagging at him in the subconscious corners of his mind.

Nearly thirteen light years away on Nazmos another scenario had been unravelling over the past week. Ritozanan had conveyed to her assistant staff that her energy was draining away and that she intended to go into a state of voluntary hibernation. This was simply euphemistic language indicating that her body was giving up its battle for life.

Since the announcement Ritozanan had relaxed her body to float in its usual sleeping position in the upper level of her sleep tank. Ritozanan's decision had been conveyed to the Nazmos governing council who had delegated a team to the house to keep a constant vigil on her in the sleep tank. Also over this period council members and their partners came at prearranged intervals to pay their last respects to a most revered member and leader.

It had been the eldest of her assistants named Nazitazat aged 230 years who had conveyed Ritozanan's decision to the governing council. Nazitazat had been with Ritozanan for 96 years and was a close confidant and friend of a lady who was a hundred years her senior.

Ritozanan floated just below the surface in her sleep tank in a spread eagled downward facing position. Her knees were angled downwards on legs that stretched back and upwards in a slightly open manner so that her feet were at the same level as her head. She had not woken or moved in three days and so had not received nourishment of any sort. She had blocked her mind from all probing when she first announced her decision.

It was shortly after Ashley and his family had begun their after dinner stroll on the habitation platform of the starship 8110-Gold that Ritozanan's life had ebbed out of her.

Nazitazat had at that very moment been standing beside the sleep tank looking at her mistress when she saw a brief spate of tiny air bubbles float to the surface from under Ritozanan's floating body. Then very slowly Ritozanan began to sink lower and lower in the sleep tank until eventually the knuckles of her hands made contact with the floor of the tank. And there she stayed for nearly twenty minutes when another brief spate of tiny bubbles rose up from under her body. Again very slowly her knees lowered and rested on the floor. Then all the breathing vanes on Ritozanan's arms, legs, face and back turned colourless and flopped limp against her body. They had shrunk to half their normal living size.

Nazitazat recognised the situation and conveyed the news to the others in the house and to the governing council. An emotion of sadness filled the room as the others came in. Ritozanan was no more and it was always a sad moment when any Oannes person died. The Oannes did not believe in an afterlife and considered that when a person's life went out of them then that was an end in itself.

The Oannes had been amused by the religious faiths of humans on Earth and had never been convinced to share in a similar concept. They had never interfered or influenced this human trait and observed with amusement the devotion that Earth's religions received from its people. However they were saddened by the divisive forces that arose from the differing religious ideologies.

Now here on Nazmos one of their respected personalities had just ceased to exist. Immediate preparations were brought into play to honour the memory of that person and also for the hygienic interment of the remains.

Ritozanan's lifeless body would be sealed in a light container and placed in one of the allocated spaceships in a far corner of the Wentazta space park. The governing council would arrange a gathering in the Great Domed Hall and a review of Ritozanan's life events would be conducted. The Domed Hall would be full of well wishers and those who knew her in her youth period. These last would be of a similar age as the deceased and would also have lived a life nearly as full.

At the start of these proceedings the spaceship bearing Ritozanan's body would lift off and accelerate directly towards Raznat some thirty million miles away. There would be no Oannes personnel aboard and Zanos on-board would be the sole controller. Its purpose would be solely to eject the container directly into Raznat from a distance of ten million miles. The ship would then slow and retreat to a safe distance and record the entry of the container into Raznat.

This was the modern Oannes way of interment that was adopted some nineteen thousand years ago when local space travel had become commonplace among the Oannes civilization.

The previous custom was different and was still adhered to by the Rimzi people. The old custom was carried out in a section of the Sea of Peruga where it was remote and deep. The body of the deceased Oannes person was taken there and placed under a domed cage. As the body began to decay and putrefy it was sensed by the Ari. These are sea creatures resembling tiny ants that live within the Peruga sea bed and feed on putrid and decaying matter. The Ari then emerge from their sea bed burrows to begin feeding on the decaying body. In a matter of a day or so only what appears to be the bony skeletal structure remains. But the Oannes bones are really an accretion of cartilage material turned hard and in the Peruga sea water this begins to soften and then also to decay. The softening period can vary from a few days to as long as a month. The Ari then come out again and devour this too so that nothing of the Oannes body remains. One of the reasons that the Sea of Peruga remains fairly clean is that when other sea creatures die and fall to the sea floor their decomposing bodies are also consumed by the Ari.

And so it was approximately at the time that Ashley had begun his after-dinner walkabout on the habitation platform of the starship 8110-Gold that Ritozanan had died on Nazmos.

He was not to know of this for another seven months when Captain Natazlat's starship 9110-Red travelled to Earth from Nazmos. Ashley would then look back to the moment of Ritozanan's passing and wonder if it was her emotion of joy and laughter that he had sensed so perfunctorily during his walkabout on Zakatanz's starship. Had Ritozanan also brushed past him in a last affectionate gesture by ruffling a lock of his hair? Ashley would have liked to believe it was so but he could not be certain.

Seven months on it would be a sad moment indeed for Ashley for he had looked upon this Oannes lady with great affection. He would remember his last meeting with her and the view of her naked form floating within her home sleep tank. She had then seemed like a great bird in majestic flight. She had confessed her emotions to Ashley and he was greatly affected by what she conveyed. He had wept when he had returned to Jazzatnit's house and had told Tania about it. And when he came to hear the news of her death he would weep again for her and the memory of her.

It was well into the walkabout on the habitation platform of Zakatanz's starship speeding towards Earth that Ashley once again encountered symptoms of fatigue that seemed to creep up on him. He realised that this could be because he had not fully completed his mental recovery. And he could only put this down to Zanos bringing him awake before time because of the impatient mindset of the captain to get Ashley to accelerate his starship again to the maximum 695 FTL cruise velocity. Now that his hunger for food had been sated Ashley's system felt the need to once again return for a sleep rest. Sirius B had taken more out of him than he had at first realised. He could complete his rest by sleeping on till the morning; as would also the others of his family group.

The time was approaching 10.pm in their simulated day period and Zanos conveyed that the starship was now at its full nominated cruise velocity of 695 FTL. Ashley returned to the captain's quarters and made polite conversation before excusing himself for the night. He conveyed that apparently he was not as yet fully recovered from his exertions against Sirius B.

The captain expressed his concern and wished Ashley a good nights rest and hoped to see him at the morning meal. The others also excused themselves and all returned to their respective apartments. Yet when Ashley and Tania shut their apartment door behind them and finally got into bed sleep seemed to elude them. Instead they lay side by side and talked. They talked about what they would do when they arrived home at the end of this journey in about six day's time.

'What day will it be when we arrive home,' Tania asked trying to do a mental calculation of their busy schedule since leaving Anztarza on January 10th which was a Monday?

Ashley too had difficulty with his own arithmetic so queried Zanos about their expected arrival in the Solar System.

'Twenty eight Earth days have elapsed since you left Earth,' conveyed Zanos, 'and expected arrival at the Solar System rendezvous position is six days from now.'

'That means we could arrive back at Aunt Brenda's B&B on the day after Valentine's Day,' said Ashley having done a quick mental calculation. 'It could have been sooner except for the fact that it takes over a day for the message to be sent to Anztarza from the starship and for their spaceships to come out to us. Then another day for them to ferry us home. That is two full days at least.'

'Our crocuses and snowdrops should be out then,' said Tania. 'I wonder what the weather has been like.'

'Cold I imagine,' said Ashley. 'It always gets colder in mid-Jan and Feb before getting milder again.'

'And wet?' added Tania.

What about snow?' from Ashley.

'Hmmm,' mumbled Tania and snuggled up to Ashley.

There was a momentary lull in their conversation.

'What are you thinking,' asked Ashley?

'I was thinking I'm glad I married you,' Tania said slowly.

'And,' Ashley prompted?

'Actually I said that wrong,' said Tania slowly, 'what I meant was I'm glad I met you.'

Ashley smiled but remained silent as he knew that Tania hadn't finished.

'I'm glad I met you because that's when I fell in love with you.'

Continued silence from Ashley.

'And because I fell in love with you I married you,' concluded Tania.

'Anything else,' asked Ashley teasing?

'Everything else,' said Tania smiling. 'I've got it all and want nothing more; except maybe more time.'

'What about excitement and adventure?'

Tania was silent for a full minute. She then rose up on one elbow and looked down at her husband's smiling face.

'Silly arse,' she exclaimed and gave him a light dig in his side. 'I think I've had enough excitement and adventure to last me ten lifetimes. If I'd known where all this might have led I may have had second thoughts about you.'

'May have?' questioned Ashley still smiling?

'Perhaps not,' said Tania, 'I don't think I would have believed any of this even if you had told me then.'

'And now?'

'And now I think I would not have missed any of this for all the tea in China,' laughed Tania as she leaned down and kissed her husband firmly on the lips. She lingered there for a moment before commencing to nibble on his lower lip.

The kiss started them on an excitement roller coaster as it had often done before. They remained cuddled together afterwards and conveyed their thoughts to each other silently. Ashley drifted off into a deep sleep first and Tania waited till his breathing had settled before extricating her arm and sliding across onto her own bed.

Ashley's deep breathing was a pleasant hum and helped lull Tania towards a drowsiness that came slowly upon her. Her thoughts were still active and were mainly of her home in Dudley and the flowers in their garden. The Tulips and daffs would soon be opening their bud-like heads. The hardy shrubs that Ashley had planted in their positions years before would also soon begin to exhibit their show. The Azaleas and Rhododendrons always did well as did the Hostas and Heucheras. There was such a variety of textures and colour that were repeated yearly without any immediate planting effort. She must remember to order her bedding plants from her usual Jersey supplier before the end of the month. The Geraniums, Begonias and Petunias always gave their best in the special container pots reserved for them. Tania's final mental image was of the view of their garden last year and its variety of colours swirled around in her head as they blended together and faded into nothing as she drifted into asleep.

PART FOUR

2015 – 2016

Chapter 20

Mazpazam

(Summer 2045)

The past winter had been a mild one with hardly a frost at night. Of course there had been some cold nights but these hardly counted for the little effect they'd had. January had been dry and sunny and the evenings had got progressively lighter. I read somewhere that 23rd January was a memorable day in Barrow up in northern Alaska. It was on this day that the Sun first popped its head above the horizon and the residents marked the occasion with a fun filled day.

Back here in the Birmingham and Dudley area, February, March and April had been wet ones with double the average rainfall. May was fairly dry in its second half and it had been so ever since. It seems that technically drought conditions are specified here in England when there's been no rainfall for fifteen days or more.

And here I am on a lovely evening in early July sitting out on my covered patio sipping a hot mug of tea and watching my lovely wife hosing the plants in their containers around our garden. Everything was in bloom but the hedges were growing too fast for my liking. I shall have to trim them again sometime soon; maybe next week.

Tania is wearing a wide brimmed floppy hat as the sun is quite high up over the far trees to the west and still strong. I have to admire her for the way she has kept her good looks and her figure. And that reminds me that I need to arrange something special for her approaching sixtieth in September. Last year we did the grand tour around Australia and New Zealand over a period of two months and Tania then said it was a fitting celebration for her approaching sixtieth birthday.

The year before that we had spent several weeks seeing Canada and then did the coast to coast rail journey. Actually the first leg from Vancouver to Banff was on the glass-topped Rocky Mountaineer train. We made visits to Calgary and Jasper with a walk on the Athabasca glacier among other exciting events. Then it was a two day trip on VIA Rail's Canadian from Jasper to Toronto.

I am sixty three now and feel pretty good about it; though Tania says that I still behave like a kid sometimes. I wonder what she means by that. I daren't ask.

Sadly my dad at ninety years of age is not very well. He has got a wheelchair but tries not to use it indoors. He prefers to walk around in the house albeit rather unsteadily while holding onto the hand rails specially fitted for him. Outdoors he tries to get by with the aid of two walking sticks but tires very quickly. We had a bedroom made up for him downstairs with a bathroom attached. It was either that or getting a stair-lift fitted. I think dad chose the better option.

Mum does a lot though a homecare assistant comes every morning to help get dad up and showered. Mum does the rest for him throughout the day. Social Services suggested a Care Home for dad but mum said 'never'; she'd do all that was necessary with a bit of homecare help. Otherwise mum is fit and well but she says that her back is not as good as it used to be.

Dad is not lonely as he can communicate with the rest of us through the Oannes badges that we all still have. He and I have long discussions about what I'm doing throughout the day.

Uncle Ron was in a bad way for a while after his stroke. He had paralysis all down his left side but has made steady progress these last two years. He can now actually walk quite well with the aid of an Ultra lightweight Aluminium Tri-Wheel Walker or Rollator as they are called. Aunt Brenda is fit and well like mum and spends all her time with Uncle Ron and both are happy living together in the B&B Annex. They are in constant communication with the family through their communication badges. I believe dad and Ron have long chats about old times and both tend to repeat themselves without realising it.

Sudzarnt, their Oannes adopted son is a young 92 and is now the proprietor of the B&B after it was made over to him when Uncle Ron had his first mini-stroke. He is a dutiful son and keeps a caring eye on his adoptive Earth parents. He runs the B&B efficiently and they want for nothing.

It was nearly a year after I got home from the Sirius trip that I learned of Ritozanan's death. Although I'd half expected it nevertheless the news saddened me and I do believe I had a little weep for the memory of that charming lady. I pictured the way she was when I'd last seen her and that vision will stay with me forever. It was solely through her efforts and arguments that she got the Nazmos Governing Council to agree to the Nazmos orbital change. She had made them accept that the Nazmos orbital change was essential in order to bring Gozmanot's vision to eventual reality. Tania was a great consolation to me in my grieving for Ritozanan as she understood exactly how I felt. She has always been there for me through thick and thin with an understanding of my psyche more than anyone else. And I love her more because of it. I only wish, - but I have to leave that thought unfinished.

Each starship arriving from Nazmos brought us fresh news about the progress and preparedness of the starship 4110-Silver in its upgrading. And three years ago our son Simon was transferred to that starship as its under-acting 3rd deputy in waiting. I'm not sure what this title meant but I believe it was a tutelage post under Captain Wastanomi. Apparently it had been a special request from the captain that Simon join his crew early. I suspect an influence from high places might have been at work. Zakatanz somehow came into my mind as did also Zazfrapiz.

Since then the communications I received from Simon showed an added exuberance and excitement of tone. It was a chance reference in a more recent communication that I learned of Mazpazam's inclusion in the starship's crew complement. I mentioned this to Tania and she smiled back at me and conveyed that she already knew that it would happen. Her manner indicated that she was pleased about it because it was what made Simon happy and definitely what he wanted. I think I was glad of it too but I wondered where their friendship might lead. I had guessed Mazpazam's age at about sixty to Simon's thirty but that was six years ago. I still had no mental image of this Oannes lady but I was confident that she must be special; and beautiful. Perhaps she was as beautiful as Muznant or even as Jazzatnit had been in her youth.

Simon's communication also stated that trials on the starship 4110-Silver had begun and that full commissioning was not too distant. Simon's last communication was about a year in the past and so I knew that I could expect a surprise arrival from him anytime. 4110-Silver could be in its commissioning stage even as I speak.

Communication with Anztarza was on a regular basis but the chief ministers could not give me any further news. I knew that I had their respect and so they would not keep anything from me.

The other piece of information that Simon had conveyed was that he had made a suggestion to his captain that the newly modified starship be reclassified and that the word 'streak' be added at the end of its designation. This would separate it from its old name and also from all the other older unmodified starships. Subsequently approval was received from the Nazmos governing council and henceforth each modified starship would be similarly designated. And so the starship 4110-Silver became the new faster starship 4110-Silverstreak. I was proud that credit for this idea went to my son. I know that he will make a name for himself in the Oannes space fleet.

Our daughter Rachel and Margaret Dutton had both gone back to Nazmos in 2041 and they spent two years there monitoring the minor climatic change that had begun to slowly manifest itself on the land areas. But these were only very minor as conditions reversed themselves each time the planet was at orbital apogee - its previous thirty one million mile distance from Raznat. However there was a very positive warm period when the Nazmos orbit was at perigee and shortly after but the cold soon returned. Rachel had sent me reports of these conditions and I was pleased that there had been no dramatic adverse climatic phenomena. These would come later I was sure when I had stabilised Nazmos in its new permanent orbit.

Margaret who was now sixty five years of age had relinquished control of her telepathic school business soon after our return to Earth in 2039 and so was officially retired. Telepathy is now a world wide accepted skill and other schools have been springing up in nearly every country. However the success rate is somewhat poor but it is still in its early stages and the human brain needs to develop considerably more to fully accommodate such a skill.

Rachel and Margaret plan to return with me to Nazmos when Simon comes to collect me in the new starship Silverstreak. I think I can dispense with its number coding in this instance. Tania of course would accompany me as she says that she will never leave my side in all of this. Jokingly she said she was addicted to adventure and there was certainly plenty of that with me around.

Katy is now the Head Teacher at her school in Yardley. She took over from the retiring head about three years ago. I've seen less of her since the appointment but I suppose that is because the job is high powered and keeps her fully occupied. I believe that there is also a lot of stress that goes with the job. But I know that she is happy and would not have it any different. Thank goodness for our communication badges.

Robin was also promoted and took over as Bank Manager in 2041 and is happy in the job. He says it fulfilled an ambition of his to be a Manager before retirement loomed. There is a retirement package being offered to those aged sixty four and over and Robin is considering taking it up next year. He is sixty three now and hopes the package is still available then. Katy says she'd like to retire on her sixtieth birthday which is only next April.

Fiona comes to see me often and asks of news about Simon. She says she is especially fond of her spaceman cousin and is looking forward to seeing him again. She knows that he is due sometime soon. Fiona still works for Revolux and was promoted to senior consultant. Meaning she doesn't travel as much but has to supervise a team of six instead. She plans to have a lot of time off when Simon returns.

Sarah and Brian got married as planned in May 2039 and are very happy together. They have a lovely son Adam who is now three years old and talking as much as he possibly can. Sarah says he can talk the hind legs off the proverbial donkey. She has given up her teaching job so that she can look after her son fulltime and she visits us often. Tania loves the little fellow and he calls us aunty and uncle. I kind of like that as it makes me feel younger. At Sarah's prompting I had to do the old trick with the buttons in my hands disappearing and reappearing as I had done with Sarah and Fiona when they were little. Sarah smiled at the thrill on Adam's face when I did my 'magic' and I'm sure it took her back to her own childhood days. When I look at Adam I too think back to the days when Simon was little. Adam however is blond haired just like Brian's mum.

Sarah and Brian have not told Adam the source of my magic but I expect they will one day when he is very much older. A sad thought came into my mind that I might never see the grown up Adam. I immediately pushed the thought from my mind. I'd do my very best to be around for all our sakes.

Tania's mum and dad, Milly and Jerry are both fit and well and in their early eighties. They only visit the shops occasionally and that too only to keep in touch with Mark, Les and Agnes. Milly has put on a bit of weight and is on pills for an under-active thyroid. She attends regularly for checkups and blood tests to regulate her medication. Her optician points out a slight brown tint in both eye lenses which hints at the start of cataracts there. But so far Milly has not noticed anything adverse in her vision.

Mark Tinman and I get on very well and I have a great respect and affection for him. He is seventy three now and keeps good health and I have made him a full partner in the business. That was three years ago and he has carte blanche to run the shop as he wishes. Mark has a young assistant named Julian Watts aged twenty six to help in the shop. Julian was a regular visitor to the main McGill's shop over several years and Mark had mentioned him to me. I approached him in 2041 and liked what I saw in his mind. He was a history graduate from Sheffield University but had done only short employment contractual jobs with a Dudley law firm. No long term job offer had been made to him and I saw a mind that was keen and full of novel ideas. So when his latest term contract expired I approached him and offered him a permanent position as assistant to Mark. His answer was an enthusiastic 'yes'. I can see a future for McGill's Antiques with Julian leading the way.

I also decided to separate the two shops into two independent companies. I wanted no clash of personalities in their functioning as Shop-One and Shop-Two McGill's Antiques. I of course remain a sleeping partner of both companies.

I made Les Gibson a full partner at the same time as I did for Mark. And I likewise gave him independent control of the business of Shop-Two. Mark had similar powers with respect to Shop-One. Les renamed his Shop Two as McGill's Antiques Annex shop and Museum. Les said that he and Agnes still plan to expand one day but not as yet. Agnes is the drive and energy behind Les and she is a great help in the business. At fifty five years of age she looks and behaves ten years younger. Rebecca their daughter joined an amateur theatre group a few years ago when she was twenty two and last year she was talent spotted and offered a minor role in a Hollywood film. She accepted and moved to Los Angeles and now shares an apartment with two other girls also in the film business. Rebecca wrote back to her parents that she was very happy there and had been given an even bigger part in another film. There was a lot of excitement in her correspondence and she was keen to continue living there. I said to Agnes that I thought Rebecca was bound to progress in the film world and might even become famous one day. She was a pretty lady and her innocent looking face would surely catch some producer's eye. I wished her the best of luck.

I continue to spend time in both shops mainly to dictate the History Cards for each new item acquired. Young Julian is quite taken by this skill of mine and says what a wonderful gift I have. It's a shame I can't pass it on as Julian would have been my perfect choice.

Poor old Mavis Chambers suffered a severe stroke four years ago. She was kept in hospital for a couple of months before being moved into a care home. Very gradually she got some mobility back on her right side but her left side remained completely paralysed. She could say a few slurred words and would carry on a conversation of sorts with Vicky who went to visit her daily. Then she developed a mild case of dementia and some days were worse than others. On one occasion she even failed to recognise Vicky which was most upsetting for Vicky.

Then last year she passed away peacefully in her sleep. She was eighty six years of age. The care home staff were very good and made all the arrangements for Mavis's funeral and we all attended. Milly and Ron managed to come down for it and were driven by Sudzarnt. They stayed with mum and dad for a few days.

Among those at the reception was retired chief superintendent Robert Black. I saw him in close conversation with Vicky and she seemed to perk up when she was with him.

Vicky is now sixty three and has put on quite a few pounds. She lives on her own in their old house and appears quite well. We have seen her quite often at my folks place as we visit there often. I asked her about Robert and she seemed happy to talk about him.

Robert is a year older than Vicky and also lives alone in central Birmingham. His wife Roberta died just over two years ago after an eighteen month battle against pancreatic cancer. She was only sixty two when she died. Robert visits his daughters up in the Aberdeen area several times a year for a week at a time. His eldest granddaughter Eliza is now eleven years of age and quite tall. Robert says that she is still a shy child but loves reading books, especially the classics.

Unknown to us at the time Robert visited Vicky at her home shortly after Roberta passed away. A general sort of friendship commenced but Vicky was for too involved with her mum to really give him any consideration. However over the past year they have got much closer in their friendship and come to visit us in Dudley quite often. I see a closeness developing between them and am glad that both have some companionship.

Obviously Robert talks about Vicky to his daughters and they said that they were glad that their dad was not moping and on his own. It took some of the worry off their minds for him to have an old flame for company. Vicky too seems to have got a sparkle in her manner and cheerfully remarked that she and Robert have a routine of seeing each other three times a week.

Tania queried Vicky if there were any plans to get closer in their friendship.

'Oh no,' replied Vicky, 'I like my independence and so does Robert. We like it just the way it is. I don't think his daughters would approve of anything more. I wouldn't want to upset their relationship. Me a stepmother? I don't think so.'

I had to smile at this and knew that a lot more was involved in their relationship than either of them were letting on. The smiles in their demeanour said it all. They looked happy and I was pleased especially for Vicky. For years she had dedicated herself to her mother's care and now deserved a life of her own.

I had a surprise one day about a year ago when a friendly face popped into the shop of an afternoon. Gary Prior, who was on a visit to Birmingham with some others from his church had broken off from them to pay us a visit. He looked good for his seventy four years and apologised profusely for not having visited more often. The church had helped him get over his wife Jill's passing and he spoke fondly of his daughter Maura, her husband Richard and their two children up in Edinburgh. Little Jacob was six and Mary was four. Gary said he went up to see them as often as he could which was at least three times a year.

It was lovely seeing Gary again after such a long time and we talked about old times. I brought him back to the house as Tania had been over with her mum that day. He was pleased to see Tania and we kept him to an early dinner. There was a lot to talk about and the time passed quickly. Somehow I don't think he'll keep his promise to visit more often so I told him to come whenever the mood took him. I knew that his main desire was to travel up to see his grandchildren as often as he could. When I queried him about relocating there he was silent for nearly a minute before giving his reply.

'Oh I don't think I could. I have too many happy memories in Mansfield and our house.'

Then after a pause he added.

'Do you know I feel that Jill is still with me? I can sense her presence strongly in the house so I could never part from it.'

I think I knew what he meant as I saw the shining wetness come to his eyes. He and Jill had been an item. I couldn't help a smile and I quickly explained to Gary that I was thinking of the pleasure on Jill's face when I made that facetious reference to strawberries and cream at her picnic.

'Yes,' he said, 'she spoke about that often. And because of it she said she would never forget you. Oh Ashley, why did she have to be taken so early?'

There was nothing I could say to that. My own fate remained silent in the deepest recesses of my mind. Tania must bear the pain all on her own if I am gone but I know the memories of our togetherness will carry her through.

Gary had to return to Birmingham before making his way to Mansfield with his church friends. He said he'd like to get back before dark. I said it was summer and light till about ten o'clock but he decided to leave at seven. It was a nice get-together with an old friend and Tania and I wished him a safe journey when he finally drove off.

'Damn Zarama,' was the curse prominent in my mind. Then I realised that but for that threat my being may not have been necessary. And my life may even have followed a very different course.

Since our return from Sirius, Tania and I have not visited Anztarza again. We are however in regular communication with several friends there. Katy keeps in constant communication with her friend Jantuzno who recently returned to Anztarza with her husband Chaztalit. They plan a fairly long stay and will return to Nazmos only when they decide to start a family. There were no plans for that as yet. Jantuzno said she'd like to stay free at least until she was about 125 years of age. She was only 91 now.

I get to communicate with Captain Bulzezatna on a fairly regular basis and she conveys all the latest news of the people we know. I believe that Puzlwat and Nogozat are doing well and have been monitoring the climate conditions on Nazmos.

Muznant and Brazjaf send me regular communication packages and always mention Jazzatnit and her husband Zazfrapiz. Sadly his health is not as it should be but at the age of 360 years that is to be expected. Yet Jazzatnit at only a year younger is full of get up and go. Muznant tells me that her aunt is planning a complete redesign of their courtyard garden. I replied that I looked forward to seeing them all again and especially the new garden.

Farzant at 29 years of age had completed her education and was now considered an adult. She featured in Muznant's communication and I was struck by her good looks. I believe she takes after her great aunt Jazzatnit and I can now visualise what that dear lady must have looked like in her youth. Farzant is truly beautiful and her parents are very proud of her. She also has a keen mind.

I have also been in communication contact with Captain Zakatanz on the occasions when he actually visits Anztarza. He now flies in his starship alone as Azatamunt stays on Nazmos to supervise their daughter Hazazamunt's further education. At his age of 261 Zakatanz had thought about spending more time with his family. He considered retiring from starship duties and transferring to a normal Nazmos based spaceship but was unable to make up his mind. He'd spent a hundred years of loneliness pining for his beloved first love Hazazamunt after she unaccountably disappeared a few days before they were due to complete a marriage contract. I had managed to clarify the reason for that disappearance when Zakatanz had confided in me. Then he had found love again in Hazazamunt's sister Azatamunt and a daughter was born to them whom they named Hazazamunt after the lost sister. The name had been chosen by Azatamunt which pleased Zakatanz immensely.

Now Zakatanz missed their company on the long starship journeys to and from Earth which was why he'd thought about retirement. Perhaps in a few years time he could offer 8110-Gold for the scheduled upgrade to 'streak' status. He had conveyed these thoughts to the Nazmos governing council through the Zanos feedback system and they would have noted it for consideration. Nazmos is an open society and no thoughts or intentions remained secret for long. A captain who was willing to give up his starship was a rarity and would make it an easy choice for the administration. Although the upgrading of 4110-Silver had been hastened considerably because of my age factor future upgrades could take well over fifty years or so. Zakatanz had finally found something precious in his Azatamunt and daughter Hazazamunt and he was impatient to spend all his remaining years beside them. He was overwhelmed by the love in his heart that he had for them.

My reverie was interrupted when Tania finished watering the containers in the garden and came and flopped down on the seat beside me. She pulled off her flowery floppy hat and placed it down so the inside was facing upwards.

'I'll let it air,' she said, 'the inner band is all sweaty.'

I looked at her and smiled. Her hair was all messy where she had carelessly pulled off the hat and I watched as she ran her fingers through each side to settle it to her liking. She then shook her head from side to side and I was surprised at how quickly it settled into a rugged neatness. She knew I was watching and turned towards me eyebrows raised.

'What?' she said.

'You look good,' was all I could say.

'Thank you,' she smiled, 'then perhaps you could get a nice cool squash for your hard working wife.'

I smiled as I stood up.

'Of course dear,' I replied, 'large or small?'

'Large please with three cubes of ice if you wouldn't mind.'

As I turned to walk through the open patio doors she reached out and caught my arm.

'Hold on,' she said, 'my tax please.'

I turned back to her and leaning down I smiled and gave her a firm kiss on the lips. It was her way of demanding a 'thank you' from me for watering my containers. The garden area was supposedly my domain while the inside of the house was hers.

'Thank you sir,' she said releasing my arm, 'you may continue with your duty.'

'Very good madam,' I mimicked in my best posh accent, 'I shall be back within the hour.'

We both laughed and I nearly tripped as I went to step over the door sill into the house.

These last few years had been glorious ones for us and we had ascended into a companionship of easy and relaxed harmony. The passion had faded but the love had grown. Our love for each other was a fulfilment into a realm that we didn't know existed which we both found surprising; but oh so wonderful.

I suppose we both felt a need for each other in the present because our future was not certain. Tania knew everything that was in my mind and my failure with Sirius B had brought home to us that if I was to succeed against Zarama then some drastic measure had to be taken. And we knew that might put me at risk. It was something we both realised had to be done which put a limit on our future together. I think it was this understanding that forced us intensely towards each other with the desire to continually feel the others presence near. I wanted to be inside her mind and she wanted to be in mine. As the physical passion gradually diminished so the calmness of togetherness and touching grew stronger. It was like the sublimation of passion into pure love. We would cuddle each other at night with a fierceness of the need to weld and maintain our pressed bodies together. And sometimes that is how we stayed much of the night. I remember one time of waking in the morning in the same position we had gone to sleep in.

There were times when our faces would be wet with tears because she had read my thoughts and I hers. One without the other would be unbearable. If the worst did happen could I keep in contact with my love afterwards just as Philip had? But things had moved on for Philip and he had phased away to somewhere where further contact had been lost. I wondered what rules applied there.

Having proved that my telekinetic gift at its very forceful best had been insufficient against Sirius B it was my belief that it would have enhanced its power over the intervening years for me to meet the Zarama challenge. Perhaps I would not need to exert my telekinetic push beyond the Pink mode level sixteen. But whatever the outcome I know that I must resort to every measure to succeed against Zarama. And succeed I must for the future of Earth and Nazmos.

The last starship 9110-Red under Captain Natazlat had set off on its return journey to Nazmos sometime in March after a stay at Earth station of four months. The last communication package had been dropped off at the Aberporth B&B sometime before that and Sudzarnt had delivered it to me on one of his frequent visits.

Sudzarnt and I had become close friends and I guess he missed some of the aspects of mental communication that could only occur between fellow Oannes. But I was a good substitute in that my telepathic prowess was nearly as good as his. I also found it a pleasure communicating with him since it took us into a dimension not possible with the ordinary human mind.

Sudzarnt liked me to convey fresh images of my experiences on Nazmos and I wondered if he was finally becoming homesick.

'Oh no,' he conveyed at my asking. 'I like myself as I am and where I am. If ever I felt a desire to visit Nazmos then I should first go to Anztarza. Currently I have no such desire. My life is here living as a human among humans which is just as I want it. I would not change one aspect of it.'

'But what about Nazmos when it begins to alter as Gozmanot envisioned it,' I asked?

He gave his practiced laugh and a shrug.

'Even by Oannes standards I shall be a very old man by then,' he said. 'I shall also be set in my ways to want to see any change. But I will look forward to hearing of the changes that come about there.'

I think I understood him perfectly.

There was still purpose in my days and I set myself a duty to spend time in both shops. Tania and I would go in about ten in the morning and stay till about two in the afternoon. We would split our time between the two shops and help out with the daily tasks. Mine was dictating the history cards but there was also the need to keep the exhibits dust free. This was a continuous chore although a cleaner came to each shop every day.

Mark sent Julian on forays for antiques and items of interest about once every week. Les from the other shop usually accompanied Julian since they all got on very well. Agnes stayed behind to mind the shop. She said it was not her scene as recognising an antique was something she did not have an eye for. She also sited her antiques memory or lack thereof as another reason.

Sometimes if it promised to be an interesting house sale or fair then Tania and I would tag along. Julian said he wished I came more often as he often chose an item because it had an interesting background. I of course could supply him with an accurate history.

The fairs were often held on open ground like the Sunday ones I attended with the Priors in Mansfield so long ago. But I never saw another Martin Brothers 'Bird Jar' item like the one displayed by Farmer Jake Pelling on his stall. That really was something to remember.

Milly and Jerry were always made welcome when they came over to us of an evening. Of course we communicated regularly through our badges but face to face contact was always preferable.

It was further for my folks but they too tried to come as often as they could. Dad likes to get out of the house but I could see it becoming more of an effort for him. He was usually asleep in our comfy recliner after about an hour of chat. Mum and Milly though liked to natter through the evening.

I worry about dad because I often pick up his thoughts through his communication badge and realise he spends a lot of his time reminiscing about his days at the MoD. At age ninety I suppose there's not much else you can do. I only hope that dad is well when Simon arrives. I noticed that of late dad had not mentioned Simon though Rachel and Katy visited him often. I tried to mention that Simon should be here any day soon but I just got a smile and a blank look in return. Dad's memory is definitely fading. I suppose that is only to be expected for each of us as we age.

And so the month of July ended and August commenced. We then finally got a few days of wet weather and very welcome it was too. It is surprising how fresh everything looks after a good downpour. Throughout August it seemed to rain on alternate days as the fronts swept in from the Atlantic. I think I've become quite an expert as I watch the weather news and its accompanying satellite pictures. The satellite images certainly make the weather forecasting easy and accurate. But the Midlands always seem to get less of the rain than other areas north and south of it.

I thought about Nazmos and according to my calculations it must be approaching the apogee of its orbit. That is at its furthest position of thirty one million miles from Raznat. I consider that it will be another five months or so before it drops to its perigee of nineteen million miles. Only then will I be able to settle it into its permanent circular orbit which I have begun to refer to as the Gozmanot orbit. It is only from then on that the realisation of her visions will commence. If Simon does come for me now then we shall have some months of leisure time together.

It was towards the latter part of August that I received communication from Anztarza that a starship had arrived at Earth station commanded by Captain Wastanomi. It was also confirmed that this was the new starship 4110-Silverstreak and that a fleet of Anztarza's spaceships had been dispatched to ferry personnel back to Earth. I knew that Simon would be one of those on board and Tania and I were elated at the news. I couldn't help but think of Mazpazam and whether I would finally get to see her. I know Tania was keen to do so.

And there would be no hurry to return to Nazmos for the reason that it would not be in the correct orbital position for a little over five months which meant about the middle of February next year. But would Simon be permitted to spend time on Earth for that long? I'm sure Simon has taken care of that.

I conveyed this information to all our family and received a joyous response especially from Fiona. Sudzarnt conveyed that as soon as Simon arrived at the B&B he would personally drive him down to us. Our son Simon was coming home and Tania and I were elated.

It was two days later that Simon actually arrived on Earth. He communicated to us the moment his ferrying spaceship entered Earth's atmosphere and he conveyed that he would see us in a few days. He had starship business to attend to in Anztarza. I believe it is Oannes etiquette and custom for a starship representative to personally convey his captain's compliments directly to the Chief Ministers. He was also directly responsible in ensuring that all the communication packages from Nazmos were formally handed over to the proper authorities. I believe that within this post from Nazmos would be one with my name on it. I had always received one whenever a starship had made Earth rendezvous. In my post package I usually received brief visual image messages and news from most of my acquaintances on Nazmos. In recent years there had been regular news from Simon. Jazzatnit and Puzlwat had always been on the regular list. Recently the news had been about the changes in the Nazmos climate. One of the major changes had been the tidal feature when Nazmos had been closest to Raznat. That would be one of the regular features that the Oannes would have to get used to after the permanent orbit had been fixed.

Another factor had been the 'Dark Wind' phenomenon. When Nazmos had been at its closest to Raznat the 'Dark Wind' had been practically non-existent. However it had returned with equal ferocity when Nazmos was at its perigee position.

Simon's conveyed communication had been concise and to the point. Tania said she thought he was saving all his news for when he was here with us. I however tend to read more into things. I thought that perhaps he had a distraction with him; namely one named Mazpazam. Perhaps he wanted to be with her on her tour of Anztarza.

'You don't know anything of the sort,' said Tania having read my mind. 'Besides it's none of our business what our grown-up son does with his time, so keep your suspicions out of it.'

I had to laugh as another thought came into my mind. Perhaps Mazpazam is here on Earth so that Simon and she are able to communicate privately whenever they wished. That way they wouldn't feel apart.

'Stop being so inquisitive and impatient,' said Tania staring at me, 'we shall meet her in due course on Silverstreak.'

I had to agree. The Oannes lady couldn't come to us so we'd just have to wait till we were on Oannes territory, namely the starship; or Anztarza.

However I was impatient to see our son again in the flesh. The imagery in his communication had shown him as a mature man and he had got broader across his shoulders. He had a wider jaw line that came with his years and a generally thickset aspect to his body and one could sense the strength in him. That fine Errol Flynn moustache had returned to adorn his upper lip.

His current communication to me started with 'Hi dad,' before going on about where he was and what he was doing. He did the same to Tania I imagine and I knew when they were having a private conversation because of Tania's smiley facial expression.

It was sad when he mentioned to me that he'd just had a strangely polite conversation with his granddad Alex. 'Granddad doesn't seem to remember who I am, dad,' he said with sadness in his tone. 'I know you warned me of his forgetfulness but never for a moment did I think he'd have forgotten me.'

'Sorry son,' I had replied, 'maybe he'll have a good day when you visit him. But don't be upset if he's the same.'

After a pause Simon added, 'I shall be with you as soon as I finish with business here in Anztarza.'

'We'll be waiting son. We are all impatient to see you again.'

And it was three days later that the diminutive Sudzarnt drove Simon after a late breakfast over into Dudley arriving at ours in the later part of the afternoon. Simon had spent a whole day with Ron and Brenda at the B&B and he promised to return there as often as he could during his fairly lengthy stay on Earth. He estimated a period of five months that he had been given 'shore leave' from his starship duties.

Sudzarnt stood back smiling as he saw Simon hug and kiss his mum. I too stood beside them with a joyful feeling awaiting my turn.

'It's so good to see you son,' said Tania in a croaky voice and eyes wet with tears.

'And you too mum,' said Simon. 'Six years is a long time.'

His voice sounded deeper and I reckon that he'd gone from a tenor to a baritone in vocal pitch. This is something that telepathic communication does not convey. It was lovely to hear him speak as the sound resonated in our ears. Telepathy is all very well but the ear's sensory perception gives a much greater personal pleasure that is quite unique.

Then it was my turn for a man hug and what a hug that was from Simon. He nearly squeezed the breath out of me. He also pressed his cheek against mine and I felt the slight wetness that he left behind. My eyes too had misted over in the silence of our affection.

I greeted Sudzarnt and mentioned that he seemed to have grown at least a couple of inches. He smiled and pointed to his heeled boots. We went indoors and I invited Sudzarnt to rest with us a while but he said he would leave us alone to enjoy our son's home-coming. He had made arrangements to visit the shops and that Les and Agnes had offered him their company and a place to stay. He would return to the B&B the next day.

So Tania and I were alone with our son and we had so much to catch up on. It was one incessant flow of chat and questions and answers. Tania and I couldn't help admiring this magnificent specimen of manhood as Simon had bulked up all over. His shoulders were broad and his chest and stomach quite flat. Or nearly flat in the loose check pattern shirt he had on.

We had tea and biscuits and I was pleased when Simon tucked into the Custard Creams. They were still his favourites from when he was a young sprite. He looked up at me and smiled knowingly with the pleasure of their taste.

'Yum,' he said as he munched away, 'I've not had one of these for ages. Thanks.'

Then he added as Tania refilled his mug of tea.

'I'm a total vegetarian now which comes from only eating Oannes food. I'm not against meat but I don't think my system could accommodate it any more,' he said.

'We got that from your communications son,' said Tania, 'so I have cooked specially to that end.'

'Thanks mum,' from Simon.

'Rachel should be over this evening and she's looking forward to seeing you again,' I said. 'There's no one else coming today. That's been put off for another day.'

'That will be great,' said Simon, 'it'll be like old times with just us four together. I look forward to meeting my little sis again. Mind you she's quite a lady now from what I remember of her communications to me.'

'Yes,' said Tania, 'she too is quite taken with the Oannes way of life and would like to settle permanently on Nazmos. She and Margaret have a yen to monitor the climate change that will come about when the Nazmos orbit is finalised.'

'I'd like to visit granddad tomorrow if that's alright,' said Simon, 'and perhaps as often as possible till he remembers me.'

'That would be lovely son,' I said quite pleased by Simon's request.

'I might be able to jog his memory with a thing I've learnt from the Oannes,' he said.

'Oh,' I said, 'and what may that be?'

He just smiled and said, 'Wait and see. It only works face to face; usually but not always. Though I shall need your help, dad.'

And so our pleasant conversation went on and on till Tania finally served up a lovely fruity salad lunch.

'I hope you don't mind sliced boiled eggs with your salad son?' asked Tania.

'That would be fine mum,' he said.

'You know that Sudzarnt has changed the B&B menu to a vegetarian one only people don't seem to notice it. He has replaced all meat dishes with their Soya equivalent,' said Tania. 'And your dad and I have adopted that same principle. We don't have the Oannes' food quality so we oldies get our protein from Soya products. We have some Soya burgers on the plate there. It's nice with ketchup.'

'I had some of Sudzarnt's dishes yesterday after he told me about the Soya,' said Simon, 'and I found it excellent. Yes mum I shall definitely have a couple of your burgers; with ketchup of course.'

Tania smiled at her son and I could see her heart nearly bursting with pride.

It was after lunch was over and we were sitting with mugs of tea and when a lull ensued in the conversation that Simon brought up the subject of Mazpazam.

'Dad, mum, I have something to tell you,' he said in a low quiet voice, 'and I think you may know what it is.'

Tania and I had the same thought and Simon read us instantly.

But we remained silent not wanting to interrupt his thought trend. His face had reddened somewhat though there was a calmness in his manner. He seemed determined to tell us about his affairs. Simon had never been secretive in his nature so nothing had changed there.

'I see you have guessed,' he said, 'so let me confirm that you are right in your assumption. Mazpazam is a beautiful Oannes lady and we like each other a lot.'

So there it was out in the open; at least to us his parents.

He paused for a moment before he conveyed images of this lady to our minds. There were moving views of a very pretty and slightly coy youthful looking Oannes lady who smiled a lot; obviously at Simon in whose memory these images rested.

I took an instant liking to her and I could sense the love in her manner.

'We met at the academy and didn't get on at all at first,' he said smiling. 'She avoided me whenever she could which didn't bother me in the least since I hardly noticed her. My one ambition then was to learn the craft of spacemanship and to impress my tutors with my skill.'

Simon paused to let this sink in.

I was reminded of my first sight of Tania aged nearly fourteen with reddish brown hair and hazel eyes at that darts match in the Navigation pub. I had hardly noticed her then.

Simon continued.

'In our second year we began our space flight projects in small syndicate groups and again she avoided me for much of that time. But eventually we were on the same space navigation test and had to work together to communicate our project plans. Here too we only communicated briefly but it was a start. I had many friends in the academy and gradually over the later years Mazpazam became a part of that group of associates. I had impressed my tutors with what to them was an uncanny navigation skill on my part. I got the reputation of knowing at all times in which direction Raznat was. My project successes drew cadets to me especially if their directional calculations were uncertain. On one occasion Mazpazam approached me for help and I explained what she needed to do rather than giving her the answer on a plate. She became curious about me and asked me about you. And so we began to talk just as I am doing now and I told her about Dudley and where we lived and the things we enjoyed. Initially our chats were quite brief but I knew that her curiosity about Earth life styles was an ever present one.'

'When she asked to know more about you I said that you were an ordinary dad at home and never showed off any of your talents. I told her about the antiques shop and how only you had the gift to make the history cards for each item on sale. She laughed when I told her of the hide-and-seek games you used to play with us as kids. And the magic tricks you performed by making buttons disappear and reappear in your hands for the benefit of Fiona and Sarah when they were little. It seemed that Mazpazam could not hear enough about you. You do know that you have a certain venerated reputation with the Oannes people in general. You especially impress them with your modesty and simplistic way of life in both thought and deed and that you only use your gifts for a specific purpose.'

I noticed a sadness emotion flit across Simon's thoughts as he said this last bit. Had he had one of his premonitions about me? Perhaps it had something to do with Zarama but I didn't probe further as I had no right to.

'Anyway I told her everything about our family, our friends and our business of the antiques shops. I told her about Sudzarnt and she expressed surprise and an interest to meet him. But when I mentioned this to Sudzarnt yesterday he said he'd rather not. So I didn't push it.'

'O yes,' he continued, 'I met her mother and father for the first time when they came for a tour of Silverstreak about two years ago. Mazpazam introduced me as a colleague and they were pleased to meet me as the son of Ashley. Everyone knows about you dad so I just basked in your shadow. But then Mazpazam told them that we were especially friendly and they didn't seem to mind. I suppose they already knew that a human was in training as a space cadet from their contacts. I've since met them a few times and they have been most welcoming. They are quite elderly with both being quite close to their third century in age. The father is Jatiztram and the mother is Hatazaton and Mazpazam is their only child. By the way, her mother has a much older sister called Latozaztan who is married to a Nazmos governing council member called Martazta. They are known friends of Muznant's aunt and uncle, Jazzatnit and Zazfrapiz. I guess if anything they must have heard about me from them. I love the Oannes dad and I love their ways and I want to emulate them.'

Simon looked at us and smiled. I think Simon was desperately trying to impress us with her background. And I was, but the Oannes people impressed me anyway.

'So tell us son when did you realise that you really liked Mazpazam as a girlfriend?' asked Tania.

'I can't answer that mum,' said Simon, 'because I just don't know. It was all a gradual process and never love at first sight as the saying goes. When our looks would meet I somehow felt that there was a communion of feelings between us - feelings of pleasure at the other's presence. It is only when I am alone I realise I miss her. My consolation is that on Nazmos as on Earth we can communicate through our badges. But out in open space the distances are far too great for that and I then miss her terribly.'

Simon then reached out to clasp each of our hands before continuing.

'Mum, dad there is something else that I can't get out of my mind. Mazpazam and I belong to different cultures and species. I am human and she is Oannes. Her lifespan will tend towards 400 years while mine will barely reach to a quarter of that. Genetically we are incompatible and so no offspring can result. I shall become old and senile while she is still in her youthful prime.'

Simon stopped because he could not go on. His eyes were glistening wet with checked emotion and I knew what he was thinking. They could not have a future together as Tania and I had though they loved each other just as much. A thought came to me.

'Have you told her that you love her?' I said.

'Not in as many words but she can read my emotions just as I can read hers,' he replied.

'It's not the same,' I said. 'Words form an indelible part of the past and once uttered can never be erased. That is why you must say it out aloud. It then goes on record and remains permanent. When we are long gone our words remain as a testament of what we felt and who we were.'

Simon was thoughtful and this time I was forced into reading his mind. His present wish was to spare Mazpazam sorrow in later years when he was no more but was uncertain as to a proper course of action. In his mindset he reckoned that they might be lucky to have forty or fifty good years of togetherness. I could see what Simon was thinking and I conveyed this to Tania.

In order to spare Mazpazam the sadness and grief when he was gone he was contemplating a plan to gradually distance himself from their current relationship. Slowly and surely he would contrive to make her see a different part of his nature by acting selfish and demanding. He intended for them to eventually go their separate ways and Simon hoped she would find love anew elsewhere.

So I asked him a question.

'But what about you, son' I asked, 'do you think you might find someone else too whom you could love as much?'

Simon was quick to reply.

'I don't think so dad,' he said, 'for me there can never be another Mazpazam.'

'And do you think you could ever be happy or even content without her?' I asked.

'It's her I'm mainly concerned about dad,' he replied, 'it doesn't matter about me.'

'Ah, but it does,' I said. 'It matters because you would be incomplete in your mind and your career as a spaceman would suffer. You would never be able to do your duty as a professional because a part of you would be missing. Your approach in the tasks set you would not be as rigorously performed by you for the same reason.'

Then a thought came to me and I put another question to our son.

'How do you know that she will outlive you? There is no guarantee of it.'

'How do you reckon that dad?' said Simon puzzled.

So I conveyed to him the sad story of Captain Zakatanz's early life and the tragic conclusion of the affair with his fiancé Hazazamunt. I conveyed the grief and sadness that Zakatanz had to live with not only at the disappearance of his love the adventurous Hazazamunt, but also with the notion that she had rejected him for some unknown reason.

Was Simon planning a similar fate of rejection for Mazpazam was a question I had to add into this tale of woe?

I then continued with the Zakatanz story. He and Hazazamunt had spent ten glorious fun years together where love overflowed in their relationship. Zakatanz had confided to me that he had never been happier and still cherished those ten wonderful years of indelible memories. Then just a week before the official certification of the sealing of their partnership Hazazamunt had suddenly disappeared. Zakatanz was grief stricken and confused not to mention puzzled.

Simon remained silent but attentive as I continued.

'For a hundred years Zakatanz mourned her memory and became a different taciturn Oannes captain. He still had no idea how and why Hazazamunt had disappeared. In fact no one else on Nazmos knew either. Then I came into the picture and on our starship journey Zakatanz and I by pure chance became friends. One day he unburdened his locked up memories and told me about Hazazamunt and conveyed images of her. She was a pretty Oannes lady but more importantly with my diagnostic gift I sensed an illness within her and the probable cause of her disappearance.'

I conveyed all this to Simon and I could see that I had his full interest.

'This eased Zakatanz's puzzled torment though his sadness remained. Then the collision of an object with his starship on a return journey to Nazmos proved a final momentous event. Through my skill of mental regression I showed him that the object that had fused into his starship's neutron shield had in fact been a small private spacecraft. The images that I conveyed to him proved to him beyond a doubt that it was the craft he had been in with Hazazamunt many times. This finally brought closure to that part of his life and subsequently in time he restarted his emotional life with Hazazamunt's sister Azatamunt. He is once again a happy Oannes starship captain.'

After a brief pause I added aloud.

'Simon, nothing is certain especially in the profession that you are in. Space is a dangerous place to be in though perhaps less for you with your premonition gift. So who can predict what accidents could or could not happen. Zakatanz had just ten years of loving memories with his love Hazazamunt. You have the rest of your life with Mazpazam and the chance to create wonderful memories. Don't throw it all away my son, I know I wouldn't.'

I let that sink in and still Simon stayed silent but there was a slight glistening of wetness in his eyes. Tania squeezed my hand to express her approval of what I had said. There was a further aspect to add.

'How would Mazpazam feel about losing you? Would she feel that she was being rejected for no reason whatsoever? It would be a terrible wounding experience from which she might never recover. The Oannes can read us humans like a book so be under no delusions that she would not know your true intention. Zakatanz had mourned for Hazazamunt for a hundred years before I eased his mind.'

I could say little more to convince him but I think Simon knew in his heart of hearts that what I had said made sense.

'There is one thing more I'd like to add son,' I said. 'If you feel that she will feel alone after you and I are long gone then it is up to you to fill the years you have together with such memories that they will give her joy for the rest of her long life. Enjoy what you have now and live your lives to the full.'

After a pause Simon looked up and smiled, albeit weakly.

'Thanks dad,' he said.

He then reached out again and taking our hands in each of his he said, 'I love you both very much and I know Mazpazam will too. And I would like you to meet her.'

Tania and I then stood up and pulling our tall son to us we got into a group hug.

'We would love to,' whispered Tania with tears in her eyes.

'But first,' said Simon with his more usual smile, 'I have a lot of catching up to do. Where is that sis of mine?'

Rachel conveyed that she was twenty five minutes away and for him not to be impatient.

When Rachel finally arrived she ran in and threw her arms around Simon's neck and hugged him fiercely. She only reached up to his shoulders in height and had to tiptoe to kiss him on his cheek.

She then stood back and said, 'Let me have a good look at you bro. Not bad, not bad at all in fact you look quite good. I see you've rekindled the moustache. I'm glad. It gives you a bit of style.'

Simon threw back his head and laughed his Errol Flynn laugh and reaching out pulled Rachel in for another hug.

I loved seeing them together like this as both seemed to be so enjoying this reunion. Rachel laughed with the joy of meeting her brother and the happiness was written all over her manner.

'Mum, dad, doesn't he look good,' she said, 'my, it'll be the luckiest girl who gets him.'

'Thanks sis,' smiled Simon. 'And on that front I've got news for you. Dad will tell you all about it as we've just finished a discussion on that topic.'

Simon looked at me and I understood that he wanted me to convey all of our discussion to Rachel as only I could do. And so I did in all of a few seconds and in full graphic detail.

I could see Rachel's immediate expression of wonder but I did not expect the response that she gave. It was quite unexpected but so welcome.

'Wow bro,' she exclaimed, 'I want to meet her. She will be my sis-in-law and I can claim residency on Nazmos. I want to spend the rest of my life there after dad does his thing. I will have to give Margaret the news. She will be thrilled.'

'Hang on sis,' said Simon, 'it may not be as simple as that.' But he was smiling broadly.

'Why, what's to prevent you and your lady Mazpazam getting together legally?' quizzed Rachel thinking of the Zakatanz story and the advice I had given Simon. 'You'd be an ass if you didn't follow your heart. And besides I'd never forgive you. I want her for a sis and you can't deny me that.'

Simon laughed and appeared pleased and relieved at Rachel's response. Another pleasurable emotion seemed to come through to me from far away and I could only conclude that Mazpazam had picked up on our conversation. And I liked that just as much.

'Since you put it like that sis,' said Simon aloud, 'how can I not do as you command.'

Rachel went back into her brother's arms and hugged him tight. Her emotion was one of happiness that was plain to see and no words were necessary.

'And what about you sis?' asked Simon.

'Oh I'm fine bro,' said Rachel. 'I have a good friend in Margaret and we get on very well together. We have the same interests and she's like an older sister to me despite our thirty year age gap. We both want to be on Nazmos to record everything that happens after the new orbital status. It'll be our life's mission to accurately record the facts from a human's perspective.'

Simon looked at Rachel with pride as he too had decided that Nazmos was to be his home from home. I could see in the way he postured that the old confidence had returned and that a doubtful decision had been resolved and put to rest – permanently. And that pleased me no end. I conveyed my thoughts to Tania and her response was immediate and pleasant as she smiled at me.

Tania and Rachel made us mugs of tea as we conversed. Simon said he wouldn't mind if the next few months were interspersed with rounds of teas and dinner events as a means of getting to meet all our friends and acquaintances.

'God knows when I shall get the chance to meet them again,' he said. 'But my present priority is for granddad Alex to get to remember me again. For that I shall need your help dad. I've asked Grandma Lillian to talk to him about me as much as possible but I don't think that's helped very much.'

'Sure son,' I said, 'I'll help in any way I can. What is it you want me to do?'

He explained and I thought, 'What a good idea.'

'It's something the Oannes do with their very aged when things become confused for them,' said Simon. 'And it is something that may need to be repeated by you each time that I visit granddad.'

What Simon wanted me to do was to implant into his granddad's mind all my visual memories of Simon from early childhood to the present and any special moments between the two of them. This would not be a problem for me since Simon and Rachel were always in the forefront of my memories. I shall keep the technique in mind for future occasions if the need arose.

Simon had conveyed to us earlier prior to his arrival that he had also communicated with Jerry and Milly and that they'd had a pleasant conversation through their badges. Ron and Brenda had been as exuberant. It was only dad with his fading memory who had disappointed Simon. But I was confident that we would remedy that at least in the short-term.

'It's because you've been away for so long that you've slipped from granddad's memory,' said Rachel. 'He has no trouble remembering me but that's because I see him several times a week and also communicate regularly. But I too can see that his memory is fading with time. I suppose that we shall all eventually get like that one day.'

'Not for a long time I hope sis,' laughed Simon.

'When do you wish to see your granddad son?' I asked.

'Tomorrow morning if that's okay,' said Simon, 'and every morning for the next week please.'

'That'll be fine,' I said, 'we'll go about ten o'clock. Dad would have breakfasted and the home help should have left by then.'

'Great,' said Simon nodding his head. It was a characteristic of his that I remember he did automatically whenever he agreed to something. It was nice to see that he hadn't changed that much in all the years. Simon was still our Simon of old.

'I'll come too,' said Rachel, 'and granddad can listen to our banter. He'll enjoy the visit more that way and it will be less tiring for him. Can I stay the night mum?'

'Of course darling, your room is always there for you,' said Tania.

Then she added as she got up to go inside. 'Dinner will be ready in about twenty minutes. I hope you are all hungry.'

I could see that brother and sister had a lot of catching up to do so I too got up, excused myself and went into the house to see if Tania needed any help.

Dinner was a nice informal meal as Tania had kept it simple. Soya burgers, mashed potatoes and assorted boiled vegetables cooked from frozen and a large jug of veggie extract gravy. Tania had decided to keep it all purely on a vegetarian basis. Sudzarnt had been our advisor in such matters for several years now. And for dessert we had plain vanilla ice-cream with all the assorted toppings in squeezy plastic bottles. There was also a can of squirty dairy cream which I quite preferred.

Later we sat out on the patio watching the evening glow in the sky and chatted easily. Although the sun was shaded by the far bank of trees the sky was still quite bright.

At about ten o'clock Tania produced a light supper of cheese and biscuits and of course mugs of tea. It was lovely having Simon home with us but by about 11:30pm I had trouble staying awake so Tania and I said our goodnights and left the young ones to stay up as long as they wished.

'I think I'll just sit out here with sis and soak in the atmosphere a bit longer,' said Simon. 'It's such a long time since I did this. It is good to be home.'

'All your things are in your rooms so you can go up whenever you are ready,' said Tania.

'Actually I think I'm ready for bye byes as well,' said Rachel, 'so I'll leave you on your own bro. Goodnight mum, dad, Simon, I'll see you in the morning.'

She kissed Simon and then walked in with us. He conveyed that he'd probably be another half hour or so.

Rachel smiled at us and gave us a goodnight peck before entering her room. In our room I conveyed a private message to Tania and she smiled. Yes, she too thought the same that Simon wished for private communication time with his Mazpazam. Tania and I do look forward to meeting her. Tania looked at me and conveyed her private thoughts to me.

'If Muznant being an Oannes could practically fall in love with you a human all those years ago then our son must just as easily have fallen for one of theirs,' she conveyed.

I had to smile and conveyed back that Muznant was not the only one. Admiration seemed to have sprung up all around and been thrown at me; but then I felt a sadness too when I thought of Ritozanan. I do believe that she truly loved, admired and respected me and that I was perhaps the only male person of both our worlds that she had held with such regard and affection. I would truly miss her on this coming visit to Nazmos. It was one of my prevailing thoughts before I finally fell asleep.

Next morning we were all up bright and early and sat around in our pyjamas drinking mugs of tea and chatting. Simon smiled and conveyed that it was a lovely feeling being home and chilling out like this.

'Yes,' I thought, 'this is nice,' but I kept the remainder of my thoughts blocked from any access. Zarama always seemed to cast its ominous shadow whenever I was enjoying myself.

We all went to see dad and I informed mum that we were on our way. It was close to 11:00am when we arrived and mum came out to meet us. Our communication badges have been indispensable and we would be lost without them. It's as though we are never apart from each other.

Simon was first out of the car and went forward to give his grandma a big cuddly hug and kiss. We followed closely behind.

'Hello grandma,' said Simon with a cheesy grin, 'the prodigal grandson has returned. It's been ages since I last saw you and you haven't changed a bit.'

'Nonsense,' said mum with a pleased smile, 'I'm as old as the hills and I can feel it too. Here let me have a good look at my gorgeous grandson.'

Mum took a step back and made a show of looking Simon up and down.

'You look as smart and debonair as ever and that fine moustache is back I see. It looks good on you Simon. And my, oh my, what broad shoulders you have.'

Simon laughed with his head up in the air.

'And what big ears I have too grandma. All the better to hear you with my dear,' said Simon in an imitation high pitched voice supposed to be that of Little Red Riding Hood at least for the first part.

Mum smiled at her grandson and taking his arm led him into the house.

'I think I managed to make your granddad understand that his one and only grandson was visiting but I don't believe that he remembers a lot about you Simon,' said mum, 'so don't be disappointed if you get some blank looks.'

'Don't worry grandma; dad and I have a plan to jog his memory,' said Simon.

At mum's puzzled expression I quickly conveyed to her what we had in mind.

'I hope it works,' she replied.

'Don't worry it will,' said Simon. 'The Oannes use it all the time with great success. I'll just let dad prepare the way.'

'Let's just go and say hello first,' I suggested.

Dad was sitting in his favourite recliner armchair facing the TV which had on one of the many programs dad liked to watch.

We filed in quietly but he must have noticed us in the corner of his vision for he quickly looked around at us. So I conveyed an immediate 'Hello dad' to his mind.

'Hello Ashley son,' he said recognising me instantly, 'nice to see you again. Is that Rachel with you? Hello Rachel.'

Then he said 'Hello Tania,' as Tania moved past me and into his view.

'Hello granddad,' said Rachel as dad switched off the TV with the remote in his hand. Dad never kept the TV on while he had visitors – a golden rule of his that he insisted upon when I was still living at home.

Then dad spied Simon and squinting at him he was desperately trying for recognition and receiving only partial success. So I immediately conveyed to dad's mind all my mental memories of my son. These included not only his growing up but also of his playing in the garden with his granddad. I transferred as much as I felt dad could absorb into his frail mind as I thought safe. I also included quite a bit about Simon's time at the Nazmos space academy and his subsequent career as a spaceman. I put visuals of his visit to us at Jazzatnit's house on Nazmos and then his arrival here in Dudley yesterday and all the conversation we'd had. All of this took me only a few seconds in real time and I immediately saw the light of recognition appear on dad's face.

'Well hello Simon,' he said with a smile on his face, 'it is nice to see my grandson again. It is lovely of you to come and visit me. You must tell me all about your adventures in the Oannes space fleet.'

'Hello granddad,' said Simon coming to stand close to dad and offering his hand which was grasped firmly and well shaken. 'It is lovely to be home and to see you again granddad. I've been away far too long but I'm here now for several months. I'll come and see you everyday if I can.'

Dad looked at me and nodded.

'My grandson is quite something, eh son?' he said to me aloud.

Then to Simon he said, 'Come, pull up a chair and sit here by me and tell me all about yourself and what you have been up to?'

Simon is quite a conversationalist in his own right and he chatted to his granddad for quite a while. But after about twenty minutes I could see dad beginning to lose concentration as his mind began to wander onto other things. Like changing the subject to the front door that needed painting again.

So I struck up a conversation to include mum and the others. We talked about our plans for the next few days and our visit to Ron and Brenda at their B&B in Aberporth. I didn't mention Anztarza as I don't think dad would have remembered it. We talked in specifics for dad's benefit and he seemed to enjoy listening to us which caused him no effort. I let Simon take the lead in much of the discussion as I wanted his voice and face to be imprinted on dad's memory. A week of this and dad would see Simon as a regular member of his immediate family. At least I hoped it would be so.

We stayed with him for another twenty minutes when we noticed his eyes growing heavy and he began to nod off into little phases of sleep. We lowered our voice tone but carried on talking till we noticed that he had fallen into quite a deep sleep. Mum nodded to us and led the way out into the dining room.

'Alex will sleep for about an hour before he wakes again and calls for me,' she whispered. 'It's a nice quiet life that we lead and we are both very content. Come and sit and I'll make us some tea. You all will stay to lunch won't you? And Simon you can tell me more of yourself.' She smiled as she said this for I had conveyed to her all that I had conveyed to dad earlier. She knew about Mazpazam and that I believe was of great interest to her. That was a woman's domain and I could see mum planning the future; or at least imagining it.

After dad woke again mum brought him to the dining table when she served up a nice hot lunch. It was a lovely meal which mum had prepared earlier and kept frozen. It consisted of a meatball mild curry dish and another of plain lentils. Then mum had made fresh boiled rice which she had coloured to a light yellow by adding a pinch of turmeric powder to the water before the rice came to the boil. I'd seen her do it many times when I lived at home.

'I knew that Simon was due sometime soon,' said mum, 'and I remembered our meals at the Kashmir Diner in Dudley and how you all liked the meatball curry and rice dishes. I've made it quite mild but I have jars of Indian pickles if you like. I think the Brinjal pickle is especially nice. Alex likes it too. Oh yes,' she quickly added, 'the meatballs are made from Soya.'

'This is great gran,' said Simon after his third mouthful, 'it tastes absolutely fab. I must visit the Kashmir Diner one of these days dad. Is that little waiter still there? You know the chatty one.'

'You mean Charlie,' I said. 'Yes he was there the last time we visited but that was quite long ago. I think it must have been around Easter time.'

Mum's meal was a pleasant affair and it was especially nice to see dad with a healthy appetite. He asked for and got a second serving though it was a much smaller one. Mum conveyed that she allowed it only occasionally. Dad kept looking up at Simon as we ate and I could see admiration in his eyes. Simon was full of the vitality of his youthfulness and dad couldn't get enough of that vision. I hope the mental imprint of Simon in dad's mind lasts the duration that Simon is home.

I read somewhere that the visual memories are the last to fade – long after the names of people and places have been forgotten. I used to worry about not being able to recall a recognisable actor's name on a TV show or movie but reading that article allayed my concerns at least for a bit. Fortunately I have my inner voice to help.

We stayed with mum for another couple of hours before leaving for Dudley. Simon promised to be back tomorrow for another chat with dad. He said he'd come later in the afternoon after spending some time at the two shops. He planned on seeing his other grandparents Milly and Jerry about then. Since Simon did not have a current licence to drive I guess it was up to Tania and me to ferry him around.

Tania and I had discussed her big day for next month. September 23rd was a Saturday as well as being her sixtieth birthday. We had decided to have a big dinner out somewhere and invite friends and family. We finally plumbed for the Lea Marsden Leisure Centre on the road to Kingsbury for an evening meal at 7:00pm. The invitations were sent out at the end of July and we were expecting about thirty to attend. Tania had wanted all from the shops as well as Vicky and Robert. Sudzarnt could bring Uncle Ron and Aunt Brenda if Ron felt up to it. They would all stay with mum and dad in Birmingham. And of course Margaret Dutton had to be invited. An invitation was sent to Gary Prior but it was doubtful if he'd be able to attend. Not to be left out were our two neighbours with whom Tania and I were on very friendly terms.

I had asked Sudzarnt to plan a special food menu based upon his B&B catering style and to liaise with the Leisure Centre staff. Everything would be done on a vegetarian basis though few would notice.

I remember when I had turned sixty in 2041 that September 8th had been a Sunday. I had not wanted a big show then and had chosen a Chinese Buffet Restaurant in Erdington not far from mum and dad's place for a Sunday 1:00pm meal. It had been just the family though Rachel and Margaret had been away on Nazmos at the time. Ron and Brenda had come down but Sudzarnt had remained at the B&B. Mum and dad had been there as dad then got about quite well with just his walking stick. Katy was there with Robin as well as Sarah and Brian. I think Sarah was just beginning to show her bump but I couldn't tell. Tania said it was so obvious. I never argue about such things. After the meal we all went back to mum's for tea and coffee and I got to open all my cards and presents.

For me Tania had specified fun presents only so I got plenty of joke books; some quite naughty ones. I have since read them all but can hardly remember any – except one or two very rude ones.

We don't talk about my 65th birthday celebrations next year as I deem it as bad luck. I think of my coming battle with Zarama and worry that I might come off second best. I block my mind to such thoughts.

As the days passed Simon visited dad nearly every day and even managed to pass a driving test first time. I put Simon onto our insurance cover and then got him a good second hand two year old Volkswagen Golf – an automatic. He took out insurance for six months only claiming that he was to emigrate abroad after that. I got my bank to issue him with a debit card on our joint account which gave our son a degree of independence.

September 8th this year was a rather wet Friday and I celebrated with just a few of us going to the Kashmir Diner for an afternoon lunch. Jerry kept joking that before I knew it I'd be catching up with him age-wise. We are a close knit family and I love it when it is just us together. Rachel had the day off and had come early as she wanted to be near her brother. She bought me a book about climate change and I thought it very apt considering that Nazmos was on a similar programmed agenda. Sadly mum and dad couldn't be with us as dad was not able to stay out for too long. But they were with us through our badge communicators and dad said he was feeling quite good today. He said he liked it when the air was wet and everything smelled fresh. Oddly enough it seemed to ease his arthritis he said. Later in the evening Brian and Sarah came to the house with little Adam, a real cutie. Of course I had to perform my little disappearing tricks for him at Sarah's insistence. Katy and Robin also came with Fiona who immediately monopolised her cousin for information about Mazpazam; not a secret anymore.

September 23rd turned out to be a glorious Indian summer type of day and Tania's party was a great success as nearly everyone came. Gary Prior sent his regrets due to a church commitment but he said he'd be down to see us sometime in early October. Mum and dad were there with dad in his wheelchair. Mum had insisted and dad had given in. As the evening progressed I think dad was grateful for it.

The meal was lovely and served expertly by the waitress staff. We all got served more or less together. And there was always someone on hand to see to any needs or requests. We had some fun with another celebratory party at another long table arrangement at the other side of the room. It was a 75th birthday party for a lady and we ribbed them about being a rowdy lot. When they found out that it was Tania's sixtieth birthday party they raised their glasses to her. Then one of them said loud and clear, 'She's only a babby,' in a brummie accent. This caused laughter on both tables and later we got to chatting with some of them. I think it turned out to be a fun evening without the need for speeches or formality of any kind. Many came over to talk to dad and said how good he looked for being ninety years of age.

After the tea and coffee was served we went into the lounge and chatted. But dad was tired out by now and mum decided to take him home. Tania and I along with Simon and Rachel walked out to the car with them. We stayed on till about midnight. The other party had all gone by then and we had a quiet last hour to ourselves.

The next day Tania phoned all her friends to say thank you for making her big day so grand. She said she would remember it always for the wonderful time she had. It was lovely how well things turned out and I think luck had a lot to do with it. Somehow I felt that perhaps my luck too would change and I'd have success with Zarama. It was funny how I did not feel uneasy about it at this moment. A certain confidence seemed to have risen up inside me and I think my face glowed outwardly at the new feeling.

Simon told us that he had made the arrangements for us to visit Anztarza in the last week of October. The plan was to spend a week with Ron and Brenda in Aberporth and then a week in Anztarza when we would meet Mazpazam. Tania got quite excited about it and felt that the news added to her birthday's celebrations. She was keen as ever to meet Simon's girl and I looked forward to it too. Simon said that the chief ministers had also arranged a banquet to welcome us all back to Anztarza after such a long interval. I immediately conveyed my thanks and acceptance of the honour to the chief ministers through my communication badge.

Something was up as I could see a sparkling glint in Simon's eyes that always warned me of a surprise in the offing. Tania read my mind and looking directly at me she conveyed a private message. I was surprised; but more than that I was surprised as to how she could even begin to guess at such a prospect.

At my query all she said was, 'I'm right and I know it, just you wait and see.'

Tania's intuition was seldom wrong and I believed she could be right. Ever since we'd had that talk with Simon about Mazpazam he'd become a changed man. And it would not have been difficult for him to organise such an event for himself. I could not broach the subject because it was currently none of my business and it might upset him. So I shall just have to wait and see if Tania is right.

Gary Prior did visit us on Thursday the 5th of October but it was a flying visit. He couldn't stay the night as he had to be back at his church for a meeting at midday on Friday. However he was with us from noon till just past 6:00pm. We visited the McGill's shops after a light snack and Gary had a good look around while chatting to Mark Tinman, Les Gibson and Agnes. Julian Watts was out somewhere at a home clearance sale so Gary missed him. We then went to the Kashmir Diner for a late afternoon meal and missed seeing Charlie who was on his day off.

We returned home for a hot drink and found Simon back from his visit to his granddad. He and Gary got on well and I smiled when Simon concocted yarns about the business he was in. Simon said he was interested in Chinese art and hoped to visit that country especially the remote central areas to see what he could discover. Yes he spoke a little Mandarin but with so many differing dialects there could be a problem though he thought he might muddle through. Tania had to leave the room at that stage and I sensed her emotion of amusement. Gary left us just after six in the evening.

Being National Trust members we took Simon to quite a few stately homes. We went on spec and on quite a few occasions Rachel came with us. Simon had left for his space academy training before we'd had the chance to do much visiting around the country and he now showed a keen interest. My guess was that he was communicating regularly with Mazpazam and conveying all these new sights to her. Sights and scenes that were very different from those on Nazmos. But hopefully it was an insight into future conditions there.

Another thing we did with Simon was to spend a week in a London hotel and visit all the popular tourist places and museums. The V&A Museum took up nearly a whole day all on its own as did the National Gallery. The Tower and Tower Bridge were interesting for him but he said he was not interested in seeing the Belfast Battleship moored on the Thames nearby. I imagine that it was an image he did not wish for Mazpazam to view.

We went as father and son to a few football matches at Villa Park, the Blues and the Albion grounds but apart from viewing the games Simon did not show a particular enthusiasm; especially as two of the matches were played in wet and cold conditions. Simon likes his comfort as I do. But it was something that fathers and sons should do together, at least once. On each occasion we left before the match ended to avoid the crowds.

On several evenings we'd drive to a nearby park and have a slow chatty stroll on the main paths while nodding 'hello' to all those with children on bikes and dogs on leads. It was a most pleasant aspect that could be conveyed to Mazpazam of how we spent some of our leisure time.

I hadn't seen Ron and Brenda for ages though we communicated regularly so I was keen to spend physical time with them prior to our Anztarza visit. Rachel was keen to meet Mazpazam but unfortunately her duties at the hospital prevented her accompanying us this time. She intended to hand in her notice soon and knew she must wait to meet Mazpazam when we embarked on the starship Silverstreak. Her last stay on Nazmos had been a two year sabbatical but this time she did not intend to return to Earth any time soon if at all. She and Margaret were quite enthusiastic about the climatic and flora studies they intended to carry out on Nazmos. The changes were likely to be dramatic but slow over a very long period of time; well beyond the lifespan of even the Oannes. Rachel had hinted to her hospital colleagues that she was interested to see how medicine was practiced in the Far East; especially China with its many herbal remedies and ancient practices.

And so on Wednesday the 18th of October we drove down in one car to the B&B at Aberporth. I drove so that Simon could enjoy the scenery along our route. We left about 10:00am and went via Shrewsbury and Welshpool to Aberystwyth. We arrived there just after 1:00pm and found a nice parking spot along the Marine Terrace sea front. We then went up the Funicular cliff railway to the top of Constitution Hill which was 500 feet above the town. The restaurant there was pleasant and we had a nice vegetarian salad lunch. Afterwards we went up into the Camera Obscura for a view of the surrounding countryside. It was a clear day and there were breathtaking views of Aberystwyth Town and the houses along the beach road. We could also see the beauty of the Welsh hills spread out inland as far as the eye could see.

We then returned down to Aberystwyth Town level and had a wander around. Simon had never been to Aberystwyth and found the town quite unique. Tania was tempted and so we had an ice cream cone each. I'm afraid I made a mess of mine as the melting ice cream trickled down the side of my cone.

'You've got to be quick and lick the sides fast,' said Tania who seemed quite expert.

She then got out her wet wipes when we finally finished and helped me clean where a drip had landed near my trouser left knee.

It was then back to the car at 4:00pm with the sun quite low and we got to the B&B in just over an hour whilst it was still quite light. Through our badge communicators Ron, Brenda and Sudzarnt knew where we were for every minute of our journey. So when we drove into the B&B car park all three were there to greet us. It was the first time I'd seen Uncle Ron using his Trike Rollator and I was amazed at how agile he was with it. Sadly he said he couldn't use it on the coastal path as some of the gradients were quite steep. I wondered if I could assist there by giving a slight telekinetic push from behind. Perhaps it was not such a bright idea after all. I'd have to walk behind him all the time.

Sudzarnt had arranged rooms for us and we were to be his special guests. He knew about the pick-up on Monday evening and was looking forward to seeing who the Bus Craft operator might be. Myzpazba had been the last one and he'd been quite a chatty fellow and Sudzarnt had enjoyed their inter Oannes style conversations in the B&B car park. But that was five days away and Simon said he'd like to visit the Seal Sanctuary and the Butterfly Centre near Cardigan. Both had connections with the Oannes. The seals were amphibious and the butterflies had their beautiful wings not too dissimilar to the vane on the back of every Oannes person. But those were my thoughts only.

Uncle Ron was more mobile than I had thought and got about very well with his Trike. We had proper verbal conversations throughout the day especially in the evenings after dinner. Simon wished to walk the coastal path and we were happy to oblige; usually in the afternoons after lunch.

On the first walk when we enquired at the Hillside Carriage house about Peter Ellis and his wife Fiona we learned that they had sold up and left years ago. The current residents were a young couple and had no idea as to their whereabouts. They had never met them since the property was vacant when they'd had their first viewing with the estate agent.

During our walks I often noticed Simon in a pensive frame of mind staring out to sea. There was probably little difference between the sailors of old and current spacemen. Both had an infinite field of vision with the unexpected just beyond the horizon.

It was a good mile to Tresaith Village and we did the walk several times. We usually returned via the upper Ffordd Tresaith Road which was a more direct route back to the B&B. On the way we passed the old church with its Lych-gate and I liked to stop under it for a brief contemplative rest. Sadly, dad had never got into his research on old churches as he had once wished though he'd kept up a lively interest. I remember that dad could never resist going into any old country church during our travels through the country. He'd always say that a stop there was good for the car as well as for the soul. Although I found these old chapels and churches dreary and damp, dad seemed to wander around inside them full of enthusiasm and wonder. He would point out the wall memorial plaques and tablets and say what a story they told. Personally as a young lad I'd found the rundown state of the interiors quite depressing. However as the antiques business interest took hold of me I reverted to my dad's feelings about such places and began to take a keener interest.

It was nice to conclude our coastal walk by returning via the Hoel Y Graig road back to the B&B to the nice tea that would be waiting for us. Sudzarnt always surprised us with his latest concoctions and I often had the feeling that I was treated as the special guest. I suppose I am special in his eyes but I like to think of myself as an ordinary fellow. I will not turn down any goodwill gesture as cakes, especially a Victoria Sponge are always welcome. Yet for all my gifts I am nothing without the benevolence of the benefactor who gave me these endowments.

We did manage to visit the Seal Sanctuary and the Butterfly Centre near Cardigan and did both on a single day's outing. Simon took everything in with a keenness that surprised me.

These last few days were a lasting pleasure for me and although Simon also enjoyed the time I could see that he was impatient for Monday to arrive. No doubt Mazpazam was as excited at the prospect of our arrival in Anztarza more so because of her reunion with Simon.

It was nice being in the company of Uncle Ron and Aunt Brenda and just chatting leisurely in the evenings. Uncle Ron tended to snooze during some of our conversations, but never if he was holding the floor about one of his national service yarns. Although these were repetitive it was nice to see how energetic he became in the telling. Aunt Brenda would roll her eyes upward when he began one of his stories.

However Monday finally arrived and it was nice to watch Simon's mood change to one of animated expectation. As usual we went for a short walk along the coastal path but turned about after half an hour to retrace our steps back to the B&B. Sudzarnt served up a sumptuous meal for us at 5:30pm and it was while we were sipping our tea and coffee that we received the communication that the pseudo bus craft 326-Red was on its way. It was nearly 8:00pm when it silently arrived in the B&B car park and Sudzarnt went out to meet it. We said our goodbyes to Ron and Brenda and slipped past the other guests to the car park. I said we'd stay a few days on our return and would keep in constant badge communication as usual. Sudzarnt communicated privately to me that the bus operator was a new one and not much of a communicator – so we'd best let him get on with his job without distraction. But when I got on I received a very friendly welcome and a big smile from the operator and I sensed an emotion of deep admiration emanating from him. So I asked him about himself and he was happy to elaborate. His name was Pazazato and he was 110 years of age and had been in Anztarza for six years. He originally came from a small town south of Wentazta and it was my regressed vision with Gozmanot that had awakened a desire to see Earth. So here he was.

Tania, Simon and I were the only passengers and without much ado were being sped over the darkness of the sea below towards the spaceship rendezvous. I must say I had half expected another passenger but Simon didn't show any such expectation. The journey was about half an hour when we slowed down and entered the shuttle bay of a somewhat smaller craft. One could estimate the size of the Oannes crafts from the shuttle bay volume and this one was about half the size we used to. We were escorted by two smart Oannes fellows to the control room where we were welcomed by a young looking Captain Miltoztona. The craft was 8854-Blue and was nearly 300 feet long and 240 feet wide with three deck levels. Captain Miltoztona had a pleasant manner and I took to him instantly. What lovely people all these Oannes are.

There was a near full moon that lit the clouds below us as we sped southwards at an altitude of about sixty miles. After a brief polite twenty minutes in the control room we were escorted to the public dining area and were served refreshments. Captain Miltoztona had conveyed that the journey would be about four hours to docking in Anztarza Bay. Two cabins had been allocated for our convenience but Simon was too keyed up and requested permission to spend the time with the crew in the control room. Of course that permission was granted and I could see that Simon was fully at home in this type of environment. He was a born spaceman and I think the captain recognised it too. The captain felt privileged that my son was also aboard. I guess reputations get passed on as Simon's must have been.

Earlier Tania and I had discussed our meeting with Mazpazam and we both expressed our concern about how we would greet the lady. I knew the Oannes etiquette but exact polite words would be hard to find.

'Why don't we just be ourselves and portray our human side,' said Tania. 'She already knows and likes everything about Simon or she wouldn't have wanted to be with him. So let's be polite and welcoming just as we would as if she were one of Rachel's friends.'

I thought it good advice and I was proud of Tania for saying it and I told her so.

I had also asked Simon about the agenda for when we were to meet Mazpazam. He said that he wasn't sure but Mazpazam would let him know. She had already changed her mind once about coming to meet us on the spaceship 8854-Blue with Captain Miltoztona. She was currently of two minds whether to meet us at the quayside or wait till the next day at our Anztarza accommodation. I guessed that the girl was quite nervous about not only meeting Simon's parents but of meeting me face to face. I was part of the legend and myth that arose from Gozmanot and so something of an anachronism to a young Oannes girl courting the son. A certain reputation was attached to my being and I must try to make Mazpazam feel comfortable in my presence. I smiled at the thought.

I knew that I felt a bit tired so decided to avail myself of the remaining journey hours for a good nap. Tania too agreed that a little sleep would be restful and refresh her before meeting her future daughter in law. While putting my head down I conveyed a quick request to Zanos on board to wake me half an hour before the craft was due to arrive in Anztarza Bay.

It seemed barely a moment before I was awake again. I queried the time and Zanos informed me of our approach to Anztarza Bay. Tania was still asleep so I gently nudged her and her eyes opened instantly.

'Is it time then?' she asked.

'Nearly,' I said, 'not long now.'

'I'd better tidy myself then,' she said and sat up to swing her legs off the bed.

I could see she was apprehensive so I conveyed a strong emotion of calm towards her. It settled her somewhat but not completely.

How could we be nervous about meeting our son's girlfriend; and yet so we were despite our recent discussion. I suppose it was for Simon's sake that we were both keen to make a good impression. I think Mazpazam must be equally nervous if not more so. I was the Ashley that every Oannes knew about and I had moved planets. And most of all I was reckoned to be the saviour of two worlds; Nazmos and Earth. If only I could communicate our good wishes I would. But I had not met her as yet so it would not be proper etiquette.

It was then that Simon conveyed to us that Mazpazam was not meeting us at the quayside after all and had decided that it was best if she was fetched by Simon later and came to meet us about mid-morning. I'm not sure if I was disappointed or relieved. I think Tania felt the same.

Twenty minutes later we were standing beside Simon in the control room. He must have sensed our apprehension and reaching out took a hand in each of his.

'Don't worry mum, she'll love you just as you are,' he said with a big smile. 'And you will love her too.'

'When do we meet her,' conveyed Tania, 'did she come to the quayside and then leave. Is she afraid of us?'

'No mum, she thought it better if you met at a private place. Anztarza Bay is too public as there will be a group of Oannes hoping to catch sight of you,' said Simon. 'We are to go to our usual accommodation for a proper nights rest. Then later about mid-morning I shall go to her and bring her back with me. It'll be just us then and we shall have all day to talk. You will like her mum and dad, I know you will. She is gentle and soft just like you mum.'

Tania smiled at this and squeezed her son's hand and I saw her shoulders relax a bit.

My own guess is that the change of plan had been Mazpazam's idea after realising that the hour would be late being well after our midnight. Not the best time to meet someone for the first time. She had probably discussed it with Simon and a daytime meeting had been agreed.

It was not long before the ship surfaced in Anztarza Bay and slowly moved to its mooring position. It was all very low key but word must have got around and there was a small group of Oannes folk gathered to see us. Humans don't visit Anztarza often especially someone of my reputation.

Simon, Tania and I took our leave of Captain Miltoztona after a brief Sewa thanking him for his hospitality and disembarked onto the quayside. We received many conveyed messages of welcome from the shore group as we walked to the waiting Deck Transporter. Once aboard and at the higher level I turned to face them and waved and thanked them for their welcoming reception. I conveyed that it was always a pleasure to visit Anztarza, an outpost of distant Nazmos.

The Transporter took us straight to Dome-7 where we alighted in the plaza area. The dome lighting had dimmed to conform to the simulated night period which as always conformed in time to GMT. We made the short walk to the dome wall near where our accommodation was located. As we approached the house we were received outside it by our old friends Laztraban and Niktukaz with beaming smiles on their faces and pleasant Sewas were exchanged. Laztraban was now 240 years of age and I noticed some age shading on his face and arms. Niktukaz at her 210 years seemed unchanged in her appearance.

We were taken inside and a light supper was provided. We sat and talked verbally for about three quarters of an hour before deciding that we must regulate our body clocks with some sleep time. It was 1:30am GMT so without much ado we retired to our usual bedroom. Our hosts were in the accommodation next door and would see us at breakfast.

Simon also said goodnight and said he'd probably miss us at breakfast as he wanted to be out early to fetch his Mazpazam to us. I guessed that he didn't want to waste much time getting back to her. He conveyed that she and other crew were housed in the usual accommodation reserved for visiting starships in the general quarters in Dome-10. Simon had requested that Mazpazam be re-housed with Niktukaz and Laztraban but only after she had met us.

I'd slept for a couple of hours on the spaceship 8854-Blue and now I had difficulty getting to sleep again. But I put this down mainly to a concern about how I would welcome my son's girlfriend. Perhaps the less said the better. I think I'll let Tania take the lead as she is good with meeting people. Eventually I dozed off but it was a restless sleep and I was glad when the dome declared daytime. I could hear movement in the dining area so I rose quietly and went to see who was there. It was Simon and Niktukaz enjoying a drink of Wazu at the table.

I sometimes wonder if I have an addiction to tea. I find it to be one of the most satisfying of drinks especially first thing in the mornings. I actually crave for that mug of sweet tea when I awake. Of course a second mug must follow the first though the law of diminishing returns seems to come into play. Later in the day I'm not too bothered and have a mug purely through habit mainly after a meal.

Niktukaz knew me well and before long I was sitting and talking to my son with a steaming mug of tea in front of me. Halfway through this we went through a momentary lull in our conversation and I suspected that a communication was being received by Simon for a smile expression appeared on his face.

'I'd better go dad,' he said, 'she's asking if I'm on my way.'

Just then Tania walked in and stood behind me. She put her hands on my shoulders before raising one hand up to her mouth to stifle a yawn. A big breathed out sigh followed this.

'Morning mum,' said Simon, 'I'm just off to fetch Mazpazam. She's keen to come over as planned. No change of plans anymore.'

'How long will you be in getting back,' asked Tania.

'Since you've just got up mum we'll make it for about an hour. So have your breakfast in peace and don't rush. I'll communicate our every movement.'

'Thanks son,' said Tania, 'I feel quite nice about it all now.'

'She's a lovely girl mum, you'll see,' he said and came and gave his mum a kiss before turning about and striding out of the room.

It was nearly an hour later that we received the communication that they were on their way. We'd showered and got into our best tunic outfits – Tania selected one for me –after we'd had a light breakfast. Tania suggested we remain indoors for the sake of privacy to which I agreed.

'We have arrived in the plaza and will be with you in about five minutes,' was the communication from Simon which brought the colour to Tania's cheeks.

Laztraban and Niktukaz conveyed that they would retreat to their own accommodation and leave us to our family affairs. They left then without another word though both had smiles on their faces. There is very little that stays private in the Oannes world.

Tania and I walked around the table and stood facing the entrance door. Tania fumbled for and caught hold of my hand and squeezed.

Simon announced their arrival with a light rat-a-tat on the door before opening it slowly and walking in ahead of his girl. Mazpazam then appeared from behind Simon with a forced smile on her face. I did not feel it odd that she was so tiny; barely five feet in height and slightly built; and what a pretty face she possessed and such a glorious smile. I was taken in by her immediately and so was Tania from the way she squeezed my hand. I looked at Tania and I could see she felt just as I did. I experienced a joy in my chest of pure emotion which must have filled the room for Mazpazam relaxed visibly. I think her smile had been a façade to hide the inner nervousness she felt.

She now took a step forward but Tania was already moving rapidly towards Mazpazam with both hands extended.

'My dear Mazpazam,' said Tania grasping both of the girls hands, 'welcome, welcome, welcome. It is so lovely to finally meet you,'

Tania looked Mazpazam up and down and then turned to me for a quick look and then back at this pretty Oannes lady. Simon's lady.

'You are the most beautiful thing ever,' she said to Mazpazam,' and what a gorgeous outfit you are wearing. The green and gold just suits you,'

'Thank you,' said Mazpazam in a voice that could have been human, 'you are very kind.'

This time her smile was genuine and I think I fell a bit in love with it. Although small, her facial features were broad and eyes wide set. I then walked forward and put a light hand on her shoulder.

'My dear Mazpazam,' I said quietly, 'Tania and I have looked forward to this moment but I never imagined what a joy it would be to actually meet you face to face. Simon has told us of you but not a lot, so I look forward to getting to know you better during our stay here in Anztarza. Simon makes us laugh and I'm sure we shall all enjoy his humour together.'

Mazpazam looked up at me and I at once noted her beautiful dusky green eyes. Most Oannes had light coloured eyes in a greyish shade with green or blue tinting. Mazpazam's were mainly green with flecks of grey. She blinked as she saw my expression and smiled with pleasure. No woman misses the look of a man who admires her.

Simon was now standing behind his lady and placed his hand on her shoulder where mine had just been.

'Mum, dad,' he said, 'please let me belatedly introduce my Mazpazam to you.'

Then to Mazpazam he said, 'Mazpazam these are my parents and I know you will come to love them as I do.'

My heart did a flip at the joyous sound of the low chuckle that emanated from Mazpazam.

'You would say that Simon,' she whispered. 'Everyone says that about their parents.'

Simon was glowing with pride and looking at him I don't know where my next words came from.

'Simon you look like someone gave you the moon and stars to hold. And I can see why, for she even takes my breath away,' I heard my voice say.

Mazpazam looked backwards up at Simon and her hand went up to her shoulder to rest on his already there. There was pure love in the glance and the wistful smile between them said more than words needed to say.

'You are most kind in your welcome of me,' she said to me in that earthy voice, 'and it is lovely to meet you. I already know of you but now I am seeing the real you. However, as Simon's parents I should like to know the manner in which I may address you. It would not be proper for me to call you by your names since Simon does not.'

I couldn't help but raise my head and give a little laugh. I suppose I must have looked a bit like Simon in that for he often threw back his head when he laughed.

'My dear Mazpazam please excuse me,' I said on a more sombre note, 'how do people on Nazmos and here in Anztarza refer to me when they discuss me?'

'Oh, you are Ashley,' she said smiling. 'Everyone knows you as Ashley.'

'Good,' I said, 'then we shall continue with the same. We shall simply be Ashley and Tania to you if you like. And there you have one up on Simon for he can never call us that. To him we are just mum and dad.'

Simon burst into loud laughter and Mazpazam gave him a stern look before also breaking into a smile. She could see the funny side of it.

It was Tania's turn to enter the fray.

'Come here you,' she said to Mazpazam, 'it's time I got a hug from my son's girl.'

Tania leaned forward and put her arms gently and carefully around Mazpazam and kissed her on both cheeks. I could see that Mazpazam also hugged Tania in return with quite a firm squeeze.

I decided to follow suit and also gave Mazpazam a light kiss on each cheek. My thoughts must have strayed for in my mind came the memory of Muznant at our first meeting in the Aberporth B&B and the kiss she bestowed on my lips then. Mazpazam must have read my thought and reaching up she pulled my head down to her level and quickly planted a light kiss on my lips.

'That is to remind you of your first Oannes kiss,' she said. 'I shall convey this to Muznant at the appropriate time.'

I was speechless and looked at Tania with embarrassment and for support. But she just smiled as did Simon. And then he threw back his head and laughed.

'Dad,' he said when he regained his composure, 'you should have seen the look on your face. It was a sight to remember. Well done Mazpazam as few have been able to throw dad off balance.'

'I'm sorry,' said a puzzled Mazpazam, 'I did not intend to offend.'

'You did nothing of the sort my girl,' said Simon still smiling, 'and I'm sure dad will remember you for it. It was nice of you to bring a little joy into an old man's heart.'

'Hold on my boy,' I said, 'a little less of the 'old man' please. And Mazpazam I am not in the least bit offended. Rather I take it as a compliment from a very pretty woman. Thank you very much.'

'I still need to decide how to address Simon's parents,' said Mazpazam in open thought.

There was a brief pause when I could see her mind working on this.

'We Oannes have studied your customs on Earth for a very long time,' she said. 'I have reviewed these and I like the way in which politeness comes across in the Asian countries especially India. When they meet their elders the young people simply refer to them as Uncle or Auntie. As familiarity grows between them a name may be added. I should very much like to do the same if that is acceptable.'

I thought about this and looking at Tania and then at Mazpazam I smiled and nodded.

'I should like that very much,' said Tania echoing my own thoughts.

'Uncle Ashley and Auntie Tania,' she rolled the words for effect, 'I will call you like that for I want to be different from other Oannes. Uncle Ashley, on Nazmos you are respected and revered by more than you can imagine. Although you have a prodigious reputation you also portray a very plain image. At one time at the academy I was against you and Simon for the influence I thought you had exerted in placing your son in an advantageous position. Entrance into the academy is by merit only and I begrudged Simon his place. But that was a wrong assumption on my part and I am sorry for it. I have since seen that Simon has a special talent and earned that place for himself. Then I learned about you from others with whom I communicated. With your tremendous gifts you could have had both worlds at your feet. But you have never sought honours or fame and I grew to admire and respect your ideals. Then I got to see Simon in a different light and he is very much like his father. We became friends and now I am here with him and he has brought me to meet you. I look forward to meeting his sister Rachel also when we are on the starship Silverstreak.'

There was no hesitancy in her manner and I could see that the academy taught its officers well. She had a certain bearing about her that reminded me of Captain Bulzezatna. She would make a good spaceship captain and partner to Simon.

'Thank you,' came from Mazpazam for again she had picked up on my thoughts.

'Gosh,' I remarked to no one in particular, 'you make me feel quite important. I feel as if a great honour has been bestowed upon me. No one has put those feelings into words quite as you have done Mazpazam and I am thankful to you for it. I hope it doesn't go to my head.'

'Dad,' said Simon, 'you are the greatest and always will be. No one knows it better than me.'

Tania snuggled up to me and we tightened our grip around each others waists. I planted a light kiss on the top of her head and she looked up at me. 'I love you Ashley Bonner,' she conveyed privately.

Mazpazam was taking all this in and I could see understanding growing in her mind about this family. I had always portrayed a low key role for my gifts and never advertised their existence. In fact dad and granddad had impressed upon me that I keep it all secret. And so I have. I have only used my gifts for good purposes and restricted its use. On Earth I have kept secret from the general public of the existence of Anztarza and Nazmos. The one thing I have desired on Earth is for more people to acquire the art of telepathy. This I believe to be the key for our eventual integration with the Oannes who are morally, culturally and scientifically far in advance of us. It was 20,000 years ago that the Oannes first ventured into space and Earth is at a comparable stage only now.

My reputation preceded me and probably drew Mazpazam towards her relationship with Simon. But she must have liked what she saw in him and the rest is history.

Quietly our hosts Laztraban and Niktukaz entered the room carrying jugs of Wazu and glasses which they placed on the table behind us.

'A family meeting such as this deserves a celebration,' said Niktukaz before they both slipped out back to their apartment.

Tania played hostess and asked us to come and sit around the table. Simon and Mazpazam sat together while Tania and I sat facing them with quite joyful expressions on our faces.

'Let me pour,' said Tania as she filled four glasses and placed one in front of each of us.

'Cheers and good health,' I said raising my glass in the air.

The others did the same as I touched my glass against Tania's. I then reached across and did the same to Simon and a smiling Mazpazam. She then clinked with Simon's glass and then Tania's.

'Cheers and good health,' I repeated as we all took a sip of our Wazu.

This was repeated in turn by Simon and Tania. I waited to see if Mazpazam wished to add something of her own. We had remained seated in proposing our toasts but Mazpazam now stood up with raised glass.

'Cheers and good health. May all our journeys together be swift, sure and safe,' she said in her earthy voice while looking at Simon.

'Well said,' came from Simon as we all took another sip of our drink.

Mazpazam had added the motto I had given long ago on my first starship journey with Captain Natazlat. I liked that she had added the word 'together' as reference to her life journey with Simon.

'Thank you Mazpazam,' I said, 'it is nice to know that what I proposed as an off the cuff toast on my first FTL journey under Captain Natazlat has become a pre-flight maxim with the Nazmos space fleet.'

Mazpazam looked at me with renewed interest before turning her gaze to Simon.

'You didn't tell me that it was your father who gave us our pre-flight motto,' she said in a soft accusing voice.

'That's because I did not know,' said Simon. 'Dad never talks about such things.'

'Simon is right,' I said, 'I never mentioned it because I did not think it important. It was October 2016 and the starship 9110-Red was about to commence its journey back to Nazmos with me as the only human aboard. The Nazmos governing council had allowed for me alone to set foot on Nazmos so my family did not accompany me. Captain Natazlat had initially been surprised at my proposal to accelerate her starship to the unthinkable velocity of 200 FTL and showed initial annoyance. So before we started the journey I proposed this toast with the captain and her deputies. It was something that I said from the top of my head that the coming journey be swift, sure and safe. The word 'swift' was mentioned because I hoped to accelerate the starship to the unheard of velocity of 200 FTL, something I had never done before. Even to me this was then an uncertainty. At first Captain Natazlat had been horrified at the proposal but Zanos had confirmed that it was compatible with its functions. The 'sure' and 'safe' meant for a direct path to our Nazmos destination that was clear of obstacles or events. So there you have it folks.'

I thought I saw a glow of pride appear on the face of Mazpazam as she continued looking directly at me. I could sense the emotion within her filling the room and I felt faintly embarrassed by it.

'Thank you Uncle Ashley,' she said aloud, 'it is nice to know that. May I relay its origin to my colleagues when I see them?'

I smiled at the manner of her address. It seemed very normal and I liked it. Only Fiona, Sarah and Brian called me that. Oh yes, and sometimes little Adam.

'Of course you may,' I replied, 'but you must remember that it was a chance expression that has become what it is.'

I think I definitely have an admirer in Simon's girl and I also know that Tania and I have taken to her in an immense way. She is straightforward in her manner which is so much like our son Simon. Mazpazam had a distinct aura of confidence about her that displayed a latent authority in her attitude. She and Simon have a lot in common character-wise and I'm certain they will never become bored of communicating with each another.

There were many general issue questions I wanted to ask regarding her likes and dislikes and Mazpazam talked freely about them all. She was quite a gossip and seemed to know a lot about other Oannes' business. She had an encyclopaedic memory of who was who in the space fleet and her historical facts went back to the initiation of the Oannes space program. We talked verbally about her ambitions and she said that when she joined the Nazmos Space Academy these had been immature. Essentially then she had simply wanted to be in charge of a spaceship of her own. But meeting Simon had changed that perspective and she knew that there were other important issues in life. She spoke frankly that she and Simon could never have a family but the same applied to many Oannes couples too.

'This way I shall have Simon all to myself,' she said smiling.

I remembered our discussion with Simon and Mazpazam must have picked up my thoughts. She had a special skill in that area.

'Although our life spans are different,' she said, 'that will not prevent us from enjoying and remembering every moment we have together.'

I did like this Oannes lady and I admired her forthright approach. She was someone who called a spade a spade.

I knew that a low-key banquet was arranged for tomorrow in Dome-4. So I queried Mazpazam and Simon if there was anything special being set up. I did not want any surprises and wondered if they knew anything about the planned events. I find fawning surprises rather embarrassing.

Simon looked at Mazpazam as if making a query and then turned to us.

'Mom, dad, it's like this,' he said slowly. 'I have asked Mazpazam to become my wife in a legal partnership contract. She has said yes and so we approached the chief ministers for their permission. This was immediately after our little talk which Mazpazam knew about.'

There was a brief moment of silence before Simon continued.

'Regretfully permission could not be granted,' said Simon, 'but this was not because they did not wish to. No, it was because they did not have the authority. There is no precedent for such a case and they must refer this to the Nazmos governing council. They will however attach a favourable recommendation. Senior chief minister Tzatzorf will announce our intentions at the banquet tomorrow. It will be a sort of local approval for everyone to know.'

At this piece of news both Tania and I were thrilled and our emotions showed it. Tania then got up and walked round the table to hug her son as well as Mazpazam.

'Congratulations to you both,' she said and I noticed her trying to blink away a tear. 'I'm so pleased for you and for us. Simon son you have chosen well because Mazpazam is perfect for you.'

'Yes,' was all I could say as I too walked around the table and gave them my hug.

I then immediately conveyed the news to all our family through my communication badge and instantly there came messages of congratulations from everyone. There was a very special one from Sudzarnt.

'You are both to be congratulated,' he conveyed, 'for it shows how compatible humans and Oannes really are. This will be marked as an historical event in the lead up to eventual deeper integration.'

Both Simon and Mazpazam conveyed their thanks to each person in turn.

The atmosphere in the house changed to one of a relaxed mood as we talked about things in general. There was no embarrassment when the subject of children was mentioned. Tania and I were not concerned that there could be no children due to the difference in the human and Oannes genome and both Simon and Mazpazam were indifferent towards it. Mazpazam conveyed the statistic that most Oannes couples remained childless through choice. And so it would have been their choice too not to have children even if it were possible.

It was Tania who raised the next issue.

'When your partnership contract has been approved and made a fact,' said Tania, 'what are your residential plans?'

Mazpazam smiled and said that they intended to live in Wentazta when not on spaceship duty.

'Because of our professional status we would be credited with certain rights,' she added. 'And these rights would allow us to choose an accommodation accordingly. In our current junior officer status we could expect a house or apartment similar to what we have here. Of course certain modifications would have to be undertaken for our sleep conditions. I cannot sleep on a bed and nor can Simon in a sleep tank. We have discussed it together and are happy with the situation. Simon's bed will be in the same room as the sleep tank and I shall be able to watch him in his slumber just as he will be able to view me in my sleep tank.'

I couldn't help thinking about Ritozanan in her sleep tank and also Gozmanot in hers. It came to me that the Oannes had a most convenient and comfortable mode for their sleep periods. To be without weight was ideal for the relaxation of ones physical body. My mind wandered to the time when Tania and I frolicked in one such sleep tank. I think it was on one of the trips to the asteroids in the spaceship 520-Green under the command of Captain Bulzezatna. I conveyed this privately to Tania and she immediately gave me a dig in the ribs though I saw her face light up in a knowing smile. I hope I had shielded my thoughts from Mazpazam's discerning mind but I could not be sure. Anyway she was too polite to indicate anything though I'm sure it would increase her understanding and perception of humans.

Subsequently we had a most pleasant day and later enjoyed an evening meal at which we insisted that our hosts Niktukaz and Laztraban be present.

The night time arrangements were in proper form with Simon in his own room and Mazpazam in a sleep tank in our hosts' house. Oannes decorum was fiercely maintained.

In the morning we assembled for breakfast at our leisure as the Dome-4 banquet with the chief ministers was not until late afternoon.

Niktukaz came in later with new outfits that had just been delivered. There were several apiece and I assumed that because of our prolonged stay in Anztarza these had been specially made. This was most considerate of the chief ministers and I immediately conveyed my thanks to them. I noticed that these were made from a different material to those supplied to us previously. Niktukaz conveyed that the material was simply that procured from shops on Earth that were more suited to our comfort. Since humans did not require clothes to be proof against wetness then it had been decided to use materials similar to what we normally wore. A stock of Earth cloths would be sent to Nazmos with us on the starship Silverstreak.

I chose my outfit from among those presented as I liked the lime green one with gold edged trim. Tania says that the colour combination quite suited me.

The banquet was a great success and we met many friends from previous visits. Everyone in Anztarza knew us but I could only name a few. The chief ministers made a great show of acknowledging Simon and Mazpazam as a couple and ceremoniously handed a large encased package to Simon as a gift from the people of Anztarza on the occasion of their intended partnership contract.

After the meal had been cleared away a general mingling of humans and Oannes took place in a very easy and congenial atmosphere. Simon took the opportunity of introducing us to several of his starship's officers and crew. I conveyed that we were pleased to meet all of them. When I enquired after his starship Captain Wastanomi I was told that he was not on Earth but that I would certainly meet him when we boarded Silverstreak for the journey to Nazmos.

Simon conveyed a private message to me and I was rather surprised by it. Some of the starship crew had requested Simon if he could persuade me to demonstrate my telekinetic gift in some small way. Perhaps moving a small object placed on a table or something similar.

Now I do not like exhibiting my gifts as they were not meant for display purposes but I also did not wish to offend by refusing their request. I had done a demonstration for Fiona, Sarah and Brian when I had first revealed myself to them so I suppose I could do something similar. I did not want to be too dramatic but then a mischievous thought occurred to me where all could actually feel the effect of a push upon their person.

I stood up and addressed the chief ministers and requested permission to proceed. They gave their enthusiastic consent so I conveyed to the entire assembly in the banquet area the tale of an incident that took place long before I knew of Anztarza and the Oannes people. I told them of the action I had taken against the three Brown Hills New Town hooligans way back in the year 2003. I remember that my sister Katy was with me at the time and she was quite pleased by the result. The three nasty boys whose average age was twelve got into a terrified panic and were forced to apologise to the residents of Park View Drive for their behaviour.

An excited buzz filled the area as I made my way to stand in front of where the chief ministers and their wives were seated. I stood with my back to their table and faced the assembly. Tania, Simon and Mazpazam came and stood beside me. I then conveyed a message for all to move to the far side of the area. This was done promptly and I could see excitement on many faces. Apprehension was also present on some.

'I now want about ten members of the starship complement to approach me,' I said.

The Oannes are extremely disciplined and without much ado exactly ten of their number stepped forward and began a slow walk towards me. When they had got about halfway up the area I willed that a gentle telekinetic push be applied upon each of them as a blanket pressure to prevent them from coming any closer. As one they all stopped where they were at that instant.

There was a surprised look on their faces as they tried to move forward but could not. Try as they might they found that an invisible barrier was keeping them at bay.

To make the demonstration more exciting for them I willed for my telekinetic effort to be increased slightly so as to cause them to be pushed backwards but for a few paces only.

There was even greater surprise on their faces as they were forced to shuffle backwards against their will. I then willed for all telekinetic effort to cease and called for them to come to me. They took hesitant steps at first before realising that there was nothing stopping them. I then told them to come and stand behind me to witness the reaction of the next batch of volunteers.

I repeated the process several times much to the amazement and amusement of the viewers. The Oannes are very contained and do not exhibit laughter like us humans. But their humorous emotional state came through to me quite clearly.

After an hour of demonstrations I conveyed that I was becoming fatigued and so must stop the performance. I could see many disappointed faces but Oannes are too polite to remonstrate. They all however conveyed their thanks for being allowed to witness such a demonstration of one of my gifts. Simon said to me that most of the Oannes present were space persons either from Silverstreak or from other local spaceships. I did not recognise any from Captain Bulzezatna's ship 520-Green.

However many of them came forward to communicate with me though they were hesitant about speaking verbally. All my replies to their queries were however verbal just to encourage them. Many subsequently did though with a great amount of hesitation when they began.

There was one Oannes gentleman who intrigued me when he asked me about my disposition after each telekinetic effort. It was the first time I had been asked such a question. It was an answer I found difficult to explain easily so communicated to him that it all depended upon the extent of the effort. I suggested to him that he read my memories especially those involved in the movement of the asteroids and then the planets Platwuz and their own Nazmos. So I put out my hand to him and he grasped it firmly like it was a handshake gesture. After several seconds he began nodding his head before commenting.

'I understand,' he said in a soft singsong of a voice, 'you have progressively increased in your telekinetic strength over the years. Let me introduce myself. I am Lazinbraz and I am a medical person. So I am what among your people you would call a doctor. I have been here in Anztarza for five years only and am required to fulfil my tenure of twenty. I am 160 years of age and I find Earth fascinating. The northern forests are an excellent recreation ground for me and I visit there at least twice each year. I would go more often but it is restricted. There is much our medical services can do for you on Earth but we are not permitted to interfere. In the past though we have given research prompts only where research was already progressing. I wish you every success with your efforts against Zarama.'

'Thank you,' I said and called Tania over to meet him.

We talked generally for a while before he politely excused himself and said he had duties to attend. I sensed he was someone I would meet again.

Tania and I then walked over to where the chief ministers and their wives sat and I expressed my thanks for a wonderful reception and a fascinating evening. They all expressed delight at my telekinetic demonstrations and wished me success with the coming events with Nazmos and then with Zarama.

'It will be our success,' I said, 'and I pray that it all works out for the best.'

'Nazmos will never be the same again,' said chief minister Rymtakza whose wife Mizpalta sat beside him, 'and there are some who do not like change. I for one am for a new Nazmos but I do not suppose that I shall see the real changes.'

'Few will who are living today,' I said, 'but the long term prospects are favourable. Gozmanot had a dream vision and we have all seen what that was.'

'Yes,' replied the chief minister, 'we can never forget Gozmanot. She will be remembered for the vision she gave us thanks to you Ashley for its revelation.'

'Thank you chief minister,' I said, 'she certainly was one very great lady.'

And I could see Mizpalta agreeing to that.

Simon and Mazpazam then came and stood to one side and slightly behind Tania and me but the chief minister Tzatzorf now aged 250 years called them forward.

'It is a great thing that has happened between you two,' he said to Simon. 'You walk in your father's footsteps and have the admiration of the Oannes people. You too have a special gift so look after your father on his trip out to Zarama and see that you bring him back safely - if that is possible.'

This last was added as an afterthought.

'That I will do chief minister,' said Simon, 'I will make it my only aim on that trip.'

'Make sure you do,' said Tzatzorf, 'make sure that you do.'

Then he turned to Mazpazam and beckoned her toward him.

'And you my young Oannes lady,' he said, 'you have a burden to bear. You must keep to this partnership with honour and fortitude. All of Nazmos will be looking upon you so behave correctly. This will be a first and must lead the way for any future integration.'

'That I will as I never want to be parted from Simon,' said Mazpazam. 'We have much in common and it is as if this too was foreseen by Gozmanot.'

'Nevertheless,' said Tzatzorf, 'taking into account the human lifespan we have recommended that your partnership contract be limited to a period of sixty years.'

Simon looked at me and nodded. He then conveyed the normal rules for an Oannes partnership which stated an unlimited period or until one or other of the participants became deceased. Simon also conveyed that this condition was acceptable to him and that if he was still fit and well at the ripe human age of ninety six then he would be happy to let Mazpazam still young at age 130 years make the necessary decision.

I think I knew exactly what Simon meant.

He then took Mazpazam's hand and conveyed a private message to her. Together they took a step forward to face the chief minister's table.

'Thank you chief minister,' Simon said, 'that is most generous. Mazpazam and I agree to participate in such a partnership contract and I hope that I live beyond normal expectations. A few humans have reached 120 years in age but that has been a rare occurrence.'

Simon and Mazpazam stepped back to their former positions as the chief ministers' entourage rose as one and slowly left the dais to walk towards the partitioned exit. This was the signal that the proceedings had ended and the hall area emptied gradually.

We four then returned to our Dome -7 lodgings and after a mug of tea and a chat retired to our rooms. Simon and Mazpazam sat alone and conversed telepathically until they also decided to retire. Mazpazam went to her sleep tank in our hosts' house and Simon to his bed in the room near ours.

The remaining days in Anztarza were spent in the constant company of our son and his lady Mazpazam while visiting friends and touring the various domes.

Finally the time came for our return home to Dudley on Saturday November 4th and Simon said that he intended to stay another week and then return to us. He conveyed that he and Mazpazam wished to visit the northern forests and that there were things they'd like to experience together.

Tania and I said we understood.

'Don't worry mum,' he said to Tania, 'I hope to spend the rest of my time on Earth with you and dad. It is years since I did any Christmas shopping and I want to experience it all anew.'

I had a funny feeling that Simon was up to something but I hadn't the slightest inkling of what that could be. But I did know that it would be a bit like old times with us all together for Christmas.

It was to be the same spacecraft 8854-Blue under Captain Miltoztona that would ferry us back to Aberporth. I was pleasantly surprised when Simon said that he and Mazpazam would accompany us for the ride. Mazpazam loved to look down at the colourful views of Earth both by day and by night. She said it was so different from Nazmos.

The journey was uneventful as usual and when we said our farewells to the captain and crew in the control room Simon conveyed that he would accompany us on the bus craft for the short trip to the B&B. There was a curious smile illuminating his face and I think I guessed what he intended. Mazpazam was nowhere to be seen so I conveyed a farewell message to her and she instantly replied likewise. She would see us again soon she also conveyed. I had the oddest impression that something was brewing but said nothing to Tania.

What we did not know was that Mazpazam was also aboard the bus craft but in the disguise that Muznant and Brazjaf were wearing at our first meeting. I wondered why Pazazato had such a broad smile on his face as we boarded. It was only when Simon went and sat beside this human looking stranger that I realised that it was someone in disguise.

'Mum, dad,' said Simon as he sat down, 'Mazpazam wished to see you right to the B&B and I agreed. However I thought it a good opportunity for her to meet the rest of the family so I contacted them all a while ago from Anztarza. Rachel, Aunty Katy and Uncle Robin and Fiona, Sarah and Brian and Adam are all there at the B&B as of now. Also there are Grandmas Lillian and Milly and Grandpa Jerry. Grandpa Alex was not able to travel so a live-in carer is staying with him till grandma Lillian gets back. Currently there is only one paying guest at the B&B but she is elderly and would have gone to her room for the night. It will be nearly midnight when we arrive at the B&B. Aunt Brenda and Uncle Ron not to mention Sudzarnt were quite excited when I asked them to arrange it all.'

Simon paused and smiled broadly before he continued.

'So you see we shall have the entire lounge to ourselves and Mazpazam can remove her disguise so all can see the wonderful girl that I love. And Mazpazam will get to meet my family too.'

I was elated at this bit of news and decided to communicate my joy. One by one they responded and it sounded like a school roll call.

'We are all here except for Alex,' conveyed Milly, 'but I think Sudzarnt is beside himself with excitement and the anticipation of meeting a fellow Oannes. He's organised everything for our comfort and keeps fussing.'

The bus craft sped over the sea at low level and I could make out lights ahead which I took to be Aberporth. We crossed the shoreline at slow speed in total darkness and quickly settled onto the roadway that led up into the houses area and made our slow way towards the B&B.

Pazazato finally drove into the car park and manoeuvred right up to the B&B entrance. After we had disembarked Pazazato conveyed that he would once again head out to sea but remain close enough to return when called. As such the bus craft turned about and left the car park by the same route towards the sea.

It was a cold chilly night with a touch of frost in the air and I could see that Mazpazam was pleasantly surprised at the conditions.

'Will Nazmos be like this even when it is closer to Raznat,' was the query from her to Simon.

Simon quickly conveyed that the seasons were both hot and cold in England mainly due to the inclination of the Earth as it orbited the Sun.

'It is what gives us our summer and winter seasons,' said Simon, 'and you will find the northern forests much colder than this at this time of year.'

It was one thing being told about what conditions were like but quite another to actually experience them in true life were the thoughts I read in Mazpazam's mind.

We then entered the B&B hallway and were welcomed first by Sudzarnt and then by the others as we progressed into the main lounge area. There was curiosity written all over their faces and Simon laughed and said for them to be patient.

Mazpazam slowly began to remove the overcoat she wore and then the loose fitting trousers to show the green and gold tunic and leggings of normal Oannes dress that we all knew so well; pale green in the main but with a gold trim at the edges. It was similar to the outfit she had worn when Tania and I first met her. The colours suited her perfectly – especially in matching her green eyes flecked with grey.

She then turned to Simon and signalled that she was ready.

Simon moved up behind her and put his hands into the thick mop of hair on her head. His hands searched for and found the hidden flap and slowly he peeled it sideways. There was a faint suction sound and then Mazpazam reached up and moved Simon's hand aside. Very slowly and carefully Mazpazam began to stretch and peel off the well fitting face mask. Gradually as the entire mask came away her own features were revealed in all its natural beauty.

The face mask was of thin flexible material and pale pink in colour. It had openings for eyes, nostrils and mouth and looked very realistic. The head had a well groomed ladies hair style that appeared quite natural. It was a vast improvement on the mask that Muznant and Brazjaf had worn that November evening in 2003.

Sudzarnt then came forward with a bowl containing a large damp towel which Mazpazam used to carefully and thoroughly wipe her face, head and neck.

'That feels better,' she said slowly in her low almost earthy human voice before looking around the room full of smiling people; and she smiled too.

'Good evening and hello to you all,' she said in the same quiet manner, 'thank you for coming to meet me. Simon has told me all about each of you and I am very pleased to be meeting you in person.'

Simon was glowing with pride as he took Mazpazam by the hand and led her to each person in turn.

Of course everyone was taller than her and she made a point of looking up into each and every face. When Mazpazam came to Rachel they put their arms around one another in a fierce hug and a lengthy communication occurred that was private of course. They then stepped back and both smiled with pleasure. Rachel then went and hugged her brother and stayed beside him smiling.

Sudzarnt was about the same height but Mazpazam was so very much lighter in build. It took a while to progress around to everyone as all wanted to converse with this beautiful Oannes lady whom Simon had chosen as his partner.

But it was when Mazpazam came to meet little Adam that she showed her sense of humour.

'Ah,' she said looking down upon Adam, 'at last I meet someone who is littler than me.'

Adam was three years old and tall for his age. He was nearly half Mazpazam's height and didn't say anything but gave Simon a big smile before turning back to hide his blond head in his mum's dress.

Everyone laughed which eased the expectant atmosphere in the room. Meeting someone new for the first time had its own bit of suspense.

The Oannes people were no strangers to my family members since all here had travelled to Nazmos and Anztarza at one time or another. Adam was the only one who had never seen an Oannes person before but for him Mazpazam's beauty would have been a captivating aspect to win him over.

Adam now shyly glanced sideways at Mazpazam to see if she were real. I noticed the hint of a smile on his cherubic face and I knew instantly that Mazpazam had his approval. I conveyed my thoughts to Mazpazam and she replied that she would wait before making any approach to Adam. Mazpazam was also captivated not only by Adam's smallness but also by the shock of blond hair on his head.

As the initial newness of meeting Simon's lady faded everyone became quite relaxed. It was Milly who then went up to Mazpazam and took hold of both her small hands in hers.

'Dear Mazpazam,' she said, 'you are truly beautiful and our Simon is a very lucky man to be chosen by you. I know that you will be very happy together.'

Then Lillian also came up beside Milly and repeated more of the same complimentary remarks.

Mazpazam looked carefully at Lillian with eyes that were full of open admiration.

'I have been fortunate in my life,' she said to Lillian and Milly. 'Firstly I meet Simon by chance when he came to the space academy. I did not like him at first. Then I got to recognise and admire his skills as a space cadet and finally got to know the person that he was. Gradually affection developed until love grew between us. Simon is unassuming and in that he is a lot like his father; someone that all of Nazmos admires. In Anztarza I met Simon's parents and I must confess with a little trepidation for Uncle Ashley's reputation of achievement is widely known. But they are ordinary in their behaviour and I came to like them very much. And now here before me I have Simon's grandparents and most of his family and I find you all most charming. You have made me feel very comfortable in your presence. Thank you.'

Then looking at Lillian she said, 'You are Ashley's mother and it must have been a great burden for you to bear when you saw the gifts he had and realised that a destiny lay before him.'

Mum could stand it no longer and her emotion broke through as she went forward with blurry eyes and hugged Mazpazam. 'I will love you as one of my own from now on. Only a mother can understand what mothers have to contend with when mystery surrounds their only son.'

Mazpazam said nothing but conveyed to Lillian an emotion of calmness and love which came through to all of us in the room.

Then Jerry stepped forward when mum had released Mazpazam. He put his arms around Milly and mum and said, 'Dear Mazpazam, I am glad you came here to meet us. I'm Jerry, Tania's father and Simon's maternal grandfather. Sadly, Ashley's father Alex could not be here today due to age and ill health but he said for me to convey has best wishes.'

'Thank you,' said Mazpazam. 'Yes, Simon has told me all about his grandfather. His is a very good age at ninety. In Oannes terms that is similar to our age of 360 years. I would be lucky to reach such an age as few achieve that number.'

I remembered Ritozanan having passed away at 333 years of age. She had become frail in her last years and my last memory of her in her sleep tank will always stay with me. There were exceptions also in Zazfrapiz and Jazzatnit who are 353 and 352 respectively and still going strong. However Zazfrapiz was showing signs of old age when I last saw him in 2039. His regular communications to me showed him needing long periods of rest during the day. Jazzatnit seemed to be faring better though she too was slowing down. Age comes to all of us sooner or later.

Gozmanot was an exception having reached five hundred years. I wondered how the Rimzi fared in their age process from living under the sea. Was it the same?

Sudzarnt brought soft drinks for us all so that a toast could be offered if need be. I know he thought it a great event when a human and an Oannes entered a legal contractual partnership as Simon and Mazpazam intended. So it was Sudzarnt who finally proposed a toast.

'Ladies and gentlemen,' he said aloud, 'please raise your glasses with me in wishing Simon and Mazpazam a marriage partnership that is full of joy and love as long as they shall live,'

After we'd all repeated the toast Simon responded with a smile.

'My dear friend Sudzarnt,' he said,' Mazpazam and I thank you for proposing this toast and we thank you for your kind wishes. As always you are a good friend and a true member of this family. Uncle Ron and Aunt Brenda have a true son in you. As such I would like to propose my own toast to you. So please ladies and gentlemen raise your glasses once again and drink to Sudzarnt.'

'Sudzarnt may you be happy and prosperous in everything you do. And may you receive as much love and affection as you give to us all.'

After we had put down our glasses I looked across at Sudzarnt and for once he seemed emotionally lost for words. However, he conveyed his thanks telepathically and presented us with a sheepish smile of appreciation.

We couldn't help but smile and I for one went to him and put an arm across his small shoulders and gave him a squeeze. As the others followed my example Mazpazam slowly moved across towards Sarah and Brian and of course little Adam. I think she communicated a pleasant emotion to the lad for he looked up at her and smiled. When I saw Adam nod I knew that Mazpazam was communicating telepathically with him and he seemed to like it. She then knelt down and Adam went right up to her.

'You're pretty,' he said and gave her his best smile.

'Thank you Adam,' said Mazpazam in her soft voice, 'and you are a very handsome boy. Shall we be friends?'

Adam nodded vigorously as he usually did when agreeing to something.

'Good, I too would like that. Shall we shake hands on that?'

Adam held out his hand and Mazpazam took it in hers.

'Thank you Adam,' she said, 'I will send you messages when I am away. Would you like that?'

Again Adam nodded vigorously.

'And will you send messages to me as well?' asked Mazpazam.

Adam suddenly went very shy and turned to his mum for an answer.

'Of course you will, won't you Adam?' said Sarah.

'Yes,' whispered Adam. He had never had so much attention from a stranger and it was new for him and quite overwhelming.

Mazpazam now stood up realising that the boy was at his communicative limit for the moment. This was another side of Mazpazam that I was getting to know – the discernment of a little boy's emotional state and the nurturing of a friendship.

Simon followed Mazpazam as she went to each person again and I listened in to her conversations with them. She had a long conversation with Rachel and they discussed Nazmos and the changes that were likely to occur after the full orbital adjustment next year. Mazpazam became interested when Rachel said that she and her friend Margaret proposed travelling to Nazmos with Simon and then living there for an indefinite period to monitor the climate changes for themselves and the possible flora development. Nothing was obviously permitted from Earth's abundance of flora variety but Rachel thought that food species thriving within the Peruga Sea might perhaps be adapted for land cultivation; in time of course.

Simon and Mazpazam moved on and finally approached Fiona.

'This is my favourite cousin,' said Simon about Fiona. 'At one time she was extremely interested in space travel and I believe she still is. Space fascinates her but time has gone by and she has had to let it go.'

'Space is a fascinating zone,' said Mazpazam, 'and few are left untouched by its beauty. When it surrounds you out there its glory makes you hold your breath, don't you think Fiona?'

'Yes,' said Fiona feeling easier now, 'that is exactly what it did to me at my first encounter. I felt I wanted to be there always. But I realised that it was not simply to be admired but one needed to have a purpose to be out there. And I did not. I enjoy my job as a medical representative and I sometimes wonder at the advances we could achieve with some of your Oannes technology.'

Mazpazam smiled before replying.

'I sometimes wish that we could help somehow but our code laws do not permit it,' she said. 'We must each develop through a process of deep learning and achievement otherwise the gain is not truly appreciated. We tend to learn more from our failures than from our successes, don't you think?'

Fiona nodded her agreement.

'Yes, it would be easy to be gifted with all your knowledge,' said Fiona, 'but a few crumbs off your ample table could not go amiss.'

Mazpazam smiled again and made no comment to that. But I knew what she was thinking. When integration did occur in say a couple of millennia from now then Earth technology would suddenly take a giant leap forward to where the Oannes currently are. I conveyed this thought to Fiona and she turned to me and smiled her thanks.

Fiona then began telling Mazpazam about the magic tricks that I used to perform when she was a child. The disappearing buttons in my hands and how she had only discovered the truth behind the magic when I had divulged my gift secrets to them for the first time in 2038 shortly before her first trip to Nazmos.

Mazpazam and Fiona stood together talking for quite some time and I was happy that they had formed a friendship of sorts. Although Fiona had thought about coming with me on this trip to Nazmos she had not quite made up her mind about it. But now after meeting Mazpazam here I think she would view it more positively. It would be nice if she did come.

After another half hour of general conversation Simon announced that he had recalled the bus craft for his and Mazpazam's return to the spacecraft. Simon conveyed that he would return after a week or so and would be in constant touch. He would speak to granddad Alex in the morning when he was awake.

He also conveyed his plans for the coming week in that he had much to show Mazpazam of the northern forests among other things. She would see it just as it was in winter.

Simon suddenly turned to mum and kissed her on both cheeks and I could swear there was a tear in his eye.

'Tell granddad I love him very much,' he said as he looked intensely at mum.

I had a sickening feeling in the pit of my stomach for some odd reason that I could not understand. I could only think that Simon had had one of his premonitions. Was it to do with dad? Perhaps. We knew that dad was old and feeble but could he be closer to the end than we thought? I conveyed my thought to Simon privately but he blocked his mind and looking at me gave a slight shake of the head. I raised my eyebrows to which he responded with an

'I don't know' signal. But I imagined it might be sometime soon for Simon's premonitions were never distant time ones. I would see dad tomorrow morning. I would also talk to mum then.

It was another half hour of pleasant talk before a communication was received from Pazazato that he had arrived in the B&B car park.

Mazpazam was nervous about her appearance so she slowly put on the loose fitting trousers and coat. She then turned to Simon who handed her the facial mask she had worn earlier. Carefully she fitted it to the front of her face and pulled it backwards for Simon to take over. She leaned forward as Simon firmly pulled the edges around to the back of her head where it overlapped and became firmly fastened. Mazpazam then massaged her face lightly so that the mask settled correctly and comfortably.

'I shall remove this as soon as we are over the sea,' she conveyed, 'it is not uncomfortable and I feel I can get used to it. Thank you for being so welcoming and I hope to see you all again soon.'

She then went around the room to each of us in turn and made a brief handshake and the word 'goodbye' came clearly through the mask mouth opening. I thought it fitted well and made her look very human though rather ordinary.

Simon too came and said his goodbyes with a kiss for the ladies and a man hug for us men. He gave Uncle Ron an extra long hug and whispered something that I couldn't quite make out. Then taking Mazpazam by the hand he led her out to the waiting bus craft.

We all trooped out behind and watched as they boarded the bus which was all darkened inside. We waved as the bus turned about and slowly made its way to the main road.

'See you soon,' was the conveyed message from Tania as the bus craft disappeared around a bend in the road.

I felt elated that most of the family had now met Mazpazam but it was now close to 2.am and we were all rather tired. There would be much discussion about Mazpazam but for now I suggested we head for bed and leave that for tomorrow.

Brenda showed us to our rooms and now that Mazpazam had left us I felt a sadness creep up on me. Tania felt the same so that when we got into bed together our emotional state would not allow sleep right away. So we cuddled up to console each other and then one thing led to another till we finally fell into an exhausted sleep.

I heard Tania's whisper of 'It's been a long time' just before sleep grabbed me into its fold.

CHAPTER 21

Starship 4110-Silverstreak

January 2046

The first thought on Ashley's mind was of his dad Alex. What had Simon sensed? Could it have been a premonition of something to do with his dad's frailty and age? Simon had blocked his mind and thoughts and Ashley puzzled over that. There was only one concern on Ashley's mind and that was for the wellbeing of his dad. He discussed it with Tania who suggested that they keep in constant open communication with his parents.

'How are you dad?' conveyed Ashley when he knew that his dad was awake.

'I'm fine son and just having my porridge,' replied Alex. 'Are you coming over later?'

'Yes dad,' said Ashley, 'Tania and I should be with you about 2 o'clock.'

'O good,' came from Lillian, 'because Milly and Jerry are also popping round about then.'

'Mum, I need to discuss something with you,' conveyed Ashley in a private communication to his mum. 'I'm a bit worried about dad,' and then related the scene as he had observed it when Simon had asked her to convey his love to his granddad. Ashley said that he'd definitely noticed a hesitation in Simon's manner as he'd said it.

'Yes, I too noticed that,' replied Lillian, 'but then it would not be unexpected. Dad is ninety and anything could happen. A simple fall could be nasty for him. We shall just enjoy each day as it comes and be thankful. Every morning I'm grateful to see him wake up. Do you know what we say to each other when we go to bed at night? We say, 'goodnight darling and hope to see you in the morning if we wake up.' Ashley darling we are both old now and we don't expect to go on forever. If it's not this year then it could be the next or the next. Alex and I have come to terms with it.'

'Thanks for that mum,' conveyed Ashley, 'but I hope you both have quite a bit longer to go.'

'And what about you son?' conveyed Lillian, 'I too worry about you for you have to deal with this Zarama thing. A lot of lives will depend on your success. You cannot fail and I remember you telling me that you will do whatever it takes. I fear for your life son and I ask you to be careful and come back to us.'

'Yes mum, that I will try to do if it is so ordained,' replied Ashley. 'But I will also do everything in my power to rid our worlds of this danger. I still say that I must do whatever it takes.'

Lillian was silent for several seconds before replying.

I understand son,' she conveyed and there was extreme sadness in her tone.

Ashley conveyed an emotion of comforting love across to his mum. That was the wonder of the Oannes communication system; words became unnecessary to convey love to the ones you loved.

'Anyway, we'll see you soon mum,' said Ashley as he cut the communication.

When Ashley and Tania went over in the afternoon Milly and Jerry were already there and Alex was holding forth from his recliner chair now in the upright position.

Ashley shook hands with his dad and quickly did a diagnostic check. There was nothing untoward or new indicated so he stood back and smiled at his dad and mum. He conveyed a private message to Lillian his mum and she nodded her thanks.

'Ah, my favourite daughter in law,' said Alex when Tania stooped to give him a kiss on his cheek.

Then to Ashley he said, 'So son, tell me about Simon's girlfriend. I'm sorry I didn't get to meet her as you all did but you can fill me in with all the visual images of yesterday. And anything else you might like to add.'

And Ashley did exactly that. He began with the moment in Anztarza when Simon brought Mazpazam to the Dome-7 house to meet them. There was a lot to convey but Ashley did it all very expertly just as an Oannes person would have. He especially concentrated on Mazpazam's face and her beautiful eyes and saw the appreciative smile come to his dad's face as he received those images. Then Ashley moved on to the B&B visit of yesterday and showed his dad a close-up of Mazpazam with her face mask on.

'She looks quite like one of our girls,' said Alex at this image. Then the wonder returned as Ashley showed Simon helping Mazpazam peel off the face mask.

'She is a very pretty Oannes lady,' said Alex aloud, 'much prettier than your Muznant, Ashley. Simon is a very lucky chap.'

'Thanks granddad,' came the communication from Simon.

'Ah, Simon hello,' said Alex, 'where are you now?'

Ashley was curious too.

'We are in Canada,' communicated Simon. 'Mazpazam was impatient about visiting the northern forests so Captain Miltoztona took the spacecraft to a rest location for the night instead of back to Anztarza. Then this morning the bus-craft ferried us to a remote location somewhere in the north region of Saskatchewan which is heavily forested with tall pines. There's deep snow everywhere and Mazpazam is thrilled. She marvels at the cold, the snow and the huge trees. We are all geared up against the cold but will return in the bus-craft to the spaceship for our night-time sleep. Mazpazam wants to return to other areas nearby over the next few days. She is in love with all this which is quite new for her. Pazazato brings us here but will not leave the luxury of the bus. He does not like the cold and said to Mazpazam that the summers are much warmer and is really the time when he likes to visit.'

Simon conveyed images of Mazpazam romping in the snow and trying to pick some up in her hands.

'We tried making a snowman,' conveyed Simon, 'but the snow is too cold and powdery and will not stick. Neither can I make snowballs to throw at Mazpazam,'

'Hello all,' came from Mazpazam. 'Simon is doing all the communication so it's my turn now. It was so lovely meeting everybody yesterday. I would have loved to meet his granddad too but the images of us here will have to do for now. Simon and I are enjoying the snow and the cold. Simon is not used to the cold as I am and he huddles up against the wind. Also his nose is very red.'

Mazpazam conveyed an image of Simon's face and Alex laughed.

'But I love it and could spend all my time here,' added Mazpazam.

'I hope they don't meet any grizzlies up there,' said Jerry.

Ashley conveyed that even if they did the Oannes telepathy would soon send it packing by conveying an emotion of fear in its mind. Jerry laughed at his imagined image of that.

'I'd love to see that,' he said. 'A bear screaming in fear with its tail between its legs scooting off for all it was worth.'

All laughed at the comical image of the running bear that Jerry portrayed.

Lillian served up some snacks later and when Alex dozed off in his chair they all left for home within minutes of each other.

Later on Rachel popped in to see her mum and dad on her way to the hospital before her shift began. Rachel worked long hours but had given her notice two months ago to leave in mid January. She was looking forward to living on Nazmos again; as was Margaret who would be up from London after Christmas.

When Ashley and Tania got home they had a private discussion about Alex and both said that they felt relieved by what Lillian had said. The dearly departed may be resting in peace but it was the ones they left behind who suffered the bitter grief of parting. Ashley worried about the effect on his mum if his dad went as they were so attached to each other. Ashley knew that he would miss his dad terribly but it was the effect on his mum that he was more concerned about.

'As long as mum is fit and well she won't want to leave the family home,' said Ashley to Tania. 'But one day as she is older I'd want her to come and live here with us.'

He nearly said 'you' but quickly corrected himself. There was no telling what might happen in his battle against Zarama.

'Yes I suppose,' said Tania, 'and the same goes for my folks. But they live close to us so that would not be as urgent.'

Ashley was glad now that they had gone for the other half of the semi and made it into one large house. Six bedrooms would be ample for the two surviving members of each family. If indeed Tania came to be on her own – after Zarama – then at least she'd have company in her later years.

It saddened Ashley to think in that way but reality always came through strongly for him. He tried to think back to Gozmanot's visions but all he could remember was her prediction that Zarama would be vanquished. How that was to be achieved was not made clear. Neither was the fate of the other party concerned.

Ashley and Tania went daily to see Alex and Lillian and stayed just a couple of hours each time. Ashley also spent a few hours each day at one or other of the McGill's shops mainly to dictate information for the history cards of the newer acquisitions. Mark Tinman had gone down with a bout of flu so Julian Watts his young assistant had kept things ticking over nicely. Ashley was impressed by the young man and spent time talking to him and giving him plenty of good advice and encouragement.

Agnes and Les Gibson were happy with their shop business and were expecting Rebecca to visit from America for a few days over Christmas. Here too Ashley spent time dictating for the history cards. Both shops were nearly up-to-date in that respect and Ashley felt he could spend more time with his dad.

The Oannes communication badges kept the family members in constant contact with one another and they also got regular reports about Mazpazam from Simon. He conveyed images of her frolicking in the snow and among the pine trees. She looked different because of the mask and the loose clothing but Simon said that it made her feel easier in her mind against any accidental human contact.

At the end of the week Simon and Mazpazam returned to Anztarza and after another week Simon returned home to Dudley. Sudzarnt drove him down from the B&B.

Simon was keen to get Christmas gifts for all his family members. He'd missed doing that for all those years that he was at the space academy and on spaceships afterwards. Tania and Ashley agreed to do a whole day's shopping at the Merry Hill Shopping Centre with Simon and the day they selected was Thursday 23rd November.

When the day arrived they left early and it was a short ride to the Merry Hill car park. They found a nice covered spot near one of the entrances at 9:45am. Simon had made a list of names and Tania had filled in a suggested type of gift beside each. Ashley liked the place because of the large number and variety of shops and everything was in an enclosed warm environment. Also the food court had an excellent choice for most tastes.

Within an hour Simon had bought six gifts and they decided to return to the car to store them away in the boot. Then they returned into the shopping area for a muffin and a hot drink.

And so the day went on and more gifts were purchased and stored in the boot of the car. At 1:30pm it was decided that another break was necessary and this time for a snack lunch in the food court. Tania went for the fish and chips deal while Simon and his dad each had the extra large Cornish veggie pasty with side chips. Needless to say Tania couldn't finish her chips so Simon helped out.

Then it was back to shopping till at 4:00pm Tania suggested they call it a day and head for home and a nice mug of home brew tea. Simon said that he was happy that he'd had got nearly everything he wanted. The three that remained he could get later in town. Besides he said that Smyth's was the shop from which he'd get Adam's present. He didn't know what to get for Sudzarnt but he'd think of something; maybe a nice flat cap perhaps.

Ashley noticed that all the gifts Simon had bought were smallish items costing not more than £20 each; some for as little as £10. But he'd put a lot of thought into them and knew that each would be appreciated by the recipient. Christmas gifts were really a token of affection rather than just material value. There is joy in giving and joy in receiving. Blessings are on both sides.

He'd bought his granddad Alex a lovely football scarf which Ashley thought was quite unique. It consisted of different sections allocated to different popular football clubs. Simon said that he'd present it personally to his granddad a few days before Christmas and before anyone else got theirs.

This gave Ashley food for thought that has dad might not make it to Christmas and conveyed the thought privately to Tania.

'We can't do the same as Simon,' conveyed Tania to her husband, 'for he might suspect that we know something.'

It was a sobering thought and Ashley agreed with his wife. Besides nothing was certain and Simon didn't seem particularly concerned.

The next couple of weeks went by in a frenzy of Christmas activity. Simon put up the old five feet tall artificial green fir tree and bought new red and gold decorations for it. He also put coloured twinkling lights on it and conveyed the images to Mazpazam when he got it all just the way he wanted. Ashley and Tania thought it looked good especially since there'd been no effort on their part.

Simon discussed what to do about the front of the house. He said he wanted it to be remembered for its gaiety and colour. So he again went out and bought lots of packs of outdoor fairy lights and put them up on the bushes and trees there. He also put some in the front porch along with a two foot real fir tree on a little coffee table. He then called time and said that was enough to give the house a festive look without being too ostentatious. He communicated the images to all of the family especially to his granddad. When Tania saw that it was all finished she invited the rest of the family to come and have a look. There would be snacks and hot drinks of course. They could also have a taste of the Christmas cake she had baked and give their approval.

Ashley thought how nice it was having Simon home especially for Christmas and realised how much he'd missed him over the years.

The weather turned cold in early December and Lillian conveyed that Alex would not be venturing out. She did not want him catching a cold or something. So everyone made a special effort to visit them whenever they could. Ashley, Tania and Simon however went daily in the afternoons.

When Simon gave his early Christmas present to his granddad it was received with amusement.

'I've not got one like it so I shall remember you especially when I wear it. Mind you I don't fancy any of those clubs there,' he said pointing to the London clubs.

As usual when 12th December arrived it was a Tuesday and the anniversary of Ashley's granddad Eric's death in 2020. Consequently a visit was made to his grave in Witton Cemetery and flowers placed on it. Again it was too cold outside so Ashley sent his dad mental images of the visit. Someone had been earlier as there was a basket of flowers already there in front of the headstone. Communication revealed that Katy and Robin had visited the previous evening as Tuesday was a working day for them and they wanted the family to see their flowers the next day.

Ashley and Tania were on tenterhooks as Christmas day approached and they communicated with Alex throughout the day. Simon went with them to sit and chat with his granddad and Ashley noticed that he seemed not to be concerned in the least. Ashley felt that he had misread what he'd seen on Simon's face during Mazpazam's visit to the B&B; so it might have had nothing to do with Alex.

On Christmas day all gathered at the 'Zoo House' as they referred to Ashley and Tania's double semi abode. And even Alex came as it had turned out to be an exceptionally mild day with a maximum forecast at 14° C. The next day was forecast as becoming colder again. The weathermen said it had all got to do with the jet-stream shifting position to the South.

Ashley had bought a recliner sofa especially for his dad and Alex said it was better than the one he had at home because the recliner control was more like a TV remote.

Tania served up Christmas dinner at 1:30pm and placed all the food on a large side table. Everyone served themselves there before going to sit at the long tables made up of two large six foot picnic tables put together lengthwise. With thirteen adults and one child there was ample seating for all.

Lillian sat next to Alex and made sure he had just enough on his plate. There was lots of chat and when Alex said he wanted to see the king give his Christmas message at 3 o'clock all got up and trooped into the living room.

It had still a few minutes to go before the speech and Alex got comfortable in the recliner sofa. Sadly he missed half the King's speech because he dozed off partway through. But Ashley had put it to record so that all could see it later. So when Alex awoke after an hour Ashley replayed it especially for him.

Then it came to the moment chosen for opening of presents. Everyone had brought theirs and placed them around the Christmas tree. Tania performed her usual duty in handing them out one by one. The first present was Adam's from Simon and it was the largest of the presents. Everyone watched as Adam eagerly ripped the wrapping off and laughed with glee when he saw that it was a big pirate ship in its box. It was what he was hoping for and Simon got a big hug from Adam at Sarah's prompting.

It then took nearly half an hour for all the presents to be handed out and for the wrapping papers to be cleared away. There were kisses and handshakes and 'thanks' mooted around the room.

Rachel got everyone involved in playing 'Headbands' and it gave them all something to laugh about. Then they went on to play Charades for a bit before someone said they'd just like to sit and chat. Games were too much of a mental effort on a Christmas night especially on a full belly.

At 6 o'clock Lillian said she'd better take Alex home before it got cold again. Simon said he'd chaperone them by following in his golf and help his granddad get into the house at the other end. Although it had been a very mild day the nights could get frosty especially with the clear skies.

Sunset was about 4 o'clock and by six it was fully night and the sky pitch-black. So Ashley, Tania and the others wholly approved of Simon following in his car. Ashley still worried about what he had reckoned as a Simon premonition. Alex had been in good form on this day and Ashley marvelled at how well he looked. So what had Simon perceived? It was obviously something else or maybe nothing at all. Time would tell.

It had been a lovely Christmas celebration for them all and on the communication front it seemed as if Ron and Brenda had been with them throughout the day. Sudzarnt had also chatted briefly and conveyed his own state of affairs at the B&B. They had a small group of pensioners booked for their Christmas do and Sudzarnt said how busy it was keeping them happy and amused.

As Simon followed Lillian and Alex in their car he gave a running commentary of the half hour journey as they progressed up the M5 and then onto the M6 towards Spaghetti Junction and finally to the house. Simon helped his granddad into the house and stayed another half hour before returning to Dudley. On the way he received a communication that Sarah and Brian were also leaving with Adam as it was well past his bedtime; so he conveyed a goodnight to them and that he would see them again soon.

Ashley began to think about what he had believed to be one of Simon's premonitions. At the outset he had thought it concerned his dad Alex. But now another thought entered his mind. Maybe it hadn't been about his dad at all but of someone else. And that someone else might just possibly be himself. Ashley knew that he must push Zarama aside from its present course and failure was not an option. So what had Simon seen if anything at all? Could this be his last Christmas with his family? Was that what the premonition was about?

Then another thought came into Ashley's mind. Had Simon seen the loss of his father's amazing powers once Zarama was vanquished? It was a possibility. Then Ashley would become an ordinary human and be very glad of it.

However he felt that his telepathic ability would remain because other humans also had that skill. It was something that the Oannes had passed on to him. He remembered Muznant's thought delivery that had primarily been meant as a gift for Simon and Rachel but which had been picked up by him and Tania. It was a visual image passed to them of a vast arrangement like a pulsating scintillating colourful ball of entangled spaghetti-like strings floating in mid-air before entering their minds. It had lasted for a micro second only. It had been Muznant's gift of telepathy way back in 2016. So Ashley was confident that at least that part of his prowess would remain.

Finally Ashley decided to give up speculating or worrying about something that he may have just misread. What mattered most was that his father Alex was still with them and doing very well considering his age. Another relief was that his mother would not have to suffer the grief that came with such a loss; at least not as yet.

After Christmas the weather changed for the worse. It got much colder with severe frosts at night. This changed again when the weather men blamed the jet-stream for moving south and drawing in several low pressure systems across the Atlantic. Severe gales gusting to nearly 100mph hit Scotland on New Years Eve bringing ice and snow with it. In Dudley this translated into high winds and torrential sleety rain. Advice from the police was that people should stay indoors and not make non-essential journeys.

Ashley had planned a little get-together but cancelled when the conditions got bad. All were advised to bring in the New Year 2046 in their own homes as individual family units. However their communication badges made it feel as if they were all together which was just as enjoyable. Even Ron and Brenda became an inclusive part of the celebrations.

Milly and Jerry came over to Ashley and Tania's at midday and planned to stay over for the night. Tania loved having her mum and dad stay nights and had prepared their usual room for them.

She prepared a nice evening meal for the five of them and a light supper for later in the night. There were also the usual snacks such as cheese and crackers and a bottle of bubbly for bringing in the New Year at midnight.

After Tania's big evening meal they all settled into comfy positions on the settees with the TV tuned to a nice musical programme on BBC1 to take them into the New Year. Simon had to smile as one by one first his grandparents dozed off and then later followed briefly by his dad. Tania winked at her son giving him a big smile before putting a finger to her lips in a conspiratorial manner. But after about an hour all woke again and looked quite refreshed.

'I needed that,' said Jerry, 'after all I'm not as young as our Simon over there.'

'I'm not immune to the odd forty winks now and then,' said Simon. 'In fact I might have one a bit later on. Though sometimes just resting your eyes can be just as beneficial.'

'Well said son,' said Ashley with a wicked smile, 'for that is just what I was doing a while ago.'

Everyone laughed and Tania came over to Ashley and gave him a kiss on the top of his head. Ashley put his arm out and gave her a little hug and said, 'Thank you darling.'

As Big Ben struck its final dozen gongs for the end of year 2045 the fireworks were initiated at the London Eye location in London. Apparently the stormy conditions were less severe further south and so the fireworks were witnessed for the 42nd year running and watched not only by all those braving the weather on the London Embankment but by the rest of the country and the world on the telly. Of course the year was old already as Ashley and the others had watched the BBC News-at-One and seen the New Year heralded in Sydney Australia with the Harbour Bridge fireworks display eleven hours previously.

Here however they interlinked with crossed arms and sang Auld Lang Syne before greeting each other with kisses and handshakes. Of course the communication badges brought each of the family members closer together and all wished each other a Happy New Year.

Secretly Ashley hoped it would be a happy year for him by giving him success against Zarama. He thought he had kept his mind blocked but obviously it hadn't been. A message came through privately from Mazpazam wishing him all success against Zarama. She conveyed nothing more. Ashley's badge must have let something through for everyone wished him the same; success against Zarama and a safe return home. They all stayed up chatting and it was nearly 2 o'clock when all said goodnight and signed off.

In the morning father and son discussed the probable departure date for Nazmos. Simon thought that the last week in January had been marked in the starship's intention log as the return agenda. And then the next day came the Oannes broadcast that all officers and crew were to be aboard the starship Silverstreak no later than January 10th. Also announced was that the starship would commence its return journey to Nazmos on January 25th.

Ashley saw a smile come to Simon's face and he knew why. Of course Simon would be happy to be back flying through space but more important at the moment was the fact that he had missed being with Mazpazam.

And so the pickup for Simon was arranged for Friday January 5th at the Aberporth B&B as usual. The spaceship would then head straight out towards the starship location. Ashley and Tania said they would drive up with Simon and spend some time with Ron and Brenda afterwards. It was expected that Mazpazam would be coming to meet

Simon but Simon said he couldn't be sure. She had not mentioned anything in their regular communications. Tania reckoned she would but that was two days away.

Simon said that he'd enjoyed putting up the Christmas decorations but now he would also help in taking them down and putting them into the boxes allocated for them. He wondered if they would be putting them up again next Christmas. Probably not as the journey to and from Zarama's location might be prolonged for whatever reason.

It was quicker taking down all the decorations as compared to putting them up. The tree and bush lights took a bit longer to roll onto the cards provided but all was eventually done and stored away. It was only the next day before they were leaving that Tania found a gold tree bauble lying in a corner of the living room. Ashley said to leave it where it could be seen for continuity for next Christmas. Tania put it on the small indoor rubber tree plant to dangle from one of its many branches.

As usual Simon went to visit his grandma and granddad on each of his last two days and went on from there to see Katy, Robin and Fiona and then also Sarah, Brian and Adam. Fiona had finally decided not to go on the trip to Nazmos for reasons of her own which Ashley accepted as probably the correct decision.

Rachel came and stayed for a couple of nights in the family home as did Jerry and Milly. It was a nice family atmosphere in the evenings chatting and watching the odd TV programs together.

The pickup for Ashley, Tania, Rachel and Margaret was planned for Sunday 21st night and would be by Captain Bulzezatna in the spaceship 520-Green. They would not be visiting Anztarza but would instead be going straight out towards the starship Silverstreak parked 9 billion miles away in the Sagittarius sector; a journey of some 22 hours in real time. Time dilation would of course make it seem nearly three hours less for the passengers.

Thursday morning arrived wet and windy. Ashley, Simon and Tania drove up to Aberporth in the one car with Simon driving his golf for the last time. Ashley and Tania would of course drive back to Dudley in it and then return it to the dealer they got it from; at a much reduced price of course.

The drive up to the B&B turned out to be easier than expected as the afternoon sky cleared and the wind eased. As usual they stopped off at Aberystwyth for a lunch break before heading down the A487 coast road to Aberporth. They arrived just as it was getting dark at 5:15pm.

They were greeted enthusiastically by Sudzarnt and tea and biscuits were waiting for them in the warm lounge. There were other guests in there and all nodded and said 'Hello' to them as they walked in. Ron and Brenda came in just as they settled down and joined them for a cuppa and a chat. The other guests looked on with interest for they didn't get too many interesting distractions.

As such Ashley and co resorted to telepathy as their main form of communication.

The pickup for Simon the next evening would be a quick one in the spaceship 11701-Red under Captain Lyzongpan which would then head straight out towards the rendezvous with the starship Silverstreak. 11701-Red would probably be carrying most of the starship's officers and crew. As such Mazpazam might not be on the shuttle bus craft when it came for Simon.

Because of the frequent ferrying to and from the B&B and also the northern forests a few of the other spaceships also had a similar bus craft as shuttles. In fact there were currently a total of five bus craft numbered from 326 to 330 and all ending with the classification of 'Red'.

It was a pleasant evening and Simon sat near his great aunt Brenda for most of the evening.

'I'd like to go for a walk on the coastal path tomorrow if I may,' said Simon aloud to the room in general.

'Well the forecast is for dry but cold weather tomorrow,' said an elderly lady who had been keenly listening to their chatter. 'Take a brolly just in case.'

'Thank you ma'am,' replied Simon to the lady, 'I shall certainly do that.'

Later they all went into the dining room for dinner where a lovely meal was served up. Simon tucked in because he knew that everything was vegetarian as per Sudzarnt's dietary rule. After the meal was over and the other guests had left they sat chatting around their table and had their tea and coffee there. It was close to 10:40pm when they returned to the lounge which was now empty of any guests.

Ron excused himself and said goodnight and Brenda went with him but returned a bit later. She said that he was settled in his bed and already snoring his head off – she smiled as she said it.

Tania said that it was late and time she too retired to bed and reaching out she pulled Ashley up off his comfy sofa seat. Brenda said she'd show them to their room and Simon if he cared to follow – which he did. Ashley reckoned that Simon would spend some private communication time with his Mazpazam before settling down for the night.

The next morning began bright and sunny but rather cold. A light frost was visible on the ground and on the cars in the B&B car park.

During breakfast Simon mentioned that Mazpazam would not be coming into the B&B lounge but would however be on the bus craft when it came for the pick-up. And of course she'd be 'in costume' as she referred to the disguise that she wore. She conveyed that she'd welcome anyone who boarded to say 'hello.' The bus craft would stop for only twenty minutes for the pick-up before returning to the waiting spaceship.

Simon said that he planned his coastal path walk for later in the morning when it was a bit warmer and would welcome anyone joining him. Ashley and Tania agreed to go with him and asked what time he had in mind.

'Oh about midday-ish,' said Simon. 'Then we could be back for about one thirty or so. I only want to walk it as far as Tresaith and then return the same way. It's the sea views that I want to enjoy and convey to Mazpazam.' Ashley thought about the walks he had as a boy way back in the eighties. He reckoned that Simon got the same enjoyment as he'd had then.

It was nearly midday when they set off. The tide was in so they had to walk around the flooded doggy beach to get to the coastal path. The weather had warmed a bit though the sky had clouded over from horizon to horizon. So just in case it rained they carried their brollies with them.

It was more of a stroll than a walk for they stopped often to look out to sea. Ashley said he was quite enjoying the walk as they stopped again to watch a steamer crossing their view from right to left. They stopped again to admire the railway carriage houses on the hillside above them.

'There seem to be more of them than I remember,' said Simon to his mum and dad.

'Yes it does seem so,' said Ashley, 'but then I don't think I ever really made a count.'

'I wonder how they got them up there in the first place,' said Tania.

'Probably by crane or something,' said Simon. 'But I can't see any proper roadway leading to them.'

'Perhaps there's one further up the hill,' said Tania.

All the carriage houses had well kept gravel paths leading to each and one could imagine a small car just about managing to drive along them.

'Do you think that they were dismantled and then assembled again on site?' asked Tania.

'I suppose that's a possibility,' said Ashley trying to probe his inner voice unsuccessfully, 'but it would be a lot of work.'

'Perhaps they have always been there and I just missed seeing so many,' said Simon which ended the discussion and they walked on.

After about forty minutes into their walk they felt a few spots of rain but which soon stopped.

'I think we ought to think about going back,' said Tania, 'we've had a good walk don't you think?'

'Good idea,' said Simon and was the first to reverse direction. However he still faced in the same direction while walking backwards and smiling at his parents.

'I hope you have shown Mazpazam all of this,' said Ashley to his son.

'I have and I am,' said Simon, 'and she conveys that she would have loved to have been here with us. That was actually the whole purpose of this walk. But you already knew that.'

Ashley nodded and smiled before he got a dig in the side from Tania.

'Why didn't you tell me I was on camera, I would have smiled more,' said Tania.

'Actually mum,' said Simon,' you haven't stopped smiling since we began the walk.'

'Thank you,' said Tania, 'and what does Mazpazam say?'

'She loved the views and hopes one day to see it all for herself,' said Simon.

'Perhaps when we return from Nazmos she can,' said Tania and quickly added, 'wearing her disguise of course.'

'I would love to do that Aunty Tania,' came the reply from Mazpazam through the communication badges, 'and I'm sure I will one day.'

'You would love it in the rain,' conveyed Ashley.

'Thank you,' conveyed Mazpazam, 'that would be a new experience for me. It snowed in the northern forests when Simon and I were there and I enjoyed the feel of it.'

'Will we see you on the bus craft tonight,' asked Tania?

'Yes I will be on it though I shall not be getting off. So please come aboard which I should like very much,' conveyed Mazpazam.

'We will see you then,' said Tania. 'I think it is starting to rain again so we had better hurry back to the B&B where Sudzarnt has lunch prepared for us.'

The rain began coming down heavily so they all put their brollies up. But after a few minutes it stopped again and the remainder of the return walk was dry. When they got indoors they removed their coats and scarves and settled down to a nice hot drink before lunch.

About 7.pm it was dark and raining again when Ashley received communication that the Bus craft was on its way to them. And it was not very long before it drove silently into the B&B car park and manoeuvred close to the entrance. The operator on the bus was new to Ashley but had a pleasant manner. He communicated a brief Sewa and the introduced himself with a big smile.

'I am pleased to meet you Ashley,' he said aloud in slightly throaty voice, 'I am Pronzipt and I can only stay here a short while. Captain Lyzongpan is impatient to get under way to deliver his passengers to their starship.'

'Thank you Pronzipt,' replied Ashley, 'we will only be a few moments.'

And Ashley was true to his word. Only Ashley and Tania followed Simon onto the bus craft and they were greeted enthusiastically by Mazpazam. In the dull glow of the red interior lighting they could see that Mazpazam was not wearing her disguise mask but she had it beside her just in case. She stood up and she and Simon touched hands before she came forward to kiss Tania and Ashley. Ashley said it was lovely seeing her again and hoped to see so much more of her when they boarded the starship soon.

Then Simon kissed his mum and gave his dad a double handshake and a man hug.

'It has been a great time for me being home after so long,' he said. 'I hope I can do it again though I don't know when. But I shall see you both aboard Silverstreak in a couple of weeks I think?'

'God Bless you son,' said Tania, 'and look after this lady.'

'That I will,' said Simon as he walked his parents to the door of the bus craft.

As soon as Ashley and Tania had alighted the door slowly closed and the bus craft turned in a wide circle and headed for the car park exit and the road beyond. It was still raining lightly and very dark so there was little chance of them being seen speeding at 100mph above the waves towards the waiting spaceship.

Ashley and Tania smiled to each other as they re-entered the B&B lounge. They were happy because of the joyous emotion they had sensed in their son's mood when he was reunited with his Mazpazam. They settled down in the lounge with Ron and Brenda and a bit later Sudzarnt served them tea and biscuits. One of the other B&B guests, an elderly lady came across to where they were sitting and looked pleasantly at Tania and Ashley.

'Was that your son who just left on that old fashioned bus?' she asked.

'Yes,' replied Tania, 'that was our son Simon and he's off on his travels to the Far East again.'

'A very handsome young man who reminds me of one of those Hollywood actors of long ago,' she said with a smile.

'Thank you kindly,' said Tania, 'and I think I know the one you mean. We thought he was a bit like that actor Errol Flynn with a similar type of fine moustache.'

'That's the one,' said the lady, 'but it was so long ago I'd forgotten. I'm 95 you know and proud of it.'

Tania stood up and invited her to join them for a cup of tea.

'Thank you very much,' was the reply, 'but no thanks for now. Early to bed and early to rise is my motto and it is already way past my bedtime. So I'll bid you goodnight and hope to see you again.'

She smiled a pleased smile as she turned and walked to the door leading out to the reception. She had obviously seen the astonished expression on their faces when she'd announced her age – and that pleased her. In her mind she was definitely aiming for a century.

'What a pleasant person,' said Ashley who had read her mind. 'She really is 95 and was widowed nearly 25 years ago. I believe she comes here regularly Aunt Brenda, though not every year.'

'Yes, that's right,' said Brenda, 'I've known Phyllis as a guest here for as long as I can remember. Since she doesn't come every year I imagine there are other haunts to visit as well. I think I vaguely remember when she visited once with her husband. Quite a short little fellow if I remember correctly.'

'Yes,' said Ashley, 'she tries to visit all the places she and her husband visited when he was with her. His name was Desmond I believe. Desmond Oakley and they were originally from Leeds.'

'That's right, she signs in as a Mrs P Oakley,' said Brenda.

'What a lovely way to keep cherished memories alive,' said Tania.

Ashley's thoughts sped miles away as he sat looking at the door through which Phyllis had gone. What was to be the outcome for him? And how would Tania cope if the worst came to the worst? Ashley's eyes misted slightly at the thought and he quickly discarded the thought and blinked away the wetness of his emotion.

'I think we'll head for home tomorrow after breakfast,' he said to Ron. 'But we shall be back here on the day of our pickup which is the evening of Sunday 21st. We shall have Rachel and Margaret with us and won't need to sleep over.'

'When do you think you might be back from Nazmos?' asked Brenda.

'Well Rachel and Margaret plan to stay long-term there to monitor any changes,' said Ashley, 'but Tania and I hope to return as soon as this Zarama business is sorted. It could be more than a year.'

They chatted on till about 10.pm before saying goodnight and retiring to their rooms.

Aboard the spaceship 11701-Red Simon and Mazpazam were recognised as being in a partnership and were placed together in one cabin. The spaceship had not quite reached the million mile distance from Earth so the neutron generators had not been operated. When they were operated the spaceship would be accelerated to 90,000 miles per second velocity for the remainder of the journey to the starship rendezvous location some 9 billion miles out at the very fringe of the solar system.

In Aberporth the next morning was sunny and bright. After a leisurely breakfast Ashley and Tania said their goodbyes and left for Dudley about 10:30am. They returned the same way they had travelled down except they did not stop in Aberystwyth. Subsequently they arrived home a little after 1:30pm. There had been heavy afternoon traffic on the M54 which had slowed their journey a bit. The house felt empty without Simon but they talked about all the eventful things they had done with Simon especially over Christmas.

'I can't believe he was home for only four months,' said Tania wistfully. 'He filled the time with so much that he made it feel as if he was here much longer.'

'And I'm so glad we met Mazpazam,' she added. 'She is just right for him don't you think darling?'

Ashley just nodded and smiled as Mazpazam's image came into his mind.

Communication with the family continued on a regular basis as did the daily visits by Ashley and Tania to Erdington to see his mum and dad. There was no change with Alex and Ashley was pleased about that.

As January progressed and the date for leaving approached Alex voiced his concern for his son's future wellbeing. He knew that the White Dwarf Star that was Zarama would be no pushover. At 431 light years away the journey would be long and possibly hazardous. But Zarama had to be moved away from its current path and Ashley was the only one given the power to do it. But was that power enough or was something more required? And at what cost to his son's life? That was a question Alex could not contemplate.

Ashley managed to get rid of Simon's VW Golf car by taking it back to the dealer they'd had it from. Of course he got back much less than he'd paid for it but that did not bother Ashley.

Tania had arranged for her parents to keep an eye on the house while they were away. She had also told her neighbour friends about going on a world tour and then they'd probably spend time with their son in the Far East for as long as he'd have them. There was so much to see of good old Earth she said.

Margaret had come up from London a couple of days earlier and had roomed with Rachel in her flat for the first night. Then both had come to stay with Tania and Ashley in Dudley in readiness for the drive up to Aberporth.

On Saturday 20th January Ashley and Tania went around to each of the family and spent a bit longer with Lillian and Alex.

'Good luck son,' said Alex as they were leaving and Ashley knew exactly what his dad meant.

The next day was overcast but dry and mild. The drive to Aberporth was uneventful and they arrived at around 4pm while it was still quite light. Sudzarnt was there to greet them with ready mugs of tea. He said that Ron and Brenda had stayed back in the Annex as Ron had been a bit under the weather since yesterday morning. Ron said that he felt an ache across his shoulders and decided that bed rest would sort it out. So later Ashley, Tania, Rachel and Margaret visited him there and he was quite happy to have them all seated around his bed.

Ashley did a quiet diagnostic and saw that nothing untoward was indicated apart from back muscle strain. Ashley conveyed this to Brenda and she nodded her thanks with a smile.

A message was then received from Captain Bulzezatna that 520-Green was on its way and the bus craft pickup was estimated for 7:20pm GMT. Ashley immediately replied that he was looking forward to meeting with his captain friend again. The reply came that so did she.

Sudzarnt conveyed that the evening meal would be served in the dining hall at 6pm as usual for all the guests and Ron quickly added for Sudzarnt to make it a table for six. Brenda smiled at Ron and knew that he was feeling better. She would of course help him get washed and dressed in time for dinner in an hour.

Sudzarnt served them on a priority basis as they had conveyed their choice of menu earlier. It was a pleasant chatty meal with Ron and Brenda present. Ron looked quite perky and he said that the bed rest had done him a world of good. The other guests had come in shortly after them and had also been served. Sudzarnt had some good young staff and he'd trained them well.

By 6:50pm they had all finished and were ready for their after-dinner hot drink of tea or coffee. Ron had not eaten very much and Brenda said that he would have a snack again a bit later on. He ate little and often. They returned to the lounge where Sudzarnt served them tea and coffee. Ashley had barely finished his first mug when the communication came that the bus craft was on its way to them. It would probably be another twenty minutes before it arrived in the B&B car park.

'Thank you Captain,' replied Ashley, 'I'll just have time for a second mug of tea before it arrives.'

'Enjoy your tea,' conveyed the captain, 'I shall see you soon.'

It was well known that Ashley loved his mugs of tea and the Oannes saw humour in it because they couldn't stand the stuff.

When the bus craft drew into the car park Ron and Brenda stood in the entrance as Ashley, Tania, Rachel and Margaret boarded. The operator was an Oannes that Ashley had not met before. A brief Sewa was exchanged with him but no smile was presented. The operator was an older Oannes male and Ashley recognised a decided nervousness in his manner. Ashley had come across this attitude before but he recognised it as one caused by an awe of the reputation that preceded him. Oannes shunned familiarity with the famous and Ashley was certainly that to those who did not know him. This was to be expected occasionally.

As Ashley walked passed into the bus central aisle he touched the operator's shoulder in a friendly gesture and conveyed his thanks for transporting them back to the spaceship 520-Green. The operator whose name was Saztazto and aged 150 years seemed to visibly relax and look more comfortable. Although his colleagues had described Ashley as a very ordinary behaved human Saztazto could not accept that someone with such gifted powers was not a proud and haughty person. But already with Ashley's simple friendly touching gesture Saztazto began to feel that his friends may have been right.

The journey to 520-Green was swift and before long Ashley, Tania, Rachel and Margaret were being greeted by Captain Bulzezatna in the magnificence of the spaceship's control room. They'd been met by 1st deputy Rubandiz in the Shuttle Bay who conducted a brief Sewa before leading them to the control room and his captain.

520-Green was already in the process of accelerating up into space and Captain Bulzezatna outlined the journey schedule to her guests. This was a matter of routine and as a reminder that the journey plans were unchanged.

It would be three hours before the spaceship progressed beyond the one million mile distance from Earth and at which the neutron generators could operate. Then it would be another 22 hours of travel at 100,000 miles per second to the rendezvous point where the starship Silverstreak was parked. To the people on the spaceship the journey would seem shorter because of the time dilation factor at the higher velocity. The 22 hour journey would register only 19 hours on the ship's time clocks. Zanos on board would however adjust this to indicate the correct time elapsed.

Ashley and Tania were now quite used to space travel with the Oannes and after exchanging pleasantries and the latest gossip with the captain decided after half an hour to retire to their allotted cabins. Rachel and Margaret would be together in one cabin and Ashley and Tania in another. Although it was only 9:30pm it had been a long day and they were all rather tired.

'Goodnight and see you at breakfast,' said Rachel to her parents as she and Margaret went into the adjoining cabin as directed by Zanos. Ashley had been informed by visual image that their dining hall was close by and just down the corridor; the same as on previous occasions.

In the cabin Tania looked inside the storage closet and saw that their clothes had been transferred there from the accommodation in Dome-7 of Anztarza. These would also be transferred to their cabin on Silverstreak and ultimately to where they were housed on Nazmos. Ashley was looking forward to seeing Jazzatnit again. So from now on they would wear the Oannes tunics and leggings provided to them. Tania conveyed this to Rachel and Margaret.

Every cabin had an inclusive sleep-tank for their Oannes passengers and when they entered Ashley looked at Tania and asked if she fancied a wallow in there. Tania's eyes sparkled when she remembered a previous occasion so she said 'Okay'.

'You go in first and I'll join you as soon as I've finished with the bathroom,' she said.

'Fine,' said Ashley, 'I can brush my teeth later,'

He then sat on the bed and began to remove first his shoes and socks and then all his clothes. The sleep-tank was small about 7 feet square with 5 feet glass panels on two sides and set into the corner of the cabin. However the base was sunken into the flooring which added another foot to its water depth.

Ashley now quite naked walked up the outer steps and then down those on the other side inside the tank. The water temperature was a mild 28°C and a bit cooler than he would have liked. But then it was meant for the Oannes who were used to cooler temperatures.

Ashley settled down with his feet on the tank floor and then floated onto his back. After several minutes of wallowing alone he saw Tania climb the steps and enter the tank. He'd had a detached view of her nude form and felt a brief thrill of excitement touch him in the pit of his stomach. There were a few saggy bits but the overall picture she presented was good for a sixty year old.

Tania had to tread water and slowly worked her way to her husband and put her arms round his neck while planting a light kiss on his lips.

'What was that for?' asked Ashley hopefully.

'That was a 'no no' signal for you my dear husband in case you got any ideas,' she said.

Ashley understood and put his own arms around his wife's waist and squeezed acknowledgement.

'Thank you' he said, 'I'm not sure if I could in here.'

They then frolicked around the tank and splashed each other occasionally too. The weightlessness caused by their buoyancy in the water leant a certain soporific effect to their relaxing muscles. At her first yawn Tania said that she'd had enough relaxation and was going to shower before getting into bed.

'I feel the same,' said Ashley and followed behind her as she stepped out of the sleep-tank. They had a quick shower and a nice rub down to dry.

Tania looked at Ashley and shook her head.

'Lets just cuddle up, I'm quite sleepy.'

'Me too,' said Ashley as they went to the bed and flopped on their respective bed sides.

They cuddled up and a couple of gentle kisses later Tania was asleep. Ashley listened to her breathing for what seemed an eternity before he too drifted into a deep sleep.

When he awoke he was alone in the bed. On querying Zanos-on-board he was informed that the time was 10:17am spaceship simulated time and his companions were in the dining hall.

'Good morning sleepy head,' was the message from Tania. 'I'm here in the dining hall with Rachel and Margaret. They were up early and called for me nearly an hour ago. We've had our breakfast but I'll have a nice hot mug of tea for you if you get here soon.'

'I'll be there in ten minutes,' conveyed Ashley. 'Can you please also get me a couple of toasts while you are at it?'

'Will do as you command my dearest hubby,' conveyed Tania and included her emotion of humour.

'Good morning dad,' conveyed Rachel, 'it's a lovely day outside with the Sun shining behind us.'

'Thank you Rachel,' conveyed Ashley, 'and good morning to you Margaret.'

'Good morning Ashley,' conveyed Margaret, 'I trust you slept well.'

'Slept well and long,' added Tania laughing.

'Just get me my tea and let me get ready in peace,' said Ashley; 'over and out.'

Ten minutes later Ashley walked into the dining hall and immediately spotted them at a table along the wall on his right. He walked to the table and sat down beside Tania. Rachel and Margaret sat facing him and he got big smiles from both. All were dressed in their Oannes outfits of tunic and leggings and quite colourful ones too.

There was a pot of tea under a cover and all the makings beside it. There was also cheese and jam to one side. Tania did the honours for her husband by pouring tea into his mug and letting him do the rest.

'I'll get your toast for you,' said Tania as she stood up. 'Two for now okay?'

'Yes thanks,' mumbled Ashley as he had just taken a sip from his mug.

The dining hall was near empty as most Oannes are early risers and like to eat first thing. There were two crew members at one table and possibly three passengers notable by their varied tunics at another. Captain Bulzezatna had stated during their chat in the control room that her ship was quite full with passengers making their way to Nazmos. Apparently the approaching final adjustment in the Nazmos orbit by Ashley was an occasion not to be missed. Then there was also the journey to faraway Zarama after that and many wished to remember the occasion for posterity. Gozmanot's vision had stated a victory over Zarama and the Oannes population were in no doubt that it would so happen.

After finishing breakfast the four of them got permission to spend an hour in the control room looking at the stars in this part of the Milky Way galaxy. When they got there the captain was not around but 1st deputy Rubandiz welcomed them and indicated for them to enjoy the views.

The stars showed up in all their brilliance as the Sun was shielded by the under-body bulk of the spaceship. The ship faced outwards towards their rendezvous location with the Sun behind.

Ashley looked out of the view panels and saw a vague familiarity in the clusters of stars laid out around them. It was like looking into a forest of trees and seeing recognition in their distribution pattern. Where once he would have felt lost he now began to feel more at ease. Ashley could understand how Simon felt when he was out in the limitlessness of space. He would feel comfortable and at peace with this environment that to him was familiarity and peace to say the least. And so it should be. The stars were momentarily fixed in their relative positions and their distribution was recognisable. Any change of relative position would be due to change of viewing location. And Simon had that natural ability common to most spacemen in understanding and interpreting those changes. And by so doing they were able to fix their location relative to home.

So far Oannes starships had only ventured to distances of approximately fifty light-years from Nazmos. But soon Ashley and Simon would be travelling much further in Silverstreak to Zarama's location. And afterwards they must find the faint star that was Raznat from that great distance of 431 light-years and travel back to it. They must do that with a certainty of navigation in order not to wander in space searching aimlessly for home. Simon's proven navigational ability would be most valuable then.

Ashley wondered if that had been the fate of the starship 2110-Blue that had set out from the Raznat system some 1400 years ago. With a full complement of 1500 Oannes it had journeyed towards an interesting star system under the leadership of Captain Chamzalt. He had taken his family with him as was the custom and since then there had been no contact or message from the starship.

Ashley's thoughts switched to his home in Dudley. If possible after all of this Zarama business was over he intended to return there and never to leave it again. A sense of nostalgia rose up in his throat but a hand on his shoulder brought him back to reality.

It was Captain Bulzezatna. She had returned quietly to her control room and had read his thoughts. She thought it wise to bring him back from a possible brink that overlooked a chasm of depression. The captain had a great affection for Ashley and knew that a great burden had been placed upon him. She conveyed a feeling of understanding and suggested that they return to their cabins and rest before the afternoon meal was served; that would be in another couple of hours. And it would then be another six hours after that to reach the rendezvous location. She suggested also that they could all return again just before the neutron generators were operated to slow the spaceship down.

She would like to see their mental reaction when they viewed the starship Silverstreak for the first time. Although she had approached this starship several times in the past months it still gave her a thrill of pride to see its sleekness and beauty of form; especially as the light from the distant Sun reflected off its long and thin smooth silver hull. The Oannes civilization had achieved another great leap in their technical progress. A starship that could achieve a hundred times light velocity was something to be proud of. And it had happened in Bulzezatna's lifetime. She conveyed her thoughts to Ashley and Ashley thanked her for it.

Ashley and the others finally left the control room and as a matter of interest made their way around the ship and ultimately towards its rear where the cargo and shuttle bays were located.

There was not much of new interest within the Cargo area so they went down a level to the Shuttle bay. From where they entered they could look down upon the craft housed together in neat rows all across the wide bay floor. It was like looking down into a large cavern but here too there was very little happening. A couple of crew members were going around to various shuttle craft and making a brief check at each with a handheld gizmo. Ashley then spied the bus-craft at a far wall position and pointed it out to Tania, Rachel and Margaret. They spent a fair while just talking and viewing all that was below them until Rachel said that she'd like to return to her cabin. Nature called she said.

'Let's all go back to our cabins,' said Tania, 'and wait for the afternoon meal call. It can't be too long now.'

All returned to their cabins and Ashley lay flat on his back on the bed and listened as Tania chatted away. He then queried Zanos and was informed that rendezvous with the starship was seven hours away.

Tania came and lay down beside Ashley and they began a discussion about Nazmos and the probable climate change effects. It was pure speculation on their part but Tania and Ashley both got a pleasant feeling thinking about the flora that could grow as a result of the orbital change. Tania was proud that her husband was the key player there.

'I suppose that one day Nazmos will have forests like ours,' said Tania.

'Not for a very long time I would think,' said Ashley.

'But it's nice to think that it will happen one day.'

The message came through from Rachel that the afternoon meal was about to be served and that she and Margaret were making their way to the dining hall. Ashley got up and replied that they too were on their way. He realised that he felt rather hungry.

The dining hall appeared full up but several places had been kept vacant at a table presumably especially for them.

'Very considerate of our Oannes hosts,' thought Ashley, but then he and his family were special guests aboard and why wouldn't places be kept for them. Perhaps the captain had had a hand in it. But anyway Ashley conveyed a brief informal Sewa along with his thanks to the Oannes at their table as the four of them sat down.

Very little attention was directed their way as it was the usual polite etiquette of the Oannes. Ashley's reputation was well known but the Oannes were much too polite to make their curiosity or their admiration a public spectacle.

Anyway all of this hidden artificiality was discarded once the meal dishes began to be placed on the buffet tables. There was an air of expectancy in the Oannes manner and Ashley realised that they were waiting for their guests to start serving themselves first. Ashley conveyed this to Tania, Rachel and Margaret as he got up and walked to the buffet table.

All the usual Oannes food dishes of Raizna, Starztal, Yaztraka, Mirzondip, Lazzonta, and Tartonta were there plus a few others that Ashley did not recognise. Ashley and Tania served themselves quite quickly and returned to their table. Rachel and Margaret took a bit longer in making their food choices before they too returned to their table places. Only then did the Oannes crew and passenger members get up and serve themselves. Such politeness was noteworthy thought Ashley.

Jugs of Wazu were already on the tables along with drinking glasses. Ashley filled a glass and gave a toast sign by raising his glass above his head and conveyed a general Sewa greeting to all before taking a long sip. This seemed to break the formality and smiles broke out as other Oannes followed suit. It turned out to be a very pleasant meal after all.

Ashley felt quite full up after his final portion of sweetened Yaztraka which he followed with his usual mug of sweet tea. As the four of them continued chatting generally Tania noticed that at one point Ashley had his eyes shut before suddenly jerking upright.

'He's sleepy,' she thought to herself and then politely suggested that she herself could do with a short nap in her cabin. After all there were nearly six hours of journey time left before they reached the starship rendezvous.

They left the dining hall and made their slow way to their own cabins. Once inside Ashley yawned and sat on the edge of the bed before removing his footwear. Then he spread himself on the bed on his back and smiled up at Tania.

'Thanks,' he said and Tania knew he was referring to her suggestion to return for a nap.

Tania smiled as his breathing changed to one with an occasional rasping snore.

'You shouldn't sleep on your back,' she said aloud, 'it restricts your airways,'

As if he'd heard her Ashley slowly turned onto his left side and eased into a more regular silent breathing.

Tania looked at her husband for a long moment taking in the sight of him asleep. She did this often and thought how like an innocent child he looked.

'One day I shall look back at this moment and remember you as you are now,' she thought to herself.

Out of curiosity she went over to the full length mirror and looked at her body – first at her front view and then her left and right side views.

'Hmmmm, age is creeping up,' she thought as she ran her hand down the front of her dress from bosom to belly. 'This belly is bigger than I'd like but then what the heck I am sixty years of age.'

Tania pottered about the cabin for a bit before going to lie down on the other side of Ashley. She looked at his back and thought many pleasant thoughts. Then she too dozed off after nuzzling closer to Ashley's broad back.

Much later Zanos slowly brought them awake to inform them that the spaceship was nearing destination and that the neutron generators would operate in twenty minutes. The captain awaited them in the control room.

Ashley conveyed this to Rachel and Margaret and fifteen minutes later they were collected by a crew member and led to the control room. They were greeted there by Captain Bulzezatna in a manner that was not quite a Sewa but rather 'a hope you are well' enquiry; a polite Earth style greeting.

The control room was brighter than normal and the captain noticing their observation explained this by simply pointing upwards. There in its spot of glory was the diminutive sized Sun appearing now like a very large and extremely bright star. Although small as seen from this nine billion miles distance it was still intense in the light that it emitted making it difficult to view directly. 520-Green had rotated about and was now travelling backwards towards the starship rendezvous position; though still travelling at 100,000 miles per second. It needed to be thus in order for the gravitational effect created by the neutron generators to slow the spaceship as necessary. Zanos on-board knew at all times the location of the starship and so would operate the neutron generators exactly as required.

The captain invited his guests to take to the split backed seats but she stood beside them in order better to gauge their response to the event. The split back seats could be reclined backwards and all made themselves comfortable. When they were all settled Zanos did a countdown before initiating the neutron generators operation.

Suddenly the sky went blank and what looked like a shower of sparks seemed to emanate from a point high above the view panel; and this was repeated several times over a couple of minutes. Then all was normal again and the bright star that was the Sun returned to view with what seemed an added brilliance. The neutron generators had produced their usual artificial degenerate mass particles ahead of the ships travel path for creating the required gravitational style acceleration towards it. Although each event lasted only micro-seconds the spaceship was accelerated tremendously after a succession of these without the occupants feeling any g-forces whatsoever. It was like falling towards the pull of a large planet mass that was very near.

Finally Zanos on-board informed the captain that the operation had been completed successfully. Zanos also gave the captain the exact position of 520-Green relative to the starship 4110-Silverstreak. In this instance 520-Green was at a position five thousand miles from it. However the spaceship was still travelling at 100 miles per second though this was slowing continually under the ship's own impulse power. It would slow considerably over the next twenty minutes when it could enter into a parking loop pattern closer to the starship. Captain Bulzezatna instructed Zanos to make this initially at a position of one thousand miles from Silverstreak and in a loop parallel to its axial length.

Zanos soon announced that this had been achieved. It was now at a distance of 900 miles from the starship and the parking loop was planned for a 150 mile traverse. The spaceship 520-Green would about face at each midpoint of the loop.

The captain then asked her guests to rise up from the recliners and to look for the starship in the view panels. Ashley and the others searched in vain for Silverstreak and it was only when the captain directed their minds did they see the tiny thin fleck of an object in the extreme distance. At 900 miles away the 2½ mile long starship was practically indiscernible from among the myriad of background stars.

But all knew of the magnification capability of the view panels so they willed for this to be done. As the magnification developed the starship Silverstreak grew in size till it filled their view. And there brilliantly displayed before them was the beauty and majesty of a sleek silver pencil-like starship. The captain had specially positioned 520-Green for this lateral full length view. Ashley marvelled at the extra length of it compared to Zakatanz's 8110-Gold and Natazlat's 9110-Red. But 4110-Silverstreak had a personality all its own. That extra half mile length gave it the sleekness that indicated speed even though it was currently just sitting out there as static as the stars in its background.

Ashley magnified further and scanned it from its head to the tail end. The fuzzy appearance at the front indicated the neutron shield there and the tail end seemed ever so distant from it. Silverstreak had no stripe markings like the other two starships Gold and Red.

'It's so beautiful,' said Rachel with wonder in her tone.

'Yes,' agreed Tania, 'it is that. And it's going to take us further than any other starship has gone.'

Ashley conveyed his agreement and turned around to look at the captain.

Bulzezatna smiled with joy at the enthralment shown by her guests. She too had been thrilled when she had first seen 4110-Silverstreak and now she took enjoyment in seeing others undergo the same reaction. Joy and pride entered her being at moments like this.

When Ashley queried when they were likely to be shuttled across to the starship the captain replied that it would not be for several hours yet. She had positioned the parking loop this far out for two reasons. One was for the distance safety margin for arrival at rendezvous and the other so that her special guests could get their first proper lengthwise view of the starship – with magnification of course. That would now change as Zanos commenced to reposition 520-Green into a parking loop that was located behind the tail end of the starship and at a distance of one hundred miles at its closest. When that had been accomplished only then could passengers from 520-Green be shuttled across to the starship.

Ashley smiled inwardly at the fact that the Oannes never seemed to be in a hurry. They were careful and meticulous in all that they did. Today was January the 22nd and the starship was not due to commence its journey to Nazmos until the morning of the 25th; another couple of days yet. So of course there was no need for any haste. But in his mind he was impatient to be aboard Silverstreak in order to meet Simon and Mazpazam again. Simon must have been of the same mind because a message came through from Zanos.

'Hi mum and dad,' he conveyed, 'welcome to starship base. Mazpazam and I are looking forward to seeing you again. Speak to you soon,'

The communication ended abruptly before Ashley could reply. He understood that Simon must have been given the special privilege of a person to person communication simply to convey his short welcome message. There would be a lot of ship to ship matters being managed and Simon as a 3rd Deputy aboard the starship would have his hands full.

Captain Bulzezatna then said that a late meal was to be served in the dining hall for all passengers before the transfer to the starship. The journey from Earth had taken twenty-five hours in total real time which included the three hours to the million mile distance. And so according to Zanos the simulated current clock time was 8:35pm GMT. The transfer to the starship would not be for another couple of hours.

The meal was the usual fare but Ashley had little appetite and only ate politely. The dining hall was quite full up though a few places were still available. Tania, Rachel and Margaret said they were famished and served themselves well. Ashley however kept nibbling away at his Yaztraka portion and when that finished even had a second small helping 'Just to keep everybody company' he said. But as he ate and the food entered his stomach he realised that he had been hungry after all and the various small portions had quite a filling effect.

There was no news from the captain regarding the transfer to the starship so Ashley, Tania and the other two stayed in the dining hall sipping mugs of hot tea.

At a little after 10.pm Zanos made a general announcement that clearance for the transfer of passengers to the starship had been given for the following simulated morning period. The first shuttle transfers would commence soon after the morning meal. All passengers were to spend this night period in their allocated cabins for a fresh start in the morning. Ashley realised that the Oannes in space adhered to a daily work schedule and it was important that rest periods and sleep times – simulated or otherwise – be properly maintained. As such to have affected a transfer now would have meant arriving on the starship at near midnight and then a further couple of hours for the passengers to settle in. Not only would this have disrupted the work pattern on the starship but that of Bulzezatna's crew as well. So the following morning was the preferred option.

Although Ashley felt disappointed at the postponement he accepted the logic behind it. Simon had said that his Captain Wastanomi was a well respected leader but a strict disciplinarian. It would have been his decision to postpone.

Before settling down for the night with Tania in their cabin Ashley requested Zanos to wake him in good time for an early breakfast. Zanos confirmed that the morning meal would be served at 8.am and that shuttle loading would commence at 10.am. Ashley would receive a mental awakening at 7.am.

There had been general acceptance among the Oannes passengers for the morning plan and all agreed that a period of night rest in their sleep tanks was better for them. It would be a long day of settling in on the starship. There was no urgency with the Oannes and there never was. The starship had two whole days before commencing its journey to the Raznat system. And with Ashley aboard they expected a short journey time; a matter of a few days at most.

Under its own impulse power 4110-Silverstreak had cruised at a little over 100 FTL velocity and made the journey to Earth rendezvous in 23 days. Simon had mentioned this way back in August. Ashley had then said to Simon that he was loath to accelerate Silverstreak to its design limit of 1200 FTL velocity on such a short run. He would decide after discussing the matter with Captain Wastanomi at the appropriate time. Not only was the distance short but the neutron generators had not been tested for slowing the starship from such a velocity.

These thoughts faded as sleep drew its curtain over Ashley's eyes and he settled into a deep and restful sleep. Ashley and Tania both had noticed that on the Oannes spaceships they'd never had any restless periods. They realised that Zanos had the ability to induce sleep for all its ship passengers to ensure they all got a proper rest.

Ashley awoke first exactly at 7.am and Tania opened her eyes as Ashley entered the bathroom to get ready for the day. She followed soon after and conveyed a message to Rachel to meet them at breakfast.

They all took their time over a leisurely tea and toast affair. Ashley had just finished his second mug of tea when Captain Bulzezatna conveyed that she awaited them in the control room if they wished to see the starship from a tail-end angle. Ashley immediately replied in the affirmative and the four of them were in the control room by 9:30am.

As before the captain directed their minds to look towards a particular section in space and upon magnification a much smaller round object was discernable. The captain explained that they were looking at the tail-end section of the starship from a position 100 miles from it. Captain Bulzezatna also explained that their parking loop pattern had a 150 mile traverse more or less at right angles to the length of the starship behind its tail end. They were currently at the mid-point of that traverse. Soon 520-Green would extend towards the loop end of its traverse when a bit more of the side of the starship would become visible.

Over the next half hour as Ashley kept looking at the back end of the starship a gradual elongation of its shape became visible till eventually a partial side view could be clearly seen. They all kept looking at the starship and soon it appeared as if 520-Green was stationary in space. The stars in the

Starship's background showed no lateral displacement.

'We are now at the end of our parking loop,' conveyed the captain, 'and will now begin our little journey to the opposite end of that loop.'

'When do you begin?' asked Ashley and the captain knew exactly what Ashley was referring to. She knew he was impatient to see his son again.

'You will be on the first shuttle group transfer,' said the captain, 'and all are being told as of now to prepare. You may do so as well. One of my crew will accompany you.'

'Thank you Captain,' said Ashley as he went forward and shook her hand. 'And I bid you farewell and I sincerely hope we shall meet again soon.'

'Go carefully Ashley,' she replied, 'and I wish for the same. Simon will be with you.'

Ashley knew what Bulzezatna was referring to. The journey to Zarama would be a long one as would the ordeal there. And then there was the journey back. There were many unknown factors to be considered which created uncertainty. As such luck would go some way towards achieving ultimate success.

For some reason the underlying emotion that Ashley sensed in Bulzezatna's manner seemed to imply that she feared she might not see him again. And she could be right thought Ashley. Gozmanot's visions implied nothing in that regard. If Zarama was indeed to be vanquished to disappear forever then was that to be Ashley's fate as well? Ashley would of course do whatever was necessary for success and at whatever cost to him.

A crew member then led them to the rear of the spaceship and into the electrostatic suiting up room. There were other Oannes passengers already there in various modes of the process of putting on the gold shuttle suits. And it was not long before Ashley, Tania, Rachel and Margaret were also fully suited up with the ladies wearing the extra head scarf adornment. The scarves would keep control of their long hair and prevent them looking like porcupines. It had been a humorous occasion on that first shuttle journey so long ago.

The first group of passengers boarded the three allocated shuttles and Ashley and co were led to one of them. The same crew member conveyed that their shuttle was designated as the lead in the group with the other two following closely behind though spaced at intervals of approximately one mile.

Ashley knew from experience that the starship airlock was large and could accommodate all three shuttles at the same time.

They boarded the shuttle in orderly fashion and settled down on the left-side front seats together. The thigh clamps slowly closed to apply a gentle pressure to keep them comfortably in place. Tania quickly re-adjusted her head scarf as she felt it not quite right. She smiled at Ashley when she was satisfied. The shuttle filled behind them and its door eventually closed. Ashley looked back to see that the same crew member was to command their shuttle journey. He was in a raised seat at the rear and catching Ashley's glance he nodded and smiled.

It was several moments later that the lights in the shuttle bay dimmed and after what seemed a long interval the rear bay doors commenced to slowly open to reveal the darkness of the outside space environment. All three shuttles rose upwards slowly and one by one they rotated to face the dark cavernous opening.

Ashley always wondered at his lack of motion sense. He peered into the black image of space that was in front of them and without any sensation of movement the shuttle had smoothly passed through the bay doors and out into its vastness.

At first all seemed like a bland blackness until the eyes adjusted and became accustomed to the ever brightening phenomena emanating from the massive congestion of points of light all around being the stars of their galaxy. The Milky Way circling across their view gave its own special glare to the darkness. After a while the bright pathway became recognisable for the twists, turns and swirls within it; a very recognisable and familiar universe zone. Suddenly loneliness departs and a vague companionship beckons as recognition of the star assembly asserted itself. Ashley felt at ease as the shuttle built its own gravity as it accelerated towards the distant starship.

After forty minutes the shuttle was just a few miles from the tail end of the starship and now its massive size became apparent. The slight gravity effect from the initial acceleration had ceased after about twenty journey minutes and Zanos on-board had countered the weightless nausea building up in some passengers with an induced emotional adjustment. Zanos was good at this. As such Ashley and the others felt quite at ease though slightly drowsy.

The shuttle was now level with the side of the lower end of the starship just a mile distant from it and moving at a relatively slow pace. The silver body of the starship filled their view as they progressed towards the forward end and the open airlock compartment. The other two shuttles were behind in a tandem fashion and Ashley could imagine the awe and pride in each Oannes passenger viewing this product of their scientific advancement and success.

'Could anyone do other than admire such an achievement,' thought Ashley as he became aware of how fiercely Tania was gripping his hand.

The shuttle soon began to rotate about its axis such that the top of it pointed toward the tail end of the starship. After several minutes a slight gravity effect made its presence felt. Ashley knew that this came from the immense gravitational effect of the starship's neutron shield.

Suddenly there before them appeared this large cavern of an airlock and Ashley looked into the large illuminated space that was in there. Within moments the shuttle had entered this and was settling upon the deck floor. Soon another shuttle settled beside them and this was followed by a third. The lighting dimmed and the airlock doors slowly shut. After several minutes the lighting went bright again which was the signal that atmosphere in the airlock was restored. The doors of the shuttles opened as one and the passengers began to disembark. Ashley and the others were the last to leave and were led by the same crew member out onto the Cargo Platform of the starship and to a large hall where they removed their electrostatic suits and handed them to one of the many Oannes attendants there. These would obviously be returned to 520-Green in time.

The crew member then led them into a large elevator about twenty feet square where they were joined by other smiling passengers and taken down one level to the Habitation Platform.

The doors to the elevator opened and there to meet them were Simon and Mazpazam. Both looked extremely smart in the uniformity of their tunics, leggings and footwear and Tania rushed forward to hug her son. She then reached out and pulled Mazpazam towards her to give her a hug too. Ashley and Rachel followed closely behind while Margaret eased up behind them with a bemused look on her face. Simon looked a bit like she remembered Ashley had that first time when he came to the Dutton Consultants' offices in Kennington, London way back in 2003.

Simon then came to Margaret and gave her a kiss on both cheeks before introducing her to Mazpazam. Mazpazam gave Margaret a Sewa welcome and added her kiss to one of Margaret's cheeks.

Ashley thought it was nice that Simon had made Margaret feel included in the family group. Simon had a lot of Oannes style in his manner for politeness and etiquette and Ashley was proud of him for it.

'It's lovely to see you all again,' said Simon in a semi official tone, 'and on behalf of our captain I welcome you all aboard the starship 4110-Silverstreak. And may all her journeys be swift, safe and sure.'

Simon had stood very straight as he said this.

Then with a big smile he added, 'Captain Wastanomi would like to meet you all so that he can convey his personal welcome and conditions of travel.'

And with an exaggerated bow and a sweeping flourish of his right arm and a wink he said, 'Follow me please.'

He then pushed in between his parents and linked arms with them and they stepped forward together. Mazpazam did the same with Rachel and Margaret. They talked and laughed as they walked the near quarter of a mile to the central column of the Habitation Platform and the captain's quarters.

As they got close a stocky Oannes figure emerged and stood awaiting their approach. Simon and Mazpazam released themselves and went forward to stand either side of their captain.

'Mum, dad,' said Simon, 'this is Captain Wastanomi of the starship Silverstreak. Captain these are my parents, my sister and a dear friend of the family.'

The captain nodded his head ever so slightly and then conveyed a Sewa which was the polite and correct thing to do.

Immediately Ashley made a slightly deeper bow from his waist and replied also telepathically to the captain's Sewa solicitation with a proper formal Sewa of his own and on behalf of their group.

The captain smiled his pleasure and looked keenly first at Ashley and then at each of the others in turn. His main interest was Ashley but Oannes politeness could not let him ignore the others of the family group. He then came forward and shook Ashley's hand.

'Welcome aboard my starship,' he said aloud looking at each in turn. 'I hope to get to know you as many of my colleagues have done. Simon is a credit to the starship as are all my officers and crew. Please enter the captain's quarters with me and drink a glass of Wazu for the success of all our ventures. Simon and Mazpazam you will join us too.'

This last was in the form of a command rather than a request.

Captain Wastanomi led the way forward and into his 'Captain's Quarters' as he put it and gestured them to places around the ample table. He then filled the glasses which had been specially placed in readiness for them. Ashley read the captain's body language and accepted that here was a person who was comfortable with formality and order and perhaps ceremony as well. The captain had obviously done research into Ashley and knew of his gifts and the history of his achievements.

But Ashley felt that he'd like to change that formal image in the captain's mind towards his more congenial life-style and unorthodox manner of thought.

'My dear Captain Wastanomi,' said Ashley with a big smile, 'I thank you for your welcome and hospitality. My family and I are grateful for the privilege of being allowed to travel aboard your starship. We have a long and hazardous journey ahead of us and I would like for us to become true friends.'

Ashley then conveyed a history of his friendship with Captains Zakatanz and Bulzezatna and also Muznant and Brazjaf. He also conveyed his past relationship with governing council member Ritozanan and her special influence in getting his wishes agreed.

'Captain I would like you to know me as they did – especially Ritozanan before she deceased,' conveyed Ashley.

Then he added, 'I am not the person as perhaps you imagine me to be.'

He then reached out his hand towards the captain and conveyed that his mind and innermost thoughts were open to him.

Captain Wastanomi hesitated before reaching out and putting his hand on Ashley's. The hesitation had been a doubt that a personage such as Ashley was willing to open his inner being to a total stranger. There must be pride and confidence within the personality of this human person from all that he could do and had achieved so far. The confidence had to be from all the power at his command. Wastanomi would soon see for himself what made this human tick.

Ashley smiled as he sensed the inner core of his mind and memories being searched and probed. It only lasted seconds before the captain withdrew his hand from Ashley's and sat back as he assimilated all that he had learned. There was no sign of pride here or sense of power within this human. On the contrary there was an inner anxiety and fear that he might not succeed in his quest to stop Zarama. Otherwise there was a lot of love, happiness and contentment and absolutely no ambition for glory. The captain had never expected Ashley to be a person such as this and before he knew what he was doing he put his own hand forward and conveyed for Ashley to do the same to him.

'Thank you Captain,' Ashley replied, 'but that will not be necessary. I have all I need to know.'

'How is that so?' asked the captain. 'I did not sense any probing from you.'

'That is because I did not,' said Ashley. 'It is another of my gifts. I call it my inner voice. It speaks to me whenever it feels so inclined and it just did. On the other hand it can remain silent too for long periods. Another Oannes also has the gift. He is Korizazit of the Nazmos governing council of ministers. He received the gift by accident through me when he was probing my mind.'

'So then you know all about me?' queried Wastanomi.

'No, not everything, only the essentials,' said Ashley. 'The inner voice is never invasive,'

Ashley smiled before he continued.

'Captain Wastanomi you graduated from the Wentazta space academy when you were aged seventy four. You were never socially minded and did not feel inclined towards the opposite sex. You were keen and out to acquire all the experience and skills of spacemanship that was possible. You transferred from spaceship to spaceship after short periods of a few years on each. The reports to the Nazmos council members stated that you were dedicated to your space duties and extremely skilled and reliable. At the age of 150 years you finally achieved your aim of joining the crew of a starship. That starship was 4110-Silver and over the years that followed you worked your way up to the responsible position of 1ˢᵗ Deputy. For a period of several years your starship was used as a passenger ferry between Nazmos and Earth. You managed to spend time in Anztarza and even visited the northern forests on several occasions. You were impressed by what you saw but expressed no views on the matter. Then at the age of 207 years you were selected to succeed your retiring captain whom you admired and respected. Captain Rozintant aged 295 years was of ill health and he gave his special recommendation to the Nazmos council that you were the best candidate to succeed him as captain.'

'I did not know that,' said Wastanomi with surprise in his manner. 'Captain Rozintant personally told me that he was surprised at my appointment as captain of his starship. He did not say much more than to wish me success in my job as its captain.'

'Like you Captain Rozintant remained a single Oannes person all his life,' continued Ashley, 'and like you he had no time for distractions of that nature. But he respected your skills and liked you as a son. If you look into the Nazmos council records you will find his glowing recommendation that there was no fitter candidate for the position of captain of the starship 4110-Silver than 1ˢᵗ Deputy Wastanomi. He detailed all his reasons for his opinion in that report.'

'How can you know all this?' said Wastanomi with a certain renewed admiration in his voice.

'I told you captain,' said Ashley smiling, 'these things are revealed to me.'

'Just as Gozmanot was revealed to you?' asked Wastanomi.

'Yes,' said Ashley simply, 'just as Gozmanot was revealed to me.'

'I thank you for this,' said Wastanomi, 'it is a revelation that means much to me. I admired Captain Rozintant and thought him a great leader and now you have enhanced that image considerably. I will drink a glass of Wazu to his memory. Sadly he is no more so I cannot convey to him what is in my mind right now.'

Ashley remained silent for a whole minute to let Wastanomi settle his thoughts with regard to the news pleasing as it was before continuing.

'You were captain of this starship for twenty three years before I came upon the Nazmos scene,' said Ashley looking keenly at the captain.

'Your Captain Rozintant had not finished with you yet,' he added with a smile. 'He and Brazjaf were known to each other and it was at Rozintant's recommendation in the Earth year date of 2005 that you and your starship be chosen for upgrading for the subsequent mission to Zarama.'

Another brief pause followed.

'The rest is history,' said Ashley. 'You Captain were then 230 years of age and became resident starship captain for the duration of the modification program. And now forty years later you are captain of the fastest operational starship of the Oannes space fleet.'

The captain nodded and then hesitated as he thought of his next question. It would be presumptuous and impolite to pose such a question but Ashley read the sign correctly and gave the answer required.

'Captain you must bear with me on this as I do not propose to push Silverstreak to its maximum 1200 FTL design velocity on our journey to Nazmos. Your neutron generators have not as yet been tested at this limit. So I propose a lesser velocity of 800FTL as a first step. Then after I have successfully completed my task of making the Nazmos orbit permanent we could perhaps arrange a trial run at maximum 1200 FTL velocity and see how the neutron generators cope with slowing the starship from that speed. If everything is as per the design and to your satisfaction then the next stage would be the journey to Zarama.'

Captain Wastanomi nodded his understanding and conveyed his agreement.

'Thank you Ashley,' he said, 'that is prudent and wise in the circumstances and I agree fully. Perhaps one day what Captain Rozintant has done for me I may in some small measure repay with respect to one of my own officers. Simon is a great spaceman and a good deputy. He will go far.'

'As far as Zarama,' said Ashley and laughed.

Captain Wastanomi looked puzzled for a moment before seeing the humour in the remark and breaking into a wide smile. Oannes rarely laugh aloud.

'Let us drink a toast,' he said. 'In fact let us drink several toasts; the first to the memory of Captain Rozintant.'

They raised their glasses and said, 'To the memory of Captain Rozintant,' and took a sip of Wazu.

'And secondly I raise a toast to you Ashley and all of your family here.' Wastanomi raised his glass alone and took a sip.

'And thirdly let us drink a toast to all our journeys in Silverstreak. May they be swift, safe and sure.'

All repeated 'swift, safe and sure' as they raised their glasses and drank.

Then Simon hesitantly stood up and walked to one side.

'May I be permitted my Captain?' he asked with deep respect in his voice.

Wastanomi frowned but then gave a brief nod to Simon.

'Captain I know that you do not like your crew to be presumptuous but I feel we have omitted one toast that I make on behalf of your crew,' said Simon.

'Continue son of Ashley,' said Wastanomi.

There was a hidden rebuke there to show Simon that he was only permitted to speak unasked because his family were present.

'I would like you all to raise your glasses in a toast to Captain Wastanomi,' said Simon in a slow measured voice. 'He is a captain who brooks no nonsense from his crew but he is wise and generous in his praise where due. He has the respect and fear of all his subordinates; the fear is that we may not measure up to his high standard. But above all he has the affection and respect of all of us who know that he cares for our welfare.'

Simon then raised his glass and looking around repeated.

'I drink to Captain Wastanomi, captain of the fastest starship in the universe.'

Ashley noticed a smile on Wastanomi's face as he looked directly at Simon and gave a slight nod of acceptance; perhaps there was approval in there as well.

Simon kept a straight face and gave his captain a bow from the waist before sitting down. His face had gone unusually red in tone as he kept his head looking downwards.

'Thank you Simon,' said Wastanomi. The use of the first name was an indication that he was forgiven. But Simon would never again speak out of turn in the presence of his captain.

After a brief interval the captain looked at Simon and Mazpazam and nodded at them and conveyed that they should go about their duties.

'Thank you Captain,' said Simon as he and Mazpazam stood up, 'we shall attend to the comfort of the new arrivals.'

Simon smiled at his parents and Rachel and Margaret and gave a brief bow before turning about and walking briskly out onto the platform – with Mazpazam following close behind.

Ashley recognised that Wastanomi was firm on discipline at least where his staff was concerned. So Ashley knew that he must express his own desires with regard to his son and Mazpazam.

'Captain,' he said in a quiet voice, 'I wish to make a request,'

Ashley had kept his mind open and was not surprised at what the captain said next.

Your request is granted Ashley,' he said, 'it shall be as you wish it. Simon and Mazpazam will be allowed to spend as much time as possible with you without infringing on their normal duties. Meal times are theirs so they will spend these with you. Arrangements will be made for your meals to be served within your accommodation and Simon and Mazpazam will come to you there.'

He paused for a moment and Ashley noticed hesitation in his manner before he continued.

'However I have a small request of you too,' he said.

'It is granted even though I do not know what it is that you wish,' said Ashley.

'Thank you,' said Wastanomi. 'It is merely this that you spend time with me here in my quarters each day that you are aboard this starship. I would like to get to know you and for you to get to know and understand me. I have few friends though many acquaintances. I would be grateful if you can indulge me in this.'

'Certainly captain it will be my pleasure,' said Ashley. 'I shall make a point of visiting your quarters each day at your convenience.'

'Thank you. Mid morning would be a most convenient time – perhaps for just an hour,' said Wastanomi. 'The journey to Zarama will be a long one and it would be nice to have pleasant company.'

Ashley was complimented that Wastanomi had taken a liking to him. And he too felt that here was a person he would like to know better. From what Ashley had seen so far he was impressed by this Oannes captain.

'Is it to be just you and me in these conversations or might I include my wife Tania?' asked Ashley not smiling this time. He did not want Tania excluded and conveyed as much by his expression.

'That is what I hoped you would say,' said Wastanomi. 'I have never been comfortable in female Oannes company but I find your wife Tania most agreeable and charming. How can I get to know the man without getting to know his partner in life? The two are as one and influence each other equally. I find you most interesting in a very pleasant way and am intrigued to know you both better. I think we shall have many interesting conversations.'

He smiled specially for Tania's benefit.

'Thank you,' said Ashley, 'you are most gracious. We too would like to know more of the captain of Silverstreak. However I have a query about my son Simon.'

Captain Wastanomi nodded for Ashley to continue. There was a hint of a smile on his face though. Ashley had kept his mind open so the captain must know the question.

'I would like to know the true reason why Simon was placed on your starship,' asked Ashley.

'All of Simon's reports were excellent especially his skill at navigation during his academy years,' said Wastanomi. 'There was also a strong recommendation for his placement here from the Nazmos governing council which I expected had been a special request from you. I supposed that you wished him to be by your side on the long journey to Zarama. So far he has done his duties well and I am pleased with his performance. He is a credit to the starship. The fact that he has chosen a legal partnership with an Oannes female does not concern me but Mazpazam's qualities as a spaceman are as good if not better than your son's. They work well together and form a good team and I am happy with that.'

'Is there anything else? Any other reason?' queried Ashley looking sideways at Tania who was smiling.

Wastanomi took on a serious air as he looked closely at Ashley and then at Tania and finally around to a smiling Rachel and Margaret. He realised that there was something he should have been told about his 3rd deputy.

'It was all I was concerned about at the time,' he said as a niggling concern arose in his mind. After all they were talking about Ashley's son. 'Is there something I should know about Simon?'

Ashley smiled and held out his hand to the captain.

'Captain you should read more deeply, particularly about my son from his childhood years,' said Ashley. 'It will tell you all you need to know about him.'

Wastanomi reached out and took hold of Ashley's hand for a brief moment and then let go of it. There was surprise and mild consternation on his face; and a questioning look.

'I was not informed,' he said huskily.

Then repeated more assertively, 'Why was I not informed?'

Ashley looked kindly at the captain before replying.

'Simon would not have wanted preferential treatment even when he was in the academy,' he said, 'and it was at his request that this secret lie hidden. His premonition gift is unique. Even I do not possess such a talent. Clairvoyance is not something that can be called upon at will. These premonition occasions are rare and come to him only at random or as a need may arise. But it supplements my own qualities and I need him to be with us on the journey to Zarama. We do not know what hazards lurk within the 431 lightyear distance between Nazmos and that dwarf star. But if there is something to impede us then Simon may be able to warn us of it and we can perhaps follow a different course. Simon's premonition instincts may be the crucial factor that leads to our success against Zarama. His presence is simply a matter of caution and safety. It was Ritozanan who was given this information and saw fit to persuade the Nazmos governing council to place Simon on your starship. I apologise if I have bent the rules for my benefit but without Simon beside me I would feel naked and vulnerable on that journey.'

There was a serious aspect on the captain's face but he remained silent for nearly a minute.

'Come, my friends,' he then said in a rather subdued tone, 'I will show you to your accommodation. All your meals will be served to you there.'

He then stood up and led the way to the door and out onto the habitation platform. They walked in silence to the first circle of housing structures and Wastanomi opened a door and led them inside.

'This is a family accommodation and you will be comfortable here,' he said, 'let me know if there is anything you desire.'

He then reached out and warmly shook Ashley's hand.

'Thank you for all that you have revealed to me,' he said. 'I am most impressed but need time to consider it all. The afternoon meal is only a couple of hours away and will be served to you here. Please remember our meeting in my quarters tomorrow mid-morning. I look forward to our conversations then.'

He then turned about and left closing the door quietly behind him.

Ashley looked at Tania and then at Rachel and Margaret.

'Well now,' he started to say but that was as far as he got. It was Tania who began first with a suppressed giggle. Then her shoulders began to shake and full blown laughter commenced. The others all couldn't help but join in. After a minute Ashley had to wipe the tears from his eyes.

'Poor chap,' said Tania, 'I think it's all been a bit much for him. I think he was in shock. What do you think he'll do about Simon?'

'Nothing I imagine,' said Ashley. 'Wastanomi is a good captain and knows an asset when he sees one. We'll see him together tomorrow after breakfast and by then it would all have sunk in I suppose. Sorry girls but you'll have to wander around on your own during these meetings.'

'That's alright dad,' said Rachel, 'I find him a bit too serious for me. Margaret and I will find lots to do I'm sure.'

It was now close to midday on the starship's simulated time. Their accommodation was in fact two apartments with inter-connecting doors. Unlike the spaceships with communal dining areas these apartments had additional space for a dining table and four split-back chairs. However it could seat upto six around it. Rachel and Margaret went through to their side which also had a similar arrangement while Tania and Ashley settled down right where they were.

For a moment Tania started her giggles again but stopped when Ashley didn't join in and gave her a frown and a shake of his head. He didn't want this flood of mirth being picked up by the captain and interpreted wrongly. But then he stepped forward with a smile and cuddled his wife in a long tight hug.

'I love you,' he whispered.

'Me too,' said Tania.

And then for some reason they both began to giggle though in a suppressed manner.

'What shall we do till lunchtime?' said Tania sporting a wicked smile.

'I can think of many things,' said Ashley, 'but we are not alone. I think I shall lie on the bed for a while and gather my thoughts regarding the captain. I'm sure we'll get to know him better as we see more of him. Our daily get-togethers should prove useful and my instinct tells me that he is quite likeable. He is perhaps a bit like Captain Zakatanz was. I remember what he was like when we first met.'

It was about an hour later and after Ashley had had a bit of a doze that there was a knock on the interconnecting door and three people walked into the room. It was Rachel, Margaret and a smiling Simon.

'The captain has delegated me to especially see to all your comforts,' said Simon as he kissed his mum. 'And also he has asked me to give you all a detailed tour of the Habitation Platform area and any other part of his starship that is not restricted to ordinary crew.'

Although Simon's presence was unexpected it did not come as a surprise to Ashley that the captain had delegated Simon in this unusual duty.

Captain Wastanomi was a wise captain and a clever one in that he considered a harmonious relationship with Ashley to be to his and to the starship's benefit. He had also drawn the inference that it was possible that Simon might be like his father with other hidden talents. As such he had instructed Zanos about Simon and for Zanos to monitor Simon's thoughts continually for any premonition revelation that might arise. Zanos would thus instantly be apprised of any necessary course of action needed which would also be brought to the attention of the Captain. Wastanomi would do whatever was necessary for the safety of his ship and its passengers. And of course the success of their mission which in this case was to reach Zarama intact.

'And where is Mazpazam,' asked Tania, 'is she not with you?'

'No mum, she has duties of her own. We have two more spaceships arriving from Anztarza loaded with passengers; one today and one tomorrow. There is a lot to oversee.'

Simon conveyed that during their meeting with the captain these rooms had been organised for the short journey to Nazmos. All clothes and toiletries had been carefully placed ready for use in each apartment. There was a lot happening behind the scenes and everything was done to a plan. Ashley had thought that he was being given preferential treatment but Simon said that all passengers on starships and spaceships were given the same privileged service. The busiest times were the transfers via the shuttles and then the meal times. With nearly two thousand passengers on a starship this required a service that needed to operate like clockwork. And most of the time it did.

They talked about what Simon planned to show them that they had not seen or been allowed to view on the other starships. Simon was not letting on about one aspect of the tour and Ashley knew that a special surprise treat was in the offing.

The afternoon meal was served about then and was delivered on floating pallets. Zanos conveyed that all the dishes should be off-loaded onto the dining table of the apartment and for them to enjoy their meal. This they did but it was not as if they were dining in the captain's quarters like they had with Captains Zakatanz and Natazlat.

Ashley reckoned that Captain Wastanomi was a very private Oannes person and preferred to dine alone unhindered by extraneous banal conversation. For this very reason Ashley was keen to get to know the captain better.

While they were busy at their meal another floating pallet arrived with hot and cold drinks. This stayed to one side out of the way and only came to the dining table when Ashley thought about his nice hot mug of sweet tea.

Apparently this was to be the pattern for their meals aboard the starship Silverstreak and Ashley's initial disappointment was picked up by Zanos and relayed to the captain. A prompt response was received that enlightened Ashley as to the purpose for this. It came in the form of a realisation that the captain had done this for a purpose. And that was to give Ashley extra family time with his son and Mazpazam.

Simon and Mazpazam had been given freedom during each mealtime while Ashley was aboard and they would spend this time with his parents. This meant that they would also have all their meals served there. The captain could not have members of his crew whether officers or otherwise to make free usage of his private quarters. Besides, freedom of conversation between father and son would be inhibited by the captain's presence among them. These thoughts had been induced in Ashley's consciousness by Zanos on the express command of Captain Wastanomi and carried out with the utmost delicacy of manner. Ashley conveyed a private thanks to the captain for setting his mind at rest about the issue.

When the meal was completed and all had been cleared away onto the floating pallets Simon led the way out onto the open Habitation Platform.

'Let us stroll around for a bit and see how the other passengers are faring,' said Simon.

They walked towards the far wall of the starship between rows upon rows of apartments but all seemed quiet and they met no one.

'These will be occupied by the new passengers who arrive tomorrow,' he said. 'However, we do have passengers arriving in a few hours and Mazpazam has been busy organising for their arrival.'

They then walked on and came to a part of the apartment blocks that were occupied. Obviously the residents knew of Ashley's presence aboard the starship and also of his usual after dinner constitution walkabout in the area. Many came out into the open and conveyed polite Sewas to Ashley and his companions. It was a pleasant way to be greeted and Ashley conveyed his own good wishes in Sewa form to all who had expressed goodness towards him. It was an emotionally uplifting experience. It made him feel special and if such a thing was possible then Ashley was smiling on the inside.

Simon led them to the elevator housing that had brought them down from the Cargo Platform earlier today. This time when they entered they were transported down another level. When they emerged and had walked forward Ashley found that they had arrived onto a balcony viewing platform. There was a walkway that led towards the central column and Ashley could see that there were three other walkways that radiated from there to outer wall positions. The ceiling was only ten feet above them.

'I think this is as good a place as any to get an idea of the layout of the food growing section of the starship,' said Simon. 'Normally passengers are not permitted here for reasons of contamination but the captain especially wished that you be shown this. It is what will sustain us on our long journey towards Zarama.'

About fifteen feet below them Ashley could see huge tanks filled with glistening clear water rippling as if something was moving within their depths. As he looked carefully he made out the occasional blurred form of an Oannes person moving underwater among the many varied coloured shapes growing further down.

'These food growing tanks are each roughly the size of a football pitch with water depths of twenty feet,' explained Simon. 'They are constructed on the same principle as are the food growing domes of Anztarza but of course on a slightly smaller scale for each tank.'

As they stood looking downwards one of the Oannes workers came up to the water surface and on seeing the visitors gave a brief wave and conveyed a welcoming Sewa. Ashley immediately conveyed a return greeting. He reckoned that there had to be a fairly large complement of starship personnel aboard for so many operations to run smoothly.

And it was Rachel who posed the question.

'How many crew are aboard the starship?' she asked.

'Because Silverstreak is a newly modified starship we have the usual complement of four hundred personnel currently supplemented by technical experts and observers. I think these add about another forty Oannes to the ship's complement.'

'And what are these extra persons supposed to do?' asked Rachel again.

'All I know is that they are monitoring every aspect of the ship and its performance,' said Simon. 'They are all very thorough and leave nothing to chance.'

'Good,' was all that Rachel had to say.

'Well then,' said Simon, 'if you've seen enough of where your dinner comes from we can proceed to your next adventure,'

Then he added with a wicked smile, 'It's only about two miles up that way,' as he pointed upwards.

'Oh,' said Tania, 'are we going outside the starship again?'

'No mum,' said Simon, 'we are staying inside it all the time. I thought I'd show you where the ship's power is housed. All two miles of it towards the tail end of Silverstreak.'

Simon then conveyed the layout of the main central shaft that ended just above the cargo platform. Above this was an empty lift shaft about twenty feet square which rose straight upwards all the way to the tail end of the starship. Along the way were floor levels at forty feet intervals upon which were fixed the numerous motors that generated the linear impulse that propelled the starship. And of course accompanying these on every alternate floor were the generators that produced the massive flow of electrons from directly stimulated atomic nuclei. These then powered the impulse motors and the starship functions. Everything was monitored by Zanos and regular status reports were conveyed to the captain and technical staff. The empty central shaft functioned as an elevator recess that permitted access to every level should the need arise.

'I'm sorry but access onto those floors is not permitted to us,' said Simon, 'but I will be able to let you view each floor from our transport platform as we rise upwards. We must remain on the transporter at all times. At the farthest position we will be about two and a quarter miles from the forward neutron shield and its gravity effect upon us will be considerably less than that on the Habitation Platform.'

'How much is less?' queried Rachel.

'Oh about a fifth of normal gravity,' said Simon. 'You will feel much lighter and may also find it rather exhilarating. I know I do.'

'I suppose it will be a bit like on the shuttle that brought us here,' said Rachel. 'It was quite nice when we began to feel gravity returning as we came close to the starship's entrance airlock.'

'I forgot about that,' said Simon smiling, 'well done sis you're quite the spaceman now.'

They all then followed Simon back into the large elevator and before long they were up on the cargo platform. Simon led the way to one side of the floor where a number of Deck Transporter types were positioned in a row along the starship's inner wall. And there waiting with a hint of a smile on her pretty face was Mazpazam. She was beside one of the transporters and Simon moved to stand beside her. There was no outward show of affection apart from the expressive glow on their faces.

The transporters were simply a dais-like platform about fifteen feet square in size and three feet in depth. There was an additional three feet of railing on three of its sides. The side with no rail had steps along its width to allow passengers to alight and disembark. It was a simple affair and Simon conveyed that the starship crew referred to them as transportation platforms for access to remote areas of the starship.

'Hello again,' said Mazpazam, 'I came as soon as Simon conveyed his message.'

'I had to send for someone to accompany us on our transporter journey up the power shaft,' said Simon. 'It is starship regulation that at least two crew members are present on the transportation platform when it rises up into the starship's power shaft. So of course I thought who better than my Mazpazam to make up our group.'

Mazpazam looked pleased that Simon had referred to her as his Mazpazam. It was an expression of his love for her. And every woman likes to be reminded of that love.

'Come with me Aunt Tania and Uncle Ashley,' said Mazpazam, 'for I shall be your guide on this little adventure. Simon will do the same for Rachel and Margaret.'

She then led the way up the few steps onto the platform and to the far side rail. Ashley and Tania followed and stood either side of her. They were followed by Simon leading Rachel and Margaret to a position at the other rail but close to them.

'Hold on,' said Mazpazam and she gave Zanos the command to take them slowly upwards to the opening in the centre of the ceiling above the cargo platform.

The ceiling was currently about a hundred feet above the cargo platform floor but it was in a fixed position and part of the starship superstructure. The Habitation, Cargo and Food platforms were fixed relative to each other but were moveable relative to the body of the starship. The movement was either towards or away from the forward neutron shield and did so on six columns around the sides and one in the central position. Under high acceleration conditions these platforms moved closer to the neutron shield. As such no extreme acceleration pressures were felt by the passengers and crew. The central and side columns then became visible on the cargo platform as if they were rising out of its floor. There were small railings around these column locations for safety reasons.

The transportation platform commanded by Mazpazam rose ever so slowly and smoothly as it proceeded up towards the central area. There was a brief hesitation as it manoeuvred to position itself correctly before entering the shaft opening. It continued upwards at the same slow and easy pace until they came level with an open floor area. The platform then came to a dead stop here and Simon took up the commentary.

'This is the first impulse power unit level,' he said. 'It extends all the way to the sides of the starship and is forty feet from floor to ceiling. Each impulse motor is twenty feet in diameter and is connected to both the floor and the ceiling. Each of the impulse motors is symmetrically positioned around this access shaft so that the starship receives a uniformity of thrust in an exact axial direction. At FTL velocities it is crucial to keep the body of the starship directionally behind the much wider neutron shield. The slightest waver could be disastrous for the starship and its inhabitants.'

Ashley looked across to the floor area and all he could see was column after neat column with nothing in between. It was like a forest of columns that were separated by a few feet on either side.

'How many impulse motors are there on this level,' asked Ashley?

'This is the widest of the floors,' said Simon, 'and there are about ten thousand individually mounted impulse motors housed here. As you know the starship tapers to eighty percent so the topmost level contains a bit less; about eight thousand impulse motors.'

'And how many levels of these are there,' asked Tania?

'There are 120 twin levels,' said Simon and paused with a smile on his face as he noticed Rachel's puzzlement.

'And what is a twin level,' asked Rachel?

'A twin level is literally two levels,' said Simon. 'One level houses the impulse motors like these here and the other is the next one above it that houses the generators that produce the electrical power for them.'

'Gosh,' said Rachel 'that is a lot of power.'

'Before modification this starship had ninety twin levels. The half mile extension to its length has added another thirty for the increased power requirement. Also the very latest development in impulse motors and generators were fitted to enhance the starship's impulse capacity by a hundred times. But this has only allowed an increase in the starship's velocity to ten times its previous max of 10 FTL. The starship must overcome the tremendously increasing rate of energy-medium being absorbed into its protective forward neutron shield.'

Rachel and Margaret both nodded to say they understood all of this; with wonder in their expressions. There was considerably more to a starship than either had at first imagined.

'What of maintenance,' asked Ashley, 'how do you go about that?'

'It is all done from within,' said Mazpazam, 'and each motor or generator can be dismantled and re-assembled right here. I know what you are thinking; with over a million power units to monitor how do we manage. Neither impulse motors nor electricity generators have any moving components so wear and tear is nil. But materials in the electrical coils can degenerate with time and so replacement eventually becomes necessary. However that time period is gauged in thousands of years and our scientists have assured us that we are not near that position.'

'Thank you for that,' said Ashley with a big grin on his face, 'I feel quite reassured.'

Mazpazam smiled back and gave her uncle Ashley a slight bow to emphasise that she appreciated the humour in his remark.

The transporter then rose upwards again and slightly above the floor level. It then moved forward onto the floor area and settled down there.

'This is how we actually get onto each floor,' said Mazpazam. 'But no one may venture onto any floor without proper purpose. So we cannot disembark or walk around – but looking is okay for you have been specially permitted by Captain Wastanomi.'

Ashley and the others looked around and Ashley conveyed an appreciative thanks to the captain for the privilege.

'We will now return to the shaft and do the same for the next level,' said Mazpazam.

The transporter lifted off the floor and floated back into the lift shaft zone. It then slowly rose upwards and stopped at the next floor level.

'This is where the electron generators are housed,' said Mazpazam. 'As you can see the generators are bulky and have a very different profile to that of the impulse motors.'

Ashley could see only those that were close to them. Each generator was again housed or attached between both floor and ceiling and was certainly very different. They blocked his view to those that were behind and further away.

'How many generators are there on this floor,' asked Rachel.

'Well each of these generates enough electricity to power upto a dozen impulse motors,' said Mazpazam, 'so of course they are proportionately fewer in number. However we keep to a fifty percent safety factor and so have thirteen hundred generators available to operate here; though not all of them need to be in operation at the same time.'

Rachel gave a silent whistle at these statistics.

Mazpazam looked at Simon who then took up the narrative of the tour.

'We've shown you as much as we can,' he said and paused.

Then he pointed upwards and said, 'Are you ready for the ride up to the tail end of Silverstreak?'

Ashley looked at Tania while Rachel looked at Margaret.

'What thrills does that entail,' asked Rachel on behalf of all of them?

'Well when the crew on duty use this lift they prefer to speed upwards quite fast,' said Simon.

'How fast,' asked a keen Rachel? She had always liked white knuckle rides when she was a kid.

'Well maybe upto forty miles per hour speed,' said Simon, 'which is nearly two floors a second.'

Simon paused and winked at Rachel.

'But we won't go that fast for mum and dad's sake,' he said smiling. 'Mazpazam will take us upwards at the slower pace of a third of that or a floor in one and a half seconds.'

'And how long will that take,' asked Rachel.

This time it was Mazpazam who answered Rachel's query.

'To reach the upper limit of our journey it will take eight minutes approximately,' she said. 'Of course the gravity will be less there as we shall be quite a bit further from the pull of the neutron shield.'

Everyone waited and Mazpazam sensed their interest.

'It will be about a fifth of normal gravity,' she said, 'so we will stop there only briefly before commencing our return. Shall we begin the ascent to the top? As a precaution I would suggest you hold onto the rails.'

At first the transporter rose slowly as before and then its ascent velocity increased gradually.

'How does that feel,' asked Mazpazam. 'We are ascending at ten miles per hour.'

'It feels fine,' said Tania.

'Good,' said Mazpazam, 'then I shall increase to fifteen miles per hour which will be our maximum ascent rate.'

Again the upward speed increased slowly till the desired rate was achieved. It took nearly two seconds for the transporter platform to rise past each floor level and it was quite easy on the eyes as they viewed what was there. The scene on each successive floor was exactly the same as they had seen lower down. A gentle breeze seemed to pass over them from head to shoulders as they travelled upwards.

When they were halfway up Ashley felt a noticeable lightness to his weight and looking at Tania and the others; he queried if they felt the same.

Rachel nodded as did Margaret and Ashley noticed that each had a firm grip on the hand rails.

Mazpazam and Simon were both smiling with satisfaction that their passengers were going through a new experience; at least within their starship and something that they had not at all expected.

Gradually the ascent rate eased as the platform reached closer to the last floor level with the end of the starship some distance above.

Ashley looked up and saw a flat ceiling about sixty feet above them.

'That is the very end of the starship,' said Simon who had been watching his parents closely.

'That's a lot of empty space there,' asked Tania the ever curious housewife. 'What is it used for?'

Mazpazam looked at Simon who nodded for her to carry on.

'Well,' said Mazpazam, 'we are at the last propulsion level here. There is another blanket floor forty feet above it which is twenty feet from that ceiling. It is used as a special storage area.'

'But isn't there enough space on the cargo platform,' asked Margaret?

'This is special,' said Simon.

'Oh,' said Margaret, 'special in what way?'

Simon looked at Mazpazam again.

'During a starship journey casualties may occur,' he said softly, 'and this is where they are placed in special sealed containers for return to Nazmos. Burial is then completed with all ceremony when the container is injected into Raznat.'

There was a long thoughtful silence at this revelation. Simon broke the spell to bring them back to the present.

'How does it feel being here near the extreme end of Silverstreak?' he asked generally.

'Very light headed,' replied Rachel glad of the change in topic.

'Yes,' said Mazpazam, 'it takes a bit of getting used to. However, Zanos monitors everyone and if there is any hint of nausea then a corrective emotion is quickly induced to alleviate the condition. So you need never worry as Zanos will ensure you are fine.'

Then very slowly the transporter platform began its descent. The downward rate remained at ten miles per hour and so the journey took longer than the ascent. At the lowest level Mazpazam got the platform to stop and let her passengers have one last look at the impulse motors arrayed there. After a couple of minutes the platform lowered again and exited the access shaft. It continued downwards to slowly settle on the cargo platform floor.

'Take your time,' said Simon, 'for even though we were at reduced gravity for a short duration you need to adjust to the full gravity conditions that exist here.'

Simon had them wait five minutes before allowing them to disembark. He led them to the floor lift before taking them down to the habitation platform level.

Simon and Mazpazam walked them to their apartment but stopped outside it.

'And that ends our tour for today,' said Simon with a flourishing bow. 'I hope it was enjoyable.

'That was wonderful son,' said Tania, 'thanks to you and to Mazpazam for showing us so much. Please thank Captain Wastanomi from all of us for letting you take us around his starship. It was quite an experience.'

'The pleasure is mine,' came the conveyed message from the captain. 'I look forward to our meeting tomorrow.'

'Thank you Captain,' conveyed Ashley, 'we shall see you tomorrow.'

'We'll leave you now,' said Simon, 'but I will meet you here for the evening meal.'

'What about Mazpazam,' asked Rachel?

'I would love to,' said Mazpazam, 'but there are allocated duties that I must attend. Another spaceship is due on station and one of us officers must be available at all times.'

She looked at Simon as she said this.

'But I will be with you at mealtimes when Silverstreak is underway to Nazmos,' she added.

'Good,' said Tania, 'that will be nice.'

Simon and Mazpazam then gave a little hand wave as they turned about and walked briskly away. Ashley noticed that Mazpazam moved her hand and placed it firmly into Simon's. She then leaned slightly against him but only for a brief instant. A public display of affection was not one of Simon's strong points.

'Well here we are back home again,' said Rachel, 'what should we do next?'

'For a start I'd like a mug of hot tea,' said Ashley, 'and I think one is on the way. Zanos must have read my mind.'

'I wonder what is available to view on our room monitors,' said Margaret, 'I wouldn't mind a refresher on a program I saw on Nazmos about its land and sea geography.'

'If you request Zanos I'm sure something could be found for you,' said Ashley.

'I think I will do exactly that,' said Margaret. 'It should fill the time until dinner.'

Ashley laughed at her expression for the evening meal. He was getting used to the Oannes terms; and lunch and dinner didn't seem to quite fit in with a spaceship's simulated clock times.

Rachel and Margaret left to enter their apartment section and Ashley took up Margaret's suggestion of watching something on their own room monitor. At first the program seemed interesting but after a while both he and Tania became bored with it and decided to chat instead.

They talked about Mazpazam and her previous discussion on her hobby interests. She was very interested in the ancient history of the Nazmos peoples. But records were either incomplete or lost and she found that she was not overly encouraged in her research.

One of Mazpazam's queries was about the Rimzi people and how they had remained separated from the land population. But this would have meant going back to a time when all of Nazmos lived in the sea. And on this aspect Mazpazam suspected that all records had been expunged from history by the then powers that be. And they had been destroyed so long ago that nothing remained even as a mythological mystery; at least among the landed Oannes population.

But what of the Rimzi people. Could they still have that information? Mazpazam suspected that they might and the reason for their behaviour and separate culture was perhaps a clue. Not in living memory had a Rimzi person come out to live among the Oannes. Nor had an Oannes been permitted to enter the Rimzi community. Was it just a matter of choice to remain in the sea or was there more to it? Mazpazam was intrigued.

Mazpazam was yet to target another source but was hesitant to do so. She thought that if Ashley could know about Gozmanot then perhaps he might be able to see back even further.

'I wish I could help Mazpazam with her history search,' said Ashley to Tania, 'but these things only come to me for a purpose. I can't just delve into the past at will though I wish I could.'

'I know dear,' said Tania, 'but something happened long ago that the Oannes do not wish to remember. Though I too like Mazpazam would like to know what that was.'

'Perhaps the past was once like our own before they settled into the pattern we see today,' said Ashley.

'Yes, but why have two civilized peoples remained separate,' said Tania. 'The Rimzi definitely wish to keep themselves to themselves.'

'There are people on Earth who wish to keep to the old ways and remain separate from the modern world,' said Ashley.

'Like the Amish,'

'Yes.'

And so the conversation went from topic to topic till eventually Rachel and Margaret came back into the room as it was nearly time for the evening meal. Margaret said she found the Nazmos documentary very good and that as they had viewed the portrayed arid landscape of Nazmos she began to imagine the flora that could eventually develop upon it. She reckoned it would become a totally transformed world. She could imagine the landscape becoming softened and much more colourful; and beautiful.

Simon arrived shortly after and it was not long before the evening meal was served. It was the usual menu with its varying choice of dishes and so one could not really become bored with it; especially when hunger played its part.

Towards the end of the meal Mazpazam entered the apartment but she said that she had already eaten. Tania said it was nice that they were all together again and perhaps they might do something afterwards. Mazpazam suggested an easy stroll across the habitation platform would enable them to meet some of the other passengers. She said this with a feigned slyness in her smile and admitted that she had in fact been approached by several of them for such a walkabout. All knew of Ashley's presence on board and many hoped for a view of him or even a chance meeting.

'An excellent idea,' said Margaret who was always in favour of meeting new Oannes faces.

There was a pleasant atmosphere all around as Ashley and his family walked past the other apartments and it seemed to be commonplace for the other passengers to do the same.

Pleasant Sewa greetings were conveyed with all those that Ashley got to meet though many others simply conveyed their pleasantries from a distance.

After about an hour Tania said she felt tired and wished to return to the apartment. In actual fact she had noticed Ashley stifle a yawn on two occasions and knew it to be a sign of his general tiredness. It had been a long and interesting day and so now Tania felt they all needed a rest. However Rachel and Margaret said they still felt fine and wished to meet more of the Oannes passengers. Simon offered to accompany them but Rachel said no thanks. She'd rather meet people on her own without a prominent ship's officer at their side.

'Thanks bro,' she said, 'but Margaret and I want it to appear informal. After all we will be living on Nazmos long term after dad does his thing. You and Mazpazam can spend some quality time together.'

'Okay sis,' said Simon, 'we'll walk mum and dad back to the apartment and then wander off too. See you at breakfast.'

'Yes, see you at breakfast,' said Rachel.

Simon and Mazpazam walked with Ashley and Tania and then bid them goodnight at their apartment door.

'Thanks for a lovely day both of you,' said Tania, 'it's been excellent. Goodnight dears and we'll see you in the morning.'

And with that Tania and Ashley entered their apartment shutting the door behind them.

'I'm ready for bed,' said Ashley, 'age must be catching me up.'

'I think I'm beginning to feel the same,' said Tania.

'Which one,' said Ashley, 'the age bit or the ready for bed bit?'

'I think a little of both actually.'

'Perhaps I'll have a wallow in the sleep-tank first to relax my muscles,' said Ashley.

Tania hid the smile that came to her face.

'And I think I might join you,' she said looking away.

It was pleasant to just float around in the cool waters of the sleep-tank; especially when the mood became playful. And it became more pleasant afterwards when they showered together.

Much later as they lay side by side on their beds Tania expressed a thought.

'Do you think we could get a sleep-tank fitted out somewhere downstairs at home,' she said as she raised herself up on one elbow. She meant in Dudley of course.

'Hmmm,' came from a dozing Ashley.

Then suddenly he was awake again.

'Why,' he said although he knew perfectly why.

'I just like the idea of one,' she replied, 'I find it so relaxing.'

'Go to sleep woman and keep those wicked thoughts in check,' he said but with laughter in his voice.

'I love you Ashley Bonner,' she said in a sudden change of mood, 'promise me you will come back to me.'

Ashley knew exactly what she meant and sadness tightened up in his chest. He found it hard to bring out the words.

After a moment of silence he whispered, 'Yes, I promise I will.' And in the inner depths of his blocked mind he said to himself, 'One way or another I will find a way my darling.'

Next morning after a late breakfast Ashley and Tania strolled over to the captain's quarters. Simon and Mazpazam had not come over and had conveyed their message about being tied up with new passenger arrivals. Rachel and Margaret planned another walk among the Oannes passengers to get to know some of them better.

Captain Wastanomi came out to meet Ashley and Tania with a firm handshake before leading them into his quarters. It was neat inside but with the barest of furniture. The seating was the split-back kind but they were well padded and looked comfortable with a slight recline angle in the backrest. Yet in spite of its Spartan appearance there was a homely feel to the room.

Ashley could see into the adjoining room which he made out to be the dining area with its long central table and well placed straight-back chairs. It was where they had talked the previous day when Rachel, Margaret, Simon and Mazpazam had also been with them. Ashley reckoned it was also the captain's meeting room for his staff and crew. There were other rooms obviously but Ashley could not make them out.

'I have six rooms in all just as for all the other starship captain's quarters. It permits families to accompany a captain should he wish it,' said a smiling Wastanomi in answer to Ashley's thoughts. 'I shall also instruct that you have more comfortable seating in your apartments; seating that you are more used to on Earth for when we make our extended trip to Zarama.'

'Thank you Captain,' said Ashley smiling across at Tania, 'that would be most welcome.'

Tania thought of Ashley sitting in front of the telly at home and falling asleep before the program had ended. The captain picked up on Tania's thought images and smiled. As a result he knew what kind of seating he must select for them. He would have these made up on Nazmos when the ship was being kitted out for the Zarama trip.

'Captain,' said Ashley, 'we had a most instructive and enjoyable day yesterday. It was kind of you to grant us the privilege.'

The captain simply nodded his head in acknowledgement as there was no need for words. His pleasant expression was reply enough.

'I trust you and yours are all comfortable in your rooms,' said the captain looking at Tania.

'Yes, thank you,' said Tania, 'most comfortable.'

The captain smiled to himself as he read Tania's thoughts about the sleep-tank.

'And the meals are to your liking?' he asked more from conversational politeness than enquiry.

This time Ashley replied.

'Very much, Captain. We have got quite used to the Oannes diet and in many ways I find it preferable to our own. As you know I am especially fond of the sweetened Yaztraka and have been ever since I first tasted it in Anztarza.'

The conversation continued in like vein for some time and each knew that it was the polite way to start a meeting. But the captain was also gauging the character of his two guests. And he liked what he saw. He was beginning to understand the make-up of this enigma person that was Ashley. Here was a human who possessed tremendous gifts of both power and knowledge and yet nothing he did or said gave him a proud appearance. Nothing exuded from him that could be remotely likened to self-pride in his attitude. In fact he behaved quite the opposite. And this at first puzzled Wastanomi. This however began to dissolve and disappear as he watched Ashley's attitude not only towards his wife but also towards his superior which was the captain himself. There was an admiration that emanated towards the captain because Ashley liked what he saw in the makeup of this Oannes captain. And Wastanomi was a captain who had achieved much by his own diligence and persistence of effort and was recognised as such by the previous captain of the starship 4110-Silver.

And so within an hour of general conversation in which Ashley described his home in Dudley and Tania mentioned how she would like to install a sleep-tank in it all began to feel at ease with one another. With Ashley and Tania the captain felt at his ease now though he continued to display what he considered the right amount of reserve in his attitude. The captain of a starship must of necessity maintain an emotional distance between himself and his passengers and crew. A clever captain knew how to balance this finely and still command the respect and affection of those he must deal with.

Yet under all of the captain's outward façade Ashley sensed an underlying question. A question that now produced a feeling of guilt and regret and was a mental burden to the captain. Ashley knew what this might be but he must get the captain to convey his feelings to Ashley before ever he could be free of them. And so Ashley conveyed his thoughts to the captain and that it was a perfectly understandable emotion.

Most Oannes questioned the reason that a human had the gift to save their world from the disaster of Zarama. Humans were an inferior backward race and surely it would have been more appropriate for an Oannes person to have had that privilege. But this was not Wastanomi's melodrama entirely. There was something else deep down inside him and Ashley intended to release him from it. And in order to do so Ashley must play the 'Father Confessor'.

'Captain,' said Ashley in a quiet voice, 'I feel there is something you wish to say to me and I am prepared to hear it.'

Wastanomi looked straight at Ashley and then looked down at his feet. But then he quickly looked up again and a new resolve lit his face. Ashley smiled encouragingly back at the captain and said nothing. Wastanomi looked at Tania and then back again at Ashley.

'You must forgive me for the words that I speak to you now,' he said looking away to one side.

Then he looked back at them.

'Firstly I want to say how ashamed I am of the thoughts I harboured before I got to meet and know you. When I heard that a human had such fantastic abilities my initial thought was one of disbelief. Then I was shown proof of your asteroids experiments and my next thought was to question how a human could do this. I did extensive research on you and found that everything said about you was true. An emotion of envy and mistrust grew in my mind that a human could achieve such things and again of this I am quite ashamed.'

Wastanomi paused while still looking directly at Ashley.

'In my mind I considered that we Oannes had evolved to a culture far in advance of humans on Earth. I considered that we were superior in mind and technology to the human race as it stands today. Oh I knew that one day you too would evolve and advance to where we Oannes are now but that is a distant prospect. We Oannes pride ourselves on our achievements and often compare our ways to yours. Sometimes, though I should say quite often, a feeling of disgust arises within us when we see what is happening in many parts of your civilization; but we quell that emotion as being improper.'

'Sadly I have to agree with everything you say,' said Ashley and Tania nodded her agreement.

Wastanomi held up his webbed hand to stop Ashley from saying anything further.

'Hear me out,' he said before continuing.

'Then you told us about Gozmanot and showed us her vision of what was to be. In your regression to her time she greeted you not only with open arms but also with an expression of love and longing. That vision haunts my thoughts even today.'

Wastanomi paused briefly.

'Gozmanot must have seen your image in her visions for she recognised you instantly when your face appeared before her. I confess I do not comprehend what is behind all this but you have appeared when both Nazmos and Earth are endangered. Not only that but you have appeared with the means to achieve the impossible; the destruction of Zarama. You must feel it as a great privilege to be able to save our worlds.'

This time Ashley held up his hand to interrupt the captain.

'I'm sorry Captain,' he said, 'it is not a privilege but rather a burden and so a duty. I did not ask for these gifts that were bestowed upon me since my infancy. At first I found it interesting and amusing that I could do certain things no other human could. My mother had a greater discernment of their purpose and was saddened by what she saw. She feared I had these gifts for a specific purpose and that I would eventually be taken away from family and home because of it. My mentor Philip had conveyed to me that a big task lay ahead of me and this was before I knew about Anztarza or Nazmos. When Zarama was revealed to me I knew that my mother's fears had been justified. If I had the choice captain I would rather that these powers and gifts had been given to another so that I could lead a normal life with my family and home. Alas, the burden is mine and I shall bear it and do my duty to the best of my ability at whatever cost to me. With Zarama I must succeed and I know I will for Gozmanot foresaw it so. But at what cost to me I do not know.'

Wastanomi read the emotion of extreme sadness in Ashley's mind and suddenly he understood how it could be. He looked across at Tania and saw tears in her eyes. She too knew about what could be. His admiration for her grew within him for she had as much a burden to bear as her husband. Wastanomi also saw that the sadness in Ashley's heart was not for himself but for the pain that his wife must endure if she lost him. Both knew it as a possibility and both had accepted it.

'Thank you Ashley and Tania,' said Wastanomi, 'I understand completely and I accept that you are the right person to possess this ability and power. I can think of no other in both our worlds who deserves it more. You are truly unique in both temperament and character and I am privileged to be associated with you in this venture.'

There was a glow of admiration in the captain's manner but he said nothing further.

After a moment of quiet the captain leaned forward with a smile on his face.

'I have enjoyed our conversation today,' he said, 'and we should continue it on future occasions. But for now let us revert to operational matters. Tomorrow at 6 o'clock GMT morning simulated time we shall begin our journey towards Nazmos. I propose that you do not become involved with accelerating the starship until Silverstreak has attained a velocity close to 60 FTL under its own power. This will take approximately four hours to achieve. Then I will call upon you to accelerate the ship further. You did mention 800 FTL as a first effort and I accepted that.'

Ashley then conveyed exactly what he planned and Wastanomi nodded his acceptance.

Ashley had indicated that his acceleration of the starship to that velocity would be done over a period of eight hours and that he could accomplish this from either within the captain's quarters or his own apartment rooms.

'I should like to witness the occasion and so if you could do it from here I should be obliged,' said Wastanomi. Ashley read this as a given command rather than a polite request.

'Very well Captain it will be as you wish,' said Ashley. 'If you would instruct Zanos to give me advance notice then I shall be here in plenty of time.'

'It shall be so,' said the captain and with that he stood up and held out his hand indicating that their meeting was over.

'Until tomorrow Captain,' said Ashley as he and Tania walked out behind Wastanomi.

'Yes,' said Wastanomi, 'swift, safe and sure.'

'Swift, safe and sure,' was repeated by Ashley and Tania together as they walked away from the captain and towards their apartment.

They had been with the captain over an hour and Ashley thought it odd that no glass of Wazu had been offered or raised during that time. Captain Wastanomi was strict on formality but perhaps he deemed it an unnecessary requirement especially since they'd only just finished their morning meal. Ashley agreed with the captain on this occasion. It also meant that the captain could dispense with formality where Ashley and Tania were concerned. Ashley took this as a compliment.

Back in their apartment Ashley put his arms around Tania and gave her a tight clinging hug. Much of what had been discussed came back into their minds and both pairs of eyes were moist with tears.

'Sshh,' said Tania when she thought Ashley was about to say something while she clung to him as fiercely. They stayed like that for some considerable time till the tightness of the effort made their arms tire. They then drew apart and looked at each other with sad smiles on their faces.

'I love you,' whispered Ashley and gave Tania a gentle kiss on the lips.

'I love you too,' she mumbled not removing her lips from his.

Tania knew that she could look back at moments like this and try to rekindle the emotion of the moment if that were possible. She also knew that were he to be alone then he too would try to do the same. But this was being maudlin and Tania pushed those thoughts aside.

The rest of the day passed in a flurry of activities with Simon attempting to entertain them. Mazpazam also spent more time in their apartment during and after each meal. Ashley thought that they would have to find additional entertainment for the long journey to Zarama. He estimated that it would take about six months of travel at the cruise velocity of 1200 FTL to cover the 431 light-years real distance to Zarama.

Ashley and Tania had never been on a spaceship for that long a duration and yet the Oannes were quite used to such journeys. The starship journeys to and from Earth took nearly eight months with the 10 FTL ships so the journey to Zarama would not feel unusually prolonged for them. Yet what of the return journey thought Ashley. Indeed what of the return journey if he paid the ultimate price of success against the rogue dwarf star. That journey would take five years to complete. There would be great speculation on Nazmos if Silverstreak did not appear back at the expected time.

Grave doubts arose in Ashley's mind about his chances of success against Zarama. And yet Gozmanot's vision clearly indicated that Zarama would be vanquished. But how was that to be accomplished when he couldn't even budge Sirius B by a fractional amount. However Ashley's instinct told him that somehow he would succeed but how would only become known nearer the time. And he had faith that his gifts would allow him to succeed.

Ashley came to another decision. From this moment on he would keep nothing from Tania. She would be privy to all his thoughts – especially his doubts; but only Tania and no one else. So now he conveyed to her his decision and all his thoughts regarding Zarama.

'I've known all along darling of the anguish in your mind,' she conveyed back. 'I could read it in your manner ever since our trip to Sirius B.'

'If I couldn't succeed there how am I to succeed with Zarama,' said Ashley more to himself than to his wife.

'Yes, but you will find a way darling,' said Tania moving close up beside him as they sat together on the edge of the bed, 'I know you will.'

Then after a moment she added.

'Ashley, you would not have been given all of this for you not to succeed now. I have faith in you darling and in whoever granted you these gifts.'

'But what if ......,' Ashley began to say before Tania stopped him with her hand on his mouth.

'If it comes to that then you would have done what needed to be done my darling and I must and will accept it,' she said.

There were tears in Ashley's eyes as he said the next few words.

'Oh Tania, my joy comes from seeing your joy and happiness when you look at my face. And that will be my sadness for when you cannot.'

The sadness was deep in Tania's eyes as she looked up at him. He was her one and only true love and companion and always would be.

'Nothing is certain,' she said. 'But if that is our destiny and is so written in the Book then so let it be. The memories of our life together will remain forever in my mind and will always be there for me to recall at will. I could relive them as a sort of vicarious adventure all over again. So far it has been a brilliant and exciting life for me. Only Ashley Bonner could have given a girl such a thrilling life of adventure; like a knight in shining armour.'

Ashley smiled then for he knew that no matter what happened the love that he and Tania shared would continue on and on and on.

At the evening meal Simon and Mazpazam looked at each other for both had noticed the glow of affection that passed between his parents. It seemed as if there had been a rekindling in the openness of their love for one another.

Mazpazam was more discerning and she conveyed to Simon what she thought. It was like the final brightness of a burning candle just before it became extinguished forever. Simon however kept these thoughts to himself.

Later that night when all had retired to their rooms Ashley and Tania lazed pleasantly in their sleep-tank. It was just afterwards that the proverbial candle was burned at both ends and extremely brightly before they fell into an exhausted sleep. It was one that Tania would certainly remember.

Ashley awoke briefly just after 6:00am and knew instantly that Silverstreak was on the move. Zanos confirmed this and that the starship was accelerating rapidly towards light speed.

When Ashley awoke again it was a couple of hours later and Tania was out of bed and in the bathroom. She peeped around the open doorway and smiled at him.

'Good morning sleepy-head,' she said, 'or should I say good morning my darling Romeo.'

'Good morning darling,' replied Ashley with a smile.

He thought of Tania last night but said nothing on that account. Let sleeping dogs lie though it was a most pleasant memory.

They were washed and dressed and ready for their breakfast shortly before 9.00am when Ashley contacted Rachel and Margaret.

'We've been waiting for your call,' said Rachel, 'Margaret and I are both starving. Simon and Mazpazam are here too.'

Ashley conveyed his wishes to Zanos and within minutes floating pallets arrived just as for the main meal times. This time they carried the breakfast items instead.

As usual Ashley had his toasts. The first with marmalade, the second with cheese and the third with strawberry jam. Accompanying these were the usual mugs of tea. It was all done in less than an hour. Simon and Mazpazam did not join in as they said they'd already eaten. When Ashley and Tania left to go to the captain's quarters they went off to see to starship business.

As Ashley approached the central shaft Zanos informed him that the starship was approaching a velocity of 50 FTL. Ashley reckoned that soon it would be time for him to apply his telekinetic push to accelerate the starship to the planned 800 FTL velocity.

The captain came out to meet them and led them into the reception area of his quarters. After a brief Sewa and exchange of polite greeting they sat down facing each other.

'The starship is currently at 50 FTL velocity and still accelerating. I will not be pedantic about the arrangement we agreed yesterday as that was an approximate consideration. You are here now and I would be happy for you to commence your telekinetic action with immediate effect.'

'Thank you Captain,' said Ashley, 'and I will do so in full conjunction with Zanos monitoring everything that I plan. So now I propose to accelerate Silverstreak from its current velocity upto a maximum of 800 FTL in a period of eight hours. I will then plan for that velocity to be maintained until Zanos instructs for it to be reduced as we near our destination. I will then coordinate with Zanos and under instruction I will gradually diminish my telekinetic push to zero over a similar period of eight hours. Silverstreak will then be wholly under its own impulse power and Zanos can operate it as normal.'

'Thank you Ashley, that is perfectly acceptable,' said Wastanomi with a pleased smile. 'Zanos has been so instructed of your intentions and will constantly monitor all your mental activity. You may commence when you feel ready.'

Ashley smiled politely at the captain and while doing so visualised that the starship's neutron shield was in the direction below where they were seated. He then willed for the starship to be accelerated uniformly through its neutron shield to a cruising velocity of 800 FTL over a period of eight hours. He conveyed this for the benefit of all and requested that Zanos provided a regular velocity status.

Almost immediately there was a whisper of sound indicating the sudden movement of the platform down the central column as a means of countering the increased acceleration of the starship.

'It is done Captain,' said Ashley, 'I need do nothing further. The starship will achieve the agreed cruise velocity in eight hours time. And I believe that the journey time to Nazmos rendezvous is approximately three days. Zanos will inform me of the plan for slowing down Silverstreak at the appropriate time.'

The captain looked at Tania with surprise on his face.

'Is that all,' he asked? 'I saw no great effort on his part and yet it is done.'

'It is all in the mind Captain,' said Tania, 'but it was not always so easy. Changes have occurred over the years and it has become easier for him. Now he simply has to wish for an accomplishment of telekinetic effort and it is fulfilled.'

'Most impressive,' said Wastanomi looking at Ashley. 'Please explain how it is done.'

'I'm sorry Captain,' said Ashley, 'I cannot do that for the simple reason that I do not fully understand it myself. All I do is to will with my mind for a velocity to be achieved with certain conditions and it happens exactly as I have desired for it to be so. I suppose my mind applies all the necessary telekinetic effort in an involuntary manner. And it will maintain that velocity until I desire a change.'

'Extraordinary' was all the captain could say.

'However there is one factor here that I must adhere to,' said Ashley, 'and that is for me to remain close to the centre of the habitation platform. My apartment is fairly centrally located and so over the next three days I will not wander beyond its radial position. Visiting you here each day of course brings me even more central.'

'I see,' said Wastanomi nodding. 'Your telekinetic force is in a direct line between you and the push target.'

'That is correct Captain,' said Ashley, 'that is exactly how it works. The push target is of course the starships neutron shield.'

'And how do you feel physically,' asked Wastanomi?

'Perfectly normal as far as I can estimate,' said Ashley. 'Though I do tend to sleep very deeply at nighttimes with my mind so actively involved.'

'And how do you think you will fare on our journey to Zarama. Then you will be pushing Silverstreak at its maximum designed velocity of 1200 FTL over a period of about six months.'

'It took eleven days to reach Sirius B from Nazmos,' said Ashley, 'and I felt no ill effects then. My telekinetic gift has become stronger with time and I think six months should not be a problem.'

Captain Wastanomi was a keen observer and he watched Ashley closely and tried to fathom the thought processes and emotions going on inside Ashley's mind. And he saw nothing that was not favourable. Ashley displayed no anxieties in relation to the starship's acceleration and the maintenance of a cruise velocity. The underlying concern of Zarama was ever present in Ashley's mind though currently it was pushed to the furthermost recesses of it.

'Captain,' said Ashley, 'I was wondering if you had given any thought to a future plan of action regarding the test trial to 1200 FTL prior to our journey to Zarama.'

'Actually I have given it some considerable thought but remain flexible as to timing,' said Wastanomi. 'My thoughts are that there must be three phases of action once we have reached Nazmos.'

'And pray what are those Captain?' asked Ashley.

'The first is your duty to Nazmos,' said Wastanomi. 'By which of course I refer to the final orbital adjustment that you must undertake. The second is our trial run in Silverstreak to maximum velocity. But that can only be undertaken when the Nazmos governing council gives permission. When that has been completed to satisfaction I will need time to prepare Silverstreak for the final phase which is the extended journey towards Zarama.'

Ashley read the captain's thoughts as he said this and a vast organisational complexity of requirements unfolded before him. There would be no incidental passengers other than the chosen few. These would include Ashley and members of his family; and of course any Oannes council members who were elected to be aboard. Then there would be the technicians and scientists and a supplementary force to assist the food growing personnel. The journey could last several years if things did not go according to plan and that eventuality must be catered for. Special additional recreational facilities had to be installed and weekly progress announcements made. At least three zero-gravity ships had to be accommodated on board and all bio-computer systems made compatible and aligned accordingly. Zanos must be able to navigate Silverstreak back to Nazmos from the Zarama location in space; a distance of 431 light-years. Such a navigational feat had not been undertaken ever before and a simulation would be required and Zanos primed with all the necessary star chart data in 3D configuration. Very briefly Simon entered into Wastanomi's thoughts on the navigation aspect. Simon's premonition gift had always brought his spaceship back towards Nazmos with an accuracy that had even surprised his academy tutors. Wastanomi looked upon Simon as a sort of backup policy in getting home on the return journey.

There were other considerations too but these were of a minor nature being made up of the finer details for long term comfort aboard the starship.

'And what will be the duration for all this preparation,' asked Ashley?

'I would need for the governing council to specify the journey date,' said Wastanomi, 'but preparations aboard Silverstreak should not take longer than two months.'

'It will be a long journey Captain,' said Ashley, 'and I hope we shall have many long discussions on both the outward as well as the return runs.'

An alarm of sorts buzzed through Wastanomi's mind but this was fleeting in duration before it melted away. Later he was to remember it and wonder that he had not taken more note of it and probed deeper as to its origin.

'Yes Ashley,' he said, 'I look forward to our journey together.'

Zanos now informed the captain privately that the starship had just achieved a velocity of 100 FTL and was continuing its acceleration towards the cruise target. Wastanomi nodded as if to an unseen guest before conveying the information to Ashley and then to his crew. The other passengers would only be informed of the ship's status when cruise velocity had been attained.

The captain then rose and thanked Ashley and Tania for their indulgence. He had been keen to see Ashley in action and although it had been quite undramatic he was pleased to have witnessed the procedure. He suggested they retire to their apartment and their family and he hoped to see them for the usual meeting tomorrow.

'Yes Captain we shall be here then,' said Ashley. 'I quite look forward to our talks.'

The captain smiled and bowed to the compliment before turning about and leading the way out onto the platform deck. He then stood to one side as Tania walked past. But Ashley stopped to face Wastanomi and held out his hand which the captain promptly took. The handshake was firm on both sides.

Ashley had begun to feel a deep admiration for this Oannes starship captain and he could sense a similar respect from the captain. Two men who admired the qualities of the other could become good friends.

When Ashley and Tania got back to their apartment there was nothing much to occupy them. For a while they discussed the captain and his command of the starship business. It was pointless asking Zanos for a velocity update since Ashley knew that for each passing hour the starship speed would have increased by another 100 FTL.

At 1:00 o'clock Margaret and Rachel came in and they seemed quite excited that Silverstreak was finally on its way to Nazmos. They seemed impatient to get there. Then a bit later Simon and Mazpazam entered and immediately announced that the afternoon meal was on its way.

The meal was served as before on the floating pallets controlled by Zanos and all ate heartily. Ashley made sure he had his extra helping of the sweetened Yaztraka.

During their conversation Simon asked his dad how the captain had reacted on witnessing his telekinetic application upon the starship. So Ashley related all the events of the morning. He especially mentioned the captain's surprise that it had seemed so undramatic. But that he was pleased to have witnessed the event anyway.

After the meal they all went for a stroll on the habitation platform and Ashley made sure he remained within the central area between the apartment and the captain's quarters. After an hour they all returned to their own apartments to pass the time viewing one of the offered programs on the room monitor.

Half an hour later Tania could see Ashley dozing in his recliner so the next time he roused himself she told him to lie on the bed and have his afternoon forty winks – which is exactly what he did.

He was awoken shortly after 4:00 o'clock evening time to be informed by Zanos that the starship was now at its cruise velocity of 800 FTL. And the time to be spent cruising at this velocity was estimated at 2 days and 18 hours; after which a slowdown must be initiated. Ashley acknowledged this and his mind registered that time as being 10:00am nearly three days from now.

Tania had gone out with Rachel and Margaret after Ashley had dozed off again but she soon returned without them. The evening meal was just an hour away and again Simon and Mazpazam conveyed that they would join them.

Back in Dudley Ashley and Tania had a library of books many of which they had not read. Ashley was an impatient reader and had subscribed to and collected a large number of the condensed books offered by The Readers Digest Association. He reckoned that one day in his retirement years he would sit down and read them. Thinking about this made him realise that he could do with something to read and pass the time here. He mentioned this to Tania and also to Simon who had just come in alone.

'Why dad,' said Simon, 'I think I can help you there. Zanos keeps a full library of most of Earth's books in all languages. You only have to request it and a section catalogue will be offered.'

'Sounds good to me,' said Ashley, 'but then what happens.'

'Well after you've chosen your book story, you may then choose how you want it presented,' said Simon smiling.

'How do you mean,' asked Tania getting interested also.

'Well,' said Simon, 'it can be as an audio book that is read to you. Or it can be a pictorial version of the book and conveyed telepathically. And then it can be presented as the print version on your room monitor. You can then read this like a book and at your leisure.'

'I like it,' said Ashley, 'I think I might try the audio version as my first choice. Do I make my request of Zanos then?'

'Yes it's as simple as that,' said Simon. 'But Zanos probably knows this already.'

'How come no one mentioned this to us before,' said Ashley.

'Perhaps you did not make such a desire known,' said Simon. 'Perhaps you were busy on other matters and the need did not arise. But the thing is that you know now.'

Then Simon added.

'There are many aspects of knowledge that the Oannes possess and they assume that all know what is available. They do not hide anything. Perhaps you would like a particular film favourite or a sporting documentary of something that was played long ago.'

'Thank you son,' said Tania, 'all this is nice to know. The long journey to Zarama does not seem so formidable now.'

Shortly after, Rachel and Margaret walked in with a smiling Mazpazam in tow.

'Hello Mazpazam,' said Tania, 'I wondered where you were when Simon came in alone.'

It was Rachel who replied.

'She has been with us for nearly an hour – girl talk and stuff,' she said and winked.

Simon was like his dad and refused to be drawn in towards the likely conversation the girls might have had.

'Don't worry bro; we were just discussing Earth dress fashion and cosmetics with Mazpazam. What do you think,' said Rachel looking towards Mazpazam.

It was only then that Simon and Ashley both noticed that Mazpazam had a softer look about her. The barest hint of blusher was on her cheeks and a very faint lip colouring had also been applied by a proud Rachel and Margaret.

It was Tania who burst out in laughter and then stopped abruptly.

'Mazpazam my dear you look absolutely lovely. It was just such a surprise to see you like this,' she said and went up to her and gave her a hug.

Mazpazam read Ashley's mind and immediately shook her head as a negative. No, she would definitely not consider wearing a lady's wig, she conveyed.

What Ashley had actually thought about was that with a little more makeup and a luxurious wig Mazpazam could pass as human on Earth and not need to wear that cumbersome face mask disguise. The northern forests on Earth would be better experienced that way. Ashley conveyed his thoughts to all.

Simon smiled at this and looking at Mazpazam threw back his head and gave his Errol Flynn laugh. He quickly raised his hand in pacification.

'Don't get me wrong darling,' he said going up to Mazpazam, 'I think you look really smashing. And next time we are on Earth you might want to consider dad's suggestion.'

Simon then went and put his arm across her shoulders and hugged her to him.

Mazpazam looked up at Simon and smiled and all could see the love and admiration in her eyes. It was pleasing for Ashley and Tania to see what they saw.

They talked for some while on general topics till the evening meal was presented. It was a pleasant meal with Simon frequently gazing at Mazpazam's new made-up look.

'She is even more beautiful than ever,' he thought to himself as he looked at the highlights that Rachel and Margaret had created to enhance Mazpazam's beauty.

'Thanks sis,' he said to Rachel, 'you and Margaret have done an excellent job. I love it.'

Earlier when Margaret had suggested a little colour Mazpazam had hesitated because she doubted if Simon would approve.

'You can always wash it off if he doesn't,' Rachel had said, 'but I know my brother well and am sure he will simply love it.'

And so he had.

Mazpazam smiled at Simon's approval which she knew was genuine. His emotional state was a clear message to her and she was pleased; and similarly aroused. They wouldn't stay too long after the meal they mutually decided. They kept their minds blocked from all but each other.

With the meal over and mugs of tea consumed Simon suggested a little walk on the platform deck.

'Dad can't wander too far so we'll just circle the central column,' he said. 'Then Mazpazam and I can leave you so we can attend to starship business.'

'In that case Margaret and I can then wander off as we please,' said Rachel. 'We've made some friends among the passengers but they are housed quite close to the outer wall. Mum and dad will be on their own then of which I'm sure they'll be relieved; none of our jabbering conversation.'

Ashley smiled at Rachel's eloquence but yes he'd like the quiet time alone with Tania.

This was to be the pattern of the next couple of days. The journey had commenced at 6:00am on Thursday Jan 25th when the starship initiated acceleration under its own impulse power. Ashley had then pushed the starship to 800 FTL by 6:00pm that evening. Zanos had estimated staying at this normal cruise velocity for two days and 18 hours. Ashley would then be required to commence a reduction in his telekinetic push to reduce the starship's velocity. This would correspond to 10:00am on Sunday 28th Jan simulated time. Ashley had agreed to do his thing in diminishing his telekinetic push in the captain's quarters as he had with the acceleration three days before.

And so just before the appointed time for slowdown Ashley and Tania walked to the captain's quarters. Ashley had had his breakfast and his two mugs of sweet tea earlier and was now ready to play his part.

Zanos had reminded the captain and Ashley of the deadline for speed reduction at regular intervals from 8:00am onwards. With the previous starships Ashley had reduced the velocity by simply diminishing his telekinetic push effort at regular one and two minute intervals. But then, as his mind became more adept, he had to simply mentally will for his telekinetic action to conform to certain parameters and it was carried out in an involuntary manner.

Ashley understood the functioning of the starship and the need to maintain normal gravity on the moveable platforms at all times. He also understood the added difficulty in maintaining this normal gravity as the starship reduced velocity. A normal gravity condition was far more difficult to maintain during deceleration than it was for acceleration. The forward neutron shield played no part in the deceleration process. It was the backward firing neutron generators operating in a continuous manner that created its own rearward gravity effect that pulled the starship and its occupants in a backward slowing down action. These neutron generators were ringed around the body of the starship at the first Impulse Motors level and sent energy medium beams backwards to focus at twenty locations in a circle a mile downstream of the tail-end of the starship. The neutron generators created their usual sparkling effect from the disintegrating mass particles but of course these were not visible from inside the starship. The subsequent massive gravity effect from these disintegrating particles pulled the starship and everything in it backwards thus slowing it down. Zanos controlled all this operation exactly right for the normal gravity comfort of all aboard. Space travel with the Oannes was about maintaining normal gravity under most conditions.

The captain was ready and waiting at the central column just outside his quarters and greeted Ashley and Tania with a brief Sewa to which Ashley replied in kind. The captain led them into his reception room and once seated comfortably Ashley conveyed that he was ready to do his part. He conveyed that he intended to reduce his telekinetic effort gradually but continuously to zero over a period of eight hours. This would allow Zanos to easily compensate with the neutron generators to reduce the starships velocity down to 100 FTL from when it would be wholly under its own impulse power.

The captain nodded his understanding and agreement and conveyed for Ashley to commence the process. Zanos was also monitoring Ashley's mind in order to control the deceleration with the neutron generators.

Ashley conveyed his intentions once again to all and opened his mind so that Zanos was fully aware of his every thought. He then closed his eyes and concentrated his mind upon the forward neutron shield. He willed for a continuous and gradual reduction in his telekinetic push effort from its current level to nil and for this to be done smoothly over a period of eight hours commencing with immediate effect. Ashley opened his eyes and looked up at the captain.

'It is done as intended,' he said in a subdued quiet voice.

Again the captain tried to hide his surprise that it had been such a simple matter of a thought command from Ashley to effect the change in the starship's velocity status.

'Thank you Ashley,' he said and this time a hint of a smile cracked his normally taciturn expression.

Ashley felt a change in the captain's outlook and he was pleased that it was happening. Perhaps it would make the captain more sociable towards other Oannes including his officers and passengers. A starship captain's life could be a lonely one as had originally been the case with Zakatanz so many years ago. He was so different now with his wife Azatamunt and daughter Hazazamunt.

Captain Wastanomi was exuberant that his starship should have travelled at eight times design speed. It was a great privilege to be in command during such a voyage. It would be the fastest journey time between Earth and Nazmos. It would look good on his recorded profile and he was pleased. He also knew that it was not his achievement alone but had been brought about by Ashley's gift of telekinesis. So now he was additionally proud to be associated with this Earth human whom he had got to look upon with admiration and respect. And somewhere mingled in between these emotions was a budding affection. Their daily conversations had allowed a mutual understanding of their personalities to develop. Ashley had come to know more of this rule-book captain and the same was true of the captain's regard for Ashley. A deep mutual respect now existed between them.

Wastanomi knew his job well and had worked hard to achieve his reputation. He had looked to his officers and crew and expected the same calibre of intenseness in their outlook. Many received his approval but so far none his respect. Then Ashley came along. The initial astonishment at Ashley's abilities had turned into an envious admiration. But on meeting this human and getting to know and understand his character and general make-up this had turned into deep respect. And Wastanomi got great satisfaction from this new emotion within him. It was as though a burden had been taken off his shoulders; a burden borne from thinking himself near perfect and superior to his fellow Oannes. He quite liked the humbling effect that this brought knowing that a far better person existed; and that was someone whom he had considered as being from an inferior race and culture. The relief came from the purification of his conscience and subsequent peace that descended with it. It was nice to feel thus and Wastanomi was grateful that his starship had been assigned to Ashley's mission. He realised that he must also be thankful to his late Captain Rozintant for recommending him to the governing council.

He now looked at Ashley and Tania seated calmly across from him and he smiled.

'There is much I must thank you for Ashley,' he said, 'and it is not just for what you have done for this journey.' Ashley had read the captain's thoughts moments earlier and knew what was being referred to.

'I understand fully Captain,' he said, 'and I am glad that I have been able to help. We humans are not all uncivilized as many would believe and I hope you can take each of us as individuals. We all have our personalities and differences. Some of us are good and some not so good.'

'I doubt that I shall have the opportunity to meet anyone like you,' said Wastanomi. 'I cannot see one even among our own Oannes. You Ashley are unique and I am proud to be associated with you and yours.' He looked at Tania as he said this. 'May our mission be a successful one.'

'Yes Captain,' said Ashley, 'may it be swift, safe and sure.'

'Swift, safe and sure,' repeated Wastanomi smiling.

'And in the very good care of Zanos too,' added Ashley.

The captain looked puzzled for a brief moment before understanding dawned. These humans had a different perspective with regard to functioning machines.

'Zanos performs well but it was an Oannes genius team who should receive the credit for its design and manufacture,' said Wastanomi. 'After all Zanos can only be as perfect as its designers have made it.'

'How long has Zanos been active,' asked Tania, 'I'm not sure whether to think of Zanos as a he or a she.'

'Zanos has always been around,' said Wastanomi. 'But history indicates a beginning with the first journey to Earth some ten thousand years ago.'

'All our seafaring ships on Earth are given the female gender,' said Ashley, 'and I would think to do the same for spaceships including starships.'

'We don't think like that,' said Wastanomi smiling. 'I find the concept difficult. For instance I couldn't classify this seat as of either gender. To me it is simply an object that serves a purpose. Its function is to allow me comfort and rest as I sit upon it. Zanos performs a function also albeit more complex.'

Ashley nodded and said, 'I get your point Captain. You have a very persuasive argument there. But I too have a point I must raise. Back in my home on Earth I possess a very comfortable seat – an armchair sofa. It is my favourite from among all the other chairs in my lounge. I would not like to dispose of it and actually have a slight emotional attachment through long term association and pleasant memories. It is not male or female but I am fond of it and mean to keep it for as long as I can.'

'Or am permitted,' he hastily added smiling across at Tania.

'I see what you mean,' said Wastanomi. 'I have a similar attachment with this starship. I am proud that it was chosen for upgrading and that I was elected to be its captain. We have a long association and many memories. I feel it belongs to me and me to it. I suppose that in itself is an emotion of connection.'

Tania laughed out aloud and both Ashley and Wastanomi turned to look at her quizzically.

'I'm sorry,' she finally said with her hand half covering the lower part of her face, 'but you both talk as if a proposal of marriage was in the offing. You Ashley and that old armchair of yours and you captain of your attachment to this magnificent starship. I'm afraid darling that the captain has the better bargain. May both of you have a long and happy relationship.'

Now it was Wastanomi's turn to smile as he nodded his head vigorously. Tania took this as laughter in the Oannes way.

'Do you know my dear lady,' said Wastanomi still smiling, 'I have never stopped to think about my little emotions. I do have preferences in many areas but I have never considered them as part of my character. I shall now review them in a very different light. I like something because it fits my make-up and vice versa. We have become friends through association. But will we continue so even when we no longer share a common goal. I think we will no matter how this business concludes. It is getting to know and understand the person that builds a friendship or not. In our case for me it is a yes and I sense a similar attitude from you and I thank you for it.'

'Captain, our daily meetings have been full of reward and I see today's as not being an exception,' said Ashley. 'We have many more interesting topics to pursue and I look forward to them.'

'As we talk Zanos informs me that Silverstreak has reduced velocity to 740 FTL,' said Wastanomi. 'Zanos also informs me that we should be at Raznat rendezvous within three hours from when it takes complete control and commences further speed reduction from the 100 FTL velocity level.'

Ashley looked at the captain with a slight degree of puzzlement before he asked.

'Does that mean that when 100 FTL is achieved at 6:00pm this evening then it would be just another three hours to rendezvous?'

The captain smiled.

'Not necessarily,' he said. 'Once the starship is at 100 FTL then Zanos will compute our position and decide when to commence further speed reductions. Reduction in velocity may not be immediate but according to Zanos' computations. It could be an hour or even longer. But hopefully it will be sometime tonight.'

The captain then stood up as usual to signify that the meeting was concluded and that he must relate to starship duties.

A spaceship captain must always have full awareness of what was happening on his ship and so show his crew he was in full control. Captain Bulzezatna was an Anztarza based spaceship captain and was quite social in her behaviour. Wastanomi was a taciturn captain by nature and very much a loner like Zakatanz had once been. Now however Wastanomi was beginning to see the view of others and towards Ashley a hint of admiration had begun. As a result Wastanomi would eventually become a likeable captain and be able to blend into Oannes society. At 230 years of age it was not too late for him to form an emotional association with an Oannes lady. But that might be taking it a bit beyond his social capabilities knowing how dedicated he was to his starship Silverstreak.

It was now approaching the noon hour and there was another six hours before Ashley could release himself from all telekinetic responsibility. He would like to walk further out on the Habitation Platform and meet more of the Oannes passengers.

Time passed and the afternoon meal was served up as usual in their apartment. Simon and Mazpazam were also there but had to leave soon afterwards as the starship officers and crew needed to make advance preparation for passenger disembarkation at the rendezvous point.

At 6:00pm simulated time Zanos informed the captain and Ashley that the starship was at 102 FTL velocity and now entirely under its own impulse power. Ashley's telekinetic push had been reduced to zero. And it was shortly after this that Zanos informed them that final speed reduction would commence in forty minutes. Subsequently estimated time of arrival at the Raznat rendezvous point was given as 9:40pm.

Ashley wondered what kind of an evening it would be. He felt excited about being on Nazmos again and meeting all his friends there. As usual Jazzatnit and Zazfrapiz were to be their hosts and Ashley was a bit concerned for the latter. In the last few communications Jazzatnit had mentioned that they were both well. But it was what she didn't say that worried Ashley. She usually referred to her husband's aches and pains but in her latest communication she had not mentioned any of this. Well, he would soon see for himself.

The evening meal was served a bit later than usual at 8:30pm and this time both Simon and Mazpazam conveyed their apologies; duties called.

With the release of Ashley's telekinetic effort he felt slightly light-headed and a lack of energy in his system; a sort of looseness in his body. Maybe it was just his imagination for otherwise he felt fine. He also felt rather hungry.

He enjoyed the meal and had extra helpings of almost everything.

Ashley had not only drunk two full glasses of Wazu during the meal but followed this with two mugs of sweet tea afterwards. Tania smiled at the bulge of his belly. She also noticed that Ashley looked droopy eyed and sleepy. He mentioned that he felt that a short kip might do him a world of good.

So at about 9:20pm when Rachel and Margaret had gone into their apartment Ashley went to his bed and lay down on his back fully clothed.

'Ah, this feels great,' he said letting out a big sigh.

He was asleep by the time Tania managed to get his footwear off. Tania gazed into her husbands face and noticed the many frown-lines on his forehead. She looked closely at these and gently ran a finger across them. He'd always had a few creases there but now they suddenly seemed more prominent. There was a huge burden upon

Ashley's shoulders and she had tried her best to support and be there for him. But realistically it was a responsibility that only he must fulfil.

Zanos announced at 9:50pm that the starship Silverstreak was now stationary and parked at its Raznat rendezvous point with an accuracy of 96% of intended location.

A message had been despatched to Nazmos informing them of Silverstreak's arrival along with the complete ship's log since leaving for Earth just over six months ago.

The rendezvous location was approximately one billion miles from Raznat and at this distance messages to and from Nazmos took ninety minutes each way.

It would be at least two or three hours before spaceships could be readied to commence the journey to the starship's location. The journey time at 80,000 miles per second would take four hours. The earliest that Wastanomi could expect spaceships to arrive here would be about 9:00am tomorrow morning; simulated time period of course.

Ashley was asleep and quite unaware of all these events and in fact he slept on for another seven hours. When he awoke it was nearly 5:00am and Tania was breathing deeply on the bed beside him fast asleep. Zanos responded to Ashley's query and filled him in with the up-to-date status of the starship. Ashley was fully awake now and decided to freshen up with a nice long hot shower. When he emerged again clean shaven Tania was awake and smiling at him.

'Good morning darling,' she said, 'how does the man feel?'

'Very rested thank you,' he replied and came and sat on the bed near her feet.

'I like you like this,' she said referring to his nakedness.

'I'm sure you do,' he said, 'but I'm really desperate for a nice hot mug of tea – or two.'

Zanos had instructions to meet Ashley's every whim and before long a floating pallet arrived in their dining area laden with tea and biscuits.

'Just the thing,' said Ashley as he put on a tunic before settling at the table.

Tania was a few minutes in the bathroom before she came to join him.

'This is nice and cosy,' she said as she came up behind her husband and put her arms around his neck in a caressing hug.

'Hmm,' said Ashley, 'I suppose it's too early for a stroll. I guess we'll just have to get back in bed after I've fed my face.'

'Yes we should,' said Tania with a twinkle in her eye, 'after all we don't want to disturb the neighbours.'

And that is what they did much to Tania's delight and amusement.

CHAPTER 22

Nazmos in transition

2046

It was nice to be back on Nazmos after nearly six years away. There does seem to be a minor change in climate but only just. I had received reports back on Earth that a brief summer season had occurred when Nazmos was at its closest to Raznat. Also a persistence of cloud formations had begun to show which I hoped to see for myself.

We were greeted warmly by Jazzatnit when we entered her domain and she took us around to show off the many new additions in her courtyard garden. I responded favourably of course. Zazfrapiz had made a prized effort to come out to see us too. His frailness was obvious and after a short while he returned to his seat on the accompanying floating pallet. It was similar to the one Ritozanan had used to attend that banquet in the Domed Hall before we had left for the Sirius B test. Jazzatnit conveyed that frailness comes inevitably with age and that Zazfrapiz now favoured the comfort of his sleep-tank more often than not.

Zazfrapiz gave us the news that Muznant and Brazjaf were now both on the Nazmos governing council. Apparently they had been council members for nearly two years and the reason I had not been informed was because communication about council members was not permitted outside of Nazmos. I said how pleased I was for them and conveyed this openly for any who wished to listen.

We had arrived in Wentazta earlier that day at around mid-afternoon aboard the spaceship 9632-Orange still under the command of Captain Rojazonto. Although we could have travelled on any one of several available ships the captain had specified his spaceship as our spaceship and that he must have me travel with him for old time's sake. I was complimented and pleased when Captain Wastanomi conveyed this message to me and I immediately agreed to the arrangement. Wastanomi was rather amused though not surprised that such a request had been made.

Captain Rojazonto had greeted us personally when we disembarked in the shuttle bay of 9632-Orange and escorted us onto the internal transporter that took us to his control room for Wazu and refreshments. It had been nice to meet an old friend and we exchanged experiences of the past few years. He was excited about Nazmos entering a permanent orbit and stated that it would again be his privilege to take me out to perform the necessary adjustment when the time was right. I said I was honoured to be on a familiar ship; his of course.

Now here we were in Jazzatnit's home conversing as if we had never been away. I did feel quite at home here with Muznant's aunt and uncle and wondered if I should see her and Brazjaf now that they had been elevated to the Nazmos council responsible for its supreme government.

Jazzatnit must have read my thoughts - I didn't mind in the least - for she immediately smiled and conveyed that Muznant, Brazjaf and daughter Farzant would be here to share our evening meal. Farzant was now in her mid thirties and a young Oannes adult, though only just. They would also accompany us onto the open upper terrace to witness Raznat-set and then stay for the night. Jazzatnit conveyed images of them and I was quite taken by Farzant's dainty little face. She was pretty in a youthful childish way. Oannes females only blossom into true womanhood after the age of fifty. Farzant was way behind Mazpazam in that respect; Mazpazam being in her seventies. I expect Farzant to become a beauty in her own right in about another thirty years or so. I conveyed as much to Jazzatnit and she seemed pleased.

We then retired to the comfort of the dining room area for light refreshments when Zazfrapiz took his leave of us for a rest in his sleep tank. He said his bones ached less in the semi-weightless conditions there. After he had left Jazzatnit explained how he had raised the temperature of the water therein because he felt the cold quite a bit especially here in the open air. I thought about Ritozanan and how she too must have had to go through similar old age related discomfiture. I couldn't help but think of her with great affection in my heart. She had been one impressive lady.

Again Jazzatnit must have read these thoughts for she briefly touched my arm in a very affectionate and consoling gesture. I looked down at her and smiled my thanks. My emotions were clear and I could have put my arms around her and hugged her. She simply nodded back in understanding with another squeeze of my arm. We understood each other perfectly and Tania smiled at me as an added comfort.

We were seated around the dining table chatting and I was on my second glass of Wazu when Jazzatnit suddenly sat upright and appeared to get quite excited.

'They're here,' was all she said and I instantly knew who she meant.

We all stood up and moved out into the courtyard again and I saw Muznant, Brazjaf and Farzant enter through the outer arched entrance. There were wide smiles all around as we got closer and Muznant reached up to put her arms around me before planting a light kiss on my lips. She did the same to Tania and then to Rachel and Margaret; to their utter amusement.

Brazjaf looked imposing in his shining outfit as befitting a member of the governing council. But he too came forward to me and we made a firm double-handed handshake which seemed to last for ages. I was very pleased to see him and said so. After all he and Muznant were the first Oannes that we had met more than forty years ago.

I then looked at Farzant and was taken aback by her coy expression and her beauty. She was so much like Muznant though her full beauty was yet to mature. I went forward not certain what was the right approach so I held out my hand and she took it.

'I'm so pleased to see you again sir,' she said and I mumbled a reply about also being pleased.

'You men,' exclaimed Tania to me, 'just give her a hug you idiot.'

So I did. I went forward smiling broadly and put my arms gingerly around Farzant and stooped to press my cheek against hers.

I then stepped back and holding her at arms length said how lovely she looked.

'Thank you,' she replied in a half whisper but with a big smile on her face.

'I think Farzant will be prettier than her mother when she is older,' said Tania looking at me. 'Don't you think so darling?'

I had to agree so just nodded my head. I didn't want to offend Muznant by saying so.

'I don't mind,' said Muznant. 'She has youth on her side and after all she is my daughter. But of course you will always love me more.'

The last bit was said with a wicked twinkle in her eye as she smiled at Tania.

Both Muznant and Brazjaf were very relaxed and I gave them my congratulations about their elevation to the Nazmos council.

'Thank you,' said Brazjaf, 'I think the council greatly feel the loss of Ritozanan. It was Korizazit who made the recommendation and we felt we must accept.'

Brazjaf then looked towards Muznant before continuing.

'Ashley, we have been commissioned to invite you and all your family members here to a closed session of the council tomorrow afternoon within the Domed Hall Chambers where such meetings are held.'

'Thank you,' I said, 'we would be happy to attend. Do you know what it is about?'

Muznant smiled.

'You will find out tomorrow Ashley,' she said smiling, 'but suffice it to say that it will be a pleasant occasion.'

I smiled back but couldn't help trying to think what could be planned. I tried to read Muznant and Brazjaf's minds but they remained closed.

Tania looked at Muznant and nodding conveyed that they looked forward to the occasion.

In the back of my mind was a worry that the council may have reversed their decision about Nazmos' new orbital location or wished a change to the agreed plan. It could still be put back to its original wider orbit but that would be months away when the planet was back at apogee. On the other hand the starship Silverstreak had brought me here a week early before Nazmos reached its perigee position in its current lopsided orbit. At that point I had intended slowing it down proportionately to fix it in its new circular orbit approximately 19 million miles from Raznat. But I need not have worried because it was a completely different agenda that was planned and nothing to do with the Nazmos orbit.

Tania came up close to me and whispered.

'Darling,' she said in quite a serious tone which I recognised as her no nonsense authoritative manner, 'you must go along and graciously accept whatever they propose. I got a glimpse into Brazjaf's mind, which I think he did intentionally, and I believe they wish to bestow upon you an honour in their own way. Don't disappoint them for it will have a bearing on Simon's future career.'

'Yes darling, okay,' I conveyed back to her, 'I'll go along with whatever is proposed.'

I would never upset Muznant by refusing something planned for I feel that she must have had a key hand in this – somewhere.

'Promise,' conveyed Tania.

'Yes, I promise,' I conveyed back.

'Good. And thank you darling I'm very proud of you.'

'Don't worry dad,' this from Rachel, 'at least they can't make you king of something. It's not in their remit.'

I had to smile at that and noticed similar smiles from all present including Oannes company.

Something came to my mind and I thought, 'Yes, why not,' and immediately conveyed it to Muznant and Brazjaf.

They smiled back at me and nodded.

'Thank you Ashley,' said Brazjaf, 'we do think alike. But it has already been done. Gozmanot's name and memory has been entered into the annals of our history records. You too are to be included alongside her for the very important part you will have played in our history. You and she have a common link in time. She knew of you and you of her.'

Then Muznant quickly added, 'Your family will also be included beside you but only those who have been here on Nazmos. They are all to be recorded as the first humans to have visited Nazmos. It will show future generations when the new era in Oannes and human relations actually began.'

Tania smiled at this but now she too wondered about tomorrow's procedure with the governing council; especially the closed session part.

However the next few hours went by pleasantly and the meal in the dining hall was a lavish one. Zazfrapiz made a show of attending the meal but clearly I could see his interest was not towards any food. But he listened to our conversation especially everything I had to say. With the meal only halfway over he politely excused himself after asking everyone if he may be allowed to retire. He was then escorted to his apartment by his wife Jazzatnit. When she returned with a worried expression she explained that Zazfrapiz seemed to tire increasingly of late so we must excuse him. I think we all understood what she was trying to say and I felt sad for her. The emotion I had read from him was of extreme tiredness along with pain in his back and legs. I reckon that Ritozanan must have had a very difficult period during the last few years of her life. There is no cure for old age and its accompanying limitations.

Afterwards we went up the zig-zag walkway onto the open terrace to witness Raznat-set and the Dark Wind effect that came with it. Raznat was very low over the distant horizon and a dull red glow emanated from it. I thought it seemed to have a slightly brighter aspect in its shine. Gradually the sky began to dull as Raznat descended lower. I noticed a sort of haze on the horizon into which the ball of Raznat slowly settled. A softening of its colour and outline fused with the haze as it gradually dissolved into it. I had been here many times before and expectantly waited for the onrush of the Dark Wind.

At first the usual darkened hush settled over the land and I listened out for the distant whispering sound to commence. I waited and nothing happened. I looked across at Jazzatnit and gave her a queried look. She simply shrugged her shoulders just like Tania often did.

'It does not always happen when Nazmos is this close to Raznat,' she said. 'Perhaps it is because there is more warmth in the upper atmosphere layers that affect us down here.'

Then suddenly I heard it. The distant whispering came as a muffled sound that very gradually grew more pronounced as it drew closer. Then a brisk breeze raced past the terrace for about a minute before diminishing again just as suddenly as it had come. I felt somewhat disappointed.

Jazzatnit smiled at me as did Muznant and Brazjaf.

'And that Ashley is what the Dark Wind has become and it is all due to you,' said Muznant. 'This is one of the first aspects of the change in our weather pattern that I quite favour. The council is pleased that its fury has finally been tamed. When Nazmos enters its new permanent orbital position we feel a new era will truly begin.'

'I'm glad you think so,' I said. 'I hope all the other aspects of your new weather will be as pleasantly received.'

'Our scientists have predicted greater energy levels building within our atmosphere and Zanos has made some model predictions,' said Brazjaf. 'Of course there will be changes but we shall have to wait and see how it all actually behaves.'

Brazjaf then conveyed what some of those predictions were. One was that the general sea surface temperature would rise initially by about one degree Centigrade over a fifty year period. Evaporation from the seas would increase causing higher levels of moisture in the atmosphere which would result in cloud formations developing. As the moisture laden clouds moved towards the Polar Regions precipitation would occur as either rain or snow. In about two hundred years the seas would have dropped by as much as a foot and the Polar Regions increased in snow cover by as much as five hundred feet. Cloud formations would absorb some of Raznat's radiation and a balance would result in the sea temperatures and the evaporation rate. Nazmos could actually become cooler as a result. After about five hundred years a complete balance in the weather system might be achieved with wind and rain patterns approaching those seen in the temperate areas of Earth. The visions of Gozmanot would begin to show up on the land areas only after another couple of hundred years had passed. And after a thousand years Nazmos might appear decidedly greener and a bit like some areas on Earth.

'Well I think that I can make a prediction of my own,' I said, 'and that is that there will be some stormy days ahead.'

'Yes, Zanos has predicted that too,' said Brazjaf, 'and I do hope that the Rimzi don't suffer too badly in their underwater domain as a result; not that they will communicate with us either way.'

I thought of Mazpazam and her research interest. She had awakened a curiosity about the Rimzi people in my mind but my inner voice remained silent on the matter.

'Perhaps one day I could visit them' was a thought that strangely entered my mind.

'And so you shall.'

It was my inner voice confirming a fact and it seemed to imply a very long stay. But the implication was confused and unclear.

'When,' I asked and repeated the question but received nothing further? A cold silence remained and I finally gave up.

We stayed up on the terrace for another half hour before the cold of night reached us and we made our way back down to the warmth of Jazzatnit's courtyard.

Eventually we all retired to our rooms when Jazzatnit said she must return to Zazfrapiz and see that all was well with him.

Next morning we had a late breakfast together. Muznant and Brazjaf who had stayed the night said that we must all dress appropriately for the council meeting later today. They were smiling as they announced this and then I knew why.

Special outfits had been commissioned for all of us and these had been delivered and stored here in Jazzatnit's house. There was great pleasure in Jazzatnit's manner when she brought out the clothes to show us.

'My goodness,' I thought, 'we are certainly going to look grand in these.'

Tania's outfit and mine both had a sort of shiny over-garment to wear on top of a special tunic and leggings affair and very much like what I had seen being worn by the governing council members.

'I think I shall feel quite regal dressed in these,' I remarked.

Rachel and Margaret also had beautiful shiny outfits but no over-garment like Tania's and mine. But I reckoned that they too would look equally as posh and regal.

It was a nice day as most days are on Nazmos and I suggested that we go up onto the terrace as I wished to look around the sky for any of the new cloud formations we'd talked about.

Jazzatnit smiled and after returning our new outfits back from where she had brought them she led the way up to the terrace; the usual zig-zag route.

The sky was blue and not a wisp of cloud to be seen above us. Then Jazzatnit pointed to the North and above the distant horizon I could make out what looked like a fuzzy mountain range – but which was actually some cloud formation.

'They tend to remain there,' said Jazzatnit, 'and craft have been sent to investigate. When they get there they can see nothing but a misty haze. However it is quite extensive which is why from here it appears so. There have been some proper clouds overhead occasionally but they dissipate after a few hours. Perhaps after the permanent new orbit is fully achieved such incidents will become more frequent and persist for longer. Zanos has made such a forecast.'

Raznat was overhead and appeared slightly larger than I remember but of course Nazmos was about a third closer now. The warmth from Raznat however seemed the same to me but then I had been away for so long and on Earth the Sun was a much hotter prospect. I thought about the general warmer climate that must come with Nazmos being permanently closer to Raznat for its entire orbital cycle.

I was brought out of my thoughts by Jazzatnit reminding us that we must not be late for the closed governing council session. She and Zazfrapiz would not be attending as it was for current council members only. I and my family had been specially invited and Margaret was considered a part of that family.

We came down into the courtyard for a while before going in for an early afternoon meal. Our council invitation was not until mid-afternoon but we needed to prepare ourselves well before that. I suggested to Tania and the girls that they apply a bit of facial make-up as if they were attending a dinner party or a Ball or some such. I too wanted to impress the council members with the beauty of my ladies. I would groom my ample hair and smarten myself up making sure I stood up straight and tall. Tania says that I tended to slouch when I was tired. There'll be none of that today.

With the meal done we went to our rooms and found that the posh outfits had been placed ready for us to wear. I conveyed this to Rachel and Margaret and they replied that theirs was also in their room.

It was about an hour later that the transporter conveyed us to the Domed Hall. Muznant and Brazjaf were with us and acted as our escort on behalf of the governing council. The transporter took us by a direct route as Raznat was directly overhead and felt quite warm. I mentioned this to Muznant but she simply smiled back. She conveyed that the Oannes had become used to the summer and were beginning to enjoy the added warmth from Raznat. But so far over the last five years the summers had been brief lasting only a couple of Nazmos months. Thereafter Nazmos had drifted back out to its apogee position. The axial tilt to the planet made little difference in the equatorial regions where Wentazta was situated.

Our arrival at the Domed Hall was an anti-climax as the place was eerily empty of the previous banqueting crowds. The transporter settled down and we disembarked. Brazjaf then led us towards where the dais was located and then veered to the right towards a large portal that I had seen the governing council enter and leave on previous occasions. As we approached the closed door Brazjaf stopped and nodded to Muznant. She came around to check on Tania and me that our over-wear was still correctly in place. She lightly adjusted Tania's over-gown at the shoulders and then briefly checked me over. She did the same to Rachel and Margaret before giving her husband a big smile and a nod.

Brazjaf then paused briefly while facing the door and I knew that he was announcing our presence to the assembly within. He pushed gently upon the door and it opened slowly as if of its own accord. He then stepped forward and we all followed with Muznant bringing up the rear.

As I entered I was at first struck by the brightness in the room. As I became accustomed to the light I saw a huge oval room before me with a domed ceiling that was made of semi-clear tinted material. The brightness came from Raznat being overhead and so lighting up the hall in glorious colour. In the central area was a very large oval table with a highly polished surface. Around it in high backed chairs were seated the council members and their wives and I could see the reflection of the members opposite mirrored in the table surface. As I walked forward I felt the soft material under my feet that covered the floor like a layer of thin sponge. I seemed to float upon it with every step that I took. Nothing like this existed upon the Domed Hall floor.

I recognised many of the faces and all seemed pleasantly disposed in their manner towards us as we approached; a welcoming lot of faces if ever I saw one. All were adorned in beautiful shiny garments similar to what Tania and I were wearing. I felt quite elevated to be dressed as they were and was suddenly immensely appreciative of my friendship with Muznant and Brazjaf.

Brazjaf then led us to a set of empty seats along one part of the table and he very formally indicated where each of us should sit. I let Tania, Rachel and Margaret go to their seats before I took my seat beside my wife. I did this slowly and with much consideration. I might as well put a bit of style into my performance while I was at it. Muznant and Brazjaf then moved to the seats beside me.

Looking up from my seated position I noticed that no one was too far away due to the ovality of our seating. Everyone had a view towards the table centre. I thought of King Arthur and his Knights at their round table and realised the wisdom of such a seating arrangement.

As I looked around at the councillors I recognised quite a few faces. There was Korizazit who must be well into his 300th year age-wise. Nerbtazwi sat further around to my right and looked good for her age; perhaps because she was so tiny at less than four feet in height. She must be at least 350 years of age now and still looked impressive. She had been leader of the representatives of the governing council and I was happy to know she was now a full member of this august body. A very well deserved promotion. She smiled across at me and I knew that all had read my thoughts.

Sitting right opposite me was Dultarzent whom I knew to be the most senior among the governing council members. He had been very close in thought to Ritozanan and had been favourable towards me and my suggested plan for Nazmos from when I first presented it. He too looked well and must be close to Nerbtazwi's age if not a bit more. I recognised Wetzarnti who was a close friend to Zazfrapiz from the time both had served on the council. I nodded across to him and conveyed my good wishes. He replied with a smile. Then there were the two scientist brothers Maztatont and Zutadintz who had accompanied me on that momentous trip to Vaz and when I had my regressed meeting with Gozmanot. We had met and talked at all of the ensuing banquets here and I held them in high regard. A friendship had built between us.

And then I got the surprise of my life for at my far right were a couple I knew and had first met in Anztarza. Smiling in my direction was Puzlwat and his lovely wife Nogozat. They were now governing council members and I immediately conveyed my joy at their presence here.

Puzlwat had been an open opponent towards me when I first went to Anztarza as he considered me to be a fraud making claim to impossible feats. Of course this all changed once he had witnessed the asteroids experiments and thereafter became a close ally. Nogozat on the other hand had liked me from the outset and played her part in reforming Puzlwat's opinion of me.

I think Puzlwat will be a good influence within the governing council as he always viewed with suspicion any plan or proposal for change. His motto was that if things were working well then it was unnecessary to make changes. If it isn't broken then why attempt to fix it. He was however in favour of a warmer and greener Nazmos. Yes, I was pleased for his inclusion in the governing council of Nazmos. One day he could be a strong influence since he was young in age compared to some of the other members. At 212 years of age I could see him making his mark and reputation in the years to come.

There were several others around this table with whom I'd had many interesting discussions at those previous banqueting sessions and came to know them well. And their wives were as interesting.

With these pleasant thoughts in my mind I reached across and put my hand in Tania's under the table. She squeezed her reassurance back to me though I noticed nervousness in the feel of her hand. We waited for the next step to be taken in the proceedings and did not have long to wait.

It was Dultarzent who while remaining seated conveyed the council's intentions.

'Ashley,' he conveyed telepathically in open mind mode so all could receive, 'it is the wish of the council that we bestow upon you our highest honour. It is not because of what you have done in achievements though these are many and highly acclaimed. Neither is it because you possess special gifts that enable you to perform those deeds. Moving a planet is no mean task but for you it becomes an ordinary process. And mentally regressing back to Gozmanot's time over 36,500 years ago and giving us all a view of her visions defies our comprehension and makes us wonder at the success you achieved. No, it is not for these accomplishments that we would honour you but rather for the fact of your character. None of what I have just stated has had any influence upon you to affect or alter your nature from that of a most decent, likeable and amenable person. You just want to be ordinary like the rest of your human and Oannes friends and to live peacefully at home with your wife and family.'

There was a pause in the communication though only briefly.

'All who meet you see someone who by reputation appears awesome yet whom they come to respect and feel affection for. And it is for this quality in you that we bestow upon you this honour, the highest that this governing body can bestow upon anyone whether Oannes or human. The honour is to be shared with your wife Tania as your partner in life. You are both offered a seat on this governing council of Nazmos as full members and we are all agreed that you will be a worthy addition to our decision making ability. We hope that you will honour us with your acceptance.'

Since I intended to respond verbally I decided that it would be appropriate that I stand up tall so all could see me. I then looked around at all the Oannes faces here and smiled.

'Thank you most gracious council members,' I began, 'it is a great honour that you offer me and Tania. To share a seat within this most august body, the Nazmos governing council of ministers is a very great privilege indeed and we gratefully accept your offer. We shall serve to the best of our ability and in every way we can. I only wish that another council member could have been present to share this moment, I refer to my dear friend Ritozanan. May her memory be forever with us to help and guide our decisions'

There was an emotional blend within the room and I knew all agreed with me. She had been a guiding light in the decisions made over the years and only a few could remember the council without her.

'However I must request that our membership as council members be considered as an honorary one,' I said. 'My reasons for this request are that much has still to be achieved by me and my absence from here may be prolonged. In a few days the Nazmos orbit must be stabilised. Then the starship Silverstreak needs to be put through its paces to achieve its maximum designed velocity of 1200 FTL and subsequent controlled slowdown. And then finally the long journey for me to tackle and defeat Zarama. The return journey may be even more prolonged and if all goes to plan then I would wish to return to Earth and live out my remaining days peacefully with my family and in my house in Dudley. I thank you most sincerely for this great honour to me and my family and we shall remain true to its fundamental principles even on Earth.'

I smiled at all present before I slowly sat down.

'We are glad of your acceptance,' conveyed Dultarzent, 'and we understand your views and accept them. However the honorary status will only be for periods when you are away from Nazmos. We value your opinion and request your attendance for the next two sessions here before the Nazmos orbital adjustment which is to be effected by you on the fifth day from now. One session is tomorrow and the next on the third day from today. We invite your attendance to both if that is convenient.'

Once again I stood up and this time conveyed telepathically to all that it would be our privilege to attend both sessions. And of course I confirmed that it would be just Tania and me. I mentioned the last bit so that there was no confusion about Rachel and Margaret. They were here today only because they were a part of my family to witness the honour that was being given to me. They had no role to play in the council's decisions.

Dultarzent then stood up and all the members followed suit. As I stood up those nearest me turned to me and shook my hand and conveyed a welcome greeting. I conveyed my appreciative thanks in return. For some reason Rachel and Margaret also received similar handshakes and congratulations though what was conveyed was slightly different. Tania and I received a special greeting from Puzlwat and Nogozat and later we talked about Anztarza times and past memories.

There was a very pleasant atmosphere here in the council chamber but I felt that the full business had not as yet concluded. And I was proved right when Dultarzent requested that all return to the council table.

'Ashley there is one other matter that must be dealt with and it concerns you,' conveyed Dultarzent who had stood up to deliver his message.

'You mentioned our late colleague Ritozanan who was a friend to you. You had a special place in her affection and it was she who had initially recommended that consideration be given to your inclusion as a member of this council. She was not certain that you would accept though she hoped you would. Since we have now passed that stage it was subsequently her wish that suitable accommodation be given to you and your family. In her last testament she offered her own residence for that purpose and so we now accede to her wishes. Her home is to be at your disposal and to any of your family who wish to stay there. Provision has been made for all your comforts within it including the continued service of Ritozanan's assistants and staff.'

I responded immediately also from a standing position.

'I thank the council and all of its members and graciously accept this gift. And I thank the Honourable Ritozanan for her thoughtfulness in making such a provision. I had a great affection for her when she was here and still hold her memory dear in my heart,' I said aloud.

I had to pause as emotion gripped me briefly and all must have noticed. I then continued.

'The gift is generous and I wish to thank Zazfrapiz and Jazzatnit for all their hospitality to me and my family during all our visits to Nazmos. As Nazmos goes into transition with its new orbit it would be nice to have somewhere that I can call home when I am not on Earth. Rachel and Margaret intend to stay on Nazmos long term to witness this transition period and I request that they be permitted to treat Ritozanan's house as their own while I am away.'

I did not add that neither of them was to accompany me on the journey to Zarama for I had not told them that as yet: but I soon would. Perhaps they had guessed already or had planned against it. After all Nazmos would be in its new permanent orbit and they would not want to miss witnessing the early changes that occurred.

After a brief pause Dultarzent conveyed that my request was granted and Rachel and Margaret were welcome to stay for as long as necessary.

I imagined that a full record of the meeting was now in the archives having been facilitated there through the Zanos system.

Dultarzent then adjourned the session and stipulated that all were free to return to their home duties. He added that a governing council session would be convened at the same time the next day and that there was only one issue for consideration. I guessed that this could be about Zarama.

It was however another half hour of meeting council members on a personal level before the Transporters took each of us back to our place of residence. Muznant and Brazjaf said they were proud of my performance before the council and both agreed that I would fit in well. When we entered the courtyard garden both Zazfrapiz and Jazzatnit were eager to receive a full report. They were overjoyed at the news and congratulated Tania and me on our elevation to the governing council. Muznant conveyed full images of the council proceedings that related to me. Anything else would not have been permitted.

The next day Muznant and Brazjaf came once again and this time took only Tania and me for the council session in the afternoon. Rachel and Margaret had earlier taken a Transporter to Ritozanan's old house. Margaret said she and Rachel needed to look it over to assess which rooms would be best for them on a long term basis since their stay on Nazmos was to be indefinite. I conveyed images of the large circular sleep tank in its specially designed room from my last visit to Ritozanan and they got quite excited for its prospect as a swim pool for them.

Tania and I were again dressed in all our finery though slightly different from yesterday and I felt quite at ease with the council members there. Jazzatnit had said that a complete wardrobe had been supplied for us so that we did not wear the same outfit twice during any week period.

Tania and I were greeted as we took our seats – all split backed of course. There were a few vacant places but apologies had been conveyed.

The session commenced and I was given the go ahead for the implementation of the new Nazmos orbit and also for the Silverstreak test run soon after. But nothing was mentioned about a timetable for the trip to tackle Zarama so I kept silent on the issue. I kept my mind open which was the prime requirement during all council sessions; as prompted earlier by Muznant.

Oddly there was no refreshment or Wazu anywhere on the table and I made the suggestion that since I often used verbal communication then at least a jug of Wazu with glasses be provided for Tania and me. This was agreed unanimously not only for me but for every seat position around the oval table. Dultarzent however conveyed that council sessions rarely lasted more than three hours. He then stipulated for my benefit that tomorrow's session would be a full and proper one.

After this session adjourned many members stood around in small groups discussing matters of interest to them. Puzlwat and Nogozat came and joined our little group consisting of Muznant, Brazjaf, Nerbtazwi and Korizazit and we all had a pleasant general discussion. Each conveyed that they would be on the spaceship 9632-Orange under Captain Rojazonto to witness the final settling in of the Nazmos orbit. At Nogozat's query I explained exactly how I would go about it. I conveyed that it would in fact be very similar to when I slowed Nazmos from its original orbit way back in January 2039.

Gradually our little group grew larger as more members sensed something of interest and approached us. But of more interest to most were the images I conveyed of my home in Dudley and of the Antiques shops in the town centre. I was happy to continue in like fashion as I enjoyed the interest shown for Earth but then Muznant prompted that our host Jazzatnit had a special meal prepared and we mustn't keep her waiting. A lame excuse but a polite one and I think all recognised it for what it was. I believe Muznant was looking out for my welfare before any embarrassing question was asked.

So once again we were greeted by Jazzatnit in her courtyard and she immediately wanted to know everything about this latest council session. Muznant began to convey this but Jazzatnit stopped her. She wanted my perspective and impressions so I passed to her all my images and thoughts of the session. I knew I was breaking council rules but both my hosts are former council members so I suppose it could be excused.

'Yes, you will do well there,' she conveyed. 'I remember it well from Zazfrapiz's time as a council member. He thought it was all bombast and of little substance at the time. But then those days were not as exciting as they are now. Ashley you have made sure of that. I wish I could be there to listen when you have something important to convey.'

I smiled at Jazzatnit and threw back my head and laughed aloud. I thought of Simon for I recognised a bit of his laughter mannerisms in mine.

'I haven't anything important to say,' I said, 'and even if I did I would never go against the wishes of the council.'

'Very well said,' came from behind me in the voice of Zazfrapiz. 'So you've attended your first council session. What did you think?'

He was seated on a floating pallet and came up behind us.

'It was worth attending,' I said, 'but I think that this session was really for my benefit to get me to see how the council conducted its business. There was nothing serious on the agenda.'

'Then nothing has changed since my time,' said Zazfrapiz with a knowing smile.

'Tania and I however quite enjoyed the session,' I said. 'It was nice to meet old friends and make new ones. They all seemed very interested in me especially of my lifestyle on Earth.'

'There will be much to contend with here on Nazmos when the weather changes begin to have effect,' he said. 'I expect new regulations of behaviour will eventually be issued to deal with those changes.'

'I hope that they will be nothing too severe,' said Jazzatnit.

'I think that all changes will be quite gradual,' I said. 'It will be many years in the making. I'm speaking of Gozmanot's visions. She saw nothing of great severity or catastrophic from what I remember.'

'The die is cast,' conveyed Zazfrapiz, 'and I for one am looking forward to these changes. Maybe my bones won't ache as much then.' He gave an inward laugh as he added the last bit.

I then asked him about tomorrow's council meeting which Dultarzent had mentioned would be a full and proper one.

Zazfrapiz explained that a full council meeting was one in which all the representatives would be present. These representatives were the real facilitators of all the decisions agreed in council. Nerbtazwi had been the leader of the representatives when I met her on my very first trip to Nazmos in 2016. I had then been invited to come alone which I did.

'They are like your own country's civil servants in a manner of speaking,' he conveyed.

'So will it be a lengthy session?' I asked.

'Not really,' said Brazjaf. 'Most matters will have been well prepared by each representative and it will simply be a matter of the council's approval or otherwise. In such a case the matter can be deferred for further investigation. Sessions seldom last more than three hours. Don't forget all proceedings are carried out telepathically and perceptions are clear and easy to comprehend. Visual images and arguments are conveyed much more strongly than verbal ones.'

And so it would prove to be.

Later that evening Rachel and Margaret returned from their visit to Ritozanan's former home. They were full of excitement and enthused about the place. They remarked how large and palatial it was. I said that I had only seen a part of it when I had been invited by Ritozanan to make that personal visit alone. Afterwards I had been too upset to notice anything about the rest of the house.

Then you must come and see it, dad,' said Rachel, 'you will love it.'

'Yes,' said Jazzatnit, 'Ritozanan's house was a grand affair. And the upper terrace is twice as large as ours here and also at a higher level.'

'Then we should visit it,' I said. 'Tomorrow is another council session and we shall be free on the day after that. Since Rachel and Margaret have already been they can be our guides.

'That we will most certainly do with pleasure,' said Margaret smiling after a quick glance towards Rachel. 'I couldn't get enough of the place.'

'We shall look forward to it,' said Tania.

After the evening meal we all went up onto the terrace but once again the Dark Wind was a meek affair.

The next day Tania and I were once again escorted to the council session by Muznant and Brazjaf. We were instructed to listen and learn the ways of the council in serious session. All matters would be conducted in the Oannes way through telepathic means. In other words I was to observe only and not convey an opinion. I would be happy to do just that.

Inside the council chamber Tania and I were pleasantly greeted as we took our seats beside Muznant. Again I felt quite resplendent in the new outfit that Jazzatnit had produced that morning.

I looked around the room and noticed how large it really was now that an additional circle of representatives were seated close to its walls.

The session commenced slowly but suddenly a buzz of telepathic information began to take place such that even I had difficulty in keeping abreast of all the issues being exchanged. I picked up most of it but after an hour my mind felt quite fatigued. Poor Tania was slightly out of her depth and looked at me with a confused look on her face. Her smile however was ever present for the sake of appearances I think.

There were jugs of Wazu in front of every member and I helped myself to some. Eventually I guessed that the meeting was about to end when the representatives began to stand up and leave the room. When there were only a few left I was jolted upright at the mention of my name.

It was Dultarzent wishing me all success in my endeavour to finalise Nazmos in its new permanent orbit.

I immediately responded and conveyed my sincere thanks to the council for its kind wishes.

'It will be our success,' I conveyed, 'and for all the people of Nazmos.'

With that the session was adjourned and as before little groups formed around the room. I had my own friends come over to me and make pleasant telepathic conversation. Again this lasted about half an hour before we dispersed.

Tomorrow was to be a free day for me and I planned to go with Rachel and Margaret to view Ritozanan's house. On the day after that my mission would begin. I would be going out into space with a full scientific team on the spaceship 9632-Orange under the command of Captain Rojazonto. I wondered how many of the council members would also be aboard to witness the occasion. I imagine quite a few though their presence would be kept private.

When we boarded the transporter and finally arrived back at Jazzatnit's house she was again anxious to hear all about the council session proceedings. I obliged her and conveyed my impressions in detail and she nodded her pleasure.

'Ashley,' she said aloud, 'I have come to think of you as if you were one of my own and I feel tremendous pride in your achievement within the council.'

She smiled as she said this and I couldn't help feeling drawn towards her. I felt great affection and love for this elderly lady. It was as if there were no 300 years difference in our ages. I considered her a very presentable lady and I conveyed this to Muznant and to Tania. I knew that Tania would understand exactly what I meant.

Later, after the evening meal all of us except Zazfrapiz went up onto the open terrace to witness how the Dark Wind of tonight's Raznat-set would perform. This was a phenomenon that the Oannes had got used to and one which I should very much miss when it became extinct. I would miss it for the thrill that it produced which at first I had found quite scary. Sarah had been startled by its ferocity when she'd first witnessed it and Brian had to put his arm around her to comfort her.

This evening however, it was a very mild affair and hardly worth mentioning.

Next morning after breakfast we took leave of Jazzatnit and Zazfrapiz and left to go to Ritozanan's house. To me it will always be her house. Rachel and Margaret walked ahead as we made our way to the plaza area where the Transporter pre-ordered by our hosts awaited us. The journey took nearly half an hour at a good pace of travel.

When we got there we were met by two assistants and after a brief Sewa were welcomed as the new owners of the property. They were Ratizdan and Statizona, both female Oannes who were aged 200 and 180 respectively. They were quite small in stature being less than five feet in height and with pleasing features and pleasant manners. They made me feel most welcome and completely at home. They conveyed they had both been very close to Ritozanan as her personal assistants for over fifty years and still missed her presence. I conveyed my own emotions about her which seemed to put them at their ease.

Ratizdan conveyed a detailed plan of the house and that they would be happy to assist us in any way that was appropriate for the comfort of me and my family. I thanked them both and conveyed that I was happy for them to continue the smooth running of the household in their own capable way. I had not met them when I had last been here because I had been brought to see Ritozanan by Korizazit and Nerbtazwi.

I looked at Rachel and conveyed a private massage and she nodded agreement. She and Margaret had met Ratizdan and Statizona on their previous visit but then had been treated formally as visitors. Today I think Tania's and my presence made all the difference.

We were taken around the house room by room and in each I expressed my delight at their appearance. It was when we entered the near circular room in which I had last seen my friend that I stopped short in semi-shock. I had expected to see a beautiful circular sleep-tank filled with clear sparkling water and with window-like view panels depicting scenes reminiscent of Earth. Instead what was before me was a barren room with blank view panels and an empty circular sleep-tank. I looked at Ratizdan with puzzlement on my face. My emotion was one of disappointment and slight annoyance.

'It was customary to empty the tank after Ritozanan died,' conveyed Ratizdan. 'We of her household had served her for many happy years and did not feel like redecorating the last room she had been in until the new owners took up residence. Now that you are here this room will be done up as you wish it to be according to your personal taste.'

I looked around very slowly and took in all that was before me.

'I honour Ritozanan's memory with affection and respect,' I said aloud, 'and would wish for her to see this room as if she were still here. So please return it to the way it was and we shall refer to it as Ritozanan's room. I shall even refer to the house as her house. I respected the lady when she was alive and I shall continue to respect her memory.'

Both Ratizdan and Statizona smiled their pleasure at this accolade from me and conveyed that it would be just as I wished.

'Everything will be as when Ritozanan occupied this sleep-tank and this room,' conveyed Ratizdan with an emotion of pleasure coming through in her telepathic tone.

When we returned to Jazzatnit's house and courtyard she was pleased at what I had done and said so. The look she gave me said a lot more.

That night the Dark Wind seemed to have an added gusto of energy as if someone was trying to tell me something. I hoped that it was an indication that she approved. And the next day would see the final part to the fulfilment of the start to Gozmanot's visions of Nazmos and also the culmination of the campaign that Ritozanan had promoted single-mindedly within the sessions of the governing council. I went to bed that night thinking of only one thing: that Nazmos would finally be entering its new permanent orbit that would usher in the new era as envisioned by that ancient lady.

I slept well through the night period and woke early before Tania. I lay there staring up at the ceiling thinking abstract thoughts. I turned hoping to see her pretty face in its sleep mode but could not as Tania habitually slept with her head under the covers. I did not want to wake her from her beauty sleep as she called it; and in her case it certainly did work. At least I thought so.

I traced back to the very first time I saw her in the Navigation Pub just after that darts match. I was eighteen then and she with her bouncy reddish brown hair a rather sparkling thirteen year old. At the time I thought nothing special of her other than that she was another pretty looking girl. How things had moved on since then I thought with a smile.

Suddenly the covers were pushed back and I saw Tania looking intensely at me – but only for an instant before she pulled the cover back up again.

But I knew she was not asleep and reading her thoughts I recognised the symptoms of an aroused mind. And a minute later she began to snake herself towards me. I felt her arm come over me as she snuggled close. Seconds later out popped her head beside mine and I got a quizzical look from her. I love to tease but this was not the time so I shifted position and cuddled her to me. We were snug as two bugs in a rug face to face. One thing led to another and passion grew to its proper fulfilment.

Afterwards we lay quietly together until I realised that Tania was in tears. She clung to me tightly and I could feel her body jerk as it was wracked with her sobbing. With telepathic mind reading nothing remains secret and I understood the source of her sadness. In her instinctive mind she was convinced that our time together was limited and that the last phase towards that end was about to begin. As the time drew nearer for me to meet with Zarama so Tania felt that it would be my end.

In my own mind I was not so sure but I knew that Zarama must be turned from its present course for Earth and Nazmos to survive. Sirius B had proved that the task was greater than my capability then. But what about now five years later; had my telekinetic power increased with time? If not then I must resort to what I had been forbidden. I would not cross that obstacle until I came to it.

I put my arms around Tania and hugged her tightly to me while placing kisses on top of her head. They were wet kisses for the emotion had got to me in quite a big way too.

We must have dozed off again for when I awoke Tania was in the shower and I could hear her humming a tune. I sent her a private message and she acknowledged. A couple of minutes later she came into the room and stood beside the bed her head wrapped in a towel. Otherwise she had not a stitch on. I conveyed that she had a very nice belly button along with the rest of her – in private mode of course. She turned and wiggled her bottom at me before walking to the chair that had her slip draped over it.

Later at breakfast Rachel said that she and Margaret were coming along to witness the final act of Nazmos being stabilised in its permanent new orbit. Rachel then added that she and Margaret would not be going on the long trip to Zarama as that would take more than a year and they didn't want to miss recording any early changes to Nazmos' climate no matter how minor.

I said I was pleased by this decision as the journey there and back would be quite monotonous to say the very least.

'I knew you would understand dad,' said Rachel smiling at me and then giving Margaret a look that said 'I told you so'.

Jazzatnit then looked at me and asked verbally, 'What are your thoughts today Ashley?'

'Well for a start,' I said, 'I'm glad I don't have to dress up and attend another governing council session. Otherwise I think it will be a successful day for all of Nazmos and for me.'

Jazzatnit looked intensely at me and shook her head. She knew that I had evaded the question and being a polite Oannes she didn't pursue it.

I knew what she was really asking. Once I had settled Nazmos in its new orbit then only Zarama remained. So my thoughts must focus upon the final phase of Gozmanot's vision that the flaming dragon must be vanquished. It was also why Tania had gone through such an emotional moment this morning. Her woman's intuition had played its part and this must have been picked up by Jazzatnit. I think Jazzatnit was concerned for me and my welfare and Tania's bout had for her shed new light on certain possibilities against Zarama. Her aspect towards me from now on would harmonise with Tania's and be tinged with a hint of sadness.

It was easy for me to put on a cheerful manner since for me nothing was certain. And it didn't worry me about the course that I might have to follow in my fight against Zarama. I only knew that these gifts had been bestowed upon me for this very purpose and therefore success was a foregone conclusion. How that success was to be achieved was as yet unresolved in my mind but I knew that I must and would do everything to succeed at whatever cost. Two worlds and too many lives were at stake so failure was not an option.

I pushed all these thoughts from my mind and focussed on the present. Today was the day I must slow Nazmos in its orbit as required. For me the task was a simple one since I had already performed a similar task on Nazmos six years earlier in 2039. I had then slowed Nazmos in its orbital velocity of 28,500 mph down to 25,792 mph. This would have gradually dropped Nazmos down from its 31 million mile orbital distance from Raznat down to 19 million miles over a period of five months. The orbital velocity would then have increased to 46,200 mph and would send it racing back up to its 31 million mile orbital apogee position over the following five month period. This elliptic orbit had continued since then.

Currently Nazmos was approaching its orbital perigee position of 19 million miles from Raznat and my task today would be to slow it down to 44,000 mph a reduction in speed of 2,200 mph. This would stabilise Nazmos into a permanent circular orbit 19 million miles from Raznat. It should take me 25 hours of constant telekinetic effort at a third of 1% of normal gravity deceleration to effect this. Of course I would break this into five stints of five hours each with normal gravity rests in between. Hopefully there would be less disruption to Nazmos' sea and atmospheric conditions than that of the previous occasion six years ago. Then I had slowed Nazmos at a deceleration rate of 0.5% of Nazmos gravity which had resulted in a tidal surge across the Peruga Sea. Also a minor gale had been reported as blowing across the land and sea and I remember feeling some concern about those conditions. However it had been reported that the conditions had not worsened so I had continued with the same deceleration level. It had taken more than a week for Nazmos to settle down back to normal.

As a direct result of that experience I discussed the aspect with the Oannes scientists team and they had recommended that the revised 0.33% of Nazmos gravity deceleration rate be applied instead to which I had immediately agreed. They also recommended that zero-gravity craft be used instead of the current smaller shuttle craft used in ferrying people to and from spaceships. Zero-g craft had much more comfortable facilities which were necessary for the longer period of use intended. Three such craft would be needed and teams of scientists would be in each. I would of course be in one of them too.

All this had been conveyed to the Oannes population on Nazmos so they were keen for it to begin. The Rimzi had not responded to any of the messages and information conveyed to them but this was not unusual. They seemed to want no contact with the land based population,

When Muznant and Brazjaf came for us about mid-morning we were walking around in Jazzatnit's courtyard. Both seemed in high energy mode and keen to get started and conveyed that this was to be an historic occasion for them all. They conveyed that Captain Rojazonto was ready with his spaceship 9632-Orange along with the one zero-g craft squeezed into its shuttle bay area. The other two zero-g craft would be on the two other accompanying spaceships.

Although zero-g craft were fully capable of flying out directly from Nazmos the nature and duration of the operation required normal gravity rest periods and nourishment after each five hour stint. This would of course be provided aboard the larger spaceships in their parking loops.

We walked to the plaza and boarded the waiting Transporter which took us directly to the space park on the outer limits of Wentazta and transferred to the spaceship's smaller internal transporter that was waiting for us. It then rose up and took us into the bowels of 9632-Orange and through a maze of shafts and corridors to the bubble of the control room. We entered the control room to a Sewa greeting from Captain Rojazonto. He conveyed that all was ready and we could rise into space as soon as Zanos had completed the checks upon all personnel aboard. Any crew or passengers with ill health symptoms or unease would not be permitted to space travel.

I think I had got used to these spaceflight procedures for within moments I noticed the other craft in the space park disappearing downwards in our view panels. We were definitely airborne and rising upwards with increasing pace. I always wondered at the smoothness and ease of the Oannes space travel process. There was never any sensation of rapid acceleration or sudden motion. If I had my eyes closed I would not have known that we were ascending rapidly.

The sky darkened to a deeper blue and then opened to the blackness of space. The stars suddenly became apparent as if they had just been awakened from their afternoon nap. One minute there were none and the next instant they were amassed all around us.

Captain Rojazonto conveyed to us that it would take about an hour to attain the 50,000 mile location where the spaceship would enter its parking loop. The two other spaceships would also arrive at safe distances from us and settle into their own parking loops. It would then be a further hour for the zero-g craft to be readied and manned up for them to exit each spaceship and to proceed to their prescribed locations. I would of course need to be downstream of Nazmos' orbital path and just less than 50,000 miles from it.

The captain suggested that we all retire to the dining hall where a good meal was to be served up shortly. It would be seven hours before our next one which would be had during the first rest break. If each rest break lasted about two hours then the entire orbit settling operation would be in the region of 38 hours including travel back and forth from the spaceships. The captain had earlier stated that depending upon the circumstances he might extend the rest periods if he found this was necessary. I think he was thinking of my comfort and the known fatigue effects upon my person from my telekinetic efforts of the past. I believe he was also thinking of the Oannes scientists who were to accompany me, not only those from 9632-Orange but from the other spaceships as well. All who spent a prolonged period at near zero gravity needed time to recover in normal gravity conditions.

He also suggested that we check our cabins after the meal since they were different from those on previous occasions. He conveyed that since I was now a governing council member the accommodation needed to suit my elevated status. I conveyed that I would have been happy with my previous accommodation which I had found most comfortable. He simply smiled at me and made no reply. The Oannes are sticklers for doing things correctly and according to form.

The internal transporter took us directly to a dining hall which had many vacant tables. We chose one located conveniently near the entrance and noticed that the place was only half full. Those that were here were probably the scientists and crew who were to accompany me on the zero-g craft.

Dishes of food were brought on floating pallets and placed by the servers on each occupied table. Jugs of Wazu and drinking glasses were already on the tables. Suddenly breakfast seemed to have been a very long time ago and I felt keen to tuck in; but I mustn't eat too much. A full belly and a zero gravity environment are not quite compatible. But I did drink plenty of Wazu. I had finished eating after half an hour and we sat discussing things in general for another half hour after that – but not about the present mission. We talked about Mazpazam and Simon and I wished that they could have been here now. But they had duties to perform aboard Silverstreak and hopefully I should see them in a few days for its test run. This past week seems to have gone by quick and it seems like ages since Silverstreak arrived at its Raznat rendezvous location and we had left it.

I had been informed that since the zero-g craft would remain semi-stationary at a fixed distance close to 50,000 miles from Nazmos that a 3% gravity level would still prevail and be felt by those on board. Better than nothing I thought.

Brazjaf suggested we retire to our cabins and rest a while as we would during the prescribed rest breaks and Zanos could induce instant sleep for a short period at least. I thought it a very good idea and we all agreed immediately.

As usual an internal transporter was waiting for us and took each of us to our allocated cabin. Rachel and Margaret had one next to ours with Muznant and Brazjaf also nearby. This was definitely different from the previous cabins in that they were larger and more luxurious. I suppose they were for special dignitaries and council members. I felt privileged to be considered thus. Tania eyed the sleep tank in the second room but I said we ought to stick to the beds provided for us here. I can read her mind like a book.

Zanos conveyed that the spaceship had reached the prescribed distance from Nazmos and was just entering its parking loop and that operations would not commence for another three hours. So Tania and I settled down on the ample beds provided and I requested Zanos to induce a restful sleep for both of us for a two hour period. I had never resorted to this before and wondered at its facilitation. I presumed that Zanos would wake me at the end of two hours when I could freshen up with a shower and comfortable clothing. An ample assortment of soft material leggings and tunics were hanging up in the cabin storage area. An assortment of footwear was also on display.

I cannot remember falling asleep but it felt as if it occurred as soon as I had got comfortable with my head on the pillow. Afterwards Tania said it was the same for her.

When I did wake it felt as if no time had passed but I did feel extraordinarily refreshed from it. Tania smiled across at me from her twin bed alongside and conveyed how good she felt. I shook my head at her hint and conveyed 'Maybe after'. Each five hour stint and following rest period totalling about thirty eight hours or so would be a long stretch for me and I did not want to be distracted.

Earlier I had suggested that Tania and the girls should stay on 9632-Orange while I performed my telekinetic push upon Nazmos but all three had refused and insisted they accompany me on the zero-g craft. It would be another adventure for them they said but I think I liked that they would be near.

Tania and I showered separately and then put on our tunics, leggings and footwear. These felt very comfortable and I felt ready for the task ahead.

Zanos conveyed that the zero-g craft were ready on all the spaceships and boarding had commenced. Muznant and Brazjaf conveyed that they would not be accompanying me as they preferred the comfort of normal gravity aboard 9632-Orange. However they came with us on the internal transporter to the shuttle bay where the single zero-g craft was sitting. This was designated with the number OG-9632-1 and was smaller than the one used for the Sirius B experiment. I should guess it was about 100 feet long and 50 feet wide which was half the size of OG-8110-1. This too had a similar single main deck layout.

Tania, Rachel, Margaret and I went towards the craft after first visiting the usual electrostatic suiting room. Also all three ladies had head scarves tied firmly under their chins to keep their hair down. We followed a group of Oannes scientists and walked up the ramp slope and into a short corridor. From here we entered the main central seating area which was also like a control room but much larger and was open plan. It was completely free of any loose items or objects and the view panels were towards the front of the craft and very similar to those on Bulzezatna's spaceship 520-Green back in Anztarza.

In all there must have been about 40 or 50 passengers and crew aboard and I imagine the scientists had direct communication with Zanos-on-board for the purpose of monitoring the deceleration conditions. Although this craft was half the size of the previous one used for Sirius B nevertheless there was ample comfortable seating within.

One of Captain Rojazonto's deputies named Sparzanzo aged 130 years and rather taller than average was in charge of the craft. He had two crew members to assist him and these ushered each passenger to their pre-designated seat. These were of the bucket type with a wide split in the back rest and were well cushioned and comfortable. Each seat had both shoulder and thigh clamps that were well padded. Our seats were positioned right at the front with an excellent space view since I was the person who needed to see Nazmos clearly in order to apply my telekinetic push upon it.

The interior of this zero-g craft was quite different from the rather smaller shuttle craft with their all around clear view panelling. I felt much more secure in this craft with its greater bulk above and below where we sat. The bucket seats were inclined slightly backwards which I found most comfortable especially with the split headrest. My head fitted there nicely and I reckon I could doze off during each five hour period.

When all had boarded and the ramp was secured the shuttle bay lights dimmed and after a minute OG-9632-1 lifted up off the deck and slowly exited through the large bay doors into the blackness of space. There was no sensation of movement until the zero gravity effect became apparent. However Zanos induced a feeling of wellbeing in our minds to counter any nausea or nil-gravity ill effects that might arise; especially as it would be a prolonged stint of five hours out here.

We moved closer to Nazmos and took up a relatively stationary position some 50,000 miles from it. At this distance Nazmos exerted 3% of its gravity upon us which made me just that tiny bit more comfortable. Also the girls did not need to wear scarves to hold down their hair but each insisted upon its use – just in case.

I was ready to commence my telekinetic effort but waited for Zanos to give me the go ahead. This could only be given when the other two zero-g craft had also got into position. And it was another twenty minutes before Zanos conveyed that all craft were in position and that I could commence my operation.

So with an open mind I stared at the half moon image that was Nazmos and willed for it to be decelerated at the rate of 0.33% of Nazmos gravity. I willed for this deceleration to be applied to every one of Nazmos' land, sea and air particles in an exact manner so as to cause a minimum of disruption. Since my mind was in open mode Zanos-on-board picked up my command thoughts and relayed them to the other spacecraft and to all of Nazmos in general.

After ten minutes Zanos reported that Nazmos was slowing very gradually and that all was near normal on its surface apart from a minor tidal swell within the Peruga Sea. After half an hour a gentle wind was reported as having commenced in the upper atmosphere. And an hour later the conditions had remained the same. Information was coming in to Zanos from the general population that everything was nearly normal apart from the Peruga Sea swell and the steady wind effect.

So then I settled back comfortably in my seat as far as the thigh and shoulder clamps would allow and let my head lean back against the headrest. Tania reached across and squeezed my hand and I looked sideways to see Rachel and Margaret smiling as they looked through the view panels at the distant Nazmos. I wondered if they had expected something dramatic though I think just being here and witnessing Nazmos' transition would have been wonder enough for anyone. They were living through an historical event at this very moment.

Regular reports of the Nazmos status kept being relayed by Zanos-on-board through communication with the other zero-g craft as well and the time just seemed to whiz by. After the third hour the reports remained consistent and a kind of monotony began to be felt. But all were alert for anything unexpected. Rachel seemed to become restless and conveyed that she could do with stretching her legs. She said that she would remain on the main spacecraft 9632-Orange for all of the next operational shifts as this zero gravity experience did not suit her. And Margaret conveyed the same. I suggested to Tania that she too would be more comfortable at normal gravity and to remain with Rachel and Margaret as I intended to sleep during the next five hour stints. But Tania gave an emphatic no. She said she wanted to be beside me because that is where she wished to be. Secretly I was pleased at her decision to remain; it was always comforting to have Tania beside me and to feel the pressure of her hand in mine. Besides she smelt nice and I could sense her thoughts and presence close beside me. I do love this woman and I can feel her love for me like an enveloping aura around me.

Zanos then conveyed that the five hours for the operation was approaching its end in five minutes. I waited for this to be up before I willed for all telekinetic action on my part to cease.

With the first shift of the operation over, Zanos confirmed that Nazmos was now orbiting Raznat at the reduced velocity of 45,760 mph. This was a reduction in its orbital velocity of 440 mph which was exactly as planned. I was pleased with this and felt quite satisfied that all had gone to plan. Tania and the others seemed pleased as well and conveyed their congratulations.

Sparzanzo then announced that the zero-g craft had begun its return journey back to the mother spacecraft 9632-Orange and we should be back in normal gravity within twenty minutes. Captain Rojazonto had shortened his ship's parking loop for it to be in a convenient position for the zero-g craft to enter its shuttle bay at an earliest. And it was nice when I felt normal gravity return as we settled down upon the shuttle bay deck exactly on time.

We earthlings waited in our seats while the other passengers disembarked. Then we slowly stood up to get used to the return of normal gravity after so long and gingerly made our way to the exit and down the shallow ramp. My legs felt a bit wobbly but the feeling soon passed. I think Tania and the others felt the same initially. Waiting for us on the deck were Muznant and Brazjaf with big smiles on their faces. Their greeting was both profuse and genuine. They went with us to the electrostatic suiting room and then to a waiting transporter that took us directly to our dining hall.

Suddenly I felt quite hungry and also very thirsty. So before I had anything to eat I drank two large glasses of Wazu in quick succession. Somehow although I felt the hunger pangs I was not in the least bit fatigued. Perhaps this would make itself felt at the end of the next operational period.

Again I ate sparingly so that I did not feel too full. But I did drink another glass of Wazu. I would make sure I used the facilities prior to going out on the zero-g craft again.

After the meal was over I decided that a twenty minute walk along the ships outer perimeter corridor would let me stretch my leg and body muscles and Tania came with me. But Rachel and Margaret returned to their cabin for a rest. I think that they'd been rather fatigued by all the inactivity aboard the zero-g craft. Boredom can be quite tiring in itself.

During our walk Tania and I stopped at the large viewing panels and chatted to some of the other passengers. After some time we called for one of the internal transporters which took us to our posh cabin. I still didn't feel tired so Tania and I just sat and chatted. We discussed about the next operational shift aboard the zero-g craft and I thought what better way to pass the time than for Zanos to put us into an induced sleep for the major part of the five hours. Tania agreed with this immediately and I conveyed the proposal to Captain Rojazonto. He liked the idea of it and would recommend it to any of the redundant crew.

Two hours on board 9632-Orange had now elapsed and Zanos announced that boarding of zero-g craft OG-9632-1 should commence forthwith.

Once again Tania and I were seated on our own at the front and in the same seats and this time I noticed that there were barely about twenty Oannes aboard. Sparzanzo conveyed that it was only the scientific personnel who were aboard. The previous lot had decided to remain aboard 9632-Orange in its normal gravity environment. The five hours and forty minutes outside at near zero gravity conditions had been a bit too much for them.

When the lights in the shuttle bay dimmed and the zero-g craft exited into open space I always felt the exhilaration of entering this vast cavern of blackness that glittered with the myriad pinpoints of light that made up our galaxy. I think there must be a bit of spaceman in my makeup which I might have passed on to Simon. I was thinking about him and Mazpazam when Zanos announced that the zero-g craft was once again in position. So I gazed at Nazmos and willed for my telekinetic action to be initiated exactly as on the previous occasion. Soon the reports came in as before and after about an hour I was pleased with the same conditions prevailing again on Nazmos. My telekinetic push that was slowing Nazmos would continue without any further attention on my part so I conveyed to Sparzanzo that I now intended to sleep for the next three and a half hours. Obviously Captain Rojazonto had informed him of my intentions and so he wished me a peaceful rest. I thanked him and then requested Zanos-on-board to induce a sleep in Tania and me and to wake us half an hour before the end of the shift.

I leaned back in the seat and settled my head and shoulders to a comfortable position. The last thing I remember before drifting into sleep was of Tania placing her hand in mine.

And that is exactly where it was when we awoke later with just half an hour of the five hour shift remaining. I felt refreshed and this time I did not feel any thirst sensation. Though thinking about it brought on feelings of mild hunger. I could do with a nibble as of now. I'm talking about the seven hours between meals and not large ones at that.

Zanos pre-warned me when there was five minutes to go and then again in the last minute. When this had elapsed I again willed for all my telekinetic action to cease and conveyed this to our craft commander Sparzanzo. He then put the craft on a course back to 9632-Orange where we arrived twenty minutes later. Rachel and Margaret were there in the shuttle bay to greet our return as also were our friends Muznant and Brazjaf. We were again congratulated on the success of the second phase of the mission and were informed that Nazmos was now orbiting at 45,320 mph exactly as planned.

Again we made a quick trip to the electrostatic suiting room before we were transported to the dining hall where a meal was being served. I first had a large glass of Wazu before tucking into a large helping of my specially sweetened Yaztraka. I think it was a well known fact on Nazmos that it was my favourite dish.

Since Tania and I had had a good sleep on the zero-g craft we didn't feel like another just yet. But many of the Oannes scientists and crew needed to get some rest so the captain extended the rest period to three hours. I agreed whole heartedly with the decision and knew that it would not make any difference to the outcome of our mission. Fine orbital adjustments can always be made if necessary.

So at the end of three hours we were once again out in open space on the zero-g craft OG-9632-1 getting into position ahead of Nazmos for the third session of orbital slowdown. I simply repeated what I had done on the previous occasions and again Tania and I were induced into a comforting sleep after about forty minutes into the operation. As before we were awakened half an hour before the end of the five hour period and I ceased my telekinetic action on the dot.

Zanos confirmed that Nazmos was now orbiting at the reduced velocity of 44,882 mph which was just a couple of miles per hour greater than planned. I should be able to correct for this at the end of the fifth and final operational shift.

The next shift went exactly as before and then as we approached the end of the fifth and final shift I requested Zanos to inform me when Nazmos was approaching the planned orbital velocity of 44,000 mph. This occurred at a full minute and a half over the five hour period and at that point I instantly ceased my telekinetic effort. For me it was a tremendous relief that all had gone so well and without large-scale disruption to the planet or its natural processes. The relief was followed by immense satisfaction on my part and as the zero-g craft made its way back to the shuttle bay of 9632-Orange for the last time messages of congratulations began to flood in. In my heart I relayed these to Gozmanot and Ritozanan wherever they might be. Somehow I felt certain they were out there and not only aware of all that had gone on but that they might be smiling as well. Zarama was still out there but for now I refused to think about it.

Nazmos was in an orbit for lasting prosperity and would continue comfortably for the next trillion years or so. Sadly our Earth would become uninhabitable after about a billion years. For then old Sol would have enlarged considerably and its heat increased some 10% causing Earth to become a barren waterless planet. Earthlings would need to migrate to Nazmos or to other as yet undiscovered worlds. Unless of course? Who knows!!

My thoughts were broken by the zero-g craft settling down upon the deck of the 9632-Orange spaceship's shuttle bay. As we disembarked we were greeted by Rachel, Margaret, Muznant and Brazjaf. We went first to the electrostatic suiting room and then were transported to the dining hall as before. It was then that I think the efforts of the last forty hours began to catch up on me; for I suddenly felt quite drained of energy. At the meal I drank two glasses of Wazu straightaway and afterwards a third. I think I ate like a horse so that the strings from my belly began to pull my eyelids closed. Tania noticed the symptoms and conveyed to the others that I needed to get to my cabin and my bed. A transporter took us post haste to our cabin and I think I must have walked like a paralytic with my two girls either side of me. I can't remember much about it. Rachel said something about coming in to help but Tania said that she could manage me on her own.

We were alone in our cabin when Tania made me undress down to my shorts and got me into the bed. I don't remember much else for I must have gone to sleep the moment my head touched the pillow.

It seemed like only a moment later that I awoke feeling quite refreshed and looked around to an empty room. I queried Zanos and I learned that I had been asleep for a little over ten hours.

'Hello, I'm awake,' I conveyed in a general manner, 'where is everyone?'

'We're in the dining hall just starting our second meal,' came back from Tania. 'You do know that you've been asleep for over ten hours. Get yourself into the shower and I'll be there presently.'

'What time is it?' I asked.

Zanos answered my query giving both Nazmos and equivalent Earth times. It was 2:00pm on Sunday 4th February 2046 Earth time. Nazmos time in Wentazta was about the same daytime period but later in the evening.

While I had been asleep Captain Rojazonto had decided to continue in the space parking loop until I had awoken. Later he joked that he had no idea how long I might remain asleep but he did not wish to disturb that rest which he deemed to be my recovery from my telekinetic exertions. He said that it was no mean feat slowing down the mass of a planet. I smiled my reply to him and thanked him for his consideration. I thought to myself that here was another true friend.

Silverstreak had left Earth orbit on Thursday January 25th 2046 and arrived at the Raznat rendezvous location on Sunday January 28th and we had been ferried to Nazmos on the following morning Monday January 29th. I had attended two governing council sessions on the following Tuesday and Wednesday and after a free day had begun the operation of slowing Nazmos into its new circular orbit about mid-morning on Friday February 2nd. It had taken a mammoth stint lasting nearly forty hours in all and then I'd slept for another ten.

Suddenly I was looking up at the pretty face of my wife smiling down at me. She had left her meal to be by my side. I think I might have been missed and smiled at the thought.

'Come on lover boy,' she conveyed, 'lets have you up and showered and then we can return to the dining hall for your breakfast. But first I've brought you this mug of tea.'

I sat up and she removed the cover off the mug and handed it to me. I gazed at her while I sipped at the tea. It was delicious.

We had begun to communicate in telepathic mode more often now and usually as a private conversation. Tania had improved in the art of it and we could say and suggest things we dared not express verbally. And I liked that very much. Also the images conveyed added so much more meaning to our conversations.

CHAPTER 23

Nazmos Business

2046

It was a week since Ashley and the others had returned to Nazmos and to the home of Jazzatnit and Zazfrapiz. The house that formerly belonged to Ritozanan was being refurbished and prepared for family use in the Earth style but it would be at least a couple of months before completion. Ratizdan and Statizona were being most particular about the decoration process and were preparing it on advice from other Oannes who had lived on Earth in Anztarza. Suitable items of furniture for the lounge and for the bedrooms were being specially made.

Rachel and Margaret had discussed particulars with the two and conveyed images of the interior of their homes on Earth. Since Rachel had loved the covered courtyard in Jazzatnit's house she had requested something similar be set up in the new place. That might take a bit longer to complete but Rachel said she didn't mind if it did.

Since Rachel and Margaret had a keen interest to follow and record climate changes on Nazmos they had requested and been granted the use of a small spacecraft with an Oannes operator for an indefinite period but on a request basis.

Margaret had drawn up charts to record the weather patterns not only around Wentazta but also in areas further north and south of it. The Oannes scientists were themselves involved in a more detailed study and intensive monitoring that would be the official analysis for onward transmission to the governing council. This included sea surface levels and temperatures and any changes in the pattern of currents within its depths. The atmosphere would also be monitored for moisture content and weather patterns using principles similar to those used on Earth. The Oannes were already familiar with Earth's weather patterns and it was their intention to detect any similarities forming on Nazmos. Nothing had been heard from the Rimzi people so it was assumed that all was well with them in their sea domain. Ashley's curiosity regarding their isolationism had been fired up by Mazpazam's interest and he believed that one day all would be revealed. Instinctively he knew that day was not too distant.

Ashley attended two governing council sessions and it was after the second that he was approached by Korizazit who appeared to possess information of interest.

'I believe that you will be returning to Earth for some duration,' he conveyed privately. 'It could be for a year if not two or even more.'

Ashley gave out a puzzled expression as if not quite believing what had just been conveyed. Seeing this Korizazit revealed that it was something that he just knew to be a fact. Again it was as a private communication between him and Ashley.

Ashley understood now. The inner voice did not always manifest itself in a very open or clear manner. Sometimes factual information was simply implanted in your mind; this had been the case for Ashley at his first meeting with the governing council and especially with Ritozanan. The information about Gozmanot had come to him out of nowhere. It was as if he had suddenly known all about her visions of so long ago.

'I must now convey this information to the governing council at its session tomorrow. I have requested it and the council have accepted that I have important information through my inner voice gift. You must attend as important factors will be revealed about your future.'

'Thank you,' conveyed Ashley, 'Tania and I will both be there.'

After Korizazit had walked away Ashley conveyed it all to Tania again in private mode. At first she appeared puzzled but her intuition brought a feeling of joy into her heart. Ashley put his finger to his lips indicating for her to keep silent. Later when they were on the transporter she could wait no longer.

'O Ashley,' she whispered, 'does this mean we are going home soon.'

'It seems like it but we shall know more tomorrow. I wonder what the overall plan will be and what Jazzatnit will make of it.'

When they were back in Jazzatnit's house and told her what Korizazit had conveyed she seemed rather subdued.

'I feel there is more to Korizazit's knowledge than he has conveyed,' she said. 'And perhaps all will be revealed at tomorrow's council session.'

They walked around the courtyard in deep discussion about Korizazit and after about an hour Rachel and Margaret made an appearance having just returned from Ritozanan's house. Tania told them what Korizazit had conveyed to Ashley and immediately Rachel said that she thought she knew what might be behind the revelation. She said that the trip back to Earth would be the velocity test for Silverstreak for a start. Then Silverstreak would need to return to Raznat rendezvous to be fitted out for the long voyage to Zarama which might take a year or longer. So what better place could Ashley be than at home in Dudley?'

Rachel smiled before she added.

'Nazmos has just entered its new permanent orbit around Raznat and everything is tentative as to how things pan out. I know that it has all been very carefully thought out but the Oannes are a cautious people. They want dad close enough where he can be easily got to if needed. And Earth is close enough. And I think that they feel kindly towards mum and dad to grant them a longish holiday before the really serious matter has to be tackled; that of sorting out Zarama.'

Tania smiled at her daughter and gave her a hug.

'Thank you for that darling,' she said, 'it has put ideas in my head but I shall wait and see what the council tells us tomorrow.'

Ashley thought about Korizazit and knew that he could keep nothing from the council as a governing body. He must convey everything that had come into his mind as a factual event and as a council member Ashley would hear it all. He was concerned about Tania and that she might draw an erroneous conclusion about any implied uncertainty surrounding his coming confrontation with Zarama. In his heart he knew that failure was not an option and that he must do with his mind force if necessary what had been forbidden him; that of exceeding push level sixteen while in pink mode. If that was the only way to push Zarama from its destructive path then so be it.

Ashley had no idea how that might affect his being and if it would cost him dear. His only sadness would be that Tania would be left on her own. It was the sadness that she must endure that was the root of his own regret and he wished that it did not have to come to that.

'Why so glum darling,' said Tania, 'it can't be as bad as that.'

Ashley jerked back to reality and was glad that he had kept his mind closed. The uncertainty in his mind would be interpreted by her as a disaster waiting to happen.

'O just curious about the total content of Korizazit's information. But I think Rachel may have guessed right that they don't want me setting off on a journey just yet from where I cannot be reached. I was also thinking about getting a sleep-tank type of thing built in one of our spare rooms in Dudley,' said Ashley.

'Silly,' said Tania, 'you must have read my mind as I was thinking the very same thing moment ago. It could be a little one about eight feet square in the conservatory like so,' as she conveyed the design she'd thought up in her head.

The image was of a glass cube six feet tall but set to half its depth in the floor.

'Looks good to me,' said Ashley.

'And what are my parents talking about,' asked Rachel, 'looks like you are planning something?'

When they told her she seemed a bit surprised until Ashley explained that he found the sleep-tanks on board the spaceships and in the apartment accommodation in Anztarza very relaxing especially after the long days of telekinetic effort.

'Actually now that you mention it I think it an excellent idea,' said Rachel, 'perhaps it will start a trend on Earth. I can see me in the circular one in Ritozanan's house with its pictorial view panels around it.'

Ashley just smiled at his daughter's sudden exuberance.

'It won't be a Jacuzzi or swim pool,' he said, 'just somewhere to wallow in. I may need to wear a float collar in case I doze off.'

'You do that dad,' said Rachel. 'Margaret and I will probably do the same in Ritozanan's one when we do eventually move in. The float collar seems a wise idea for we don't want any one getting drowned do we?'

The conversation moved on and again the Nazmos weather or lack of it remained a prominent topic – on and off of course.

Every evening just before Raznat-set Rachel and Margaret went up onto Jazzatnit's terrace to witness the Dark Wind phenomena. It hadn't changed from its previous milder flow and Margaret said it was early days yet. After all Nazmos was about the same distance from Raznat that it had been just before Ashley had slowed it into this new orbit a week ago. A lot would change eventually and Margaret reckoned that the Dark Wind, several years from now might be a thing of the past. Time would tell.

'You are right you know,' said Ashley somehow knowing how it would be.

The moisture in the atmosphere would gradually increase and extensive cloud formations would develop. Weather not too dissimilar to Earth's would eventually begin to be experienced causing Raznat to be often hidden from view at its setting times. The Dark Wind would simply not be initiated though other weather winds would take its place; but not necessarily at the same Raznat setting time. These winds could be quite severe and prolonged. There were other factors also involved and Ashley conveyed all of these to Rachel and Margaret.

'Yes of course,' said Margaret, 'that is so logical and obvious. How long do you think all this might take to develop?'

'Look at it this way,' said Ashley. 'If I gave you a large tin bathtub full of cold water and you placed it on a cradle about two feet above a single lighted candle how long would it take for the water to become hot enough to bathe in?'

'Probably never,' said Margaret.

'Exactly right,' replied Ashley. 'So the answer to your question is years, decades or even centuries. The weather is a very slow coach and atmospheric rebuilding for weather like on Earth could take anywhere from a few hundred to a thousand years if not more. You might have a long wait.'

Margaret looked crestfallen.

'I shan't be around that long,' she said.

'Oh, but I think you just might see the odd anomaly now and then,' said Ashley. 'I do hope we see a few changes at least before age gets the better of us.'

'Would you like to return to Earth again then,' asked Tania.

'Yes, I think I should like to. But then I should miss Nazmos and wonder what was happening here,' said Margaret.

'Plenty of time to decide,' said Rachel, 'but whatever you decide I shall come along too.'

Margaret looked at Rachel and smiled.

'You are a true friend Rachel,' she said reaching out and touching Rachel on her shoulder, 'and I thank you for it.'

They exchanged knowing looks with pleasant smiles on their faces.

Tania saw and approved. Rachel had always been so independent in herself but now she seemed to have found a good friend and companion in Margaret.

The day passed and after the evening meal and another stint up on the terrace witnessing the remnants of the enfeebled Dark Wind they all retired to their rooms. Ashley and Tania lazed for a while in their sleep-tank before drowsiness overcame them and they too went to bed.

'It would be nice to be able to breathe underwater like the Oannes,' said Tania aiming the remark at a very sleepy Ashley, 'then I could sleep in a weightless condition which I expect must be most relaxing.'

'Hmmmm,' responded Ashley as he drifted into a deep sleep. His main thought had been about Korizazit and the information that had been given to him.

In the morning Ashley and Tania had dressed in their favourite posh outfits including over garment to be as presentable as possible for the afternoon session with the governing council. Muznant and Brazjaf came later to the house as was their custom to escort the two new council members to the meeting and also to prompt them on any procedures to follow.

The journey by transporter to the Domed Hall was in calm weather conditions though Tania often peered up at the sky for any visible change. There was none.

The council chamber was quite full when Ashley and Tania took their seats and shortly after the session was commenced with Dultarzent in the Chair. The agenda was conveyed to all and it was a short one with Korizazit as the third and last item on the listing. It was after nearly an hour into the proceedings that Korizazit was called upon to convey his information in full. He did not stand while he did this.

He began slowly and conveyed that he did not know how he came upon this information but that in his mind it was a realisation of a positive fact. The council members understood that he had the gift of inner voice and that it came in subtle guises. As such they did not doubt what Korizazit conveyed.

'I do not understand the workings of Ashley's inner voice but I do know that I was endowed by chance with the same gift,' he conveyed. 'However this time it was different for I did not hear a voice in my mind speaking of certain things. Yet when I awoke two mornings ago my mind was filled with this knowledge which I deemed as factual.'

He paused as if debating what to convey next.

'I know that Ashley is required to spend the next two years or more near his parents on Earth. I do not know the reason for this but my conviction on the matter is clear.'

He made another brief pause to separate this from the next item of information.

'The next matter is that Silverstreak requires a more reliable and greater food growing capability to cover an indefinite period in space. Again I don't understand this need but I accept that the requirement must be met.'

Again Korizazit paused but only for a few seconds. He then smiled at those near him before continuing.

'And lastly I can confirm that Nazmos is on course to fulfil all of Gozmanot's visions. And that is the full extent of the information I am able to submit to this council. I thank you for your attention.'

Dultarzent as the senior most council member at the ripe old age of 350 years thanked Korizazit for his revelation and then conveyed that he had something to communicate. Immediately a telepathic silence descended within the room.

'Firstly I must enquire of Ashley if he has any matter he wishes to communicate.'

Ashley was taken by surprise but rallied quickly.

'I thank Korizazit for his revelation,' Ashley said aloud, 'but I have nothing to add or to comment upon. My own inner voice remains silent and I am pleased that Korizazit has received a communication from that quarter. The information he imparts is not controversial and in fact makes good sense. I was under the impression that all starships had a limitless food growing capability for supply. If this is not the case then it would be wise to make it so. I shall be pleased to be back on Earth and near my family if that is the wish of the council. I am also pleased that Korizazit has confirmed that Gozmanot's visions for Nazmos are on course to be realised in time.'

'Then let us discuss the issue of Korizazit's information and decide upon a course of action,' conveyed Dultarzent. 'Let us be split into small mental groups and then convey our conclusions to the session as a whole.'

Ashley and Tania looked at each other and smiled their pleasure that they might be going home soon. Tania reached over and taking Ashley's hand in hers squeezed it tightly. It reflected how they both felt.

Ashley opened his mind and picked up a hive of buzzing telepathic communications. Apparently communication was also taking place between council members and their representatives seated behind them. Some representatives left the room and Ashley assumed that they had been sent on an errand of sorts; perhaps to check or gather information.

Finally, after about twenty minutes a telepathic silence once again descended during which single communications were made in turn. And it was after another few minutes that Dultarzent finally stood to command the attention of all. He then sat down and conveyed the results of the discussions.

'This session has reached a unanimous conclusion and I thank the members for all their suggestions,' he conveyed. 'When it is convenient Silverstreak will convey Ashley and Tania back to Earth, and enroute it is suggested that Silverstreak be put through its maximum speed trial if Ashley is agreeable.'

Dultarzent paused and Ashley quickly conveyed to all members that he was agreeable and would comply as suggested.

'Thank you Ashley,' conveyed Dultarzent, 'Captain Wastanomi will be informed of our decision. And if it is not too soon you may leave for Earth whenever it is convenient for you and for the captain. Perhaps you would like to spend some time with your son aboard Silverstreak before then.'

'Thank you that is most considerate,' said Ashley. 'And may Silverstreak be allowed to remain at Earth rendezvous for a suitable period so that Simon can meet his grandparents again. My father remains in poor health and it would be nice for him to see his grandson for a while again.'

'It is usual for starships to stay at Earth rendezvous for a period of three months before initiating the return journey,' conveyed Dultarzent, 'and there is no reason to alter the routine.'

Ashley once again conveyed his gratitude to the council and then enquired about the time scale for the enhancement to Silverstreak's food growing capability.

Dultarzent looked around at the other council members and again it became obvious that an intense telepathic discussion was taking place. Such matters usually came to a conclusion within minutes as the communication also involved the representatives for the provision of relevant facts. And so it did.

'The exact nature of the food growing enhancement has yet to be determined,' conveyed Dultarzent, 'but Korizazit's information may be implying that a complete overhaul of the food growing tank system is required for its longer term efficient capability. 4110-Silver was one of the very early starships and it is good that Korizazit has brought this matter to our attention. A broad estimate is that it could require between three to five years for this to be accomplished. Time is not a factor here and it is a good point to consider for our other starships when they are also taken out of commission to be modified to 100 FTL capabilities. You will be informed of the progress while you are on Earth.'

'Thank you honourable council member,' said Ashley aloud, 'it is with joy in my heart that I know I shall spend time with my family on Earth. Perhaps this is providence in that it gives time for the enhancement of my telekinetic ability for when I tackle Zarama. I will be ready when Silverstreak calls for me.'

'Captain Wastanomi will be informed of our decision and will contact you accordingly,' conveyed Dultarzent. Then he announced that the council session was now concluded.

Ashley realised that Tania's hand was still in his but now she was holding it even tighter and when he looked across at her he couldn't help but notice the cherubic smile on her face. He was happy too though much more for her than for himself.

When they got back to Jazzatnit's house Rachel and Margaret were there eagerly awaiting their news. And when they heard the full extent of the council's decision they were quite elated.

'So when do you plan to leave dad?' asked Rachel.

'By that I assume Margaret and you are staying here,' said Ashley.

'Yep, that's right. There's a lot of stuff we want to witness and you could be gone for years. We don't want to miss what happens here.'

'Then look after yourselves and keep in contact with us via Anztarza. When Silverstreak eventually comes for me I imagine it would make sense to go straight out to where Zarama is if the council has so decreed. I expect we won't see you then till after,' said Ashley.

'I imagine we shall see quite a bit of Simon when the food growing refurbishment is underway,' said Rachel.

'I shall pass the message on to him,' said Ashley.

'So then when are you planning to leave for home?' asked Rachel again.

'Well there's nothing for us really to do here now,' said Ashley, 'so it might as well be sooner than later. The council will be informing Captain Wastanomi about the trip being used as a speed trial as well so I expect we shall be hearing from him soon.'

In fact it was a couple of days later that they were surprised and pleased to get the message telling them that Simon and Mazpazam were on their way to Nazmos. The journey to Earth was to be arranged sometime after that. The message was rather terse and divulged nothing more. Ashley thought it typical of Captain Wastanomi.

And it was on the following morning that Simon and Mazpazam entered Jazzatnit's house as Ashley and the others were finishing with breakfast. Ashley was on his final mug of tea when Simon entered the room followed closely by a smiling Mazpazam. They looked a very happy couple.

'Hi everybody,' said Simon cheerily, 'I hope there's some breakfast left for us.'

'Do come and sit with us and I will get you something,' said Jazzatnit.

'I'm only joking,' said Simon laughing, 'Mazpazam and I have already eaten with Captain Rojazonto on the journey here. But thank you.'

Tania and Ashley got up and gave Simon and Mazpazam a big hug each. Then Rachel and Margaret followed suit.

'So bro,' said Rachel, 'how are you both. How is my big brother adjusting to married life?'

'We are just fine,' smiled Simon. 'Mazpazam and I are just great together. Oh yes, Captain Wastanomi sends his best wishes dad. He is pleased that the period of inactivity is to end and that the speed trial is imminent. He reckons that Silverstreak should be ready for the trip to Earth in ten days. All crew who are on leave on Nazmos are to be informed to return for duty within seven days. And that includes Mazpazam and me.'

'Can you be allowed to stay here in my house,' asked Jazzatnit for she knew of the strict rules that applied to starship crew members about accommodation. They were not normally allowed to use other than the prescribed accommodation already allocated to them.

'We would love to stay here with you,' said Simon apologetically, 'but a Nazmos accommodation has already been set up for us.'

Jazzatnit smiled her understanding for she knew what it was like for newly bonded couples. And the legal partnership of Simon and Mazpazam had been confirmed by the Nazmos governing council and recognised in a broadcast.

'But we will spend all our day periods here with you' said Mazpazam.

She looked at Simon with eyes that seemed to plead at which Simon threw his head back and laughed in his typical fashion.

'Mazpazam is shy to ask in case you disapprove,' he said, 'but she has a desire to visit the site on the island of Vaz where dad regressed to meet with Gozmanot. There are some things that we have talked about and she wants to see this for herself; including to sit upon that cairn of stones at the site.'

'What a wonderful idea,' said Rachel. 'That is something that Margaret and I have talked about for a possible visit. Do you mind if we came with you?'

'Thank you Rachel,' said Mazpazam, 'it would be nice to have company and especially you beside me. Perhaps Uncle Ashley wouldn't mind being our guide on the day.'

'It would be my pleasure,' said Ashley smiling, 'and perhaps we could tour the rest of the island while we are there.'

'That would be one day only,' said Simon, 'how are we to fill the rest of the week.'

'Well Margaret and I had planned an extensive aerial tour of Nazmos aboard the private craft allocated to us,' said Rachel, 'you could accompany us on that. We want to see things on the land areas before any major changes occur. I think that was planned for tomorrow or is it the day after,'

'Definitely tomorrow,' said Margaret, 'but not till noon. There's plenty of room aboard for us all. We intend making similar trips at intervals of five or six weeks depending on how things progress. But I expect it will be years before we even notice any changes if at all.'

'Great,' said Simon. 'And how about showing us around the house allocated to you by the governing council. It was once lived in by one of the senior council members.'

'Yes, she was a great lady was Ritozanan,' said Ashley conveying all his images of her to Simon and Mazpazam. 'It was she who ultimately persuaded the council to accede to the fulfilment of Gozmanot's dream for Nazmos. Without her I do believe the council might have rejected my proposals for the orbital change. We owe much to her.'

'Sorry dad,' said Simon in a quiet voice, 'I meant no disrespect. I shall revere her in my memory now I know how much she meant to you. Nazmos owes her everything.'

Tania conveyed a private message to her son. She explained about the love that the old lady had for Ashley and of his sadness that came with her death. Simon acknowledged the information and conveyed it to Mazpazam. But Mazpazam already knew of this from Muznant who had confided to her that Ashley often became the object of adoration by many of those he met – females of course. Mazpazam recognised this and she too had experienced a bit of what those ladies had felt. But what was surprising to her was that Ashley was quite oblivious to the fact of it.

'We could show you around the house on our return from the Vaz visit the day after tomorrow,' said Rachel casting a quick glance towards Margaret who nodded her head in agreement.

'That would be excellent,' said Simon, 'providing it does not get too late.'

Then Tania came up with one of her quick-fire ideas.

'On one of the days why don't we ladies have a day out visiting the shops in the Wentazta bazaars? We had a quick look around some years back and it would be nice to browse around again this time at our leisure.'

'I'd like that very much,' said Mazpazam, 'but couldn't we persuade the men to come along too if only for us to see how bored they get.'

'I like window shopping as much as any of you,' said Simon, 'as long as you don't expect me to give an opinion for you. I hate it if someone can't make up their mind about what they prefer.'

'Don't worry son,' said Ashley, 'live and learn. If you're asked which is better say the first thing that comes to mind as a choice? One item always looks better than another but don't get involved beyond that; especially if asked for a reason.'

Simon smiled his understanding. Sadly few men on Earth did.

Jazzatnit had been listening to all of this and she smiled to herself.

'Humans are not too unlike us,' she thought and that it was a shame that any program for integration with the Oannes people was such a long way off in time.

Mazpazam was quite relaxed towards Simon's family and Tania's affection for her grew tremendously. However Rachel seemed to be drawn especially towards her brother's wife and they were often in intense conversation. Mazpazam wanted to know as much as possible about her husband and Rachel was just the person to provide it. Growing up was an important part of life and the character of the child is reflected in the man. And Mazpazam liked what she heard about Simon as a boy.

The day passed in pleasant conversation and it was after they had witnessed another feeble event that was the Dark Wind that Simon and Mazpazam left Jazzatnit's house saying they would return the next day for the Nazmos aerial tour.

In the morning Simon and Mazpazam came in a bit later than previously and in fact arrived just in time for them all to walk out together to the transporter for the trip to the space park. They were taken to one side of it where a smaller craft was stationed. This was 16034-Green Private Class and awaiting beside it was a very slim built Oannes male who came forward and introduced himself as their craft pilot for the day. His name was Taturtiz and he was part of the pool of small craft operators for allocation to specific Nazmos aerial operations. He was aged 110 years and had served on several spaceships over a period of two decades. Commanding a small craft such as this one was very similar to operating the shuttles that were used on the larger spaceships; and Taturtiz had done his fair share of shuttling. He had a pleasant manner and showed his pleasure in meeting Ashley and family. For him this was a great honour too. Ashley felt his person being visually scrutinised and he offered an open mind to Taturtiz who subsequently showed his embarrassment and apologised for his rude behaviour.

Both Ashley and Simon laughed at this and said he was forgiven on the condition that he told them all about himself and of his career ambitions. Taturtiz was doubly smitten in his admiration and thought of what he could tell his parents about the events of that day.

And when Ashley introduced him to Rachel and Margaret and requested that Taturtiz look after their interests especially after he returned to Earth he was over the moon with delight.

'I shall request specifically to be their pilot chauffeur for all their Nazmos flights whenever that might be,' he conveyed.

'Well tomorrow is another trip to Vaz,' said Ashley. 'Will it be the same craft and you as its commander?'

'The craft will always be the same,' Taturtiz conveyed smiling at his elevation to commander. '16034-Green Private Class has been allocated to Margaret and Rachel on the explicit orders of the governing council. The operator for it is drawn from those available at the pool but I shall ensure that I am the one allocated to you. After that it depends upon where I am sent.'

'Good,' said Ashley, 'then we shall get to know each other well.'

Taturtiz then led them onto the craft and after securing the entrance door got airborne almost immediately.

The craft was about twice the size of the late Hazazamunt's private craft 17426-Black which had disappeared with her only to collide with her lover's starship a hundred years later. 16034-Green could seat a dozen passengers and perhaps another few at a squeeze. There were large view panels in a semi-circle at the front half of the craft which curved down low to allow good views of the ground passing below.

Simon and Mazpazam were very interested in Taturtiz's career history and queried why he had not applied for a placement at the Space Academy.

'I had no one to sponsor me,' he replied, 'but it was also not my wish as I preferred to be Nazmos based. My parents are old and I am their only child.'

Simon said he understood as it would have taken him away from friends and family.

'I would however like to visit Anztarza having heard and seen so much about it,' he conveyed to continue the conversation.

'Then you should make your desire known,' said Mazpazam, 'and perhaps one day you will. Earth is beautiful and hopefully Nazmos will also become the same –though perhaps not in our lifetime. Once in Anztarza you must visit the northern forests to see what lies in store for Nazmos.'

Mazpazam conveyed her memory images of when she was there.

Taturtiz's eyes sparkled at the thought but also sadness as he definitely did not fancy the trip into outer space.

Margaret then excused herself and asked if Taturtiz could generate the tour of Nazmos over the main land areas. She requested that they venture towards the northern polar region before doing the same for the south staying in the day zone all the while.

Taturtiz suggested flying at 10,000 feet if that was alright and he would slow down whenever requested. Margaret agreed and the tour began in earnest. She also suggested varying the height as well as the speed to cover the distances more conveniently.

Ashley had seen all this before and realised that nothing had changed. It was a very arid grey coloured landscape but some views also had their own peculiar beauty.

Taturtiz repeatedly slowed the craft and brought it down to a lower altitude when any of his passengers drew his attention to some feature below like a town or small grouped habitation. Then he would return to altitude and speed up again. The extreme north region was completely arid with nothing of interest. But Margaret said she had noted its appearance for future reference and comparison.

Taturtiz then circled around over a different land area so as to begin the journey southwards. The southern region seemed no different to the north but it had to be seen by Rachel and Margaret simply for the record and future comparison.

It was five hours from the start of the trip when they landed back at the space park. They all thanked Taturtiz for an excellent tour and hoped to see him again the next day for the trip to Vaz. Before disembarking Ashley shook hands with Taturtiz and exchanged a brief though formal Sewa – which really pleased him.

Back at the house Jazzatnit had refreshments waiting including tea and biscuits. After a walk around the courtyard Margaret announced that the trip today had been a great success as she now had a benchmark from which to gauge any changes that might show up in time. And she hoped to restrict her attention to a few selected areas in particular which she had chosen during the tour. She added that she would discuss these with Rachel later.

Simon and Mazpazam did not stay long saying that they had promised to meet up with some other crew members for a meal in a restaurant in the town. They would however return in the morning for the Vaz trip. Mazpazam was specially looking forward to it.

Next morning the routine was repeated and the private class craft 16034-Green operated by the pleasant faced Taturtiz was making its way across the Peruga Sea and cruising towards the island of Vaz at an altitude of sixty miles.

There were several large islands dotted around at fair intervals. One of these was particularly larger than any of the others and was pointed out as the island of Ventrazta. Ashley remembered it from the last time he had been over it when Muznant had informed him that Nuztazm a cousin of Captain Bulzezatna came originally from a town near its centre. Ashley conveyed this to the others.

Once across the island they continued over the sea for quite some distance until another island appeared below them. This island was Vaz and was about half the size of Ventrazta and was rather oddly shaped. It was oval in shape but with a large bite taken out at one side. It had the form of a child's mitten with the fat thumb jutting outwards. It was about eighty miles at its widest stretch and maybe forty miles across at its central part. The peninsular was like a fat thumb ten miles at its base which extended out to about twenty miles. It narrowed near its end. There were no steep cliffs anywhere on this peninsular section and it had pleasant shallow beaches all along it. The island itself was a mixture of soil and rock and the central part rose to several hundred feet above the sea.

All knew about the events of Ashley's visit here in 561-Silverlake with Nerbtazwi and Ritozanan some thirty years ago. He had then mentally regressed and come face to face with Gozmanot. What a momentous occasion that had been not only for him but also for all of Nazmos with whom he had shared the entire experience immediately afterwards.

Taturtiz knew well the details of that trip and he brought our craft down towards the top of the peninsular of land and settled down more or less exactly on the spot that 561-Silverlake had occupied.

All disembarked and stood looking at the cairn of flat rocks that was about two hundred feet away.

'Uncle Ashley,' said Mazpazam in a very quiet voice, 'please could you talk us through what happened on your previous visit here.'

'Gladly,' said Ashley and went on to describe how Korizazit while walking along had somehow got a bit of grit inside his footwear. So looking for a place to sit he had settled down upon this same cairn of rocks but became dizzy in his head soon afterwards. Noticing this Ashley had gone to help him and felt the same dizziness. Together they walked back towards Silverlake and the feeling disappeared with distance from the cairn.

'An analysis was conducted from the air by the brothers Maztatont and Zutadintz but nothing unusual was picked up,' said Ashley.

Ashley then led the way to the cairn with Tania, Mazpazam and the others following and this time all seemed quite normal. Mazpazam went and sat upon the cairn of flat rocks and closed her eyes trying to visualise the previous events.

'I feel nothing,' she said, 'but I'm glad to be here.'

Ashley then pointed to the other side of the cairn and the shallow dip in the ground.

'I believe that is where Gozmanot lived in her house,' he said.

Ashley then conveyed how he and the others with him had walked into this dip and he had gone into pink mode hoping to regress to Gozmanot's time.

It had all happened like in a dream. He had then suddenly become a spectator viewing the events of the past. He felt himself suspended over the island and could see a small village of some forty or fifty block type houses. The name of the village that was sent into his mind was Rasfarrant. He was somehow attracted towards one of the houses near the seaward edge of the village. His floating consciousness was drawn into this house and he came face to face with Gozmanot in her sleep tank. She recognised his presence and greeted him with open arms. Afterwards Ashley had felt emotionally drained by the experience and had wept for a long gone Gozmanot.

'The last thing she said to me was and I quote, *'at last I am satisfied and can go in peace,'* said Ashley aloud to the others.

Mazpazam looked at Ashley and smiling said, 'Thank you.'

'Gozmanot was one very gifted lady,' said Ashley to no one in particular.

Mazpazam was in deep thought and Simon guessed that her curiosity for Vaz had not been completely satisfied. He conveyed a querying thought.

'What is it that puzzles you my dear,' conveyed Simon in open mode for all to receive.

'It is Gozmanot,' said Mazpazam. 'How was it possible for her to reach across time and guide Uncle Ashley towards her house and into her sleep tank? And then how could she have recognised someone who was from Earth and not an Oannes at all. And then to convey all her vision images into his mind she had to literally span 36,520 years to give us information in our time. I find it hard to believe let alone comprehend. And yet it is all fact.'

Ashley went over to Mazpazam and put his hand on her shoulder.

'It is a difficult concept to grasp for an Oannes person,' he said and then conveyed to her his gift of regression and of his first experience of it on his eighteenth birthday at the Navigation pub after the darts match. How he had been guided by his inner voice to view the past antics of the pub crooks Quigley Thorn and Johnny Price. From then he had progressed to helping solve crime cases in the Birmingham law courts by conveying images of what really happened to the judge and jury. And he had helped solve the mystery for Captain Zakatanz of his missing love Hazazamunt and confirming that it was her small spacecraft 17426-Black that had collided with his starship 8110-Gold a hundred years later.

But for Gozmanot to recognise and welcome him when she saw him was a bit different. Perhaps Ashley was a part of her visions. Everything she had seen had yet to come to pass. Nazmos would not become green for another millennium at least – and Zarama had yet to be overcome. But Gozmanot had seen it all as if it had occurred in her time.

Ashley then quoted something that a famous sage had described about what went on in the universe. He had said that not only was it more complex and stranger than we imagined but it was more complex and stranger than we *could* imagine.

'Humans are superstitious,' he said, 'and anything unusual is ascribed to the power of an invisible Super-Being. To this Being is attributed the creation of everything around us. This is the basis of all religions on Earth. There is no tangible proof of this apart from a general and universal acceptance of it. It is the root of religious faith within the human race.'

'Does no one question this?' asked Mazpazam.

'Of course they do,' said Ashley, 'and many discard association with it. But for most it is the foundation that remains as an underlying concept whether discarded or not.'

'And how do you feel personally about it all,' asked Mazpazam.

'I think I must feel differently because of all the gifts I have been given,' said Ashley.

Mazpazam waited for more.

'Different because I know that these gifts were given specially to me for a specific purpose.'

Mazpazam still waited.

'Someone very great gave me these gifts and power and I firmly believe that it is through Divine intervention. Someone who does not want to see Nazmos or Earth destroyed. Just as Gozmanot was given her gift of vision into the future so I have been given my gifts to help fulfil those visions for her. Neither of our gifts could have resulted through a natural evolutionary process so another factor must be put into the equation – that of an invisible, intangible to us Supreme Being whom I call the Great Giver,' concluded Ashley with a smile.

'I have studied all of Earth's religions but I cannot find or see any such connection,' said Mazpazam.

'No, you could not and never will,' said Ashley. 'It is what separates the religious from the non-religious. Seeing the connection in ones mind is called faith, which is what I have in abundance.'

Mazpazam remained silent and in apparent deep thought. Simon looked at his father with a smile and twitched his eyebrows up and down and conveyed a private 'Well done dad.'

Ashley decided not to pursue the topic any further. Mazpazam was a good researcher and would one day draw her own conclusions. She might even find an answer as to why the Rimzi people had kept themselves in the sea and apart from the land based Oannes population.

Ashley intuitively felt that there was a sinister undertone somewhere there and that one day he would be told all. For now however it remained a puzzle.

Rachel interrupted with, 'Come on folks I'd like to see the rest of this island of Vaz from the air. You never know what other secrets lie waiting to be discovered.'

'There are no records of anyone living on Vaz,' said Mazpazam now smiling, 'but the topography of the island should prove interesting.'

All returned to the small craft and Taturtiz then took it up to an altitude of several miles before flying across towards the centre of the island.

When seen from the air Vaz was like any other piece of land on Nazmos. It was grey and desolate across its entire 80 by 40 mile area. Hopefully the image Ashley had seen briefly of a forested landscape was a vision of the future and he conveyed this to Mazpazam and the others.

'I wonder how long that will take to become reality,' asked Margaret. 'Anyway if it doesn't happen in my lifetime then at least I've had a glimpse of it in the future.'

The landscape was smooth with very little erosion and the central area rose in a sort of hump. To Ashley it looked like a turtle's shell with one of its legs extended forward. The extended bit would be the peninsular of land upon which Gozmanot had last resided. There was an area near the centre of the island that had quite a large depression that resembled a shallow bowl about a mile across. Everything was smoothed out at its edges such that at ground level it was hardly noticeable and could have been missed. The bowl shape was a shallow one being hardly fifteen feet lower than the outer edge. A fifteen feet drop in half a mile was a gradient of just half a degree.

Anyway Rachel got Taturtiz to settle the craft at the edge of the dip and all disembarked and walked the distance down to its centre. It was all sand and was gritty to walk on and very similar to where Gozmanot had lived.

Ashley closed his eyes and tried to sense the mood of the place but nothing appeared in his mind. After about a minute he opened his eyes again and smiling at the others shook his head to convey that he'd drawn a blank. But then a thought occurred to him which he conveyed to them all.

'If ever there is a need for research into the island's history I would suggest that you begin with this place,' he said. 'I sense that something of interest exists deep under our feet.'

Back on 16034-Green private class Taturtiz went up to a much higher altitude of close to sixty miles and remained stationary over the island's centre. The day was clear and the view exhilarating and the interesting thing was that Rachel and Margaret began to point to several other smaller dip-like features dotted around the island.

'So the depression at the centre of the island is not the only one down there,' said Rachel. 'I wonder if there is a connection.'

Rachel looked at her dad but he only shrugged his shoulders and shook his head. She then looked towards Simon.

'Sorry sis, I wouldn't know where to begin,' he said. 'I'm a spaceman not an archaeologist.'

'Perhaps we should pass our findings on to the governing council for them to look into,' said Margaret.

'No one has ever been permitted to settle on Vaz. It is a law that has been passed down the ages,' said Mazpazam. 'The reason is obscure and that is all I know. The governing council is unlikely to see any purpose to your thoughts other than a vain curiosity.'

Ashley conveyed that the day was drawing on and that they should return to base. Tania and the others agreed and so Taturtiz turned the craft in the direction of Wentazta and accelerated towards its space park.

The plan had been to tour Rachel and Margaret's newly allocated house after seeing Vaz.

'Could we visit Ritozanan's house another day,' said Tania. 'I think we've all had a long day and have much to think about.'

'Perhaps we could visit on the day after tomorrow,' said Mazpazam. 'Simon and I must leave for our starship duties on the day after that.'

'Excellent,' said Margaret, 'we could spend more time there then,'

And all agreed to the new plan.

They were all soon back in Jazzatnit's house enjoying refreshments prior to the evening meal. They had not eaten since late morning and so were quite hungry. Jazzatnit showed an interest in what they had discovered about Vaz. She could offer nothing about the many shallow dips across its normally smooth contours. And yet Ashley sensed a slight worrying thought within her mind about the matter though she kept it well hidden and blocked from the others.

That night Ashley conveyed privately his thoughts to Tania about Vaz and reckoned they should not upset the status quo of opinion about it. Let sleeping dogs lie and keep their secrets,

In his heart he knew that Mazpazam not only had her questions about the Rimzi but now also about Vaz as well. Nazmos was very much older than Earth by about a factor of ten so its history went back even further. Events may have been lost in its distant history.

When Ashley awoke next morning Tania had already showered and dressed and was ready with his favourite mug of tea which he drank sitting up in bed. She sat on the edge of the bed facing him looking at him as he cupped his hands around the mug. She thought what he must have been like as a little boy. And she liked the comparison that came into her mind especially from having seen him in the old family albums at his mums.

Ashley did the same and reading her mind thought of a particular photo that came into his mind – that of a freckled faced girl in pigtails.

'I hated those pigtails and made sure mum never did my hair like that again,' Tania said. 'I actually had them tugged by a boy. It was his shy way of expressing that he liked me I suppose.'

Then on impulse Tania leaned forward avoiding the mug and kissed Ashley lightly on the lips.

'I love you,' she said huskily and stopped as tears came to her eyes.

Ashley reached over with one hand touching her cheek and nodding his head.

'Me too,' he said simply and then took another sip of his tea.

They smiled at each other until suddenly Tania began to giggle.

'What's so funny?' asked Ashley.

'It's you, you idiot,' she blurted. 'Everyone seems to fall for you so easily,'

'So who's it now?' asked Ashley.

'Why Margaret of course,' said Tania.

'Nonsense,' said Ashley, 'that's not new. She fell for me when I first went to meet her dad at their consultancy offices in London. That's when I got the 'thinking stone' from him.'

'Well then there's been a rekindling of the old love as I see it,' said Tania, 'poor old thing.'

'Oh dear, O dear,' said Ashley feigning distress and putting palm to forehead, 'what shall I do. Will you protect me from these conniving damsels?'

'Ashley Bonner you are such an idiot and I love you for it.'

'Good, I'm glad,' said Ashley handing her his empty mug.

'Right, up you get and into the shower with you,' said Tania standing up. 'I'll see you at the dining table. I think us girls want to make an early start for our shopping spree, so don't be long.'

Later Muznant and Brazjaf arrived and joined them at the breakfast table. Rachel had asked Muznant and Brazjaf to come with them knowing that it was their old haunt and where they had originally met each other. Farzant had come along with her parents and Ashley noticed how much she resembled her mother. She was now in her middle thirties and had the assurance of an adult. She was seated next to Mazpazam and the two seemed to be in continued communication. Farzant had as yet not chosen a career and was querying Mazpazam about life in space aboard spacecraft. There were so many options available to her.

'Why not spend some time on Earth,' suggested Margaret. 'Anztarza is lovely and you could visit the Northern Forests too. It will give you an idea of how Nazmos will look one day.'

Farzant looked across at her parents but they were no help. Both were keen that Farzant find her own path. But Muznant conveyed that it could be a part of her education and life experience if she did go there.

'Then I shall go there one day but not just yet,' said Farzant.

Muznant smiled and conveyed privately to Ashley that Farzant had never made a hasty decision in her life. She would think about Margaret's suggestion and consider all the issues before making her decision of whether or not to visit Anztarza and Earth. And if so when.

Ashley smiled to himself and gave his reply; privately of course. It made Muznant look away in semi-embarrassment. Ashley had simply reminded her of the manner in which she and Brazjaf had first met. She had decided then and there that he was the one for her. In that respect Farzant was quite unlike her mother – or was she?

Muznant then reminded them that there was much to see today and so they had better get started. She refused to look directly at Ashley and Tania tugged his arm mainly from instinct and conveyed for him to behave himself. She had seen Muznant's embarrassment and put it down to something he must have conveyed. And of course she was right.

They all walked to the plaza and boarded the transporter. The operator was a pleasant looking Oannes male and smiled at each of them as they climbed the few steps onto the platform. As soon as all were aboard the transporter lifted up smoothly and rose to a good height. As it increased its forward momentum glass panels rose up all around its perimeter to shield the passengers from the wind effect. From an initial leisurely pace the speed had increased to about 50mph. After twenty minutes they once again slowed and then settled down in a plaza area a few miles from the Domed Hall which was clearly visible in the distance.

Muznant seemed to take charge then and led the way towards some buildings on one side. They entered a street and Ashley recognised it as one he had visited before way back in 2016. He'd had the whole family with him then and both Rachel and Simon were children.

The street was decorated with ornate pictorial representations for each establishment shop. The street itself was about a mile long with other streets branching off on either side.

There were shops displaying all sorts of things and Ashley thought he recognised a few from his last visit. Many had goods that he had seen in Jazzatnit's house and courtyard. There were restaurants too and Ashley felt sure that they'd sample something in one of them later.

There were clothes stores too and he noticed how Rachel and Margaret pointed at specific items on display. Since they intended living on Nazmos long-term Ashley could see their intention to return here often. Earth obviously had had its influence on Oannes fashion or was it the other way around?

Ashley thought back in time and knew that the Oannes must have had a tremendous influence on human consciousness over the ages and Earth civilization must have been given many prompts in its development.

Facial adornment had recently become quite a fashion among the young Oannes females which was definitely an Earth influence. Although they had known of Earth fashions it had all become reality for them with Ashley and his family visiting Nazmos. Ashley wondered if wigs and hairpieces might also become fashionable one day; perhaps not. Those that wandered Earth's northern forests from Anztarza definitely had worn them but for disguise purposes only.

As they walked along they passed many Oannes wandering around looking in the shops too. These gave the group their greetings as they walked by.

They turned into one of the side streets and found this similar to the one they had just left. It too was full of stores showing a good variety. Some seemed strange and Ashley thought these might be specific to the Oannes lifestyle. They walked on for a fair distance before Muznant stopped them.

'This is where Brazjaf and I first met,' she conveyed. 'He was about there with his two friends when I saw him. I too was with my friends when I sensed that I was being stared at by this person. I looked to see who it was and when I saw him I think I liked him from that moment. It must have been love at first sight for both of us and I'm glad of it. That was a very long time ago and we come regularly to this street just to remember.'

Ashley could see Farzant roll her eyes upward in such a human gesture that it endeared her to him even more. She conveyed that she knew the story well and that it had ceased to cause her embarrassment – well not much anyway.

Ashley thought that the Oannes were similar to humans in their emotions and he couldn't help remembering his own first glimpse of Tania in the Navigation pub so very long ago. It was a month after his 18th birthday and he'd just taken part in a darts match. He remembered the evening well.

His mum had called him over and introduced him to Jerry Marsh's wife Milly and their daughter Tania. For a very brief moment Ashley had the weirdest sensation as though he was about to receive a message of some sort. Nothing happened and the moment passed without incident. Something about that thirteen year old had struck a chord in the very core of his being. For Tania however it had been different. She had seen Ashley and for her it was love at first sight. But Ashley never realised any of this till years later.

The group continued to spend time wandering the street shops before someone mentioned resting for a bit. So Muznant took them into one of the restaurants and chose a table by a window. They had a nice view of the street outside and refreshments were soon brought to the table. Muznant had pre-arranged for them to have a meal here but a bit later on. They would return after a bit more of a wander around. But it was nice to sit for a while and drink a refreshing cool glass of Wazu. Rachel helped herself to the squash that had been specially ordered for her. Muznant knew her well.

Leaving here they returned to the plaza and boarded the transporter as it was too far to walk to the next area Muznant wanted them to see. It was only a few minutes before they settled back down in another plaza which Ashley remembered too from his previous visit. It was a cross between Trafalgar Square and the Piazza Novona in Rome. The adornment of the fountains was accurate and gave a feeling of being back on Earth. In fact as they progressed further Ashley recognised the next street as being a good copy of Oxford Street in London.

Ashley knew that there were more streets in this area that were also representative of other famous streets around the big cities of Earth. Of course they just had to walk into some of the shops for a look around and Ashley and Tania reckoned that everything in them had been imported from Earth. Rachel and Margaret were quite intrigued by what they saw and could be seen discussing what they could put into their new home.

After this they walked into another side street that had an India theme to it with jewellery displays in abundance. Another street had a market place atmosphere with open stalls which was something that especially enthralled the ladies in the group. Mazpazam and Simon looked on with amazement written all over their faces.

Brazjaf then conveyed that the time had arrived for the afternoon meal and led the way back to the plaza and the transporter waiting there. They were all quite hungry now and looked forward to the approaching meal and accompanying seated rest. After all they had done some extensive walking. The transporter took them back to the initial area and they were soon seated in the restaurant again where Muznant had arranged their afternoon meal. They sat at the same window table and before long the usual Oannes fare was laid out before them. All ate and drank well and Ashley had a good helping of his favourite Yaztraka sweetened as usual for him. The Milsony was not to Tania's liking though Ashley thought it okay. Tania said that the taste of it lingered on for too long afterwards.

A good hour and a half was spent sitting down in the restaurant as a form of recovery from all the walking and Muznant read the mood and conveyed that the remainder of the tour would not involve much walking and would be conducted from the comfortable deck of the transporter. She indicated that there were many other different shopping zones that represented other cultures on Earth. There were Japanese, Chinese and most of the other Asian nations represented not to mention African and South American as well. Paris was represented in miniature though the Eiffel Tower was not a part of it. Many other Shopping Malls would be recognisable if visited. Muznant conveyed that about a tenth of Wentazta was occupied by these representations. As Earth modernised with time so did these.

When the meal was over Ashley thanked the restaurant staff with a brief Sewa and patted his belly area to indicate how much he had liked the meal. They then returned to the plaza and boarded the transporter. The operator took them up quite a bit higher so that Muznant could point out the various Earth cities represented. The operator read his passengers thoughts and brought them lower for a better view of a particular interest. At a hundred feet up the styles in the Chinese zone were clearly visible. There were not many shoppers in this area and Ashley suggested that if another visit were possible he'd like it to be to one of these exotic representations.

Muznant then explained that all of these areas shown were for the benefit of the Oannes population in an educational aspect. Many were projects initiated by groups of individuals interested in Earth lifestyles and based upon information and images received from starship despatches.

With windshields raised once again the transporter lifted upwards and sped towards a distant location. They travelled beyond the city limits and over barren land before approaching a vast complex of building structures. Alongside this was a large space-park containing spacecraft in a variety of shapes and sizes; some quite large.

'Aha,' exclaimed Simon, 'we approach my old academy, the one and only Nazmos Space Academy.'

He and Mazpazam conveyed something to Muznant and she agreed.

'We do not have clearance to land here,' she conveyed, 'but I brought you here for you to see the extent of the expansion of facilities that has and is taking place to the whole establishment. The academy intake has increased by half again because of the greater interest among young Oannes. This is mainly as a result of humans from Earth arriving on Nazmos. Many feel that a new era may be about to unfold with inter-planetary travel playing a major role.'

Muznant then gave a description of the main areas of expansion and hinted that even more might be added.

Simon and Mazpazam became quite excited about something and Ashley realised that they were pointing to one of the larger spacecraft parked to one side of the space-park.

'That is Academy craft 686-Blue32,' said Simon. 'Don't ask me the reason for the academy's odd identification numbers but that is a very important craft as far as I am concerned.'

He looked at Mazpazam but she quickly looked away and blocked her mind.

'I was in my fifth year at the academy and a group of us cadets were sent out on a major navigation exercise,' said Simon. 'We were flown blind at half light speed for three months. At the end of the period Zanos-on-board slowed the craft and placed it in a parking loop and our space visibility was restored in all view panels. Zanos was programmed not to respond to any queries from anyone on board for a further period of three months. Basically we cadets were expected to extrapolate our spatial location and then set a course for Nazmos. We all had our star charts and relevant star parallax variations.'

Simon smiled again and this time Mazpazam smiled back. She knew what was coming.

'Well after a week of analysis by the group as a whole the consensus for Nazmos' location could not be ascertained with a greater than 70% certainty. Opinion was divided until Mazpazam came to me and asked what my navigation recommendation was. I had three assets in my favour that the others did not. These were firstly my extensive spatial insight into the positioning of stars with their parallax shifts with respect to varying space locations. Secondly, I had a natural directional instinct even though we had been flying blind. Thirdly, my instinctive awareness of where Nazmos was located. I could not rely on my premonitions as these only occurred at random. The three factors made it relatively straightforward for me to pinpoint the faint star that was Raznat.'

'I thought Ashley liked to show off his navigation skills by pointing out our return direction,' said Mazpazam, 'and initially none of us was convinced that he was right. The rules allow for a course to be agreed and then set and for the ship to cruise towards a return. If the course is incorrect then after a full day of cruising Zanos-on-board would automatically slow the craft and once again enter a parking loop.'

'On previous exercises I didn't explain my navigational conclusions,' said Simon, 'but with Mazpazam I made an exception on this occasion mainly because she had approached me on her own. She had never asked my opinion before when we had been on similar exercises together.'

'What he did impressed me and changed my opinion of him in an instant,' said Mazpazam. 'He put his arm across my shoulders and I felt an electrostatic charge flash between us. This was not unusual but then he conveyed with such detail all his star parallax extrapolations and the spatial configuration of our current vicinity that I became convinced. Then as a conclusion he directed my focus towards the bright star Vega and there nestling right alongside it and as if hiding in its brightness was a dim star which of course was Raznat. Vega was much more distant and the Academy plan had been to confuse us by choosing a direction that positioned Raznat nearly in front of it. I was convinced Simon was right and so it proved to be. I managed to convince the others to follow Simon's calculations and accept that he was correct. We set his course for Raznat and after a week of cruising at half light speed we were informed by Zanos that the course was correct and full recognition given to Simon for the achievement.'

Simon threw back his head and laughed in his familiar style.

'That was when Mazpazam let her guard down and I saw her staring in my direction a number of times. I also received a full blast of her emotions which included tons of admiration for me. I think the admiration included my looks as well. So then to her I was not just a pretty face.'

Mazpazam looked up at Simon and smiled.

'I had an emotional dislike for Simon from his first day at the academy. I felt naturally that he was not an Oannes person and therefore shouldn't be there. And I also felt sure that because his father was famous he had been shown favouritism in being granted admission to the academy. But all that changed in an instant when he put his arm upon my shoulders and sparked something new into my being. Yes it was at that moment that I fell under his spell and totally came to love this human creature.'

'And it was the same for me,' said Simon. 'When a girl throws all her emotions at you how can you fail to respond? I had always thought Mazpazam was pretty but from that moment I saw her as simply beautiful.'

'Thank you Simon,' said Mazpazam softly.

Ashley and Tania looked at one another and both felt comfortable with what they had just heard.

After a moment of thoughts flowing back and forth Simon thanked Muznant for bringing them here and suggested that the tour be concluded and they return to Jazzatnit's house. This was agreed by all.

At the house when they were alone Tania put her arms around Mazpazam and gave her a silent hug. She then conveyed her thanks to Mazpazam and Simon for sharing a very private moment of their lives; one she would always remember with affection.

'With your uncle Ashley and me it was a bit different,' said Tania. 'I knew he was the one for me the moment I saw him when I was only thirteen. But it took him a long time to realise his love for me. He says he was in the middle of it before he realised he loved me. Men are like that I suppose.'

The next day they all went to see Rachel and Margaret's proposed new home. Although it was still in good décor order nevertheless it was to be done up to suit the new occupants' particular tastes; something that would be as good but special.

When Ashley entered the circular sleep-tank room he immediately thought of Ritozanan and the image she had projected at him at his last visit. It had been her bit of flirtation with him and Ashley felt the sadness of that moment and that he had been unable to respond. Ritozanan had not expected anything from him other than his respect and friendship. And that he certainly had for her in abundance. She was an amazing Oannes lady and he remembered her with fondness. Nazmos owed her much.

Ratizdan acted as their guide and took them around the house explaining what was planned. Work had yet to begin though some materials had arrived and had been stored away carefully. The outside courtyard would not be built until the main house rooms had been done up to satisfaction. Ratizdan gave a two month time scale for the interior to be completed and then a further three months for the courtyard structure to be built from scratch. Special furniture suitable for human habitation had been ordered and should be delivered in time.

As they processed from room to room Rachel and Margaret kept conveying information to the others about how they intended to utilise the space therein. Ashley could see that both were quite excited about when they finally moved in. Of course by then he and Tania would be in Dudley in their own happy home environment. Thinking about that was fulfilling in its own unique way.

While they had been going around the house with Ratizdan her associate Statizona had been busy setting up refreshments and snacks in the old dining area which was still very presentable but in the former style for Ritozanan. Raznat was shining brightly through the window panels so that this room was awash with light and looked quite glorious. Statizona conveyed that this had been Ritozanan's evening room from where she could watch the setting Raznat in comfort. Also that she liked to hear the rattling of the window panels when the Dark Wind made its presence felt.

They all sat down around the table as requested and Ratizdan and Statizona then served up a rather nice meal for them saying it was quite late in the day and it was nice for the house to entertain once again. It was the usual fare but with only five different dish types. And Ashley was happy to see that the sweet Yaztraka was one of them.

Ratizdan said that it was nice to have visitors after so long and they looked forward to when Rachel and Margaret moved in permanently. A house needed to be lived in to make it feel alive. Ashley wondered if Ritozanan could see what was going on in her house and he hoped that she approved.

Later after the meal Ratizdan took them outside and conveyed images of the planned courtyard feature yet to be constructed there. The clear flat top was to be quite high up with a slight slant to it. Ashley could imagine that this was meant so that future rain could drain away easily. With the expected weather changes many structural changes might be needed in the houses all over Nazmos.

Eventually they thanked Ratizdan and Statizona for making them feel so welcome and Ashley conveyed a special farewell Sewa on behalf of himself and Tania since he was soon to return to Earth.

The transporter then took them back to Jazzatnit's house although it was still early evening. She apologised for Zazfrapiz's absence stating that he had not been well today and so stayed in the comfort of his sleep tank. Hopefully he would feel better tomorrow.

They strolled around the courtyard with Rachel and Margaret still on the theme of the features they hoped to incorporate in their house. Simon and Mazpazam stayed on for just an hour before taking their leave with goodbyes to all, especially Rachel and Margaret. They were due to rejoin the crew on their starship Silverstreak this very night as per Captain Wastanomi's recall instructions. Ashley and Tania were to be ferried to Silverstreak also but not until late tomorrow.

Before that Ashley and Tania were to attend a council session in the early afternoon. This was the customary goodwill meeting among council members when one of their members was due to leave for a long-term away appointment.

Rachel got an extra special hug from Simon and she clung to him briefly before letting go. Mazpazam did the same but in a much more polite manner.

'Look after yourself sis,' said Simon, 'hopefully I shall see you in a few months time when I return from Earth.'

Then turning to his parents he said, 'Mum, dad we shall see you tomorrow aboard Silverstreak. I think the run home will probably be a day or so later depending upon what the captain has planned.'

Of course Ashley knew that home was Dudley and Dudley was Earth. Then Simon and Mazpazam left Jazzatnit's house and walked to the plaza for their transporter.

Muznant and Brazjaf stayed till quite late and even sat at the dining table and partook of Jazzatnit's late evening meal. They stayed on to witness the Dark Wind phenomena but which failed to deliver anything of prominence. When they were leaving they conveyed that they would return in the early afternoon to escort Ashley and Tania to the special council session. Muznant hinted for them to wear their very best finery and to get Jazzatnit's approval. Ashley simply smiled and nodded his appreciation for the advice. He knew it was given with the best of intentions.

Later that night Rachel sat close to her parents and they spoke of a variety of things. Rachel was a bit like Simon and had a strong instinct about the future in respect of her family. She could not be certain about when she might see or meet her parents again. This Zarama thing had her worried.

Finally it was close to midnight before they all went to their rooms in deep thought. That night Tania again wept quietly in Ashley's arms before dropping into a troubled sleep. 'Damn Zarama to Hell' was her last thought.

The next morning all was bright and cheery and later Zazfrapiz made an appearance with Jazzatnit lending her arm for support. She led him to his usual seat at the head of the table where he smiled at them all before setting down as best he could.

'I'm sorry I could not be with you yesterday,' he said in a quiet husky voice, 'but I shall make up for it today. I decided that I must see you at least once before you leave for Earth. Perhaps we shall meet again and then perhaps we might not. Ashley, you go to Earth for a long duration and then onward from there to do battle with Zarama. I wish you success in that which I'm sure you will achieve. Gozmanot forecast it and I know it will be so. I have been fortunate to have met you and known you over the years and I look upon you all as if you were my own children – though Jazzatnit and I had none of our own. I thank you for staying here with us and making this your home while on Nazmos. It has been a pleasure and a privilege for Jazzatnit and me.'

Ashley stood up, walked around to stand beside Zazfrapiz and put a hand on his shoulder.

'Tania and I and all my family including those who are not with us would like to thank you for your sincere friendship and advice over the years. From the start when Muznant brought us to you we felt most welcome and I include my parents in this. I go now to be with them for a while before venturing out again on the big task. Yes, I will do my utmost to succeed and I thank you for your good wishes on that score.'

Zazfrapiz reached up and put his hand upon Ashley's and gave it a gentle squeeze.

'And now,' he said, 'I should like a glass of Wazu and also something to eat if that can be arranged.'

Jazzatnit looked at the others, raised her forehead wrinkles and smiled as if to say, 'He's getting grumpier as the days go on.' She then poured him some Wazu and went to get him his breakfast.

Ashley returned to his seat and his mug of tea. Jazzatnit then came and put a plate of food in front of her husband. The way he ate it though made it appear as if he was not particularly hungry. Jazzatnit stood beside him with concern written all over her face. She conveyed privately to Ashley only that moments like this had been increasing of late. He was she conveyed 360 years of age and had enjoyed life to the full.

Ashley thought of Ritozanan who had been 333 years of age when she had died. But she had been frail for a long while before that. Yet Jazzatnit at 359 years of age looked fit and able.

Ashley couldn't help comparing this to his own family situation. His mum Lillian was fit and well at 85 while his dad at 90 needed daily help. The same was true of Uncle Ron and Aunt Brenda. After his stroke Ron needed constant care from his very able wife Brenda. Tania's parents however were the exception in that both were in good health; though Milly had to have constant medication and checkups for her under-active thyroid condition. For this very reason Ashley was glad that he would be home again and for a good few years by the look of things. He felt that this was providence and was obliged to the Nazmos governing council for taking note of Korizazit's inner voice messages and granting him the extra time on Earth. The journey home would commence later today and it would not be long before he and Tania would see their parents again.

Zazfrapiz made polite conversation with his guests but they could see that he was growing visibly more tired from the effort. They all stood up when he asked to be excused so that he could return to his room for a rest in the comfort of his sleep tank. They remained standing while he made his way back to his rooms assisted by Jazzatnit.

When Jazzatnit returned alone they all went for a stroll in her courtyard area and made polite conversation. Jazzatnit expressed her regret that Zazfrapiz could not be with his guests but that she would make up for it on her own.

After about an hour Muznant and Brazjaf arrived and said that they had come early to ensure that Ashley and Tania were appropriately adorned in their governing council outfits. She said that since it would be their last session for some time then it would be nice to attend in a blaze of glory. The session was flexible as far as time was concerned since early afternoon had a wide interpretation.

'But it is better to be early than late,' said Muznant.

'We didn't want to partake of the midday meal in our finery,' said Tania, 'but all is chosen and ready in our rooms. Jazzatnit helped in our selection but you may come and approve if you wish.'

'That won't be necessary,' said Muznant. 'I'm certain you have chosen well. I'll advise on minor adjustments with my practiced eye just before we enter the council chambers.'

The midday meal was an hour later and afterwards Tania and Ashley put on their outfits and came out to show themselves to their host and escorts. Tania had done her hair up in a bunch and put on subtle amounts of make-up. Ashley thought she looked stunning.

'You both look perfect,' said Jazzatnit and turning around she asked for Muznant's opinion.

Muznant made an exaggerated show of walking around Tania first and then Ashley before she nodded.

'Yes excellent,' she said. 'Tania is pretty as Ashley is handsome. Come, the council chamber beckons.'

The transporter with glass panel shields fully raised took them directly to the Domed Hall. They walked from the large hall area towards the door leading to the council chamber. When they entered only a few other members were seen to have arrived. But it was not long before the room filled and the session was fully attended; except for the administrative assistants who were not required for this particular session. Muznant explained privately to Ashley and Tania that this was not an official sitting but rather an honorary one solely for the council to bid farewell to Ashley and to wish him all success in the big task of moving Zarama out of the way. She explained that the council had agreed the plan for the trip to Zarama to commence directly from Earth rather than from Nazmos.

Dultarzent stood up to draw everyone's attention and then conveyed to all that the purpose of this session was to bid farewell to Ashley and Tania and to wish them a happy and satisfying period on Earth with their families.

'On my own behalf I do wish you a fulfilling time on Earth with your family and when the moment approaches for all success against Zarama. I hope that when all has been successfully accomplished that you will once again grace us with your presence here. We thank you for all that you have achieved for us from the day that you first arrived on Nazmos. If Ritozanan were with us today I'm certain she would express her good wishes to you. We know that she favoured you especially and I am pleased that she did. Without her guidance the council might not have acceded to all that you rightly intended. And now the council members would each like to convey their personal good wishes to you. Ashley, whatever does happen you will always be remembered with great respect and affection by me and the people of Nazmos. I bid you a personal farewell.'

Dultarzent smiled and sat down. Then one by one in a pre-arranged manner each council member conveyed his good wishes and farewell. It only took a few seconds of telepathic communication per message and Tania knew that although Ashley was the principal object of their address that she as his wife was automatically included.

When all messages had been delivered Dultarzent conveyed a private message asking Ashley if he wished to respond. Ashley immediately replied in the affirmative and at once stood up and looked around at the assembly with a wide pleased smile on his face.

'My dear fellow council members,' he said in a loud clear voice, 'I thank each of you for your kind and generous messages to me and my wife Tania. Your sentiments are very much appreciated.'

Ashley paused and made a show of looking at all seated around the large table and nodding his head ever so slightly as he smiled. Then he drew a deep breath and continued.

'Ever since I came in contact with the Oannes people, first in Anztarza and later here on Nazmos, I have received nothing but friendship and affection from all. Your good wishes have meant a lot to me and have given me strength to pursue my aims. And when my family also visited Anztarza and Nazmos they too received the same affection and friendship from all. The Nazmos governing council have always been fair and just and my requests were listened to and wishes granted. For that I give thanks to the late Ritozanan and I honour her memory. She was a great Oannes lady and as far as I am concerned second only to Gozmanot whose vision for Nazmos is nearing fulfilment.'

Here Ashley paused for a couple of seconds to let his words sink in.

'And now I too must bid you farewell and wish all goodness for the future of Nazmos as envisioned by Gozmanot. Zarama will be defeated and pushed aside so that both Earth and Nazmos may continue on indefinitely. I do not know if I will ever grace this table again but I am sure others of my race will do so at some time in the distant future. There is one thing I leave behind with you and that is my lasting good will and affection. And may Nazmos and Earth be blessed with a long life of peace and mutual prosperity. Thank you.'

Ashley sat down and gradually a clapping began. First from just a few members and then the whole table erupted in sonorous applause. Then Dultarzent stood up as he clapped and all the others followed suit. The first standing ovation in the Nazmos governing council chamber had just been delivered and that for a human. Tania's face filled with pride for her husband. When Ashley looked towards Muznant and Brazjaf he saw that they too were glowing with pride just as much as Tania and his heart filled with love for them all.

In the mingling that followed many additional pleasant messages were conveyed to Ashley and Tania along with the accepted handshake that had become part of the farewell ritual with the Sewa. That would of course always be there.

Korizazit came forward towards the latter part of this mingling of council members to convey his own special message to Ashley. He did this in a very private and singular fashion.

'Thank you my friend for all that you have done for us,' he conveyed. 'You have shown to us a way of life that is possible between our two cultures and you will be in my thoughts even after Zarama is a distant memory. You will however return to Nazmos one day but not as you are now – which puzzles me since I do not know what is meant. But that is the nature of the information that came to me which I now pass on to you. May peace be with you my friend and I wish you goodbye.'

Ashley wondered what this could mean. Was he to be disfigured in some way by his confrontation with Zarama? Would Zarama explode in front of him? Or was there some other interpretation to Korizazit's message?

When Ashley mentioned this to Tania she seemed to find relief in the thought that he was to return to Nazmos one day. To her it meant that Ashley would survive the ordeal of Zarama and return to her. Her earlier instincts had been that Ashley would not survive and that had filled her with dread. Now somehow Korizazit's message had given her new hope.

They were accompanied by Muznant and Brazjaf on their return journey to Jazznatnit's house. It was a most pleasant journey for Tania as she felt that a heavy burden had been lifted from her thoughts. She looked at her husband anew and involuntarily exuded emotional pheromones in an aroused state. Thoughts of frolicking in their sleep-tank awakened in her mind ideas of experimentation that had only been a distant memory of her youth. Throughout this she held his hand firmly giving the odd squeeze and smiling up at him. Ashley was not unaffected by her emotional excitement which induced in him a similar stimulation. He conveyed a very private message to her and she responded immediately in the affirmative and gave his hand an extra firm squeeze.

At Jazzatnit's house their host wanted to know how the council session had gone and she was pleased that Ashley had been honoured so. A personal farewell from a full chamber of members was not an everyday occurrence; but then Ashley was special.

The evening meal was served at the usual time but Zazfrapiz did not make an appearance. Jazzatnit apologised on his behalf and said that the morning session had tired him out. It would be rare now for him to leave his sleep-tank apart from the essential occasions. The meal was good and Ashley ate well knowing that his next would be aboard Rojazonto's spaceship 9632-Orange. Their cabin had an excellent sleep-tank which he intended to make good use of.

Later Ashley and Tania changed into their more usual tunic and leggings clothes in preparation for the journey to the starship Silverstreak. The starship was parked at a distance of 800 million miles from Raznat. This was closer than the previous one billion mile distance due to the relocation of Platwuz. The journey time from Nazmos would be approximately five and a half hours. It would take two and a half hours to accelerate to the million mile distance from Nazmos before the neutron generators could be brought into operation to accelerate the spaceship to 80,000 mps. Then it would be just under three hours to rendezvous with the starship Silverstreak.

Ashley and Tania said their final goodbyes to Jazzatnit and to this Ashley added a special formal Sewa which was much appreciated. They then walked to the plaza and were accompanied by Rachel, Margaret, Muznant and Brazjaf. Ashley's thought was that he was parting from one member of his family only to be reunited with another. Rachel would remain here on Nazmos while Simon was coming with him to Earth.

The journey to the space park was a short one and there was a momentary sadness in Rachel's mind as she said farewell to her mum and dad.

'Give my love to all at home and tell them how we are here,' said Rachel. 'We shall send regular reports to Anztarza about our work and you must do the same from there. I think it is going to be quite an interesting period for Margaret and me when changes start to happen.'

Ashley smiled as he hugged his daughter and told her to look after herself. Tania got a big hug and kiss from Rachel too and both had tears in their eyes as they separated. It was then Margaret's turn and she got the same treatment.

Muznant said her own style farewell as she kissed Ashley lightly on the lips and did the same to Tania. Brazjaf shook hands with both as was now the adopted format between humans and Oannes.

Ashley and Tania then disembarked off the large transporter and boarded the much smaller internal one to Rojazonto's spaceship. They waved one last time to the others as the internal transporter rose off the ground and moved towards the parked spaceship. Daylight vanished as it rose up underneath 9632-Orange and entered the bowels of Rojazonto's large spaceship.

Uppermost in Ashley's thoughts was the fact that once again he was heading for home; home to Dudley and home to his family. Tania and he would have many joyous years of peaceful living and perhaps a little excitement in the sleep-tank feature that Tania wanted installed. Tania squeezed her husband's hand repeatedly each time she picked up these thoughts from him. For them the journey home had truly begun.

PART FIVE

2046 — 2052

CHAPTER 24

Home Affairs

Summer 2051

So far the summer has been great temperature-wise. The balmy days began towards the end of May and continued all through June apart from one rainy weekend. And here we were in early July with the warm days continuing. There's been very little rain since May and it is lucky for us that we had a very wet winter so that all the reservoirs are at near full capacity. Because there'd been no rain for a month there was talk of drought conditions being announced and I expect the councils in the Midlands to eventually consider a hosepipe ban. Leaflets had already been posted around our area for the sparing use of tap water to conserve supplies.

And here I am luxuriating in our very own sleep-tank pool. The afternoon sun is bright in the western sky and it shines straight onto me through the Plexiglas sides of the tank. Tania had originally wanted it inside the house but the architect suggested a wiser option; that of building a purpose-built extension at the back of the house. It would be a sort of conservatory with large glass panels on three sides but with a proper tiled roof. The architect said that a higher ceiling was recommended since west facing conservatories could become unbearable on hot summer days. A height of thirteen feet was agreed which rose up to just under the sills of the upstairs bedroom windows, which were modified to suit. When completed our friends thought it was an odd looking Jacuzzi. It took some explaining but they grew to the idea of having a relaxing deep tub eight feet square inside the house. Word got around and many of our neighbours popped in just to view it. The construction was simple. Its base was three feet below floor level and four feet above. The four feet above the floor was of inch thick Plexiglas on three sides. The fourth side was the side of the house wall but with a two foot wide and four foot high walled section. Steps went up this so that one could climb up and then step down into the sleep-tank via a swimming pool type ladder with curved hand rails. A wise addition was the overhead monorail electric hoist with its suspended metal chair for lifting a person over the Plexiglas and into the pool. I said I was planning ahead for my old age but really I was thinking of dad and Uncle Ron. None of us was getting any younger.

The conservatory itself was much larger being twenty five feet along the house back wall and extending twelve feet out into the back garden space. Tania had bought new furniture for this room and I often relaxed on the comfy sofas reading one of my many Readers Digest condensed books. I had been collecting these for many years now. We sometimes sat in here and had our supper at the small table and chairs that Tania had managed to fit in.

After our return from Nazmos in the spring of 2046 Tania had kept on and on about her sleep-tank. So that summer after Simon and Mazpazam had left again for Nazmos Tania got things moving. It took months of design work and submitting of plans for planning permission before work could begin. This started just before Christmas. The building work took six months to complete and the builders were excellent and only over-ran by a few weeks.

Tania and I were nervous about trying it but our first frolic in the new pool was a thrilling one I shall always remember. We decided not to call it a sleep-tank anymore and after some consideration named it as our indoor wallowing pool. I found that an hour of wallowing in the warmth of the pool was most relaxing around the mid-afternoon period. Our house is on the west side of Paganel Drive and so has an East-West aspect. The front has the morning sun while the back gets the full force of the afternoon sun from one o'clock onwards; when it's not raining or overcast of course.

Tania was seated on the larger sofa in bright sun reading one of her detective novels and as I looked admiringly at her she too glanced up towards me and smiled. We tend to automatically sense each others thoughts whenever we are together and it is a comfort to me to have her near.

I had on my sleep collar and it was quite a boon since I often dosed off. Then my legs drop downwards but my head stays above the surface. Except one time when I must have rolled over while asleep and woke instantly coughing like mad. I must have swallowed a mouthful. Since then I have had the sleep collar modified and enlarged and I've not had a repeat. I don't normally use the collar while wallowing or frolicking with Tania in the pool and only use it when I'm alone and feeling drowsy. Nowadays that is quite often.

My emotional state today was calmness itself and Tania read me clearly. No chance of a frolic she knew. Over the years my libido seems to have diminished somewhat so our frolics are less often. With Tania it seems to be the reverse and she knows exactly when and how to get me going.

I saw Tania's book slip onto her lap and her head tilt backwards into a comfortable position against the sofa back. She had dozed off and I couldn't help admiring her profile. Even when her jaw slackened and her mouth fell slightly open she still looked good.

I shall be seventy this September and Tania sixty-six a couple of weeks later. We have been through a heap of good times, not to mention adventures, and it will be fifty-two years ago that we first met. I still call it our brief encounter. I remember it was a month after my eighteenth birthday and I'd just played in a darts match in the Navigation Pub.

My thoughts then flashed across to Nazmos and the latest news from Rachel and Margaret said that not much had altered; however the sunsets or Raznat sets had become quite colourful. Moisture levels in the atmosphere must have risen somewhat.

Jazzatnit's news was that nothing had changed with regard to Zazfrapiz. He still spent long hours in his sleep-tank. There was a sad tone in Jazzatnit's message.

Other news was from the Nazmos governing council. They informed me that all work on the food growing assemblies on Silverstreak had been completed and that the first crops were close to being harvested. This news was over six months old so I expect that Silverstreak might be Earth bound quite soon. I looked forward to seeing Simon again after nearly six years. His and Mazpazam's communications show that neither of them has changed much in appearance. I hope they come in time for Simon to see dad again.

When Tania and I left Jazzatnit's house we were ferried off Nazmos and to the Silverstreak rendezvous on board Rojazonto's ship 9632-Orange. The journey time had been the usual six hours and we arrived in the early hours. Silverstreak did not leave for Earth until late the following day. I remember the delay was to Tania's advantage because we retired to our allotted accommodation almost immediately after having presented ourselves formally to Captain Wastanomi. We'd been given an excellent meal aboard 9632-Orange and so we just drank the polite glass of Wazu with the captain before retiring.

It was Tania's idea of fun and she certainly capitalised on our private time in the apartment. It was first a frolic in the sleep-tank to energise events which then progressed and culminated in our bed. We missed breakfast which was mainly Tania's fault because she wanted another session in the sleep-tank. However we finally made it to the midday meal specially laid on for us. I think Simon and Mazpazam quite understood for they never mentioned anything then or later.

The journey to Earth rendezvous had taken two and a half days only and the speed trial had been most successful. It had taken me twelve hours of telekinetic effort to accelerate Silverstreak to its design velocity of 1200 FTL. Silverstreak had cruised at this speed for the next thirty-four and a half hours after which I began the deceleration process again over a similar twelve hour period under advice from Zanos of course. Captain Wastanomi was pleased not only that his starship had performed exceptionally but also that his ship had set a record for the journey time between Nazmos and Earth. Our homecoming had been a pleasant surprise to all the family and dad was especially pleased to see Simon again so soon. Mazpazam had stayed in Anztarza and she and Simon kept in constant communication throughout each day. Simon stayed the allotted three months and then had to leave for Silverstreak's journey back to Nazmos and the planned overhaul of its entire food growing system.

After our sleep-tank pool had been installed we had our friends and relatives come to try it out. Chief among these was dad. Tania turned the water temperature up to a nice warm 30 centigrade for him and he revelled in its warmth. He said it really took the load off his joints and wished he'd had one installed at home long ago. His arthritic pains had increased over the last few years and the sleep-tank pool did a lot to ease that pain. He called it his hydro-therapy session. He said he remembered the times he had used one but that was on Nazmos years ago when he was a lot younger and fitter. As a result mum brought him over nearly every week.

However I could see that he became quite exhausted after each session. It was the stress for him of being lifted in and out of the pool. Perhaps we should have built it as a normal ground level pool instead. But I liked the way the afternoon sun came through the sides which added that extra bit of warmth to my wallowing. I am indebted to the Nazmos governing council for giving me these enjoyable years with my family and so I always include a message thanks to them in all of my correspondence to Nazmos.

Uncle Ron and Aunt Brenda came to visit too but only for a short holiday the following summer. Uncle Ron still had partial feeling on his left side and although he enjoyed the pool experience he said it was too much bother being hoisted in and out of it. They had visited again but only once in the last three years. The journeying from Aberporth was a rather long and tiring one for him Aunt Brenda said. Tania and I made weekend trips to visit them at least once every six weeks or so. Communication with our badges still continued between us all which I thought was a tremendous boon. Aberporth has many pleasant memories for me especially its coastal path walks.

Milly and Jerry were over often usually in the evenings as they were not too far from us in Dudley. They sampled the indoor pool but Milly felt embarrassed by the fact that we on the outside had a clear view of her on the inside. So it was usually Jerry and me wallowing when we could. Both were doing reasonably well in spite of their advanced ages. Milly was eighty eight and Jerry a year older. Milly had the cataract in her right eye sorted at the hospital over a year ago and had come home the same evening. The left eye was fine and didn't need anything done to it as yet.

More often than not we just sat on the settees and enjoyed the afternoon sun when the weather was clear; with our mugs of tea of course. Tania had told them about my return to Nazmos one day as foretold by Korizazit in his last message to me and they were happy that this meant I would survive Zarama. At least that was one interpretation. I had other thoughts on the matter but didn't convey any of them.

I spent about three mornings a week at the shops and helped with the history cards. I enjoyed the time there and Tania often came with me. Jerry and Milly popped in only occasionally and that was just for a chat with Mark, Les and the others. They were all good company and gave time to their visitors since the antiques business usually operates at a relaxed pace. However we leave the house clearance visits to the younger generation.

Mark Tinman was talking about retiring and letting Julian Watts take over all his work. I had agreed with Mark in 2048 that Julian be made a partner and this was done that same year. I mentioned that perhaps taking on another assistant might be a wise move but so far no one suitable had been found.

Les Gibson and his wife Agnes were doing well also in the second shop. Out in Hollywood their daughter Rebecca had fallen in love with a theatre agent several years her senior. She had got pregnant by him but he had stepped back and denied paternity. It turned out that he was already married. Rebecca was heart broken and decided to return to England and her parents. Both Les and Agnes gave her loving support and eventually on 8th July 2049 Rebecca was delivered of a beautiful baby girl whom she named Maisy Agnes Gibson. The birth was duly registered with the father's details omitted. One day Rebecca would tell Maisy the truth about her father including his name.

My sis Katy and Robin are both retired now. Katy retired in early 2050 and Robin a couple of years before. They bought an apartment in Tenerife in the Los Americanos area close to and facing the beach there. They go there just after Christmas every year for about three months and usually get back for Easter. And then they go again for a month at a time in early July and also in October. Tania and I went with them once in the summer for a fortnight but it was not our cup of tea. I wanted to stay close to mum and dad for as long as I could. I have this gut feeling that I don't talk about.

Sarah and Brian had another son on Christmas day in '46 and named him Noel. He has dark hair but otherwise looks a lot like Adam in his facial makeup. They are now aged 8 and 4 respectively and both are quite mischievous in their behaviour. Though I must say they are polite towards visitors and other members of the family. Brian and I get on well and talk a lot about Nazmos and the Oannes people. When they do come over we take Noel and Adam into the wallowing pool with us; it being one of the first things they usually ask for. Adam learnt to swim when he was six and says he loves our little indoor pool because he can see through the sides when he's underwater and make faces at us. Of course if I am around I make a face back at him which usually makes him surface for a good giggle. I like the way he refers to us as Uncle Ashley and Auntie Tania. Sarah and Brian try to see us about once a month though communication is regular through our badges.

Fiona is still with Revolux and has met a chap six years her senior. His name is Michael Rotherham and he is a divorcee. His wife Marjorie left him for another chap whom she married as soon as the divorce came through. Michael and Marjorie had two girls in the six years they were together and she had custody of them. Michael sees them every other weekend and they stay over for just the one night only. Veronica is eleven and Mary is nine now and they are quite happy with their mum and new dad Richard.

Michael and Fiona are thinking of moving in together but haven't decided whether to live in his flat or her apartment. Time will tell as Michael's two daughters have to be considered as well for accommodation when they stay over. Fiona has met them and they all seem to get on okay.

Fiona has brought Michael over to meet us and I felt a natural reserve to his personality. But I have heard him laugh on occasion and he will need time to get used to new faces. Fiona hasn't told him anything about me and my gifts. Fiona and I have a very special relationship and we communicate often through our badges. She always queries me about Simon but in a nice way. She is pleased that he is married to an Oannes lady and I got a 'wow' from her when I first conveyed images of Mazpazam to her. She said Mazpazam was a real beauty and she and Simon made a perfect couple.

Robert Black and Vicky are still very friendly and see each other three times each week. Vicky told me that they have a set routine for Tuesdays, Thursdays and Saturdays. They each like their independence but do go abroad for their holidays about three times a year, usually for a week at a time. They arrange with Katy and Robin for the renting of the Tenerife apartment when it is available. They try for either June or September. Robin had thought about getting an agent to look after the hiring of the place but Katy persuaded him not to. She didn't fancy strangers sharing her apartment. She said that she wanted it for family and friends only and for free. She said it was not as if they needed the money and Robin agreed.

I communicate with dad everyday though first with mum. Mum tells me when he is awake and dressed and the homecare chap has left. Dad is now 97 and when I visit most days I find him thinner in the face. He has gradually got frailer and some days mum has to hold his tea mug up for him. He says it is rather too heavy for him when it's full. But I'm pleased that his mind is still clear and alert though I can see concern written all over mum's face. I read her thoughts and she knows that it is just a matter of time.

Mum is nearly 92, still driving her car and very fit for her age. But looking after dad is wearing her down. It's not just the physical side but the worry as well. She refuses to consider a nursing home even for a bit of respite care. She says she can't bear to be apart from him even for a day. So long as she can manage she says she will continue to look after his needs. I understand fully and Tania and I have talked about getting a live-in carer to assist mum. I said I knew my dad and it would have to be someone young and pretty. But we haven't mentioned this to mum as yet.

Enough of my thoughts as I wallow in our sleep-tank pool so I decide to get out before I melt. I notice that Tania is in full sun and still fast asleep. I climb up out of the pool, take the bath robe off the hook and put it on before stepping down to normal floor level. I creep past Tania and head upstairs to the bathroom. A nice hot shower followed by a mug of tea would do me wonders. I'm not sure what Tania has got planned for our evening meal which we have around 5:30 to 6:00pm. And afterwards we usually go for a stroll in one of the parks near us if it is reasonably dry.

Priory Park borders the back of our house but there is no access that way. The Wrens Nest Nature Reserve is a bit further away about half a mile to the north west of us. This is quite an adventurous walk up a hilly area and the views from some of the high points are great. Its geological make-up is mainly limestone which was quarried when the Priory was constructed way back in the twelfth century. When Simon and Rachel were little they enjoyed our walks there and called it their adventure playground. On a good day you could walk the paths all the way to the Sedgley Road well over a mile away.

Dudley zoo is on the opposite side of us and we went there often with Rachel and Simon though both decided that they didn't like the animals in cages. But there were plenty of other enclosures where the animals were less confined. The otters' enclosure was one of their favourites.

When I came down after my shower I put the kettle on and its singing noise woke Tania.

'I'll have one if you're making yourself a cuppa,' she said looking across at me.

I walked out to her and looked down at her still reclined figure.

'Tea or soup,' I asked?

She looked across at the wall clock showing half past three.

'Gosh, have I been asleep that long?' she said. 'I think soup dear.'

'Any preference?'

'What did I have yesterday? I think it was the Potato and Leak so I'll have one of the others. Perhaps Asparagus if there's still some in the packet.'

I looked up at the packets displayed and spied the one Tania wanted.

'Yep you're in luck we still have some,' I said.

I brought the two mugs of hot soup to the settee and placed them on the coffee table in front and then got her to sit up and I settled down beside her. I felt refreshed from my wallow in the sleep-tank pool and then the hot shower afterwards. Tania smiled at me and touched my still damp hair.

We discussed what to do after our evening meal and a stroll in Priory Park was agreed.

We had visited mum and dad in Birmingham earlier that morning and had stayed only about an hour. Dad had fallen asleep partway through our chat and mum indicated that she too would rest up while dad slept. Mum tended to doze in the recliner beside dad with half her mind alert to his waking up again. So we left them and went to each of the McGill's Antique shops on the way home. Milly and Jerry were also at the shop so we stayed for a mug of tea and a chat. We talked about many things including the Oannes and Anztarza.

I thought back to those earlier days well before Anztarza came on the scene. It seemed like everything had happened in a set orchestrated manner; as if to a preordained pattern. There seemed to be a guiding hand keeping control of things and I wondered if this long stay on Earth was included in that plan. Was I being made stronger in my telekinetic ability as a form of grooming for my confrontation with Zarama? I certainly hoped that was the case. I felt in excellent physical fettle and surely strength of body had to be matched by strength of mind.

Sitting on the settee beside Tania I felt I didn't have a care in the world as I sipped my mug of soup. I preferred Tomato soup every time to Tania's varied choices. We sat and chatted and then with the sun still bright and strong I shut my eyes against the glare. It was a peaceful scene of comfort and homeliness. I think Tania went upstairs to do a spot of ironing. When we go for our strolls she irons the clothes she plans to wear. She says that even though they hang in her cupboard they tend to get crease marks from being pushed against the other clothes in there. I joke and tell her she should get another wardrobe to space out all her stuff. I never get an answer to that.

I then heard her go into the kitchen to prepare dinner. I've always called our evening meal dinner from mum's time. She always said the afternoon meal was lunch except for Sunday when we had a late afternoon Sunday Roast Dinner. Then we had supper in the evening but later than usual at about seven o'clock.

'We are having lamb chops with boiled potatoes tossed in margarine just as you like them along with boiled veggies and gravy,' she said from the adjoining room.

'Fine,' I said, 'that will be lovely.'

After dinner we had our little tubs of flavoured yogurt followed by our usual mugs of tea. We then watched the six o'clock news but switched off halfway through. It was all the same old political stuff from earlier in the day.

As it was still bright and sunny we thought to have our usual after dinner stroll. Today we thought that a walk around Priory Park behind our house would be sufficient. It is more of a stroll really since we often stop for a brief chat with some of the other people who also happen to be out and about. People we recognise from the local area.

After a last minute visit to the loo we walked out the front of the house and turned left. It was a couple of minutes to Woodland Avenue and we turned left again for the North entrance to Priory Park. The walk within the park was a pleasant one and the place had a couple of dog walkers who said hello as they passed us. There were some youths playing tennis in the enclosed courts to our right. They seemed to be having fun from the joyous sounds that came across to us. Tania remarked that they didn't need to be so noisy. Further along we stopped to admire the blooms in the rose garden which was more or less behind where our house was. I could just see the upper part of our row of houses as we strolled along.

We continued slowly and walked passed the shelter on our left which stood empty today. In the distant past on cloudy and wet days we had used this shelter as a sort of outdoor covered picnic area with Simon and Rachel. We'd make up a bag of eats and a hot flask and have sandwiches and cupcakes which they found very exciting. After the eats they would race out to the Priory Ruins and run along the protruding foundations and jump the gaps to the next one. They would stand under one of the two archways and see who could get to the next arch by running in opposite directions. Rachel said the small one was hers because it was cosier and more near her size. Those were good memories and now we have newer ones. How times change.

Priory Park is nearly half a mile in length and is a popular recreation area for us locals of Dudley. On other days we would take the kids into the zoo. Tania had invested in an annual family pass so that we could just go in whenever we wanted for a walk around as a recreational event rather than a proper zoo visit. Of course a visit to the café restaurant inside there for an ice cream cone was a must for the kids before we could be allowed to exit for home which was barely ten minutes walk away.

Today as we strolled towards the tall ruins we saw a young mother with a pushchair and her two little children around a park bench close beside the ruins' foundations. One was a little girl aged about two or three and I could hear her crying. The other child was a boy of about six who was standing to one side with his hands on his hips and looking on with a smug expression on his face.

'I've told you a hundred times not to put your hand in there,' said the mother to the girl. 'Now see what you've got yourself into. I shall have to ring for help if you don't get your hand out right away.'

'But mummy it won't come out,' cried the little girl, 'it always did before.'

By now Tania and I had got up to them and I could see straight away that the child's wrist was in the gap between two of the wooden slats of the bench's seating area.

'Can we help,' said Tania to the mother who must have been in her late twenties. She was slim and well dressed but at the moment quite annoyed with her little girl.

'She keeps doing it,' said the mum, 'and I've told her time and again not to because of all the splinters she might get. But she just won't listen and now she's got her hand well and truly trapped and can't get it out. I've a mind to give it a good tug.'

'Can she move it along the gap to perhaps where it might be wider,' I asked?

'Oh she can move it along alright but her hand has puffed up a bit and she can't get it out, silly girl. We've tried everything but its no use. I shall have to ring the Fire Brigade if nought else works,' said the mum still angry at the child.

'We live on Priory Road and come here often. Now it's getting near the time for her bottle and then bed and God only knows how long we'll be stuck here,' she added.

'Let me see if I can help to widen the gap,' I said. 'If I push my fingers hard into the same gap maybe the slats will move just enough for her to pull her hand out.'

I put my right hand fingers into the gap well away from where the child's hand was and then went into pink mode. I used my fingers to compress the wood by pushing my hand in a bit further. The wood felt soft to me and I created a much wider gap pattern. I then returned to normal and pulled my hand away.

'There,' I said, 'I think I felt the wood give a bit so it might have got a bit wider here. Let's see if it is wide enough.'

The mother got the child to move her hand to the side I had indicated and straightway the hand pulled out easily. I could see the relief in the mother's expression as well as the little girl's. She smiled up at me and a very pretty smile it was too.

'Thank you,' said the mum,' I'm sure we tried that side before but you must have pushed really hard and widened the gap. Thanks very much.'

Then to the girl she said, 'Well Tracy my darling I hope you've learned your lesson and will stop putting your hand in there in future. Say thank you to these nice people.'

Tracy looked up at Tania and me and whispered a shy 'Thank you.'

'You're very welcome Tracy,' said Tania smiling at the little girl, 'I hope you haven't picked up any splinters from the wood.'

Tracy looked up at her mum and held up the guilty hand.

'It feels okay mummy,' she said.

'Good girl,' said the mum. 'Now hop into the pushchair and we'll get you home and put some cream on that wrist.'

She then strapped the little girl into the pushchair while her brother quietly looked on. She then wheeled it off the grass area and onto the tarmac path. As she moved away she turned to us as we stood beside the bench and once again said a loud 'Thank you.'

'You're very welcome,' I conveyed without realising I'd done it in telepathic mode.

The mother stopped suddenly and turned to look at me. She knew of the Dutton Telepathic Institutes but had never met anyone with the skill. She nodded her head as if to say she understood.

'You're very good,' she it in her mind only. But I read her thought as if she had sent me a message.

So I replied again telepathically.

'You are very kind,' I conveyed. 'One day perhaps you too might learn the skill. Good luck when you do.'

She waved and smiled before she turned around and carried on walking. We watched as they made their way past the shelter and headed towards the tennis courts area. They probably lived across on the other side of the Priory Road. I had given the mum something to think about for her future learning.

Progress in the Dutton Telepathic Institutes had continued but recently attendance had fallen away due to a low success rate. I had expected this when Margaret left but a small nucleus of skilled practitioners remained and that in itself was progress for future generations.

Tania must have sensed that something was on my mind for she looked at me and said, 'What is it?'

'You know,' I conveyed telepathically, 'when I was in pink mode widening the gap for the child I thought I saw a hooded figure from the corner of my eye standing in that large archway. Only it wasn't a ruin as it is now but it was a complete structure as the Priory was in its heyday. It was only a fleeting glimpse but I'm sure I saw something.'

'Then why not go into pink mode again,' suggested Tania, 'and this time look directly towards where you saw the figure. It could mean something.'

'I'd rather not,' I said. 'Regression is one thing but this was rather spooky.'

A sudden slight dizziness came over me and I reached out to Tania for support. I don't think I made it for the next instant I felt my subconscious mind transported to a time when the Priory was alive in all its glory. I could view all that went on in the Priory but in a detached manner. It was as if I was an ethereal entity without body or form and could go wherever I willed. From what I gathered of the thoughts in the minds of the residents the period was in the time of King John youngest son of Henry the second. This would make it the early part of the twelfth century AD. The thoughts were of the King's excommunication for refusing to accept the Pope's choice of an Archbishop of Canterbury and of the interdict placed over the entire country as a result. The monks were concerned about the effect this might have on their living and their future pilgrimage travels. I was surprised that their thoughts and prayers were known clearly to me as if on an individual basis. It was more an awareness of all these thoughts and desires than actually hearing them. Yet there must have been hundreds of minds invoking thoughts and requests of their God at the same time.

My mind shifted to a curiosity of their living conditions and immediately I drifted into and through the entire priory. I was not just in one room but seemed to be everywhere within the priory at the same time. I seemed to encompass the whole of the structure with my ethereal form and could see into every nook and cranny. The priory was well furnished in all its rooms with wood fires burning in the grates of every room. There was thickly woven rush matting on nearly all the floor spaces including the monks' private chambers. Although the monks were allowed to eat meat they were encouraged towards a fish diet which was in plentiful supply within the moats surrounding the Priory buildings. These moats had been the scene of a few disastrous drownings from monks slipping in while trying to harvest a few extra fish. My conscious conveyed to me that not all of these mishaps were entirely accidental. Also around the priory were large areas of cultivation and well tended orchards of apple, pear, fig and quince.

I somehow knew that all monks carried daggers in scabbards under their cassocks. These were used mainly for eating purposes and for cutting fruit. It was an essential item for them all. It was also a well known fact and as such monks who visited the poor in Dudley and the surrounding villages were unlikely to be accosted or attacked. At meal times in the priory hall all daggers came out and were placed alongside the wooden plates on which the food was served.

My conscious moved to the areas surrounding the priory. There on the hill were the ruins of Dudley Castle and my subconscious moved to overlook it. There were some areas that had an overhanging stonework and these were converted by some villagers into makeshift shelters against the frequent wet weather. Sheriff's men came on a regular basis to evict those who could not pay the penny tariff demanded. I sensed a great sadness among these poor squatters who had nowhere else to go.

My subconscious then moved across to a rugged hill some distance on the other side which I knew to be made up mainly of limestone and used as the quarry for the stone that built the castle. Today it is called Wren's Nest. Here too I saw villagers living in the shallow rock caves that had resulted from recent quarry work as well as from ancient times dating back to the Stone Age. It looked very different from its present day appearance.

Making up the third side of this three pointed triangle was a gentle rise of land upon which were amassed about forty cottage type dwellings that made up the village of Dudley. Here too I seemed to instantly hover above and at the same time in amongst the people living here. I became immediately conscious of all the thoughts and cravings, sadness and joys of this complex community. Yet it all looked tranquilly peaceful from the outside with figures going about what was their normal everyday business of survival. I noticed a child about to fall into a ditch and I tried to warn it but found I could not. I was simply an observer to this scene of the past and it was impossible for me to interfere or even communicate with these ghostly representations. I had no interaction with them but I did know what they were thinking and what they were praying for in their hopeful desires.

The next thing I knew was that I was once again standing beside my Tania and staring at the Priory ruins of today. My little subconscious journey into the past had taken barely a second but Tania sensed my thoughts and knew something odd had taken place.

'What?' she queried staring at me wide eyed.

'What is what?' I replied smiling. We played these games of tease occasionally.

'Tell me what you saw just now silly,' she said. 'I know something happened.'

So I told her and conveyed to her mind all the mental images of my experience including the monk's thoughts and all of the others too.

'Wow,' exclaimed Tania. 'They lived well these monks. No wonder so many went into holy orders.'

There was puzzlement in my thoughts and I realised why and conveyed this to Tania.

'I'm not sure why I was taken into and through this review of the past,' I said. 'I'm puzzled as to the meaning behind it. Was there some reason I was shown this?'

That meaning became clear to me some time later and it had to do with dad.

The next few days passed in leisurely fashion with our daily morning visits to mum and dad. Dad and I had some nice chats and when I conveyed the incident of the child's hand being wedged in the park bench he seemed quite interested. When I finished recounting the story he asked if there was more.

'Why do you say that dad?' I asked.

'Well it's too simple an event so I thought there must be something else,' he said.

Tania laughed then.

'Tell him the rest darling,' she said.

'Yes,' said dad, 'tell me all. Convey everything exactly as it happened.'

And so I did in vivid colourful imagery.

Dad was silent for a long time looking down at his feet. I knew he was in deep thought and going over in his mind what I had just conveyed.

Then out of the blue he said, 'So that is what it is going to be like.'

Then after a moment he added in a slow manner, 'So, our thoughts can be heard.'

There seemed a new calmness in his demeanour and he reached out and took my hand.

'It won't be too long now, son,' he said with a smile.

I thought he meant about Zarama since it was a frequently discussed subject.

So I said, 'I expect Silverstreak to arrive back at Earth rendezvous any time now dad. So Simon should be here to see you again quite soon.'

Dad looked at me, smiled and nodded.

'Take care, son,' he said, 'I shall be watching with interest.'

It was a couple of weeks later that dad passed away during his afternoon nap. Mum conveyed through her communication badge how it had happened.

'It was a warm sunny day as you know when you were here this morning. After you and Tania left us I gave dad his usual snack lunch and we had tea together. Dad suggested we go out into the garden and enjoy the weather while it lasted. Dad was in his wheelchair with the back raised high and slightly inclined so he could rest his head. The sun was lovely and warm and we chatted pleasantly. Dad talked about when we'd gone to Blackpool when you were a baby and how he'd carried you around in his arms. Dad said that you got heavier by the minute and he had to lock his arms together to keep a hold of you. It was nice to see him smiling as he talked. After a bit I noticed him dozing off as usual but I carried on talking because I knew he liked that. I think I was talking about you and Tania and your sleep-tank pool. I noticed a smile appear on his face so he must have heard me chattering away. The smile stayed and it was only a couple of minutes later when I noticed him not breathing anymore. Only then it came to me that he was gone.' Mum stopped for a moment full of sad emotion.

'I moved up close to him and put my arms around him and kissed his still warm face before my tears came flooding out. He was a good man son and a devoted husband and father and I miss him already.'

She stopped then and could convey no more but her emotions came through to me strongly such that my tears also flowed freely. Tania who had also received mum's message came and put her arms around me in a tight hug. Words were unnecessary.

I then remembered what dad had said to me that morning just as were leaving. He repeated what he had said to me after I'd related the park bench incident and conveyed in detail my subsequent subconscious ethereal journey into the past.

'Take care son,' he had said, 'I shall be watching with interest.'

And those were his last words to me and suddenly I knew what he really meant.

I looked upwards and said aloud, 'Cheers dad, enjoy floating around.'

Or perhaps he had flitted to another time period. I sensed that an emotional smile must be out there somewhere.

I tried to convey these thoughts to mum but I don't think it registered. Not as yet anyway.

'I do miss him,' was all she said.

I conveyed the sad news to all the family and said that Tania and I were going over to be with mum.

When we got there Katy was already with mum. The family doctor had been and sent for an ambulance to take dad to the hospital mortuary. Procedures had to be followed which upset mum quite a bit.

I had managed to see dad before they took him away and was surprised how cold his face had become in so short a time. I had kissed his forehead then and whispered 'Goodbye dad,' as I squeezed his cold hand. I remembered when granddad Eric had passed away in December 2020. He too had died in his sleep and aged ninety six. Dad had been a year older. We seem to have a long lived family tradition and I wonder if I shall reach such an age too.

A few days later Tania and I went with mum to see dad in the Chapel of Rest at the funeral parlour on Gravelly Hill. It was our first visit there and the funeral director was very sympathetic and patient. He showed us where dad 'was in repose' and then left us on our own. For several moments mum stood in the doorway to the Chapel unable to move. Only when I came up behind her and put my hand on her shoulder did she take a step forward. I was beside mum on her right with Tania on her other side as we moved forward towards the open mahogany coloured polished coffin. It was the only one in the room so it had to be dad. Mum again stopped a few feet from the coffin.

I was reading mum's thoughts and she was thinking back to the words she had last spoken to him in the garden just before he fell asleep. Again mum stepped forward but very slowly while keeping her head bowed downwards as if afraid to look at her husband. As she came up closer to the coffin she raised her eyes and looked straight at dad's face. And she smiled.

They had done well with dad and made him look just the way he had in life. I was pleased that dad's smile had remained. Mum looked up at me still smiling though with a slightly crooked quivering slant at the edges of her lips.

'They've combed his hair just right,' she said as if talking to herself. 'And it's the same smile he left me with when he fell asleep. They've done well.'

It was my turn to gaze at dad's face and I resisted an urge to touch him with the intention of waking him like I had done so often when on some of my visits to the house in Erdington. For to my senses of sight and smell dad was simply asleep – and at peace I hoped. Or was he flitting around across time and space? I looked upwards in case he was peering down at us.

Mum wept openly now though quietly as she moved right up against dad's coffin. She reached her hand up and pressed the tops of her three middle fingers to her lips and then touched them to dad's lips, cheeks and forehead. An audible sob escaped her lips but she immediately checked herself. She stood stiffly erect and looking up at me nodded ever so slightly. She looked stronger and more resilient than a moment ago when we'd walked in.

Mum and I changed places and I then reached out to touch dad's cheek now so cold and lifeless. No message came back to me. He was truly gone unlike when Philip Stevens had died in the hospital. Where was Philip now? He had given me a message initially but that was all. He had moved on. Also perhaps he and dad might be chatting now and exchanging stories as at that last Christmas. My eyes were blurry with wetness after watching mum go through her farewell ritual with her hand kisses. Tania too was in tears crying quietly into my folded handkerchief.

We stood quietly together beside dad and I knew he must be reading our thoughts as I had of all those people at the priory during my subconscious fleeting flighty hovering. Eventually mum turned around and we walked out of the chapel and into the bright sunshine once again.

The funeral was set for a week later and in that time we came three times to see dad again. It was the same but mum seemed better prepared each time. She even spoke to him once saying 'We're here to see you again Alex'.

With all of the family's help mum gave dad a touching send off. I'm sure he was watching. He could always do a repeat visit if he wished. I am convinced that all earthly events are locked into our past and access to it is possible for the subconscious of those allowed a visit as I was. And for those who have passed on into that unknown sphere when "we have shuffled of this mortal coil".

Over the following weeks mum often talked about dad and much of it I'd not heard before. They were her memories and they brought her comfort and I was glad to listen.

Yes, it was good to talk. Sometimes a sad person can talk the sadness right out through their mouth. Yet every now and then mum would blink vigorously, put her head down and fight a desire to weep. I'm sure she did a lot of that while on her own, especially in bed at night. Tears are a release for the emotion of sadness that comes from a permanent parting from a loved one.

The communication badges were a godsend and mum was never alone through the day. She kept her communication mode open and so was in constant touch with all of us. There were also frequent chats with one or another member of the family no matter how far away. So in amongst all the talking there was one from Aunt Brenda in Aberporth who conveyed a wisdom that I shall always remember.

'Oh Lillian,' she had conveyed one morning, 'life must go on must it not? The clock still ticks and measures out the hours, minutes and seconds even though Alex is gone. We who remain are all here for you with our love. So when you think of Alex think also of all that he has left us with. Your children and grandchildren are all part of what Alex was. And I thank him and you for all of them.'

Tania and I visited mum every day as if dad were still at home. Katy and Robin came too as did some of the others. Robert and Vicky visited a couple of times when we were there and I think mum liked having a house full. It reminded her of old times. She even began to smile again.

'I think I might downsize,' mum said one day and I wondered at her for thinking so.

But then she explained.

'Alex won't be needing any of his stuff now so I might as well pass it all on to the charity shops,' she said, 'there are quite a few on the High Street.'

I didn't comment as I felt if that was her decision I'd let her get on with it. But a few days later I don't think that she even remembered saying it.

Then on another day she said she'd like to de-clutter the house of excess items that she would never use anymore. This saddened me as I felt she was preparing herself to follow dad. She must have sensed my mood for she instantly went on to explain her reasons for wanting to do so.

'There's just too much in the house that I shan't need,' she said. 'What's the point of bookshelves without books or wardrobes without clothes or linen? I'd just like to simplify things for myself in this house. That old piano can go for a start.'

Again I made no comment and as the days went by nothing changed. The house was still the same and I was glad that it was.

Our daily visits and chats continued as ever and mum began to talk of old times something she had never done while dad was around. She talked about how she and dad had met and often repeated the telling though with a slightly different slant each time.

Mum had been a teacher in a secondary school teaching the sciences while dad worked in the main railway offices in Birmingham as a computer technician. Computers were a recent addition to the railways in those days so Alex went on frequent courses.

'We first met at a Christmas dance in '79,' said mum wistfully. 'It was the Forget-Me-Not Club on the Tyburn Road. Brenda and I were with mum and dad and I think Alex was with his folks. Both our parents were good dancers and our dads were ex-servicemen and had met at the Club often.'

She then smiled as she remembered something.

'Alex had two left feet when it came to dancing but he had a good go at it,' said mum. 'We just shuffled backwards, forwards and sideways to the rhythm of the music. I didn't mind at all that Alex couldn't dance as I liked him from the start. We went out together and met every Saturday after that. It was usually the pictures in the afternoons and Alex was the perfect gentleman in there. He just wanted to be with me and I with him. We got married that October in St. Barnabas' church. It was the year of the Moscow Olympics. I was twenty one and Alex five years older. Our first place was a small flat at the lower end of Church Road and was conveniently close to the shops; but when you decided to make your presence felt we got this house, Alex arranged it all with a mortgage and a small deposit. Things were cheaper in those days.'

Mum then went silent but the smile remained on her face. I could see that she was thinking back to those times with all their pleasant memories.

In the ensuing days she repeated herself while adding little details to her memories. Like it rained on the day they got married and had continued as a light drizzle all day. Then she mentioned that the wedding was at two o'clock in the afternoon. Another time mum said that they'd gone to Blackpool for the honeymoon but only for a week which was all the time-off Alex was allowed as he had another course to attend.

I didn't mind listening to mum's memories even though Tania and I knew most of it. Memories are everpresent in ones mind and can be picked out frequently and at any time. It's good to do that for it keeps the love fresh that you hold so dear.

Mum had many visitors and I think she enjoyed her sister's visit immensely. Aunt Brenda spent a week and it was nice seeing them talk of the old times that they had in common. They'd sit talking pleasantly and occasionally I'd hear a chuckle and even light laughter. Brenda said that Ron was fine and not on his own as he had Sudzarnt to look after his needs. The communication badges kept us all in touch and sometimes I felt as if the whole family were with us in the room. These badges were an immense boon to a person living alone.

Time went by and on Friday 8th September Tania did a party for my seventieth. It was a low key affair as dad was missing and that so recently. Mum was there as were all of the family and when I gave my little speech of thanks I also conveyed once again the images of my subconscious visit to the priory of the past. I then raised a toast to dad and said that he was probably looking on and smiling.

Mum smiled at this and I think she finally accepted that dad was up there somewhere looking down on these proceedings and hearing all our thoughts just as I had.

'Wonderful,' I thought to myself, 'this is a big step forward for mum.'

Afterwards on another one of our visits mum asked me to convey again to her mind the images of that priory subconscious visit. Mum began to believe more and more of what life might be like after death and I think she took on a vicarious joy out of accompanying me on my relived subconscious priory visit. I was to repeat the process for her many times at her request. And I was pleased that she did and was happy for her.

A couple of weeks later on Saturday 23rd September Tania celebrated her sixty sixth birthday. I called her my equinox baby just as a tease. Although it was meant to be a low key affair it actually turned out to be quite a joyous occasion when news came in from Anztarza that Silverstreak had arrived at Earth rendezvous. This meant that Simon would be here with us soon.

That night we had a special frolic in our indoor pool. We cuddled and chatted as we floated around and Tania said she couldn't wait for Simon to arrive. She said she also wished that Mazpazam could come too but we both knew that was not practical.

'Then why don't we visit Anztarza instead. We could stay some time with our son and his wife and then later Simon could come back home with us,' said Tania. 'Then after a month here we could all return to Anztarza again. What do you think darling?'

'Yes why not,' I said. I tended to agree to all of Tania's ideas.

And then I suggested that we could perhaps spend a final week in Anztarza and commence our scheduled trip up to Silverstreak directly from there. That would make it probably sometime in January of the New Year.

'I'd like that a lot,' said Tania and I noticed sadness in her tone.

I think the mention of Silverstreak brought Zarama to her mind and she still harboured doubts in that region. In my own mind I was impatient to get to grips with my foe. I was somehow confident that I would prevail at whatever cost to me. I had no fears there not since I knew how I should be if the worst scenario were to occur. That subconscious journey I had been taken on around the Priory had given me a new mental confidence and strength.

The next three months were an especially memorable time for Tania and me.

After the news of the arrival of Silverstreak it was a week later that Simon arrived at Aberporth. The world still has no knowledge of Anztarza or of the Oannes existence there or of Nazmos. I suspect that this could be in part due to a mild form of corrective brainwash of any form of curiosity that might be initiated in a particular human. Prior to Simon's arrival here his communication with all family members had been frequent and news of his granddad's passing so recently had saddened him. But then he said that granddad had lived to a great age having done all the things he'd wished for. Simon said he only hoped he himself could reach such an age.

'We are not like the Oannes,' he had conveyed, 'but hopefully the trend for us humans will head in a similar direction.'

Tania and I had studied the Oannes histories and learnt that for them illnesses and accidents were few and far between. Human medical science was uncovering new cures and the treatments of difficult diseases were achieving progressive successes. But we still had a long way to go before we could even approach the longevity of the Oannes people.

Sudzarnt drove Simon down to us in Dudley and it was nice seeing him face to face. One forgets the pleasure that physical contact brings. It is all very well with telepathic communication with all its imagery and emotions relayed but who can beat a physical hug or a handshake. Sudzarnt stayed over for one night only before returning to Aberporth. He said he was concerned for Uncle Ron – especially now that he was beginning to forget things. Some were inconsequent but others more serious. Like taking his medication repeatedly and not realising he had just done so. Brenda had made a chart to prove to him he'd had a particular pill at a particular time. Sometimes he accepted this but at other times he got quite agitated and argumentative. Only Sudzarnt had the mental ability of inducing calm and conveying to his mind the image of him actually taking the medicine or pill. As such Ron became quite dependant on his adopted son and Brenda was grateful for it.

Simon stayed with us a full month and visited his grandmother Lillian nearly every day. He accompanied us on our daily visits and sometimes made a visit on his own of an evening by driving himself using his old licence. With Simon here we made arrangements for mum to spend her weekends with us in Dudley.

I hadn't mentioned to Simon about the subconscious journey I had been taken on around the Priory in any of my communications and he was surprised when mum raised the topic. Subsequently he wanted to know the full detail of the episode. So I gave him the whole scenario including how his grandfather Alex had responded to the imagery. Mum said that after repeated viewing of the event she had found peace and consolation with regard to her husband Alex. As a result Simon walked to the priory ruins where it had all taken place and stood there quietly in a most contemplative mode.

'Dad,' he then said to me, 'you must convey all this to Mazpazam; not now but when you see her in Anztarza.'

I nodded my agreement though I wondered at the impact it might cause if the imagery spread to the Oannes in general. They had all viewed my visit to Gozmanot when I had regressed to her time but this was different. The Oannes are not religious and I wondered if this might be a sort of initiation in that direction. I conveyed these thoughts to Simon but he said that the Oannes psyche would need a lot more factual evidence before they could be convinced of any religious connotations. Monitoring of Earth's numerous varied beliefs would have created its own scepticism among them. But then who can predict what direction the future might take.

I had requested and agreed arrangements with the council of chief ministers in Anztarza for us to visit there along with Katy and Robin accompanied by our Simon. We all had a great desire to meet Mazpazam again in person. And so it was that in the first week of November 2051 Simon accompanied us to Anztarza. We all travelled up a day earlier to spend time with Ron and Brenda. Ron seemed fine although he got Katy mixed up with Tania. But no one made an issue of it or even tried to correct Uncle Ron.

The Bus Craft came as usual to pick us up late in the dark evening of the second day and the operator was once again a different Oannes male person. He was on his own which gave Tania a slight disappointment not to see Mazpazam on it. But this was short-lived for shortly after we alighted in the shuttle bay of the spacecraft 11701-Red there was the lady in question coming forward to greet us. She followed protocol by doing so in seniority order which put me first. My goodness I thought at sight of her, she is certainly one beautiful Oannes woman.

Mazpazam still addressed Tania and me as aunt and uncle which I found most agreeable. Tania had secretly hoped that it might eventually become mum and dad. I thought it unlikely though Tania simply said, 'Perhaps one day.'

Katy and Mazpazam were old friends and Robin smilingly looked on as the two got on famously. All the while Simon was at his wife's side holding her hand. She and Simon had greeted each other with smiles and that was all. Not a hug or a kiss but simply smiling up at him then coming close to get hold of his hand. I could see a private communication going on between them and knew that any outward show of affection in public was not the Oannes way. I liked that and both Tania and I could feel the emotion of intense love radiating between them. Tania looked up at me and smiled with pleasure at her son's happiness.

I had not visited Anztarza for nearly three years so the chief ministers made it a celebratory occasion with a banquet in Dome-4 on the day after our arrival. It was a grand affair and no mention was made of the impending trip to Zarama. It was a lovely celebration in which only a welcoming speech was made by chief minister Rymtakza who was there with his wife Mizpalto; both in their 228th year and looking well for it. After that everyone mingled and came to greet and talk to us on a personal basis. Invitations to dine were given but which Tania and I politely declined since we had just a week here and wished every moment to be with our son and his lovely wife. Tania and Mazpazam got to know one another even better with Katy for additional company doing what three women did best; swapping stories I believe. The same applied to us men though our subject matter was rather different. Robin was good company and helped our discussions to flow easily. Looking at Simon and Robin discussing a topic allowed me to view my son from a different perspective. Here was a content and confident man and I have to say that I came to admire what I saw. Mazpazam was fortunate in him and he in her which was plain for me to see.

At the end of our planned week together in Anztarza, Tania, Katy, Robin and I returned home via Aberporth while Simon remained behind. He and Mazpazam had things to do and see and Simon said he'd return to us again in early December to spend Christmas with the family. He said he and Mazpazam intended to visit the northern forests of Canada once again which this year were having an unusually cold spell. Mazpazam was keen to renew her experience of her earlier first trip there in January 2046. Simon wanted for just the two of them to spend time alone deep in a remote part of the forests and for her to experience a real blizzard or at least heavy snowfall conditions. They would need to stay there for several days and just so we could appreciate Mazpazam's sensory emotions of the forest conditions Simon would keep us regularly updated with events.

It was a couple of days later that Simon conveyed through his badge that they were deep in a forested area and that the weather was extremely cold and snowfall was continuous – sometimes heavy and at other times not so heavy; sadly no blizzard as yet. He was well clothed like an Eskimo from head to his foot against the bitter cold. Mazpazam didn't feel the cold as much but was nevertheless also well covered like Simon though mainly for disguise purposes to hide her Oannes features.

I was a bit concerned for them but Simon assured me that their living conditions were comfortable and warm. A shuttle type craft had been put at their disposal and it had been camouflaged to appear like a campervan. Mazpazam was its logged on operator with the Zanos on-board system under her sole command. They spent two days and nights at their first location and then moved further north for a further three days. The wonder for Mazpazam was that she was experiencing here on Earth the conditions that might prevail on Nazmos one day perhaps a thousand years in the future. She conveyed her emotional joy of the experience and said what an enchanting place Earth was. I had to agree and I conveyed as much. I also conveyed that it had been my aim from the very beginning of my awareness that Nazmos share in the conditions of Earth and it was the reason I had pushed so hard for the orbital change of Nazmos. I was grateful that Ritozanan had shared my vision.

At the second location on one of the mornings Mazpazam awoke inside their warm shuttle abode to see a furry face peering in through a side view panel. Simon conveyed that it had startled Mazpazam but he had told her it was simply a curious young grizzly bear. Mazpazam had gone up to the panel to stand face to face with the creature when it became agitated and commenced to paw and scratch at the panel trying to get inside. Without thinking Mazpazam sent a calming emotion to the bear's mind and it immediately stopped scratching at the panel. After a brief hesitation it simply turned about and calmly walked off into the trees of the forest. Simon conveyed all this to us and added that he thought Mazpazam was most clever to have been able to do what she did.

So, I thought, the Oannes can mentally influence our animals as well. She is not just a pretty face as the saying goes.

She and Simon went out of their shuttle-campervan to enjoy the falling snow whenever they could. He sent us images of Mazpazam's exhilarating joy of the weather conditions. She would pull her hood back and let the snow settle on her smooth skin. The view was of her outspread arms with gloves removed and palms facing upward feeling the snow.

'One day Nazmos will be like this thanks to Uncle Ashley,' she had said to Simon, 'but I feel sad that it will not be soon enough for me to enjoy. Perhaps in a thousand years from now others on Nazmos will feel this like I am now.'

I remember when I first laid eyes on Mazpazam as she walked in behind Simon at Jazzatnit's house. My first thought was that she was a very beautiful woman. Then I looked around at Tania and saw the look of wonder and admiration on her face too. Her thoughts were open and the words that were conveyed abroad were 'What a beautiful woman.' They were the exact same thoughts that had been evoked in my own mind.

Since then I realised that those were also the thoughts that came to the minds of all who met her, male and female. And Simon basked in the aura that Mazpazam's beauty radiated. There was no jealousy there simply a matter of pride of possession and belonging. And above all it was clear to see that he loved her with the same intensity of love that she too bestowed upon him. It was a mutual thing between them that became magnified like two inward facing mirrors reflecting repeatedly into infinity.

I knew of Mazpazam's interest in the history search for the reason that had kept the Rimzi people of her planet aloof from their land based fellow Oannes. Recorded history did not go back far enough to give any hints. Or it had been expunged from the records for a reason. But Mazpazam felt that I could help her in her quest at discovering the truth. Sadly it was one area about which my inner voice remained exceptionally silent. Nor was I willing to try a regression for fear of what I might find. My own instincts gave me a bad feeling about the whole affair and I decided that perhaps it was best left alone. One could stir up a hornet's nest of unnecessary emotions good and bad. But my curiosity had been aroused and I could not help but think about it. And Mazpazam remained intense in her quest.

Simon told me that Mazpazam had initially discussed the subject with him. She had hoped that he might have some notions about the matter from his premonition gift. But Simon could not shed light on the matter either. In fact he said that he'd never even given it a thought.

When Mazpazam had discussed the Rimzi with me she said that her instincts told her that at the very beginning of life on Nazmos creatures had all lived in the cold but habitable seas. One half progressed to live on the land while the other half had remained within the sea. And since then nothing had changed – or had it? For some strange reason Korizazit's prediction flashed across my mind momentarily. Then it was gone leaving no meaning behind and I soon forgot about it.

Apart from the Ari surviving within the sea bed no other creatures existed on Nazmos.

'Surely, Uncle Ashley,' she had said to me, 'evolution on Nazmos must have produced other creatures similar to what had occurred on Earth?'

I could give no answer to this. What was the intent of Korizazit's prediction?

I knew that there was definitely an attitude within the Rimzi that wished to have nothing to do with their scientifically advanced land based neighbours the Oannes. What had occurred for it to come to this state of affairs? And also how did the Rimzi live so well in their sea domain?

Mazpazam had asked how they had survived when nothing else did. It remained a mystery that baffled her and which made her even more determined to discover the truth. Thankfully her mind was distracted by the beauty of the snowy scenes of the northern forests around her. She especially enjoyed it when the snowflakes were large fluffy ones. She so revelled in the present. I could imagine Simon just staring at her enjoyment of it all. His joy was seeing her joy.

Back on Nazmos the redecorating of Ritozanan's house and the courtyard extension had been completed a year after I had left there and now it was a truly beautiful abode that Rachel and Margaret could call home. The furnishings were Earth orientated in their approach and Rachel had been the chief architect in its design and layout. Simon and Mazpazam had visited whenever the opportunity arose for them to get leave from Silverstreak during the refurbishment of its food-growing systems and Rachel and Margaret had made them very welcome. Mazpazam liked the style and layout that had been affected but she especially liked the colours that Rachel and Margaret had incorporated. Rachel said that Jazzatnit had been a great influence and guiding hand in much of the colourful design.

My thoughts turned to Zarama and I wondered if the Rimzi knew of its approach or even cared at what might happen to them if Zarama was not defeated. With a mass slightly greater than our Sun this dense White Dwarf Star compressed to the size of Earth was speeding on its inexorable path directly towards Nazmos and Earth. It was travelling close to 33,000 miles per second or nearly 18% of the speed of light.

The Oannes scientists had calculated its path direction as approaching Raznat first and then continuing on towards Earth. It was estimated to come within two billion miles of Raznat if it continued on its current path.

At this estimated distance Raznat would certainly be drawn up towards Zarama. It is possible that they would combine as a twin star system with Raznat orbiting the more massive Zarama. The planets might or might not survive the transition. All this was well known to the Oannes but as yet Earth's people had no knowledge of it and probably never would if I was successful in altering Zarama's path.

The scenario that might develop if I did nothing was that Zarama would next approach to within eight billion miles of Earth and its Sun after another twenty years to adversely affect the orbits of our planets. The scenario could be infinitely more complex if Zarama came with Raznat as its twin. Some planets might be pulled away to drift into space or into orbit around Zarama. Whether Earth was one of those would depend upon its orbital position at that critical moment.

These were thoughts that raced through my mind every so often and made me ever more determined to succeed against Zarama. And I just knew that I would since Gozmanot had seen it happen so. I have great faith in that venerable lady's visionary predictions.

But for now back to the present.

Simon and Mazpazam made an additional shorter trip to another part of the northern forests early in December after which Simon came home on his own to spend Christmas with us.

My Tania made that Christmas day a special occasion and invited all of the family over for a grand afternoon buffet lunch. Tania had been out shopping and bought each and every one a small gimmicky gift. She called them fun gifts and tried to get something that the person had loved as a child. I know what I had liked and that was those little die-cast windup racing cars. Sadly I remember that the windup spring hadn't lasted very long but I'd had fun playing with it anyway.

Simon and I drove to Birmingham in the morning and brought mum back with us. We planned for her to stay on till after the New Year. Ron and Brenda couldn't come as it was very difficult for Ron to travel the distance from Aberporth. But we had them with us in spirit since they kept in constant badge communication. I felt as if they were here with me in Dudley. But it was Brenda who did most of the communicating since Ron's forgetfulness was becoming serious. Some days were worse than others though he still recognised faces. Or so Brenda said.

Katy and Robin came followed closely by Sarah, Brian and their two lovely kids Adam and Noel now eight and four respectively.

Jerry and Millie came too but then they only lived a short distance away.

Fiona had communicated her desire to bring her man friend Michael with her since otherwise he would spend Christmas alone. Fiona had just celebrated her fortieth birthday on November 19th and we had all been invited to a restaurant function and had met Michael there. It was Fiona's way of introducing Michael to the rest of the family.

He was a tall man at about six feet and a bit and had quite prominent features. He had a thin large nose that dominated the face topped by a full head of dark wavy hair. He was pleasant in manner and got on well with the men of the family. He did not initiate conversation but soon joined in once a topic got going. He was into politics but did not push for any particular party. However he did express an opinion regarding what the government or the opposition were doing. Some things he was for and some he was against. He had a clear uncluttered mind and I liked him straight away. Fiona said that although he was six years her senior she found him very compatible in thought pattern. When he came over for Tania's Christmas lunch he brought us a little house gift as thanks for having him. Tania was impressed by the kind thought.

After everyone had eaten their fill and Tania had cleared things away helped by the girls of course, we all sat down to listen to the King's Speech on Telly. Soon the older generation including myself had begun to doze off where we sat.

Sarah and Brian then took their two youngsters into the sleep tank pool for a play around in the warm water. Fiona and Michael joined them in the conservatory but sat on the sofa there just watching. They didn't hold hands but sat with shoulders touching as they smiled and talked. Fortunately for them the sofa was far enough away from the sleep tank pool for them not to get splashed; even though the mischievous Adam tried his utmost to fling water in their direction. Little Noel couldn't swim so Sarah had come prepared with arm floats for him.

Adam would go underwater up against the clear side panel and wave to his aunty Fiona – and she would wave back in a sort of fun game. When I woke after my little doze I too went into the conservatory to see how the kids were enjoying themselves. Four in the pool was just right; any more and it would be a crowd. I watched Adam and thought he was very good at holding his breath underwater for such a long time. I estimated it to be nearly a full minute. It was nice to see Sarah and Brian enjoying their Christmas here. Everyone seemed really relaxed.

New Year's Eve was a much quieter affair. We had just Millie, Jerry and mum with Tania, Simon and me to bring in the New Year together. We had a nice sit down evening meal at about seven o'clock and then sat in the lounge with our drinks chatting pleasantly. Later about ten thirty Tania put out some snacks which she called nibbles and a bottle of fizzy wine to bring in the New Year. The youngsters were out with their friends' to bring in the New Year in their own style. Katy and Robin were staying in just like us and had done so for years. They said that after watching the fireworks at midnight they tended to doze and eventually wander up to bed; which is exactly what we also planned to do.

During the course of the evening Millie and mum dozed off while Jerry, Tania, Simon and I chatted. I don't think anyone had any nibbles apart from me picking at the peanuts. A bowl of peanuts seems to send out a telepathic message saying 'please eat me.' Although I say 'no more' to myself I find that a few minutes later I'm automatically reaching out for more.

Of course all were wide awake when Big Ben sounded out at midnight and the countdown on BBC1 began. No one wanted to miss the fireworks display from the London Eye. The fireworks lasted longer than usual and well over the usual fifteen minutes. I reckon it was nearer to twenty minutes this year and quite spectacular. 2052 came in on a clear night and a cold one. We kept the old tradition of exiting from the back door and coming in via the front door carrying a piece of coal and a silver coin. These Tania had placed in a convenient spot by the front door. The tradition was supposed to bring good luck and prosperity to the house over the coming year. It being a very chilly night only Tania, Simon and I did the honours of going out and then coming in again.

During the fireworks we formed a circle of crossed arms and sang Auld Lang Syne repeating the first verse twice. After the fireworks ended Millie and Jerry left for their own home.

'Nothing like your own bed,' said Jerry and I agreed with that.

And it wasn't long before mum too said good night and went up to her room.

Tania, Simon and I sat and chatted till well after one when we too decided on our beds.

Simon had mentioned the Silverstreak plans sometime earlier. He would return to Anztarza on January 2nd and then the entire crew were to report for duty by the seventh. The plan was for Tania and me to be picked up from Aberporth on the evening of Sunday 14th January for the direct trip to Silverstreak. Captain Wastanomi planned on beginning the long journey towards Zarama about a day or so after we had settled in.

My initial suggestion that Tania and I spend a last week in Anztarza with Simon and Mazpazam had been altered because of Simon's extended stay with us for the New Year celebrations. Not enough time remained before Silverstreak's crew had to report for duty. Tania consoled herself with the thought that we would be spending over five months with Simon and Mazpazam in close proximity aboard the starship while journeying to Zarama. I had estimated around 160 days for the journey which I conveyed to Tania.

'And don't forget we shall have the same time again for the return journey,' said Tania.

I hesitated fractionally before I replied.

'Yes of course,' I said.

Tania looked at me suspiciously as if she had sensed something in my manner.

Something in my gut feeling told me not to bank on it. Leaving Earth this time might be my final farewell.

CHAPTER 25

Journey towards Zarama

Early 2052

The journey on 520-Green commanded by Captain Bulzezatna from Earth to the Silverstreak rendezvous position went like clockwork. The pickup at Aberporth on the Sunday evening of January 14th 2052 was on time and 22 hours later 520-Green arrived at its initial parking loop location 9,000 miles from the starship Silverstreak and at a lateral position.

As before Ashley and Tania were summoned up to the control room for their first sighting of Silverstreak which was a star-like speck in the distance. Captain Bulzezatna said she always got an inward thrill of pride at the sight of this magnificent starship; a truly phenomenal spaceship not only in its sleek length but also in its simplistic beauty. It reflected the nature of the Oannes people as an advanced and widely achieved civilization. And it made Captain Bulzezatna proud of her place within that frame.

Ashley had to agree with her as he brought Silverstreak into magnified focus and scanned its length from shield to tail. And to think he and Tania had travelled up through that bank of generators and impulse motors with Simon and Mazpazam. When he conveyed this to the captain she seemed amazed that he and Tania had been permitted such an access.

'But then you are Ashley and Captain Wastanomi must have been pleased to allow you such a privilege,' said Bulzezatna smiling, 'I know I would have.'

After having made contact with Silverstreak, Captain Bulzezatna manoeuvred 520-Green closer to the starship. The new parking loop was at a symmetrically central position 100 miles astern of it and perpendicular to the starship's axis. The loop itself was just 100 miles in travel distance.

It was late on the evening of Monday 15th January and so the transfers to the starship were not scheduled until the following morning. Having only just arrived at the rendezvous location Captain Bulzezatna thought a restful night period and a good morning breakfast aboard 520-Green would give her guests a fresh start for their next journey; a journey of immense importance to all.

Ashley and Tania then left the control room and retired to their cabin. They had already partaken of the evening meal just prior to arriving at the Silverstreak rendezvous. However they were disappointed that no messages had been received from Simon or Mazpazam but they knew that this did not mean that they were being ignored. Far from it as Ashley was to learn later. Official spaceship protocol had to be strictly observed at all times unless their captains allowed different.

Next morning after a leisurely breakfast the transfer schedule was announced. Three shuttles at a time would make the short journey from 520-Green to Silverstreak.

Captain Bulzezatna came personally to the dining hall to see Ashley and Tania and to bid them farewell. She knew what the ultimate journey entailed and it was thinly veiled in the message she spoke.

'May your onward journey to Zarama be swift, safe and sure my friends,' she said with emotion in her tone, 'and may you return to us again soon. And please convey my best good wishes to your son Simon and his wife Mazpazam. I am proud of that young man as I am of you Ashley.'

As per standard practice all transferees had to put on the loose fitting gold electrostatic suits prior to boarding the shuttles. As usual this was accomplished in the large hall adjacent to the shuttle bay area. When all shuttles were boarded and sealed shut they had to wait till 520-Green was at one end of its parking loop when the spaceship was practically stationary.

The three shuttles then left in line-astern formation with Ashley and Tania in the lead shuttle. It took about forty minutes for the shuttles to get abreast of the stern of Silverstreak and from there they proceeded at a slower pace up towards its forward section. The shuttles kept to a distance of a few hundred yards from the side of the starship.

Gradually a slight gravity began to be felt from the forward shield of Silverstreak and the shuttle commander rotated the shuttle so that the gravity effect came up through its floor. Looking upwards Ashley got a good view of the tail-end of the starship and its gigantic length. It seemed to grow into the distance. The word awesome came into his mind.

The shuttle began to slow its downward motion until it became stationary in front of the brightly lit cavern of the starship's airlock chamber. Ashley's shuttle proceeded slowly forward into the airlock for it to then gently settle on the deck floor within. The two other shuttles were not far behind as they too settled down progressively onto the deck to one side. The lighting then dimmed as the outer airlock doors closed to firmly shut out the darkness of outer space. After several minutes the airlock brightened again indicating that normal atmospheric air pressure had been restored within.

Shuttle doors were opened and passengers near the rear disembarked first. When all passengers were out a starship crew member led them onto the cargo platform and thence to a large hall at one side against the starship inner wall. Here everyone divested themselves of the bulky electrostatic suits and handed them to the waiting Oannes attendants. No doubt thought Ashley to be returned via the same shuttles to Bulzezatna's spaceship 520-Green.

They were all then led into a large elevator about twenty feet square which descended down one level to the habitation platform. As the doors opened the smiling faces of Simon and Mazpazam were there to greet them. Tania felt a thrill to see her son and daughter-in-law in their natural surroundings. Greetings were profuse though correct because protocol so demanded this in open company; but Mazpazam did plant a kiss on Ashley's cheek. Simon gave his mum a special hug and a cheek kiss and conveyed that a special surprise awaited them in the captain's quarters.

While the other passengers dispersed to their assigned accommodation destinations Ashley and Tania were led by Simon and Mazpazam to the central pillar area. There Ashley recognised the stocky figure of Captain Wastanomi. He had a welcoming smile on his usually grim face for he had an affectionate spot in his being for his special guests Ashley and Tania.

Captain Wastanomi strode two steps forward when they came close and stretched both his hands out towards them; one to Ashley and the other to Tania. It wasn't quite a handshake but was a much more meaningful one that expressed the familiarity of friendship. A brief goodwill Sewa was exchanged as they met. Ashley responded in kind.

'Welcome my friends,' Wastanomi then said, 'it is good to see you again. You both look well and I am pleased for you. But come inside my quarters for there is another friend who wishes to greet you also.'

Wastanomi gave a nod to Simon and Mazpazam and conveyed an instruction. They both stood back as Ashley and Tania followed the captain into his suite of rooms. This was to be a strictly private meeting and Simon and Mazpazam as crew members had been instructed to wait outside.

As Ashley entered the large main room where the captain held his official meetings he saw a face that he would never have expected there in a thousand years. For sitting calmly there with a broad smile on his face was Korizazit a fellow Nazmos governing council member.

Ashley smiled in return and looked around half expecting to see Muznant and Brazjaf. Korizazit read his thought and conveyed that they could not leave their daughter Farzant alone for too long. She was at that crucial developmental stage of adulthood at the age of thirty-five years and the journey to Zarama was into uncharted territory against a foe containing too many unknown factors.

Korizazit then stood up and held out his hand in greeting. Again a mutual Sewa was exchanged.

'Greetings my friends,' he said in his husky voice, 'it is good that we meet again.'

'And you too,' said Ashley, 'this is an unexpected surprise indeed. And a very pleasant one if I may add. But what brought you on this trip.'

'Well at my age of 325 years I felt that I should like to add at least one great episode to my rather easy life before restrictions prevented me from starship travel,' he conveyed. 'And Zarama will be that ultimate event entering into an adventure category as you humans put it.'

'But we had no inkling that you were aboard Silverstreak,' said Ashley.

'It was the Nazmos governing council's decision that this trip undertaken by me was of a private nature and that absolutely no contact be made with the Anztarza administration. In fact they deemed it fitting that Anztarza must not be informed of my presence here. Which is why it has appeared so,' he concluded.

'I see,' said Ashley, 'but I still don't understand what made you really decide to come in the first place?'

'You are very discerning Ashley,' said Korizazit looking hesitant. 'Yes, I had another purpose for wanting to be with you.'

'Please go on,' said Ashley expectantly.

'I think Gozmanot has entered into my head,' said Korizazit looking extremely foolish. 'I know it sounds hard to believe but I have seen parts of her visions when I am asleep. This has recurred many times over the past year and when I mentioned it to the governing council they did not know what to make of it. They could only suggest that I present the situation to you which is one of the reasons that I am here.'

Ashley was quiet in deep thought for a moment and then asked.

'As a part of these visions have you by chance also seen a golden globe-like object the size of a football moving near to the ground and sucking up all the plant-life that it passes over?'

'Yes,' he exclaimed, 'but how did you know this?'

'Because when I was a young boy I too had a dream of a glowing golden ball moving low to the ground and sucking up everything in its path and I sensed the menace of it,' said Ashley. 'And this was before ever I had met Muznant and Brazjaf or even knew of Nazmos let alone Zarama.'

'But there is more to my dream,' said Korizazit, 'for I felt happiness at the end of it.'

Ashley waited in silence as did Tania and Wastanomi.

'Out of the corner of my dream vision I saw a hand, a human hand, with a finger pointing at the golden ball and I knew that a command was being given to it,' said Korizazit. 'I then saw the ball move as if it was being pushed violently aside. It moved further and further away and then vanished into the distance. I was pleased to see it gone and then my dream ended,'

'So your dream ended on a happy note,' smiled Ashley. 'I pray that it relates to Zarama and foretells of the outcome of my efforts against it. I did not know how my own dream ended but you have shown me how it could end.'

'Do you think that Gozmanot has shown me this as a message for you?' asked Korizazit.

'Possibly,' said Ashley, 'though she had already seen the fiery dragon in the sky defeated by a man from another world. And she recognised me when I regressed into her time-period.'

Captain Wastanomi intervened at this point with great deference towards Korizazit.

'Esteemed council member,' he said aloud, 'as a detached spectator to this conversation I can come to only one conclusion. And that is that Ashley here will do to Zarama what was done to the golden ball in your dreams. For Gozmanot's visions to come true then so must your dream. It is an omen that foretells the future. But first let us drink a glass of Wazu with our new guests as is our welcoming custom.'

Glasses were filled, raised and sips taken.

Then as if in a trance Korizazit recited the spaceman's motto.

'So may our journey to Zarama be swift, safe and sure. And may we be rid of the menace of it forever.'

'Hear, hear to that,' said Tania in an undertone whisper. But she was only partly relieved by Korizazit's dream. There was still an uncertainty of the outcome especially for Ashley. Korizazit's private message to Ashley just before they had left Nazmos way back in 2046 had always remained at the back of her mind.

'*You will however return to Nazmos one day but not as you are now,*' he had said.

Therein lay the puzzle for her. What was to happen to him that he would be altered somehow? She could only think of injury and or deformity from his battle with Zarama. All she wanted was for her beloved Ashley to be at home with her in Dudley.

Captain Wastanomi then conveyed the information that the Nazmos governing council had seen fit to issue instructions early on for the zero-gravity ships aboard Silverstreak to be upgraded with shielding to lock out the radiation that emanated from white dwarf stars such as Zarama. This had been facilitated by ferrying them to Nazmos for the work to be done before returning them to Silverstreak. It was understood that Ashley wished to get as close to Zarama as was physically possible. The intended distance had been speculated at four million miles as the closest position for Ashley to be. The heat however been proved as extreme in the case of Sirius B and Captain Wastanomi had specific instructions for alternatives since Zarama was a third more massive. Zanos on board Silverstreak had also been given action instructions for emergencies; all as a last resort only. All work on the zero-g ships had been completed well before the food growing tank refurbishment had been accomplished. It was a revelation that gave Tania just a tiny modicum of additional consolation.

The Oannes scientists had first analysed Zarama some 244 Earth years earlier. The Red Shift of the lines within its spectrum indicated its motion as being directly towards Nazmos. That motion was also indicated as being extremely large. In fact this velocity was calculated as 33,000 miles per second which was just over a sixth of light speed towards Nazmos. At that time Zarama was calculated as being 566 light years distant. As to accuracy of distance the Oannes scientists could footprint any ray of light to determine the total time from when it was originally emitted. A bit like carbon dating is done on Earth. Today in 2052 Zarama was checked out as being 476 light years distant according to its footprint. It was still travelling towards Nazmos but at an increased velocity of 33,093 miles per second. In 244 years Zarama had accelerated its velocity by 93 miles per second. Ashley had explained to the Oannes in Anztarza during his first visit there in 2003 how this was possible.

Although the light seen in 2003 had left Zarama 525 years earlier it was known that because of Zarama's velocity it was really closer to Nazmos than that. Zanos had worked out that Zarama would have traversed a distance of 93.6 light years towards Nazmos in that 525 year period that its light took to reach Nazmos. So in reality in 2003 Zarama was at an approximate invisible location of 431.8 light years from Nazmos. This had then put the star's arrival at Nazmos some 2,421 years in the future; or in the Earth year of 4424 AD

Now, a mere 49 years later, Zarama would have travelled an additional 8.7 light years closer to Nazmos; which put its real distance from Nazmos at about 423 light years.

Ashley knew that the journey distance to Zarama was without precedent because the precise location of Zarama could not be visibly ascertained; mainly due to its inherent velocity towards Nazmos. Also there was the fact that unknown factors could develop along the way.

With Simon beside him however Ashley felt that these might be predicted. And now Korizazit was to accompany them as well which was good for he too might foresee any potential dangers to the mission. His inner voice seemed to be quite active of late.

The Oannes on Nazmos had scanned the spatial path all the way to Zarama in a wide angle of observation and had analysed that there were no obvious hazards to endanger the starship enroute to its mission. Zarama remained on its same course though images were 476 years in the past. Space is vast and most stars tend to exist in predictable isolation with little unexpected movement. If however there was anything nearby then the Oannes scientists would have observed it. No, the path to Zarama was clear as far as could be determined.

Korizazit had also received another inner voice message that the return journey back to Nazmos would be very different from the outbound one. He did not understand what this meant and therefore did not mention it to anyone, not even to Ashley. In fact he put it to the back of his mind and then quite forgot about it.

At his age he found that he did tend to forget things that were said to him rather more often than he would have liked. He had thought about resigning from the Nazmos governing council but had not got around to discussing it with any of the other members. He decided that he would definitely initiate his resignation upon return to Nazmos. The discussion then moved on to consider the journey time to Zarama.

Captain Wastanomi conveyed the journey plan as had been discussed and approved by the Nazmos governing council. The safety of the starship was of paramount importance and so the journey to Zarama would be carried out in two stages. As a safety margin Captain Wastanomi planned to rendezvous at a position two light years short of Zarama's estimated position. This would therefore entail a first stage journey of 421 light years. At an average velocity of 1200 FTL and taking account of average acceleration and deceleration periods this should take just over 130 Earth days.

Zanos would then accurately fix onto Zarama's course and proceed to a rendezvous at a transverse position ten million miles from Zarama on a course parallel to it and at the same velocity. This second stage of the journey would be entirely under Silverstreak's own impulse power and would take approximately another eight days. Then in stages Silverstreak would progress ever closer to a position that was safe in terms of radiation emissions and the intense heat from the Dwarf star. Ashley could then execute his push effort upon Zarama from there. The direction of that push would be transverse to the direction of travel and directly away from the centre of the galaxy to deflect Zarama towards Rasalgethi.

Captain Wastanomi joined in here again to state that the routines would be no different from those currently in place for the journeys between Nazmos and Earth in the older 10 FTL starships which took approximately seven and a half months each way. The journey to Zarama in Silverstreak would be about two months shorter.

The captain stated that during the journey he would like daily meetings in his quarters preferably about an hour before the midday meal. He would also have some of his officers in attendance on occasion for a varied routine. Otherwise all were free to roam the entire Habitation Platform to meet other travellers. There were few passengers aboard as most were Oannes scientists and analysts of one kind or another. Yet all were interested in Zarama. The total number aboard was slightly less than a thousand persons including starship crew; this was half of the usual maximum.

'We received your request Ashley so plenty of book-style reading material has been placed within your apartment,' said Wastanomi. 'There are also thousands of hours of monitor viewing available on request from Zanos. Four and a half months aboard Silverstreak is a long duration for you but not unusual for us. Then there is the return journey to also contend with.'

Over the five years of leisure living in Dudley while Silverstreak was having its food-growing tanks refurbished Ashley had conveyed many requests for his and Tania's entertainment while on the journeys to and from Zarama. These had all been acceded to with the diligence and care for detail that the Oannes were so renowned for. As such there was more than enough reading, viewing and music entertainment to keep a 'human' entertained for years. A thought flashed through Ashley's mind that such might be the case for one of them at least. It was a puzzling thought that seemed to have the phrase 'what if' attached to it. At the moment it signified little so he made no mention of it to Tania or for that matter to Simon or anyone else. Later it would prove to be of great significance.

For the Oannes people on the trip it would be no great hardship in time since the routine journeys to Earth took longer. Yet they too had their own style of entertainment for such periods.

'And of course,' added Captain Wastanomi, 'you will have the company of your son Simon and his partner Mazpazam. They will look after your every need and be with you as a family as often as you would wish. Simon's mind is open to Zanos so if anything of note is received by him on the premonition front then I will be informed of it. This starship's safety is of paramount importance.

'Thank you Captain,' said Ashley with a respectful bow of his head, 'that is very kind and most considerate. Tania and I have looked forward to spending this time aboard with Simon and Mazpazam. But we shall not take them away from their official duties as it is important that they remain integral to the starship's functioning and that their fellow officers see them as such.'

Captain Wastanomi stood up and bowed slightly to Ashley.

'You are wise to make such a fine distinction,' he said, 'it will be just as you have said.'

He then conveyed that the journey to Zarama was to commence the next morning at 6:00am starship simulated time. Everything was in place and it would be pointless to delay proceedings unnecessarily. The journey would initially be entirely under the starship's own impulse power and the approach to 100FTL velocity should be achieved over a six hour period.

'I would be obliged if you Ashley could come here to my quarters sometime before noon to apply your particular telekinetic effort just as you did to accelerate the starship at the last trial five years ago. 1200FTL would be a good journey velocity to see us approach within two light years of Zarama in 130 days time. Zarama is nearly in a direct line the other side of Nazmos so Zanos will set a course accordingly to avoid Raznat. The angle of deviation is minor and Zanos will make the necessary adjustment in the following 130 day period.'

Ashley replied in the affirmative and added that he too would keep his mind open to Zanos at all times.

'Thank you,' said the captain and then walked to the door and led the way out towards the deck.

'I will let your son show you to your allotted accommodation,' said Captain Wastanomi. 'It is the same as before and always will be. I shall personally see to council member Korizazit after we have discussed further matters. His apartment is adjacent to your own as I thought it best for two esteemed Nazmos governing council members be in close proximity to one another.'

A smiling Korizazit remained seated as Ashley and Tania followed the captain and were politely handed over to the patiently waiting Simon and Mazpazam.

Once inside their apartment Tania looked around with approval. There had been some additions to the furniture in the living area. A large monitor screen partially covered one wall and facing it were a set of reclining armchair settees. They looked extremely comfortable with their soft fabric puffed up appearance. There were also other armchairs positioned to one side with side tables placed beside them. But what caught Ashley's eye was the wall to wall shelving at one side and it was filled with books of the sort Ashley liked. He could see that these had all been imported from Earth bookshops and among them were the condensed book volumes that Ashley was particularly fond of. He went up to the shelving and read through some of the book titles and gave his nod of approval. Yes he thought I shall certainly go through a few of these.

Below the monitor screen was a mantel feature with an ornamental surround enclosing an imitation fireplace. It gave the room a very homely appearance especially as it emitted a faint reddish glow.

'This is very cosy,' said Tania with delight, 'I just love it.'

Ashley noticed that the walls were all covered in a pale pink wall paper with faded roses on single stems interspersed at regular intervals as the main pattern. It looked warm and homely.

'Simon chose the décor in here especially for you aunt Tania,' said Mazpazam, 'and I agreed with all his choices.'

'I thought of having panel scenes in hologram form showing Earth scenes like Rachel and Margaret have around their pool room but we both thought it would be extreme and not to your taste,' said Simon. 'I thought this would remind you of Dudley more than anything else.'

'It certainly does,' said Ashley. 'All I shall need is a pipe and my slippers.'

Mazpazam looked quickly at Simon with a horrified expression. She hadn't realised that Ashley smoked.

'He doesn't,' conveyed Simon privately, 'it just a sort of joking expression that everything is perfect.'

Mazpazam kept the relief to herself. She had never understood what humans found in the inhalation of tobacco smoke.

They then progressed into the bedroom with its adjoining sleep-tank. And here too it had all been done in pale colours. Except this was a pale apple green and left quite plain but with a raised embossed design of oak leaves evenly dispersed. Ashley remarked that he liked it very much.

Tania sat on the bed which was a king-size similar to the one in their Dudley bedroom.

'This is nice,' she said as she bounced on it to feel the firmness of the foam mattress, 'it seems just about right.' She blushed as she realised what she had just said as she bounced. Simon pretended to examine the sleep tank to hide his smile but Mazpazam felt puzzled. She would ask later what it was about.

'I mean that Ashley needs a firm support for his back now that he is of that age,' Tania quickly corrected.

'Can we have a little less of the age reference please my dear,' said Ashley smiling too at Tania's earlier remark. 'But yes, a comfy bed is essential to a good nights rest.'

Mazpazam listened and smiled. She hoped that she and Simon would have a similar camaraderie and fellowship as they too advanced in their marriage years.

It was now past noon on the ship's simulated time and close to the midday meal. Simon suggested that it be taken here in their apartment and that they could then go for a walkabout over the entire habitation platform area and meet up with some of the other travellers. Most would have some role to fulfil and would make interesting conversation. The Oannes did not like to keep secrets and would happily discuss their functional status within the starship.

'That would be excellent,' said Ashley. 'I shall be able to walk anywhere today as I have no telekinetic action in place. Tomorrow will be another matter of course.'

They all knew that once Ashley's telekinetic push was being exerted upon the forward shield that he must remain within a limited central zone area of the habitation platform.

For some reason when the meal was served up in the apartment Ashley said that he was not feeling particularly hungry at that time. Tania looked worried for it was most unusual for Ashley to have a loss of appetite. Something must be on his mind she thought. She conveyed her concern privately.

'I can't understand it,' conveyed Ashley back to Tania.

There was an empty feeling at the pit of his belly which he knew must be from some form of hidden anxiety. Yet he felt none of that at the moment so what was it he thought. Perhaps it was a subconscious sense of foreboding? Again nothing like that seemed prominent in his mind. Zarama was a concern but not a worry as such. There was something niggling at the back of his mind but it was just a notion. A notion built upon a feeling that food would be a non-essential part of his life.

However as the meal progressed and Ashley tried a nibble here and there at the Starztal and mashed Raizna his appetite seemed to revive and the food notion faded. It was the spicy Milsony however that finally brought his taste buds to life and the full return of his appetite. Tania smiled as she saw him help himself to a large portion of his favourite dish; the much sweetened Yaztraka. He was back into his usual eating form.

After Simon and Mazpazam had left she asked Ashley again about his sudden loss of appetite.

'Are you okay darling,' she said. 'I was a bit concerned back there when you said you didn't feel like eating.'

'I know,' he replied slowly. 'For a minute I felt that food was quite an unnecessary item. I don't know why but the silly notion seemed to enter my head. Then when I got to eat a bit, the taste felt good and suddenly I was hungry again. I'm glad that initial feeling passed quickly.'

'So am I,' said Tania wistfully with deeply worrying thoughts about their future.

Ashley having read her mood and thoughts stood up and pulled her up with him.

'Come on darling, lets have a frolic in the sleep tank before bed,' he said half laughing, 'you never know I might even feel invigorated for some fun and games.'

Tania knew exactly what he meant but those moments were few and far between these days.

But she hoped for the best, always.

'Yes lets,' she said as she came close to him and wrapped her arms around his waist and raised her mouth to his.

It was a nice soft loving kiss full of the pureness of the love that existed between them. A love that coursed through her body to envelop her being in the warmth of an emotion that was impossible to describe. She had loved him from the first moment she'd set eyes on him not knowing then of the powers that lay dormant within him. She loved him even more as the days and years passed because he remained so unassuming about himself. He never displayed any emotion to advertise his gifts and capabilities. And because of this trait he was loved instantly by all who met and came to know him. In turn this filled her with such immense all consuming pride that at times she felt that her tiny heart could not retain it all and must surely burst.

Tania looked upon her husband as an unassuming gentle character who saw nothing in himself other than to love his family and to fulfil his destiny; a destiny that would save worlds.

Tania felt a stirring in the core of her being that awakened passions partially forgotten. So in the sleep tank she did things to Ashley only a wife would dare. Afterwards they lay together in their large bed arms wrapped tightly around each other with Ashley the first to fall asleep. His face was wet from the tears that flowed from Tania's eyes.

'O God, please let Ashley be alright,' she prayed over and over again till she too fell into a tired sleep still locked in his embrace.

Next morning Ashley awoke feeling rested and full of renewed energy. Today was to be the start of the journey towards his destiny. In fact Zanos informed him that Silverstreak was already on its way and had been accelerating under its own impulse power since 6:00am starship simulated time. It was strange that the Oannes in Anztarza had opted to adhere to GMT as their set time. Of course any time zone would have sufficed but the Earth's zero meridian time had been adopted as a logical option. Zanos informed him that Silverstreak was already at several times light speed and Ashley felt keen to provide his own contribution in taking the starship to its full cruise velocity of 1200FTL. Twelve hundred times light speed was the maximum design velocity permitted for Silverstreak.

Ashley suddenly remembered that he'd had a very odd dream last night but couldn't remember what it had been about. The one thing that he did remember was that it had something to do with being under water. This was an alien environment for him and try as he might he could not remember more. Of one thing he was sure and that was that it was not a dream that had upset him. In fact he'd felt a calmness about its general content. Since he couldn't put a story or theme to the dream he gave up and put it aside. As it was soon forgotten he made no mention of it to anyone.

Later Simon came on his own to have his breakfast with his mum and dad.

'Mazpazam has some ship duties to fulfil but will be here as soon as she can,' said Simon. 'But I suspect that she wants me to spend private time with you.'

'She is very discerning,' said Tania. 'A son cannot always be himself when his wife is at his shoulder.'

During their breakfast of tea, toast, marmalade, jam and cheese they talked about Simon's career prospects and also what he hoped for Mazpazam.

'We have chosen that our life will be aboard Silverstreak,' said Simon. 'We have our quarters that are not too dissimilar to this one and we find it comfortable. Both of us feel happy aboard Silverstreak with our officer status as it is. I can never become a captain of a ship like this because of my short human lifespan. One day I hope that Mazpazam will have a starship of her own to command but that will be a matter of chance selection at the time.'

'What about a house on Nazmos,' asked Tania? 'With the climate improving you could enjoy a courtyard garden like Jazzatnit's.'

Simon smiled at his mum. He knew what she was implying. She wanted for him and Mazpazam to have a home with a life around it.

'Mum, the life I have chosen is to be out in space. I could not be happy anywhere else. I'm lucky to have found Mazpazam. She fulfils my life like I could never have expected from anyone. She caters to my every need and desire and I love her more than I can describe. She too would suffocate away from this lifestyle. We are space people and that is the way I like and want it. I am happy here and always will be. Perhaps one day far in the future when I am old and tatty we might have to live on Nazmos. Something will be provided which is the way of the Oannes.'

'I understand son,' said Tania. 'I'm being an interfering old mother but I just wanted to know how you felt.'

'We are fine mum,' said Simon. 'We visit Rachel and Margaret as often as we can. Nazmos is home to me because it is where Mazpazam can also be. Earth is out of bounds to us as a couple except Anztarza of course.'

Tania reached across the table and squeezed Simon's hand. Ashley had been listening to the conversation and quite agreed with everything Simon had said so eloquently. While Simon had been talking Ashley had been nodding his head in agreement.

The topic changed to other things and it was not long after they had finished breakfast that Mazpazam announced her arrival and came in to join them.

She looked keenly at Simon and then from Tania to Ashley. She knew that by holding back Simon had been able to say things to his parents in an open manner. She could see that there were no embarrassment issues hanging loose so their talk had to have been a pleasant one she thought.

'We talked about you Mazpazam,' said Tania, 'and I think that Simon and you are good for each other. It makes me happy to see you both as you are. Ashley and I wish you a good life in all that you do and we hope you fulfil all your desires. You have made Simon happy and we see you as a wonderful couple and can see that you are meant for each other. May your love grow and keep you happy together.'

'Thank you Aunt Tania and Uncle Ashley, it is very nice of you to say it,' said Mazpazam.' But I think I am the fortunate one to have the love of your son. I could never be happy with anyone else.'

Mazpazam glowed radiantly as she said this and emotion filled her words.

And it was nice for Tania especially to see Simon move around beside his wife and put an arm around her shoulders. She in turn rested her head sideways against him while smiling at Ashley and Tania. And that was the view that Tania would carry with her forever; the sight of her son and daughter in law in an affectionate pose.

'Well it is coming close to 11:30am so Tania and I had better think about making our way to the captain's quarters,' said Ashley as a general announcement.

'Silverstreak is now at 76 FTL,' said Simon having just consulted with Zanos. Then he added, 'Just in case you wanted to know dad.'

'Thank you son,' said Ashley. 'I think I might surprise the captain with something that has just come into my head.'

They all looked at Ashley in a puzzled manner but waited for him to clarify.

'I don't see why I have to wait to be in the captain's quarters to begin my telekinetic acceleration of the starship towards its full cruising velocity,' said Ashley. 'I can do it from here. After all the push effort during the journey will be done mostly from this apartment.'

Ashley communicated his intentions with Zanos before beginning his action. He then looked down at the floor between his knees and after a brief moment looked up again smiling.

'It is done,' he said in a factual manner.

Ashley had willed for his telekinetic gift to push upon the forward shield of the starship to uniformly accelerate Silverstreak to its cruise velocity of 1200 FTL over a period of 24 hours. Again this prolonged period of acceleration had come into his head with the earlier thought. Zanos conveyed what Ashley had done not only to the captain but also to the entire starships personnel.

Since this was not a trial but the start of the 130 days first stage journey to Zarama, Ashley felt that an easier acceleration would be less stressful not only for the starship but also on his own person.

Simon smiled his approval. But inwardly he was pleased that his dad had taken charge of his actions without first being told to do so by Captain Wastanomi.

When Ashley and Tania arrived at the captain's quarters they were greeted formally by a serious faced captain but a very smiling Korizazit. There were none of the ship's other officers present.

'You have pre-empted my orders for the acceleration of my starship,' said Wastanomi. 'I had desired that you did so while you were here in my quarters. You have also extended the acceleration period to 24 hours from the original planned 12 hours as per the trial.'

'Forgive me Captain,' said Ashley while still standing, 'but I had not pre-planned for this. The plan was put into my mind just before I came to your quarters. It may have been that inner voice of mine but I cannot be certain. It was simply a matter of a thought from me willing the acceleration to occur which only took a second in time. It was done in the privacy of my apartment which I found preferable to a public display. After all the push effort during the journey will be done mostly from within my apartment. Your starship will attain its cruising velocity of 1200FTL over a period of 24 hours and I communicated my full intentions to Zanos. The acceleration will be less fatiguing on me.'

Captain Wastanomi was annoyed that he had not been informed prior to Ashley's action in addition to the fact that it had been done outside of his chain of command. This was something new to him and he did not like it.

'Thank you Ashley,' he said, 'but as captain of this starship you must let me know of any action you intend to take before you do it. Everything that is done on this ship is my responsibility and mine alone. I hope that is understood.'

'I understand Captain,' said Ashley in a serious tone and a bit louder than he intended. 'However in this case you had already asked me to take the action I did. It is just that you wanted me to do it here in your presence for your personal gratification. Or should I say a performance for your edification?'

Ashley then stepped back beside Tania and put an arm across her shoulders. He then raised his head higher and looked directly at Wastanomi.

'Captain I am not some circus act to perform in front of an audience. You wanted something done and I did it more or less precisely as required. However I did it in the privacy of my apartment because that is where I like to be. I did follow protocol and Zanos was kept fully informed of my actions. The task I go to fulfil is my responsibility and mine alone. Yours is to get me as close to Zarama as possible and with my assistance. We are a team captain with the same goal and I pray that we function as such.'

Korizazit conveyed a private message to Captain Wastanomi which was to remind the captain that Ashley was a Nazmos governing council member and that to exercise caution in his attitude.

The captain knew immediately that he had overstepped his authority in regard to Ashley. But he also recognised the strength in Ashley's character just as Ritozanan had found to her dismay at her first confrontation with Ashley. But it had drawn her to respect this man from Earth and a similar feeling went through to Captain Wastanomi. A new respect for this human came into his conscious mingled with a wariness that he should step carefully in his dealings with Ashley. Here was a man not to be taken lightly even by a starship captain.

'I am sorry Ashley,' said Wastanomi, 'please forgive a captain who forgot himself for a moment. You and Korizazit are both honourable Nazmos governing council members and I shall give you the respect that is your due. We shall function as the team that defeated Zarama.'

Along with his newfound respect for Ashley came a realisation of the privilege that would be his in having Ashley as an ally. He would go down in history as the starship captain who ferried Ashley to his victory over Zarama. A pride of association filled his mind. It said much about the captain that he could also weigh up the benefits to his reputation that this mission would bring for him. He realised suddenly that he had much to learn about the character of this human. He would also learn much about his own make-up, both the positive and negative facets, when comparing himself to that of Ashley's character.

Before leaving Nazmos, Captain Wastanomi had been summoned to a special meeting with the Nazmos governing council. Specific instructions had been conveyed regarding the mission to Zarama. He was to do exactly all that Ashley required but without endangering his starship or to delay the return journey to Nazmos once Zarama had been dealt with.

Later when all this was over Wastanomi would analyse his feelings for his fellow Oannes and he would try to make adjustments in his behaviour towards them. He would then not only become a more content captain but a likeable Oannes person as well.

Now Captain Wastanomi softened his attitude as he looked around him.

'Let us meet again here tomorrow at the noon hour,' he said. 'The starship will by then be at its cruise velocity and I shall ask my officers to attend as well. It will be a short meeting and we can discuss any other issues that you might like to raise.'

Ashley assumed correctly that Simon and Mazpazam would be among the officers listed to attend.

'I expect that councillor Korizazit will also be attending,' said Ashley.

'Of course,' said the captain, 'that is clearly understood. Councillor Korizazit is welcome to attend all our meetings.'

This meeting was over as signalled by the captain rising and offering his hand to Ashley and then bowing to Korizazit and Tania.

Korizazit smiled at Ashley and asked if he could accompany him out since he had some matters to discuss. So Tania, Ashley and Korizazit left the room and were joined outside by a waiting Simon and Mazpazam. Simon informed them that Silverstreak was now at 122 FTL velocity and accelerating.

Ashley looked at Korizazit with an enquiring expression on his face. He wondered what it was that needed to be discussed and conveyed his query.

'Ah,' said Korizazit, 'I found it rather formal in there so it was my way of coming out with you without offending the captain. He is not a conversationalist on social matters and time does drag very slowly in his presence. But have no doubt that he is an excellent starship captain and perfectly suited to Silverstreak. It is just that he does take his role very seriously. But enough said about Captain Wastanomi for now. The midday meal is close and I would be honoured if the four of you could see fit to partake of it with me as my guests in my quarters. I have arranged it as a special occasion for the start of our journey to Zarama.'

'Thank you,' said Tania, 'this is most gracious of you and we gladly accept.'

'Then since it is just past the noon hour perhaps we could go straight to my apartments right now, unless of course you would wish to freshen up first.'

'Yes,' said Tania, 'I think I would prefer that. We could come to you in half an hour if that is alright.'

'That would be excellent,' said Korizazit. 'All will be ready when you enter. I shall leave the door unlocked so please just walk in and choose your seat at the table. I myself will be seated and waiting.'

'Thank you,' said Tania.

Simon and Mazpazam conveyed that they too would freshen up in their own apartment and return for the meal.

Since Ashley's apartment was adjacent to Korizazit's they all parted company outside the entrance doors. Simon and Mazpazam went in an opposite direction and towards their own apartment.

Ashley sat on his bed and thought about all that had occurred so far.

Although it was he who was pushing the starship onward, he was held by an inner conviction that somehow he was also heading towards his fate from which there was to be no alternative or escape. His mind was resigned to it such that he felt no fear or sadness. Rather he had an overwhelming sense of anticipation that something extraordinary and wonderful might be about to happen.

Until recently a seed of foreboding and unease had been fermenting inside his every thought just as it had also been doing in Tania's mind. But now for him that was replaced by this feeling of elation of things to come. It was as if some joyful event was to be unveiled though he did not know what that might be. This had the result of building within Ashley a new inner strength and confidence.

When he conveyed all this to Tania she immediately felt a boost to her own mental awareness and was uplifted by Ashley's revelations. And so for the first time in a very long time she felt confident for their future.

'Oh Ashley,' she exclaimed with happiness in her voice. 'It is going to be alright for us after all isn't it?'

'Yes my darling,' he replied, 'I think and hope so.'

She sat beside him and they hugged each other. Then they kissed each other lightly on their lips. She drew her face back from his and stared unblinking into his eyes.

'Later,' she whispered and then quickly stood up. 'We must get ready for dinner.'

The meal with Korizazit was a happy one with Tania the focus of the pleasant atmosphere. Simon and Mazpazam sensed her mood and joined in to supplement it with their own sense of emotional belonging.

Korizazit was pleased that his meal was being enjoyed so much that he suggested they repeat the occasion more often during this journey.

'Perhaps we could do this about once every week over the coming months,' he said. 'I confess that I have an ulterior motive in asking this. It is a long journey and you are very pleasant company.'

'Thank you that would be nice,' said Tania. 'And may I suggest that we could also do this in our apartment sometimes.'

'Yes of course,' said Korizazit. 'Except of course I believe that Captain Wastanomi intends to invite us for a meal in his quarters on occasion.'

'I'm afraid that Mazpazam and I could not dine with the captain as we have with you today honourable councillor,' said Simon. 'If we are indeed invited then so must several of the other officers. It is a matter of protocol and that would make it a more formal occasion.'

Mazpazam conveyed her agreement to this statement and Korizazit responded that of course he understood.

It was much later when they all left to return to their own apartments after having thanked Korizazit profusely.

That night Tania slept peacefully with Ashley's arms snugly around her and this time there were no tears to spill onto Ashley cheeks.

'I feel like I want to wrap my arms around you and stay like this forever, among other things,' was just one of her thoughts before sleep enveloped her.

Next morning Ashley and Tania sat in bed talking while they drank their mugs of tea. They reckoned that for the next several months this could be the start pattern of their daily routine. It would be a waiting game. From a young age Ashley had always been an early riser because that was how his body clock functioned. His eyes would open at dawn summer or winter and he would get up and dress and move to a position in his mum and dad's front porch to look at the sky changing gradually into the various hues of the approaching day.

As age had crept up on him he had mellowed and the dawn failed to awaken him fully. In the last session in Dudley he had begun to enjoy the leisure of wallowing in bed with Tania even when fully awake. To hear her breathe beside him brought inner peace to his being. And Tania was relieved that she could at last keep her head under the covers for a bit longer without feeling that niggling guilt when she heard him busy elsewhere in the house.

And so it was now with Ashley having reached the age of seventy. After a while he got up for a leisurely wash and shave followed by a hot shower. When Tania had also showered and dressed they had a breakfast of buttered toast with jam and cheese. Tania often smiled at her husband's fad of jam with everything. Back home he would add jam to his plate when having a breakfast of fried eggs with toast. He said the taste was enhanced. The debated arguments regarding Ashley's strawberry jam preferences had ceased early on in their longstanding marriage.

'What's the difference between strawberry jam with my eggs and cranberry sauce with your turkey,' he often reasoned with success.

And about Ashley's other amazing gifts; these had never been a matter for discussion. It was all just taken as factual reality. Like the sunshine making the day bright.

It was now approaching the midday hour so Ashley queried Zanos regarding the starship's velocity status.

'Silverstreak is now speeding towards its first Zarama rendezvous at maximum cruise velocity of 1200 FTL,' was the response.

'Thank you,' said Ashley, 'and please inform the captain that Tania and I are on our way to his quarters.'

When they entered they were met by a smiling captain, councillor Korizazit and several of the ship's officers with Simon being among them.

Ashley was told that the meeting had commenced earlier in order to deal with essential starship business. Mazpazam was not present as many others were not either. The captain repeated the information that Zanos had provided earlier and thanked Ashley for making it possible.

'This is unknown territory that we enter,' said the captain, 'and we must execute our mission with careful consideration and planning.'

The captain then repeated for Ashley and Tania the two stage journey plan to Zarama.

'Captain, may I ask you to go over the second stage of our journey to Zarama,' said Ashley. 'I'm not clear about when my role commences.'

'Very well,' said the captain. 'Having ascertained the precise location of Zarama from our first rendezvous position we shall then travel the remaining two light year distance entirely under Silverstreak's own impulse power of 100 FTL capability. Silverstreak will drop to half light speed some two billion miles from Zarama. Zanos would then accurately fix onto Zarama's course and proceed to rendezvous at a transverse position ten million miles from it and on a parallel course at the same velocity. All this will take another eight days. So we are talking of a total journey time of about 140 simulated Earth days.'

The captain paused and looked around at his officers with whom he had repeatedly discussed these procedures. He then continued for Ashley's benefit.

'We already know a lot about the emissions from Zarama but from Nazmos we could not be certain about the intensity and diversity of those emissions at close range. Although White Dwarf stars have a minimal core activity Zarama may prove the exception. We cannot discount the presence of extreme gamma and x-ray emissions. These must not be allowed to affect life aboard Silverstreak. What Zanos finds will determine how close to Zarama we may approach. The starship will be positioned so that the forward shield faces towards Zarama. We shall then in planned stages attempt for a closer position as was the case in your trial attempt on Sirius B while taking account of the heat intensity on the zero-g ships. Only then can we decide on the safe distance for you to be.'

'Thank you Captain,' said Ashley, 'that is very clear and precise.'

He then had a thought which he conveyed to the captain privately. He stressed that he did not want Tania to know of his plan just yet. The captain replied that he would consult on the matter before he gave Ashley a reply. It was not in their protocol but exceptions were always possible. Especially in extreme circumstances such as was the case here.

Ashley had been considering his options regarding his approach to Zarama in the specially modified zero-gravity spaceships. What he had requested of the captain was the possibility of the command of a zero-gravity ship being under his sole control. Although Zanos-on-board would be the initiator of all operational commands Ashley wanted his mind to be linked directly to the zero-g ship's functioning for an instant response were his inner voice or senses to imply it. And if he were to become incapacitated for any reason then Zanos would automatically return the zero-g ship to Silverstreak.

There was also further discussion about the deflection of Zarama from its present course for it to be directed into Rasalgethi. The starship must be positioned with its back to the Milky Way pathway where the centre of the galaxy lay. A precise 5.4° of deflection was required in Zarama's course.

When and if it was confirmed that Zarama had been diverted as required then Silverstreak must shadow it for a month at least to verify its proper course. During that period any necessary corrections could be made. Zarama's present location put it at 142 light years from Rasalgethi meaning that it would take approximately eight hundred years to get there.

A visual image momentarily flashed through Ashley's mind just then. It was like a firework burst of bright yellow and orange which quickly faded into nothing. It was a confusing image but oddly it left Ashley with a peaceful emotion. Ashley couldn't help but smile.

Tania was the only one in the room who noticed this and immediately conveyed a 'What' query in private mode.

Ashley reached across under the table and caught her hand and transmitted the brief image privately to her. Later when they were back alone in their apartment she asked about it and what it could mean.

'I don't know exactly but could it somehow be connected to Zarama?' said Ashley.

'You mean its destruction?' asked Tania.

'The thought had crossed my mind,' said Ashley.

'Maybe it does,' said Tania, 'but Korizazit said that he saw a hand pointing at the golden ball and that it disappeared into the distance.'

'Hmmm,' came from Ashley. 'In that case I'm not sure what it could mean.'

After about a minute of thought Tania's head came up and she smiled.

'Wait a second,' she exclaimed, 'Korizazit's dream only saw it disappearing into the distance. But that doesn't mean it ends there. Perhaps the next bit is where Zarama explodes like in your flashing image.'

'Possibly,' said Ashley, 'but my image seemed quite close at hand and prominent in its blaze of colours. Korizazit's dream would indicate it could only have exploded after he lost sight of it.'

'Well then,' said Tania refusing to give up hope, 'what if you have been shown what happens to Zarama after his dream ended. It doesn't mean that it couldn't happen at all.'

Ashley smiled at his wife's interpretation and exuberance. He drew her into his arms and gave her a tight hug and kissed her neck while entwined close.

'Oh I do love you so my darling and now I just got to love you that little bit more,' he whispered. 'You are incorrigible that's what you are and I hope you are right.'

And so another day and night went by taking Silverstreak closer to its destination. Speeding through space at 1200 FTL velocity Silverstreak was by far the fastest object in the Milky Way galaxy. Its speed through space equated to 223 million miles per second. This would take it just 46 hours to traverse the 6.3 light years distance between

Nazmos and Earth. And within the solar system at this velocity Silverstreak would traverse the 3.8 billion miles form the Sun to Pluto in 170 seconds or 2.8 minutes. Such was the wonder of the Oannes spaceship technology.

At the next midday meeting there was just the captain, Korizazit, Ashley and Tania in attendance.

'I have given your request much consideration and discussed it with my senior officers,' said the captain as politely as was possible for him. 'Unfortunately your wish cannot be granted. Not because of any regulation but because Zanos would need to be programmed to accept an operational command from you. And that programming can only be done through the auspices of the Nazmos space academy. Subsequently one of my officers will have to be aboard the zero-g spaceship. Any requirement from you can be instantly communicated through him to Zanos-on-board. The time lag would be negligible.'

'Thank you Captain, I understand fully,' said Ashley. 'What you suggest is acceptable to me. However I request that the officer in question be other that either Simon or Mazpazam. I wish them out of the equation in this instance.'

'It shall be as you wish,' said Wastanomi. 'We will talk further on the matter more near the event.'

Korizazit looked at Ashley and smiled but said nothing.

That evening Ashley, Tania, Simon and Mazpazam dined together as one family. The conversational topics were varied and pleasant with Tania telling Mazpazam about their life on Earth. Included were some tales of the things Simon did as a child and Mazpazam showed a lot of interest and wanted to know more.

Afterwards when Ashley and Tania were alone Ashley selected one of the condensed books and settled down in his comfortable armchair for a read. He was asleep before he'd completed the first chapter with the book flopped open on his lap. Tania who had been watching him smiled and studied her husband with his head slanted sideways against the headrest. He still looked good with the wrinkles partly spreading across his face. The jaw was firm as were the cheek bones. His jowls had a slight sag building in them. He was seventy after all she thought. She wondered that even though he was asleep his telekinetic powers were still actively pushing the starship at full steam.

'I'm lucky that I have him,' she thought as the power of her love for him exploded little pangs of delicious orgasmic pain inside her chest. She took a deep breath and then sighed as she continued to gaze upon the face of this man of hers. A gentle person and yet so gifted with power. The wonder of it was an enigma in itself.

It was an hour and a bit before Ashley stirred awake and looking up met Tania's eyes.

'Lets to bed darling,' said Tania and Ashley nodded.

'Yes, lets,' he agreed.

The next morning and afternoon was spent in the usual routine. Their late breakfast was followed at noon by the meeting with Captain Wastanomi and Korizazit. It was a short meeting as all was going to plan and Wastanomi expressed his satisfaction. They then returned to their apartment for the afternoon snack meal at which Simon and Mazpazam joined them. Afterwards they took a stroll around the inner platform together and then parted company to return to their apartment for a relaxing read and nap. Before he left them Korizazit had invited them all to join him again for the evening meal but Simon and Mazpazam had politely declined as they had duties to attend to.

Later that evening it was just the three of them in Korizazit's apartment for the meal. It was pleasant as usual and throughout it Ashley felt that there was something on Korizazit's mind.

So after the meal as they sat conversing Ashley finally queried his friend and fellow councillor.

'Something is on your mind,' said Ashley, 'what is it?'

'I think you might have seen what I saw the other day,' he said. 'A bursting array of light as if something bright had exploded.'

'Yes,' said Ashley. 'I saw a momentary vision of a bursting firework and it seemed to be quite close to me. Is that what you saw?'

And Ashley conveyed his flashing mental image across to Korizazit's mind.

'That is exactly what came into my vision,' said Korizazit. 'What does it imply?'

Ashley smiled and reached out to take Tania's hand in his.

'This lady thinks that it is a vision foretelling the destruction of Zarama,' he said. 'But I said that it does not conform to your earlier dream.'

'Tania may be right in her interpretation,' said Korizazit. 'My dream was rather indistinct towards its end with the golden ball fading from my view. Dreams are often hazy and end abruptly and this was no different. Although it was clear at first I remember it as not so prominent towards the end part. But then it was only a dream and might have no meaning whatsoever.'

Ashley thought about it and came to the conclusion that he knew the pattern of action he would follow. These dream visions could play no part in the decision that he must make. The future was not set in stone.

An object is pulled to the ground by the pull of gravity; there could be no question of the outcome there. And as such Zarama would be pushed aside by the power given to Ashley. Ashley had a contingency plan in mind just in case his initial telekinetic effort did not work. And in his mind he was prepared to accept the resulting consequences; whatever they might be. Long ago his inner voice had advised that he must never exceed push level sixteen of his telekinetic effort when in pink mode. The implied implication had been hinted at then and a sadness emotion had prevailed within him. But for Ashley his objective was to deflect Zarama from its current path and Ashley had decided that he would exceed this level if that is what was required. It would be as a final resort and he would accept whatever consequences arose from it.

After four days of 1200 FTL travel Silverstreak sped past the Raznat –Nazmos system but at the safe distance of one and a half a light years from it. No information could be conveyed as the velocity distortion was deemed too great. The next 126 simulated days to the first rendezvous location would soon elapse and the Oannes personnel aboard had quickly settled into their normal Earth to Nazmos shuttle routine. As Captain Wastanomi had stated earlier that for them this was not an exceptionally long voyage. In fact it was a bit shorter than their usual interplanetary run.

However this was Ashley and Tania's first such trip and the Oannes had provided well to keep them entertained throughout the journey. Ashley planned to catch up on a lot of reading while Tania found a limitless catalogue of Earth features and films for the monitor screens that would hold her interest. Besides she just loved being with her husband even if it was just them sitting and dozing together. Talk was unnecessary; being in each others company was satisfaction enough. Tania remembered the times on a long car journey with Ashley driving; the quietness of their togetherness was pleasant and fulfilling. And so it was here in their apartment on Silverstreak.

Chapter 26

Towards Journey's end

May 2052

Silverstreak was now stationary in space at the planned first rendezvous location nearly two light years short of Zarama's position. All had gone exactly as planned and Captain Wastanomi was pleased with their progress so far. For some reason I liked to equate my days in space with actual days elapsing on Earth. I had requested Zanos to do this for me and as Silverstreak also adhered to a 24 hour period for the simulation of its days it was not difficult to count the days as they elapsed. Tania had a diary with her and she had continually informed me of the month and day we were at. We had arrived at this rendezvous sometime during our simulated night period and this morning Tania proudly announced that according to her diary log today was the morning of Monday 27th May 2052. And Zanos confirmed this to be correct. So it was full marks to Tania.

At a previous noon meeting several days ago Captain Wastanomi had raised the issue of the soon to be initiated deceleration of Silverstreak. Zanos would convey the exact time when the slowing down process was to commence and the captain said that I could initiate my action from the comfort of my apartment if I so wished.

'Thank you Captain,' I had said, 'but if it pleases you I should like to do it in your presence and here in your quarters. If I could be given advance notice of the exact moment for the commencement of the deceleration process then I could make my way here just prior to it.'

The captain seemed pleased by this and smiled his agreement and then conveyed to me that Zanos had already set the moment in time for the deceleration to commence. And this was to be in two days time at approximately the noon hour. The first rendezvous selected was not a precise location in space but rather a safe convenient distance short of Zarama's estimated position. The deceleration timing was not critical but then Zanos always worked towards an exact formula. Thus my initiation of the deceleration had all taken place as planned but with a slight difference.

On that occasion Captain Wastanomi had all his senior officers around the meeting table in his quarters when Tania and I arrived there. Simon and Mazpazam who had accompanied us had a prior invitation from the captain to also attend this session. We exchanged our greetings and took our places as indicated. There was a pleasant welcoming atmosphere in the room with smiles all around.

The captain who was seated at a far end had stood up when we entered.

'Welcome Ashley and Tania,' he had said in his low authoritarian voice, 'I have asked my officers here to witness for themselves the force that you carry within you. Please feel free to commence the deceleration process when it is convenient.'

'Thank you Captain,' I had replied. 'For the benefit of your officers I can state that it is no great thing that I do. I will simply will my mind to carry out the process and the action is taken. What happens afterwards becomes an involuntary process and I need consciously do nothing further. So here goes.'

Looking straight ahead I closed my eyes for a second and willed for my mind to decelerate the starship down to 100 FTL in 24 hours commencing from this moment. I kept my mind open so Zanos could correlate all actions accordingly. Also I had let my thoughts be transmitted to not only all in this room but also to all on the starship.

'It is done Captain,' was all I then said.

The captain smiled at the surprised expressions on the faces of his officers. He too had been so taken when he'd first witnessed the simple manner with which I had initiated my telekinetic skills. But now the captain took great pleasure in seeing the wonder expressed in his officers faces. I think his purpose was for them to see me in action and also for them to witness that great things could be done in a quiet and self effacing manner. This he conveyed to them was the path to true greatness.

The captain glowed with pride that I was on his starship. But an even greater pride glowed in the breast of Tania because her own dear husband could impress others with such simplicity of manner. I just thought that all of this was not really me but the one who had bestowed upon me all that I did and could do.

After I'd said 'It is done Captain' I had simply shrugged my shoulders. I showed an obvious self conscious embarrassment at all this sudden attention. For me it had been a simple mental command to will my telekinetic action that was pushing Silverstreak at 1200 FTL to be reduced in a progressive manner over the next 24 hour period. I could not see anything special in that.

Tania thought that after this deceleration command I might like to rest for a period. But I conveyed to her that it would not be finished till the starship dropped to 100 FTL velocity and I was released from all action. Besides I also conveyed that I'd had a very good sleep the night before and felt in excellent fettle. And so it had been.

For the final six hours of Silverstreak's deceleration from 100 FTL to zero I had felt quite unburdened. It seemed that my telekinetic powers had improved considerably and the effect upon my physical wellbeing was less than it once used to be. That gave me confidence for when I tackled Zarama. At least I hoped so.

Here we were at the first rendezvous location and Captain Wastanomi showed his pleasure in the achievement. He informed us that the starship would stay on site for 24 hours while the Zero-g spaceships ventured outside for the scientists to get precise readings on Zarama's state of affairs. When he asked me if I might like to accompany one of these ships I jumped at the chance.

'Yes please Captain,' I had said and added, 'and may Tania accompany me too?'

'If you wish,' said the captain and so it was agreed.

Tania was pleased that she would be beside me on the Zero-g ship. Of late she had become rather possessive and wanted to be wherever I went and I understood why. As the confrontation with Zarama drew closer her old qualms had resurfaced.

At one of the earlier noon meetings Captain Wastanomi had stated that for the final confrontation only I and one other crew member would be permitted aboard the Zero-g ship. The other two ships would be at strategic locations outside to gauge any change in Zarama's direction of motion. Tania had said she wanted to be with me then but the captain had refused her permission which had upset her and brought back some of the old fears. Unknown to Tania the captain was simply acceding to my wishes.

Simon had been directed to take us down for the Zero-g ships trip outside Silverstreak. He would be accompanying us for which I was grateful to the captain. We went down to the cargo platform and donned our electrostatic suits as normal before being led to our seats on one of the Zero-g ships in the huge airlock. We had good vantage seats at one of the many view panel spots. These Zero-g ships were large being about 200 feet long, 90 feet wide and about 35 feet in height. They had just the one deck for crew called the central habitation deck and were circled with seating and view panels on three sides. All seats had thigh clamping to ensure we stayed seated. Also everything aboard was secured in place and no liquids in open containers; hence their purpose as zero gravity ships.

The anticipation was always great when one of these was about to exit the airlock for outer space. The lights dimmed and the outer airlock doors opened fully. The three ships then rose up slowly and went out one after the other into the blackness that was space. They rapidly went towards the tail end of Silverstreak before diverging to triangular positions some 100 miles apart. They stayed in these respective positions for nearly an hour. Any queasiness from the gravity-free conditions was allayed by Zanos-on-board inducing a feeling of mental wellbeing.

While out there Zanos answered my query and gave me the exact location of Zarama. It was a fairly bright star but not exceptionally so. It blended in with all the myriad of stars in our view. However the star Vega was of outstanding brightness but well towards the Milky Way side of Zarama. Zanos indicated for Vega to be used as a benchmark even though it was nowhere near Zarama.

Zanos had positioned the Zero-g ship such that Vega was in the centre of the view panel in front of us. Then it directed our vision towards the right side of Vega and for our vision to continue coursing sideways until we came upon a small cluster of uniquely grouped stars. We recognised this easily. Zanos directed us to continue our scanning along the same direct line but for only a third of the initial distance till we came to a star that was slightly brighter than the others in the background. This was the white dwarf Zarama.

As this star came into my and Tania's vision we got it magnified in the view panel at our request. At just under two light years away Zarama appeared enlarged to about half the size of Earth's full moon but much brighter. The bright white light that came from it gave it a slightly hazy appearance and I was unable to make out any particular features. Zanos informed us that this was because Zarama had a rotation period of just over one revolution per minute. This was not considered excessive in astronomical terms but neither was it deemed as minor. Zarama was now measured as travelling at 33,111 miles per second in the direction of Nazmos. This was a further velocity increase of 18 miles per second in the last 49 year period.

I continued to stare at the bright image of Zarama and mixed thoughts went through my mind. For some reason I did not hate it or find it repugnant. It had been thrown out into space when its twin star exploded and it was here by pure circumstance. Had its direction been only slightly different then it would not have been a threat to anyone. Perhaps then I might not have been given this task and neither might I have known about Anztarza or Nazmos; or Gozmanot for that matter. Who knows? Yet I have to be glad of all that has passed in my life. And I have this weird feeling that the future has set something even more for me to accomplish.

It was then announced that all measurements were complete and the Zero-g ships were to return to Silverstreak. It took another hour before all three ships were settled safely back on the floor of the airlock chamber. It was nice to feel full gravity once again. We disembarked in slow order after the pressure in the airlock chamber had been normalised.

We changed out of the electrostatic suits before Simon took Tania and me down to the habitation platform; and at my suggestion straight to the captain's quarters. I wanted to express my thanks for the privilege of being allowed out on a Zero-gravity ship and my first direct view of Zarama. We were met by a smiling Captain Wastanomi and Korizazit who always seemed to gravitate there.

'Thank you Captain,' I said in my sincerest voice, 'that was truly amazing. Both Tania and I found the trip most enlightening. And I was glad that we had Simon as our guide.'

'I'm glad you think so Ashley,' said the captain. 'That was really a rehearsal for you of what is planned when we are at the actual ten million mile or less rendezvous from Zarama. Tania will not be beside you then nor will Officer Simon. But they will both know of the conditions you will be in from your trip today. The only difference being that you will of course be much closer to Zarama.'

Korizazit then asked me a question about what I thought of Zarama under magnification.

I had to smile at this before I answered.

'Well it looked quite like Earth's moon only much brighter. I had many thoughts but the one that stayed with me was that somehow I felt sorry for it. I know it is not a living thing but it does have a natural aging cycle. Were it not for the fact of its directional velocity we would not be in this position. But then so many other thoughts came into my mind as well which I now convey to you.'

'Yes I see,' said Korizazit, 'so I suppose it all came about because of Zarama. And I must say that I'm glad of it. If it were not for you I would not have had the experience of my inner voice. It is a gift I could never have imagined as possible and I thank you for it.'

I looked at the captain and he seemed to be deep in thought. I don't suppose starship captains tend to speculate on what might have been. But it did give him food for thought I could see.

We had missed the noonday meal by a good couple of hours and the captain invited us to partake of a delayed meal here with him. Korizazit was of course invited but Simon was not as per the captain's protocol. Simon didn't seem to mind and smiled as he took his leave. I knew Mazpazam was on his mind.

It was a pleasant meal but I noticed that both the captain and Korizazit ate sparingly. It would have been impolite to enquire why and I reckoned that they may have had a small snack earlier while awaiting our return from our space trip outside Silverstreak.

Both Tania and I were rather hungry but we ate at a measured pace while carrying on a conversation with the captain and Korizazit. For some reason I felt unusually thirsty and downed two glasses of Wazu during the meal.

'And when do we continue our journey Captain?' asked Tania in her politest tone.

The captain smiled back at Tania. I think he quite liked being addressed by her.

'Well,' he said, 'as soon as all data collected has been analysed and Zanos is satisfied I will be given a full report. So far it seems that Zarama is not the fierce emitter of radiation that we first suspected. But I must wait for the full report. I had planned a 24 hour wait at this rendezvous but that may seem unnecessary now that all external readings and measurements have been completed. But I am a cautious captain and I like to adhere to a preset time table. Thus we shall continue our journey tomorrow morning at 6: 00am as planned.'

'Thank you Captain,' said Tania.

The captain then added as an afterthought mainly to me.

'We shall be cruising solely under Silverstreak's own impulse power so you will be free to wander around the habitation platform as you please Ashley. With acceleration and deceleration periods taken into account our journey time to final rendezvous will be approximately eight days. This will of course include the final manoeuvring of Silverstreak into its planned position of ten million miles or less from Zarama. We shall then keep pace with Zarama's velocity but with Silverstreak's forward shield facing directly towards it. All three Zero-g ships will then exit the airlock and proceed into a triangular configuration with Silverstreak as the radial centre. Each Zero-g ship will locate to a position of 200 miles from the starship and hold position there. You Ashley will be in one of those Zero-g ships as requested. One of my senior officers Voortazin will be in sole command and you and he will be the only ones on that ship. He has been instructed to follow your orders explicitly without endangering the ship.'

'Thank you Captain,' I said, 'that is very clear. Would it be possible for me to meet with this officer before hand?'

'Yes of course,' said the captain. 'When would you like to meet him?'

I thought for a bit and then decided that I'd like to meet this officer Voortazin without the captain being present. I'd like to get to know the officer in a congenial informal setting.

'I thought perhaps Simon and Mazpazam could bring him to my apartment to join us at an evening meal. We would talk informally then and I could get to know the real person,' I said.

The captain recognised my purpose and smiled his agreement. He knew that a simple introduction in his presence would not be conducive to informal discourse.

'Yes that will be fine,' said the captain. 'I will let Voortazin know of your invitation plan and perhaps Simon can complete the arrangement.'

'Thank you once again captain, you are most understanding,' I said. 'I'm sure Simon will oblige. Would tomorrow evening be too early for the officer if it does not interfere with his duties?'

'I shall instruct Voortazin to make himself available as per your request,' said the captain. I noticed a hint of amusement in his voice when he added.

'You may have seen Voortazin in my quarters. He was here when you initiated the deceleration of Silverstreak from 1200 FTL. You may have noticed him as a slightly older officer amongst all the other younger ones. I think he was seated two spaces away from me on my left. You may remember him if you cast your mind back.'

The captain then conveyed a visual image of Voortazin. I put his age from this view of him as about 200 years. In fact I learned later that he was 209 years of age.

I tried to review the meeting in my mind but I could not actually see him among all those present.

'Sorry Captain, but I cannot place the officer at that meeting,' I said. 'Perhaps I didn't pay full attention to all those present. But I do look forward to meeting him again.'

The captain smiled and said that all the officers had been very impressed by the simplicity of my telekinetic control. And they were keen to meet with me on a more informal basis. They would be quite envious of Voortazin.

'Then perhaps I could get to meet the other officers as well sometime during this second phase journey to Zarama. If it is agreeable to you I could ask Simon and Mazpazam to take me around to meet some of them.'

'Yes of course,' said the captain. 'That will be perfectly in order. I shall inform them to expect your visits.'

'Thank you Captain,' I said, 'you are most kind.'

After some further light conversation we excused ourselves and returned to our apartment to rest.

Next morning I awoke a bit later than usual. Tania was already up and washed and dressed. I think she must have given me a gentle nudge or else made the appropriate noises to get me awake. I used to be a very light sleeper once but I think with age I tend to sleep more deeply. Also I try to get as much sleep as I can whenever I can. That's my excuse anyway. Tania had my mug of tea ready and I thanked her with a grateful smile. It was close to 11:00am when I finally was ready and got started on my breakfast.

Simon and Mazpazam arrived when I had finished my toast and was having a second mug of tea. They stated that Silverstreak was now well on its way to its final rendezvous position with Zarama. I could see that they were in a joyous mood and I couldn't help thinking what a lovely couple they made.

'Hi dad,' said Simon. 'We thought that when you and mum have finished your meeting with the captain we could go far a walkabout and you could see where the officer's quarters are located. Mazpazam and I would like to show you our home from home living accommodation.'

'Sounds excellent,' I replied. 'I don't imagine there is much that the captain will want to discuss today so we shouldn't be very long with him. It is a good routine and I look forward to it and wouldn't want to disappoint. I think Korizazit likes our chats too.'

And so it was. Tania and I were with the captain and Korizazit all of half an hour before we took our leave. The captain seemed to know of Simon's plan for our walkabout and I'm sure he knew more than he let on.

'Have a nice day,' were his final words to us said with a wide smile on his face.

Simon was waiting outside the captains' quarters with Mazpazam beside him.

'Silverstreak has attained its 100 FTL cruise velocity and all is smooth sailing at the moment,' he said. 'Shall we go this way?'

Tania squeezed my hand as we stepped up beside our son and his wife. Simon led the way in a slow stroll while giving us a verbal idea of the apartments we passed. The technical personnel were grouped together in order of their specialist skill and they certainly were a varied lot. But I found it most interesting when Simon described how many food growing specialists were aboard.

When we came to the outer wall of the starship we walked along its perimeter for some distance before turning inwards again between a different row of apartments. We were halfway along these when Mazpazam stopped and looked at Simon.

'Here we are mom and dad,' said Simon and gestured to the door of the adjacent apartment. 'This is home from home where Mazpazam and I live. Our humble quarters are open for your inspection.'

He then led the way in and the interior was very similar to ours. The decoration was simple but all the amenities were there. Simon's bed was beside the sleep tank and I'm sure that was by design so he could sleep close to Mazpazam while she slept in the sleep-tank.

We spent several minutes walking around the apartment with Mazpazam showing us some of the special features when Simon remarked that it was about that time for the midday meal.

'Yes, so it is,' I said.

'In that case would you and mum care to dine with us,' said Simon with a smile that seemed to stretch from one ear to the other.

'That would be lovely,' said Tania thinking as I did that we would have it here in Simon and Mazpazam's apartment.

Simon smiled.

'Actually I use the term loosely,' he said. 'By us I mean me and my fellow officers. The officers' dining hall is just near here and it was their idea mainly. They are all keen to meet you dad. And mum too of course.' The last bit added hastily but Tania understood that no offence was meant.

'Lead on son,' I said. 'Let us go and meet your colleagues.'

So we walked back out and across to the other side of the row of apartments. I conveyed the comparison of walking into a lions den at which Simon laughed. Mazpazam seemed puzzled until Simon explained it to her.

We then walked up to a double fronted apartment facia and Simon opened the rather large door for us to enter. Tania and I stepped inside and found ourselves in a sort of hallway.

Simon walked passed us and another sliding door opened automatically. I could see a large hall with a long central table with about twenty or so split backed chairs around it. And standing behind each chair was an Oannes officer dressed in space academy uniform. A very smart looking lot I thought. We walked in and Simon led us towards one end of the table before he made a verbal announcement.

'Fellow starship officers,' he said in his quiet low tone voice of formality, 'my mother and father have graciously accepted your offer of this midday meal here with us and thank you for your kind invitation.'

I noticed that among them were three other female Oannes officers. With Mazpazam that made four in all. So the gender difference was much the same as on Earth.

'I am very pleased to be here and meet you all,' I said with a smile.

I then conveyed a brief Sewa to them all in general which was responded to immediately. I replied that Tania and I were in good health and excellent spirits and quite hungry.

There were smiles and nodding looks all around as I had just set the pace for informality.

'Then do let us be seated and begin our meal,' said the officer I recognised as Voortazin.

'Thank you officer Voortazin,' I said. 'The captain has spoken to me about you and I am pleased that we finally meet face to face. We shall face Zarama together.'

Voortazin seemed to glow with pride at the mention of his name as we all began to take our seats.

I looked around the table and smiled as I said, 'I hope to get to know all of you by name over the next few days and hope we can become good friends. So let us now eat before my stomach thinks my throat has been cut.'

Everyone smiled and visibly relaxed in attitude. My reputation had obviously preceded me and it must have been daunting for some of them meeting me face to face. I hope they get to know me as the informal person that I am.

The usual Oannes fare was soon brought to the table and dishes were passed around as requested. I was rather hungry so served myself well especially to the very sweet Yaztraka. I think they all knew of my preference for it and so a full dish was made available close to me at all times. Finally I was quite sated and said so.

'No more for me thank you,' I said. 'That was a most enjoyable meal among the most excellent of company. I feel wonderful thanks to you all.'

'Would you like a mug of your favourite tea?' asked one of the officers near me.

'I would love one,' I said. 'You all know a lot about me but I know so little of you. We must change that.'

It wasn't long before a hot mug of tea was placed before me. I picked it up and took a sip.

'Ah, this is beautiful,' I said looking up, 'just the way I like it, hot and sweet.'

After another few sips I put the mug down and looked around at the seated officers. There was an expectant expression on some of the faces and I knew they were keen to ask some of their prepared questions. And I was in just the right mood to grant them anything.

At a whim I stood up and raised my mug of tea in a sort of toast.

'Officers, I drink to you all and to Silverstreak,' I said. 'Let us drink to her and may all her journeys be swift, safe and sure and may all aboard her enjoy the comfort that she provides.'

'Hear, hear,' said Simon standing up with a raised glass of Wazu in an uplifted hand. 'I'll drink to that.'

There was a rustling of chairs as all the assembly of officers stood with glasses in their hands. Then as if to a signal all raised their glasses to their mouths and took a sip of Wazu. I then sat down again as did everyone too.

I sensed their curiosity and I was happy to oblige.

'Now starship officers,' I said, 'what may I do for you? Please feel free to ask me any questions that may be pertinent to my purpose here.'

It was Voortazin who stood up and asked if they could really ask me anything.

'Yes of course,' I said, 'apart from the secrets between Tania and me.'

I nodded sideways repeatedly indicating Tania seated beside me as I winked several times. Tania laughed and pretended to punch me on my shoulder. They all knew the humour of my gesture and smiled.

'May we convey our questions telepathically,' asked one of the younger looking officers, 'it is just that I am more comfortable communicating that way.'

'Yes of course.' I conveyed back telepathically and with my mind open to all. 'Please proceed as you wish.'

'I am officer Ventezto and I would like to know when you first knew of your special gifts,' he conveyed.

'Well I seemed to discover the gifts one at a time by pure chance over a long period of time,' I conveyed. 'I was about four years of age when I found that I could see things happening as if in slow motion if I wished it.'

I then conveyed the games I played with granddad Eric and how it was he who realised that I had something special when I kept catching a ball he threw into different areas. I mentioned that the sky looked pink when I did so. I could go into this pink mode whenever I wished for it to happen.

'My father and grandfather then put me through a series of tests to see what I could actually do. In pink mode I could bend steel bars which became rather hot. My father expressly told me to keep all of this from other humans and I have done so ever since. I think it was good advice.'

I conveyed that although I realised all this at age four I must have been able to do things from a much younger age as indicated by the teeth marks left on the railings around the toddlers play area in the park and the holes I had made for birds in nearby tree trunks. I then conveyed about the school cricket match and how I automatically went into pink mode when the fast moving ball struck at my chest. This was realisation of another one of my gifts. I mentioned the subsequent tests I did on myself in falling from a tall building and then the airgun pellets fired into my hand by my father as a test. How while on holiday at my aunt Brenda's B&B in Aberporth I found I could understand people speaking another language. I told them of Jan Bogdan and Sarul Kwaitkowski, the Polish plumbers. And how I could look into their minds and know their history and speak to them in their own language too.

I then conveyed many of the instances when I taught naughty boys or vandals a lesson. Like the lime tree vandals and the Brownhills New Town hooligans. I smiled inwardly as I conveyed all this.

Then I came to the all important pub darts match on my eighteenth birthday and how my father had discerned that I could move objects with my mind; and the subsequent sandbag suspended in our garage for me to practice this new telekinetic gift. Also how my mind had automatically regressed in the pub at that darts match when thieves had stolen peoples handbags and wallets. I mentioned how I had through my skill of mental regression been able to assist in solving criminal cases in the law courts. Much later I had used that gift to regress to meet Gozmanot and also to solve Captain Zakatanz's 100 year old mystery of his betrothed's disappearance.

Then of course I added how by accidentally touching someone like Oliver Ramirez I had discovered that I could diagnose their illness condition. He had a brain tumour.

I conveyed how I could move around in pink mode without being seen and the games I played with Simon and Katy in our garden. And how Simon seemed to be able to guess or know precisely where I would appear next. We then learned of his premonition gift.

An officer named Tiptizat then interrupted as he conveyed who he was and how he had been on several navigation exercises with Simon aboard.

'I was always impressed by Simon's navigational skill in correctly determining our exact location relative to Nazmos. He was the only space cadet to get 100% in all his navigation tests over the course's six year period. Now I know why and how it was achieved. So it all began with the games he played with you when he was a child.'

'I had also to learn how to control the strength of my telekinetic push since the asteroid tests of 2004 in which Asteroid 2867 Steins had been pulverised by the excessive force used upon it. The rest is all on Oannes records as to what I have done.'

I paused for a moment before I added.

'However one further aspect came to light when I was about to demonstrate my telekinetic power to my nieces Fiona and Sarah. Before this I had always had to specify the force of my telekinetic push by concentrating my mind for a particular push level. But suddenly I discovered that my telekinesis had become an involuntary act of will. I simply had to will for a particular push to occur and it was done exactly to the detail I had expressed for it. Subsequently it became less of a burden to me especially in the movement of starships and planet bodies. But I do feel rather exhausted and very thirsty after all my telekinetic exertions. However that seems to be reducing with time. Does that tell you what you wanted to know Ventezto?'

'Yes, thank you,' conveyed Voortazin who seemed to be the elected spokesperson for the officers. But I could see that he hesitated before his next question. And instead he relayed it to Simon.

'Dad,' said Simon aloud, 'the officers would like a small demonstration of a telekinetic push upon an object if you don't mind their forwardness in asking.'

'Not at all,' I said, 'it will be a pleasure just as I did for Fiona and Sarah. But let me move to the top of the table for a longer motion. Now if I may have an object placed in front of me I shall demonstrate.'

The officers quickly cleared away all the meal dishes leaving the table a free and open surface. Then an empty dish was positioned just in front of me.

'Are you ready officers,' I said, 'here is what I propose to do. I shall will for this empty dish to commence a slow movement down the centre of the table. And to be polite I shall will it to stop for two seconds alongside each paired place before continuing on to the next. The movement is to be at an average walking pace only and for all movement to stop when it reaches close to the end of the table. Will that be acceptable?'

'Perfectly,' said Simon smiling.

'Well then here goes,' I said.

So I willed for the dish to move exactly as I had stated and then sat back with a smile.

As if of its own accord the empty dish slid along the table directly away from me for about two feet. It then stopped for two seconds opposite the first place setting nearest to me. Then it moved on as before to the next place before stopping again for the same two second interval. This was repeated several times for each place setting before finally stopping near the other end of the long table.

While this had been going on I looked at the expressions of wonder on the faces of the officers. Even Mazpazam looked quite enthralled with Simon smiling as he watched her. She was even lovelier with that expression on her face and Simon gazed at her with his own expression of love and wonder.

'There you are officers,' I said, 'I trust that was a satisfactory demonstration. I hope that Zarama will be as easy to move.'

'Thank you,' conveyed Voortazin, 'that was fascinating. Our science cannot explain how it is done. It is a topic that we often discuss.'

'You will notice that I can only apply my telekinetic force as a push directly away from me,' I conveyed. 'It is the only direction in which it works.'

Another officer from further down the table introduced himself as Tropitazon and conveyed that he was interested in my bending of steel bars and making holes in tree trunks for the birds when I was very young. Was I still able to do that now he asked?

'Yes I still can,' I conveyed. 'I suppose you would like a demonstration.'

'Yes please,' was generally conveyed by several of the officers.

'And what is it that you would like me to bend?' I asked aloud.

There was a general discussion lasting barely a second before another officer I got to know as Vaztanizat excused himself from the table and left the room. I was informed that he had gone to fetch a bar of stiff material. He must have been gone about two minutes and returned carrying a heavy silvery metal rod about two inches in diameter and two feet long. Slowly he came around to me and placed it with a gentle thud on the table in front of me.

'Will this be acceptable?' he conveyed with a smile as he looked around at his fellow officers who were also smiling in anticipation.

I suspect that they had done their homework on me and pre-prepared these requests.

I stood up and looked at the large piece of metal and tested it for weight by lifting it off the table.

'Ooof,' I said, 'this is quite a weight. It must be twenty or twenty five pounds at least and an excellent prop for the experiment. I haven't done anything like this since those early tests with my father. But I shall give it a try. I will need to go into my pink mode so you won't actually see me bending it,'

'Yes we understand,' said Natozita a young looking female Oannes officer sitting halfway along the table. She had a pleasant face and with a highly intelligent expression. Her gaze towards me was quite intense and I conveyed my favourable impression of her as I nodded in her direction. She looked away at once and then back again with a smile on her face. Tania kicked me under the table.

'Okay here goes,' I said and went into pink mode. I thought to impress them by adding something to the test.

In pink mode the metal bar proved light and of a soft material in my hands. So I gripped the round bar near each end and squeezed a fair amount to leave the impression of my fingers and palm in the bar. Then I bent it into a horseshoe shape and gently placed it back on the table before returning to normal mode.

'There you are,' I said, 'a souvenir for the officers' hall. Don't touch it with your bare hands just yet as it may feel rather warm.'

'Please may I see it,' said Natozita as she stood up and began to walk around the table.

'Yes of course,' I said as I stepped back and moved my chair seat back as well.

She first looked at the bent bar and then gingerly put her hand over the bar to feel its heat. Then she lightly tapped it with one finger and repeated the process again after a few seconds. Then after about a minute she picked it up and conveyed that it was still quite warm but okay to handle. She examined it carefully and then looked again at me with wonder in her eyes. She then looked away and passed the bent bar to the next officer to my left. Each officer examined it intensely before passing it on. I kept getting admiring looks to which I merely shrugged my shoulders to indicate I had done nothing very special.

'Thank you for that sir,' said another officers aloud. He was shorter than the others and rather stocky in build and reminded me of Captain Wastanomi. He conveyed that he was Wistuzab and had been a colleague of Simon's during the same academy years. I said I was pleased to know him.

He then conveyed that he noticed I had left my hand prints at the bar ends. Was that a result of the bending pressure on the bar he asked?

'No,' I said, 'I thought to add another dimension to the experiment so I first squeezed the bar to create those impressions before I did the actual bending. When I am in pink mode most materials feel soft to my touch. It is how I made the holes in the tree trunks when I was a young child.'

By now I could sense that most of the officers had relaxed and felt easier in my presence and so many more questions were asked. The one I thought most relevant was that put by Natozita who by the way had a lovely smile.

'Have you wondered how and why you acquired these powers of yours,' she asked.

'I have never thought much about how I got these talents or powers as you call them,' I said aloud. 'As I discovered each gift I just accepted it as something normal. I do believe that my mother was saddened by the fact and thought that these gifts must have been given to me for a purpose. Perhaps for some special task and she feared for my wellbeing. She had some notion that I would be expendable in having to fulfil that task. Personally I believe that these powers were endowed upon me by a greater Being. We humans acknowledge and believe that all creation is by a Supreme Being whom we refer to as the Creator or the one and only God. It is a concept within our religions no matter how differing they may appear in outward concept.'

I paused to let my meaning sink in before I continued to answer the question.

'As to the why part of your question Natozita I didn't know for a long while. The first time I knew about some special task was when it was mentioned by my friend Philip Stevens. Perhaps I was chosen to fulfil Gozmanot's vision for Nazmos. Or perhaps it was to deal with Zarama as we now plan to do. Perhaps all the other gifts are supplementary and are there to complement the main gift of telekinesis in order to preserve me for the approaching moment.'

Natozita had another question.

'What happens after you have dealt with Zarama,' she asked?

'I really don't know,' I said,' but I have thought about it. What I would like is for me to be released from all these gifts as they are quite a responsibility and burden to me. I would just like to live an ordinary life in peace with my wife Tania in my home on Earth. I sometimes do hope that my powers will cease once Zarama has been successfully dealt with.'

I hope that all I've said goes on record and proves to those present and others elsewhere that I am no megalomaniac greedy for power and influence. I could see many of them nodding their understanding and being sympathetic to my argument.

Another one of the questions I thought relevant to Earth was by a young Oannes male officer named Waltazat who asked it.

'I lived in Anztarza for several years before I was selected for the space academy,' he conveyed. 'It was stressed as a general rule that on no account must there be any contact between humans and Oannes. It was important that humans did not know of our existence. Yet some of our people moved among then in disguise for commercial purposes such as obtaining food supplies on a regular basis. What is your view on this isolationism between our peoples? Do you think that integration may occur one day?'

I had to smile as I looked at Waltazat.

'I don't have a definitive answer to that,' I replied. 'But I do know that a start towards integration has already been made. I am human and you are Oannes and yet here we are in affable communication. My family members were accepted by your governing council mainly because of me. Gozmanot foresaw this moment so maybe she had a part to play in it. The path that history takes can be thrilling as well as mysterious. There are many people on Earth who are gentle and likeable. But there are others also who are not. Greed and avarice are still abundant among the human race but I would say these are not the majority.'

I could see that there was general agreement to my words.

'I introduced telepathic communication among a small group of humans and schools for teaching its skills were set up in selected places,' I continued. 'But it has not as yet achieved extensive practice. The human brain is not as developed as the Oannes brain and it is difficult to acquire the skill. Our society may alter for the good when telepathy has become universal as it is with you. Until then you would be wise to maintain the status quo as it is today. Our civilizations are bound by closer ties than you would think. With Nazmos eventually becoming more like Earth I think it inevitable for integration to take place one day; perhaps in a thousand years or so from now. And when the first steps are about to be taken then it will require careful process not to cause alarm among humans. The general public on Earth know nothing of your existence or of Anztarza and Nazmos. For them the notion is that people from outer space are to be feared'

I could see agreement on many of the officer's faces; but Mazpazam's smile of approval towards me was filled with pride and brought a welling up of my affection for her; like a pang of pain within my chest. An emotion that was like what you feel at first sight of your new born child. I smiled back at her and nodded.

The one question I feared was about my plans for tackling Zarama. I think they knew how I felt and that it was a delicate issue for Tania, and so the topic was not mentioned.

It was Simon who suggested that they return to starship duties during a lull in the conversation. So Tania and I took our leave with many thanks to all the officers for their kind hospitality. They in turn through their spokesperson Voortazin thanked Tania and me for gracing their hall and answering all their questions. No mention was made of a further visit but I have no doubt that an arrangement would be made through Simon.

Simon and Mazpazam walked with us back to our apartment via a circuitous route that took in other residential areas. It was only when I entered the apartment that I realised that I had missed the afternoon nap that I was getting into the habit of.

Next morning we went for our daily meeting with the captain and he seemed pleased to see us. He conveyed that he was glad that his officers had had the opportunity to socialise with me and Tania. He said that they were impressed by my easy manner and had been most comfortable and relaxed during our time together. I gathered that the captain had received full imagery of the entire event.

As usual Korizazit was present and he too must have received all the details.

'I was very pleased to meet your officers Captain,' I said. 'They are a most interesting group. I am honoured that Simon is one of that elite band of starship officers. He certainly fits in well and I see him as one of them.'

'Simon is an asset to my crew,' said Captain Wastanomi. 'As long as Simon is aboard we know that we can never really be lost. He has a unique ability of instinctively knowing where he is in space relative to Nazmos. His record at the space academy was exemplary in every respect with 100% success in his navigation tests. Of course we have Zanos to guide us but it is nice to know that we can rely elsewhere also.'

As Silverstreak drew closer to its destination I began to review my plans in attempting to push it aside. I could not discuss or convey my thoughts to anyone not even to Tania. In my heart of hearts instinct I knew that I might and probably would exceed that sixteen push level limit I had been set. I kept thinking of Sirius B and the abject failure of my effort there. I had been warned not to exceed that push level limit but I knew that I could do so if I wanted. What dire consequences would result I did not know? Was there a danger to my person? Was I slowing Time too much or was I going too fast as Brian had thought? Whatever the result I simply had to go through with it if that was the only recourse for me to push Zarama aside to a different path.

It was nice walking around the habitation platform and meeting technicians, engineers and scientists going about there daily duties. And yet all would stop and politely converse with me. But it was the officers who were the most affable in their manner.

Halfway into this final leg of Silverstreak's journey to Zarama Tania and I were invited again to an evening meal with the officers. This time there were no curious questions but rather a healthy discussion about Gozmanot and what Nazmos would be like in the far distant future.

'Just visit Earth and you will get an idea of how Nazmos may eventually look,' I conveyed, 'but we will not see it in our lifetime.'

'Yes,' said Waltazat from the end of the table, 'I spent several years in Anztarza and during that time I visited the northern forests of Canada several times. It gets very cold there in its winter period, even colder than Nazmos in its northern region. I did enjoy the experience and had wished for Nazmos to be like that.'

It was Mazpazam who broached the question of what the flora and possible fauna might be on a future Nazmos. I read her mind and knew she still queried the fact of why the Rimzi lived totally separate from the land based Oannes population. The mystery remained since the reasons for it appeared lost in distant history. I also caught a glimpse of another question forming in her mind. Why had not other creatures evolved within the seas alongside the then water-living Oannes and Rimzi? Had they lived peaceably together or had something arisen to displease either side? Were they originally one people separated by their preference of land or water? I somehow felt that perhaps the Rimzi had preserved their own account in history and were still anti-Oannes about it. One had to be Rimzi to find out. Prophetic words that sprang out to surprise me. Good luck to Mazpazam in her quest.

It was a most pleasant meal with the officers and getting to know them better was a highly rewarding experience for Tania and me. It was especially satisfying for us to know the good company that Simon kept. He was happy with his wife Mazpazam, with his career and with his colleagues; and we were happy for him. We mentioned this as he and Mazpazam walked us back to our apartment after we had once again thanked the officers for their generous hospitality.

It was when we were nearing the end of our journey with but a day of travel left that we were invited to a meal with the captain and Korizazit in the captain's quarters.

It turned out to be a most pleasant meal and the conversation was light-hearted and approached the jovial. The captain led the conversation more than once and I wondered what could have made him feel so congenial. Perhaps he had an insight of Tania and me from what had been revealed of us by his officers.

Towards the end of the meal it was Korizazit who turned the topic back to business. He raised the subject of Zarama and the likely duration of our stay in its vicinity. He looked at me questioningly.

'I suppose all I need is a day or so for my attempt at pushing it aside as planned,' I said with a hint of a smile.

'It may take a bit longer than that,' said the captain. 'There are other factors to consider.'

He then conveyed what those considerations were.

'Firstly a team of scientists must venture out of Silverstreak and get measurements of all the emissions that are emanating from the Dwarf star at our initial ten million miles position. Then they must return to the starship to assess whether it is feasible and safe to proceed to a closer position to Zarama. It is known that White Dwarf stars are degenerate and have few emissions and which are mainly of x-rays. There is no fusion reaction within Zarama so it has no source of energy but it is extremely hot. In time this heat is radiated away causing it to cool. We do not know how young or old Zarama is but for it to be this hot it cannot be very old in astronomical terms. And so we must precisely measure the level of its x-ray emissions to assess how safe it is to be approached in a Zero-g spaceship like the one you Ashley will be in. Heat conditions will also be assessed. For the best possible chance of success we must try for the safest close position for you. If it is the scientists' recommendation then Silverstreak will move closer to Zarama by another few million miles. A further assessment will be made by the scientists venturing out again and we shall repeat this sequence of events till they are satisfied that we can go no closer in safety. The whole process may require several days which I am prepared to allow. We will be guided by the closest distance of five million miles limit that Sirius B was approached. My intention is not to get closer than this for Zarama. Only then will I allow you and Voortazin to prepare yourselves for the attempt at pushing Zarama aside.'

I realised that Captain Wastanomi was being extremely thorough in his approach to the mission and he was not prepared to endanger me or his starship in any way. He and I both felt that the closer I was to Zarama the greater would be the effect of my telekinetic push upon it. I was glad that the captain had stated his plan in such detail and I'm sure he exerted the same influence for safety upon all of his crew including the scientists functioning under his command.

'And when would it be appropriate to commence the return journey?' asked Korizazit.

'Once Ashley has completed his mission and returned to Silverstreak we must shadow Zarama to ensure that its course has been rightly changed and that it is on a correct path towards Rasalgethi,' said the captain. 'My plan is to shadow Zarama for a couple of weeks at least until our scientists are confident that its course is as planned. Only then would I be willing to commence the journey back to Nazmos.'

'And what time-span do you estimate for the return journey?' asked Korizazit.

'I have yet to instruct Zanos for a detailed plan,' said the captain, 'but with Ashley's assistance I imagine about the same time as it took to get here; or perhaps a little less than that. I shall convey the question to Zanos as a direct enquiry from me for full logistics of the journey. It will only take a moment.'

I knew that the captain always planned well ahead of anticipated events so now he requested a full report from Zanos on Silverstreak's return journey to Nazmos. He received a reply instantly but not what he had expected. Zanos had given a reply that the computation and its probabilities were in progress.

With his mind open the captain conveyed all this to us and also that he thought it odd because Zanos usually analysed a situation and gave an inference more or less instantly.

It was a few moments later that Zanos presented the analysed conclusion to the captain which I could see came to him as a shock. Zanos had predicted the journey back to Nazmos to take four years and eighty three days; all in equivalent Earth time.

I watched Korizazit and he seemed to accept the truth of it. He now realised why his inner voice had asked that Silverstreak's food growing systems be completely overhauled. Somehow the future requirements for it had been predicted and Korizazit was the instrument for that forward planning. Whatever may have been the shortcomings in the previous food system these had been made good by its renewal. Food growing systems in all starships cope well for long term periods in space and have done so ever since being installed when the starships were initially constructed. And since 4110-Silver was one of the earlier 10 FTL starships its systems would predate most of those currently in service. Now of course its conversion to 100 FTL had seen most of its generators and impulse motors modified but the food systems had not then been considered. Korizazit had seen that they were.

Korizazit conveyed all his thoughts to the captain who I could see remained puzzled by the Zanos predicted journey time.

Then Korizazit also conveyed to the captain about another inner voice massage he had received back on Nazmos which he had mentioned to me before our journey began. And that was that I, Ashley would return to Nazmos but not as I was then – whatever that meant.

When Tania heard about it she had thought that I might get injured or somehow affected by the confrontation with Zarama. And now Zanos had picked up on all these thoughts and come to the conclusion that there was a high probability that my telekinetic ability to accelerate the starship would not be available.

The captain asked me for a comment and what my thoughts on the matter might be.

'I don't know Captain,' I said. 'I can only think of two things which I thought about when Korizazit here first mentioned it to me on Nazmos. The first was that once I had achieved success with Zarama that my gifts would no longer be necessary and that I might then become as ordinary humans are. I feel that these gifts were bestowed upon me for a purpose. I believe that purpose was to defeat Zarama by altering its course. The second is that in my efforts against Zarama I may have to resort to an extreme action against which I had been warned that dire consequences might subsequently result. Zanos knows all of my thoughts so either way it has made a fairly correct assumption.'

'What is this extreme action that you talk about?' asked Wastanomi.

So I conveyed about how I had used my telekinetic push force at successive levels beginning at the first level of one. I had used this system in the early asteroid experiments. I explained that it was then that I had been warned by my inner voice not to exceed a telekinetic push level of sixteen when in pink mode. I added that in the push trial against Sirius B I had not achieved any success. Therefore if I could not alter Zarama's path by a normal maximum push then I was resolved to exceed the said push level sixteen no matter what the consequences to myself.

'Captain,' I said in a serious voice, 'whatever the outcome of my battle against Zarama you may confidently set your plans for the return journey according to Zanos' predicted time scale.'

The captain looked at me intensely and I thought he might say something like an admonishment. But then he smiled and began to nod his head in understanding.

'Thank you for that Ashley,' he said. 'I shall put my plans for this into effect right away. No starship has spent more than a year travelling at FTL velocity in a current Oannes' lifetime. So this will be another record for Silverstreak and that too solely under its own impulse power.'

'You never know Captain,' said Tania, 'Zanos might be mistaken regarding Ashley.'

'I rely on Zanos utterly for all judgements,' said Wastanomi as a matter of fact and without adding anything further.

I could see the captain planning in his mind for this new development. I knew the captain to be thorough in his mind approach to all eventualities and this would be no exception. I read his mind which was open to me and he had already summoned all his officers for a meeting here later in the afternoon today. I could see that his thoughts were about putting into motion plans for the rotational growing and harvesting of food supply crops over the next five year period.

The captain was also considering a check of all the generators and impulse motors for the prolonged run to Nazmos. However, Silverstreak's propulsion systems had only recently received their upgrade for its new 100 FTL status so here everything should be in prime condition. But Captain Wastanomi would still get Zanos to check out all the systems.

Tania and I then took our leave of the captain but Korizazit said that he had matters to discuss and would stay on for a while.

That evening when Simon and Mazpazam came to join us for our evening meal we learned that the captain had given command instructions to his officers to initiate checks upon all the propulsion motors and generators under Zanos' supervisory analysis of them when at Zarama rendezvous.

'I don't think Captain Wastanomi is overly concerned that no other starship has done a four and a half year continuous FTL stint in living memory. He knows that Silverstreak is in prime condition and sees this as more of a challenge than a risk to his ship,' said Simon.

It was Tania who raised a new issue.

'I feel sorry for Rachel and Margaret,' she said, 'and also all of Nazmos when they receive no news of us for year after year. And the word will spread to Earth with the next starship arriving there and our parents will also worry. They will not know what could have happened to Silverstreak and us for Zarama will still be a visible image on their monitoring screens.'

'Silverstreak will not be like 2110-Blue under Captain Chamzalt,' said Mazpazam. 'Five years of waiting is not 1400 years.'

'Yes,' said Simon, 'for at least we shall know that we are heading home and can look forward to the joyous reception when we finally do arrive.'

It was a pleasant thought and I felt easier. Rachel and Margaret knew me well and would never give up hope of our return and I'm sure they would convince others too.

It was Mazpazam who made the comparison.

'We know that Zanos on Silverstreak looked at all the thought aspects within our minds. Korizazit's prediction that you Uncle Ashley would return to Nazmos in a different state and your willingness to do whatever was necessary to defeat Zarama brought Zanos to its current conclusion. But all of this must certainly also have been picked up by Zanos on Nazmos. And the governing council there would most certainly consult Zanos for the probabilities of our non-arrival as initially expected. I feel certain that Zanos on Nazmos will make a similar analysis and as such predict a new arrival date based upon Silverstreak's 100 FTL capabilities alone. If that date were to be exceeded by a large margin only then would it show cause for concern.'

A sudden thought raced through my head. Was it my inner voice? I think not, but it was certainly something predicted. But how would it be possible: unless. I hesitated at the aspect of it. But then I thought of Philip Stevens. He had managed to contact us just as he had passed on. There was also Ritozanan. I'm sure it was her who whisked my hair with a puff of air as she passed on her way to wherever she was heading. I decided to keep my mind blocked on this matter and keep it hidden away in the deepest recesses of my mind. Tania would not understand or accept it.

Mazpazam was staring at me with an odd expression on her face. I shook my head ever so slightly and conveyed a private request. She nodded an understanding and I closed my eyes with relief. She would keep my secret but would Zanos. Unless the captain specifically requested it Zanos was programmed to maintain total privacy of the thoughts it picked up from Oannes or human. I could not put Tania through any more pain.

Simon and Mazpazam stayed later than usual and I suspect it was at Mazpazam's instigation. Earlier Mazpazam had conveyed a plan with full agreement from Simon. I thought it a brilliant idea and contacted Zanos as often as necessary to convey my innermost thoughts and feelings. Plus messages and things I'd like to convey in response to questions; including my sense of humour and accompanying laughter. If anything happened to me Zanos would act as a surrogate for me. Tania knows nothing about this nor will she ever.

It was the last night of our journey because on the morrow Silverstreak would arrive at its first rendezvous position ten million miles from Zarama. The analysis of Zarama's emissions would then be made by the scientists on board Silverstreak and the corresponding assessment of danger to life outside the starship. The intense heat generated by the Dwarf Star would be a major factor.

The captain had earlier detailed his plan of trying to get as close to Zarama as was safely possible; to give me the best chance of success. So it might be a while before Silverstreak was in a position that satisfied the captain. Only then would he allow me to venture out against Zarama. Of course the closer I got to Zarama the greater would be the effect of my telekinetic push upon it; at least that is what I thought.

That night when we were alone and together in bed Tania snuggled up to me and repeatedly kissed me with light kisses. When she finally slept I once again felt the wetness on her cheeks. I felt saddened for her and what she might have to go through and my own tears flowed to mix with hers. I thought about dad and how he had accepted the fact of my regression in Priory Park when I seemed to float above it. I had been transported back in time to the 12th century period of King John youngest son of Henry the second. It was as if I was an ethereal entity without body or form and could go wherever I willed. When I had given dad the full visual imagery of my experience he had been quite thoughtful. Then out of the blue he had said, 'So that is what it is going to be like.' It didn't mean anything to me till much later and I was glad that I had given him comfort.

I was approaching my own Zarama confrontation and whatever happened I hoped I'd still be able to view those I loved. But it might be a one way thing and that is what brought forth my sadness. My tears were for Tania. Perhaps I might be allowed a final communication like I'd had from Philip. I would be happy if I could though I can now rely on Zanos to cover for me.

Chapter 27

The Final confrontation

June 2052

Three simulated Earth day periods had elapsed since Silverstreak had arrived at the Zarama rendezvous as planned. Captain Wastanomi had played it safe by revising this first rendezvous distance to ten and a half million miles from the rogue Dwarf Star. This was because the arrival distance was being shortened at the rate of just over thirty three thousand miles per second; the velocity of Zarama in the direction of Nazmos.

Silverstreak had then manoeuvred to a lateral position and on a parallel course with Zarama. The starship had its neutron shield facing directly towards it at a distance of ten million miles with its tail end pointed in the direction of the Milky Way centre. This was so that Ashley's telekinetic push would be in the correct direction to deflect Zarama onto a course towards Rasalgethi the Red Giant star 400 times the size of Earth's Sun.

The first environment tests were conducted by the Oannes scientists some twelve hours later using two of the Zero-g ships. Their analysis of the x-ray emissions showed them not to be a serious threat at this distance. Subsequently they made their recommendation to the captain for Silverstreak to be moved closer to Zarama by another two million miles. This had been achieved over a period of several hours and no further tests were conducted that day.

On the following day period about midday the scientists had once again ventured out in the two Zero-g ships and though they found the emissions from Zarama to be slightly more intense it was not enough to threaten life aboard their ships. Their recommendation again to captain Wastanomi was to reposition Silverstreak still closer to Zarama by another two million miles and for further tests to be carried out later. And so the starship was repositioned as before but at six million miles from Zarama.

The tests were again repeated the next day with the result that Silverstreak was repositioned again but at five million miles from Zarama; the emissions were considered to be border-line but the heat intensity was nearly as great as it had been for Sirius B. The scientists however considered that it was safe to bring Silverstreak another million miles closer to Zarama. Ashley thought this final distance of four million miles was better than what he had initially hoped for and he expressed this to the captain. This was achieved the following day.

On each of the days since Silverstreak's arrival at the initial Zarama location Ashley and Tania had kept to their noon meetings with Captain Wastanomi and Korizazit. These had been important meetings as the captain had kept them fully informed of the Oannes scientists' emission and heat intensity findings and of their recommendations that had brought Silverstreak to the final four million mile distance from Zarama. This compared favourably with the Sirius B trial distance.

At the last meeting Korizazit had made a unique request of his captain. He conveyed that he would like to venture out in one of the Zero-g ships to have a direct visual experience of Zarama. He stated that he was curious to see if it matched the image of the golden ball that he had seen in his dream vision. Although he could see the image on the viewing screens it was another matter to see it directly face to face in an outer space environment.

Captain Wastanomi was a happy captain. He was pleased that his mission had so far achieved all its objectives. Silverstreak was in that unique position from which Ashley could exercise his telekinetic push upon Zarama. And so being in a pleasant frame of mind he gave his permission not only for Korizazit to venture outside the starship but also for any others on board who wished to see the rogue Dwarf Star at first hand. The captain conveyed that he would put in place for a relay of trips aboard the Zero-g ships for the next day. Ashley said that he too would like to accompany Korizazit along with Tania beside him.

'Perhaps you would like your son Simon and his wife Mazpazam to accompany you,' said the captain. 'I shall arrange for their temporary release from duties.'

'Thank you Captain, you are most understanding and generous,' said a smiling and happy Tania.

The captain bowed slightly to acknowledge the compliment and gave Tania a fleeting smile.

'Of course I must stipulate that the Zero-g ships will only venture out as far as ten miles from the body of Silverstreak and then remain at location for just twenty minutes rotating slowly before returning to the airlock,' said

Captain Wastanomi. 'By this process most of the inhabitants and crew who so wish would have the opportunity to venture out to see Zarama face to face.'

Ashley was curious to know beforehand what Zarama might look like from this close distance. And so at a later moment he queried one of the scientists who had already been out checking the emissions. The scientists name was Mazazta and he was about 200 years of age and had served with Brajam aboard Captain Bulzezatna's spaceship 520-Green in Anztarza.

'It has a unique appearance,' said Mazazta. 'It appears featureless because of its spin but overall it glows with the ferocity of a very bright star. However it also has a faint yellow colouring which becomes apparent only after gazing at it for a prolonged period.'

'And what about its image size,' asked Ashley. 'I mean how large is its appearance?'

'It is just a large bright star,' he said, 'but under magnification has a round sphere shape.'

'Is there a corona type of glow around it,' asked Ashley?

Mazazta became thoughtful for a second or two before he replied.

'I don't think so,' he said, 'but let me convey the image of it to you.'

Ashley saw the image clearly and drew his personal conclusions about Zarama. It was certainly the same glowing ball of his vision that now appeared as the large star that Mazazta had implied. But of course Ashley knew that he would see it for himself when he ventured out the next day. At least now he knew what to expect. Tania had been at Ashley's side when he had spoken to Mazazta so she too saw the image of Zarama that was conveyed.

She thought about the asteroids experiment of so long ago when Ashley showed the Oannes what he was capable of. And she saw how that first asteroid Steins had been so fiercely pushed by Ashley's telekinetic power that it had exploded to smithereens. She wished that Ashley did the same to Zarama but doubted if he could. Zarama was far too massive for that and like Sirius B would be exceedingly difficult to budge.

Later during the evening meal in their apartment Ashley and Tania played host to Simon, Mazpazam and Korizazit. They had a lively discussion regarding Zarama and also about their venture outside the starship the next day. Korizazit said he was pleased that the captain had agreed for the five of them to be together on the same Zero-g ship. They would be among the first group of three ships venturing out for the viewing. It was to be an early start so that they could return in time for their usual midday meeting with the captain. Much later when their guests had finally left them Tania suggested bedtime as it had been a tense day for her.

But sleep didn't come easily to Ashley or Tania that night and at the midnight hour both were still wide awake. Tania made the first move and suggested that a frolic in the sleep-tank might help them to relax. A wise suggestion because an hour later they were both asleep in their bed snuggled up tight in the 'spoons' position; Ashley being tight up against Tania's back. He felt the wetness on Tania's cheeks when she'd kissed his hand just before she'd fallen asleep. Feeling the warmth of her naked back against his chest he thought how he would miss all this physical contact. He wondered where the thought had come from unless it was a reminder of a probable outcome. He thought it was a reference to his experience in Priory Park when he was in that floating ethereal state as he witnessed the people of a long gone era. He remembered the experience as if it were yesterday. And now he too echoed his father's words of 'So that is what it is going to be like'. An out of body experience but would it be of a permanent nature?

Suddenly he received an emotional consolation in the thought that came with Korizazit's prediction that he would 'return to Nazmos but not as he was now.' Was reincarnation possible? Or was there some other meaning to the prediction. Surely it was not possible; or was it?

Next morning Ashley awoke to find he was alone in the bed. He had eventually fallen into a deep sleep and now felt fully refreshed. The sadness and the thoughts of last night were a faded memory and he felt exhilarated by the prospect of what lay ahead of him today. He was keen to view Zarama at first hand though he knew what to expect from Mazazta's conveyed images. He felt like a combatant setting out to view the opposition.

Ashley thought Tania might be somewhere in the apartment but she was not. However she responded to his query to let him know that she had been up quite early and had decided to go for a stroll around the Habitation Platform on her own. There had been few Oannes about and it had been an enjoyable bit of exercise but she was now on her way back to the apartment.

'I shall be with you in about five minutes or so,' she conveyed.

So Ashley just lay in the bed and thought his usual thoughts and found them all very pleasant. Tania, Rachel, Simon, Mazpazam, Muznant and Jazzatnit were but a few of the images that raced through his mind. All in all he was grateful for the life given to him and the fulfilling emotions that came from all who loved him. Vicky also came into his thoughts and he wondered how she was getting on. She and Robert had made a good couple - eventually. Other thoughts were of Mrs Burns and Mrs Preston his Reception and Year 1 teachers; of little Barclay, his Aunt Brenda's King Charles Cavalier spaniel and the loving fun they'd enjoyed together; Jimmy Marshall and Mike Marrs who both became his school friends. He especially remembered that famous cricket match between the upper and lower school and what a close thing it had been for the senior team. Then his granddad Eric appeared in his minds eye and he realised what a tremendous influence he had been. It was granddad's vision and nurturing that had made the family aware of the first gift that Ashley had. And it was from there that he had progressed to discovering his other gifts.

The door of the apartment opened and Tania's cheery voice brought Ashley back to the present.

'Okay, my sleepy-head Romeo,' came Tania's dulcet tones, 'sits you up and I shall get you a mug of tea pronto.'

The tea and chat was followed by Ashley shaving and showering and then a speedy breakfast. Towards the end they were joined by Simon and Mazpazam. And before Ashley could be given a final mug of tea Simon interrupted to say that the Zero-g ships were ready and waiting.

'They are all being loaded up as we speak and I have been sent especially by Korizazit and the captain to escort you there,' said Simon.

'Right then, lets not keep everybody waiting,' said Ashley smiling and rising up from his seat.

Korizazit met them outside the apartment and the five of them proceeded towards the lift up to the cargo platform. Once up there they went straight to the room for donning the electrostatic suits. Putting these on was easy since they were a loose fitting item. And it was not long before the five of them were seated in an advantageous position opposite a large view panel at one side of the Zero-g ship. Korizazit sat beside Ashley with Tania on the other side together with Simon and Mazpazam.

The ship's door was sealed shut soon after and a few minutes later the lights within the airlock dimmed. Then the large outer doors in the side of Silverstreak opened slowly to reveal the sinister blackness of space. Ashley always thought of space as a dangerous place but Simon and Mazpazam revelled in the glory of it. To them nothing was as enchanting or as beautiful.

One by one each Zero-g ship floated off the airlock deck and proceeded to exit the starship. Ashley's ship went straight out from the airlock to a position ten miles distant. As the gravity effect from Silverstreak was lost the gravity effect from Zarama took over. This was at the much reduced level of a quarter of Nazmos gravity but nevertheless most welcome; as were the thigh and shoulder clamps. The other two Zero-g ships went to positions at right angles to the path of Ashley's ship and both to the ten miles distance from Silverstreak.

All the Zero-g ships pointed themselves towards Zarama before commencing a slow flat rotation. This would enable all of the view panels to face towards Zarama in turn so that each passenger got a good view of it. Since Ashley and Tania were near the forward part of the ship it was not long before Zarama appeared within their view panel. As it moved slowly across from one side of their window panel to the other Ashley got a very good sighting of it for about three minutes. Ashley's impression of Zarama was that of a very large bright star and with magnification appeared exactly like the image Mazazta had conveyed. The intense heat of Zarama was well shielded inside the ship.

However as Ashley stared at the distant Dwarf Star he again felt a sympathy towards it for some strange reason and yet at the same time he knew what had to be done. Zarama had either to be deflected from its current path or else destroyed altogether. An instinctive sense came into Ashley's mind that it might have to be the latter – remembering his failed experience with Sirius B.

While staring keenly at Zarama Ashley gained the impression that it was not as bright as Sirius B and the image of that glowing ball of his dream came into his mind. He concluded that Zarama was a much older White Dwarf star and possibly twice as ancient as Sirius B. The Oannes scientists would probably have come to a similar conclusion and have ascribed a precise age to it.

As it neared the end of the window traverse Ashley willed a further magnification of the Dwarf Star. Now he could see Zarama really close up so that it filled his vision as a large disc but again Ashley could not discern any specific features upon its surface. There was a corona glow around its edges which lent fuzziness to its appearance. And then it was gone from his window view.

Within the cabin there was a hushed silence as others took in their own viewing of Zarama. Simon, Mazpazam and Korizazit sitting alongside Ashley and Tania were also silent as there was nothing really to comment upon. They'd come to see Zarama at first hand and that is just what had been achieved. Zarama was what it was being neither spectacular nor disappointing. Silverstreak had journeyed 423 light years to be here and now confronted by Zarama at the close up distance of just four million miles was a great achievement. The initial objective had been achieved.

The trip back to the airlock took fifteen minutes and soon all three Zero-g ships were settled comfortably upon its deck with full gravity restored. This was a relief for Ashley and Tania. Apparently the Oannes weren't as prone to the effects of low gravity as were their human counterparts. However Korizazit expressed an opinion that he did not like being in space with little or no gravity sensation and had never liked the shuttle transfers between spaceships.

The entire viewing operation outside of Silverstreak had lasted just over an hour and Ashley thought it long enough. The reduced gravity level was not something he relished at the best of times and it always required Zanos to settle his mind to the new conditions.

Having disembarked off the Zero-g ship and then divested themselves of the electrostatic suits, Simon and Mazpazam guided their little group to the elevators and down to the Habitation Platform. They then made their way towards the captain's quarters. They were greeted by a smiling Wastanomi who took charge by thanking Simon and Mazpazam for performing their duty. It was his form of polite dismissal and for his officers to resume their ship duties. He then ushered Ashley, Tania and Korizazit into his quarters where a glass of Wazu was provided as they sat down. The captain seemed to expect a comment from them and it was Korizazit who gave the first response.

'We must thank you captain for allowing us to make this momentous viewing trip,' he said with great feeling in his voice. 'It will be an experience that I shall remember and I will convey it all to my fellow governing council members when I see them. Just as we treasure the images of Gozmanot from Ashley's regression experience so shall this close viewing encounter with Zarama also become part of our history.'

The captain nodded and smiled as he turned towards Ashley.

'I too must thank you captain for allowing this viewing excursion outside Silverstreak,' said Ashley. 'We had a tremendous sighting of Zarama. As a stellar object a White Dwarf Star is quite a thing of beauty. It is another added pinpoint of shining light among the vast array of galaxy stars. One has to admire it. Yet this one moves along a sinister path which must be altered and sent to its destruction in the giant star Rasalgethi. One way or another Zarama must cease to exist and I somehow felt sympathetic towards its plight. But what needs to be done must be done.'

The captain nodded his understanding of what Ashley had said.

'Well spoken Ashley,' he said. 'I feel much as you do. There is beauty in the universe of stars all around us and we of the Space Academy institution have chosen to live in its environment. It is natural for us. With Zarama gone there will be one less bright light to see. But then stars are being born and are dying on a regular basis; so Zarama will become just another statistic.'

'Yes Captain that is so true and I shall remember your words when I tackle Zarama,' said Ashley.

'Good,' said the captain returning to a business footing. 'And if it is alright with you perhaps we can discuss the timetable for when you wish to proceed with the main task in hand. It is for you to make that decision but I would prefer that an agenda be set in time.'

'Yes Captain, I have been thinking about this moment for a very long time,' said Ashley, 'and there is no preparation time that I need except in my mindset. However I must think of others; namely my wife and my son and the scientists and crew on board Silverstreak. There are some unknowns about this mission that chiefly concern me so I would like to give them all a few days to accept the idea of me finally going out to deal with Zarama. The reality of the immensity of my task and of its finality must be allowed to germinate. I think a two day interval would not come as too much of a shock to their minds. Voortazin has no idea of the real challenge facing me so he too needs to prepare mentally.'

Ashley paused for a several seconds before continuing.

'So Captain, may I suggest that Voortazin and I venture out against Zarama at about midday on the third day from today.'

Tania had gripped Ashley's hand in a fierce hold and her face had gone a lighter shade of pale with her lips tightly compressed. If Ashley had suggested a week from today her reaction would have been the same. Her husband of forty six years was about to carry out the Big Task that had been in the offing since the day he was born. He had been designed for this and it was his destiny; so why did she feel so sad about it. Was it her woman's intuition telling her inner mind of something disastrous? Perhaps. Was he about to leave her or be changed according to Korizazit's inner voice message?

'You will however return to Nazmos one day but not as you are now.'

Ashley squeezed Tania's hand in return and conveyed a private message. She looked back up at him through blurry eyes and conveyed back that she would be strong – for Simon and Rachel's sakes.

'A brave decision Ashley,' said Korizazit and then conveyed his own private message.

'Thank you for that Ashley,' said the captain, 'I shall formulate a detailed agenda and then get Zanos to convey it to everyone on board Silverstreak. On the day in question you will do me the honour of coming here first and I shall accompany you and Voortazin to the Zero-g ship assigned to you. The other two ships will also go out with you to monitor any change in Zarama's path.'

He then looked at Tania with an intensity that Ashley had not seen from him before.

'I realise that it will be difficult for you to see Ashley leaving Silverstreak,' said Wastanomi in a soft polite voice. 'I have thought about this for some time now and feel that you would like to be out there not too far from him. So if it be your wish I can arrange for you to be aboard one of the accompanying Zero-g ships. In that way you will have sight of Ashley's ship and the consolation that he will know that you are watching him out there.'

Tania visibly relaxed her grip of Ashley's hand and smiled at the captain.

'Oh Captain that would be wonderful,' she said. 'I am ever so grateful. And may I request that my son and his wife be beside me as well. I shall need their support. Ashley is their father too.'

The captain was smiling as broadly as he could.

'That would be perfectly in order,' he said. 'I shall instruct for it to be so. It is only right, for you are one family. I shall delegate one of the scientists on board to continually update you with the reports of Ashley's progress against Zarama.'

'Thank you Captain,' was all Tania could manage in a whisper.

'And I thank you personally,' said Ashley to Wastanomi. 'To know that Tania and Simon are also out there watching me will give me added resolve.'

Korizazit conveyed a private message to Wastanomi and received a smile in return.

'Yes of course honourable council member it will be as you wish,' said the captain to Korizazit.

Then to Ashley he said. 'It appears that our honourable Korizazit would also like to accompany your wife and son on the day. And so it shall be. Unfortunately as captain of Silverstreak I cannot be out there with you much as I would like to be. But a captain cannot leave his ship when not in port so to speak. But I shall be kept aware of progress as it happens through updates from Zanos.'

There was not much more to be said so Korizazit, Ashley and Tania took their leave of the captain and conveyed that they would keep to the regular noon meetings as usual – at least for the next two days.

The next day only one Zero-g ship ventured outside Silverstreak with a group of Oannes scientists. Their purpose was not clear but they had their own agenda which was to record and analyse data pertaining to White Dwarf stars. Being this close to one gave them an opportunity to look into its depths and perhaps establish a timeline of its history. The Zero-g ship spent just over an hour probing Zarama's secrets before returning to Silverstreak.

The midday meeting in Captain Wastanomi's quarters took place as usual and lasted only half an hour as there was nothing new to discuss. Thereafter Ashley, Tania and Korizazit took a stroll about the Habitation Platform and met with several scientists and civilian passengers. Most had set duties aboard Silverstreak to do mainly with this Zarama based mission. At the moment there was little essential work that needed doing so a general relaxed atmosphere prevailed aboard the starship. The only real effort was concentrated on the food growing level where intense planning was in progress. This was because of the fresh orders that the captain had issued with regard to the lengthy return journey. The Oannes were always well prepared for every eventuality and ample supplies were available aboard for long term crop cultivation in the refurbished food growing tanks. It was just a matter of planning the changes required for efficient rotational crop cultivation patterns.

Simon and Mazpazam came to his parent's apartment for the evening meal and stayed till late. Korizazit felt that these final days before Ashley confronted Zarama should be spent privately with his family. So after the midday meal with the captain he did not see Ashley again for the remainder of the day period. In fact he spent the time alone in his apartment trying to analyse and draw his own conclusions with regard to what he considered was a likely outcome of future events for Ashley. There was nothing definite to cling to and Korizazit did not like uncertainty. Yet in his mind he could not shake off the feeling that it was not going to be a good result for Ashley. He gave no indication of this outwardly either in his looks or his manner.

Tania too had arrived at a similar conclusion and yet neither had conveyed their thoughts to each other about it. Although Tania felt sadness for herself she also had a feeling of exultation at what Ashley was going out to achieve. She was confident that Ashley would not fail against Zarama and knew that he had set his mind on a certain course. It was a plan of action for success no matter what it would cost him. He had been born for this – 'the big task' as Philip had put it – and Tania was proud that for forty six beautiful years she had been blessed as his wife. Whatever happened out there his name would be remembered forever. Seventy years was a good lifespan for a human and Tania felt that the memories of their years together were brilliantly imprinted in her mind. Nothing and no one could erase that.

On the night before he was to tackle Zarama Ashley and Tania decided to have an early night alone. Simon and Mazpazam left for their own apartment on instinct and both had wistful expressions as they walked out of the apartment door.

'See you in the morning dad,' said Simon. 'We have been invited by the captain to attend the meeting with you tomorrow. We were surprised but quite pleased. We can go together from here after your breakfast.'

'Goodnight son,' said Tania and she went and hugged and kissed Mazpazam as well.

When the door had shut Tania turned around and put her arms around Ashley and kissed him firmly mouth against mouth. They clung to each other for what seemed an eternity.

'I love you husband,' she said in a whisper, 'and I will love you always forever and ever.'

Ashley then made his decision and conveyed everything that was in his heart and mind including all that he had kept hidden from her; except about the Zanos surrogate thing.

'I already knew,' said Tania, 'a woman always does. It is a wonderful thing that you must do darling and I gladly let you go because of that. I release you to it but I shall still talk to you as if you are here.'

'And I shall be listening,' said Ashley. And then he began to laugh which puzzled Tania until he conveyed his thoughts. Then she too gave a giggle before bursting into peals of laughter. Their imagination ran wild as they communicated their thoughts. It had to do with Korizazit's inner voice prediction that Ashley would return to Nazmos but not as he was now. Could it mean a reincarnation or something similar?

'A Koala bear would be cute,' conveyed Tania.

'Or a Barclay,' responded Ashley. 'woof, woof.'

'Meow, meow,' conveyed Tania.

'An eagle would be great.'

'How about a dolphin?'

'Or even an Oannes.'

Suddenly this brought a halt to the mirth. It seemed a serious consideration and both went quietly pensive.

'Cheer up darling,' said Ashley, 'it might never happen.'

'Let's spend some time in the sleep-tank,' suggested Tania, 'we can relax in there.'

So for the next hour and a half they sat and floated in the sleep-tank and talked of their past memories and about all the things they'd done. Every now and then Ashley kissed Tania's hand which brought calmness to their emotions. This was the peace and calm of the love that had existed from the moment Tania had first laid eyes on Ashley. The passion may have faded but the love and feeling of belonging remained strong and would do forever.

'If this was to be our last night together,' thought Tania to herself, 'then let it be the most memorable one.'

The love they made was with their minds and the fulfilment far exceeded anything physical.

Back in their bed sleep came gradually with Ashley going first. Tania looked at him with keen eyes and kissed him a dozen times before she too drifted into sleep.

They slept late and it was Ashley who woke first to find Tania still entwined within his arms. Their bodies were warm and each was damp with their combined perspiration of the night. He looked into her face and knew he would miss seeing it like this. To hold her would be a pleasant memory only. Would he be able to regress to a previous time? Was it a possibility? He did not know since his gifts might no longer be his to command.

Tania opened her eyes suddenly – his thoughts had penetrated her conscious and awakened her. How could they not have? She tightened her squeeze on him and felt the moistness of their bodies.

'We should shower,' she said.

'Yes,' as he tried to untangle himself out of her embrace.

'In a moment,' she said as she clung tightly to him.

Ashley smiled and kissed her lips gently. She responded in kind and then her ferocity built until she had climbed onto him. Their passion lasted only minutes before subsiding into a calm nuzzling cuddle.

'Come on darling, lets shower together,' said Tania with a hint of sadness in her voice.

An hour later they were seated at their table having breakfast when Simon and Mazpazam communicated their arrival outside their door and were invited in.

'How are you dad?' asked Simon.

Ashley knew what he meant.

'As ready as I'll ever be son,' he replied and smiled at Mazpazam too.

Ashley normally had two mugs of tea with his breakfast; one after the other. But today he asked for a third just before they were due to see Captain Wastanomi.

This put them slightly behind in their visit schedule to the captain's quarters. When they did arrive a pleasant faced Wastanomi gestured for Simon and Mazpazam to precede them inside. Then Ashley and Tania followed the captain in and were surprised by the reception they received. All of the starship's officers were assembled inside and were standing two deep around the centre table. Ashley recognised the faces and greeted each telepathically by name.

'My officers expressed the desire to see you before you ventured out against Zarama,' said the captain. 'They wanted to wish you success personally and I could not deny them the privilege.'

'Thank you,' said Ashley aloud to the assembled Oannes officers, 'thank you very much indeed. This is a great honour you convey and it will give me confidence and strength in my push against Zarama.'

Korizazit had been beside the door when Ashley came in and now he approached and put a hand on Ashley's shoulder.

'You have all the strength you need my friend,' he said. 'You will succeed. I have seen it.'

'Thank you honourable Korizazit,' said Ashley turning to his friend, 'I am glad you came on this journey.'

'As am I,' he replied.

And then Ashley did a very strange and out of character thing. In an involuntary gesture he blew a cool puff of his breath across Korizazit's forehead while conveying a private message. 'Remember this,' was the gist of it.

On the table were jugs filled with Wazu and rows of glasses alongside. Several officers then stepped forward and began pouring Wazu into the glasses but to half levels only.

'Officers,' said Voortazin who was to command Ashley's Zero-g ship, 'let us drink to the fulfilment of this venture before us. May Ashley achieve all that he desires against Zarama. May his success be swift, safe and sure as always.'

'Hear, hear,' added Simon, 'and may it be a speedy one at that.'

They all watched as Captain Wastanomi picked up a glass, raised it in Ashley's direction and slowly brought it to his lips. He smiled and then with a rapid tilting action he poured the Wazu down his throat in one large gulp. He then replaced the empty glass back on the table with a resounding smack. His officers followed suit in similar fashion but randomly such that a staccato of table tapping filled the room as the glasses were forcefully placed back on the table.

There was a brief moment of smiles all around before Ashley too picked up a glass and held it aloft.

'As always,' he said, 'may it be swift, safe and sure.'

Then putting the glass to his lips he drank the Wazu in two quick gulps before tapping it back onto the table.

Then Tania slowly picked up a glass and was the last to do so. She moved towards her husband while moving the glass into her left hand. Stopping in front of him she dipped two fingers of her right hand into the Wazu, kissed her fingers and then reached up and made a sign on his forehead.

'I bless you my husband with all that is holy and venerated by all religions both here and on Earth,' she said barely above a whisper.

Once again she dipped her fingers in the glass of Wazu and repeated the gesture.

'And may all success come to you my dearest,' she added.

Then she slowly drank what was left in her glass and gently placed it back on the table with hardly a sound. There were tears in her eyes for all to see.

It was an emotional moment and all were drawn in to the feeling. How could they not?

It was the captain who then broke the spell.

'My fellow officers,' he said in his usual commanding tone, 'let us proceed with the task in hand. We shall escort Ashley to his ship and I will lead the way.'

Ashley recognised this as a great honour from the captain of a starship.

'You do me a great honour Captain,' said Ashley, 'and if you will permit it then Tania and I would like to walk beside you.'

Wastanomi smiled and nodded. It would have been embarrassing to walk alone ahead of his officers. And so they went as a group towards the lift to take them up to the cargo platform. Once there they went straight to the room for the electrostatic suits. The captain waited outside with half of his officers while the electrostatic suits were being put on. Several of his officers also put on the suits. Putting them on was easy since they were a loose fitting garment and took a few minutes only. They then proceeded on towards the adjacent airlock chamber which had its inner doors fully open. Ashley was always taken by surprise at the size of the airlock chamber and at what could be accommodated within.

There the three Zero-g ships sat serenely spaced apart from one another and the captain led them to the nearest one which was quite empty. The other two seemed to be flush with many Oannes already on board.

'Ashley,' said the captain, 'this is the ship allocated to you and officer Voortazin. The other ships are already loaded up with our scientists and their equipment. However seats have been reserved for your family members and honourable Korizazit on this second ship. Some of my officers wish to accompany you and so they shall on the other ships. You may all board when you are ready.'

'Thank you Captain,' said Ashley. 'I hope to see you before long.'

The captain then nodded and reached out and shook Ashley's hand.

'May you succeed in this task,' he conveyed privately to Ashley only.

He then turned about and strode purposefully out of the airlock and he was followed by just over half of his officers. Those who stayed behind had been given permission to ride on the other Zero-g ships as observers.

Ashley turned to Tania and put his arms around her and hugged her for quite a while and conveyed a very private message. She smiled and whispered softly 'I love you'. Then just as he stepped back he gently flicked the hair on her forehead with a finger and she gave an understanding smile.

He then walked to Simon and gave his son a firm prolonged man hug. His private message to Simon was simply 'You know don't you son, so look after your mum.'

Simon nodded his understanding.

Then it was Mazpazam's turn. He put his arms partly around her in a gentle caress and conveyed another private message. 'I love you as my own, take care of my son.'

She nodded her understanding and Ashley knew that Simon had discussed the future with her.

'You will meet her again,' came the message from his inner voice and Ashley had a vague understanding of it. But how could that be?

Finally he came to Korizazit and reached out with his hand. Korizazit took it in both of his and held on tightly as he smiled.

'You have been a good friend to me,' said Ashley. 'I hope all your visions come true.'

Korizazit replied in a private message and Ashley acknowledged it with a nod and a smile.

Ashley then turned to Voortazin and said, 'I am ready, shall we board our ship?'

'Yes,' said Voortazin with a smile, 'I am yours to command for those are my instructions. You will be captain of the ship and I will do as you wish.'

Ashley nodded with a returned smile and turned to board the zZro-g ship. Inside he walked along to the very front area and took a seat where he was central to a view panel facing forward. Voortazin followed behind but walked towards the rear area in a direct line behind Ashley's position.

Communication between Ashley and Voortazin would be done telepathically from now on as agreed between them earlier. When the thigh and shoulder clamps were in place Voortazin issued the command for the ship's door to close. He then had to await instructions from the airlock system.

In the meantime Simon, Mazpazam, Tania, Korizazit and several of the officers walked to the second Zero-g ship and boarded. The remaining officers boarded the third ship in the airlock. Seats had been reserved for Tania, Simon, Mazpazam and Korizazit at the very front similar to the seat area that Ashley occupied in the other ship. When all were seated and thighs had been gently clamped the doors of the Zero-g ships were slowly closed.

There was a period of about five minutes before the lighting in the air lock dimmed. All its doors were now closed both inner and outer. Then slowly without a sound the outer airlock doors commenced to open to expose the vast blackness of space. The dim lighting in the airlock gave it a sinister effect.

With the outer doors fully open the first Zero-g ship lifted off the airlock deck and smoothly moved through and out into space. The second ship followed at a safe distance and finally Ashley's ship also rose up and moved through the airlock door. Once outside Silverstreak the blank space effect was replaced by the universe of stars appearing as if by magic. Their brilliancy never ceased to amaze.

'Isn't it beautiful,' was a remark that he recognised as Tania's.

'Yes, we are just coming out now,' he conveyed back as an open remark to all.

Ashley directed Voortazin to take the ship straight outwards to a position ten miles from Silverstreak. The other two Zero-g ships had by arrangement each gone to positions about five miles out but in directions above and below the starship. Tania watched as Ashley's ship had continued travelling to its further-out position. She felt relief when she saw it eventually stop and turn to face in the direction of Zarama. Although it was a small image in the distance she applied for magnification to get a close-up view. She wondered what Ashley was planning to do and alternately looked from Zarama to his Zero-g ship expecting something to happen. There was no communication from him and she realised there could be none if he was in pink mode.

Meanwhile Ashley looked back at the commander of his ship and conveyed a request to which Voortazin agreed with a nod. Very slowly their ship began a movement towards Zarama and then gradually increased its pace. When its velocity reached 100 mph all acceleration ceased but its movement towards Zarama continued. It was then that Ashley decided to proceed with his planned action.

He concentrated his gaze upon the Dwarf Star and willed for it to be pushed in the away direction with the maximum possible force of his telekinetic ability. He waited five minutes but his instinct told him that it was not enough just like when he had tried against Sirius B. He decided to go to the next stage of his plan but which he first conveyed to Voortazin.

He went into pink mode and concentrating his mind exerted a telekinetic force upon Zarama at the push level of sixteen. This was the push level he had been warned not to exceed all those years ago. He waited another few moments and again his mind told him that it had not been enough. What must he do he thought and a plan to up the push level crossed his mind.

'Don't waste time stepping your push level in stages – you must go straight to the very maximum level of thirty with your telekinetic ability.'

Ashley's inner voice had finally spoken or was it someone else? The thought of Philip came into his mind. Philip had said he would be there when the need arose. In his mind Ashley knew now that there was no higher level than thirty but from his puny human mind would it be enough for the big task. Then suddenly as if a brilliant new plan had been revealed he knew that beyond the barrier level sixteen his mind would enter another sphere both in size and power.

And so Ashley performed his final task in his human form. Looking directly at Zarama he increased his pink mode push to the instructed level of thirty. For a brief instant nothing seemed to change. Then Ashley felt like he was extending outside his human body and suddenly he was outside of the ship but in mind only. And as his consciousness billowed ever larger he felt a tremendous power building inside him. Although the human body of Ashley sat slumped lifeless in the Zero-g ship seat his mental consciousness filled the space all the way to Silverstreak.

He felt that the power of the universe was being given to him and he grasped it with meaningful pleasure. As his expanding self sped towards Zarama he looked with pity upon it for it seemed to shrink before him like a bully cowering at the approach of a giant. Suddenly Ashley found himself alongside a diminutive Zarama and the power of his mind gave it his mightiest telekinetic push – like a proverbial kick up the backside but an almighty one.

What happened next was the fulfilling of Korizazit's dream vision. Zarama jerked away from Ashley's vicinity with such tremendous acceleration that all of its internal gravity was not enough to sustain the cohesive bonding of its atomic structure. It burst open as if shattered by an internal explosive force like a mini-supernova. Zarama's speed away from its former position kept its shattered remnants away from Silverstreak. The image that Tania got from her Zero-g ship position was of Zarama rapidly diminishing from sight before its explosive display occurred. The showery display was huge filling a good part of her forward view. It was clearly visible in the distance and Tania was reminded of a bonfire night firework rocket exploding high up in the night sky. But Zarama's explosion far exceeded anything she had ever seen before. Also watching beside her were Simon, Mazpazam and Korizazit. A shocked telepathic silence existed within their ship.

'Gozmanot's vision is fulfilled,' said an excited Korizazit. 'The fiery dragon has been vanquished by a being from another planet.'

Then he added, 'It is just as I saw it in my dream. Ashley has done some great things for Nazmos but this last is his greatest achievement. Nazmos and Earth are safe now. Zarama is pulverised just like what Ashley did to the asteroid Steins when he first demonstrated his telekinetic ability all those years ago.'

'But what of my Ashley,' asked Tania with tears in her eyes?

Ashley in his ephemeral state turned back towards Voortazin who seemed transfixed with his mouth open by what he had just witnessed; and Ashley conveyed his message.

'Return to Silverstreak,' was all he conveyed as a terse command.

Ashley then directed his thoughts to the Zero-g ship carrying Tania and the others. He willed for a puff of air to blow onto Korizazit's forehead. He then caused the large curl of hair at the front of Tania's head to be flicked up with another puff of wind while conveying an emotion of his love for her. She smiled an understanding and looked upwards.

Then he was inside Silverstreak and willed for a strong breeze to blow momentarily across the Habitation Platform causing the Oannes there including Captain Wastanomi to wonder at this strange phenomenon. Zanos reported nothing unusual; there was no leak or drop in air pressure.

While the captain was still in puzzlement Ashley conveyed a simple message to him.

'Return to Nazmos, they will know,' was all it said.

Ashley now felt his conscious begin to expand again as if something was pulling at him.

'Is it time to go,' he thought?

But he had a couple of things to do and wished for more time.

He first willed to be on Nazmos and was there in an instant and inside Ritozanan's old home where Rachel and Margaret were having a meal. Here again he caused the hair at the front of their heads to be flicked by a gentle puff of air while conveying a thought of love and wellbeing along with a short message to Rachel.

'Its dad,' cried Rachel as she burst into tears. 'He's done it Margaret, he's done it.'

'I love you dad,' she sobbed and then added, 'yes I will, I will. I will tell them.'

She would go to the governing council and tell them all that Ashley had conveyed.

Now Ashley had his final task. He willed himself on Earth and to the home he had grown up in. He went to his mother Lillian's bedside - for it was the middle of the night there. He looked down upon her sleeping form and instantly knew what he must do. He would induce a dream into her sleep domain to carry his message of farewell to her.

In the dream Lillian saw her son Ashley standing in front of her in a large outdoor garden like those in a stately home. He leaned forward and kissed her on each cheek in turn smiling all the while. She then saw him turn and walk towards some nearby garden steps. The ten steps led up a grassy embankment to the next garden level above. She saw Ashley reach the top of the steps and slowly turn to look down at her and smile. Then she saw him raise an arm and wave to her in a farewell gesture. The emotion of love poured down upon her and she saw him turn and walk away and sink from her sight.

She would remember this dream and later when the news reached her she would realise that her son had come to her to say his final goodbye. Something so dramatic would remain with her forever. She would remember the night of Friday June 14th 2052 for this very reason.

Ashley now felt drawn back towards Silverstreak and he watched the proceedings with regard to his human body with a detached interest. His lifeless body being taken from the Zero-g ship after it had docked in the airlock compartment, put onto a floating pallet and taken to one of the side rooms in the Cargo Bay. He watched as Tania, Simon and Mazpazam sat beside him as his body lay there. He was looking down at things happening below like when he had regressed and floated around that time at Priory Park. He saw Tania take one of his hands in hers and stroke it and whisper that she loved him. She spoke as if she knew he was there and listening and she was right for he immediately conveyed his own emotion of love for her. Ashley knew that she recognised that he was there when she nodded and smiled as she looked upwards. She remembered the images of his Priory Park experience that he had conveyed then and knew he must be looking down at her. Tania conveyed her thoughts to Simon and Mazpazam and they nodded as they too had sensed the emotion.

Ashley kept his presence in a hover near Tania when the container arrived and his body was placed within it. He stayed when the lid was placed to seal the container permanently. He also stayed till the coffin was finally placed in its storage receptacle at the very tail end of the starship and the portal door was shut.

'It is finished,' thought Ashley's conscious mind which now began to expand and he felt as if something was definitely pulling him away.

Spread out before him was The Milky Way galaxy as if in miniature form. Everything he knew was being left behind. The reality of his new phase crowded upon him – the end of a spectacular material life. All those gifts for one purpose he thought. He would never see his family again or his friends both human and Oannes. No spring or beautiful summers to be seen. And as he thought these thoughts a tremendous feeling of loneliness, vulnerability, nakedness and helplessness overcame him.

Then a warm comforting emotion enveloped him and he sensed the essence of a great power, greater than anything he could imagine drawing him into its haven. And he was not alone. He felt the consciousness of others who came close in and around him. His dad Alex was among these giving him comforting thoughts. They also conveyed infinite knowledge and suddenly Ashley realised that what had been told him about man being created in the likeness of the Supreme Being was true but not as he had initially thought. Man was an image of God's mind – and therein was the mystery of it. It was the soul that was of God, for God and from God.

Ashley continued his journey growing ever larger as he did so. He moved about at will through the universe until it seemed to end in nothingness. He was in an immense blank though comforting void. It was a void so vast and empty of substance that there was nothing to compare. Yet he did not feel alone. A vast presence surrounded and comforted him. There were other universes comparable to the one he had left speeding past on some predestined journey. Each seemed to move in a set direction and it was only when he traced backwards was he able to discern their origin; an origin of light which seemed to draw him in that direction. He willed his consciousness towards it and immediately he was there. He sensed too that he had moved into a new dimension and this confused him. Was Zarama here too he thought? No this was like a vast ocean of glorious light only a billion times brighter. The light had a glow of calmness about it and from it came an outpouring of goodness and love that filled Ashley to the core.

The love coming into him was so immense that the love he felt in return for it was a million fold greater than any love he had experienced during his lifetime as a human being on Earth. It was beyond imagination and he wanted to stay like this forever. Ashley realised that the love that he had felt on Earth had been but a taster of the immense love he now experienced. Love, peace, wellbeing, goodness, generosity and caring were but facets within this greatest of gifts – being near to the Divine Being he knew to be his Creator and God.

Ashley reached out and tried to enter this wonderful domain but he could not. Something prevented him and he knew not why. Then he understood. His turn had not yet come. Something more needed to be done. Gradually a dark fog descended upon him and his consciousness was pulled in another direction – back towards the universe he had left. Total darkness enveloped him – yet the feeling of peace, love and happiness remained as his mind faded into a deep dark sleep format.

'Wow,' exclaimed Simon and Tania together when they saw Zarama first speed away from its stationary position and then its explosive disintegration. The massive firework type showery display was quite impressive before it disappeared into the distance and oblivion.

The Zero-g ships as well as Silverstreak had to adjust for the sudden lack of gravitational pull from what was formerly a nearby White Dwarf Star. Zanos made a general announcement that an adjustment had been made for the lack of any gravitational pull from Zarama.

It was a short while later that Captain Wastanomi felt the sudden flow of air blow across the Habitation Platform. It was strange for such a movement of air to blow as it did unless the starship had sprung a massive leak. Zanos confirmed that there was no such malfunction. Then the message 'Return to Nazmos' was conveyed to him loud and clear and he knew it was not from Zanos.

'He has been successful,' thought Wastanomi and it was not long before full communications began arriving from the Zero-g ships.

'Zarama is no more – it is totally destroyed,' was the message that came through repeatedly. There was an emotion of jubilation mixed in the messages.

Then the message from Voortazin also came through filled with an emotion of extreme sadness.

'I am returning to the airlock with the body of Ashley on board,' was all it conveyed.

When all three Zero-g ships were safely settled upon the deck of the airlock and the usual procedures completed, air pressure was restored and the ships doors were opened. As soon as the cargo platform large door opened Captain Wastanomi was in there and issued the command that no one was to disembark except Tania, Simon and Mazpazam. He went to their ship and reached out to assist Tania down even though Simon was there beside her. Then together the four of them walked to Voortazin's zero-g ship. He was still within but was now standing right behind where Ashley sat with his head slumped forward.

Simon, Tania, Mazpazam and the captain climbed aboard but at a prompt from Simon they stopped there to let Tania alone go forward to her husband. She stepped to where Ashley was sitting and slowly kneeled down in front of him. She leaned forward with his knees against her breasts as she reached up and lifted his face in the palms of her cupped hands. His eyes were closed but the hint of a smile remained on his lips.

'Oh my beautiful, beautiful Ashley,' she whispered, 'I knew the instant you flicked my hair when we were still out there. You have achieved everything that you set out to do. The big task is completed and you can rest easy. Thank you for my wonderful life darling, you will always be in my heart. The memories of us together will sustain me.'

She then put her head down into his lap and wept quietly with her tears soaking into his electrostatic suit. She still wore hers. Then she felt a hand on her shoulder and looked up with tear-filled eyes at her son's moist eyes. Mazpazam was on her other side but stood there silently her arms down at her sides. An emotion of grief exuded from her. She conveyed a calm understanding of Tania's loss and how they were all sad at Ashley's sacrifice and glad that he had destroyed Zarama.

The captain gave the command for the thigh and shoulder clamps on Ashley to be released and nodded to Simon.

'Wait,' said Tania. She then leaned forward; raised Ashley's face and kissed him on his forehead before stepping back and nodding that she was ready.

Simon put his right arm under his father's knees and the other behind his lower back and lifted him up without difficulty. With his mother and wife either side of him he carried his father to the door and off the Zero-g ship. Waiting there were a group of the starship's officers with a floating pallet ready for Ashley. The pallet was well cushioned and Simon gently laid his father upon it with a little assistance from one of the officers. Then as if they were a guard of honour some walked ahead of and some behind the pallet. Tania, Simon and Mazpazam walked beside it on the one side while the captain and a row of officers were on the other. They walked to a side room not far from the airlock chamber and positioned the pallet upon a table. There was seating either side of it.

Simon knew the starship protocol for a death on board during a space mission. The body had to be encapsulated within a sealed container and kept at a special location on the starship. This had to be done as soon as was conveniently possible. Accidents could and did happen and the Oannes were always prepared.

Ashley's family would be allowed a couple of hours beside him. Anyone else would also be permitted to pay their respects but only briefly.

Tania asked Simon about the electrostatic suit and he conveyed that this would be removed soon. And it was shortly after this that four of the ships crew came forward and cut the electrostatic suit into slices and gently pulled the pieces clear. Tania was pleased at the way it was done without disturbing the body unnecessarily. Ashley's eyes remained closed and the hint of that smile was still there.

'How majestic he looks,' thought Tania. She gazed upon her husband and her heart swelled with pride as she held his hand.

Korizazit came forward and stood beside Tania and conveyed his emotions to her. She looked around and smiled up at him. He also conveyed to her details of the protocol and ceremony that must be followed when a member of the Nazmos governing council dies. Ashley must be taken back to Nazmos and all ceremonies conducted. Then his final destination would be into Raznat itself as was the custom for all Oannes.

Tania nodded. She was not sentimental about where her husband's final resting place should be. He had given his life for the Oannes people and Raznat would be a fitting crematorium. Yes, all of Nazmos knew him or of him while on Earth few did.

Ashley's hand is cold she thought so I know he is not in there. She looked upwards and smiled. Was he seeing her as he had in his Priory Park experience? Very likely he was. She conveyed her thoughts to him and felt consolation in the process. She did not expect a reply and none came.

Only this morning he had asked her what tunic and leggings he should wear. She had suggested the pale yellow tunic with bright green borders. And the leggings also of pale green but with a pale yellow bottom cuff with moccasin footwear in a light tan colour. She looked at him now lying silent and still and visualised him getting dressed in their apartment. He had smiled at her as he put the leggings on over his underwear. She had chosen these because they were similar to the very first Oannes clothes he had worn on their first trip to Anztarza.

What lovely memories she could look back upon were some of her thoughts.

Ashley had then said something to her which she hadn't understood at the time.

'Remember this day,' he had said.

'June 14th 2052 it is and so it will remain.'

Now she knew what he had meant. It was to be the date on which he had left this life.

'It is time to say goodbye to dad, mum,' conveyed Simon. 'The container will be arriving soon.'

But it was Korizazit who came in instead. He conveyed that a container was being specially modified to accommodate Ashley's longer body length. The Oannes were shorter by about a foot and all the standard containers were too small. Starships had workshop facilities and the special body container for Ashley would be ready in about an hour.

Tania looked up and smiled. She would have a little extra time beside her Ashley for which she was grateful. So she spoke softly to his lifeless form expressing her innermost thoughts and memories. She just knew he was watching though unable to communicate. However he did manage to convey his own emotion of love for her which Tania sensed immediately. The hour sped by and Korizazit finally conveyed that the coffin container had entered the room.

It was a simple block shape made from the same material as for most spaceships and dome structures and hollow along its central internal length. All its surfaces were smooth and flat. The internal area was dressed in soft pale cream material to act as a cushion for Ashley's body.

Four starship officers including Simon then lifted Ashley's body and gently positioned it inside the container upon the cushioning within. They then stood aside and waited.

Tania went forward and took Ashley's hand nearest her and lifting it placed it across his chest. She then nodded to Simon and he did the same with the other arm. Tania then touched her fingers to her lips and gently placed them upon Ashley's own before stepping back with the softly spoken words, 'Goodbye darling.'

An emotion of love filled the room and Tania smiled because she knew he was watching.

Six officers came forward carrying a large flat four inch thick slab which they carefully placed on top of the container. The fit was perfect. It would take about an hour for the seal to be completed though initial fusion of the base and lid commenced the moment material contact was made.

Tania sensed a change in the atmosphere around her but didn't think anything of it. It was just another feeling within her grief she thought.

Simon then came to his mum and explained the procedure that was about to take place with regard to the container coffin.

'Remember how Mazpazam and I took you up the shaft to show you and dad all the impulse motors and generators at their various levels,' he said.

'Yes I remember,' said Tania.

'Well we will now put dad's coffin on a floating platform and take him up the same shaft but this time we shall go to the topmost point,' said Simon. 'Up there at the very tail end of Silverstreak is an empty platform level. This is reserved for situations like this; contingencies that must be planned for. There are horizontal cubicles specially designed to accommodate container coffins like dads much like the mortuaries have on Earth. Dad's coffin will be placed within one of these until we reach Nazmos. Then a proper ceremony will take place before dad's coffin will be taken into space and ejected towards and into Raznat.'

'May I come up with you son,' said Tania, 'I should like to see this resting place. After all we shan't arrive at Nazmos for the next four and a quarter years. I can think of him while I am down here and feel that he is not far away.'

'The captain expected you to ask that and since the ship is in port - so to speak – he had already anticipated your request and agreed it,' said Simon.

'I wish to attend as well,' said Korizazit and immediately received permission from the captain.

The float pallet carrying Ashley's coffin now lifted up and was guided by one of the ship's officers towards the central area of the Cargo Platform. Two officers had gone ahead to where several Deck Transporters were parked and had brought one to the central area. They didn't have long to wait for Ashley's container coffin which arrived with its entourage. There was ample room on the fifteen feet square transporter deck for the pallet and a dozen or so persons.

Tania stood beside the coffin with Simon and Mazpazam either side of her. The officers lined the rail on three sides when it began its ascent slowly towards the central power access shaft. The ceiling was a hundred feet above the current cargo platform floor and was part of the starship's permanent structure. When the deck transporter reached the power shaft opening there was a brief pause as it manoeuvred to position itself correctly before entering the twenty feet square shaft opening. Then it continued upwards at a steady 10 mph rising velocity for the next ten minutes until it neared the end of the starship. It slowed and then stopped when the ceiling was just twenty feet overhead. It then proceeded sideways and settled on what appeared to be an empty deck floor.

Ashley's coffin was again raised up off the transporter and floated towards the wall area.

An officer got Zanos to open a rectangular portal in the wall which was in fact the door to a recess to accommodate the container coffin. It was a bare chamber with recessed clamps on either side within it. A base plate then came outwards and four officers transferred Ashley's coffin onto it. Gravity here was very low about a fifth of normal so weight was not an issue. The plate supporting the coffin then retracted back into the recess and the portal door was shut. The inner clamps were activated to hold the container firmly in position under all conditions of acceleration. It would remain securely in place during the entire return journey to Nazmos.

Tania went forward and placed her open hand against the closed portal door and whispered her farewell. She then turned briskly around and followed the officers back to the deck transporter with Simon and Mazpazam either side of her. The rest was a blur for her until she found herself back in her apartment with her son and his wife for company only.

They sat and talked for a while and had a drink. Then Simon suggested that it was time for an overdue meal but Tania said not just yet – perhaps later in the evening. After an hour Simon could see that his mum was growing restless in her mind and body and wanted to be left alone.

'We'll leave you now mum and you can be alone with dad here,' Simon said. 'But we will be back and have our evening meal with you.'

'That will be fine son. Your dad is always with me of that I am sure,' said Tania.

When the door closed and Tania was alone she stood for a while just looking around the apartment. He had been here this morning putting on his favourite tunic and leggings she thought. Such a short time ago and now he's gone. She then went to the bed and lay down on her back and stared at the ceiling.

'O Ashley, Ashley,' she whispered, 'I miss you. O how I miss you darling.'

And then the storm burst and an avalanche of grief poured through her being. She turned over and sank her face into the soft pillow and wept like never before. Wracking sobs pulsed through her body as she kept repeating his name over and over. The pillow was soaked with her tears and raising her head she turned it over. Again she sank her face into the pillow but now the sobs came less but the ache in her chest remained.

Then suddenly love flooded the room and she sensed someone laughing. The mood caught on and turning onto her back she smiled a little. Then a bigger smile grew on her face.

'You silly arse,' she said aloud and again she sensed his laughter and she couldn't help a little giggle herself.

She sat up and wiped her eyes with the palms of her hands. Something Ashley would have done himself if needed. She knew he was out there somewhere but then a realisation broke into her thoughts.

'He's not out there,' she thought, 'he's here inside me and will be forever and I can live with that.'

When Simon and Mazpazam came back later in the evening they found her fresh faced and glowing. She had showered and changed into fresh apparel. They looked at each other and smiled. It had worked.

At Mazpazam's insistence Ashley had spent long private mental sessions with Zanos transferring all that he wished to say to his wife after he had gone and would no longer be able to communicate. It was important that Tania felt his presence during those early days for some while at least.

So during the first year of the journey back to Nazmos, Zanos would convey many of Ashley thoughts and emotions to Tania as if Ashley himself was doing so – silly remarks, laughter and all.

The next morning at precisely 6:00am simulated time Silverstreak commenced accelerating towards its 100 FTL cruise velocity for the long journey home. Zanos' estimate of four years and eighty days was to be accurate and the journey itself was uneventful and for Tania it proved not to be an unpleasant one. She was regularly feted in the officer's mess with Simon and Mazpazam always beside her. Ashley too was near and ever-present in her thoughts and Zanos proved an excellent surrogate in his place. However the connection was allowed to fade after about a year – by design – and then Tania understood that he must have needed to move on. Simon and Mazpazam were her chief concerns now and she was looking forward to her reunion with Rachel on Nazmos. They were her family and Nazmos would be her home. Looking back she was grateful for the wonderful life that she'd had with her Ashley. Ashley had been and still was her knight in shining armour. His armour had been that tremendous gift to go into pink mode and slow time. He had been her fabulous Pink Knight. No one could have asked for more.

ABOUT THE AUTHOR

C J Harvey was born in 1940 in Peshawar in the North West Frontier Province of then British India. He went to English-run boarding schools till the age of sixteen and continued his education at university to graduate in Mechanical Engineering in 1962 from the Peshawar University in Pakistan.

His working life started as part of the maintenance team in a Hydro-Electric Power Station for seven years before he emigrated to Birmingham in England in 1970 with his wife and infant daughters. He then joined the British Steel Works at Bromford in Birmingham that same year as a Work Study Engineer and worked his way up to Safety Adviser and Training Officer. He took early retirement in 1993 when the works was shutdown.

He has always maintained an interest in physics and cosmology with a wide ranging study of Texts by the world's prominent physicists such as Einstein, George Gamow, Narlikar, Otto Frisch, Schrödinger, John Gibbin, Michio Kaku etc to name a few.

Out of all this he developed his own concept for the 'Life Cycle' of our universe in his 'Seven Circles Theory' but this remains unpublished.

He finally decided on a work of science fiction but with factual science included where relevant. Pink Knight is the result of twelve years of researched writing and is his only venture into the fiction writing field. A sequel to Pink Knight is however being considered.